15 Books in 1: L. Frank Baum's Original "Oz" Series

The Wonderful Wizard of Oz,
The Marvelous Land of Oz,
Ozma of Oz,
Dorothy and the Wizard in Oz,
The Road to Oz,
The Emerald City of Oz,
The Patchwork Girl Of Oz,
Little Wizard Stories of Oz,
Tik-Tok of Oz,
The Scarecrow Of Oz,
Rinkitink In Oz,
The Lost Princess Of Oz,
The Tin Woodman Of Oz,
The Magic of Oz,
and
Glinda Of Oz

Published by Shoes and Ships and Sealing Wax

Visit our website, ShoesAndShipsAndSealingWax.com, for more great books!

This omnibus edition first published in the UK in 2005

Published by Shoes and Ships and Sealing Wax Ltd
Registered in the UK, company number 5180917

ISBN 0-9548401-3-5

Edits to 'The Patchwork Girl': 'coal-black' has been deleted from the phonograph's song; part of the description of the Tottenhots has been deleted. Edit to 'Rinkitink in Oz': part of the description of the Tottenhots has been deleted.

      "The time has come," the Walrus said,
      "To talk of many things:
        Of shoes — and ships — and sealing-wax —
        Of cabbages — and kings —
        And why the sea is boiling hot —
        And whether pigs have wings."
              Lewis Carroll, The Walrus and The Carpenter, 1872

Contents

The Wonderful Wizard of Oz

by L. Frank Baum

Introduction

Folklore, legends, myths and fairy tales have followed childhood through the ages, for every healthy youngster has a wholesome and instinctive love for stories fantastic, marvelous and manifestly unreal. The winged fairies of Grimm and Andersen have brought more happiness to childish hearts than all other human creations.

Yet the old time fairy tale, having served for generations, may now be classed as "historical" in the children's library; for the time has come for a series of newer "wonder tales" in which the stereotyped genie, dwarf and fairy are eliminated, together with all the horrible and blood-curdling incidents devised by their authors to point a fearsome moral to each tale. Modern education includes morality; therefore the modern child seeks only entertainment in its wonder tales and gladly dispenses with all disagreeable incident.

Having this thought in mind, the story of "The Wonderful Wizard of Oz" was written solely to please children of today. It aspires to being a modernized fairy tale, in which the wonderment and joy are retained and the heartaches and nightmares are left out.

L. Frank Baum
Chicago, April, 1900.

1. The Cyclone

Dorothy lived in the midst of the great Kansas prairies, with Uncle Henry, who was a farmer, and Aunt Em, who was the farmer's wife. Their house was small, for the lumber to build it had to be carried by wagon many miles. There were four walls, a floor and a roof, which made one room; and this room contained a rusty looking cookstove, a cupboard for the dishes, a table, three or four chairs, and the beds. Uncle Henry and Aunt Em had a big bed in one corner, and Dorothy a little bed in another corner. There was no garret at all, and no cellar—except a small hole dug in the ground, called a cyclone cellar, where the family could go in case one of those great whirlwinds arose, mighty enough to crush any building in its path. It was reached by a trap door in the middle of the floor, from which a ladder led down into the small, dark hole.

When Dorothy stood in the doorway and looked around, she could see nothing but the great gray prairie on every side. Not a tree nor a house broke the broad sweep of flat country that reached to the edge of the sky in all directions. The sun had baked the plowed land into a gray mass, with little cracks running through it. Even the grass was not green, for the sun had burned the tops of the long blades until they were the same gray color to be seen everywhere. Once the house had been painted, but the sun blistered the paint and the rains washed it away, and now the house was as dull and gray as everything else.

When Aunt Em came there to live she was a young, pretty wife. The sun and wind had changed her, too. They had taken the sparkle from her eyes and left them a sober gray; they had taken the red from her cheeks and lips, and they were gray also. She was thin and gaunt, and never smiled now. When Dorothy, who was an orphan, first came to her, Aunt Em had been so startled by the child's laughter that she would scream and press her hand upon her heart whenever Dorothy's merry voice reached her ears; and she still looked at the little girl with wonder that she could find anything to laugh at.

Uncle Henry never laughed. He worked hard from morning till night and did not know what joy was. He was gray also, from his long beard to his rough boots, and he looked stern and solemn, and rarely spoke.

It was Toto that made Dorothy laugh, and saved her from growing as gray as her other surroundings. Toto was not gray; he was a little black dog, with long silky hair and small black eyes that twinkled merrily on either side of his funny, wee nose. Toto played all day long, and Dorothy played with him, and loved him dearly.

Today, however, they were not playing. Uncle Henry sat upon the doorstep and looked anxiously at the sky, which was even grayer than usual. Dorothy stood in the door with Toto in her arms, and looked at the sky too. Aunt Em was washing the dishes.

From the far north they heard a low wail of the wind, and Uncle Henry and Dorothy could see where the long grass bowed in waves before the coming storm. There now came a sharp whistling in the air from the south, and as they turned their eyes that way they saw ripples in the grass coming from that direction also.

Suddenly Uncle Henry stood up.

"There's a cyclone coming, Em," he called to his wife. "I'll go look after the stock." Then he ran toward the sheds where the cows and horses were kept.

Aunt Em dropped her work and came to the door. One glance told her of the danger close at hand.

"Quick, Dorothy!" she screamed. "Run for the cellar!"

Toto jumped out of Dorothy's arms and hid under the bed, and the girl started to get him. Aunt Em, badly frightened, threw open the trap door in the floor and climbed down the ladder into the small, dark hole. Dorothy caught Toto at last and started to follow her aunt. When she was halfway across the room there came a great shriek from the wind, and the house shook so hard that she lost her footing and sat down suddenly upon the floor.

Then a strange thing happened.

The house whirled around two or three times and rose slowly through the air. Dorothy felt as if she were going up in a balloon.

The north and south winds met where the house stood, and made it the exact center of the cyclone. In the middle of a cyclone the air is generally still, but the great pressure of the wind on every side of the house raised it up higher and higher, until it was at the very top of the cyclone; and there it remained and was carried miles and miles away as easily as you could carry a feather.

It was very dark, and the wind howled horribly around her, but Dorothy found she was riding quite easily. After the first few whirls around, and one other time when the house tipped badly, she felt as if she were being rocked gently, like a baby in a cradle.

Toto did not like it. He ran about the room, now here, now there, barking loudly; but Dorothy sat quite still on the floor and waited to see what would happen.

Once Toto got too near the open trap door, and fell in; and at first the little girl thought she had lost him. But soon she saw one of his ears sticking up through the hole, for the strong pressure of the air was keeping him up so that he could not fall. She crept to the hole, caught Toto by the ear, and dragged him into the room again, afterward closing the trap door so that no more accidents could happen.

Hour after hour passed away, and slowly Dorothy got over her fright; but she felt quite lonely, and the wind shrieked so loudly all about her that she nearly became deaf. At first she had wondered if she would be dashed to pieces when the house fell again; but as the hours passed and nothing terrible happened, she stopped worrying and resolved to wait calmly and see what the future would bring. At last she crawled over the swaying floor to her bed, and lay down upon it; and Toto followed and lay down beside her.

In spite of the swaying of the house and the wailing of the wind, Dorothy soon closed her eyes and fell fast asleep.

2. The Council with the Munchkins

She was awakened by a shock, so sudden and severe that if Dorothy had not been lying on the soft bed she might have been hurt. As it was, the jar made her catch her breath and wonder what had happened; and Toto put his cold little nose into her face and whined dismally. Dorothy sat up and noticed that the house was not moving; nor was it dark, for the bright sunshine came in at the window, flooding the little room. She sprang from her bed and with Toto at her heels ran and opened the door.

The little girl gave a cry of amazement and looked about her, her eyes growing bigger and bigger at the wonderful sights she saw.

The cyclone had set the house down very gently—for a cyclone—in the midst of a country of marvelous beauty. There were lovely patches of greensward all about, with stately trees bearing rich and luscious fruits. Banks of gorgeous flowers were on every hand, and birds with rare and brilliant plumage sang and fluttered in the trees and bushes. A little way off was a small brook, rushing and sparkling along between green banks, and murmuring in a voice very grateful to a little girl who had lived so long on the dry, gray prairies.

While she stood looking eagerly at the strange and beautiful sights, she noticed coming toward her a group of the queerest people she had ever seen. They were not as big as the grown folk she had always been used to; but neither were they very small. In fact, they seemed about as tall as Dorothy, who was a well-grown child for her age, although they were, so far as looks go, many years older.

Three were men and one a woman, and all were oddly dressed. They wore round hats that rose to a small point a foot above their heads, with little bells around the brims that tinkled sweetly as they moved. The hats of the men were blue; the little woman's hat was white, and she wore a white gown that hung in pleats from her shoulders. Over it were sprinkled little stars that glistened in the sun like diamonds. The men were dressed in blue, of the same shade as their hats, and wore well-polished boots with a deep roll of blue at the tops. The men, Dorothy thought, were about as old as Uncle Henry, for two of them had beards. But the little woman was doubtless much older. Her face was covered with wrinkles, her hair was nearly white, and she walked rather stiffly.

When these people drew near the house where Dorothy was standing in the doorway, they paused and whispered among themselves, as if afraid to come farther. But the little old woman walked up to Dorothy, made a low bow and said, in a sweet voice:

"You are welcome, most noble Sorceress, to the land of the Munchkins. We are so grateful to you for having killed the Wicked Witch of the East, and for setting our people free from bondage."

Dorothy listened to this speech with wonder. What could the little woman possibly mean by calling her a sorceress, and saying she had killed the Wicked Witch of the East? Dorothy was an innocent, harmless little girl, who had been carried by a cyclone many miles from home; and she had never killed anything in all her life.

But the little woman evidently expected her to answer; so Dorothy said, with hesitation, "You are very kind, but there must be some mistake. I have not killed anything."

"Your house did, anyway," replied the little old woman, with a laugh, "and that is the same thing. See!" she continued, pointing to the corner of the house. "There are her two feet, still sticking out from under a block of wood."

Dorothy looked, and gave a little cry of fright. There, indeed, just under the corner of the great beam the house rested on, two feet were sticking out, shod in silver shoes with pointed toes.

"Oh, dear! Oh, dear!" cried Dorothy, clasping her hands together in dismay. "The house must have fallen on her. Whatever shall we do?"

"There is nothing to be done," said the little woman calmly.

"But who was she?" asked Dorothy.

"She was the Wicked Witch of the East, as I said," answered the little woman. "She has held all the Munchkins in bondage for many years, making them slave for her night and day. Now they are all set free, and are grateful to you for the favor."

"Who are the Munchkins?" inquired Dorothy.

"They are the people who live in this land of the East where the Wicked Witch ruled."

"Are you a Munchkin?" asked Dorothy.

"No, but I am their friend, although I live in the land of the North. When they saw the Witch of the East was dead the Munchkins sent a swift messenger to me, and I came at once. I am the Witch of the North."

"Oh, gracious!" cried Dorothy. "Are you a real witch?"

"Yes, indeed," answered the little woman. "But I am a good witch, and the people love me. I am not as powerful as the Wicked Witch was who ruled here, or I should have set the people free myself."

"But I thought all witches were wicked," said the girl, who was half frightened at facing a real witch. "Oh, no, that is a great mistake. There were only four witches in all the Land of Oz, and two of them, those who live in the North and the South, are good witches. I know this is true, for I am one of them myself, and cannot be mistaken. Those who dwelt in the East and the West were, indeed, wicked witches; but now that you have killed one of them, there is but one Wicked Witch in all the Land of Oz—the one who lives in the West."

"But," said Dorothy, after a moment's thought, "Aunt Em has told me that the witches were all dead—years and years ago."

"Who is Aunt Em?" inquired the little old woman.

"She is my aunt who lives in Kansas, where I came from."

The Witch of the North seemed to think for a time, with her head bowed and her eyes upon the ground. Then she looked up and said, "I do not know where Kansas is, for I have never heard that country mentioned before. But tell me, is it a civilized country?"

"Oh, yes," replied Dorothy.

"Then that accounts for it. In the civilized countries I believe there are no witches left, nor wizards, nor sorceresses, nor magicians. But, you see, the Land of Oz has never been civilized, for we are cut off from all the rest of the world. Therefore we still have witches and wizards amongst us."

"Who are the wizards?" asked Dorothy.

"Oz himself is the Great Wizard," answered the Witch, sinking her voice to a whisper. "He is more powerful than all the rest of us together. He lives in the City of Emeralds."

Dorothy was going to ask another question, but just then the Munchkins, who had been standing silently by, gave a loud shout and pointed to the corner of the house where the Wicked Witch had been lying.

"What is it?" asked the little old woman, and looked, and began to laugh. The feet of the dead Witch had disappeared entirely, and nothing was left but the silver shoes.

"She was so old," explained the Witch of the North, "that she dried up quickly in the sun. That is the end of her. But the silver shoes are yours, and you shall have them to wear." She reached down and picked up the shoes, and after shaking the dust out of them handed them to Dorothy.

"The Witch of the East was proud of those silver shoes," said one of the Munchkins, "and there is some charm connected with them; but what it is we never knew."

Dorothy carried the shoes into the house and placed them on the table. Then she came out again to the Munchkins and said:

"I am anxious to get back to my aunt and uncle, for I am sure they will worry about me. Can you help me find my way?"

The Munchkins and the Witch first looked at one another, and then at Dorothy, and then shook their heads.

"At the East, not far from here," said one, "there is a great desert, and none could live to cross it."

"It is the same at the South," said another, "for I have been there and seen it. The South is the country of the Quadlings."

"I am told," said the third man, "that it is the same at the West. And that country, where the Winkies live, is ruled by the Wicked Witch of the West, who would make you her slave if you passed her way."

"The North is my home," said the old lady, "and at its edge is the same great desert that surrounds this Land of Oz. I'm afraid, my dear, you will have to live with us."

Dorothy began to sob at this, for she felt lonely among all these strange people. Her tears seemed to grieve the kind-hearted Munchkins, for they immediately took out their handkerchiefs and began to weep also. As for the little old woman, she took off her cap and balanced the point on the end of her nose, while she counted "One, two, three" in a solemn voice. At once the cap changed to a slate, on which was written in big, white chalk marks:

"LET DOROTHY GO TO THE CITY OF EMERALDS"

The little old woman took the slate from her nose, and having read the words on it, asked, "Is your name Dorothy, my dear?"

"Yes," answered the child, looking up and drying her tears.

"Then you must go to the City of Emeralds. Perhaps Oz will help you."

"Where is this city?" asked Dorothy.

"It is exactly in the center of the country, and is ruled by Oz, the Great Wizard I told you of."

"Is he a good man?" inquired the girl anxiously.

"He is a good Wizard. Whether he is a man or not I cannot tell, for I have never seen him."

"How can I get there?" asked Dorothy.

"You must walk. It is a long journey, through a country that is sometimes pleasant and sometimes dark and terrible. However, I will use all the magic arts I know of to keep you from harm."

"Won't you go with me?" pleaded the girl, who had begun to look upon the little old woman as her only friend.

"No, I cannot do that," she replied, "but I will give you my kiss, and no one will dare injure a person who has been kissed by the Witch of the North."

She came close to Dorothy and kissed her gently on the forehead. Where her lips touched the girl they left a round, shining mark, as Dorothy found out soon after.

"The road to the City of Emeralds is paved with yellow brick," said the Witch, "so you cannot miss it. When you get to Oz do not be afraid of him, but tell your story and ask him to help you. Good-bye, my dear."

The three Munchkins bowed low to her and wished her a pleasant journey, after which they walked away through the trees. The Witch gave Dorothy a friendly little nod, whirled around on her left heel three times, and straightway disappeared, much to the surprise of little Toto, who barked after her loudly enough when she had gone, because he had been afraid even to growl while she stood by.

But Dorothy, knowing her to be a witch, had expected her to disappear in just that way, and was not surprised in the least.

3. How Dorothy Saved the Scarecrow

When Dorothy was left alone she began to feel hungry. So she went to the cupboard and cut herself some bread, which she spread with butter. She gave some to Toto, and taking a pail from the shelf she carried it down to the little brook and filled it with clear, sparkling water. Toto ran over to the trees and began to bark at the birds sitting there. Dorothy went to get him, and saw such delicious fruit hanging from the branches that she gathered some of it, finding it just what she wanted to help out her breakfast.

Then she went back to the house, and having helped herself and Toto to a good drink of the cool, clear water, she set about making ready for the journey to the City of Emeralds.

Dorothy had only one other dress, but that happened to be clean and was hanging on a peg beside her bed. It was gingham, with checks of white and blue; and although the blue was somewhat faded with many washings, it was still a pretty frock. The girl washed herself carefully, dressed herself in the clean gingham, and tied her pink sunbonnet on her head. She took a little basket and filled it with bread from the cupboard, laying a white cloth over the top. Then she looked down at her feet and noticed how old and worn her shoes were.

"They surely will never do for a long journey, Toto," she said. And Toto looked up into her face with his little black eyes and wagged his tail to show he knew what she meant.

At that moment Dorothy saw lying on the table the silver shoes that had belonged to the Witch of the East.

"I wonder if they will fit me," she said to Toto. "They would be just the thing to take a long walk in, for they could not wear out."

She took off her old leather shoes and tried on the silver ones, which fitted her as well as if they had been made for her.

Finally she picked up her basket.

"Come along, Toto," she said. "We will go to the Emerald City and ask the Great Oz how to get back to Kansas again."

She closed the door, locked it, and put the key carefully in the pocket of her dress. And so, with Toto trotting along soberly behind her, she started on her journey.

There were several roads near by, but it did not take her long to find the one paved with yellow bricks. Within a short time she was walking briskly toward the Emerald City, her silver shoes tinkling merrily on the hard, yellow road-bed. The sun shone bright and the birds sang sweetly, and Dorothy did not feel nearly so bad as you might think a little girl would who had been suddenly whisked away from her own country and set down in the midst of a strange land.

She was surprised, as she walked along, to see how pretty the country was about her. There were neat fences at the sides of the road, painted a dainty blue color, and beyond them were fields of grain and vegetables in abundance. Evidently the Munchkins were good farmers and able to raise large crops. Once in a while she would pass a house, and the people came out to look at her and bow low as she went by; for everyone knew she had been the means of destroying the Wicked Witch and setting them free from bondage. The houses of the Munchkins were odd-looking dwellings, for each was round, with a big dome for a roof. All were painted blue, for in this country of the East blue was the favorite color.

Toward evening, when Dorothy was tired with her long walk and began to wonder where she should pass the night, she came to a house rather larger than the rest. On the green lawn before it many men and women were dancing. Five little fiddlers played as loudly as possible, and the people were laughing and singing, while a big table near by was loaded with delicious fruits and nuts, pies and cakes, and many other good things to eat.

The people greeted Dorothy kindly, and invited her to supper and to pass the night with them; for this was the home of one of the richest Munchkins in the land, and his friends were gathered with him to celebrate their freedom from the bondage of the Wicked Witch.

Dorothy ate a hearty supper and was waited upon by the rich Munchkin himself, whose name was Boq. Then she sat upon a settee and watched the people dance.

When Boq saw her silver shoes he said, "You must be a great sorceress."

"Why?" asked the girl.

"Because you wear silver shoes and have killed the Wicked Witch. Besides, you have white in your frock, and only witches and sorceresses wear white."

"My dress is blue and white checked," said Dorothy, smoothing out the wrinkles in it.

"It is kind of you to wear that," said Boq. "Blue is the color of the Munchkins, and white is the witch color. So we know you are a friendly witch."

Dorothy did not know what to say to this, for all the people seemed to think her a witch, and she knew very well she was only an ordinary little girl who had come by the chance of a cyclone into a strange land.

When she had tired watching the dancing, Boq led her into the house, where he gave her a room with a pretty bed in it. The sheets were made of blue cloth, and Dorothy slept soundly in them till morning, with Toto curled up on the blue rug beside her.

She ate a hearty breakfast, and watched a wee Munchkin baby, who played with Toto and pulled his tail and crowed and laughed in a way that greatly amused Dorothy. Toto was a fine curiosity to all the people, for they had never seen a dog before.

"How far is it to the Emerald City?" the girl asked.

"I do not know," answered Boq gravely, "for I have never been there. It is better for people to keep away from Oz, unless they have business with him. But it is a long way to the Emerald City, and it will take you many days. The country here is rich and pleasant, but you must pass through rough and dangerous places before you reach the end of your journey."

This worried Dorothy a little, but she knew that only the Great Oz could help her get to Kansas again, so she bravely resolved not to turn back.

She bade her friends good-bye, and again started along the road of yellow brick. When she had gone several miles she thought she would stop to rest, and so climbed to the top of the fence beside the road and sat down. There was a great cornfield beyond the fence, and not far away she saw a Scarecrow, placed high on a pole to keep the birds from the ripe corn.

Dorothy leaned her chin upon her hand and gazed thoughtfully at the Scarecrow. Its head was a small sack stuffed with straw, with eyes, nose, and mouth painted on it to represent a face. An old, pointed blue hat, that had belonged to some Munchkin, was perched on his head, and the rest of the figure was a blue suit of clothes, worn and faded, which had also been stuffed with straw. On the feet were some old boots with blue tops, such as every man wore in this country, and the figure was raised above the stalks of corn by means of the pole stuck up its back.

While Dorothy was looking earnestly into the queer, painted face of the Scarecrow, she was surprised to see one of the eyes slowly wink at her. She thought she must have been mistaken at first, for none of the scarecrows in Kansas ever wink; but presently the figure nodded its head to her in a friendly way. Then she climbed down from the fence and walked up to it, while Toto ran around the pole and barked.

"Good day," said the Scarecrow, in a rather husky voice.

"Did you speak?" asked the girl, in wonder.

"Certainly," answered the Scarecrow. "How do you do?"

"I'm pretty well, thank you," replied Dorothy politely. "How do you do?"

"I'm not feeling well," said the Scarecrow, with a smile, "for it is very tedious being perched up here night and day to scare away crows."

"Can't you get down?" asked Dorothy.

"No, for this pole is stuck up my back. If you will please take away the pole I shall be greatly obliged to you."

Dorothy reached up both arms and lifted the figure off the pole, for, being stuffed with straw, it was quite light.

"Thank you very much," said the Scarecrow, when he had been set down on the ground. "I feel like a new man."

Dorothy was puzzled at this, for it sounded queer to hear a stuffed man speak, and to see him bow and walk along beside her.

"Who are you?" asked the Scarecrow when he had stretched himself and yawned. "And where are you going?"

"My name is Dorothy," said the girl, "and I am going to the Emerald City, to ask the Great Oz to send me back to Kansas."

"Where is the Emerald City?" he inquired. "And who is Oz?"

"Why, don't you know?" she returned, in surprise.

"No, indeed. I don't know anything. You see, I am stuffed, so I have no brains at all," he answered sadly.

"Oh," said Dorothy, "I'm awfully sorry for you."

"Do you think," he asked, "if I go to the Emerald City with you, that Oz would give me some brains?"

"I cannot tell," she returned, "but you may come with me, if you like. If Oz will not give you any brains you will be no worse off than you are now."

"That is true," said the Scarecrow. "You see," he continued confidentially, "I don't mind my legs and arms and body being stuffed, because I cannot get hurt. If anyone treads on my toes or sticks a pin into me, it doesn't matter, for I can't feel it. But I do not want people to call me a fool, and if my head stays stuffed with straw instead of with brains, as yours is, how am I ever to know anything?"

"I understand how you feel," said the little girl, who was truly sorry for him. "If you will come with me I'll ask Oz to do all he can for you."

"Thank you," he answered gratefully.

They walked back to the road. Dorothy helped him over the fence, and they started along the path of yellow brick for the Emerald City.

Toto did not like this addition to the party at first. He smelled around the stuffed man as if he suspected there might be a nest of rats in the straw, and he often growled in an unfriendly way at the Scarecrow.

"Don't mind Toto," said Dorothy to her new friend. "He never bites."

"Oh, I'm not afraid," replied the Scarecrow. "He can't hurt the straw. Do let me carry that basket for you. I shall not mind it, for I can't get tired. I'll tell you a secret," he continued, as he walked along. "There is only one thing in the world I am afraid of."

"What is that?" asked Dorothy; "the Munchkin farmer who made you?"

"No," answered the Scarecrow; "it's a lighted match."

4. The Road Through the Forest

After a few hours the road began to be rough, and the walking grew so difficult that the Scarecrow often stumbled over the yellow bricks, which were here very uneven. Sometimes, indeed, they were broken or missing altogether, leaving holes that Toto jumped across and Dorothy walked around. As for the Scarecrow, having no brains, he walked straight ahead, and so stepped into the holes and fell at full length on the hard bricks. It never hurt him, however, and Dorothy would pick him up and set him upon his feet again, while he joined her in laughing merrily at his own mishap.

The farms were not nearly so well cared for here as they were farther back. There were fewer houses and fewer fruit trees, and the farther they went the more dismal and lonesome the country became.

At noon they sat down by the roadside, near a little brook, and Dorothy opened her basket and got out some bread. She offered a piece to the Scarecrow, but he refused.

"I am never hungry," he said, "and it is a lucky thing I am not, for my mouth is only painted, and if I should cut a hole in it so I could eat, the straw I am stuffed with would come out, and that would spoil the shape of my head."

Dorothy saw at once that this was true, so she only nodded and went on eating her bread.

Tell me something about yourself and the country you came from," said the Scarecrow, when she had finished her dinner. So she told him all about Kansas, and how gray everything was there, and how the cyclone had carried her to this queer Land of Oz.

The Scarecrow listened carefully, and said, "I cannot understand why you should wish to leave this beautiful country and go back to the dry, gray place you call Kansas."

That is because you have no brains" answered the girl. "No matter how dreary and gray our homes are, we people of flesh and blood would rather live there than in any other country, be it ever so beautiful. There is no place like home."

The Scarecrow sighed.

Of course I cannot understand it," he said. "If your heads were stuffed with straw, like mine, you would probably all live in the beautiful places, and then Kansas would have no people at all. It is fortunate for Kansas that you have brains."

Won't you tell me a story, while we are resting?" asked the child.

The Scarecrow looked at her reproachfully, and answered:

My life has been so short that I really know nothing whatever. I was only made day before yesterday. What happened in the world before that time is all unknown to me. Luckily, when the farmer made my head, one of the first things he did was to paint my ears, so that I heard what was going on. There was another Munchkin with him, and the first thing I heard was the farmer saying, `How do you like those ears?'

`They aren't straight,'" answered the other.

`Never mind,'" said the farmer. "`They are ears just the same,'" which was true enough.

`Now I'll make the eyes,'" said the farmer. So he painted my right eye, and as soon as it was finished I found myself looking at him and at everything around me with a great deal of curiosity, for this was my first glimpse of the world.

`That's a rather pretty eye,'" remarked the Munchkin who was watching the farmer. "`Blue paint is just the color for eyes.'

`I think I'll make the other a little bigger,'" said the farmer. And when the second eye was done I could see much better than before. Then he made my nose and my mouth. But I did not speak, because at that time I didn't know what a mouth was for. I had the fun of watching them make my body and my arms and legs; and when they fastened on my head, at last, I felt very proud, for I thought I was just as good a man as anyone.

`This fellow will scare the crows fast enough,' said the farmer. He looks just like a man.'

`Why, he is a man,' said the other, and I quite agreed with him. The farmer carried me under his arm to the cornfield, and set me up on a tall stick, where you found me. He and his friend soon after walked away and left me alone.

I did not like to be deserted this way. So I tried to walk after them. But my feet would not touch the ground, and I was forced to stay on that pole. It was a lonely life to lead, for I had nothing to think of, having been made such a little while before. Many crows and other birds flew into the cornfield, but as soon as they saw me they flew away again, thinking I was a Munchkin; and this pleased me and made me feel that I was quite an important person. By and by an old crow flew near me, and after looking at me carefully he perched upon my shoulder and said:

"`I wonder if that farmer thought to fool me in this clumsy manner. Any crow of sense could see that you are only stuffed with straw.' Then he hopped down at my feet and ate all the corn he wanted. The other birds, seeing he was not harmed by me, came to eat the corn too, so in a short time there was a great flock of them about me.

"I felt sad at this, for it showed I was not such a good Scarecrow after all; but the old crow comforted me, saying, `If you only had brains in your head you would be as good a man as any of them, and a better man than some of them. Brains are the only things worth having in this world, no matter whether one is a crow or a man.'

"After the crows had gone I thought this over, and decided I would try hard to get some brains. By good luck you came along and pulled me off the stake, and from what you say I am sure the Great Oz will give me brains as soon as we get to the Emerald City."

"I hope so," said Dorothy earnestly, "since you seem anxious to have them."

"Oh, yes; I am anxious," returned the Scarecrow. "It is such an uncomfortable feeling to know one is a fool."

"Well," said the girl, "let us go." And she handed the basket to the Scarecrow.

There were no fences at all by the roadside now, and the land was rough and untilled. Toward evening they came to a great forest, where the trees grew so big and close together that their branches met over the road of yellow brick. It was almost dark under the trees, for the branches shut out the daylight; but the travelers did not stop, and went on into the forest.

"If this road goes in, it must come out," said the Scarecrow, "and as the Emerald City is at the other end of the road, we must go wherever it leads us."

"Anyone would know that," said Dorothy.

"Certainly; that is why I know it," returned the Scarecrow. "If it required brains to figure it out, I never should have said it."

After an hour or so the light faded away, and they found themselves stumbling along in the darkness. Dorothy could not see at all, but Toto could, for some dogs see very well in the dark; and the Scarecrow declared he could see as well as by day. So she took hold of his arm and managed to get along fairly well.

"If you see any house, or any place where we can pass the night," she said, "you must tell me; for it is very uncomfortable walking in the dark."

Soon after the Scarecrow stopped.

"I see a little cottage at the right of us," he said, "built of logs and branches. Shall we go there?"

"Yes, indeed," answered the child. "I am all tired out."

So the Scarecrow led her through the trees until they reached the cottage, and Dorothy entered and found a bed of dried leaves in one corner. She lay down at once, and with Toto beside her soon fell into a sound sleep. The Scarecrow, who was never tired, stood up in another corner and waited patiently until morning came.

5. The Rescue of the Tin Woodman

When Dorothy awoke the sun was shining through the trees and Toto had long been out chasing birds around him and squirrels. She sat up and looked around her. Scarecrow, still standing patiently in his corner, waiting for her.

"We must go and search for water," she said to him.

"Why do you want water?" he asked.

"To wash my face clean after the dust of the road, and to drink, so the dry bread will not stick in my throat."

"It must be inconvenient to be made of flesh," said the Scarecrow thoughtfully, "for you must sleep, and eat and drink. However, you have brains, and it is worth a lot of bother to be able to think properly."

They left the cottage and walked through the trees until they found a little spring of clear water, where Dorothy drank and bathed and ate her breakfast. She saw there was not much bread left in the basket, and the girl was thankful the Scarecrow did not have to eat anything, for there was scarcely enough for herself and Toto for the day.

When she had finished her meal, and was about to go back to the road of yellow brick, she was startled to hear a deep groan near by.

"What was that?" she asked timidly.

"I cannot imagine," replied the Scarecrow; "but we can go and see."

Just then another groan reached their ears, and the sound seemed to come from behind them. They turned and walked through the forest a few steps, when Dorothy discovered something shining in a ray of sunshine that fell between the trees. She ran to the place and then stopped short, with a little cry of surprise.

One of the big trees had been partly chopped through, and standing beside it, with an uplifted axe in his hands, was a man made entirely of tin. His head and arms and legs were jointed upon his body, but he stood perfectly motionless, as if he could not stir at all.

Dorothy looked at him in amazement, and so did the Scarecrow, while Toto barked sharply and made a snap at the tin legs, which hurt his teeth.

"Did you groan?" asked Dorothy.

"Yes," answered the tin man, "I did. I've been groaning for more than a year, and no one has ever heard me before or come to help me."

"What can I do for you?" she inquired softly, for she was moved by the sad voice in which the man spoke.

"Get an oil-can and oil my joints," he answered. "They are rusted so badly that I cannot move them at all; if I am well oiled I shall soon be all right again. You will find an oil-can on a shelf in my cottage."

Dorothy at once ran back to the cottage and found the oil-can and then she returned and asked anxiously, "Where are your joints?"

"Oil my neck, first," replied the Tin Woodman. So she oiled it and as it was quite badly rusted the Scarecrow took hold of the tin head and moved it gently from side to side until it worked freely, and then the man could turn it himself.

"Now oil the joints in my arms," he said. And Dorothy oiled them and the Scarecrow bent them carefully until they were quite free from rust and as good as new.

The Tin Woodman gave a sigh of satisfaction and lowered his axe, which he leaned against the tree.

"This is a great comfort," he said. "I have been holding that axe in the air ever since I rusted, and I'm glad to be able to put it down at last. Now, if you will oil the joints of my legs, I shall be all right once more."

So they oiled his legs until he could move them freely; and he thanked them again and again for his release, for he seemed very polite creature, and very grateful.

"I might have stood there always if you had not come along," he said; "so you have certainly saved my life. How did you happen to be here?"

"We are on our way to the Emerald City to see the Great Oz," she answered, "and we stopped at your cottage to pass the night."

"Why do you wish to see Oz?" he asked.

"I want him to send me back to Kansas, and the Scarecrow wants him to put a few brains into his head," she replied.

The Tin Woodman appeared to think deeply for a moment. Then he said:

"Do you suppose Oz could give me a heart?"

"Why, I guess so," Dorothy answered. "It would be as easy as to give the Scarecrow brains."

"True," the Tin Woodman returned. "So, if you will allow me to join your party, I will also go to the Emerald City and ask Oz to help me."

"Come along," said the Scarecrow heartily, and Dorothy added that she would be pleased to have his company. So the Tin Woodman shouldered his axe and they all passed through the forest until they came to the road that was paved with yellow brick.

The Tin Woodman had asked Dorothy to put the oil-can in her basket. "For," he said, "if I should get caught in the rain, and rust again, I would need the oil-can badly."

It was a bit of good luck to have their new comrade join the party, for soon after they had begun their journey again they came to a place where the trees and branches grew so thick over the road that the travelers could not pass. But the Tin Woodman set to work with his axe and chopped so well that soon he cleared a passage for the entire party.

Dorothy was thinking so earnestly as they walked along that she did not notice when the Scarecrow stumbled into a hole and rolled over to the side of the road. Indeed he was obliged to call to her to help him up again.

"Why didn't you walk around the hole?" asked the Tin Woodman.

"I don't know enough," replied the Scarecrow cheerfully. "My head is stuffed with straw, you know, and that is why I am going to Oz to ask him for some brains."

"Oh, I see," said the Tin Woodman. "But, after all, brains are not the best things in the world."

"Have you any?" inquired the Scarecrow.

"No, my head is quite empty," answered the Woodman. "But once I had brains, and a heart also; so, having tried them both, I should much rather have a heart."

"And why is that?" asked the Scarecrow.

"I will tell you my story, and then you will know."

So, while they were walking through the forest, the Tin Woodman told the following story:

"I was born the son of a woodman who chopped down trees in the forest and sold the wood for a living. When I grew up, I too became a woodchopper, and after my father died I took care of my old mother as long as she lived. Then I made up my mind that instead of living alone I would marry, so that I might not become lonely.

"There was one of the Munchkin girls who was so beautiful that I soon grew to love her with all my heart. She, on her part, promised to marry me as soon as I could earn enough money to build a better house for her; so I set to work harder than ever. But the girl lived with an old woman who did not want her to marry anyone, for she was so lazy she wished the girl to remain with her and do the cooking and the housework. So the old woman went to the Wicked Witch of the East, and promised her two sheep and a cow if she would prevent the marriage. Thereupon the Wicked Witch enchanted my axe, and when I was chopping away at my best one day, for I was anxious to get the new house and my wife as soon as possible, the axe slipped all at once and cut off my left leg.

"This at first seemed a great misfortune, for I knew a one-legged man could not do very well as a wood-chopper. So I went to a tinsmith and had him make me a new leg out of tin. The leg worked very well, once I was used to it. But my action angered the Wicked Witch of the East, for she had promised the old woman I should not marry the pretty Munchkin girl. When I began chopping again, my axe slipped and cut off my right leg. Again I went to the tinsmith, and again he made me a leg out of tin. After this the enchanted axe cut off my arms, one after the other; but, nothing daunted, I had them replaced with tin ones. The Wicked Witch then made the axe slip and cut off my head, and at first I thought that was the end of me. But the tinsmith happened to come along, and he made me a new head out of tin.

"I thought I had beaten the Wicked Witch then, and I worked harder than ever; but I little knew how cruel my enemy could be. She thought of a new way to kill my love for the beautiful Munchkin maiden, and made my axe slip again, so that it cut right through my body, splitting me into two halves. Once more the tinsmith came to my help and made me a body of tin, fastening my tin arms and legs and head to it, by means of joints, so that I could move around as well as ever. But, alas! I had now no heart, so that I lost all my love for the Munchkin girl, and did not care whether I married her or not. I suppose she is still living with the old woman, waiting for me to come after her.

"My body shone so brightly in the sun that I felt very proud of it and it did not matter now if my axe slipped, for it could not cut me. There was only one danger—that my joints would rust; but I kept an oil-can in my cottage and took care to oil myself whenever I needed it. However, there came a day when I forgot to do this, and, being caught in a rainstorm, before I thought of the danger my joints had rusted, and I was left to stand in the woods until you came to help me. It was a terrible thing to undergo, but during the year I stood there I had time to think that the greatest loss I had known was the loss of my heart. While I was in love I was the happiest man on earth; but no one can love who has not a heart, and so I am resolved to ask Oz to give me one. If he does, I will go back to the Munchkin maiden and marry her."

Both Dorothy and the Scarecrow had been greatly interested in the story of the Tin Woodman, and now they knew why he was so anxious to get a new heart.

"All the same," said the Scarecrow, "I shall ask for brains instead of a heart; for a fool would not know what to do with a heart if he had one."

"I shall take the heart," returned the Tin Woodman; "for brains do not make one happy, and happiness is the best thing in the world."

Dorothy did not say anything, for she was puzzled to know which of her two friends was right, and she decided if she could only get back to Kansas and Aunt Em, it did not matter so much whether the Woodman had no brains and the Scarecrow no heart, or each got what he wanted.

What worried her most was that the bread was nearly gone, and another meal for herself and Toto would empty the basket. To be sure neither the Woodman nor the Scarecrow ever ate anything, but she was not made of tin nor straw, and could not live unless she was fed.

6. The Cowardly Lion

All this time Dorothy and her companions had been walking through the thick woods. The road was still paved with yellow brick, but these were much covered by dried branches and dead leaves from the trees, and the walking was not at all good.

There were few birds in this part of the forest, for birds love the open country where there is plenty of sunshine. But now and then there came a deep growl from some wild animal hidden among the trees. These sounds made the little girl's heart beat fast, for she did not know what made them; but Toto knew, and he walked close to Dorothy's side, and did not even bark in return.

"How long will it be," the child asked of the Tin Woodman, "before we are out of the forest?"

"I cannot tell," was the answer, "for I have never been to the Emerald City. But my father went there once, when I was a boy, and he said it was a long journey through a dangerous country, although nearer to the city where Oz dwells the country is beautiful. But I am not afraid so long as I have my oil-can, and nothing can hurt the Scarecrow, while you bear upon your forehead the mark of the Good Witch's kiss, and that will protect you from harm."

"But Toto!" said the girl anxiously. "What will protect him?"

"We must protect him ourselves if he is in danger," replied the Tin Woodman.

Just as he spoke there came from the forest a terrible roar, and the next moment a great Lion bounded into the road. With one blow of his paw he sent the Scarecrow spinning over and over to the edge of the road, and then he struck at the Tin Woodman with his sharp claws. But, to the Lion's surprise, he could make no impression on the tin, although the Woodman fell over in the road and lay still.

Little Toto, now that he had an enemy to face, ran barking toward the Lion, and the great beast had opened his mouth to bite the dog, when Dorothy, fearing Toto would be killed, and heedless of danger, rushed forward and slapped the Lion upon his nose as hard as she could, while she cried out:

"Don't you dare to bite Toto! You ought to be ashamed of yourself, a big beast like you, to bite a poor little dog!"

"I didn't bite him," said the Lion, as he rubbed his nose with his paw where Dorothy had hit it.

"No, but you tried to," she retorted. "You are nothing but a big coward."

"I know it," said the Lion, hanging his head in shame. "I've always known it. But how can I help it?"

"I don't know, I'm sure. To think of your striking a stuffed man, like the poor Scarecrow!"

"Is he stuffed?" asked the Lion in surprise, as he watched her pick up the Scarecrow and set him upon his feet, while she patted him into shape again.

"Of course he's stuffed," replied Dorothy, who was still angry.

"That's why he went over so easily," remarked the Lion. "It astonished me to see him whirl around so. Is the other one stuffed also?"

"No," said Dorothy, "he's made of tin." And she helped the Woodman up again.

"That's why he nearly blunted my claws," said the Lion. "When they scratched against the tin it made a cold shiver run down my back. What is that little animal you are so tender of?"

"He is my dog, Toto," answered Dorothy.

"Is he made of tin, or stuffed?" asked the Lion.

"Neither. He's a—a—a meat dog," said the girl.

"Oh! He's a curious animal and seems remarkably small, now that I look at him. No one would think of biting such a little thing, except a coward like me," continued the Lion sadly.

"What makes you a coward?" asked Dorothy, looking at the great beast in wonder, for he was as big as a small horse.

"It's a mystery," replied the Lion. "I suppose I was born that way. All the other animals in the forest naturally expect me to be brave, for the Lion is everywhere thought to be the King of Beasts. I learned that if I roared very loudly every living thing was frightened and got out of my way. Whenever I've met a man I've been awfully scared; but I just roared at him, and he has always run away as fast as he could go. If the elephants and the tigers and the bears had ever tried to fight me, I should have run myself—I'm such a coward; but just as soon as they hear me roar they all try to get away from me, and of course I let them go."

"But that isn't right. The King of Beasts shouldn't be a coward," said the Scarecrow.

"I know it," returned the Lion, wiping a tear from his eye with the tip of his tail. "It is my great sorrow, and makes my life very unhappy. But whenever there is danger, my heart begins to beat fast."

"Perhaps you have heart disease," said the Tin Woodman.

"It may be," said the Lion.

"If you have," continued the Tin Woodman, "you ought to be glad, for it proves you have a heart. For my part, I have no heart; so I cannot have heart disease."

"Perhaps," said the Lion thoughtfully, "if I had no heart I should not be a coward."

"Have you brains?" asked the Scarecrow.

"I suppose so. I've never looked to see," replied the Lion.

"I am going to the Great Oz to ask him to give me some," remarked the Scarecrow, "for my head is stuffed with straw."

"And I am going to ask him to give me a heart," said the Woodman.

"And I am going to ask him to send Toto and me back to Kansas," added Dorothy.

"Do you think Oz could give me courage?" asked the Cowardly Lion.

"Just as easily as he could give me brains," said the Scarecrow.

"Or give me a heart," said the Tin Woodman.

"Or send me back to Kansas," said Dorothy.

"Then, if you don't mind, I'll go with you," said the Lion, "for my life is simply unbearable without a bit of courage."

"You will be very welcome," answered Dorothy, "for you will help to keep away the other wild beasts. It seems to me they must be more cowardly than you are if they allow you to scare them so easily."

"They really are," said the Lion, "but that doesn't make me any braver, and as long as I know myself to be a coward I shall be unhappy."

So once more the little company set off upon the journey, the Lion walking with stately strides at Dorothy's side. Toto did not approve this new comrade at first, for he could not forget how nearly he had been crushed between the Lion's great jaws. But after a time he became more at ease, and presently Toto and the Cowardly Lion had grown to be good friends.

During the rest of that day there was no other adventure to mar the peace of their journey. Once, indeed, the Tin Woodman stepped upon a beetle that was crawling along the road, and killed the poor little thing. This made the Tin Woodman very unhappy, for he was always careful not to hurt any living creature; and as he walked along he wept several tears of sorrow and regret. These tears ran slowly down his face and over the hinges of his jaw, and there they rusted. When Dorothy presently asked him a question the Tin Woodman could not open his mouth, for his jaws were tightly rusted together. He became greatly frightened at this and made many motions to Dorothy to relieve him, but she could not understand. The Lion was also puzzled to know what was wrong. But the Scarecrow seized the oil-can from Dorothy's basket and oiled the Woodman's jaws, so that after a few moments he could talk as well as before.

"This will serve me a lesson," said he, "to look where I step. For if I should kill another bug or beetle I should surely cry again, and crying rusts my jaws so that I cannot speak."

Thereafter he walked very carefully, with his eyes on the road, and when he saw a tiny ant toiling by he would step over it, so as not to harm it. The Tin Woodman knew very well he had no heart, and therefore he took great care never to be cruel or unkind to anything.

"You people with hearts," he said, "have something to guide you, and need never do wrong; but I have no heart, and so I must be very careful. When Oz gives me a heart of course I needn't mind so much."

7. The Journey to the Great Oz

They were obliged to camp out that night under a large tree in the forest, for there were no houses near. The tree made a good, thick covering to protect them from the dew, and the Tin Woodman chopped a great pile of wood with his axe and Dorothy built a splendid fire that warmed her and made her feel less lonely. She and Toto ate the last of their bread, and now she did not know what they would do for breakfast.

"If you wish," said the Lion, "I will go into the forest and kill a deer for you. You can roast it by the fire, since your tastes are so peculiar that you prefer cooked food, and then you will have a very good breakfast."

"Don't! Please don't," begged the Tin Woodman. "I should certainly weep if you killed a poor deer, and then my jaws would rust again."

But the Lion went away into the forest and found his own supper, and no one ever knew what it was, for he didn't mention it. And the Scarecrow found a tree full of nuts and filled Dorothy's basket with them, so that she would not be hungry for a long time. She thought this was very kind and thoughtful of the Scarecrow, but she laughed heartily at the awkward way in which the poor creature picked up the nuts. His padded hands were so clumsy and the nuts were so small that he dropped almost as many as he put in the basket. But the Scarecrow did not mind how long it took him to fill the basket, for it enabled him to keep away from the fire, as he feared a spark might get into his straw and burn him up. So he kept a good distance away from the flames, and only came near to cover Dorothy with dry leaves when she lay down to sleep. These kept her very snug and warm, and she slept soundly until morning.

When it was daylight, the girl bathed her face in a little rippling brook, and soon after they all started toward the Emerald City.

This was to be an eventful day for the travelers. They had hardly been walking an hour when they saw before them a great ditch that crossed the road and divided the forest as far as they could see on either side. It was a very wide ditch, and when they crept up to the edge and looked into it they could see it was also very deep, and there were many big, jagged rocks at the bottom. The sides were so steep that none of them could climb down, and for a moment it seemed that their journey must end.

"What shall we do?" asked Dorothy despairingly.

"I haven't the faintest idea," said the Tin Woodman, and the Lion shook his shaggy mane and looked thoughtful.

But the Scarecrow said, "We cannot fly, that is certain. Neither can we climb down into this great ditch. Therefore, if we cannot jump over it, we must stop where we are."

"I think I could jump over it," said the Cowardly Lion, after measuring the distance carefully in his mind.

"Then we are all right," answered the Scarecrow, "for you can carry us all over on your back, one at a time."

"Well, I'll try it," said the Lion. "Who will go first?"

"I will," declared the Scarecrow, "for, if you found that you could not jump over the gulf, Dorothy would be killed, or the Tin Woodman badly dented on the rocks below. But if I am on your back it will not matter so much, for the fall would not hurt me at all."

"I am terribly afraid of falling, myself," said the Cowardly Lion, "but I suppose there is nothing to do but try it. So get on my back and we will make the attempt."

The Scarecrow sat upon the Lion's back, and the big beast walked to the edge of the gulf and crouched down.

"Why don't you run and jump?" asked the Scarecrow.

"Because that isn't the way we Lions do these things," he replied. Then giving a great spring, he shot through the air and landed safely on the other side. They were all greatly pleased to see how easily he did it, and after the Scarecrow had got down from his back the Lion sprang across the ditch again.

Dorothy thought she would go next; so she took Toto in her arms and climbed on the Lion's back, holding tightly to his mane with one hand. The next moment it seemed as if she were flying through the air; and then, before she had time to think about it, she was safe on the other side. The Lion went back a third time and got the Tin Woodman, and then they all sat down for a few moments to give the beast a chance to rest, for his great leaps had made his breath short, and he panted like a big dog that has been running too long.

They found the forest very thick on this side, and it looked dark and gloomy. After the Lion had rested they started along the road of yellow brick, silently wondering, each in his own mind, if ever they would come to the end of the woods and reach the bright sunshine again. To add to their discomfort, they soon heard strange noises in the depths of the forest, and the Lion whispered to them that it was in this part of the country that the Kalidahs lived.

"What are the Kalidahs?" asked the girl.

"They are monstrous beasts with bodies like bears and heads like tigers," replied the Lion, "and with claws so long and sharp that they could tear me in two as easily as I could kill Toto. I'm terribly afraid of the Kalidahs."

"I'm not surprised that you are," returned Dorothy. "They must be dreadful beasts."

The Lion was about to reply when suddenly they came to another gulf across the road. But this one was so broad and deep that the Lion knew at once he could not leap across it.

So they sat down to consider what they should do, and after serious thought the Scarecrow said:

"Here is a great tree, standing close to the ditch. If the Tin Woodman can chop it down, so that it will fall to the other side, we can walk across it easily."

"That is a first-rate idea," said the Lion. "One would almost suspect you had brains in your head, instead of straw."

The Woodman set to work at once, and so sharp was his axe that the tree was soon chopped nearly through. Then the Lion put his strong front legs against the tree and pushed with all his might, and slowly the big tree tipped and fell with a crash across the ditch, with its top branches on the other side.

They had just started to cross this queer bridge when a sharp growl made them all look up, and to their horror they saw running toward them two great beasts with bodies like bears and heads like tigers.

"They are the Kalidahs!" said the Cowardly Lion, beginning to tremble.

"Quick!" cried the Scarecrow. "Let us cross over."

So Dorothy went first, holding Toto in her arms, the Tin Woodman followed, and the Scarecrow came next. The Lion, although he was certainly afraid, turned to face the Kalidahs, and then he gave so loud and terrible a roar that Dorothy screamed and the Scarecrow fell over backward, while even the fierce beasts stopped short and looked at him in surprise.

But, seeing they were bigger than the Lion, and remembering that there were two of them and only one of him, the Kalidahs again rushed forward, and the Lion crossed over the tree and turned to see what they would do next. Without stopping an instant the fierce beasts also began to cross the tree. And the Lion said to Dorothy:

"We are lost, for they will surely tear us to pieces with their sharp claws. But stand close behind me, and I will fight them as long as I am alive."

"Wait a minute!" called the Scarecrow. He had been thinking what was best to be done, and now he asked the Woodman to chop away the end of the tree that rested on their side of the ditch. The Tin Woodman began to use his axe at once, and, just as the two Kalidahs were nearly across, the tree fell with a crash into the gulf, carrying the ugly, snarling brutes with it, and both were dashed to pieces on the sharp rocks at the bottom.

"Well," said the Cowardly Lion, drawing a long breath of relief, "I see we are going to live a little while longer, and I am glad of it for it must be a very uncomfortable thing not to be alive. Those creatures frightened me so badly that my heart is beating yet."

"Ah," said the Tin Woodman sadly, "I wish I had a heart to beat."

This adventure made the travelers more anxious than ever to get out of the forest, and they walked so fast that Dorothy became tired, and had to ride on the Lion's back. To their great joy the trees became thinner the farther they advanced, and in the afternoon they suddenly came upon a broad river, flowing swiftly just before them. On the other side of the water they could see the road of yellow brick running through a beautiful country with green meadows dotted with bright flowers and all the road bordered with trees hanging full of delicious fruits. They were greatly pleased to see this delightful country before them.

"How shall we cross the river?" asked Dorothy.

"That is easily done," replied the Scarecrow. "The Tin Woodman must build us a raft, so we can float to the other side."

So the Woodman took his axe and began to chop down small trees to make a raft, and while he was busy at this the Scarecrow found on the riverbank a tree full of fine fruit. This pleased Dorothy, who had eaten nothing but nuts all day, and she made a hearty meal of the ripe fruit.

But it takes time to make a raft, even when one is as industrious and untiring as the Tin Woodman, and when night came the work was not done. So they found a cozy place under the trees where they slept well until the morning; and Dorothy dreamed of the Emerald City, and of the good Wizard Oz, who would soon send her back to her own home again.

8. The Deadly Poppy Field

Our little party of travelers awakened the next morning, refreshed and full of hope, and Dorothy breakfasted like a princess off peaches and plums from the trees beside the river. Behind them was the dark forest they had passed safely through, although they had suffered many discouragements; but before them was a lovely, sunny country that seemed to beckon them on to the Emerald City.

To be sure, the broad river now cut them off from this beautiful land. But the raft was nearly done, and after the Tin Woodman had cut a few more logs and fastened them together with wooden pins, they were ready to start. Dorothy sat down in the middle of the raft and held Toto in her arms. When the Cowardly Lion stepped upon the raft it tipped badly, for he was big and heavy; but the Scarecrow and the Tin Woodman stood upon the other end to steady it, and they had long poles in their hands to push the raft through the water.

They got along quite well at first, but when they reached the middle of the river the swift current swept the raft downstream, farther and farther away from the road of yellow brick. And the water grew so deep that the long poles would not touch the bottom.

"This is bad," said the Tin Woodman, "for if we cannot get to the land we shall be carried into the country of the Wicked Witch of the West, and she will enchant us and make us her slaves."

"And then I should get no brains," said the Scarecrow.

"And I should get no courage," said the Cowardly Lion.

"And I should get no heart," said the Tin Woodman.

"And I should never get back to Kansas," said Dorothy.

"We must certainly get to the Emerald City if we can," the Scarecrow continued, and he pushed so hard on his long pole that it stuck fast in the mud at the bottom of the river. Then, before he could pull it out again—or let go—the raft was swept away, and the poor Scarecrow left clinging to the pole in the middle of the river.

"Good-bye!" he called after them, and they were very sorry to leave him. Indeed, the Tin Woodman began to cry, but fortunately remembered that he might rust, and so dried his tears on Dorothy's apron.

Of course this was a bad thing for the Scarecrow.

"I am now worse off than when I first met Dorothy," he thought. "Then, I was stuck on a pole in a cornfield, where I could make-believe scare the crows, at any rate. But surely there is no use for a Scarecrow stuck on a pole in the middle of a river. I am afraid I shall never have any brains, after all!"

Down the stream the raft floated, and the poor Scarecrow was left far behind. Then the Lion said:

"Something must be done to save us. I think I can swim to the shore and pull the raft after me, if you will only hold fast to the tip of my tail."

So he sprang into the water, and the Tin Woodman caught fast hold of his tail. Then the Lion began to swim with all his might toward the shore. It was hard work, although he was so big; but by and by they were drawn out of the current, and then Dorothy took the Tin Woodman's long pole and helped push the raft to the land.

They were all tired out when they reached the shore at last and stepped off upon the pretty green grass, and they also knew that the stream had carried them a long way past the road of yellow brick that led to the Emerald City.

"What shall we do now?" asked the Tin Woodman, as the Lion lay down on the grass to let the sun dry him.

"We must get back to the road, in some way," said Dorothy.

"The best plan will be to walk along the riverbank until we come to the road again," remarked the Lion.

So, when they were rested, Dorothy picked up her basket and they started along the grassy bank, to the road from which the river had carried them. It was a lovely country, with plenty of flowers and fruit trees and sunshine to cheer them, and had they not felt so sorry for the poor Scarecrow, they could have been very happy.

They walked along as fast as they could, Dorothy only stopping once to pick a beautiful flower; and after a time the Tin Woodman cried out: "Look!"

Then they all looked at the river and saw the Scarecrow perched upon his pole in the middle of the water, looking very lonely and sad.

"What can we do to save him?" asked Dorothy.

The Lion and the Woodman both shook their heads, for they did not know. So they sat down upon the bank and gazed wistfully at the Scarecrow until a Stork flew by, who, upon seeing them, stopped to rest at the water's edge.

"Who are you and where are you going?" asked the Stork.

"I am Dorothy," answered the girl, "and these are my friends, the Tin Woodman and the Cowardly Lion; and we are going to the Emerald City."

"This isn't the road," said the Stork, as she twisted her long neck and looked sharply at the queer party.

"I know it," returned Dorothy, "but we have lost the Scarecrow, and are wondering how we shall get him again."

"Where is he?" asked the Stork.

"Over there in the river," answered the little girl.

"If he wasn't so big and heavy I would get him for you," remarked the Stork.

"He isn't heavy a bit," said Dorothy eagerly, "for he is stuffed with straw; and if you will bring him back to us, we shall thank you ever and ever so much."

"Well, I'll try," said the Stork, "but if I find he is too heavy to carry I shall have to drop him in the river again."

So the big bird flew into the air and over the water till she came to where the Scarecrow was perched upon his pole. Then the Stork with her great claws grabbed the Scarecrow by the arm and carried him up into the air and back to the bank, where Dorothy and the Lion and the Tin Woodman and Toto were sitting.

When the Scarecrow found himself among his friends again, he was so happy that he hugged them all, even the Lion and Toto; and as they walked along he sang "Tol-de-ri-de-oh!" at every step, he felt so gay.

"I was afraid I should have to stay in the river forever," he said, "but the kind Stork saved me, and if I ever get any brains I shall find the Stork again and do her some kindness in return."

"That's all right," said the Stork, who was flying along beside them. "I always like to help anyone in trouble. But I must go now, for my babies are waiting in the nest for me. I hope you will find the Emerald City and that Oz will help you."

"Thank you," replied Dorothy, and then the kind Stork flew into the air and was soon out of sight.

They walked along listening to the singing of the brightly colored birds and looking at the lovely flowers which now became so thick that the ground was carpeted with them. There were big yellow and white and blue and purple blossoms, besides great clusters of scarlet poppies, which were so brilliant in color they almost dazzled Dorothy's eyes.

"Aren't they beautiful?" the girl asked, as she breathed in the spicy scent of the bright flowers.

"I suppose so," answered the Scarecrow. "When I have brains, I shall probably like them better."

"If I only had a heart, I should love them," added the Tin Woodman.

"I always did like flowers," said the Lion. "They of seem so helpless and frail. But there are none in the forest so bright as these."

They now came upon more and more of the big scarlet poppies, and fewer and fewer of the other flowers; and soon they found themselves in the midst of a great meadow of poppies. Now it is well known that when there are many of these flowers together their odor is so powerful that anyone who breathes it falls asleep, and if the sleeper is not carried away from the scent of the flowers, he sleeps on and on forever. But Dorothy did not know this, nor could she get away from the bright red flowers that were everywhere about; so presently her eyes grew heavy and she felt she must sit down to rest and to sleep.

But the Tin Woodman would not let her do this.

"We must hurry and get back to the road of yellow brick before dark," he said; and the Scarecrow agreed with him. So they kept walking until Dorothy could stand no longer. Her eyes closed in spite of herself and she forgot where she was and fell among the poppies, fast asleep.

"What shall we do?" asked the Tin Woodman.

"If we leave her here she will die," said the Lion. "The smell of the flowers is killing us all. I myself can scarcely keep my eyes open, and the dog is asleep already."

It was true; Toto had fallen down beside his little mistress. But the Scarecrow and the Tin Woodman, not being made of flesh, were not troubled by the scent of the flowers.

"Run fast," said the Scarecrow to the Lion, "and get out of this deadly flower bed as soon as you can. We will bring the little girl with us, but if you should fall asleep you are too big to be carried."

So the Lion aroused himself and bounded forward as fast as he could go. In a moment he was out of sight.

"Let us make a chair with our hands and carry her," said the Scarecrow. So they picked up Toto and put the dog in Dorothy's lap, and then they made a chair with their hands for the seat and their arms for the arms and carried the sleeping girl between them through the flowers.

On and on they walked, and it seemed that the great carpet of deadly flowers that surrounded them would never end. They followed the bend of the river, and at last came upon their friend the Lion, lying fast asleep among the poppies. The flowers had been too strong for the huge beast and he had given up at last, and fallen only a short distance from the end of the poppy bed, where the sweet grass spread in beautiful green fields before them.

"We can do nothing for him," said the Tin Woodman, sadly; "for he is much too heavy to lift. We must leave him here to sleep on forever, and perhaps he will dream that he has found courage at last."

"I'm sorry," said the Scarecrow. "The Lion was a very good comrade for one so cowardly. But let us go on."

They carried the sleeping girl to a pretty spot beside the river, far enough from the poppy field to prevent her breathing any more of the poison of the flowers, and here they laid her gently on the soft grass and waited for the fresh breeze to waken her.

9. The Queen of the Field Mice

"We cannot be far from the road of yellow brick, now," remarked the Scarecrow, as he stood beside the girl, "for we have come nearly as far as the river carried us away."

The Tin Woodman was about to reply when he heard a low growl, and turning his head (which worked beautifully on hinges) he saw a strange beast come bounding over the grass toward them. It was, indeed, a great yellow Wildcat, and the Woodman thought it must be chasing something, for its ears were lying close to its head and its mouth was wide open, showing two rows of ugly teeth, while its red eyes glowed like balls of fire. As it came nearer the Tin Woodman saw that running before the beast was a little gray field mouse, and although he had no heart he knew it was wrong for the Wildcat to try to kill such a pretty, harmless creature.

So the Woodman raised his axe, and as the Wildcat ran by he gave it a quick blow that cut the beast's head clean off from its body, and it rolled over at his feet in two pieces.

The field mouse, now that it was freed from its enemy, stopped short; and coming slowly up to the Woodman it said, in a squeaky little voice:

"Oh, thank you! Thank you ever so much for saving my life."

"Don't speak of it, I beg of you," replied the Woodman. "I have no heart, you know, so I am careful to help all those who may need a friend, even if it happens to be only a mouse."

"Only a mouse!" cried the little animal, indignantly. "Why, I am a Queen—the Queen of all the Field Mice!"

"Oh, indeed," said the Woodman, making a bow.

"Therefore you have done a great deed, as well as a brave one, in saving my life," added the Queen.

At that moment several mice were seen running up as fast as their little legs could carry them, and when they saw their Queen they exclaimed:

"Oh, your Majesty, we thought you would be killed! How did you manage to escape the great Wildcat?" They all bowed so low to the little Queen that they almost stood upon their heads.

"This funny tin man," she answered, "killed the Wildcat and saved my life. So hereafter you must all serve him, and obey his slightest wish."

"We will!" cried all the mice, in a shrill chorus. And then they scampered in all directions, for Toto had awakened from his sleep, and seeing all these mice around him he gave one bark of delight and jumped right into the middle of the group. Toto had always loved to chase mice when he lived in Kansas, and he saw no harm in it.

But the Tin Woodman caught the dog in his arms and held him tight, while he called to the mice, "Come back! Come back! Toto shall not hurt you."

At this the Queen of the Mice stuck her head out from underneath a clump of grass and asked, in a timid voice, "Are you sure he will not bite us?"

"I will not let him," said the Woodman; "so do not be afraid."

One by one the mice came creeping back, and Toto did not bark again, although he tried to get out of the Woodman's arms, and would have bitten him had he not known very well he was made of tin. Finally one of the biggest mice spoke.

"Is there anything we can do," it asked, "to repay you for saving the life of our Queen?"

"Nothing that I know of," answered the Woodman; but the Scarecrow, who had been trying to think, but could not because his head was stuffed with straw, said, quickly, "Oh, yes; you can save our friend, the Cowardly Lion, who is asleep in the poppy bed."

"A Lion!" cried the little Queen. "Why, he would eat us all up."

"Oh, no," declared the Scarecrow; "this Lion is a coward."

"Really?" asked the Mouse.

"He says so himself," answered the Scarecrow, "and he would never hurt anyone who is our friend. If you will help us to save him I promise that he shall treat you all with kindness."

"Very well," said the Queen, "we trust you. But what shall we do?"

"Are there many of these mice which call you Queen and are willing to obey you?"

"Oh, yes; there are thousands," she replied.

"Then send for them all to come here as soon as possible, and let each one bring a long piece of string."

The Queen turned to the mice that attended her and told them to go at once and get all her people. As soon as they heard her orders they ran away in every direction as fast as possible.

"Now," said the Scarecrow to the Tin Woodman, "you must go to those trees by the riverside and make a truck that will carry the Lion."

So the Woodman went at once to the trees and began to work; and he soon made a truck out of the limbs of trees, from which he chopped away all the leaves and branches. He fastened it together with wooden pegs and made the four wheels out of short pieces of a big tree trunk. So fast and so well did he work that by the time the mice began to arrive the truck was all ready for them.

They came from all directions, and there were thousands of them: big mice and little mice and middle-sized mice; and each one brought a piece of string in his mouth. It was about this time that Dorothy woke from her long sleep and opened her eyes. She was greatly astonished to find herself lying upon the grass, with thousands of mice standing around and looking at her timidly.

But the Scarecrow told her about everything, and turning to the dignified little Mouse, he said:

"Permit me to introduce to you her Majesty, the Queen."

Dorothy nodded gravely and the Queen made a curtsy, after which she became quite friendly with the little girl.

The Scarecrow and the Woodman now began to fasten the mice to the truck, using the strings they had brought. One end of a string was tied around the neck of each mouse and the other end to the truck. Of course the truck was a thousand times bigger than any of the mice who were to draw it; but when all the mice had been harnessed, they were able to pull it quite easily. Even the Scarecrow and the Tin Woodman could sit on it, and were drawn swiftly by their queer little horses to the place where the Lion lay asleep.

After a great deal of hard work, for the Lion was heavy, they managed to get him up on the truck. Then the Queen hurriedly gave her people the order to start, for she feared if the mice stayed among the poppies too long they also would fall asleep.

At first the little creatures, many though they were, could hardly stir the heavily loaded truck; but the Woodman and the Scarecrow both pushed from behind, and they got along better. Soon they rolled the Lion out of the poppy bed to the green fields, where he could breathe the sweet, fresh air again, instead of the poisonous scent of the flowers.

Dorothy came to meet them and thanked the little mice warmly for saving her companion from death. She had grown so fond of the big Lion she was glad he had been rescued.

Then the mice were unharnessed from the truck and scampered away through the grass to their homes. The Queen of the Mice was the last to leave.

"If ever you need us again," she said, "come out into the field and call, and we shall hear you and come to your assistance. Good-bye!"

"Good-bye!" they all answered, and away the Queen ran, while Dorothy held Toto tightly lest he should run after her and frighten her.

After this they sat down beside the Lion until he should awaken; and the Scarecrow brought Dorothy some fruit from a tree near by, which she ate for her dinner.

10. The Guardian of the Gate

It was some time before the Cowardly Lion awakened, for he had lain among the poppies a long while, breathing in their deadly fragrance; but when he did open his eyes and roll off the truck he was very glad to find himself still alive.

"I ran as fast as I could," he said, sitting down and yawning, "but the flowers were too strong for me. How did you get me out?"

Then they told him of the field mice, and how they had generously saved him from death; and the Cowardly Lion laughed, and said:

"I have always thought myself very big and terrible; yet such little things as flowers came near to killing me, and such small animals as mice have saved my life. How strange it all is! But, comrades, what shall we do now?"

"We must journey on until we find the road of yellow brick again," said Dorothy, "and then we can keep on to the Emerald City."

So, the Lion being fully refreshed, and feeling quite himself again, they all started upon the journey, greatly enjoying the walk through the soft, fresh grass; and it was not long before they reached the road of yellow brick and turned again toward the Emerald City where the Great Oz dwelt.

The road was smooth and well paved, now, and the country about was beautiful, so that the travelers rejoiced in leaving the forest far behind, and with it the many dangers they had met in its gloomy shades. Once more they could see fences built beside the road; but these were painted green, and when they came to a small house, in which a farmer evidently lived, that also was painted green. They passed by several of these houses during the afternoon, and sometimes people came to the doors and looked at them as if they would like to ask questions; but no one came near them nor spoke to them because of the great Lion, of which they were very much afraid. The people were all dressed in clothing of a lovely emerald-green color and wore peaked hats like those of the Munchkins.

"This must be the Land of Oz," said Dorothy, "and we are surely getting near the Emerald City."

"Yes," answered the Scarecrow. "Everything is green here, while in the country of the Munchkins blue was the favorite color. But the people do not seem to be as friendly as the Munchkins, and I'm afraid we shall be unable to find a place to pass the night."

"I should like something to eat besides fruit," said the girl, "and I'm sure Toto is nearly starved. Let us stop at the next house and talk to the people."

So, when they came to a good-sized farmhouse, Dorothy walked boldly up to the door and knocked.

A woman opened it just far enough to look out, and said, "What do you want, child, and why is that great Lion with you?"

"We wish to pass the night with you, if you will allow us," answered Dorothy; "and the Lion is my friend and comrade, and would not hurt you for the world."

"Is he tame?" asked the woman, opening the door a little wider.

"Oh, yes," said the girl, "and he is a great coward, too. He will be more afraid of you than you are of him."

"Well," said the woman, after thinking it over and taking another peep at the Lion, "if that is the case you may come in, and I will give you some supper and a place to sleep."

So they all entered the house, where there were, besides the woman, two children and a man. The man had hurt his leg, and was lying on the couch in a corner. They seemed greatly surprised to see so strange a company, and while the woman was busy laying the table the man asked:

"Where are you all going?"

"To the Emerald City," said Dorothy, "to see the Great Oz."

"Oh, indeed!" exclaimed the man. "Are you sure that Oz will see you?"

"Why not?" she replied.

"Why, it is said that he never lets anyone come into his presence. I have been to the Emerald City many times, and it is a beautiful and wonderful place; but I have never been permitted to see the Great Oz, nor do I know of any living person who has seen him."

"Does he never go out?" asked the Scarecrow.

"Never. He sits day after day in the great Throne Room of his Palace, and even those who wait upon him do not see him face to face."

"What is he like?" asked the girl.

"That is hard to tell," said the man thoughtfully. "You see, Oz is a Great Wizard, and can take on any form he wishes. So that some say he looks like a bird; and some say he looks like an elephant; and some say he looks like a cat. To others he appears as a beautiful fairy, or a brownie, or in any other form that pleases him. But who the real Oz is, when he is in his own form, no living person can tell."

"That is very strange," said Dorothy, "but we must try, in some way, to see him, or we shall have made our journey for nothing."

"Why do you wish to see the terrible Oz?" asked the man.

"I want him to give me some brains," said the Scarecrow eagerly.

"Oh, Oz could do that easily enough," declared the man. "He has more brains than he needs."

"And I want him to give me a heart," said the Tin Woodman.

"That will not trouble him," continued the man, "for Oz has a large collection of hearts, of all sizes and shapes."

"And I want him to give me courage," said the Cowardly Lion.

"Oz keeps a great pot of courage in his Throne Room," said the man, "which he has covered with a golden plate, to keep it from running over. He will be glad to give you some."

"And I want him to send me back to Kansas," said Dorothy.

"Where is Kansas?" asked the man, with surprise.

"I don't know," replied Dorothy sorrowfully, "but it is my home, and I'm sure it's somewhere."

"Very likely. Well, Oz can do anything; so I suppose he will find Kansas for you. But first you must get to see him, and that will be a hard task; for the Great Wizard does not like to see anyone, and he usually has his own way. But what do YOU want?" he continued, speaking to Toto. Toto only wagged his tail; for strange to say, he could not speak.

The woman now called to them that supper was ready, so they gathered around the table and Dorothy ate some delicious porridge and a dish of scrambled eggs and a plate of nice white bread, and enjoyed her meal. The Lion ate some of the porridge, but did not care for it, saying it was made from oats and oats were food for horses, not for lions. The Scarecrow and the Tin Woodman ate nothing at all. Toto ate a little of everything, and was glad to get a good supper again.

The woman now gave Dorothy a bed to sleep in, and Toto lay down beside her, while the Lion guarded the door of her room so she might not be disturbed. The Scarecrow and the Tin Woodman stood up in a corner and kept quiet all night, although of course they could not sleep.

The next morning, as soon as the sun was up, they started on their way, and soon saw a beautiful green glow in the sky just before them.

"That must be the Emerald City," said Dorothy.

As they walked on, the green glow became brighter and brighter, and it seemed that at last they were nearing the end of their travels. Yet it was afternoon before they came to the great wall that surrounded the City. It was high and thick and of a bright green color.

In front of them, and at the end of the road of yellow brick, was a big gate, all studded with emeralds that glittered so in the sun that even the painted eyes of the Scarecrow were dazzled by their brilliancy.

There was a bell beside the gate, and Dorothy pushed the button and heard a silvery tinkle sound within. Then the big gate swung slowly open, and they all passed through and found themselves in a high arched room, the walls of which glistened with countless emeralds.

Before them stood a little man about the same size as the Munchkins. He was clothed all in green, from his head to his feet, and even his skin was of a greenish tint. At his side was a large green box.

When he saw Dorothy and her companions the man asked, "What do you wish in the Emerald City?"

"We came here to see the Great Oz," said Dorothy.

The man was so surprised at this answer that he sat down to think it over.

"It has been many years since anyone asked me to see Oz," he said, shaking his head in perplexity. "He is powerful and terrible, and if you come on an idle or foolish errand to bother the wise reflections of the Great Wizard, he might be angry and destroy you all in an instant."

"But it is not a foolish errand, nor an idle one," replied the Scarecrow; "it is important. And we have been told that Oz is a good Wizard."

"So he is," said the green man, "and he rules the Emerald City wisely and well. But to those who are not honest, or who approach him from curiosity, he is most terrible, and few have ever dared ask to see his face. I am the Guardian of the Gates, and since you demand to see the Great Oz I must take you to his Palace. But first you must put on the spectacles."

"Why?" asked Dorothy.

"Because if you did not wear spectacles the brightness and glory of the Emerald City would blind you. Even those who live in the City must wear spectacles night and day. They are all locked on, for Oz so ordered it when the City was first built, and I have the only key that will unlock them."

He opened the big box, and Dorothy saw that it was filled with spectacles of every size and shape. All of them had green glasses in them. The Guardian of the Gates found a pair that would just fit Dorothy and put them over her eyes. There were two golden bands fastened to them that passed around the back of her head, where they were locked together by a little key that was at the end of a chain the Guardian of the Gates wore around his neck. When they were on, Dorothy could not take them off had she wished, but of course she did not wish to be blinded by the glare of the Emerald City, so she said nothing.

Then the green man fitted spectacles for the Scarecrow and the Tin Woodman and the Lion, and even on little Toto; and all were locked fast with the key.

Then the Guardian of the Gates put on his own glasses and told them he was ready to show them to the Palace. Taking a big golden key from a peg on the wall, he opened another gate, and they all followed him through the portal into the streets of the Emerald City.

11. The Wonderful City of Oz

Even with eyes protected by the green spectacles, Dorothy and her friends were at first dazzled by the brilliancy of the wonderful City. The streets were lined with beautiful houses all built of green marble and studded everywhere with sparkling emeralds. They walked over a pavement of the same green marble, and where the blocks were joined together were rows of emeralds, set closely, and glittering in the brightness of the sun. The window panes were of green glass; even the sky above the City had a green tint, and the rays of the sun were green.

There were many people—men, women, and children—walking about, and these were all dressed in green clothes and had greenish skins. They looked at Dorothy and her strangely assorted company with wondering eyes, and the children all ran away and hid behind their mothers when they saw the Lion; but no one spoke to them. Many shops stood in the street, and Dorothy saw that everything in them was green. Green candy and green pop corn were offered for sale, as well as green shoes, green hats, and green clothes of all sorts. At one place a man was selling green lemonade, and when the children bought it Dorothy could see that they paid for it with green pennies.

There seemed to be no horses nor animals of any kind; the men carried things around in little green carts, which they pushed before them. Everyone seemed happy and contented and prosperous.

The Guardian of the Gates led them through the streets until they came to a big building, exactly in the middle of the City, which was the Palace of Oz, the Great Wizard. There was a soldier before the door, dressed in a green uniform and wearing a long green beard.

"Here are strangers," said the Guardian of the Gates to him, "and they demand to see the Great Oz."

"Step inside," answered the soldier, "and I will carry your message to him."

So they passed through the Palace Gates and were led into a big room with a green carpet and lovely green furniture set with emeralds. The soldier made them all wipe their feet upon a green mat before entering this room, and when they were seated he said politely:

"Please make yourselves comfortable while I go to the door of the Throne Room and tell Oz you are here."

They had to wait a long time before the soldier returned. When, at last, he came back, Dorothy asked:

"Have you seen Oz?"

"Oh, no," returned the soldier; "I have never seen him. But I spoke to him as he sat behind his screen and gave him your message. He said he will grant you an audience, if you so desire; but each one of you must enter his presence alone, and he will admit but one each day. Therefore, as you must remain in the Palace for several days, I will have you shown to rooms where you may rest in comfort after your journey."

"Thank you," replied the girl; "that is very kind of Oz."

The soldier now blew upon a green whistle, and at once a young girl, dressed in a pretty green silk gown, entered the room. She had lovely green hair and green eyes, and she bowed low before Dorothy as she said, "Follow me and I will show you your room."

So Dorothy said good-bye to all her friends except Toto, and taking the dog in her arms followed the green girl through seven passages and up three flights of stairs until they came to a room at the front of the Palace. It was the sweetest little room in the world, with a soft comfortable bed that had sheets of green silk and a green velvet counterpane. There was a tiny fountain in the middle of the room, that shot a spray of green perfume into the air, to fall back into a beautifully carved green marble basin. Beautiful green flowers stood in the windows, and there was a shelf with a row of little green books. When Dorothy had time to open these books she found them full of queer green pictures that made her laugh, they were so funny.

In a wardrobe were many green dresses, made of silk and satin and velvet; and all of them fitted Dorothy exactly.

"Make yourself perfectly at home," said the green girl, "and if you wish for anything ring the bell. Oz will send for you tomorrow morning."

She left Dorothy alone and went back to the others. These she also led to rooms, and each one of them found himself lodged in a very pleasant part of the Palace. Of course this politeness was wasted on the Scarecrow; for when he found himself alone in his room he stood stupidly in one spot, just within the doorway, to wait till morning. It would not rest him to lie down, and he could not close his eyes; so he remained all night staring at a little spider which was weaving its web in a corner of the room, just as if it were not one of the most wonderful rooms in the world. The Tin Woodman lay down on his bed from force of habit, for he remembered when he was made of flesh; but not being able to sleep, he passed the night moving his joints up and down to make sure they kept in good working order. The Lion would have preferred a bed of dried leaves in the forest, and did not like being shut up in a room; but he had too much sense to let this worry him, so he sprang upon the bed and rolled himself up like a cat and purred himself asleep in a minute.

The next morning, after breakfast, the green maiden came to fetch Dorothy, and she dressed her in one of the prettiest gowns, made of green brocaded satin. Dorothy put on a green silk apron and tied a green ribbon around Toto's neck, and they started for the Throne Room of the Great Oz.

First they came to a great hall in which were many ladies and gentlemen of the court, all dressed in rich costumes. These

people had nothing to do but talk to each other, but they always came to wait outside the Throne Room every morning, although they were never permitted to see Oz. As Dorothy entered they looked at her curiously, and one of them whispered:

"Are you really going to look upon the face of Oz the Terrible?"

"Of course," answered the girl, "if he will see me."

"Oh, he will see you," said the soldier who had taken her message to the Wizard, "although he does not like to have people ask to see him. Indeed, at first he was angry and said I should send you back where you came from. Then he asked me what you looked like, and when I mentioned your silver shoes he was very much interested. At last I told him about the mark upon your forehead, and he decided he would admit you to his presence."

Just then a bell rang, and the green girl said to Dorothy, "That is the signal. You must go into the Throne Room alone."

She opened a little door and Dorothy walked boldly through and found herself in a wonderful place. It was a big, round room with a high arched roof, and the walls and ceiling and floor were covered with large emeralds set closely together. In the center of the roof was a great light, as bright as the sun, which made the emeralds sparkle in a wonderful manner.

But what interested Dorothy most was the big throne of green marble that stood in the middle of the room. It was shaped like a chair and sparkled with gems, as did everything else. In the center of the chair was an enormous Head, without a body to support it or any arms or legs whatever. There was no hair upon this head, but it had eyes and a nose and mouth, and was much bigger than the head of the biggest giant.

As Dorothy gazed upon this in wonder and fear, the eyes turned slowly and looked at her sharply and steadily. Then the mouth moved, and Dorothy heard a voice say:

"I am Oz, the Great and Terrible. Who are you, and why do you seek me?"

It was not such an awful voice as she had expected to come from the big Head; so she took courage and answered:

"I am Dorothy, the Small and Meek. I have come to you for help."

The eyes looked at her thoughtfully for a full minute. Then said the voice:

"Where did you get the silver shoes?"

"I got them from the Wicked Witch of the East, when my house fell on her and killed her," she replied.

"Where did you get the mark upon your forehead?" continued the voice.

"That is where the Good Witch of the North kissed me when she bade me good-bye and sent me to you," said the girl.

Again the eyes looked at her sharply, and they saw she was telling the truth. Then Oz asked, "What do you wish me to do?"

"Send me back to Kansas, where my Aunt Em and Uncle Henry are," she answered earnestly. "I don't like your country, although it is so beautiful. And I am sure Aunt Em will be dreadfully worried over my being away so long."

The eyes winked three times, and then they turned up to the ceiling and down to the floor and rolled around so queerly that they seemed to see every part of the room. And at last they looked at Dorothy again.

"Why should I do this for you?" asked Oz.

"Because you are strong and I am weak; because you are a Great Wizard and I am only a little girl."

"But you were strong enough to kill the Wicked Witch of the East," said Oz.

"That just happened," returned Dorothy simply; "I could not help it."

"Well," said the Head, "I will give you my answer. You have no right to expect me to send you back to Kansas unless you do something for me in return. In this country everyone must pay for everything he gets. If you wish me to use my magic power to send you home again you must do something for me first. Help me and I will help you."

"What must I do?" asked the girl.

"Kill the Wicked Witch of the West," answered Oz.

"But I cannot!" exclaimed Dorothy, greatly surprised.

"You killed the Witch of the East and you wear the silver shoes, which bear a powerful charm. There is now but one Wicked Witch left in all this land, and when you can tell me she is dead I will send you back to Kansas—but not before."

The little girl began to weep, she was so much disappointed; and the eyes winked again and looked upon her anxiously, as if the Great Oz felt that she could help him if she would.

"I never killed anything, willingly," she sobbed. "Even if I wanted to, how could I kill the Wicked Witch? If you, who are Great and Terrible, cannot kill her yourself, how do you expect me to do it?"

"I do not know," said the Head; "but that is my answer, and until the Wicked Witch dies you will not see your uncle and aunt again. Remember that the Witch is Wicked—tremendously Wicked -and ought to be killed. Now go, and do not ask to see me again until you have done your task."

Sorrowfully Dorothy left the Throne Room and went back where the Lion and the Scarecrow and the Tin Woodman were waiting to hear what Oz had said to her. "There is no hope for me," she said sadly, "for Oz will not send me home until I have killed the Wicked Witch of the West; and that I can never do."

Her friends were sorry, but could do nothing to help her; so Dorothy went to her own room and lay down on the bed and cried herself to sleep.

The next morning the soldier with the green whiskers came to the Scarecrow and said:

"Come with me, for Oz has sent for you."

So the Scarecrow followed him and was admitted into the great Throne Room, where he saw, sitting in the emerald throne, a most lovely Lady. She was dressed in green silk gauze and wore upon her flowing green locks a crown of jewels. Growing from her shoulders were wings, gorgeous in color and so light that they fluttered if the slightest breath of air reached them.

When the Scarecrow had bowed, as prettily as his straw stuffing would let him, before this beautiful creature, she looked upon him sweetly, and said:

"I am Oz, the Great and Terrible. Who are you, and why do you seek me?"

Now the Scarecrow, who had expected to see the great Head Dorothy had told him of, was much astonished; but he answered her bravely.

"I am only a Scarecrow, stuffed with straw. Therefore I have no brains, and I come to you praying that you will put brains in my head instead of straw, so that I may become as much a man as any other in your dominions."

"Why should I do this for you?" asked the Lady.

"Because you are wise and powerful, and no one else can help me," answered the Scarecrow.

"I never grant favors without some return," said Oz; "but this much I will promise. If you will kill for me the Wicked Witch of the West, I will bestow upon you a great many brains, and such good brains that you will be the wisest man in all the Land of Oz."

"I thought you asked Dorothy to kill the Witch," said the Scarecrow, in surprise.

"So I did. I don't care who kills her. But until she is dead I will not grant your wish. Now go, and do not seek me again until you have earned the brains you so greatly desire."

The Scarecrow went sorrowfully back to his friends and told them what Oz had said; and Dorothy was surprised to find that the Great Wizard was not a Head, as she had seen him, but a lovely Lady.

"All the same," said the Scarecrow, "she needs a heart as much as the Tin Woodman."

On the next morning the soldier with the green whiskers came to the Tin Woodman and said:

"Oz has sent for you. Follow me."

So the Tin Woodman followed him and came to the great Throne Room. He did not know whether he would find Oz a lovely Lady or a Head, but he hoped it would be the lovely Lady. "For," he said to himself, "if it is the head, I am sure I shall not be given a heart, since a head has no heart of its own and therefore cannot feel for me. But if it is the lovely Lady I shall beg hard for a heart, for all ladies are themselves said to be kindly hearted."

But when the Woodman entered the great Throne Room he saw neither the Head nor the Lady, for Oz had taken the shape of a most terrible Beast. It was nearly as big as an elephant, and the green throne seemed hardly strong enough to hold its weight. The Beast had a head like that of a rhinoceros, only there were five eyes in its face. There were five long arms growing out of its body, and it also had five long, slim legs. Thick, woolly hair covered every part of it, and a more dreadful-looking monster could not be imagined. It was fortunate the Tin Woodman had no heart at that moment, for it would have beat loud and fast from terror. But being only tin, the Woodman was not at all afraid, although he was much disappointed.

"I am Oz, the Great and Terrible," spoke the Beast, in a voice that was one great roar. "Who are you, and why do you seek me?"

"I am a Woodman, and made of tin. Therefore I have no heart, and cannot love. I pray you to give me a heart that I may be as other men are."

"Why should I do this?" demanded the Beast.

"Because I ask it, and you alone can grant my request," answered the Woodman.

Oz gave a low growl at this, but said, gruffly: "If you indeed desire a heart, you must earn it."

"How?" asked the Woodman.

"Help Dorothy to kill the Wicked Witch of the West," replied the Beast. "When the Witch is dead, come to me, and I will then give you the biggest and kindest and most loving heart in all the Land of Oz."

So the Tin Woodman was forced to return sorrowfully to his friends and tell them of the terrible Beast he had seen. They all wondered greatly at the many forms the Great Wizard could take upon himself, and the Lion said:

"If he is a Beast when I go to see him, I shall roar my loudest, and so frighten him that he will grant all I ask. And if he is the lovely Lady, I shall pretend to spring upon her, and so compel her to do my bidding. And if he is the great Head, he will be at my mercy; for I will roll this head all about the room until he promises to give us what we desire. So be of good cheer, my friends, for all will yet be well."

The next morning the soldier with the green whiskers led the Lion to the great Throne Room and bade him enter the presence of Oz.

The Lion at once passed through the door, and glancing around saw, to his surprise, that before the throne was a Ball of Fire, so fierce and glowing he could scarcely bear to gaze upon it. His first thought was that Oz had by accident caught on fire and was burning up; but when he tried to go nearer, the heat was so intense that it singed his whiskers, and he crept back tremblingly to a spot nearer the door.

Then a low, quiet voice came from the Ball of Fire, and these were the words it spoke:

"I am Oz, the Great and Terrible. Who are you, and why do you seek me?"

And the Lion answered, "I am a Cowardly Lion, afraid of everything. I came to you to beg that you give me courage, so that in reality I may become the King of Beasts, as men call me."

"Why should I give you courage?" demanded Oz.

"Because of all Wizards you are the greatest, and alone have power to grant my request," answered the Lion.

The Ball of Fire burned fiercely for a time, and the voice said,

"Bring me proof that the Wicked Witch is dead, and that moment I will give you courage. But as long as the Witch lives you must remain a coward."

The Lion was angry at this speech, but could say nothing in reply, and while he stood silently gazing at the Ball of Fire it became so furiously hot that he turned tail and rushed from the room. He was glad to find his friends waiting for him, and told them of his terrible interview with the Wizard.

"What shall we do now?" asked Dorothy sadly.

"There is only one thing we can do," returned the Lion, "and that is to go to the land of the Winkies, seek out the Wicked Witch and destroy her."

"But suppose we cannot?" said the girl.

"Then I shall never have courage," declared the Lion.

"And I shall never have brains," added the Scarecrow.

"And I shall never have a heart," spoke the Tin of Woodman.

"And I shall never see Aunt Em and Uncle Henry," said Dorothy beginning to cry.

"Be careful!" cried the green girl. "The tears will fall on your green silk gown and spot it."

So Dorothy dried her eyes and said, "I suppose we must try it but I am sure I do not want to kill anybody, even to see Aunt Em again."

"I will go with you; but I'm too much of a coward to kill the Witch," said the Lion.

"I will go too," declared the Scarecrow; "but I shall not be of much help to you, I am such a fool."

"I haven't the heart to harm even a Witch," remarked the Tin Woodman; "but if you go I certainly shall go with you."

Therefore it was decided to start upon their journey the next morning, and the Woodman sharpened his axe on a green grindstone and had all his joints properly oiled. The Scarecrow stuffed himself with fresh straw and Dorothy put new paint on his eyes that he might see better. The green girl, who was very kind to them, filled Dorothy's basket with good things to eat, and fastened a little bell around Toto's neck with a green ribbon.

They went to bed quite early and slept soundly until daylight when they were awakened by the crowing of a green cock that lived in the back yard of the Palace, and the cackling of a hen that had laid a green egg.

12. The Search for the Wicked Witch

The soldier with the green whiskers led them through the streets of the Emerald City until they reached the room where the Guardian of the Gates lived. This officer unlocked their spectacles to put them back in his great box, and then he politely opened the gate for our friends.

"Which road leads to the Wicked Witch of the West?" asked Dorothy.

"There is no road," answered the Guardian of the Gates. "No one ever wishes to go that way."

"How, then, are we to find her?" inquired the girl.

"That will be easy," replied the man, "for when she knows you are in the country of the Winkies she will find you, and make you all her slaves."

"Perhaps not," said the Scarecrow, "for we mean to destroy her."

"Oh, that is different," said the Guardian of the Gates. "No one has ever destroyed her before, so I naturally thought she would make slaves of you, as she has of the rest. But take care; for she is wicked and fierce, and may not allow you to destroy her. Keep to the West, where the sun sets, and you cannot fail to find her."

They thanked him and bade him good-bye, and turned toward the West, walking over fields of soft grass dotted here and there with daisies and buttercups. Dorothy still wore the pretty silk dress she had put on in the palace, but now, to her surprise, she found it was no longer green, but pure white. The ribbon around Toto's neck had also lost its green color and was as white as Dorothy's dress.

The Emerald City was soon left far behind. As they advanced the ground became rougher and hillier, for there were no farms nor houses in this country of the West, and the ground was untilled.

In the afternoon the sun shone hot in their faces, for there were no trees to offer them shade; so that before night Dorothy and Toto and the Lion were tired, and lay down upon the grass and fell asleep, with the Woodman and the Scarecrow keeping watch.

Now the Wicked Witch of the West had but one eye, yet that was as powerful as a telescope, and could see everywhere. So, as she sat in the door of her castle, she happened to look around and saw Dorothy lying asleep, with her friends all about her. They were a long distance off, but the Wicked Witch was angry to find them in her country; so she blew upon a silver whistle that hung around her neck.

At once there came running to her from all directions a pack of great wolves. They had long legs and fierce eyes and sharp teeth.

"Go to those people," said the Witch, "and tear them to pieces."

"Are you not going to make them your slaves?" asked the leader of the wolves.

"No," she answered, "one is of tin, and one of straw; one is a girl and another a Lion. None of them is fit to work, so you may tear them into small pieces."

"Very well," said the wolf, and he dashed away at full speed, followed by the others.

It was lucky the Scarecrow and the Woodman were wide awake and heard the wolves coming.

"This is my fight," said the Woodman, "so get behind me and I will meet them as they come."

He seized his axe, which he had made very sharp, and as the leader of the wolves came on the Tin Woodman swung his arm and chopped the wolf's head from its body, so that it immediately died. As soon as he could raise his axe another wolf came up, and he also fell under the sharp edge of the Tin Woodman's weapon. There were forty wolves, and forty times a wolf was killed, so that at last they all lay dead in a heap before the Woodman.

Then he put down his axe and sat beside the Scarecrow, who said, "It was a good fight, friend."

They waited until Dorothy awoke the next morning. The little girl was quite frightened when she saw the great pile of shaggy wolves, but the Tin Woodman told her all. She thanked him for saving them and sat down to breakfast, after which they started again upon their journey.

Now this same morning the Wicked Witch came to the door of her castle and looked out with her one eye that could see far off. She saw all her wolves lying dead, and the strangers still traveling through her country. This made her angrier than before, and she blew her silver whistle twice.

Straightway a great flock of wild crows came flying toward her, enough to darken the sky.

And the Wicked Witch said to the King Crow, "Fly at once to the strangers; peck out their eyes and tear them to pieces."

The wild crows flew in one great flock toward Dorothy and her companions. When the little girl saw them coming she was afraid.

But the Scarecrow said, "This is my battle, so lie down beside me and you will not be harmed."

So they all lay upon the ground except the Scarecrow, and he stood up and stretched out his arms. And when the crows saw him they were frightened, as these birds always are by scarecrows, and did not dare to come any nearer. But the King Crow said:

"It is only a stuffed man. I will peck his eyes out."

The King Crow flew at the Scarecrow, who caught it by the head and twisted its neck until it died. And then another crow flew at him, and the Scarecrow twisted its neck also. There were forty crows, and forty times the Scarecrow twisted a neck, until at last all were lying dead beside him. Then he called to his companions to rise, and again they went upon their journey.

When the Wicked Witch looked out again and saw all her crows lying in a heap, she got into a terrible rage, and blew three times upon her silver whistle.

Forthwith there was heard a great buzzing in the air, and a swarm of black bees came flying toward her.

"Go to the strangers and sting them to death!" commanded the Witch, and the bees turned and flew rapidly until they came to where Dorothy and her friends were walking. But the Woodman had seen them coming, and the Scarecrow had decided what to do.

"Take out my straw and scatter it over the little girl and the dog and the Lion," he said to the Woodman, "and the bees cannot sting them." This the Woodman did, and as Dorothy lay close beside the Lion and held Toto in her arms, the straw covered them entirely.

The bees came and found no one but the Woodman to sting, so they flew at him and broke off all their stings against the tin, without hurting the Woodman at all. And as bees cannot live when their stings are broken that was the end of the black bees, and they lay scattered thick about the Woodman, like little heaps of fine coal.

Then Dorothy and the Lion got up, and the girl helped the Tin Woodman put the straw back into the Scarecrow again, until he was as good as ever. So they started upon their journey once more.

The Wicked Witch was so angry when she saw her black bees in little heaps like fine coal that she stamped her foot and tore her hair and gnashed her teeth. And then she called a dozen of her slaves, who were the Winkies, and gave them sharp spears, telling them to go to the strangers and destroy them.

The Winkies were not a brave people, but they had to do as they were told. So they marched away until they came near to Dorothy. Then the Lion gave a great roar and sprang towards them, and the poor Winkies were so frightened that they ran back as fast as they could.

When they returned to the castle the Wicked Witch beat them well with a strap, and sent them back to their work, after which she sat down to think what she should do next. She could not understand how all her plans to destroy these strangers had failed; but she was a powerful Witch, as well as a wicked one, and she soon made up her mind how to act.

There was, in her cupboard, a Golden Cap, with a circle of diamonds and rubies running round it. This Golden Cap had a charm. Whoever owned it could call three times upon the Winged Monkeys, who would obey any order they were given. But no person could command these strange creatures more than three times. Twice already the Wicked Witch had used the charm of the Cap. Once was when she had made the Winkies her slaves, and set herself to rule over their country. The Winged Monkeys had helped her do this. The second time was when she had fought against the Great Oz himself, and driven him out of the land of the West. The Winged Monkeys had also helped her in doing this. Only once more could she use this Golden Cap, for which reason she did not like to do so until all her other powers were exhausted. But now that her fierce wolves and her wild crows and her stinging bees were gone, and her slaves had been scared away by the Cowardly Lion, she saw there was only one way left to destroy Dorothy and her friends.

So the Wicked Witch took the Golden Cap from her cupboard and placed it upon her head. Then she stood upon her left foot and said slowly:

"Ep-pe, pep-pe, kak-ke!"

Next she stood upon her right foot and said:

"Hil-lo, hol-lo, hel-lo!"

After this she stood upon both feet and cried in a loud voice:

"Ziz-zy, zuz-zy, zik!"

Now the charm began to work. The sky was darkened, and a low rumbling sound was heard in the air. There was a rushing of many wings, a great chattering and laughing, and the sun came out of the dark sky to show the Wicked Witch surrounded by a crowd of monkeys, each with a pair of immense and powerful wings on his shoulders.

One, much bigger than the others, seemed to be their leader. He flew close to the Witch and said, "You have called us for the third and last time. What do you command?"

"Go to the strangers who are within my land and destroy them all except the Lion," said the Wicked Witch. "Bring that beast to me, for I have a mind to harness him like a horse, and make him work."

"Your commands shall be obeyed," said the leader. Then, with a great deal of chattering and noise, the Winged Monkeys flew away to the place where Dorothy and her friends were walking.

Some of the Monkeys seized the Tin Woodman and carried him through the air until they were over a country thickly covered with sharp rocks. Here they dropped the poor Woodman, who fell a great distance to the rocks, where he lay so battered and dented that he could neither move nor groan.

Others of the Monkeys caught the Scarecrow, and with their long fingers pulled all of the straw out of his clothes and head. They made his hat and boots and clothes into a small bundle and threw it into the top branches of a tall tree.

The remaining Monkeys threw pieces of stout rope around the Lion and wound many coils about his body and head and legs, until he was unable to bite or scratch or struggle in any way. Then they lifted him up and flew away with him to the Witch's castle, where he was placed in a small yard with a high iron fence around it, so that he could not escape.

But Dorothy they did not harm at all. She stood, with Toto in her arms, watching the sad fate of her comrades and thinking it would soon be her turn. The leader of the Winged Monkeys flew up to her, his long, hairy arms stretched out and his ugly face grinning terribly; but he saw the mark of the Good Witch's kiss upon her forehead and stopped short, motioning the others not to touch her.

"We dare not harm this little girl," he said to them, "for she is protected by the Power of Good, and that is greater than the Power of Evil. All we can do is to carry her to the castle of the Wicked Witch and leave her there."

So, carefully and gently, they lifted Dorothy in their arms and carried her swiftly through the air until they came to the castle, where they set her down upon the front doorstep. Then the leader said to the Witch:

"We have obeyed you as far as we were able. The Tin Woodman and the Scarecrow are destroyed, and the Lion is tied up in your yard. The little girl we dare not harm, nor the dog she carries in her arms. Your power over our band is now ended, and you will never see us again."

Then all the Winged Monkeys, with much laughing and chattering and noise, flew into the air and were soon out of sight.

The Wicked Witch was both surprised and worried when she saw the mark on Dorothy's forehead, for she knew well that neither the Winged Monkeys nor she, herself, dare hurt the girl in any way. She looked down at Dorothy's feet, and seeing the Silver Shoes, began to tremble with fear, for she knew what a powerful charm belonged to them. At first the Witch was tempted to run away from Dorothy; but she happened to look into the child's eyes and saw how simple the soul behind them was, and that the little girl did not know of the wonderful power the Silver Shoes gave her. So the Wicked Witch laughed to herself, and thought, "I can still make her my slave, for she does not know how to use her power." Then she said to Dorothy, harshly and severely:

"Come with me; and see that you mind everything I tell you, for if you do not I will make an end of you, as I did of the Tin Woodman and the Scarecrow."

Dorothy followed her through many of the beautiful rooms in her castle until they came to the kitchen, where the Witch bade her clean the pots and kettles and sweep the floor and keep the fire fed with wood.

Dorothy went to work meekly, with her mind made up to work as hard as she could; for she was glad the Wicked Witch had decided not to kill her.

With Dorothy hard at work, the Witch thought she would go into the courtyard and harness the Cowardly Lion like a horse; it would amuse her, she was sure, to make him draw her chariot whenever she wished to go to drive. But as she opened the gate the Lion gave a loud roar and bounded at her so fiercely that the Witch was afraid, and ran out and shut the gate again.

"If I cannot harness you," said the Witch to the Lion, speaking through the bars of the gate, "I can starve you. You shall have nothing to eat until you do as I wish."

So after that she took no food to the imprisoned Lion; but every day she came to the gate at noon and asked, "Are you ready to be harnessed like a horse?"

And the Lion would answer, "No. If you come in this yard, I will bite you."

The reason the Lion did not have to do as the Witch wished was that every night, while the woman was asleep, Dorothy carried him food from the cupboard. After he had eaten he would lie down on his bed of straw, and Dorothy would lie beside him and put her head on his soft, shaggy mane, while they talked of their troubles and tried to plan some way to escape. But they could find no way to get out of the castle, for it was constantly guarded by the yellow Winkies, who were the slaves of the Wicked Witch and too afraid of her not to do as she told them.

The girl had to work hard during the day, and often the Witch threatened to beat her with the same old umbrella she always carried in her hand. But, in truth, she did not dare to strike Dorothy, because of the mark upon her forehead. The child did not know this, and was full of fear for herself and Toto. Once the Witch struck Toto a blow with her umbrella and the brave little dog flew at her and bit her leg in return. The Witch did not bleed where she was bitten, for she was so wicked that the blood in her had dried up many years before.

Dorothy's life became very sad as she grew to understand that it would be harder than ever to get back to Kansas and Aunt Em again. Sometimes she would cry bitterly for hours, with Toto sitting at her feet and looking into her face, whining dismally to show how sorry he was for his little mistress. Toto did not really care whether he was in Kansas or the Land of Oz so long as Dorothy was with him; but he knew the little girl was unhappy, and that made him unhappy too.

Now the Wicked Witch had a great longing to have for her own the Silver Shoes which the girl always wore. Her bees and her crows and her wolves were lying in heaps and drying up, and she had used up all the power of the Golden Cap; but if she could only get hold of the Silver Shoes, they would give her more power than all the other things she had lost. She watched Dorothy carefully, to see if she ever took off her shoes, thinking she might steal them. But the child was so proud of her pretty shoes that she never took them off except at night and when she took her bath. The Witch was too much afraid of the dark to dare go in Dorothy's room at night to take the shoes, and her dread of water was greater than her fear of the dark, so she never came near when Dorothy was bathing. Indeed, the old Witch never touched water, nor ever let water touch her in any way.

But the wicked creature was very cunning, and she finally thought of a trick that would give her what she wanted. She placed a bar of iron in the middle of the kitchen floor, and then by her magic arts made the iron invisible to human eyes. So that when Dorothy walked across the floor she stumbled over the bar, not being able to see it, and fell at full length. She was not much hurt, but in her fall one of the Silver Shoes came off; and before she could reach it, the Witch had snatched it away and put it on her own skinny foot.

The wicked woman was greatly pleased with the success of her trick, for as long as she had one of the shoes she owned half the power of their charm, and Dorothy could not use it against her, even had she known how to do so.

The little girl, seeing she had lost one of her pretty shoes, grew angry, and said to the Witch, "Give me back my shoe!"

"I will not," retorted the Witch, "for it is now my shoe, and not yours."

"You are a wicked creature!" cried Dorothy. "You have no right to take my shoe from me."

"I shall keep it, just the same," said the Witch, laughing at her, "and someday I shall get the other one from you, too."

This made Dorothy so very angry that she picked up the bucket of water that stood near and dashed it over the Witch, wetting her from head to foot.

Instantly the wicked woman gave a loud cry of fear, and then, as Dorothy looked at her in wonder, the Witch began to shrink and fall away.

"See what you have done!" she screamed. "In a minute I shall melt away."

"I'm very sorry, indeed," said Dorothy, who was truly frightened to see the Witch actually melting away like brown sugar before her very eyes.

"Didn't you know water would be the end of me?" asked the Witch, in a wailing, despairing voice.

"Of course not," answered Dorothy. "How should I?"

"Well, in a few minutes I shall be all melted, and you will have the castle to yourself. I have been wicked in my day, but I never thought a little girl like you would ever be able to melt me and end my wicked deeds. Look out—here I go!"

With these words the Witch fell down in a brown, melted, shapeless mass and began to spread over the clean boards of the kitchen floor. Seeing that she had really melted away to nothing, Dorothy drew another bucket of water and threw it over the mess. She then swept it all out the door. After picking out the silver shoe, which was all that was left of the old woman, she cleaned and dried it with a cloth, and put it on her foot again.

Then, being at last free to do as she chose, she ran out to the courtyard to tell the Lion that the Wicked Witch of the West had come to an end, and that they were no longer prisoners in a strange land.

13. The Rescue

The Cowardly Lion was much pleased to hear that the Wicked Witch had been melted by a bucket of water, and Dorothy at once unlocked the gate of his prison and set him free. They went in together to the castle, where Dorothy's first act was to call all the Winkies together and tell them that they were no longer slaves.

There was great rejoicing among the yellow Winkies, for they had been made to work hard during many years for the Wicked Witch, who had always treated them with great cruelty. They kept this day as a holiday, then and ever after, and spent the time in feasting and dancing.

"If our friends, the Scarecrow and the Tin Woodman, were only with us," said the Lion, "I should be quite happy."

"Don't you suppose we could rescue them?" asked the girl anxiously.

"We can try," answered the Lion.

So they called the yellow Winkies and asked them if they would help to rescue their friends, and the Winkies said that they would be delighted to do all in their power for Dorothy, who had set them free from bondage. So she chose a number of the Winkies who looked as if they knew the most, and they all started away. They traveled that day and part of the next until they came to the rocky plain where the Tin Woodman lay, all battered and bent. His axe was near him, but the blade was rusted and the handle broken off short.

The Winkies lifted him tenderly in their arms, and carried him back to the Yellow Castle again, Dorothy shedding a few tears by the way at the sad plight of her old friend, and the Lion looking sober and sorry. When they reached the castle Dorothy said to the Winkies:

"Are any of your people tinsmiths?"

"Oh, yes. Some of us are very good tinsmiths," they told her.

"Then bring them to me," she said. And when the tinsmiths came, bringing with them all their tools in baskets, she inquired, "Can you straighten out those dents in the Tin Woodman, and bend him back into shape again, and solder him together where he is broken?"

The tinsmiths looked the Woodman over carefully and then answered that they thought they could mend him so he would be as good as ever. So they set to work in one of the big yellow rooms of the castle and worked for three days and four nights, hammering and twisting and bending and soldering and polishing and pounding at the legs and body and head of the Tin Woodman, until at last he was straightened out into his old form, and his joints worked as well as ever. To be sure, there were several patches on him, but the tinsmiths did a good job, and as the Woodman was not a vain man he did not mind the patches at all.

When, at last, he walked into Dorothy's room and thanked her for rescuing him, he was so pleased that he wept tears of joy, and

Dorothy had to wipe every tear carefully from his face with her apron, so his joints would not be rusted. At the same time her own tears fell thick and fast at the joy of meeting her old friend again, and these tears did not need to be wiped away. As for the Lion, he wiped his eyes so often with the tip of his tail that it became quite wet, and he was obliged to go out into the courtyard and hold it in the sun till it dried.

"If we only had the Scarecrow with us again," said the Tin Woodman, when Dorothy had finished telling him everything that had happened, "I should be quite happy."

"We must try to find him," said the girl.

So she called the Winkies to help her, and they walked all that day and part of the next until they came to the tall tree in the branches of which the Winged Monkeys had tossed the Scarecrow's clothes.

It was a very tall tree, and the trunk was so smooth that no one could climb it; but the Woodman said at once, "I'll chop it down, and then we can get the Scarecrow's clothes."

Now while the tinsmiths had been at work mending the Woodman himself, another of the Winkies, who was a goldsmith, had made an axe-handle of solid gold and fitted it to the Woodman's axe, instead of the old broken handle. Others polished the blade until all the rust was removed and it glistened like burnished silver.

As soon as he had spoken, the Tin Woodman began to chop, and in a short time the tree fell over with a crash, whereupon the Scarecrow's clothes fell out of the branches and rolled off on the ground.

Dorothy picked them up and had the Winkies carry them back to the castle, where they were stuffed with nice, clean straw; and behold! here was the Scarecrow, as good as ever, thanking them over and over again for saving him.

Now that they were reunited, Dorothy and her friends spent a few happy days at the Yellow Castle, where they found everything they needed to make them comfortable.

But one day the girl thought of Aunt Em, and said, "We must go back to Oz, and claim his promise."

"Yes," said the Woodman, "at last I shall get my heart."

"And I shall get my brains," added the Scarecrow joyfully.

"And I shall get my courage," said the Lion thoughtfully.

"And I shall get back to Kansas," cried Dorothy, clapping her hands. "Oh, let us start for the Emerald City tomorrow!"

This they decided to do. The next day they called the Winkies together and bade them good-bye. The Winkies were sorry to have them go, and they had grown so fond of the Tin Woodman that they begged him to stay and rule over them and the Yellow Land of the West. Finding they were determined to go, the Winkies gave Toto and the Lion each a golden collar; and to Dorothy they presented a beautiful bracelet studded with diamonds; and to the Scarecrow they gave a gold-headed walking stick, to keep him from stumbling; and to the Tin Woodman they offered a silver oil-can, inlaid with gold and set with precious jewels.

Every one of the travelers made the Winkies a pretty speech in return, and all shook hands with them until their arms ached.

Dorothy went to the Witch's cupboard to fill her basket with food for the journey, and there she saw the Golden Cap. She tried it on her own head and found that it fitted her exactly. She did not know anything about the charm of the Golden Cap, but she saw that it was pretty, so she made up her mind to wear it and carry her sunbonnet in the basket.

Then, being prepared for the journey, they all started for the Emerald City; and the Winkies gave them three cheers and many good wishes to carry with them.

14. The Winged Monkeys

You will remember there was no road—not even a pathway—between the castle of the Wicked Witch and the Emerald City. When the four travelers went in search of the Witch she had seen them coming, and so sent the Winged Monkeys to bring them to her. It was much harder to find their way back through the big fields of buttercups and yellow daisies than it was being carried. They knew, of course, they must go straight east, toward the rising sun; and they started off in the right way. But at noon, when the sun was over their heads, they did not know which was east and which was west, and that was the reason they were lost in the great fields. They kept on walking, however, and at night the moon came out and shone brightly. So they lay down among the sweet smelling yellow flowers and slept soundly until morning— all but the Scarecrow and the Tin Woodman.

The next morning the sun was behind a cloud, but they started on, as if they were quite sure which way they were going.

"If we walk far enough," said Dorothy, "I am sure we shall sometime come to some place."

But day by day passed away, and they still saw nothing before them but the scarlet fields. The Scarecrow began to grumble a bit.

"We have surely lost our way," he said, "and unless we find it again in time to reach the Emerald City, I shall never get my brains."

"Nor I my heart," declared the Tin Woodman. "It seems to me I can scarcely wait till I get to Oz, and you must admit this is a very long journey."

"You see," said the Cowardly Lion, with a whimper, "I haven't the courage to keep tramping forever, without getting anywhere at all."

Then Dorothy lost heart. She sat down on the grass and looked at her companions, and they sat down and looked at her, and Toto found that for the first time in his life he was too tired to chase a butterfly that flew past his head. So he put out his tongue and panted and looked at Dorothy as if to ask what they should do next.

"Suppose we call the field mice," she suggested. "They could probably tell us the way to the Emerald City."

"To be sure they could," cried the Scarecrow. "Why didn't we think of that before?"

Dorothy blew the little whistle she had always carried about her neck since the Queen of the Mice had given it to her. In a few minutes they heard the pattering of tiny feet, and many of the small gray mice came running up to her. Among them was the Queen herself, who asked, in her squeaky little voice:

"What can I do for my friends?"

"We have lost our way," said Dorothy. "Can you tell us where the Emerald City is?"

"Certainly," answered the Queen; "but it is a great way off, for you have had it at your backs all this time." Then she noticed Dorothy's Golden Cap, and said, "Why don't you use the charm of the Cap, and call the Winged Monkeys to you? They will carry you to the City of Oz in less than an hour."

"I didn't know there was a charm," answered Dorothy, in surprise. "What is it?"

"It is written inside the Golden Cap," replied the Queen of the Mice. "But if you are going to call the Winged Monkeys we must run away, for they are full of mischief and think it great fun to plague us."

"Won't they hurt me?" asked the girl anxiously.

"Oh, no. They must obey the wearer of the Cap. Good-bye!" And she scampered out of sight, with all the mice hurrying after her.

Dorothy looked inside the Golden Cap and saw some words written upon the lining. These, she thought, must be the charm, so she read the directions carefully and put the Cap upon her head.

"Ep-pe, pep-pe, kak-ke!" she said, standing on her left foot.

"What did you say?" asked the Scarecrow, who did not know what she was doing.

"Hil-lo, hol-lo, hel-lo!" Dorothy went on, standing this time on her right foot.

"Hello!" replied the Tin Woodman calmly.

"Ziz-zy, zuz-zy, zik!" said Dorothy, who was now standing on both feet. This ended the saying of the charm, and they heard a great chattering and flapping of wings, as the band of Winged Monkeys flew up to them.

The King bowed low before Dorothy, and asked, "What is your command?"

"We wish to go to the Emerald City," said the child, "and we have lost our way."

"We will carry you," replied the King, and no sooner had he spoken than two of the Monkeys caught Dorothy in their arms and flew away with her. Others took the Scarecrow and the Woodman and the Lion, and one little Monkey seized Toto and flew after them, although the dog tried hard to bite him.

The Scarecrow and the Tin Woodman were rather frightened at first, for they remembered how badly the Winged Monkeys had treated them before; but they saw that no harm was intended, so they rode through the air quite cheerfully, and had a fine time looking at the pretty gardens and woods far below them.

Dorothy found herself riding easily between two of the biggest Monkeys, one of them the King himself. They had made a chair of their hands and were careful not to hurt her.

"Why do you have to obey the charm of the Golden Cap?" she asked.

"That is a long story," answered the King, with a Winged laugh; "but as we have a long journey before us, I will pass the time by telling you about it, if you wish."

"I shall be glad to hear it," she replied.

"Once," began the leader, "we were a free people, living happily in the great forest, flying from tree to tree, eating nuts and fruit, and doing just as we pleased without calling anybody master. Perhaps some of us were rather too full of mischief at times, flying down to pull the tails of the animals that had no wings, chasing birds, and throwing nuts at the people who walked in the forest. But we were careless and happy and full of fun, and enjoyed every minute of the day. This was many years ago, long before Oz came out of the clouds to rule over this land.

"There lived here then, away at the North, a beautiful princess, who was also a powerful sorceress. All her magic was used to help the people, and she was never known to hurt anyone who was good. Her name was Gayelette, and she lived in a handsome palace built from great blocks of ruby. Everyone loved her, but her greatest sorrow was that she could find no one to love in return, since all the men were much too stupid and ugly to mate with one so beautiful and wise. At last, however, she found a boy who was handsome and manly and wise beyond his years. Gayelette made up her mind that when he grew to be a man she would make him her husband, so she took him to her ruby palace and used all her magic powers to make him as strong and good and lovely as any woman could wish. When he grew to manhood, Quelala, as he was called, was said to be the best and wisest man in all the land, while his manly beauty was so great that Gayelette loved him dearly, and hastened to make everything ready for the wedding.

"My grandfather was at that time the King of the Winged Monkeys which lived in the forest near Gayelette's palace, and the old fellow loved a joke better than a good dinner. One day, just before the wedding, my grandfather was flying out with his band when he saw Quelala walking beside the river. He was dressed in a rich costume of pink silk and purple velvet, and my grandfather thought he would see what he could do. At his word the band flew down and seized Quelala, carried him in their arms until they were over the middle of the river, and then dropped him into the water.

"`Swim out, my fine fellow,' cried my grandfather, `and see if the water has spotted your clothes.' Quelala was much too wise not to swim, and he was not in the least spoiled by all his good fortune. He laughed, when he came to the top of the water, and swam in to shore. But when Gayelette came running out to him she found his silks and velvet all ruined by the river.

"The princess was angry, and she knew, of course, who did it. She had all the Winged Monkeys brought before her, and she said at first that their wings should be tied and they should be treated as they had treated Quelala, and dropped in the river. But my grandfather pleaded hard, for he knew the Monkeys would drown in the river with their wings tied, and Quelala said a kind word for them also; so that Gayelette finally spared them, on condition that the Winged Monkeys should ever after do three times the bidding of the owner of the Golden Cap. This Cap had been made for a wedding present to Quelala, and it is said to have cost the princess half her kingdom. Of course my

grandfather and all the other Monkeys at once agreed to the condition, and that is how it happens that we are three times the slaves of the owner of the Golden Cap, whosoever he may be."

"And what became of them?" asked Dorothy, who had been greatly interested in the story.

"Quelala being the first owner of the Golden Cap," replied the Monkey, "he was the first to lay his wishes upon us. As his bride could not bear the sight of us, he called us all to him in the forest after he had married her and ordered us always to keep where she could never again set eyes on a Winged Monkey, which we were glad to do, for we were all afraid of her.

"This was all we ever had to do until the Golden Cap fell into the hands of the Wicked Witch of the West, who made us enslave the Winkies, and afterward drive Oz himself out of the Land of the West. Now the Golden Cap is yours, and three times you have the right to lay your wishes upon us."

As the Monkey King finished his story Dorothy looked down and saw the green, shining walls of the Emerald City before them. She wondered at the rapid flight of the Monkeys, but was glad the journey was over. The strange creatures set the travelers down carefully before the gate of the City, the King bowed low to Dorothy, and then flew swiftly away, followed by all his band.

"That was a good ride," said the little girl.

"Yes, and a quick way out of our troubles," replied the Lion. "How lucky it was you brought away that wonderful Cap!"

15. The Discovery of Oz, the Terrible

The four travelers walked up to the great gate of Emerald City and rang the bell. After ringing several times, it was opened by the same Guardian of the Gates they had met before.

"What! are you back again?" he asked, in surprise.

"Do you not see us?" answered the Scarecrow.

"But I thought you had gone to visit the Wicked Witch of the West."

"We did visit her," said the Scarecrow.

"And she let you go again?" asked the man, in wonder.

"She could not help it, for she is melted," explained the Scarecrow.

"Melted! Well, that is good news, indeed," said the man. "Who melted her?"

"It was Dorothy," said the Lion gravely.

"Good gracious!" exclaimed the man, and he bowed very low indeed before her.

Then he led them into his little room and locked the spectacles from the great box on all their eyes, just as he had done before. Afterward they passed on through the gate into the Emerald City. When the people heard from the Guardian of the Gates that Dorothy had melted the Wicked Witch of the West, they all gathered around the travelers and followed them in a great crowd to the Palace of Oz.

The soldier with the green whiskers was still on guard before the door, but he let them in at once, and they were again met by the beautiful green girl, who showed each of them to their old rooms at once, so they might rest until the Great Oz was ready to receive them.

The soldier had the news carried straight to Oz that Dorothy and the other travelers had come back again, after destroying the Wicked Witch; but Oz made no reply. They thought the Great Wizard would send for them at once, but he did not. They had no word from him the next day, nor the next, nor the next. The waiting was tiresome and wearing, and at last they grew vexed that Oz should treat them in so poor a fashion, after sending them to undergo hardships and slavery. So the Scarecrow at last asked the green girl to take another message to Oz, saying if he did not let them in to see him at once they would call the Winged Monkeys to help them, and find out whether he kept his promises or not. When the Wizard was given this message he was so frightened that he sent word for them to come to the Throne Room at four minutes after nine o'clock the next morning. He had once met the Winged Monkeys in the Land of the West, and he did not wish to meet them again.

The four travelers passed a sleepless night, each thinking of the gift Oz had promised to bestow on him. Dorothy fell asleep only once, and then she dreamed she was in Kansas, where Aunt Em was telling her how glad she was to have her little girl at home again.

Promptly at nine o'clock the next morning the green-whiskered soldier came to them, and four minutes later they all went into the Throne Room of the Great Oz.

Of course each one of them expected to see the Wizard in the shape he had taken before, and all were greatly surprised when they looked about and saw no one at all in the room. They kept close to the door and closer to one another, for the stillness of the empty room was more dreadful than any of the forms they had seen Oz take.

Presently they heard a solemn Voice, that seemed to come from somewhere near the top of the great dome, and it said:

I am Oz, the Great and Terrible. Why do you seek me?"

They looked again in every part of the room, and then, seeing no one, Dorothy asked, "Where are you?"

I am everywhere," answered the Voice, "but to the eyes of common mortals I am invisible. I will now seat myself upon my throne, that you may converse with me." Indeed, the Voice seemed just then to come straight from the throne itself; so they walked toward it and stood in a row while Dorothy said:

We have come to claim our promise, O Oz."

What promise?" asked Oz.

You promised to send me back to Kansas when the Wicked Witch was destroyed," said the girl.

And you promised to give me brains," said the Scarecrow.

And you promised to give me a heart," said the Tin Woodman.

And you promised to give me courage," said the Cowardly Lion.

Is the Wicked Witch really destroyed?" asked the Voice, and

Dorothy thought it trembled a little.

"Yes," she answered, "I melted her with a bucket of water."

"Dear me," said the Voice, "how sudden! Well, come to me tomorrow, for I must have time to think it over."

"You've had plenty of time already," said the Tin Woodman angrily.

"We shan't wait a day longer," said the Scarecrow.

"You must keep your promises to us!" exclaimed Dorothy.

The Lion thought it might be as well to frighten the Wizard, so he gave a large, loud roar, which was so fierce and dreadful that Toto jumped away from him in alarm and tipped over the screen that stood in a corner. As it fell with a crash they looked that way, and the next moment all of them were filled with wonder. For they saw, standing in just the spot the screen had hidden, a little old man, with a bald head and a wrinkled face, who seemed to be as much surprised as they were. The Tin Woodman, raising his axe, rushed toward the little man and cried out, "Who are you?"

"I am Oz, the Great and Terrible," said the little man, in a trembling voice. "But don't strike me—please don't—and I'll do anything you want me to."

Our friends looked at him in surprise and dismay.

"I thought Oz was a great Head," said Dorothy.

"And I thought Oz was a lovely Lady," said the Scarecrow.

"And I thought Oz was a terrible Beast," said the Tin Woodman.

"And I thought Oz was a Ball of Fire," exclaimed the Lion.

"No, you are all wrong," said the little man meekly. "I have been making believe."

"Making believe!" cried Dorothy. "Are you not a Great Wizard?"

"Hush, my dear," he said. "Don't speak so loud, or you will be overheard—and I should be ruined. I'm supposed to be a Great Wizard."

"And aren't you?" she asked.

"Not a bit of it, my dear; I'm just a common man."

"You're more than that," said the Scarecrow, in a grieved tone; "you're a humbug."

"Exactly so!" declared the little man, rubbing his hands together as if it pleased him. "I am a humbug."

"But this is terrible," said the Tin Woodman. "How shall I ever get my heart?"

"Or I my courage?" asked the Lion.

"Or I my brains?" wailed the Scarecrow, wiping the tears from his eyes with his coat sleeve.

"My dear friends," said Oz, "I pray you not to speak of these little things. Think of me, and the terrible trouble I'm in at being found out."

"Doesn't anyone else know you're a humbug?" asked Dorothy.

"No one knows it but you four—and myself," replied Oz. "I have fooled everyone so long that I thought I should never be found out. It was a great mistake my ever letting you into the Throne Room. Usually I will not see even my subjects, and so they believe I am something terrible."

"But, I don't understand," said Dorothy, in bewilderment. "How was it that you appeared to me as a great Head?"

"That was one of my tricks," answered Oz. "Step this way, please, and I will tell you all about it."

He led the way to a small chamber in the rear of the Throne Room, and they all followed him. He pointed to one corner, in which lay the great Head, made out of many thicknesses of paper, and with a carefully painted face.

"This I hung from the ceiling by a wire," said Oz. "I stood behind the screen and pulled a thread, to make the eyes move and the mouth open."

"But how about the voice?" she inquired.

"Oh, I am a ventriloquist," said the little man. "I can throw the sound of my voice wherever I wish, so that you thought it was coming out of the Head. Here are the other things I used to deceive you." He showed the Scarecrow the dress and the mask he had worn when he seemed to be the lovely Lady. And the Tin Woodman saw that his terrible Beast was nothing but a lot of skins, sewn together, with slats to keep their sides out. As for the Ball of Fire, the false Wizard had hung that also from the ceiling. It was really a ball of cotton, but when oil was poured upon it the ball burned fiercely.

"Really," said the Scarecrow, "you ought to be ashamed of yourself for being such a humbug."

"I am—I certainly am," answered the little man sorrowfully; "but it was the only thing I could do. Sit down, please, there are plenty of chairs; and I will tell you my story."

So they sat down and listened while he told the following tale.

"I was born in Omaha—"

"Why, that isn't very far from Kansas!" cried Dorothy.

"No, but it's farther from here," he said, shaking his head at her sadly. "When I grew up I became a ventriloquist, and at that I was very well trained by a great master. I can imitate any kind of a bird or beast." Here he mewed so like a kitten that Toto pricked up his ears and looked everywhere to see where she was. "After a time," continued Oz, "I tired of that, and became a balloonist."

"What is that?" asked Dorothy.

"A man who goes up in a balloon on circus day, so as to draw a crowd of people together and get them to pay to see the circus," he explained.

"Oh," she said, "I know."

"Well, one day I went up in a balloon and the ropes got twisted, so that I couldn't come down again. It went way up above the clouds, so far that a current of air struck it and carried it many many miles away. For a day and a night I traveled through the air, and on the morning of the second day I awoke and found the balloon floating over a strange and beautiful country.

"It came down gradually, and I was not hurt a bit. But I found myself in the midst of a strange people, who, seeing me come from the clouds, thought I was a great Wizard. Of course I let them think so, because they were afraid of me, and promised to do anything I wished them to.

"Just to amuse myself, and keep the good people busy, I ordered them to build this City, and my Palace; and they did it all willingly and well. Then I thought, as the country was so green and beautiful, I would call it the Emerald City; and to make the name fit better I put green spectacles on all the people, so that everything they saw was green."

"But isn't everything here green?" asked Dorothy.

"No more than in any other city," replied Oz; "but when you wear green spectacles, why of course everything you see looks green to you. The Emerald City was built a great many years ago, for I was a young man when the balloon brought me here, and am a very old man now. But my people have worn green glasses on their eyes so long that most of them think it really is an Emerald City, and it certainly is a beautiful place, abounding in jewels and precious metals, and every good thing that is needed to make one happy. I have been good to the people, and they like me; but ever since this Palace was built, I have shut myself up and would not see any of them.

"One of my greatest fears was the Witches, for while I had no magical powers at all I soon found out that the Witches were really able to do wonderful things. There were four of them in this country, and they ruled the people who live in the North and South and East and West. Fortunately, the Witches of the North and South were good, and I knew they would do me no harm; but the Witches of the East and West were terribly wicked, and had they not thought I was more powerful than they themselves, they would surely have destroyed me. As it was, I lived in deadly fear of them for many years; so you can imagine how pleased I was when I heard your house had fallen on the Wicked Witch of the East. When you came to me, I was willing to promise anything if you would only do away with the other Witch; but now that you have melted her, I am ashamed to say that I cannot keep my promises."

"I think you are a very bad man," said Dorothy.

"Oh, no, my dear; I'm really a very good man, but I'm a very bad Wizard, I must admit."

"Can't you give me brains?" asked the Scarecrow.

"You don't need them. You are learning something every day. A baby has brains, but it doesn't know much. Experience is the only thing that brings knowledge, and the longer you are on earth the more experience you are sure to get."

"That may all be true," said the Scarecrow, "but I shall be very unhappy unless you give me brains."

The false Wizard looked at him carefully.

"Well," he said with a sigh, "I'm not much of a magician, as I said; but if you will come to me tomorrow morning, I will stuff your head with brains. I cannot tell you how to use them however; you must find that out for yourself."

"Oh, thank you—thank you!" cried the Scarecrow. "I'll find a way to use them, never fear!"

"But how about my courage?" asked the Lion anxiously.

"You have plenty of courage, I am sure," answered Oz. "All you need is confidence in yourself. There is no living thing that is not afraid when it faces danger. The True courage is in facing danger when you are afraid, and that kind of courage you have in plenty."

"Perhaps I have, but I'm scared just the same," said the Lion. "I shall really be very unhappy unless you give me the sort of courage that makes one forget he is afraid."

"Very well, I will give you that sort of courage tomorrow," replied Oz.

"How about my heart?" asked the Tin Woodman.

"Why, as for that," answered Oz, "I think you are wrong to want a heart. It makes most people unhappy. If you only knew it, you are in luck not to have a heart."

"That must be a matter of opinion," said the Tin Woodman. "For my part, I will bear all the unhappiness without a murmur, if you will give me the heart."

"Very well," answered Oz meekly. "Come to me tomorrow and you shall have a heart. I have played Wizard for so many years that I may as well continue the part a little longer."

"And now," said Dorothy, "how am I to get back to Kansas?"

"We shall have to think about that," replied the little man. "Give me two or three days to consider the matter and I'll try to find a way to carry you over the desert. In the meantime you shall all be treated as my guests, and while you live in the Palace my people will wait upon you and obey your slightest wish. There is only one thing I ask in return for my help—such as it is. You must keep my secret and tell no one I am a humbug."

They agreed to say nothing of what they had learned, and went back to their rooms in high spirits. Even Dorothy had hope that "The Great and Terrible Humbug," as she called him, would find a way to send her back to Kansas, and if he did she was willing to forgive him everything.

16. The Magic Art of the Great Humbug

Next morning the Scarecrow said to his friends:

"Congratulate me. I am going to Oz to get my brains at last. When I return I shall be as other men are."

"I have always liked you as you were," said Dorothy simply.

"It is kind of you to like a Scarecrow," he replied. "But surely you will think more of me when you hear the splendid thoughts my new brain is going to turn out." Then he said good-bye to them all in a cheerful voice and went to the Throne Room, where he rapped upon the door.

"Come in," said Oz.

The Scarecrow went in and found the little man sitting down by the window, engaged in deep thought.

"I have come for my brains," remarked the Scarecrow, a little uneasily.

"Oh, yes; sit down in that chair, please," replied Oz. "You must excuse me for taking your head off, but I shall have to do it in order to put your brains in their proper place."

"That's all right," said the Scarecrow. "You are quite welcome to take my head off, as long as it will be a better one when you put it on again."

So the Wizard unfastened his head and emptied out the straw. Then he entered the back room and took up a measure of bran, which he mixed with a great many pins and needles. Having shaken them together thoroughly, he filled the top of the Scarecrow's head with the mixture and stuffed the rest of the space with straw, to hold it in place.

When he had fastened the Scarecrow's head on his body again he said to him, "Hereafter you will be a great man, for I have given you a lot of bran-new brains."

The Scarecrow was both pleased and proud at the fulfillment of his greatest wish, and having thanked Oz warmly he went back to his friends.

Dorothy looked at him curiously. His head was quite bulged out at the top with brains.

"How do you feel?" she asked.

"I feel wise indeed," he answered earnestly. "When I get used to my brains I shall know everything."

"Why are those needles and pins sticking out of your head?" asked the Tin Woodman.

"That is proof that he is sharp," remarked the Lion.

"Well, I must go to Oz and get my heart," said the Woodman. So he walked to the Throne Room and knocked at the door.

"Come in," called Oz, and the Woodman entered and said, "I have come for my heart."

"Very well," answered the little man. "But I shall have to cut a hole in your breast, so I can put your heart in the right place. I hope it won't hurt you."

"Oh, no," answered the Woodman. "I shall not feel it at all."

So Oz brought a pair of tinsmith's shears and cut a small, square hole in the left side of the Tin Woodman's breast. Then, going to a chest of drawers, he took out a pretty heart, made entirely of silk and stuffed with sawdust.

"Isn't it a beauty?" he asked.

"It is, indeed!" replied the Woodman, who was greatly pleased. "But is it a kind heart?"

"Oh, very!" answered Oz. He put the heart in the Woodman's breast and then replaced the square of tin, soldering it neatly together where it had been cut.

"There," said he; "now you have a heart that any man might be proud of. I'm sorry I had to put a patch on your breast, but it really couldn't be helped."

"Never mind the patch," exclaimed the happy Woodman. "I am very grateful to you, and shall never forget your kindness."

"Don't speak of it," replied Oz.

Then the Tin Woodman went back to his friends, who wished him every joy on account of his good fortune.

The Lion now walked to the Throne Room and knocked at the door.

"Come in," said Oz.

"I have come for my courage," announced the Lion, entering the room.

"Very well," answered the little man; "I will get it for you."

He went to a cupboard and reaching up to a high shelf took down a square green bottle, the contents of which he poured into a green-gold dish, beautifully carved. Placing this before the Cowardly Lion, who sniffed at it as if he did not like it, the Wizard said:

"Drink."

"What is it?" asked the Lion.

"Well," answered Oz, "if it were inside of you, it would be courage. You know, of course, that courage is always inside one; so that this really cannot be called courage until you have swallowed it. Therefore I advise you to drink it as soon as possible."

The Lion hesitated no longer, but drank till the dish was empty.

"How do you feel now?" asked Oz.

"Full of courage," replied the Lion, who went joyfully back to his friends to tell them of his good fortune.

Oz, left to himself, smiled to think of his success in giving the Scarecrow and the Tin Woodman and the Lion exactly what they thought they wanted. "How can I help being a humbug," he said, "when all these people make me do things that everybody knows can't be done? It was easy to make the Scarecrow and the Lion and the Woodman happy, because they imagined I could do anything. But it will take more than imagination to carry Dorothy back to Kansas, and I'm sure I don't know how it can be done."

17. How the Balloon Was Launched

For three days Dorothy heard nothing from Oz. These were sad days for the little girl, although her friends were all quite happy and contented. The Scarecrow told them there were wonderful thoughts in his head; but he would not say what they were because he knew no one could understand them but himself. When the Tin Woodman walked about he felt his heart rattling around in his breast; and he told Dorothy he had discovered it to be a kinder and more tender heart than the one he had owned when he was made of flesh. The Lion declared he was afraid of nothing on earth, and would gladly face an army or a dozen of the fierce Kalidahs.

Thus each of the little party was satisfied except Dorothy, who longed more than ever to get back to Kansas.

On the fourth day, to her great joy, Oz sent for her, and when she entered the Throne Room he greeted her pleasantly:

"Sit down, my dear; I think I have found the way to get you out of this country."

"And back to Kansas?" she asked eagerly.

"Well, I'm not sure about Kansas," said Oz, "for I haven't the faintest notion which way it lies. But the first thing to do is to cross the desert, and then it should be easy to find your way home."

"How can I cross the desert?" she inquired.

"Well, I'll tell you what I think," said the little man. "You see, when I came to this country it was in a balloon. You also came through the air, being carried by a cyclone. So I believe the best way to get across the desert will be through the air. Now, it is quite beyond my powers to make a cyclone; but I've been thinking the matter over, and I believe I can make a balloon."

"How?" asked Dorothy.

"A balloon," said Oz, "is made of silk, which is coated with glue to keep the gas in it. I have plenty of silk in the Palace, so it will be no trouble to make the balloon. But in all this country there is no gas to fill the balloon with, to make it float."

"If it won't float," remarked Dorothy, "it will be of no use to us."

"True," answered Oz. "But there is another way to make it float, which is to fill it with hot air. Hot air isn't as good as gas, for if the air should get cold the balloon would come down in the desert, and we should be lost."

"We!" exclaimed the girl. "Are you going with me?"

"Yes, of course," replied Oz. "I am tired of being such a humbug. If I should go out of this Palace my people would soon discover I am not a Wizard, and then they would be vexed with me for having deceived them. So I have to stay shut up in these rooms all day, and it gets tiresome. I'd much rather go back to Kansas with you and be in a circus again."

"I shall be glad to have your company," said Dorothy.

"Thank you," he answered. "Now, if you will help me sew the silk together, we will begin to work on our balloon."

So Dorothy took a needle and thread, and as fast as Oz cut the strips of silk into proper shape the girl sewed them neatly together. First there was a strip of light green silk, then a strip of dark green and then a strip of emerald green; for Oz had a fancy to make the balloon in different shades of the color about them. It took three days to sew all the strips together, but when it was finished they had a big bag of green silk more than twenty feet long.

Then Oz painted it on the inside with a coat of thin glue, to make it airtight, after which he announced that the balloon was ready.

"But we must have a basket to ride in," he said. So he sent the soldier with the green whiskers for a big clothes basket, which he fastened with many ropes to the bottom of the balloon.

When it was all ready, Oz sent word to his people that he was going to make a visit to a great brother Wizard who lived in the clouds. The news spread rapidly throughout the city and everyone came to see the wonderful sight.

Oz ordered the balloon carried out in front of the Palace, and the people gazed upon it with much curiosity. The Tin Woodman had chopped a big pile of wood, and now he made a fire of it, and Oz held the bottom of the balloon over the fire so that the hot air that arose from it would be caught in the silken bag. Gradually the balloon swelled out and rose into the air, until finally the basket just touched the ground.

Then Oz got into the basket and said to all the people in a loud voice:

"I am now going away to make a visit. While I am gone the Scarecrow will rule over you. I command you to obey him as you would me."

The balloon was by this time tugging hard at the rope that held it to the ground, for the air within it was hot, and this made it so much lighter in weight than the air without that it pulled hard to rise into the sky.

"Come, Dorothy!" cried the Wizard. "Hurry up, or the balloon will fly away."

"I can't find Toto anywhere," replied Dorothy, who did not wish to leave her little dog behind. Toto had run into the crowd to bark at a kitten, and Dorothy at last found him. She picked him up and ran towards the balloon.

She was within a few steps of it, and Oz was holding out his hands to help her into the basket, when, crack! went the ropes, and the balloon rose into the air without her.

"Come back!" she screamed. "I want to go, too!"

"I can't come back, my dear," called Oz from the basket. "Good-bye!"

"Good-bye!" shouted everyone, and all eyes were turned upward to where the Wizard was riding in the basket, rising every moment farther and farther into the sky.

And that was the last any of them ever saw of Oz, the Wonderful Wizard, though he may have reached Omaha safely, and be there now, for all we know. But the people remembered him lovingly, and said to one another:

"Oz was always our friend. When he was here he built for us this beautiful Emerald City, and now he is gone he has left the Wise Scarecrow to rule over us."

Still, for many days they grieved over the loss of the Wonderful Wizard, and would not be comforted.

18. Away to the South

Dorothy wept bitterly at the passing of her hope to get home to Kansas again; but when she thought it all over she was glad she had not gone up in a balloon. And she also felt sorry at losing Oz, and so did her companions.

The Tin Woodman came to her and said:

"Truly I should be ungrateful if I failed to mourn for the man who gave me my lovely heart. I should like to cry a little because Oz is gone, if you will kindly wipe away my tears, so that I shall not rust."

"With pleasure," she answered, and brought a towel at once. Then the Tin Woodman wept for several minutes, and she watched the tears carefully and wiped them away with the towel. When he had finished, he thanked her kindly and oiled himself thoroughly with his jeweled oil-can, to guard against mishap.

The Scarecrow was now the ruler of the Emerald City, and although he was not a Wizard the people were proud of him. "For," they said, "there is not another city in all the world that is ruled by a stuffed man." And, so far as they knew, they were quite right.

The morning after the balloon had gone up with Oz, the four travelers met in the Throne Room and talked matters over. The Scarecrow sat in the big throne and the others stood respectfully before him.

"We are not so unlucky," said the new ruler, "for this Palace and the Emerald City belong to us, and we can do just as we please. When I remember that a short time ago I was up on a pole in a farmer's cornfield, and that now I am the ruler of this beautiful City, I am quite satisfied with my lot."

"I also," said the Tin Woodman, "am well-pleased with my new heart; and, really, that was the only thing I wished in all the world."

"For my part, I am content in knowing I am as brave as any beast that ever lived, if not braver," said the Lion modestly.

"If Dorothy would only be contented to live in the Emerald City," continued the Scarecrow, "we might all be happy together."

"But I don't want to live here," cried Dorothy. "I want to go to Kansas, and live with Aunt Em and Uncle Henry."

"Well, then, what can be done?" inquired the Woodman.

The Scarecrow decided to think, and he thought so hard that the pins and needles began to stick out of his brains. Finally he said:

"Why not call the Winged Monkeys, and ask them to carry you over the desert?"

"I never thought of that!" said Dorothy joyfully. "It's just the thing. I'll go at once for the Golden Cap."

When she brought it into the Throne Room she spoke the magic words, and soon the band of Winged Monkeys flew in through the open window and stood beside her.

"This is the second time you have called us," said the Monkey King, bowing before the little girl. "What do you wish?"

"I want you to fly with me to Kansas," said Dorothy.

But the Monkey King shook his head.

"That cannot be done," he said. "We belong to this country alone, and cannot leave it. There has never been a Winged Monkey in Kansas yet, and I suppose there never will be, for they don't belong there. We shall be glad to serve you in any way in our power, but we cannot cross the desert. Good-bye."

And with another bow, the Monkey King spread his wings and flew away through the window, followed by all his band.

Dorothy was ready to cry with disappointment. "I have wasted the charm of the Golden Cap to no purpose," she said, "for the Winged Monkeys cannot help me."

"It is certainly too bad!" said the tender-hearted Woodman.

The Scarecrow was thinking again, and his head bulged out so horribly that Dorothy feared it would burst.

"Let us call in the soldier with the green whiskers," he said, "and ask his advice."

So the soldier was summoned and entered the Throne Room timidly, for while Oz was alive he never was allowed to come farther than the door.

"This little girl," said the Scarecrow to the soldier, "wishes to cross the desert. How can she do so?"

"I cannot tell," answered the soldier, "for nobody has ever crossed the desert, unless it is Oz himself."

"Is there no one who can help me?" asked Dorothy earnestly.

"Glinda might," he suggested.

"Who is Glinda?" inquired the Scarecrow.

"The Witch of the South. She is the most powerful of all the Witches, and rules over the Quadlings. Besides, her castle stands on the edge of the desert, so she may know a way to cross it."

"Glinda is a Good Witch, isn't she?" asked the child.

"The Quadlings think she is good," said the soldier, "and she is kind to everyone. I have heard that Glinda is a beautiful woman, who knows how to keep young in spite of the many years she has lived."

"How can I get to her castle?" asked Dorothy.

"The road is straight to the South," he answered, "but it is said to be full of dangers to travelers. There are wild beasts in the woods, and a race of queer men who do not like strangers to cross their country. For this reason none of the Quadlings ever come to the Emerald City."

The soldier then left them and the Scarecrow said:

"It seems, in spite of dangers, that the best thing Dorothy can do is to travel to the Land of the South and ask Glinda to help her. For, of course, if Dorothy stays here she will never get back to Kansas."

"You must have been thinking again," remarked the Tin Woodman.

"I have," said the Scarecrow.

"I shall go with Dorothy," declared the Lion, "for I am tired of your city and long for the woods and the country again. I am really a wild beast, you know. Besides, Dorothy will need someone to protect her."

"That is true," agreed the Woodman. "My axe may be of servic to her; so I also will go with her to the Land of the South."

"When shall we start?" asked the Scarecrow.

"Are you going?" they asked, in surprise.

"Certainly. If it wasn't for Dorothy I should never have ha brains. She lifted me from the pole in the cornfield and brough me to the Emerald City. So my good luck is all due to her, and shall never leave her until she starts back to Kansas for good an all."

"Thank you," said Dorothy gratefully. "You are all very kind t me. But I should like to start as soon as possible."

"We shall go tomorrow morning," returned the Scarecrow. "S now let us all get ready, for it will be a long journey."

19. Attacked by the Fighting Trees

The next morning Dorothy kissed the pretty green girl good-by and they all shook hands with the soldier with the gree whiskers, who had walked with them as far as the gate. When th Guardian of the Gate saw them again he wondered greatly tha they could leave the beautiful City to get into new trouble. But h at once unlocked their spectacles, which he put back into th green box, and gave them many good wishes to carry with them.

"You are now our ruler," he said to the Scarecrow; "so you mu come back to us as soon as possible."

"I certainly shall if I am able," the Scarecrow replied; "but I mu help Dorothy to get home, first."

As Dorothy bade the good-natured Guardian a last farewell sh said:

"I have been very kindly treated in your lovely City, and everyor has been good to me. I cannot tell you how grateful I am."

"Don't try, my dear," he answered. "We should like to keep yc with us, but if it is your wish to return to Kansas, I hope you wi find a way." He then opened the gate of the outer wall, and the walked forth and started upon their journey.

The sun shone brightly as our friends turned their faces towar the Land of the South. They were all in the best of spirits, ar laughed and chatted together. Dorothy was once more filled wit the hope of getting home, and the Scarecrow and the Ti Woodman were glad to be of use to her. As for the Lion, h sniffed the fresh air with delight and whisked his tail from side side in pure joy at being in the country again, while Toto ra around them and chased the moths and butterflies, barkir merrily all the time.

"City life does not agree with me at all," remarked the Lion, a they walked along at a brisk pace. "I have lost much flesh since lived there, and now I am anxious for a chance to show the oth beasts how courageous I have grown."

They now turned and took a last look at the Emerald City. A they could see was a mass of towers and steeples behind th green walls, and high up above everything the spires and dom of the Palace of Oz.

"Oz was not such a bad Wizard, after all," said the Ti Woodman, as he felt his heart rattling around in his breast.

"He knew how to give me brains, and very good brains, too," said the Scarecrow.

"If Oz had taken a dose of the same courage he gave me," added the Lion, "he would have been a brave man."

Dorothy said nothing. Oz had not kept the promise he made her, but he had done his best, so she forgave him. As he said, he was a good man, even if he was a bad Wizard.

The first day's journey was through the green fields and bright flowers that stretched about the Emerald City on every side. They slept that night on the grass, with nothing but the stars over them; and they rested very well indeed.

In the morning they traveled on until they came to a thick wood. There was no way of going around it, for it seemed to extend to the right and left as far as they could see; and, besides, they did not dare change the direction of their journey for fear of getting lost. So they looked for the place where it would be easiest to get into the forest.

The Scarecrow, who was in the lead, finally discovered a big tree with such wide-spreading branches that there was room for the party to pass underneath. So he walked forward to the tree, but just as he came under the first branches they bent down and twined around him, and the next minute he was raised from the ground and flung headlong among his fellow travelers.

This did not hurt the Scarecrow, but it surprised him, and he looked rather dizzy when Dorothy picked him up.

"Here is another space between the trees," called the Lion.

"Let me try it first," said the Scarecrow, "for it doesn't hurt me to get thrown about." He walked up to another tree, as he spoke, but its branches immediately seized him and tossed him back again.

"This is strange," exclaimed Dorothy. "What shall we do?"

"The trees seem to have made up their minds to fight us, and stop our journey," remarked the Lion.

"I believe I will try it myself," said the Woodman, and shouldering his axe, he marched up to the first tree that had handled the Scarecrow so roughly. When a big branch bent down to seize him the Woodman chopped at it so fiercely that he cut it in two. At once the tree began shaking all its branches as if in pain, and the Tin Woodman passed safely under it.

"Come on!" he shouted to the others. "Be quick!" They all ran forward and passed under the tree without injury, except Toto, who was caught by a small branch and shaken until he howled. But the Woodman promptly chopped off the branch and set the little dog free.

The other trees of the forest did nothing to keep them back, so they made up their minds that only the first row of trees could bend down their branches, and that probably these were the policemen of the forest, and given this wonderful power in order to keep strangers out of it.

The four travelers walked with ease through the trees until they came to the farther edge of the wood. Then, to their surprise, they found before them a high wall which seemed to be made of white china. It was smooth, like the surface of a dish, and higher than their heads.

"What shall we do now?" asked Dorothy.

"I will make a ladder," said the Tin Woodman, "for we certainly must climb over the wall."

20. The Dainty China Country

While the Woodman was making a ladder from wood which he found in the forest Dorothy lay down and slept, for she was tired by the long walk. The Lion also curled himself up to sleep and Toto lay beside him.

The Scarecrow watched the Woodman while he worked, and said to him:

"I cannot think why this wall is here, nor what it is made of."

"Rest your brains and do not worry about the wall," replied the Woodman. "When we have climbed over it, we shall know what is on the other side."

After a time the ladder was finished. It looked clumsy, but the Tin Woodman was sure it was strong and would answer their purpose. The Scarecrow waked Dorothy and the Lion and Toto, and told them that the ladder was ready. The Scarecrow climbed up the ladder first, but he was so awkward that Dorothy had to follow close behind and keep him from falling off. When he got his head over the top of the wall the Scarecrow said, "Oh, my!"

"Go on," exclaimed Dorothy.

So the Scarecrow climbed farther up and sat down on the top of the wall, and Dorothy put her head over and cried, "Oh, my!" just as the Scarecrow had done.

Then Toto came up, and immediately began to bark, but Dorothy made him be still.

The Lion climbed the ladder next, and the Tin Woodman came last; but both of them cried, "Oh, my!" as soon as they looked over the wall. When they were all sitting in a row on the top of the wall, they looked down and saw a strange sight.

Before them was a great stretch of country having a floor as smooth and shining and white as the bottom of a big platter. Scattered around were many houses made entirely of china and painted in the brightest colors. These houses were quite small, the biggest of them reaching only as high as Dorothy's waist. There were also pretty little barns, with china fences around them; and many cows and sheep and horses and pigs and chickens, all made of china, were standing about in groups.

But the strangest of all were the people who lived in this queer country. There were milkmaids and shepherdesses, with brightly colored bodices and golden spots all over their gowns; and princesses with most gorgeous frocks of silver and gold and purple; and shepherds dressed in knee breeches with pink and yellow and blue stripes down them, and golden buckles on their shoes; and princes with jeweled crowns upon their heads, wearing ermine robes and satin doublets; and funny clowns in ruffled gowns, with round red spots upon their cheeks and tall, pointed caps. And, strangest of all, these people were all made of china, even to their clothes, and were so small that the tallest of them was no higher than Dorothy's knee.

No one did so much as look at the travelers at first, except one little purple china dog with an extra-large head, which came to the wall and barked at them in a tiny voice, afterwards running away again.

"How shall we get down?" asked Dorothy.

They found the ladder so heavy they could not pull it up, so the Scarecrow fell off the wall and the others jumped down upon him so that the hard floor would not hurt their feet. Of course they took pains not to light on his head and get the pins in their feet. When all were safely down they picked up the Scarecrow, whose body was quite flattened out, and patted his straw into shape again.

"We must cross this strange place in order to get to the other side," said Dorothy, "for it would be unwise for us to go any other way except due South."

They began walking through the country of the china people, and the first thing they came to was a china milkmaid milking a china cow. As they drew near, the cow suddenly gave a kick and kicked over the stool, the pail, and even the milkmaid herself, and all fell on the china ground with a great clatter.

Dorothy was shocked to see that the cow had broken her leg off, and that the pail was lying in several small pieces, while the poor milkmaid had a nick in her left elbow.

"There!" cried the milkmaid angrily. "See what you have done! My cow has broken her leg, and I must take her to the mender's shop and have it glued on again. What do you mean by coming here and frightening my cow?"

"I'm very sorry," returned Dorothy. "Please forgive us."

But the pretty milkmaid was much too vexed to make any answer. She picked up the leg sulkily and led her cow away, the poor animal limping on three legs. As she left them the milkmaid cast many reproachful glances over her shoulder at the clumsy strangers, holding her nicked elbow close to her side.

Dorothy was quite grieved at this mishap.

"We must be very careful here," said the kind-hearted Woodman, "or we may hurt these pretty little people so they will never get over it."

A little farther on Dorothy met a most beautifully dressed young Princess, who stopped short as she saw the strangers and started to run away.

Dorothy wanted to see more of the Princess, so she ran after her. But the china girl cried out:

"Don't chase me! Don't chase me!"

She had such a frightened little voice that Dorothy stopped and said, "Why not?"

"Because," answered the Princess, also stopping, a safe distance away, "if I run I may fall down and break myself."

"But could you not be mended?" asked the girl.

"Oh, yes; but one is never so pretty after being mended, you know," replied the Princess.

"I suppose not," said Dorothy.

"Now there is Mr. Joker, one of our clowns," continued the china lady, "who is always trying to stand upon his head. He has broken himself so often that he is mended in a hundred places, and doesn't look at all pretty. Here he comes now, so you can see for yourself."

Indeed, a jolly little clown came walking toward them, and Dorothy could see that in spite of his pretty clothes of red and yellow and green he was completely covered with cracks, running every which way and showing plainly that he had been mended in many places.

The Clown put his hands in his pockets, and after puffing out his cheeks and nodding his head at them saucily, he said:

"My lady fair, Why do you stare At poor old Mr. Joker? You're quite as stiff And prim as if You'd eaten up a poker!"

"Be quiet, sir!" said the Princess. "Can't you see these are strangers, and should be treated with respect?"

"Well, that's respect, I expect," declared the Clown, and immediately stood upon his head.

"Don't mind Mr. Joker," said the Princess to Dorothy. "He is considerably cracked in his head, and that makes him foolish."

"Oh, I don't mind him a bit," said Dorothy. "But you are so beautiful," she continued, "that I am sure I could love you dearly. Won't you let me carry you back to Kansas, and stand you on Aunt Em's mantel? I could carry you in my basket."

"That would make me very unhappy," answered the china Princess. "You see, here in our country we live contentedly, and can talk and move around as we please. But whenever any of us are taken away our joints at once stiffen, and we can only stand straight and look pretty. Of course that is all that is expected of us when we are on mantels and cabinets and drawing-room tables, but our lives are much pleasanter here in our own country."

"I would not make you unhappy for all the world!" exclaimed Dorothy. "So I'll just say good-bye."

"Good-bye," replied the Princess.

They walked carefully through the china country. The little animals and all the people scampered out of their way, fearing the strangers would break them, and after an hour or so the travelers reached the other side of the country and came to another china wall.

It was not so high as the first, however, and by standing upon the Lion's back they all managed to scramble to the top. Then the Lion gathered his legs under him and jumped on the wall; but just as he jumped, he upset a china church with his tail and smashed it all to pieces.

"That was too bad," said Dorothy, "but really I think we were lucky in not doing these little people more harm than breaking a cow's leg and a church. They are all so brittle!"

"They are, indeed," said the Scarecrow, "and I am thankful I am made of straw and cannot be easily damaged. There are worse things in the world than being a Scarecrow."

21. The Lion Becomes the King of Beasts

After climbing down from the china wall the travelers found themselves in a disagreeable country, full of bogs and marshes and covered with tall, rank grass. It was difficult to walk without falling into muddy holes, for the grass was so thick that it hid them from sight. However, by carefully picking their way, they got safely along until they reached solid ground. But here the country seemed wilder than ever, and after a long and tiresome walk through the underbrush they entered another forest, where the trees were bigger and older than any they had ever seen.

"This forest is perfectly delightful," declared the Lion, looking around him with joy. "Never have I seen a more beautiful place."

"It seems gloomy," said the Scarecrow.

"Not a bit of it," answered the Lion. "I should like to live here all my life. See how soft the dried leaves are under your feet and how rich and green the moss is that clings to these old trees. Surely no wild beast could wish a pleasanter home."

"Perhaps there are wild beasts in the forest now," said Dorothy.

"I suppose there are," returned the Lion, "but I do not see any of them about."

They walked through the forest until it became too dark to go any farther. Dorothy and Toto and the Lion lay down to sleep, while the Woodman and the Scarecrow kept watch over them as usual.

When morning came, they started again. Before they had gone far they heard a low rumble, as of the growling of many wild animals. Toto whimpered a little, but none of the others was frightened, and they kept along the well-trodden path until they came to an opening in the wood, in which were gathered hundreds of beasts of every variety. There were tigers and elephants and bears and wolves and foxes and all the others in the natural history, and for a moment Dorothy was afraid. But the Lion explained that the animals were holding a meeting, and he judged by their snarling and growling that they were in great trouble.

As he spoke several of the beasts caught sight of him, and at once the great assemblage hushed as if by magic. The biggest of the tigers came up to the Lion and bowed, saying:

"Welcome, O King of Beasts! You have come in good time to fight our enemy and bring peace to all the animals of the forest once more."

"What is your trouble?" asked the Lion quietly.

"We are all threatened," answered the tiger, "by a fierce enemy which has lately come into this forest. It is a most tremendous monster, like a great spider, with a body as big as an elephant and legs as long as a tree trunk. It has eight of these long legs, and as the monster crawls through the forest he seizes an animal with a leg and drags it to his mouth, where he eats it as a spider does a fly. Not one of us is safe while this fierce creature is alive, and we had called a meeting to decide how to take care of ourselves when you came among us."

The Lion thought for a moment.

"Are there any other lions in this forest?" he asked.

"No; there were some, but the monster has eaten them all. And,

besides, they were none of them nearly so large and brave as you."

"If I put an end to your enemy, will you bow down to me and obey me as King of the Forest?" inquired the Lion.

"We will do that gladly," returned the tiger; and all the other beasts roared with a mighty roar: "We will!"

"Where is this great spider of yours now?" asked the Lion.

"Yonder, among the oak trees," said the tiger, pointing with his forefoot.

"Take good care of these friends of mine," said the Lion, "and I will go at once to fight the monster."

He bade his comrades good-bye and marched proudly away to do battle with the enemy.

The great spider was lying asleep when the Lion found him, and it looked so ugly that its foe turned up his nose in disgust. Its legs were quite as long as the tiger had said, and its body covered with coarse black hair. It had a great mouth, with a row of sharp teeth a foot long; but its head was joined to the pudgy body by a neck as slender as a wasp's waist. This gave the Lion a hint of the best way to attack the creature, and as he knew it was easier to fight it asleep than awake, he gave a great spring and landed directly upon the monster's back. Then, with one blow of his heavy paw, all armed with sharp claws, he knocked the spider's head from its body. Jumping down, he watched it until the long legs stopped wiggling, when he knew it was quite dead.

The Lion went back to the opening where the beasts of the forest were waiting for him and said proudly:

"You need fear your enemy no longer."

Then the beasts bowed down to the Lion as their King, and he promised to come back and rule over them as soon as Dorothy was safely on her way to Kansas.

22. The Country of the Quadlings

The four travelers passed through the rest of the forest in safety, and when they came out from its gloom saw before them a steep hill, covered from top to bottom with great pieces of rock.

"That will be a hard climb," said the Scarecrow, "but we must get over the hill, nevertheless."

So he led the way and the others followed. They had nearly reached the first rock when they heard a rough voice cry out, "Keep back!"

"Who are you?" asked the Scarecrow.

Then a head showed itself over the rock and the same voice said, "This hill belongs to us, and we don't allow anyone to cross it."

"But we must cross it," said the Scarecrow. "We're going to the country of the Quadlings."

"But you shall not!" replied the voice, and there stepped from behind the rock the strangest man the travelers had ever seen.

He was quite short and stout and had a big head, which was flat at the top and supported by a thick neck full of wrinkles. But he had no arms at all, and, seeing this, the Scarecrow did not fear that so helpless a creature could prevent them from climbing the hill. So he said, "I'm sorry not to do as you wish, but we must pass over your hill whether you like it or not," and he walked boldly forward.

As quick as lightning the man's head shot forward and his neck stretched out until the top of the head, where it was flat, struck the Scarecrow in the middle and sent him tumbling, over and over, down the hill. Almost as quickly as it came the head went back to the body, and the man laughed harshly as he said, "It isn't as easy as you think!"

A chorus of boisterous laughter came from the other rocks, and Dorothy saw hundreds of the armless Hammer-Heads upon the hillside, one behind every rock.

The Lion became quite angry at the laughter caused by the Scarecrow's mishap, and giving a loud roar that echoed like thunder, he dashed up the hill.

Again a head shot swiftly out, and the great Lion went rolling down the hill as if he had been struck by a cannon ball.

Dorothy ran down and helped the Scarecrow to his feet, and the Lion came up to her, feeling rather bruised and sore, and said, "It is useless to fight people with shooting heads; no one can withstand them."

"What can we do, then?" she asked.

"Call the Winged Monkeys," suggested the Tin Woodman. "You have still the right to command them once more."

"Very well," she answered, and putting on the Golden Cap she uttered the magic words. The Monkeys were as prompt as ever, and in a few moments the entire band stood before her.

"What are your commands?" inquired the King of the Monkeys, bowing low.

"Carry us over the hill to the country of the Quadlings," answered the girl.

"It shall be done," said the King, and at once the Winged Monkeys caught the four travelers and Toto up in their arms and flew away with them. As they passed over the hill the Hammer-Heads yelled with vexation, and shot their heads high in the air, but they could not reach the Winged Monkeys, which carried Dorothy and her comrades safely over the hill and set them down in the beautiful country of the Quadlings.

"This is the last time you can summon us," said the leader to Dorothy; "so good-bye and good luck to you."

"Good-bye, and thank you very much," returned the girl; and the Monkeys rose into the air and were out of sight in a twinkling.

The country of the Quadlings seemed rich and happy. There was field upon field of ripening grain, with well-paved roads running between, and pretty rippling brooks with strong bridges across them. The fences and houses and bridges were all painted bright red, just as they had been painted yellow in the country of the Winkies and blue in the country of the Munchkins. The Quadlings themselves, who were short and fat and looked chubby and good-natured, were dressed all in red, which showed bright against the green grass and the yellowing grain.

The Monkeys had set them down near a farmhouse, and the four travelers walked up to it and knocked at the door. It was opened by the farmer's wife, and when Dorothy asked for something to eat the woman gave them all a good dinner, with three kinds of cake and four kinds of cookies, and a bowl of milk for Toto.

"How far is it to the Castle of Glinda?" asked the child.

"It is not a great way," answered the farmer's wife. "Take the road to the South and you will soon reach it."

Thanking the good woman, they started afresh and walked by the fields and across the pretty bridges until they saw before them a very beautiful Castle. Before the gates were three young girls, dressed in handsome red uniforms trimmed with gold braid; and as Dorothy approached, one of them said to her:

"Why have you come to the South Country?"

"To see the Good Witch who rules here," she answered. "Will you take me to her?"

"Let me have your name, and I will ask Glinda if she will receive you." They told who they were, and the girl soldier went into the Castle. After a few moments she came back to say that Dorothy and the others were to be admitted at once.

23. Glinda The Good Witch Grants Dorothy's Wish

Before they went to see Glinda, however, they were taken to a room of the Castle, where Dorothy washed her face and combed her hair, and the Lion shook the dust out of his mane, and the Scarecrow patted himself into his best shape, and the Woodman polished his tin and oiled his joints.

When they were all quite presentable they followed the soldier girl into a big room where the Witch Glinda sat upon a throne of rubies.

She was both beautiful and young to their eyes. Her hair was a rich red in color and fell in flowing ringlets over her shoulders. Her dress was pure white but her eyes were blue, and they looked kindly upon the little girl.

"What can I do for you, my child?" she asked.

Dorothy told the Witch all her story: how the cyclone had brought her to the Land of Oz, how she had found her companions, and of the wonderful adventures they had met with.

"My greatest wish now," she added, "is to get back to Kansas, for Aunt Em will surely think something dreadful has happened to me, and that will make her put on mourning; and unless the crops are better this year than they were last, I am sure Uncle Henry cannot afford it."

Glinda leaned forward and kissed the sweet, upturned face of the loving little girl.

"Bless your dear heart," she said, "I am sure I can tell you of a way to get back to Kansas." Then she added, "But, if I do, you must give me the Golden Cap."

"Willingly!" exclaimed Dorothy; "indeed, it is of no use to me now, and when you have it you can command the Winged Monkeys three times."

"And I think I shall need their service just those three times," answered Glinda, smiling.

Dorothy then gave her the Golden Cap, and the Witch said to the Scarecrow, "What will you do when Dorothy has left us?"

"I will return to the Emerald City," he replied, "for Oz has made me its ruler and the people like me. The only thing that worries me is how to cross the hill of the Hammer-Heads."

"By means of the Golden Cap I shall command the Winged Monkeys to carry you to the gates of the Emerald City," said Glinda, "for it would be a shame to deprive the people of so wonderful a ruler."

"Am I really wonderful?" asked the Scarecrow.

"You are unusual," replied Glinda.

Turning to the Tin Woodman, she asked, "What will become of you when Dorothy leaves this country?"

He leaned on his axe and thought a moment. Then he said, "The Winkies were very kind to me, and wanted me to rule over them after the Wicked Witch died. I am fond of the Winkies, and if I could get back again to the Country of the West, I should like nothing better than to rule over them forever."

"My second command to the Winged Monkeys," said Glinda "will be that they carry you safely to the land of the Winkies. Your brain may not be so large to look at as those of the Scarecrow, but you are really brighter than he is—when you are well polished— and I am sure you will rule the Winkies wisely and well."

Then the Witch looked at the big, shaggy Lion and asked, "When Dorothy has returned to her own home, what will become of you?"

"Over the hill of the Hammer-Heads," he answered, "lies a grand old forest, and all the beasts that live there have made me their King. If I could only get back to this forest, I would pass my life very happily there."

"My third command to the Winged Monkeys," said Glinda, "shall be to carry you to your forest. Then, having used up the powers of the Golden Cap, I shall give it to the King of the Monkeys, that he and his band may thereafter be free for evermore."

The Scarecrow and the Tin Woodman and the Lion now thanked the Good Witch earnestly for her kindness; and Dorothy exclaimed:

"You are certainly as good as you are beautiful! But you have not yet told me how to get back to Kansas."

"Your Silver Shoes will carry you over the desert," replied Glinda. "If you had known their power you could have gone back to your Aunt Em the very first day you came to this country."

"But then I should not have had my wonderful brains!" cried the Scarecrow. "I might have passed my whole life in the farmer's cornfield."

"And I should not have had my lovely heart," said the Tin Woodman. "I might have stood and rusted in the forest till the end of the world."

"And I should have lived a coward forever," declared the Lion, "and no beast in all the forest would have had a good word to say to me."

"This is all true," said Dorothy, "and I am glad I was of use to these good friends. But now that each of them has had what he most desired, and each is happy in having a kingdom to rule besides, I think I should like to go back to Kansas."

"The Silver Shoes," said the Good Witch, "have wonderful powers. And one of the most curious things about them is that they can carry you to any place in the world in three steps, and each step will be made in the wink of an eye. All you have to do is to knock the heels together three times and command the shoes to carry you wherever you wish to go."

"If that is so," said the child joyfully, "I will ask them to carry me back to Kansas at once."

She threw her arms around the Lion's neck and kissed him, patting his big head tenderly. Then she kissed the Tin Woodman, who was weeping in a way most dangerous to his joints. But she hugged the soft, stuffed body of the Scarecrow in her arms instead of kissing his painted face, and found she was crying herself at this sorrowful parting from her loving comrades.

Glinda the Good stepped down from her ruby throne to give the little girl a good-bye kiss, and Dorothy thanked her for all the kindness she had shown to her friends and herself.

Dorothy now took Toto up solemnly in her arms, and having said one last good-bye she clapped the heels of her shoes together three times, saying:

"Take me home to Aunt Em!"

Instantly she was whirling through the air, so swiftly that all she could see or feel was the wind whistling past her ears.

The Silver Shoes took but three steps, and then she stopped so suddenly that she rolled over upon the grass several times before she knew where she was.

At length, however, she sat up and looked about her.

"Good gracious!" she cried.

For she was sitting on the broad Kansas prairie, and just before her was the new farmhouse Uncle Henry built after the cyclone had carried away the old one. Uncle Henry was milking the cows in the barnyard, and Toto had jumped out of her arms and was running toward the barn, barking furiously.

Dorothy stood up and found she was in her stocking-feet. For the Silver Shoes had fallen off in her flight through the air, and were lost forever in the desert.

24. Home Again

Aunt Em had just come out of the house to water the cabbages when she looked up and saw Dorothy running toward her.

"My darling child!" she cried, folding the little girl in her arms and covering her face with kisses. "Where in the world did you come from?"

"From the Land of Oz," said Dorothy gravely. "And here is Toto, too. And oh, Aunt Em! I'm so glad to be at home again!"

The Marvelous Land of Oz
by L. Frank Baum

The Marvelous Land of Oz, being an account of the further adventures of the Scarecrow and Tin Woodman and also the strange experiences of the highly magnified Woggle-Bug, Jack Pumpkin-head, the Animated Saw-Horse and the Gump; the story being A Sequel to The Wizard of Oz.
By L. Frank Baum, Author of Father Goose-His Book; The Wizard of Oz; The Magical Monarch of Mo; The Enchanted Isle of Yew; The Life and Adventures of Santa Claus; Dot and Tot of Merryland etc. etc.

Author's Note

AFTER the publication of "The Wonderful Wizard of Oz" I began to receive letters from children, telling me of their pleasure in reading the story and asking me to "write something more" about the Scarecrow and the Tin Woodman. At first I considered these little letters, frank and earnest though they were, in the light of pretty compliments; but the letters continued to come during succeeding months, and even years.

Finally I promised one little girl, who made a long journey to see me and proffer her request, — and she is a "Dorothy," by the way — that when a thousand little girls had written me a thousand little letters asking for the Scarecrow and the Tin Woodman I would write the book. Either little Dorothy was a fairy in disguise, and waved her magic wand, or the success of the stage production of "The Wizard of Oz" made new friends for the story, for the thousand letters reached their destination long since — and many more followed them.

And now, although pleading guilty to long delay, I have kept my promise in this book.

L. Frank Baum.
Chicago, June, 1904

To those excellent good fellows and comedians David C. Montgomery and Frank A. Stone whose clever personations of the Tin Woodman and the Scarecrow have delighted thousands of children throughout the land, this book is gratefully dedicated by the author.

Tip Manufactures a Pumpkinhead

In the Country of the Gillikins, which is at the North of the Land of Oz, lived a youth called Tip. There was more to his name than that, for old Mombi often declared that his whole name was Tippetarius; but no one was expected to say such a long word when "Tip" would do just as well.

This boy remembered nothing of his parents, for he had been brought when quite young to be reared by the old woman known as Mombi, whose reputation, I am sorry to say, was none of the best. For the Gillikin people had reason to suspect her of indulging in magical arts, and therefore hesitated to associate with her.

Mombi was not exactly a Witch, because the Good Witch who ruled that part of the Land of Oz had forbidden any other Witch to exist in her dominions. So Tip's guardian, however much she might aspire to working magic, realized it was unlawful to be more than a Sorceress, or at most a Wizardess.

Tip was made to carry wood from the forest, that the old woman might boil her pot. He also worked in the corn-fields, hoeing and husking; and he fed the pigs and milked the four-horned cow that was Mombi's especial pride.

But you must not suppose he worked all the time, for he felt that would be bad for him. When sent to the forest Tip often climbed trees for birds' eggs or amused himself chasing the fleet white rabbits or fishing in the brooks with bent pins. Then he would hastily gather his armful of wood and carry it home. And when he was supposed to be working in the corn-fields, and the tall stalks hid him from Mombi's view, Tip would often dig in the gopher holes, or if the mood seized him lie upon his back between the rows of corn and take a nap. So, by taking care not to exhaust his strength, he grew as strong and rugged as a boy may be.

Mombi's curious magic often frightened her neighbors, and they treated her shyly, yet respectfully, because of her weird powers. But Tip frankly hated her, and took no pains to hide his feelings. Indeed, he sometimes showed less respect for the old woman than he should have done, considering she was his guardian.

There were pumpkins in Mombi's corn-fields, lying golden red among the rows of green stalks; and these had been planted and carefully tended that the four-horned cow might eat of them in the winter time. But one day, after the corn had all been cut and stacked, and Tip was carrying the pumpkins to the stable, he took a notion to make a "Jack Lantern" and try to give the old woman a fright with it.

So he selected a fine, big pumpkin — one with a lustrous, orange-red color — and began carving it. With the point of his knife he made two round eyes, a three-cornered nose, and a mouth shaped like a new moon. The face, when completed, could not have been considered strictly beautiful; but it wore a smile so big and broad, and was so jolly in expression, that even Tip laughed as he looked admiringly at his work.

The child had no playmates, so he did not know that boys often dig out the inside of a "pumpkin-jack," and in the space thus made put a lighted candle to render the face more startling; but he conceived an idea of his own that promised to be quite as effective. He decided to manufacture the form of a man, who would wear this pumpkin head, and to stand it in a place where old Mombi would meet it face to face.

"And then," said Tip to himself, with a laugh, "she'll squeal louder than the brown pig does when I pull her tail, and shiver with fright worse than I did last year when I had the ague!"

He had plenty of time to accomplish this task, for Mombi had gone to a village — to buy groceries, she said — and it was a journey of at least two days.

So he took his axe to the forest, and selected some stout, straight saplings, which he cut down and trimmed of all their twigs and leaves. From these he would make the arms, and legs, and feet of his man. For the body he stripped a sheet of thick bark from around a big tree, and with much labor fashioned it into a cylinder of about the right size, pinning the edges together with wooden pegs. Then, whistling happily as he worked, he carefully jointed the limbs and fastened them to the body with pegs whittled into shape with his knife.

By the time this feat had been accomplished it began to grow dark, and Tip remembered he must milk the cow and feed the pigs. So he picked up his wooden man and carried it back to the house with him.

During the evening, by the light of the fire in the kitchen, Tip carefully rounded all the edges of the joints and smoothed the rough places in a neat and workmanlike manner. Then he stood the figure up against the wall and admired it. It seemed remarkably tall, even for a full-grown man; but that was a good point in a small boy's eyes, and Tip did not object at all to the size of his creation.

Next morning, when he looked at his work again, Tip saw he had forgotten to give the dummy a neck, by means of which he might fasten the pumpkinhead to the body. So he went again to the forest, which was not far away, and chopped from a tree several pieces of wood with which to complete his work. When he returned he fastened a cross-piece to the upper end of the body, making a hole through the center to hold upright the neck. The bit of wood which formed this neck was also sharpened at the upper end, and when all was ready Tip put on the pumpkin head, pressing it well down onto the neck, and found that it fitted very well. The head could be turned to one side or the other, as he pleased, and the hinges of the arms and legs allowed him to place the dummy in any position he desired.

"Now, that," declared Tip, proudly, "is really a very fine man, and it ought to frighten several screeches out of old Mombi! But it would be much more lifelike if it were properly dressed."

To find clothing seemed no easy task; but Tip boldly ransacked the great chest in which Mombi kept all her keepsakes and treasures, and at the very bottom he discovered some purple trousers, a red shirt and a pink vest which was dotted with white spots. These he carried away to his man and succeeded, although the garments did not fit very well, in dressing the creature in a jaunty fashion. Some knit stockings belonging to Mombi and a much worn pair of his own shoes completed the man's apparel, and Tip was so delighted that he danced up and down and laughed aloud in boyish ecstacy.

"I must give him a name!" he cried. "So good a man as this must surely have a name. I believe," he added, after a moment's thought, "I will name the fellow 'Jack Pumpkinhead!'"

The Marvelous Powder of Life

After considering the matter carefully, Tip decided that the best place to locate Jack would be at the bend in the road, a little way from the house. So he started to carry his man there, but found him heavy and rather awkward to handle. After dragging the creature a short distance Tip stood him on his feet, and by first bending the joints of one leg, and then those of the other, at the same time pushing from behind, the boy managed to induce Jack to walk to the bend in the road. It was not accomplished without a few tumbles, and Tip really worked harder than he ever had in the fields or forest; but a love of mischief urged him on, and it pleased him to test the cleverness of his workmanship.

"Jack's all right, and works fine!" he said to himself, panting with the unusual exertion. But just then he discovered the man's left arm had fallen off in the journey so he went back to find it, and afterward, by whittling a new and stouter pin for the shoulder-joint, he repaired the injury so successfully that the arm was stronger than before. Tip also noticed that Jack's pumpkin head had twisted around until it faced his back; but this was easily remedied. When, at last, the man was set up facing the turn in the path where old Mombi was to appear, he looked natural enough to be a fair imitation of a Gillikin farmer, — and unnatural enough to startle anyone that came on him unawares.

As it was yet too early in the day to expect the old woman to return home, Tip went down into the valley below the farmhouse and began to gather nuts from the trees that grew there.

However, old Mombi returned earlier than usual. She had met a crooked wizard who resided in a lonely cave in the mountains, and had traded several important secrets of magic with him. Having in this way secured three new recipes, four magical powders and a selection of herbs of wonderful power and potency, she hobbled home as fast as she could, in order to test her new sorceries.

So intent was Mombi on the treasures she had gained that when she turned the bend in the road and caught a glimpse of the man, she merely nodded and said:

"Good evening, sir."

But, a moment after, noting that the person did not move or reply, she cast a shrewd glance into his face and discovered his pumpkin head elaborately carved by Tip's jack-knife.

"Heh!" ejaculated Mombi, giving a sort of grunt; "that rascally boy has been playing tricks again! Very good! ve — ry good! I'll beat him black- and-blue for trying to scare me in this fashion!"

Angrily she raised her stick to smash in the grinning pumpkin head of the dummy; but a sudden thought made her pause, the uplifted stick left motionless in the air.

"Why, here is a good chance to try my new powder!" said she, eagerly. "And then I can tell whether that crooked wizard has fairly traded secrets, or whether he has fooled me as wickedly as I fooled him."

So she set down her basket and began fumbling in it for one of the precious powders she had obtained.

While Mombi was thus occupied Tip strolled back, with his pockets full of nuts, and discovered the old woman standing beside her man and apparently not the least bit frightened by it.

At first he was generally disappointed; but the next moment he became curious to know what Mombi was going to do. So he hid behind a hedge, where he could see without being seen, and prepared to watch.

After some search the woman drew from her basket an old pepper-box, upon the faded label of which the wizard had written with a lead-pencil:

"Powder of Life."

"Ah — here it is!" she cried, joyfully. "And now let us see if it is potent. The stingy wizard didn't give me much of it, but I guess there's enough for two or three doses."

Tip was much surprised when he overheard this speech. Then he saw old Mombi raise her arm and sprinkle the powder from the box over the pumpkin head of his man Jack. She did this in the same way one would pepper a baked potato, and the powder sifted down from Jack's head and scattered over the red shirt and pink waistcoat and purple trousers Tip had dressed him in, and a portion even fell upon the patched and worn shoes.

Then, putting the pepper-box back into the basket, Mombi lifted her left hand, with its little finger pointed upward, and said:

"Weaugh!"

Then she lifted her right hand, with the thumb pointed upward, and said:

"Teaugh!"

Then she lifted both hands, with all the fingers and thumbs spread out, and cried:

"Peaugh!"

Jack Pumpkinhead stepped back a pace, at this, and said in a reproachful voice:

"Don't yell like that! Do you think I'm deaf?"

Old Mombi danced around him, frantic with delight.

"He lives!" she screamed: "He lives! he lives!"

Then she threw her stick into the air and caught it as it came down; and she hugged herself with both arms, and tried to do a step of a jig; and all the time she repeated, rapturously:

"He lives! — he lives! — he lives!"

Now you may well suppose that Tip observed all this with amazement.

At first he was so frightened and horrified that he wanted to run away, but his legs trembled and shook so badly that he couldn't. Then it struck him as a very funny thing for Jack to come to life, especially as the expression on his pumpkin face was so droll and comical it excited laughter on the instant. So, recovering from his first fear, Tip began to laugh; and the merry peals reached old Mombi's ears and made her hobble quickly to the hedge, where she seized Tip's collar and dragged him back to where she had left her basket and the pumpkinheaded man.

"You naughty, sneaking, wicked boy!" she exclaimed, furiously:" I'll teach you to spy out my secrets and to make fun of me!"

"I wasn't making fun of you," protested Tip. "I was laughing at old Pumpkinhead! Look at him! Isn't he a picture, though?"

"I hope you are not reflecting on my personal appearance," said Jack; and it was so funny to hear his grave voice, while his face continued to wear its jolly smile, that Tip again burst into a peal of laughter.

Even Mombi was not without a curious interest in the man her magic had brought to life; for, after staring at him intently, she presently asked:

"What do you know?"

"Well, that is hard to tell," replied Jack. "For although I feel that I know a tremendous lot, I am not yet aware how much there is in the world to find out about. It will take me a little time to discover whether I am very wise or very foolish."

"To be sure," said Mombi, thoughtfully.

"But what are you going to do with him, now he is alive?" asked Tip, wondering.

"I must think it over," answered Mombi. "But we must get home at once, for it is growing dark. Help the Pumpkinhead to walk."

"Never mind me," said Jack; "I can walk as well as you can. Haven't I got legs and feet, and aren't they jointed?"

"Are they?" asked the woman, turning to Tip.

"Of course they are; I made 'em myself," returned the boy, with pride.

So they started for the house, but when they reached the farm yard old Mombi led the pumpkin man to the cow stable and shut him up in an empty stall, fastening the door securely on the outside.

"I've got to attend to you, first," she said, nodding her head at Tip.

Hearing this, the boy became uneasy; for he knew Mombi had a bad and revengeful heart, and would not hesitate to do any evil thing.

They entered the house. It was a round, domeshaped structure, as are nearly all the farm houses in the Land of Oz.

Mombi bade the boy light a candle, while she put her basket in a cupboard and hung her cloak on a peg. Tip obeyed quickly, for he was afraid of her.

After the candle had been lighted Mombi ordered him to build a fire in the hearth, and while Tip was thus engaged the old woman ate her supper. When the flames began to crackle the boy came to her and asked a share of the bread and cheese; but Mombi refused him.

"I'm hungry!" said Tip, in a sulky tone.

"You won't be hungry long," replied Mombi, with a grim look.

The boy didn't like this speech, for it sounded like a threat; but he happened to remember he had nuts in his pocket, so he cracked some of those and ate them while the woman rose, shook the crumbs from her apron, and hung above the fire a small black kettle.

Then she measured out equal parts of milk and vinegar and poured them into the kettle. Next she produced several packets of herbs and powders and began adding a portion of each to the contents of the kettle. Occasionally she would draw near the candle and read from a yellow paper the recipe of the mess she was concocting.

As Tip watched her his uneasiness increased.

"What is that for?" he asked.

"For you," returned Mombi, briefly.

Tip wriggled around upon his stool and stared awhile at the kettle, which was beginning to bubble. Then he would glance at the stern and wrinkled features of the witch and wish he were any place but in that dim and smoky kitchen, where even the shadows cast by the candle upon the wall were enough to give one the horrors. So an hour passed away, during which the silence was only broken by the bubbling of the pot and the hissing of the flames.

Finally, Tip spoke again.

"Have I got to drink that stuff?" he asked, nodding toward the pot.

"Yes," said Mombi.

"What'll it do to me?" asked Tip.

"If it's properly made," replied Mombi, "it will change or transform you into a marble statue."

Tip groaned, and wiped the perspiration from his forehead with his sleeve.

"I don't want to be a marble statue!" he protested.

"That doesn't matter I want you to be one," said the old woman, looking at him severely.

"What use'll I be then?" asked Tip. "There won't be any one to work for you."

"I'll make the Pumpkinhead work for me," said Mombi.

Again Tip groaned.

"Why don't you change me into a goat, or a chicken?" he asked, anxiously. "You can't do anything with a marble statue."

"Oh, yes, I can," returned Mombi. "I'm going to plant a flower garden, next Spring, and I'll put you in the middle of it, for an ornament. I wonder I haven't thought of that before; you've been a bother to me for years."

At this terrible speech Tip felt the beads of perspiration starting all over his body. but he sat still and shivered and looked anxiously at the kettle.

"Perhaps it won't work," he muttered, in a voice that sounded weak and discouraged.

"Oh, I think it will," answered Mombi, cheerfully. "I seldom make a mistake."

Again there was a period of silence a silence so long and gloomy that when Mombi finally lifted the kettle from the fire it was close to midnight.

"You cannot drink it until it has become quite cold," announced the old witch, for in spite of the law she had acknowledged practising witchcraft. "We must both go to bed now, and at daybreak I will call you and at once complete your transformation into a marble statue."

With this she hobbled into her room, bearing the steaming kettle with her, and Tip heard her close and lock the door.

The boy did not go to bed, as he had been commanded to do, but still sat glaring at the embers of the dying fire.

Tip reflected.

"It's a hard thing, to be a marble statue," he thought, rebelliously, "and I'm not going to stand it. For years I've been a bother to her, she says; so she's going to get rid of me. Well, there's an easier way than to become a statue. No boy could have any fun forever standing in the middle of a flower garden! I'll run away, that's what I'll do — and I may as well go before she makes me drink that nasty stuff in the kettle." He waited until the snores of the old witch announced she was fast asleep, and then he arose softly and went to the cupboard to find something to eat.

"No use starting on a journey without food," he decided, searching upon the narrow shelves.

He found some crusts of bread; but he had to look into Mombi's basket to find the cheese she had brought from the village. While turning over the contents of the basket he came upon the pepper-box which contained the "Powder of Life."

"I may as well take this with me," he thought, "or Mombi'll be using it to make more mischief with." So he put the box in his pocket, together with the bread and cheese.

Then he cautiously left the house and latched the door behind him. Outside both moon and stars shone brightly, and the night seemed peaceful and inviting after the close and ill-smelling kitchen.

"I'll be glad to get away," said Tip, softly; "for I never did like that old woman. I wonder how I ever came to live with her."

He was walking slowly toward the road when a thought made him pause.

"I don't like to leave Jack Pumpkinhead to the tender mercies of old Mombi," he muttered. "And Jack belongs to me, for I made him even if the old witch did bring him to life."

He retraced his steps to the cow-stable and opened the door of the stall where the pumpkin-headed man had been left.

Jack was standing in the middle of the stall, and by the moonlight Tip could see he was smiling just as jovially as ever.

"Come on!" said the boy, beckoning."

"Where to?" asked Jack.

"You'll know as soon as I do," answered Tip, smiling sympathetically into the pumpkin face. "All we've got to do now is to tramp."

"Very well," returned Jack, and walked awkwardly out of the stable and into the moonlight.

Tip turned toward the road and the man followed him. Jack walked with a sort of limp, and occasionally one of the joints of his legs would turn backward, instead of frontwise, almost causing him to tumble. But the Pumpkinhead was quick to notice this, and began to take more pains to step carefully; so that he met with few accidents.

Tip led him along the path without stopping an instant. They could not go very fast, but they walked steadily; and by the time the moon sank away and the sun peeped over the hills they had travelled so great a distance that the boy had no reason to fear pursuit from the old witch. Moreover, he had turned first into one path, and then into another, so that should anyone follow them it would prove very difficult to guess which way they had gone, or where to seek them.

Fairly satisfied that he had escaped — for a time, at least — being turned into a marble statue, the boy stopped his companion and seated himself upon a rock by the roadside.

"Let's have some breakfast," he said.

Jack Pumpkinhead watched Tip curiously, but refused to join in the repast. "I don't seem to be made the same way you are," he said.

"I know you are not," returned Tip; "for I made you."

"Oh! Did you?" asked Jack.

"Certainly. And put you together. And carved your eyes and nose and ears and mouth," said Tip proudly. "And dressed you."

Jack looked at his body and limbs critically.

"It strikes me you made a very good job of it," he remarked.

"Just so-so," replied Tip, modestly; for he began to see certain defects in the construction of his man. "If I'd known we were going to travel together I might have been a little more particular."

"Why, then," said the Pumpkinhead, in a tone that expressed surprise, "you must be my creator — my parent — my father!"

"Or your inventor," replied the boy with a laugh. "Yes, my son; I really believe I am!"

"Then I owe you obedience," continued the man, "and you owe me — support."

"That's it, exactly", declared Tip, jumping up. "So let us be off."

"Where are we going?" asked Jack, when they had resumed their journey.

"I'm not exactly sure," said the boy; "but I believe we are headed South, and that will bring us, sooner or later, to the Emerald City."

"What city is that?" enquired the Pumpkinhead.

"Why, it's the center of the Land of Oz, and the biggest town in all the country. I've never been there, myself, but I've heard all about its history. It was built by a mighty and wonderful Wizard named Oz, and everything there is of a green color — just as everything in this Country of the Gillikins is of a purple color."

"Is everything here purple?" asked Jack.

"Of course it is. Can't you see?" returned the boy.

"I believe I must be color-blind," said the Pumpkinhead, after staring about him.

"Well, the grass is purple, and the trees are purple, and the houses and fences are purple," explained Tip. "Even the mud in the roads is purple. But in the Emerald City everything is green that is purple here. And in the Country of the Munchkins, over at the East, everything is blue; and in the South country of the Quadlings everything is red; and in the West country of the Winkies, where the Tin Woodman rules, everything is yellow."

"Oh!" said Jack. Then, after a pause, he asked: "Did you say a Tin Woodman rules the Winkies?"

"Yes; he was one of those who helped Dorothy to destroy the Wicked Witch of the West, and the Winkies were so grateful that they invited him to become their ruler, — just as the people of the Emerald City invited the Scarecrow to rule them."

"Dear me!" said Jack. "I'm getting confused with all this history. Who is the Scarecrow?"

"Another friend of Dorothy's," replied Tip.

"And who is Dorothy?"

"She was a girl that came here from Kansas, a place in the big, outside World. She got blown to the Land of Oz by a cyclone, and while she was here the Scarecrow and the Tin Woodman accompanied her on her travels."

"And where is she now?" inquired the Pumpkinhead.

"Glinda the Good, who rules the Quadlings, sent her home again," said the boy.

"Oh. And what became of the Scarecrow?"

"I told you. He rules the Emerald City," answered Tip.

"I thought you said it was ruled by a wonderful Wizard," objected Jack, seeming more and more confused.

"Well, so I did. Now, pay attention, and I'll explain it," said Tip, speaking slowly and looking the smiling Pumpkinhead squarely in the eye. "Dorothy went to the Emerald City to ask the Wizard to send her back to Kansas; and the Scarecrow and the Tin Woodman went with her. But the Wizard couldn't send her back, because he wasn't so much of a Wizard as he might have been. And then they got angry at the Wizard, and threatened to expose him; so the Wizard made a big balloon and escaped in it, and no one has ever seen him since."

"Now, that is very interesting history," said Jack, well pleased; "and I understand it perfectly — all but the explanation."

"I'm glad you do," responded Tip. "After the Wizard was gone, the people of the Emerald City made His Majesty, the Scarecrow, their King; "and I have heard that he became a very popular ruler."

"Are we going to see this queer King?" asked Jack, with interest.

"I think we may as well," replied the boy; "unless you have something better to do."

"Oh, no, dear father," said the Pumpkinhead. "I am quite willing to go wherever you please."

The boy, small and rather delicate in appearance seemed somewhat embarrassed at being called "father" by the tall, awkward, pumpkinheaded man, but to deny the relationship would involve another long and tedious explanation; so he changed the subject by asking, abruptly:

"Are you tired?"

"Of course not!" replied the other. "But," he continued, after a pause, "it is quite certain I shall wear out my wooden joints if I keep on walking."

Tip reflected, as they journeyed on, that this was true. He began to regret that he had not constructed the wooden limbs more carefully and substantially. Yet how could he ever have guessed that the man he had made merely to scare old Mombi with would be brought to life by means of a magical powder contained in an old pepper-box?

So he ceased to reproach himself, and began to think how he might yet remedy the deficiencies of Jack's weak joints.

While thus engaged they came to the edge of a wood, and the boy sat down to rest upon an old sawhorse that some woodcutter had left there.

"Why don't you sit down?" he asked the Pumpkinhead.

"Won't it strain my joints?" inquired the other.

"Of course not. It'll rest them," declared the boy.

So Jack tried to sit down; but as soon as he bent his joints farther than usual they gave way altogether, and he came clattering to the ground with such a crash that Tip feared he was entirely ruined.

He rushed to the man, lifted him to his feet, straightened his arms and legs, and felt of his head to see if by chance it had become cracked. But Jack seemed to be in pretty good shape, after all, and Tip said to him:

I guess you'd better remain standing, hereafter. It seems the safest way."

Very well, dear father, just as you say", replied the smiling Jack, who had been in no wise confused by his tumble.

Tip sat down again. Presently the Pumpkinhead asked: "What is that thing you are sitting on?"

Oh, this is a horse," replied the boy, carelessly.

What is a horse?" demanded Jack.

A horse? Why, there are two kinds of horses," returned Tip, lightly puzzled how to explain. "One kind of horse is alive, and has four legs and a head and a tail. And people ride upon its back."

I understand," said Jack, cheerfully "That's the kind of horse you are now sitting on."

No, it isn't," answered Tip, promptly.

Why not? That one has four legs, and a head, and a tail." Tip looked at the saw-horse more carefully, and found that the Pumpkinhead was right. The body had been formed from a tree-trunk, and a branch had been left sticking up at one end that looked very much like a tail. In the other end were two big knots that resembled eyes, and a place had been chopped away that might easily be mistaken for the horse's mouth. As for the legs, they were four straight limbs cut from trees and stuck fast into the body, being spread wide apart so that the saw-horse would stand firmly when a log was laid across it to be sawed.

This thing resembles a real horse more than I imagined," said Tip, trying to explain. "But a real horse is alive, and trots and prances and eats oats, while this is nothing more than a dead horse, made of wood, and used to saw logs upon."

If it were alive, wouldn't it trot, and prance, and eat oats?" inquired the Pumpkinhead.

"It would trot and prance, perhaps; but it wouldn't eat oats," replied the boy, laughing at the idea." And of course it can't ever be alive, because it is made of wood."

"So am I," answered the man.

Tip looked at him in surprise.

"Why, so you are!" he exclaimed. "And the magic powder that brought you to life is here in my pocket."

He brought out the pepper box, and eyed it curiously.

"I wonder," said he, musingly, "if it would bring the saw-horse to life."

"If it would," returned Jack, calmly for nothing seemed to surprise him" I could ride on its back, and that would save my joints from wearing out."

"I'll try it!" cried the boy, jumping up. "But I wonder if I can remember the words old Mombi said, and the way she held her hands up."

He thought it over for a minute, and as he had watched carefully from the hedge every motion of the old witch, and listened to her words, he believed he could repeat exactly what she had said and done.

So he began by sprinkling some of the magic Powder of Life from the pepper-box upon the body of the saw-horse. Then he lifted his left hand, with the little finger pointing upward, and said: "Weaugh!"

"What does that mean, dear father?" asked Jack, curiously.

"I don't know," answered Tip. Then he lifted his right hand, with the thumb pointing upward and said: "Teaugh!"

"What's that, dear father?" inquired Jack.

"It means you must keep quiet!" replied the boy, provoked at being interrupted at so important a moment.

"How fast I am learning!" remarked the Pumpkinhead, with his eternal smile.

Tip now lifted both hands above his head, with all the fingers and thumbs spread out, and cried in a loud voice: "Peaugh!"

Immediately the saw-horse moved, stretched its legs, yawned with its chopped-out mouth, and shook a few grains of the powder off its back. The rest of the powder seemed to have vanished into the body of the horse.

"Good!" called Jack, while the boy looked on in astonishment. "You are a very clever sorcerer, dear father!"

The Awakening of the Saw-horse

The Saw-Horse, finding himself alive, seemed even more astonished than Tip. He rolled his knotty eyes from side to side, taking a first wondering view of the world in which he had now so important an existence. Then he tried to look at himself; but he had, indeed, no neck to turn; so that in the endeavor to see his body he kept circling around and around, without catching even a glimpse of it. His legs were stiff and awkward, for there were no knee-joints in them; so that presently he bumped against Jack Pumpkinhead and sent that personage tumbling upon the moss that lined the roadside.

Tip became alarmed at this accident, as well as at the persistence of the Saw-Horse in prancing around in a circle; so he called out:

"Whoa! Whoa, there!"

The Saw-Horse paid no attention whatever to this command, and the next instant brought one of his wooden legs down upon Tip's foot so forcibly that the boy danced away in pain to a safer distance, from where he again yelled:

"Whoa! Whoa, I say!"

Jack had now managed to raise himself to a sitting position, and he looked at the Saw-Horse with much interest.

"I don't believe the animal can hear you," he remarked.

"I shout loud enough, don't I?" answered Tip, angrily.

"Yes; but the horse has no ears," said the smiling Pumpkinhead.

"Sure enough!" exclaimed Tip, noting the fact for the first time. "How, then, am I going to stop him?"

But at that instant the Saw-Horse stopped himself, having concluded it was impossible to see his own body. He saw Tip, however, and came close to the boy to observe him more fully.

It was really comical to see the creature walk; for it moved the legs on its right side together, and those on its left side together, as a pacing horse does; and that made its body rock sidewise, like a cradle.

Tip patted it upon the head, and said "Good boy! Good Boy!" in a coaxing tone; and the Saw-Horse pranced away to examine with its bulging eyes the form of Jack Pumpkinhead.

"I must find a halter for him," said Tip; and having made a search in his pocket he produced a roll of strong cord. Unwinding this, he approached the Saw-Horse and tied the cord around its neck, afterward fastening the other end to a large tree. The Saw-Horse, not understanding the action, stepped backward and snapped the string easily; but it made no attempt to run away.

"He's stronger than I thought," said the boy, "and rather obstinate, too."

"Why don't you make him some ears?" asked Jack. "Then you can tell him what to do."

"That's a splendid idea!" said Tip. "How did you happen to think of it?"

"Why, I didn't think of it," answered the Pumpkinhead; "I didn't need to, for it's the simplest and easiest thing to do."

So Tip got out his knife and fashioned some ears out of the bark of a small tree.

"I mustn't make them too big," he said, as he whittled, "or our horse would become a donkey."

"How is that?" inquired Jack, from the roadside.

"Why, a horse has bigger ears than a man; and a donkey has bigger ears than a horse," explained Tip.

"Then, if my ears were longer, would I be a horse?" asked Jack.

"My friend," said Tip, gravely, "you'll never be anything but a Pumpkinhead, no matter how big your ears are."

"Oh," returned Jack, nodding; "I think I understand."

"If you do, you're a wonder," remarked the boy "but there's no harm in thinking you understand. I guess these ears are ready now. Will you hold the horse while I stick them on?"

"Certainly, if you'll help me up," said Jack.

So Tip raised him to his feet, and the Pumpkinhead went to the horse and held its head while the boy bored two holes in it with his knife-blade and inserted the ears.

"They make him look very handsome," said Jack, admiringly.

But those words, spoken close to the Saw-Horse, and being the first sounds he had ever heard, so startled the animal that he made a bound forward and tumbled Tip on one side and Jack on the other. Then he continued to rush forward as if frightened by the clatter of his own foot-steps.

"Whoa!" shouted Tip, picking himself up; "whoa! you idiot, whoa!" The Saw-Horse would probably have paid no attention to this, but just then it stepped a leg into a gopher-hole and stumbled head-over-heels to the ground, where it lay upon its back, frantically waving its four legs in the air.

Tip ran up to it.

"You're a nice sort of a horse, I must say!" he exclaimed. "Why didn't you stop when I yelled 'whoa?'"

"Does 'whoa' mean to stop?" asked the Saw-Horse, in a surprised voice, as it rolled its eyes upward to look at the boy.

"Of course it does," answered Tip.

"And a hole in the ground means to stop, also, doesn't it?" continued the horse.

"To be sure; unless you step over it," said Tip.

"What a strange place this is," the creature exclaimed, as amazed. "What am I doing here, anyway?"

"Why, I've brought you to life," answered the boy "but it won't hurt you any, if you mind me and do as I tell you."

"Then I will do as you tell me," replied the Saw-Horse, humbly. "But what happened to me, a moment ago? I don't seem to be just right, someway."

"You're upside down," explained Tip. "But just keep those legs still a minute and I'll set you right side up again."

"How many sides have I?" asked the creature, wonderingly.

"Several," said Tip, briefly. "But do keep those legs still."

The Saw-Horse now became quiet, and held its legs rigid; so that Tip, after several efforts, was able to roll him over and set him upright.

"Ah, I seem all right now," said the queer animal, with a sigh.

"One of your ears is broken," Tip announced, after a careful examination. "I'll have to make a new one."

Then he led the Saw-Horse back to where Jack was vainly struggling to regain his feet, and after assisting the Pumpkinhead to stand upright Tip whittled out a new ear and fastened it to the horse's head.

"Now," said he, addressing his steed, "pay attention to what I'm going to tell you. 'Whoa!' means to stop; 'Get-Up!' means to walk forward; 'Trot!' means to go as fast as you can. Understand?"

"I believe I do," returned the horse.

"Very good. We are all going on a journey to the Emerald City, to see His Majesty, the Scarecrow; and Jack Pumpkinhead is going to ride on your back, so he won't wear out his joints."

"I don't mind," said the Saw-Horse. "Anything that suits you suits me."

Then Tip assisted Jack to get upon the horse.

"Hold on tight," he cautioned, "or you may fall off and crack your pumpkin head."

"That would be horrible!" said Jack, with a shudder. "What shall I hold on to?"

"Why, hold on to his ears," replied Tip, after a moment's hesitation.

"Don't do that!" remonstrated the Saw-Horse; "for then I can't hear."

That seemed reasonable, so Tip tried to think of something else.

"I'll fix it!" said he, at length. He went into the wood and cut a short length of limb from a young, stout tree. One end of this he sharpened to a point, and then he dug a hole in the back of the Saw-Horse, just behind its head. Next he brought a piece of rock from the road and hammered the post firmly into the animal's back.

"Stop! Stop!" shouted the horse; "you're jarring me terribly."

"Does it hurt?" asked the boy.

"Not exactly hurt," answered the animal; "but it makes me quite nervous to be jarred."

"Well, it's all over now" said Tip, encouragingly. "Now, Jack, be sure to hold fast to this post and then you can't fall off and get smashed."

So Jack held on tight, and Tip said to the horse:

"Get up."

The obedient creature at once walked forward, rocking from side to side as he raised his feet from the ground.

Tip walked beside the Saw-Horse, quite content with this addition to their party. Presently he began to whistle.

"What does that sound mean?" asked the horse.

"Don't pay any attention to it," said Tip. "I'm just whistling, and that only means I'm pretty well satisfied."

"I'd whistle myself, if I could push my lips together," remarked Jack. "I fear, dear father, that in some respects I am sadly lacking."

After journeying on for some distance the narrow path they were following turned into a broad roadway, paved with yellow brick. By the side of the road Tip noticed a sign-post that read:

"NINE MILES TO THE EMERALD CITY."

But it was now growing dark, so he decided to camp for the night by the roadside and to resume the journey next morning by daybreak. He led the Saw-Horse to a grassy mound upon which grew several bushy trees, and carefully assisted the Pumpkinhead to alight.

"I think I'll lay you upon the ground, overnight," said the boy. "You will be safer that way."

"How about me?" asked the Saw-Horse.

"It won't hurt you to stand," replied Tip; "and, as you can't sleep, you may as well watch out and see that no one comes near to disturb us."

Then the boy stretched himself upon the grass beside the Pumpkinhead, and being greatly wearied by the journey was soon fast asleep.

Jack Pumpkinhead's Ride to the Emerald City

At daybreak Tip was awakened by the Pumpkinhead. He rubbed the sleep from his eyes, bathed in a little brook, and then ate a portion of his bread and cheese. Having thus prepared for a new day the boy said:

"Let us start at once. Nine miles is quite a distance, but we ought to reach the Emerald City by noon if no accidents happen." So the Pumpkinhead was again perched upon the back of the Saw-Horse and the journey was resumed.

Tip noticed that the purple tint of the grass and trees had now faded to a dull lavender, and before long this lavender appeared to take on a greenish tinge that gradually brightened as they drew nearer to the great City where the Scarecrow ruled.

The little party had traveled but a short two miles upon their way when the road of yellow brick was parted by a broad and swift river. Tip was puzzled how to cross over; but after a time he discovered a man in a ferry-boat approaching from the other side of the stream.

When the man reached the bank Tip asked:

"Will you row us to the other side?"

"Yes, if you have money," returned the ferryman, whose face looked cross and disagreeable.

"But I have no money," said Tip.

"None at all?" inquired the man.

"None at all," answered the boy.

"Then I'll not break my back rowing you over," said the ferryman, decidedly.

"What a nice man!" remarked the Pumpkinhead, smilingly.

The ferryman stared at him, but made no reply. Tip was trying to think, for it was a great disappointment to him to find his journey so suddenly brought to an end.

"I must certainly get to the Emerald City," he said to the boatman; "but how can I cross the river if you do not take me?"

The man laughed, and it was not a nice laugh.

"That wooden horse will float," said he; "and you can ride him across. As for the pumpkinheaded loon who accompanies you, let him sink or swim — it won't matter greatly which."

"Don't worry about me," said Jack, smiling pleasantly upon the crabbed ferryman; "I'm sure I ought to float beautifully."

Tip thought the experiment was worth making, and the Saw-Horse, who did not know what danger meant, offered no objections whatever. So the boy led it down into the water and climbed upon its back. Jack also waded in up to his knees and grasped the tail of the horse so that he might keep his pumpkin head above the water.

"Now," said Tip, instructing the Saw-Horse, "if you wiggle your legs you will probably swim; and if you swim we shall probably reach the other side."

The Saw-Horse at once began to wiggle its legs, which acted as oars and moved the adventurers slowly across the river to the opposite side. So successful was the trip that presently they were climbing, wet and dripping, up the grassy bank.

Tip's trouser-legs and shoes were thoroughly soaked; but the Saw-Horse had floated so perfectly that from his knees up the boy was entirely dry. As for the Pumpkinhead, every stitch of his gorgeous clothing dripped water.

"The sun will soon dry us," said Tip "and, anyhow, we are now safely across, in spite of the ferryman, and can continue our journey.

"I didn't mind swimming, at all," remarked the horse.

"Nor did I," added Jack.

They soon regained the road of yellow brick, which proved to be a continuation of the road they had left on the other side, and then Tip once more mounted the Pumpkinhead upon the back of the Saw-Horse.

"If you ride fast," said he, "the wind will help to dry your clothing. I will hold on to the horse's tail and run after you. In this way we all will become dry in a very short time."

"Then the horse must step lively," said Jack.

"I'll do my best," returned the Saw-Horse, cheerfully.

Tip grasped the end of the branch that served as tail to the Saw-Horse, and called loudly: "Get-up!"

The horse started at a good pace, and Tip followed behind. Then he decided they could go faster, so he shouted: "Trot!"

Now, the Saw-Horse remembered that this word was the command to go as fast as he could; so he began rocking along the road at a tremendous pace, and Tip had hard work — running faster than he ever had before in his life — to keep his feet.

Soon he was out of breath, and although he wanted to call "Whoa!" to the horse, he found he could not get the word out of his throat. Then the end of the tail he was clutching, being nothing more than a dead branch, suddenly broke away, and the next minute the boy was rolling in the dust of the road, while the horse and its pumpkin-headed rider dashed on and quickly disappeared in the distance.

By the time Tip had picked himself up and cleared the dust from his throat so he could say "Whoa!" there was no further need of saying it, for the horse was long since out of sight.

So he did the only sensible thing he could do. He sat down and took a good rest, and afterward began walking along the road.

"Some time I will surely overtake them," he reflected; "for the road will end at the gates of the Emerald City, and they can go no further than that."

Meantime Jack was holding fast to the post and the Saw-Horse was tearing along the road like a racer. Neither of them knew Tip was left behind, for the Pumpkinhead did not look around and the Saw-Horse couldn't.

As he rode, Jack noticed that the grass and trees had become a bright emerald-green in color, so he guessed they were nearing the Emerald City even before the tall spires and domes came into sight.

At length a high wall of green stone, studded thick with emeralds, loomed up before them; and fearing the Saw-Horse would not know enough to stop and so might smash them both against this wall, Jack ventured to cry "Whoa!" as loud as he could.

So suddenly did the horse obey that had it not been for his post Jack would have been pitched off head foremost, and his beautiful face ruined.

"That was a fast ride, dear father!" he exclaimed; and then, hearing no reply, he turned around and discovered for the first time that Tip was not there.

This apparent desertion puzzled the Pumpkinhead, and made him uneasy. And while he was wondering what had become of the boy, and what he ought to do next under such trying circumstances, the gateway in the green wall opened and a man came out.

This man was short and round, with a fat face that seemed remarkably good- natured. He was clothed all in green and wore a high, peaked green hat upon his head and green spectacles over his eyes. Bowing before the Pumpkinhead he said:

"I am the Guardian of the Gates of the Emerald City. May I inquire who you are, and what is your business?"

"My name is Jack Pumpkinhead," returned the other, smilingly; "but as to my business, I haven't the least idea in the world what it is."

The Guardian of the Gates looked surprised, and shook his head as if dissatisfied with the reply.

"What are you, a man or a pumpkin?" he asked, politely.

"Both, if you please," answered Jack.

"And this wooden horse — is it alive?" questioned the Guardian.

The horse rolled one knotty eye upward and winked at Jack. Then it gave a prance and brought one leg down on the Guardian's toes.

"Ouch!" cried the man; "I'm sorry I asked that question. But the answer is most convincing. Have you any errand, sir, in the Emerald City?"

"It seems to me that I have," replied the Pumpkinhead, seriously; "but I cannot think what it is. My father knows all about it, but he is not here."

"This is a strange affair very strange!" declared the Guardian. "But you seem harmless. Folks do not smile so delightfully when they mean mischief."

"As for that," said Jack, "I cannot help my smile, for it is carved on my face with a jack-knife."

"Well, come with me into my room," resumed the Guardian, "and I will see what can be done for you."

So Jack rode the Saw-Horse through the gateway into a little room built into the wall. The Guardian pulled a bell-cord, and presently a very tall soldier — clothed in a green uniform — entered from the opposite door. This soldier carried a long green gun over his shoulder and had lovely green whiskers that fell quite to his knees. The Guardian at once addressed him, saying:

Here is a strange gentleman who doesn't know why he has come to the Emerald City, or what he wants. Tell me, what shall we do with him?"

The Soldier with the Green Whiskers looked at Jack with much care and curiosity. Finally he shook his head so positively that little waves rippled down his whiskers, and then he said:

I must take him to His Majesty, the Scarecrow."

But what will His Majesty, the Scarecrow, do with him?" asked the Guardian of the Gates.

That is His Majesty's business," returned the soldier. "I have troubles enough of my own. All outside troubles must be turned over to His Majesty. So put the spectacles on this fellow, and I'll take him to the royal palace."

So the Guardian opened a big box of spectacles and tried to fit a pair to Jack's great round eyes.

I haven't a pair in stock that will really cover those eyes up," said the little man, with a sigh; "and your head is so big that I shall be obliged to tie the spectacles on."

But why need I wear spectacles?" asked Jack.

"It's the fashion here," said the Soldier, "and they will keep you from being blinded by the glitter and glare of the gorgeous Emerald City."

"Oh!" exclaimed Jack. "Tie them on, by all means. I don't wish to be blinded."

"Nor I!" broke in the Saw-Horse; so a pair of green spectacles was quickly fastened over the bulging knots that served it for eyes.

Then the Soldier with the Green Whiskers led them through the inner gate and they at once found themselves in the main street of the magnificent Emerald City.

Sparkling green gems ornamented the fronts of the beautiful houses and the towers and turrets were all faced with emeralds. Even the green marble pavement glittered with precious stones, and it was indeed a grand and marvelous sight to one who beheld it for the first time.

However, the Pumpkinhead and the Saw-Horse, knowing nothing of wealth and beauty, paid little attention to the wonderful sights they saw through their green spectacles. They calmly followed after the green soldier and scarcely noticed the crowds of green people who stared at them in surprise. When a green dog ran out and barked at them the Saw-Horse promptly kicked at it with its wooden leg and sent the little animal howling into one of the houses; but nothing more serious than this happened to interrupt their progress to the royal palace.

The Pumpkinhead wanted to ride up the green marble steps and straight into the Scarecrow's presence; but the soldier would not permit that. So Jack dismounted, with much difficulty, and a servant led the Saw-Horse around to the rear while the Soldier with the Green Whiskers escorted the Pumpkinhead into the palace, by the front entrance.

The stranger was left in a handsomely furnished waiting room while the soldier went to announce him. It so happened that at this hour His Majesty was at leisure and greatly bored for want of something to do, so he ordered his visitor to be shown at once into his throne room.

Jack felt no fear or embarrassment at meeting the ruler of this magnificent city, for he was entirely ignorant of all worldly customs. But when he entered the room and saw for the first time His Majesty the Scarecrow seated upon his glittering throne, he stopped short in amazement.

His Majesty the Scarecrow

I suppose every reader of this book knows what a scarecrow is; but Jack Pumpkinhead, never having seen such a creation, was more surprised at meeting the remarkable King of the Emerald City than by any other one experience of his brief life.

His Majesty the Scarecrow was dressed in a suit of faded blue clothes, and his head was merely a small sack stuffed with straw, upon which eyes, ears, a nose and a mouth had been rudely painted to represent a face. The clothes were also stuffed with straw, and that so unevenly or carelessly that his Majesty's legs and arms seemed more bumpy than was necessary. Upon his hands were gloves with long fingers, and these were padded with cotton. Wisps of straw stuck out from the monarch's coat and also from his neck and boot-tops. Upon his head he wore a heavy golden crown set thick with sparkling jewels, and the weight of this crown caused his brow to sag in wrinkles, giving a thoughtful expression to the painted face. Indeed, the crown alone betokened majesty; in all else the, Scarecrow King was but a simple scarecrow — flimsy, awkward, and unsubstantial.

But if the strange appearance of his Majesty the Scarecrow seemed startling to Jack, no less wonderful was the form of the Pumpkinhead to the Scarecrow. The purple trousers and pink waistcoat and red shirt hung loosely over the wooden joints Tip had manufactured, and the carved face on the pumpkin grinned perpetually, as if its wearer considered life the jolliest thing imaginable.

At first, indeed, His Majesty thought his queer visitor was laughing at him, and was inclined to resent such a liberty; but it was not without reason that the Scarecrow had attained the reputation of being the wisest personage in the Land of Oz. He made a more careful examination of his visitor, and soon discovered that Jack's features were carved into a smile and that he could not look grave if he wished to.

The King was the first to speak. After regarding Jack for some minutes he said, in a tone of wonder:

"Where on earth did you come from, and how do you happen to be alive?"

"I beg your Majesty's pardon," returned the Pumpkinhead; "but I do not understand you."

"What don't you understand?" asked the Scarecrow.

"Why, I don't understand your language. You see, I came from the Country of the Gillikins, so that I am a foreigner."

"Ah, to be sure!" exclaimed the Scarecrow. "I myself speak the language of the Munchkins, which is also the language of the Emerald City. But you, I suppose, speak the language of the Pumpkinheads?"

"Exactly so, your Majesty" replied the other, bowing; "so it will be impossible for us to understand one another."

"That is unfortunate, certainly," said the Scarecrow, thoughtfully. "We must have an interpreter."

"What is an interpreter?" asked Jack.

"A person who understands both my language and your own. When I say anything, the interpreter can tell you what I mean; and when you say anything the interpreter can tell me what you mean. For the interpreter can speak both languages as well as understand them."

"That is certainly clever," said Jack, greatly pleased at finding so simple a way out of the difficulty.

So the Scarecrow commanded the Soldier with the Green Whiskers to search among his people until he found one who understood the language of the Gillikins as well as the language of the Emerald City, and to bring that person to him at once.

When the Soldier had departed the Scarecrow said:

"Won't you take a chair while we are waiting?"

"Your Majesty forgets that I cannot understand you," replied the Pumpkinhead. "If you wish me to sit down you must make a sign

for me to do so." The Scarecrow came down from his throne and rolled an armchair to a position behind the Pumpkinhead. Then he gave Jack a sudden push that sent him sprawling upon the cushions in so awkward a fashion that he doubled up like a jackknife, and had hard work to untangle himself.

"Did you understand that sign?" asked His Majesty, politely.

"Perfectly," declared Jack, reaching up his arms to turn his head to the front, the pumpkin having twisted around upon the stick that supported it.

"You seem hastily made," remarked the Scarecrow, watching Jack's efforts to straighten himself.

"Not more so than your Majesty," was the frank reply.

"There is this difference between us," said the Scarecrow, "that whereas I will bend, but not break, you will break, but not bend."

At this moment the soldier returned leading a young girl by the hand. She seemed very sweet and modest, having a pretty face and beautiful green eyes and hair. A dainty green silk skirt reached to her knees, showing silk stockings embroidered with pea-pods, and green satin slippers with bunches of lettuce for decorations instead of bows or buckles. Upon her silken waist clover leaves were embroidered, and she wore a jaunty little jacket trimmed with sparkling emeralds of a uniform size.

"Why, it's little Jellia Jamb!" exclaimed the Scarecrow, as the green maiden bowed her pretty head before him. "Do you understand the language of the Gillikins, my dear?"

"Yes, your Majesty, she answered, "for I was born in the North Country."

"Then you shall be our interpreter," said the Scarecrow, "and explain to this Pumpkinhead all that I say, and also explain to me all that he says. Is this arrangement satisfactory?" he asked turning toward his guest.

"Very satisfactory indeed," was the reply.

"Then ask him, to begin with," resumed the Scarecrow, turning to Jellia, "what brought him to the Emerald City"

But instead of this the girl, who had been staring at Jack, said to him:

"You are certainly a wonderful creature. Who made you?"

"A boy named Tip," answered Jack.

"What does he say?" inquired the Scarecrow. "My ears must have deceived me. What did he say?"

"He says that your Majesty's brains seem to have come loose," replied the girl, demurely.

The Scarecrow moved uneasily upon his throne, and felt of his head with his left hand.

"What a fine thing it is to understand two different languages," he said, with a perplexed sigh. "Ask him, my dear, if he has any objection to being put in jail for insulting the ruler of the Emerald City."

"I didn't insult you!" protested Jack, indignantly.

"Tut — tut!" cautioned the Scarecrow "wait, until Jellia translates my speech. What have we got an interpreter for, if you break out in this rash way?"

"All right, I'll wait," replied the Pumpkinhead, in a surly tone — although his face smiled as genially as ever. "Translate the speech, young woman."

"His Majesty inquires if you are hungry, said Jellia.

"Oh, not at all!" answered Jack, more pleasantly, "for it is impossible for me to eat."

"It's the same way with me," remarked the Scarecrow. "What did he say, Jellia, my dear?"

"He asked if you were aware that one of your eyes is painted larger than the other," said the girl, mischievously.

"Don't you believe her, your Majesty, cried Jack.

"Oh, I don't," answered the Scarecrow, calmly. Then, casting a sharp look at the girl, he asked:

"Are you quite certain you understand the languages of both the Gillikins and the Munchkins?"

"Quite certain, your Majesty," said Jellia Jamb, trying hard not to laugh in the face of royalty.

"Then how is it that I seem to understand them myself?" inquired the Scarecrow.

"Because they are one and the same!" declared the girl, now laughing merrily. "Does not your Majesty know that in all the land of Oz but one language is spoken?"

"Is it indeed so?" cried the Scarecrow, much relieved to hear this; "then I might easily have been my own interpreter!"

"It was all my fault, your Majesty," said Jack, looking rather foolish," I thought we must surely speak different languages, since we came from different countries."

"This should be a warning to you never to think," returned the Scarecrow, severely. "For unless one can think wisely it is better to remain a dummy — which you most certainly are."

"I am! — I surely am!" agreed the Pumpkinhead.

"It seems to me," continued the Scarecrow, more mildly, "that your manufacturer spoiled some good pies to create an indifferent man."

"I assure your Majesty that I did not ask to be created," answered Jack.

"Ah! It was the same in my case," said the King, pleasantly. And so, as we differ from all ordinary people, let us become friends."

"With all my heart!" exclaimed Jack.

"What! Have you a heart?" asked the Scarecrow, surprised.

"No; that was only imaginative — I might say, a figure of speech," said the other.

"Well, your most prominent figure seems to be a figure of wood; so I must beg you to restrain an imagination which, having no brains, you have no right to exercise," suggested the Scarecrow, warningly.

"To be sure!" said Jack, without in the least comprehending.

His Majesty then dismissed Jellia Jamb and the Soldier with the Green Whiskers, and when they were gone he took his new friend by the arm and led him into the courtyard to play a game of quoits.

Gen. Jinjur's Army of Revolt

Tip was so anxious to rejoin his man Jack and the Saw-Horse that he walked a full half the distance to the Emerald City without stopping to rest. Then he discovered that he was hungry and the crackers and cheese he had provided for the Journey had all been eaten.

While wondering what he should do in this emergency he came upon a girl sitting by the roadside. She wore a costume that struck the boy as being remarkably brilliant: her silken waist being of emerald green and her skirt of four distinct colors — blue in front, yellow at the left side, red at the back and purple at the right side. Fastening the waist in front were four buttons — the top one blue, the next yellow, a third red and the last purple.

The splendor of this dress was almost barbaric; so Tip was fully justified in staring at the gown for some moments before his eyes were attracted by the pretty face above it. Yes, the face was pretty enough, he decided; but it wore an expression of discontent coupled to a shade of defiance or audacity.

While the boy stared the girl looked upon him calmly. A lunch basket stood beside her, and she held a dainty sandwich in one hand and a hard-boiled egg in the other, eating with an evident appetite that aroused Tip's sympathy.

He was just about to ask a share of the luncheon when the girl stood up and brushed the crumbs from her lap.

"There!" said she; "it is time for me to go. Carry that basket for me and help yourself to its contents if you are hungry."

Tip seized the basket eagerly and began to eat, following for a time the strange girl without bothering to ask questions. She walked along before him with swift strides, and there was about her an air of decision and importance that led him to suspect she was some great personage.

Finally, when he had satisfied his hunger, he ran up beside her and tried to keep pace with her swift footsteps — a very difficult feat, for she was much taller than he, and evidently in a hurry.

"Thank you very much for the sandwiches," said Tip, as he trotted along. "May I ask your name?"

"I am General Jinjur," was the brief reply.

"Oh!" said the boy surprised. "What sort of a General?"

"I command the Army of Revolt in this war," answered the General, with unnecessary sharpness.

"Oh!" he again exclaimed. "I didn't know there was a war."

"You were not supposed to know it," she returned, "for we have kept it a secret; and considering that our army is composed entirely of girls," she added, with some pride, "it is surely a remarkable thing that our Revolt is not yet discovered."

"It is, indeed," acknowledged Tip. "But where is your army?"

"About a mile from here," said General Jinjur. "The forces have assembled from all parts of the Land of Oz, at my express command. For this is the day we are to conquer His Majesty the Scarecrow, and wrest from him the throne. The Army of Revolt only awaits my coming to march upon the Emerald City."

"Well!" declared Tip, drawing a long breath, "this is certainly a surprising thing! May I ask why you wish to conquer His Majesty the Scarecrow?"

"Because the Emerald City has been ruled by men long enough, for one reason," said the girl.

"Moreover, the City glitters with beautiful gems, which might far better be used for rings, bracelets and necklaces; and there is enough money in the King's treasury to buy every girl in our Army a dozen new gowns. So we intend to conquer the City and run the government to suit ourselves."

Jinjur spoke these words with an eagerness and decision that proved she was in earnest.

"But war is a terrible thing," said Tip, thoughtfully.

"This war will be pleasant," replied the girl, cheerfully.

"Many of you will be slain!" continued the boy, in an awed voice.

"Oh, no", said Jinjur. "What man would oppose a girl, or dare to harm her? And there is not an ugly face in my entire Army."

Tip laughed.

"Perhaps you are right," said he. "But the Guardian of the Gate is considered a faithful Guardian, and the King's Army will not let the City be conquered without a struggle."

"The Army is old and feeble," replied General Jinjur, scornfully. "His strength has all been used to grow whiskers, and his wife has such a temper that she has already pulled more than half of them out by the roots. When the Wonderful Wizard reigned the Soldier with the Green Whiskers was a very good Royal Army, for people feared the Wizard. But no one is afraid of the Scarecrow, so his Royal Army don't count for much in time of war."

After this conversation they proceeded some distance in silence, and before long reached a large clearing in the forest where fully four hundred young women were assembled. These were laughing and talking together as gaily as if they had gathered for a picnic instead of a war of conquest.

They were divided into four companies, and Tip noticed that all were dressed in costumes similar to that worn by General Jinjur. The only real difference was that while those girls from the Munchkin country had the blue strip in front of their skirts, those from the country of the Quadlings had the red strip in front; and those from the country of the Winkies had the yellow strip in front, and the Gillikin girls wore the purple strip in front. All had green waists, representing the Emerald City they intended to conquer, and the top button on each waist indicated by its color which country the wearer came from. The uniforms

were jaunty and becoming, and quite effective when massed together.

Tip thought this strange Army bore no weapons whatever; but in this he was wrong. For each girl had stuck through the knot of her back hair two long, glittering knitting-needles.

General Jinjur immediately mounted the stump of a tree and addressed her army.

"Friends, fellow-citizens, and girls!" she said; "we are about to begin our great Revolt against the men of Oz! We march to conquer the Emerald City — to dethrone the Scarecrow King — to acquire thousands of gorgeous gems — to rifle the royal treasury — and to obtain power over our former oppressors!"

"Hurrah!" said those who had listened; but Tip thought most of the Army was too much engaged in chattering to pay attention to the words of the General.

The command to march was now given, and the girls formed themselves into four bands, or companies, and set off with eager strides toward the Emerald City.

The boy followed after them, carrying several baskets and wraps and packages which various members of the Army of Revolt had placed in his care. It was not long before they came to the green granite walls of the City and halted before the gateway.

The Guardian of the Gate at once came out and looked at them curiously, as if a circus had come to town. He carried a bunch of keys swung round his neck by a golden chain; his hands were thrust carelessly into his pockets, and he seemed to have no idea at all that the City was threatened by rebels. Speaking pleasantly to the girls, he said:

"Good morning, my dears! What can I do for you?"

"Surrender instantly!" answered General Jinjur, standing before him and frowning as terribly as her pretty face would allow her to.

"Surrender!" echoed the man, astounded. "Why, it's impossible. It's against the law! I never heard of such a thing in my life."

"Still, you must surrender!" exclaimed the General, fiercely. "We are revolting!"

"You don't look it," said the Guardian, gazing from one to another, admiringly.

"But we are!" cried Jinjur, stamping her foot, impatiently; "and we mean to conquer the Emerald City!"

"Good gracious!" returned the surprised Guardian of the Gates; "what a nonsensical idea! Go home to your mothers, my good girls, and milk the cows and bake the bread. Don't you know it's a dangerous thing to conquer a city?"

"We are not afraid!" responded the General; and she looked so determined that it made the Guardian uneasy.

So he rang the bell for the Soldier with the Green Whiskers, and the next minute was sorry he had done it. For immediately he was surrounded by a crowd of girls who drew the knitting-needles from their hair and began jabbing them at the Guardian with the sharp points dangerously near his fat cheeks and blinking eyes.

The poor man howled loudly for mercy and made no resistance when Jinjur drew the bunch of keys from around his neck.

Followed by her Army the General now rushed to the gateway, where she was confronted by the Royal Army of Oz — which was the other name for the Soldier with the Green Whiskers.

"Halt!" he cried, and pointed his long gun full in the face of the leader.

Some of the girls screamed and ran back, but General Jinjur bravely stood her ground and said, reproachfully:

"Why, how now? Would you shoot a poor, defenceless girl?"

"No," replied the soldier. "for my gun isn't loaded."

"Not loaded?"

"No; for fear of accidents. And I've forgotten where I hid the powder and shot to load it with. But if you'll wait a short time I'll try to hunt them up."

"Don't trouble yourself," said Jinjur, cheerfully. Then she turned to her Army and cried:

"Girls, the gun isn't loaded!"

"Hooray," shrieked the rebels, delighted at this good news, and they proceeded to rush upon the Soldier with the Green Whiskers in such a crowd that it was a wonder they didn't stick the knitting-needles into one another.

But the Royal Army of Oz was too much afraid of women to meet the onslaught. He simply turned about and ran with all his might through the gate and toward the royal palace, while General Jinjur and her mob flocked into the unprotected City.

In this way was the Emerald City captured without a drop of blood being spilled. The Army of Revolt had become an Army of Conquerors!

The Scarecrow Plans an Escape

Tip slipped away from the girls and followed swiftly after the Soldier with the Green Whiskers. The invading army entered the City more slowly, for they stopped to dig emeralds out of the walls and paving-stones with the points of their knitting-needles. So the Soldier and the boy reached the palace before the news had spread that the City was conquered.

The Scarecrow and Jack Pumpkinhead were still playing at quoits in the courtyard when the game was interrupted by the abrupt entrance of the Royal Army of Oz, who came flying in without his hat or gun, his clothes in sad disarray and his long beard floating a yard behind him as he ran.

"Tally one for me," said the Scarecrow, calmly "What's wrong, my man?" he added, addressing the Soldier.

"Oh! your Majesty — your Majesty! The City is conquered!" gasped the Royal Army, who was all out of breath.

"This is quite sudden," said the Scarecrow. "But please go and bar all the doors and windows of the palace, while I show this Pumpkinhead how to throw a quoit."

The Soldier hastened to do this, while Tip, who had arrived at his heels, remained in the courtyard to look at the Scarecrow with wondering eyes.

His Majesty continued to throw the quoits as coolly as if no danger threatened his throne, but the Pumpkinhead, having caught sight of Tip, ambled toward the boy as fast as his wooden legs would go.

"Good afternoon, noble parent!" he cried, delightedly. "I'm glad to see you are here. That terrible Saw-Horse ran away with me."

"I suspected it," said Tip. "Did you get hurt? Are you cracked at all?"

"No, I arrived safely," answered Jack, "and his Majesty has been very kind indeed to me.

At this moment the Soldier with the Green Whiskers returned, and the Scarecrow asked:

"By the way, who has conquered me?"

"A regiment of girls, gathered from the four corners of the Land of Oz," replied the Soldier, still pale with fear.

"But where was my Standing Army at the time?" inquired his Majesty, looking at the Soldier, gravely.

"Your Standing Army was running," answered the fellow, honestly; "for no man could face the terrible weapons of the invaders."

"Well," said the Scarecrow, after a moment's thought, "I don't mind much the loss of my throne, for it's a tiresome job to rule over the Emerald City. And this crown is so heavy that it makes my head ache. But I hope the Conquerors have no intention of injuring me, just because I happen to be the King."

"I heard them, say" remarked Tip, with some hesitation, "that they intend to make a rag carpet of your outside and stuff their sofa-cushions with your inside."

"Then I am really in danger," declared his Majesty, positively, "and it will be wise for me to consider a means to escape."

"Where can you go?" asked Jack Pumpkinhead.

"Why, to my friend the Tin Woodman, who rules over the Winkies, and calls himself their Emperor," was the answer. "I am sure he will protect me."

Tip was looking out the window.

"The palace is surrounded by the enemy," said he "It is too late to escape. They would soon tear you to pieces."

The Scarecrow sighed.

"In an emergency," he announced, "it is always a good thing to pause and reflect. Please excuse me while I pause and reflect."

"But we also are in danger," said the Pumpkinhead, anxiously." If any of these girls understand cooking, my end is not far off!"

"Nonsense!" exclaimed the Scarecrow. "they're too busy to cook, even if they know how!"

"But should I remain here a prisoner for any length of time," protested Jack, "I'm liable to spoil."

"Ah! then you would not be fit to associate with," returned the Scarecrow. "The matter is more serious than I suspected."

"You," said the Pumpkinhead, gloomily, "are liable to live for many years. My life is necessarily short. So I must take advantage of the few days that remain to me."

"There, there! Don't worry," answered the Scarecrow soothingly; "if you'll keep quiet long enough for me to think, I'll try to find some way for us all to escape."

So the others waited in patient silence while the Scarecrow walked to a corner and stood with his face to the wall for a good five minutes. At the end of that time he faced them with a more cheerful expression upon his painted face.

"Where is the Saw-Horse you rode here?" he asked the Pumpkinhead.

"Why, I said he was a jewel, and so your man locked him up in the royal treasury," said Jack.

"It was the only place I could think of your Majesty," added the Soldier, fearing he had made a blunder.

"It pleases me very much," said the Scarecrow. "Has the animal been fed?"

"Oh, yes; I gave him a heaping peck of sawdust."

"Excellent!" cried the Scarecrow. "Bring the horse here at once."

The Soldier hastened away, and presently they heard the clattering of the horse's wooden legs upon the pavement as he was led into the courtyard.

His Majesty regarded the steed critically. "He doesn't seem especially graceful!" he remarked, musingly. "but I suppose he can run?"

"He can, indeed," said Tip, gazing upon the Saw-Horse admiringly.

"Then, bearing us upon his back, he must make a dash through the ranks of the rebels and carry us to my friend the Tin Woodman," announced the Scarecrow.

"He can't carry four!" objected Tip.

"No, but he may be induced to carry three," said his Majesty. "I shall therefore leave my Royal Army Behind. For, from the ease with which he was conquered, I have little confidence in his powers."

"Still, he can run," declared Tip, laughing.

"I expected this blow" said the Soldier, sulkily; "but I can bear it. I shall disguise myself by cutting off my lovely green whiskers. And, after all, it is no more dangerous to face those reckless girls than to ride this fiery, untamed wooden horse!"

"Perhaps you are right," observed his Majesty. "But, for my part, not being a soldier, I am fond of danger. Now, my boy, you must mount first. And please sit as close to the horse's neck as possible."

Tip climbed quickly to his place, and the Soldier and the Scarecrow managed to hoist the Pumpkinhead to a seat just behind him. There remained so little space for the King that he was liable to fall off as soon as the horse started.

"Fetch a clothesline," said the King to his Army, "and tie us all together. Then if one falls off we will all fall off."

And while the Soldier was gone for the clothesline his Majesty continued, "it is well for me to be careful, for my very existence is in danger."

"I have to be as careful as you do," said Jack.

"Not exactly," replied the Scarecrow. "for if anything happened to me, that would be the end of me. But if anything happened to you, they could use you for seed."

The Soldier now returned with a long line and tied all three firmly together, also lashing them to the body of the Saw-Horse so there seemed little danger of their tumbling off.

"Now throw open the gates," commanded the Scarecrow, "and we will make a dash to liberty or to death."

The courtyard in which they were standing was located in the center of the great palace, which surrounded it on all sides. But in one place a passage led to an outer gateway, which the Soldier had barred by order of his sovereign. It was through this gateway his Majesty proposed to escape, and the Royal Army now led the Saw-Horse along the passage and unbarred the gate, which swung backward with a loud crash.

"Now," said Tip to the horse, "you must save us all. Run as fast as you can for the gate of the City, and don't let anything stop you."

"All right!" answered the Saw-Horse, gruffly, and dashed away so suddenly that Tip had to gasp for breath and hold firmly to the post he had driven into the creature's neck.

Several of the girls, who stood outside guarding the palace, were knocked over by the Saw-Horse's mad rush. Others ran screaming out of the way, and only one or two jabbed their knitting-needles frantically at the escaping prisoners. Tip got one small prick in his left arm, which smarted for an hour afterward; but the needles had no effect upon the Scarecrow or Jack Pumpkinhead, who never even suspected they were being prodded.

As for the Saw-Horse, he made a wonderful record, upsetting a fruit cart, overturning several meek looking men, and finally bowling over the new Guardian of the Gate — a fussy little fat woman appointed by General Jinjur.

Nor did the impetuous charger stop then. Once outside the walls of the Emerald City he dashed along the road to the West with fast and violent leaps that shook the breath out of the boy and filled the Scarecrow with wonder.

Jack had ridden at this mad rate once before, so he devoted every effort to holding, with both hands, his pumpkin head upon its stick, enduring meantime the dreadful jolting with the courage of a philosopher.

"Slow him up! Slow him up!" shouted the Scarecrow. "My straw is all shaking down into my legs."

But Tip had no breath to speak, so the Saw-Horse continued his wild career unchecked and with unabated speed.

Presently they came to the banks of a wide river, and without a pause the wooden steed gave one final leap and launched them all in mid-air.

A second later they were rolling, splashing and bobbing about in the water, the horse struggling frantically to find a rest for its feet and its riders being first plunged beneath the rapid current and then floating upon the surface like corks.

The Journey to the Tin Woodman

Tip was well soaked and dripping water from every angle of his body. But he managed to lean forward and shout in the ear of the Saw-Horse:

"Keep still, you fool! Keep still!"

The horse at once ceased struggling and floated calmly upon the surface, its wooden body being as buoyant as a raft.

"What does that word 'fool' mean?" enquired the horse.

"It is a term of reproach," answered Tip, somewhat ashamed of the expression. "I only use it when I am angry."

"Then it pleases me to be able to call you a fool, in return," said the horse. "For I did not make the river, nor put it in our way; so only a term of reproach is fit for one who becomes angry with me for falling into the water."

"That is quite evident," replied Tip; "so I will acknowledge myself in the wrong." Then he called out to the Pumpkinhead: "are you all right, Jack?"

There was no reply. So the boy called to the King "are you all right, your majesty?"

The Scarecrow groaned.

"I'm all wrong, somehow," he said, in a weak voice. "How very wet this water is!"

Tip was bound so tightly by the cord that he could not turn his head to look at his companions; so he said to the Saw-Horse:

"Paddle with your legs toward the shore."

The horse obeyed, and although their progress was slow they finally reached the opposite river bank at a place where it was low enough to enable the creature to scramble upon dry land.

With some difficulty the boy managed to get his knife out of his pocket and cut the cords that bound the riders to one another and to the wooden horse. He heard the Scarecrow fall to the ground with a mushy sound, and then he himself quickly dismounted and looked at his friend Jack.

The wooden body, with its gorgeous clothing, still sat upright upon the horse's back; but the pumpkin head was gone, and only the sharpened stick that served for a neck was visible. As for the Scarecrow, the straw in his body had shaken down with the jolting and packed itself into his legs and the lower part of his body — which appeared very plump and round while his upper half seemed like an empty sack. Upon his head the Scarecrow still wore the heavy crown, which had been sewed on to prevent his losing it; but the head was now so damp and limp that the weight of the gold and jewels sagged forward and crushed the painted face into a mass of wrinkles that made him look exactly like a Japanese pug dog.

Tip would have laughed — had he not been so anxious about his man Jack. But the Scarecrow, however damaged, was all there, while the pumpkin head that was so necessary to Jack's existence was missing; so the boy seized a long pole that fortunately lay near at hand and anxiously turned again toward the river.

Far out upon the waters he sighted the golden hue of the pumpkin, which gently bobbed up and down with the motion of the waves. At that moment it was quite out of Tip's reach, but after a time it floated nearer and still nearer until the boy was able to reach it with his pole and draw it to the shore. Then he brought it to the top of the bank, carefully wiped the water from its pumpkin face with his handkerchief, and ran with it to Jack and replaced the head upon the man's neck.

"Dear me!" were Jack's first words. "What a dreadful experience! I wonder if water is liable to spoil pumpkins?"

Tip did not think a reply was necessary, for he knew that the Scarecrow also stood in need of his help. So he carefully removed the straw from the King's body and legs, and spread it out in the sun to dry. The wet clothing he hung over the body of the Saw-Horse.

"If water spoils pumpkins," observed Jack, with a deep sigh, "then my days are numbered."

"I've never noticed that water spoils pumpkins," returned Tip; "unless the water happens to be boiling. If your head isn't cracked, my friend, you must be in fairly good condition."

"Oh, my head isn't cracked in the least," declared Jack, more cheerfully.

"Then don't worry," retorted the boy. "Care once killed a cat."

"Then," said Jack, seriously, "I am very glad indeed that I am not a cat."

The sun was fast drying their clothing, and Tip stirred up his Majesty's straw so that the warm rays might absorb the moisture and make it as crisp and dry as ever. When this had been accomplished he stuffed the Scarecrow into symmetrical shape and smoothed out his face so that he wore his usual gay and charming expression.

"Thank you very much," said the monarch, brightly, as he walked about and found himself to be well balanced. "There are several distinct advantages in being a Scarecrow. For if one has friends near at hand to repair damages, nothing very serious can happen to you."

"I wonder if hot sunshine is liable to crack pumpkins," said Jack, with an anxious ring in his voice.

"Not at all — not at all!" replied the Scarecrow, gaily. "All you need fear, my boy, is old age. When your golden youth has decayed we shall quickly part company — but you needn't look forward to it; we'll discover the fact ourselves, and notify you. But come! Let us resume our journey. I am anxious to greet my friend the Tin Woodman."

So they remounted the Saw-Horse, Tip holding to the post, the Pumpkinhead clinging to Tip, and the Scarecrow with both arms around the wooden form of Jack.

"Go slowly, for now there is no danger of pursuit," said Tip to his steed.

"All right!" responded the creature, in a voice rather gruff.

"Aren't you a little hoarse?" asked the Pumpkinhead politely.

The Saw-Horse gave an angry prance and rolled one knotty eye backward toward Tip.

"See here," he growled, "can't you protect me from insult?"

"To be sure!" answered Tip, soothingly. "I am sure Jack meant no harm. And it will not do for us to quarrel, you know; we must all remain good friends."

"I'll have nothing more to do with that Pumpkinhead," declared the Saw-Horse, viciously, "he loses his head too easily to suit me."

There seemed no fitting reply to this speech, so for a time they rode along in silence.

After a while the Scarecrow remarked:

"This reminds me of old times. It was upon this grassy knoll that I once saved Dorothy from the Stinging Bees of the Wicked Witch of the West."

"Do Stinging Bees injure pumpkins?" asked Jack, glancing around fearfully.

"They are all dead, so it doesn't matter," replied the Scarecrow." And here is where Nick Chopper destroyed the Wicked Witch's Grey Wolves."

"Who was Nick Chopper?" asked Tip.

"That is the name of my friend the Tin Woodman, answered his Majesty. And here is where the Winged Monkeys captured and bound us, and flew away with little Dorothy," he continued, after they had traveled a little way farther.

"Do Winged Monkeys ever eat pumpkins?" asked Jack, with a shiver of fear.

"I do not know; but you have little cause to, worry, for the Winged Monkeys are now the slaves of Glinda the Good, who owns the Golden Cap that commands their services," said the Scarecrow, reflectively.

Then the stuffed monarch became lost in thought recalling the days of past adventures. And the Saw-Horse rocked and rolled over the flower-strewn fields and carried its riders swiftly upon their way.

* * * * * * * *

Twilight fell, bye and bye, and then the dark shadows of night. So Tip stopped the horse and they all proceeded to dismount.

"I'm tired out," said the boy, yawning wearily; "and the grass is soft and cool. Let us lie down here and sleep until morning."

"I can't sleep," said Jack.

"I never do," said the Scarecrow.

"I do not even know what sleep is," said the Saw-Horse.

"Still, we must have consideration for this poor boy, who is made of flesh and blood and bone, and gets tired," suggested the Scarecrow, in his usual thoughtful manner. "I remember it was the same way with little Dorothy. We always had to sit through the night while she slept."

"I'm sorry," said Tip, meekly, "but I can't help it. And I'm dreadfully hungry, too!"

"Here is a new danger!" remarked Jack, gloomily. "I hope you are not fond of eating pumpkins."

"Not unless they're stewed and made into pies," answered the boy, laughing. "So have no fears of me, friend Jack."

"What a coward that Pumpkinhead is!" said the Saw-Horse, scornfully.

"You might be a coward yourself, if you knew you were liable to spoil!" retorted Jack, angrily.

"There! — there!" interrupted the Scarecrow; "don't let us quarrel. We all have our weaknesses, dear friends; so we must strive to be considerate of one another. And since this poor boy is hungry and has nothing whatever to eat, let us all remain quiet and allow him to sleep; for it is said that in sleep a mortal may forget even hunger."

"Thank you!" exclaimed Tip, gratefully. "Your Majesty is fully as good as you are wise — and that is saying a good deal!"

He then stretched himself upon the grass and, using the stuffed form of the Scarecrow for a pillow, was presently fast asleep.

A Nickel-Plated Emperor

Tip awoke soon after dawn, but the Scarecrow had already risen and plucked, with his clumsy fingers, a double-handful of ripe berries from some bushes near by. These the boy ate greedily, finding them an ample breakfast, and afterward the little party resumed its Journey.

After an hour's ride they reached the summit of a hill from whence they espied the City of the Winkies and noted the tall domes of the Emperor's palace rising from the clusters of more modest dwellings.

The Scarecrow became greatly animated at this sight, and exclaimed:

"How delighted I shall be to see my old friend the Tin Woodman again! I hope that he rules his people more successfully than I have ruled mine!"

Is the Tin Woodman the Emperor of the Winkies?" asked the horse.

"Yes, indeed. They invited him to rule over them soon after the Wicked Witch was destroyed; and as Nick Chopper has the best heart in all the world I am sure he has proved an excellent and able emperor."

I thought that 'Emperor' was the title of a person who rules an empire," said Tip, "and the Country of the Winkies is only a Kingdom."

Don't mention that to the Tin Woodman!" exclaimed the Scarecrow, earnestly. "You would hurt his feelings terribly. He is a proud man, as he has every reason to be, and it pleases him to be termed Emperor rather than King."

I'm sure it makes no difference to me," replied the boy.

The Saw-Horse now ambled forward at a pace so fast that its riders had hard work to stick upon its back; so there was little further conversation until they drew up beside the palace steps.

An aged Winkie, dressed in a uniform of silver cloth, came forward to assist them to alight. Said the Scarecrow to his personage:

Show us at once to your master, the Emperor."

The man looked from one to another of the party in an embarrassed way, and finally answered:

I fear I must ask you to wait for a time. The Emperor is not receiving this morning."

How is that?" enquired the Scarecrow, anxiously." I hope nothing has happened to him."

Oh, no; nothing serious," returned the man. "But this is his Majesty's day for being polished; and just now his august presence is thickly smeared with putz-pomade."

Oh, I see!" cried the Scarecrow, greatly reassured. "My friend was ever inclined to be a dandy, and I suppose he is now more proud than ever of his personal appearance."

He is, indeed," said the man, with a polite bow. "Our mighty Emperor has lately caused himself to be nickel-plated."

Good Gracious!" the Scarecrow exclaimed at hearing this. "If his wit bears the same polish, how sparkling it must be! But show us in — I'm sure the Emperor will receive us, even in his present state"

The Emperor's state is always magnificent," said the man. "But I will venture to tell him of your arrival, and will receive his commands concerning you."

So the party followed the servant into a splendid ante-room, and the Saw-Horse ambled awkwardly after them, having no knowledge that a horse might be expected to remain outside.

The travelers were at first somewhat awed by their surroundings, and even the Scarecrow seemed impressed as he examined the rich hangings of silver cloth caught up into knots and fastened with tiny silver axes. Upon a handsome center-table stood a large silver oil-can, richly engraved with scenes from the past adventures of the Tin Woodman, Dorothy, the Cowardly Lion and the Scarecrow: the lines of the engraving being traced upon the silver in yellow gold. On the walls hung several portraits, that of the Scarecrow seeming to be the most prominent and carefully executed, while a the large painting of the famous Wizard of Oz, in act of presenting the Tin Woodman with a heart, covered almost one entire end of the room.

While the visitors gazed at these things in silent admiration they suddenly heard a loud voice in the next room exclaim:

"Well! well! well! What a great surprise!"

And then the door burst open and Nick Chopper rushed into their midst and caught the Scarecrow in a close and loving embrace that creased him into many folds and wrinkles.

"My dear old friend! My noble comrade!" cried the Tin Woodman, joyfully, "how delighted I am to meet you once again!"

And then he released the Scarecrow and held him at arms' length while he surveyed the beloved, painted features.

But, alas! the face of the Scarecrow and many portions of his body bore great blotches of putz-pomade; for the Tin Woodman, in his eagerness to welcome his friend, had quite forgotten the condition of his toilet and had rubbed the thick coating of paste from his own body to that of his comrade.

"Dear me!" said the Scarecrow dolefully. "What a mess I'm in!"

"Never mind, my friend," returned the Tin Woodman," I'll send you to my Imperial Laundry, and you'll come out as good as new."

"Won't I be mangled?" asked the Scarecrow.

"No, indeed!" was the reply. "But tell me, how came your Majesty here? and who are your companions?"

The Scarecrow, with great politeness, introduced Tip and Jack Pumpkinhead, and the latter personage seemed to interest the Tin Woodman greatly.

"You are not very substantial, I must admit," said the Emperor. "but you are certainly unusual, and therefore worthy to become a member of our select society."

"I thank your Majesty, said Jack, humbly.

"I hope you are enjoying good health?" continued the Woodman.

"At present, yes;" replied the Pumpkinhead, with a sigh; "but I am in constant terror of the day when I shall spoil."

"Nonsense!" said the Emperor — but in a kindly, sympathetic tone. "Do not, I beg of you, dampen today's sun with the showers of tomorrow. For before your head has time to spoil you can have it canned, and in that way it may be preserved indefinitely."

Tip, during this conversation, was looking at the Woodman with undisguised amazement, and noticed that the celebrated Emperor of the Winkies was composed entirely of pieces of tin, neatly soldered and riveted together into the form of a man. He rattled and clanked a little, as he moved, but in the main he seemed to be most cleverly constructed, and his appearance was only marred by the thick coating of polishing-paste that covered him from head to foot.

The boy's intent gaze caused the Tin Woodman to remember that he was not in the most presentable condition, so he begged his friends to excuse him while he retired to his private apartment and allowed his servants to polish him. This was accomplished in a short time, and when the emperor returned his nickel-plated body shone so magnificently that the Scarecrow heartily congratulated him on his improved appearance.

"That nickel-plate was, I confess, a happy thought," said Nick; "and it was the more necessary because I had become somewhat scratched during my adventurous experiences. You will observe this engraved star upon my left breast. It not only indicates where my excellent heart lies, but covers very neatly the patch made by the Wonderful Wizard when he placed that valued organ in my breast with his own skillful hands."

"Is your heart, then, a hand-organ?" asked the Pumpkinhead, curiously.

"By no means," responded the emperor, with dignity. "It is, I am convinced, a strictly orthodox heart, although somewhat larger and warmer than most people possess."

Then he turned to the Scarecrow and asked:

"Are your subjects happy and contented, my dear friend?"

"I cannot, say" was the reply. "for the girls of Oz have risen in revolt and driven me out of the emerald City."

"Great Goodness!" cried the Tin Woodman, "What a calamity! They surely do not complain of your wise and gracious rule?"

"No; but they say it is a poor rule that don't work both ways," answered the Scarecrow; "and these females are also of the opinion that men have ruled the land long enough. So they have captured my city, robbed the treasury of all its jewels, and are running things to suit themselves."

"Dear me! What an extraordinary idea!" cried the Emperor, who was both shocked and surprised.

"And I heard some of them say," said Tip, "that they intend to march here and capture the castle and city of the Tin Woodman."

"Ah! we must not give them time to do that," said the Emperor, quickly; "we will go at once and recapture the Emerald City and place the Scarecrow again upon his throne."

"I was sure you would help me," remarked the Scarecrow in a pleased voice. "How large an army can you assemble?"

"We do not need an army," replied the Woodman. "We four, with the aid of my gleaming axe, are enough to strike terror into the hearts of the rebels."

"We five," corrected the Pumpkinhead.

"Five?" repeated the Tin Woodman.

"Yes; the Saw-Horse is brave and fearless," answered Jack, forgetting his recent quarrel with the quadruped.

The Tin Woodman looked around him in a puzzled way, for the Saw-Horse had until now remained quietly standing in a corner, where the Emperor had not noticed him. Tip immediately called the odd-looking creature to them, and it approached so awkwardly that it nearly upset the beautiful center-table and the engraved oil-can.

"I begin to think," remarked the Tin Woodman as he looked earnestly at the Saw-Horse, "that wonders will never cease! How came this creature alive?"

"I did it with a magic powder," modestly asserted the boy, "and the Saw-Horse has been very useful to us."

"He enabled us to escape the rebels," added the Scarecrow.

"Then we must surely accept him as a comrade," declared the emperor. "A live Saw-Horse is a distinct novelty, and should prove an interesting study. Does he know anything?"

"Well, I cannot claim any great experience in life," the Saw-Horse answered for himself. "but I seem to learn very quickly, and often it occurs to me that I know more than any of those around me."

"Perhaps you do," said the emperor; "for experience does not always mean wisdom. But time is precious just now, so let us quickly make preparations to start upon our journey."

The emperor called his Lord High Chancellor and instructed him how to run the kingdom during his absence. Meanwhile the Scarecrow was taken apart and the painted sack that served him for a head was carefully laundered and restuffed with the brains originally given him by the great Wizard. His clothes were also cleaned and pressed by the Imperial tailors, and his crown polished and again sewed upon his head, for the Tin Woodman insisted he should not renounce this badge of royalty. The Scarecrow now presented a very respectable appearance, and although in no way addicted to vanity he was quite pleased with himself and strutted a trifle as he walked. While this was being done Tip mended the wooden limbs of Jack Pumpkinhead and made them stronger than before, and the Saw-Horse was also inspected to see if he was in good working order.

Then bright and early the next morning they set out upon their return journey to the emerald City, the Tin Woodman bearing upon his shoulder a gleaming axe and leading the way, while the Pumpkinhead rode upon the Saw-Horse and Tip and the Scarecrow walked upon either side to make sure that he didn't fall off or become damaged.

Mr. H. M. Woggle-Bug, T. E.

Now, General Jinjur — who, you will remember, commanded the Army of Revolt — was rendered very uneasy by the escape of the Scarecrow from the Emerald City. She feared, and with good reason, that if his Majesty and the Tin Woodman joined forces, it would mean danger to her and her entire army; for the people of Oz had not yet forgotten the deeds of these famous heroes, who had passed successfully through so many startling adventures.

So Jinjur sent post-haste for old Mombi, the witch, and promised her large rewards if she would come to the assistance of the rebel army.

Mombi was furious at the trick Tip had played upon her as well as at his escape and the theft of the precious Powder of Life; so she needed no urging to induce her to travel to the Emerald City to assist Jinjur in defeating the Scarecrow and the Tin Woodman, who had made Tip one of their friends.

Mombi had no sooner arrived at the royal palace than she discovered, by means of her secret magic, that the adventurers were starting upon their journey to the Emerald City; so she retired to a small room high up in a tower and locked herself in while she practised such arts as she could command to prevent the return of the Scarecrow and his companions.

That was why the Tin Woodman presently stopped and said:

"Something very curious has happened. I ought to know by heart and every step of this Journey, yet I fear we have already lost our way."

"That is quite impossible!" protested the Scarecrow. "Why do you think, my dear friend, that we have gone astray?"

"Why, here before us is a great field of sunflowers — and I never saw this field before in all my life."

At these words they all looked around, only to find that they were indeed surrounded by a field of tall stalks, every stalk bearing at its top a gigantic sunflower. And not only were these flowers almost blinding in their vivid hues of red and gold, but each one whirled around upon its stalk like a miniature wind-mill, completely dazzling the vision of the beholders and so mystifying them that they knew not which way to turn.

"It's witchcraft!" exclaimed Tip.

While they paused, hesitating and wondering, the Tin Woodman uttered a cry of impatience and advanced with swinging axe to cut down the stalks before him. But now the sunflowers suddenly stopped their rapid whirling, and the travelers plainly saw a girl's face appear in the center of each flower. These lovely faces looked upon the astonished band with mocking smiles, and then burst into a chorus of merry laughter at the dismay their appearance caused.

"Stop! stop!" cried Tip, seizing the Woodman's arm; "they're alive! they're girls!"

At that moment the flowers began whirling again, and the faces faded away and were lost in the rapid revolutions.

The Tin Woodman dropped his axe and sat down upon the ground.

"It would be heartless to chop down those pretty creatures," said he, despondently. "and yet I do not know how else we can proceed upon our way"

"They looked to me strangely like the faces of the Army of Revolt," mused the Scarecrow. "But I cannot conceive how the girls could have followed us here so quickly."

"I believe it's magic," said Tip, positively, "and that someone is playing a trick upon us. I've known old Mombi do things like that before. Probably it's nothing more than an illusion, and there are no sunflowers here at all."

"Then let us shut our eyes and walk forward," suggested the Woodman.

"Excuse me," replied the Scarecrow. "My eyes are not painted to shut. Because you happen to have tin eyelids, you must not imagine we are all built in the same way."

"And the eyes of the Saw-Horse are knot eyes," said Jack, leaning forward to examine them.

"Nevertheless, you must ride quickly forward," commanded Tip, "and we will follow after you and so try to escape. My eyes are already so dazzled that I can scarcely see."

So the Pumpkinhead rode boldly forward, and Tip grasped the stub tail of the Saw-Horse and followed with closed eyes. The Scarecrow and the Tin Woodman brought up the rear, and before they had gone many yards a joyful shout from Jack announced that the way was clear before them.

Then all paused to look backward, but not a trace of the field of sunflowers remained.

More cheerfully, now they proceeded upon their Journey; but old Mombi had so changed the appearance of the landscape that they would surely have been lost had not the Scarecrow wisely concluded to take their direction from the sun. For no witchcraft could change the course of the sun, and it was therefore a safe guide.

However, other difficulties lay before them. The Saw-Horse stepped into a rabbit hole and fell to the ground. The Pumpkinhead was pitched high into the air, and his history would probably have ended at that exact moment had not the Tin Woodman skillfully caught the pumpkin as it descended and saved it from injury.

Tip soon had it fitted to the neck again and replaced Jack upon his feet. But the Saw-Horse did not escape so easily. For when his leg was pulled from the rabbit hole it was found to be broken short off, and must be replaced or repaired before he could go a step farther.

"This is quite serious," said the Tin Woodman." If there were trees near by I might soon manufacture another leg for this animal; but I cannot see even a shrub for miles around."

"And there are neither fences nor houses in this part of the land of Oz," added the Scarecrow, disconsolately.

"Then what shall we do?" enquired the boy.

"I suppose I must start my brains working," replied his Majesty the Scarecrow; "for experience has taught me that I can do anything if I but take time to think it out."

"Let us all think," said Tip; "and perhaps we shall find a way to repair the Saw-Horse."

So they sat in a row upon the grass and began to think, while the Saw-Horse occupied itself by gazing curiously upon its broken limb.

"Does it hurt?" asked the Tin Woodman, in a soft, sympathetic voice.

"Not in the least," returned the Saw-Horse; "but my pride is injured to find that my anatomy is so brittle."

For a time the little group remained in silent thought. Presently the Tin Woodman raised his head and looked over the fields.

"What sort of creature is that which approaches us?" he asked, wonderingly.

The others followed his gaze, and discovered coming toward them the most extraordinary object they had ever beheld. It advanced quickly and noiselessly over the soft grass and in a few minutes stood before the adventurers and regarded them with an astonishment equal to their own.

The Scarecrow was calm under all circumstances.

"Good morning!" he said, politely.

The stranger removed his hat with a flourish, bowed very low, and then responded:

"Good morning, one and all. I hope you are, as an aggregation, enjoying excellent health. Permit me to present my card."

With this courteous speech it extended a card toward the Scarecrow, who accepted it, turned it over and over, and handed it with a shake of his head to Tip.

The boy read aloud:

"MR. H. M. WOGGLE-BUG, T. E."

"Dear me!" ejaculated the Pumpkinhead, staring somewhat intently.

"How very peculiar!" said the Tin Woodman.

Tip's eyes were round and wondering, and the Saw-Horse uttered a sigh and turned away its head.

"Are you really a Woggle-Bug?" enquired the Scarecrow.

"Most certainly, my dear sir!" answered the stranger, briskly. "Is not my name upon the card?"

"It is," said the Scarecrow. "But may I ask what 'H. M.' stands for?"

"'H. M.' means Highly Magnified," returned the Woggle-Bug, proudly.

"Oh, I see." The Scarecrow viewed the stranger critically. "And are you, in truth, highly magnified?"

"Sir," said the Woggle-Bug, "I take you for a gentleman of judgment and discernment. Does it not occur to you that I am several thousand times greater than any Woggle-Bug you ever saw before? Therefore it is plainly evident that I am Highly Magnified, and there is no good reason why you should doubt the fact."

"Pardon me," returned the Scarecrow. "My brains are slightly mixed since I was last laundered. Would it be improper for me to ask, also, what the 'T.E.' at the end of your name stands for?"

"Those letters express my degree," answered the Woggle-Bug, with a condescending smile. "To be more explicit, the initials mean that I am Thoroughly Educated."

"Oh!" said the Scarecrow, much relieved.

Tip had not yet taken his eyes off this wonderful personage. What he saw was a great, round, buglike body supported upon two slender legs which ended in delicate feet — the toes curling upward. The body of the Woggle-Bug was rather flat, and judging from what could be seen of it was of a glistening dark brown color upon the back, while the front was striped with alternate bands of light brown and white, blending together at the edges. Its arms were fully as slender as its legs, and upon a rather long neck was perched its head — not unlike the head of a man, except that its nose ended in a curling antenna, or "feeler," and its ears from the upper points bore antennae that decorated the sides of its head like two miniature, curling pig tails. It must be admitted that the round, black eyes were rather bulging in

appearance; but the expression upon the Woggle-Bug's face was by no means unpleasant.

For dress the insect wore a dark-blue swallowtail coat with a yellow silk lining and a flower in the button-hole; a vest of white duck that stretched tightly across the wide body; knickerbockers of fawn-colored plush, fastened at the knees with gilt buckles; and, perched upon its small head, was jauntily set a tall silk hat.

Standing upright before our amazed friends the Woggle-Bug appeared to be fully as tall as the Tin Woodman; and surely no bug in all the Land of Oz had ever before attained so enormous a size.

"I confess," said the Scarecrow, "that your abrupt appearance has caused me surprise, and no doubt has startled my companions. I hope, however, that this circumstance will not distress you. We shall probably get used to you in time."

"Do not apologize, I beg of you!" returned the Woggle-Bug, earnestly. "It affords me great pleasure to surprise people; for surely I cannot be classed with ordinary insects and am entitled to both curiosity and admiration from those I meet."

"You are, indeed," agreed his Majesty.

"If you will permit me to seat myself in your august company," continued the stranger, "I will gladly relate my history, so that you will be better able to comprehend my unusual — may I say remarkable? — appearance."

"You may say what you please," answered the Tin Woodman, briefly.

So the Woggle-Bug sat down upon the grass, facing the little group of wanderers, and told them the following story:

A Highly Magnified History

"It is but honest that I should acknowledge at the beginning of my recital that I was born an ordinary Woggle-Bug," began the creature, in a frank and friendly tone. "Knowing no better, I used my arms as well as my legs for walking, and crawled under the edges of stones or hid among the roots of grasses with no thought beyond finding a few insects smaller than myself to feed upon.

The chill nights rendered me stiff and motionless, for I wore no clothing, but each morning the warm rays of the sun gave me new life and restored me to activity. A horrible existence is this, but you must remember it is the regular ordained existence of Woggle-Bugs, as well as of many other tiny creatures that inhabit the earth.

But Destiny had singled me out, humble though I was, for a grander fate! One day I crawled near to a country school house, and my curiosity being excited by the monotonous hum of the students within, I made bold to enter and creep along a crack between two boards until I reached the far end, where, in front of a hearth of glowing embers, sat the master at his desk.

No one noticed so small a creature as a Woggle-Bug, and when I found that the hearth was even warmer and more comfortable than the sunshine, I resolved to establish my future home beside it. So I found a charming nest between two bricks and hid myself therein for many, many months.

Professor Nowitall is, doubtless, the most famous scholar in the land of Oz, and after a few days I began to listen to the lectures and discourses he gave his pupils. Not one of them was more attentive than the humble, unnoticed Woggle-Bug, and I acquired in this way a fund of knowledge that I will myself confess is simply marvelous. That is why I place 'T.E.' Thoroughly Educated upon my cards; for my greatest pride lies in the fact that the world cannot produce another Woggle-Bug with a tenth part of my own culture and erudition."

"I do not blame you," said the Scarecrow. "Education is a thing to be proud of. I'm educated myself. The mess of brains given me by the Great Wizard is considered by my friends to be unexcelled."

"Nevertheless," interrupted the Tin Woodman, "a good heart is, I believe, much more desirable than education or brains."

"To me," said the Saw-Horse, "a good leg is more desirable than either."

"Could seeds be considered in the light of brains?" enquired the Pumpkinhead, abruptly.

"Keep quiet!" commanded Tip, sternly.

"Very well, dear father," answered the obedient Jack.

The Woggle-Bug listened patiently — even respectfully — to these remarks, and then resumed his story.

"I must have lived fully three years in that secluded school-house hearth," said he, "drinking thirstily of the ever-flowing fount of limpid knowledge before me."

"Quite poetical," commented the Scarecrow, nodding his head approvingly.

"But one, day" continued the Bug, "a marvelous circumstance occurred that altered my very existence and brought me to my present pinnacle of greatness. The Professor discovered me in the act of crawling across the hearth, and before I could escape he had caught me between his thumb and forefinger.

'My dear children,' said he, 'I have captured a Woggle-Bug — a very rare and interesting specimen. Do any of you know what a Woggle-Bug is?'

'No!' yelled the scholars, in chorus.

'Then,' said the Professor, 'I will get out my famous magnifying-glass and throw the insect upon a screen in a highly-magnified condition, that you may all study carefully its peculiar construction and become acquainted with its habits and manner of life.'

He then brought from a cupboard a most curious instrument, and before I could realize what had happened I found myself thrown upon a screen in a highly-magnified state — even as you now behold me.

The students stood up on their stools and craned their heads forward to get a better view of me, and two little girls jumped upon the sill of an open window where they could see more plainly.

'Behold!' cried the Professor, in a loud voice, 'this highly-magnified Woggle-Bug; one of the most curious insects in existence!'

Being Thoroughly Educated, and knowing what is required of a cultured gentleman, at this juncture I stood upright and, placing my hand upon my bosom, made a very polite bow. My action, being unexpected, must have startled them, for one of the little girls perched upon the window-sill gave a scream and fell backward out the window, drawing her companion with her as she disappeared.

The Professor uttered a cry of horror and rushed away through the door to see if the poor children were injured by the fall. The scholars followed after him in a wild mob, and I was left alone in the school-room, still in a Highly-Magnified state and free to do as I pleased.

It immediately occurred to me that this was a good opportunity to escape. I was proud of my great size, and realized that now I could safely travel anywhere in the world, while my superior culture would make me a fit associate for the most learned person I might chance to meet.

So, while the Professor picked the little girls — who were more frightened than hurt — off the ground, and the pupils clustered around him closely grouped, I calmly walked out of the school-house, turned a corner, and escaped unnoticed to a grove of trees that stood near"

"Wonderful!" exclaimed the Pumpkinhead, admiringly.

"It was, indeed," agreed the Woggle-Bug. "I have never ceased to congratulate myself for escaping while I was Highly Magnified; for even my excessive knowledge would have proved of little use to me had I remained a tiny, insignificant insect."

"I didn't know before," said Tip, looking at the Woggle-Bug with a puzzled expression, "that insects wore clothes."

"Nor do they, in their natural state," returned the stranger. "But in the course of my wanderings I had the good fortune to save the ninth life of a tailor — tailors having, like cats, nine lives, as you probably know. The fellow was exceedingly grateful, for had he lost that ninth life it would have been the end of him; so he begged permission to furnish me with the stylish costume I now wear. It fits very nicely, does it not?" and the Woggle-Bug stood up and turned himself around slowly, that all might examine his person.

"He must have been a good tailor," said the Scarecrow, somewhat enviously.

"He was a good-hearted tailor, at any rate," observed Nick Chopper.

"But where were you going, when you met us?" Tip asked the Woggle-Bug.

"Nowhere in particular," was the reply, "although it is my intention soon to visit the Emerald City and arrange to give a course of lectures to select audiences on the 'Advantages of Magnification.'"

"We are bound for the Emerald City now," said the Tin Woodman; "so, if it pleases you to do so, you are welcome to travel in our company."

The Woggle-Bug bowed with profound grace.

"It will give me great pleasure," said he "to accept your kind invitation; for nowhere in the Land of Oz could I hope to meet with so congenial a company."

"That is true," acknowledged the Pumpkinhead. "We are quite as congenial as flies and honey."

"But — pardon me if I seem inquisitive — are you not all rather — ahem! rather unusual?" asked the Woggle-Bug, looking from one to another with unconcealed interest.

"Not more so than yourself," answered the Scarecrow. "Everything in life is unusual until you get accustomed to it."

"What rare philosophy!" exclaimed the Woggle-Bug, admiringly.

"Yes; my brains are working well today," admitted the Scarecrow, an accent of pride in his voice.

"Then, if you are sufficiently rested and refreshed, let us bend our steps toward the Emerald City," suggested the magnified one.

"We can't," said Tip. "The Saw-Horse has broken a leg, so he can't bend his steps. And there is no wood around to make him a new limb from. And we can't leave the horse behind because the Pumpkinhead is so stiff in his Joints that he has to ride."

"How very unfortunate!" cried the Woggle-Bug. Then he looked the party over carefully and said:

"If the Pumpkinhead is to ride, why not use one of his legs to make a leg for the horse that carries him? I judge that both are made of wood."

"Now, that is what I call real cleverness," said the Scarecrow, approvingly. "I wonder my brains did not think of that long ago! Get to work, my dear Nick, and fit the Pumpkinhead's leg to the Saw-Horse."

Jack was not especially pleased with this idea; but he submitted to having his left leg amputated by the Tin Woodman and whittled down to fit the left leg of the Saw-Horse. Nor was the Saw-Horse especially pleased with the operation, either; for he growled a good deal about being "butchered," as he called it, and afterward declared that the new leg was a disgrace to a respectable Saw-Horse.

"I beg you to be more careful in your speech," said the Pumpkinhead, sharply. "Remember, if you please, that it is my leg you are abusing."

"I cannot forget it," retorted the Saw-Horse, "for it is quite as flimsy as the rest of your person."

"Flimsy! me flimsy!" cried Jack, in a rage. "How dare you call me flimsy?"

"Because you are built as absurdly as a jumping-jack," sneered the horse, rolling his knotty eyes in a vicious manner. "Even your head won't stay straight, and you never can tell whether you are looking backwards or forwards!"

"Friends, I entreat you not to quarrel!" pleaded the Tin Woodman, anxiously. "As a matter of fact, we are none of us above criticism; so let us bear with each others' faults."

"An excellent suggestion," said the Woggle-Bug, approvingly. "You must have an excellent heart, my metallic friend."

"I have," returned Nick, well pleased. "My heart is quite the best part of me. But now let us start upon our Journey.

They perched the one-legged Pumpkinhead upon the Saw-Horse, and tied him to his seat with cords, so that he could not possibly fall off.

And then, following the lead of the Scarecrow, they all advanced in the direction of the Emerald City.

Old Mombi Indulges in Witchcraft

They soon discovered that the Saw-Horse limped, for his new leg was a trifle too long. So they were obliged to halt while the Tin Woodman chopped it down with his axe, after which the wooden steed paced along more comfortably. But the Saw-Horse was not entirely satisfied, even yet.

"It was a shame that I broke my other leg!" it growled.

"On the contrary," airily remarked the Woggle-Bug, who was walking alongside, "you should consider the accident most fortunate. For a horse is never of much use until he has been broken."

"I beg your pardon," said Tip, rather provoked, for he felt a warm interest in both the Saw-Horse and his man Jack; "but permit me to say that your joke is a poor one, and as old as it is poor."

"Still, it is a joke," declared the Woggle-Bug; firmly, "and a joke derived from a play upon words is considered among educated people to be eminently proper."

"What does that mean?" enquired the Pumpkinhead, stupidly.

"It means, my dear friend," explained the Woggle-Bug, "that our language contains many words having a double meaning; and that to pronounce a joke that allows both meanings of a certain word, proves the joker a person of culture and refinement, who has, moreover, a thorough command of the language."

"I don't believe that," said Tip, plainly; "anybody can make a pun."

"Not so," rejoined the Woggle-Bug, stiffly. "It requires education of a high order. Are you educated, young sir?"

"Not especially," admitted Tip.

"Then you cannot judge the matter. I myself am Thoroughly Educated, and I say that puns display genius. For instance, were I to ride upon this Saw-Horse, he would not only be an animal, he would become an equipage. For he would then be a horse-and-buggy."

At this the Scarecrow gave a gasp and the Tin Woodman stopped short and looked reproachfully at the Woggle-Bug. At the same time the Saw-Horse loudly snorted his derision; and even the Pumpkinhead put up his hand to hide the smile which, because it was carved upon his face, he could not change to a frown.

But the Woggle-Bug strutted along as if he had made some brilliant remark, and the Scarecrow was obliged to say:

"I have heard, my dear friend, that a person can become over-educated; and although I have a high respect for brains, no matter how they may be arranged or classified, I begin to suspect that yours are slightly tangled. In any event, I must beg you to restrain your superior education while in our society."

"We are not very particular," added the Tin Woodman; "and we are exceedingly kind hearted. But if your superior culture gets leaky again — " He did not complete the sentence, but he twirled his gleaming axe so carelessly that the Woggle-Bug looked frightened, and shrank away to a safe distance.

The others marched on in silence, and the Highly Magnified one, after a period of deep thought, said in an humble voice:

"I will endeavor to restrain myself."

"That is all we can expect," returned the Scarecrow pleasantly; and good nature being thus happily restored to the party, they proceeded upon their way.

When they again stopped to allow Tip to rest — the boy being the only one that seemed to tire — the Tin Woodman noticed many small, round holes in the grassy meadow.

"This must be a village of the Field Mice," he said to the Scarecrow." I wonder if my old friend, the Queen of the Mice, is in this neighborhood."

"If she is, she may be of great service to us," answered the Scarecrow, who was impressed by a sudden thought. "See if you can call her, my dear Nick."

So the Tin Woodman blew a shrill note upon a silver whistle that hung around his neck, and presently a tiny grey mouse popped from a near-by hole and advanced fearlessly toward them. For the Tin Woodman had once saved her life, and the Queen of the Field Mice knew he was to be trusted."

"Good day, your Majesty", said Nick, politely addressing the mouse; "I trust you are enjoying good health?"

"Thank you, I am quite well," answered the Queen, demurely, as she sat up and displayed the tiny golden crown upon her head. "Can I do anything to assist my old friends?"

"You can, indeed," replied the Scarecrow, eagerly. "Let me, I intreat you, take a dozen of your subjects with me to the Emerald City."

"Will they be injured in any way?" asked the Queen, doubtfully.

"I think not," replied the Scarecrow. "I will carry them hidden in the straw which stuffs my body, and when I give them the signal by unbuttoning my jacket, they have only to rush out and scamper home again as fast as they can. By doing this they will assist me to regain my throne, which the Army of Revolt has taken from me."

"In that case," said the Queen, "I will not refuse your request. Whenever you are ready, I will call twelve of my most intelligent subjects."

"I am ready now" returned the Scarecrow. Then he lay flat upon the ground and unbuttoned his jacket, displaying the mass of straw with which he was stuffed.

The Queen uttered a little piping call, and in an instant a dozen pretty field mice had emerged from their holes and stood before their ruler, awaiting her orders.

What the Queen said to them none of our travelers could understand, for it was in the mouse language; but the field mice obeyed without hesitation, running one after the other to the Scarecrow and hiding themselves in the straw of his breast.

When all of the twelve mice had thus concealed themselves, the Scarecrow buttoned his Jacket securely and then arose and thanked the Queen for her kindness.

"One thing more you might do to serve us," suggested the Tin Woodman; "and that is to run ahead and show us the way to the Emerald City. For some enemy is evidently trying to prevent us from reaching it."

"I will do that gladly," returned the Queen. "Are you ready?"

The Tin Woodman looked at Tip.

"I'm rested," said the boy. "Let us start."

Then they resumed their journey, the little grey Queen of the Field Mice running swiftly ahead and then pausing until the travelers drew near, when away she would dart again.

Without this unerring guide the Scarecrow and his comrades might never have gained the Emerald City; for many were the obstacles thrown in their way by the arts of old Mombi. Yet not one of the obstacles really existed — all were cleverly contrived deceptions. For when they came to the banks of a rushing river that threatened to bar their way the little Queen kept steadily on, passing through the seeming flood in safety; and our travelers followed her without encountering a single drop of water.

Again, a high wall of granite towered high above their heads and opposed their advance. But the grey Field Mouse walked straight through it, and the others did the same, the wall melting into mist as they passed it.

Afterward, when they had stopped for a moment to allow Tip to rest, they saw forty roads branching off from their feet in forty different directions; and soon these forty roads began whirling around like a mighty wheel, first in one direction and then in the other, completely bewildering their vision.

But the Queen called for them to follow her and darted off in a straight line; and when they had gone a few paces the whirling pathways vanished and were seen no more.

Mombi's last trick was the most fearful of all. She sent a sheet of crackling flame rushing over the meadow to consume them; and for the first time the Scarecrow became afraid and turned to fly.

"If that fire reaches me I will be gone in no time!" said he, trembling until his straw rattled. "It's the most dangerous thing I ever encountered."

"I'm off, too!" cried the Saw-Horse, turning and prancing with agitation; "for my wood is so dry it would burn like kindlings."

"Is fire dangerous to pumpkins?" asked Jack, fearfully.

"You'll be baked like a tart — and so will I!" answered the Woggle-Bug, getting down on all fours so he could run the faster.

But the Tin Woodman, having no fear of fire, averted the stampede by a few sensible words.

"Look at the Field Mouse!" he shouted. "The fire does not burn her in the least. In fact, it is no fire at all, but only a deception."

Indeed, to watch the little Queen march calmly through the advancing flames restored courage to every member of the party, and they followed her without being even scorched.

"This is surely a most extraordinary adventure," said the Woggle-Bug, who was greatly amazed; "for it upsets all the Natural Laws that I heard Professor Nowitall teach in the school-house."

"Of course it does," said the Scarecrow, wisely. "All magic is unnatural, and for that reason is to be feared and avoided. But I see before us the gates of the Emerald City, so I imagine we have now overcome all the magical obstacles that seemed to oppose us."

Indeed, the walls of the City were plainly visible, and the Queen of the Field Mice, who had guided them so faithfully, came near to bid them goodbye.

"We are very grateful to your Majesty for your kind assistance," said the Tin Woodman, bowing before the pretty creature.

"I am always pleased to be of service to my friends," answered the Queen, and in a flash she had darted away upon her journey home.

The Prisoners of the Queen

Approaching the gateway of the Emerald City the travelers found it guarded by two girls of the Army of Revolt, who opposed their entrance by drawing the knitting-needles from their hair and threatening to prod the first that came near.

But the Tin Woodman was not afraid. "At the worst they can but scratch my beautiful nickel-plate," he said. "But there will be no 'worst,' for I think I can manage to frighten these absurd soldiers very easily. Follow me closely, all of you!"

Then, swinging his axe in a great circle to right and left before him, he advanced upon the gate, and the others followed him without hesitation.

The girls, who had expected no resistance whatever, were terrified by the sweep of the glittering axe and fled screaming into the city; so that our travelers passed the gates in safety and marched down the green marble pavement of the wide street toward the royal palace.

"At this rate we will soon have your Majesty upon the throne again," said the Tin Woodman, laughing at his easy conquest of the guards.

"Thank you, friend Nick," returned the Scarecrow, gratefully. "Nothing can resist your kind heart and your sharp axe."

As they passed the rows of houses they saw through the open doors that men were sweeping and dusting and washing dishes, while the women sat around in groups, gossiping and laughing.

"What has happened?" the Scarecrow asked a sad-looking man with a bushy beard, who wore an apron and was wheeling a baby-carriage along the sidewalk.

"Why, we've had a revolution, your Majesty as you ought to know very well," replied the man; "and since you went away the women have been running things to suit themselves. I'm glad

you have decided to come back and restore order, for doing housework and minding the children is wearing out the strength of every man in the Emerald City."

"Hm!" said the Scarecrow, thoughtfully. "If it is such hard work as you say, how did the women manage it so easily?"

"I really do not know" replied the man, with a deep sigh. "Perhaps the women are made of cast iron."

No movement was made, as they passed along the street, to oppose their progress. Several of the women stopped their gossip long enough to cast curious looks upon our friends, but immediately they would turn away with a laugh or a sneer and resume their chatter. And when they met with several girls belonging to the Army of Revolt, those soldiers, instead of being alarmed or appearing surprised, merely stepped out of the way and allowed them to advance without protest.

This action rendered the Scarecrow uneasy. "I'm afraid we are walking into a trap," said he.

"Nonsense!" returned Nick Chopper, confidently; "the silly creatures are conquered already!"

But the Scarecrow shook his head in a way that expressed doubt, and Tip said: "It's too easy, altogether. Look out for trouble ahead."

"I will," returned his Majesty. Unopposed they reached the royal palace and marched up the marble steps, which had once been thickly crusted with emeralds but were now filled with tiny holes where the jewels had been ruthlessly torn from their settings by the Army of Revolt. And so far not a rebel barred their way.

Through the arched hallways and into the magnificent throne room marched the Tin Woodman and his followers, and here, when the green silken curtains fell behind them, they saw a curious sight.

Seated within the glittering throne was General Jinjur, with the Scarecrow's second-best crown upon her head, and the royal sceptre in her right hand. A box of caramels, from which she was eating, rested in her lap, and the girl seemed entirely at ease in her royal surroundings.

The Scarecrow stepped forward and confronted her, while the Tin Woodman leaned upon his axe and the others formed a half-circle back of his Majesty's person.

"How dare you sit in my throne?" demanded the Scarecrow, sternly eyeing the intruder. "Don't you know you are guilty of treason, and that there is a law against treason?"

"The throne belongs to whoever is able to take it," answered Jinjur, as she slowly ate another caramel. "I have taken it, as you see; so just now I am the Queen, and all who oppose me are guilty of treason, and must be punished by the law you have just mentioned."

This view of the case puzzled the Scarecrow.

"How is it, friend Nick?" he asked, turning to the Tin Woodman.

"Why, when it comes to Law, I have nothing to, say" answered that personage. "for laws were never meant to be understood, and it is foolish to make the attempt."

Then what shall we do?" asked the Scarecrow, in dismay.

Why don't you marry the Queen? And then you can both rule," suggested the Woggle-Bug.

Jinjur glared at the insect fiercely. "Why don't you send her back to her mother, where she belongs?" asked Jack Pumpkinhead.

Jinjur frowned.

Why don't you shut her up in a closet until she behaves herself, and promises to be good?" enquired Tip. Jinjur's lip curled scornfully.

Or give her a good shaking!" added the Saw-Horse.

"No," said the Tin Woodman, "we must treat the poor girl with gentleness. Let us give her all the jewels she can carry, and send her away happy and contented."

At this Queen Jinjur laughed aloud, and the next minute clapped her pretty hands together thrice, as if for a signal.

You are very absurd creatures," said she; "but I am tired of your nonsense and have no time to bother with you longer."

While the monarch and his friends listened in amazement to this impudent speech, a startling thing happened. The Tin Woodman's axe was snatched from his grasp by some person behind him, and he found himself disarmed and helpless. At the same instant a shout of laughter rang in the ears of the devoted band, and turning to see whence this came they found themselves surrounded by the Army of Revolt, the girls bearing in either hand their glistening knitting-needles. The entire throne room seemed to be filled with the rebels, and the Scarecrow and his comrades realized that they were prisoners.

You see how foolish it is to oppose a woman's wit," said Jinjur, gaily; "and this event only proves that I am more fit to rule the Emerald City than a Scarecrow. I bear you no ill will, I assure you; but lest you should prove troublesome to me in the future I shall order you all to be destroyed. That is, all except the boy, who belongs to old Mombi and must be restored to her keeping. The rest of you are not human, and therefore it will not be wicked to demolish you. The Saw-Horse and the Pumpkinhead's body I will have chopped up for kindling-wood; and the pumpkin shall be made into tarts. The Scarecrow will do nicely to start a bonfire, and the tin man can be cut into small pieces and fed to the goats. As for this immense Woggle-Bug —"

Highly Magnified, if you please!" interrupted the insect.

I think I will ask the cook to make green-turtle soup of you," continued the Queen, reflectively.

The Woggle-Bug shuddered.

Or, if that won't do, we might use you for a Hungarian goulash, stewed and highly spiced," she added, cruelly.

This programme of extermination was so terrible that the prisoners looked upon one another in a panic of fear. The Scarecrow alone did not give way to despair. He stood quietly before the Queen and his brow was wrinkled in deep thought as he strove to find some means to escape.

While thus engaged he felt the straw within his breast move gently. At once his expression changed from sadness to joy, and raising his hand he quickly unbuttoned the front of his jacket.

This action did not pass unnoticed by the crowd of girls clustering about him, but none of them suspected what he was doing until a tiny grey mouse leaped from his bosom to the floor and scampered away between the feet of the Army of Revolt. Another mouse quickly followed; then another and another, in rapid succession. And suddenly such a scream of terror went up from the Army that it might easily have filled the stoutest heart with consternation. The flight that ensued turned to a stampede, and the stampede to a panic.

For while the startled mice rushed wildly about the room the Scarecrow had only time to note a whirl of skirts and a twinkling of feet as the girls disappeared from the palace — pushing and crowding one another in their mad efforts to escape.

The Queen, at the first alarm, stood up on the cushions of the throne and began to dance frantically upon her tiptoes. Then a mouse ran up the cushions, and with a terrified leap poor Jinjur shot clear over the head of the Scarecrow and escaped through an archway — never pausing in her wild career until she had reached the city gates.

So, in less time than I can explain, the throne room was deserted by all save the Scarecrow and his friends, and the Woggle-Bug heaved a deep sigh of relief as he exclaimed:

"Thank goodness, we are saved!"

"For a time, yes;" answered the Tin Woodman. "But the enemy will soon return, I fear."

"Let us bar all the entrances to the palace!" said the Scarecrow. "Then we shall have time to think what is best to be done."

So all except Jack Pumpkinhead, who was still tied fast to the Saw-Horse, ran to the various entrances of the royal palace and closed the heavy doors, bolting and locking them securely. Then, knowing that the Army of Revolt could not batter down the barriers in several days, the adventurers gathered once more in the throne room for a council of war.

The Scarecrow Takes Time to Think

"It seems to me," began the Scarecrow, when all were again assembled in the throne room, "that the girl Jinjur is quite right in claiming to be Queen. And if she is right, then I am wrong, and we have no business to be occupying her palace."

"But you were the King until she came," said the Woggle-Bug, strutting up and down with his hands in his pockets; "so it appears to me that she is the interloper instead of you."

"Especially as we have just conquered her and put her to flight," added the Pumpkinhead, as he raised his hands to turn his face toward the Scarecrow.

"Have we really conquered her?" asked the Scarecrow, quietly. "Look out of the window, and tell me what you see."

Tip ran to the window and looked out.

"The palace is surrounded by a double row of girl soldiers," he announced.

"I thought so," returned the Scarecrow. "We are as truly their prisoners as we were before the mice frightened them from the palace."

"My friend is right," said Nick Chopper, who had been polishing his breast with a bit of chamois-leather. "Jinjur is still the Queen, and we are her prisoners."

"But I hope she cannot get at us," exclaimed the Pumpkinhead, with a shiver of fear. "She threatened to make tarts of me, you know."

"Don't worry," said the Tin Woodman. "It cannot matter greatly. If you stay shut up here you will spoil in time, anyway. A good tart is far more admirable than a decayed intellect."

"Very true," agreed the Scarecrow.

"Oh, dear!" moaned Jack; "what an unhappy lot is mine! Why, dear father, did you not make me out of tin — or even out of straw — so that I would keep indefinitely."

"Shucks!" returned Tip, indignantly. "You ought to be glad that I made you at all." Then he added, reflectively, "everything has to come to an end, some time."

"But I beg to remind you," broke in the Woggle-Bug, who had a distressed look in his bulging, round eyes, "that this terrible Queen Jinjur suggested making a goulash of me — Me! the only Highly Magnified and Thoroughly Educated Woggle-Bug in the wide, wide world!"

"I think it was a brilliant idea," remarked the Scarecrow, approvingly.

"Don't you imagine he would make a better soup?" asked the Tin Woodman, turning toward his friend.

"Well, perhaps," acknowledged the Scarecrow.

The Woggle-Bug groaned.

"I can see, in my mind's eye," said he, mournfully, "the goats eating small pieces of my dear comrade, the Tin Woodman, while my soup is being cooked on a bonfire built of the Saw-Horse and Jack Pumpkinhead's body, and Queen Jinjur watches me boil while she feeds the flames with my friend the Scarecrow!"

This morbid picture cast a gloom over the entire party, making them restless and anxious.

"It can't happen for some time," said the Tin Woodman, trying to speak cheerfully; "for we shall be able to keep Jinjur out of the palace until she manages to break down the doors."

"And in the meantime I am liable to starve to death, and so is the Woggle-Bug," announced Tip.

"As for me," said the Woggle-Bug, "I think that I could live for some time on Jack Pumpkinhead. Not that I prefer pumpkins for food; but I believe they are somewhat nutritious, and Jack's head is large and plump."

"How heartless!" exclaimed the Tin Woodman, greatly shocked. "Are we cannibals, let me ask? Or are we faithful friends?"

"I see very clearly that we cannot stay shut up in this palace," said the Scarecrow, with decision. "So let us end this mournful talk and try to discover a means to escape."

At this suggestion they all gathered eagerly around the throne wherein was seated the Scarecrow, and as Tip sat down upon a stool there fell from his pocket a pepper-box, which rolled upon the floor.

"What is this?" asked Nick Chopper, picking up the box.

"Be careful!" cried the boy. "That's my Powder of Life. Don't spill it, for it is nearly gone."

"And what is the Powder of Life?" enquired the Scarecrow, as Tip replaced the box carefully in his pocket.

"It's some magical stuff old Mombi got from a crooked sorcerer," explained the boy. "She brought Jack to life with it, and afterward I used it to bring the Saw-Horse to life. I guess it will make anything live that is sprinkled with it; but there's only about one dose left."

"Then it is very precious," said the Tin Woodman.

"Indeed it is," agreed the Scarecrow. "It may prove our best means of escape from our difficulties. I believe I will think for a few minutes; so I will thank you, friend Tip, to get out your knife and rip this heavy crown from my forehead."

Tip soon cut the stitches that had fastened the crown to the Scarecrow's head, and the former monarch of the Emerald City removed it with a sigh of relief and hung it on a peg beside the throne.

"That is my last memento of royalty" said he; "and I'm glad to get rid of it. The former King of this City, who was named Pastoria, lost the crown to the Wonderful Wizard, who passed it on to me. Now the girl Jinjur claims it, and I sincerely hope it will not give her a headache."

"A kindly thought, which I greatly admire," said the Tin Woodman, nodding approvingly.

"And now I will indulge in a quiet think," continued the Scarecrow, lying back in the throne.

The others remained as silent and still as possible, so as not to disturb him; for all had great confidence in the extraordinary brains of the Scarecrow.

And, after what seemed a very long time indeed to the anxious watchers, the thinker sat up, looked upon his friends with his most whimsical expression, and said:

"My brains work beautifully today. I'm quite proud of them. Now, listen! If we attempt to escape through the doors of the palace we shall surely be captured. And, as we can't escape through the ground, there is only one other thing to be done. We must escape through the air!"

He paused to note the effect of these words; but all his hearers seemed puzzled and unconvinced.

"The Wonderful Wizard escaped in a balloon," he continued. "We don't know how to make a balloon, of course; but any sort of thing that can fly through the air can carry us easily. So I suggest that my friend the Tin Woodman, who is a skillful mechanic, shall build some sort of a machine, with good strong wings, to carry us; and our friend Tip can then bring the Thing to life with his magical powder."

"Bravo!" cried Nick Chopper.

"What splendid brains!" murmured Jack.

"Really quite clever!" said the Educated Woggle-Bug.

"I believe it can be done," declared Tip; "that is, if the Tin Woodman is equal to making the Thing."

"I'll do my best," said Nick, cheerily; "and, as a matter of fact, I do not often fail in what I attempt. But the Thing will have to be built on the roof of the palace, so it can rise comfortably into the air."

"To be sure," said the Scarecrow.

"Then let us search through the palace," continued the Tin Woodman, "and carry all the material we can find to the roof, where I will begin my work."

"First, however," said the Pumpkinhead, "I beg you will release me from this horse, and make me another leg to walk with. For in my present condition I am of no use to myself or to anyone else."

So the Tin Woodman knocked a mahogany center-table to pieces with his axe and fitted one of the legs, which was beautifully carved, on to the body of Jack Pumpkinhead, who was very proud of the acquisition.

"It seems strange," said he, as he watched the Tin Woodman work, "that my left leg should be the most elegant and substantial part of me."

"That proves you are unusual," returned the Scarecrow, "and I am convinced that the only people worthy of consideration in this world are the unusual ones. For the common folks are like the leaves of a tree, and live and die unnoticed."

"Spoken like a philosopher!" cried the Woggle-Bug, as he assisted the Tin Woodman to set Jack upon his feet.

"How do you feel now?" asked Tip, watching the Pumpkinhead stump around to try his new leg."

As good as new" answered Jack, joyfully, "and quite ready to assist you all to escape."

"Then let us get to work," said the Scarecrow, in a business-like tone.

So, glad to be doing anything that might lead to the end of their captivity, the friends separated to wander over the palace in search of fitting material to use in the construction of their aerial machine.

The Astonishing Flight of the Gump

When the adventurers reassembled upon the roof it was found that a remarkably queer assortment of articles had been selected by the various members of the party. No one seemed to have a very clear idea of what was required, but all had brought something.

The Woggle-Bug had taken from its position over the mantle-piece in the great hallway the head of a Gump, which was adorned with wide-spreading antlers; and this, with great care

and greater difficulty, the insect had carried up the stairs to the roof. This Gump resembled an Elk's head, only the nose turned upward in a saucy manner and there were whiskers upon its chin, like those of a billy-goat. Why the Woggle-Bug selected this article he could not have explained, except that it had aroused his curiosity.

Tip, with the aid of the Saw-Horse, had brought a large, upholstered sofa to the roof. It was an oldfashioned piece of furniture, with high back and ends, and it was so heavy that even by resting the greatest weight upon the back of the Saw-Horse, the boy found himself out of breath when at last the clumsy sofa was dumped upon the roof.

The Pumpkinhead had brought a broom, which was the first thing he saw. The Scarecrow arrived with a coil of clothes-lines and ropes which he had taken from the courtyard, and in his trip up the stairs he had become so entangled in the loose ends of the ropes that both he and his burden tumbled in a heap upon the roof and might have rolled off if Tip had not rescued him.

The Tin Woodman appeared last. He also had been to the courtyard, where he had cut four great, spreading leaves from a huge palm-tree that was the pride of all the inhabitants of the Emerald City.

"My dear Nick!" exclaimed the Scarecrow, seeing what his friend had done; "you have been guilty of the greatest crime any person can commit in the Emerald City. If I remember rightly, the penalty for chopping leaves from the royal palm-tree is to be killed seven times and afterward imprisoned for life."

"It cannot be helped now" answered the Tin Woodman, throwing down the big leaves upon the roof. "But it may be one more reason why it is necessary for us to escape. And now let us see what you have found for me to work with."

Many were the doubtful looks cast upon the heap of miscellaneous material that now cluttered the roof, and finally the Scarecrow shook his head and remarked:

"Well, if friend Nick can manufacture, from this mess of rubbish, a Thing that will fly through the air and carry us to safety, then I will acknowledge him to be a better mechanic than I suspected."

But the Tin Woodman seemed at first by no means sure of his powers, and only after polishing his forehead vigorously with the chamois-leather did he resolve to undertake the task.

"The first thing required for the machine," said he, "is a body big enough to carry the entire party. This sofa is the biggest thing we have, and might be used for a body. But, should the machine ever tip sideways, we would all slide off and fall to the ground."

"Why not use two sofas?" asked Tip. "There's another one just like this down stairs."

"That is a very sensible suggestion," exclaimed the Tin Woodman. "You must fetch the other sofa at once."

So Tip and the Saw-Horse managed, with much labor, to get the second sofa to the roof; and when the two were placed together, edge to edge, the backs and ends formed a protecting rampart all around the seats.

"Excellent!" cried the Scarecrow. "We can ride within this snug nest quite at our ease."

The two sofas were now bound firmly together with ropes and clothes-lines, and then Nick Chopper fastened the Gump's head to one end.

"That will show which is the front end of the Thing," said he, greatly pleased with the idea." And, really, if you examine it critically, the Gump looks very well as a figure-head. These great palm-leaves, for which I have endangered my life seven times, must serve us as wings."

"Are they strong enough?" asked the boy.

"They are as strong as anything we can get," answered the Woodman; "and although they are not in proportion to the Thing's body, we are not in a position to be very particular."

So he fastened the palm-leaves to the sofas, two on each side.

Said the Woggle-Bug, with considerable admiration: "The Thing is now complete, and only needs to be brought to life."

"Stop a moment!" exclaimed Jack." Are you not going to use my broom?"

"What for?" asked the Scarecrow.

"Why, it can be fastened to the back end for a tail," answered the Pumpkinhead. "Surely you would not call the Thing complete without a tail."

"Hm!" said the Tin Woodman, "I do not see the use of a tail. We are not trying to copy a beast, or a fish, or a bird. All we ask of the Thing is to carry us through the air.

"Perhaps, after the Thing is brought to life, it can use a tail to steer with," suggested the Scarecrow. "For if it flies through the air it will not be unlike a bird, and I've noticed that all birds have tails, which they use for a rudder while flying."

"Very well," answered Nick, "the broom shall be used for a tail," and he fastened it firmly to the back end of the sofa body.

Tip took the pepper-box from his pocket.

"The Thing looks very big," said he, anxiously; "and I am not sure there is enough powder left to bring all of it to life. But I'll make it go as far as possible."

"Put most on the wings," said Nick Chopper; "for they must be made as strong as possible."

"And don't forget the head!" exclaimed the Woggle-Bug.

"Or the tail!" added Jack Pumpkinhead.

"Do be quiet," said Tip, nervously; "you must give me a chance to work the magic charm in the proper manner."

Very carefully he began sprinkling the Thing with the precious powder. Each of the four wings was first lightly covered with a layer. then the sofas were sprinkled, and the broom given a slight coating.

"The head! The head! Don't, I beg of you, forget the head!" cried the Woggle-Bug, excitedly.

"There's only a little of the powder left," announced Tip, looking within the box." And it seems to me it is more important to bring

the legs of the sofas to life than the head."

"Not so," decided the Scarecrow. "Every thing must have a head to direct it; and since this creature is to fly, and not walk, it is really unimportant whether its legs are alive or not."

So Tip abided by this decision and sprinkled the Gump's head with the remainder of the powder.

"Now" said he, "keep silent while I work the charm!"

Having heard old Mombi pronounce the magic words, and having also succeeded in bringing the Saw-Horse to life, Tip did not hesitate an instant in speaking the three cabalistic words, each accompanied by the peculiar gesture of the hands.

It was a grave and impressive ceremony.

As he finished the incantation the Thing shuddered throughout its huge bulk, the Gump gave the screeching cry that is familiar to those animals, and then the four wings began flopping furiously.

Tip managed to grasp a chimney, else he would have been blown off the roof by the terrible breeze raised by the wings. The Scarecrow, being light in weight, was caught up bodily and borne through the air until Tip luckily seized him by one leg and held him fast. The Woggle-Bug lay flat upon the roof and so escaped harm, and the Tin Woodman, whose weight of tin anchored him firmly, threw both arms around Jack Pumpkinhead and managed to save him. The Saw-Horse toppled over upon its back and lay with its legs waving helplessly above him.

And now, while all were struggling to recover themselves, the Thing rose slowly from the roof and mounted into the air.

"Here! Come back!" cried Tip, in a frightened voice, as he clung to the chimney with one hand and the Scarecrow with the other. "Come back at once, I command you!"

It was now that the wisdom of the Scarecrow, in bringing the head of the Thing to life instead of the legs, was proved beyond a doubt. For the Gump, already high in the air, turned its head at Tip's command and gradually circled around until it could view the roof of the palace.

"Come back!" shouted the boy, again.

And the Gump obeyed, slowly and gracefully waving its four wings in the air until the Thing had settled once more upon the roof and become still.

In the Jackdaw's Nest

"This," said the Gump, in a squeaky voice not at all proportioned to the size of its great body, "is the most novel experience I ever heard of. The last thing I remember distinctly is walking through the forest and hearing a loud noise. Something probably killed me then, and it certainly ought to have been the end of me. Yet here I am, alive again, with four monstrous wings and a body which I venture to say would make any respectable animal or fowl weep with shame to own. What does it all mean? Am I a Gump, or am I a juggernaut?" The creature, as it spoke, wiggled its chin whiskers in a very comical manner.

"You're just a Thing," answered Tip, "with a Gump's head on it. And we have made you and brought you to life so that you may carry us through the air wherever we wish to go."

Very good!" said the Thing. "As I am not a Gump, I cannot have a Gump's pride or independent spirit. So I may as well become your servant as anything else. My only satisfaction is that I do not seem to have a very strong constitution, and am not likely to live long in a state of slavery."

Don't say that, I beg of you!" cried the Tin Woodman, whose excellent heart was strongly affected by this sad speech." Are you not feeling well today?"

Oh, as for that," returned the Gump, "it is my first day of existence; so I cannot judge whether I am feeling well or ill." And it waved its broom tail to and fro in a pensive manner.

Come, come!" said the Scarecrow, kindly. "do try, to be more cheerful and take life as you find it. We shall be kind masters, and will strive to render your existence as pleasant as possible. Are you willing to carry us through the air wherever we wish to go?"

Certainly," answered the Gump. "I greatly prefer to navigate the air. For should I travel on the earth and meet with one of my own species, my embarrassment would be something awful!"

I can appreciate that," said the Tin Woodman, sympathetically.

And yet," continued the Thing, "when I carefully look you over, my masters, none of you seems to be constructed much more artistically than I am."

Appearances are deceitful," said the Woggle-Bug, earnestly. "I am both Highly Magnified and Thoroughly Educated."

Indeed!" murmured the Gump, indifferently.

And my brains are considered remarkably rare specimens," added the Scarecrow, proudly.

How strange!" remarked the Gump.

Although I am of tin," said the Woodman, "I own a heart altogether the warmest and most admirable in the whole world."

I'm delighted to hear it," replied the Gump, with a slight cough.

My smile," said Jack Pumpkinhead, "is worthy your best attention. It is always the same."

Semper idem," explained the Woggle-Bug, pompously; and the Gump turned to stare at him.

And I," declared the Saw-Horse, filling in an awkward pause, am only remarkable because I can't help it."

I am proud, indeed, to meet with such exceptional masters," said the Gump, in a careless tone. "If I could but secure so complete an introduction to myself, I would be more than satisfied."

That will come in time," remarked the Scarecrow. "To 'Know thyself' is considered quite an accomplishment, which it has taken us, who are your elders, months to perfect. But now," he added, turning to the others, "let us get aboard and start upon our journey."

Where shall we go?" asked Tip, as he clambered to a seat on the sofas and assisted the Pumpkinhead to follow him.

"In the South Country rules a very delightful Queen called Glinda the Good, who I am sure will gladly receive us," said the Scarecrow, getting into the Thing clumsily. "Let us go to her and ask her advice."

"That is cleverly thought of," declared Nick Chopper, giving the Woggle-Bug a boost and then toppling the Saw-Horse into the rear end of the cushioned seats." I know Glinda the Good, and believe she will prove a friend indeed."

"Are we all ready?" asked the boy.

"Yes," announced the Tin Woodman, seating himself beside the Scarecrow.

"Then," said Tip, addressing the Gump, "be kind enough to fly with us to the Southward; and do not go higher than to escape the houses and trees, for it makes me dizzy to be up so far."

"All right," answered the Gump, briefly.

It flopped its four huge wings and rose slowly into the air; and then, while our little band of adventurers clung to the backs and sides of the sofas for support, the Gump turned toward the South and soared swiftly and majestically away.

"The scenic effect, from this altitude, is marvelous," commented the educated Woggle-Bug, as they rode along.

"Never mind the scenery," said the Scarecrow. "Hold on tight, or you may get a tumble. The Thing seems to rock badly.'

"It will be dark soon," said Tip, observing that the sun was low on the horizon. "Perhaps we should have waited until morning. I wonder if the Gump can fly in the night."

"I've been wondering that myself," returned the Gump quietly. "You see, this is a new experience to me. I used to have legs that carried me swiftly over the ground. But now my legs feel as if they were asleep."

"They are," said Tip. "We didn't bring 'em to life."

"You're expected to fly," explained the Scarecrow. "not to walk."

"We can walk ourselves," said the Woggle-Bug."

I begin to understand what is required of me," remarked the Gump; "so I will do my best to please you," and he flew on for a time in silence.

Presently Jack Pumpkinhead became uneasy. "I wonder if riding through the air is liable to spoil pumpkins," he said.

"Not unless you carelessly drop your head over the side," answered the Woggle-Bug. "In that event your head would no longer be a pumpkin, for it would become a squash."

"Have I not asked you to restrain these unfeeling jokes?" demanded Tip, looking at the Woggle-Bug with a severe expression.

"You have; and I've restrained a good many of them," replied the insect. "But there are opportunities for so many excellent puns in our language that, to an educated person like myself, the temptation to express them is almost irresistible."

"People with more or less education discovered those puns centuries ago," said Tip.

"Are you sure?" asked the Woggle-Bug, with a startled look.

"Of course I am," answered the boy. "An educated Woggle-Bug may be a new thing; but a Woggle-Bug education is as old as the hills, judging from the display you make of it."

The insect seemed much impressed by this remark, and for a time maintained a meek silence.

The Scarecrow, in shifting his seat, saw upon the cushions the pepper-box which Tip had cast aside, and began to examine it.

"Throw it overboard," said the boy; "it's quite empty now, and there's no use keeping it."

"Is it really empty?" asked the Scarecrow, looking curiously into the box.

"Of course it is," answered Tip. "I shook out every grain of the powder.

"Then the box has two bottoms," announced the Scarecrow, "for the bottom on the inside is fully an inch away from the bottom on the outside."

"Let me see," said the Tin Woodman, taking the box from his friend. "Yes," he declared, after looking it over, "the thing certainly has a false bottom. Now, I wonder what that is for?"

"Can't you get it apart, and find out?" enquired Tip, now quite interested in the mystery.

"Why, yes; the lower bottom unscrews," said the Tin Woodman. "My fingers are rather stiff; please see if you can open it."

He handed the pepper-box to Tip, who had no difficulty in unscrewing the bottom. And in the cavity below were three silver pills, with a carefully folded paper lying underneath them.

This paper the boy proceeded to unfold, taking care not to spill the pills, and found several lines clearly written in red ink.

"Read it aloud," said the Scarecrow. so Tip read, as follows:

"DR. NIKIDIK'S CELEBRATED WISHING PILLS. Directions for Use: Swallow one pill; count seventeen by twos; then make a Wish. The Wish will immediately be granted. CAUTION: Keep in a Dry and Dark Place."

"Why, this is a very valuable discovery!" cried the Scarecrow.

"It is, indeed," replied Tip, gravely. "These pills may be of great use to us. I wonder if old Mombi knew they were in the bottom of the pepper-box. I remember hearing her say that she got the Powder of Life from this same Nikidik."

"He must be a powerful Sorcerer!" exclaimed the Tin Woodman; "and since the powder proved a success we ought to have confidence in the pills."

"But how," asked the Scarecrow, "can anyone count seventeen by twos? Seventeen is an odd number."

"That is true," replied Tip, greatly disappointed. "No one can possibly count seventeen by twos."

"Then the pills are of no use to us," wailed the Pumpkinhead "and this fact overwhelms me with grief. For I had intended wishing that my head would never spoil."

"Nonsense!" said the Scarecrow, sharply. "If we could use th pills at all we would make far better wishes than that."

"I do not see how anything could be better," protested poor Jack "If you were liable to spoil at any time you could understand m anxiety."

"For my part," said the Tin Woodman, "I sympathize with you i every respect. But since we cannot count seventeen by two sympathy is all you are liable to get."

By this time it had become quite dark, and the voyagers foun above them a cloudy sky, through which the rays of the moo could not penetrate.

The Gump flew steadily on, and for some reason the huge sofa body rocked more and more dizzily every hour.

The Woggle-Bug declared he was sea-sick; and Tip was also pal and somewhat distressed. But the others clung to the backs o the sofas and did not seem to mind the motion as long as the were not tipped out.

Darker and darker grew the night, and on and on sped the Gum through the black heavens. The travelers could not even see on another, and an oppressive silence settled down upon them.

After a long time Tip, who had been thinking deeply, spoke.

"How are we to know when we come to the palace of Glinda th Good?" he asked.

"It's a long way to Glinda's palace," answered the Woodma "I've traveled it."

"But how are we to know how fast the Gump is flying?" persiste the boy. "We cannot see a single thing down on the earth, an before morning we may be far beyond the place we want t reach."

"That is all true enough," the Scarecrow replied, a little uneasi "But I do not see how we can stop just now; for we might aligh in a river, or on, the top of a steeple; and that would be a grea disaster."

So they permitted the Gump to fly on, with regular flops of i great wings, and waited patiently for morning.

Then Tip's fears were proven to be well founded; for with th first streaks of gray dawn they looked over the sides of the sof and discovered rolling plains dotted with queer villages, whe the houses, instead of being dome-shaped — as they all are in th Land of Oz — had slanting roofs that rose to a peak in the cente Odd looking animals were also moving about upon the ope plains, and the country was unfamiliar to both the Tin Woodma and the Scarecrow, who had formerly visited Glinda the Goo domain and knew it well.

"We are lost!" said the Scarecrow, dolefully. "The Gump mu have carried us entirely out of the Land of Oz and over the san deserts and into the terrible outside world that Dorothy told about."

"We must get back," exclaimed the Tin Woodman, earnestly. "we must get back as soon as possible!"

"Turn around!" cried Tip to the Gump. "turn as quickly as you can!"

"If I do I shall upset," answered the Gump. "I'm not at all used to flying, and the best plan would be for me to alight in some place, and then I can turn around and take a fresh start."

Just then, however, there seemed to be no stopping-place that would answer their purpose. They flew over a village so big that the Woggle-Bug declared it was a city. and then they came to a range of high mountains with many deep gorges and steep cliffs showing plainly.

"Now is our chance to stop," said the boy, finding they were very close to the mountain tops. Then he turned to the Gump and commanded: "Stop at the first level place you see!"

"Very well," answered the Gump, and settled down upon a table of rock that stood between two cliffs.

But not being experienced in such matters, the Gump did not judge his speed correctly; and instead of coming to a stop upon the flat rock he missed it by half the width of his body, breaking off both his right wings against the sharp edge of the rock and then tumbling over and over down the cliff.

Our friends held on to the sofas as long as they could, but when the Gump caught on a projecting rock the Thing stopped suddenly — bottom side up — and all were immediately dumped out.

By good fortune they fell only a few feet; for underneath them was a monster nest, built by a colony of Jackdaws in a hollow ledge of rock; so none of them — not even the Pumpkinhead — was injured by the fall. For Jack found his precious head resting on the soft breast of the Scarecrow, which made an excellent cushion; and Tip fell on a mass of leaves and papers, which saved him from injury. The Woggle-Bug had bumped his round head against the Saw-Horse, but without causing him more than a moment's inconvenience.

The Tin Woodman was at first much alarmed; but finding he had escaped without even a scratch upon his beautiful nickle-plate he at once regained his accustomed cheerfulness and turned to address his comrades.

"Our journey had ended rather suddenly," said he; "and we cannot justly blame our friend the Gump for our accident, because he did the best he could under the circumstances. But how we are ever to escape from this nest I must leave to someone with better brains than I possess."

Here he gazed at the Scarecrow; who crawled to the edge of the nest and looked over. Below them was a sheer precipice several hundred feet in depth. Above them was a smooth cliff unbroken save by the point of rock where the wrecked body of the Gump still hung suspended from the end of one of the sofas. There really seemed to be no means of escape, and as they realized their helpless plight the little band of adventurers gave way to their bewilderment.

"This is a worse prison than the palace," sadly remarked the Woggle-Bug.

"I wish we had stayed there," moaned Jack. "I'm afraid the mountain air isn't good for pumpkins."

"It won't be when the Jackdaws come back," growled the Saw-Horse, which lay waving its legs in a vain endeavor to get upon its feet again. "Jackdaws are especially fond of pumpkins."

"Do you think the birds will come here?" asked Jack, much distressed.

"Of course they will," said Tip; "for this is their nest. And there must be hundreds of them," he continued, "for see what a lot of things they have brought here!"

Indeed, the nest was half filled with a most curious collection of small articles for which the birds could have no use, but which the thieving Jackdaws had stolen during many years from the homes of men. And as the nest was safely hidden where no human being could reach it, this lost property would never be recovered.

The Woggle-Bug, searching among the rubbish — for the Jackdaws stole useless things as well as valuable ones — turned up with his foot a beautiful diamond necklace. This was so greatly admired by the Tin Woodman that the Woggle-Bug presented it to him with a graceful speech, after which the Woodman hung it around his neck with much pride, rejoicing exceedingly when the big diamonds glittered in the sun's rays.

But now they heard a great jabbering and flopping of wings, and as the sound grew nearer to them Tip exclaimed:

"The Jackdaws are coming! And if they find us here they will surely kill us in their anger."

"I was afraid of this!" moaned the Pumpkinhead. "My time has come!"

"And mine, also!" said the Woggle-Bug; "for Jackdaws are the greatest enemies of my race."

The others were not at all afraid; but the Scarecrow at once decided to save those of the party who were liable to be injured by the angry birds. So he commanded Tip to take off Jack's head and lie down with it in the bottom of the nest, and when this was done he ordered the Woggle-Bug to lie beside Tip. Nick Chopper, who knew from past experience just what to do, then took the Scarecrow to pieces (all except his head) and scattered the straw over Tip and the Woggle-Bug, completely covering their bodies.

Hardly had this been accomplished when the flock of Jackdaws reached them. Perceiving the intruders in their nest the birds flew down upon them with screams of rage.

Dr. Nikidik's Famous Wishing Pills

The Tin Woodman was usually a peaceful man, but when occasion required he could fight as fiercely as a Roman gladiator. So, when the Jackdaws nearly knocked him down in their rush of wings, and their sharp beaks and claws threatened to damage his brilliant plating, the Woodman picked up his axe and made it whirl swiftly around his head.

But although many were beaten off in this way, the birds were so numerous and so brave that they continued the attack as furiously as before. Some of them pecked at the eyes of the Gump, which hung over the nest in a helpless condition; but the Gump's eyes were of glass and could not be injured. Others of the Jackdaws rushed at the Saw-Horse; but that animal, being still upon his back, kicked out so viciously with his wooden legs that he beat off as many assailants as did the Woodman's axe.

Finding themselves thus opposed, the birds fell upon the Scarecrow's straw, which lay at the center of the nest, covering Tip and the Woggle-Bug and Jack's pumpkin head, and began tearing it away and flying off with it, only to let it drop, straw by straw into the great gulf beneath.

The Scarecrow's head, noting with dismay this wanton destruction of his interior, cried to the Tin Woodman to save him; and that good friend responded with renewed energy. His axe fairly flashed among the Jackdaws, and fortunately the Gump began wildly waving the two wings remaining on the left side of its body. The flutter of these great wings filled the Jackdaws with terror, and when the Gump by its exertions freed itself from the peg of rock on which it hung, and sank flopping into the nest, the alarm of the birds knew no bounds and they fled screaming over the mountains.

When the last foe had disappeared, Tip crawled from under the sofas and assisted the Woggle-Bug to follow him.

"We are saved!" shouted the boy, delightedly.

"We are, indeed!" responded the Educated Insect, fairly hugging the stiff head of the Gump in his joy. "and we owe it all to the flopping of the Thing, and the good axe of the Woodman!"

"If I am saved, get me out of here!" called Jack; whose head was still beneath the sofas; and Tip managed to roll the pumpkin out and place it upon its neck again. He also set the Saw-Horse upright, and said to it:

"We owe you many thanks for the gallant fight you made."

"I really think we have escaped very nicely," remarked the Tin Woodman, in a tone of pride.

"Not so!" exclaimed a hollow voice.

At this they all turned in surprise to look at the Scarecrow's head, which lay at the back of the nest.

"I am completely ruined!" declared the Scarecrow, as he noted their astonishment. "For where is the straw that stuffs my body?"

The awful question startled them all. They gazed around the nest with horror, for not a vestige of straw remained. The Jackdaws had stolen it to the last wisp and flung it all into the chasm that yawned for hundreds of feet beneath the nest.

"My poor, poor friend!" said the Tin Woodman, taking up the Scarecrow's head and caressing it tenderly; "whoever could imagine you would come to this untimely end?"

"I did it to save my friends," returned the head; "and I am glad that I perished in so noble and unselfish a manner."

"But why are you all so despondent?" inquired the Woggle-Bug. "The Scarecrow's clothing is still safe."

"Yes," answered the Tin Woodman; "but our friend's clothes are useless without stuffing."

"Why not stuff him with money?" asked Tip.

"Money!" they all cried, in an amazed chorus.

"To be sure," said the boy. "In the bottom of the nest are thousands of dollar bills — and two-dollar bills — and five-dollar bills — and tens, and twenties, and fifties. There are enough of them to stuff a dozen Scarecrows. Why not use the money?"

The Tin Woodman began to turn over the rubbish with the handle of his axe; and, sure enough, what they had first thought only worthless papers were found to be all bills of various denominations, which the mischievous Jackdaws had for years been engaged in stealing from the villages and cities they visited.

There was an immense fortune lying in that inaccessible nest; and Tip's suggestion was, with the Scarecrow's consent, quickly acted upon.

They selected all the newest and cleanest bills and assorted them into various piles. The Scarecrow's left leg and boot were stuffed with five- dollar bills; his right leg was stuffed with ten-dollar bills, and his body so closely filled with fifties, one-hundreds and one-thousands that he could scarcely button his jacket with comfort.

"You are now" said the Woggle-Bug, impressively, when the task had been completed, "the most valuable member of our party; and as you are among faithful friends there is little danger of your being spent."

"Thank you," returned the Scarecrow, gratefully. "I feel like a new man; and although at first glance I might be mistaken for a Safety Deposit Vault, I beg you to remember that my Brains are still composed of the same old material. And these are the possessions that have always made me a person to be depended upon in an emergency."

"Well, the emergency is here," observed Tip; "and unless your brains help us out of it we shall be compelled to pass the remainder of our lives in this nest."

"How about these wishing pills?" enquired the Scarecrow, taking the box from his jacket pocket. "Can't we use them to escape?"

"Not unless we can count seventeen by twos," answered the Tin Woodman. "But our friend the Woggle-Bug claims to be highly educated, so he ought easily to figure out how that can be done."

"It isn't a question of education," returned the Insect; "it's merely a question of mathematics. I've seen the professor work lots of sums on the blackboard, and he claimed anything could be done with x's and y's and a's, and such things, by mixing them up with plenty of plusses and minuses and equals, and so forth. But he never said anything, so far as I can remember, about counting up to the odd number of seventeen by the even numbers of twos."

"Stop! stop!" cried the Pumpkinhead. "You're making my head ache."

"And mine," added the Scarecrow. "Your mathematics seem to me very like a bottle of mixed pickles — the more you fish for what you want the less chance you have of getting it. I am certain that if the thing can be accomplished at all, it is in a very simple manner."

"Yes," said Tip. "old Mombi couldn't use x's and minuses, for she never went to school."

"Why not start counting at a half of one?" asked the Saw-Horse, abruptly. "Then anyone can count up to seventeen by twos very easily."

They looked at each other in surprise, for the Saw-Horse was considered the most stupid of the entire party.

"You make me quite ashamed of myself," said the Scarecrow, bowing low to the Saw-Horse.

"Nevertheless, the creature is right," declared the Woggle-Bug; "for twice one-half is one, and if you get to one it is easy to count from one up to seventeen by twos."

"I wonder I didn't think of that myself," said the Pumpkinhead.

"I don't," returned the Scarecrow. "You're no wiser than the rest of us, are you? But let us make a wish at once. Who will swallow the first pill?"

"Suppose you do it," suggested Tip.

"I can't," said the Scarecrow.

"Why not? You've a mouth, haven't you?" asked the boy.

"Yes; but my mouth is painted on, and there's no swallow connected with it,' answered the Scarecrow. "In fact," he continued, looking from one to another critically, "I believe the boy and the Woggle-Bug are the only ones in our party that are able to swallow."

Observing the truth of this remark, Tip said:

"Then I will undertake to make the first wish. Give me one of the Silver Pills."

This the Scarecrow tried to do; but his padded gloves were too clumsy to clutch so small an object, and he held the box toward the boy while Tip selected one of the pills and swallowed it.

"Count!" cried the Scarecrow.

"One-half, one, three, five, seven, nine, eleven!" counted Tip, "thirteen, fifteen, seventeen."

"Now wish!" said the Tin Woodman anxiously:

But just then the boy began to suffer such fearful pains that he became alarmed.

"The pill has poisoned me!" he gasped; "O — h! O-o-o-o-o! Ouch! Murder! Fire! O-o-h!" and here he rolled upon the bottom of the nest in such contortions that he frightened them all.

"What can we do for you. Speak, I beg!" entreated the Tin Woodman, tears of sympathy running down his nickel cheeks.

"I — I don't know!" answered Tip. "O — h! I wish I'd never swallowed that pill!"

Then at once the pain stopped, and the boy rose to his feet again and found the Scarecrow looking with amazement at the end of the pepper-box.

"What's happened?" asked the boy, a little ashamed of his recent exhibition.

"Why, the three pills are in the box again!" said the Scarecrow.

"Of course they are," the Woggle-Bug declared. "Didn't Tip wish that he'd never swallowed one of them? Well, the wish came true, and he didn't swallow one of them. So of course they are all three in the box."

"That may be; but the pill gave me a dreadful pain, just the same," said the boy.

"Impossible!" declared the Woggle-Bug. "If you have never swallowed it, the pill can not have given you a pain. And as your wish, being granted, proves you did not swallow the pill, it is also plain that you suffered no pain."

"Then it was a splendid imitation of a pain," retorted Tip, angrily. "Suppose you try the next pill yourself. We've wasted one wish already."

"Oh, no, we haven't!" protested the Scarecrow. "Here are still three pills in the box, and each pill is good for a wish."

"Now you're making my head ache," said Tip. "I can't understand the thing at all. But I won't take another pill, I promise you!" and with this remark he retired sulkily to the back of the nest.

"Well," said the Woggle-Bug, "it remains for me to save us in my most Highly Magnified and Thoroughly Educated manner; for I seem to be the only one able and willing to make a wish. Let me have one of the pills."

He swallowed it without hesitation, and they all stood admiring his courage while the Insect counted seventeen by twos in the same way that Tip had done. And for some reason — perhaps because Woggle-Bugs have stronger stomachs than boys — the silver pellet caused it no pain whatever.

"I wish the Gump's broken wings mended, and as good as new!" said the Woggle-Bug, in a slow; impressive voice.

All turned to look at the Thing, and so quickly had the wish been granted that the Gump lay before them in perfect repair, and as well able to fly through the air as when it had first been brought to life on the roof of the palace.

The Scarecrow Appeals to Glenda the Good

"Hooray!" shouted the Scarecrow, gaily. "We can now leave this miserable Jackdaws' nest whenever we please."

"But it is nearly dark," said the Tin Woodman; "and unless we wait until morning to make our flight we may get into more trouble. I don't like these night trips, for one never knows what will happen."

So it was decided to wait until daylight, and the adventurers amused themselves in the twilight by searching the Jackdaws' nest for treasures.

The Woggle-Bug found two handsome bracelets of wrought gold, which fitted his slender arms very well. The Scarecrow took a fancy for rings, of which there were many in the nest. Before long he had fitted a ring to each finger of his padded gloves, and not being content with that display he added one more to each thumb. As he carefully chose those rings set with sparkling stones, such as rubies, amethysts and sapphires, the Scarecrow's hands now presented a most brilliant appearance.

"This nest would be a picnic for Queen Jinjur," said he, musingly. "for as nearly as I can make out she and her girls conquered me merely to rob my city of its emeralds."

The Tin Woodman was content with his diamond necklace and refused to accept any additional decorations; but Tip secured a fine gold watch, which was attached to a heavy fob, and placed it in his pocket with much pride. He also pinned several jeweled brooches to Jack Pumpkinhead's red waistcoat, and attached a lorgnette, by means of a fine chain, to the neck of the Saw-Horse.

"It's very pretty," said the creature, regarding the lorgnette approvingly; "but what is it for?"

None of them could answer that question, however; so the Saw-Horse decided it was some rare decoration and became very fond of it.

That none of the party might be slighted, they ended by placing several large seal rings upon the points of the Gump's antlers, although that odd personage seemed by no means gratified by the attention.

Darkness soon fell upon them, and Tip and the Woggle-Bug went to sleep while the others sat down to wait patiently for the day.

Next morning they had cause to congratulate themselves upon the useful condition of the Gump; for with daylight a great flock of Jackdaws approached to engage in one more battle for the possession of the nest.

But our adventurers did not wait for the assault. They tumbled into the cushioned seats of the sofas as quickly as possible, and Tip gave the word to the Gump to start.

At once it rose into the air, the great wings flopping strongly and with regular motions, and in a few moments they were so far from the nest that the chattering Jackdaws took possession without any attempt at pursuit.

The Thing flew due North, going in the same direction from whence it had come. At least, that was the Scarecrow's opinion, and the others agreed that the Scarecrow was the best judge of direction. After passing over several cities and villages the Gump carried them high above a broad plain where houses became more and more scattered until they disappeared altogether. Next came the wide, sandy desert separating the rest of the world from the Land of Oz, and before noon they saw the dome-shaped houses that proved they were once more within the borders of their native land.

"But the houses and fences are blue," said the Tin Woodman, "and that indicates we are in the land of the Munchkins, and therefore a long distance from Glinda the Good."

"What shall we do?" asked the boy, turning to their guide.

"I don't know" replied the Scarecrow, frankly. "If we were at the Emerald City we could then move directly southward, and so reach our destination. But we dare not go to the Emerald City, and the Gump is probably carrying us further in the wrong direction with every flop of its wings."

"Then the Woggle-Bug must swallow another pill," said Tip, decidedly, "and wish us headed in the right direction."

"Very well," returned the Highly Magnified one; "I'm willing."

But when the Scarecrow searched in his pocket for the pepper box containing the two silver Wishing Pills, it was not to be found. Filled with anxiety, the voyagers hunted throughout every inch of the Thing for the precious box; but it had disappeared entirely.

And still the Gump flew onward, carrying them they knew no where.

"I must have left the pepper-box in the Jackdaws' nest," said the Scarecrow, at length.

"It is a great misfortune," the Tin Woodman declared. "But we are no worse off than before we discovered the Wishing Pills."

"We are better off," replied Tip. "for the one pill we used has enabled us to escape from that horrible nest."

"Yet the loss of the other two is serious, and I deserve a good scolding for my carelessness," the Scarecrow rejoined penitently. "For in such an unusual party as this accidents are liable to happen any moment, and even now we may be approaching a new danger."

No one dared contradict this, and a dismal silence ensued.

The Gump flew steadily on.

Suddenly Tip uttered an exclamation of surprise. "We must have reached the South Country," he cried, "for below us everything is red!"

Immediately they all leaned over the backs of the sofas to look — all except Jack, who was too careful of his pumpkin head to risk its slipping off his neck. Sure enough; the red houses and fences and trees indicated they were within the domain of Glinda the Good; and presently, as they glided rapidly on, the Tin Woodman recognized the roads and buildings they passed, and altered slightly the flight of the Gump so that they might reach the palace of the celebrated Sorceress.

"Good!" cried the Scarecrow, delightedly. "We do not need the lost Wishing Pills now, for we have arrived at our destination."

Gradually the Thing sank lower and nearer to the ground until at length it came to rest within the beautiful gardens of Glinda, settling upon a velvety green lawn close by a fountain which sent sprays of flashing gems, instead of water, high into the air whence they fell with a soft, tinkling sound into the carved marble basin placed to receive them.

Everything was very gorgeous in Glinda's gardens, and while our voyagers gazed about with admiring eyes a company of soldiers silently appeared and surrounded them. But these soldiers of the great Sorceress were entirely different from those of Jinjur's Army of Revolt, although they were likewise girls. For Glinda's soldiers wore neat uniforms and bore swords and spears; and they marched with a skill and precision that proved them well trained in the arts of war.

The Captain commanding this troop — which was Glinda's private Body Guard — recognized the Scarecrow and the Tin Woodman at once, and greeted them with respectful salutations.

"Good day!" said the Scarecrow, gallantly removing his hat, while the Woodman gave a soldierly salute; "we have come to request an audience with your fair Ruler."

"Glinda is now within her palace, awaiting you," returned the Captain; "for she saw you coming long before you arrived."

"That is strange!" said Tip, wondering.

"Not at all," answered the Scarecrow, "for Glinda the Good is a mighty Sorceress, and nothing that goes on in the Land of Oz escapes her notice. I suppose she knows why we came as well as we do ourselves."

"Then what was the use of our coming?" asked Jack, stupidly.

"To prove you are a Pumpkinhead!" retorted the Scarecrow. "But, if the Sorceress expects us, we must not keep her waiting."

So they all clambered out of the sofas and followed the Captain toward the palace — even the Saw-Horse taking his place in the queer procession.

Upon her throne of finely wrought gold sat Glinda, and she could scarcely repress a smile as her peculiar visitors entered and bowed before her. Both the Scarecrow and the Tin Woodman she knew and liked; but the awkward Pumpkinhead and Highly Magnified Woggle-Bug were creatures she had never seen before, and they seemed even more curious than the others. As for the Saw-Horse, he looked to be nothing more than an animated chunk of wood; and he bowed so stiffly that his head bumped against the floor, causing a ripple of laughter among the soldiers, in which Glinda frankly joined.

"I beg to announce to your glorious highness," began the Scarecrow, in a solemn voice, "that my Emerald City has been overrun by a crowd of impudent girls with knitting-needles, who have enslaved all the men, robbed the streets and public buildings of all their emerald jewels, and usurped my throne."

"I know it," said Glinda.

"They also threatened to destroy me, as well as all the good friends and allies you see before you," continued the Scarecrow, "and had we not managed to escape their clutches our days would long since have ended."

"I know it," repeated Glinda.

"Therefore I have come to beg your assistance," resumed the Scarecrow, "for I believe you are always glad to succor the unfortunate and oppressed."

"That is true," replied the Sorceress, slowly. "But the Emerald City is now ruled by General Jinjur, who has caused herself to be proclaimed Queen. What right have I to oppose her?"

"Why, she stole the throne from me," said the Scarecrow.

"And how came you to possess the throne?" asked Glinda.

"I got it from the Wizard of Oz, and by the choice of the people," returned the Scarecrow, uneasy at such questioning.

"And where did the Wizard get it?" she continued gravely.

"I am told he took it from Pastoria, the former King," said the Scarecrow, becoming confused under the intent look of the Sorceress.

"Then," declared Glinda, "the throne of the Emerald City belongs neither to you nor to Jinjur, but to this Pastoria from whom the Wizard usurped it."

"That is true," acknowledged the Scarecrow, humbly; "but Pastoria is now dead and gone, and some one must rule in his place."

"Pastoria had a daughter, who is the rightful heir to the throne of the Emerald City. Did you know that?" questioned the Sorceress.

"No," replied the Scarecrow. "But if the girl still lives I will not stand in her way. It will satisfy me as well to have Jinjur turned out, as an impostor, as to regain the throne myself. In fact, it isn't much fun to be King, especially if one has good brains. I have known for some time that I am fitted to occupy a far more exalted position. But where is the girl who owns the throne, and what is her name?"

"Her name is Ozma," answered Glinda. "But where she is I have tried in vain to discover. For the Wizard of Oz, when he stole the throne from Ozma's father, hid the girl in some secret place; and by means of a magical trick with which I am not familiar he also managed to prevent her being discovered — even by so experienced a Sorceress as myself."

"That is strange," interrupted the Woggle-Bug, pompously. "I have been informed that the Wonderful Wizard of Oz was nothing more than a humbug!"

"Nonsense!" exclaimed the Scarecrow, much provoked by this speech. "Didn't he give me a wonderful set of brains?"

"There's no humbug about my heart," announced the Tin Woodman, glaring indignantly at the Woggle-Bug.

"Perhaps I was misinformed," stammered the Insect, shrinking back; "I never knew the Wizard personally."

"Well, we did," retorted the Scarecrow, "and he was a very great Wizard, I assure you. It is true he was guilty of some slight impostures, but unless he was a great Wizard how — let me ask — could he have hidden this girl Ozma so securely that no one can find her?"

"I — I give it up!" replied the Woggle-Bug, meekly.

"That is the most sensible speech you've made," said the Tin Woodman.

"I must really make another effort to discover where this girl is hidden," resumed the Sorceress, thoughtfully. "I have in my library a book in which is inscribed every action of the Wizard while he was in our land of Oz — or, at least, every action that could be observed by my spies. This book I will read carefully tonight, and try to single out the acts that may guide us in discovering the lost Ozma. In the meantime, pray amuse yourselves in my palace and command my servants as if they were your own. I will grant you another audience tomorrow."

With this gracious speech Glinda dismissed the adventurers, and they wandered away through the beautiful gardens, where they passed several hours enjoying all the delightful things with which the Queen of the Southland had surrounded her royal palace.

On the following morning they again appeared before Glinda, who said to them:

"I have searched carefully through the records of the Wizard's actions, and among them I can find but three that appear to have been suspicious. He ate beans with a knife, made three secret visits to old Mombi, and limped slightly on his left foot."

"Ah! that last is certainly suspicious!" exclaimed the Pumpkinhead.

"Not necessarily," said the Scarecrow. "he may, have had corns. Now, it seems to me his eating beans with a knife is more suspicious."

"Perhaps it is a polite custom in Omaha, from which great country the Wizard originally came," suggested the Tin Woodman.

"It may be," admitted the Scarecrow.

"But why," asked Glinda, "did he make three secret visits to old Mombi?"

"Ah! Why, indeed!" echoed the Woggle-Bug, impressively.

"We know that the Wizard taught the old woman many of his tricks of magic," continued Glinda; "and this he would not have done had she not assisted him in some way. So we may suspect with good reason that Mombi aided him to hide the girl Ozma, who was the real heir to the throne of the Emerald City, and a constant danger to the usurper. For, if the people knew that she lived, they would quickly make her their Queen and restore her to her rightful position."

"An able argument!" cried the Scarecrow. "I have no doubt that Mombi was mixed up in this wicked business. But how does that knowledge help us?"

"We must find Mombi," replied Glinda, "and force her to tell where the girl is hidden."

"Mombi is now with Queen Jinjur, in the Emerald City" said Tip. "It was she who threw so many obstacles in our pathway, and made Jinjur threaten to destroy my friends and give me back into the old witch's power."

"Then," decided Glinda, "I will march with my army to the Emerald City, and take Mombi prisoner. After that we can, perhaps, force her to tell the truth about Ozma."

"She is a terrible old woman!" remarked Tip, with a shudder at the thought of Mombi's black kettle; "and obstinate, too."

"I am quite obstinate myself," returned the Sorceress, with a sweet smile. "so I do not fear Mombi in the least. Today I will make all necessary preparations, and we will march upon the Emerald City at daybreak tomorrow."

The Tin-Woodman Plucks a Rose

The Army of Glinda the Good looked very grand and imposing when it assembled at daybreak before the palace gates. The uniforms of the girl soldiers were pretty and of gay colors, and their silver-tipped spears were bright and glistening, the long shafts being inlaid with mother-of-pearl. All the officers wore sharp, gleaming swords, and shields edged with peacock feathers; and it really seemed that no foe could by any possibility defeat such a brilliant army.

The Sorceress rode in a beautiful palanquin which was like the body of a coach, having doors and windows with silken curtains; but instead of wheels, which a coach has, the palanquin rested upon two long, horizontal bars, which were borne upon the shoulders of twelve servants.

The Scarecrow and his comrades decided to ride in the Gump, in order to keep up with the swift march of the army; so, as soon as Glinda had started and her soldiers had marched away to the inspiring strains of music played by the royal band, our friends climbed into the sofas and followed. The Gump flew along slowly at a point directly over the palanquin in which rode the Sorceress.

"Be careful," said the Tin Woodman to the Scarecrow, who was leaning far over the side to look at the army below. "You might fall."

"It wouldn't matter," remarked the educated Woggle-Bug. "he can't get broke so long as he is stuffed with money."

"Didn't I ask you," began Tip, in a reproachful voice.

"You did!" said the Woggle-Bug, promptly. "And I beg your pardon. I will really try to restrain myself."

"You'd better," declared the boy. "That is, if you wish to travel in our company."

"Ah! I couldn't bear to part with you now," murmured the Insect, feelingly; so Tip let the subject drop.

The army moved steadily on, but night had fallen before they came to the walls of the Emerald City. By the dim light of the new moon, however, Glinda's forces silently surrounded the city and pitched their tents of scarlet silk upon the greensward. The tent of the Sorceress was larger than the others, and was composed of pure white silk, with scarlet banners flying above it. A tent was also pitched for the Scarecrow's party; and when these preparations had been made, with military precision and quickness, the army retired to rest.

Great was the amazement of Queen Jinjur next morning when her soldiers came running to inform her of the vast army surrounding them. She at once climbed to a high tower of the royal palace and saw banners waving in every direction and the great white tent of Glinda standing directly before the gates.

"We are surely lost!" cried Jinjur, in despair; "for how can our knitting needles avail against the long spears and terrible swords of our foes?"

"The best thing we can do," said one of the girls, "is to surrender as quickly as possible, before we get hurt."

"Not so," returned Jinjur, more bravely. "The enemy is still outside the walls, so we must try to gain time by engaging them in parley. Go you with a flag of truce to Glinda and ask her why she has dared to invade my dominions, and what are her demands."

So the girl passed through the gates, bearing a white flag to show she was on a mission of peace, and came to Glinda's tent. "Tell your Queen," said the Sorceress to the girl, "that she must deliver up to me old Mombi, to be my prisoner. If this is done I will not molest her farther."

Now when this message was delivered to the Queen it filled her with dismay, for Mombi was her chief counsellor, and Jinjur was erribly afraid of the old hag. But she sent for Mombi, and told her what Glinda had said.

I see trouble ahead for all of us," muttered the old witch, after glancing into a magic mirror she carried in her pocket. "But we may even yet escape by deceiving this sorceress, clever as she thinks herself."

"Don't you think it will be safer for me to deliver you into her hands?" asked Jinjur, nervously.

If you do, it will cost you the throne of the Emerald City!" answered the witch, positively. "But if you will let me have my own way, I can save us both very easily."

"Then do as you please," replied Jinjur, "for it is so aristocratic to be a Queen that I do not wish to be obliged to return home again, to make beds and wash dishes for my mother."

So Mombi called Jellia Jamb to her, and performed a certain magical rite with which she was familiar. As a result of the enchantment Jellia took on the form and features of Mombi, while the old witch grew to resemble the girl so closely that it seemed impossible anyone could guess the deception.

Now," said old Mombi to the Queen, "let your soldiers deliver up this girl to Glinda. She will think she has the real Mombi in her power, and so will return immediately to her own country in the South."

Therefore Jellia, hobbling along like an aged woman, was led from the city gates and taken before Glinda.

Here is the person you demanded," said one of the guards, "and our Queen now begs you will go away, as you promised, and leave us in peace."

That I will surely do," replied Glinda, much pleased; "if this is really the person she seems to be."

It is certainly old Mombi," said the guard, who believed she was speaking the truth; and then Jinjur's soldiers returned within the city's gates.

The Sorceress quickly summoned the Scarecrow and his friends to her tent, and began to question the supposed Mombi about the lost girl Ozma. But Jellia knew nothing at all of this affair, and presently she grew so nervous under the questioning that she gave way and began to weep, to Glinda's great astonishment.

Here is some foolish trickery!" said the Sorceress, her eyes flashing with anger. "This is not Mombi at all, but some other person who has been made to resemble her! Tell me," she demanded, turning to the trembling girl, "what is your name?"

This Jellia dared not tell, having been threatened with death by the witch if she confessed the fraud. But Glinda, sweet and fair though she was, understood magic better than any other person in the Land of Oz. So, by uttering a few potent words and making peculiar gesture, she quickly transformed the girl into her proper shape, while at the same time old Mombi, far away in Jinjur's palace, suddenly resumed her own crooked form and evil features.

Why, it's Jellia Jamb!" cried the Scarecrow, recognizing in the girl one of his old friends.

It's our interpreter!" said the Pumpkinhead, smiling pleasantly.

Then Jellia was forced to tell of the trick Mombi had played and she also begged Glinda's protection, which the Sorceress readily granted. But Glinda was now really angry, and sent word to Jinjur that the fraud was discovered and she must deliver up the real Mombi or suffer terrible consequences. Jinjur was prepared for this message, for the witch well understood, when her natural form was thrust upon her, that Glinda had discovered her trickery. But the wicked old creature had already thought up a new deception, and had made Jinjur promise to carry it out. So the Queen said to Glinda's messenger:

"Tell your mistress that I cannot find Mombi anywhere, but that Glinda is welcome to enter the city and search herself for the old woman. She may also bring her friends with her, if she likes; but if she does not find Mombi by sundown, the Sorceress must promise to go away peaceably and bother us no more."

Glinda agreed to these terms, well knowing that Mombi was somewhere within the city walls. So Jinjur caused the gates to be thrown open, and Glinda marched in at the head of a company of soldiers, followed by the Scarecrow and the Tin Woodman, while Jack Pumpkinhead rode astride the Saw-Horse, and the Educated, Highly Magnified Woggle-Bug sauntered behind in a dignified manner. Tip walked by the side of the Sorceress, for Glinda had conceived a great liking for the boy.

Of course old Mombi had no intention of being found by Glinda; so, while her enemies were marching up the street, the witch transformed herself into a red rose growing upon a bush in the garden of the palace. It was a clever idea, and a trick Glinda did not suspect; so several precious hours were spent in a vain search for Mombi.

As sundown approached the Sorceress realized she had been defeated by the superior cunning of the aged witch; so she gave the command to her people to march out of the city and back to their tents.

The Scarecrow and his comrades happened to be searching in the garden of the palace just then, and they turned with disappointment to obey Glinda's command. But before they left the garden the Tin Woodman, who was fond of flowers, chanced to espy a big red rose growing upon a bush; so he plucked the flower and fastened it securely in the tin buttonhole of his tin bosom.

As he did this he fancied he heard a low moan proceed from the rose; but he paid no attention to the sound, and Mombi was thus carried out of the city and into Glinda's camp without anyone having a suspicion that they had succeeded in their quest.

The Transformation of Old Mombi

The Witch was at first frightened at finding herself captured by the enemy; but soon she decided that she was exactly as safe in the Tin Woodman's button-hole as growing upon the bush. For no one knew the rose and Mombi to be one, and now that she was without the gates of the City her chances of escaping altogether from Glinda were much improved.

"But there is no hurry," thought Mombi. "I will wait awhile and enjoy the humiliation of this Sorceress when she finds I have outwitted her." So throughout the night the rose lay quietly on the Woodman's bosom, and in the morning, when Glinda summoned our friends to a consultation, Nick Chopper carried his pretty flower with him to the white silk tent.

"For some reason," said Glinda, "we have failed to find this cunning old Mombi; so I fear our expedition will prove a failure. And for that I am sorry, because without our assistance little Ozma will never be rescued and restored to her rightful position as Queen of the Emerald City"

"Do not let us give up so easily," said the Pumpkinhead. "Let us do something else."

"Something else must really be done," replied Glinda, with a smile. "yet I cannot understand how I have been defeated so easily by an old Witch who knows far less of magic than I do myself."

"While we are on the ground I believe it would be wise for us to conquer the Emerald City for Princess Ozma, and find the girl afterward," said the Scarecrow." And while the girl remains hidden I will gladly rule in her place, for I understand the business of ruling much better than Jinjur does."

"But I have promised not to molest Jinjur," objected Glinda.

"Suppose you all return with me to my kingdom — or Empire, rather," said the Tin Woodman, politely including the entire party in a royal wave of his arm. "It will give me great pleasure to entertain you in my castle, where there is room enough and to spare. And if any of you wish to be nickel-plated, my valet will do it free of all expense."

While the Woodman was speaking Glinda's eyes had been noting the rose in his button-hole, and now she imagined she saw the big red leaves of the flower tremble slightly. This quickly aroused her suspicions, and in a moment more the Sorceress had decided that the seeming rose was nothing else than a transformation of old Mombi. At the same instant Mombi knew she was discovered and must quickly plan an escape, and as transformations were easy to her she immediately took the form of a Shadow and glided along the wall of the tent toward the entrance, thinking thus to disappear.

But Glinda had not only equal cunning, but far more experience than the Witch. So the Sorceress reached the opening of the tent before the Shadow, and with a wave of her hand closed the entrance so securely that Mombi could not find a crack big enough to creep through. The Scarecrow and his friends were greatly surprised at Glinda's actions; for none of them had noted the Shadow. But the Sorceress said to them:

"Remain perfectly quiet, all of you! For the old Witch is even now with us in this tent, and I hope to capture her."

These words so alarmed Mombi that she quickly transformed herself from a shadow to a Black Ant, in which shape she crawled along the ground, seeking a crack or crevice in which to hide her tiny body.

Fortunately, the ground where the tent had been pitched, being just before the city gates, was hard and smooth; and while the Ant still crawled about, Glinda discovered it and ran quickly forward to effect its capture. But, just as her hand was descending, the Witch, now fairly frantic with fear, made her last transformation, and in the form of a huge Griffin sprang through the wall of the tent — tearing the silk asunder in her rush — and in a moment had darted away with the speed of a whirlwind.

Glinda did not hesitate to follow. She sprang upon the back of the Saw-Horse and cried:

"Now you shall prove that you have a right to be alive! Run — run — run!"

The Saw-Horse ran. Like a flash he followed the Griffin, his wooden legs moving so fast that they twinkled like the rays of a star. Before our friends could recover from their surprise both the Griffin and the Saw-Horse had dashed out of sight.

"Come! Let us follow!" cried the Scarecrow.

They ran to the place where the Gump was lying and quickly tumbled aboard.

"Fly!" commanded Tip, eagerly.

"Where to?" asked the Gump, in its calm voice.

"I don't know," returned Tip, who was very nervous at the delay "but if you will mount into the air I think we can discover which way Glinda has gone."

"Very well," returned the Gump, quietly; and it spread its great wings and mounted high into the air.

Far away, across the meadows, they could now see two tiny specks, speeding one after the other; and they knew these specks must be the Griffin and the Saw-Horse. So Tip called the Gump's attention to them and bade the creature try to overtake the Witch and the Sorceress. But, swift as was the Gump's flight, the pursued and pursuer moved more swiftly yet, and within a few moments were blotted out against the dim horizon.

"Let us continue to follow them, nevertheless," said the Scarecrow. "for the Land of Oz is of small extent, and sooner or later they must both come to a halt."

Old Mombi had thought herself very wise to choose the form of a Griffin, for its legs were exceedingly fleet and its strength more enduring than that of other animals. But she had not reckoned on the untiring energy of the Saw-Horse, whose wooden limbs could run for days without slacking their speed. Therefore, after an hour's hard running, the Griffin's breath began to fail, and it panted and gasped painfully, and moved more slowly than before. Then it reached the edge of the desert and began racing across the deep sands. But its tired feet sank far into the sand and in a few minutes the Griffin fell forward, completely exhausted, and lay still upon the desert waste.

Glinda came up a moment later, riding the still vigorous Saw-Horse; and having unwound a slender golden thread from her girdle the Sorceress threw it over the head of the panting and helpless Griffin, and so destroyed the magical power of Mombi's transformation.

For the animal, with one fierce shudder, disappeared from view while in its place was discovered the form of the old Witch glaring savagely at the serene and beautiful face of the Sorceress

Princess Ozma of Oz

"You are my prisoner, and it is useless for you to struggle any longer," said Glinda, in her soft, sweet voice. "Lie still a moment and rest yourself, and then I will carry you back to my tent."

"Why do you seek me?" asked Mombi, still scarce able to speak plainly for lack of breath. "What have I done to you, to be so persecuted?"

"You have done nothing to me," answered the gentle Sorceress; "but I suspect you have been guilty of several wicked actions; and if I find it is true that you have so abused your knowledge of magic, I intend to punish you severely."

"I defy you!" croaked the old hag. "You dare not harm me!"

Just then the Gump flew up to them and alighted upon the desert sands beside Glinda. Our friends were delighted to find that Mombi had finally been captured, and after a hurried consultation it was decided they should all return to the camp in the Gump. So the Saw-Horse was tossed aboard, and then Glinda still holding an end of the golden thread that was around Mombi's neck, forced her prisoner to climb into the sofas. The others now followed, and Tip gave the word to the Gump to return.

The Journey was made in safety, Mombi sitting in her place with a grim and sullen air; for the old hag was absolutely helpless so long as the magical thread encircled her throat. The army hailed Glinda's return with loud cheers, and the party of friends soon gathered again in the royal tent, which had been neatly repaired during their absence.

"Now," said the Sorceress to Mombi, "I want you to tell us why the Wonderful Wizard of Oz paid you three visits, and what became of the child, Ozma, which so curiously disappeared."

The Witch looked at Glinda defiantly, but said not a word.

"Answer me!" cried the Sorceress.

But still Mombi remained silent.

"Perhaps she doesn't know," remarked Jack.

"I beg you will keep quiet," said Tip. "You might spoil everything with your foolishness."

"Very well, dear father!" returned the Pumpkinhead, meekly.

"How glad I am to be a Woggle-Bug!" murmured the Highly Magnified Insect, softly. "No one can expect wisdom to flow from a pumpkin."

"Well," said the Scarecrow, "what shall we do to make Mombi speak? Unless she tells us what we wish to know her capture will do us no good at all."

"Suppose we try kindness," suggested the Tin Woodman. "I've heard that anyone can be conquered with kindness, no matter how ugly they may be."

At this the Witch turned to glare upon him so horribly that the Tin Woodman shrank back abashed.

Glinda had been carefully considering what to do, and now she turned to Mombi and said:

"You will gain nothing, I assure you, by thus defying us. For I am determined to learn the truth about the girl Ozma, and unless you tell me all that you know, I will certainly put you to death."

"Oh, no! Don't do that!" exclaimed the Tin Woodman. "It would be an awful thing to kill anyone — even old Mombi!"

"But it is merely a threat," returned Glinda. "I shall not put Mombi to death, because she will prefer to tell me the truth."

"Oh, I see!" said the tin man, much relieved.

"Suppose I tell you all that you wish to know,". said Mombi, speaking so suddenly that she startled them all. "What will you do with me then?"

"In that case," replied Glinda, "I shall merely ask you to drink a powerful draught which will cause you to forget all the magic you have ever learned."

"Then I would become a helpless old woman!"

"But you would be alive," suggested the Pumpkinhead, consolingly.

"Do try to keep silent!" said Tip, nervously.

"I'll try," responded Jack; "but you will admit that it's a good thing to be alive."

"Especially if one happens to be Thoroughly Educated," added the Woggle-Bug, nodding approval.

"You may make your choice," Glinda said to old Mombi, "between death if you remain silent, and the loss of your magical powers if you tell me the truth. But I think you will prefer to live.

Mombi cast an uneasy glance at the Sorceress, and saw that she was in earnest, and not to be trifled with. So she replied, slowly:

"I will answer your questions."

"That is what I expected," said Glinda, pleasantly. "You have chosen wisely, I assure you."

She then motioned to one of her Captains, who brought her a beautiful golden casket. From this the Sorceress drew an immense white pearl, attached to a slender chain which she placed around her neck in such a way that the pearl rested upon her bosom, directly over her heart.

"Now," said she, "I will ask my first question: Why did the Wizard pay you three visits?"

"Because I would not come to him," answered Mombi.

"That is no answer," said Glinda, sternly. "Tell me the truth."

"Well," returned Mombi, with downcast eyes, "he visited me to learn the way I make tea-biscuits."

"Look up!" commanded the Sorceress.

Mombi obeyed.

"What is the color of my pearl?" demanded Glinda.

"Why — it is black!" replied the old Witch, in a tone of wonder.

"Then you have told me a falsehood!" cried Glinda, angrily. "Only when the truth is spoken will my magic pearl remain a pure white in color."

Mombi now saw how useless it was to try to deceive the Sorceress; so she said, meanwhile scowling at her defeat:

"The Wizard brought to me the girl Ozma, who was then no

more than a baby, and begged me to conceal the child."

"That is what I thought," declared Glinda, calmly. "What did he give you for thus serving him?"

"He taught me all the magical tricks he knew. Some were good tricks, and some were only frauds; but I have remained faithful to my promise."

"What did you do with the girl?" asked Glinda; and at this question everyone bent forward and listened eagerly for the reply.

"I enchanted her," answered Mombi.

"In what way?"

"I transformed her into — into — "

"Into what?" demanded Glinda, as the Witch hesitated.

"Into a boy!" said Mombi, in a low tone."

A boy!" echoed every voice; and then, because they knew that this old woman had reared Tip from childhood, all eyes were turned to where the boy stood.

"Yes," said the old Witch, nodding her head; "that is the Princess Ozma — the child brought to me by the Wizard who stole her father's throne. That is the rightful ruler of the Emerald City!" and she pointed her long bony finger straight at the boy.

"I!" cried Tip, in amazement. "Why, I'm no Princess Ozma — I'm not a girl!"

Glinda smiled, and going to Tip she took his small brown hand within her dainty white one.

"You are not a girl just now" said she, gently, "because Mombi transformed you into a boy. But you were born a girl, and also a Princess; so you must resume your proper form, that you may become Queen of the Emerald City."

"Oh, let Jinjur be the Queen!" exclaimed Tip, ready to cry. "I want to stay a boy, and travel with the Scarecrow and the Tin Woodman, and the Woggle-Bug, and Jack — yes! and my friend the Saw-Horse — and the Gump! I don't want to be a girl!"

"Never mind, old chap," said the Tin Woodman, soothingly; "it don't hurt to be a girl, I'm told; and we will all remain your faithful friends just the same. And, to be honest with you, I've always considered girls nicer than boys."

"They're just as nice, anyway," added the Scarecrow, patting Tip affectionately upon the head.

"And they are equally good students," proclaimed the Woggle-Bug. "I should like to become your tutor, when you are transformed into a girl again."

"But — see here!" said Jack Pumpkinhead, with a gasp: "if you become a girl, you can't be my dear father any more!"

"No," answered Tip, laughing in spite of his anxiety. "and I shall not be sorry to escape the relationship." Then he added, hesitatingly, as he turned to Glinda: "I might try it for a while — just to see how it seems, you know. But if I don't like being a girl you must promise to change me into a boy again."

"Really," said the Sorceress, "that is beyond my magic. I never deal in transformations, for they are not honest, and no respectable sorceress likes to make things appear to be what they are not. Only unscrupulous witches use the art, and therefore I must ask Mombi to effect your release from her charm, and restore you to your proper form. It will be the last opportunity she will have to practice magic."

Now that the truth about Princes Ozma had been discovered, Mombi did not care what became of Tip; but she feared Glinda's anger, and the boy generously promised to provide for Mombi in her old age if he became the ruler of the Emerald City. So the Witch consented to effect the transformation, and preparations for the event were at once made.

Glinda ordered her own royal couch to be placed in the center of the tent. It was piled high with cushions covered with rose-colored silk, and from a golden railing above hung many folds of pink gossamer, completely concealing the interior of the couch.

The first act of the Witch was to make the boy drink a potion which quickly sent him into a deep and dreamless sleep. Then the Tin Woodman and the Woggle-Bug bore him gently to the couch, placed him upon the soft cushions, and drew the gossamer hangings to shut him from all earthly view.

The Witch squatted upon the ground and kindled a tiny fire of dried herbs, which she drew from her bosom. When the blaze shot up and burned clearly old Mombi scattered a handful of magical powder over the fire, which straightway gave off a rich violet vapor, filling all the tent with its fragrance and forcing the Saw-Horse to sneeze — although he had been warned to keep quiet.

Then, while the others watched her curiously, the hag chanted a rhythmical verse in words which no one understood, and bent her lean body seven times back and forth over the fire. And now the incantation seemed complete, for the Witch stood upright and cried the one word "Yeowa!" in a loud voice.

The vapor floated away; the atmosphere became, clear again; a whiff of fresh air filled the tent, and the pink curtains of the couch trembled slightly, as if stirred from within.

Glinda walked to the canopy and parted the silken hangings. Then she bent over the cushions, reached out her hand, and from the couch arose the form of a young girl, fresh and beautiful as a May morning. Her eyes sparkled as two diamonds, and her lips were tinted like a tourmaline. All adown her back floated tresses of ruddy gold, with a slender jeweled circlet confining them at the brow. Her robes of silken gauze floated around her like a cloud, and dainty satin slippers shod her feet.

At this exquisite vision Tip's old comrades stared in wonder for the space of a full minute, and then every head bent low in honest admiration of the lovely Princess Ozma. The girl herself cast one look into Glinda's bright face, which glowed with pleasure and satisfaction, and then turned upon the others. Speaking the words with sweet diffidence, she said:

"I hope none of you will care less for me than you did before. I'm just the same Tip, you know; only — only — "

"Only you're different!" said the Pumpkinhead; and everyone thought it was the wisest speech he had ever made.

The Riches of Content

When the wonderful tidings reached the ears of Queen Jinjur — how Mombi the Witch had been captured; how she had confessed her crime to Glinda; and how the long-lost Princess Ozma had been discovered in no less a personage than the boy Tip — she wept real tears of grief and despair.

"To think," she moaned, "that after having ruled as Queen, and lived in a palace, I must go back to scrubbing floors and churning butter again! It is too horrible to think of! I will never consent!"

So when her soldiers, who spent most of their time making fudge in the palace kitchens, counseled Jinjur to resist, she listened to their foolish prattle and sent a sharp defiance to Glinda the Good and the Princess Ozma. The result was a declaration of war, and the very next day Glinda marched upon the Emerald City with pennants flying and bands playing, and a forest of shining spears, sparkling brightly beneath the sun's rays.

But when it came to the walls this brave assembly made a sudden halt; for Jinjur had closed and barred every gateway, and the walls of the Emerald City were builded high and thick with many blocks of green marble. Finding her advance thus baffled, Glinda bent her brows in deep thought, while the Woggle-Bug said, in his most positive tone:

"We must lay siege to the city, and starve it into submission. It is the only thing we can do."

"Not so," answered the Scarecrow. "We still have the Gump, and the Gump can still fly"

The Sorceress turned quickly at this speech, and her face now wore a bright smile.

"You are right," she exclaimed, "and certainly have reason to be proud of your brains. Let us go to the Gump at once!"

So they passed through the ranks of the army until they came to the place, near the Scarecrow's tent, where the Gump lay. Glinda and Princess Ozma mounted first, and sat upon the sofas. Then the Scarecrow and his friends climbed aboard, and still there was room for a Captain and three soldiers, which Glinda considered sufficient for a guard.

Now, at a word from the Princess, the queer Thing they had called the Gump flopped its palm-leaf wings and rose into the air, carrying the party of adventurers high above the walls. They hovered over the palace, and soon perceived Jinjur reclining in a hammock in the courtyard, where she was comfortably reading a novel with a green cover and eating green chocolates, confident that the walls would protect her from her enemies. Obeying a quick command, the Gump alighted safely in this very courtyard, and before Jinjur had time to do more than scream, the Captain and three soldiers leaped out and made the former Queen a prisoner, locking strong chains upon both her wrists.

That act really ended the war; for the Army of Revolt submitted as soon as they knew Jinjur to be a captive, and the Captain marched in safety through the streets and up to the gates of the city, which she threw wide open. Then the bands played their most stirring music while Glinda's army marched into the city, and heralds proclaimed the conquest of the audacious Jinjur and the accession of the beautiful Princess Ozma to the throne of her royal ancestors.

At once the men of the Emerald City cast off their aprons. And it is said that the women were so tired eating of their husbands' cooking that they all hailed the conquest of Jinjur with joy. Certain it is that, rushing one and all to the kitchens of their houses, the good wives prepared so delicious a feast for the weary men that harmony was immediately restored in every family.

Ozma's first act was to oblige the Army of Revolt to return to her every emerald or other gem stolen from the public streets and buildings; and so great was the number of precious stones picked from their settings by these vain girls, that every one of the royal jewelers worked steadily for more than a month to replace them in their settings.

Meanwhile the Army of Revolt was disbanded and the girls sent home to their mothers. On promise of good behavior Jinjur was likewise released.

Ozma made the loveliest Queen the Emerald City had ever known; and, although she was so young and inexperienced, she ruled her people with wisdom and Justice. For Glinda gave her good advice on all occasions; and the Woggle-Bug, who was appointed to the important post of Public Educator, was quite helpful to Ozma when her royal duties grew perplexing.

The girl, in her gratitude to the Gump for its services, offered the creature any reward it might name.

"Then," replied the Gump, "please take me to pieces. I did not wish to be brought to life, and I am greatly ashamed of my conglomerate personality. Once I was a monarch of the forest, as my antlers fully prove; but now, in my present upholstered condition of servitude, I am compelled to fly through the air — my legs being of no use to me whatever. Therefore I beg to be dispersed."

So Ozma ordered the Gump taken apart. The antlered head was again hung over the mantle-piece in the hall, and the sofas were untied and placed in the reception parlors. The broom tail resumed its accustomed duties in the kitchen, and finally, the Scarecrow replaced all the clotheslines and ropes on the pegs from which he had taken them on the eventful day when the Thing was constructed.

You might think that was the end of the Gump; and so it was, as a flying-machine. But the head over the mantle-piece continued to talk whenever it took a notion to do so, and it frequently startled, with its abrupt questions, the people who waited in the hall for an audience with the Queen.

The Saw-Horse, being Ozma's personal property, was tenderly cared for; and often she rode the queer creature along the streets of the Emerald City. She had its wooden legs shod with gold, to keep them from wearing out, and the tinkle of these golden shoes upon the pavement always filled the Queen's subjects with awe as they thought upon this evidence of her magical powers.

"The Wonderful Wizard was never so wonderful as Queen Ozma," the people said to one another, in whispers; "for he claimed to do many things he could not do; whereas our new Queen does many things no one would ever expect her to accomplish."

Jack Pumpkinhead remained with Ozma to the end of his days; and he did not spoil as soon as he had feared, although he always remained as stupid as ever. The Woggle-Bug tried to teach him several arts and sciences; but Jack was so poor a student that any attempt to educate him was soon abandoned.

After Glinda's army had marched back home, and peace was restored to the Emerald City, the Tin Woodman announced his intention to return to his own Kingdom of the Winkies.

"It isn't a very big Kingdom," said he to Ozma, "but for that very reason it is easier to rule; and I have called myself an Emperor because I am an Absolute Monarch, and no one interferes in any way with my conduct of public or personal affairs. When I get home I shall have a new coat of nickel plate; for I have become somewhat marred and scratched lately; and then I shall be glad to have you pay me a visit."

"Thank you," replied Ozma. "Some day I may accept the invitation. But what is to become of the Scarecrow?"

"I shall return with my friend the Tin Woodman," said the stuffed one, seriously. "We have decided never to be parted in the future."

"And I have made the Scarecrow my Royal Treasurer," explained the Tin Woodman." For it has occurred to me that it is a good thing to have a Royal Treasurer who is made of money. What do you think?"

"I think," said the little Queen, smiling, "that your friend must be the richest man in all the world."

"I am," returned the Scarecrow. "but not on account of my money. For I consider brains far superior to money, in every way. You may have noticed that if one has money without brains, he cannot use it to advantage; but if one has brains without money, they will enable him to live comfortably to the end of his days."

"At the same time," declared the Tin Woodman, "you must acknowledge that a good heart is a thing that brains can not create, and that money can not buy. Perhaps, after all, it is I who am the richest man in all the world."

"You are both rich, my friends," said Ozma, gently; "and your riches are the only riches worth having — the riches of content!"

Ozma of Oz
by L. Frank Baum

A Record of Her Adventures with Dorothy Gale of Kansas, the Yellow Hen, the Scarecrow, the Tin Woodman, Tiktok, the Cowardly Lion and the Hungry Tiger; Besides Other Good People too Numerous to Mention Faithfully Recorded Herein.
By L. Frank Baum, The Author of The Wizard of Oz, The Land of Oz, etc.

Author's Note

My friends the children are responsible for this new "Oz Book," as they were for the last one, which was called The Land of Oz. Their sweet little letters plead to know "more about Dorothy"; and they ask: "What became of the Cowardly Lion?" and "What did Ozma do afterward?"—meaning, of course, after she became the Ruler of Oz. And some of them suggest plots to me, saying: "Please have Dorothy go to the Land of Oz again"; or, "Why don't you make Ozma and Dorothy meet, and have a good time together?" Indeed, could I do all that my little friends ask, I would be obliged to write dozens of books to satisfy their demands. And I wish I could, for I enjoy writing these stories just as much as the children say they enjoy reading them.

Well, here is "more about Dorothy," and about our old friends the Scarecrow and the Tin Woodman, and about the Cowardly Lion, and Ozma, and all the rest of them; and here, likewise, is a good deal about some new folks that are queer and unusual. One little friend, who read this story before it was printed, said to me: "Billina is REAL OZZY, Mr. Baum, and so are Tiktok and the Hungry Tiger."

If this judgment is unbiased and correct, and the little folks find this new story "real Ozzy," I shall be very glad indeed that I wrote it. But perhaps I shall get some more of those very welcome letters from my readers, telling me just how they like "Ozma of Oz." I hope so, anyway.

L. Frank Baum.
Macatawa, 1907.

1. The Girl in the Chicken Coop

The wind blew hard and joggled the water of the ocean, sending ripples across its surface. Then the wind pushed the edges of the ripples until they became waves, and shoved the waves around until they became billows. The billows rolled dreadfully high: higher even than the tops of houses. Some of them, indeed, rolled as high as the tops of tall trees, and seemed like mountains; and the gulfs between the great billows were like deep valleys.

All this mad dashing and splashing of the waters of the big ocean, which the mischievous wind caused without any good reason whatever, resulted in a terrible storm, and a storm on the ocean is liable to cut many queer pranks and do a lot of damage.

At the time the wind began to blow, a ship was sailing far out upon the waters. When the waves began to tumble and toss and to grow bigger and bigger the ship rolled up and down, and tipped sidewise—first one way and then the other—and was jostled around so roughly that even the sailor-men had to hold fast to the ropes and railings to keep themselves from being swept away by the wind or pitched headlong into the sea.

And the clouds were so thick in the sky that the sunlight couldn't get through them; so that the day grew dark as night, which added to the terrors of the storm.

The Captain of the ship was not afraid, because he had seen storms before, and had sailed his ship through them in safety; but he knew that his passengers would be in danger if they tried to stay on deck, so he put them all into the cabin and told them to stay there until after the storm was over, and to keep brave hearts and not be scared, and all would be well with them.

Now, among these passengers was a little Kansas girl named Dorothy Gale, who was going with her Uncle Henry to Australia, to visit some relatives they had never before seen. Uncle Henry, you must know, was not very well, because he had been working so hard on his Kansas farm that his health had given way and left him weak and nervous. So he left Aunt Em at home to watch after the hired men and to take care of the farm, while he traveled far away to Australia to visit his cousins and have a good rest.

Dorothy was eager to go with him on this journey, and Uncle Henry thought she would be good company and help cheer him up; so he decided to take her along. The little girl was quite an experienced traveller, for she had once been carried by a cyclone as far away from home as the marvelous Land of Oz, and she had met with a good many adventures in that strange country before she managed to get back to Kansas again. So she wasn't easily frightened, whatever happened, and when the wind began to howl and whistle, and the waves began to tumble and toss, our little girl didn't mind the uproar the least bit.

"Of course we'll have to stay in the cabin," she said to Uncle Henry and the other passengers, "and keep as quiet as possible until the storm is over. For the Captain says if we go on deck we may be blown overboard."

No one wanted to risk such an accident as that, you may be sure; so all the passengers stayed huddled up in the dark cabin, listening to the shrieking of the storm and the creaking of the masts and rigging and trying to keep from bumping into one another when the ship tipped sidewise.

Dorothy had almost fallen asleep when she was aroused with a start to find that Uncle Henry was missing. She couldn't imagine where he had gone, and as he was not very strong she began to worry about him, and to fear he might have been careless enough to go on deck. In that case he would be in great danger unless he instantly came down again.

The fact was that Uncle Henry had gone to lie down in his little sleeping-berth, but Dorothy did not know that. She only remembered that Aunt Em had cautioned her to take good care of her uncle, so at once she decided to go on deck and find him, in spite of the fact that the tempest was now worse than ever, and the ship was plunging in a really dreadful manner. Indeed, the little girl found it was as much as she could do to mount the stairs to the deck, and as soon as she got there the wind struck her so fiercely that it almost tore away the skirts of her dress. Yet Dorothy felt a sort of joyous excitement in defying the storm, and while she held fast to the railing she peered around through the gloom and thought she saw the dim form of a man clinging to a mast not far away from her. This might be her uncle, so she called as loudly as she could:

"Uncle Henry! Uncle Henry!"

But the wind screeched and howled so madly that she scarce heard her own voice, and the man certainly failed to hear her, for he did not move.

Dorothy decided she must go to him; so she made a dash forward, during a lull in the storm, to where a big square chicken-coop had been lashed to the deck with ropes. She reached this place in safety, but no sooner had she seized fast hold of the slats of the big box in which the chickens were kept than the wind, as if enraged because the little girl dared to resist its power, suddenly redoubled its fury. With a scream like that of an angry giant it tore away the ropes that held the coop and lifted it high into the air, with Dorothy still clinging to the slats. Around and over it whirled, this way and that, and a few moments later the chicken-coop dropped far away into the sea, where the big waves caught it and slid it up-hill to a foaming crest and then down-hill into a deep valley, as if it were nothing more than a plaything to keep them amused.

Dorothy had a good ducking, you may be sure, but she didn't lose her presence of mind even for a second. She kept tight hold of the stout slats and as soon as she could get the water out of her eyes she saw that the wind had ripped the cover from the coop, and the poor chickens were fluttering away in every direction, being blown by the wind until they looked like feather dusters without handles. The bottom of the coop was made of thick boards, so Dorothy found she was clinging to a sort of raft, with sides of slats, which readily bore up her weight. After coughing the water out of her throat and getting her breath again, she managed to climb over the slats and stand upon the firm wooden bottom of the coop, which supported her easily enough.

"Why, I've got a ship of my own!" she thought, more amused than frightened at her sudden change of condition; and then, as the coop climbed up to the top of a big wave, she looked eagerly around for the ship from which she had been blown.

It was far, far away, by this time. Perhaps no one on board had yet missed her, or knew of her strange adventure. Down into a valley between the waves the coop swept her, and when she climbed another crest the ship looked like a toy boat, it was such a long way off. Soon it had entirely disappeared in the gloom, and then Dorothy gave a sigh of regret at parting with Uncle Henry and began to wonder what was going to happen to her next.

Just now she was tossing on the bosom of a big ocean, with nothing to keep her afloat but a miserable wooden hen-coop that had a plank bottom and slatted sides, through which the water constantly splashed and wetted her through to the skin! And there was nothing to eat when she became hungry—as she was sure to do before long—and no fresh water to drink and no dry clothes to put on.

"Well, I declare!" she exclaimed, with a laugh. "You're in a pretty fix, Dorothy Gale, I can tell you! and I haven't the least idea how you're going to get out of it!"

As if to add to her troubles the night was now creeping on, and the gray clouds overhead changed to inky blackness. But the wind, as if satisfied at last with its mischievous pranks, stopped blowing this ocean and hurried away to another part of the world to blow something else; so that the waves, not being joggled any more, began to quiet down and behave themselves.

It was lucky for Dorothy, I think, that the storm subsided; otherwise, brave though she was, I fear she might have perished. Many children, in her place, would have wept and given way to despair; but because Dorothy had encountered so many adventures and come safely through them it did not occur to her at this time to be especially afraid. She was wet and uncomfortable, it is true; but, after sighing that one sigh I told you of, she managed to recall some of her customary cheerfulness and decided to patiently await whatever her fate might be.

By and by the black clouds rolled away and showed a blue sky overhead, with a silver moon shining sweetly in the middle of it and little stars winking merrily at Dorothy when she looked their way. The coop did not toss around any more, but rode the waves more gently—almost like a cradle rocking—so that the floor upon which Dorothy stood was no longer swept by water coming through the slats. Seeing this, and being quite exhausted by the excitement of the past few hours, the little girl decided that sleep would be the best thing to restore her strength and the easiest way in which she could pass the time. The floor was damp and she was herself wringing wet, but fortunately this was a warm climate and she did not feel at all cold.

So she sat down in a corner of the coop, leaned her back against the slats, nodded at the friendly stars before she closed her eyes, and was asleep in half a minute.

2. The Yellow Hen

A strange noise awoke Dorothy, who opened her eyes to find that day had dawned and the sun was shining brightly in a clear sky. She had been dreaming that she was back in Kansas again, and playing in the old barn-yard with the calves and pigs and chickens all around her; and at first, as she rubbed the sleep from her eyes, she really imagined she was there.

"Kut-kut-kut, ka-daw-kut! Kut-kut-kut, ka-daw-kut!"

Ah; here again was the strange noise that had awakened her. Surely it was a hen cackling! But her wide-open eyes first saw, through the slats of the coop, the blue waves of the ocean, now calm and placid, and her thoughts flew back to the past night, so full of danger and discomfort. Also she began to remember that she was a waif of the storm, adrift upon a treacherous and unknown sea.

"Kut-kut-kut, ka-daw-w-w—kut!"

"What's that?" cried Dorothy, starting to her feet.

"Why, I've just laid an egg, that's all," replied a small, but sharp and distinct voice, and looking around her the little girl discovered a yellow hen squatting in the opposite corner of the coop.

"Dear me!" she exclaimed, in surprise; "have YOU been here all night, too?"

"Of course," answered the hen, fluttering her wings and yawning. "When the coop blew away from the ship I clung fast to this corner, with claws and beak, for I knew if I fell into the water I'd surely be drowned. Indeed, I nearly drowned, as it was, with all that water washing over me. I never was so wet before in my life!"

"Yes," agreed Dorothy, "it was pretty wet, for a time, I know. But do you feel comfor'ble now?"

"Not very. The sun has helped to dry my feathers, as it has your dress, and I feel better since I laid my morning egg. But what's to become of us, I should like to know, afloat on this big pond?"

"I'd like to know that, too," said Dorothy. "But, tell me; how does it happen that you are able to talk? I thought hens could only cluck and cackle."

"Why, as for that," answered the yellow hen thoughtfully, "I've clucked and cackled all my life, and never spoken a word before this morning, that I can remember. But when you asked a question, a minute ago, it seemed the most natural thing in the world to answer you. So I spoke, and I seem to keep on speaking, just as you and other human beings do. Strange, isn't it?"

"Very," replied Dorothy. "If we were in the Land of Oz, I wouldn't think it so queer, because many of the animals can talk in that fairy country. But out here in the ocean must be a good long way from Oz."

"How is my grammar?" asked the yellow hen, anxiously. "Do I speak quite properly, in your judgment?"

"Yes," said Dorothy, "you do very well, for a beginner."

"I'm glad to know that," continued the yellow hen, in a confidential tone; "because, if one is going to talk, it's best to talk correctly. The red rooster has often said that my cluck and my cackle were quite perfect; and now it's a comfort to know I am talking properly."

"I'm beginning to get hungry," remarked Dorothy. "It's breakfast time; but there's no breakfast."

"You may have my egg," said the yellow hen. "I don't care for it, you know."

"Don't you want to hatch it?" asked the little girl, in surprise.

"No, indeed; I never care to hatch eggs unless I've a nice snug nest, in some quiet place, with a baker's dozen of eggs under me. That's thirteen, you know, and it's a lucky number for hens. So you may as well eat this egg."

"Oh, I couldn't POSS'BLY eat it, unless it was cooked," exclaimed Dorothy. "But I'm much obliged for your kindness, just the same."

"Don't mention it, my dear," answered the hen, calmly, and began preening her feathers.

For a moment Dorothy stood looking out over the wide sea. She was still thinking of the egg, though; so presently she asked:

"Why do you lay eggs, when you don't expect to hatch them?"

"It's a habit I have," replied the yellow hen. "It has always been my pride to lay a fresh egg every morning, except when I'm moulting. I never feel like having my morning cackle till the egg is properly laid, and without the chance to cackle I would not be happy."

"It's strange," said the girl, reflectively; "but as I'm not a hen I can't be 'spected to understand that."

"Certainly not, my dear."

Then Dorothy fell silent again. The yellow hen was some company, and a bit of comfort, too; but it was dreadfully lonely out on the big ocean, nevertheless.

After a time the hen flew up and perched upon the topmost slat of the coop, which was a little above Dorothy's head when she was sitting upon the bottom, as she had been doing for some moments past.

"Why, we are not far from land!" exclaimed the hen.

"Where? Where is it?" cried Dorothy, jumping up in great excitement.

"Over there a little way," answered the hen, nodding her head in a certain direction. "We seem to be drifting toward it, so that before noon we ought to find ourselves upon dry land again."

"I shall like that!" said Dorothy, with a little sigh, for her feet and legs were still wetted now and then by the sea-water that came through the open slats.

"So shall I," answered her companion. "There is nothing in the world so miserable as a wet hen."

The land, which they seemed to be rapidly approaching, since it grew more distinct every minute, was quite beautiful as viewed by the little girl in the floating hen-coop. Next to the water was a broad beach of white sand and gravel, and farther back were several rocky hills, while beyond these appeared a strip of green trees that marked the edge of a forest. But there were no houses to be seen, nor any sign of people who might inhabit this unknown land.

"I hope we shall find something to eat," said Dorothy, looking eagerly at the pretty beach toward which they drifted. "It's long past breakfast time, now."

"I'm a trifle hungry, myself," declared the yellow hen.

"Why don't you eat the egg?" asked the child. "You don't need to have your food cooked, as I do."

"Do you take me for a cannibal?" cried the hen, indignantly. "I do not know what I have said or done that leads you to insult me!"

"I beg your pardon, I'm sure Mrs.—Mrs.—by the way, may I inquire your name, ma'am?" asked the little girl.

"My name is Bill," said the yellow hen, somewhat gruffly.

"Bill! Why, that's a boy's name."

"What difference does that make?"

"You're a lady hen, aren't you?"

"Of course. But when I was first hatched out no one could tell whether I was going to be a hen or a rooster; so the little boy at the farm where I was born called me Bill, and made a pet of me because I was the only yellow chicken in the whole brood. When I grew up, and he found that I didn't crow and fight, as all the roosters do, he did not think to change my name, and every creature in the barn-yard, as well as the people in the house, knew me as 'Bill.' So Bill I've always been called, and Bill is my name."

"But it's all wrong, you know," declared Dorothy, earnestly; "and, if you don't mind, I shall call you 'Billina.' Putting the 'eena' on the end makes it a girl's name, you see."

"Oh, I don't mind it in the least," returned the yellow hen. "It doesn't matter at all what you call me, so long as I know the name means ME."

"Very well, Billina. MY name is Dorothy Gale—just Dorothy to my friends and Miss Gale to strangers. You may call me Dorothy, if you like. We're getting very near the shore. Do you suppose it is too deep for me to wade the rest of the way?"

"Wait a few minutes longer. The sunshine is warm and pleasant, and we are in no hurry."

"But my feet are all wet and soggy," said the girl. "My dress is dry enough, but I won't feel real comfor'ble till I get my feet dried."

She waited, however, as the hen advised, and before long the big wooden coop grated gently on the sandy beach and the dangerous voyage was over.

It did not take the castaways long to reach the shore, you may be sure. The yellow hen flew to the sands at once, but Dorothy had to climb over the high slats. Still, for a country girl, that was not much of a feat, and as soon as she was safe ashore Dorothy drew off her wet shoes and stockings and spread them upon the sun-warmed beach to dry.

Then she sat down and watched Billina, who was pick-pecking away with her sharp bill in the sand and gravel, which she scratched up and turned over with her strong claws.

"What are you doing?" asked Dorothy.

"Getting my breakfast, of course," murmured the hen, busily pecking away.

"What do you find?" inquired the girl, curiously.

"Oh, some fat red ants, and some sand-bugs, and once in a while a tiny crab. They are very sweet and nice, I assure you."

"How dreadful!" exclaimed Dorothy, in a shocked voice.

"What is dreadful?" asked the hen, lifting her head to gaze with one bright eye at her companion.

"Why, eating live things, and horrid bugs, and crawly ants. You ought to be 'SHAMED of yourself!"

"Goodness me!" returned the hen, in a puzzled tone; "how queer you are, Dorothy! Live things are much fresher and more wholesome than dead ones, and you humans eat all sorts of dead creatures."

"We don't!" said Dorothy.

"You do, indeed," answered Billina. "You eat lambs and sheep and cows and pigs and even chickens."

"But we cook 'em," said Dorothy, triumphantly.

"What difference does that make?"

"A good deal," said the girl, in a graver tone. "I can't just 'splain the diff'rence, but it's there. And, anyhow, we never eat such dreadful things as BUGS."

"But you eat the chickens that eat the bugs," retorted the yellow hen, with an odd cackle. "So you are just as bad as we chickens are."

This made Dorothy thoughtful. What Billina said was true enough, and it almost took away her appetite for breakfast. As for the yellow hen, she continued to peck away at the sand busily, and seemed quite contented with her bill-of-fare.

Finally, down near the water's edge, Billina stuck her bill deep into the sand, and then drew back and shivered.

"Ow!" she cried. "I struck metal, that time, and it nearly broke my beak."

"It prob'bly was a rock," said Dorothy, carelessly.

"Nonsense. I know a rock from metal, I guess," said the hen. "There's a different feel to it."

"But there couldn't be any metal on this wild, deserted seashore," persisted the girl. "Where's the place? I'll dig it up, and prove to you I'm right."

Billina showed her the place where she had "stubbed her bill," as she expressed it, and Dorothy dug away the sand until she felt something hard. Then, thrusting in her hand, she pulled the thing out, and discovered it to be a large sized golden key—rather old, but still bright and of perfect shape.

"What did I tell you?" cried the hen, with a cackle of triumph. "Can I tell metal when I bump into it, or is the thing a rock?"

"It's metal, sure enough," answered the child, gazing thoughtfully at the curious thing she had found. "I think it is pure gold, and it must have lain hidden in the sand for a long time. How do you suppose it came there, Billina? And what do you suppose this mysterious key unlocks?"

"I can't say," replied the hen. "You ought to know more about locks and keys than I do."

Dorothy glanced around. There was no sign of any house in that part of the country, and she reasoned that every key must fit a lock and every lock must have a purpose. Perhaps the key had been lost by somebody who lived far away, but had wandered on this very shore.

Musing on these things the girl put the key in the pocket of her dress and then slowly drew on her shoes and stockings, which the sun had fully dried.

"I b'lieve, Billina," she said, "I'll have a look 'round, and see if I can find some breakfast."

3. Letters in the Sand

Walking a little way back from the water's edge, toward the grove of trees, Dorothy came to a flat stretch of white sand that seemed to have queer signs marked upon its surface, just as one would write upon sand with a stick.

"What does it say?" she asked the yellow hen, who trotted along beside her in a rather dignified fashion.

"How should I know?" returned the hen. "I cannot read."

"Oh! Can't you?"

"Certainly not; I've never been to school, you know."

"Well, I have," admitted Dorothy; "but the letters are big and far apart, and it's hard to spell out the words."

But she looked at each letter carefully, and finally discovered that these words were written in the sand:

"BEWARE THE WHEELERS!"

"That's rather strange," declared the hen, when Dorothy had read aloud the words. "What do you suppose the Wheelers are?"

"Folks that wheel, I guess. They must have wheelbarrows, or baby-cabs or hand-carts," said Dorothy.

"Perhaps they're automobiles," suggested the yellow hen. "There is no need to beware of baby-cabs and wheelbarrows; but automobiles are dangerous things. Several of my friends have been run over by them."

"It can't be auto'biles," replied the girl, "for this is a new, wild country, without even trolley-cars or tel'phones. The people here haven't been discovered yet, I'm sure; that is, if there ARE any people. So I don't b'lieve there CAN be any auto'biles, Billina."

"Perhaps not," admitted the yellow hen. "Where are you going now?"

"Over to those trees, to see if I can find some fruit or nuts," answered Dorothy.

She tramped across the sand, skirting the foot of one of the little rocky hills that stood near, and soon reached the edge of the forest.

At first she was greatly disappointed, because the nearer trees were all punita, or cotton-wood or eucalyptus, and bore no fruit or nuts at all. But, bye and bye, when she was almost in despair, the little girl came upon two trees that promised to furnish her with plenty of food.

One was quite full of square paper boxes, which grew in clusters on all the limbs, and upon the biggest and ripest boxes the word "Lunch" could be read, in neat raised letters. This tree seemed to bear all the year around, for there were lunch-box blossoms on some of the branches, and on others tiny little lunch-boxes that were as yet quite green, and evidently not fit to eat until they had grown bigger.

The leaves of this tree were all paper napkins, and it presented a very pleasing appearance to the hungry little girl.

But the tree next to the lunch-box tree was even more wonderful, for it bore quantities of tin dinner-pails, which were so full and heavy that the stout branches bent underneath their weight. Some were small and dark-brown in color; those larger were of a dull tin color; but the really ripe ones were pails of bright tin that shone and glistened beautifully in the rays of sunshine that touched them.

Dorothy was delighted, and even the yellow hen acknowledged that she was surprised.

The little girl stood on tip-toe and picked one of the nicest and biggest lunch-boxes, and then she sat down upon the ground and eagerly opened it. Inside she found, nicely wrapped in white papers, a ham sandwich, a piece of sponge-cake, a pickle, a slice of new cheese and an apple. Each thing had a separate stem, and so had to be picked off the side of the box; but Dorothy found

them all to be delicious, and she ate every bit of luncheon in the box before she had finished.

"A lunch isn't 'zactly breakfast," she said to Billina, who sat beside her curiously watching. "But when one is hungry one can eat even supper in the morning, and not complain."

"I hope your lunch-box was perfectly ripe," observed the yellow hen, in a anxious tone. "So much sickness is caused by eating green things."

"Oh, I'm sure it was ripe," declared Dorothy, "all, that is, 'cept the pickle, and a pickle just HAS to be green, Billina. But everything tasted perfectly splendid, and I'd rather have it than a church picnic. And now I think I'll pick a dinner-pail, to have when I get hungry again, and then we'll start out and 'splore the country, and see where we are."

"Haven't you any idea what country this is?" inquired Billina.

"None at all. But listen: I'm quite sure it's a fairy country, or such things as lunch-boxes and dinner-pails wouldn't be growing upon trees. Besides, Billina, being a hen, you wouldn't be able to talk in any civ'lized country, like Kansas, where no fairies live at all."

"Perhaps we're in the Land of Oz," said the hen, thoughtfully.

"No, that can't be," answered the little girl; because I've been to the Land of Oz, and it's all surrounded by a horrid desert that no one can cross."

"Then how did you get away from there again?" asked Billina.

"I had a pair of silver shoes, that carried me through the air; but I lost them," said Dorothy.

"Ah, indeed," remarked the yellow hen, in a tone of unbelief.

"Anyhow," resumed the girl, "there is no seashore near the Land of Oz, so this must surely be some other fairy country."

While she was speaking she selected a bright and pretty dinner-pail that seemed to have a stout handle, and picked it from its branch. Then, accompanied by the yellow hen, she walked out of the shadow of the trees toward the sea-shore.

They were part way across the sands when Billina suddenly cried, in a voice of terror:

"What's that?"

Dorothy turned quickly around, and saw coming out of a path that led from between the trees the most peculiar person her eyes had ever beheld.

It had the form of a man, except that it walked, or rather rolled, upon all fours, and its legs were the same length as its arms, giving them the appearance of the four legs of a beast. Yet it was no beast that Dorothy had discovered, for the person was clothed most gorgeously in embroidered garments of many colors, and wore a straw hat perched jauntily upon the side of its head. But it differed from human beings in this respect, that instead of hands and feet there grew at the end of its arms and legs round wheels, and by means of these wheels it rolled very swiftly over the level ground. Afterward Dorothy found that these odd wheels were of the same hard substance that our finger-nails and toe-nails are composed of, and she also learned that creatures of this strange race were born in this queer fashion. But when our little girl first caught sight of the first individual of a race that was destined to cause her a lot of trouble, she had an idea that the brilliantly-clothed personage was on roller-skates, which were attached to his hands as well as to his feet.

"Run!" screamed the yellow hen, fluttering away in great fright. "It's a Wheeler!"

"A Wheeler?" exclaimed Dorothy. "What can that be?"

"Don't you remember the warning in the sand: 'Beware the Wheelers'? Run, I tell you—run!"

So Dorothy ran, and the Wheeler gave a sharp, wild cry and came after her in full chase.

Looking over her shoulder as she ran, the girl now saw a great procession of Wheelers emerging from the forest—dozens and dozens of them—all clad in splendid, tight-fitting garments and all rolling swiftly toward her and uttering their wild, strange cries.

"They're sure to catch us!" panted the girl, who was still carrying the heavy dinner-pail she had picked. "I can't run much farther, Billina."

"Climb up this hill,—quick!" said the hen; and Dorothy found she was very near to the heap of loose and jagged rocks they had passed on their way to the forest. The yellow hen was even now fluttering among the rocks, and Dorothy followed as best she could, half climbing and half tumbling up the rough and rugged steep.

She was none too soon, for the foremost Wheeler reached the hill a moment after her; but while the girl scrambled up the rocks the creature stopped short with howls of rage and disappointment.

Dorothy now heard the yellow hen laughing, in her cackling, henny way.

"Don't hurry, my dear," cried Billina. "They can't follow us among these rocks, so we're safe enough now."

Dorothy stopped at once and sat down upon a broad boulder, for she was all out of breath.

The rest of the Wheelers had now reached the foot of the hill, but it was evident that their wheels would not roll upon the rough and jagged rocks, and therefore they were helpless to follow Dorothy and the hen to where they had taken refuge. But they circled all around the little hill, so the child and Billina were fast prisoners and could not come down without being captured.

Then the creatures shook their front wheels at Dorothy in a threatening manner, and it seemed they were able to speak as well as to make their dreadful outcries, for several of them shouted:

"We'll get you in time, never fear! And when we do get you, we'll tear you into little bits!"

"Why are you so cruel to me?" asked Dorothy. "I'm a stranger in your country, and have done you no harm."

"No harm!" cried one who seemed to be their leader. "Did you not pick our lunch-boxes and dinner-pails? Have you not a stolen dinner-pail still in your hand?"

"I only picked one of each," she answered. "I was hungry, and I didn't know the trees were yours."

"That is no excuse," retorted the leader, who was clothed in a most gorgeous suit. "It is the law here that whoever picks a dinner-pail without our permission must die immediately."

"Don't you believe him," said Billina. "I'm sure the trees do not belong to these awful creatures. They are fit for any mischief, and it's my opinion they would try to kill us just the same if you hadn't picked a dinner-pail."

"I think so, too," agreed Dorothy. "But what shall we do now?"

"Stay where we are," advised the yellow hen. "We are safe from the Wheelers until we starve to death, anyhow; and before that time comes a good many things can happen."

4. Tiktok the Machine Man

After an hour or so most of the band of Wheelers rolled back into the forest, leaving only three of their number to guard the hill. These curled themselves up like big dogs and pretended to go to sleep on the sands; but neither Dorothy nor Billina were fooled by this trick, so they remained in security among the rocks and paid no attention to their cunning enemies.

Finally the hen, fluttering over the mound, exclaimed: "Why, here's a path!"

So Dorothy at once clambered to where Billina sat, and there, sure enough, was a smooth path cut between the rocks. It seemed to wind around the mound from top to bottom, like a cork-screw, twisting here and there between the rough boulders but always remaining level and easy to walk upon.

Indeed, Dorothy wondered at first why the Wheelers did not roll up this path; but when she followed it to the foot of the mound she found that several big pieces of rock had been placed directly across the end of the way, thus preventing any one outside from seeing it and also preventing the Wheelers from using it to climb up the mound.

Then Dorothy walked back up the path, and followed it until she came to the very top of the hill, where a solitary round rock stood that was bigger than any of the others surrounding it. The path came to an end just beside this great rock, and for a moment it puzzled the girl to know why the path had been made at all. But the hen, who had been gravely following her around and was now perched upon a point of rock behind Dorothy, suddenly remarked:

"It looks something like a door, doesn't it?"

"What looks like a door?" enquired the child.

"Why, that crack in the rock, just facing you," replied Billina, whose little round eyes were very sharp and seemed to see everything. "It runs up one side and down the other, and across the top and the bottom."

"What does?"

"Why, the crack. So I think it must be a door of rock, although I do not see any hinges."

"Oh, yes," said Dorothy, now observing for the first time the crack in the rock. "And isn't this a key-hole, Billina?" pointing to a round, deep hole at one side of the door.

"Of course. If we only had the key, now, we could unlock it and see what is there," replied the yellow hen. "May be it's a treasure chamber full of diamonds and rubies, or heaps of shining gold, or—"

"That reminds me," said Dorothy, "of the golden key I picked up on the shore. Do you think that it would fit this key-hole, Billina?"

"Try it and see," suggested the hen.

So Dorothy searched in the pocket of her dress and found the golden key. And when she had put it into the hole of the rock, and turned it, a sudden sharp snap was heard; then, with a solemn creak that made the shivers run down the child's back, the face of the rock fell outward, like a door on hinges, and revealed a small dark chamber just inside.

"Good gracious!" cried Dorothy, shrinking back as far as the narrow path would let her.

For, standing within the narrow chamber of rock, was the form of a man—or, at least, it seemed like a man, in the dim light. He was only about as tall as Dorothy herself, and his body was round as a ball and made out of burnished copper. Also his head and limbs were copper, and these were jointed or hinged to his body in a peculiar way, with metal caps over the joints, like the armor worn by knights in days of old. He stood perfectly still, and where the light struck upon his form it glittered as if made of pure gold.

"Don't be frightened," called Billina, from her perch. "It isn't alive."

"I see it isn't," replied the girl, drawing a long breath.

"It is only made out of copper, like the old kettle in the barn-yard at home," continued the hen, turning her head first to one side and then to the other, so that both her little round eyes could examine the object.

"Once," said Dorothy, "I knew a man made out of tin, who was a woodman named Nick Chopper. But he was as alive as we are, 'cause he was born a real man, and got his tin body a little at a time—first a leg and then a finger and then an ear—for the reason that he had so many accidents with his axe, and cut himself up in a very careless manner."

"Oh," said the hen, with a sniff, as if she did not believe the story.

"But this copper man," continued Dorothy, looking at it with big eyes, "is not alive at all, and I wonder what it was made for, and why it was locked up in this queer place."

"That is a mystery," remarked the hen, twisting her head to arrange her wing-feathers with her bill.

Dorothy stepped inside the little room to get a back view of the copper man, and in this way discovered a printed card that hung between his shoulders, it being suspended from a small copper peg at the back of his neck. She unfastened this card and returned to the path, where the light was better, and sat herself down upon a slab of rock to read the printing.

"What does it say?" asked the hen, curiously.

Dorothy read the card aloud, spelling out the big words with some difficulty; and this is what she read:

SMITH & TINKER'S
Patent Double-Action, Extra-Responsive,
Thought-Creating, Perfect-Talking
MECHANICAL MAN
Fitted with our Special Clock-Work Attachment.
Thinks, Speaks, Acts, and Does Everything but Live.
Manufactured only at our Works at Evna, Land of Ev.
All infringements will be promptly
Prosecuted according to Law.

"How queer!" said the yellow hen. "Do you think that is all true, my dear?"

"I don't know," answered Dorothy, who had more to read. "Listen to this, Billina:"

DIRECTIONS FOR USING:
For THINKING: Wind the Clock-work Man under his left arm, (marked No. 1.)
For SPEAKING: Wind the Clock-work Man under his right arm, (marked No. 2.)
For WALKING and ACTION: Wind Clock-work in the middle of his back, (marked No. 3.)
N.B. This Mechanism is guaranteed to work perfectly for a thousand years.

"Well, I declare!" gasped the yellow hen, in amazement; "if the copper man can do half of these things he is a very wonderful machine. But I suppose it is all humbug, like so many other patented articles."

"We might wind him up," suggested Dorothy, "and see what he'll do."

"Where is the key to the clock-work?" asked Billina.

"Hanging on the peg where I found the card."

"Then," said the hen, "let us try him, and find out if he will go. He is warranted for a thousand years, it seems; but we do not know how long he has been standing inside this rock."

Dorothy had already taken the clock key from the peg.

"Which shall I wind up first?" she asked, looking again at the directions on the card.

"Number One, I should think," returned Billina. "That makes him think, doesn't it?"

"Yes," said Dorothy, and wound up Number One, under the left arm.

"He doesn't seem any different," remarked the hen, critically.

"Why, of course not; he is only thinking, now," said Dorothy.

"I wonder what he is thinking about."

"I'll wind up his talk, and then perhaps he can tell us," said the girl.

So she wound up Number Two, and immediately the clock-work man said, without moving any part of his body except his lips:

"Good morn-ing, lit-tle girl. Good morn-ing, Mrs. Hen."

The words sounded a little hoarse and creaky, and they were uttered all in the same tone, without any change of expression whatever; but both Dorothy and Billina understood them perfectly.

"Good morning, sir," they answered, politely.

"Thank you for res-cu-ing me," continued the machine, in the same monotonous voice, which seemed to be worked by a bellows inside of him, like the little toy lambs and cats the children squeeze so that they will make a noise.

"Don't mention it," answered Dorothy. And then, being very curious, she asked: "How did you come to be locked up in this place?"

"It is a long sto-ry," replied the copper man; "but I will tell it to you brief-ly. I was pur-chased from Smith & Tin-ker, my man-u-fac-tur-ers, by a cru-el King of Ev, named Ev-ol-do, who used to beat all his serv-ants un-til they died. How-ev-er, he was not a-ble to kill me, be-cause I was not a-live, and one must first live in or-der to die. So that all his beat-ing did me no harm, and mere-ly kept my cop-per bod-y well pol-ished.

"This cru-el king had a love-ly wife and ten beau-ti-ful chil-dren—five boys and five girls—but in a fit of an-ger he sold them all to the Nome King, who by means of his mag-ic arts changed them all in-to oth-er forms and put them in his un-der-ground pal-ace to or-na-ment the rooms.

"Af-ter-ward the King of Ev re-gret-ted his wick-ed ac-tion, and tried to get his wife and chil-dren a-way from the Nome King, but with-out a-vail. So, in de-spair, he locked me up in this rock, threw the key in-to the o-cean, and then jumped in af-ter it and was drowned."

"How very dreadful!" exclaimed Dorothy.

"It is, in-deed," said the machine. "When I found my-self im-pris-oned I shout-ed for help un-til my voice ran down; and then I walked back and forth in this lit-tle room un-til my ac-tion ran down; and then I stood still and thought un-til my thoughts ran down. Af-ter that I re-mem-ber noth-ing un-til you wound me up a-gain."

"It's a very wonderful story," said Dorothy, "and proves that the Land of Ev is really a fairy land, as I thought it was."

"Of course it is," answered the copper man. "I do not sup-pose such a per-fect ma-chine as I am could be made in an-y place but a fair-y land."

"I've never seen one in Kansas," said Dorothy.

"But where did you get the key to un-lock this door?" asked the clock-work voice.

"I found it on the shore, where it was prob'ly washed up by the waves," she answered. "And now, sir, if you don't mind, I'll wind up your action."

"That will please me ve-ry much," said the machine.

So she wound up Number Three, and at once the copper man in a somewhat stiff and jerky fashion walked out of the rocky cavern, took off his copper hat and bowed politely, and then kneeled before Dorothy. Said he:

"From this time forth I am your o-be-di-ent ser-vant. What-ev-er you com-mand, that I will do will-ing-ly—if you keep me wound up."

"What is your name?" she asked.

"Tik-tok," he replied. "My for-mer mas-ter gave me that name be-cause my clock-work al-ways ticks when it is wound up."

"I can hear it now," said the yellow hen.

"So can I," said Dorothy. And then she added, with some anxiety, "You don't strike, do you?"

"No," answered Tiktok; "and there is no a-larm con-nec-ted with my ma-chin-er-y. I can tell the time, though, by speak-ing, and as I nev-er sleep I can wak-en you at an-y hour you wish to get up in the morn-ing."

"That's nice," said the little girl; "only I never wish to get up in the morning."

"You can sleep until I lay my egg," said the yellow hen. "Then when I cackle, Tiktok will know it is time to waken you."

"Do you lay your egg very early?" asked Dorothy.

"About eight o'clock," said Billina. "And everybody ought to be up by that time, I'm sure."

5. Dorothy Opens the Dinner Pail

"Now Tiktok," said Dorothy, "the first thing to be done is to find a way for us to escape from these rocks. The Wheelers are down below, you know, and threaten to kill us."

"There is no rea-son to be a-fraid of the Wheel-ers," said Tiktok, the words coming more slowly than before.

"Why not?" she asked.

"Be-cause they are ag-g-g—gr-gr-r-r-"

He gave a sort of gurgle and stopped short, waving his hand frantically until suddenly he became motionless, with one arm in the air and the other held stiffly before him with all the copper fingers of the hand spread out like a fan.

"Dear me!" said Dorothy, in a frightened tone. "What can the matter be?"

"He's run down, I suppose," said the hen, calmly. "You couldn't have wound him up very tight."

"I didn't know how much to wind him," replied the girl; "but I'll try to do better next time."

She ran around the copper man to take the key from the peg at the back of his neck, but it was not there.

"It's gone!" cried Dorothy, in dismay.

"What's gone?" asked Billina.

"The key."

"It probably fell off when he made that low bow to you," returned the hen. "Look around, and see if you cannot find it again."

Dorothy looked, and the hen helped her, and by and by the girl discovered the clock-key, which had fallen into a crack of the rock.

At once she wound up Tiktok's voice, taking care to give the key as many turns as it would go around. She found this quite a task, as you may imagine if you have ever tried to wind a clock, but the machine man's first words were to assure Dorothy that he would now run for at least twenty-four hours.

"You did not wind me much, at first," he calmly said, "and I told you that long sto-ry a-bout King Ev-ol-do; so it is no won-der that I ran down."

She next rewound the action clock-work, and then Billina advised her to carry the key to Tiktok in her pocket, so it would not get lost again.

"And now," said Dorothy, when all this was accomplished, "tell me what you were going to say about the Wheelers."

"Why, they are noth-ing to be fright-en'd at," said the machine. "They try to make folks be-lieve that they are ver-y ter-ri-ble, but as a mat-ter of fact the Wheel-ers are harm-less e-nough to an-y one that dares to fight them. They might try to hurt a lit-tle girl like you, per-haps, be-cause they are ver-y mis-chiev-ous. But if I had a club they would run a-way as soon as they saw me."

"Haven't you a club?" asked Dorothy.

"No," said Tiktok.

"And you won't find such a thing among these rocks, either," declared the yellow hen.

"Then what shall we do?" asked the girl.

"Wind up my think-works tight-ly, and I will try to think of some oth-er plan," said Tiktok.

So Dorothy rewound his thought machinery, and while he was thinking she decided to eat her dinner. Billina was already pecking away at the cracks in the rocks, to find something to eat, so Dorothy sat down and opened her tin dinner-pail.

In the cover she found a small tank that was full of very nice lemonade. It was covered by a cup, which might also, when removed, be used to drink the lemonade from. Within the pail were three slices of turkey, two slices of cold tongue, some lobster salad, four slices of bread and butter, a small custard pie, an orange and nine large strawberries, and some nuts and raisins. Singularly enough, the nuts in this dinner-pail grew already cracked, so that Dorothy had no trouble in picking out their meats to eat.

She spread the feast upon the rock beside her and began her dinner, first offering some of it to Tiktok, who declined because, as he said, he was merely a machine. Afterward she offered to share with Billina, but the hen murmured something about "dead things" and said she preferred her bugs and ants.

"Do the lunch-box trees and the dinner-pail trees belong to the Wheelers?" the child asked Tiktok, while engaged in eating her meal.

"Of course not," he answered. "They be-long to the roy-al fam-il-y of Ev, on-ly of course there is no roy-al fam-il-y just now be-cause King Ev-ol-do jumped in-to the sea and his wife and ten chil-dren have been trans-formed by the Nome King. So there is no one to rule the Land of Ev, that I can think of. Per-haps it is for this rea-son that the Wheel-ers claim the trees for their own, and pick the lunch-eons and din-ners to eat them-selves. But they be-long to the King, and you will find the roy-al "E" stamped up-on the bot-tom of ev-er-y din-ner pail."

Dorothy turned the pail over, and at once discovered the royal mark upon it, as Tiktok had said.

"Are the Wheelers the only folks living in the Land of Ev?" enquired the girl.

"No; they on-ly in-hab-it a small por-tion of it just back of the woods," replied the machine. "But they have al-ways been mis-chiev-ous and im-per-ti-nent, and my old mas-ter, King Ev-ol-do, used to car-ry a whip with him, when he walked out, to keep the crea-tures in or-der. When I was first made the Wheel-ers tried to run o-ver me, and butt me with their heads; but they soon found I was built of too sol-id a ma-ter-i-al for them to in-jure."

"You seem very durable," said Dorothy. "Who made you?"

"The firm of Smith & Tin-ker, in the town of Evna, where the roy-al pal-ace stands," answered Tiktok.

"Did they make many of you?" asked the child.

"No; I am the on-ly au-to-mat-ic me-chan-i-cal man they ev-er com-plet-ed," he replied. "They were ver-y won-der-ful in-ven-tors, were my mak-ers, and quite ar-tis-tic in all they did."

"I am sure of that," said Dorothy. "Do they live in the town of Evna now?"

"They are both gone," replied the machine. "Mr. Smith was an art-ist, as well as an in-vent-or, and he paint-ed a pic-ture of a riv-er which was so nat-ur-al that, as he was reach-ing a-cross it to paint some flow-ers on the op-po-site bank, he fell in-to the wa-ter and was drowned."

"Oh, I'm sorry for that!" exclaimed the little girl.

"Mis-ter Tin-ker," continued Tiktok, "made a lad-der so tall that he could rest the end of it a-gainst the moon, while he stood on the high-est rung and picked the lit-tle stars to set in the points of the king's crown. But when he got to the moon Mis-ter Tin-ker found it such a love-ly place that he de-cid-ed to live there, so he pulled up the lad-der af-ter him and we have nev-er seen him since."

"He must have been a great loss to this country," said Dorothy, who was by this time eating her custard pie.

"He was," acknowledged Tiktok. "Also he is a great loss to me. For if I should get out of or-der I do not know of an-y one a-ble to re-pair me, be-cause I am so com-pli-cat-ed. You have no i-de-a how full of ma-chin-er-y I am."

"I can imagine it," said Dorothy, readily.

"And now," continued the machine, "I must stop talk-ing and be-gin think-ing a-gain of a way to es-cape from this rock." So he turned half way around, in order to think without being disturbed.

"The best thinker I ever knew," said Dorothy to the yellow hen, "was a scarecrow."

"Nonsense!" snapped Billina.

"It is true," declared Dorothy. "I met him in the Land of Oz, and he traveled with me to the city of the great Wizard of Oz, so as to get some brains, for his head was only stuffed with straw. But it seemed to me that he thought just as well before he got his brains as he did afterward."

"Do you expect me to believe all that rubbish about the Land of Oz?" enquired Billina, who seemed a little cross—perhaps because bugs were scarce.

"What rubbish?" asked the child, who was now finishing her nuts and raisins.

"Why, your impossible stories about animals that can talk, and a tin woodman who is alive, and a scarecrow who can think."

"They are all there," said Dorothy, "for I have seen them."

"I don't believe it!" cried the hen, with a toss of her head.

"That's 'cause you're so ign'rant," replied the girl, who was a little offended at her friend Billina's speech.

"In the Land of Oz," remarked Tiktok, turning toward them, "any-thing is pos-si-ble. For it is a won-der-ful fair-y coun-try."

"There, Billina! what did I say?" cried Dorothy. And then she turned to the machine and asked in an eager tone: "Do you know the Land of Oz, Tiktok?"

"No; but I have heard a-bout it," said the cop-per man. "For it is on-ly sep-a-ra-ted from this Land of Ev by a broad des-ert."

Dorothy clapped her hands together delightedly.

"I'm glad of that!" she exclaimed. "It makes me quite happy to be so near my old friends. The scarecrow I told you of, Billina, is the King of the Land of Oz."

"Par-don me. He is not the king now," said Tiktok.

"He was when I left there," declared Dorothy.

"I know," said Tiktok, "but there was a rev-o-lu-tion in the Land of Oz, and the Scare-crow was de-posed by a sol-dier wo-man named Gen-er-al Jin-jur. And then Jin-jur was de-posed by a lit-tle girl named Oz-ma, who was the right-ful heir to the throne and now rules the land un-der the ti-tle of Oz-ma of Oz."

"That is news to me," said Dorothy, thoughtfully. "But I s'pose lots of things have happened since I left the Land of Oz. I wonder what has become of the Scarecrow, and of the Tin Woodman, and the Cowardly Lion. And I wonder who this girl Ozma is, for I never heard of her before."

But Tiktok did not reply to this. He had turned around again to resume his thinking.

Dorothy packed the rest of the food back into the pail, so as not to be wasteful of good things, and the yellow hen forgot her dignity far enough to pick up all of the scattered crumbs, which she ate rather greedily, although she had so lately pretended to despise the things that Dorothy preferred as food.

By this time Tiktok approached them with his stiff bow.

"Be kind e-nough to fol-low me," he said, "and I will lead you a-way from here to the town of Ev-na, where you will be more com-for-ta-ble, and al-so I will pro-tect you from the Wheel-ers."

"All right," answered Dorothy, promptly. "I'm ready!"

6. The Heads of Langwidere

They walked slowly down the path between the rocks, Tiktok going first, Dorothy following him, and the yellow hen trotting along last of all.

At the foot of the path the copper man leaned down and tossed aside with ease the rocks that encumbered the way. Then he turned to Dorothy and said:

"Let me car-ry your din-ner-pail."

She placed it in his right hand at once, and the copper fingers closed firmly over the stout handle.

Then the little procession marched out upon the level sands.

As soon as the three Wheelers who were guarding the mound saw them, they began to shout their wild cries and rolled swiftly toward the little group, as if to capture them or bar their way. But when the foremost had approached near enough, Tiktok swung the tin dinner-pail and struck the Wheeler a sharp blow over its head with the queer weapon. Perhaps it did not hurt very much, but it made a great noise, and the Wheeler uttered a howl and tumbled over upon its side. The next minute it scrambled to its wheels and rolled away as fast as it could go, screeching with fear at the same time.

"I told you they were harm-less," began Tiktok; but before he could say more another Wheeler was upon them. Crack! went the dinner-pail against its head, knocking its straw hat a dozen feet away; and that was enough for this Wheeler, also. It rolled away after the first one, and the third did not wait to be pounded with the pail, but joined its fellows as quickly as its wheels would whirl.

The yellow hen gave a cackle of delight, and flying to a perch upon Tiktok's shoulder, she said:

"Bravely done, my copper friend! and wisely thought of, too. Now we are free from those ugly creatures."

But just then a large band of Wheelers rolled from the forest, and relying upon their numbers to conquer, they advanced fiercely upon Tiktok. Dorothy grabbed Billina in her arms and held her tight, and the machine embraced the form of the little girl with his left arm, the better to protect her. Then the Wheelers were upon them.

Rattlety, bang! bang! went the dinner-pail in every direction, and it made so much clatter bumping against the heads of the Wheelers that they were much more frightened than hurt and fled in a great panic. All, that is, except their leader. This Wheeler had stumbled against another and fallen flat upon his back, and before he could get his wheels under him to rise again, Tiktok had fastened his copper fingers into the neck of the gorgeous jacket of his foe and held him fast.

"Tell your peo-ple to go a-way," commanded the machine.

The leader of the Wheelers hesitated to give this order, so Tiktok shook him as a terrier dog does a rat, until the Wheeler's teeth rattled together with a noise like hailstones on a window pane. Then, as soon as the creature could get its breath, it shouted to the others to roll away, which they immediately did.

"Now," said Tiktok, "you shall come with us and tell me what I want to know."

"You'll be sorry for treating me in this way," whined the Wheeler. "I'm a terribly fierce person."

"As for that," answered Tiktok, "I am only a ma-chine, and can-not feel sor-row or joy, no mat-ter what hap-pens. But you are wrong to think your-self ter-ri-ble or fierce."

"Why so?" asked the Wheeler.

"Be-cause no one else thinks as you do. Your wheels make you help-less to in-jure an-y one. For you have no fists and can not scratch or e-ven pull hair. Nor have you an-y feet to kick with. All you can do is to yell and shout, and that does not hurt an-y one at all."

The Wheeler burst into a flood of tears, to Dorothy's great surprise.

"Now I and my people are ruined forever!" he sobbed; "for you have discovered our secret. Being so helpless, our only hope is to make people afraid of us, by pretending we are very fierce and terrible, and writing in the sand warnings to Beware the Wheelers. Until now we have frightened everyone, but since you have discovered our weakness our enemies will fall upon us and make us very miserable and unhappy."

"Oh, no," exclaimed Dorothy, who was sorry to see this beautifully dressed Wheeler so miserable; "Tiktok will keep your secret, and so will Billina and I. Only, you must promise not to try to frighten children any more, if they come near to you."

"I won't—indeed I won't!" promised the Wheeler, ceasing to cry and becoming more cheerful. "I'm not really bad, you know; but we have to pretend to be terrible in order to prevent others from attacking us."

"That is not ex-act-ly true," said Tiktok, starting to walk toward the path through the forest, and still holding fast to his prisoner, who rolled slowly along beside him. "You and your peo-ple are full of mis-chief, and like to both-er those who fear you. And you are of-ten im-pu-dent and dis-a-gree-a-ble, too. But if you will try to cure those faults I will not tell any-one how help-less you are."

"I'll try, of course," replied the Wheeler, eagerly. "And thank you, Mr. Tiktok, for your kindness."

"I am on-ly a ma-chine," said Tiktok. "I can not be kind an-y more than I can be sor-ry or glad. I can on-ly do what I am wound up to do."

"Are you wound up to keep my secret?" asked the Wheeler, anxiously.

"Yes; if you be-have your-self. But tell me: who rules the Land of Ev now?" asked the machine.

"There is no ruler," was the answer, "because every member of the royal family is imprisoned by the Nome King. But the Princess Langwidere, who is a niece of our late King Evoldo, lives in a part of the royal palace and takes as much money out of the royal treasury as she can spend. The Princess Langwidere is not exactly a ruler, you see, because she doesn't rule; but she is the nearest approach to a ruler we have at present."

"I do not re-mem-ber her," said Tiktok. "What does she look like?"

"That I cannot say," replied the Wheeler, "although I have seen her twenty times. For the Princess Langwidere is a different person every time I see her, and the only way her subjects can recognize her at all is by means of a beautiful ruby key which she always wears on a chain attached to her left wrist. When we see the key we know we are beholding the Princess."

"That is strange," said Dorothy, in astonishment. "Do you mean to say that so many different princesses are one and the same person?"

"Not exactly," answered the Wheeler. "There is, of course, but one princess; but she appears to us in many forms, which are all more or less beautiful."

"She must be a witch," exclaimed the girl.

"I do not think so," declared the Wheeler. "But there is some mystery connected with her, nevertheless. She is a very vain creature, and lives mostly in a room surrounded by mirrors, so that she can admire herself whichever way she looks."

No one answered this speech, because they had just passed out of the forest and their attention was fixed upon the scene before them—a beautiful vale in which were many fruit trees and green fields, with pretty farm-houses scattered here and there and broad, smooth roads that led in every direction.

In the center of this lovely vale, about a mile from where our friends were standing, rose the tall spires of the royal palace, which glittered brightly against their background of blue sky. The palace was surrounded by charming grounds, full of flowers and shrubbery. Several tinkling fountains could be seen, and there were pleasant walks bordered by rows of white marble statuary.

All these details Dorothy was, of course, unable to notice or admire until they had advanced along the road to a position quite near to the palace, and she was still looking at the pretty sights when her little party entered the grounds and approached the big front door of the king's own apartments. To their disappointment they found the door tightly closed. A sign was tacked to the panel which read as follows:

> OWNER ABSENT.
> Please Knock at the Third Door in the Left Wing.

"Now," said Tiktok to the captive Wheeler, "you must show us the way to the Left Wing."

"Very well," agreed the prisoner, "it is around here at the right."

"How can the left wing be at the right?" demanded Dorothy, who feared the Wheeler was fooling them.

"Because there used to be three wings, and two were torn down, so the one on the right is the only one left. It is a trick of the Princess Langwidere to prevent visitors from annoying her."

Then the captive led them around to the wing, after which the machine man, having no further use for the Wheeler, permitted him to depart and rejoin his fellows. He immediately rolled away at a great pace and was soon lost to sight.

Tiktok now counted the doors in the wing and knocked loudly upon the third one.

It was opened by a little maid in a cap trimmed with gay ribbons, who bowed respectfully and asked:

"What do you wish, good people?"

"Are you the Princess Langwidere?" asked Dorothy.

"No, miss; I am her servant," replied the maid.

"May I see the Princess, please?"

"I will tell her you are here, miss, and ask her to grant you an audience," said the maid. "Step in, please, and take a seat in the drawing-room."

So Dorothy walked in, followed closely by the machine. But as the yellow hen tried to enter after them, the little maid cried "Shoo!" and flapped her apron in Billina's face.

"Shoo, yourself!" retorted the hen, drawing back in anger and ruffling up her feathers. "Haven't you any better manners than that?"

"Oh, do you talk?" enquired the maid, evidently surprised.

"Can't you hear me?" snapped Billina. "Drop that apron, and get out of the doorway, so that I may enter with my friends!"

"The Princess won't like it," said the maid, hesitating.

"I don't care whether she likes it or not," replied Billina, and fluttering her wings with a loud noise she flew straight at the maid's face. The little servant at once ducked her head, and the hen reached Dorothy's side in safety.

"Very well," sighed the maid; "if you are all ruined because of this obstinate hen, don't blame me for it. It isn't safe to annoy the Princess Langwidere."

"Tell her we are waiting, if you please," Dorothy requested, with dignity. "Billina is my friend, and must go wherever I go."

Without more words the maid led them to a richly furnished drawing-room, lighted with subdued rainbow tints that came in through beautiful stained-glass windows.

"Remain here," she said. "What names shall I give the Princess?"

"I am Dorothy Gale, of Kansas," replied the child; "and this gentleman is a machine named Tiktok, and the yellow hen is my friend Billina."

The little servant bowed and withdrew, going through several passages and mounting two marble stairways before she came to the apartments occupied by her mistress.

Princess Langwidere's sitting-room was paneled with great mirrors, which reached from the ceiling to the floor; also the ceiling was composed of mirrors, and the floor was of polished silver that reflected every object upon it. So when Langwidere sat in her easy chair and played soft melodies upon her mandolin, her form was mirrored hundreds of times, in walls and ceiling and floor, and whichever way the lady turned her head she could see and admire her own features. This she loved to do, and just as the maid entered she was saying to herself:

"This head with the auburn hair and hazel eyes is quite attractive. I must wear it more often than I have done of late, although it may not be the best of my collection."

"You have company, Your Highness," announced the maid, bowing low.

"Who is it?" asked Langwidere, yawning.

"Dorothy Gale of Kansas, Mr. Tiktok and Billina," answered the maid.

"What a queer lot of names!" murmured the Princess, beginning to be a little interested. "What are they like? Is Dorothy Gale of Kansas pretty?"

"She might be called so," the maid replied.

"And is Mr. Tiktok attractive?" continued the Princess.

"That I cannot say, Your Highness. But he seems very bright. Will Your Gracious Highness see them?"

"Oh, I may as well, Nanda. But I am tired admiring this head, and if my visitor has any claim to beauty I must take care that she does not surpass me. So I will go to my cabinet and change to No. 17, which I think is my best appearance. Don't you?"

"Your No. 17 is exceedingly beautiful," answered Nanda, with another bow.

Again the Princess yawned. Then she said:

"Help me to rise."

So the maid assisted her to gain her feet, although Langwidere was the stronger of the two; and then the Princess slowly walked across the silver floor to her cabinet, leaning heavily at every step upon Nanda's arm.

Now I must explain to you that the Princess Langwidere had thirty heads—as many as there are days in the month. But of course she could only wear one of them at a time, because she had but one neck. These heads were kept in what she called her "cabinet," which was a beautiful dressing-room that lay just between Langwidere's sleeping-chamber and the mirrored sitting-room. Each head was in a separate cupboard lined with velvet. The cupboards ran all around the sides of the dressing-room, and had elaborately carved doors with gold numbers on the outside and jeweled-framed mirrors on the inside of them.

When the Princess got out of her crystal bed in the morning she went to her cabinet, opened one of the velvet-lined cupboards, and took the head it contained from its golden shelf. Then, by the aid of the mirror inside the open door, she put on the head—as neat and straight as could be—and afterward called her maid to robe her for the day. She always wore a simple white costume that suited all the heads. For, being able to change her face whenever she liked, the Princess had no interest in wearing a variety of gowns, as have other ladies who are compelled to wear the same face constantly.

Of course the thirty heads were in great variety, no two formed alike but all being of exceeding loveliness. There were heads with golden hair, brown hair, rich auburn hair and black hair; but none with gray hair. The heads had eyes of blue, of gray, of hazel, of brown and of black; but there were no red eyes among them, and all were bright and handsome. The noses were Grecian, Roman, retrousse and Oriental, representing all types of beauty; and the mouths were of assorted sizes and shapes, displaying pearly teeth when the heads smiled. As for dimples, they appeared in cheeks and chins, wherever they might be most charming, and one or two heads had freckles upon the faces to contrast the better with the brilliancy of their complexions.

One key unlocked all the velvet cupboards containing these treasures—a curious key carved from a single blood-red ruby—and this was fastened to a strong but slender chain which the Princess wore around her left wrist.

When Nanda had supported Langwidere to a position in front of cupboard No. 17, the Princess unlocked the door with her ruby key and after handing head No. 9, which she had been wearing, to the maid, she took No. 17 from its shelf and fitted it to her neck. It had black hair and dark eyes and a lovely pearl-and-white complexion, and when Langwidere wore it she knew she was remarkably beautiful in appearance.

There was only one trouble with No. 17; the temper that went with it (and which was hidden somewhere under the glossy black hair) was fiery, harsh and haughty in the extreme, and it often led the Princess to do unpleasant things which she regretted when she came to wear her other heads.

But she did not remember this today, and went to meet her guests in the drawing-room with a feeling of certainty that she would surprise them with her beauty.

However, she was greatly disappointed to find that her visitors were merely a small girl in a gingham dress, a copper man that would only go when wound up, and a yellow hen that was sitting contentedly in Langwidere's best work-basket, where there was a china egg used for darning stockings. (It may surprise you to learn that a princess ever does such a common thing as darn stockings. But, if you will stop to think, you will realize that a princess is sure to wear holes in her stockings, the same as other people; only it isn't considered quite polite to mention the matter.)

"Oh!" said Langwidere, slightly lifting the nose of No. 17. "I thought some one of importance had called."

"Then you were right," declared Dorothy. "I'm a good deal of 'portance myself, and when Billina lays an egg she has the proudest cackle you ever heard. As for Tiktok, he's the—"

"Stop—Stop!" commanded the Princess, with an angry flash of her splendid eyes. "How dare you annoy me with your senseless chatter?"

"Why, you horrid thing!" said Dorothy, who was not accustomed to being treated so rudely.

The Princess looked at her more closely.

"Tell me," she resumed, "are you of royal blood?"

"Better than that, ma'am," said Dorothy. "I came from Kansas."

"Huh!" cried the Princess, scornfully. "You are a foolish child, and I cannot allow you to annoy me. Run away, you little goose, and bother some one else."

Dorothy was so indignant that for a moment she could find no words to reply. But she rose from her chair, and was about to leave the room when the Princess, who had been scanning the girl's face, stopped her by saying, more gently:

"Come nearer to me."

Dorothy obeyed, without a thought of fear, and stood before the Princess while Langwidere examined her face with careful attention.

"You are rather attractive," said the lady, presently. "Not at all beautiful, you understand, but you have a certain style of prettiness that is different from that of any of my thirty heads. So I believe I'll take your head and give you No. 26 for it."

"Well, I b'lieve you won't!" exclaimed Dorothy.

"It will do you no good to refuse," continued the Princess; "for I need your head for my collection, and in the Land of Ev my will is law. I never have cared much for No. 26, and you will find that it is very little worn. Besides, it will do you just as well as the one you're wearing, for all practical purposes."

"I don't know anything about your No. 26, and I don't want to," said Dorothy, firmly. "I'm not used to taking cast-off things, so I'll just keep my own head."

"You refuse?" cried the Princess, with a frown.

"Of course I do," was the reply.

"Then," said Langwidere, "I shall lock you up in a tower until you decide to obey me. Nanda," turning to her maid, "call my army."

Nanda rang a silver bell, and at once a big fat colonel in a bright red uniform entered the room, followed by ten lean soldiers, who all looked sad and discouraged and saluted the princess in a very melancholy fashion.

"Carry that girl to the North Tower and lock her up!" cried the Princess, pointing to Dorothy.

"To hear is to obey," answered the big red colonel, and caught the child by her arm. But at that moment Tiktok raised his dinner-pail and pounded it so forcibly against the colonel's head that the big officer sat down upon the floor with a sudden bump, looking both dazed and very much astonished.

"Help!" he shouted, and the ten lean soldiers sprang to assist their leader.

There was great excitement for the next few moments, and Tiktok had knocked down seven of the army, who were sprawling in every direction upon the carpet, when suddenly the machine paused, with the dinner-pail raised for another blow, and remained perfectly motionless.

"My ac-tion has run down," he called to Dorothy. "Wind me up, quick."

She tried to obey, but the big colonel had by this time managed to get upon his feet again, so he grabbed fast hold of the girl and she was helpless to escape.

"This is too bad," said the machine. "I ought to have run six hours lon-ger, at least, but I sup-pose my long walk and my fight with the Wheel-ers made me run down fast-er than us-u-al."

"Well, it can't be helped," said Dorothy, with a sigh.

"Will you exchange heads with me?" demanded the Princess.

"No, indeed!" cried Dorothy.

"Then lock her up," said Langwidere to her soldiers, and they led Dorothy to a high tower at the north of the palace and locked her securely within.

The soldiers afterward tried to lift Tiktok, but they found the machine so solid and heavy that they could not stir it. So they left him standing in the center of the drawing-room.

"People will think I have a new statue," said Langwidere, "so it won't matter in the least, and Nanda can keep him well polished."

"What shall we do with the hen?" asked the colonel, who had just discovered Billina in the work-basket.

"Put her in the chicken-house," answered the Princess. "Someday I'll have her fried for breakfast."

"She looks rather tough, Your Highness," said Nanda, doubtfully.

"That is a base slander!" cried Billina, struggling frantically in the colonel's arms. "But the breed of chickens I come from is said to be poison to all princesses."

"Then," remarked Langwidere, "I will not fry the hen, but keep her to lay eggs; and if she doesn't do her duty I'll have her drowned in the horse trough."

7. Ozma of Oz to the Rescue

Nanda brought Dorothy bread and water for her supper, and she slept upon a hard stone couch with a single pillow and a silken coverlet.

In the morning she leaned out of the window of her prison in the tower to see if there was any way to escape. The room was not so very high up, when compared with our modern buildings, but it was far enough above the trees and farm houses to give her a good view of the surrounding country.

To the east she saw the forest, with the sands beyond it and the ocean beyond that. There was even a dark speck upon the shore that she thought might be the chicken-coop in which she had arrived at this singular country.

Then she looked to the north, and saw a deep but narrow valley lying between two rocky mountains, and a third mountain that shut off the valley at the further end.

Westward the fertile Land of Ev suddenly ended a little way from the palace, and the girl could see miles and miles of sandy desert that stretched further than her eyes could reach. It was this desert, she thought, with much interest, that alone separated her from the wonderful Land of Oz, and she remembered

sorrowfully that she had been told no one had ever been able to cross this dangerous waste but herself. Once a cyclone had carried her across it, and a magical pair of silver shoes had carried her back again. But now she had neither a cyclone nor silver shoes to assist her, and her condition was sad indeed. For she had become the prisoner of a disagreeable princess who insisted that she must exchange her head for another one that she was not used to, and which might not fit her at all.

Really, there seemed no hope of help for her from her old friends in the Land of Oz. Thoughtfully she gazed from her narrow window. On all the desert not a living thing was stirring.

Wait, though! Something surely WAS stirring on the desert—something her eyes had not observed at first. Now it seemed like a cloud; now it seemed like a spot of silver; now it seemed to be a mass of rainbow colors that moved swiftly toward her.

What COULD it be, she wondered?

Then, gradually, but in a brief space of time nevertheless, the vision drew near enough to Dorothy to make out what it was.

A broad green carpet was unrolling itself upon the desert, while advancing across the carpet was a wonderful procession that made the girl open her eyes in amazement as she gazed.

First came a magnificent golden chariot, drawn by a great Lion and an immense Tiger, who stood shoulder to shoulder and trotted along as gracefully as a well-matched team of thoroughbred horses. And standing upright within the chariot was a beautiful girl clothed in flowing robes of silver gauze and wearing a jeweled diadem upon her dainty head. She held in one hand the satin ribbons that guided her astonishing team, and in the other an ivory wand that separated at the top into two prongs, the prongs being tipped by the letters "O" and "Z", made of glistening diamonds set closely together.

The girl seemed neither older nor larger than Dorothy herself, and at once the prisoner in the tower guessed that the lovely driver of the chariot must be that Ozma of Oz of whom she had so lately heard from Tiktok.

Following close behind the chariot Dorothy saw her old friend the Scarecrow, riding calmly astride a wooden Saw-Horse, which pranced and trotted as naturally as any meat horse could have done.

And then came Nick Chopper, the Tin Woodman, with his funnel-shaped cap tipped carelessly over his left ear, his gleaming axe over his right shoulder, and his whole body sparkling as brightly as it had ever done in the old days when first she knew him.

The Tin Woodman was on foot, marching at the head of a company of twenty-seven soldiers, of whom some were lean and some fat, some short and some tall; but all the twenty-seven were dressed in handsome uniforms of various designs and colors, no two being alike in any respect.

Behind the soldiers the green carpet rolled itself up again, so that there was always just enough of it for the procession to walk upon, in order that their feet might not come in contact with the deadly, life-destroying sands of the desert.

Dorothy knew at once it was a magic carpet she beheld, and her heart beat high with hope and joy as she realized she was soon to be rescued and allowed to greet her dearly beloved friends of

Oz—the Scarecrow, the Tin Woodman and the Cowardly Lion.

Indeed, the girl felt herself as good as rescued as soon as she recognized those in the procession, for she well knew the courage and loyalty of her old comrades, and also believed that any others who came from their marvelous country would prove to be pleasant and reliable acquaintances.

As soon as the last bit of desert was passed and all the procession, from the beautiful and dainty Ozma to the last soldier, had reached the grassy meadows of the Land of Ev, the magic carpet rolled itself together and entirely disappeared.

Then the chariot driver turned her Lion and Tiger into a broad roadway leading up to the palace, and the others followed, while Dorothy still gazed from her tower window in eager excitement.

They came quite close to the front door of the palace and then halted, the Scarecrow dismounting from his Saw-Horse to approach the sign fastened to the door, that he might read what it said.

Dorothy, just above him, could keep silent no longer.

"Here I am!" she shouted, as loudly as she could. "Here's Dorothy!"

"Dorothy who?" asked the Scarecrow, tipping his head to look upward until he nearly lost his balance and tumbled over backward.

"Dorothy Gale, of course. Your friend from Kansas," she answered.

"Why, hello, Dorothy!" said the Scarecrow. "What in the world are you doing up there?"

"Nothing," she called down, "because there's nothing to do. Save me, my friend—save me!"

"You seem to be quite safe now," replied the Scarecrow.

"But I'm a prisoner. I'm locked in, so that I can't get out," she pleaded.

"That's all right," said the Scarecrow. "You might be worse off, little Dorothy. Just consider the matter. You can't get drowned, or be run over by a Wheeler, or fall out of an apple-tree. Some folks would think they were lucky to be up there."

"Well, I don't," declared the girl, "and I want to get down immed'i'tly and see you and the Tin Woodman and the Cowardly Lion."

"Very well," said the Scarecrow, nodding. "It shall be just as you say, little friend. Who locked you up?"

"The princess Langwidere, who is a horrid creature," she answered.

At this Ozma, who had been listening carefully to the conversation, called to Dorothy from her chariot, asking:

"Why did the Princess lock you up, my dear?"

"Because," exclaimed Dorothy, "I wouldn't let her have my head for her collection, and take an old, cast-off head in exchange for it."

"I do not blame you," exclaimed Ozma, promptly. "I will see the Princess at once, and oblige her to liberate you."

"Oh, thank you very, very much!" cried Dorothy, who as soon as she heard the sweet voice of the girlish Ruler of Oz knew that she would soon learn to love her dearly.

Ozma now drove her chariot around to the third door of the wing, upon which the Tin Woodman boldly proceeded to knock.

As soon as the maid opened the door Ozma, bearing in her hand her ivory wand, stepped into the hall and made her way at once to the drawing-room, followed by all her company, except the Lion and the Tiger. And the twenty-seven soldiers made such a noise and a clatter that the little maid Nanda ran away screaming to her mistress, whereupon the Princess Langwidere, roused to great anger by this rude invasion of her palace, came running into the drawing-room without any assistance whatever.

There she stood before the slight and delicate form of the little girl from Oz and cried out;—

"How dare you enter my palace unbidden? Leave this room at once, or I will bind you and all your people in chains, and throw you into my darkest dungeons!"

"What a dangerous lady!" murmured the Scarecrow, in a soft voice.

"She seems a little nervous," replied the Tin Woodman.

But Ozma only smiled at the angry Princess.

"Sit down, please," she said, quietly. "I have traveled a long way to see you, and you must listen to what I have to say."

"Must!" screamed the Princess, her black eyes flashing with fury—for she still wore her No. 17 head. "Must, to ME!"

"To be sure," said Ozma. "I am Ruler of the Land of Oz, and I am powerful enough to destroy all your kingdom, if I so wish. Yet I did not come here to do harm, but rather to free the royal family of Ev from the thrall of the Nome King, the news having reached me that he is holding the Queen and her children prisoners."

Hearing these words, Langwidere suddenly became quiet.

"I wish you could, indeed, free my aunt and her ten royal children," said she, eagerly. "For if they were restored to their proper forms and station they could rule the Kingdom of Ev themselves, and that would save me a lot of worry and trouble. At present there are at least ten minutes every day that I must devote to affairs of state, and I would like to be able to spend my whole time in admiring my beautiful heads."

"Then we will presently discuss this matter," said Ozma, "and try to find a way to liberate your aunt and cousins. But first you must liberate another prisoner—the little girl you have locked up in your tower."

"Of course," said Langwidere, readily. "I had forgotten all about her. That was yesterday, you know, and a Princess cannot be expected to remember today what she did yesterday. Come with me, and I will release the prisoner at once."

So Ozma followed her, and they passed up the stairs that led to the room in the tower.

While they were gone Ozma's followers remained in the drawing-room, and the Scarecrow was leaning against a form that he had mistaken for a copper statue when a harsh, metallic voice said suddenly in his ear:

"Get off my foot, please. You are scratch-ing my pol-ish."

"Oh, excuse me!" he replied, hastily drawing back. "Are you alive?"

"No," said Tiktok, "I am on-ly a ma-chine. But I can think and speak and act, when I am pro-per-ly wound up. Just now my ac-tion is run down, and Dor-o-thy has the key to it."

"That's all right," replied the Scarecrow. "Dorothy will soon be free, and then she'll attend to your works. But it must be a great misfortune not to be alive. I'm sorry for you."

"Why?" asked Tiktok.

"Because you have no brains, as I have," said the Scarecrow.

"Oh, yes, I have," returned Tiktok. "I am fit-ted with Smith & Tin-ker's Im-proved Com-bi-na-tion Steel Brains. They are what make me think. What sort of brains are you fit-ted with?"

"I don't know," admitted the Scarecrow. "They were given to me by the great Wizard of Oz, and I didn't get a chance to examine them before he put them in. But they work splendidly and my conscience is very active. Have you a conscience?"

"No," said Tiktok.

"And no heart, I suppose?" added the Tin Woodman, who had been listening with interest to this conversation.

"No," said Tiktok.

"Then," continued the Tin Woodman, "I regret to say that you are greatly inferior to my friend the Scarecrow, and to myself. For we are both alive, and he has brains which do not need to be wound up, while I have an excellent heart that is continually beating in my bosom."

"I con-grat-u-late you," replied Tiktok. "I can-not help be-ing your in-fer-i-or for I am a mere ma-chine. When I am wound up I do my du-ty by go-ing just as my ma-chin-er-y is made to go. You have no i-de-a how full of ma-chin-er-y I am."

"I can guess," said the Scarecrow, looking at the machine man curiously. "Some day I'd like to take you apart and see just how you are made."

"Do not do that, I beg of you," said Tiktok; "for you could not put me to-geth-er a-gain, and my use-ful-ness would be de-stroyed."

"Oh! are you useful?" asked the Scarecrow, surprised.

"Ve-ry," said Tiktok.

"In that case," the Scarecrow kindly promised, "I won't fool with your interior at all. For I am a poor mechanic, and might mix you up."

"Thank you," said Tiktok.

Just then Ozma re-entered the room, leading Dorothy by the hand and followed closely by the Princess Langwidere.

8. The Hungry Tiger

The first thing Dorothy did was to rush into the embrace of the Scarecrow, whose painted face beamed with delight as he pressed her form to his straw-padded bosom. Then the Tin Woodman embraced her—very gently, for he knew his tin arms might hurt her if he squeezed too roughly.

These greetings having been exchanged, Dorothy took the key to Tiktok from her pocket and wound up the machine man's action so that he could bow properly when introduced to the rest of the company. While doing this she told them how useful Tiktok had been to her, and both the Scarecrow and the Tin Woodman shook hands with the machine once more and thanked him for protecting their friend.

Then Dorothy asked: "Where is Billina?"

"I don't know," said the Scarecrow. "Who is Billina?"

"She's a yellow hen who is another friend of mine," answered the girl, anxiously. "I wonder what has become of her?"

"She is in the chicken house, in the back yard," said the Princess. "My drawing-room is no place for hens."

Without waiting to hear more Dorothy ran to get Billina, and just outside the door she came upon the Cowardly Lion, still hitched to the chariot beside the great Tiger. The Cowardly Lion had a big bow of blue ribbon fastened to the long hair between his ears, and the Tiger wore a bow of red ribbon on his tail, just in front of the bushy end.

In an instant Dorothy was hugging the huge Lion joyfully.

"I'm SO glad to see you again!" she cried.

"I am also glad to see you, Dorothy," said the Lion. "We've had some fine adventures together, haven't we?"

"Yes, indeed," she replied. "How are you?"

"As cowardly as ever," the beast answered in a meek voice. "Every little thing scares me and makes my heart beat fast. But let me introduce to you a new friend of mine, the Hungry Tiger."

"Oh! Are you hungry?" she asked, turning to the other beast, who was just then yawning so widely that he displayed two rows of terrible teeth and a mouth big enough to startle anyone.

"Dreadfully hungry," answered the Tiger, snapping his jaws together with a fierce click.

"Then why don't you eat something?" she asked.

"It's no use," said the Tiger sadly. "I've tried that, but I always get hungry again."

"Why, it is the same with me," said Dorothy. "Yet I keep on eating."

"But you eat harmless things, so it doesn't matter," replied the Tiger. "For my part, I'm a savage beast, and have an appetite for all sorts of poor little living creatures, from a chipmunk to fat babies."

"How dreadful!" said Dorothy.

"Isn't it, though?" returned the Hungry Tiger, licking his lips with his long red tongue. "Fat babies! Don't they sound delicious? But I've never eaten any, because my conscience tells me it is wrong. If I had no conscience I would probably eat the babies and then get hungry again, which would mean that I had sacrificed the poor babies for nothing. No; hungry I was born, and hungry I shall die. But I'll not have any cruel deeds on my conscience to be sorry for."

"I think you are a very good tiger," said Dorothy, patting the huge head of the beast.

"In that you are mistaken," was the reply. "I am a good beast, perhaps, but a disgracefully bad tiger. For it is the nature of tigers to be cruel and ferocious, and in refusing to eat harmless living creatures I am acting as no good tiger has ever before acted. That is why I left the forest and joined my friend the Cowardly Lion."

"But the Lion is not really cowardly," said Dorothy. "I have seen him act as bravely as can be."

"All a mistake, my dear," protested the Lion gravely. "To others I may have seemed brave, at times, but I have never been in any danger that I was not afraid."

"Nor I," said Dorothy, truthfully. "But I must go and set free Billina, and then I will see you again."

She ran around to the back yard of the palace and soon found the chicken house, being guided to it by a loud cackling and crowing and a distracting hubbub of sounds such as chickens make when they are excited.

Something seemed to be wrong in the chicken house, and when Dorothy looked through the slats in the door she saw a group of hens and roosters huddled in one corner and watching what appeared to be a whirling ball of feathers. It bounded here and there about the chicken house, and at first Dorothy could not tell what it was, while the screeching of the chickens nearly deafened her.

But suddenly the bunch of feathers stopped whirling, and then, to her amazement, the girl saw Billina crouching upon the prostrate form of a speckled rooster. For an instant they both remained motionless, and then the yellow hen shook her wings to settle the feathers and walked toward the door with a strut of proud defiance and a cluck of victory, while the speckled rooster limped away to the group of other chickens, trailing his crumpled plumage in the dust as he went.

"Why, Billina!" cried Dorothy, in a shocked voice; "have you been fighting?"

"I really think I have," retorted Billina. "Do you think I'd let that speckled villain of a rooster lord it over ME, and claim to run this chicken house, as long as I'm able to peck and scratch? Not if my name is Bill!"

"It isn't Bill, it's Billina; and you're talking slang, which is very undig'n'fied," said Dorothy, reprovingly. "Come here, Billina, and I'll let you out; for Ozma of Oz is here, and has set us free."

So the yellow hen came to the door, which Dorothy unlatched for her to pass through, and the other chickens silently watched them from their corner without offering to approach nearer.

The girl lifted her friend in her arms and exclaimed: "Oh, Billina! how dreadful you look. You've lost a lot of feathers, and one of your eyes is nearly pecked out, and your comb is bleeding!"

"That's nothing," said Billina. "Just look at the speckled rooster! Didn't I do him up brown?"

Dorothy shook her head.

"I don't 'prove of this, at all," she said, carrying Billina away toward the palace. "It isn't a good thing for you to 'sociate with those common chickens. They would soon spoil your good manners, and you wouldn't be respec'able any more."

"I didn't ask to associate with them," replied Billina. "It is that cross old Princess who is to blame. But I was raised in the United States, and I won't allow any one-horse chicken of the Land of Ev to run over me and put on airs, as long as I can lift a claw in self-defense."

"Very well, Billina," said Dorothy. "We won't talk about it any more."

Soon they came to the Cowardly Lion and the Hungry Tiger to whom the girl introduced the Yellow Hen.

"Glad to meet any friend of Dorothy's," said the Lion, politely. "To judge by your present appearance, you are not a coward, as I am."

"Your present appearance makes my mouth water," said the Tiger, looking at Billina greedily. "My, my! how good you would taste if I could only crunch you between my jaws. But don't worry. You would only appease my appetite for a moment; so it isn't worth while to eat you."

"Thank you," said the hen, nestling closer in Dorothy's arms.

"Besides, it wouldn't be right," continued the Tiger, looking steadily at Billina and clicking his jaws together.

"Of course not," cried Dorothy, hastily. "Billina is my friend, and you mustn't ever eat her under any circ'mstances."

"I'll try to remember that," said the Tiger; "but I'm a little absent-minded, at times."

Then Dorothy carried her pet into the drawing-room of the palace, where Tiktok, being invited to do so by Ozma, had seated himself between the Scarecrow and the Tin Woodman. Opposite to them sat Ozma herself and the Princess Langwidere, and beside them there was a vacant chair for Dorothy.

Around this important group was ranged the Army of Oz, and as Dorothy looked at the handsome uniforms of the Twenty-Seven she said:

"Why, they seem to be all officers."

"They are, all except one," answered the Tin Woodman. "I have in my Army eight Generals, six Colonels, seven Majors and five Captains, besides one private for them to command. I'd like to promote the private, for I believe no private should ever be in public life; and I've also noticed that officers usually fight better and are more reliable than common soldiers. Besides, the officers are more important looking, and lend dignity to our army."

"No doubt you are right," said Dorothy, seating herself beside Ozma.

"And now," announced the girlish Ruler of Oz, "we will hold a solemn conference to decide the best manner of liberating the royal family of this fair Land of Ev from their long imprisonment."

9. The Royal Family of Ev

The Tin Woodman was the first to address the meeting.

"To begin with," said he, "word came to our noble and illustrious Ruler, Ozma of Oz, that the wife and ten children—five boys and five girls—of the former King of Ev, by name Evoldo, have been enslaved by the Nome King and are held prisoners in his underground palace. Also that there was no one in Ev powerful enough to release them. Naturally our Ozma wished to undertake the adventure of liberating the poor prisoners; but for a long time she could find no way to cross the great desert between the two countries. Finally she went to a friendly sorceress of our land named Glinda the Good, who heard the story and at once presented Ozma a magic carpet, which would continually unroll beneath our feet and so make a comfortable path for us to cross the desert. As soon as she had received the carpet our gracious Ruler ordered me to assemble our army, which I did. You behold in these bold warriors the pick of all the finest soldiers of Oz; and, if we are obliged to fight the Nome King, every officer as well as the private, will battle fiercely unto death."

Then Tiktok spoke.

"Why should you fight the Nome King?" he asked. "He has done no wrong."

"No wrong!" cried Dorothy. "Isn't it wrong to imprison a queen mother and her ten children?"

"They were sold to the Nome King by King Ev-ol-do," replied Tiktok. "It was the King of Ev who did wrong, and when he re-al-ized what he had done he jumped in-to the sea and drowned him-self."

"This is news to me," said Ozma, thoughtfully. "I had supposed the Nome King was all to blame in the matter. But, in any case, he must be made to liberate the prisoners."

"My uncle Evoldo was a very wicked man," declared the Princess Langwidere. "If he had drowned himself before he sold his family, no one would have cared. But he sold them to the powerful Nome King in exchange for a long life, and afterward destroyed the life by jumping into the sea."

"Then," said Ozma, "he did not get the long life, and the Nome King must give up the prisoners. Where are they confined?"

"No one knows, exactly," replied the Princess. "For the king, whose name is Roquat of the Rocks, owns a splendid palace underneath the great mountain which is at the north end of this kingdom, and he has transformed the queen and her children into ornaments and bric-a-brac with which to decorate his rooms."

"I'd like to know," said Dorothy, "who this Nome King is?"

"I will tell you," replied Ozma. "He is said to be the Ruler of the Underground World, and commands the rocks and all that the rocks contain. Under his rule are many thousands of the Nomes, who are queerly shaped but powerful sprites that labor at the furnaces and forges of their king, making gold and silver and other metals which they conceal in the crevices of the rocks, so that those living upon the earth's surface can only find them with great difficulty. Also they make diamonds and rubies and emeralds, which they hide in the ground; so that the kingdom of the Nomes is wonderfully rich, and all we have of precious stones and silver and gold is what we take from the earth and rocks where the Nome King has hidden them."

"I understand," said Dorothy, nodding her little head wisely.

"For the reason that we often steal his treasures," continued Ozma, "the Ruler of the Underground World is not fond of those who live upon the earth's surface, and never appears among us. If we wish to see King Roquat of the Rocks, we must visit his own country, where he is all powerful, and therefore it will be a dangerous undertaking."

"But, for the sake of the poor prisoners," said Dorothy, "we ought to do it."

"We shall do it," replied the Scarecrow, "although it requires a lot of courage for me to go near to the furnaces of the Nome King. For I am only stuffed with straw, and a single spark of fire might destroy me entirely."

"The furnaces may also melt my tin," said the Tin Woodman; "but I am going."

"I can't bear heat," remarked the Princess Langwidere, yawning lazily, "so I shall stay at home. But I wish you may have success in your undertaking, for I am heartily tired of ruling this stupid kingdom, and I need more leisure in which to admire my beautiful heads."

"We do not need you," said Ozma. "For, if with the aid of my brave followers I cannot accomplish my purpose, then it would be useless for you to undertake the journey."

"Quite true," sighed the Princess. "So, if you'll excuse me, I will now retire to my cabinet. I've worn this head quite awhile, and I want to change it for another."

When she had left them (and you may be sure no one was sorry to see her go) Ozma said to Tiktok: "Will you join our party?"

"I am the slave of the girl Dor-oth-y, who rescued me from pris-on," replied the machine. "Where she goes I will go."

"Oh, I am going with my friends, of course," said Dorothy, quickly. "I wouldn't miss the fun for anything. Will you go, too, Billina?"

"To be sure," said Billina in a careless tone. She was smoothing down the feathers of her back and not paying much attention.

"Heat is just in her line," remarked the Scarecrow. "If she is nicely roasted, she will be better than ever."

"Then" said Ozma, "we will arrange to start for the Kingdom of the Nomes at daybreak tomorrow. And, in the meantime, we will rest and prepare ourselves for the journey."

Although Princess Langwidere did not again appear to her guests, the palace servants waited upon the strangers from Oz and did everything in their power to make the party comfortable. There were many vacant rooms at their disposal, and the brave Army of twenty-seven was easily provided for and liberally feasted.

The Cowardly Lion and the Hungry Tiger were unharnessed from the chariot and allowed to roam at will throughout the palace, where they nearly frightened the servants into fits, although they did no harm at all. At one time Dorothy found the little maid Nanda crouching in terror in a corner, with the Hungry Tiger standing before her.

"You certainly look delicious," the beast was saying. "Will you kindly give me permission to eat you?"

"No, no, no!" cried the maid in reply.

"Then," said the Tiger, yawning frightfully, "please to get me about thirty pounds of tenderloin steak, cooked rare, with a peck of boiled potatoes on the side, and five gallons of ice-cream for dessert."

"I—I'll do the best I can!" said Nanda, and she ran away as fast as she could go.

"Are you so very hungry?" asked Dorothy, in wonder.

"You can hardly imagine the size of my appetite," replied the Tiger, sadly. "It seems to fill my whole body, from the end of my throat to the tip of my tail. I am very sure the appetite doesn't fit me, and is too large for the size of my body. Some day, when I meet a dentist with a pair of forceps, I'm going to have it pulled."

"What, your tooth?" asked Dorothy.

"No, my appetite," said the Hungry Tiger.

The little girl spent most of the afternoon talking with the Scarecrow and the Tin Woodman, who related to her all that had taken place in the Land of Oz since Dorothy had left it. She was much interested in the story of Ozma, who had been, when a baby, stolen by a wicked old witch and transformed into a boy. She did not know that she had ever been a girl until she was restored to her natural form by a kind sorceress. Then it was found that she was the only child of the former Ruler of Oz, and was entitled to rule in his place. Ozma had many adventures, however, before she regained her father's throne, and in these she was accompanied by a pumpkin-headed man, a highly magnified and thoroughly educated Woggle-Bug, and a wonderful sawhorse that had been brought to life by means of a magic powder. The Scarecrow and the Tin Woodman had also assisted her; but the Cowardly Lion, who ruled the great forest as the King of Beasts, knew nothing of Ozma until after she became the reigning princess of Oz. Then he journeyed to the Emerald City to see her, and on hearing she was about to visit the Land of Ev to set free the royal family of that country, the Cowardly Lion begged to go with her, and brought along his friend, the Hungry Tiger, as well.

Having heard this story, Dorothy related to them her own adventures, and then went out with her friends to find the Sawhorse, which Ozma had caused to be shod with plates of gold, so that its legs would not wear out.

They came upon the Sawhorse standing motionless beside the garden gate, but when Dorothy was introduced to him he bowed politely and blinked his eyes, which were knots of wood, and wagged his tail, which was only the branch of a tree.

"What a remarkable thing, to be alive!" exclaimed Dorothy.

"I quiet agree with you," replied the Sawhorse, in a rough but not unpleasant voice. "A creature like me has no business to live, as we all know. But it was the magic powder that did it, so I cannot justly be blamed."

"Of course not," said Dorothy. "And you seem to be of some use, 'cause I noticed the Scarecrow riding upon your back."

"Oh, yes; I'm of use," returned the Sawhorse; "and I never tire, never have to be fed, or cared for in any way."

"Are you intel'gent?" asked the girl.

"Not very," said the creature. "It would be foolish to waste intelligence on a common Sawhorse, when so many professors need it. But I know enough to obey my masters, and to gid-dup, or whoa, when I'm told to. So I'm pretty well satisfied."

That night Dorothy slept in a pleasant little bed-chamber next to that occupied by Ozma of Oz, and Billina perched upon the foot of the bed and tucked her head under her wing and slept as soundly in that position as did Dorothy upon her soft cushions.

But before daybreak every one was awake and stirring, and soon the adventurers were eating a hasty breakfast in the great dining-room of the palace. Ozma sat at the head of a long table, on a raised platform, with Dorothy on her right hand and the Scarecrow on her left. The Scarecrow did not eat, of course; but Ozma placed him near her so that she might ask his advice about the journey while she ate.

Lower down the table were the twenty-seven warriors of Oz, and at the end of the room the Lion and the Tiger were eating out of a kettle that had been placed upon the floor, while Billina fluttered around to pick up any scraps that might be scattered.

It did not take long to finish the meal, and then the Lion and the Tiger were harnessed to the chariot and the party was ready to start for the Nome King's Palace.

First rode Ozma, with Dorothy beside her in the golden chariot and holding Billina fast in her arms. Then came the Scarecrow on the Sawhorse, with the Tin Woodman and Tiktok marching side by side just behind him. After these tramped the Army, looking brave and handsome in their splendid uniforms. The generals commanded the colonels and the colonels commanded the majors and the majors commanded the captains and the captains commanded the private, who marched with an air of proud importance because it required so many officers to give him his orders.

And so the magnificent procession left the palace and started along the road just as day was breaking, and by the time the sun came out they had made good progress toward the valley that led to the Nome King's domain.

10. The Giant with the Hammer

The road led for a time through a pretty farm country, and then past a picnic grove that was very inviting. But the procession continued to steadily advance until Billina cried in an abrupt and commanding manner: "Wait—wait!"

Ozma stopped her chariot so suddenly that the Scarecrow's Sawhorse nearly ran into it, and the ranks of the army tumbled over one another before they could come to a halt. Immediately the yellow hen struggled from Dorothy's arms and flew into a clump of bushes by the roadside.

"What's the matter?" called the Tin Woodman, anxiously.

"Why, Billina wants to lay her egg, that's all," said Dorothy.

"Lay her egg!" repeated the Tin Woodman, in astonishment.

"Yes; she lays one every morning, about this time; and it's quite fresh," said the girl.

"But does your foolish old hen suppose that this entire cavalcade, which is bound on an important adventure, is going to stand still while she lays her egg?" enquired the Tin Woodman, earnestly.

"What else can we do?" asked the girl. "It's a habit of Billina's and she can't break herself of it."

"Then she must hurry up," said the Tin Woodman, impatiently.

"No, no!" exclaimed the Scarecrow. "If she hurries she may lay scrambled eggs."

"That's nonsense," said Dorothy. "But Billina won't be long, I'm sure."

So they stood and waited, although all were restless and anxious to proceed. And by and by the yellow hen came from the bushes saying: "Kut-kut, kut, ka-daw-kutt! Kut, kut, kut—ka-daw-kut!"

"What is she doing—singing her lay?" asked the Scarecrow.

"For-ward—march!" shouted the Tin Woodman, waving his axe, and the procession started just as Dorothy had once more grabbed Billina in her arms.

"Isn't anyone going to get my egg?" cried the hen, in great excitement.

"I'll get it," said the Scarecrow; and at his command the Sawhorse pranced into the bushes. The straw man soon found the egg, which he placed in his jacket pocket. The cavalcade, having moved rapidly on, was even then far in advance; but it did not take the Sawhorse long to catch up with it, and presently the Scarecrow was riding in his accustomed place behind Ozma's chariot.

"What shall I do with the egg?" he asked Dorothy.

"I do not know," the girl answered. "Perhaps the Hungry Tiger would like it."

"It would not be enough to fill one of my back teeth," remarked the Tiger. "A bushel of them, hard boiled, might take a little of the edge off my appetite; but one egg isn't good for anything at all, that I know of."

"No; it wouldn't even make a sponge cake," said the Scarecrow, thoughtfully. "The Tin Woodman might carry it with his axe and hatch it; but after all I may as well keep it myself for a souvenir." So he left it in his pocket.

They had now reached that part of the valley that lay between the two high mountains which Dorothy had seen from her tower window. At the far end was the third great mountain, which blocked the valley and was the northern edge of the Land of Ev.

It was underneath this mountain that the Nome King's palace was said to be; but it would be some time before they reached that place.

The path was becoming rocky and difficult for the wheels of the chariot to pass over, and presently a deep gulf appeared at their feet which was too wide for them to leap. So Ozma took a small square of green cloth from her pocket and threw it upon the ground. At once it became the magic carpet, and unrolled itself far enough for all the cavalcade to walk upon. The chariot now advanced, and the green carpet unrolled before it, crossing the gulf on a level with its banks, so that all passed over in safety.

"That's easy enough," said the Scarecrow. "I wonder what will happen next."

He was not long in making the discovery, for the sides of the mountain came closer together until finally there was but a narrow path between them, along which Ozma and her party were forced to pass in single file.

They now heard a low and deep "thump!—thump!—thump!" which echoed throughout the valley and seemed to grow louder as they advanced. Then, turning a corner of rock, they saw before them a huge form, which towered above the path for more than a hundred feet. The form was that of a gigantic man built out of plates of cast iron, and it stood with one foot on either side of the narrow road and swung over its right shoulder an immense iron mallet, with which it constantly pounded the earth. These resounding blows explained the thumping sounds they had heard, for the mallet was much bigger than a barrel, and where it struck the path between the rocky sides of the mountain it filled all the space through which our travelers would be obliged to pass.

Of course they at once halted, a safe distance away from the terrible iron mallet. The magic carpet would do them no good in this case, for it was only meant to protect them from any danger upon the ground beneath their feet, and not from dangers that appeared in the air above them.

"Wow!" said the Cowardly Lion, with a shudder. "It makes me dreadfully nervous to see that big hammer pounding so near my head. One blow would crush me into a door-mat."

"The ir-on gi-ant is a fine fel-low," said Tiktok, "and works stead-i-ly as a clock. He was made for the Nome King by Smith Tin-ker, who made me, and his du-ty is to keep folks from find-ing the un-der-ground pal-ace. Is he not a great work of art?"

"Can he think, and speak, as you do?" asked Ozma, regarding the giant with wondering eyes.

"No," replied the machine; "he is on-ly made to pound the road, and has no think-ing or speak-ing at-tach-ment. But he pounds ve-ry well, I think."

"Too well," observed the Scarecrow. "He is keeping us from going farther. Is there no way to stop his machinery?"

"On-ly the Nome King, who has the key, can do that," answered Tiktok.

"Then," said Dorothy, anxiously, "what shall we do?"

"Excuse me for a few minutes," said the Scarecrow, "and I will think it over."

He retired, then, to a position in the rear, where he turned his painted face to the rocks and began to think.

Meantime the giant continued to raise his iron mallet high in the air and to strike the path terrific blows that echoed through the mountains like the roar of a cannon. Each time the mallet lifted, however, there was a moment when the path beneath the monster was free, and perhaps the Scarecrow had noticed this, for when he came back to the others he said:

"The matter is a very simple one, after all. We have but to run under the hammer, one at a time, when it is lifted, and pass to the other side before it falls again."

"It will require quick work, if we escape the blow," said the Tin Woodman, with a shake of his head. "But it really seems the only thing to be done. Who will make the first attempt?"

They looked at one another hesitatingly for a moment. Then the Cowardly Lion, who was trembling like a leaf in the wind, said to them:

"I suppose the head of the procession must go first—and that's me. But I'm terribly afraid of the big hammer!"

"What will become of me?" asked Ozma. "You might rush under the hammer yourself, but the chariot would surely be crushed."

"We must leave the chariot," said the Scarecrow. "But you two girls can ride upon the backs of the Lion and the Tiger."

So this was decided upon, and Ozma, as soon as the Lion was unfastened from the chariot, at once mounted the beast's back and said she was ready.

"Cling fast to his mane," advised Dorothy. "I used to ride him myself, and that's the way I held on."

So Ozma clung fast to the mane, and the lion crouched in the path and eyed the swinging mallet carefully until he knew just the instant it would begin to rise in the air.

Then, before anyone thought he was ready, he made a sudden leap straight between the iron giant's legs, and before the mallet struck the ground again the Lion and Ozma were safe on the other side.

The Tiger went next. Dorothy sat upon his back and locked her arms around his striped neck, for he had no mane to cling to. He made the leap straight and true as an arrow from a bow, and ere Dorothy realized it she was out of danger and standing by Ozma's side.

Now came the Scarecrow on the Sawhorse, and while they made the dash in safety they were within a hair's breadth of being caught by the descending hammer.

Tiktok walked up to the very edge of the spot the hammer struck, and as it was raised for the next blow he calmly stepped forward and escaped its descent. That was an idea for the Tin Woodman to follow, and he also crossed in safety while the great hammer was in the air. But when it came to the twenty-six officers and the private, their knees were so weak that they could not walk a step.

"In battle we are wonderfully courageous," said one of the generals, "and our foes find us very terrible to face. But war is one thing and this is another. When it comes to being pounded

upon the head by an iron hammer, and smashed into pancakes, we naturally object."

"Make a run for it," urged the Scarecrow.

"Our knees shake so that we cannot run," answered a captain. "If we should try it we would all certainly be pounded to a jelly."

"Well, well," sighed the Cowardly Lion, "I see, friend Tiger, that we must place ourselves in great danger to rescue this bold army. Come with me, and we will do the best we can."

So, Ozma and Dorothy having already dismounted from their backs, the Lion and the Tiger leaped back again under the awful hammer and returned with two generals clinging to their necks. They repeated this daring passage twelve times, when all the officers had been carried beneath the giant's legs and landed safely on the further side. By that time the beasts were very tired, and panted so hard that their tongues hung out of their great mouths.

"But what is to become of the private?" asked Ozma.

"Oh, leave him there to guard the chariot," said the Lion. "I'm tired out, and won't pass under that mallet again."

The officers at once protested that they must have the private with them, else there would be no one for them to command. But neither the Lion or the Tiger would go after him, and so the Scarecrow sent the Sawhorse.

Either the wooden horse was careless, or it failed to properly time the descent of the hammer, for the mighty weapon caught it squarely upon its head, and thumped it against the ground so powerfully that the private flew off its back high into the air, and landed upon one of the giant's cast-iron arms. Here he clung desperately while the arm rose and fell with each one of the rapid strokes.

The Scarecrow dashed in to rescue his Sawhorse, and had his left foot smashed by the hammer before he could pull the creature out of danger. They then found that the Sawhorse had been badly dazed by the blow; for while the hard wooden knot of which his head was formed could not be crushed by the hammer, both his ears were broken off and he would be unable to hear a sound until some new ones were made for him. Also his left knee was cracked, and had to be bound up with a string.

Billina having fluttered under the hammer, it now remained only to rescue the private who was riding upon the iron giant's arm, high in the air.

The Scarecrow lay flat upon the ground and called to the man to jump down upon his body, which was soft because it was stuffed with straw. This the private managed to do, waiting until a time when he was nearest the ground and then letting himself drop upon the Scarecrow. He accomplished the feat without breaking any bones, and the Scarecrow declared he was not injured in the least.

Therefore, the Tin Woodman having by this time fitted new ears to the Sawhorse, the entire party proceeded upon its way, leaving the giant to pound the path behind them.

11. The Nome King

By and by, when they drew near to the mountain that blocked their path and which was the furthermost edge of the Kingdom of Ev, the way grew dark and gloomy for the reason that the high peaks on either side shut out the sunshine. And it was very silent, too, as there were no birds to sing or squirrels to chatter, the trees being left far behind them and only the bare rocks remaining.

Ozma and Dorothy were a little awed by the silence, and all the others were quiet and grave except the Sawhorse, which, as it trotted along with the Scarecrow upon his back, hummed a queer song, of which this was the chorus:

"Would a wooden horse in a woodland go?
Aye, aye! I sigh, he would, although
Had he not had a wooden head
He'd mount the mountain top instead."

But no one paid any attention to this because they were now close to the Nome King's dominions, and his splendid underground palace could not be very far away.

Suddenly they heard a shout of jeering laughter, and stopped short. They would have to stop in a minute, anyway, for the huge mountain barred their further progress and the path ran close up to a wall of rock and ended.

"Who was that laughing?" asked Ozma.

There was no reply, but in the gloom they could see strange forms flit across the face of the rock. Whatever the creations might be they seemed very like the rock itself, for they were the color of rocks and their shapes were as rough and rugged as if they had been broken away from the side of the mountain. They kept close to the steep cliff facing our friends, and glided up and down, and this way and that, with a lack of regularity that was quite confusing. And they seemed not to need places to rest their feet, but clung to the surface of the rock as a fly does to a window-pane, and were never still for a moment.

"Do not mind them," said Tiktok, as Dorothy shrank back. "They are on-ly the Nomes."

"And what are Nomes?" asked the girl, half frightened.

"They are rock fair-ies, and serve the Nome King," replied the machine. "But they will do us no harm. You must call for the King, be-cause with-out him you can ne-ver find the en-trance to the pal-ace."

"YOU call," said Dorothy to Ozma.

Just then the Nomes laughed again, and the sound was so weird and disheartening that the twenty-six officers commanded the private to "right-about-face!" and they all started to run as fast as they could.

The Tin Woodman at once pursued his army and cried "halt!" and when they had stopped their flight he asked: "Where are you going?"

"I—I find I've forgotten the brush for my whiskers," said a general, trembling with fear. "S-s-so we are g-going back after it!"

"That is impossible," replied the Tin Woodman. "For the giant with the hammer would kill you all if you tried to pass him."

"Oh! I'd forgotten the giant," said the general, turning pale.

"You seem to forget a good many things," remarked the Tin Woodman. "I hope you won't forget that you are brave men."

"Never!" cried the general, slapping his gold-embroidered chest.

"Never!" cried all the other officers, indignantly slapping their chests.

"For my part," said the private, meekly, "I must obey my officers; so when I am told to run, I run; and when I am told to fight, I fight."

"That is right," agreed the Tin Woodman. "And now you must all come back to Ozma, and obey HER orders. And if you try to run away again I will have her reduce all the twenty-six officers to privates, and make the private your general."

This terrible threat so frightened them that they at once returned to where Ozma was standing beside the Cowardly Lion.

Then Ozma cried out in a loud voice: "I demand that the Nome King appear to us!"

There was no reply, except that the shifting Nomes upon the mountain laughed in derision.

"You must not command the Nome King," said Tiktok, "for you do not rule him, as you do your own peo-ple."

So Ozma called again, saying:

"I request the Nome King to appear to us."

Only the mocking laughter replied to her, and the shadowy Nomes continued to flit here and there upon the rocky cliff.

"Try en-treat-y," said Tiktok to Ozma. "If he will not come at your re-quest, then the Nome King may list-en to your plead-ing."

Ozma looked around her proudly.

"Do you wish your ruler to plead with this wicked Nome King?" she asked. "Shall Ozma of Oz humble herself to a creature who lives in an underground kingdom?"

"No!" they all shouted, with big voices; and the Scarecrow added:

"If he will not come, we will dig him out of his hole, like a fox, and conquer his stubbornness. But our sweet little ruler must always maintain her dignity, just as I maintain mine."

"I'm not afraid to plead with him," said Dorothy. "I'm only a little girl from Kansas, and we've got more dignity at home than we know what to do with. I'LL call the Nome King."

"Do," said the Hungry Tiger; "and if he makes hash of you I'll willingly eat you for breakfast tomorrow morning."

So Dorothy stepped forward and said:

"PLEASE Mr. Nome King, come here and see us."

The Nomes started to laugh again; but a low growl came from the mountain, and in a flash they had all vanished from sight and were silent.

Then a door in the rock opened, and a voice cried:

"Enter!"

"Isn't it a trick?" asked the Tin Woodman.

"Never mind," replied Ozma. "We came here to rescue the poor Queen of Ev and her ten children, and we must run some risks to do so."

"The Nome King is hon-est and good na-tured," said Tiktok. "You can trust him to do what is right."

So Ozma led the way, hand in hand with Dorothy, and they passed through the arched doorway of rock and entered a long passage which was lighted by jewels set in the walls and having lamps behind them. There was no one to escort them, or to show them the way, but all the party pressed through the passage until they came to a round, domed cavern that was grandly furnished.

In the center of this room was a throne carved out of a solid boulder of rock, rude and rugged in shape but glittering with great rubies and diamonds and emeralds on every part of its surface. And upon the throne sat the Nome King.

This important monarch of the Underground World was a little fat man clothed in gray-brown garments that were the exact color of the rock throne in which he was seated. His bushy hair and flowing beard were also colored like the rocks, and so was his face. He wore no crown of any sort, and his only ornament was a broad, jewel-studded belt that encircled his fat little body. As for his features, they seemed kindly and good humored, and his eyes were turned merrily upon his visitors as Ozma and Dorothy stood before him with their followers ranged in close order behind them.

"Why, he looks just like Santa Claus—only he isn't the same color!" whispered Dorothy to her friend; but the Nome King heard the speech, and it made him laugh aloud.

"'He had a red face and a round little belly
That shook when he laughed like a bowl full of jelly!'"
quoth the monarch, in a pleasant voice; and they could all see that he really did shake like jelly when he laughed.

Both Ozma and Dorothy were much relieved to find the Nome King so jolly, and a minute later he waved his right hand and the girls each found a cushioned stool at her side.

"Sit down, my dears," said the King, "and tell me why you have come all this way to see me, and what I can do to make you happy."

While they seated themselves the Nome King picked up a pipe, and taking a glowing red coal out of his pocket he placed it in the bowl of the pipe and began puffing out clouds of smoke that curled in rings above his head. Dorothy thought this made the little monarch look more like Santa Claus than ever; but Ozma now began speaking, and every one listened intently to her words.

"Your Majesty," said she, "I am the ruler of the Land of Oz, and I have come here to ask you to release the good Queen of Ev and her ten children, whom you have enchanted and hold as your prisoners."

"Oh, no; you are mistaken about that," replied the King. "They are not my prisoners, but my slaves, whom I purchased from the King of Ev."

"But that was wrong," said Ozma.

"According to the laws of Ev, the king can do no wrong," answered the monarch, eying a ring of smoke he had just blown from his mouth; "so that he had a perfect right to sell his family to me in exchange for a long life."

"You cheated him, though," declared Dorothy; "for the King of Ev did not have a long life. He jumped into the sea and was drowned."

"That was not my fault," said the Nome King, crossing his legs and smiling contentedly. "I gave him the long life, all right; but he destroyed it."

"Then how could it be a long life?" asked Dorothy.

"Easily enough," was the reply. "Now suppose, my dear, that I gave you a pretty doll in exchange for a lock of your hair, and that after you had received the doll you smashed it into pieces and destroyed it. Could you say that I had not given you a pretty doll?"

"No," answered Dorothy.

"And could you, in fairness, ask me to return to you the lock of hair, just because you had smashed the doll?"

"No," said Dorothy, again.

"Of course not," the Nome King returned. "Nor will I give up the Queen and her children because the King of Ev destroyed his long life by jumping into the sea. They belong to me and I shall keep them."

"But you are treating them cruelly," said Ozma, who was much distressed by the King's refusal.

"In what way?" he asked.

"By making them your slaves," said she.

"Cruelty," remarked the monarch, puffing out wreathes of smoke and watching them float into the air, "is a thing I can't abide. So, as slaves must work hard, and the Queen of Ev and her children were delicate and tender, I transformed them all into articles of ornament and bric-a-brac and scattered them around the various rooms of my palace. Instead of being obliged to labor, they merely decorate my apartments, and I really think I have treated them with great kindness."

"But what a dreadful fate is theirs!" exclaimed Ozma, earnestly. "And the Kingdom of Ev is in great need of its royal family to govern it. If you will liberate them, and restore them to their proper forms, I will give you ten ornaments to replace each one you lose."

The Nome King looked grave.

"Suppose I refuse?" he asked.

"Then," said Ozma, firmly, "I am here with my friends and my army to conquer your kingdom and oblige you to obey my wishes."

The Nome King laughed until he choked; and he choked until he coughed; and he coughed until his face turned from grayish-brown to bright red. And then he wiped his eyes with a rock-colored handkerchief and grew grave again.

"You are as brave as you are pretty, my dear," he said to Ozma. "But you have little idea of the extent of the task you have undertaken. Come with me for a moment."

He arose and took Ozma's hand, leading her to a little door at one side of the room. This he opened and they stepped out upon a balcony, from whence they obtained a wonderful view of the Underground World.

A vast cave extended for miles and miles under the mountain, and in every direction were furnaces and forges glowing brightly and Nomes hammering upon precious metals or polishing gleaming jewels. All around the walls of the cave were thousands of doors of silver and gold, built into the solid rock, and these extended in rows far away into the distance, as far as Ozma's eyes could follow them.

While the little maid from Oz gazed wonderingly upon this scene the Nome King uttered a shrill whistle, and at once all the silver and gold doors flew open and solid ranks of Nome soldiers marched out from every one. So great were their numbers that they quickly filled the immense underground cavern and forced the busy workmen to abandon their tasks.

Although this tremendous army consisted of rock-colored Nomes, all squat and fat, they were clothed in glittering armor of polished steel, inlaid with beautiful gems. Upon his brow each wore a brilliant electric light, and they bore sharp spears and swords and battle-axes of solid bronze. It was evident they were perfectly trained, for they stood in straight rows, rank after rank, with their weapons held erect and true, as if awaiting but the word of command to level them upon their foes.

"This," said the Nome King, "is but a small part of my army. No ruler upon Earth has ever dared to fight me, and no ruler ever will, for I am too powerful to oppose."

He whistled again, and at once the martial array filed through the silver and gold doorways and disappeared, after which the workmen again resumed their labors at the furnaces.

Then, sad and discouraged, Ozma of Oz turned to her friends, and the Nome King calmly reseated himself on his rock throne.

"It would be foolish for us to fight," the girl said to the Tin Woodman. "For our brave Twenty-Seven would be quickly destroyed. I'm sure I do not know how to act in this emergency."

"Ask the King where his kitchen is," suggested the Tiger. "I'm hungry as a bear."

"I might pounce upon the King and tear him in pieces," remarked the Cowardly Lion.

"Try it," said the monarch, lighting his pipe with another hot coal which he took from his pocket.

The Lion crouched low and tried to spring upon the Nome King; but he hopped only a little way into the air and came down again in the same place, not being able to approach the throne by even an inch.

"It seems to me," said the Scarecrow, thoughtfully, "that our best plan is to wheedle his Majesty into giving up his slaves, since he is too great a magician to oppose."

"This is the most sensible thing any of you have suggested," declared the Nome King. "It is folly to threaten me, but I'm s[o] kind-hearted that I cannot stand coaxing or wheedling. If yo[u] really wish to accomplish anything by your journey, my dea[r] Ozma, you must coax me."

"Very well," said Ozma, more cheerfully. "Let us be friends, an[d] talk this over in a friendly manner."

"To be sure," agreed the King, his eyes twinkling merrily.

"I am very anxious," she continued, "to liberate the Queen of E[v] and her children who are now ornaments and bric-a-brac in you[r] Majesty's palace, and to restore them to their people. Tell m[e] sir, how this may be accomplished."

The king remained thoughtful for a moment, after which h[e] asked:

"Are you willing to take a few chances and risks yourself, in orde[r] to set free the people of Ev?"

"Yes, indeed!" answered Ozma, eagerly.

"Then," said the Nome King, "I will make you this offer: Yo[u] shall go alone and unattended into my palace and examin[e] carefully all that the rooms contain. Then you shall hav[e] permission to touch eleven different objects, pronouncing at th[e] time the word 'Ev,' and if any one of them, or more than on[e] proves to be the transformation of the Queen of Ev or any of he[r] ten children, then they will instantly be restored to their tru[e] forms and may leave my palace and my kingdom in you[r] company, without any objection whatever. It is possible for yo[u] in this way, to free the entire eleven; but if you do not guess a[ll] the objects correctly, and some of the slaves remai[n] transformed, then each one of your friends and followers may, i[n] turn, enter the palace and have the same privileges I grant you."

"Oh, thank you! thank you for this kind offer!" said Ozm[a] eagerly.

"I make but one condition," added the Nome King, his eye[s] twinkling.

"What is it?" she enquired.

"If none of the eleven objects you touch proves to be th[e] transformation of any of the royal family of Ev, then, instead [of] freeing them, you will yourself become enchanted, an[d] transformed into an article of bric-a-brac or an ornament. This [is] only fair and just, and is the risk you declared you were willing t[o] take."

12. The Eleven Guesses

Hearing this condition imposed by the Nome King, Ozm[a] became silent and thoughtful, and all her friends looked at he[r] uneasily.

"Don't you do it!" exclaimed Dorothy. "If you guess wrong, yo[u] will be enslaved yourself."

"But I shall have eleven guesses," answered Ozma. "Surely [I] ought to guess one object in eleven correctly; and, if I do, I sha[ll] rescue one of the royal family and be safe myself. Then the re[st] of you may attempt it, and soon we shall free all those who a[re] enslaved."

"What if we fail?" enquired the Scarecrow. "I'd look nice as a piece of bric-a-brac, wouldn't I?"

"We must not fail!" cried Ozma, courageously. "Having come all this distance to free these poor people, it would be weak and cowardly in us to abandon the adventure. Therefore I will accept the Nome King's offer, and go at once into the royal palace."

"Come along, then, my dear," said the King, climbing down from his throne with some difficulty, because he was so fat; "I'll show you the way."

He approached a wall of the cave and waved his hand. Instantly an opening appeared, through which Ozma, after a smiling farewell to her friends, boldly passed.

She found herself in a splendid hall that was more beautiful and grand than anything she had ever beheld. The ceilings were composed of great arches that rose far above her head, and all the walls and floors were of polished marble exquisitely tinted in many colors. Thick velvet carpets were on the floor and heavy silken draperies covered the arches leading to the various rooms of the palace. The furniture was made of rare old woods richly carved and covered with delicate satins, and the entire palace was lighted by a mysterious rosy glow that seemed to come from no particular place but flooded each apartment with its soft and pleasing radiance.

Ozma passed from one room to another, greatly delighted by all she saw. The lovely palace had no other occupant, for the Nome King had left her at the entrance, which closed behind her, and in all the magnificent rooms there appeared to be no other person.

Upon the mantels, and on many shelves and brackets and tables, were clustered ornaments of every description, seemingly made out of all sorts of metals, glass, china, stones and marbles. There were vases, and figures of men and animals, and graven platters and bowls, and mosaics of precious gems, and many other things. Pictures, too, were on the walls, and the underground palace was quite a museum of rare and curious and costly objects.

After her first hasty examination of the rooms Ozma began to wonder which of all the numerous ornaments they contained were the transformations of the royal family of Ev. There was nothing to guide her, for everything seemed without a spark of life. So she must guess blindly; and for the first time the girl came to realize how dangerous was her task, and how likely she was to lose her own freedom in striving to free others from the bondage of the Nome King. No wonder the cunning monarch laughed good naturedly with his visitors, when he knew how easily they might be entrapped.

But Ozma, having undertaken the venture, would not abandon it. She looked at a silver candelabra that had ten branches, and thought: "This may be the Queen of Ev and her ten children." So she touched it and uttered aloud the word "Ev," as the Nome King had instructed her to do when she guessed. But the candelabra remained as it was before.

Then she wandered into another room and touched a china lamb, thinking it might be one of the children she sought. But again she was unsuccessful. Three guesses; four guesses; five, six, seven, eight, nine and ten she made, and still not one of them was right!

The girl shivered a little and grew pale even under the rosy light; for now but one guess remained, and her own fate depended upon the result.

She resolved not to be hasty, and strolled through all the rooms once more, gazing earnestly upon the various ornaments and trying to decide which she would touch. Finally, in despair, she decided to leave it entirely to chance. She faced the doorway of a room, shut her eyes tightly, and then, thrusting aside the heavy draperies, she advanced blindly with her right arm outstretched before her.

Slowly, softly she crept forward until her hand came in contact with an object upon a small round table. She did not know what it was, but in a low voice she pronounced the word "Ev."

The rooms were quite empty of life after that. The Nome King had gained a new ornament. For upon the edge of the table rested a pretty grasshopper, that seemed to have been formed from a single emerald. It was all that remained of Ozma of Oz.

In the throne room just beyond the palace the Nome King suddenly looked up and smiled.

"Next!" he said, in his pleasant voice.

Dorothy, the Scarecrow, and the Tin Woodman, who had been sitting in anxious silence, each gave a start of dismay and stared into one another's eyes.

"Has she failed?" asked Tiktok.

"So it seems," answered the little monarch, cheerfully. "But that is no reason one of you should not succeed. The next may have twelve guesses, instead of eleven, for there are now twelve persons transformed into ornaments. Well, well! Which of you goes next?"

"I'll go," said Dorothy.

"Not so," replied the Tin Woodman. "As commander of Ozma's army, it is my privilege to follow her and attempt her rescue."

"Away you go, then," said the Scarecrow. "But be careful, old friend."

"I will," promised the Tin Woodman; and then he followed the Nome King to the entrance to the palace and the rock closed behind him.

13. The Nome King Laughs

In a moment the King returned to his throne and relighted his pipe, and the rest of the little band of adventurers settled themselves for another long wait. They were greatly disheartened by the failure of their girl Ruler, and the knowledge that she was now an ornament in the Nome King's palace—a dreadful, creepy place in spite of all its magnificence. Without their little leader they did not know what to do next, and each one, down to the trembling private of the army, began to fear he would soon be more ornamental than useful.

Suddenly the Nome King began laughing.

"Ha, ha, ha! He, he, he! Ho, ho, ho!"

"What's happened?" asked the Scarecrow.

"Why, your friend, the Tin Woodman, has become the funniest thing you can imagine," replied the King, wiping the tears of merriment from his eyes. "No one would ever believe he could make such an amusing ornament. Next!"

They gazed at each other with sinking hearts. One of the generals began to weep dolefully.

"What are you crying for?" asked the Scarecrow, indignant at such a display of weakness.

"He owed me six weeks back pay," said the general, "and I hate to lose him."

"Then you shall go and find him," declared the Scarecrow.

"Me!" cried the general, greatly alarmed.

"Certainly. It is your duty to follow your commander. March!"

"I won't," said the general. "I'd like to, of course; but I just simply WON'T."

The Scarecrow looked enquiringly at the Nome King.

"Never mind," said the jolly monarch. "If he doesn't care to enter the palace and make his guesses I'll throw him into one of my fiery furnaces."

"I'll go!—of course I'm going," yelled the general, as quick as scat. "Where is the entrance—where is it? Let me go at once!"

So the Nome King escorted him into the palace, and again returned to await the result. What the general did, no one can tell; but it was not long before the King called for the next victim, and a colonel was forced to try his fortune.

Thus, one after another, all of the twenty-six officers filed into the palace and made their guesses— and became ornaments.

Meantime the King ordered refreshments to be served to those waiting, and at his command a rudely shaped Nome entered, bearing a tray. This Nome was not unlike the others that Dorothy had seen, but he wore a heavy gold chain around his neck to show that he was the Chief Steward of the Nome King, and he assumed an air of much importance, and even told his majesty not to eat too much cake late at night, or he would be ill.

Dorothy, however, was hungry, and she was not afraid of being ill; so she ate several cakes and found them good, and also she drank a cup of excellent coffee made of a richly flavored clay, browned in the furnaces and then ground fine, and found it most refreshing and not at all muddy.

Of all the party which had started upon this adventure, the little Kansas girl was now left alone with the Scarecrow, Tiktok, and the private for counsellors and companions. Of course the Cowardly Lion and the Hungry Tiger were still there, but they, having also eaten some of the cakes, had gone to sleep at one side of the cave, while upon the other side stood the Sawhorse, motionless and silent, as became a mere thing of wood. Billina had quietly walked around and picked up the crumbs of cake which had been scattered, and now, as it was long after bed-time, she tried to find some dark place in which to go to sleep.

Presently the hen espied a hollow underneath the King's rocky throne, and crept into it unnoticed. She could still hear the chattering of those around her, but it was almost dark underneath the throne, so that soon she had fallen fast asleep.

"Next!" called the King, and the private, whose turn it was to enter the fatal palace, shook hands with Dorothy and the Scarecrow and bade them a sorrowful good-bye, and passed through the rocky portal.

They waited a long time, for the private was in no hurry to become an ornament and made his guesses very slowly. The Nome King, who seemed to know, by some magical power, all that took place in his beautiful rooms of his palace, grew impatient finally and declared he would sit up no longer.

"I love ornaments," said he, "but I can wait until tomorrow to get more of them; so, as soon as that stupid private is transformed, we will all go to bed and leave the job to be finished in the morning."

"Is it so very late?" asked Dorothy.

"Why, it is after midnight," said the King, "and that strikes me as being late enough. It is neither night nor day in my kingdom, because it is under the earth's surface, where the sun does not shine. But we have to sleep, just the same as the up-stairs people do, and for my part I'm going to bed in a few minutes."

Indeed, it was not long after this that the private made his last guess. Of course he guessed wrongly, and of course he at once became an ornament. So the King was greatly pleased, and clapped his hands to summon his Chief Steward.

"Show these guests to some of the sleeping apartments," he commanded, "and be quick about it, too, for I'm dreadfully sleepy myself."

"You've no business to sit up so late," replied the Steward, gruffly. "You'll be as cross as a griffin tomorrow morning."

His Majesty made no answer to this remark, and the Chief Steward led Dorothy through another doorway into a long hall, from which several plain but comfortable sleeping rooms opened. The little girl was given the first room, and the Scarecrow and Tiktok the next—although they never slept—and the Lion and the Tiger the third. The Sawhorse hobbled after the Steward into a fourth room, to stand stiffly in the center of it until morning. Each night was rather a bore to the Scarecrow, Tiktok and the Sawhorse; but they had learned from experience to pass the time patiently and quietly, since all their friends who were made of flesh had to sleep and did not like to be disturbed.

When the Chief Steward had left them alone the Scarecrow remarked, sadly:

"I am in great sorrow over the loss of my old comrade, the Tin Woodman. We have had many dangerous adventures together, and escaped them all, and now it grieves me to know he has become an ornament, and is lost to me forever."

"He was al-ways an or-na-ment to so-ci-e-ty," said Tiktok.

"True; but now the Nome King laughs at him, and calls him the funniest ornament in all the palace. It will hurt my poor friend's pride to be laughed at," continued the Scarecrow, sadly.

"We will make rath-er ab-surd or-na-ments, our-selves, to-mor-row," observed the machine, in his monotonous voice.

Just then Dorothy ran into their room, in a state of great anxiety, rying:

Where's Billina? Have you seen Billina? Is she here?"

No," answered the Scarecrow.

Then what has become of her?" asked the girl.

Why, I thought she was with you," said the Scarecrow. "Yet I do not remember seeing the yellow hen since she picked up the crumbs of cake."

We must have left her in the room where the King's throne is," decided Dorothy, and at once she turned and ran down the hall to the door through which they had entered. But it was fast closed and locked on the other side, and the heavy slab of rock proved to be so thick that no sound could pass through it. So Dorothy was forced to return to her chamber.

The Cowardly Lion stuck his head into her room to try to console the girl for the loss of her feathered friend.

The yellow hen is well able to take care of herself," said he; "so don't worry about her, but try to get all the sleep you can. It has been a long and weary day, and you need rest."

I'll prob'ly get lots of rest tomorrow, when I become an orn'ment," said Dorothy, sleepily. But she lay down upon her couch, nevertheless, and in spite of all her worries was soon in the land of dreams.

4. Dorothy Tries to be Brave

Meantime the Chief Steward had returned to the throne room, where he said to the King:

You are a fool to waste so much time upon these people."

What!" cried his Majesty, in so enraged a voice that it awoke Billina, who was asleep under his throne. "How dare you call me a fool?"

Because I like to speak the truth," said the Steward. "Why didn't you enchant them all at once, instead of allowing them to go one by one into the palace and guess which ornaments are the Queen of Ev and her children?"

Why, you stupid rascal, it is more fun this way," returned the King, "and it serves to keep me amused for a long time."

But suppose some of them happen to guess aright," persisted the Steward; "then you would lose your old ornaments and these new ones, too."

There is no chance of their guessing aright," replied the monarch, with a laugh. "How could they know that the Queen of Ev and her family are all ornaments of a royal purple color?"

But there are no other purple ornaments in the palace," said the Steward.

There are many other colors, however, and the purple ones are scattered throughout the rooms, and are of many different shapes and sizes. Take my word for it, Steward, they will never think of choosing the purple ornaments."

Billina, squatting under the throne, had listened carefully to all this talk, and now chuckled softly to herself as she heard the King disclose his secret.

"Still, you are acting foolishly by running the chance," continued the Steward, roughly; "and it is still more foolish of you to transform all those people from Oz into green ornaments."

"I did that because they came from the Emerald City," replied the King; "and I had no green ornaments in my collection until now. I think they will look quite pretty, mixed with the others. Don't you?"

The Steward gave an angry grunt.

"Have your own way, since you are the King," he growled. "But if you come to grief through your carelessness, remember that I told you so. If I wore the magic belt which enables you to work all your transformations, and gives you so much other power, I am sure I would make a much wiser and better King than you are."

"Oh, cease your tiresome chatter!" commanded the King, getting angry again. "Because you are my Chief Steward you have an idea you can scold me as much as you please. But the very next time you become impudent, I will send you to work in the furnaces, and get another Nome to fill your place. Now follow me to my chamber, for I am going to bed. And see that I am wakened early tomorrow morning. I want to enjoy the fun of transforming the rest of these people into ornaments."

"What color will you make the Kansas girl?" asked the Steward.

"Gray, I think," said his Majesty.

"And the Scarecrow and the machine man?"

"Oh, they shall be of solid gold, because they are so ugly in real life."

Then the voices died away, and Billina knew that the King and his Steward had left the room. She fixed up some of her tail feathers that were not straight, and then tucked her head under her wing again and went to sleep.

In the morning Dorothy and the Lion and Tiger were given their breakfast in their rooms, and afterward joined the King in his throne room. The Tiger complained bitterly that he was half starved, and begged to go into the palace and become an ornament, so that he would no longer suffer the pangs of hunger.

"Haven't you had your breakfast?" asked the Nome King.

"Oh, I had just a bite," replied the beast. "But what good is a bite, to a hungry tiger?"

"He ate seventeen bowls of porridge, a platter full of fried sausages, eleven loaves of bread and twenty-one mince pies," said the Steward.

"What more do you want?" demanded the King.

"A fat baby. I want a fat baby," said the Hungry Tiger. "A nice, plump, juicy, tender, fat baby. But, of course, if I had one, my conscience would not allow me to eat it. So I'll have to be an ornament and forget my hunger."

"Impossible!" exclaimed the King. "I'll have no clumsy beasts enter my palace, to overturn and break all my pretty nick-nacks. When the rest of your friends are transformed you can return to the upper world, and go about your business."

"As for that, we have no business, when our friends are gone," said the Lion. "So we do not care much what becomes of us."

Dorothy begged to be allowed to go first into the palace, but Tiktok firmly maintained that the slave should face danger before the mistress. The Scarecrow agreed with him in that, so the Nome King opened the door for the machine man, who tramped into the palace to meet his fate. Then his Majesty returned to his throne and puffed his pipe so contentedly that a small cloud of smoke formed above his head.

Bye and bye he said:

"I'm sorry there are so few of you left. Very soon, now, my fun will be over, and then for amusement I shall have nothing to do but admire my new ornaments."

"It seems to me," said Dorothy, "that you are not so honest as you pretend to be."

"How's that?" asked the King.

"Why, you made us think it would be easy to guess what ornaments the people of Ev were changed into."

"It IS easy," declared the monarch, "if one is a good guesser. But it appears that the members of your party are all poor guessers."

"What is Tiktok doing now?" asked the girl, uneasily.

"Nothing," replied the King, with a frown. "He is standing perfectly still, in the middle of a room."

"Oh, I expect he's run down," said Dorothy. "I forgot to wind him up this morning. How many guesses has he made?"

"All that he is allowed except one," answered the King. "Suppose you go in and wind him up, and then you can stay there and make your own guesses."

"All right," said Dorothy.

"It is my turn next," declared the Scarecrow.

"Why, you don't want to go away and leave me all alone, do you?" asked the girl. "Besides, if I go now I can wind up Tiktok, so that he can make his last guess."

"Very well, then," said the Scarecrow, with a sigh. "Run along, little Dorothy, and may good luck go with you!"

So Dorothy, trying to be brave in spite of her fears, passed through the doorway into the gorgeous rooms of the palace. The stillness of the place awed her, at first, and the child drew short breaths, and pressed her hand to her heart, and looked all around with wondering eyes.

Yes, it was a beautiful place; but enchantments lurked in every nook and corner, and she had not yet grown accustomed to the wizardries of these fairy countries, so different from the quiet and sensible common-places of her own native land.

Slowly she passed through several rooms until she came upon Tiktok, standing motionless. It really seemed, then, that she had found a friend in this mysterious palace, so she hastened to wind up the machine man's action and speech and thoughts.

"Thank you, Dor-oth-y," were his first words. "I have now on more guess to make."

"Oh, be very careful, Tiktok; won't you?" cried the girl.

"Yes. But the Nome King has us in his power, and he has set trap for us. I fear we are all lost." he answered.

"I fear so, too," said Dorothy, sadly.

"If Smith & Tin-ker had giv-en me a guess-ing clock-work at tach-ment," continued Tiktok, "I might have de-fied the Nom King. But my thoughts are plain and sim-ple, and are not much use in this case."

"Do the best you can," said Dorothy, encouragingly, "and if yo fail I will watch and see what shape you are changed into."

So Tiktok touched a yellow glass vase that had daisies painted o one side, and he spoke at the same time the word "Ev."

In a flash the machine man had disappeared, and although th girl looked quickly in every direction, she could not tell which the many ornaments the room contained had a moment befor been her faithful friend and servant.

So all she could do was to accept the hopeless task set her, an make her guesses and abide by the result.

"It can't hurt very much," she thought, "for I haven't heard any them scream or cry out—not even the poor officers. Dear me! wonder if Uncle Henry or Aunt Em will ever know I have becom an orn'ment in the Nome King's palace, and must stand foreve and ever in one place and look pretty—'cept when I'm moved t be dusted. It isn't the way I thought I'd turn out, at all; but s'pose it can't be helped."

She walked through all the rooms once more, and examined wit care all the objects they contained; but there were so many, the bewildered her, and she decided, after all, as Ozma had don that it could be only guess work at the best, and that the chance were much against her guessing aright.

Timidly she touched an alabaster bowl and said: "Ev."

"That's one failure, anyhow," she thought. "But how am I t know which thing is enchanted, and which is not?"

Next she touched the image of a purple kitten that stood on th corner of a mantel, and as she pronounced the word "Ev" th kitten disappeared, and a pretty, fair-haired boy stood besid her. At the same time a bell rang somewhere in the distance, an as Dorothy started back, partly in surprise and partly in joy, th little one exclaimed:

"Where am I? And who are you? And what has happened t me?"

"Well, I declare!" said Dorothy. "I've really done it."

"Done what?" asked the boy.

"Saved myself from being an ornament," replied the girl, with laugh, "and saved you from being forever a purple kitten."

"A purple kitten?" he repeated. "There IS no such thing."

"I know," she answered. "But there was, a minute ago. Don't you remember standing on a corner of the mantel?"

"Of course not. I am a Prince of Ev, and my name is Evring," the little one announced, proudly. "But my father, the King, sold my mother and all her children to the cruel ruler of the Nomes, and after that I remember nothing at all."

"A purple kitten can't be 'spected to remember, Evring," said Dorothy. "But now you are yourself again, and I'm going to try to save some of your brothers and sisters, and perhaps your mother, as well. So come with me."

She seized the child's hand and eagerly hurried here and there, trying to decide which object to choose next. The third guess was another failure, and so was the fourth and the fifth.

Little Evring could not imagine what she was doing, but he trotted along beside her very willingly, for he liked the new companion he had found.

Dorothy's further quest proved unsuccessful; but after her first disappointment was over, the little girl was filled with joy and thankfulness to think that after all she had been able to save one member of the royal family of Ev, and could restore the little Prince to his sorrowing country. Now she might return to the terrible Nome King in safety, carrying with her the prize she had won in the person of the fair-haired boy.

So she retraced her steps until she found the entrance to the palace, and as she approached, the massive doors of rock opened of their own accord, allowing both Dorothy and Evring to pass the portals and enter the throne room.

15. Billina Frightens the Nome King

Now when Dorothy had entered the palace to make her guesses and the Scarecrow was left with the Nome King, the two sat in moody silence for several minutes. Then the monarch exclaimed, in a tone of satisfaction:

"Very good!"

"Who is very good?" asked the Scarecrow.

"The machine man. He won't need to be wound up any more, for he has now become a very neat ornament. Very neat, indeed."

"How about Dorothy?" the Scarecrow enquired.

"Oh, she will begin to guess, pretty soon," said the King, cheerfully. "And then she will join my collection, and it will be your turn."

The good Scarecrow was much distressed by the thought that his little friend was about to suffer the fate of Ozma and the rest of their party; but while he sat in gloomy reverie a shrill voice suddenly cried: "Kut, kut, kut—ka-daw-kutt! Kut, kut, kut—ka-daw-kutt!"

The Nome King nearly jumped off his seat, he was so startled.

"Good gracious! What's that?" he yelled.

"Why, it's Billina," said the Scarecrow.

"What do you mean by making a noise like that?" shouted the King, angrily, as the yellow hen came from under the throne and strutted proudly about the room.

"I've got a right to cackle, I guess," replied Billina. "I've just laid my egg."

"What! Laid an egg! In my throne room! How dare you do such a thing?" asked the King, in a voice of fury.

"I lay eggs wherever I happen to be," said the hen, ruffling her feathers and then shaking them into place.

"But—thunder-ation! Don't you know that eggs are poison?" roared the King, while his rock-colored eyes stuck out in great terror.

"Poison! well, I declare," said Billina, indignantly. "I'll have you know all my eggs are warranted strictly fresh and up to date. Poison, indeed!"

"You don't understand," retorted the little monarch, nervously. "Eggs belong only to the outside world—to the world on the earth's surface, where you came from. Here, in my underground kingdom, they are rank poison, as I said, and we Nomes can't bear them around."

"Well, you'll have to bear this one around," declared Billina; "for I've laid it."

"Where?" asked the King.

"Under your throne," said the hen.

The King jumped three feet into the air, so anxious was he to get away from the throne.

"Take it away! Take it away at once!" he shouted.

"I can't," said Billina. "I haven't any hands."

"I'll take the egg," said the Scarecrow. "I'm making a collection of Billina's eggs. There's one in my pocket now, that she laid yesterday."

Hearing this, the monarch hastened to put a good distance between himself and the Scarecrow, who was about to reach under the throne for the egg when the hen suddenly cried:

"Stop!"

"What's wrong?" asked the Scarecrow.

"Don't take the egg unless the King will allow me to enter the palace and guess as the others have done," said Billina.

"Pshaw!" returned the King. "You're only a hen. How could you guess my enchantments?"

"I can try, I suppose," said Billina. "And, if I fail, you will have another ornament."

"A pretty ornament you'd make, wouldn't you?" growled the King. "But you shall have your way. It will properly punish you for daring to lay an egg in my presence. After the Scarecrow is enchanted you shall follow him into the palace. But how will you touch the objects?"

"With my claws," said the hen; "and I can speak the word 'Ev' as plainly as anyone. Also I must have the right to guess the enchantments of my friends, and to release them if I succeed."

"Very well," said the King. "You have my promise."

"Then," said Billina to the Scarecrow, "you may get the egg."

He knelt down and reached underneath the throne and found the egg, which he placed in another pocket of his jacket, fearing that if both eggs were in one pocket they would knock together and get broken.

Just then a bell above the throne rang briskly, and the King gave another nervous jump.

"Well, well!" said he, with a rueful face; "the girl has actually done it."

"Done what?" asked the Scarecrow.

"She has made one guess that is right, and broken one of my neatest enchantments. By ricketty, it's too bad! I never thought she would do it."

"Do I understand that she will now return to us in safety?" enquired the Scarecrow, joyfully wrinkling his painted face into a broad smile.

"Of course," said the King, fretfully pacing up and down the room. "I always keep my promises, no matter how foolish they are. But I shall make an ornament of the yellow hen to replace the one I have just lost."

"Perhaps you will, and perhaps you won't," murmured Billina, calmly. "I may surprise you by guessing right."

"Guessing right?" snapped the King. "How could you guess right, where your betters have failed, you stupid fowl?"

Billina did not care to answer this question, and a moment later the doors flew open and Dorothy entered, leading the little Prince Evring by the hand.

The Scarecrow welcomed the girl with a close embrace, and he would have embraced Evring, too, in his delight. But the little Prince was shy, and shrank away from the painted Scarecrow because he did not yet know his many excellent qualities.

But there was little time for the friends to talk, because the Scarecrow must now enter the palace. Dorothy's success had greatly encouraged him, and they both hoped he would manage to make at least one correct guess.

However, he proved as unfortunate as the others except Dorothy, and although he took a good deal of time to select his objects, not one did the poor Scarecrow guess aright.

So he became a solid gold card-receiver, and the beautiful but terrible palace awaited its next visitor.

"It's all over," remarked the King, with a sigh of satisfaction; "and it has been a very amusing performance, except for the one good guess the Kansas girl made. I am richer by a great many pretty ornaments."

"It is my turn, now," said Billina, briskly.

"Oh, I'd forgotten you," said the King. "But you needn't go if you don't wish to. I will be generous, and let you off."

"No you won't," replied the hen. "I insist upon having my guesses, as you promised."

"Then go ahead, you absurd feathered fool!" grumbled the King, and he caused the opening that led to the palace to appear once more.

"Don't go, Billina," said Dorothy, earnestly. "It isn't easy to guess those orn'ments, and only luck saved me from being one myself. Stay with me and we'll go back to the Land of Ev together. I'm sure this little Prince will give us a home."

"Indeed I will," said Evring, with much dignity.

"Don't worry, my dear," cried Billina, with a cluck that was meant for a laugh. "I may not be human, but I'm no fool, if I AM a chicken."

"Oh, Billina!" said Dorothy, "you haven't been a chicken in a long time. Not since you—you've been—grown up."

"Perhaps that's true," answered Billina, thoughtfully. "But if a Kansas farmer sold me to some one, what would he call me?—a hen or a chicken!"

"You are not a Kansas farmer, Billina," replied the girl, "and you said—"

"Never mind that, Dorothy. I'm going. I won't say good-bye, because I'm coming back. Keep up your courage, for I'll see you a little later."

Then Billina gave several loud "cluck-clucks" that seemed to make the fat little King MORE nervous than ever, and marched through the entrance into the enchanted palace.

"I hope I've seen the last of THAT bird," declared the monarch, seating himself again in his throne and mopping the perspiration from his forehead with his rock-colored handkerchief. "Hens are bothersome enough at their best, but when they can talk they're simply dreadful."

"Billina's my friend," said Dorothy quietly. "She may not always be 'zactly polite; but she MEANS well, I'm sure."

16. Purple, Green, and Gold

The yellow hen, stepping high and with an air of vast importance, walked slowly over the rich velvet carpets of the splendid palace, examining everything she met with her sharp little eyes.

Billina had a right to feel important; for she alone shared the Nome King's secret and knew how to tell the objects that were transformations from those that had never been alive. She was very sure that her guesses would be correct, but before she began to make them she was curious to behold all the magnificence of this underground palace, which was perhaps one of the most splendid and beautiful places in any fairyland.

As she went through the rooms she counted the purple ornaments; and although some were small and hidden in queer places, Billina spied them all, and found the entire ten scattered about the various rooms. The green ornaments she did not bother to count, for she thought she could find them all when the time came.

Finally, having made a survey of the entire palace and enjoyed its splendor, the yellow hen returned to one of the rooms where she had noticed a large purple footstool. She placed a claw upon this and said "Ev," and at once the footstool vanished and a lovely lady, tall and slender and most beautifully robed, stood before her.

The lady's eyes were round with astonishment for a moment, for she could not remember her transformation, nor imagine what had restored her to life.

"Good morning, ma'am," said Billina, in her sharp voice. "You're looking quite well, considering your age."

"Who speaks?" demanded the Queen of Ev, drawing herself up proudly.

"Why, my name's Bill, by rights," answered the hen, who was now perched upon the back of a chair; "although Dorothy has put scollops on it and made it Billina. But the name doesn't matter. I've saved you from the Nome King, and you are a slave no longer."

"Then I thank you for the gracious favor," said the Queen, with a graceful courtesy. "But, my children—tell me, I beg of you— where are my children?" and she clasped her hands in anxious entreaty.

"Don't worry," advised Billina, pecking at a tiny bug that was crawling over the chair back. "Just at present they are out of mischief and perfectly safe, for they can't even wiggle."

"What mean you, O kindly stranger?" asked the Queen, striving to repress her anxiety.

"They're enchanted," said Billina, "just as you have been—all, that is, except the little fellow Dorothy picked out. And the chances are that they have been good boys and girls for some time, because they couldn't help it."

"Oh, my poor darlings!" cried the Queen, with a sob of anguish.

"Not at all," returned the hen. "Don't let their condition make you unhappy, ma'am, because I'll soon have them crowding round to bother and worry you as naturally as ever. Come with me, if you please, and I'll show you how pretty they look."

She flew down from her perch and walked into the next room, the Queen following. As she passed a low table a small green grasshopper caught her eye, and instantly Billina pounced upon it and snapped it up in her sharp bill. For grasshoppers are a favorite food with hens, and they usually must be caught quickly, before they can hop away. It might easily have been the end of Ozma of Oz, had she been a real grasshopper instead of an emerald one. But Billina found the grasshopper hard and lifeless, and suspecting it was not good to eat she quickly dropped it instead of letting it slide down her throat.

"I might have known better," she muttered to herself, "for where there is no grass there can be no live grasshoppers. This is probably one of the King's transformations."

A moment later she approached one of the purple ornaments, and while the Queen watched her curiously the hen broke the Nome King's enchantment and a sweet-faced girl, whose golden hair fell in a cloud over her shoulders, stood beside them.

"Evanna!" cried the Queen, "my own Evanna!" and she clasped the girl to her bosom and covered her face with kisses.

"That's all right," said Billina, contentedly. "Am I a good guesser, Mr. Nome King? Well, I guess!"

Then she disenchanted another girl, whom the Queen addressed as Evrose, and afterwards a boy named Evardo, who was older than his brother Evring. Indeed, the yellow hen kept the good Queen exclaiming and embracing for some time, until five Princesses and four Princes, all looking very much alike except for the difference in size, stood in a row beside their happy mother.

The Princesses were named, Evanna, Evrose, Evella, Evirene and Evedna, while the Princes were Evrob, Evington, Evardo and Evroland. Of these Evardo was the eldest and would inherit his father's throne and be crowned King of Ev when he returned to his own country. He was a grave and quiet youth, and would doubtless rule his people wisely and with justice.

Billina, having restored all of the royal family of Ev to their proper forms, now began to select the green ornaments which were the transformations of the people of Oz. She had little trouble in finding these, and before long all the twenty-six officers, as well as the private, were gathered around the yellow hen, joyfully congratulating her upon their release. The thirty-seven people who were now alive in the rooms of the palace knew very well that they owed their freedom to the cleverness of the yellow hen, and they were earnest in thanking her for saving them from the magic of the Nome King.

"Now," said Billina, "I must find Ozma. She is sure to be here, somewhere, and of course she is green, being from Oz. So look around, you stupid soldiers, and help me in my search."

For a while, however, they could discover nothing more that was green. But the Queen, who had kissed all her nine children once more and could now find time to take an interest in what was going on, said to the hen:

"Mayhap, my gentle friend, it is the grasshopper whom you seek."

"Of course it's the grasshopper!" exclaimed Billina. "I declare, I'm nearly as stupid as these brave soldiers. Wait here for me, and I'll go back and get it."

So she went into the room where she had seen the grasshopper, and presently Ozma of Oz, as lovely and dainty as ever, entered and approached the Queen of Ev, greeting her as one high born princess greets another.

"But where are my friends, the Scarecrow and the Tin Woodman?" asked the girl Ruler, when these courtesies had been exchanged.

"I'll hunt them up," replied Billina. "The Scarecrow is solid gold, and so is Tiktok; but I don't exactly know what the Tin Woodman is, because the Nome King said he had been transformed into something funny."

Ozma eagerly assisted the hen in her quest, and soon the Scarecrow and the machine man, being ornaments of shining gold, were discovered and restored to their accustomed forms. But, search as they might, in no place could they find a funny ornament that might be the transformation of the Tin Woodman.

"Only one thing can be done," said Ozma, at last, "and that is to return to the Nome King and oblige him to tell us what has become of our friend."

"Perhaps he won't," suggested Billina.

"He must," returned Ozma, firmly. "The King has not treated us honestly, for under the mask of fairness and good nature he entrapped us all, and we would have been forever enchanted had not our wise and clever friend, the yellow hen, found a way to save us."

"The King is a villain," declared the Scarecrow.

"His laugh is worse than another man's frown," said the private, with a shudder.

"I thought he was hon-est, but I was mis-tak-en," remarked Tiktok. "My thoughts are us-u-al-ly cor-rect, but it is Smith & Tin-ker's fault if they some-times go wrong or do not work prop-er-ly."

"Smith & Tinker made a very good job of you," said Ozma, kindly. "I do not think they should be blamed if you are not quite perfect."

"Thank you," replied Tiktok.

"Then," said Billina, in her brisk little voice, "let us all go back to the Nome King, and see what he has to say for himself."

So they started for the entrance, Ozma going first, with the Queen and her train of little Princes and Princesses following. Then came Tiktok, and the Scarecrow with Billina perched upon his straw-stuffed shoulder. The twenty-seven officers and the private brought up the rear.

As they reached the hall the doors flew open before them; but then they all stopped and stared into the domed cavern with faces of astonishment and dismay. For the room was filled with the mail-clad warriors of the Nome King, rank after rank standing in orderly array. The electric lights upon their brows gleamed brightly, their battle-axes were poised as if to strike down their foes; yet they remained motionless as statues, awaiting the word of command.

And in the center of this terrible army sat the little King upon his throne of rock. But he neither smiled nor laughed. Instead, his face was distorted with rage, and most dreadful to behold.

17. The Scarecrow Wins the Fight

After Billina had entered the palace Dorothy and Evring sat down to await the success or failure of her mission, and the Nome King occupied his throne and smoked his long pipe for a while in a cheerful and contented mood.

Then the bell above the throne, which sounded whenever an enchantment was broken, began to ring, and the King gave a start of annoyance and exclaimed, "Rocketty-ricketts!"

When the bell rang a second time the King shouted angrily, "Smudge and blazes!" and at a third ring he screamed in a fury, "Hippikaloric!" which must be a dreadful word because we don't know what it means.

After that the bell went on ringing time after time; but the King was now so violently enraged that he could not utter a word, but hopped out of his throne and all around the room in a mad frenzy, so that he reminded Dorothy of a jumping-jack.

The girl was, for her part, filled with joy at every peal of the bell, for it announced the fact that Billina had transformed one more ornament into a living person. Dorothy was also amazed at Billina's success, for she could not imagine how the yellow hen was able to guess correctly from all the bewildering number of articles clustered in the rooms of the palace. But after she had counted ten, and the bell continued to ring, she knew that not only the royal family of Ev, but Ozma and her followers also, were being restored to their natural forms, and she was so delighted that the antics of the angry King only made her laugh merrily.

Perhaps the little monarch could not be more furious than he was before, but the girl's laughter nearly drove him frantic, and he roared at her like a savage beast. Then, as he found that all his enchantments were likely to be dispelled and his victims every one set free, he suddenly ran to the little door that opened upon the balcony and gave the shrill whistle that summoned his warriors.

At once the army filed out of the gold and silver doors in great numbers, and marched up a winding stairs and into the throne room, led by a stern featured Nome who was their captain. When they had nearly filled the throne room they formed ranks in the big underground cavern below, and then stood still until they were told what to do next.

Dorothy had pressed back to one side of the cavern when the warriors entered, and now she stood holding little Prince Evring's hand while the great Lion crouched upon one side and the enormous Tiger crouched on the other side.

"Seize that girl!" shouted the King to his captain, and a group of warriors sprang forward to obey. But both the Lion and Tiger snarled so fiercely and bared their strong, sharp teeth so threateningly, that the men drew back in alarm.

"Don't mind them!" cried the Nome King; "they cannot leap beyond the places where they now stand."

"But they can bite those who attempt to touch the girl," said the captain.

"I'll fix that," answered the King. "I'll enchant them again, so that they can't open their jaws."

He stepped out of the throne to do this, but just then the Sawhorse ran up behind him and gave the fat monarch a powerful kick with both his wooden hind legs.

"Ow! Murder! Treason!" yelled the King, who had been hurled against several of his warriors and was considerably bruised. "Who did that?"

"I did," growled the Sawhorse, viciously. "You let Dorothy alone or I'll kick you again."

"We'll see about that," replied the King, and at once he waved his hand toward the Sawhorse and muttered a magical word. "Aha!" he continued; "NOW let us see you move, you wooden mule!"

But in spite of the magic the Sawhorse moved; and he moved so quickly toward the King, that the fat little man could not get out of his way. Thump—BANG! came the wooden heels, right against his round body, and the King flew into the air and fell upon the head of his captain, who let him drop flat upon the ground.

"Well, well!" said the King, sitting up and looking surprised. "Why didn't my magic belt work, I wonder?"

"The creature is made of wood," replied the captain. "Your magic will not work on wood, you know."

"Ah, I'd forgotten that," said the King, getting up and limping to his throne. "Very well, let the girl alone. She can't escape us, anyway."

The warriors, who had been rather confused by these incidents, now formed their ranks again, and the Sawhorse pranced across the room to Dorothy and took a position beside the Hungry Tiger.

At that moment the doors that led to the palace flew open and the people of Ev and the people of Oz were disclosed to view. They paused, astonished, at sight of the warriors and the angry Nome King, seated in their midst.

"Surrender!" cried the King, in a loud voice. "You are my prisoners."

"Go 'long!" answered Billina, from the Scarecrow's shoulder. "You promised me that if I guessed correctly my friends and I might depart in safety. And you always keep your promises."

"I said you might leave the palace in safety," retorted the King; "and so you may, but you cannot leave my dominions. You are my prisoners, and I will hurl you all into my underground dungeons, where the volcanic fires glow and the molten lava flows in every direction, and the air is hotter than blue blazes."

"That will be the end of me, all right," said the Scarecrow, sorrowfully. "One small blaze, blue or green, is enough to reduce me to an ash-heap."

"Do you surrender?" demanded the King.

Billina whispered something in the Scarecrow's ear that made him smile and put his hands in his jacket pockets.

"No!" returned Ozma, boldly answering the King. Then she said to her army:

"Forward, my brave soldiers, and fight for your Ruler and yourselves, unto death!"

"Pardon me, Most Royal Ozma," replied one of her generals; "but I find that I and my brother officers all suffer from heart disease, and the slightest excitement might kill us. If we fight we may get excited. Would it not be well for us to avoid this grave danger?"

"Soldiers should not have heart disease," said Ozma.

"Private soldiers are not, I believe, afflicted that way," declared another general, twirling his moustache thoughtfully. "If your Royal Highness desires, we will order our private to attack yonder warriors."

"Do so," replied Ozma.

"For-ward—march!" cried all the generals, with one voice. "For-ward—march!" yelled the colonels. "For-ward—march!" shouted the majors. "For-ward—march!" commanded the captains.

And at that the private leveled his spear and dashed furiously upon the foe.

The captain of the Nomes was so surprised by this sudden onslaught that he forgot to command his warriors to fight, so that the ten men in the first row, who stood in front of the private's spear, fell over like so many toy soldiers. The spear could not go through their steel armor, however, so the warriors scrambled to their feet again, and by that time the private had knocked over another row of them.

Then the captain brought down his battle-axe with such a strong blow that the private's spear was shattered and knocked from his grasp, and he was helpless to fight any longer.

The Nome King had left his throne and pressed through his warriors to the front ranks, so he could see what was going on; but as he faced Ozma and her friends the Scarecrow, as if aroused to action by the valor of the private, drew one of Billina's eggs from his right jacket pocket and hurled it straight at the little monarch's head.

It struck him squarely in his left eye, where the egg smashed and scattered, as eggs will, and covered his face and hair and beard with its sticky contents.

"Help, help!" screamed the King, clawing with his fingers at the egg, in a struggle to remove it.

"An egg! an egg! Run for your lives!" shouted the captain of the Nomes, in a voice of horror.

And how they DID run! The warriors fairly tumbled over one another in their efforts to escape the fatal poison of that awful egg, and those who could not rush down the winding stair fell off the balcony into the great cavern beneath, knocking over those who stood below them.

Even while the King was still yelling for help his throne room became emptied of every one of his warriors, and before the monarch had managed to clear the egg away from his left eye the Scarecrow threw the second egg against his right eye, where it smashed and blinded him entirely. The King was unable to flee because he could not see which way to run; so he stood still and howled and shouted and screamed in abject fear.

While this was going on, Billina flew over to Dorothy, and perching herself upon the Lion's back the hen whispered eagerly to the girl:

"Get his belt! Get the Nome King's jeweled belt! It unbuckles in the back. Quick, Dorothy—quick!"

18. The Fate of the Tin Woodman

Dorothy obeyed. She ran at once behind the Nome King, who was still trying to free his eyes from the egg, and in a twinkling she had unbuckled his splendid jeweled belt and carried it away with her to her place beside the Tiger and Lion, where, because she did not know what else to do with it, she fastened it around her own slim waist.

Just then the Chief Steward rushed in with a sponge and a bowl of water, and began mopping away the broken eggs from his master's face. In a few minutes, and while all the party stood looking on, the King regained the use of his eyes, and the first thing he did was to glare wickedly upon the Scarecrow and exclaim:

"I'll make you suffer for this, you hay-stuffed dummy! Don't you know eggs are poison to Nomes?"

"Really," said the Scarecrow, "they DON'T seem to agree with you, although I wonder why."

"They were strictly fresh and above suspicion," said Billina. "You ought to be glad to get them."

"I'll transform you all into scorpions!" cried the King, angrily, and began waving his arms and muttering magic words.

But none of the people became scorpions, so the King stopped and looked at them in surprise.

"What's wrong?" he asked.

"Why, you are not wearing your magic belt," replied the Chief Steward, after looking the King over carefully. "Where is it? What have you done with it?"

The Nome King clapped his hand to his waist, and his rock colored face turned white as chalk.

"It's gone," he cried, helplessly. "It's gone, and I am ruined!"

Dorothy now stepped forward and said:

"Royal Ozma, and you, Queen of Ev, I welcome you and your people back to the land of the living. Billina has saved you from your troubles, and now we will leave this drea'ful place, and return to Ev as soon as poss'ble."

While the child spoke they could all see that she wore the magic belt, and a great cheer went up from all her friends, which was led by the voices of the Scarecrow and the private. But the Nome King did not join them. He crept back onto his throne like a whipped dog, and lay there bitterly bemoaning his defeat.

"But we have not yet found my faithful follower, the Tin Woodman," said Ozma to Dorothy, "and without him I do not wish to go away."

"Nor I," replied Dorothy, quickly. "Wasn't he in the palace?"

"He must be there," said Billina; "but I had no clue to guide me in guessing the Tin Woodman, so I must have missed him."

"We will go back into the rooms," said Dorothy. "This magic belt, I am sure, will help us to find our dear old friend."

So she re-entered the palace, the doors of which still stood open, and everyone followed her except the Nome King, the Queen of Ev and Prince Evring. The mother had taken the little Prince in her lap and was fondling and kissing him lovingly, for he was her youngest born.

But the others went with Dorothy, and when she came to the middle of the first room the girl waved her hand, as she had seen the King do, and commanded the Tin Woodman, whatever form he might then have, to resume his proper shape. No result followed this attempt, so Dorothy went into another room and repeated it, and so through all the rooms of the palace. Yet the Tin Woodman did not appear to them, nor could they imagine which among the thousands of ornaments was their transformed friend.

Sadly they returned to the throne room, where the King, seeing that they had met with failure, jeered at Dorothy, saying:

"You do not know how to use my belt, so it is of no use to you. Give it back to me and I will let you go free—you and all the people who came with you. As for the royal family of Ev, they are my slaves, and shall remain here."

"I shall keep the belt," said Dorothy.

"But how can you escape, without my consent?" asked the King.

"Easily enough," answered the girl. "All we need to do is to walk out the way that we came in."

"Oh, that's all, is it?" sneered the King. "Well, where is the passage through which you entered this room?"

They all looked around, but could not discover the place, for it had long since been closed. Dorothy, however, would not be dismayed. She waved her hand toward the seemingly solid wall of the cavern and said:

"I command the passage to open!"

Instantly the order was obeyed; the opening appeared and the passage lay plainly before them.

The King was amazed, and all the others overjoyed.

"Why, then, if the belt obeys you, were we unable to discover the Tin Woodman?" asked Ozma.

"I can't imagine," said Dorothy.

"See here, girl," proposed the King, eagerly; "give me the belt, and I will tell you what shape the Tin Woodman was changed into, and then you can easily find him."

Dorothy hesitated, but Billina cried out:

"Don't you do it! If the Nome King gets the belt again he will make every one of us prisoners, for we will be in his power. Only by keeping the belt, Dorothy, will you ever be able to leave this place in safety."

"I think that is true," said the Scarecrow. "But I have another idea, due to my excellent brains. Let Dorothy transform the King into a goose-egg unless he agrees to go into the palace and bring out to us the ornament which is our friend Nick Chopper, the Tin Woodman."

"A goose-egg!" echoed the horrified King. "How dreadful!"

"Well, a goose-egg you will be unless you go and fetch us the ornament we want," declared Billina, with a joyful chuckle.

"You can see for yourself that Dorothy is able to use the magic belt all right," added the Scarecrow.

The Nome King thought it over and finally consented, for he did not want to be a goose-egg. So he went into the palace to get the ornament which was the transformation of the Tin Woodman, and they all awaited his return with considerable impatience, for they were anxious to leave this underground cavern and see the sunshine once more. But when the Nome King came back he brought nothing with him except a puzzled and anxious expression upon his face.

"He's gone!" he said. "The Tin Woodman is nowhere in the palace."

"Are you sure?" asked Ozma, sternly.

"I'm very sure," answered the King, trembling, "for I know just what I transformed him into, and exactly where he stood. But he is not there, and please don't change me into a goose-egg, because I've done the best I could."

They were all silent for a time, and then Dorothy said:

"There is no use punishing the Nome King any more, and I'm afraid we'll have to go away without our friend."

"If he is not here, we cannot rescue him," agreed the Scarecrow, sadly. "Poor Nick! I wonder what has become of him."

"And he owed me six weeks back pay!" said one of the generals, wiping the tears from his eyes with his gold-laced coat sleeve.

Very sorrowfully they determined to return to the upper world without their former companion, and so Ozma gave the order to begin the march through the passage.

The army went first, and then the royal family of Ev, and afterward came Dorothy, Ozma, Billina, the Scarecrow and Tiktok.

They left the Nome King scowling at them from his throne, and had no thought of danger until Ozma chanced to look back and saw a large number of the warriors following them in full chase, with their swords and spears and axes raised to strike down the fugitives as soon as they drew near enough.

Evidently the Nome King had made this last attempt to prevent their escaping him; but it did him no good, for when Dorothy saw the danger they were in she stopped and waved her hand and whispered a command to the magic belt.

Instantly the foremost warriors became eggs, which rolled upon the floor of the cavern in such numbers that those behind could not advance without stepping upon them. But, when they saw the eggs, all desire to advance departed from the warriors, and they turned and fled madly into the cavern, and refused to go back again.

Our friends had no further trouble in reaching the end of the passage, and soon were standing in the outer air upon the gloomy path between the two high mountains. But the way to Ev lay plainly before them, and they fervently hoped that they had seen the last of the Nome King and of his dreadful palace.

The cavalcade was led by Ozma, mounted on the Cowardly Lion, and the Queen of Ev, who rode upon the back of the Tiger. The children of the Queen walked behind her, hand in hand. Dorothy rode the Sawhorse, while the Scarecrow walked and commanded the army in the absence of the Tin Woodman.

Presently the way began to lighten and more of the sunshine to come in between the two mountains. And before long they heard the "thump! thump! thump!" of the giant's hammer upon the road.

"How may we pass the monstrous man of iron?" asked the Queen, anxious for the safety of her children. But Dorothy solved the problem by a word to the magic belt.

The giant paused, with his hammer held motionless in the air, thus allowing the entire party to pass between his cast-iron legs in safety.

19. The King of Ev

If there were any shifting, rock-colored Nomes on the mountain side now, they were silent and respectful, for our adventurers were not annoyed, as before, by their impudent laughter. Really the Nomes had nothing to laugh at, since the defeat of their King.

On the other side they found Ozma's golden chariot, standing as they had left it. Soon the Lion and the Tiger were harnessed to the beautiful chariot, in which was enough room for Ozma and the Queen and six of the royal children.

Little Evring preferred to ride with Dorothy upon the Sawhorse, which had a long back. The Prince had recovered from his shyness and had become very fond of the girl who had rescued him, so they were fast friends and chatted pleasantly together as they rode along. Billina was also perched upon the head of the wooden steed, which seemed not to mind the added weight in the least, and the boy was full of wonder that a hen could talk, and say such sensible things.

When they came to the gulf, Ozma's magic carpet carried them all over in safety; and now they began to pass the trees, in which birds were singing; and the breeze that was wafted to them from the farms of Ev was spicy with flowers and new-mown hay; and the sunshine fell full upon them, to warm them and drive away from their bodies the chill and dampness of the underground kingdom of the Nomes.

"I would be quite content," said the Scarecrow to Tiktok, "were only the Tin Woodman with us. But it breaks my heart to leave him behind."

"He was a fine fel-low," replied Tiktok, "al-though his ma-ter-i-al was not ve-ry du-ra-ble."

"Oh, tin is an excellent material," the Scarecrow hastened to say; "and if anything ever happened to poor Nick Chopper he was always easily soldered. Besides, he did not have to be wound up, and was not liable to get out of order."

"I some-times wish," said Tiktok, "that I was stuffed with straw, as you are. It is hard to be made of cop-per."

"I have no reason to complain of my lot," replied the Scarecrow. "A little fresh straw, now and then, makes me as good as new. But I can never be the polished gentleman that my poor departed friend, the Tin Woodman, was."

You may be sure the royal children of Ev and their Queen mother were delighted at seeing again their beloved country; and when the towers of the palace of Ev came into view they could not forbear cheering at the sight. Little Evring, riding in front of Dorothy, was so overjoyed that he took a curious tin whistle from his pocket and blew a shrill blast that made the Sawhorse leap and prance in sudden alarm.

"What is that?" asked Billina, who had been obliged to flutter her wings in order to keep her seat upon the head of the frightened Sawhorse.

"That's my whistle," said Prince Evring, holding it out upon his hand.

It was in the shape of a little fat pig, made of tin and painted green. The whistle was in the tail of the pig.

"Where did you get it?" asked the yellow hen, closely examining the toy with her bright eyes.

"Why, I picked it up in the Nome King's palace, while Dorothy was making her guesses, and I put it in my pocket," answered the little Prince.

Billina laughed; or at least she made the peculiar cackle that served her for a laugh.

"No wonder I couldn't find the Tin Woodman," she said; "and no wonder the magic belt didn't make him appear, or the King couldn't find him, either!"

"What do you mean?" questioned Dorothy.

"Why, the Prince had him in his pocket," cried Billina, cackling again.

"I did not!" protested little Evring. "I only took the whistle."

"Well, then, watch me," returned the hen, and reaching out a claw she touched the whistle and said "Ev."

Swish!

"Good afternoon," said the Tin Woodman, taking off his funnel cap and bowing to Dorothy and the Prince. "I think I must have been asleep for the first time since I was made of tin, for I do not remember our leaving the Nome King."

"You have been enchanted," answered the girl, throwing an arm around her old friend and hugging him tight in her joy. "But it's all right, now."

"I want my whistle!" said the little Prince, beginning to cry.

"Hush!" cautioned Billina. "The whistle is lost, but you may have another when you get home."

The Scarecrow had fairly thrown himself upon the bosom of his old comrade, so surprised and delighted was he to see him again, and Tiktok squeezed the Tin Woodman's hand so earnestly that he dented some of his fingers. Then they had to make way for Ozma to welcome the tin man, and the army caught sight of him and set up a cheer, and everybody was delighted and happy.

For the Tin Woodman was a great favorite with all who knew him, and his sudden recovery after they had thought he was lost to them forever was indeed a pleasant surprise.

Before long the cavalcade arrived at the royal palace, where a great crowd of people had gathered to welcome their Queen and her ten children. There was much shouting and cheering, and the people threw flowers in their path, and every face wore a happy smile.

They found the Princess Langwidere in her mirrored chamber, where she was admiring one of her handsomest heads—one with rich chestnut hair, dreamy walnut eyes and a shapely hickorynut nose. She was very glad to be relieved of her duties to the people of Ev, and the Queen graciously permitted her to retain her rooms and her cabinet of heads as long as she lived.

Then the Queen took her eldest son out upon a balcony that overlooked the crowd of subjects gathered below, and said to them:

"Here is your future ruler, King Evardo Fifteenth. He is fifteen years of age, has fifteen silver buckles on his jacket and is the fifteenth Evardo to rule the land of Ev."

The people shouted their approval fifteen times, and even the Wheelers, some of whom were present, loudly promised to obey the new King.

So the Queen placed a big crown of gold, set with rubies, upon Evardo's head, and threw an ermine robe over his shoulders, and proclaimed him King; and he bowed gratefully to all his subjects and then went away to see if he could find any cake in the royal pantry.

Ozma of Oz and her people, as well as Dorothy, Tiktok and Billina, were splendidly entertained by the Queen mother, who owed all her happiness to their kind offices; and that evening the yellow hen was publicly presented with a beautiful necklace of pearls and sapphires, as a token of esteem from the new King.

20. The Emerald City

Dorothy decided to accept Ozma's invitation to return with her to the Land of Oz. There was no greater chance of her getting home from Ev than from Oz, and the little girl was anxious to see once more the country where she had encountered such wonderful adventures. By this time Uncle Henry would have reached Australia in his ship, and had probably given her up for lost; so he couldn't worry any more than he did if she stayed away from him a while longer. So she would go to Oz.

They bade good-bye to the people of Ev, and the King promised Ozma that he would ever be grateful to her and render the Land of Oz any service that might lie within his power.

And then they approached the edge of the dangerous desert, and Ozma threw down the magic carpet, which at once unrolled far enough for all of them to walk upon it without being crowded.

Tiktok, claiming to be Dorothy's faithful follower because he belonged to her, had been permitted to join the party, and before they started the girl wound up his machinery as far as possible and the copper man stepped off as briskly as any one of them.

Ozma also invited Billina to visit the Land of Oz, and the yellow hen was glad enough to go where new sights and scenes awaited her.

They began the trip across the desert early in the morning, and as they stopped only long enough for Billina to lay her daily egg before sunset they espied the green slopes and wooded hills of the beautiful Land of Oz. They entered it in the Munchkin territory, and the King of the Munchkins met them at the border and welcomed Ozma with great respect, being very pleased by her safe return. For Ozma of Oz ruled the King of the Munchkins, the King of the Winkies, the King of the Quadlings and the King of the Gillikins just as those kings ruled their own people; and this supreme ruler of the Land of Oz lived in a great town of her own, called the Emerald City, which was in the exact center of the four kingdoms of the Land of Oz.

The Munchkin king entertained them at his palace that night and in the morning they set out for the Emerald City, travelling over a road of yellow brick that led straight to the jewel-studded gates. Everywhere the people turned out to greet their beloved Ozma, and to hail joyfully the Scarecrow, the Tin Woodman and the Cowardly Lion, who were popular favorites. Dorothy, too, remembered some of the people, who had befriended her on the occasion of her first visit to Oz, and they were well pleased to see the little Kansas girl again, and showered her with compliments and good wishes.

At one place, where they stopped to refresh themselves, Ozma accepted a bowl of milk from the hands of a pretty dairy-maid. Then she looked at the girl more closely, and exclaimed:

"Why, it's Jinjur—isn't it!"

"Yes, your Highness," was the reply, as Jinjur dropped a low curtsy. And Dorothy looked wonderingly at this lively appearing person, who had once assembled an army of women and driven the Scarecrow from the throne of the Emerald City, and even fought a battle with the powerful army of Glinda the Sorceress.

"I've married a man who owns nine cows," said Jinjur to Ozma, "and now I am happy and contented and willing to lead a quiet life and mind my own business."

"Where is your husband?" asked Ozma.

"He is in the house, nursing a black eye," replied Jinjur, calmly. "The foolish man would insist upon milking the red cow when I wanted him to milk the white one; but he will know better next time, I am sure."

Then the party moved on again, and after crossing a broad river on a ferry and passing many fine farm houses that were dome shaped and painted a pretty green color, they came in sight of a large building that was covered with flags and bunting.

"I don't remember that building," said Dorothy. "What is it?"

"That is the College of Art and Athletic Perfection," replied Ozma. "I had it built quite recently, and the Woggle-Bug is its president. It keeps him busy, and the young men who attend the college are no worse off than they were before. You see, in this country are a number of youths who do not like to work, and the college is an excellent place for them."

And now they came in sight of the Emerald City, and the people flocked out to greet their lovely ruler. There were several bands and many officers and officials of the realm, and a crowd of citizens in their holiday attire.

Thus the beautiful Ozma was escorted by a brilliant procession to her royal city, and so great was the cheering that she was obliged to constantly bow to the right and left to acknowledge the greetings of her subjects.

That evening there was a grand reception in the royal palace, attended by the most important persons of Oz, and Jack Pumpkinhead, who was a little overripe but still active, read an address congratulating Ozma of Oz upon the success of her generous mission to rescue the royal family of a neighboring kingdom.

Then magnificent gold medals set with precious stones were presented to each of the twenty-six officers; and the Tin Woodman was given a new axe studded with diamonds; and the Scarecrow received a silver jar of complexion powder. Dorothy was presented with a pretty coronet and made a Princess of Oz,

and Tiktok received two bracelets set with eight rows of very clear and sparkling emeralds.

Afterward they sat down to a splendid feast, and Ozma put Dorothy at her right and Billina at her left, where the hen sat upon a golden roost and ate from a jeweled platter. Then were placed the Scarecrow, the Tin Woodman and Tiktok, with baskets of lovely flowers before them, because they did not require food. The twenty-six officers were at the lower end of the table, and the Lion and the Tiger also had seats, and were served on golden platters, that held a half a bushel at one time.

The wealthiest and most important citizens of the Emerald City were proud to wait upon these famous adventurers, and they were assisted by a sprightly little maid named Jellia Jamb, whom the Scarecrow pinched upon her rosy cheeks and seemed to know very well.

During the feast Ozma grew thoughtful, and suddenly she asked:

"Where is the private?"

"Oh, he is sweeping out the barracks," replied one of the generals, who was busy eating a leg of a turkey. "But I have ordered him a dish of bread and molasses to eat when his work is done."

"Let him be sent for," said the girl ruler.

While they waited for this command to be obeyed, she enquired:

"Have we any other privates in the armies?"

"Oh, yes," replied the Tin Woodman, "I believe there are three, altogether."

The private now entered, saluting his officers and the royal Ozma very respectfully.

"What is your name, my man?" asked the girl.

"Omby Amby," answered the private.

"Then, Omby Amby," said she, "I promote you to be Captain General of all the armies of my kingdom, and especially to be Commander of my Body Guard at the royal palace."

"It is very expensive to hold so many offices," said the private, hesitating. "I have no money with which to buy uniforms."

"You shall be supplied from the royal treasury," said Ozma.

Then the private was given a seat at the table, where the other officers welcomed him cordially, and the feasting and merriment were resumed.

Suddenly Jellia Jamb exclaimed:

"There is nothing more to eat! The Hungry Tiger has consumed everything!"

"But that is not the worst of it," declared the Tiger, mournfully. "Somewhere or somehow, I've actually lost my appetite!"

21. Dorothy's Magic Belt

Dorothy passed several very happy weeks in the Land of Oz as the guest of the royal Ozma, who delighted to please and interest the little Kansas girl. Many new acquaintances were formed and many old ones renewed, and wherever she went Dorothy found herself among friends.

One day, however, as she sat in Ozma's private room, she noticed hanging upon the wall a picture which constantly changed in appearance, at one time showing a meadow and at another time a forest, a lake or a village.

"How curious!" she exclaimed, after watching the shifting scenes for a few moments.

"Yes," said Ozma, "that is really a wonderful invention in magic. If I wish to see any part of the world or any person living, I need only express the wish and it is shown in the picture."

"May I use it?" asked Dorothy, eagerly.

"Of course, my dear."

"Then I'd like to see the old Kansas farm, and Aunt Em," said the girl.

Instantly the well remembered farmhouse appeared in the picture, and Aunt Em could be seen quite plainly. She was engaged in washing dishes by the kitchen window and seemed quite well and contented. The hired men and the teams were in the harvest fields behind the house, and the corn and wheat seemed to the child to be in prime condition. On the side porch Dorothy's pet dog, Toto, was lying fast asleep in the sun, and to her surprise old Speckles was running around with a brood of twelve new chickens trailing after her.

"Everything seems all right at home," said Dorothy, with a sigh of relief. "Now I wonder what Uncle Henry is doing."

The scene in the picture at once shifted to Australia, where, in a pleasant room in Sydney, Uncle Henry was seated in an easy chair, solemnly smoking his briar pipe. He looked sad and lonely, and his hair was now quite white and his hands and face thin and wasted.

"Oh!" cried Dorothy, in an anxious voice, "I'm sure Uncle Henry isn't getting any better, and it's because he is worried about me. Ozma, dear, I must go to him at once!"

"How can you?" asked Ozma.

"I don't know," replied Dorothy; "but let us go to Glinda the Good. I'm sure she will help me, and advise me how to get to Uncle Henry."

Ozma readily agreed to this plan and caused the Sawhorse to be harnessed to a pretty green and pink phaeton, and the two girls rode away to visit the famous sorceress.

Glinda received them graciously, and listened to Dorothy's story with attention.

"I have the magic belt, you know," said the little girl. "If I buckled it around my waist and commanded it to take me to Uncle Henry, wouldn't it do it?"

"I think so," replied Glinda, with a smile.

"And then," continued Dorothy, "if I ever wanted to come back here again, the belt would bring me."

"In that you are wrong," said the sorceress. "The belt has magical powers only while it is in some fairy country, such as the Land of Oz, or the Land of Ev. Indeed, my little friend, were you to wear it and wish yourself in Australia, with your uncle, the wish would doubtless be fulfilled, because it was made in fairyland. But you would not find the magic belt around you when you arrived at your destination."

"What would become of it?" asked the girl.

"It would be lost, as were your silver shoes when you visited Oz before, and no one would ever see it again. It seems too bad to destroy the use of the magic belt in that way, doesn't it?"

"Then," said Dorothy, after a moment's thought, "I will give the magic belt to Ozma, for she can use it in her own country. And she can wish me transported to Uncle Henry without losing the belt."

"That is a wise plan," replied Glinda.

So they rode back to the Emerald City, and on the way it was arranged that every Saturday morning Ozma would look at Dorothy in her magic picture, wherever the little girl might chance to be. And, if she saw Dorothy make a certain signal, then Ozma would know that the little Kansas girl wanted to revisit the Land of Oz, and by means of the Nome King's magic belt would wish that she might instantly return.

This having been agreed upon, Dorothy bade good-bye to all her friends. Tiktok wanted to go to Australia; too, but Dorothy knew that the machine man would never do for a servant in a civilized country, and the chances were that his machinery wouldn't work at all. So she left him in Ozma's care.

Billina, on the contrary, preferred the Land of Oz to any other country, and refused to accompany Dorothy.

"The bugs and ants that I find here are the finest flavored in the world," declared the yellow hen, "and there are plenty of them. So here I shall end my days; and I must say, Dorothy, my dear, that you are very foolish to go back into that stupid, humdrum world again."

"Uncle Henry needs me," said Dorothy, simply; and every one except Billina thought it was right that she should go.

All Dorothy's friends of the Land of Oz—both old and new— gathered in a group in front of the palace to bid her a sorrowful good-bye and to wish her long life and happiness. After much hand shaking, Dorothy kissed Ozma once more, and then handed her the Nome King's magic belt, saying:

"Now, dear Princess, when I wave my handkerchief, please wish me with Uncle Henry. I'm aw'fly sorry to leave you—and the Scarecrow—and the Tin Woodman—and the Cowardly Lion— and Tiktok—and—and everybody—but I do want my Uncle Henry! So good-bye, all of you."

Then the little girl stood on one of the big emeralds which decorated the courtyard, and after looking once again at each of her friends, waved her handkerchief.

* * * * *

"No," said Dorothy, "I wasn't drowned at all. And I've come to nurse you and take care of you, Uncle Henry, and you must promise to get well as soon as poss'ble."

Uncle Henry smiled and cuddled his little niece close in his lap.

"I'm better already, my darling," said he.

Dorothy and the Wizard in Oz
by L. Frank Baum

A Faithful Record of Their Amazing Adventures in an Underground World; and How with the Aid of Their Friends Zeb Hugson, Eureka the Kitten, and Jim the Cab-Horse, They Finally Reached the Wonderful Land of Oz, by L. Frank Baum, "Royal Historian of Oz"

To My Readers

It's no use; no use at all. The children won't let me stop telling tales of the Land of Oz. I know lots of other stories, and I hope to tell them, some time or another; but just now my loving tyrants won't allow me. They cry: "Oz—Oz! more about Oz, Mr. Baum!" and what can I do but obey their commands?

This is Our Book—mine and the children's. For they have flooded me with thousands of suggestions in regard to it, and I have honestly tried to adopt as many of these suggestions as could be fitted into one story.

After the wonderful success of "Ozma of Oz" it is evident that Dorothy has become a firm fixture in these Oz stories. The little ones all love Dorothy, and as one of my small friends aptly states: "It isn't a real Oz story without her." So here she is again, as sweet and gentle and innocent as ever, I hope, and the heroine of another strange adventure.

There were many requests from my little correspondents for "more about the Wizard." It seems the jolly old fellow made hosts of friends in the first Oz book, in spite of the fact that he frankly acknowledged himself "a humbug." The children had heard how he mounted into the sky in a balloon and they were all waiting for him to come down again. So what could I do but tell "what happened to the Wizard afterward"? You will find him in these pages, just the same humbug Wizard as before.

There was one thing the children demanded which I found it impossible to do in this present book: they bade me introduce Toto, Dorothy's little black dog, who has many friends among my readers. But you will see, when you begin to read the story, that Toto was in Kansas while Dorothy was in California, and so she had to start on her adventure without him. In this book Dorothy had to take her kitten with her instead of her dog; but in the next Oz book, if I am permitted to write one, I intend to tell a good deal about Toto's further history.

Princess Ozma, whom I love as much as my readers do, is again introduced in this story, and so are several of our old friends of Oz. You will also become acquainted with Jim the Cab-Horse, the Nine Tiny Piglets, and Eureka, the Kitten. I am sorry the kitten was not as well behaved as she ought to have been; but perhaps she wasn't brought up properly. Dorothy found her, you see, and who her parents were nobody knows.

I believe, my dears, that I am the proudest story-teller that ever lived. Many a time tears of pride and joy have stood in my eyes while I read the tender, loving, appealing letters that came to me in almost every mail from my little readers. To have pleased you, to have interested you, to have won your friendship, and perhaps your love, through my stories, is to my mind as great an achievement as to become President of the United States. Indeed, I would much rather be your story-teller, under these conditions, than to be the President. So you have helped me to fulfill my life's ambition, and I am more grateful to you, my dears, than I can express in words.

I try to answer every letter of my young correspondents; yet sometimes there are so many letters that a little time must pass before you get your answer. But be patient, friends, for the answer will surely come, and by writing to me you more than repay me for the pleasant task of preparing these books. Besides, I am proud to acknowledge that the books are partly yours, for your suggestions often guide me in telling the stories, and I am sure they would not be half so good without your clever and thoughtful assistance.

L. Frank Baum
Coronado, 1908.

1. The Earthquake

The train from 'Frisco was very late. It should have arrived at Hugson's Siding at midnight, but it was already five o'clock and the gray dawn was breaking in the east when the little train slowly rumbled up to the open shed that served for the station house. As it came to a stop the conductor called out in a loud voice:

"Hugson's Siding!"

At once a little girl rose from her seat and walked to the door of the car, carrying a wicker suit-case in one hand and a round bird-cage covered up with newspapers in the other, while a parasol was tucked under her arm. The conductor helped her off the car and then the engineer started his train again, so that it puffed and groaned and moved slowly away up the track. The reason he was so late was because all through the night there were times when the solid earth shook and trembled under him, and the engineer was afraid that at any moment the rails might spread apart and an accident happen to his passengers. So he moved the cars slowly and with caution.

The little girl stood still to watch until the train had disappeared around a curve; then she turned to see where she was.

The shed at Hugson's Siding was bare save for an old wooden bench, and did not look very inviting. As she peered through the soft gray light not a house of any sort was visible near the station, nor was any person in sight; but after a while the child discovered a horse and buggy standing near a group of trees a short distance away. She walked toward it and found the horse tied to a tree and standing motionless, with its head hanging down almost to the ground. It was a big horse, tall and bony, with long legs and large knees and feet. She could count his ribs easily where they showed through the skin of his body, and his head was long and seemed altogether too big for him, as if it did not fit. His tail was short and scraggly, and his harness had been broken in many places and fastened together again with cord and bits of wire. The buggy seemed almost new, for it had a shiny top and side curtains. Getting around in front, so that she could look inside, the girl saw a boy curled up on the seat, fast asleep.

She set down the bird-cage and poked the boy with her parasol. Presently he woke up, rose to a sitting position and rubbed his eyes briskly.

"Hello!" he said, seeing her, "are you Dorothy Gale?"

"Yes," she answered, looking gravely at his tousled hair and blinking gray eyes. "Have you come to take me to Hugson's Ranch?"

"Of course," he answered. "Train in?"

"I couldn't be here if it wasn't," she said.

He laughed at that, and his laugh was merry and frank. Jumping out of the buggy he put Dorothy's suit-case under the seat and her bird-cage on the floor in front.

"Canary-birds?" he asked.

"Oh no; it's just Eureka, my kitten. I thought that was the best way to carry her."

The boy nodded.

"Eureka's a funny name for a cat," he remarked.

"I named my kitten that because I found it," she explained. "Uncle Henry says 'Eureka' means 'I have found it.'"

"All right; hop in."

She climbed into the buggy and he followed her. Then the boy picked up the reins, shook them, and said "Gid-dap!"

The horse did not stir. Dorothy thought he just wiggled one of his drooping ears, but that was all.

"Gid-dap!" called the boy, again.

The horse stood still.

"Perhaps," said Dorothy, "if you untied him, he would go."

The boy laughed cheerfully and jumped out.

"Guess I'm half asleep yet," he said, untying the horse. "But Jim knows his business all right—don't you, Jim?" patting the long nose of the animal.

Then he got into the buggy again and took the reins, and the horse at once backed away from the tree, turned slowly around, and began to trot down the sandy road which was just visible in the dim light.

"Thought that train would never come," observed the boy. "I've waited at that station for five hours."

"We had a lot of earthquakes," said Dorothy. "Didn't you feel the ground shake?"

"Yes; but we're used to such things in California," he replied. "They don't scare us much."

"The conductor said it was the worst quake he ever knew."

"Did he? Then it must have happened while I was asleep," he said thoughtfully.

"How is Uncle Henry?" she enquired, after a pause during which the horse continued to trot with long, regular strides.

"He's pretty well. He and Uncle Hugson have been having a fine visit."

"Is Mr. Hugson your uncle?" she asked.

"Yes. Uncle Bill Hugson married your Uncle Henry's wife's sister; so we must be second cousins," said the boy, in an amused tone. "I work for Uncle Bill on his ranch, and he pays me six dollars a month and my board."

"Isn't that a great deal?" she asked, doubtfully.

"Why, it's a great deal for Uncle Hugson, but not for me. I'm a splendid worker. I work as well as I sleep," he added, with a laugh.

"What is your name?" said Dorothy, thinking she liked the boy's manner and the cheery tone of his voice.

"Not a very pretty one," he answered, as if a little ashamed. "My whole name is Zebediah; but folks just call me 'Zeb.' You've been to Australia, haven't you?"

"Yes; with Uncle Henry," she answered. "We got to San Francisco a week ago, and Uncle Henry went right on to Hugson's Ranch for a visit while I stayed a few days in the city with some friends we had met."

"How long will you be with us?" he asked.

"Only a day. Tomorrow Uncle Henry and I must start back for Kansas. We've been away for a long time, you know, and so we're anxious to get home again."

The boy flicked the big, boney horse with his whip and looked thoughtful. Then he started to say something to his little companion, but before he could speak the buggy began to sway dangerously from side to side and the earth seemed to rise up before them. Next minute there was a roar and a sharp crash, and at her side Dorothy saw the ground open in a wide crack and then come together again.

"Goodness!" she cried, grasping the iron rail of the seat. "What was that?"

"That was an awful big quake," replied Zeb, with a white face. "It almost got us that time, Dorothy."

The horse had stopped short, and stood firm as a rock. Zeb shook the reins and urged him to go, but Jim was stubborn. Then the boy cracked his whip and touched the animal's flanks with it, and after a low moan of protest Jim stepped slowly along the road.

Neither the boy nor the girl spoke again for some minutes. There was a breath of danger in the very air, and every few moments the earth would shake violently. Jim's ears were standing erect upon his head and every muscle of his big body was tense as he trotted toward home. He was not going very fast, but on his flanks specks of foam began to appear and at times he would tremble like a leaf.

The sky had grown darker again and the wind made queer sobbing sounds as it swept over the valley.

Suddenly there was a rending, tearing sound, and the earth split into another great crack just beneath the spot where the horse was standing. With a wild neigh of terror the animal fell bodily into the pit, drawing the buggy and its occupants after him.

Dorothy grabbed fast hold of the buggy top and the boy did the same. The sudden rush into space confused them so that they could not think.

Blackness engulfed them on every side, and in breathless silence they waited for the fall to end and crush them against jagged rocks or for the earth to close in on them again and bury them forever in its dreadful depths.

The horrible sensation of falling, the darkness and the terrifying noises, proved more than Dorothy could endure and for a few moments the little girl lost consciousness. Zeb, being a boy, did not faint, but he was badly frightened, and clung to the buggy seat with a tight grip, expecting every moment would be his last.

2. The Glass City

When Dorothy recovered her senses they were still falling, but not so fast. The top of the buggy caught the air like a parachute or an umbrella filled with wind, and held them back so that they floated downward with a gentle motion that was not so very disagreeable to bear. The worst thing was their terror of reaching the bottom of this great crack in the earth, and the natural fear that sudden death was about to overtake them at any moment. Crash after crash echoed far above their heads, as the earth came together where it had split, and stones and chunks of clay rattled around them on every side. These they could not see, but they could feel them pelting the buggy top, and Jim screamed almost like a human being when a stone overtook him and struck his boney body. They did not really hurt the poor horse, because everything was falling together; only the stones and rubbish fell faster than the horse and buggy, which were held back by the pressure of the air, so that the terrified animal was actually more frightened than he was injured.

How long this state of things continued Dorothy could not even guess, she was so greatly bewildered. But bye and bye, as she stared ahead into the black chasm with a beating heart, she began to dimly see the form of the horse Jim—his head up in the air, his ears erect and his long legs sprawling in every direction as he tumbled through space. Also, turning her head, she found that she could see the boy beside her, who had until now remained as still and silent as she herself.

Dorothy sighed and commenced to breathe easier. She began to realize that death was not in store for her, after all, but that she had merely started upon another adventure, which promised to be just as queer and unusual as were those she had before encountered.

With this thought in mind the girl took heart and leaned her head over the side of the buggy to see where the strange light was coming from. Far below her she found six great glowing balls suspended in the air. The central and largest one was white, and reminded her of the sun. Around it were arranged, like the five points of a star, the other five brilliant balls; one being rose colored, one violet, one yellow, one blue and one orange. This splendid group of colored suns sent rays darting in every direction, and as the horse and buggy—with Dorothy and Zeb—sank steadily downward and came nearer to the lights, the rays began to take on all the delicate tintings of a rainbow, growing more and more distinct every moment until all the space was brilliantly illuminated.

Dorothy was too dazed to say much, but she watched one of Jim's big ears turn to violet and the other to rose, and wondered that his tail should be yellow and his body striped with blue and orange like the stripes of a zebra. Then she looked at Zeb, whose face was blue and whose hair was pink, and gave a little laugh that sounded a bit nervous.

"Isn't it funny?" she said.

The boy was startled and his eyes were big. Dorothy had a green streak through the center of her face where the blue and yellow lights came together, and her appearance seemed to add to his fright.

"I—I don't s-s-see any-thing funny—'bout it!" he stammered.

Just then the buggy tipped slowly over upon its side, the body of the horse tipping also. But they continued to fall, all together, and the boy and girl had no difficulty in remaining upon the seat, just as they were before. Then they turned bottom side up, and continued to roll slowly over until they were right side up again. During this time Jim struggled frantically, all his legs kicking the air; but on finding himself in his former position the horse said, in a relieved tone of voice:

"Well, that's better!"

Dorothy and Zeb looked at one another in wonder.

"Can your horse talk?" she asked.

"Never knew him to, before," replied the boy.

"Those were the first words I ever said," called out the horse, who had overheard them, "and I can't explain why I happened to speak then. This is a nice scrape you've got me into, isn't it?"

"As for that, we are in the same scrape ourselves," answered Dorothy, cheerfully. "But never mind; something will happen pretty soon."

"Of course," growled the horse, "and then we shall be sorry it happened."

Zeb gave a shiver. All this was so terrible and unreal that he could not understand it at all, and so had good reason to be afraid.

Swiftly they drew near to the flaming colored suns, and passed close beside them. The light was then so bright that it dazzled their eyes, and they covered their faces with their hands to escape being blinded. There was no heat in the colored suns, however, and after they had passed below them the top of the buggy shut out many of the piercing rays so that the boy and girl could open their eyes again.

"We've got to come to the bottom some time," remarked Zeb, with a deep sigh. "We can't keep falling forever, you know."

"Of course not," said Dorothy. "We are somewhere in the middle of the earth, and the chances are we'll reach the other side of it before long. But it's a big hollow, isn't it?"

"Awful big!" answered the boy.

"We're coming to something now," announced the horse.

At this they both put their heads over the side of the buggy and looked down. Yes; there was land below them; and not so very far away, either. But they were floating very, very slowly—so slowly that it could no longer be called a fall—and the children had ample time to take heart and look about them.

They saw a landscape with mountains and plains, lakes and rivers, very like those upon the earth's surface; but all the scene was splendidly colored by the variegated lights from the six suns. Here and there were groups of houses that seemed made of clear glass, because they sparkled so brightly.

"I'm sure we are in no danger," said Dorothy, in a sober voice. "We are falling so slowly that we can't be dashed to pieces when we land, and this country that we are coming to seems quite pretty."

"We'll never get home again, though!" declared Zeb, with a groan.

"Oh, I'm not so sure of that," replied the girl. "But don't let us worry over such things, Zeb; we can't help ourselves just now, you know, and I've always been told it's foolish to borrow trouble."

The boy became silent, having no reply to so sensible a speech, and soon both were fully occupied in staring at the strange scenes spread out below them. They seemed to be falling right into the middle of a big city which had many tall buildings with glass domes and sharp-pointed spires. These spires were like great spear-points, and if they tumbled upon one of them they were likely to suffer serious injury.

Jim the horse had seen these spires, also, and his ears stood straight up with fear, while Dorothy and Zeb held their breaths in suspense. But no; they floated gently down upon a broad, flat roof, and came to a stop at last.

When Jim felt something firm under his feet the poor beast's legs trembled so much that he could hardly stand; but Zeb at once leaped out of the buggy to the roof, and he was so awkward and hasty that he kicked over Dorothy's bird-cage, which rolled out upon the roof so that the bottom came off. At once a pink kitten crept out of the upset cage, sat down upon the glass roof, and yawned and blinked its round eyes.

"Oh," said Dorothy. "There's Eureka."

"First time I ever saw a pink cat," said Zeb.

"Eureka isn't pink; she's white. It's this queer light that gives her hat color."

"Where's my milk?" asked the kitten, looking up into Dorothy's face. "I'm 'most starved to death."

"Oh, Eureka! Can you talk?"

"Talk! Am I talking? Good gracious, I believe I am. Isn't it funny?" asked the kitten.

"It's all wrong." said Zeb, gravely. "Animals ought not to talk. But even old Jim has been saying things since we had our accident."

"I can't see that it's wrong," remarked Jim, in his gruff tones. "At least, it isn't as wrong as some other things. What's going to become of us now?"

"I don't know," answered the boy, looking around him curiously.

The houses of the city were all made of glass, so clear and transparent that one could look through the walls as easily as through a window. Dorothy saw, underneath the roof on which she stood, several rooms used for rest chambers, and even thought she could make out a number of queer forms huddled into the corners of these rooms.

The roof beside them had a great hole smashed through it, and

pieces of glass were lying scattered in every direction. A nearby steeple had been broken off short and the fragments lay heaped beside it. Other buildings were cracked in places or had corners chipped off from them; but they must have been very beautiful before these accidents had happened to mar their perfection. The rainbow tints from the colored suns fell upon the glass city softly and gave to the buildings many delicate, shifting hues which were very pretty to see.

But not a sound had broken the stillness since the strangers had arrived, except that of their own voices. They began to wonder if there were no people to inhabit this magnificent city of the inner world.

Suddenly a man appeared through a hole in the roof next to the one they were on and stepped into plain view. He was not a very large man, but was well formed and had a beautiful face—calm and serene as the face of a fine portrait. His clothing fitted his form snugly and was gorgeously colored in brilliant shades of green, which varied as the sunbeams touched them but was not wholly influenced by the solar rays.

The man had taken a step or two across the glass roof before he noticed the presence of the strangers; but then he stopped abruptly. There was no expression of either fear or surprise upon his tranquil face, yet he must have been both astonished and afraid; for after his eyes had rested upon the ungainly form of the horse for a moment he walked rapidly to the furthest edge of the roof, his head turned back over his shoulder to gaze at the strange animal.

"Look out!" cried Dorothy, who noticed that the beautiful man did not look where he was going; "be careful, or you'll fall off!"

But he paid no attention to her warning. He reached the edge of the tall roof, stepped one foot out into the air, and walked into space as calmly as if he were on firm ground.

The girl, greatly astonished, ran to lean over the edge of the roof, and saw the man walking rapidly through the air toward the ground. Soon he reached the street and disappeared through a glass doorway into one of the glass buildings.

"How strange!" she exclaimed, drawing a long breath.

"Yes; but it's lots of fun, if it IS strange," remarked the small voice of the kitten, and Dorothy turned to find her pet walking in the air a foot or so away from the edge of the roof.

"Come back, Eureka!" she called, in distress, "you'll certainly be killed."

"I have nine lives," said the kitten, purring softly as it walked around in a circle and then came back to the roof; "but I can't lose even one of them by falling in this country, because I really couldn't manage to fall if I wanted to."

"Does the air bear up your weight?" asked the girl.

"Of course; can't you see?" and again the kitten wandered into the air and back to the edge of the roof.

"It's wonderful!" said Dorothy.

"Suppose we let Eureka go down to the street and get some one to help us," suggested Zeb, who had been even more amazed than Dorothy at these strange happenings.

"Perhaps we can walk on the air ourselves," replied the girl.

Zeb drew back with a shiver.

"I wouldn't dare try," he said.

"Maybe Jim will go," continued Dorothy, looking at the horse.

"And maybe he won't!" answered Jim. "I've tumbled through the air long enough to make me contented on this roof."

"But we didn't tumble to the roof," said the girl; "by the time we reached here we were floating very slowly, and I'm almost sure we could float down to the street without getting hurt. Eureka walks on the air all right."

"Eureka weights only about half a pound," replied the horse, in a scornful tone, "while I weigh about half a ton."

"You don't weigh as much as you ought to, Jim," remarked the girl, shaking her head as she looked at the animal. "You're dreadfully skinny."

"Oh, well; I'm old," said the horse, hanging his head despondently, "and I've had lots of trouble in my day, little one. For a good many years I drew a public cab in Chicago, and that's enough to make anyone skinny."

"He eats enough to get fat, I'm sure," said the boy, gravely.

"Do I? Can you remember any breakfast that I've had today?" growled Jim, as if he resented Zeb's speech.

"None of us has had breakfast," said the boy; "and in a time of danger like this it's foolish to talk about eating."

"Nothing is more dangerous than being without food," declared the horse, with a sniff at the rebuke of his young master; "and just at present no one can tell whether there are any oats in this queer country or not. If there are, they are liable to be glass oats!"

"Oh, no!" exclaimed Dorothy. "I can see plenty of nice gardens and fields down below us, at the edge of this city. But I wish we could find a way to get to the ground."

"Why don't you walk down?" asked Eureka. "I'm as hungry as the horse is, and I want my milk."

"Will you try it, Zeb" asked the girl, turning to her companion.

Zeb hesitated. He was still pale and frightened, for this dreadful adventure had upset him and made him nervous and worried. But he did not wish the little girl to think him a coward, so he advanced slowly to the edge of the roof.

Dorothy stretched out a hand to him and Zeb put one foot out and let it rest in the air a little over the edge of the roof. It seemed firm enough to walk upon, so he took courage and put out the other foot. Dorothy kept hold of his hand and followed him, and soon they were both walking through the air, with the kitten frisking beside them.

"Come on, Jim!" called the boy. "It's all right."

Jim had crept to the edge of the roof to look over, and being a sensible horse and quite experienced, he made up his mind that he could go where the others did. So, with a snort and a neigh

and a whisk of his short tail he trotted off the roof into the air and at once began floating downward to the street. His great weight made him fall faster than the children walked, and he passed them on the way down; but when he came to the glass pavement he alighted upon it so softly that he was not even jarred.

"Well, well!" said Dorothy, drawing a long breath, "What a strange country this is."

People began to come out of the glass doors to look at the new arrivals, and pretty soon quite a crowd had assembled. There were men and women, but no children at all, and the folks were all beautifully formed and attractively dressed and had wonderfully handsome faces. There was not an ugly person in all the throng, yet Dorothy was not especially pleased by the appearance of these people because their features had no more expression than the faces of dolls. They did not smile nor did they frown, or show either fear or surprise or curiosity or friendliness. They simply started at the strangers, paying most attention to Jim and Eureka, for they had never before seen either a horse or a cat and the children bore an outward resemblance to themselves.

Pretty soon a man joined the group who wore a glistening star in the dark hair just over his forehead. He seemed to be a person of authority, for the others pressed back to give him room. After turning his composed eyes first upon the animals and then upon the children he said to Zeb, who was a little taller than Dorothy:

"Tell me, intruder, was it you who caused the Rain of Stones?"

For a moment the boy did not know what he meant by this question. Then, remembering the stones that had fallen with them and passed them long before they had reached this place he answered:

"No, sir; we didn't cause anything. It was the earthquake."

The man with the star stood for a time quietly thinking over this speech. Then he asked:

"What is an earthquake?"

"I don't know," said Zeb, who was still confused. But Dorothy, seeing his perplexity, answered:

"It's a shaking of the earth. In this quake a big crack opened and we fell through—horse and buggy, and all—and the stones got loose and came down with us."

The man with the star regarded her with his calm, expressionless eyes.

"The Rain of Stones has done much damage to our city," he said, "and we shall hold you responsible for it unless you can prove your innocence."

"How can we do that?" asked the girl.

"That I am not prepared to say. It is your affair, not mine. You must go to the House of the Sorcerer, who will soon discover the truth."

"Where is the House of the Sorcerer?" the girl enquired.

"I will lead you to it. Come!"

He turned and walked down the street, and after a moment's hesitation Dorothy caught Eureka in her arms and climbed into the buggy. The boy took his seat beside her and said: "Gid-dap Jim."

As the horse ambled along, drawing the buggy, the people of the glass city made way for them and formed a procession in their rear. Slowly they moved down one street and up another, turning first this way and then that, until they came to an open square in the center of which was a big glass palace having a central dome and four tall spires on each corner.

3. The Arrival Of The Wizard

The doorway of the glass palace was quite big enough for the horse and buggy to enter, so Zeb drove straight through it and the children found themselves in a lofty hall that was very beautiful. The people at once followed and formed a circle around the sides of the spacious room, leaving the horse and buggy and the man with the star to occupy the center of the hall.

"Come to us, oh, Gwig!" called the man, in a loud voice.

Instantly a cloud of smoke appeared and rolled over the floor; then it slowly spread and ascended into the dome, disclosing a strange personage seated upon a glass throne just before Jim's nose. He was formed just as were the other inhabitants of this land and his clothing only differed from theirs in being bright yellow. But he had no hair at all, and all over his bald head and face and upon the backs of his hands grew sharp thorns like those found on the branches of rose-bushes. There was even a thorn upon the tip of his nose and he looked so funny that Dorothy laughed when she saw him.

The Sorcerer, hearing the laugh, looked toward the little girl with cold, cruel eyes, and his glance made her grow sober in an instant.

"Why have you dared to intrude your unwelcome persons into the secluded Land of the Mangaboos?" he asked, sternly.

"'Cause we couldn't help it," said Dorothy.

"Why did you wickedly and viciously send the Rain of Stones to crack and break our houses?" he continued.

"We didn't," declared the girl.

"Prove it!" cried the Sorcerer.

"We don't have to prove it," answered Dorothy, indignantly. "If you had any sense at all you'd known it was the earthquake."

"We only know that yesterday came a Rain of Stones upon us, which did much damage and injured some of our people. Today came another Rain of Stones, and soon after it you appeared among us."

"By the way," said the man with the star, looking steadily at the Sorcerer, "you told us yesterday that there would not be a second Rain of Stones. Yet one has just occurred that was even worse than the first. What is your sorcery good for if it cannot tell us the truth?"

"My sorcery does tell the truth!" declared the thorn-covered man. "I said there would be but one Rain of Stones. This second one was a Rain of People-and-Horse-and-Buggy. And some stones came with them."

"Will there be any more Rains?" asked the man with the star.

"No, my Prince."

"Neither stones nor people?"

"No, my Prince."

"Are you sure?"

"Quite sure, my Prince. My sorcery tells me so."

Just then a man came running into the hall and addressed the Prince after making a low bow.

"More wonders in the air, my Lord," said he.

Immediately the Prince and all of his people flocked out of the hall into the street, that they might see what was about to happen. Dorothy and Zeb jumped out of the buggy and ran after them, but the Sorcerer remained calmly in his throne.

Far up in the air was an object that looked like a balloon. It was not so high as the glowing star of the six colored suns, but was descending slowly through the air—so slowly that at first it scarcely seemed to move.

The throng stood still and waited. It was all they could do, for to go away and leave that strange sight was impossible; nor could they hurry its fall in any way. The earth children were not noticed, being so near the average size of the Mangaboos, and the horse had remained in the House of the Sorcerer, with Eureka curled up asleep on the seat of the buggy.

Gradually the balloon grew bigger, which was proof that it was settling down upon the Land of the Mangaboos. Dorothy was surprised to find how patient the people were, for her own little heart was beating rapidly with excitement. A balloon meant to her some other arrival from the surface of the earth, and she hoped it would be some one able to assist her and Zeb out of their difficulties.

In an hour the balloon had come near enough for her to see a basket suspended below it; in two hours she could see a head looking over the side of the basket; in three hours the big balloon settled slowly into the great square in which they stood and came to rest on the glass pavement.

Then a little man jumped out of the basket, took off his tall hat, and bowed very gracefully to the crowd of Mangaboos around him. He was quite an old little man and his head was long and entirely bald.

"Why," cried Dorothy, in amazement, "it's Oz!"

The little man looked toward her and seemed as much surprised as she was. But he smiled and bowed as he answered:

"Yes, my dear; I am Oz, the Great and Terrible. Eh? And you are little Dorothy, from Kansas. I remember you very well."

"Who did you say it was?" whispered Zeb to the girl.

"It's the wonderful Wizard of Oz. Haven't you heard of him?"

Just then the man with the star came and stood before the Wizard.

"Sir," said he, "why are you here, in the Land of the Mangaboos?"

"Didn't know what land it was, my son," returned the other, with a pleasant smile; "and, to be honest, I didn't mean to visit you when I started out. I live on top of the earth, your honor, which is far better than living inside it; but yesterday I went up in a balloon, and when I came down I fell into a big crack in the earth, caused by an earthquake. I had let so much gas out of my balloon that I could not rise again, and in a few minutes the earth closed over my head. So I continued to descend until I reached this place, and if you will show me a way to get out of it, I'll go with pleasure. Sorry to have troubled you; but it couldn't be helped."

The Prince had listened with attention. Said he: "This child, who is from the crust of the earth, like yourself, called you a Wizard. Is not a Wizard something like a Sorcerer?"

"It's better," replied Oz, promptly. "One Wizard is worth three Sorcerers."

"Ah, you shall prove that," said the Prince. "We Mangaboos have, at the present time, one of the most wonderful Sorcerers that ever was picked from a bush; but he sometimes makes mistakes. Do you ever make mistakes?"

"Never!" declared the Wizard, boldly.

"Oh, Oz!" said Dorothy; "you made a lot of mistakes when you were in the marvelous Land of Oz."

"Nonsense!" said the little man, turning red—although just then a ray of violet sunlight was on his round face.

"Come with me," said the Prince to him. "I wish you to meet our Sorcerer."

The Wizard did not like this invitation, but he could not refuse to accept it. So he followed the Prince into the great domed hall, and Dorothy and Zeb came after them, while the throng of people trooped in also.

There sat the thorny Sorcerer in his chair of state, and when the Wizard saw him he began to laugh, uttering comical little chuckles.

"What an absurd creature!" he exclaimed.

"He may look absurd," said the Prince, in his quiet voice; "but he is an excellent Sorcerer. The only fault I find with him is that he is so often wrong."

"I am never wrong," answered the Sorcerer.

"Only a short time ago you told me there would be no more Rain of Stones or of People," said the Prince.

"Well, what then?"

"Here is another person descended from the air to prove you were wrong."

"One person cannot be called 'people,'" said the Sorcerer. "If two should come out of the sky you might with justice say I was wrong; but unless more than this one appears I will hold that I was right."

"Very clever," said the Wizard, nodding his head as if pleased. "I am delighted to find humbugs inside the earth, just the same as on top of it. Were you ever with a circus, brother?"

"No," said the Sorcerer.

"You ought to join one," declared the little man seriously. "I belong to Bailum & Barney's Great Consolidated Shows—three rings in one tent and a menagerie on the side. It's a fine aggregation, I assure you."

"What do you do?" asked the Sorcerer.

"I go up in a balloon, usually, to draw the crowds to the circus. But I've just had the bad luck to come out of the sky, skip the solid earth, and land lower down than I intended. But never mind. It isn't everybody who gets a chance to see your Land of the Gabazoos."

"Mangaboos," said the Sorcerer, correcting him. "If you are a Wizard you ought to be able to call people by their right names."

"Oh, I'm a Wizard; you may be sure of that. Just as good a Wizard as you are a Sorcerer."

"That remains to be seen," said the other.

"If you are able to prove that you are better," said the Prince to the little man, "I will make you the Chief Wizard of this domain. Otherwise—"

"What will happen otherwise?" asked the Wizard.

"I will stop you from living and forbid you to be planted," returned the Prince.

"That does not sound especially pleasant," said the little man, looking at the one with the star uneasily. "But never mind. I'll beat Old Prickly, all right."

"My name is Gwig," said the Sorcerer, turning his heartless, cruel eyes upon his rival. "Let me see you equal the sorcery I am about to perform."

He waved a thorny hand and at once the tinkling of bells was heard, playing sweet music. Yet, look where she would, Dorothy could discover no bells at all in the great glass hall.

The Mangaboo people listened, but showed no great interest. It was one of the things Gwig usually did to prove he was a sorcerer.

Now was the Wizard's turn, so he smiled upon the assemblage and asked: "Will somebody kindly loan me a hat?"

No one did, because the Mangaboos did not wear hats, and Zeb had lost his, somehow, in his flight through the air.

"Ahem!" said the Wizard, "will somebody please loan me a handkerchief?"

But they had no handkerchiefs, either.

"Very good," remarked the Wizard. "I'll use my own hat, if you please. Now, good people, observe me carefully. You see, there is nothing up my sleeve and nothing concealed about my person. Also, my hat is quite empty." He took off his hat and held it upside down, shaking it briskly.

"Let me see it," said the Sorcerer.

He took the hat and examined it carefully, returning it afterward to the Wizard.

"Now," said the little man, "I will create something out of nothing."

He placed the hat upon the glass floor, made a pass with his hand, and then removed the hat, displaying a little white piglet no bigger than a mouse, which began to run around here and there and to grunt and squeal in a tiny, shrill voice.

The people watched it intently, for they had never seen a pig before, big or little. The Wizard reached out, caught the wee creature in his hand, and holding its head between one thumb and finger and its tail between the other thumb and finger he pulled it apart, each of the two parts becoming a whole and separate piglet in an instant.

He placed one upon the floor, so that it could run around, and pulled apart the other, making three piglets in all; and then one of these was pulled apart, making four piglets. The Wizard continued this surprising performance until nine tiny piglets were running about at his feet, all squealing and grunting in a very comical way.

"Now," said the Wizard of Oz, "having created something from nothing, I will make something nothing again."

With this he caught up two of the piglets and pushed them together, so that the two were one. Then he caught up another piglet and pushed it into the first, where it disappeared. And so, one by one, the nine tiny piglets were pushed together until but a single one of the creatures remained. This the Wizard placed underneath his hat and made a mystic sign above it. When he removed his hat the last piglet had disappeared entirely.

The little man gave a bow to the silent throng that had watched him, and then the Prince said, in his cold, calm voice:

"You are indeed a wonderful Wizard, and your powers are greater than those of my Sorcerer."

"He will not be a wonderful Wizard long," remarked Gwig.

"Why not?" enquired the Wizard.

"Because I am going to stop your breath," was the reply. "I perceive that you are curiously constructed, and that if you cannot breathe you cannot keep alive."

The little man looked troubled.

"How long will it take you to stop my breath?" he asked.

"About five minutes. I'm going to begin now. Watch me carefully."

He began making queer signs and passes toward the Wizard; but the little man did not watch him long. Instead, he drew a leathern case from his pocket and took from it several sharp knives, which he joined together, one after another, until they made a long sword. By the time he had attached a handle to this sword he was having much trouble to breathe, as the charm of the Sorcerer was beginning to take effect.

So the Wizard lost no more time, but leaping forward he raised the sharp sword, whirled it once or twice around his head, and then gave a mighty stroke that cut the body of the Sorcerer exactly in two.

Dorothy screamed and expected to see a terrible sight; but as the two halves of the Sorcerer fell apart on the floor she saw that he had no bones or blood inside of him at all, and that the place where he was cut looked much like a sliced turnip or potato.

"Why, he's vegetable!" cried the Wizard, astonished.

"Of course," said the Prince. "We are all vegetable, in this country. Are you not vegetable, also?"

"No," answered the Wizard. "People on top of the earth are all meat. Will your Sorcerer die?"

"Certainly, sir. He is really dead now, and will wither very quickly. So we must plant him at once, that other Sorcerers may grow upon his bush," continued the Prince.

"What do you mean by that?" asked the little Wizard, greatly puzzled.

"If you will accompany me to our public gardens," replied the Prince, "I will explain to you much better than I can here the mysteries of our Vegetable Kingdom."

4. The Vegetable Kingdom

After the Wizard had wiped the dampness from his sword and taken it apart and put the pieces into their leathern case again, the man with the star ordered some of his people to carry the two halves of the Sorcerer to the public gardens.

Jim pricked up his ears when he heard they were going to the gardens, and wanted to join the party, thinking he might find something proper to eat; so Zeb put down the top of the buggy and invited the Wizard to ride with them. The seat was amply wide enough for the little man and the two children, and when Jim started to leave the hall the kitten jumped upon his back and sat there quite contentedly.

So the procession moved through the streets, the bearers of the Sorcerer first, the Prince next, then Jim drawing the buggy with the strangers inside of it, and last the crowd of vegetable people who had no hearts and could neither smile nor frown.

The glass city had several fine streets, for a good many people lived there; but when the procession had passed through these it came upon a broad plain covered with gardens and watered by many pretty brooks that flowed through it. There were paths through these gardens, and over some of the brooks were ornamental glass bridges.

Dorothy and Zeb now got out of the buggy and walked beside the Prince, so that they might see and examine the flowers and plants better.

"Who built these lovely bridges?" asked the little girl.

"No one built them," answered the man with the star. "They grow."

"That's queer," said she. "Did the glass houses in your city grow, too?"

"Of course," he replied. "But it took a good many years for them to grow as large and fine as they are now. That is why we are so angry when a Rain of Stones comes to break our towers and crack our roofs."

"Can't you mend them?" she enquired.

"No; but they will grow together again, in time, and we must wait until they do."

They first passed through many beautiful gardens of flowers, which grew nearest the city; but Dorothy could hardly tell what kind of flowers they were, because the colors were constantly changing under the shifting lights of the six suns. A flower would be pink one second, white the next, then blue or yellow; and it was the same way when they came to the plants, which had broad leaves and grew close to the ground.

When they passed over a field of grass Jim immediately stretched down his head and began to nibble.

"A nice country this is," he grumbled, "where a respectable horse has to eat pink grass!"

"It's violet," said the Wizard, who was in the buggy.

"Now it's blue," complained the horse. "As a matter of fact, I'm eating rainbow grass."

"How does it taste?" asked the Wizard.

"Not bad at all," said Jim. "If they give me plenty of it I'll not complain about its color."

By this time the party had reached a freshly plowed field, and the Prince said to Dorothy:

"This is our planting-ground."

Several Mangaboos came forward with glass spades and dug a hole in the ground. Then they put the two halves of the Sorcerer into it and covered him up. After that other people brought water from a brook and sprinkled the earth.

"He will sprout very soon," said the Prince, "and grow into a large bush, from which we shall in time be able to pick several very good sorcerers."

"Do all your people grow on bushes?" asked the boy.

"Certainly," was the reply. "Do not all people grow upon bushes where you came from, on the outside of the earth?"

"Not that I ever hear of."

"How strange! But if you will come with me to one of our folk gardens I will show you the way we grow in the Land of the Mangaboos."

It appeared that these odd people, while they were able to walk through the air with ease, usually moved upon the ground in the ordinary way. There were no stairs in their houses, because they did not need them, but on a level surface they generally walked just as we do.

The little party of strangers now followed the Prince across a few more of the glass bridges and along several paths until they came to a garden enclosed by a high hedge. Jim had refused to leave the field of grass, where he was engaged in busily eating; so the Wizard got out of the buggy and joined Zeb and Dorothy, and the kitten followed demurely at their heels.

Inside the hedge they came upon row after row of large and handsome plants with broad leaves gracefully curving until their points nearly reached the ground. In the center of each plant grew a daintily dressed Mangaboo, for the clothing of all these creatures grew upon them and was attached to their bodies.

The growing Mangaboos were of all sizes, from the blossom that had just turned into a wee baby to the full-grown and almost ripe man or woman. On some of the bushes might be seen a bud, a blossom, a baby, a half-grown person and a ripe one; but even those ready to pluck were motionless and silent, as if devoid of life. This sight explained to Dorothy why she had seen no children among the Mangaboos, a thing she had until now been unable to account for.

"Our people do not acquire their real life until they leave their bushes," said the Prince. "You will notice they are all attached to the plants by the soles of their feet, and when they are quite ripe they are easily separated from the stems and at once attain the powers of motion and speech. So while they grow they cannot be said to really live, and they must be picked before they can become good citizens."

"How long do you live, after you are picked?" asked Dorothy.

"That depends upon the care we take of ourselves," he replied. "If we keep cool and moist, and meet with no accidents, we often live for five years. I've been picked over six years, but our family is known to be especially long lived."

"Do you eat?" asked the boy.

"Eat! No, indeed. We are quite solid inside our bodies, and have no need to eat, any more than does a potato."

"But the potatoes sometimes sprout," said Zeb.

"And sometimes we do," answered the Prince; "but that is considered a great misfortune, for then we must be planted at once."

"Where did you grow?" asked the Wizard.

"I will show you," was the reply. "Step this way, please."

He led them within another but smaller circle of hedge, where grew one large and beautiful bush.

"This," said he, "is the Royal Bush of the Mangaboos. All of our Princes and Rulers have grown upon this one bush from time immemorial."

They stood before it in silent admiration. On the central stalk stood poised the figure of a girl so exquisitely formed and colored and so lovely in the expression of her delicate features that Dorothy thought she had never seen so sweet and adorable a creature in all her life. The maiden's gown was soft as satin and fell about her in ample folds, while dainty lace-like traceries trimmed the bodice and sleeves. Her flesh was fine and smooth as polished ivory, and her poise expressed both dignity and grace.

"Who is this?" asked the Wizard, curiously.

The Prince had been staring hard at the girl on the bush. Now he answered, with a touch of uneasiness in his cold tones:

"She is the Ruler destined to be my successor, for she is a Royal Princess. When she becomes fully ripe I must abandon the sovereignty of the Mangaboos to her."

"Isn't she ripe now?" asked Dorothy.

He hesitated.

"Not quite," said he, finally. "It will be several days before she needs to be picked, or at least that is my judgment. I am in no hurry to resign my office and be planted, you may be sure."

"Probably not," declared the Wizard, nodding.

"This is one of the most unpleasant things about our vegetable lives," continued the Prince, with a sigh, "that while we are in our full prime we must give way to another, and be covered up in the ground to sprout and grow and give birth to other people."

"I'm sure the Princess is ready to be picked," asserted Dorothy, gazing hard at the beautiful girl on the bush. "She's as perfect as she can be."

"Never mind," answered the Prince, hastily, "she will be all right for a few days longer, and it is best for me to rule until I can dispose of you strangers, who have come to our land uninvited and must be attended to at once."

"What are you going to do with us?" asked Zeb.

"That is a matter I have not quite decided upon," was the reply. "I think I shall keep this Wizard until a new Sorcerer is ready to pick, for he seems quite skillful and may be of use to us. But the rest of you must be destroyed in some way, and you cannot be planted, because I do not wish horses and cats and meat people growing all over our country."

"You needn't worry," said Dorothy. "We wouldn't grow under ground, I'm sure."

"But why destroy my friends?" asked the little Wizard. "Why not let them live?"

"They do not belong here," returned the Prince. "They have no right to be inside the earth at all."

"We didn't ask to come down here; we fell," said Dorothy.

"That is no excuse," declared the Prince, coldly.

The children looked at each other in perplexity, and the Wizard sighed. Eureka rubbed her paw on her face and said in her soft, purring voice: "He won't need to destroy ME, for if I don't get something to eat pretty soon I shall starve to death, and so save him the trouble."

"If he planted you, he might grow some cat-tails," suggested the Wizard.

"Oh, Eureka! perhaps we can find you some milk-weeds to eat," said the boy.

"Phoo!" snarled the kitten; "I wouldn't touch the nasty things!"

"You don't need milk, Eureka," remarked Dorothy; "you are big enough now to eat any kind of food."

"If I can get it," added Eureka.

"I'm hungry myself," said Zeb. "But I noticed some strawberries growing in one of the gardens, and some melons in another place. These people don't eat such things, so perhaps on our way back they will let us get them."

"Never mind your hunger," interrupted the Prince. "I shall order you destroyed in a few minutes, so you will have no need to ruin our pretty melon vines and berry bushes. Follow me, please, to meet your doom."

5. Dorothy Picks the Princess

The words of the cold and moist vegetable Prince were not very comforting, and as he spoke them he turned away and left the enclosure. The children, feeling sad and despondent, were about to follow him when the Wizard touched Dorothy softly on her shoulder.

"Wait!" he whispered.

"What for?" asked the girl.

"Suppose we pick the Royal Princess," said the Wizard. "I'm quite sure she's ripe, and as soon as she comes to life she will be the Ruler, and may treat us better than that heartless Prince intends to."

"All right!" exclaimed Dorothy, eagerly. "Let's pick her while we have the chance, before the man with the star comes back."

So together they leaned over the great bush and each of them seized one hand of the lovely Princess.

"Pull!" cried Dorothy, and as they did so the royal lady leaned toward them and the stems snapped and separated from her feet. She was not at all heavy, so the Wizard and Dorothy managed to lift her gently to the ground.

The beautiful creature passed her hands over her eyes an instant, tucked in a stray lock of hair that had become disarranged, and after a look around the garden made those present a gracious bow and said, in a sweet but even toned voice:

"I thank you very much."

"We salute your Royal Highness!" cried the Wizard, kneeling and kissing her hand.

Just then the voice of the Prince was heard calling upon them to hasten, and a moment later he returned to the enclosure, followed by a number of his people.

Instantly the Princess turned and faced him, and when he saw that she was picked the Prince stood still and began to tremble.

"Sir," said the Royal Lady, with much dignity, "you have wronged me greatly, and would have wronged me still more had not these strangers come to my rescue. I have been ready for picking all the past week, but because you were selfish and desired to continue your unlawful rule, you left me to stand silent upon my bush."

"I did not know that you were ripe," answered the Prince, in a low voice.

"Give me the Star of Royalty!" she commanded.

Slowly he took the shining star from his own brow and placed it upon that of the Princess. Then all the people bowed low to her, and the Prince turned and walked away alone. What became of him afterward our friends never knew.

The people of Mangaboo now formed themselves into a procession and marched toward the glass city to escort their new ruler to her palace and to perform those ceremonies proper to the occasion. But while the people in the procession walked upon the ground the Princess walked in the air just above their heads, to show that she was a superior being and more exalted than her subjects.

No one now seemed to pay any attention to the strangers, so Dorothy and Zeb and the Wizard let the train pass on and then wandered by themselves into the vegetable gardens. They did not bother to cross the bridges over the brooks, but when they came to a stream they stepped high and walked in the air to the other side. This was a very interesting experience to them, and Dorothy said:

"I wonder why it is that we can walk so easily in the air."

"Perhaps," answered the Wizard, "it is because we are close to the center of the earth, where the attraction of gravitation is very slight. But I've noticed that many queer things happen in fairy countries."

"Is this a fairy country?" asked the boy.

"Of course it is," returned Dorothy promptly. "Only a fairy country could have veg'table people; and only in a fairy country could Eureka and Jim talk as we do."

"That's true," said Zeb, thoughtfully.

In the vegetable gardens they found the strawberries and melons, and several other unknown but delicious fruits, of which they ate heartily. But the kitten bothered them constantly by demanding milk or meat, and called the Wizard names because he could not bring her a dish of milk by means of his magical arts.

As they sat upon the grass watching Jim, who was still busily eating, Eureka said: "I don't believe you are a Wizard at all!"

"No," answered the little man, "you are quite right. In the strict sense of the word I am not a Wizard, but only a humbug."

"The Wizard of Oz has always been a humbug," agreed Dorothy. "I've known him for a long time."

"If that is so," said the boy, "how could he do that wonderful trick with the nine tiny piglets?"

"Don't know," said Dorothy, "but it must have been humbug."

"Very true," declared the Wizard, nodding at her. "It was necessary to deceive that ugly Sorcerer and the Prince, as well as their stupid people; but I don't mind telling you, who are my friends, that the thing was only a trick."

"But I saw the little pigs with my own eyes!" exclaimed Zeb.

"So did I," purred the kitten.

"To be sure," answered the Wizard. "You saw them because they were there. They are in my inside pocket now. But the pulling of them apart and pushing them together again was only a sleight-of-hand trick."

"Let's see the pigs," said Eureka, eagerly.

The little man felt carefully in his pocket and pulled out the tiny piglets, setting them upon the grass one by one, where they ran around and nibbled the tender blades.

"They're hungry, too," he said.

"Oh, what cunning things!" cried Dorothy, catching up one and petting it.

"Be careful!" said the piglet, with a squeal, "you're squeezing me!"

"Dear me!" murmured the Wizard, looking at his pets in astonishment. "They can actually talk!"

"May I eat one of them?" asked the kitten, in a pleading voice. "I'm awfully hungry."

"Why, Eureka," said Dorothy, reproachfully, "what a cruel question! It would be dreadful to eat these dear little things."

"I should say so!" grunted another of the piglets, looking uneasily at the kitten; "cats are cruel things."

"I'm not cruel," replied the kitten, yawning. "I'm just hungry."

"You cannot eat my piglets, even if you are starving," declared the little man, in a stern voice. "They are the only things I have to prove I'm a wizard."

"How did they happen to be so little?" asked Dorothy. "I never saw such small pigs before."

"They are from the Island of Teenty-Weent," said the Wizard, "where everything is small because it's a small island. A sailor brought them to Los Angeles and I gave him nine tickets to the circus for them."

"But what am I going to eat?" wailed the kitten, sitting in front of Dorothy and looking pleadingly into her face. "There are no cows here to give milk; or any mice, or even grasshoppers. And if I can't eat the piglets you may as well plant me at once and raise catsup."

"I have an idea," said the Wizard, "that there are fishes in these brooks. Do you like fish?"

"Fish!" cried the kitten. "Do I like fish? Why, they're better than piglets—or even milk!"

"Then I'll try to catch you some," said he.

"But won't they be veg'table, like everything else here?" asked the kitten.

"I think not. Fishes are not animals, and they are as cold and moist as the vegetables themselves. There is no reason, that I can see, why they may not exist in the waters of this strange country."

Then the Wizard bent a pin for a hook and took a long piece of string from his pocket for a fish-line. The only bait he could find was a bright red blossom from a flower; but he knew fishes are easy to fool if anything bright attracts their attention, so he decided to try the blossom. Having thrown the end of his line in the water of a nearby brook he soon felt a sharp tug that told him a fish had bitten and was caught on the bent pin; so the little man drew in the string and, sure enough, the fish came with it and was landed safely on the shore, where it began to flop around in great excitement.

The fish was fat and round, and its scales glistened like beautifully cut jewels set close together; but there was no time to examine it closely, for Eureka made a jump and caught it between her claws, and in a few moments it had entirely disappeared.

"Oh, Eureka!" cried Dorothy, "did you eat the bones?"

"If it had any bones, I ate them," replied the kitten, composedly, as it washed its face after the meal. "But I don't think that fish had any bones, because I didn't feel them scratch my throat."

"You were very greedy," said the girl.

"I was very hungry," replied the kitten.

The little pigs had stood huddled in a group, watching this scene with frightened eyes.

"Cats are dreadful creatures!" said one of them.

"I'm glad we are not fishes!" said another.

"Don't worry," Dorothy murmured, soothingly, "I'll not let the kitten hurt you."

Then she happened to remember that in a corner of her suit-case were one or two crackers that were left over from her luncheon on the train, and she went to the buggy and brought them. Eureka stuck up her nose at such food, but the tiny piglets squealed delightedly at the sight of the crackers and ate them up in a jiffy.

"Now let us go back to the city," suggested the Wizard. "That is, if Jim has had enough of the pink grass."

The cab-horse, who was browsing near, lifted his head with a sigh.

"I've tried to eat a lot while I had the chance," said he, "for it's likely to be a long while between meals in this strange country. But I'm ready to go, now, at any time you wish."

So, after the Wizard had put the piglets back into his inside pocket, where they cuddled up and went to sleep, the three climbed into the buggy and Jim started back to the town.

"Where shall we stay?" asked the girl.

"I think I shall take possession of the House of the Sorcerer," replied the Wizard; "for the Prince said in the presence of his people that he would keep me until they picked another sorcerer, and the new Princess won't know but that we belong here."

They agreed to this plan, and when they reached the great square

Jim drew the buggy into the big door of the domed hall.

"It doesn't look very homelike," said Dorothy, gazing around at the bare room. "But it's a place to stay, anyhow."

"What are those holes up there?" enquired the boy, pointing to some openings that appeared near the top of the dome.

"They look like doorways," said Dorothy; "only there are no stairs to get to them."

"You forget that stairs are unnecessary," observed the Wizard. "Let us walk up, and see where the doors lead to."

With this he began walking in the air toward the high openings, and Dorothy and Zeb followed him. It was the same sort of climb one experiences when walking up a hill, and they were nearly out of breath when they came to the row of openings, which they perceived to be doorways leading into halls in the upper part of the house. Following these halls they discovered many small rooms opening from them, and some were furnished with glass benches, tables and chairs. But there were no beds at all.

"I wonder if these people never sleep," said the girl.

"Why, there seems to be no night at all in this country," Zeb replied. "Those colored suns are exactly in the same place they were when we came, and if there is no sunset there can be no night."

"Very true," agreed the Wizard. "But it is a long time since I have had any sleep, and I'm tired. So I think I shall lie down upon one of these hard glass benches and take a nap."

"I will, too," said Dorothy, and chose a little room at the end of the hall.

Zeb walked down again to unharness Jim, who, when he found himself free, rolled over a few times and then settled down to sleep, with Eureka nestling comfortably beside his big, boney body. Then the boy returned to one of the upper rooms, and in spite of the hardness of the glass bench was soon deep in slumberland.

6. The Mangaboos Prove Dangerous

When the Wizard awoke the six colored suns were shining down upon the Land of the Mangaboos just as they had done ever since his arrival. The little man, having had a good sleep, felt rested and refreshed, and looking through the glass partition of the room he saw Zeb sitting up on his bench and yawning. So the Wizard went in to him.

"Zeb," said he, "my balloon is of no further use in this strange country, so I may as well leave it on the square where it fell. But in the basket-car are some things I would like to keep with me. I wish you would go and fetch my satchel, two lanterns, and a can of kerosene oil that is under the seat. There is nothing else that I care about."

So the boy went willingly upon the errand, and by the time he had returned Dorothy was awake. Then the three held a counsel to decide what they should do next, but could think of no way to better their condition.

"I don't like these veg'table people," said the little girl. "They're cold and flabby, like cabbages, in spite of their prettiness."

"I agree with you. It is because there is no warm blood in them," remarked the Wizard.

"And they have no hearts; so they can't love anyone—not even themselves," declared the boy.

"The Princess is lovely to look at," continued Dorothy, thoughtfully; "but I don't care much for her, after all. If there was any other place to go, I'd like to go there."

"But IS there any other place?" asked the Wizard.

"I don't know," she answered.

Just then they heard the big voice of Jim the cab-horse calling to them, and going to the doorway leading to the dome they found the Princess and a throng of her people had entered the House of the Sorcerer.

So they went down to greet the beautiful vegetable lady, who said to them:

"I have been talking with my advisors about you meat people, and we have decided that you do not belong in the Land of the Mangaboos and must not remain here."

"How can we go away?" asked Dorothy.

"Oh, you cannot go away, of course; so you must be destroyed," was the answer.

"In what way?" enquired the Wizard.

"We shall throw you three people into the Garden of the Twining Vines," said the Princess, "and they will soon crush you and devour your bodies to make themselves grow bigger. The animals you have with you we will drive to the mountains and put into the Black Pit. Then our country will be rid of all its unwelcome visitors."

"But you are in need of a Sorcerer," said the Wizard, "and not one of those growing is yet ripe enough to pick. I am greater than any thorn-covered sorcerer that every grew in your garden. Why destroy me?"

"It is true we need a Sorcerer," acknowledged the Princess, "but I am informed that one of our own will be ready to pick in a few days, to take the place of Gwig, whom you cut in two before it was time for him to be planted. Let us see your arts, and the sorceries you are able to perform. Then I will decide whether to destroy you with the others or not."

At this the Wizard made a bow to the people and repeated his trick of producing the nine tiny piglets and making them disappear again. He did it very cleverly, indeed, and the Princess looked at the strange piglets as if she were as truly astonished as any vegetable person could be. But afterward she said: "I have heard of this wonderful magic. But it accomplishes nothing of value. What else can you do?"

The Wizard tried to think. Then he jointed together the blades of his sword and balanced it very skillfully upon the end of his nose. But even that did not satisfy the Princess.

Just then his eye fell upon the lanterns and the can of kerosene oil which Zeb had brought from the car of his balloon, and he got a clever idea from those commonplace things.

"Your Highness," said he, "I will now proceed to prove my magic by creating two suns that you have never seen before; also I will exhibit a Destroyer much more dreadful that your Clinging Vines."

So he placed Dorothy upon one side of him and the boy upon the other and set a lantern upon each of their heads.

"Don't laugh," he whispered to them, "or you will spoil the effect of my magic."

Then, with much dignity and a look of vast importance upon his wrinkled face, the Wizard got out his match-box and lighted the two lanterns. The glare they made was very small when compared with the radiance of the six great colored suns; but still they gleamed steadily and clearly. The Mangaboos were much impressed because they had never before seen any light that did not come directly from their suns.

Next the Wizard poured a pool of oil from the can upon the glass floor, where it covered quite a broad surface. When he lighted the oil a hundred tongues of flame shot up, and the effect was really imposing.

"Now, Princess," exclaimed the Wizard, "those of your advisors who wished to throw us into the Garden of Clinging Vines must step within this circle of light. If they advised you well, and were in the right, they will not be injured in any way. But if any advised you wrongly, the light will wither him."

The advisors of the Princess did not like this test; but she commanded them to step into the flame and one by one they did so, and were scorched so badly that the air was soon filled with an odor like that of baked potatoes. Some of the Mangaboos fell down and had to be dragged from the fire, and all were so withered that it would be necessary to plant them at once.

"Sir," said the Princess to the Wizard, "you are greater than any Sorcerer we have ever known. As it is evident that my people have advised me wrongly, I will not cast you three people into the dreadful Garden of the Clinging Vines; but your animals must be driven into the Black Pit in the mountain, for my subjects cannot bear to have them around."

The Wizard was so pleased to have saved the two children and himself that he said nothing against this decree; but when the Princess had gone both Jim and Eureka protested they did not want to go to the Black Pit, and Dorothy promised she would do all that she could to save them from such a fate.

For two or three days after this—if we call days the period between sleep, there being no night to divide the hours into days—our friends were not disturbed in any way. They were even permitted to occupy the House of the Sorcerer in peace, as if it had been their own, and to wander in the gardens in search of food.

Once they came near to the enclosed Garden of the Clinging Vines, and walking high into the air looked down upon it with much interest. They saw a mass of tough green vines all matted together and writhing and twisting around like a nest of great snakes. Everything the vines touched they crushed, and our adventurers were indeed thankful to have escaped being cast among them.

Whenever the Wizard went to sleep he would take the nine tiny piglets from his pocket and let them run around on the floor of his room to amuse themselves and get some exercise; and one time they found his glass door ajar and wandered into the hall and then into the bottom part of the great dome, walking through the air as easily as Eureka could. They knew the kitten, by this time, so they scampered over to where she lay beside Jim and commenced to frisk and play with her.

The cab-horse, who never slept long at a time, sat upon his haunches and watched the tiny piglets and the kitten with much approval.

"Don't be rough!" he would call out, if Eureka knocked over one of the round, fat piglets with her paw; but the pigs never minded, and enjoyed the sport very greatly.

Suddenly they looked up to find the room filled with the silent, solemn-eyed Mangaboos. Each of the vegetable folks bore a branch covered with sharp thorns, which was thrust defiantly toward the horse, the kitten and the piglets.

"Here—stop this foolishness!" Jim roared, angrily; but after being pricked once or twice he got upon his four legs and kept out of the way of the thorns.

The Mangaboos surrounded them in solid ranks, but left an opening to the doorway of the hall; so the animals slowly retreated until they were driven from the room and out upon the street. Here were more of the vegetable people with thorns, and silently they urged the now frightened creatures down the street. Jim had to be careful not to step upon the tiny piglets, who scampered under his feet grunting and squealing, while Eureka, snarling and biting at the thorns pushed toward her, also tried to protect the pretty little things from injury. Slowly but steadily the heartless Mangaboos drove them on, until they had passed through the city and the gardens and come to the broad plains leading to the mountain.

"What does all this mean, anyhow?" asked the horse, jumping to escape a thorn.

"Why, they are driving us toward the Black Pit, into which they threatened to cast us," replied the kitten. "If I were as big as you are, Jim, I'd fight these miserable turnip-roots!"

"What would you do?" enquired Jim.

"I'd kick out with those long legs and iron-shod hoofs."

"All right," said the horse; "I'll do it."

An instant later he suddenly backed toward the crowd of Mangaboos and kicked out his hind legs as hard as he could. A dozen of them smashed together and tumbled to the ground, and seeing his success Jim kicked again and again, charging into the vegetable crowd, knocking them in all directions and sending the others scattering to escape his iron heels. Eureka helped him by flying into the faces of the enemy and scratching and biting furiously, and the kitten ruined so many vegetable complexions that the Mangaboos feared her as much as they did the horse.

But the foes were too many to be repulsed for long. They tired Jim and Eureka out, and although the field of battle was thickly covered with mashed and disabled Mangaboos, our animal friends had to give up at last and allow themselves to be driven to the mountain.

7. Into the Black Pit and Out Again

When they came to the mountain it proved to be a rugged, towering chunk of deep green glass, and looked dismal and forbidding in the extreme. Half way up the steep side was a yawning cave, black as night beyond the point where the rainbow rays of the colored suns reached into it.

The Mangaboos drove the horse and the kitten and the piglets into this dark hole and then, having pushed the buggy in after them—for it seemed some of them had dragged it all the way from the domed hall—they began to pile big glass rocks within the entrance, so that the prisoners could not get out again.

"This is dreadful!" groaned Jim. "It will be about the end of our adventures, I guess."

"If the Wizard was here," said one of the piglets, sobbing bitterly, "he would not see us suffer so."

"We ought to have called him and Dorothy when we were first attacked," added Eureka. "But never mind; be brave, my friends, and I will go and tell our masters where you are, and get them to come to your rescue."

The mouth of the hole was nearly filled up now, but the kitten gave a leap through the remaining opening and at once scampered up into the air. The Mangaboos saw her escape, and several of them caught up their thorns and gave chase, mounting through the air after her. Eureka, however, was lighter than the Mangaboos, and while they could mount only about a hundred feet above the earth the kitten found she could go nearly two hundred feet. So she ran along over their heads until she had left them far behind and below and had come to the city and the House of the Sorcerer. There she entered in at Dorothy's window in the dome and aroused her from her sleep.

As soon as the little girl knew what had happened she awakened the Wizard and Zeb, and at once preparations were made to go to the rescue of Jim and the piglets. The Wizard carried his satchel, which was quite heavy, and Zeb carried the two lanterns and the oil can. Dorothy's wicker suit-case was still under the seat of the buggy, and by good fortune the boy had also placed the harness in the buggy when he had taken it off from Jim to let the horse lie down and rest. So there was nothing for the girl to carry but the kitten, which she held close to her bosom and tried to comfort, for its little heart was still beating rapidly.

Some of the Mangaboos discovered them as soon as they left the House of the Sorcerer; but when they started toward the mountain the vegetable people allowed them to proceed without interference, yet followed in a crowd behind them so that they could not go back again.

Before long they neared the Black Pit, where a busy swarm of Mangaboos, headed by their Princess, was engaged in piling up glass rocks before the entrance.

"Stop, I command you!" cried the Wizard, in an angry tone, and at once began pulling down the rocks to liberate Jim and the piglets. Instead of opposing him in this they stood back in silence until he had made a good-sized hole in the barrier, when by order of the Princess they all sprang forward and thrust out their sharp thorns.

Dorothy hopped inside the opening to escape being pricked, and Zeb and the Wizard, after enduring a few stabs from the thorns, were glad to follow her. At once the Mangaboos began piling up the rocks of glass again, and as the little man realized that they were all about to be entombed in the mountain he said to the children:

"My dears, what shall we do? Jump out and fight?"

"What's the use?" replied Dorothy. "I'd as soon die here as live much longer among these cruel and heartless people."

"That's the way I feel about it," remarked Zeb, rubbing his wounds. "I've had enough of the Mangaboos."

"All right," said the Wizard; "I'm with you, whatever you decide. But we can't live long in this cavern, that's certain."

Noticing that the light was growing dim he picked up his nine piglets, patted each one lovingly on its fat little head, and placed them carefully in his inside pocket.

Zeb struck a match and lighted one of the lanterns. The rays of the colored suns were now shut out from them forever, for the last chinks had been filled up in the wall that separated their prison from the Land of the Mangaboos.

"How big is this hole?" asked Dorothy.

"I'll explore it and see," replied the boy.

So he carried the lantern back for quite a distance, while Dorothy and the Wizard followed at his side. The cavern did not come to an end, as they had expected it would, but slanted upward through the great glass mountain, running in a direction that promised to lead them to the side opposite the Mangaboo country.

"It isn't a bad road," observed the Wizard, "and if we followed it it might lead us to some place that is more comfortable than this black pocket we are now in. I suppose the vegetable folk were always afraid to enter this cavern because it is dark; but we have our lanterns to light the way, so I propose that we start out and discover where this tunnel in the mountain leads to."

The others agreed readily to this sensible suggestion, and at once the boy began to harness Jim to the buggy. When all was in readiness the three took their seats in the buggy and Jim started cautiously along the way, Zeb driving while the Wizard and Dorothy each held a lighted lantern so the horse could see where to go.

Sometimes the tunnel was so narrow that the wheels of the buggy grazed the sides; then it would broaden out as wide as a street; but the floor was usually smooth, and for a long time they travelled on without any accident. Jim stopped sometimes to rest, for the climb was rather steep and tiresome.

"We must be nearly as high as the six colored suns, by this time," said Dorothy. "I didn't know this mountain was so tall."

"We are certainly a good distance away from the Land of the Mangaboos," added Zeb; "for we have slanted away from it ever since we started."

But they kept steadily moving, and just as Jim was about tired out with his long journey the way suddenly grew lighter, and Zeb put out the lanterns to save the oil.

To their joy they found it was a white light that now greeted them, for all were weary of the colored rainbow lights which, after a time, had made their eyes ache with their constantly shifting rays. The sides of the tunnel showed before them like the inside of a long spy-glass, and the floor became more level. Jim

hastened his lagging steps at this assurance of a quick relief from the dark passage, and in a few moments more they had emerged from the mountain and found themselves face to face with a new and charming country.

8. The Valley of Voices

By journeying through the glass mountain they had reached a delightful valley that was shaped like the hollow of a great cup, with another rugged mountain showing on the other side of it, and soft and pretty green hills at the ends. It was all laid out into lovely lawns and gardens, with pebble paths leading through them and groves of beautiful and stately trees dotting the landscape here and there. There were orchards, too, bearing luscious fruits that are all unknown in our world. Alluring brooks of crystal water flowed sparkling between their flower-strewn banks, while scattered over the valley were dozens of the quaintest and most picturesque cottages our travelers had ever beheld. None of them were in clusters, such as villages or towns, but each had ample grounds of its own, with orchards and gardens surrounding it.

As the new arrivals gazed upon this exquisite scene they were enraptured by its beauties and the fragrance that permeated the soft air, which they breathed so gratefully after the confined atmosphere of the tunnel. Several minutes were consumed in silent admiration before they noticed two very singular and unusual facts about this valley. One was that it was lighted from some unseen source; for no sun or moon was in the arched blue sky, although every object was flooded with a clear and perfect light. The second and even more singular fact was the absence of any inhabitant of this splendid place. From their elevated position they could overlook the entire valley, but not a single moving object could they see. All appeared mysteriously deserted.

The mountain on this side was not glass, but made of a stone similar to granite. With some difficulty and danger Jim drew the buggy over the loose rocks until he reached the green lawns below, where the paths and orchards and gardens began. The nearest cottage was still some distance away.

"Isn't it fine?" cried Dorothy, in a joyous voice, as she sprang out of the buggy and let Eureka run frolicking over the velvety grass.

"Yes, indeed!" answered Zeb. "We were lucky to get away from those dreadful vegetable people."

"It wouldn't be so bad," remarked the Wizard, gazing around him, "if we were obliged to live here always. We couldn't find a prettier place, I'm sure."

He took the piglets from his pocket and let them run on the grass, and Jim tasted a mouthful of the green blades and declared he was very contented in his new surroundings.

"We can't walk in the air here, though," called Eureka, who had tried it and failed; but the others were satisfied to walk on the ground, and the Wizard said they must be nearer the surface of the earth then they had been in the Mangaboo country, for everything was more homelike and natural.

"But where are the people?" asked Dorothy.

The little man shook his bald head.

"Can't imagine, my dear," he replied.

They heard the sudden twittering of a bird, but could not find the creature anywhere. Slowly they walked along the path toward the nearest cottage, the piglets racing and gambolling beside them and Jim pausing at every step for another mouthful of grass.

Presently they came to a low plant which had broad, spreading leaves, in the center of which grew a single fruit about as large as a peach. The fruit was so daintily colored and so fragrant, and looked so appetizing and delicious that Dorothy stopped and exclaimed: "What is it, do you s'pose?"

The piglets had smelled the fruit quickly, and before the girl could reach out her hand to pluck it every one of the nine tiny ones had rushed in and commenced to devour it with great eagerness.

"It's good, anyway," said Zeb, "or those little rascals wouldn't have gobbled it up so greedily."

"Where are they?" asked Dorothy, in astonishment.

They all looked around, but the piglets had disappeared.

"Dear me!" cried the Wizard; "they must have run away. But I didn't see them go; did you?"

"No!" replied the boy and the girl, together.

"Here,—piggy, piggy, piggy!" called their master, anxiously.

Several squeals and grunts were instantly heard at his feet, but the Wizard could not discover a single piglet.

"Where are you?" he asked.

"Why, right beside you," spoke a tiny voice. "Can't you see us?"

"No," answered the little man, in a puzzled tone.

"We can see you," said another of the piglets.

The Wizard stooped down and put out his hand, and at once felt the small fat body of one of his pets. He picked it up, but could not see what he held.

"It is very strange," said he, soberly. "The piglets have become invisible, in some curious way."

"I'll bet it's because they ate that peach!" cried the kitten.

"It wasn't a peach, Eureka," said Dorothy. "I only hope it wasn't poison."

"It was fine, Dorothy," called one of the piglets.

"We'll eat all we can find of them," said another.

"But WE mus'n't eat them," the Wizard warned the children, "or we too may become invisible, and lose each other. If we come across another of the strange fruit we must avoid it."

Calling the piglets to him he picked them all up, one by one, and put them away in his pocket; for although he could not see them he could feel them, and when he had buttoned his coat he knew they were safe for the present.

The travellers now resumed their walk toward the cottage, which they presently reached. It was a pretty place, with vines growing thickly over the broad front porch. The door stood open and a table was set in the front room, with four chairs drawn up to it. On the table were plates, knives and forks, and dishes of bread, meat and fruits. The meat was smoking hot and the knives and forks were performing strange antics and jumping here and there in quite a puzzling way. But not a single person appeared to be in the room.

"How funny!" exclaimed Dorothy, who with Zeb and the Wizard now stood in the doorway.

A peal of merry laughter answered her, and the knives and forks fell to the plates with a clatter. One of the chairs pushed back from the table, and this was so astonishing and mysterious that Dorothy was almost tempted to run away in fright.

"Here are strangers, mama!" cried the shrill and childish voice of some unseen person.

"So I see, my dear," answered another voice, soft and womanly.

"What do you want?" demanded a third voice, in a stern, gruff accent.

"Well, well!" said the Wizard; "are there really people in this room?"

"Of course," replied the man's voice.

"And—pardon me for the foolish question—but, are you all invisible?"

"Surely," the woman answered, repeating her low, rippling laughter. "Are you surprised that you are unable to see the people of Voe?"

"Why, yes," stammered the Wizard. "All the people I have ever met before were very plain to see."

"Where do you come from, then?" asked the woman, in a curious tone.

"We belong upon the face of the earth," explained the Wizard, "but recently, during an earthquake, we fell down a crack and landed in the Country of the Mangaboos."

"Dreadful creatures!" exclaimed the woman's voice. "I've heard of them."

"They walled us up in a mountain," continued the Wizard; "but we found there was a tunnel through to this side, so we came here. It is a beautiful place. What do you call it?"

"It is the Valley of Voe."

"Thank you. We have seen no people since we arrived, so we came to this house to enquire our way."

"Are you hungry?" asked the woman's voice.

"I could eat something," said Dorothy.

"So could I," added Zeb.

"But we do not wish to intrude, I assure you," the Wizard hastened to say.

"That's all right," returned the man's voice, more pleasantly than before. "You are welcome to what we have."

As he spoke the voice came so near to Zeb that he jumped back in alarm. Two childish voices laughed merrily at this action, and Dorothy was sure they were in no danger among such light-hearted folks, even if those folks couldn't be seen.

"What curious animal is that which is eating the grass on my lawn?" enquired the man's voice.

"That's Jim," said the girl. "He's a horse."

"What is he good for?" was the next question.

"He draws the buggy you see fastened to him, and we ride in the buggy instead of walking," she explained.

"Can he fight?" asked the man's voice.

"No! he can kick pretty hard with his heels, and bite a little; but Jim can't 'zactly fight," she replied.

"Then the bears will get him," said one of the children's voices.

"Bears!" exclaimed Dorothy. "Are these bears here?"

"That is the one evil of our country," answered the invisible man. "Many large and fierce bears roam in the Valley of Voe, and when they can catch any of us they eat us up; but as they cannot see us, we seldom get caught."

"Are the bears invis'ble, too?" asked the girl.

"Yes; for they eat of the dama-fruit, as we all do, and that keeps them from being seen by any eye, whether human or animal."

"Does the dama-fruit grow on a low bush, and look something like a peach?" asked the Wizard.

"Yes," was the reply.

"If it makes you invis'ble, why do you eat it?" Dorothy enquired.

"For two reasons, my dear," the woman's voice answered. "The dama-fruit is the most delicious thing that grows, and when it makes us invisible the bears cannot find us to eat us up. But now, good wanderers, your luncheon is on the table, so please sit down and eat as much as you like."

9. They Fight the Invisible Bears

The strangers took their seats at the table willingly enough, for they were all hungry and the platters were now heaped with good things to eat. In front of each place was a plate bearing one of the delicious dama-fruit, and the perfume that rose from these was so enticing and sweet that they were sorely tempted to eat of them and become invisible.

But Dorothy satisfied her hunger with other things, and her companions did likewise, resisting the temptation.

"Why do you not eat the damas?" asked the woman's voice.

"We don't want to get invis'ble," answered the girl.

"But if you remain visible the bears will see you and devour you," said a girlish young voice, that belonged to one of the children.

"We who live here much prefer to be invisible; for we can still hug and kiss one another, and are quite safe from the bears."

"And we do not have to be so particular about our dress," remarked the man.

"And mama can't tell whether my face is dirty or not!" added the other childish voice, gleefully.

"But I make you wash it, every time I think of it," said the mother; "for it stands to reason your face is dirty, Ianu, whether I can see it or not."

Dorothy laughed and stretched out her hands.

"Come here, please—Ianu and your sister—and let me feel of you," she requested.

They came to her willingly, and Dorothy passed her hands over their faces and forms and decided one was a girl of about her own age and the other a boy somewhat smaller. The girl's hair was soft and fluffy and her skin as smooth as satin. When Dorothy gently touched her nose and ears and lips they seemed to be well and delicately formed.

"If I could see you I am sure you would be beautiful," she declared.

The girl laughed, and her mother said:

"We are not vain in the Valley of Voe, because we can not display our beauty, and good actions and pleasant ways are what make us lovely to our companions. Yet we can see and appreciate the beauties of nature, the dainty flowers and trees, the green fields and the clear blue of the sky."

"How about the birds and beasts and fishes?" asked Zeb.

"The birds we cannot see, because they love to eat of the dama as much as we do; yet we hear their sweet songs and enjoy them. Neither can we see the cruel bears, for they also eat the fruit. But the fishes that swim in our brooks we can see, and often we catch them to eat."

"It occurs to me you have a great deal to make you happy, even while invisible," remarked the Wizard. "Nevertheless, we prefer to remain visible while we are in your valley."

Just then Eureka came in, for she had been until now wandering outside with Jim; and when the kitten saw the table set with food she cried out:

"Now you must feed me, Dorothy, for I'm half starved."

The children were inclined to be frightened by the sight of the small animal, which reminded them of the bears; but Dorothy reassured them by explaining that Eureka was a pet and could do no harm even if she wished to. Then, as the others had by this time moved away from the table, the kitten sprang upon the chair and put her paws upon the cloth to see what there was to eat. To her surprise an unseen hand clutched her and held her suspended in the air. Eureka was frantic with terror, and tried to scratch and bite, so the next moment she was dropped to the floor,

"Did you see that, Dorothy?" she gasped.

"Yes, dear," her mistress replied; "there are people living in this house, although we cannot see them. And you must have better manners, Eureka, or something worse will happen to you."

She placed a plate of food upon the floor and the kitten ate greedily.

"Give me that nice-smelling fruit I saw on the table," she begged, when she had cleaned the plate.

"Those are damas," said Dorothy, "and you must never even taste them, Eureka, or you'll get invis'ble, and then we can't see you at all."

The kitten gazed wistfully at the forbidden fruit.

"Does it hurt to be invis'ble?" she asked.

"I don't know," Dorothy answered; "but it would hurt me dre'fully to lose you."

"Very well, I won't touch it," decided the kitten; "but you must keep it away from me, for the smell is very tempting."

"Can you tell us, sir or ma'am," said the Wizard, addressing the air because he did not quite know where the unseen people stood, "if there is any way we can get out of your beautiful Valley, and on top of the Earth again."

"Oh, one can leave the Valley easily enough," answered the man's voice; "but to do so you must enter a far less pleasant country. As for reaching the top of the earth, I have never heard that it is possible to do that, and if you succeeded in getting there you would probably fall off."

"Oh, no," said Dorothy, "we've been there, and we know."

"The Valley of Voe is certainly a charming place," resumed the Wizard; "but we cannot be contented in any other land than our own, for long. Even if we should come to unpleasant places on our way it is necessary, in order to reach the earth's surface, to keep moving on toward it."

"In that case," said the man, "it will be best for you to cross our Valley and mount the spiral staircase inside the Pyramid Mountain. The top of that mountain is lost in the clouds, and when you reach it you will be in the awful Land of Naught, where the Gargoyles live."

"What are Gargoyles?" asked Zeb.

"I do not know, young sir. Our greatest Champion, Overman-Anu, once climbed the spiral stairway and fought nine days with the Gargoyles before he could escape them and come back; but he could never be induced to describe the dreadful creatures, and soon afterward a bear caught him and ate him up."

The wanders were rather discouraged by this gloomy report, but Dorothy said with a sigh: "If the only way to get home is to meet the Gurgles, then we've got to meet 'em. They can't be worse than the Wicked Witch or the Nome King."

"But you must remember you had the Scarecrow and the Tin Woodman to help you conquer those enemies," suggested the Wizard. "Just now, my dear, there is not a single warrior in your company."

"Oh, I guess Zeb could fight if he had to. Couldn't you, Zeb?" asked the little girl.

"Perhaps; if I had to," answered Zeb, doubtfully.

"And you have the jointed sword that you chopped the veg'table Sorcerer in two with," the girl said to the little man.

"True," he replied; "and in my satchel are other useful things to fight with."

"What the Gargoyles most dread is a noise," said the man's voice. "Our Champion told me that when he shouted his battle-cry the creatures shuddered and drew back, hesitating to continue the combat. But they were in great numbers, and the Champion could not shout much because he had to save his breath for fighting."

"Very good," said the Wizard; "we can all yell better than we can fight, so we ought to defeat the Gargoyles."

"But tell me," said Dorothy, "how did such a brave Champion happen to let the bears eat him? And if he was invis'ble, and the bears invis'ble, who knows that they really ate him up?"

"The Champion had killed eleven bears in his time," returned the unseen man; "and we know this is true because when any creature is dead the invisible charm of the dama-fruit ceases to be active, and the slain one can be plainly seen by all eyes. When the Champion killed a bear everyone could see it; and when the bears killed the Champion we all saw several pieces of him scattered about, which of course disappeared again when the bears devoured them."

They now bade farewell to the kind but unseen people of the cottage, and after the man had called their attention to a high, pyramid-shaped mountain on the opposite side of the Valley, and told them how to travel in order to reach it, they again started upon their journey.

They followed the course of a broad stream and passed several more pretty cottages; but of course they saw no one, nor did any one speak to them. Fruits and flowers grew plentifully all about, and there were many of the delicious damas that the people of Voe were so fond of.

About noon they stopped to allow Jim to rest in the shade of a pretty orchard, and while they plucked and ate some of the cherries and plums that grew there a soft voice suddenly said to them: "There are bears near by. Be careful."

The Wizard got out his sword at once, and Zeb grabbed the horse-whip. Dorothy climbed into the buggy, although Jim had been unharnessed from it and was grazing some distance away.

The owner of the unseen voice laughed lightly and said: "You cannot escape the bears that way."

"How CAN we 'scape?" asked Dorothy, nervously, for an unseen danger is always the hardest to face.

"You must take to the river," was the reply. "The bears will not venture upon the water."

"But we would be drowned!" exclaimed the girl.

"Oh, there is no need of that," said the voice, which from its gentle tones seemed to belong to a young girl. "You are strangers in the Valley of Voe, and do not seem to know our ways; so I will try to save you."

The next moment a broad-leaved plant was jerked from the ground where it grew and held suspended in the air before the Wizard.

"Sir," said the voice, "you must rub these leaves upon the soles of all your feet, and then you will be able to walk upon the water without sinking below the surface. It is a secret the bears do not know, and we people of Voe usually walk upon the water when we travel, and so escape our enemies."

"Thank you!" cried the Wizard, joyfully, and at once rubbed a leaf upon the soles of Dorothy's shoes and then upon his own. The girl took a leaf and rubbed it upon the kitten's paws, and the rest of the plant was handed to Zeb, who, after applying it to his own feet, carefully rubbed it upon all four of Jim's hoofs and then upon the tires of the buggy-wheels. He had nearly finished this last task when a low growling was suddenly heard and the horse began to jump around and kick viciously with his heels.

"Quick! To the water or you are lost!" cried their unseen friend, and without hesitation the Wizard drew the buggy down the bank and out upon the broad river, for Dorothy was still seated in it with Eureka in her arms. They did not sink at all, owing to the virtues of the strange plant they had used, and when the buggy was in the middle of the stream the Wizard returned to the bank to assist Zeb and Jim.

The horse was plunging madly about, and two or three deep gashes appeared upon its flanks, from which the blood flowed freely.

"Run for the river!" shouted the Wizard, and Jim quickly freed himself from his unseen tormenters by a few vicious kicks and then obeyed. As soon as he trotted out upon the surface of the river he found himself safe from pursuit, and Zeb was already running across the water toward Dorothy.

As the little Wizard turned to follow them he felt a hot breath against his cheek and heard a low, fierce growl. At once he began stabbing at the air with his sword, and he knew that he had struck some substance because when he drew back the blade it was dripping with blood. The third time that he thrust out the weapon there was a loud roar and a fall, and suddenly at his feet appeared the form of a great red bear, which was nearly as big as the horse and much stronger and fiercer. The beast was quite dead from the sword thrusts, and after a glance at its terrible claws and sharp teeth the little man turned in a panic and rushed out upon the water, for other menacing growls told him more bears were near.

On the river, however, the adventurers seemed to be perfectly safe. Dorothy and the buggy had floated slowly down stream with the current of the water, and the others made haste to join her. The Wizard opened his satchel and got out some sticking-plaster with which he mended the cuts Jim had received from the claws of the bears.

"I think we'd better stick to the river, after this," said Dorothy. "If our unknown friend hadn't warned us, and told us what to do, we would all be dead by this time."

"That is true," agreed the Wizard, "and as the river seems to be flowing in the direction of the Pyramid Mountain it will be the easiest way for us to travel."

Zeb hitched Jim to the buggy again, and the horse trotted along and drew them rapidly over the smooth water. The kitten was at first dreadfully afraid of getting wet, but Dorothy let her down and soon Eureka was frisking along beside the buggy without being scared a bit. Once a little fish swam too near the surface, and the kitten grabbed it in her mouth and ate it up as quick as a wink; but Dorothy cautioned her to be careful what she ate in this valley of enchantments, and no more fishes were careless enough to swim within reach.

After a journey of several hours they came to a point where the river curved, and they found they must cross a mile or so of the Valley before they came to the Pyramid Mountain. There were few houses in this part, and few orchards or flowers; so our friends feared they might encounter more of the savage bears, which they had learned to dread with all their hearts.

"You'll have to make a dash, Jim," said the Wizard, "and run as fast as you can go."

"All right," answered the horse; "I'll do my best. But you must remember I'm old, and my dashing days are past and gone."

All three got into the buggy and Zeb picked up the reins, though Jim needed no guidance of any sort. The horse was still smarting from the sharp claws of the invisible bears, and as soon as he was on land and headed toward the mountain the thought that more of those fearsome creatures might be near acted as a spur and sent him galloping along in a way that made Dorothy catch her breath.

Then Zeb, in a spirit of mischief, uttered a growl like that of the bears, and Jim pricked up his ears and fairly flew. His boney legs moved so fast they could scarcely be seen, and the Wizard clung fast to the seat and yelled "Whoa!" at the top of his voice.

"I—I'm 'fraid he's—he's running away!" gasped Dorothy.

"I KNOW he is," said Zeb; "but no bear can catch him if he keeps up that gait—and the harness or the buggy don't break."

Jim did not make a mile a minute; but almost before they were aware of it he drew up at the foot of the mountain, so suddenly that the Wizard and Zeb both sailed over the dashboard and landed in the soft grass—where they rolled over several times before they stopped. Dorothy nearly went with them, but she was holding fast to the iron rail of the seat, and that saved her. She squeezed the kitten, though, until it screeched; and then the old cab-horse made several curious sounds that led the little girl to suspect he was laughing at them all.

10. The Braided Man of Pyramid Mountain

The mountain before them was shaped like a cone and was so tall that its point was lost in the clouds. Directly facing the place where Jim had stopped was an arched opening leading to a broad stairway. The stairs were cut in the rock inside the mountain, and they were broad and not very steep, because they circled around like a cork-screw, and at the arched opening where the flight began the circle was quite big. At the foot of stairs was a sign reading:

WARNING. These steps lead to the Land of the Gargoyles. DANGER! KEEP OUT.

"I wonder how Jim is ever going to draw the buggy up so many stairs," said Dorothy, gravely.

"No trouble at all," declared the horse, with a contemptuous neigh. "Still, I don't care to drag any passengers. You'll all have to walk."

"Suppose the stairs get steeper?" suggested Zeb, doubtfully.

"Then you'll have to boost the buggy-wheels, that's all," answered Jim.

"We'll try it, anyway," said the Wizard. "It's the only way to get out of the Valley of Voe."

So they began to ascend the stairs, Dorothy and the Wizard first, Jim next, drawing the buggy, and then Zeb to watch that nothing happened to the harness.

The light was dim, and soon they mounted into total darkness, so that the Wizard was obliged to get out his lanterns to light the way. But this enabled them to proceed steadily until they came to a landing where there was a rift in the side of the mountain that let in both light and air. Looking through this opening they could see the Valley of Voe lying far below them, the cottages seeming like toy houses from that distance.

After resting a few moments they resumed their climb, and still the stairs were broad and low enough for Jim to draw the buggy easily after him. The old horse panted a little, and had to stop often to get his breath. At such times they were all glad to wait for him, for continually climbing up stairs is sure to make one's legs ache.

They wound about, always going upward, for some time. The lights from the lanterns dimly showed the way, but it was a gloomy journey, and they were pleased when a broad streak of light ahead assured them they were coming to a second landing.

Here one side of the mountain had a great hole in it, like the mouth of a cavern, and the stairs stopped at the near edge of the floor and commenced ascending again at the opposite edge.

The opening in the mountain was on the side opposite to the Valley of Voe, and our travellers looked out upon a strange scene. Below them was a vast space, at the bottom of which was a black sea with rolling billows, through which little tongues of flame constantly shot up. Just above them, and almost on a level with their platform, were banks of rolling clouds which constantly shifted position and changed color. The blues and greys were very beautiful, and Dorothy noticed that on the cloud banks sat or reclined fleecy, shadowy forms of beautiful beings who must have been the Cloud Fairies. Mortals who stand upon the earth and look up at the sky cannot often distinguish these forms, but our friends were now so near to the clouds that they observed the dainty fairies very clearly.

"Are they real?" asked Zeb, in an awed voice.

"Of course," replied Dorothy, softly. "They are the Cloud Fairies."

"They seem like open-work," remarked the boy, gazing intently. "If I should squeeze one, there wouldn't be anything left of it."

In the open space between the clouds and the black, bubbling sea far beneath, could be seen an occasional strange bird winging its way swiftly through the air. These birds were of enormous size, and reminded Zeb of the rocs he had read about in the Arabian Nights. They had fierce eyes and sharp talons and beaks, and the children hoped none of them would venture into the cavern.

"Well, I declare!" suddenly exclaimed the little Wizard. "What in the world is this?"

They turned around and found a man standing on the floor in the center of the cave, who bowed very politely when he saw he had attracted their attention. He was a very old man, bent nearly double; but the queerest thing about him was his white hair and beard. These were so long that they reached to his feet, and both the hair and the beard were carefully plaited into many braids, and the end of each braid fastened with a bow of colored ribbon.

"Where did you come from?" asked Dorothy, wonderingly.

"No place at all," answered the man with the braids; "that is, not recently. Once I lived on top the earth, but for many years I have had my factory in this spot—half way up Pyramid Mountain."

"Are we only half way up?" enquired the boy, in a discouraged tone.

"I believe so, my lad," replied the braided man. "But as I have never been in either direction, down or up, since I arrived, I cannot be positive whether it is exactly half way or not."

"Have you a factory in this place?" asked the Wizard, who had been examining the strange personage carefully.

"To be sure," said the other. "I am a great inventor, you must know, and I manufacture my products in this lonely spot."

"What are your products?" enquired the Wizard.

"Well, I make Assorted Flutters for flags and bunting, and a superior grade of Rustles for ladies' silk gowns."

"I thought so," said the Wizard, with a sigh. "May we examine some of these articles?"

"Yes, indeed; come into my shop, please," and the braided man turned and led the way into a smaller cave, where he evidently lived. Here, on a broad shelf, were several cardboard boxes of various sizes, each tied with cotton cord.

"This," said the man, taking up a box and handling it gently, "contains twelve dozen rustles—enough to last any lady a year. Will you buy it, my dear?" he asked, addressing Dorothy.

"My gown isn't silk," she said, smiling.

"Never mind. When you open the box the rustles will escape, whether you are wearing a silk dress or not," said the man, seriously. Then he picked up another box. "In this," he continued, "are many assorted flutters. They are invaluable to make flags flutter on a still day, when there is no wind. You, sir," turning to the Wizard, "ought to have this assortment. Once you have tried my goods I am sure you will never be without them."

"I have no money with me," said the Wizard, evasively.

"I do not want money," returned the braided man, "for I could not spend it in this deserted place if I had it. But I would like very much a blue hair-ribbon. You will notice my braids are tied with yellow, pink, brown, red, green, white and black; but I have no blue ribbons."

"I'll get you one!" cried Dorothy, who was sorry for the poor man; so she ran back to the buggy and took from her suit-case a pretty blue ribbon. It did her good to see how the braided man's eyes sparkled when he received this treasure.

"You have made me very, very happy, my dear!" he exclaimed; and then he insisted on the Wizard taking the box of flutters and the little girl accepting the box of rustles.

"You may need them, some time," he said, "and there is really no use in my manufacturing these things unless somebody uses them."

"Why did you leave the surface of the earth?" enquired the Wizard.

"I could not help it. It is a sad story, but if you will try to restrain your tears I will tell you about it. On earth I was a manufacturer of Imported Holes for American Swiss Cheese, and I will acknowledge that I supplied a superior article, which was in great demand. Also I made pores for porous plasters and high-grade holes for doughnuts and buttons. Finally I invented a new Adjustable Post-hole, which I thought would make my fortune. I manufactured a large quantity of these post-holes, and having no room in which to store them I set them all end to end and put the top one in the ground. That made an extraordinary long hole, as you may imagine, and reached far down into the earth; and, as I leaned over it to try to see to the bottom, I lost my balance and tumbled in. Unfortunately, the hole led directly into the vast space you see outside this mountain; but I managed to catch a point of rock that projected from this cavern, and so saved myself from tumbling headlong into the black waves beneath, where the tongues of flame that dart out would certainly have consumed me. Here, then, I made my home; and although it is a lonely place I amuse myself making rustles and flutters, and so get along very nicely."

When the braided man had completed this strange tale Dorothy nearly laughed, because it was all so absurd; but the Wizard tapped his forehead significantly, to indicate that he thought the poor man was crazy. So they politely bade him good day, and went back to the outer cavern to resume their journey.

11. They Meet the Wooden Gargoyles

Another breathless climb brought our adventurers to a third landing where there was a rift in the mountain. On peering out all they could see was rolling banks of clouds, so thick that they obscured all else.

But the travellers were obliged to rest, and while they were sitting on the rocky floor the Wizard felt in his pocket and brought out the nine tiny piglets. To his delight they were now plainly visible, which proved that they had passed beyond the influence of the magical Valley of Voe.

"Why, we can see each other again!" cried one, joyfully.

"Yes," sighed Eureka; "and I also can see you again, and the sight makes me dreadfully hungry. Please, Mr. Wizard, may I eat just one of the fat little piglets? You'd never miss ONE of them, I'm sure!"

"What a horrid, savage beast!" exclaimed a piglet; "and after we've been such good friends, too, and played with one another!"

"When I'm not hungry, I love to play with you all," said the kitten, demurely; "but when my stomach is empty it seems that nothing would fill it so nicely as a fat piglet."

"And we trusted you so!" said another of the nine, reproachfully.

"And thought you were respectable!" said another.

"It seems we were mistaken," declared a third, looking at the kitten timorously, "no one with such murderous desires should belong to our party, I'm sure."

"You see, Eureka," remarked Dorothy, reprovingly, "you are making yourself disliked. There are certain things proper for kitten to eat; but I never heard of a kitten eating a pig, under ANY cir'stances."

"Did you ever see such little pigs before?" asked the kitten. "They are no bigger than mice, and I'm sure mice are proper for me to eat."

"It isn't the bigness, dear; its the variety," replied the girl. "These are Mr. Wizard's pets, just as you are my pet, and it wouldn't be any more proper for you to eat them than it would be for Jim to eat you."

"And that's just what I shall do if you don't let those little balls of pork alone," said Jim, glaring at the kitten with his round, big eyes. "If you injure any one of them I'll chew you up instantly."

The kitten looked at the horse thoughtfully, as if trying to decide whether he meant it or not.

"In that case," she said, "I'll leave them alone. You haven't many teeth left, Jim, but the few you have are sharp enough to make me shudder. So the piglets will be perfectly safe, hereafter, as far as I am concerned."

"That is right, Eureka," remarked the Wizard, earnestly. "Let us all be a happy family and love one another."

Eureka yawned and stretched herself.

"I've always loved the piglets," she said; "but they don't love me."

"No one can love a person he's afraid of," asserted Dorothy. "If you behave, and don't scare the little pigs, I'm sure they'll grow very fond of you."

The Wizard now put the nine tiny ones back into his pocket and the journey was resumed.

"We must be pretty near the top, now," said the boy, as they climbed wearily up the dark, winding stairway.

"The Country of the Gurgles can't be far from the top of the earth," remarked Dorothy. "It isn't very nice down here. I'd like to get home again, I'm sure."

No one replied to this, because they found they needed all their breath for the climb. The stairs had become narrower and Zeb and the Wizard often had to help Jim pull the buggy from one step to another, or keep it from jamming against the rocky walls.

At last, however, a dim light appeared ahead of them, which grew clearer and stronger as they advanced.

"Thank goodness we're nearly there!" panted the little Wizard.

Jim, who was in advance, saw the last stair before him and stuck his head above the rocky sides of the stairway. Then he halted, ducked down and began to back up, so that he nearly fell with the buggy onto the others.

"Let's go down again!" he said, in his hoarse voice.

"Nonsense!" snapped the tired Wizard. "What's the matter with you, old man?"

"Everything," grumbled the horse. "I've taken a look at this place, and it's no fit country for real creatures to go to. Everything's dead, up there—no flesh or blood or growing thing anywhere."

"Never mind;. we can't turn back," said Dorothy; "and we don't intend to stay there, anyhow."

"It's dangerous," growled Jim, in a stubborn tone.

"See here, my good steed," broke in the Wizard, "little Dorothy and I have been in many queer countries in our travels, and always escaped without harm. We've even been to the marvelous Land of Oz—haven't we, Dorothy?—so we don't much care what the Country of the Gargoyles is like. Go ahead, Jim, and whatever happens we'll make the best of it."

"All right," answered the horse; "this is your excursion, and not mine; so if you get into trouble don't blame me."

With this speech he bent forward and dragged the buggy up the remaining steps. The others followed and soon they were all standing upon a broad platform and gazing at the most curious and startling sight their eyes had ever beheld.

"The Country of the Gargoyles is all wooden!" exclaimed Zeb; and so it was. The ground was sawdust and the pebbles scattered around were hard knots from trees, worn smooth in course of time. There were odd wooden houses, with carved wooden flowers in the front yards. The tree-trunks were of coarse wood, but the leaves of the trees were shavings. The patches of grass were splinters of wood, and where neither grass nor sawdust showed was a solid wooden flooring. Wooden birds fluttered among the trees and wooden cows were browsing upon the wooden grass; but the most amazing things of all were the wooden people—the creatures known as Gargoyles.

These were very numerous, for the place was thickly inhabited, and a large group of the queer people clustered near, gazing sharply upon the strangers who had emerged from the long spiral stairway.

The Gargoyles were very small of stature, being less than three feet in height. Their bodies were round, their legs short and thick and their arms extraordinarily long and stout. Their heads were too big for their bodies and their faces were decidedly ugly to look upon. Some had long, curved noses and chins, small eyes and wide, grinning mouths. Others had flat noses, protruding eyes, and ears that were shaped like those of an elephant. There were many types, indeed, scarcely two being alike; but all were equally disagreeable in appearance. The tops of their heads had no hair, but were carved into a variety of fantastic shapes, some having a row of points or balls around the top, others designs resembling flowers or vegetables, and still others having squares that looked like waffles cut criss-cross on their heads. They all wore short wooden wings which were fastened to their wooden bodies by means of wooden hinges with wooden screws, and with these wings they flew swiftly and noiselessly here and there, their legs being of little use to them.

This noiseless motion was one of the most peculiar things about the Gargoyles. They made no sounds at all, either in flying or trying to speak, and they conversed mainly by means of quick signals made with their wooden fingers or lips. Neither was there any sound to be heard anywhere throughout the wooden country. The birds did not sing, nor did the cows moo; yet there was more than ordinary activity everywhere.

The group of these queer creatures which was discovered clustered near the stairs at first remained staring and motionless, glaring with evil eyes at the intruders who had so suddenly appeared in their land. In turn the Wizard and the children, the horse and the kitten, examined the Gargoyles with the same silent attention.

"There's going to be trouble, I'm sure," remarked the horse. "Unhitch those tugs, Zeb, and set me free from the buggy, so I can fight comfortably."

"Jim's right," sighed the Wizard. "There's going to be trouble, and my sword isn't stout enough to cut up those wooden bodies—so I shall have to get out my revolvers."

He got his satchel from the buggy and, opening it, took out two deadly looking revolvers that made the children shrink back in alarm just to look at.

"What harm can the Gurgles do?" asked Dorothy. "They have no weapons to hurt us with."

"Each of their arms is a wooden club," answered the little man, "and I'm sure the creatures mean mischief, by the looks of their eyes. Even these revolvers can merely succeed in damaging a few of their wooden bodies, and after that we will be at their mercy."

"But why fight at all, in that case?" asked the girl.

"So I may die with a clear conscience," returned the Wizard, gravely. "It's every man's duty to do the best he knows how; and I'm going to do it."

"Wish I had an axe," said Zeb, who by now had unhitched the horse.

"If we had known we were coming we might have brought along several other useful things," responded the Wizard. "But we dropped into this adventure rather unexpectedly."

The Gargoyles had backed away a distance when they heard the sound of talking, for although our friends had spoken in low tones their words seemed loud in the silence surrounding them. But as soon as the conversation ceased, the grinning, ugly creatures arose in a flock and flew swiftly toward the strangers, their long arms stretched out before them like the bowsprits of a fleet of sail-boats. The horse had especially attracted their notice, because it was the biggest and strangest creature they had ever seen; so it became the center of their first attack.

But Jim was ready for them, and when he saw them coming he turned his heels toward them and began kicking out as hard as he could. Crack! crash! bang! went his iron-shod hoofs against the wooden bodies of the Gargoyles, and they were battered right and left with such force that they scattered like straws in the wind. But the noise and clatter seemed as dreadful to them as Jim's heels, for all who were able swiftly turned and flew away to a great distance. The others picked themselves up from the ground one by one and quickly rejoined their fellows, so for a moment the horse thought he had won the fight with ease.

But the Wizard was not so confident.

"Those wooden things are impossible to hurt," he said, "and all the damage Jim has done to them is to knock a few splinters from their noses and ears. That cannot make them look any uglier, I'm sure, and it is my opinion they will soon renew the attack."

"What made them fly away?" asked Dorothy.

"The noise, of course. Don't you remember how the Champion escaped them by shouting his battle-cry?"

"Suppose we escape down the stairs, too," suggested the boy. "We have time, just now, and I'd rather face the invis'ble bears than those wooden imps."

"No," returned Dorothy, stoutly, "it won't do to go back, for then we would never get home. Let's fight it out."

"That is what I advise," said the Wizard. "They haven't defeated us yet, and Jim is worth a whole army."

But the Gargoyles were clever enough not to attack the horse the next time. They advanced in a great swarm, having been joined by many more of their kind, and they flew straight over Jim's head to where the others were standing.

The Wizard raised one of his revolvers and fired into the throng of his enemies, and the shot resounded like a clap of thunder in that silent place.

Some of the wooden beings fell flat upon the ground, where they quivered and trembled in every limb; but most of them managed to wheel and escape again to a distance.

Zeb ran and picked up one of the Gargoyles that lay nearest to him. The top of its head was carved into a crown and the Wizard's bullet had struck it exactly in the left eye, which was a hard wooden knot. Half of the bullet stuck in the wood and half stuck out, so it had been the jar and the sudden noise that had knocked the creature down, more than the fact that it was really hurt. Before this crowned Gargoyle had recovered himself Zeb had wound a strap several times around its body, confining its wings and arms so that it could not move. Then, having tied the wooden creature securely, the boy buckled the strap and tossed his prisoner into the buggy. By that time the others had all retired.

12. A Wonderful Escape

For a while the enemy hesitated to renew the attack. Then a few of them advanced until another shot from the Wizard's revolver made them retreat.

"That's fine," said Zeb. "We've got 'em on the run now, sure enough."

"But only for a time," replied the Wizard, shaking his head gloomily. "These revolvers are good for six shots each, but when those are gone we shall be helpless."

The Gargoyles seemed to realize this, for they sent a few of their band time after time to attack the strangers and draw the fire from the little man's revolvers. In this way none of them was shocked by the dreadful report more than once, for the main band kept far away and each time a new company was sent into the battle. When the Wizard had fired all of his twelve bullets he had caused no damage to the enemy except to stun a few by the noise, and so he as no nearer to victory than in the beginning of the fray.

"What shall we do now?" asked Dorothy, anxiously.

"Let's yell—all together," said Zeb.

"And fight at the same time," added the Wizard. "We will get near Jim, so that he can help us, and each one must take some weapon and do the best he can. I'll use my sword, although it isn't much account in this affair. Dorothy must take her parasol and open it suddenly when the wooden folks attack her. I haven't anything for you, Zeb."

"I'll use the king," said the boy, and pulled his prisoner out of the buggy. The bound Gargoyle's arms extended far out beyond its head, so by grasping its wrists Zeb found the king made a very good club. The boy was strong for one of his years, having always worked upon a farm; so he was likely to prove more dangerous to the enemy than the Wizard.

When the next company of Gargoyles advanced, our adventurers began yelling as if they had gone mad. Even the kitten gave a dreadfully shrill scream and at the same time Jim the cab-horse neighed loudly. This daunted the enemy for a time, but the defenders were soon out of breath. Perceiving this, as well as the fact that there were no more of the awful "bangs" to come from the revolvers, the Gargoyles advanced in a swarm as thick as bees, so that the air was filled with them.

Dorothy squatted upon the ground and put up her parasol, which nearly covered her and proved a great protection. The Wizard's sword-blade snapped into a dozen pieces at the first blow he struck against the wooden people. Zeb pounded away with the Gargoyle he was using as a club until he had knocked down dozens of foes; but at the last they clustered so thickly about him that he no longer had room in which to swing his arms. The horse performed some wonderful kicking and even Eureka assisted when she leaped bodily upon the Gargoyles and scratched and bit at them like a wild-cat.

But all this bravery amounted to nothing at all. The wooden things wound their long arms around Zeb and the Wizard and held them fast. Dorothy was captured in the same way, and numbers of the Gargoyles clung to Jim's legs, so weighting him down that the poor beast was helpless. Eureka made a desperate dash to escape and scampered along the ground like a streak; but a grinning Gargoyle flew after her and grabbed her before she had gone very far.

All of them expected nothing less than instant death; but to their surprise the wooden creatures flew into the air with them and bore them far away, over miles and miles of wooden country, until they came to a wooden city. The houses of this city had many corners, being square and six-sided and eight-sided. They were tower-like in shape and the best of them seemed old and weather-worn; yet all were strong and substantial.

To one of these houses which had neither doors nor windows, but only one broad opening far up underneath the roof, the prisoners were brought by their captors. The Gargoyles roughly pushed them into the opening, where there was a platform, and then flew away and left them. As they had no wings the strangers could not fly away, and if they jumped down from such a height they would surely be killed. The creatures had sense enough to reason that way, and the only mistake they made was in supposing the earth people were unable to overcome such ordinary difficulties.

Jim was brought with the others, although it took a good many Gargoyles to carry the big beast through the air and land him on the high platform, and the buggy was thrust in after him because it belonged to the party and the wooden folks had no idea what it was used for or whether it was alive or not. When Eureka's captor had thrown the kitten after the others the last Gargoyle silently disappeared, leaving our friends to breathe freely once more.

"What an awful fight!" said Dorothy, catching her breath in little gasps.

"Oh, I don't know," purred Eureka, smoothing her ruffled fur with her paw; "we didn't manage to hurt anybody, and nobody managed to hurt us."

"Thank goodness we are together again, even if we are prisoners," sighed the little girl.

"I wonder why they didn't kill us on the spot," remarked Zeb, who had lost his king in the struggle.

"They are probably keeping us for some ceremony," the Wizard answered, reflectively; "but there is no doubt they intend to kill us as dead as possible in a short time."

"As dead as poss'ble would be pretty dead, wouldn't it?" asked Dorothy.

"Yes, my dear. But we have no need to worry about that just now. Let us examine our prison and see what it is like."

The space underneath the roof, where they stood, permitted them to see on all sides of the tall building, and they looked with much curiosity at the city spread out beneath them. Everything visible was made of wood, and the scene seemed stiff and extremely unnatural.

From their platform a stair descended into the house, and the children and the Wizard explored it after lighting a lantern to show them the way. Several stories of empty rooms rewarded their search, but nothing more; so after a time they came back to the platform again. Had there been any doors or windows in the lower rooms, or had not the boards of the house been so thick and stout, escape could have been easy; but to remain down below was like being in a cellar or the hold of a ship, and they did not like the darkness or the damp smell.

In this country, as in all others they had visited underneath the earth's surface, there was no night, a constant and strong light coming from some unknown source. Looking out, they could see into some of the houses near them, where there were open windows in abundance, and were able to mark the forms of the wooden Gargoyles moving about in their dwellings.

"This seems to be their time of rest," observed the Wizard. "All people need rest, even if they are made of wood, and as there is no night here they select a certain time of the day in which to sleep or doze."

"I feel sleepy myself," remarked Zeb, yawning.

"Why, where's Eureka?" cried Dorothy, suddenly.

They all looked around, but the kitten was no place to be seen.

"She's gone out for a walk," said Jim, gruffly.

"Where? On the roof?" asked the girl.

"No; she just dug her claws into the wood and climbed down the sides of this house to the ground."

"She couldn't climb DOWN, Jim," said Dorothy. "To climb means to go up."

"Who said so?" demanded the horse.

"My school-teacher said so; and she knows a lot, Jim."

"To 'climb down' is sometimes used as a figure of speech," remarked the Wizard.

"Well, this was a figure of a cat," said Jim, "and she WENT down, anyhow, whether she climbed or crept."

"Dear me! how careless Eureka is," exclaimed the girl, much distressed. "The Gurgles will get her, sure!"

"Ha, ha!" chuckled the old cab-horse; "they're not 'Gurgles,' little maid; they're Gargoyles."

"Never mind; they'll get Eureka, whatever they're called."

"No they won't," said the voice of the kitten, and Eureka herself crawled over the edge of the platform and sat down quietly upon the floor.

"Wherever have you been, Eureka?" asked Dorothy, sternly.

"Watching the wooden folks. They're too funny for anything, Dorothy. Just now they are all going to bed, and—what do you think?—they unhook the hinges of their wings and put them in a corner until they wake up again."

"What, the hinges?"

"No; the wings."

"That," said Zeb, "explains why this house is used by them for a prison. If any of the Gargoyles act badly, and have to be put in jail, they are brought here and their wings unhooked and taken away from them until they promise to be good."

The Wizard had listened intently to what Eureka had said.

"I wish we had some of those loose wings," he said.

"Could we fly with them?" asked Dorothy.

"I think so. If the Gargoyles can unhook the wings then the power to fly lies in the wings themselves, and not in the wooden bodies of the people who wear them. So, if we had the wings, we could probably fly as well as they do—as least while we are in their country and under the spell of its magic."

"But how would it help us to be able to fly?" questioned the girl.

"Come here," said the little man, and took her to one of the corners of the building. "Do you see that big rock standing on the hillside yonder?" he continued, pointing with his finger.

"Yes; it's a good way off, but I can see it," she replied.

"Well, inside that rock, which reaches up into the clouds, is an archway very much like the one we entered when we climbed the spiral stairway from the Valley of Voe. I'll get my spy-glass, and then you can see it more plainly."

He fetched a small but powerful telescope, which had been in his satchel, and by its aid the little girl clearly saw the opening.

"Where does it lead to?" she asked.

"That I cannot tell," said the Wizard; "but we cannot now be far below the earth's surface, and that entrance may lead to another stairway that will bring us on top of our world again, where we belong. So, if we had the wings, and could escape the Gargoyles, we might fly to that rock and be saved."

"I'll get you the wings," said Zeb, who had thoughtfully listened to all this. "That is, if the kitten will show me where they are."

"But how can you get down?" enquired the girl, wonderingly.

For answer Zeb began to unfasten Jim's harness, strap by strap, and to buckle one piece to another until he had made a long leather strip that would reach to the ground.

"I can climb down that, all right," he said.

"No you can't," remarked Jim, with a twinkle in his round eyes. "You may GO down, but you can only CLIMB up."

"Well, I'll climb up when I get back, then," said the boy, with a laugh. "Now, Eureka, you'll have to show me the way to those wings."

"You must be very quiet," warned the kitten; "for if you make the least noise the Gargoyles will wake up. They can hear a pin drop."

"I'm not going to drop a pin," said Zeb.

He had fastened one end of the strap to a wheel of the buggy, and now he let the line dangle over the side of the house.

"Be careful," cautioned Dorothy, earnestly.

"I will," said the boy, and let himself slide over the edge.

The girl and the Wizard leaned over and watched Zeb work his way carefully downward, hand over hand, until he stood upon the ground below. Eureka clung with her claws to the wooden side of the house and let herself down easily. Then together they crept away to enter the low doorway of a neighboring dwelling.

The watchers waited in breathless suspense until the boy again appeared, his arms now full of the wooden wings.

When he came to where the strap was hanging he tied the wings all in a bunch to the end of the line, and the Wizard drew them up. Then the line was let down again for Zeb to climb up by. Eureka quickly followed him, and soon they were all standing together upon the platform, with eight of the much prized wooden wings beside them.

The boy was no longer sleepy, but full of energy and excitement. He put the harness together again and hitched Jim to the buggy. Then, with the Wizard's help, he tried to fasten some of the wings to the old cab-horse.

This was no easy task, because half of each one of the hinges of the wings was missing, it being still fastened to the body of the

Gargoyle who had used it. However, the Wizard went once more to his satchel— which seemed to contain a surprising variety of odds and ends—and brought out a spool of strong wire, by means of which they managed to fasten four of the wings to Jim's harness, two near his head and two near his tail. They were a bit wiggley, but secure enough if only the harness held together.

The other four wings were then fastened to the buggy, two on each side, for the buggy must bear the weight of the children and the Wizard as it flew through the air.

These preparations had not consumed a great deal of time, but the sleeping Gargoyles were beginning to wake up and move around, and soon some of them would be hunting for their missing wings. So the prisoners resolved to leave their prison at once.

They mounted into the buggy, Dorothy holding Eureka safe in her lap. The girl sat in the middle of the seat, with Zeb and the Wizard on each side of her. When all was ready the boy shook the reins and said:

"Fly away, Jim!"

"Which wings must I flap first?" asked the cab-horse undecidedly.

"Flap them all together," suggested the Wizard.

"Some of them are crooked," objected the horse.

"Never mind; we will steer with the wings on the buggy," said Zeb. "Just you light out and make for that rock, Jim; and don't waste any time about it, either."

So the horse gave a groan, flapped its four wings all together and flew away from the platform. Dorothy was a little anxious about the success of their trip, for the way Jim arched his long neck and spread out his bony legs as he fluttered and floundered through the air was enough to make anybody nervous. He groaned, too, as if frightened, and the wings creaked dreadfully because the Wizard had forgotten to oil them; but they kept fairly good time with the wings of the buggy, so that they made excellent progress from the start. The only thing that anyone could complain of with justice was the fact that they wobbled first up and then down, as if the road were rocky instead of being as smooth as the air could make it.

The main point, however, was that they flew, and flew swiftly, if a bit unevenly, toward the rock for which they had headed.

Some of the Gargoyles saw them, presently, and lost no time in collecting a band to pursue the escaping prisoners; so that when Dorothy happened to look back she saw them coming in a great cloud that almost darkened the sky.

13. The Den of the Dragonettes

Our friends had a good start and were able to maintain it, for with their eight wings they could go just as fast as could the Gargoyles. All the way to the great rock the wooden people followed them, and when Jim finally alighted at the mouth of the cavern the pursuers were still some distance away.

"But, I'm afraid they'll catch us yet," said Dorothy, greatly excited.

"No; we must stop them," declared the Wizard. "Quick Zeb, help me pull off these wooden wings!"

They tore off the wings, for which they had no further use, and the Wizard piled them in a heap just outside the entrance to the cavern. Then he poured over them all the kerosene oil that was left in his oil-can, and lighting a match set fire to the pile.

The flames leaped up at once and the bonfire began to smoke and roar and crackle just as the great army of wooden Gargoyles arrived. The creatures drew back at once, being filled with fear and horror; for such as dreadful thing as a fire they had never before known in all the history of their wooden land.

Inside the archway were several doors, leading to different rooms built into the mountain, and Zeb and the Wizard lifted these wooden doors from their hinges and tossed them all on the flames.

"That will prove a barrier for some time to come," said the little man, smiling pleasantly all over his wrinkled face at the success of their stratagem. "Perhaps the flames will set fire to all that miserable wooden country, and if it does the loss will be very small and the Gargoyles never will be missed. But come, my children; let us explore the mountain and discover which way we must go in order to escape from this cavern, which is getting to be almost as hot as a bake-oven."

To their disappointment there was within this mountain no regular flight of steps by means of which they could mount to the earth's surface. A sort of inclined tunnel led upward for a way, and they found the floor of it both rough and steep. Then a sudden turn brought them to a narrow gallery where the buggy could not pass. This delayed and bothered them for a while, because they did not wish to leave the buggy behind them. It carried their baggage and was useful to ride in wherever there were good roads, and since it had accompanied them so far in their travels they felt it their duty to preserve it. So Zeb and the Wizard set to work and took off the wheels and the top, and then they put the buggy edgewise, so it would take up the smallest space. In this position they managed, with the aid of the patient cab-horse, to drag the vehicle through the narrow part of the passage. It was not a great distance, fortunately, and when the path grew broader they put the buggy together again and proceeded more comfortably. But the road was nothing more than a series of rifts or cracks in the mountain, and it went zig-zag in every direction, slanting first up and then down until they were puzzled as to whether they were any nearer to the top of the earth than when they had started, hours before.

"Anyhow," said Dorothy, "we've 'scaped those awful Gurgles, and that's ONE comfort!"

"Probably the Gargoyles are still busy trying to put out the fire," returned the Wizard. "But even if they succeeded in doing that it would be very difficult for them to fly amongst these rocks; so I am sure we need fear them no longer."

Once in a while they would come to a deep crack in the floor, which made the way quite dangerous; but there was still enough oil in the lanterns to give them light, and the cracks were not so wide but that they were able to jump over them. Sometimes they had to climb over heaps of loose rock, where Jim could scarcely drag the buggy. At such times Dorothy, Zeb and the Wizard all pushed behind, and lifted the wheels over the roughest places; so they managed, by dint of hard work, to keep going. But the little party was both weary and discouraged when at last, on turning a sharp corner, the wanderers found themselves in a vast cave arching high over their heads and having a smooth, level floor.

The cave was circular in shape, and all around its edge, near to the ground, appeared groups of dull yellow lights, two of them being always side by side. These were motionless at first, but soon began to flicker more brightly and to sway slowly from side to side and then up and down.

"What sort of place is this?" asked the boy, trying to see more clearly through the gloom.

"I cannot imagine, I'm sure," answered the Wizard, also peering about.

"Woogh!" snarled Eureka, arching her back until her hair stood straight on end; "it's den of alligators, or crocodiles, or some other dreadful creatures! Don't you see their terrible eyes?"

"Eureka sees better in the dark than we can," whispered Dorothy. "Tell us, dear, what do the creatures look like?" she asked, addressing her pet.

"I simply can't describe 'em," answered the kitten, shuddering. "Their eyes are like pie-plates and their mouths like coal-scuttles. But their bodies don't seem very big."

"Where are they?" enquired the girl.

"They are in little pockets all around the edge of this cavern. Oh, Dorothy—you can't imagine what horrid things they are! They're uglier than the Gargoyles."

"Tut-tut! be careful how you criticise your neighbors," spoke a rasping voice near by. "As a matter of fact you are rather ugly-looking creatures yourselves, and I'm sure mother has often told us we were the loveliest and prettiest things in all the world."

Hearing these words our friends turned in the direction of the sound, and the Wizard held his lanterns so that their light would flood one of the little pockets in the rock.

"Why, it's a dragon!" he exclaimed.

"No," answered the owner of the big yellow eyes which were blinking at them so steadily; "you are wrong about that. We hope to grow to be dragons some day, but just now we're only dragonettes."

"What's that?" asked Dorothy, gazing fearfully at the great scaley head, the yawning mouth and the big eyes.

"Young dragons, of course; but we are not allowed to call ourselves real dragons until we get our full growth," was the reply. "The big dragons are very proud, and don't think children amount to much; but mother says that some day we will all be very powerful and important."

"Where is your mother?" asked the Wizard, anxiously looking around.

"She has gone up to the top of the earth to hunt for our dinner. If she has good luck she will bring us an elephant, or a brace of rhinoceri, or perhaps a few dozen people to stay our hunger."

"Oh; are you hungry?" enquired Dorothy, drawing back.

"Very," said the dragonette, snapping its jaws.

"And—and—do you eat people?"

"To be sure, when we can get them. But they've been very scarce for a few years and we usually have to be content with elephants or buffaloes," answered the creature, in a regretful tone.

"How old are you?" enquired Zeb, who stared at the yellow eyes as if fascinated.

"Quite young, I grieve to say; and all of my brothers and sisters that you see here are practically my own age. If I remember rightly, we were sixty-six years old the day before yesterday."

"But that isn't young!" cried Dorothy, in amazement.

"No?" drawled the dragonette; "it seems to me very babyish."

"How old is your mother?" asked the girl.

"Mother's about two thousand years old; but she carelessly lost track of her age a few centuries ago and skipped several hundreds. She's a little fussy, you know, and afraid of growing old, being a widow and still in her prime."

"I should think she would be," agreed Dorothy. Then, after a moment's thought, she asked: "Are we friends or enemies? I mean, will you be good to us, or do you intend to eat us?"

"As for that, we dragonettes would love to eat you, my child; but unfortunately mother has tied all our tails around the rocks at the back of our individual caves, so that we can not crawl out to get you. If you choose to come nearer we will make a mouthful of you in a wink; but unless you do you will remain quite safe."

There was a regretful accent in the creature's voice, and at the words all the other dragonettes sighed dismally.

Dorothy felt relieved. Presently she asked:

"Why did your mother tie your tails?"

"Oh, she is sometimes gone for several weeks on her hunting trips, and if we were not tied we would crawl all over the mountain and fight with each other and get into a lot of mischief. Mother usually knows what she is about, but she made a mistake this time; for you are sure to escape us unless you come too near, and you probably won't do that."

"No, indeed!" said the little girl. "We don't wish to be eaten by such awful beasts."

"Permit me to say," returned the dragonette, "that you are rather impolite to call us names, knowing that we cannot resent your insults. We consider ourselves very beautiful in appearance, for mother has told us so, and she knows. And we are of an excellent family and have a pedigree that I challenge any humans to equal, as it extends back about twenty thousand years, to the time of the famous Green Dragon of Atlantis, who lived in a time when humans had not yet been created. Can you match that pedigree, little girl?"

"Well," said Dorothy, "I was born on a farm in Kansas, and I guess that's being just as 'spectable and haughty as living in a cave with your tail tied to a rock. If it isn't I'll have to stand it, that's all."

"Tastes differ," murmured the dragonette, slowly drooping its scaley eyelids over its yellow eyes, until they looked like half-moons.

Being reassured by the fact that the creatures could not crawl out of their rock-pockets, the children and the Wizard now took time to examine them more closely. The heads of the dragonettes were as big as barrels and covered with hard, greenish scales that glittered brightly under the light of the lanterns. Their front legs, which grew just back of their heads, were also strong and big; but their bodies were smaller around than their heads, and dwindled away in a long line until their tails were slim as a shoe-string. Dorothy thought, if it had taken them sixty-six years to grow to this size, that it would be fully a hundred years more before they could hope to call themselves dragons, and that seemed like a good while to wait to grow up.

"It occurs to me," said the Wizard, "that we ought to get out of this place before the mother dragon comes back."

"Don't hurry," called one of the dragonettes; "mother will be glad to meet you, I'm sure."

"You may be right," replied the Wizard, "but we're a little particular about associating with strangers. Will you kindly tell us which way your mother went to get on top the earth?"

"That is not a fair question to ask us," declared another dragonette. "For, if we told you truly, you might escape us altogether; and if we told you an untruth we would be naughty and deserve to be punished."

"Then," decided Dorothy, "we must find our way out the best we can."

They circled all around the cavern, keeping a good distance away from the blinking yellow eyes of the dragonettes, and presently discovered that there were two paths leading from the wall opposite to the place where they had entered. They selected one of these at a venture and hurried along it as fast as they could go, for they had no idea when the mother dragon would be back and were very anxious not to make her acquaintance.

14. Ozma Uses the Magic Belt

For a considerable distance the way led straight upward in a gentle incline, and the wanderers made such good progress that they grew hopeful and eager, thinking they might see sunshine at any minute. But at length they came unexpectedly upon a huge rock that shut off the passage and blocked them from proceeding a single step farther.

This rock was separate from the rest of the mountain and was in motion, turning slowly around and around as if upon a pivot. When first they came to it there was a solid wall before them; but presently it revolved until there was exposed a wide, smooth path across it to the other side. This appeared so unexpectedly that they were unprepared to take advantage of it at first, and allowed the rocky wall to swing around again before they had decided to pass over. But they knew now that there was a means of escape and so waited patiently until the path appeared for the second time.

The children and the Wizard rushed across the moving rock and sprang into the passage beyond, landing safely though a little out of breath. Jim the cab-horse came last, and the rocky wall almost caught him; for just as he leaped to the floor of the further passage the wall swung across it and a loose stone that the buggy wheels knocked against fell into the narrow crack where the rock turned, and became wedged there.

They heard a crunching, grinding sound, a loud snap, and the turn-table came to a stop with its broadest surface shutting off the path from which they had come.

"Never mind," said Zeb, "we don't want to get back, anyhow."

"I'm not so sure of that," returned Dorothy. "The mother dragon may come down and catch us here."

"It is possible," agreed the Wizard, "if this proves to be the path she usually takes. But I have been examining this tunnel, and I do not see any signs of so large a beast having passed through it."

"Then we're all right," said the girl, "for if the dragon went the other way she can't poss'bly get to us now."

"Of course not, my dear. But there is another thing to consider. The mother dragon probably knows the road to the earth's surface, and if she went the other way then we have come the wrong way," said the Wizard, thoughtfully.

"Dear me!" cried Dorothy. "That would be unlucky, wouldn't it?"

"Very. Unless this passage also leads to the top of the earth," said Zeb. "For my part, if we manage to get out of here I'll be glad it isn't the way the dragon goes."

"So will I," returned Dorothy. "It's enough to have your pedigree flung in your face by those saucy dragonettes. No one knows what the mother might do."

They now moved on again, creeping slowly up another steep incline. The lanterns were beginning to grow dim, and the Wizard poured the remaining oil from one into the other, so that the one light would last longer. But their journey was almost over, for in a short time they reached a small cave from which there was no further outlet.

They did not realize their ill fortune at first, for their hearts were gladdened by the sight of a ray of sunshine coming through a small crack in the roof of the cave, far overhead. That meant that their world—the real world—was not very far away, and that the succession of perilous adventures they had encountered had at last brought them near the earth's surface, which meant home to them. But when the adventurers looked more carefully around them they discovered that there were in a strong prison from which there was no hope of escape.

"But we're ALMOST on earth again," cried Dorothy, "for there is the sun—the most BEAU'FUL sun that shines!" and she pointed eagerly at the crack in the distant roof.

"Almost on earth isn't being there," said the kitten, in a discontented tone. "It wouldn't be possible for even me to get up to that crack—or through it if I got there."

"It appears that the path ends here," announced the Wizard, gloomily.

"And there is no way to go back," added Zeb, with a low whistle of perplexity.

"I was sure it would come to this, in the end," remarked the old cab-horse. "Folks don't fall into the middle of the earth and then get back again to tell of their adventures—not in real life. And the whole thing has been unnatural because that cat and I are both able to talk your language, and to understand the words you say."

"And so can the nine tiny piglets," added Eureka. "Don't forget them, for I may have to eat them, after all."

"I've heard animals talk before," said Dorothy, "and no harm came of it."

"Were you ever before shut up in a cave, far under the earth, with no way of getting out?" enquired the horse, seriously.

"No," answered Dorothy. "But don't you lose heart, Jim, for I'm sure this isn't the end of our story, by any means."

The reference to the piglets reminded the Wizard that his pets had not enjoyed much exercise lately, and must be tired of their prison in his pocket. So he sat down upon the floor of the cave, brought the piglets out one by one, and allowed them to run around as much as they pleased.

"My dears," he said to them, "I'm afraid I've got you into a lot of trouble, and that you will never again be able to leave this gloomy cave."

"What's wrong?" asked a piglet. "We've been in the dark quite a while, and you may as well explain what has happened."

The Wizard told them of the misfortune that had overtaken the wanderers.

"Well," said another piglet, "you are a wizard, are you not?"

"I am," replied the little man.

"Then you can do a few wizzes and get us out of this hole," declared the tiny one, with much confidence.

"I could if I happened to be a real wizard," returned the master sadly. "But I'm not, my piggy-wees; I'm a humbug wizard."

"Nonsense!" cried several of the piglets, together.

"You can ask Dorothy," said the little man, in an injured tone.

"It's true enough," returned the girl, earnestly. "Our friend Oz is merely a humbug wizard, for he once proved it to me. He can do several very wonderful things—if he knows how. But he can't wiz a single thing if he hasn't the tools and machinery to work with."

"Thank you, my dear, for doing me justice," responded the Wizard, gratefully. "To be accused of being a real wizard, when I'm not, is a slander I will not tamely submit to. But I am one of the greatest humbug wizards that ever lived, and you will realize this when we have all starved together and our bones are scattered over the floor of this lonely cave."

"I don't believe we'll realize anything, when it comes to that," remarked Dorothy, who had been deep in thought. "But I'm not going to scatter my bones just yet, because I need them, and you prob'ly need yours, too."

"We are helpless to escape," sighed the Wizard.

"WE may be helpless," answered Dorothy, smiling at him, "but there are others who can do more than we can. Cheer up, friends. "I'm sure Ozma will help us."

"Ozma!" exclaimed the Wizard. "Who is Ozma?"

"The girl that rules the marvelous Land of Oz," was the reply. "She's a friend of mine, for I met her in the Land of Ev, not long ago, and went to Oz with her."

"For the second time?" asked the Wizard, with great interest.

"Yes. The first time I went to Oz I found you there, ruling the Emerald City. After you went up in a balloon, and escaped us, I got back to Kansas by means of a pair of magical silver shoes."

"I remember those shoes," said the little man, nodding. "They once belonged to the Wicked Witch. Have you them here with you?"

"No; I lost them somewhere in the air," explained the child. "But the second time I went to the Land of Oz I owned the Nome King's Magic Belt, which is much more powerful than were the Silver Shoes."

"Where is that Magic Belt?" enquired the Wizard, who had listened with great interest.

"Ozma has it; for its powers won't work in a common, ordinary country like the United States. Anyone in a fairy country like the Land of Oz can do anything with it; so I left it with my friend the Princess Ozma, who used it to wish me in Australia with Uncle Henry."

"And were you?" asked Zeb, astonished at what he heard.

"Of course; in just a jiffy. And Ozma has an enchanted picture hanging in her room that shows her the exact scene where any of her friends may be, at any time she chooses. All she has to do is to say: 'I wonder what So-and-so is doing,' and at once the picture shows where her friend is and what the friend is doing. That's REAL magic, Mr. Wizard; isn't it? Well, every day at four o'clock Ozma has promised to look at me in that picture, and if I am in need of help I am to make her a certain sign and she will put on the Nome King's Magic Belt and wish me to be with her in Oz."

"Do you mean that Princess Ozma will see this cave in her enchanted picture, and see all of us here, and what we are doing?" demanded Zeb.

"Of course; when it is four o'clock," she replied, with a laugh at his startled expression.

"And when you make a sign she will bring you to her in the Land of Oz?" continued the boy.

"That's it, exactly; by means of the Magic Belt."

"Then," said the Wizard, "you will be saved, little Dorothy; and I am very glad of it. The rest of us will die much more cheerfully when we know you have escaped our sad fate."

"I won't die cheerfully!" protested the kitten. "There's nothing cheerful about dying that I could ever see, although they say a cat has nine lives, and so must die nine times."

"Have you ever died yet?" enquired the boy.

"No, and I'm not anxious to begin," said Eureka.

"Don't worry, dear," Dorothy exclaimed, "I'll hold you in my arms, and take you with me."

"Take us, too!" cried the nine tiny piglets, all in one breath.

"Perhaps I can," answered Dorothy. "I'll try."

"Couldn't you manage to hold me in your arms?" asked the cab-horse.

Dorothy laughed.

"I'll do better than that," she promised, "for I can easily save you all, once I am myself in the Land of Oz."

"How?" they asked.

"By using the Magic Belt. All I need do is to wish you with me, and there you'll be—safe in the royal palace!"

"Good!" cried Zeb.

"I built that palace, and the Emerald City, too," remarked the Wizard, in a thoughtful tone, "and I'd like to see them again, for I was very happy among the Munchkins and Winkies and Quadlings and Gillikins."

"Who are they?" asked the boy.

"The four nations that inhabit the Land of Oz," was the reply. "I wonder if they would treat me nicely if I went there again."

"Of course they would!" declared Dorothy. "They are still proud of their former Wizard, and often speak of you kindly."

"Do you happen to know whatever became of the Tin Woodman and the Scarecrow?" he enquired.

"They live in Oz yet," said the girl, "and are very important people."

"And the Cowardly Lion?"

"Oh, he lives there too, with his friend the Hungry Tiger; and Billina is there, because she liked the place better than Kansas and wouldn't go with me to Australia."

"I'm afraid I don't know the Hungry Tiger and Billina," said the Wizard, shaking his head. "Is Billina a girl?"

"No; she's a yellow hen, and a great friend of mine. You're sure to like Billina, when you know her," asserted Dorothy.

"Your friends sound like a menagerie," remarked Zeb, uneasily. "Couldn't you wish me in some safer place than Oz."

"Don't worry," replied the girl. "You'll just love the folks in Oz when you get acquainted. What time is it, Mr. Wizard?"

The little man looked at his watch—a big silver one that he carried in his vest pocket.

"Half-past three," he said.

"Then we must wait for half an hour," she continued; "but it won't take long, after that, to carry us all to the Emerald City."

They sat silently thinking for a time. Then Jim suddenly asked:

"Are there any horses in Oz?"

"Only one," replied Dorothy, "and he's a sawhorse."

"A what?"

"A sawhorse. Princess Ozma once brought him to life with a witch-powder, when she was a boy."

"Was Ozma once a boy?" asked Zeb, wonderingly.

"Yes; a wicked witch enchanted her, so she could not rule her kingdom. But she's a girl now, and the sweetest, loveliest girl in all the world."

"A sawhorse is a thing they saw boards on," remarked Jim, with a sniff.

"It is when it's not alive," acknowledged the girl. "But this sawhorse can trot as fast as you can, Jim; and he's very wise, too."

"Pah! I'll race the miserable wooden donkey any day in the week!" cried the cab-horse.

Dorothy did not reply to that. She felt that Jim would know more about the Saw-Horse later on.

The time dragged wearily enough to the eager watchers, but finally the Wizard announced that four o'clock had arrived, and Dorothy caught up the kitten and began to make the signal that had been agreed upon to the far-away invisible Ozma.

"Nothing seems to happen," said Zeb, doubtfully.

"Oh, we must give Ozma time to put on the Magic Belt," replied the girl.

She had scarcely spoken the words then she suddenly disappeared from the cave, and with her went the kitten. There had been no sound of any kind and no warning. One moment Dorothy sat beside them with the kitten in her lap, and a moment later the horse, the piglets, the Wizard and the boy were all that remained in the underground prison.

"I believe we will soon follow her," announced the Wizard, in a tone of great relief; "for I know something about the magic of the fairyland that is called the Land of Oz. Let us be ready, for we may be sent for any minute."

He put the piglets safely away in his pocket again and then he and Zeb got into the buggy and sat expectantly upon the seat.

"Will it hurt?" asked the boy, in a voice that trembled a little.

"Not at all," replied the Wizard. "It will all happen as quick as a wink."

And that was the way it did happen.

The cab-horse gave a nervous start and Zeb began to rub his eyes to make sure he was not asleep. For they were in the streets of a beautiful emerald-green city, bathed in a grateful green light that was especially pleasing to their eyes, and surrounded by merry faced people in gorgeous green-and-gold costumes of many extraordinary designs.

Before them were the jewel-studded gates of a magnificent palace, and now the gates opened slowly as if inviting them to enter the courtyard, where splendid flowers were blooming and pretty fountains shot their silvery sprays into the air.

Zeb shook the reins to rouse the cab-horse from his stupor of amazement, for the people were beginning to gather around and stare at the strangers.

"Gid-dap!" cried the boy, and at the word Jim slowly trotted into the courtyard and drew the buggy along the jewelled driveway to the great entrance of the royal palace.

15. Old Friends are Reunited

Many servants dressed in handsome uniforms stood ready to welcome the new arrivals, and when the Wizard got out of the buggy a pretty girl in a green gown cried out in surprise:

"Why, it's Oz, the Wonderful Wizard, come back again!"

The little man looked at her closely and then took both the maiden's hands in his and shook them cordially.

"On my word," he exclaimed, "it's little Jellia Jamb—as pert and pretty as ever!"

"Why not, Mr. Wizard?" asked Jellia, bowing low. "But I'm afraid you cannot rule the Emerald City, as you used to, because we now have a beautiful Princess whom everyone loves dearly."

"And the people will not willingly part with her," added a tall soldier in a Captain-General's uniform.

The Wizard turned to look at him.

"Did you not wear green whiskers at one time?" he asked.

"Yes," said the soldier; "but I shaved them off long ago, and since then I have risen from a private to be the Chief General of the Royal Armies."

"That's nice," said the little man. "But I assure you, my good people, that I do not wish to rule the Emerald City," he added, earnestly.

"In that case you are very welcome!" cried all the servants, and it pleased the Wizard to note the respect with which the royal retainers bowed before him. His fame had not been forgotten in the Land of Oz, by any means.

"Where is Dorothy?" enquired Zeb, anxiously, as he left the buggy and stood beside his friend the little Wizard.

"She is with the Princess Ozma, in the private rooms of the palace," replied Jellia Jamb. "But she has ordered me to make you welcome and to show you to your apartments."

The boy looked around him with wondering eyes. Such magnificence and wealth as was displayed in this palace was more than he had ever dreamed of, and he could scarcely believe that all the gorgeous glitter was real and not tinsel.

"What's to become of me?" asked the horse, uneasily. He had seen considerable of life in the cities in his younger days, and knew that this regal palace was no place for him.

It perplexed even Jellia Jamb, for a time, to know what to do with the animal. The green maiden was much astonished at the sight of so unusual a creature, for horses were unknown in this

Land; but those who lived in the Emerald City were apt to be astonished by queer sights, so after inspecting the cab-horse and noting the mild look in his big eyes the girl decided not to be afraid of him.

"There are no stables here," said the Wizard, "unless some have been built since I went away."

"We have never needed them before," answered Jellia; "for the Sawhorse lives in a room of the palace, being much smaller and more natural in appearance than this great beast you have brought with you."

"Do you mean that I'm a freak?" asked Jim, angrily.

"Oh, no," she hastened to say, "there may be many more like you in the place you came from, but in Oz any horse but a Sawhorse is unusual."

This mollified Jim a little, and after some thought the green maiden decided to give the cab-horse a room in the palace, such a big building having many rooms that were seldom in use.

So Zeb unharnessed Jim, and several of the servants then led the horse around to the rear, where they selected a nice large apartment that he could have all to himself.

Then Jellia said to the Wizard: "Your own room—which was back of the great Throne Room—has been vacant ever since you left us. Would you like it again?"

"Yes, indeed!" returned the little man. "It will seem like being at home again, for I lived in that room for many, many years."

He knew the way to it, and a servant followed him, carrying his satchel. Zeb was also escorted to a room—so grand and beautiful that he almost feared to sit in the chairs or lie upon the bed, lest he might dim their splendor. In the closets he discovered many fancy costumes of rich velvets and brocades, and one of the attendants told him to dress himself in any of the clothes that pleased him and to be prepared to dine with the Princess and Dorothy in an hour's time.

Opening from the chamber was a fine bathroom having a marble tub with perfumed water; so the boy, still dazed by the novelty of his surroundings, indulged in a good bath and then selected a maroon velvet costume with silver buttons to replace his own soiled and much worn clothing. There were silk stockings and soft leather slippers with diamond buckles to accompany his new costume, and when he was fully dressed Zeb looked much more dignified and imposing than ever before in his life.

He was all ready when an attendant came to escort him to the presence of the Princess; he followed bashfully and was ushered into a room more dainty and attractive than it was splendid. Here he found Dorothy seated beside a young girl so marvelously beautiful that the boy stopped suddenly with a gasp of admiration.

But Dorothy sprang up and ran to seize her friend's hand drawing him impulsively toward the lovely Princess, who smiled most graciously upon her guest. Then the Wizard entered, and his presence relieved the boy's embarrassment. The little man was clothed in black velvet, with many sparkling emerald ornaments decorating his breast; but his bald head and wrinkled features made him appear more amusing than impressive.

Ozma had been quite curious to meet the famous man who had built the Emerald City and united the Munchkins, Gillikins, Quadlings and Winkies into one people; so when they were all four seated at the dinner table the Princess said:

"Please tell me, Mr. Wizard, whether you called yourself Oz after this great country, or whether you believe my country is called Oz after you. It is a matter that I have long wished to enquire about, because you are of a strange race and my own name is Ozma. No, one, I am sure, is better able to explain this mystery than you."

"That is true," answered the little Wizard; "therefore it will give me pleasure to explain my connection with your country. In the first place, I must tell you that I was born in Omaha, and my father, who was a politician, named me Oscar Zoroaster Phadrig Isaac Norman Henkle Emmannuel Ambroise Diggs, Diggs being the last name because he could think of no more to go before it. Taken altogether, it was a dreadfully long name to weigh down a poor innocent child, and one of the hardest lessons I ever learned was to remember my own name. When I grew up I just called myself O. Z., because the other initials were P-I-N-H-E-A-D; and that spelled 'pinhead,' which was a reflection on my intelligence."

"Surely no one could blame you for cutting your name short," said Ozma, sympathetically. "But didn't you cut it almost too short?"

"Perhaps so," replied the Wizard. "When a young man I ran away from home and joined a circus. I used to call myself a Wizard, and do tricks of ventriloquism."

"What does that mean?" asked the Princess.

"Throwing my voice into any object I pleased, to make it appear that the object was speaking instead of me. Also I began to make balloon ascensions. On my balloon and on all the other articles I used in the circus I painted the two initials: 'O. Z.', to show that those things belonged to me.

"One day my balloon ran away with me and brought me across the deserts to this beautiful country. When the people saw me come from the sky they naturally thought me some superior creature, and bowed down before me. I told them I was a Wizard, and showed them some easy tricks that amazed them; and when they saw the initials painted on the balloon they called me Oz."

"Now I begin to understand," said the Princess, smiling.

"At that time," continued the Wizard, busily eating his soup while talking, "there were four separate countries in this Land, each one of the four being ruled by a Witch. But the people thought my power was greater than that of the Witches; and perhaps the Witches thought so too, for they never dared oppose me. I ordered the Emerald City to be built just where the four countries cornered together, and when it was completed I announced myself the Ruler of the Land of Oz, which included all the four countries of the Munchkins, the Gillikins, the Winkies and the Quadlings. Over this Land I ruled in peace for many years, until I grew old and longed to see my native city once again. So when Dorothy was first blown to this place by a cyclone I arranged to go away with her in a balloon; but the balloon escaped too soon and carried me back alone. After many adventures I reached Omaha, only to find that all my old friends were dead or had moved away. So, having nothing else to do, I joined a circus again, and made my balloon ascensions until the earthquake caught me."

"That is quite a history," said Ozma; "but there is a little more history about the Land of Oz that you do not seem to understand—perhaps for the reason that no one ever told it you. Many years before you came here this Land was united under one Ruler, as it is now, and the Ruler's name was always 'Oz,' which means in our language 'Great and Good'; or, if the Ruler happened to be a woman, her name was always 'Ozma.' But once upon a time four Witches leagued together to depose the king and rule the four parts of the kingdom themselves; so when the Ruler, my grandfather, was hunting one day, one Wicked Witch named Mombi stole him and carried him away, keeping him a close prisoner. Then the Witches divided up the kingdom, and ruled the four parts of it until you came here. That was why the people were so glad to see you, and why they thought from your initials that you were their rightful ruler."

"But, at that time," said the Wizard, thoughtfully, "there were two Good Witches and two Wicked Witches ruling in the land."

"Yes," replied Ozma, "because a good Witch had conquered Mombi in the North and Glinda the Good had conquered the evil Witch in the South. But Mombi was still my grandfather's jailor, and afterward my father's jailor. When I was born she transformed me into a boy, hoping that no one would ever recognize me and know that I was the rightful Princess of the Land of Oz. But I escaped from her and am now the Ruler of my people."

"I am very glad of that," said the Wizard, "and hope you will consider me one of your most faithful and devoted subjects."

"We owe a great deal to the Wonderful Wizard," continued the Princess, "for it was you who built this splendid Emerald City."

"Your people built it," he answered. "I only bossed the job, as we say in Omaha."

"But you ruled it wisely and well for many years," said she, "and made the people proud of your magical art. So, as you are now too old to wander abroad and work in a circus, I offer you a home here as long as you live. You shall be the Official Wizard of my kingdom, and be treated with every respect and consideration."

"I accept your kind offer with gratitude, gracious Princess," the little man said, in a soft voice, and they could all see that tear-drops were standing in his keen old eyes. It meant a good deal to him to secure a home like this.

"He's only a humbug Wizard, though," said Dorothy, smiling at him.

"And that is the safest kind of a Wizard to have," replied Ozma, promptly.

"Oz can do some good tricks, humbug or no humbug," announced Zeb, who was now feeling more at ease.

"He shall amuse us with his tricks tomorrow," said the Princess. "I have sent messengers to summon all of Dorothy's old friends to meet her and give her welcome, and they ought to arrive very soon, now."

Indeed, the dinner was no sooner finished than in rushed the Scarecrow, to hug Dorothy in his padded arms and tell her how glad he was to see her again. The Wizard was also most heartily welcomed by the straw man, who was an important personage in the Land of Oz.

"How are your brains?" enquired the little humbug, as he grasped the soft, stuffed hands of his old friend.

"Working finely," answered the Scarecrow. "I'm very certain, Oz, that you gave me the best brains in the world, for I can think with them day and night, when all other brains are fast asleep."

"How long did you rule the Emerald City, after I left here?" was the next question.

"Quite a while, until I was conquered by a girl named General Jinjur. But Ozma soon conquered her, with the help of Glinda the Good, and after that I went to live with Nick Chopper, the Tin Woodman."

Just then a loud cackling was heard outside; and, when a servant threw open the door with a low bow, a yellow hen strutted in. Dorothy sprang forward and caught the fluffy fowl in her arms, uttering at the same time a glad cry.

"Oh, Billina!" she said; "how fat and sleek you've grown."

"Why shouldn't I?" asked the hen, in a sharp, clear voice. "I live on the fat of the land—don't I, Ozma?"

"You have everything you wish for," said the Princess.

Around Billina's neck was a string of beautiful pearls, and on her legs were bracelets of emeralds. She nestled herself comfortably in Dorothy's lap until the kitten gave a snarl of jealous anger and leaped up with a sharp claw fiercely bared to strike Billina a blow. But the little girl gave the angry kitten such a severe cuff that it jumped down again without daring to scratch.

"How horrid of you, Eureka!" cried Dorothy. "Is that the way to treat my friends?"

"You have queer friends, seems to me," replied the kitten, in a surly tone.

"Seems to me the same way," said Billina, scornfully, "if that beastly cat is one of them."

"Look here!" said Dorothy, sternly. "I won't have any quarrelling in the Land of Oz, I can tell you! Everybody lives in peace here, and loves everybody else; and unless you two, Billina and Eureka, make up and be friends, I'll take my Magic Belt and wish you both home again, IMMEJITLY. So, there!"

They were both much frightened at the threat, and promised meekly to be good. But it was never noticed that they became very warm friends, for all of that.

And now the Tin Woodman arrived, his body most beautifully nickle-plated, so that it shone splendidly in the brilliant light of the room. The Tin Woodman loved Dorothy most tenderly, and welcomed with joy the return of the little old Wizard.

"Sir," said he to the latter, "I never can thank you enough for the excellent heart you once gave me. It has made me many friends, I assure you, and it beats as kindly and lovingly today as it every did."

"I'm glad to hear that," said the Wizard. "I was afraid it would get moldy in that tin body of yours."

"Not at all," returned Nick Chopper. "It keeps finely, being preserved in my air-tight chest."

Zeb was a little shy when first introduced to these queer people; but they were so friendly and sincere that he soon grew to admire them very much, even finding some good qualities in the yellow hen. But he became nervous again when the next visitor was announced.

"This," said Princess Ozma, "is my friend Mr. H. M. Woggle-Bug, T. E., who assisted me one time when I was in great distress, and is now the Dean of the Royal College of Athletic Science."

"Ah," said the Wizard; "I'm pleased to meet so distinguished a personage."

"H. M.," said the Woggle-Bug, pompously, "means Highly Magnified; and T. E. means Thoroughly Educated. I am, in reality, a very big bug, and doubtless the most intelligent being in all this broad domain."

"How well you disguise it," said the Wizard. "But I don't doubt your word in the least."

"Nobody doubts it, sir," replied the Woggle-Bug, and drawing a book from its pocket the strange insect turned its back on the company and sat down in a corner to read.

Nobody minded this rudeness, which might have seemed more impolite in one less thoroughly educated; so they straightway forgot him and joined in a merry conversation that kept them well amused until bed-time arrived.

16. Jim, The Cab-Horse

Jim the Cab-horse found himself in possession of a large room with a green marble floor and carved marble wainscoting, which was so stately in its appearance that it would have awed anyone else. Jim accepted it as a mere detail, and at his command the attendants gave his coat a good rubbing, combed his mane and tail, and washed his hoofs and fetlocks. Then they told him dinner would be served directly and he replied that they could not serve it too quickly to suit his convenience. First they brought him a steaming bowl of soup, which the horse eyed in dismay.

"Take that stuff away!" he commanded. "Do you take me for a salamander?"

They obeyed at once, and next served a fine large turbot on a silver platter, with drawn gravy poured over it.

"Fish!" cried Jim, with a sniff. "Do you take me for a tom-cat? Away with it!"

The servants were a little discouraged, but soon they brought in a great tray containing two dozen nicely roasted quail on toast.

"Well, well!" said the horse, now thoroughly provoked. "Do you take me for a weasel? How stupid and ignorant you are, in the Land of Oz, and what dreadful things you feed upon! Is there nothing that is decent to eat in this palace?"

The trembling servants sent for the Royal Steward, who came in haste and said: "What would your Highness like for dinner?"

"Highness!" repeated Jim, who was unused to such titles.

"You are at least six feet high, and that is higher than any other animal in this country," said the Steward.

"Well, my Highness would like some oats," declared the horse.

"Oats? We have no whole oats," the Steward replied, with much deference. "But there is any quantity of oatmeal, which we often cook for breakfast. Oatmeal is a breakfast dish," added the Steward, humbly.

"I'll make it a dinner dish," said Jim. "Fetch it on, but don't cook it, as you value your life."

You see, the respect shown the worn-out old cab-horse made him a little arrogant, and he forgot he was a guest, never having been treated otherwise than as a servant since the day he was born, until his arrival in the Land of Oz. But the royal attendants did not heed the animal's ill temper. They soon mixed a tub of oatmeal with a little water, and Jim ate it with much relish.

Then the servants heaped a lot of rugs upon the floor and the old horse slept on the softest bed he had ever known in his life.

In the morning, as soon as it was daylight, he resolved to take a walk and try to find some grass for breakfast; so he ambled calmly through the handsome arch of the doorway, turned the corner of the palace, wherein all seemed asleep, and came face to face with the Sawhorse.

Jim stopped abruptly, being startled and amazed. The Sawhorse stopped at the same time and stared at the other with its queer protruding eyes, which were mere knots in the log that formed its body. The legs of the Sawhorse were four sticks driving into holes bored in the log; its tail was a small branch that had been left by accident and its mouth a place chopped in one end of the body which projected a little and served as a head. The ends of the wooden legs were shod with plates of solid gold, and the saddle of the Princess Ozma, which was of red leather set with sparkling diamonds, was strapped to the clumsy body.

Jim's eyes stuck out as much as those of the Sawhorse, and he stared at the creature with his ears erect and his long head drawn back until it rested against his arched neck.

In this comical position the two horses circled slowly around each other for a while, each being unable to realize what the singular thing might be which it now beheld for the first time. Then Jim exclaimed: "For goodness sake, what sort of a being are you?"

"I'm a Sawhorse," replied the other.

"Oh; I believe I've heard of you," said the cab-horse; "but you are unlike anything that I expected to see."

"I do not doubt it," the Sawhorse observed, with a tone of pride. "I am considered quite unusual."

"You are, indeed. But a rickety wooden thing like you has no right to be alive."

"I couldn't help it," returned the other, rather crestfallen. "Ozma sprinkled me with a magic powder, and I just had to live. I know I'm not much account; but I'm the only horse in all the Land of Oz, so they treat me with great respect."

"You, a horse!"

"Oh, not a real one, of course. There are no real horses here at all. But I'm a splendid imitation of one."

Jim gave an indignant neigh.

"Look at me!" he cried. "Behold a real horse!"

The wooden animal gave a start, and then examined the other intently.

"Is it possible that you are a Real Horse?" he murmured.

"Not only possible, but true," replied Jim, who was gratified by the impression he had created. "It is proved by my fine points. For example, look at the long hairs on my tail, with which I can whisk away the flies."

"The flies never trouble me," said the Saw-Horse.

"And notice my great strong teeth, with which I nibble the grass."

"It is not necessary for me to eat," observed the Sawhorse.

"Also examine my broad chest, which enables me to draw deep, full breaths," said Jim, proudly.

"I have no need to breathe," returned the other.

"No; you miss many pleasures," remarked the cab-horse, pityingly. "You do not know the relief of brushing away a fly that has bitten you, nor the delight of eating delicious food, nor the satisfaction of drawing a long breath of fresh, pure air. You may be an imitation of a horse, but you're a mighty poor one."

"Oh, I cannot hope ever to be like you," sighed the Sawhorse. "But I am glad to meet a last a Real Horse. You are certainly the most beautiful creature I ever beheld."

This praise won Jim completely. To be called beautiful was a novelty in his experience. Said he: "Your chief fault, my friend, is in being made of wood, and that I suppose you cannot help. Real horses, like myself, are made of flesh and blood and bones."

"I can see the bones all right," replied the Sawhorse, "and they are admirable and distinct. Also I can see the flesh. But the blood, I suppose is tucked away inside."

"Exactly," said Jim.

"What good is it?" asked the Sawhorse.

Jim did not know, but he would not tell the Sawhorse that.

"If anything cuts me," he replied, "the blood runs out to show where I am cut. You, poor thing! cannot even bleed when you are hurt."

"But I am never hurt," said the Sawhorse. "Once in a while I get broken up some, but I am easily repaired and put in good order again. And I never feel a break or a splinter in the least."

Jim was almost tempted to envy the wooden horse for being unable to feel pain; but the creature was so absurdly unnatural that he decided he would not change places with it under any circumstances.

"How did you happen to be shod with gold?" he asked.

"Princess Ozma did that," was the reply; "and it saves my legs from wearing out. We've had a good many adventures together, Ozma and I, and she likes me."

The cab-horse was about to reply when suddenly he gave a start and a neigh of terror and stood trembling like a leaf. For around the corner had come two enormous savage beasts, treading so lightly that they were upon him before he was aware of their presence. Jim was in the act of plunging down the path to escape when the Sawhorse cried out: "Stop, my brother! Stop, Real Horse! These are friends, and will do you no harm."

Jim hesitated, eyeing the beasts fearfully. One was an enormous Lion with clear, intelligent eyes, a tawney mane bushy and well kept, and a body like yellow plush. The other was a great Tiger with purple stripes around his lithe body, powerful limbs, and eyes that showed through the half closed lids like coals of fire. The huge forms of these monarchs of the forest and jungle were enough to strike terror to the stoutest heart, and it is no wonder Jim was afraid to face them.

But the Sawhorse introduced the stranger in a calm tone, saying: "This, noble Horse, is my friend the Cowardly Lion, who is the valiant King of the Forest, but at the same time a faithful vassal of Princess Ozma. And this is the Hungry Tiger, the terror of the jungle, who longs to devour fat babies but is prevented by his conscience from doing so. These royal beasts are both warm friends of little Dorothy and have come to the Emerald City this morning to welcome her to our fairyland."

Hearing these words Jim resolved to conquer his alarm. He bowed his head with as much dignity as he could muster toward the savage looking beasts, who in return nodded in a friendly way.

"Is not the Real Horse a beautiful animal?" asked the Sawhorse admiringly.

"That is doubtless a matter of taste," returned the Lion. "In the forest he would be thought ungainly, because his face is stretched out and his neck is uselessly long. His joints, I notice, are swollen and overgrown, and he lacks flesh and is old in years."

"And dreadfully tough," added the Hungry Tiger, in a sad voice. "My conscience would never permit me to eat so tough a morsel as the Real Horse."

"I'm glad of that," said Jim; "for I, also, have a conscience, and it tells me not to crush in your skull with a blow of my powerful hoof."

If he thought to frighten the striped beast by such language he was mistaken. The Tiger seemed to smile, and winked one eye slowly.

"You have a good conscience, friend Horse," it said, "and if you attend to its teachings it will do much to protect you from harm. Some day I will let you try to crush in my skull, and afterward you will know more about tigers than you do now."

"Any friend of Dorothy," remarked the Cowardly Lion, "must be our friend, as well. So let us cease this talk of skull crushing and converse upon more pleasant subjects. Have you breakfasted, Sir Horse?"

"Not yet," replied Jim. "But here is plenty of excellent clover, so if you will excuse me I will eat now."

"He's a vegetarian," remarked the Tiger, as the horse began to munch the clover. "If I could eat grass I would not need a conscience, for nothing could then tempt me to devour babies and lambs."

Just then Dorothy, who had risen early and heard the voices of the animals, ran out to greet her old friends. She hugged both the Lion and the Tiger with eager delight, but seemed to love the King of Beasts a little better than she did his hungry friend, having known him longer.

By this time they had indulged in a good talk and Dorothy had told them all about the awful earthquake and her recent adventures, the breakfast bell rang from the palace and the little girl went inside to join her human comrades. As she entered the great hall a voice called out, in a rather harsh tone: "What! are YOU here again?"

"Yes, I am," she answered, looking all around to see where the voice came from.

"What brought you back?" was the next question, and Dorothy's eye rested on an antlered head hanging on the wall just over the fireplace, and caught its lips in the act of moving.

"Good gracious!" she exclaimed. "I thought you were stuffed."

"So I am," replied the head. "But once on a time I was part of the Gump, which Ozma sprinkled with the Powder of Life. I was then for a time the Head of the finest Flying Machine that was ever known to exist, and we did many wonderful things. Afterward the Gump was taken apart and I was put back on this wall; but I can still talk when I feel in the mood, which is not often."

"It's very strange," said the girl. "What were you when you were first alive?"

"That I have forgotten," replied the Gump's Head, "and I do not think it is of much importance. But here comes Ozma; so I'd better hush up, for the Princess doesn't like me to chatter since she changed her name from Tip to Ozma."

Just then the girlish Ruler of Oz opened the door and greeted Dorothy with a good-morning kiss. The little Princess seemed fresh and rosy and in good spirits.

"Breakfast is served, dear," she said, "and I am hungry. So don't let us keep it waiting a single minute."

17. The Nine Tiny Piglets

After breakfast Ozma announced that she had ordered a holiday to be observed throughout the Emerald City, in honor of her visitors. The people had learned that their old Wizard had returned to them and all were anxious to see him again, for he had always been a rare favorite. So first there was to be a grand procession through the streets, after which the little old man was requested to perform some of his wizardries in the great Throne Room of the palace. In the afternoon there were to be games and races.

The procession was very imposing. First came the Imperial Cornet Band of Oz, dressed in emerald velvet uniforms with slashes of pea-green satin and buttons of immense cut emeralds. They played the National air called "The Oz Spangled Banner,"

and behind them were the standard bearers with the Royal flag. This flag was divided into four quarters, one being colored sky-blue, another pink, a third lavender and a fourth white. In the center was a large emerald-green star, and all over the four quarters were sewn spangles that glittered beautifully in the sunshine. The colors represented the four countries of Oz, and the green star the Emerald City.

Just behind the royal standard-bearers came the Princess Ozma in her royal chariot, which was of gold encrusted with emeralds and diamonds set in exquisite designs. The chariot was drawn on this occasion by the Cowardly Lion and the Hungry Tiger, who were decorated with immense pink and blue bows. In the chariot rode Ozma and Dorothy, the former in splendid raiment and wearing her royal coronet, while the little Kansas girl wore around her waist the Magic Belt she had once captured from the Nome King.

Following the chariot came the Scarecrow mounted on the Sawhorse, and the people cheered him almost as loudly as they did their lovely Ruler. Behind him stalked with regular, jerky steps, the famous machine-man called Tik-tok, who had been wound up by Dorothy for the occasion. Tik-tok moved by clockwork, and was made all of burnished copper. He really belonged to the Kansas girl, who had much respect for his thoughts after they had been properly wound and set going; but as the copper man would be useless in any place but a fairy country Dorothy had left him in charge of Ozma, who saw that he was suitably cared for.

There followed another band after this, which was called the Royal Court Band, because the members all lived in the palace. They wore white uniforms with real diamond buttons and played "What is Oz without Ozma" very sweetly.

Then came Professor Woggle-Bug, with a group of students from the Royal College of Scientific Athletics. The boys wore long hair and striped sweaters and yelled their college yell every other step they took, to the great satisfaction of the populace, which was glad to have this evidence that their lungs were in good condition.

The brilliantly polished Tin Woodman marched next, at the head of the Royal Army of Oz which consisted of twenty-eight officers, from Generals down to Captains. There were no privates in the army because all were so courageous and skillful that they had been promoted one by one until there were no privates left. Jim and the buggy followed, the old cab-horse being driven by Zeb while the Wizard stood up on the seat and bowed his bald head right and left in answer to the cheers of the people, who crowded thick about him.

Taken altogether the procession was a grand success, and when it had returned to the palace the citizens crowded into the great Throne Room to see the Wizard perform his tricks.

The first thing the little humbug did was to produce a tiny white piglet from underneath his hat and pretend to pull it apart, making two. This act he repeated until all of the nine tiny piglets were visible, and they were so glad to get out of his pocket that they ran around in a very lively manner. The pretty little creatures would have been a novelty anywhere, so the people were as amazed and delighted at their appearance as even the Wizard could have desired. When he had made them all disappear again Ozma declared she was sorry they were gone, for she wanted one of them to pet and play with. So the Wizard pretended to take one of the piglets out of the hair of the Princess (while really he slyly took it from his inside pocket) and

Ozma smiled joyously as the creature nestled in her arms, and she promised to have an emerald collar made for its fat neck and to keep the little squealer always at hand to amuse her.

Afterward it was noticed that the Wizard always performed his famous trick with eight piglets, but it seemed to please the people just as well as if there had been nine of them.

In his little room back of the Throne Room the Wizard had found a lot of things he had left behind him when he went away in the balloon, for no one had occupied the apartment in his absence. There was enough material there to enable him to prepare several new tricks which he had learned from some of the jugglers in the circus, and he had passed part of the night in getting them ready. So he followed the trick of the nine tiny piglets with several other wonderful feats that greatly delighted his audience and the people did not seem to care a bit whether the little man was a humbug Wizard or not, so long as he succeeded in amusing them. They applauded all his tricks and at the end of the performance begged him earnestly not to go away again and leave them.

"In that case," said the little man, gravely, "I will cancel all of my engagements before the crowned heads of Europe and America and devote myself to the people of Oz, for I love you all so well that I can deny you nothing."

After the people had been dismissed with this promise our friends joined Princess Ozma at an elaborate luncheon in the palace, where even the Tiger and the Lion were sumptuously fed and Jim the Cab-horse ate his oatmeal out of a golden bowl with seven rows of rubies, sapphires and diamonds set around the rim of it.

In the afternoon they all went to a great field outside the city gates where the games were to be held. There was a beautiful canopy for Ozma and her guests to sit under and watch the people run races and jump and wrestle. You may be sure the folks of Oz did their best with such a distinguished company watching them, and finally Zeb offered to wrestle with a little Munchkin who seemed to be the champion. In appearance he was twice as old as Zeb, for he had long pointed whiskers and wore a peaked hat with little bells all around the brim of it, which tinkled gaily as he moved. But although the Munchkin was hardly tall enough to come to Zeb's shoulder he was so strong and clever that he laid the boy three times on his back with apparent ease.

Zeb was greatly astonished at his defeat, and when the pretty Princess joined her people in laughing at him he proposed a boxing-match with the Munchkin, to which the little Ozite readily agreed. But the first time that Zeb managed to give him a sharp box on the ears the Munchkin sat down upon the ground and cried until the tears ran down his whiskers, because he had been hurt. This made Zeb laugh, in turn, and the boy felt comforted to find that Ozma laughed as merrily at her weeping subject as she had at him.

Just then the Scarecrow proposed a race between the Sawhorse and the Cab-horse; and although all the others were delighted at the suggestion the Sawhorse drew back, saying: "Such a race would not be fair."

"Of course not," added Jim, with a touch of scorn; "those little wooden legs of yours are not half as long as my own."

"It isn't that," said the Sawhorse, modestly; "but I never tire, and you do."

"Bah!" cried Jim, looking with great disdain at the other; "do you imagine for an instant that such a shabby imitation of a horse as you are can run as fast as I?"

"I don't know, I'm sure," replied the Sawhorse.

"That is what we are trying to find out," remarked the Scarecrow. "The object of a race is to see who can win it—or at least that is what my excellent brains think."

"Once, when I was young," said Jim, "I was a race horse, and defeated all who dared run against me. I was born in Kentucky, you know, where all the best and most aristocratic horses come from."

"But you're old, now, Jim," suggested Zeb.

"Old! Why, I feel like a colt today," replied Jim. "I only wish there was a real horse here for me to race with. I'd show the people a fine sight, I can tell you."

"Then why not race with the Sawhorse?" enquired the Scarecrow.

"He's afraid," said Jim.

"Oh, no," answered the Sawhorse. "I merely said it wasn't fair. But if my friend the Real Horse is willing to undertake the race I am quite ready."

So they unharnessed Jim and took the saddle off the Sawhorse, and the two queerly matched animals were stood side by side for the start.

"When I say 'Go!'" Zeb called to them, "you must dig out and race until you reach those three trees you see over yonder. Then circle 'round them and come back again. The first one that passes the place where the Princess sits shall be named the winner. Are you ready?"

"I suppose I ought to give the wooden dummy a good start of me," growled Jim.

"Never mind that," said the Sawhorse. "I'll do the best I can."

"Go!" cried Zeb; and at the word the two horses leaped forward and the race was begun.

Jim's big hoofs pounded away at a great rate, and although he did not look very graceful he ran in a way to do credit to his Kentucky breeding. But the Sawhorse was swifter than the wind. Its wooden legs moved so fast that their twinkling could scarcely be seen, and although so much smaller than the cab-horse it covered the ground much faster. Before they had reached the trees the Sawhorse was far ahead, and the wooden animal returned to the starting place as was being lustily cheered by the Ozites before Jim came panting up to the canopy where the Princess and her friends were seated.

I am sorry to record the fact that Jim was not only ashamed of his defeat but for a moment lost control of his temper. As he looked at the comical face of the Sawhorse he imagined that the creature was laughing at him; so in a fit of unreasonable anger he turned around and made a vicious kick that sent his rival tumbling head over heels upon the ground, and broke off one of its legs and its left ear.

An instant later the Tiger crouched and launched its huge body through the air swift and resistless as a ball from a cannon. The beast struck Jim full on his shoulder and sent the astonished cab-horse rolling over and over, amid shouts of delight from the spectators, who had been horrified by the ungracious act he had been guilty of.

When Jim came to himself and sat upon his haunches he found the Cowardly Lion crouched on one side of him and the Hungry Tiger on the other, and their eyes were glowing like balls of fire.

"I beg your pardon, I'm sure," said Jim, meekly. "I was wrong to kick the Sawhorse, and I am sorry I became angry at him. He has won the race, and won it fairly; but what can a horse of flesh do against a tireless beast of wood?"

Hearing this apology the Tiger and the Lion stopped lashing their tails and retreated with dignified steps to the side of the Princess.

"No one must injure one of our friends in our presence," growled the Lion; and Zeb ran to Jim and whispered that unless he controlled his temper in the future he would probably be torn to pieces.

Then the Tin Woodman cut a straight and strong limb from a tree with his gleaming axe and made a new leg and a new ear for the Sawhorse; and when they had been securely fastened in place Princess Ozma took the coronet from her own head and placed it upon that of the winner of the race. Said she:

"My friend, I reward you for your swiftness by proclaiming you Prince of Horses, whether of wood or of flesh; and hereafter all other horses—in the Land of Oz, at least—must be considered imitations, and you the real Champion of your race."

There was more applause at this, and then Ozma had the jewelled saddle replaced upon the Sawhorse and herself rode the victor back to the city at the head of the grand procession.

"I ought to be a fairy," grumbled Jim, as he slowly drew the buggy home; "for to be just an ordinary horse in a fairy country is to be of no account whatever. It's no place for us, Zeb."

"It's lucky we got here, though," said the boy; and Jim thought of the dark cave, and agreed with him.

18. The Trial of Eureka the Kitten

Several days of festivity and merry-making followed, for such old friends did not often meet and there was much to be told and talked over between them, and many amusements to be enjoyed in this delightful country.

Ozma was happy to have Dorothy beside her, for girls of her own age with whom it was proper for the Princess to associate were very few, and often the youthful Ruler of Oz was lonely for lack of companionship.

It was the third morning after Dorothy's arrival, and she was sitting with Ozma and their friends in a reception room, talking over old times, when the Princess said to her maid:

"Please go to my boudoir, Jellia, and get the white piglet I left on the dressing-table. I want to play with it."

Jellia at once departed on the errand, and she was gone so long that they had almost forgotten her mission when the green robed maiden returned with a troubled face.

"The piglet is not there, your Highness," said she.

"Not there!" exclaimed Ozma. "Are you sure?"

"I have hunted in every part of the room," the maid replied.

"Was not the door closed?" asked the Princess.

"Yes, your Highness; I am sure it was; for when I opened it Dorothy's white kitten crept out and ran up the stairs."

Hearing this, Dorothy and the Wizard exchanged startled glances, for they remembered how often Eureka had longed to eat a piglet. The little girl jumped up at once.

"Come, Ozma," she said, anxiously; "let us go ourselves to search for the piglet."

So the two went to the dressing-room of the Princess and searched carefully in every corner and among the vases and baskets and ornaments that stood about the pretty boudoir. But not a trace could they find of the tiny creature they sought.

Dorothy was nearly weeping, by this time, while Ozma was angry and indignant. When they returned to the others the Princess said: "There is little doubt that my pretty piglet has been eaten by that horrid kitten, and if that is true the offender must be punished."

"I don't b'lieve Eureka would do such a dreadful thing!" cried Dorothy, much distressed. "Go and get my kitten, please, Jellia, and we'll hear what she has to say about it."

The green maiden hastened away, but presently returned and said: "The kitten will not come. She threatened to scratch my eyes out if I touched her."

"Where is she?" asked Dorothy.

"Under the bed in your own room," was the reply.

So Dorothy ran to her room and found the kitten under the bed.

"Come here, Eureka!" she said.

"I won't," answered the kitten, in a surly voice.

"Oh, Eureka! Why are you so bad?"

The kitten did not reply.

"If you don't come to me, right away," continued Dorothy, getting provoked, "I'll take my Magic Belt and wish you in the Country of the Gurgles."

"Why do you want me?" asked Eureka, disturbed by this threat.

"You must go to Princess Ozma. She wants to talk to you."

"All right," returned the kitten, creeping out. "I'm not afraid of Ozma—or anyone else."

Dorothy carried her in her arms back to where the others sat in grieved and thoughtful silence.

"Tell me, Eureka," said the Princess, gently: "did you eat my pretty piglet?"

"I won't answer such a foolish question," asserted Eureka, with a snarl.

"Oh, yes you will, dear," Dorothy declared. "The piglet is gone, and you ran out of the room when Jellia opened the door. So, if you are innocent, Eureka, you must tell the Princess how you came to be in her room, and what has become of the piglet."

"Who accuses me?" asked the kitten, defiantly.

"No one," answered Ozma. "Your actions alone accuse you. The fact is that I left my little pet in my dressing-room lying asleep upon the table; and you must have stolen in without my knowing it. When next the door was opened you ran out and hid yourself—and the piglet was gone."

"That's none of my business," growled the kitten.

"Don't be impudent, Eureka," admonished Dorothy.

"It is you who are impudent," said Eureka, "for accusing me of such a crime when you can't prove it except by guessing."

Ozma was now greatly incensed by the kitten's conduct. She summoned her Captain-General, and when the long, lean officer appeared she said: "Carry this cat away to prison, and keep her in safe confinement until she is tried by law for the crime of murder."

So the Captain-General took Eureka from the arms of the now weeping Dorothy and in spite of the kitten's snarls and scratches carried it away to prison.

"What shall we do now?" asked the Scarecrow, with a sigh, for such a crime had cast a gloom over all the company.

"I will summon the Court to meet in the Throne Room at three o'clock," replied Ozma. "I myself will be the judge, and the kitten shall have a fair trial."

"What will happen if she is guilty?" asked Dorothy.

"She must die," answered the Princess.

"Nine times?" enquired the Scarecrow.

"As many times as is necessary," was the reply. "I will ask the Tin Woodman to defend the prisoner, because he has such a kind heart I am sure he will do his best to save her. And the Woggle-Bug shall be the Public Accuser, because he is so learned that no one can deceive him."

"Who will be the jury?" asked the Tin Woodman.

"There ought to be several animals on the jury," said Ozma, "because animals understand each other better than we people understand them. So the jury shall consist of the Cowardly Lion, the Hungry Tiger, Jim the Cab-horse, the Yellow Hen, the Scarecrow, the Wizard, Tik-tok the Machine Man, the Sawhorse and Zeb of Hugson's Ranch. That makes the nine which the law requires, and all my people shall be admitted to hear the testimony."

They now separated to prepare for the sad ceremony; for whenever an appeal is made to law sorrow is almost certain to follow—even in a fairyland like Oz. But is must be stated that the people of that Land were generally so well-behaved that there was not a single lawyer amongst them, and it had been years since any Ruler had sat in judgment upon an offender of the law. The crime of murder being the most dreadful crime of all, tremendous excitement prevailed in the Emerald City when the news of Eureka's arrest and trial became known.

The Wizard, when he returned to his own room, was exceedingly thoughtful. He had no doubt Eureka had eaten his piglet, but he realized that a kitten cannot be depended upon at all times to act properly, since its nature is to destroy small animals and even birds for food, and the tame cat that we keep in our houses today is descended from the wild cat of the jungle—a very ferocious creature, indeed. The Wizard knew that if Dorothy's pet was found guilty and condemned to death the little girl would be made very unhappy; so, although he grieved over the piglet's sad fate as much as any of them, he resolved to save Eureka's life.

Sending for the Tin Woodman the Wizard took him into a corner and whispered:

"My friend, it is your duty to defend the white kitten and try to save her, but I fear you will fail because Eureka has long wished to eat a piglet, to my certain knowledge, and my opinion is that she has been unable to resist the temptation. Yet her disgrace and death would not bring back the piglet, but only serve to make Dorothy unhappy. So I intend to prove the kitten's innocence by a trick."

He drew from his inside pocket one of the eight tiny piglets that were remaining and continued:

"This creature you must hide in some safe place, and if the jury decides that Eureka is guilty you may then produce this piglet and claim it is the one that was lost. All the piglets are exactly alike, so no one can dispute your word. This deception will save Eureka's life, and then we may all be happy again."

"I do not like to deceive my friends," replied the Tin Woodman; "still, my kind heart urges me to save Eureka's life, and I can usually trust my heart to do the right thing. So I will do as you say, friend Wizard."

After some thought he placed the little pig inside his funnel-shaped hat, and then put the hat upon his head and went back to his room to think over his speech to the jury.

19. The Wizard Performs Another Trick

At three o'clock the Throne Room was crowded with citizens, men, women and children being eager to witness the great trial.

Princess Ozma, dressed in her most splendid robes of state, sat in the magnificent emerald throne, with her jewelled sceptre in her hand and her sparkling coronet upon her fair brow. Behind her throne stood the twenty-eight officers of her army and many officials of the royal household. At her right sat the queerly assorted Jury—animals, animated dummies and people—all gravely prepared to listen to what was said. The kitten had been placed in a large cage just before the throne, where she sat upon her haunches and gazed through the bars at the crowds around her, with seeming unconcern.

And now, at a signal from Ozma, the Woggle-Bug arose and addressed the jury. His tone was pompous and he strutted up and down in an absurd attempt to appear dignified.

"Your Royal Highness and Fellow Citizens," he began; "the small cat you see a prisoner before you is accused of the crime of first murdering and then eating our esteemed Ruler's fat piglet—or else first eating and then murdering it. In either case a grave crime has been committed which deserves a grave punishment."

"Do you mean my kitten must be put in a grave?" asked Dorothy.

"Don't interrupt, little girl," said the Woggle-Bug. "When I get my thoughts arranged in good order I do not like to have anything upset them or throw them into confusion."

"If your thoughts were any good they wouldn't become confused," remarked the Scarecrow, earnestly. "My thoughts are always—"

"Is this a trial of thoughts, or of kittens?" demanded the Woggle-Bug.

"It's a trial of one kitten," replied the Scarecrow; "but your manner is a trial to us all."

"Let the Public Accuser continue," called Ozma from her throne, "and I pray you do not interrupt him."

"The criminal who now sits before the court licking her paws," resumed the Woggle-Bug, "has long desired to unlawfully eat the fat piglet, which was no bigger than a mouse. And finally she made a wicked plan to satisfy her depraved appetite for pork. I can see her, in my mind's eye—"

"What's that?" asked the Scarecrow.

"I say I can see her in my mind's eye—"

"The mind has no eye," declared the Scarecrow. "It's blind."

"Your Highness," cried the Woggle-Bug, appealing to Ozma, "have I a mind's eye, or haven't I?"

"If you have, it is invisible," said the Princess.

"Very true," returned the Woggle-Bug, bowing. "I say I see the criminal, in my mind's eye, creeping stealthily into the room of our Ozma and secreting herself, when no one was looking, until the Princess had gone away and the door was closed. Then the murderer was alone with her helpless victim, the fat piglet, and I see her pounce upon the innocent creature and eat it up—"

"Are you still seeing with your mind's eye?" enquired the Scarecrow.

"Of course; how else could I see it? And we know the thing is true, because since the time of that interview there is no piglet to be found anywhere."

"I suppose, if the cat had been gone, instead of the piglet, your mind's eye would see the piglet eating the cat," suggested the Scarecrow.

"Very likely," acknowledged the Woggle-Bug. "And now, Fellow Citizens and Creatures of the Jury, I assert that so awful a crime deserves death, and in the case of the ferocious criminal before you—who is now washing her face—the death penalty should be inflicted nine times."

There was great applause when the speaker sat down. Then the Princess spoke in a stern voice:

"Prisoner, what have you to say for yourself? Are you guilty, or not guilty?"

"Why, that's for you to find out," replied Eureka. "If you can prove I'm guilty, I'll be willing to die nine times, but a mind's eye is no proof, because the Woggle-Bug has no mind to see with."

"Never mind, dear," said Dorothy.

Then the Tin Woodman arose and said:

"Respected Jury and dearly beloved Ozma, I pray you not to judge this feline prisoner unfeelingly. I do not think the innocent kitten can be guilty, and surely it is unkind to accuse a luncheon of being a murder. Eureka is the sweet pet of a lovely little girl whom we all admire, and gentleness and innocence are her chief virtues. Look at the kitten's intelligent eyes;" (here Eureka closed her eyes sleepily) "gaze at her smiling countenance!" (here Eureka snarled and showed her teeth) "mark the tender pose of her soft, padded little hands!" (Here Eureka bared her sharp claws and scratched at the bars of the cage.) "Would such a gentle animal be guilty of eating a fellow creature? No; a thousand times, no!"

"Oh, cut it short," said Eureka; "you've talked long enough."

"I'm trying to defend you," remonstrated the Tin Woodman.

"Then say something sensible," retorted the kitten. "Tell them it would be foolish for me to eat the piglet, because I had sense enough to know it would raise a row if I did. But don't try to make out I'm too innocent to eat a fat piglet if I could do it and not be found out. I imagine it would taste mighty good."

"Perhaps it would, to those who eat," remarked the Tin Woodman. "I myself, not being built to eat, have no personal experience in such matters. But I remember that our great poet once said:
"'To eat is sweet
When hunger's seat
Demands a treat
Of savory meat.'

"Take this into consideration, friends of the Jury, and you will readily decide that the kitten is wrongfully accused and should be set at liberty."

When the Tin Woodman sat down no one applauded him, for his arguments had not been very convincing and few believed that he had proved Eureka's innocence. As for the Jury, the members whispered to each other for a few minutes and then they appointed the Hungry Tiger their spokesman. The huge beast slowly arose and said: "Kittens have no consciences, so they eat whatever pleases them. The jury believes the white kitten known as Eureka is guilty of having eaten the piglet owned by Princess Ozma, and recommends that she be put to death in punishment of the crime."

The judgment of the jury was received with great applause, although Dorothy was sobbing miserably at the fate of her pet. The Princess was just about to order Eureka's head chopped off with the Tin Woodman's axe when that brilliant personage once more arose and addressed her.

"Your Highness," said he, "see how easy it is for a jury to be mistaken. The kitten could not have eaten your piglet—for here it is!"

He took off his funnel hat and from beneath it produced a tiny white piglet, which he held aloft that all might see it clearly.

Ozma was delighted and exclaimed, eagerly:

"Give me my pet, Nick Chopper!"

And all the people cheered and clapped their hands, rejoicing that the prisoner had escaped death and been proved to be innocent.

As the Princess held the white piglet in her arms and stroked its soft hair she said: "Let Eureka out of the cage, for she is no longer a prisoner, but our good friend. Where did you find my missing pet, Nick Chopper?"

"In a room of the palace," he answered.

"Justice," remarked the Scarecrow, with a sigh, "is a dangerous thing to meddle with. If you hadn't happened to find the piglet, Eureka would surely have been executed."

"But justice prevailed at the last," said Ozma, "for here is my pet, and Eureka is once more free."

"I refuse to be free," cried the kitten, in a sharp voice, "unless the Wizard can do his trick with eight piglets. If he can produce but seven, then this is not the piglet that was lost, but another one."

"Hush, Eureka!" warned the Wizard.

"Don't be foolish," advised the Tin Woodman, "or you may be sorry for it."

"The piglet that belonged to the Princess wore an emerald collar," said Eureka, loudly enough for all to hear.

"So it did!" exclaimed Ozma. "This cannot be the one the Wizard gave me."

"Of course not; he had nine of them, altogether," declared Eureka; "and I must say it was very stingy of him not to let me eat just a few. But now that this foolish trial is ended, I will tell you what really became of your pet piglet."

At this everyone in the Throne Room suddenly became quiet, and the kitten continued, in a calm, mocking tone of voice:

"I will confess that I intended to eat the little pig for my breakfast; so I crept into the room where it was kept while the Princess was dressing and hid myself under a chair. When Ozma went away she closed the door and left her pet on the table. At once I jumped up and told the piglet not to make a fuss, for he would be inside of me in half a second; but no one can teach one of these creatures to be reasonable. Instead of keeping still, so I could eat him comfortably, he trembled so with fear that he fell off the table into a big vase that was standing on the floor. The vase had a very small neck, and spread out at the top like a bowl. At first the piglet stuck in the neck of the vase and I thought I should get him, after all, but he wriggled himself through and fell down into the deep bottom part—and I suppose he's there yet."

All were astonished at this confession, and Ozma at once sent an officer to her room to fetch the vase. When he returned the Princess looked down the narrow neck of the big ornament and discovered her lost piglet, just as Eureka had said she would.

There was no way to get the creature out without breaking the vase, so the Tin Woodman smashed it with his axe and set the little prisoner free.

Then the crowd cheered lustily and Dorothy hugged the kitten in her arms and told her how delighted she was to know that she was innocent.

"But why didn't you tell us at first?" she asked.

"It would have spoiled the fun," replied the kitten, yawning.

Ozma gave the Wizard back the piglet he had so kindly allowed Nick Chopper to substitute for the lost one, and then she carried her own into the apartments of the palace where she lived. And now, the trial being over, the good citizens of the Emerald City scattered to their homes, well content with the day's amusement.

20. Zeb Returns to the Ranch

Eureka was much surprised to find herself in disgrace; but she was, in spite of the fact that she had not eaten the piglet. For the folks of Oz knew the kitten had tried to commit the crime, and that only an accident had prevented her from doing so; therefore even the Hungry Tiger preferred not to associate with her. Eureka was forbidden to wander around the palace and was made to stay in confinement in Dorothy's room; so she began to beg her mistress to send her to some other place where she could enjoy herself better.

Dorothy was herself anxious to get home, so she promised Eureka they would not stay in the Land of Oz much longer.

The next evening after the trial the little girl begged Ozma to allow her to look in the enchanted picture, and the Princess readily consented. She took the child to her room and said: "Make your wish, dear, and the picture will show the scene you desire to behold."

Then Dorothy found, with the aid of the enchanted picture, that Uncle Henry had returned to the farm in Kansas, and she also saw that both he and Aunt Em were dressed in mourning, because they thought their little niece had been killed by the earthquake.

"Really," said the girl, anxiously, "I must get back as soon as poss'ble to my own folks."

Zeb also wanted to see his home, and although he did not find anyone mourning for him, the sight of Hugson's Ranch in the picture made him long to get back there.

"This is a fine country, and I like all the people that live in it," he told Dorothy. "But the fact is, Jim and I don't seem to fit into a fairyland, and the old horse has been begging me to go home again ever since he lost the race. So, if you can find a way to fix it, we'll be much obliged to you."

"Ozma can do it, easily," replied Dorothy. "Tomorrow morning I'll go to Kansas and you can go to Californy."

That last evening was so delightful that the boy will never forget it as long as he lives. They were all together (except Eureka) in the pretty rooms of the Princess, and the Wizard did some new tricks, and the Scarecrow told stories, and the Tin Woodman sang a love song in a sonorous, metallic voice, and everybody laughed and had a good time. Then Dorothy wound up Tik-tok and he danced a jig to amuse the company, after which the Yellow Hen related some of her adventures with the Nome King in the Land of Ev.

The Princess served delicious refreshments to those who were in the habit of eating, and when Dorothy's bed time arrived the company separated after exchanging many friendly sentiments.

Next morning they all assembled for the final parting, and many of the officials and courtiers came to look upon the impressive ceremonies.

Dorothy held Eureka in her arms and bade her friends a fond good-bye.

"You must come again, some time," said the little Wizard; and she promised she would if she found it possible to do so.

"But Uncle Henry and Aunt Em need me to help them," she added, "so I can't ever be very long away from the farm in Kansas."

Ozma wore the Magic Belt; and, when she had kissed Dorothy farewell and had made her wish, the little girl and her kitten disappeared in a twinkling.

"Where is she?" asked Zeb, rather bewildered by the suddenness of it.

"Greeting her uncle and aunt in Kansas, by this time," returned Ozma, with a smile.

Then Zeb brought out Jim, all harnessed to the buggy, and took his seat.

"I'm much obliged for all your kindness," said the boy, "and very grateful to you for saving my life and sending me home again after all the good times I've had. I think this is the loveliest country in the world; but not being fairies Jim and I feel we ought to be where we belong—and that's at the ranch. Good-bye, everybody!"

He gave a start and rubbed his eyes. Jim was trotting along the well-known road, shaking his ears and whisking his tail with a contented motion. Just ahead of them were the gates of Hugson's Ranch, and Uncle Hugson now came out and stood with uplifted arms and wide open mouth, staring in amazement.

"Goodness gracious! It's Zeb—and Jim, too!" he exclaimed. "Where in the world have you been, my lad?"

"Why, in the world, Uncle," answered Zeb, with a laugh.

The Road to Oz
by L. Frank Baum

In which is related how Dorothy Gale of Kansas, The Shaggy Man, Button Bright, and Polychrome the Rainbow's Daughter met on an Enchanted Road and followed it all the way to the Marvelous Land of Oz, by L. Frank Baum "Royal Historian of Oz"

To My Readers

Well, my dears, here is what you have asked for: another "Oz Book" about Dorothy's strange adventures. Toto is in this story, because you wanted him to be there, and many other characters which you will recognize are in the story, too. Indeed, the wishes of my little correspondents have been considered as carefully as possible, and if the story is not exactly as you would have written it yourselves, you must remember that a story has to be a story before it can be written down, and the writer cannot change it much without spoiling it.

In the preface to "Dorothy and the Wizard of Oz" I said I would like to write some stories that were not "Oz" stories, because I thought I had written about Oz long enough; but since that volume was published I have been fairly deluged with letters from children imploring me to "write more about Dorothy," and "more about Oz," and since I write only to please the children I shall try to respect their wishes.

There are some new characters in this book that ought to win your love. I'm very fond of the shaggy man myself, and I think you will like him, too. As for Polychrome—the Rainbow's Daughter—and stupid little Button-Bright, they seem to have brought a new element of fun into these Oz stories, and I am glad I discovered them. Yet I am anxious to have you write and tell me how you like them.

Since this book was written I have received some very remarkable News from The Land of Oz, which has greatly astonished me. I believe it will astonish you, too, my dears, when you hear it. But it is such a long and exciting story that it must be saved for another book—and perhaps that book will be the last story that will ever be told about the Land of Oz.

L. Frank Baum
Coronado, 1909.

1. The Way to Butterfield

"Please, miss," said the shaggy man, "can you tell me the road to Butterfield?"

Dorothy looked him over. Yes, he was shaggy, all right, but there was a twinkle in his eye that seemed pleasant.

"Oh yes," she replied; "I can tell you. But it isn't this road at all."

"No?"

"You cross the ten-acre lot, follow the lane to the highway, go north to the five branches, and take—let me see—"

"To be sure, miss; see as far as Butterfield, if you like," said the shaggy man.

"You take the branch next the willow stump, I b'lieve; or else the branch by the gopher holes; or else—"

"Won't any of 'em do, miss?"

"'Course not, Shaggy Man. You must take the right road to get to Butterfield."

"And is that the one by the gopher stump, or—"

"Dear me!" cried Dorothy. "I shall have to show you the way, you're so stupid. Wait a minute till I run in the house and get my sunbonnet."

The shaggy man waited. He had an oat-straw in his mouth, which he chewed slowly as if it tasted good; but it didn't. There was an apple-tree beside the house, and some apples had fallen to the ground. The shaggy man thought they would taste better than the oat-straw, so he walked over to get some. A little black dog with bright brown eyes dashed out of the farm-house and ran madly toward the shaggy man, who had already picked up three apples and put them in one of the big wide pockets of his shaggy coat. The little dog barked and made a dive for the shaggy man's leg; but he grabbed the dog by the neck and put it in his big pocket along with the apples. He took more apples, afterward, for many were on the ground; and each one that he tossed into his pocket hit the little dog somewhere upon the head or back, and made him growl. The little dog's name was Toto, and he was sorry he had been put in the shaggy man's pocket.

Pretty soon Dorothy came out of the house with her sunbonnet, and she called out:

"Come on, Shaggy Man, if you want me to show you the road to Butterfield." She climbed the fence into the ten-acre lot and he followed her, walking slowly and stumbling over the little hillocks in the pasture as if he was thinking of something else and did not notice them.

"My, but you're clumsy!" said the little girl. "Are your feet tired?"

"No, miss; it's my whiskers; they tire very easily in this warm weather," said he. "I wish it would snow, don't you?"

"'Course not, Shaggy Man," replied Dorothy, giving him a severe look. "If it snowed in August it would spoil the corn and the oats and the wheat; and then Uncle Henry wouldn't have any crops; and that would make him poor; and—"

"Never mind," said the shaggy man. "It won't snow, I guess. Is this the lane?"

"Yes," replied Dorothy, climbing another fence; "I'll go as far as the highway with you."

"Thankee, miss; you're very kind for your size, I'm sure," said he gratefully.

"It isn't everyone who knows the road to Butterfield," Dorothy remarked as she tripped along the lane; "but I've driven there many a time with Uncle Henry, and so I b'lieve I could find it blindfolded."

"Don't do that, miss," said the shaggy man earnestly; "you might make a mistake."

"I won't," she answered, laughing. "Here's the highway. Now it's the second—no, the third turn to the left—or else it's the fourth. Let's see. The first one is by the elm tree, and the second is by the gopher holes; and then—"

"Then what?" he inquired, putting his hands in his coat pockets. Toto grabbed a finger and bit it; the shaggy man took his hand out of that pocket quickly, and said "Oh!"

Dorothy did not notice. She was shading her eyes from the sun with her arm, looking anxiously down the road.

"Come on," she commanded. "It's only a little way farther, so I may as well show you."

After a while, they came to the place where five roads branched in different directions; Dorothy pointed to one, and said:

"That's it, Shaggy Man."

"I'm much obliged, miss," he said, and started along another road.

"Not that one!" she cried; "you're going wrong."

He stopped.

"I thought you said that other was the road to Butterfield," said he, running his fingers through his shaggy whiskers in a puzzled way.

"So it is."

"But I don't want to go to Butterfield, miss."

"You don't?"

"Of course not. I wanted you to show me the road, so I shouldn't go there by mistake."

"Oh! Where DO you want to go, then?"

"I'm not particular, miss."

This answer astonished the little girl; and it made her provoked, too, to think she had taken all this trouble for nothing.

"There are a good many roads here," observed the shaggy man, turning slowly around, like a human windmill. "Seems to me a person could go 'most anywhere, from this place."

Dorothy turned around too, and gazed in surprise. There WERE a good many roads; more than she had ever seen before. She tried to count them, knowing there ought to be five, but when she had counted seventeen she grew bewildered and stopped, for the roads were as many as the spokes of a wheel and ran in every direction from the place where they stood; so if she kept on counting she was likely to count some of the roads twice.

"Dear me!" she exclaimed. "There used to be only five roads, highway and all. And now—why, where's the highway, Shaggy Man?"

"Can't say, miss," he responded, sitting down upon the ground as if tired with standing. "Wasn't it here a minute ago?"

"I thought so," she answered, greatly perplexed. "And I saw the gopher holes, too, and the dead stump; but they're not here now. These roads are all strange—and what a lot of them there are! Where do you suppose they all go to?"

"Roads," observed the shaggy man, "don't go anywhere. They stay in one place, so folks can walk on them."

He put his hand in his side-pocket and drew out an apple—quick, before Toto could bite him again. The little dog got his head out this time and said "Bow-wow!" so loudly that it made Dorothy jump.

"O, Toto!" she cried; "where did you come from?"

"I brought him along," said the shaggy man.

"What for?" she asked.

"To guard these apples in my pocket, miss, so no one would steal them."

With one hand the shaggy man held the apple, which he began eating, while with the other hand he pulled Toto out of his pocket and dropped him to the ground. Of course Toto made for Dorothy at once, barking joyfully at his release from the dark pocket. When the child had patted his head lovingly, he sat down before her, his red tongue hanging out one side of his mouth, and looked up into her face with his bright brown eyes, as if asking her what they should do next.

Dorothy didn't know. She looked around her anxiously for some familiar landmark; but everything was strange. Between the branches of the many roads were green meadows and a few shrubs and trees, but she couldn't see anywhere the farm-house from which she had just come, or anything she had ever seen before—except the shaggy man and Toto. Besides this, she had turned around and around so many times trying to find out where she was, that now she couldn't even tell which direction the farm-house ought to be in; and this began to worry her and make her feel anxious.

"I'm 'fraid, Shaggy Man," she said, with a sigh, "that we're lost!"

"That's nothing to be afraid of," he replied, throwing away the core of his apple and beginning to eat another one. "Each of these roads must lead somewhere, or it wouldn't be here. So what does it matter?"

"I want to go home again," she said.

"Well, why don't you?" said he.

"I don't know which road to take."

"That is too bad," he said, shaking his shaggy head gravely. "I wish I could help you; but I can't. I'm a stranger in these parts."

"Seems as if I were, too," she said, sitting down beside him. "It's funny. A few minutes ago I was home, and I just came to show you the way to Butterfield—"

"So I shouldn't make a mistake and go there—"

"And now I'm lost myself and don't know how to get home!"

"Have an apple," suggested the shaggy man, handing her one with pretty red cheeks.

"I'm not hungry," said Dorothy, pushing it away.

"But you may be, to-morrow; then you'll be sorry you didn't eat the apple," said he.

"If I am, I'll eat the apple then," promised Dorothy.

"Perhaps there won't be any apple then," he returned, beginning to eat the red-cheeked one himself. "Dogs sometimes can find their way home better than people," he went on; "perhaps your dog can lead you back to the farm."

"Will you, Toto?" asked Dorothy.

Toto wagged his tail vigorously.

"All right," said the girl; "let's go home."

Toto looked around a minute and dashed up one of the roads.

"Good-bye, Shaggy Man," called Dorothy, and ran after Toto. The little dog pranced briskly along for some distance; when he turned around and looked at his mistress questioningly.

"Oh, don't 'spect ME to tell you anything; I don't know the way," she said. "You'll have to find it yourself."

But Toto couldn't. He wagged his tail, and sneezed, and shook his ears, and trotted back where they had left the shaggy man. From here he started along another road; then came back and tried another; but each time he found the way strange and decided it would not take them to the farm-house. Finally, when Dorothy had begun to tire with chasing after him, Toto sat down panting beside the shaggy man and gave up.

Dorothy sat down, too, very thoughtful. The little girl had encountered some queer adventures since she came to live at the farm; but this was the queerest of them all. To get lost in fifteen minutes, so near to her home and in the unromantic State of Kansas, was an experience that fairly bewildered her.

"Will your folks worry?" asked the shaggy man, his eyes twinkling in a pleasant way.

"I s'pose so," answered Dorothy with a sigh. "Uncle Henry says there's ALWAYS something happening to me; but I've always come home safe at the last. So perhaps he'll take comfort and think I'll come home safe this time."

"I'm sure you will," said the shaggy man, smilingly nodding at her. "Good little girls never come to any harm, you know. For my part, I'm good, too; so nothing ever hurts me."

Dorothy looked at him curiously. His clothes were shaggy, his boots were shaggy and full of holes, and his hair and whiskers were shaggy. But his smile was sweet and his eyes were kind.

"Why didn't you want to go to Butterfield?" she asked.

"Because a man lives there who owes me fifteen cents, and if I went to Butterfield and he saw me he'd want to pay me the money. I don't want money, my dear."

"Why not?" she inquired.

"Money," declared the shaggy man, "makes people proud and haughty. I don't want to be proud and haughty. All I want is to have people love me; and as long as I own the Love Magnet, everyone I meet is sure to love me dearly."

"The Love Magnet! Why, what's that?"

"I'll show you, if you won't tell any one," he answered, in a low, mysterious voice.

"There isn't any one to tell, 'cept Toto," said the girl.

The shaggy man searched in one pocket, carefully; and in another pocket; and in a third. At last he drew out a small parcel wrapped in crumpled paper and tied with a cotton string. He unwound the string, opened the parcel, and took out a bit of metal shaped like a horseshoe. It was dull and brown, and not very pretty.

"This, my dear," said he, impressively, "is the wonderful Love Magnet. It was given me by an Eskimo in the Sandwich Islands— where there are no sandwiches at all—and as long as I carry it every living thing I meet will love me dearly."

"Why didn't the Eskimo keep it?" she asked, looking at the Magnet with interest.

"He got tired of being loved and longed for some one to hate him. So he gave me the Magnet and the very next day a grizzly bear ate him."

"Wasn't he sorry then?" she inquired.

"He didn't say," replied the shaggy man, wrapping and tying the Love Magnet with great care and putting it away in another pocket. "But the bear didn't seem sorry a bit," he added.

"Did you know the bear?" asked Dorothy.

"Yes; we used to play ball together in the Caviar Islands. The bear loved me because I had the Love Magnet. I couldn't blame him for eating the Eskimo, because it was his nature to do so."

"Once," said Dorothy, "I knew a Hungry Tiger who longed to eat fat babies, because it was his nature to; but he never ate any because he had a Conscience."

"This bear," replied the shaggy man, with a sigh, "had no Conscience, you see."

The shaggy man sat silent for several minutes, apparently considering the cases of the bear and the tiger, while Toto watched him with an air of great interest. The little dog was doubtless thinking of his ride in the shaggy man's pocket and planning to keep out of reach in the future.

At last the shaggy man turned and inquired, "What's your name, little girl?"

"My name's Dorothy," said she, jumping up again, "but what are we going to do? We can't stay here forever, you know."

"Let's take the seventh road," he suggested. "Seven is a lucky number for little girls named Dorothy."

"The seventh from where?"

"From where you begin to count."

So she counted seven roads, and the seventh looked just like all the others; but the shaggy man got up from the ground where he had been sitting and started down this road as if sure it was the best way to go; and Dorothy and Toto followed him.

2. Dorothy Meets Button-Bright

The seventh road was a good road, and curved this way and

that— winding through green meadows and fields covered with daisies and buttercups and past groups of shady trees. There were no houses of any sort to be seen, and for some distance they met with no living creature at all.

Dorothy began to fear they were getting a good way from the farm-house, since here everything was strange to her; but it would do no good at all to go back where the other roads all met, because the next one they chose might lead her just as far from home.

She kept on beside the shaggy man, who whistled cheerful tunes to beguile the journey, until by and by they followed a turn in the road and saw before them a big chestnut tree making a shady spot over the highway. In the shade sat a little boy dressed in sailor clothes, who was digging a hole in the earth with a bit of wood. He must have been digging some time, because the hole was already big enough to drop a football into.

Dorothy and Toto and the shaggy man came to a halt before the little boy, who kept on digging in a sober and persistent fashion.

"Who are you?" asked the girl.

He looked up at her calmly. His face was round and chubby and his eyes were big, blue and earnest.

"I'm Button-Bright," said he.

"But what's your real name?" she inquired.

"Button-Bright."

"That isn't a really-truly name!" she exclaimed.

"Isn't it?" he asked, still digging.

"'Course not. It's just a—a thing to call you by. You must have a name."

"Must I?"

"To be sure. What does your mama call you?"

He paused in his digging and tried to think.

"Papa always said I was bright as a button; so mama always called me Button-Bright," he said.

"What is your papa's name?"

"Just Papa."

"What else?"

"Don't know."

"Never mind," said the shaggy man, smiling. "We'll call the boy Button-Bright, as his mama does. That name is as good as any, and better than some."

Dorothy watched the boy dig.

"Where do you live?" she asked.

"Don't know," was the reply.

"How did you come here?"

"Don't know," he said again.

"Don't you know where you came from?"

"No," said he.

"Why, he must be lost," she said to the shaggy man. She turned to the boy once more.

"What are you going to do?" she inquired.

"Dig," said he.

"But you can't dig forever; and what are you going to do then?" she persisted.

"Don't know," said the boy.

"But you MUST know SOMETHING," declared Dorothy, getting provoked.

"Must I?" he asked, looking up in surprise.

"Of course you must."

"What must I know?"

"What's going to become of you, for one thing," she answered.

"Do YOU know what's going to become of me?" he asked.

"Not—not 'zactly," she admitted.

"Do you know what's going to become of YOU?" he continued earnestly.

"I can't say I do," replied Dorothy, remembering her present difficulties.

The shaggy man laughed.

"No one knows everything, Dorothy," he said.

"But Button-Bright doesn't seem to know ANYthing," she declared. "Do you, Button-Bright?"

He shook his head, which had pretty curls all over it, and replied with perfect calmness: "Don't know."

Never before had Dorothy met with anyone who could give her so little information. The boy was evidently lost, and his people would be sure to worry about him. He seemed two or three years younger than Dorothy, and was prettily dressed, as if someone loved him dearly and took much pains to make him look well. How, then, did he come to be in this lonely road? she wondered.

Near Button-Bright, on the ground, lay a sailor hat with a gilt anchor on the band. His sailor trousers were long and wide at the bottom, and the broad collar of his blouse had gold anchors sewed on its corners. The boy was still digging at his hole.

"Have you ever been to sea?" asked Dorothy.

"To see what?" answered Button-Bright.

"I mean, have you ever been where there's water?"

"Yes," said Button-Bright; "there's a well in our back yard."

"You don't understand," cried Dorothy. "I mean, have you ever been on a big ship floating on a big ocean?"

"Don't know," said he.

"Then why do you wear sailor clothes?"

"Don't know," he answered, again.

Dorothy was in despair.

"You're just AWFUL stupid, Button-Bright," she said.

"Am I?" he asked.

"Yes, you are."

"Why?" looking up at her with big eyes.

She was going to say: "Don't know," but stopped herself in time.

"That's for you to answer," she replied.

"It's no use asking Button-Bright questions," said the shaggy man, who had been eating another apple; "but someone ought to take care of the poor little chap, don't you think? So he'd better come along with us."

Toto had been looking with great curiosity in the hole which the boy was digging, and growing more and more excited every minute, perhaps thinking that Button-Bright was after some wild animal. The little dog began barking loudly and jumped into the hole himself, where he began to dig with his tiny paws, making the earth fly in all directions. It spattered over the boy. Dorothy seized him and raised him to his feet, brushing his clothes with her hand.

"Stop that, Toto!" she called. "There aren't any mice or woodchucks in that hole, so don't be foolish."

Toto stopped, sniffed at the hole suspiciously, and jumped out of it, wagging his tail as if he had done something important.

"Well," said the shaggy man, "let's start on, or we won't get anywhere before night comes."

"Where do you expect to get to?" asked Dorothy.

"I'm like Button-Bright. I don't know," answered the shaggy man, with a laugh. "But I've learned from long experience that every road leads somewhere, or there wouldn't be any road; so it's likely that if we travel long enough, my dear, we will come to some place or another in the end. What place it will be we can't even guess at this moment, but we're sure to find out when we get there."

"Why, yes," said Dorothy; "that seems reas'n'ble, Shaggy Man."

3. A Queer Village

Button-Bright took the shaggy man's hand willingly; for the shaggy man had the Love Magnet, you know, which was the reason Button-Bright had loved him at once. They started on, with Dorothy on one side, and Toto on the other, the little party trudging along more cheerfully than you might have supposed. The girl was getting used to queer adventures, which interested her very much. Wherever Dorothy went Toto was sure to go, like Mary's little lamb. Button-Bright didn't seem a bit afraid or worried because he was lost, and the shaggy man had no home, perhaps, and was as happy in one place as in another.

Before long they saw ahead of them a fine big arch spanning the road, and when they came nearer they found that the arch was beautifully carved and decorated with rich colors. A row of peacocks with spread tails ran along the top of it, and all the feathers were gorgeously painted. In the center was a large fox's head, and the fox wore a shrewd and knowing expression and had large spectacles over its eyes and a small golden crown with shiny points on top of its head.

While the travelers were looking with curiosity at this beautiful arch there suddenly marched out of it a company of soldiers—only the soldiers were all foxes dressed in uniforms. They wore green jackets and yellow pantaloons, and their little round caps and their high boots were a bright red color. Also, there was a big red bow tied about the middle of each long, bushy tail. Each soldier was armed with a wooden sword having an edge of sharp teeth set in a row, and the sight of these teeth at first caused Dorothy to shudder.

A captain marched in front of the company of fox-soldiers, his uniform embroidered with gold braid to make it handsomer than the others.

Almost before our friends realized it the soldiers had surrounded them on all sides, and the captain was calling out in a harsh voice: "Surrender! You are our prisoners."

"What's a pris'ner?" asked Button-Bright.

"A prisoner is a captive," replied the fox-captain, strutting up and down with much dignity.

"What's a captive?" asked Button-Bright.

"You're one," said the captain.

That made the shaggy man laugh

"Good afternoon, captain," he said, bowing politely to all the foxes and very low to their commander. "I trust you are in good health, and that your families are all well?"

The fox-captain looked at the shaggy man, and his sharp features grew pleasant and smiling.

"We're pretty well, thank you, Shaggy Man," said he; and Dorothy knew that the Love Magnet was working and that all the foxes now loved the shaggy man because of it. But Toto didn't know this, for he began barking angrily and tried to bite the captain's hairy leg where it showed between his red boots and his yellow pantaloons.

"Stop, Toto!" cried the little girl, seizing the dog in her arms. "These are our friends."

"Why, so we are!" remarked the captain in tones of astonishment. "I thought at first we were enemies, but it seems you are friends instead. You must come with me to see King Dox."

"Who's he?" asked Button-Bright, with earnest eyes.

"King Dox of Foxville; the great and wise sovereign who rules over our community."

"What's sov'rin, and what's c'u'nity?" inquired Button-Bright.

"Don't ask so many questions, little boy."

"Why?"

"Ah, why indeed?" exclaimed the captain, looking at Button-Bright admiringly. "If you don't ask questions you will learn nothing. True enough. I was wrong. You're a very clever little boy, come to think of it—very clever indeed. But now, friends, please come with me, for it is my duty to escort you at once to the royal palace."

The soldiers marched back through the arch again, and with them marched the shaggy man, Dorothy, Toto, and Button-Bright. Once through the opening they found a fine, big city spread out before them, all the houses of carved marble in beautiful colors. The decorations were mostly birds and other fowl, such as peacocks, pheasants, turkeys, prairie-chickens, ducks, and geese. Over each doorway was carved a head representing the fox who lived in that house, this effect being quite pretty and unusual.

As our friends marched along, some of the foxes came out on the porches and balconies to get a view of the strangers. These foxes were all handsomely dressed, the girl-foxes and women-foxes wearing gowns of feathers woven together effectively and colored in bright hues which Dorothy thought were quite artistic and decidedly attractive.

Button-Bright stared until his eyes were big and round, and he would have stumbled and fallen more than once had not the shaggy man grasped his hand tightly. They were all interested, and Toto was so excited he wanted to bark every minute and to chase and fight every fox he caught sight of; but Dorothy held his little wiggling body fast in her arms and commanded him to be good and behave himself. So he finally quieted down, like a wise doggy, deciding there were too many foxes in Foxville to fight at one time.

By-and-by they came to a big square, and in the center of the square stood the royal palace. Dorothy knew it at once because it had over its great door the carved head of a fox just like the one she had seen on the arch, and this fox was the only one who wore a golden crown.

There were many fox-soldiers guarding the door, but they bowed to the captain and admitted him without question. The captain led them through many rooms, where richly dressed foxes were sitting on beautiful chairs or sipping tea, which was being passed around by fox-servants in white aprons. They came to a big doorway covered with heavy curtains of cloth of gold.

Beside this doorway stood a huge drum. The fox-captain went to this drum and knocked his knees against it— first one knee and then the other—so that the drum said: "Boom-boom."

"You must all do exactly what I do," ordered the captain; so the shaggy man pounded the drum with his knees, and so did Dorothy and so did Button-Bright. The boy wanted to keep on pounding it with his little fat knees, because he liked the sound of it; but the captain stopped him. Toto couldn't pound the drum with his knees and he didn't know enough to wag his tail against it, so Dorothy pounded the drum for him and that made him bark, and when the little dog barked the fox-captain scowled.

The golden curtains drew back far enough to make an opening, through which marched the captain with the others.

The broad, long room they entered was decorated in gold with stained-glass windows of splendid colors. In the corner of the room upon a richly carved golden throne, sat the fox-king, surrounded by a group of other foxes, all of whom wore great spectacles over their eyes, making them look solemn and important.

Dorothy knew the King at once, because she had seen his head carved on the arch and over the doorway of the palace. Having met with several other kings in her travels, she knew what to do, and at once made a low bow before the throne. The shaggy man bowed, too, and Button-Bright bobbed his head and said "Hello."

"Most wise and noble Potentate of Foxville," said the captain, addressing the King in a pompous voice, "I humbly beg to report that I found these strangers on the road leading to your Foxy Majesty's dominions, and have therefore brought them before you, as is my duty."

"So—so," said the King, looking at them keenly. "What brought you here, strangers?"

"Our legs, may it please your Royal Hairiness," replied the shaggy man.

"What is your business here?" was the next question.

"To get away as soon as possible," said the shaggy man.

The King didn't know about the Magnet, of course; but it made him love the shaggy man at once.

"Do just as you please about going away," he said; "but I'd like to show you the sights of my city and to entertain your party while you are here. We feel highly honored to have little Dorothy with us, I assure you, and we appreciate her kindness in making us a visit. For whatever country Dorothy visits is sure to become famous."

This speech greatly surprised the little girl, who asked:

"How did your Majesty know my name?"

"Why, everybody knows you, my dear," said the Fox-King. "Don't you realize that? You are quite an important personage since Princess Ozma of Oz made you her friend."

"Do you know Ozma?" she asked, wondering.

"I regret to say that I do not," he answered, sadly; "but I hope to meet her soon. You know the Princess Ozma is to celebrate her birthday on the twenty-first of this month."

"Is she?" said Dorothy. "I didn't know that."

"Yes; it is to be the most brilliant royal ceremony ever held in any city in Fairyland, and I hope you will try to get me an invitation."

Dorothy thought a moment.

"I'm sure Ozma would invite you if I asked her," she said; "but how could you get to the Land of Oz and the Emerald City? It's a good way from Kansas."

"Kansas!" he exclaimed, surprised.

"Why, yes; we are in Kansas now, aren't we?" she returned.

"What a queer notion!" cried the Fox-King, beginning to laugh. "Whatever made you think this is Kansas?"

"I left Uncle Henry's farm only about two hours ago; that's the reason," she said, rather perplexed.

"But, tell me, my dear, did you ever see so wonderful a city as Foxville in Kansas?" he questioned.

"No, your Majesty."

"And haven't you traveled from Oz to Kansas in less than half a jiffy, by means of the Silver Shoes and the Magic Belt?"

"Yes, your Majesty," she acknowledged.

"Then why do you wonder that an hour or two could bring you to Foxville, which is nearer to Oz than it is to Kansas?"

"Dear me!" exclaimed Dorothy; "is this another fairy adventure?"

"It seems to be," said the Fox-King, smiling.

Dorothy turned to the shaggy man, and her face was grave and reproachful.

"Are you a magician? or a fairy in disguise?" she asked. "Did you enchant me when you asked the way to Butterfield?"

The shaggy man shook his head.

"Who ever heard of a shaggy fairy?" he replied. "No, Dorothy, my dear; I'm not to blame for this journey in any way, I assure you. There's been something strange about me ever since I owned the Love Magnet; but I don't know what it is any more than you do. I didn't try to get you away from home, at all. If you want to find your way back to the farm I'll go with you willingly, and do my best to help you."

"Never mind," said the little girl, thoughtfully. "There isn't so much to see in Kansas as there is here, and I guess Aunt Em won't be VERY much worried; that is, if I don't stay away too long."

"That's right," declared the Fox-King, nodding approval. "Be contented with your lot, whatever it happens to be, if you are wise. Which reminds me that you have a new companion on this adventure—he looks very clever and bright."

"He is," said Dorothy; and the shaggy man added: "That's his name, your Royal Foxiness—Button-Bright."

4. King Dox

It was amusing to note the expression on the face of King Dox as he looked the boy over, from his sailor hat to his stubby shoes, and it was equally diverting to watch Button-Bright stare at the King in return. No fox ever beheld a fresher, fairer child's face, and no child had ever before heard a fox talk, or met with one who dressed so handsomely and ruled so big a city. I am sorry to say that no one had ever told the little boy much about fairies of any kind; this being the case, it is easy to understand how much his strange experience startled and astonished him.

"How do you like us?" asked the King.

"Don't know," said Button-Bright.

"Of course you don't. It's too short an acquaintance," returned his Majesty. "What do you suppose my name is?"

"Don't know," said Button-Bright.

"How should you? Well, I'll tell you. My private name is Dox, but a King can't be called by his private name; he has to take one that is official. Therefore my official name is King Renard the Fourth. Ren-ard with the accent on the 'Ren'."

"What's 'ren'?" asked Button-Bright.

"How clever!" exclaimed the King, turning a pleased face toward his counselors. "This boy is indeed remarkably bright. 'What's 'ren'?' he asks; and of course 'ren' is nothing at all, all by itself. Yes, he's very bright indeed."

"That question is what your Majesty might call foxy," said one of the counselors, an old grey fox.

"So it is," declared the King. Turning again to Button-Bright, he asked:

"Having told you my name, what would you call me?"

"King Dox," said the boy.

"Why?"

"'Cause 'ren''s nothing at all," was the reply.

"Good! Very good indeed! You certainly have a brilliant mind. Do you know why two and two make four?"

"No," said Button-Bright.

"Clever! clever indeed! Of course you don't know. Nobody knows why; we only know it's so, and can't tell why it's so. Button-Bright, those curls and blue eyes do not go well with so much wisdom. They make you look too youthful, and hide your real cleverness. Therefore, I will do you a great favor. I will confer upon you the head of a fox, so that you may hereafter look as bright as you really are."

As he spoke the King waved his paw toward the boy, and at once the pretty curls and fresh round face and big blue eyes were gone, while in their place a fox's head appeared upon Button-Bright's shoulders—a hairy head with a sharp nose, pointed ears, and keen little eyes.

"Oh, don't do that!" cried Dorothy, shrinking back from her transformed companion with a shocked and dismayed face.

"Too late, my dear; it's done. But you also shall have a fox's head if you can prove you're as clever as Button-Bright."

"I don't want it; it's dreadful!" she exclaimed; and, hearing this verdict, Button-Bright began to boo-hoo just as if he were still a little boy.

"How can you call that lovely head dreadful?" asked the King. "It's a much prettier face than he had before, to my notion, and my wife says I'm a good judge of beauty. Don't cry, little fox-boy. Laugh and be proud, because you are so highly favored. How do you like the new head, Button-Bright?"

"D-d-don't n-n-know!" sobbed the child.

"Please, PLEASE change him back again, your Majesty!" begged Dorothy.

King Renard IV shook his head.

"I can't do that," he said; "I haven't the power, even if I wanted to. No, Button-Bright must wear his fox head, and he'll be sure to love it dearly as soon as he gets used to it."

Both the shaggy man and Dorothy looked grave and anxious, for they were sorrowful that such a misfortune had overtaken their little companion. Toto barked at the fox-boy once or twice, not realizing it was his former friend who now wore the animal head; but Dorothy cuffed the dog and made him stop. As for the foxes, they all seemed to think Button-Bright's new head very becoming and that their King had conferred a great honor on this little stranger. It was funny to see the boy reach up to feel of his sharp nose and wide mouth, and wail afresh with grief. He wagged his ears in a comical manner and tears were in his little black eyes. But Dorothy couldn't laugh at her friend just yet, because she felt so sorry.

Just then three little fox-princesses, daughters of the King, entered the room, and when they saw Button-Bright one exclaimed: "How lovely he is!" and the next one cried in delight: "How sweet he is!" and the third princess clapped her hands with pleasure and said, "How beautiful he is!"

Button-Bright stopped crying and asked timidly: "Am I?"

"In all the world there is not another face so pretty," declared the biggest fox-princess.

"You must live with us always, and be our brother," said the next.

"We shall all love you dearly," the third said.

This praise did much to comfort the boy, and he looked around and tried to smile. It was a pitiful attempt, because the fox face was new and stiff, and Dorothy thought his expression more stupid than before the transformation.

"I think we ought to be going now," said the shaggy man, uneasily, for he didn't know what the King might take into his head to do next.

"Don't leave us yet, I beg of you," pleaded King Renard. "I intend to have several days of feasting and merry-making in honor of your visit."

"Have it after we're gone, for we can't wait," said Dorothy, decidedly. But seeing this displeased the King, she added: "If I'm going to get Ozma to invite you to her party I'll have to find her as soon as poss'ble, you know."

In spite of all the beauty of Foxville and the gorgeous dresses of its inhabitants, both the girl and the shaggy man felt they were not quite safe there, and would be glad to see the last of it.

"But it is now evening," the King reminded them, "and you must stay with us until morning, anyhow. Therefore, I invite you to be my guests at dinner, and to attend the theater afterward and sit in the royal box. To-morrow morning, if you really insist upon it,

you may resume your journey."

They consented to this, and some of the fox-servants led them to a suite of lovely rooms in the big palace.

Button-Bright was afraid to be left alone, so Dorothy took him into her own room. While a maid-fox dressed the little girl's hair—which was a bit tangled—and put some bright, fresh ribbons in it, another maid-fox combed the hair on poor Button-Bright's face and head and brushed it carefully, tying a pink bow to each of his pointed ears. The maids wanted to dress the children in fine costumes of woven feathers, such as all the foxes wore; but neither of them consented to that.

"A sailor suit and a fox head do not go well together," said one of the maids, "for no fox was ever a sailor that I can remember."

"I'm not a fox!" cried Button-Bright.

"Alas, no," agreed the maid. "But you've got a lovely fox head on your skinny shoulders, and that's ALMOST as good as being a fox."

The boy, reminded of his misfortune, began to cry again. Dorothy petted and comforted him and promised to find some way to restore him his own head.

"If we can manage to get to Ozma," she said, "the Princess will change you back to yourself in half a second; so you just wear that fox head as comf't'bly as you can, dear, and don't worry about it at all. It isn't nearly as pretty as your own head, no matter what the foxes say; but you can get along with it for a little while longer, can't you?"

"Don't know," said Button-Bright, doubtfully; but he didn't cry any more after that.

Dorothy let the maids pin ribbons to her shoulders, after which they were ready for the King's dinner. When they met the shaggy man in the splendid drawing room of the palace they found him just the same as before. He had refused to give up his shaggy clothes for new ones, because if he did that he would no longer be the shaggy man, he said, and he might have to get acquainted with himself all over again.

He told Dorothy he had brushed his shaggy hair and whiskers, but she thought he must have brushed them the wrong way, for they were quite as shaggy as before.

As for the company of foxes assembled to dine with the strangers, they were most beautifully costumed, and their rich dresses made Dorothy's simple gown and Button-Bright's sailor suit and the shaggy man's shaggy clothes look commonplace. But they treated their guests with great respect and the King's dinner was a very good dinner indeed. Foxes, as you know, are fond of chicken and other fowl; so they served chicken soup and roasted turkey and stewed duck and fried grouse and broiled quail and goose pie, and as the cooking was excellent the King's guests enjoyed the meal and ate heartily of the various dishes.

The party went to the theater, where they saw a play acted by foxes dressed in costumes of brilliantly colored feathers. The play was about a fox-girl who was stolen by some wicked wolves and carried to their cave; and just as they were about to kill her and eat her a company of fox-soldiers marched up, saved the girl, and put all the wicked wolves to death.

"How do you like it?" the King asked Dorothy.

"Pretty well," she answered. "It reminds me of one of Mr. Aesop's fables."

"Don't mention Aesop to me, I beg of you!" exclaimed King Dox. "I hate that man's name. He wrote a good deal about foxes, but always made them out cruel and wicked, whereas we are gentle and kind, as you may see."

"But his fables showed you to be wise and clever, and more shrewd than other animals," said the shaggy man, thoughtfully.

"So we are. There is no question about our knowing more than men do," replied the King, proudly. "But we employ our wisdom to do good, instead of harm; so that horrid Aesop did not know what he was talking about."

They did not like to contradict him, because they felt he ought to know the nature of foxes better than men did; so they sat still and watched the play, and Button-Bright became so interested that for the time he forgot he wore a fox head.

Afterward they went back to the palace and slept in soft beds stuffed with feathers; for the foxes raised many fowl for food, and used their feathers for clothing and to sleep upon.

Dorothy wondered why the animals living in Foxville did not wear just their own hairy skins as wild foxes do; when she mentioned it to King Dox he said they clothed themselves because they were civilized.

"But you were born without clothes," she observed, "and you don't seem to me to need them."

"So were human beings born without clothes," he replied; "and until they became civilized they wore only their natural skins. But to become civilized means to dress as elaborately and prettily as possible, and to make a show of your clothes so your neighbors will envy you, and for that reason both civilized foxes and civilized humans spend most of their time dressing themselves."

"I don't," declared the shaggy man.

"That is true," said the King, looking at him carefully; "but perhaps you are not civilized."

After a sound sleep and a good night's rest they had their breakfast with the King and then bade his Majesty good-bye.

"You've been kind to us—'cept poor Button-Bright," said Dorothy, "and we've had a nice time in Foxville."

"Then," said King Dox, "perhaps you'll be good enough to get me an invitation to Princess Ozma's birthday celebration."

"I'll try," she promised; "if I see her in time."

"It's on the twenty-first, remember," he continued; "and if you'll just see that I'm invited I'll find a way to cross the Dreadful Desert into the marvelous Land of Oz. I've always wanted to visit the Emerald City, so I'm sure it was fortunate you arrived here just when you did, you being Princess Ozma's friend and able to assist me in getting the invitation."

"If I see Ozma I'll ask her to invite you," she replied.

The Fox-King had a delightful luncheon put up for them, which the shaggy man shoved in his pocket, and the fox-captain escorted them to an arch at the side of the village opposite the one by which they had entered. Here they found more soldiers guarding the road.

"Are you afraid of enemies?" asked Dorothy.

"No; because we are watchful and able to protect ourselves," answered the captain. "But this road leads to another village peopled by big, stupid beasts who might cause us trouble if they thought we were afraid of them."

"What beasts are they?" asked the shaggy man.

The captain hesitated to answer. Finally, he said:

"You will learn all about them when you arrive at their city. But do not be afraid of them. Button-Bright is so wonderfully clever and has now such an intelligent face that I'm sure he will manage to find a way to protect you."

This made Dorothy and the shaggy man rather uneasy, for they had not so much confidence in the fox-boy's wisdom as the captain seemed to have. But as their escort would say no more about the beasts, they bade him good-bye and proceeded on their journey.

5. The Rainbow's Daughter

Toto, now allowed to run about as he pleased, was glad to be free again and able to bark at the birds and chase the butterflies. The country around them was charming, yet in the pretty fields of wild-flowers and groves of leafy trees were no houses whatever, or sign of any inhabitants. Birds flew through the air and cunning white rabbits darted amongst the tall grasses and green bushes; Dorothy noticed even the ants toiling busily along the roadway, bearing gigantic loads of clover seed; but of people there were none at all.

They walked briskly on for an hour or two, for even little Button-Bright was a good walker and did not tire easily. At length as they turned a curve in the road they beheld just before them a curious sight.

A little girl, radiant and beautiful, shapely as a fairy and exquisitely dressed, was dancing gracefully in the middle of the lonely road, whirling slowly this way and that, her dainty feet twinkling in sprightly fashion. She was clad in flowing, fluffy robes of soft material that reminded Dorothy of woven cobwebs, only it was colored in soft tintings of violet, rose, topaz, olive, azure, and white, mingled together most harmoniously in stripes which melted one into the other with soft blendings. Her hair was like spun gold and flowed around her in a cloud, no strand being fastened or confined by either pin or ornament or ribbon.

Filled with wonder and admiration our friends approached and stood watching this fascinating dance. The girl was no taller than Dorothy, although more slender; nor did she seem any older than our little heroine.

Suddenly she paused and abandoned the dance, as if for the first time observing the presence of strangers. As she faced them, shy as a frightened fawn, poised upon one foot as if to fly the next instant, Dorothy was astonished to see tears flowing from her violet eyes and trickling down her lovely rose-hued cheeks. That the dainty maiden should dance and weep at the same time was indeed surprising; so Dorothy asked in a soft, sympathetic voice: "Are you unhappy, little girl?"

"Very!" was the reply; "I am lost."

"Why, so are we," said Dorothy, smiling; "but we don't cry about it."

"Don't you? Why not?"

"'Cause I've been lost before, and always got found again," answered Dorothy simply.

"But I've never been lost before," murmured the dainty maiden, "and I'm worried and afraid."

"You were dancing," remarked Dorothy, in a puzzled tone of voice.

"Oh, that was just to keep warm," explained the maiden, quickly. "It was not because I felt happy or gay, I assure you."

Dorothy looked at her closely. Her gauzy flowing robes might not be very warm, yet the weather wasn't at all chilly, but rather mild and balmy, like a spring day.

"Who are you, dear?" she asked, gently.

"I'm Polychrome," was the reply.

"Polly whom?"

"Polychrome. I'm the Daughter of the Rainbow."

"Oh!" said Dorothy with a gasp; "I didn't know the Rainbow had children. But I MIGHT have known it, before you spoke. You couldn't really be anything else."

"Why not?" inquired Polychrome, as if surprised.

"Because you're so lovely and sweet."

The little maiden smiled through her tears, came up to Dorothy, and placed her slender fingers in the Kansas girl's chubby hand.

"You'll be my friend—won't you?" she said, pleadingly.

"Of course."

"And what is your name?"

"I'm Dorothy; and this is my friend Shaggy Man, who owns the Love Magnet; and this is Button-Bright—only you don't see him as he really is because the Fox-King carelessly changed his head into a fox head. But the real Button-Bright is good to look at, and I hope to get him changed back to himself, some time."

The Rainbow's Daughter nodded cheerfully, no longer afraid of her new companions.

"But who is this?" she asked, pointing to Toto, who was sitting before her wagging his tail in the most friendly manner and admiring the pretty maid with his bright eyes. "Is this, also, some enchanted person?"

"Oh no, Polly—I may call you Polly, mayn't I? Your whole name's awful hard to say."

"Call me Polly if you wish, Dorothy."

"Well, Polly, Toto's just a dog; but he has more sense than Button-Bright, to tell the truth; and I'm very fond of him."

"So am I," said Polychrome, bending gracefully to pat Toto's head.

"But how did the Rainbow's Daughter ever get on this lonely road, and become lost?" asked the shaggy man, who had listened wonderingly to all this.

"Why, my father stretched his rainbow over here this morning, so that one end of it touched this road," was the reply; "and I was dancing upon the pretty rays, as I love to do, and never noticed I was getting too far over the bend in the circle. Suddenly I began to slide, and I went faster and faster until at last I bumped on the ground, at the very end. Just then father lifted the rainbow again, without noticing me at all, and though I tried to seize the end of it and hold fast, it melted away entirely and I was left alone and helpless on the cold, hard earth!"

"It doesn't seem cold to me, Polly," said Dorothy; "but perhaps you're not warmly dressed."

"I'm so used to living nearer the sun," replied the Rainbow's Daughter, "that at first I feared I would freeze down here. But my dance has warmed me some, and now I wonder how I am ever to get home again."

"Won't your father miss you, and look for you, and let down another rainbow for you?"

"Perhaps so, but he's busy just now because it rains in so many parts of the world at this season, and he has to set his rainbow in a lot of different places. What would you advise me to do, Dorothy?"

"Come with us," was the answer. "I'm going to try to find my way to the Emerald City, which is in the fairy Land of Oz. The Emerald City is ruled by a friend of mine, the Princess Ozma, and if we can manage to get there I'm sure she will know a way to send you home to your father again."

"Do you really think so?" asked Polychrome, anxiously.

"I'm pretty sure."

"Then I'll go with you," said the little maid; "for travel will help keep me warm, and father can find me in one part of the world as well as another—if he gets time to look for me."

"Come along, then," said the shaggy man, cheerfully; and they started on once more. Polly walked beside Dorothy a while, holding her new friend's hand as if she feared to let it go; but her nature seemed as light and buoyant as her fleecy robes, for suddenly she darted ahead and whirled round in a giddy dance. Then she tripped back to them with sparkling eyes and smiling cheeks, having regained her usual happy mood and forgotten all her worry about being lost.

They found her a charming companion, and her dancing and laughter— for she laughed at times like the tinkling of a silver bell—did much to enliven their journey and keep them contented.

6. The City Of Beasts

When noon came they opened the Fox-King's basket of luncheon, and found a nice roasted turkey with cranberry sauce and some slices of bread and butter. As they sat on the grass by the roadside the shaggy man cut up the turkey with his pocket-knife and passed slices of it around.

"Haven't you any dewdrops, or mist-cakes, or cloudbuns?" asked Polychrome, longingly.

"Course not," replied Dorothy. "We eat solid things, down here on the earth. But there's a bottle of cold tea. Try some, won't you?"

The Rainbow's Daughter watched Button-Bright devour one leg of the turkey.

"Is it good?" she asked.

He nodded.

"Do you think I could eat it?"

"Not this," said Button-Bright.

"But I mean another piece?"

"Don't know," he replied.

"Well, I'm going to try, for I'm very hungry," she decided, and took a thin slice of the white breast of turkey which the shaggy man cut for her, as well as a bit of bread and butter. When she tasted it Polychrome thought the turkey was good—better even than mist-cakes; but a little satisfied her hunger and she finished with a tiny sip of cold tea.

"That's about as much as a fly would eat," said Dorothy, who was making a good meal herself. "But I know some people in Oz who eat nothing at all."

"Who are they?" inquired the shaggy man.

"One is a scarecrow who's stuffed with straw, and the other a woodman made out of tin. They haven't any appetites inside of 'em, you see; so they never eat anything at all."

"Are they alive?" asked Button-Bright.

"Oh yes," replied Dorothy; "and they're very clever and very nice, too. If we get to Oz I'll introduce them to you."

"Do you really expect to get to Oz?" inquired the shaggy man, taking a drink of cold tea.

"I don't know just what to 'spect," answered the child, seriously; "but I've noticed if I happen to get lost I'm almost sure to come to the Land of Oz in the end, somehow 'r other; so I may get there this time. But I can't promise, you know; all I can do is wait and see."

"Will the Scarecrow scare me?" asked Button-Bright.

"No; 'cause you're not a crow," she returned. "He has the loveliest smile you ever saw—only it's painted on and he can't help it."

Luncheon being over they started again upon their journey, the shaggy man, Dorothy and Button-Bright walking soberly along, side by side, and the Rainbow's Daughter dancing merrily before them.

Sometimes she darted along the road so swiftly that she was nearly out of sight, then she came tripping back to greet them with her silvery laughter. But once she came back more sedately, to say: "There's a city a little way off."

"I 'spected that," returned Dorothy; "for the fox-people warned us there was one on this road. It's filled with stupid beasts of some sort, but we musn't be afraid of 'em 'cause they won't hurt us."

"All right," said Button-Bright; but Polychrome didn't know whether it was all right or not.

"It's a big city," she said, "and the road runs straight through it."

"Never mind," said the shaggy man; "as long as I carry the Love Magnet every living thing will love me, and you may be sure I shan't allow any of my friends to be harmed in any way."

This comforted them somewhat, and they moved on again. Pretty soon they came to a signpost that read:

HAF A MYLE TO DUNKITON

"Oh," said the shaggy man, "if they're donkeys, we've nothing to fear at all."

"They may kick," said Dorothy, doubtfully.

"Then we will cut some switches, and make them behave," he replied. At the first tree he cut himself a long, slender switch from one of the branches, and shorter switches for the others.

"Don't be afraid to order the beasts around," he said; "they're used to it."

Before long the road brought them to the gates of the city. There was a high wall all around, which had been whitewashed, and the gate just before our travelers was a mere opening in the wall, with no bars across it. No towers or steeples or domes showed above the enclosure, nor was any living thing to be seen as our friends drew near.

Suddenly, as they were about to boldly enter through the opening, there arose a harsh clamor of sound that swelled and echoed on every side, until they were nearly deafened by the racket and had to put their fingers to their ears to keep the noise out.

It was like the firing of many cannon, only there were no cannon-balls or other missiles to be seen; it was like the rolling of mighty thunder, only no cloud was in the sky; it was like the roar of countless breakers on a rugged seashore, only there was no sea or other water anywhere about.

They hesitated to advance; but, as the noise did no harm, they entered through the whitewashed wall and quickly discovered the cause of the turmoil. Inside were suspended many sheets of tin or thin iron, and against these metal sheets a row of donkeys were pounding their heels with vicious kicks.

The shaggy man ran up to the nearest donkey and gave the beast a sharp blow with his switch.

"Stop that noise!" he shouted; and the donkey stopped kicking the metal sheet and turned its head to look with surprise at the shaggy man. He switched the next donkey, and made him stop, and then the next, so that gradually the rattling of heels ceased and the awful noise subsided. The donkeys stood in a group and eyed the strangers with fear and trembling.

"What do you mean by making such a racket?" asked the shaggy man, sternly.

"We were scaring away the foxes," said one of the donkeys, meekly. "Usually they run fast enough when they hear the noise, which makes them afraid."

"There are no foxes here," said the shaggy man.

"I beg to differ with you. There's one, anyhow," replied the donkey, sitting upright on its haunches and waving a hoof toward Button-Bright. "We saw him coming and thought the whole army of foxes was marching to attack us."

"Button-Bright isn't a fox," explained the shaggy man. "He's only wearing a fox head for a time, until he can get his own head back."

"Oh, I see," remarked the donkey, waving its left ear reflectively. "I'm sorry we made such a mistake, and had all our work and worry for nothing."

The other donkeys by this time were sitting up and examining the strangers with big, glassy eyes. They made a queer picture, indeed; for they wore wide, white collars around their necks and the collars had many scallops and points. The gentlemen-donkeys wore high pointed caps set between their great ears, and the lady-donkeys wore sunbonnets with holes cut in the top for the ears to stick through. But they had no other clothing except their hairy skins, although many wore gold and silver bangles on their front wrists and bands of different metals on their rear ankles. When they were kicking they had braced themselves with their front legs, but now they all stood or sat upright on their hind legs and used the front ones as arms. Having no fingers or hands the beasts were rather clumsy, as you may guess; but Dorothy was surprised to observe how many things they could do with their stiff, heavy hoofs.

Some of the donkeys were white, some were brown, or gray, or black, or spotted; but their hair was sleek and smooth and their broad collars and caps gave them a neat, if whimsical, appearance.

"This is a nice way to welcome visitors, I must say!" remarked the shaggy man, in a reproachful tone.

"Oh, we did not mean to be impolite," replied a grey donkey which had not spoken before. "But you were not expected, nor did you send in your visiting cards, as it is proper to do."

"There is some truth in that," admitted the shaggy man; "but, now you are informed that we are important and distinguished travelers, I trust you will accord us proper consideration."

These big words delighted the donkeys, and made them bow to the shaggy man with great respect. Said the grey one: "You shall be taken before his great and glorious Majesty King Kik-a-bray, who will greet you as becomes your exalted stations."

"That's right," answered Dorothy. "Take us to some one who knows something."

"Oh, we all know something, my child, or we shouldn't be donkeys," asserted the grey one, with dignity. "The word 'donkey' means 'clever,' you know."

"I didn't know it," she replied. "I thought it meant 'stupid'."

"Not at all, my child. If you will look in the Encyclopedia Donkaniara you will find I'm correct. But come; I will myself lead you before our splendid, exalted, and most intellectual ruler."

All donkeys love big words, so it is no wonder the grey one used so many of them.

7. The Shaggy Man's Transformation

They found the houses of the town all low and square and built of bricks, neatly whitewashed inside and out. The houses were not set in rows, forming regular streets, but placed here and there in a haphazard manner which made it puzzling for a stranger to find his way.

"Stupid people must have streets and numbered houses in their cities, to guide them where to go," observed the grey donkey, as he walked before the visitors on his hind legs, in an awkward but comical manner; "but clever donkeys know their way about without such absurd marks. Moreover, a mixed city is much prettier than one with straight streets."

Dorothy did not agree with this, but she said nothing to contradict it. Presently she saw a sign on a house that read "Madam de Fayke, Hoofist," and she asked their conductor:

"What's a 'hoofist,' please?"

"One who reads your fortune in your hoofs," replied the grey donkey.

"Oh, I see," said the little girl. "You are quite civilized here."

"Dunkiton," he replied, "is the center of the world's highest civilization."

They came to a house where two youthful donkeys were whitewashing the wall, and Dorothy stopped a moment to watch them. They dipped the ends of their tails, which were much like paint-brushes, into a pail of whitewash, backed up against the house, and wagged their tails right and left until the whitewash was rubbed on the wall, after which they dipped these funny brushes in the pail again and repeated the performance.

"That must be fun," said Button-Bright.

"No, it's work," replied the old donkey; "but we make our youngsters do all the whitewashing, to keep them out of mischief."

"Don't they go to school?" asked Dorothy.

"All donkeys are born wise," was the reply, "so the only school we need is the school of experience. Books are only for those who know nothing, and so are obliged to learn things from other people."

"In other words, the more stupid one is, the more he thinks he knows," observed the shaggy man. The grey donkey paid no attention to this speech because he had just stopped before a house which had painted over the doorway a pair of hoofs, with a donkey tail between them and a rude crown and sceptre above.

"I'll see if his magnificent Majesty King Kik-a-bray is at home, said he. He lifted his head and called "Whee-haw! whee-haw! whee-haw!" three times, in a shocking voice, turning about and kicking with his heels against the panel of the door. For a time there was no reply; then the door opened far enough to permit a donkey's head to stick out and look at them.

It was a white head, with big, awful ears and round, solemn eyes.

"Have the foxes gone?" it asked, in a trembling voice.

"They haven't been here, most stupendous Majesty," replied the grey one. "The new arrivals prove to be travelers of distinction."

"Oh," said the King, in a relieved tone of voice. "Let them come in."

He opened the door wide, and the party marched into a big room, which, Dorothy thought, looked quite unlike a king's palace. There were mats of woven grasses on the floor and the place was clean and neat; but his Majesty had no other furniture at all—perhaps because he didn't need it. He squatted down in the center of the room and a little brown donkey ran and brought a big gold crown which it placed on the monarch's head, and a golden staff with a jeweled ball at the end of it, which the King held between his front hoofs as he sat upright.

"Now then," said his Majesty, waving his long ears gently to and fro, "tell me why you are here, and what you expect me to do for you." He eyed Button-Bright rather sharply, as if afraid of the little boy's queer head, though it was the shaggy man who undertook to reply.

"Most noble and supreme ruler of Dunkiton," he said, trying not to laugh in the solemn King's face, "we are strangers traveling through your dominions and have entered your magnificent city because the road led through it, and there was no way to go around. All we desire is to pay our respects to your Majesty—the cleverest king in all the world, I'm sure—and then to continue on our way."

This polite speech pleased the King very much; indeed, it pleased him so much that it proved an unlucky speech for the shaggy man. Perhaps the Love Magnet helped to win his Majesty's affections as well as the flattery, but however this may be, the white donkey looked kindly upon the speaker and said:

"Only a donkey should be able to use such fine, big words, and you are too wise and admirable in all ways to be a mere man. Also, I feel that I love you as well as I do my own favored people, so I will bestow upon you the greatest gift within my power—a donkey's head."

As he spoke he waved his jeweled staff. Although the shaggy man cried out and tried to leap backward and escape, it proved of no use. Suddenly his own head was gone and a donkey head appeared in its place—a brown, shaggy head so absurd and droll that Dorothy and Polly both broke into merry laughter, and even Button-Bright's fox face wore a smile.

"Dear me! dear me!" cried the shaggy man, feeling of his shaggy new head and his long ears. "What a misfortune—what a great misfortune! Give me back my own head, you stupid king—if you love me at all!"

"Don't you like it?" asked the King, surprised.

"Hee-haw! I hate it! Take it away, quick!" said the shaggy man.

"But I can't do that," was the reply. "My magic works only one way. I can DO things, but I can't UNdo them. You'll have to find the Truth Pond, and bathe in its water, in order to get back your own head. But I advise you not to do that. This head is much more beautiful than the old one."

"That's a matter of taste," said Dorothy.

"Where is the Truth Pond?" asked the shaggy man, earnestly.

"Somewhere in the Land of Oz; but just the exact location of it I can not tell," was the answer.

"Don't worry, Shaggy Man," said Dorothy, smiling because her friend wagged his new ears so comically. "If the Truth Pond is in Oz, we'll be sure to find it when we get there."

"Oh! Are you going to the Land of Oz?" asked King Kik-a-bray.

"I don't know," she replied, "but we've been told we are nearer the Land of Oz than to Kansas, and if that's so, the quickest way for me to get home is to find Ozma."

"Haw-haw! Do you know the mighty Princess Ozma?" asked the King, his tone both surprised and eager.

"'Course I do; she's my friend," said Dorothy.

"Then perhaps you'll do me a favor," continued the white donkey, much excited.

"What is it?" she asked.

"Perhaps you can get me an invitation to Princess Ozma's birthday celebration, which will be the grandest royal function ever held in Fairyland. I'd love to go."

"Hee-haw! You deserve punishment, rather than reward, for giving me this dreadful head," said the shaggy man, sorrowfully.

"I wish you wouldn't say 'hee-haw' so much," Polychrome begged him; "it makes cold chills run down my back."

"But I can't help it, my dear; my donkey head wants to bray continually," he replied. "Doesn't your fox head want to yelp every minute?" he asked Button-Bright.

"Don't know," said the boy, still staring at the shaggy man's ears. These seemed to interest him greatly, and the sight also made him forget his own fox head, which was a comfort.

"What do you think, Polly? Shall I promise the donkey king an invitation to Ozma's party?" asked Dorothy of the Rainbow's Daughter, who was flitting about the room like a sunbeam because she could never keep still.

"Do as you please, dear," answered Polychrome. "He might help to amuse the guests of the Princess."

"Then, if you will give us some supper and a place to sleep to-night, and let us get started on our journey early to-morrow morning," said Dorothy to the King, "I'll ask Ozma to invite you—if I happen to get to Oz."

"Good! Hee-haw! Excellent!" cried Kik-a-bray, much pleased. "You shall all have fine suppers and good beds. What food would you prefer, a bran mash or ripe oats in the shell?"

"Neither one," replied Dorothy, promptly.

"Perhaps plain hay, or some sweet juicy grass would suit you better," suggested Kik-a-bray, musingly.

"Is that all you have to eat?" asked the girl.

"What more do you desire?"

"Well, you see we're not donkeys," she explained, "and so we're used to other food. The foxes gave us a nice supper in Foxville."

"We'd like some dewdrops and mist-cakes," said Polychrome.

"I'd prefer apples and a ham sandwich," declared the shaggy man, "for although I've a donkey head, I still have my own particular stomach."

"I want pie," said Button-Bright.

"I think some beefsteak and chocolate layer-cake would taste best," said Dorothy.

"Hee-haw! I declare!" exclaimed the King. "It seems each one of you wants a different food. How queer all living creatures are, except donkeys!"

"And donkeys like you are queerest of all," laughed Polychrome.

"Well," decided the King, "I suppose my Magic Staff will produce the things you crave; if you are lacking in good taste it is not my fault."

With this, he waved his staff with the jeweled ball, and before them instantly appeared a tea-table, set with linen and pretty dishes, and on the table were the very things each had wished for. Dorothy's beefsteak was smoking hot, and the shaggy man's apples were plump and rosy-cheeked. The King had not thought to provide chairs, so they all stood in their places around the table and ate with good appetite, being hungry. The Rainbow's Daughter found three tiny dewdrops on a crystal plate, and Button-Bright had a big slice of apple pie, which he devoured eagerly.

Afterward the King called the brown donkey, which was his favorite servant, and bade it lead his guests to the vacant house where they were to pass the night. It had only one room and no furniture except beds of clean straw and a few mats of woven grasses; but our travelers were contented with these simple things because they realized it was the best the Donkey-King had to offer them. As soon as it was dark they lay down on the mats and slept comfortably until morning.

At daybreak there was a dreadful noise throughout the city. Every donkey in the place brayed. When he heard this the shaggy man woke up and called out "Hee-haw!" as loud as he could.

"Stop that!" said Button-Bright, in a cross voice. Both Dorothy and Polly looked at the shaggy man reproachfully.

"I couldn't help it, my dears," he said, as if ashamed of his bray; "but I'll try not to do it again."

Of coursed they forgave him, for as he still had the Love Magnet in his pocket they were all obliged to love him as much as ever.

They did not see the King again, but Kik-a-bray remembered them; for a table appeared again in their room with the same food upon it as on the night before.

"Don't want pie for breakfus'," said Button-Bright.

"I'll give you some of my beefsteak," proposed Dorothy; "there's plenty for us all."

That suited the boy better, but the shaggy man said he was content with his apples and sandwiches, although he ended the meal by eating Button-Bright's pie. Polly liked her dewdrops and mist-cakes better than any other food, so they all enjoyed an excellent breakfast. Toto had the scraps left from the beefsteak, and he stood up nicely on his hind legs while Dorothy fed them to him.

Breakfast ended, they passed through the village to the side opposite that by which they had entered, the brown servant-donkey guiding them through the maze of scattered houses. There was the road again, leading far away into the unknown country beyond.

"King Kik-a-bray says you must not forget his invitation," said the brown donkey, as they passed through the opening in the wall.

"I shan't," promised Dorothy.

Perhaps no one ever beheld a more strangely assorted group than the one which now walked along the road, through pretty green fields and past groves of feathery pepper-trees and fragrant mimosa. Polychrome, her beautiful gauzy robes floating around her like a rainbow cloud, went first, dancing back and forth and darting now here to pluck a wild-flower or there to watch a beetle crawl across the path. Toto ran after her at times, barking joyously the while, only to become sober again and trot along at Dorothy's heels. The little Kansas girl walked holding Button-Bright's hand clasped in her own, and the wee boy with his fox head covered by the sailor hat presented an odd appeaance. Strangest of all, perhaps, was the shaggy man, with his shaggy donkey head, who shuffled along in the rear with his hands thrust deep in his big pockets.

None of the party was really unhappy. All were straying in an unknown land and had suffered more or less annoyance and discomfort; but they realized they were having a fairy adventure in a fairy country, and were much interested in finding out what would happen next.

8. The Musicker

About the middle of the forenoon they began to go up a long hill. By-and-by this hill suddenly dropped down into a pretty valley, where the travelers saw, to their surprise, a small house standing by the road-side.

It was the first house they had seen, and they hastened into the valley to discover who lived there. No one was in sight as they approached, but when they began to get nearer the house they heard queer sounds coming from it. They could not make these out at first, but as they became louder our friends thought they heard a sort of music like that made by a wheezy hand-organ; the music fell upon their ears in this way: "Tiddle-widdle-iddle oom pom-pom! Oom, pom-pom! oom, pom-pom! Tiddle-tiddle-tiddle oom pom-pom! Oom, pom-pom—pah!"

"What is it, a band or a mouth-organ?" asked Dorothy.

"Don't know," said Button-Bright.

Sounds to me like a played-out phonograph," said the shaggy man, lifting his enormous ears to listen.

Oh, there just COULDN'T be a funnygraf in Fairyland!" cried Dorothy.

It's rather pretty, isn't it?" asked Polychrome, trying to dance to the strains.

Tiddle-widdle-iddle, oom pom-pom, Oom pom-pom; oom pom-pom! "

came the music to their ears, more distinctly as they drew nearer the house. Presently, they saw a little fat man sitting on a bench before the door. He wore a red, braided jacket that reached to his waist, a blue waistcoat, and white trousers with gold stripes down the sides. On his bald head was perched a little, round, red cap held in place by a rubber elastic underneath his chin. His face was round, his eyes a faded blue, and he wore white cotton gloves. The man leaned on a stout gold-headed cane, bending forward on his seat to watch his visitors approach.

Singularly enough, the musical sounds they had heard seemed to come from the inside of the fat man himself; for he was playing no instrument nor was any to be seen near him.

They came up and stood in a row, staring at him, and he stared back while the queer sounds came from him as before: "Tiddle-iddle-iddle, oom pom-pom, Oom, pom-pom; oom pom-pom! Tiddle-widdle-iddle, oom pom-pom, Oom, pom-pom—pah!"

Why, he's a reg'lar musicker!" said Button-Bright.

What's a musicker?" asked Dorothy.

Him!" said the boy.

Hearing this, the fat man sat up a little stiffer than before, as if he had received a compliment, and still came the sounds: "Tiddle-widdle-iddle, oom pom-pom, Oom pom-pom, oom—"

Stop it!" cried the shaggy man, earnestly. "Stop that dreadful noise."

The fat man looked at him sadly and began his reply. When he spoke the music changed and the words seemed to accompany the notes. He said—or rather sang:
It isn't a noise that you hear,
But Music, harmonic and clear.
My breath makes me play
Like an organ, all day—
That bass note is in my left ear."

How funny!" exclaimed Dorothy; "he says his breath makes the music."

That's all nonsense," declared the shaggy man; but now the music began again, and they all listened carefully.

My lungs are full of reeds like those
In organs, therefore I suppose,
If I breathe in or out my nose,
The reeds are bound to play.

So as I breathe to live, you know,
I squeeze out music as I go;
I'm very sorry this is so—

Forgive my piping, pray!"

"Poor man," said Polychrome; "he can't help it. What a great misfortune it is!"

"Yes," replied the shaggy man; "we are only obliged to hear this music a short time, until we leave him and go away; but the poor fellow must listen to himself as long as he lives, and that is enough to drive him crazy. Don't you think so?"

"Don't know," said Button-Bright. Toto said, "Bow-wow!" and the others laughed.

"Perhaps that's why he lives all alone," suggested Dorothy.

"Yes; if he had neighbors, they might do him an injury," responded the shaggy man.

All this while the little fat musicker was breathing the notes: "Tiddle-tiddle-iddle, oom, pom-pom," and they had to speak loud in order to hear themselves. The shaggy man said:

"Who are you, sir?"

The reply came in the shape of this sing-song:
"I'm Allegro da Capo, a very famous man;
Just find another, high or low, to match me if you can.
Some people try, but can't, to play
And have to practice every day;
But I've been musical always, since first my life began. "

"Why, I b'lieve he's proud of it," exclaimed Dorothy; "and seems to me I've heard worse music than he makes."

"Where?" asked Button-Bright.

"I've forgotten, just now. But Mr. Da Capo is certainly a strange person—isn't he?—and p'r'aps he's the only one of his kind in all the world."

This praise seemed to please the little fat musicker, for he swelled out his chest, looked important and sang as follows:
"I wear no band around me,
And yet I am a band!
I do not strain to make my strains
But, on the other hand,
My toot is always destitute
Of flats or other errors;
To see sharp and be natural are
For me but minor terrors."

"I don't quite understand that," said Polychrome, with a puzzled look; "but perhaps it's because I'm accustomed only to the music of the spheres."

"What's that?" asked Button-Bright.

"Oh, Polly means the atmosphere and hemisphere, I s'pose," explained Dorothy.

"Oh," said Button-Bright.

"Bow-wow!" said Toto.

But the musicker was still breathing his constant "Oom, pom-pom; Oom pom-pom—" and it seemed to jar on the shaggy man's nerves.

"Stop it, can't you?" he cried angrily; "or breathe in a whisper; or put a clothes-pin on your nose. Do something, anyhow!"

But the fat one, with a sad look, sang this answer:
"Music hath charms, and it may
Soothe even the savage, they say;
So if savage you feel
Just list to my reel,
For sooth to say that's the real way."

The shaggy man had to laugh at this, and when he laughed he stretched his donkey mouth wide open. Said Dorothy: "I don't know how good his poetry is, but it seems to fit the notes, so that's all that can be 'xpected."

"I like it," said Button-Bright, who was staring hard at the musicker, his little legs spread wide apart. To the surprise of his companions, the boy asked this long question: "If I swallowed a mouth-organ, what would I be?"

"An organette," said the shaggy man. "But come, my dears; I think the best thing we can do is to continue on our journey before Button-Bright swallows anything. We must try to find that Land of Oz, you know."

Hearing this speech the musicker sang, quickly:
"If you go to the Land of Oz
Please take me along, because
On Ozma's birthday I'm anxious to play
The loveliest song ever was."

"No thank you," said Dorothy; "we prefer to travel alone. But if I see Ozma I'll tell her you want to come to her birthday party."

"Let's be going," urged the shaggy man, anxiously.

Polly was already dancing along the road, far in advance, and the others turned to follow her. Toto did not like the fat musicker and made a grab for his chubby leg. Dorothy quickly caught up the growling little dog and hurried after her companions, who were walking faster than usual in order to get out of hearing. They had to climb a hill, and until they got to the top they could not escape the musicker's monotonous piping: "Oom, pom-pom; oom, pom-pom; Tiddle-iddle-widdle, oom, pom-pom; Oom, pom-pom—pah!"

As they passed the brow of the hill, however, and descended on the other side, the sounds gradually died away, whereat they all felt much relieved.

"I'm glad I don't have to live with the organ-man; aren't you, Polly?" said Dorothy.

"Yes indeed," answered the Rainbow's Daughter.

"He's nice," declared Button-Bright, soberly.

"I hope your Princess Ozma won't invite him to her birthday celebration," remarked the shaggy man; "for the fellow's music would drive her guests all crazy. You've given me an idea, Button-Bright; I believe the musicker must have swallowed an accordion in his youth."

"What's 'cordeon?" asked the boy.

"It's a kind of pleating," explained Dorothy, putting down the dog.

"Bow-wow!" said Toto, and ran away at a mad gallop to chase a bumble-bee.

9. Facing the Scoodlers

The country wasn't so pretty now. Before the travelers appeared a rocky plain covered with hills on which grew nothing green. They were nearing some low mountains, too, and the road which before had been smooth and pleasant to walk upon, grew rough and uneven.

Button-Bright's little feet stumbled more than once, and Polychrome ceased her dancing because the walking was now so difficult that she had no trouble to keep warm.

It had become afternoon, yet there wasn't a thing for their luncheon except two apples which the shaggy man had taken from the breakfast table. He divided these into four pieces and gave a portion to each of his companions. Dorothy and Button-Bright were glad to get theirs; but Polly was satisfied with a small bite, and Toto did not like apples.

"Do you know," asked the Rainbow's Daughter, "if this is the right road to the Emerald City?"

"No, I don't," replied Dorothy, "but it's the only road in this part of the country, so we may as well go to the end of it."

"It looks now as if it might end pretty soon," remarked the shaggy man; "and what shall we do if it does?"

"Don't know," said Button-Bright.

"If I had my Magic Belt," replied Dorothy, thoughtfully, "it could do us a lot of good just now."

"What is your Magic Belt?" asked Polychrome.

"It's a thing I captured from the Nome King one day, and it can do 'most any wonderful thing. But I left it with Ozma, you know, 'cause magic won't work in Kansas, but only in fairy countries."

"Is this a fairy country?" asked Button-Bright.

"I should think you'd know," said the little girl, gravely. "If it wasn't a fairy country you couldn't have a fox head and the shaggy man couldn't have a donkey head, and the Rainbow's Daughter would be invis'ble."

"What's that?" asked the boy.

"You don't seem to know anything, Button-Bright. Invis'ble is a thing you can't see."

"Then Toto's invis'ble," declared the boy, and Dorothy found he was right. Toto had disappeared from view, but they could hear him barking furiously among the heaps of grey rock ahead of them.

They moved forward a little faster to see what the dog was barking at, and found perched upon a point of rock by the roadside a curious creature. It had the form of a man, middle sized and rather slender and graceful; but as it sat silent and motionless upon the peak they could see that its face was black as ink, and it wore a black cloth costume made like a union suit and fitting tight to its skin. Its hands were black, too, and its toes curled down, like a bird's. The creature was black all over except its hair, which was fine, and yellow, banged in front across the black forehead and cut close at the sides. The eyes, which were fixed steadily upon the barking dog, were small and sparkling and looked like the eyes of a weasel.

"What in the world do you s'pose that is?" asked Dorothy in a hushed voice, as the little group of travelers stood watching the strange creature.

"Don't know," said Button-Bright.

The thing gave a jump and turned half around, sitting in the same place but with the other side of its body facing them. Instead of being black, it was now pure white, with a face like that of a clown in a circus and hair of a brilliant purple. The creature could bend either way, and its white toes now curled the same way the black ones on the other side had done.

"It has a face both front and back," whispered Dorothy, wonderingly; "only there's no back at all, but two fronts."

Having made the turn, the being sat motionless as before, while Toto barked louder at the white man than he had done at the black one.

"Once," said the shaggy man, "I had a jumping jack like that, with two faces."

"Was it alive?" asked Button-Bright.

"No," replied the shaggy man; "it worked on strings and was made of wood."

"Wonder if this works with strings," said Dorothy; but Polychrome cried "Look!" for another creature just like the first had suddenly appeared sitting on another rock, its black side toward them. The two twisted their heads around and showed a black face on the white side of one and a white face on the black side of the other.

"How curious," said Polychrome; "and how loose their heads seem to be! Are they friendly to us, do you think?"

"Can't tell, Polly," replied Dorothy. "Let's ask 'em."

The creatures flopped first one way and then the other, showing black or white by turns; and now another joined them, appearing on another rock. Our friends had come to a little hollow in the hills, and the place where they now stood was surrounded by jagged peaks of rock, except where the road ran through.

"Now there are four of them," said the shaggy man.

"Five," declared Polychrome.

"Six," said Dorothy.

"Lots of 'em!" cried Button-Bright; and so there were—quite a row of the two-sided black and white creatures sitting on the rocks all around.

Toto stopped barking and ran between Dorothy's feet, where he crouched down as if afraid. The creatures did not look pleasant or friendly, to be sure, and the shaggy man's donkey face became solemn, indeed.

"Ask 'em who they are, and what they want," whispered Dorothy; so the shaggy man called out in a loud voice: "Who are you?"

"Scoodlers!" they yelled in chorus, their voices sharp and shrill.

"What do you want?" called the shaggy man.

"You!" they yelled, pointing their thin fingers at the group; and they all flopped around, so they were white, and then all flopped back again, so they were black.

"But what do you want us for?" asked the shaggy man, uneasily.

"Soup!" they all shouted, as if with one voice.

"Goodness me!" said Dorothy, trembling a little; "the Scoodlers must be reg'lar cannibals."

"Don't want to be soup," protested Button-Bright, beginning to cry.

"Hush, dear," said the little girl, trying to comfort him; "we don't any of us want to be soup. But don't worry; the shaggy man will take care of us."

"Will he?" asked Polychrome, who did not like the Scoodlers at all, and kept close to Dorothy.

"I'll try," promised the shaggy man; but he looked worried.

Happening just then to feel the Love Magnet in his pocket, he said to the creatures, with more confidence: "Don't you love me?"

"Yes!" they shouted, all together.

"Then you mustn't harm me, or my friends," said the shaggy man, firmly.

"We love you in soup!" they yelled, and in a flash turned their white sides to the front.

"How dreadful!" said Dorothy. "This is a time, Shaggy Man, when you get loved too much."

"Don't want to be soup!" wailed Button-Bright again; and Toto began to whine dismally, as if he didn't want to be soup, either.

"The only thing to do," said the shaggy man to his friends, in a low tone, "is to get out of this pocket in the rocks as soon as we can, and leave the Scoodlers behind us. Follow me, my dears, and don't pay any attention to what they do or say."

With this, he began to march along the road to the opening in the rocks ahead, and the others kept close behind him. But the Scoodlers closed up in front, as if to bar their way, and so the shaggy man stooped down and picked up a loose stone, which he threw at the creatures to scare them from the path.

At this the Scoodlers raised a howl. Two of them picked their heads from their shoulders and hurled them at the shaggy man with such force that he fell over in a heap, greatly astonished. The two now ran forward with swift leaps, caught up their heads, and put them on again, after which they sprang back to their positions on the rocks.

10. Escaping the Soup-Kettle

The shaggy man got up and felt of himself to see if he was hurt; but he was not. One of the heads had struck his breast and the other his left shoulder; yet though they had knocked him down, the heads were not hard enough to bruise him.

"Come on," he said firmly; "we've got to get out of here some way," and forward he started again.

The Scoodlers began yelling and throwing their heads in great numbers at our frightened friends. The shaggy man was knocked over again, and so was Button-Bright, who kicked his heels against the ground and howled as loud as he could, although he was not hurt a bit. One head struck Toto, who first yelped and then grabbed the head by an ear and started running away with it.

The Scoodlers who had thrown their heads began to scramble down and run to pick them up, with wonderful quickness; but the one whose head Toto had stolen found it hard to get it back again. The head couldn't see the body with either pair of its eyes, because the dog was in the way, so the headless Scoodler stumbled around over the rocks and tripped on them more than once in its effort to regain its top. Toto was trying to get outside the rocks and roll the head down the hill; but some of the other Scoodlers came to the rescue of their unfortunate comrade and pelted the dog with their own heads until he was obliged to drop his burden and hurry back to Dorothy.

The little girl and the Rainbow's Daughter had both escaped the shower of heads, but they saw now that it would be useless to try to run away from the dreadful Scoodlers.

"We may as well submit," declared the shaggy man, in a rueful voice, as he got upon his feet again. He turned toward their foes and asked:

"What do you want us to do?"

"Come!" they cried, in a triumphant chorus, and at once sprang from the rocks and surrounded their captives on all sides. One funny thing about the Scoodlers was they could walk in either direction, coming or going, without turning around; because they had two faces and, as Dorothy said, "two front sides," and their feet were shaped like the letter T upside down. They moved with great rapidity and there was something about their glittering eyes and contrasting colors and removable heads that inspired the poor prisoners with horror, and made them long to escape.

But the creatures led their captives away from the rocks and the road, down the hill by a side path until they came before a low mountain of rock that looked like a huge bowl turned upside down. At the edge of this mountain was a deep gulf—so deep that when you looked into it there was nothing but blackness below. Across the gulf was a narrow bridge of rock, and at the other end of the bridge was an arched opening that led into the mountain.

Over this bridge the Scoodlers led their prisoners, through the opening into the mountain, which they found to be an immense hollow dome lighted by several holes in the roof. All around the circular space were built rock houses, set close together, each with a door in the front wall. None of these houses was more than six feet wide, but the Scoodlers were thin people sidewise and did not need much room. So vast was the dome that there was a large space in the middle of the cave, in front of all these houses, where the creatures might congregate as in a great hall.

It made Dorothy shudder to see a huge iron kettle suspended by a stout chain in the middle of the place, and underneath the kettle a great heap of kindling wood and shavings, ready to light.

"What's that?" asked the shaggy man, drawing back as they approached this place, so that they were forced to push him forward.

"The Soup Kettle!" yelled the Scoodlers, and then they shouted in the next breath: "We're hungry!"

Button-Bright, holding Dorothy's hand in one chubby fist and Polly's hand in the other, was so affected by this shout that he began to cry again, repeating the protest: "Don't want to be soup, I don't!"

"Never mind," said the shaggy man, consolingly; "I ought to make enough soup to feed them all, I'm so big; so I'll ask them to put me in the kettle first."

"All right," said Button-Bright, more cheerfully.

But the Scoodlers were not ready to make soup yet. They led the captives into a house at the farthest side of the cave—a house somewhat wider than the others.

"Who lives here?" asked the Rainbow's Daughter. The Scoodlers nearest her replied: "The Queen."

It made Dorothy hopeful to learn that a woman ruled over these fierce creatures, but a moment later they were ushered by two or three of the escort into a gloomy, bare room—and her hope died away.

For the Queen of the Scoodlers proved to be much more dreadful in appearance than any of her people. One side of her was fiery red, with jet-black hair and green eyes and the other side of her was bright yellow, with crimson hair and black eyes. She wore a short skirt of red and yellow and her hair, instead of being banged, was a tangle of short curls upon which rested a circular crown of silver—much dented and twisted because the Queen had thrown her head at so many things so many times. Her form was lean and bony and both her faces were deeply wrinkled.

"What have we here?" asked the Queen sharply, as our friends were made to stand before her.

"Soup!" cried the guard of Scoodlers, speaking together.

"We're not!" said Dorothy, indignantly; "we're nothing of the sort."

"Ah, but you will be soon," retorted the Queen, a grim smile making her look more dreadful than before.

"Pardon me, most beautiful vision," said the shaggy man, bowing before the queen politely. "I must request your Serene Highness to let us go our way without being made into soup. For I own the Love Magnet, and whoever meets me must love me and all my friends."

"True," replied the Queen. "We love you very much; so much that we intend to eat your broth with real pleasure. But tell me, do you think I am so beautiful?"

"You won't be at all beautiful if you eat me," he said, shaking his head sadly. "Handsome is as handsome does, you know."

The Queen turned to Button-Bright.

"Do YOU think I'm beautiful?" she asked.

"No," said the boy; "you're ugly."

"I think you're a fright," said Dorothy.

"If you could see yourself you'd be terribly scared," added Polly.

The Queen scowled at them and flopped from her red side to her yellow side.

"Take them away," she commanded the guard, "and at six o'clock run them through the meat chopper and start the soup kettle boiling. And put plenty of salt in the broth this time, or I'll punish the cooks severely."

"Any onions, your Majesty?" asked one of the guard.

"Plenty of onions and garlic and a dash of red pepper. Now, go!"

The Scoodlers led the captives away and shut them up in one of the houses, leaving only a single Scoodler to keep guard.

The place was a sort of store-house; containing bags of potatoes and baskets of carrots, onions and turnips.

"These," said their guard, pointing to the vegetables, "we use to flavor our soups with."

The prisoners were rather disheartened by this time, for they saw no way to escape and did not know how soon it would be six o'clock and time for the meatchopper to begin work. But the shaggy man was brave and did not intend to submit to such a horrid fate without a struggle.

"I'm going to fight for our lives," he whispered to the children, "for if I fail we will be no worse off than before, and to sit here quietly until we are made into soup would be foolish and cowardly."

The Scoodler on guard stood near the doorway, turning first his white side toward them and then his black side, as if he wanted to show to all of his greedy four eyes the sight of so many fat prisoners. The captives sat in a sorrowful group at the other end of the room—except Polychrome, who danced back and forth in the little place to keep herself warm, for she felt the chill of the cave. Whenever she approached the shaggy man he would whisper something in her ear, and Polly would nod her pretty head as if she understood.

The shaggy man told Dorothy and Button-Bright to stand before him while he emptied the potatoes out of one of the sacks. When this had been secretly done, little Polychrome, dancing near to the guard, suddenly reached out her hand and slapped his face, the next instant whirling away from him quickly to rejoin her friends.

The angry Scoodler at once picked off his head and hurled it at the Rainbow's Daughter; but the shaggy man was expecting that, and caught the head very neatly, putting it in the sack, which he tied at the mouth. The body of the guard, not having the eyes of its head to guide it, ran here and there in an aimless manner, and the shaggy man easily dodged it and opened the door. Fortunately, there was no one in the big cave at that moment, so he told Dorothy and Polly to run as fast as they could for the entrance, and out across the narrow bridge.

"I'll carry Button-Bright," he said, for he knew the little boy's legs were too short to run fast.

Dorothy picked up Toto and then seized Polly's hand and ran swiftly toward the entrance to the cave. The shaggy man perched Button-Bright on his shoulders and ran after them. They moved so quickly and their escape was so wholly unexpected that they had almost reached the bridge when one of the Scoodlers looked out of his house and saw them.

The creature raised a shrill cry that brought all of its fellows bounding out of the numerous doors, and at once they started in chase. Dorothy and Polly had reached the bridge and crossed it when the Scoodlers began throwing their heads. One of the queer missiles struck the shaggy man on his back and nearly knocked him over; but he was at the mouth of the cave now, so he set down Button-Bright and told the boy to run across the bridge to Dorothy.

Then the shaggy man turned around and faced his enemies, standing just outside the opening, and as fast as they threw their heads at him he caught them and tossed them into the black gulf below. The headless bodies of the foremost Scoodlers kept the others from running close up, but they also threw their heads in an effort to stop the escaping prisoners. The shaggy man caught them all and sent them whirling down into the black gulf. Among them he noticed the crimson and yellow head of the Queen, and this he tossed after the others with right good will.

Presently every Scoodler of the lot had thrown its head, and every head was down in the deep gulf, and now the helpless bodies of the creatures were mixed together in the cave and wriggling around in a vain attempt to discover what had become of their heads. The shaggy man laughed and walked across the bridge to rejoin his companions.

"It's lucky I learned to play baseball when I was young," he remarked, "for I caught all those heads easily and never missed one. But come along, little ones; the Scoodlers will never bother us or anyone else any more."

Button-Bright was still frightened and kept insisting, "I don't want to be soup!" for the victory had been gained so suddenly that the boy could not realize they were free and safe. But the shaggy man assured him that all danger of their being made into soup was now past, as the Scoodlers would be unable to eat soup for some time to come.

So now, anxious to get away from the horrid gloomy cave as soon as possible, they hastened up the hillside and regained the road just beyond the place where they had first met the Scoodlers; and you may be sure they were glad to find their feet on the old familiar path again.

11. Johnny Dooit Does It

"It's getting awful rough walking," said Dorothy, as they trudged along. Button-Bright gave a deep sigh and said he was hungry. Indeed, all were hungry, and thirsty, too; for they had eaten nothing but the apples since breakfast; so their steps lagged and they grew silent and weary. At last they slowly passed over the crest of a barren hill and saw before them a line of green trees with a strip of grass at their feet. An agreeable fragrance was wafted toward them.

Our travelers, hot and tired, ran forward on beholding this refreshing sight and were not long in coming to the trees. Here they found a spring of pure bubbling water, around which the grass was full of wild strawberry plants, their pretty red berries ripe and ready to eat. Some of the trees bore yellow oranges and some russet pears, so the hungry adventurers suddenly found themselves provided with plenty to eat and to drink. They lost no time in picking the biggest strawberries and ripest oranges and soon had feasted to their hearts' content. Walking beyond the line of trees they saw before them a fearful, dismal desert, everywhere gray sand. At the edge of this awful waste was a large, white sign with black letters neatly painted upon it and the letters made these words:

ALL PERSONS ARE WARNED NOT
TO VENTURE UPON THIS DESERT

For the Deadly Sands will Turn Any Living Flesh
to Dust in an instant. Beyond This Barrier is the

LAND OF OZ

But no one can Reach that Beautiful Country
because of these Destroying Sands

"Oh," said Dorothy, when the shaggy man had read the sign aloud; "I've seen this desert before, and it's true no one can live who tries to walk upon the sands."

"Then we musn't try it," answered the shaggy man thoughtfully. "But as we can't go ahead and there's no use going back, what shall we do next?"

"Don't know," said Button-Bright.

"I'm sure I don't know, either," added Dorothy, despondently.

"I wish father would come for me," sighed the pretty Rainbow's Daughter, "I would take you all to live upon the rainbow, where you could dance along its rays from morning till night, without a care or worry of any sort. But I suppose father's too busy just now to search the world for me."

"Don't want to dance," said Button-Bright, sitting down wearily upon the soft grass.

"It's very good of you, Polly," said Dorothy; "but there are other things that would suit me better than dancing on rainbows. I'm 'fraid they'd be kind of soft an' squashy under foot, anyhow, although they're so pretty to look at."

This didn't help to solve the problem, and they all fell silent and looked at one another questioningly.

"Really, I don't know what to do," muttered the shaggy man, gazing hard at Toto; and the little dog wagged his tail and said "Bow-wow!" just as if he could not tell, either, what to do. Button-Bright got a stick and began to dig in the earth, and the others watched him for a while in deep thought. Finally, the shaggy man said:

"It's nearly evening, now; so we may as well sleep in this pretty place and get rested; perhaps by morning we can decide what is best to be done."

There was little chance to make beds for the children, but the leaves of the trees grew thickly and would serve to keep off the night dews, so the shaggy man piled soft grasses in the thickest shade and when it was dark they lay down and slept peacefully until morning.

Long after the others were asleep, however, the shaggy man sat in the starlight by the spring, gazing thoughtfully into its bubbling waters. Suddenly he smiled and nodded to himself as if

he had found a good thought, after which he, too, laid himself down under a tree and was soon lost in slumber.

In the bright morning sunshine, as they ate of the strawberries and sweet juicy pears, Dorothy said: "Polly, can you do any magic?"

"No dear," answered Polychrome, shaking her dainty head.

"You ought to know SOME magic, being the Rainbow's Daughter," continued Dorothy, earnestly.

"But we who live on the rainbow among the fleecy clouds have no use for magic," replied Polychrome.

"What I'd like," said Dorothy, "is to find some way to cross the desert to the Land of Oz and its Emerald City. I've crossed it already, you know, more than once. First a cyclone carried my house over, and some Silver Shoes brought me back again—in half a second. Then Ozma took me over on her Magic Carpet and the Nome King's Magic Belt took me home that time. You see it was magic that did it every time 'cept the first, and we can' 'spect a cyclone to happen along and take us to the Emerald City now."

"No indeed," returned Polly, with a shudder, "I hate cyclones anyway."

"That's why I wanted to find out if you could do any magic," said the little Kansas girl. "I'm sure I can't; and I'm sure Button Bright can't; and the only magic the shaggy man has is the Love Magnet, which won't help us much."

"Don't be too sure of that, my dear," spoke the shaggy man, a smile on his donkey face. "I may not be able to do magic myself but I can call to us a powerful friend who loves me because I own the Love Magnet, and this friend surely will be able to help us."

"Who is your friend?" asked Dorothy.

"Johnny Dooit."

"What can Johnny do?"

"Anything," answered the shaggy man, with confidence.

"Ask him to come," she exclaimed, eagerly.

The shaggy man took the Love Magnet from his pocket and unwrapped the paper that surrounded it. Holding the charm in the palm of his hand he looked at it steadily and said these words:
"Dear Johnny Dooit, come to me.
I need you bad as bad can be."

"Well, here I am," said a cheery little voice; "but you shouldn't say you need me bad, 'cause I'm always, ALWAYS, good."

At this they quickly whirled around to find a funny little man sitting on a big copper chest, puffing smoke from a long pipe. His hair was grey, his whiskers were grey; and these whiskers were so long that he had wound the ends of them around his waist and tied them in a hard knot underneath the leather apron that reached from his chin nearly to his feet, and which was soiled and scratched as if it had been used a long time. His nose was broad, and stuck up a little; but his eyes were twinkling and merry. The little man's hands and arms were as hard and tough as the leather in his apron, and Dorothy thought Johnny Dooit looked as if he had done a lot of hard work in his lifetime.

"Good morning, Johnny," said the shaggy man. "Thank you for coming to me so quickly."

"I never waste time," said the newcomer, promptly. "But what's happened to you? Where did you get that donkey head? Really, I wouldn't have known you at all, Shaggy Man, if I hadn't looked at your feet."

The shaggy man introduced Johnny Dooit to Dorothy and Toto and Button-Bright and the Rainbow's Daughter, and told him the story of their adventures, adding that they were anxious now to reach the Emerald City in the Land of Oz, where Dorothy had friends who would take care of them and send them safe home again.

"But," said he, "we find that we can't cross this desert, which turns all living flesh that touches it into dust; so I have asked you to come and help us."

Johnny Dooit puffed his pipe and looked carefully at the dreadful desert in front of them—stretching so far away they could not see its end.

"You must ride," he said, briskly.

"What in?" asked the shaggy man.

"In a sand-boat, which has runners like a sled and sails like a ship. The wind will blow you swiftly across the desert and the sand cannot touch your flesh to turn it into dust."

"Good!" cried Dorothy, clapping her hands delightedly. "That was the way the Magic Carpet took us across. We didn't have to touch the horrid sand at all."

"But where is the sand-boat?" asked the shaggy man, looking all around him.

"I'll make you one," said Johnny Dooit.

As he spoke, he knocked the ashes from his pipe and put it in his pocket. Then he unlocked the copper chest and lifted the lid, and Dorothy saw it was full of shining tools of all sorts and shapes.

Johnny Dooit moved quickly now—so quickly that they were astonished at the work he was able to accomplish. He had in his chest a tool for everything he wanted to do, and these must have been magic tools because they did their work so fast and so well.

The man hummed a little song as he worked, and Dorothy tried to listen to it. She thought the words were something like these:
"The only way to do a thing
Is do it when you can,
And do it cheerfully, and sing
And work and think and plan.

The only real unhappy one
Is he who dares to shirk;
The only really happy one
Is he who cares to work. "

Whatever Johnny Dooit was singing he was certainly doing things, and they all stood by and watched him in amazement.

He seized an axe and in a couple of chops felled a tree. Next he took a saw and in a few minutes sawed the tree-trunk into broad,

long boards. He then nailed the boards together into the shape of a boat, about twelve feet long and four feet wide. He cut from another tree a long, slender pole which, when trimmed of its branches and fastened upright in the center of the boat, served as a mast. From the chest he drew a coil of rope and a big bundle of canvas, and with these—still humming his song—he rigged up a sail, arranging it so it could be raised or lowered upon the mast.

Dorothy fairly gasped with wonder to see the thing grow so speedily before her eyes, and both Button-Bright and Polly looked on with the same absorbed interest.

"It ought to be painted," said Johnny Dooit, tossing his tools back into the chest, "for that would make it look prettier. But 'though I can paint it for you in three seconds it would take an hour to dry, and that's a waste of time."

"We don't care how it looks," said the shaggy man, "if only it will take us across the desert."

"It will do that," declared Johnny Dooit. "All you need worry about is tipping over. Did you ever sail a ship?"

"I've seen one sailed," said the shaggy man.

"Good. Sail this boat the way you've seen a ship sailed, and you'll be across the sands before you know it."

With this he slammed down the lid of the chest, and the noise made them all wink. While they were winking the workman disappeared, tools and all.

12. The Deadly Desert Crossed

"Oh, that's too bad!" cried Dorothy; "I wanted to thank Johnny Dooit for all his kindness to us."

"He hasn't time to listen to thanks," replied the shaggy man; "but I'm sure he knows we are grateful. I suppose he is already at work in some other part of the world."

They now looked more carefully at the sand-boat, and saw that the bottom was modeled with two sharp runners which would glide through the sand. The front of the sand-boat was pointed like the bow of a ship, and there was a rudder at the stern to steer by.

It had been built just at the edge of the desert, so that all its length lay upon the gray sand except the after part, which still rested on the strip of grass.

"Get in, my dears," said the shaggy man; "I'm sure I can manage this boat as well as any sailor. All you need do is sit still in your places."

Dorothy got in, Toto in her arms, and sat on the bottom of the boat just in front of the mast. Button-Bright sat in front of Dorothy, while Polly leaned over the bow. The shaggy man knelt behind the mast. When all were ready he raised the sail half-way. The wind caught it. At once the sand-boat started forward—slowly at first, then with added speed. The shaggy man pulled the sail way up, and they flew so fast over the Deadly Desert that every one held fast to the sides of the boat and scarcely dared to breathe.

The sand lay in billows, and was in places very uneven, so that the boat rocked dangerously from side to side; but it never quite tipped over, and the speed was so great that the shaggy man himself became frightened and began to wonder how he could make the ship go slower.

"It we're spilled in this sand, in the middle of the desert," Dorothy thought to herself, "we'll be nothing but dust in a few minutes, and that will be the end of us."

But they were not spilled, and by-and-by Polychrome, who was clinging to the bow and looking straight ahead, saw a dark line before them and wondered what it was. It grew plainer every second, until she discovered it to be a row of jagged rocks at the end of the desert, while high above these rocks she could see a tableland of green grass and beautiful trees.

"Look out!" she screamed to the shaggy man. "Go slowly, or we shall smash into the rocks."

He heard her, and tried to pull down the sail; but the wind would not let go of the broad canvas and the ropes had become tangled.

Nearer and nearer they drew to the great rocks, and the shaggy man was in despair because he could do nothing to stop the wild rush of the sand-boat.

They reached the edge of the desert and bumped squarely into the rocks. There was a crash as Dorothy, Button-Bright, Toto and Polly flew up in the air in a curve like a skyrocket's, one after another landing high upon the grass, where they rolled and tumbled for a time before they could stop themselves.

The shaggy man flew after them, head first, and lighted in a heap beside Toto, who, being much excited at the time, seized one of the donkey ears between his teeth and shook and worried it as hard as he could, growling angrily. The shaggy man made the little dog let go, and sat up to look around him.

Dorothy was feeling one of her front teeth, which was loosened by knocking against her knee as she fell. Polly was looking sorrowfully at a rent in her pretty gauze gown, and Button-Bright's fox head had stuck fast in a gopher hole and he was wiggling his little fat legs frantically in an effort to get free.

Otherwise they were unhurt by the adventure; so the shaggy man stood up and pulled Button-Bright out of the hole and went to the edge of the desert to look at the sand-boat. It was a mere mass of splinters now, crushed out of shape against the rocks. The wind had torn away the sail and carried it to the top of a tall tree, where the fragments of it fluttered like a white flag.

"Well," he said, cheerfully, "we're here; but where the here is I don't know."

"It must be some part of the Land of Oz," observed Dorothy, coming to his side.

"Must it?"

"'Course it must. We're across the desert, aren't we? And somewhere in the middle of Oz is the Emerald City."

"To be sure," said the shaggy man, nodding. "Let's go there."

"But I don't see any people about, to show us the way," she continued.

"Let's hunt for them," he suggested. "There must be people somewhere; but perhaps they did not expect us, and so are not at hand to give us a welcome."

13. The Truth Pond

They now made a more careful examination of the country around them. All was fresh and beautiful after the sultriness of the desert, and the sunshine and sweet, crisp air were delightful to the wanderers. Little mounds of yellowish green were away at the right, while on the left waved a group of tall leafy trees bearing yellow blossoms that looked like tassels and pompoms. Among the grasses carpeting the ground were pretty buttercups and cowslips and marigolds. After looking at these a moment Dorothy said reflectively: "We must be in the Country of the Winkies, for the color of that country is yellow, and you will notice that 'most everything here is yellow that has any color at all."

"But I thought this was the Land of Oz," replied the shaggy man, as if greatly disappointed.

"So it is," she declared; "but there are four parts to the Land of Oz. The North Country is purple, and it's the Country of the Gillikins. The East Country is blue, and that's the Country of the Munchkins. Down at the South is the red Country of the Quadlings, and here, in the West, the yellow Country of the Winkies. This is the part that is ruled by the Tin Woodman, you know."

"Who's he?" asked Button-Bright.

"Why, he's the tin man I told you about. His name is Nick Chopper, and he has a lovely heart given him by the wonderful Wizard."

"Where does HE live?" asked the boy.

"The Wizard? Oh, he lives in the Emerald City, which is just in the middle of Oz, where the corners of the four countries meet."

"Oh," said Button-Bright, puzzled by this explanation.

"We must be some distance from the Emerald City," remarked the shaggy man.

"That's true," she replied; "so we'd better start on and see if we can find any of the Winkies. They're nice people," she continued, as the little party began walking toward the group of trees, "and I came here once with my friends the Scarecrow, and the Tin Woodman, and the Cowardly Lion, to fight a wicked witch who had made all the Winkies her slaves."

"Did you conquer her?" asked Polly.

"Why, I melted her with a bucket of water, and that was the end of her," replied Dorothy. "After that the people were free, you know, and they made Nick Chopper—that's the Tin Woodman— their Emp'ror."

"What's that?" asked Button-Bright.

"Emp'ror? Oh, it's something like an alderman, I guess."

"Oh," said the boy.

"But I thought Princess Ozma ruled Oz," said the shaggy man.

"So she does; she rules the Emerald City and all the four countries of Oz; but each country has another little ruler, not so big as Ozma. It's like the officers of an army, you see; the little rulers are all captains, and Ozma's the general."

By this time they had reached the trees, which stood in a perfect circle and just far enough apart so that their thick branches touched—or "shook hands," as Button-Bright remarked. Under the shade of the trees they found, in the center of the circle, a crystal pool, its water as still as glass. It must have been deep, too, for when Polychrome bent over it she gave a little sigh of pleasure.

"Why, it's a mirror!" she cried; for she could see all her pretty face and fluffy, rainbow-tinted gown reflected in the pool, as natural as life.

Dorothy bent over, too, and began to arrange her hair, blown by the desert wind into straggling tangles. Button-Bright leaned over the edge next, and then began to cry, for the sight of his fox head frightened the poor little fellow.

"I guess I won't look," remarked the shaggy man, sadly, for he didn't like his donkey head, either. While Polly and Dorothy tried to comfort Button-Bright, the shaggy man sat down near the edge of the pool, where his image could not be reflected, and stared at the water thoughtfully. As he did this he noticed a silver plate fastened to a rock just under the surface of the water, and on the silver plate was engraved these words:

THE TRUTH POND

"Ah!" cried the shaggy man, springing to his feet with eager joy; "we've found it at last."

"Found what?" asked Dorothy, running to him.

"The Truth Pond. Now, at last, I may get rid of this frightful head; for we were told, you remember, that only the Truth Pond could restore to me my proper face."

"Me, too!" shouted Button-Bright, trotting up to them.

"Of course," said Dorothy. "It will cure you both of your bad heads, I guess. Isn't it lucky we found it?"

"It is, indeed," replied the shaggy man. "I hated dreadfully to go to Princess Ozma looking like this; and she's to have a birthday celebration, too."

Just then a splash startled them, for Button-Bright, in his anxiety to see the pool that would "cure" him, had stepped too near the edge and tumbled heels over head into the water. Down he went, out of sight entirely, so that only his sailor hat floated on the top of the Truth Pond.

He soon bobbed up, and the shaggy man seized him by his sailor collar and dragged him to the shore, dripping and gasping for breath. They all looked upon the boy wonderingly, for the fox head with its sharp nose and pointed ears was gone, and in its place appeared the chubby round face and blue eyes and pretty curls that had belonged to Button-Bright before King Dox of Foxville transformed him.

"Oh, what a darling!" cried Polly, and would have hugged the little one had he not been so wet.

Their joyful exclamations made the child rub the water out of his eyes and look at his friends questioningly.

"You're all right now, dear," said Dorothy. "Come and look at yourself." She led him to the pool, and although there were still a few ripples on the surface of the water he could see his reflection plainly.

"It's me!" he said, in a pleased yet awed whisper.

"'Course it is," replied the girl, "and we're all as glad as you are, Button-Bright."

"Well," announced the shaggy man, "it's my turn next." He took off his shaggy coat and laid it on the grass and dived head first into the Truth Pond.

When he came up the donkey head had disappeared, and the shaggy man's own shaggy head was in its place, with the water dripping in little streams from his shaggy whiskers. He scrambled ashore and shook himself to get off some of the wet, and then leaned over the pool to look admiringly at his reflected face.

"I may not be strictly beautiful, even now," he said to his companions, who watched him with smiling faces; "but I'm so much handsomer than any donkey that I feel as proud as I can be."

"You're all right, Shaggy Man," declared Dorothy. "And Button-Bright is all right, too. So let's thank the Truth Pond for being so nice, and start on our journey to the Emerald City."

"I hate to leave it," murmured the shaggy man, with a sigh. "A truth pond wouldn't be a bad thing to carry around with us." But he put on his coat and started with the others in search of some one to direct them on their way.

14. Tik-Tok and Billina

They had not walked far across the flower-strewn meadows when they came upon a fine road leading toward the northwest and winding gracefully among the pretty yellow hills.

"That way," said Dorothy, "must be the direction of the Emerald City. We'd better follow the road until we meet some one or come to a house."

The sun soon dried Button-Bright's sailor suit and the shaggy man's shaggy clothes, and so pleased were they at regaining their own heads that they did not mind at all the brief discomfort of getting wet.

"It's good to be able to whistle again," remarked the shaggy man, "for those donkey lips were so thick I could not whistle a note with them." He warbled a tune as merrily as any bird.

"You'll look more natural at the birthday celebration, too," said Dorothy, happy in seeing her friends so happy.

Polychrome was dancing ahead in her usual sprightly manner, whirling gaily along the smooth, level road, until she passed from sight around the curve of one of the mounds. Suddenly they heard her exclaim "Oh!" and she appeared again, running toward them at full speed.

"What's the matter, Polly?" asked Dorothy, perplexed.

There was no need for the Rainbow's Daughter to answer, for turning the bend in the road there came advancing slowly toward them a funny round man made of burnished copper, gleaming brightly in the sun. Perched on the copper man's shoulder sat a yellow hen, with fluffy feathers and a pearl necklace around her throat.

"Oh, Tik-tok!" cried Dorothy, running forward. When she came to him, the copper man lifted the little girl in his copper arms and kissed her cheek with his copper lips.

"Oh, Billina!" cried Dorothy, in a glad voice, and the yellow hen flew to her arms, to be hugged and petted by turns.

The others were curiously crowding around the group, and the girl said to them: "It's Tik-tok and Billina; and oh! I'm so glad to see them again."

"Wel-come to Oz," said the copper man in a monotonous voice.

Dorothy sat right down in the road, the yellow hen in her arms, and began to stroke Billina's back. Said the hen: "Dorothy, dear, I've got some wonderful news to tell you."

"Tell it quick, Billina!" said the girl.

Just then Toto, who had been growling to himself in a cross way, gave a sharp bark and flew at the yellow hen, who ruffled her feathers and let out such an angry screech that Dorothy was startled.

"Stop, Toto! Stop that this minute!" she commanded. "Can't you see that Billina is my friend?" In spite of this warning had she not grabbed Toto quickly by the neck the little dog would have done the yellow hen a mischief, and even now he struggled madly to escape Dorothy's grasp. She slapped his ears once or twice and told him to behave, and the yellow hen flew to Tik-tok's shoulder again, where she was safe.

"What a brute!" croaked Billina, glaring down at the little dog.

"Toto isn't a brute," replied Dorothy, "but at home Uncle Henry has to whip him sometimes for chasing the chickens. Now look here, Toto," she added, holding up her finger and speaking sternly to him, "you've got to understand that Billina is one of my dearest friends, and musn't be hurt—now or ever."

Toto wagged his tail as if he understood.

"The miserable thing can't talk," said Billina, with a sneer.

"Yes, he can," replied Dorothy; "he talks with his tail, and I know everything he says. If you could wag your tail, Billina, you wouldn't need words to talk with."

"Nonsense!" said Billina.

"It isn't nonsense at all. Just now Toto says he's sorry, and that he'll try to love you for my sake. Don't you, Toto?"

"Bow-wow!" said Toto, wagging his tail again.

"But I've such wonderful news for you, Dorothy," cried the yellow hen; "I've—"

"Wait a minute, dear," interrupted the little girl; "I've got to introduce you all, first. That's manners, Billina. This," turning to her traveling companions, "is Mr. Tik-tok, who works by machinery 'cause his thoughts wind up, and his talk winds up, and his action winds up—like a clock."

"Do they all wind up together?" asked the shaggy man.

"No; each one separate. But he works just lovely, and Tik-tok was a good friend to me once, and saved my life—and Billina's life, too."

"Is he alive?" asked Button-Bright, looking hard at the copper man.

"Oh, no, but his machinery makes him just as good as alive." She turned to the copper man and said politely: "Mr. Tik-tok, these are my new friends: the shaggy man, and Polly the Rainbow's Daughter, and Button-Bright, and Toto. Only Toto isn't a new friend, 'cause he's been to Oz before."

The copper man bowed low, removing his copper hat as he did so.

"I'm ve-ry pleased to meet Dor-o-thy's fr-r-r-r—" Here he stopped short.

"Oh, I guess his speech needs winding!" said the little girl, running behind the copper man to get the key off a hook at his back. She wound him up at a place under his right arm and he went on to say: "Par-don me for run-ning down. I was a-bout to say I am pleased to meet Dor-o-thy's friends, who must be my friends." The words were somewhat jerky, but plain to understand.

"And this is Billina," continued Dorothy, introducing the yellow hen, and they all bowed to her in turn.

"I've such wonderful news," said the hen, turning her head so that one bright eye looked full at Dorothy.

"What is it, dear?" asked the girl.

"I've hatched out ten of the loveliest chicks you ever saw."

"Oh, how nice! And where are they, Billina?"

"I left them at home. But they're beauties, I assure you, and all wonderfully clever. I've named them Dorothy."

"Which one?" asked the girl.

"All of them," replied Billina.

"That's funny. Why did you name them all with the same name?"

"It was so hard to tell them apart," explained the hen. "Now when I call 'Dorothy,' they all come running to me in a bunch; it's much easier, after all, than having a separate name for each."

"I'm just dying to see 'em, Billina," said Dorothy, eagerly. "But tell me, my friends, how did you happen to be here, in the Country of the Winkies, the first of all to meet us?"

"I'll tell you," answered Tik-tok, in his monotonous voice, all the sounds of his words being on one level—"Prin-cess Oz-ma saw you in her mag-ic pic-ture, and knew you were com-ing here; so she sent Bil-lin-a and me to wel-come you as she could not come her-self; so that—fiz-i-dig-le cum-so-lut-ing hy-ber-gob-ble in-tu-zib-ick—"

"Good gracious! Whatever's the matter now?" cried Dorothy, as the copper man continued to babble these unmeaning words, which no one could understand at all because they had no sense.

"Don't know," said Button-Bright, who was half scared. Polly whirled away to a distance and turned to look at the copper man in a fright.

"His thoughts have run down, this time," remarked Billina composedly, as she sat on Tik-tok's shoulder and pruned her sleek feathers. "When he can't think, he can't talk properly, any more than you can. You'll have to wind up his thoughts, Dorothy, or else I'll have to finish his story myself."

Dorothy ran around and got the key again and wound up Tik-tok under his left arm, after which he could speak plainly again.

"Par-don me," he said, "but when my thoughts run down, my speech has no mean-ing, for words are formed on-ly by thought. I was a-bout to say that Oz-ma sent us to wel-come you and in-vite you to come straight to the Em-er-ald Ci-ty. She was too bus-y to come her-self, for she is pre-par-ing for her birth-day cel-e-bra-tion, which is to be a grand af-fair."

"I've heard of it," said Dorothy, "and I'm glad we've come in time to attend. Is it far from here to the Emerald City?"

"Not ve-ry far," answered Tik-tok, "and we have plen-ty of time. To-night we will stop at the pal-ace of the Tin Wood-man, and to-mor-row night we will ar-rive at the Em-er-ald Ci-ty."

"Goody!" cried Dorothy. "I'd like to see dear Nick Chopper again. How's his heart?"

"It's fine," said Billina; "the Tin Woodman says it gets softer and kindlier every day. He's waiting at his castle to welcome you, Dorothy; but he couldn't come with us because he's getting polished as bright as possible for Ozma's party."

"Well then," said Dorothy, "let's start on, and we can talk more as we go."

They proceeded on their journey in a friendly group, for Polychrome had discovered that the copper man was harmless and was no longer afraid of him. Button-Bright was also reassured, and took quite a fancy to Tik-tok. He wanted the clockwork man to open himself, so that he might see the wheels go round; but that was a thing Tik-tok could not do. Button-Bright then wanted to wind up the copper man, and Dorothy promised he should do so as soon as any part of the machinery ran down. This pleased Button-Bright, who held fast to one of Tik-tok's copper hands as he trudged along the road, while Dorothy walked on the other side of her old friend and Billina perched by turns upon his shoulder or his copper hat. Polly once more joyously danced ahead and Toto ran after her, barking with glee. The shaggy man was left to walk behind; but he didn't seem to mind that a bit, and whistled merrily or looked curiously upon the pretty scenes they passed.

At last they came to a hilltop from which the tin castle of Nick Chopper could plainly be seen, its towers glistening magnificently under the rays of the declining sun.

"How pretty!" exclaimed Dorothy. "I've never seen the Emp'ror's new house before."

"He built it because the old castle was damp, and likely to rust his tin body," said Billina. "All those towers and steeples and domes and gables took a lot of tin, as you can see."

"Is it a toy?" asked Button-Bright softly.

"No, dear," answered Dorothy; "it's better than that. It's the fairy dwelling of a fairy prince."

15. The Emperor's Tin Castle

The grounds around Nick Chopper's new house were laid out in pretty flower-beds, with fountains of crystal water and statues of tin representing the Emperor's personal friends. Dorothy was astonished and delighted to find a tin statue of herself standing on a tin pedestal at a bend in the avenue leading up to the entrance. It was life-size and showed her in her sunbonnet with her basket on her arm, just as she had first appeared in the Land of Oz.

"Oh, Toto—you're there too!" she exclaimed; and sure enough there was the tin figure of Toto lying at the tin Dorothy's feet.

Also, Dorothy saw figures of the Scarecrow, and the Wizard, and Ozma, and of many others, including Tik-tok. They reached the grand tin entrance to the tin castle, and the Tin Woodman himself came running out of the door to embrace little Dorothy and give her a glad welcome. He welcomed her friends as well, and the Rainbow's Daughter he declared to be the loveliest vision his tin eyes had ever beheld. He patted Button-Bright's curly head tenderly, for he was fond of children, and turned to the shaggy man and shook both his hands at the same time.

Nick Chopper, the Emperor of the Winkies, who was also known throughout the Land of Oz as the Tin Woodman, was certainly a remarkable person. He was neatly made, all of tin, nicely soldered at the joints, and his various limbs were cleverly hinged to his body so that he could use them nearly as well as if they had been common flesh. Once, he told the shaggy man, he had been made all of flesh and bones, as other people are, and then he chopped wood in the forests to earn his living. But the axe slipped so often and cut off parts of him—which he had replaced with tin—that finally there was no flesh left, nothing but tin; so he became a real tin woodman. The wonderful Wizard of Oz had given him an excellent heart to replace his old one, and he didn't at all mind being tin. Every one loved him, he loved every one; and he was therefore as happy as the day was long.

The Emperor was proud of his new tin castle, and showed his visitors through all the rooms. Every bit of the furniture was made of brightly polished tin—the tables, chairs, beds, and all—even the floors and walls were of tin.

"I suppose," said he, "that there are no cleverer tinsmiths in all the world than the Winkies. It would be hard to match this castle in Kansas; wouldn't it, little Dorothy?"

"Very hard," replied the child, gravely.

"It must have cost a lot of money," remarked the shaggy man.

"Money! Money in Oz!" cried the Tin Woodman. "What a queer idea! Did you suppose we are so vulgar as to use money here?"

"Why not?" asked the shaggy man.

"If we used money to buy things with, instead of love and kindness and the desire to please one another, then we should be no better than the rest of the world," declared the Tin Woodman. "Fortunately money is not known in the Land of Oz at all. We have no rich, and no poor; for what one wishes the others all try to give him, in order to make him happy, and no one in all Oz cares to have more than he can use."

"Good!" cried the shaggy man, greatly pleased to hear this. "I also despise money—a man in Butterfield owes me fifteen cents, and I will not take it from him. The Land of Oz is surely the most favored land in all the world, and its people the happiest. I should like to live here always."

The Tin Woodman listened with respectful attention. Already he loved the shaggy man, although he did not yet know of the Love Magnet. So he said: "If you can prove to the Princess Ozma that you are honest and true and worthy of our friendship, you may indeed live here all your days, and be as happy as we are."

"I'll try to prove that," said the shaggy man, earnestly.

"And now," continued the Emperor, "you must all go to your rooms and prepare for dinner, which will presently be served in the grand tin dining-hall. I am sorry, Shaggy Man, that I can not offer you a change of clothing; but I dress only in tin, myself, and I suppose that would not suit you."

"I care little about dress," said the shaggy man, indifferently.

"So I should imagine," replied the Emperor, with true politeness.

They were shown to their rooms and permitted to make such toilets as they could, and soon they assembled again in the grand tin dining-hall, even Toto being present. For the Emperor was fond of Dorothy's little dog, and the girl explained to her friends that in Oz all animals were treated with as much consideration as the people—"if they behave themselves," she added.

Toto behaved himself, and sat in a tin high-chair beside Dorothy and ate his dinner from a tin platter.

Indeed, they all ate from tin dishes, but these were of pretty shapes and brightly polished; Dorothy thought they were just as good as silver.

Button-Bright looked curiously at the man who had "no appetite inside him," for the Tin Woodman, although he had prepared so fine a feast for his guests, ate not a mouthful himself, sitting patiently in his place to see that all built so they could eat were well and plentifully served.

What pleased Button-Bright most about the dinner was the tin orchestra that played sweet music while the company ate. The players were not tin, being just ordinary Winkies; but the instruments they played upon were all tin—tin trumpets, tin fiddles, tin drums and cymbals and flutes and horns and all. They played so nicely the "Shining Emperor Waltz," composed expressly in honor of the Tin Woodman by Mr. H. M. Wogglebug, T.E., that Polly could not resist dancing to it. After she had tasted a few dewdrops, freshly gathered for her, she danced gracefully to the music while the others finished their repast; and when she whirled until her fleecy draperies of rainbow hues enveloped her like a cloud, the Tin Woodman was so delighted that he clapped his tin hands until the noise of them drowned the sound of the cymbals.

Altogether it was a merry meal, although Polychrome ate little and the host nothing at all.

"I'm sorry the Rainbow's Daughter missed her mist-cakes," said the Tin Woodman to Dorothy; "but by a mistake Miss Polly's mist-cakes were mislaid and not missed until now. I'll try to have some for her breakfast."

They spent the evening telling stories, and the next morning left the splendid tin castle and set out upon the road to the Emerald City. The Tin Woodman went with them, of course, having by this time been so brightly polished that he sparkled like silver. His axe, which he always carried with him, had a steel blade that was tin plated and a handle covered with tin plate beautifully engraved and set with diamonds.

The Winkies assembled before the castle gates and cheered their Emperor as he marched away, and it was easy to see that they all loved him dearly.

16. Visiting the Pumpkin-Field

Dorothy let Button-Bright wind up the clock-work in the copper man this morning—his thinking machine first, then his speech, and finally his action; so he would doubtless run perfectly until they had reached the Emerald City. The copper man and the tin man were good friends, and not so much alike as you might think. For one was alive and the other moved by means of machinery; one was tall and angular and the other short and round. You could love the Tin Woodman because he had a fine nature, kindly and simple; but the machine man you could only admire without loving, since to love such a thing as he was as impossible as to love a sewing-machine or an automobile. Yet Tik-tok was popular with the people of Oz because he was so trustworthy, reliable and true; he was sure to do exactly what he was wound up to do, at all times and in all circumstances. Perhaps it is better to be a machine that does its duty than a flesh-and-blood person who will not, for a dead truth is better than a live falsehood.

About noon the travelers reached a large field of pumpkins—a vegetable quite appropriate to the yellow country of the Winkies—and some of the pumpkins which grew there were of remarkable size. Just before they entered upon this field they saw three little mounds that looked like graves, with a pretty headstone to each one of them.

"What is this?" asked Dorothy, in wonder.

"It's Jack Pumpkinhead's private graveyard," replied the Tin Woodman.

"But I thought nobody ever died in Oz," she said.

"Nor do they; although if one is bad, he may be condemned and killed by the good citizens," he answered.

Dorothy ran over to the little graves and read the words engraved upon the tombstones. The first one said:

Here Lies the Mortal Part of JACK PUMPKINHEAD
Which Spoiled April 9th.

She then went to the next stone, which read:

Here Lies the Mortal Part of JACK PUMPKINHEAD
Which Spoiled October 2nd.

On the third stone were carved these words:

Here Lies the Mortal Part of JACK PUMPKINHEAD
Which Spoiled January 24th.

"Poor Jack!" sighed Dorothy. "I'm sorry he had to die in three parts, for I hoped to see him again."

"So you shall," declared the Tin Woodman, "since he is still alive. Come with me to his house, for Jack is now a farmer and lives in this very pumpkin field."

They walked over to a monstrous big, hollow pumpkin which had a door and windows cut through the rind. There was a stovepipe running through the stem, and six steps had been built leading up to the front door.

They walked up to this door and looked in. Seated on a bench was a man clothed in a spotted shirt, a red vest, and faded blue trousers, whose body was merely sticks of wood, jointed clumsily together. On his neck was set a round, yellow pumpkin, with a face carved on it such as a boy often carves on a jack-lantern.

This queer man was engaged in snapping slippery pumpkin-seeds with his wooden fingers, trying to hit a target on the other side of the room with them. He did not know he had visitors until Dorothy exclaimed: "Why, it's Jack Pumpkinhead himself!"

He turned and saw them, and at once came forward to greet the little Kansas girl and Nick Chopper, and to be introduced to their new friends.

Button-Bright was at first rather shy with the quaint Pumpkinhead, but Jack's face was so jolly and smiling—being carved that way—that the boy soon grew to like him.

"I thought a while ago that you were buried in three parts," said Dorothy, "but now I see you're just the same as ever."

"Not quite the same, my dear, for my mouth is a little more one-sided than it used to be; but pretty nearly the same. I've a new head, and this is the fourth one I've owned since Ozma first made me and brought me to life by sprinkling me with the Magic Powder."

"What became of the other heads, Jack?"

"They spoiled and I buried them, for they were not even fit for pies. Each time Ozma has carved me a new head just like the old one, and as my body is by far the largest part of me, I am still Jack Pumpkinhead, no matter how often I change my upper end. Once we had a dreadful time to find another pumpkin, as they were out of season, and so I was obliged to wear my old head a little longer than was strictly healthy. But after this sad experience I resolved to raise pumpkins myself, so as never to be caught again without one handy; and now I have this fine field that you see before you. Some grow pretty big—too big to be used for heads—so I dug out this one and use it for a house."

"Isn't it damp?" asked Dorothy.

"Not very. There isn't much left but the shell, you see, and it will last a long time yet."

"I think you are brighter than you used to be, Jack," said the Tin Woodman. "Your last head was a stupid one."

"The seeds in this one are better," was the reply.

"Are you going to Ozma's party?" asked Dorothy.

"Yes," said he, "I wouldn't miss it for anything. Ozma's my parent, you know, because she built my body and carved my pumpkin head. I'll follow you to the Emerald City to-morrow, where we shall meet again. I can't go to-day, because I have to plant fresh pumpkin-seeds and water the young vines. But give my love to Ozma, and tell her I'll be there in time for the jubilation."

"We will," she promised; and then they all left him and resumed their journey.

17. The Royal Chariot Arrives

The neat yellow houses of the Winkies were now to be seen standing here and there along the roadway, giving the country a more cheerful and civilized look. They were farm-houses, though, and set far apart; for in the Land of Oz there were no towns or villages except the magnificent Emerald City in its center.

Hedges of evergreen or of yellow roses bordered the broad highway and the farms showed the care of their industrious inhabitants. The nearer the travelers came to the great city the more prosperous the country became, and they crossed many bridges over the sparkling streams and rivulets that watered the lands.

As they walked leisurely along the shaggy man said to the Tin Woodman: "What sort of a Magic Powder was it that made your friend the Pumpkinhead live?"

"It was called the Powder of Life," was the answer; "and it was invented by a crooked Sorcerer who lived in the mountains of the North Country. A Witch named Mombi got some of this powder from the crooked Sorcerer and took it home with her. Ozma lived with the Witch then, for it was before she became our Princess, while Mombi had transformed her into the shape of a boy. Well, while Mombi was gone to the crooked Sorcerer's, the boy made this pumpkin-headed man to amuse himself, and also with the hope of frightening the Witch with it when she returned. But Mombi was not scared, and she sprinkled the Pumpkinhead with her Magic Powder of Life, to see if the Powder would work. Ozma was watching, and saw the Pumpkinhead come to life; so that night she took the pepper-box containing the Powder and ran away with it and with Jack, in search of adventures.

"Next day they found a wooden Saw-Horse standing by the roadside, and sprinkled it with the Powder. It came to life at once, and Jack Pumpkinhead rode the Saw-Horse to the Emerald City."

"What became of the Saw-Horse, afterward?" asked the shaggy man, much interested in this story.

"Oh, it's alive yet, and you will probably meet it presently in the Emerald City. Afterward, Ozma used the last of the Powder to bring the Flying Gump to life; but as soon as it had carried her away from her enemies the Gump was taken apart, so it doesn't exist any more."

"It's too bad the Powder of Life was all used up," remarked the shaggy man; "it would be a handy thing to have around."

"I am not so sure of that, sir," answered the Tin Woodman. "A while ago the crooked Sorcerer who invented the Magic Powder fell down a precipice and was killed. All his possessions went to a relative—an old woman named Dyna, who lives in the Emerald City. She went to the mountains where the Sorcerer had lived and brought away everything she thought of value. Among them was a small bottle of the Powder of Life; but of course Dyna didn't know it was a Magic Powder, at all. It happened she had once had a big blue bear for a pet; but the bear choked to death on a fishbone one day, and she loved it so dearly that Dyna made a rug of its skin, leaving the head and four paws on the hide. She kept the rug on the floor of her front parlor."

"I've seen rugs like that," said the shaggy man, nodding, "but never one made from a blue bear."

"Well," continued the Tin Woodman, "the old woman had an idea that the Powder in the bottle must be moth-powder, because it smelled something like moth-powder; so one day she sprinkled it on her bear rug to keep the moths out of it. She said, looking lovingly at the skin: 'I wish my dear bear were alive again!' To her horror, the bear rug at once came to life, having been sprinkled with the Magic Powder; and now this live bear rug is a great trial to her, and makes her a lot of trouble."

"Why?" asked the shaggy man.

"Well, it stands up on its four feet and walks all around, and gets in the way; and that spoils it for a rug. It can't speak, although it is alive; for, while its head might say words, it has no breath in a solid body to push the words out of its mouth. It's a very slimpsy affair altogether, that bear rug, and the old woman is sorry it came to life. Every day she has to scold it, and make it lie down flat on the parlor floor to be walked upon; but sometimes when she goes to market the rug will hump up its back skin, and stand on its four feet, and trot along after her."

"I should think Dyna would like that," said Dorothy.

"Well, she doesn't; because every one knows it isn't a real bear, but just a hollow skin, and so of no actual use in the world except for a rug," answered the Tin Woodman. "Therefore I believe it is a good thing that all the Magic Powder of Life is now used up, as it can not cause any more trouble."

"Perhaps you're right," said the shaggy man, thoughtfully.

At noon they stopped at a farmhouse, where it delighted the farmer and his wife to be able to give them a good luncheon. The farm people knew Dorothy, having seen her when she was in the country before, and they treated the little girl with as much respect as they did the Emperor, because she was a friend of the powerful Princess Ozma.

They had not proceeded far after leaving this farm-house before coming to a high bridge over a broad river. This river, the Tin Woodman informed them, was the boundary between the Country of the Winkies and the territory of the Emerald City. The city itself was still a long way off, but all around it was a green meadow as pretty as a well-kept lawn, and in this were neither houses nor farms to spoil the beauty of the scene.

From the top of the high bridge they could see far away the magnificent spires and splendid domes of the superb city, sparkling like brilliant jewels as they towered above the emerald walls. The shaggy man drew a deep breath of awe and amazement, for never had he dreamed that such a grand and beautiful place could exist—even in the fairyland of Oz.

Polly was so pleased that her violet eyes sparkled like amethysts, and she danced away from her companions across the bridge and into a group of feathery trees lining both the roadsides. These trees she stopped to look at with pleasure and surprise, for their leaves were shaped like ostrich plumes, their feather edges beautifully curled; and all the plumes were tinted in the same dainty rainbow hues that appeared in Polychrome's own pretty gauze gown.

"Father ought to see these trees," she murmured; "they are almost as lovely as his own rainbows."

Then she gave a start of terror, for beneath the trees came stalking two great beasts, either one big enough to crush the little Daughter of the Rainbow with one blow of his paws, or to eat her up with one snap of his enormous jaws. One was a tawny lion, as tall as a horse, nearly; the other a striped tiger almost the same size.

Polly was too frightened to scream or to stir; she stood still with a wildly beating heart until Dorothy rushed past her and with a glad cry threw her arms around the huge lion's neck, hugging and kissing the beast with evident joy.

"Oh, I'm SO glad to see you again!" cried the little Kansas girl. "And the Hungry Tiger, too! How fine you're both looking. Are you well and happy?"

"We certainly are, Dorothy," answered the Lion, in a deep voice that sounded pleasant and kind; "and we are greatly pleased that you have come to Ozma's party. It's going to be a grand affair, I promise you."

"There will be lots of fat babies at the celebration, I hear," remarked the Hungry Tiger, yawning so that his mouth opened dreadfully wide and showed all his big, sharp teeth; "but of course I can't eat any of 'em."

"Is your Conscience still in good order?" asked Dorothy anxiously.

"Yes; it rules me like a tyrant," answered the Tiger, sorrowfully. "I can imagine nothing more unpleasant than to own a Conscience," and he winked slyly at his friend the Lion.

"You're fooling me!" said Dorothy, with a laugh. "I don't b'lieve you'd eat a baby if you lost your Conscience. Come here, Polly," she called, "and be introduced to my friends."

Polly advanced rather shyly.

"You have some queer friends, Dorothy," she said.

"The queerness doesn't matter so long as they're friends," was the answer. "This is the Cowardly Lion, who isn't a coward at all, but just thinks he is. The Wizard gave him some courage once, and he has part of it left."

The Lion bowed with great dignity to Polly.

"You are very lovely, my dear," said he. "I hope we shall be friends when we are better acquainted."

"And this is the Hungry Tiger," continued Dorothy. "He says he longs to eat fat babies; but the truth is he is never hungry at all 'cause he gets plenty to eat; and I don't s'pose he'd hurt anybody, even if he WAS hungry."

"Hush, Dorothy," whispered the Tiger; "you'll ruin my reputation if you are not more discreet. It isn't what we are, but what folks think we are, that counts in this world. And come to think of it Miss Polly would make a fine variegated breakfast, I'm sure."

18. The Emerald City

The others now came up, and the Tin Woodman greeted the Lion and the Tiger cordially. Button-Bright yelled with fear when

Dorothy first took his hand and led him toward the great beasts; but the girl insisted they were kind and good, and so the boy mustered up courage enough to pat their heads; after they had spoken to him gently and he had looked into their intelligent eyes his fear vanished entirely and he was so delighted with the animals that he wanted to keep close to them and stroke their soft fur every minute.

As for the shaggy man, he might have been afraid if he had met the beasts alone, or in any other country, but so many were the marvels in the Land of Oz that he was no longer easily surprised, and Dorothy's friendship for the Lion and Tiger was enough to assure him they were safe companions. Toto barked at the Cowardly Lion in joyous greeting, for he knew the beast of old and loved him, and it was funny to see how gently the Lion raised his huge paw to pat Toto's head. The little dog smelled of the Tiger's nose, and the Tiger politely shook paws with him; so they were quite likely to become firm friends.

Tik-tok and Billina knew the beasts well, so merely bade them good day and asked after their healths and inquired about the Princess Ozma.

Now it was seen that the Cowardly Lion and the Hungry Tiger were drawing behind them a splendid golden chariot, to which they were harnessed by golden cords. The body of the chariot was decorated on the outside with designs in clusters of sparkling emeralds, while inside it was lined with a green and gold satin, and the cushions of the seats were of green plush embroidered in gold with a crown, underneath which was a monogram.

"Why, it's Ozma's own royal chariot!" exclaimed Dorothy.

"Yes," said the Cowardly Lion; "Ozma sent us to meet you here, for she feared you would be weary with your long walk and she wished you to enter the City in a style becoming your exalted rank."

"What!" cried Polly, looking at Dorothy curiously. "Do you belong to the nobility?"

"Just in Oz I do," said the child, "'cause Ozma made me a Princess, you know. But when I'm home in Kansas I'm only a country girl, and have to help with the churning and wipe the dishes while Aunt Em washes 'em. Do you have to help wash dishes on the rainbow, Polly?"

"No, dear," answered Polychrome, smiling.

"Well, I don't have to work any in Oz, either," said Dorothy. "It's kind of fun to be a Princess once in a while; don't you think so?"

"Dorothy and Polychrome and Button-Bright are all to ride in the chariot," said the Lion. "So get in, my dears, and be careful not to mar the gold or put your dusty feet on the embroidery."

Button-Bright was delighted to ride behind such a superb team, and he told Dorothy it made him feel like an actor in a circus. As the strides of the animals brought them nearer to the Emerald City every one bowed respectfully to the children, as well as to the Tin Woodman, Tik-tok, and the shaggy man, who were following behind.

The Yellow Hen had perched upon the back of the chariot, where she could tell Dorothy more about her wonderful chickens as they rode. And so the grand chariot came finally to the high wall surrounding the City, and paused before the magnificent jewel-studded gates.

These were opened by a cheerful-looking little man who wore green spectacles over his eyes. Dorothy introduced him to her friends as the Guardian of the Gates, and they noticed a big bunch of keys suspended on the golden chain that hung around his neck. The chariot passed through the outer gates into a fine arched chamber built in the thick wall, and through the inner gates into the streets of the Emerald City.

Polychrome exclaimed in rapture at the wondrous beauty that met her eyes on every side as they rode through this stately and imposing City, the equal of which has never been discovered, even in Fairyland. Button-Bright could only say "My!" so amazing was the sight; but his eyes were wide open and he tried to look in every direction at the same time, so as not to miss anything.

The shaggy man was fairly astounded at what he saw, for the graceful and handsome buildings were covered with plates of gold and set with emeralds so splendid and valuable that in any other part of the world any one of them would have been worth a fortune to its owner. The sidewalks were superb marble slabs polished as smooth as glass, and the curbs that separated the walks from the broad street were also set thick with clustered emeralds. There were many people on these walks—men, women and children—all dressed in handsome garments of silk or satin or velvet, with beautiful jewels. Better even than this: all seemed happy and contented, for their faces were smiling and free from care, and music and laughter might be heard on every side.

"Don't they work at all?" asked the shaggy man.

"To be sure they work," replied the Tin Woodman; "this fair city could not be built or cared for without labor, nor could the fruit and vegetables and other food be provided for the inhabitants to eat. But no one works more than half his time, and the people of Oz enjoy their labors as much as they do their play."

"It's wonderful!" declared the shaggy man. "I do hope Ozma will let me live here."

The chariot, winding through many charming streets, paused before a building so vast and noble and elegant that even Button-Bright guessed at once that it was the Royal Palace. Its gardens and ample grounds were surrounded by a separate wall, not so high or thick as the wall around the City, but more daintily designed and built all of green marble. The gates flew open as the chariot appeared before them, and the Cowardly Lion and Hungry Tiger trotted up a jeweled driveway to the front door of the palace and stopped short.

"Here we are!" said Dorothy, gaily, and helped Button-Bright from the chariot. Polychrome leaped out lightly after them, and they were greeted by a crowd of gorgeously dressed servants who bowed low as the visitors mounted the marble steps. At their head was a pretty little maid with dark hair and eyes, dressed all in green embroidered with silver. Dorothy ran up to her with evident pleasure, and exclaimed: "O, Jellia Jamb! I'm so glad to see you again. Where's Ozma?"

"In her room, your Highness," replied the little maid demurely, for this was Ozma's favorite attendant. "She wishes you to come to her as soon as you have rested and changed your dress, Princess Dorothy. And you and your friends are to dine with her this evening."

"When is her birthday, Jellia?" asked the girl.

"Day after to-morrow, your Highness."

"And where's the Scarecrow?"

"He's gone into the Munchkin country to get some fresh straw to stuff himself with, in honor of Ozma's celebration," replied the maid. "He returns to the Emerald City to-morrow, he said."

By this time, Tok-tok, the Tin Woodman, and the shaggy man had arrived and the chariot had gone around to the back of the palace, Billina going with the Lion and Tiger to see her chickens after her absence from them. But Toto stayed close beside Dorothy.

"Come in, please," said Jellia Jamb; "it shall be our pleasant duty to escort all of you to the rooms prepared for your use."

The shaggy man hesitated. Dorothy had never known him to be ashamed of his shaggy looks before, but now that he was surrounded by so much magnificence and splendor the shaggy man felt sadly out of place.

Dorothy assured him that all her friends were welcome at Ozma's palace, so he carefully dusted his shaggy shoes with his shaggy handkerchief and entered the grand hall after the others.

Tik-tok lived at the Royal Palace and the Tin Woodman always had the same room whenever he visited Ozma, so these two went at once to remove the dust of the journey from their shining bodies. Dorothy also had a pretty suite of rooms which she always occupied when in the Emerald City; but several servants walked ahead politely to show the way, although she was quite sure she could find the rooms herself. She took Button-Bright with her, because he seemed too small to be left alone in such a big palace; but Jellia Jamb herself ushered the beautiful Daughter of the Rainbow to her apartments, because it was easy to see that Polychrome was used to splendid palaces and was therefore entitled to especial attention.

19. The Shaggy Man's Welcome

The shaggy man stood in the great hall, his shaggy hat in his hands, wondering what would become of him. He had never been a guest in a fine palace before; perhaps he had never been a guest anywhere. In the big, cold, outside world people did not invite shaggy men to their homes, and this shaggy man of ours had slept more in hay-lofts and stables than in comfortable rooms. When the others left the great hall he eyed the splendidly dressed servants of the Princess Ozma as if he expected to be ordered out; but one of them bowed before him as respectfully as if he had been a prince, and said: "Permit me, sir, to conduct you to your apartments."

The shaggy man drew a long breath and took courage.

"Very well," he answered. "I'm ready."

Through the big hall they went, up the grand staircase carpeted thick with velvet, and so along a wide corridor to a carved doorway. Here the servant paused, and opening the door said with polite deference: "Be good enough to enter, sir, and make yourself at home in the rooms our Royal Ozma has ordered prepared for you. Whatever you see is for you to use and enjoy, as if your own. The Princess dines at seven, and I shall be here in time to lead you to the drawing-room, where you will be privileged to meet the lovely Ruler of Oz. Is there any command, in the meantime, with which you desire to honor me?"

"No," said the shaggy man; "but I'm much obliged."

He entered the room and shut the door, and for a time stood in bewilderment, admiring the grandeur before him.

He had been given one of the handsomest apartments in the most magnificent palace in the world, and you can not wonder that his good fortune astonished and awed him until he grew used to his surroundings.

The furniture was upholstered in cloth of gold, with the royal crown embroidered upon it in scarlet. The rug upon the marble floor was so thick and soft that he could not hear the sound of his own footsteps, and upon the walls were splendid tapestries woven with scenes from the Land of Oz. Books and ornaments were scattered about in profusion, and the shaggy man thought he had never seen so many pretty things in one place before. In one corner played a tinkling fountain of perfumed water, and in another was a table bearing a golden tray loaded with freshly gathered fruit, including several of the red-cheeked apples that the shaggy man loved.

At the farther end of this charming room was an open doorway, and he crossed over to find himself in a bedroom containing more comforts than the shaggy man had ever before imagined. The bedstead was of gold and set with many brilliant diamonds, and the coverlet had designs of pearls and rubies sewed upon it. At one side of the bedroom was a dainty dressing-room with closets containing a large assortment of fresh clothing; and beyond this was the bath—a large room having a marble pool big enough to swim in, with white marble steps leading down to the water. Around the edge of the pool were set rows of fine emeralds as large as door-knobs, while the water of the bath was clear as crystal.

For a time the shaggy man gazed upon all this luxury with silent amazement. Then he decided, being wise in his way, to take advantage of his good fortune. He removed his shaggy boots and his shaggy clothing, and bathed in the pool with rare enjoyment. After he had dried himself with the soft towels he went into the dressing-room and took fresh linen from the drawers and put it on, finding that everything fitted him exactly. He examined the contents of the closets and selected an elegant suit of clothing. Strangely enough, everything about it was shaggy, although so new and beautiful, and he sighed with contentment to realize that he could now be finely dressed and still be the shaggy man. His coat was of rose-colored velvet, trimmed with shags and bobtails, with buttons of blood-red rubies and golden shags around the edges. His vest was a shaggy satin of a delicate cream color, and his knee-breeches of rose velvet trimmed like the coat. Shaggy creamy stockings of silk, and shaggy slippers of rose leather with ruby buckles, completed his costume, and when he was thus attired the shaggy man looked at himself in a long mirror with great admiration. On a table he found a mother-of-pearl chest decorated with delicate silver vines and flowers of clustered rubies, and on the cover was a silver plate engraved with these words:

THE SHAGGY MAN: HIS BOX OF ORNAMENTS

The chest was not locked, so he opened it and was almost dazzled by the brilliance of the rich jewels it contained. After admiring the pretty things, he took out a fine golden watch with a big chain, several handsome finger-rings, and an ornament of rubies to pin upon the breast of his shaggy shirt-bosom. Having carefully brushed his hair and whiskers all the wrong way to make them look as shaggy as possible, the shaggy man breathed a deep sigh of joy and decided he was ready to meet the Royal Princess as soon as she sent for him. While he waited he returned to the beautiful sitting room and ate several of the red-cheeked apples to pass away the time.

Meanwhile, Dorothy had dressed herself in a pretty gown of soft grey embroidered with silver, and put a blue-and-gold suit of satin upon little Button-Bright, who looked as sweet as a cherub in it. Followed by the boy and Toto—the dog with a new green ribbon around his neck—she hastened down to the splendid drawing-room of the palace, where, seated upon an exquisite throne of carved malachite and nestled amongst its green satin cushions was the lovely Princess Ozma, waiting eagerly to welcome her friend.

20. Princess Ozma Of Oz

The royal historians of Oz, who are fine writers and know any number of big words, have often tried to describe the rare beauty of Ozma and failed because the words were not good enough. So of course I cannot hope to tell you how great was the charm of this little Princess, or how her loveliness put to shame all the sparkling jewels and magnificent luxury that surrounded her in this her royal palace. Whatever else was beautiful or dainty or delightful of itself faded to dullness when contrasted with Ozma's bewitching face, and it has often been said by those who know that no other ruler in all the world can ever hope to equal the gracious charm of her manner.

Everything about Ozma attracted one, and she inspired love and the sweetest affection rather than awe or ordinary admiration. Dorothy threw her arms around her little friend and hugged and kissed her rapturously, and Toto barked joyfully and Button-Bright smiled a happy smile and consented to sit on the soft cushions close beside the Princess.

"Why didn't you send me word you were going to have a birthday party?" asked the little Kansas girl, when the first greetings were over.

"Didn't I?" asked Ozma, her pretty eyes dancing with merriment.

"Did you?" replied Dorothy, trying to think.

"Who do you imagine, dear, mixed up those roads, so as to start you wandering in the direction of Oz?" inquired the Princess.

"Oh! I never 'spected YOU of that," cried Dorothy.

"I've watched you in my Magic Picture all the way here," declared Ozma, "and twice I thought I should have to use the Magic Belt to save you and transport you to the Emerald City. Once was when the Scoodlers caught you, and again when you reached the Deadly Desert. But the shaggy man was able to help you out both times, so I did not interfere."

"Do you know who Button-Bright is?" asked Dorothy.

"No; I never saw him until you found him in the road, and then only in my Magic Picture."

"And did you send Polly to us?"

"No, dear; the Rainbow's Daughter slid from her father's pretty arch just in time to meet you."

"Well," said Dorothy, "I've promised King Dox of Foxville and King Kik-a-bray of Dunkiton that I'd ask you to invite them to your party."

"I have already done that," returned Ozma, "because I thought it would please you to favor them."

"Did you 'vite the Musicker?" asked Button-Bright.

"No; because he would be too noisy, and might interfere with the comfort of others. When music is not very good, and is indulged in all the time, it is better that the performer should be alone," said the Princess.

"I like the Musicker's music," declared the boy, gravely.

"But I don't," said Dorothy.

"Well, there will be plenty of music at my celebration," promised Ozma; "so I've an idea Button-Bright won't miss the Musicker at all."

Just then Polychrome danced in, and Ozma rose to greet the Rainbow's Daughter in her sweetest and most cordial manner.

Dorothy thought she had never seen two prettier creatures together than these lovely maidens; but Polly knew at once her own dainty beauty could not match that of Ozma, yet was not a bit jealous because this was so.

The Wizard of Oz was announced, and a dried-up, little, old man, clothed all in black, entered the drawing-room. His face was cheery and his eyes twinkling with humor, so Polly and Button-Bright were not at all afraid of the wonderful personage whose fame as a humbug magician had spread throughout the world. After greeting Dorothy with much affection, he stood modestly behind Ozma's throne and listened to the lively prattle of the young people.

Now the shaggy man appeared, and so startling was his appearance, all clad in shaggy new rainment, that Dorothy cried "Oh!" and clasped her hands impulsively as she examined her friend with pleased eyes.

"He's still shaggy, all right," remarked Button-Bright; and Ozma nodded brightly because she had meant the shaggy man to remain shaggy when she provided his new clothes for him.

Dorothy led him toward the throne, as he was shy in such fine company, and presented him gracefully to the Princess, saying: "This, your Highness, is my friend, the shaggy man, who owns the Love Magnet."

"You are welcome to Oz," said the girl Ruler, in gracious accents. "But tell me, sir, where did you get the Love Magnet which you say you own?"

The shaggy man grew red and looked downcast, as he answered in a low voice: "I stole it, your Majesty."

"Oh, Shaggy Man!" cried Dorothy. "How dreadful! And you told me the Eskimo gave you the Love Magnet."

He shuffled first on one foot and then on the other, much embarrassed.

"I told you a falsehood, Dorothy," he said; "but now, having bathed in the Truth Pond, I must tell nothing but the truth."

"Why did you steal it?" asked Ozma, gently.

"Because no one loved me, or cared for me," said the shaggy man, "and I wanted to be loved a great deal. It was owned by a girl in Butterfield who was loved too much, so that the young men quarreled over her, which made her unhappy. After I had stolen the Magnet from her, only one young man continued to love the girl, and she married him and regained her happiness."

"Are you sorry you stole it?" asked the Princess.

"No, your Highness; I'm glad," he answered; "for it has pleased me to be loved, and if Dorothy had not cared for me I could not have accompanied her to this beautiful Land of Oz, or met its kind-hearted Ruler. Now that I'm here, I hope to remain, and to become one of your Majesty's most faithful subjects."

"But in Oz we are loved for ourselves alone, and for our kindness to one another, and for our good deeds," she said.

"I'll give up the Love Magnet," said the shaggy man, eagerly; "Dorothy shall have it."

"But every one loves Dorothy already," declared the Wizard.

"Then Button-Bright shall have it."

"Don't want it," said the boy, promptly.

"Then I'll give it to the Wizard, for I'm sure the lovely Princess Ozma does not need it."

"All my people love the Wizard, too," announced the Princess, laughing; "so we will hang the Love Magnet over the gates of the Emerald City, that whoever shall enter or leave the gates may be loved and loving."

"That is a good idea," said the shaggy man; "I agree to it most willingly."

Those assembled now went in to dinner, which you can imagine was a grand affair; and afterward Ozma asked the Wizard to give them an exhibition of his magic.

The Wizard took eight tiny white piglets from an inside pocket and set them on the table. One was dressed like a clown, and performed funny antics, and the others leaped over the spoons and dishes and ran around the table like race-horses, and turned hand-springs and were so sprightly and amusing that they kept the company in one roar of merry laughter. The Wizard had trained these pets to do many curious things, and they were so little and so cunning and soft that Polychrome loved to pick them up as they passed near her place and fondle them as if they were kittens.

It was late when the entertainment ended, and they separated to go to their rooms.

"To-morrow," said Ozma, "my invited guests will arrive, and you will find among them some interesting and curious people, I promise you. The next day will be my birthday, and the festivities will be held on the broad green just outside the gates of the City, where all my people can assemble without being crowded."

"I hope the Scarecrow won't be late," said Dorothy, anxiously.

"Oh, he is sure to return to-morrow," answered Ozma. "He wanted new straw to stuff himself with, so he went to the Munchkin Country, where straw is plentiful."

With this the Princess bade her guests good night and went to her own room.

21. Dorothy Receives the Guests

Next morning Dorothy's breakfast was served in her own pretty sitting room, and she sent to invite Polly and the shaggy man to join her and Button-Bright at the meal. They came gladly, and Toto also had breakfast with them, so that the little party that had traveled together to Oz was once more reunited.

No sooner had they finished eating than they heard the distant blast of many trumpets, and the sound of a brass band playing martial music; so they all went out upon the balcony. This was at the front of the palace and overlooked the streets of the City, being higher than the wall that shut in the palace grounds. They saw approaching down the street a band of musicians, playing as hard and loud as they could, while the people of the Emerald City crowded the sidewalks and cheered so lustily that they almost drowned the noise of the drums and horns.

Dorothy looked to see what they were cheering at, and discovered that behind the band was the famous Scarecrow riding proudly upon the back of a wooden Saw-Horse which pranced along the street almost as gracefully as if it had been made of flesh. Its hoofs, or rather the ends of its wooden legs, were shod with plates of solid gold, and the saddle strapped to the wooden body was richly embroidered and glistened with jewels.

As he reached the palace the Scarecrow looked up and saw Dorothy, and at once waved his peaked hat at her in greeting. He rode up to the front door and dismounted, and the band stopped playing and went away and the crowds of people returned to their dwellings.

By the time Dorothy and her friends had re-entered her room the Scarecrow was there, and he gave the girl a hearty embrace and shook the hands of the others with his own squashy hands, which were white gloves filled with straw.

The shaggy man, Button-Bright, and Polychrome stared hard at this celebrated person, who was acknowledged to be the most popular and most beloved man in all the Land of Oz.

"Why, your face has been newly painted!" exclaimed Dorothy, when the first greetings were over.

"I had it touched up a bit by the Munchkin farmer who first made me," answered the Scarecrow, pleasantly. "My complexion had become a bit grey and faded, you know, and the paint had peeled off one end of my mouth, so I couldn't talk quite straight. Now I feel like myself again, and I may say without immodesty that my body is stuffed with the loveliest oat-straw in all Oz." He pushed against his chest. "Hear me crunkle?" he asked.

"Yes," said Dorothy; "you sound fine."

Button-Bright was wonderfully attracted by the strawman, and so was Polly. The shaggy man treated him with great respect, because he was so queerly made.

Jellia Jamb now came to say that Ozma wanted Princess Dorothy to receive the invited guests in the Throne-Room, as they arrived. The Ruler was herself busy ordering the preparations for the morrow's festivities, so she wished her friend to act in her place.

Dorothy willingly agreed, being the only other Princess in the Emerald City; so she went to the great Throne-Room and sat in Ozma's seat, placing Polly on one side of her and Button-Bright on the other. The Scarecrow stood at the left of the throne and the Tin Woodman at the right, while the Wonderful Wizard and the shaggy man stood behind.

The Cowardly Lion and the Hungry Tiger came in, with bright new bows of ribbon on their collars and tails. After greeting Dorothy affectionately the huge beasts lay down at the foot of the throne.

While they waited, the Scarecrow, who was near the little boy, asked: "Why are you called Button-Bright?"

"Don't know," was the answer.

"Oh yes, you do, dear," said Dorothy. "Tell the Scarecrow how you got your name."

"Papa always said I was bright as a button, so mama always called me Button-Bright," announced the boy.

"Where is your mama?" asked the Scarecrow.

"Don't know," said Button-Bright.

"Where is your home?" asked the Scarecrow.

"Don't know," said Button-Bright.

"Don't you want to find your mama again?" asked the Scarecrow.

"Don't know," said Button-Bright, calmly.

The Scarecrow looked thoughtful.

"Your papa may have been right," he observed; "but there are many kinds of buttons, you see. There are silver and gold buttons, which are highly polished and glitter brightly. There are pearl and rubber buttons, and other kinds, with surfaces more or less bright. But there is still another sort of button which is covered with dull cloth, and that must be the sort your papa meant when he said you were bright as a button. Don't you think so?"

"Don't know," said Button-Bright.

Jack Pumpkinhead arrived, wearing a pair of new, white kid gloves; and he brought a birthday present for Ozma consisting of a necklace of pumpkin-seeds. In each seed was set a sparkling carolite, which is considered the rarest and most beautiful gem that exists. The necklace was in a plush case and Jellia Jamb put it on a table with the Princess Ozma's other presents.

Next came a tall, beautiful woman clothed in a splendid trailing gown, trimmed with exquisite lace as fine as cobweb. This was the important Sorceress known as Glinda the Good, who had been of great assistance to both Ozma and Dorothy. There was no humbug about her magic, you may be sure, and Glinda was as kind as she was powerful. She greeted Dorothy most lovingly, and kissed Button-Bright and Polly, and smiled upon the shaggy man, after which Jellia Jamb led the Sorceress to one of the most magnificent rooms of the royal palace and appointed fifty servants to wait upon her.

The next arrival was Mr. H. M. Woggle-Bug, T.E.; the "H. M." meaning Highly Magnified and the "T.E." meaning Thoroughly Educated. The Woggle-Bug was head professor at the Royal College of Oz, and he had composed a fine Ode in honor of Ozma's birthday. This he wanted to read to them; but the Scarecrow wouldn't let him.

Soon they heard a clucking sound and a chorus of "cheep! cheep!" and a servant threw open the door to allow Billina and her ten fluffy chicks to enter the Throne-Room. As the Yellow Hen marched proudly at the head of her family, Dorothy cried, "Oh, you lovely things!" and ran down from her seat to pet the little yellow downy balls. Billina wore a pearl necklace, and around the neck of each chicken was a tiny gold chain holding a locket with the letter "D" engraved upon the outside.

"Open the lockets, Dorothy," said Billina. The girl obeyed and found a picture of herself in each locket. "They were named after you, my dear," continued the Yellow Hen, "so I wanted all my chickens to wear your picture. Cluck—cluck! come here, Dorothy—this minute!" she cried, for the chickens were scattered and wandering all around the big room.

They obeyed the call at once, and came running as fast as they could, fluttering their fluffy wings in a laughable way.

It was lucky that Billina gathered the little ones under her soft breast just then, for Tik-tok came in and tramped up to the throne on his flat copper feet.

"I am all wound up and work-ing fine-ly," said the clock-work man to Dorothy.

"I can hear him tick," declared Button-Bright.

"You are quite the polished gentleman," said the Tin Woodman. "Stand up here beside the shaggy man, Tik-tok, and help receive the company."

Dorothy placed soft cushions in a corner for Billina and her chicks, and had just returned to the Throne and seated herself when the playing of the royal band outside the palace announced the approach of distinguished guests.

And my, how they did stare when the High Chamberlain threw open the doors and the visitors entered the Throne-Room!

First walked a gingerbread man neatly formed and baked to a lovely brown tint. He wore a silk hat and carried a candy cane prettily striped with red and yellow. His shirt-front and cuffs were white frosting, and the buttons on his coat were licorice drops.

Behind the gingerbread man came a child with flaxen hair and merry blue eyes, dressed in white pajamas, with sandals on the soles of its pretty bare feet. The child looked around smiling and thrust its hands into the pockets of the pajamas. Close after it came a big rubber bear, walking erect on its hind feet. The bear had twinkling black eyes, and its body looked as if it had been pumped full of air.

Following these curious visitors were two tall, thin men and two short, fat men, all four dressed in gorgeous uniforms.

Ozma's High Chamberlain now hurried forward to announce the names of the new arrivals, calling out in a loud voice: "His Gracious and Most Edible Majesty, King Dough the First, Ruler of the Two Kingdoms of Hiland and Loland. Also the Head Boolywag of his Majesty, known as Chick the Cherub, and their faithful friend Para Bruin, the rubber bear."

These great personages bowed low as their names were called, and Dorothy hastened to introduce them to the assembled company. They were the first foreign arrivals, and the friends of Princess Ozma were polite to them and tried to make them feel that they were welcome.

Chick the Cherub shook hands with every one, including Billina, and was so joyous and frank and full of good spirits that John Dough's Head Booleywag at once became a prime favorite.

"Is it a boy or a girl?" whispered Dorothy.

"Don't know," said Button-Bright.

"Goodness me! what a queer lot of people you are," exclaimed the rubber bear, looking at the assembled company.

"So're you," said Button-Bright, gravely. "Is King Dough good to eat?"

"He's too good to eat," laughed Chick the Cherub.

"I hope none of you are fond of gingerbread," said the King, rather anxiously.

"We should never think of eating our visitors, if we were," declared the Scarecrow; "so please do not worry, for you will be perfectly safe while you remain in Oz."

"Why do they call you Chick?" the Yellow Hen asked the child.

"Because I'm an Incubator Baby, and never had any parents," replied the Head Booleywag.

"My chicks have a parent, and I'm it," said Billina.

"I'm glad of that," answered the Cherub, "because they'll have more fun worrying you than if they were brought up in an Incubator. The Incubator never worries, you know."

King John Dough had brought for Ozma's birthday present a lovely gingerbread crown, with rows of small pearls around it and a fine big pearl in each of its five points. After this had been received by Dorothy with proper thanks and placed on the table with the other presents, the visitors from Hiland and Loland were escorted to their rooms by the High Chamberlain.

They had no sooner departed than the band before the palace began to play again, announcing more arrivals, and as these were doubtless from foreign parts the High Chamberlain hurried back to receive them in his most official manner.

22. Important Arrivals

First entered a band of Ryls from the Happy Valley, all merry little sprites like fairy elves. A dozen crooked Knooks followed from the great Forest of Burzee. They had long whiskers and pointed caps and curling toes, yet were no taller than Button-Bright's shoulder. With this group came a man so easy to recognize and so important and dearly beloved throughout the known world, that all present rose to their feet and bowed their heads in respectful homage, even before the High Chamberlain knelt to announce his name.

"The most Mighty and Loyal Friend of Children, His Supreme Highness—Santa Claus!" said the Chamberlain, in an awed voice.

"Well, well, well! Glad to see you—glad to meet you all!" cried Santa Claus, briskly, as he trotted up the long room.

He was round as an apple, with a fresh rosy face, laughing eyes, and a bushy beard as white as snow. A red cloak trimmed with beautiful ermine hung from his shoulders and upon his back was a basket filled with pretty presents for the Princess Ozma.

"Hello, Dorothy; still having adventures?" he asked in his jolly way, as he took the girl's hand in both his own.

"How did you know my name, Santa?" she replied, feeling more shy in the presence of this immortal saint than she ever had before in her young life.

"Why, don't I see you every Christmas Eve, when you're asleep?" he rejoined, pinching her blushing cheek.

"Oh, do you?"

"And here's Button-Bright, I declare!" cried Santa Claus, holding up the boy to kiss him. "What a long way from home you are; dear me!"

"Do you know Button-Bright, too?" questioned Dorothy, eagerly.

"Indeed I do. I've visited his home several Christmas Eves."

"And do you know his father?" asked the girl.

"Certainly, my dear. Who else do you suppose brings him his Christmas neckties and stockings?" with a sly wink at the Wizard.

"Then where does he live? We're just crazy to know, 'cause Button-Bright's lost," she said.

Santa laughed and laid his finger aside of his nose as if thinking what to reply. He leaned over and whispered something in the Wizard's ear, at which the Wizard smiled and nodded as if he understood.

Now Santa Claus spied Polychrome, and trotted over to where she stood.

"Seems to me the Rainbow's Daughter is farther from home than any of you," he observed, looking at the pretty maiden admiringly. "I'll have to tell your father where you are, Polly, and send him to get you."

"Please do, dear Santa Claus," implored the little maid, beseechingly.

"But just now we must all have a jolly good time at Ozma's party," said the old gentleman, turning to put his presents on the table with the others already there. "It isn't often I find time to leave my castle, as you know; but Ozma invited me and I just couldn't help coming to celebrate the happy occasion."

"I'm so glad!" exclaimed Dorothy.

"These are my Ryls," pointing to the little sprites squatting around him. "Their business is to paint the colors of the flowers when they bud and bloom; but I brought the merry fellows along to see Oz, and they've left their paint-pots behind them. Also I brought these crooked Knooks, whom I love. My dears, the Knooks are much nicer than they look, for their duty is to water and care for the young trees of the forest, and they do their work faithfully and well. It's hard work, though, and it makes my Knooks crooked and gnarled, like the trees themselves; but their hearts are big and kind, as are the hearts of all who do good in our beautiful world."

"I've read of the Ryls and Knooks," said Dorothy, looking upon these little workers with interest.

Santa Claus turned to talk with the Scarecrow and the Tin Woodman, and he also said a kind word to the shaggy man, and afterward went away to ride the Saw-Horse around the Emerald City. "For," said he, "I must see all the grand sights while I am here and have the chance, and Ozma has promised to let me ride the Saw-Horse because I'm getting fat and short of breath."

"Where are your reindeer?" asked Polychrome.

"I left them at home, for it is too warm for them in this sunny country," he answered. "They're used to winter weather when they travel."

In a flash he was gone, and the Ryls and Knooks with him; but they could all hear the golden hoofs of the Saw-Horse ringing on the marble pavement outside, as he pranced away with his noble rider.

Presently the band played again, and the High Chamberlain announced: "Her Gracious Majesty, the Queen of Merryland."

They looked earnestly to discover whom this queen might be, and saw advancing up the room an exquisite wax doll dressed in dainty fluffs and ruffles and spangled gown. She was almost as big as Button-Bright, and her cheeks and mouth and eyebrows were prettily painted in delicate colors. Her blue eyes stared a bit, being of glass, yet the expression upon her Majesty's face was quite pleasant and decidedly winning. With the Queen of Merryland were four wooden soldiers, two stalking ahead of her with much dignity and two following behind, like a royal bodyguard. The soldiers were painted in bright colors and carried wooden guns, and after them came a fat little man who attracted attention at once, although he seemed modest and retiring. For he was made of candy, and carried a tin sugar-sifter filled with powdered sugar, with which he dusted himself frequently so that he wouldn't stick to things if he touched them. The High Chamberlain had called him "The Candy Man of Merryland," and Dorothy saw that one of his thumbs looked as if it had been bitten off by some one who was fond of candy and couldn't resist the temptation.

The wax doll Queen spoke prettily to Dorothy and the others, and sent her loving greetings to Ozma before she retired to the rooms prepared for her. She had brought a birthday present wrapped in tissue paper and tied with pink and blue ribbons, and one of the wooden soldiers placed it on the table with the other gifts. But the Candy Man did not go to his room, because he said he preferred to stay and talk with the Scarecrow and Tik-tok and the Wizard and Tin Woodman, whom he declared the queerest people he had ever met. Button-Bright was glad the Candy Man stayed in the Throne Room, because the boy thought this guest smelled deliciously of wintergreen and maple sugar.

The Braided Man now entered the room, having been fortunate enough to receive an invitation to the Princess Ozma's party. He was from a cave halfway between the Invisible Valley and the Country of the Gargoyles, and his hair and whiskers were so long that he was obliged to plait them into many braids that hung to his feet, and every braid was tied with a bow of colored ribbon.

"I've brought Princess Ozma a box of flutters for her birthday," said the Braided Man, earnestly; "and I hope she will like them, for they are the finest quality I have ever made."

"I'm sure she will be greatly pleased," said Dorothy, who remembered the Braided Man well; and the Wizard introduced the guest to the rest of the company and made him sit down in a chair and keep quiet, for, if allowed, he would talk continually about his flutters.

The band then played a welcome to another set of guests, and into the Throne-Room swept the handsome and stately Queen of Ev. Beside her was young King Evardo, and following them came the entire royal family of five Princesses and four Princes of Ev. The Kingdom of Ev lay just across the Deadly Desert to the North of Oz, and once Ozma and her people had rescued the Queen of Ev and her ten children from the Nome King, who had enslaved them. Dorothy had been present on this adventure, so she greeted the royal family cordially; and all the visitors were delighted to meet the little Kansas girl again. They knew Tik-tok and Billina, too, and the Scarecrow and Tin Woodman, as well as the Lion and Tiger; so there was a joyful reunion, as you may imagine, and it was fully an hour before the Queen and her train retired to their rooms. Perhaps they would not have gone then had not the band begun to play to announce new arrivals; but before they left the great Throne-Room King Evardo added to Ozma's birthday presents a diadem of diamonds set in radium.

The next comer proved to be King Renard of Foxville; or King Dox, as he preferred to be called. He was magnificently dressed in a new feather costume and wore white kid mittens over his paws and a flower in his button-hole and had his hair parted in the middle.

King Dox thanked Dorothy fervently for getting him the invitation to come to Oz, which he all his life longed to visit. He strutted around rather absurdly as he was introduced to all the famous people assembled in the Throne-Room, and when he learned that Dorothy was a Princess of Oz the Fox King insisted on kneeling at her feet and afterward retired backward—a dangerous thing to do, as he might have stubbed his paw and tumbled over.

No sooner was he gone than the blasts of bugles and clatter of drums and cymbals announced important visitors, and the High Chamberlain assumed his most dignified tone as he threw open the door and said proudly: "Her Sublime and Resplendent Majesty, Queen Zixi of Ix! His Serene and Tremendous Majesty, King Bud of Noland. Her Royal Highness, the Princess Fluff."

That three such high and mighty royal personages should arrive at once was enough to make Dorothy and her companions grow solemn and assume their best company manners; but when the exquisite beauty of Queen Zixi met their eyes they thought they had never beheld anything so charming. Dorothy decided that Zixi must be about sixteen years old, but the Wizard whispered to her that this wonderful queen had lived thousands of years, but knew the secret of remaining always fresh and beautiful.

King Bud of Noland and his dainty fair-haired sister, the Princess Fluff, were friends of Zixi, as their kingdoms were adjoining, so they had traveled together from their far-off domains to do honor to Ozma of Oz on the occasion of her birthday. They brought many splendid gifts; so the table was now fairly loaded down with presents.

Dorothy and Polly loved the Princess Fluff the moment they saw her, and little King Bud was so frank and boyish that Button-Bright accepted him as a chum at once and did not want him to go away. But it was after noon now, and the royal guests must prepare their toilets for the grand banquet at which they were to assemble that evening to meet the reigning Princess of this Fairyland; so Queen Zixi was shown to her room by a troop of maidens led by Jellia Jamb, and Bud and Fluff presently withdrew to their own apartments.

"My! what a big party Ozma is going to have," exclaimed Dorothy. "I guess the palace will be chock full, Button-Bright; don't you think so?"

"Don't know," said the boy.

"But we must go to our rooms, pretty soon, to dress for the banquet," continued the girl.

"I don't have to dress," said the Candy Man from Merryland. "All I need do is to dust myself with fresh sugar."

"Tik-tok always wears the same suits of clothes," said the Tin Woodman; "and so does our friend the Scarecrow."

"My feathers are good enough for any occasion," cried Billina, from her corner.

"Then I shall leave you four to welcome any new guests that come," said Dorothy; "for Button-Bright and I must look our very best at Ozma's banquet."

"Who is still to come?" asked the Scarecrow.

"Well, there's King Kik-a-bray of Dunkiton, and Johnny Dooit, and the Good Witch of the North. But Johnny Dooit may not get here until late, he's so very busy."

"We will receive them and give them a proper welcome," promised the Scarecrow. "So run along, little Dorothy, and get yourself dressed."

23. The Grand Banquet

I wish I could tell you how fine the company was that assembled that evening at Ozma's royal banquet. A long table was spread in the center of the great dining-hall of the palace and the splendor of the decorations and the blaze of lights and jewels was acknowledged to be the most magnificent sight that any of the guests had ever seen.

The jolliest person present, as well as the most important, was of course old Santa Claus; so he was given the seat of honor at one end of the table while at the other end sat Princess Ozma, the hostess.

John Dough, Queen Zixi, King Bud, the Queen of Ev and her son Evardo, and the Queen of Merryland had golden thrones to sit in, while the others were supplied with beautiful chairs.

At the upper end of the banquet room was a separate table provided for the animals. Toto sat at one end of this table with a bib tied around his neck and a silver platter to eat from. At the other end was placed a small stand, with a low rail around the edge of it, for Billina and her chicks. The rail kept the ten little Dorothys from falling off the stand, while the Yellow Hen could easily reach over and take her food from her tray upon the table. At other places sat the Hungry Tiger, the Cowardly Lion, the Saw-Horse, the Rubber Bear, the Fox King and the Donkey King;

they made quite a company of animals.

At the lower end of the great room was another table, at which sat the Ryls and Knooks who had come with Santa Claus, the wooden soldiers who had come with the Queen of Merryland, and the Hilanders and Lolanders who had come with John Dough. Here were also seated the officers of the royal palace and of Ozma's army.

The splendid costumes of those at the three tables made a gorgeous and glittering display that no one present was ever likely to forget; perhaps there has never been in any part of the world at any time another assemblage of such wonderful people as that which gathered this evening to honor the birthday of the Ruler of Oz.

When all members of ethe company were in their places an orchestra of five hundred pieces, in a balcony overlooking the banquet room, began to play sweet and delightful music. Then a door draped with royal green opened, and in came the fair and girlish Princess Ozma, who now greeted her guests in person for the first time.

As she stood by her throne at the head of the banquet table every eye was turned eagerly upon the lovely Princess, who was as dignified as she was bewitching, and who smiled upon all her old and new friends in a way that touched their hearts and brough an answering smile to every face.

Each guest had been served with a crystal goblet filled with lacasa, which is a sort of nectar famous in Oz and nicer to drink than soda-water or lemonade. Santa now made a pretty speech in verse, congratulating Ozma on having a birthday, and asking every one present to drink to the health and happiness of their dearly beloved hostess. This was done with great enthusiasm by those who were made so they could drink at all, and those who could not drink politely touched the rims of their goblets to their lips. All seated themselves at the tables and the servants of the Princess began serving the feast.

I am quite sure that only in Fairyland could such a delicious repast be prepared. The dishes were of precious metals set with brilliant jewels and the good things to eat which were placed upon them were countless in number and of exquisite flavor. Several present, such as the Candy Man, the Rubber Bear, Tik tok, and the Scarecrow, were not made so they could eat, and the Queen of Merryland contented herself with a small dish of sawdust; but these enjoyed the pomp and glitter of the gorgeous scene as much as did those who feasted.

The Woggle-Bug read his "Ode to Ozma," which was written in very good rhythm and was well received by the company. The Wizard added to the entertainment by making a big pie appear before Dorothy, and when the little girl cut the pie the nine tiny piglets leaped out of it and danced around the table, while the orchestra played a merry tune. This amused the company very much, but they were even more pleased when Polychrome, whose hunger had been easily satisfied, rose from the table and performed her graceful and bewildering Rainbow Dance for them. When it was ended, the people clapped their hands and the animals clapped their paws, while Billina cackled and the Donkey King brayed approval.

Johnny Dooit was present, and of course he proved he could do wonders in the way of eating, as well as in everything else that he undertook to do; the Tin Woodman sang a love song, every one joining in the chorus; and the wooden soldiers from Merryland gave an exhibition of a lightning drill with their wooden muskets; the Ryls and Knooks danced the Fairy Circle; and the Rubber Bear bounced himself all around the room. There was laughter and merriment on every side, and everybody was having a royal good time. Button-Bright was so excited and interested that he paid little attention to his fine dinner and a great deal of attention to his queer companions; and perhaps he was wise to do this, because he could eat at any other time.

The feasting and merrymaking continued until late in the evening, when they separated to meet again the next morning and take part in the birthday celebration, to which this royal banquet was merely the introduction.

24. The Birthday Celebration

A clear, perfect day, with a gentle breeze and a sunny sky, greeted Princess Ozma as she wakened next morning, the anniversary of her birth. While it was yet early all the city was astir and crowds of people came from all parts of the Land of Oz to witness the festivities in honor of their girl Ruler's birthday.

The noted visitors from foreign countries, who had all been transported to the Emerald City by means of the Magic Belt, were as much a show to the Ozites as were their own familiar celebrities, and the streets leading from the royal palace to the jeweled gates were thronged with men, women, and children to see the procession as it passed out to the green fields where the ceremonies were to take place.

And what a great procession it was!

First came a thousand young girls—the prettiest in the land— dressed in white muslin, with green sashes and hair ribbons, bearing green baskets of red roses. As they walked they scattered these flowers upon the marble pavements, so that the way was carpeted thick with roses for the procession to walk upon.

Then came the Rulers of the four Kingdoms of Oz: the Emperor of the Winkies, the Monarch of the Munchkins, the King of the Quadlings and the Sovereign of the Gillikins, each wearing a long chain of emeralds around his neck to show that he was a vassal of the Ruler of the Emerald City.

Next marched the Emerald City Cornet Band, clothed in green-and-gold uniforms and playing the "Ozma Two-Step." The Royal Army of Oz followed, consisting of twenty-seven officers, from the Captain-General down to the Lieutenants. There were no privates in Ozma's Army because soldiers were not needed to fight battles, but only to look important, and an officer always looks more imposing than a private.

While the people cheered and waved their hats and handkerchiefs, there came walking the Royal Princess Ozma, looking so pretty and sweet that it is no wonder her people love her so dearly. She had decided she would not ride in her chariot that day, as she preferred to walk in the procession with her favored subjects and her guests. Just in front of her trotted the living Blue Bear Rug owned by old Dyna, which wobbled clumsily on its four feet because there was nothing but the skin to support them, with a stuffed head at one end and a stubby tail at the other. But whenever Ozma paused in her walk the Bear Rug would flop down flat upon the ground for the princess to stand upon until she resumed her progress.

Following the Princess stalked her two enormous beasts, the Cowardly Lion and the Hungry Tiger, and even if the Army had not been there these two would have been powerful enough to guard their mistress from any harm.

Next marched the invited guests, who were loudly cheered by the people of Oz along the road, and were therefore obliged to bow to right and left almost every step of the way. First was Santa Claus, who, because he was fat and not used to walking, rode the wonderful Saw-Horse. The merry old gentleman had a basket of small toys with him, and he tossed the toys one by one to the children as he passed by. His Ryls and Knooks marched close behind him.

Queen Zixi of Ix came after; then John Dough and the Cherub, with the rubber bear named Para Bruin strutting between them on its hind legs; then the Queen of Merryland, escorted by her wooden soldiers; then King Bud of Noland and his sister, the Princess Fluff; then the Queen of Ev and her ten royal children; then the Braided Man and the Candy Man, side by side; then King Dox of Foxville and King Kik-a-bray of Dunkiton, who by this time had become good friends; and finally Johnny Dooit, in his leather apron, smoking his long pipe.

These wonderful personages were not more heartily cheered by the people than were those who followed after them in the procession. Dorothy was a general favorite, and she walked arm in arm with the Scarecrow, who was beloved by all. Then came Polychrome and Button-Bright, and the people loved the Rainbow's pretty Daughter and the beautiful blue-eyed boy as soon as they saw them. The shaggy man in his shaggy new suit attracted much attention because he was such a novelty. With regular steps tramped the machine-man Tik-tok, and there was more cheering when the Wizard of Oz followed in the procession. The Woggle-Bug and Jack Pumpkinhead were next, and behind them Glinda the Sorceress and the Good Witch of the North. Finally came Billina, with her brood of chickens to whom she clucked anxiously to keep them together and to hasten them along so they would not delay the procession.

Another band followed, this time the Tin Band of the Emperor of the Winkies, playing a beautiful march called, "There's No Plate Like Tin." Then came the servants of the Royal Palace, in a long line, and behind them all the people joined the procession and marched away through the emerald gates and out upon the broad green.

Here had been erected a splendid pavilion, with a grandstand big enough to seat all the royal party and those who had taken part in the procession. Over the pavilion, which was of green silk and cloth of gold, countless banners waved in the breeze. Just in front of this, and connected with it by a runway had been built a broad platform, so that all the spectators could see plainly the entertainment provided for them.

The Wizard now became Master of Ceremonies, as Ozma had placed the conduct of the performance in his hands. After the people had all congregated about the platform and the royal party and the visitors were seated in the grandstand, the Wizard skillfully performed some feats of juggling glass balls and lighted candles. He tossed a dozen or so of them high in the air and caught them one by one as they came down, without missing any.

Then he introduced the Scarecrow, who did a sword-swallowing act that aroused much interest. After this the Tin Woodman gave an exhibition of Swinging the Axe, which he made to whirl around him so rapidly that the eye could scarcely follow the motion of the gleaming blade. Glinda the Sorceress then stepped upon the platform, and by her magic made a big tree grow in the middle of the space, made blossoms appear upon the tree, and made the blossoms become delicious fruit called tamornas, and so great was the quantity of fruit produced that when the servants climbed the tree and tossed it down to the crowd, there was enough to satisfy every person present.

Para Bruin, the rubber bear, climbed to a limb of the big tree, rolled himself into a ball, and dropped to the platform, whence he bounded up again to the limb. He repeated this bouncing act several times, to the great delight of all the children present. After he had finished, and bowed, and returned to his seat, Glinda waved her wand and the tree disappeared; but its fruit still remained to be eaten.

The Good Witch of the North amused the people by transforming ten stones into ten birds, the ten birds into ten lambs, and the ten lambs into ten little girls, who gave a pretty dance and were then transformed into ten stones again, just as they were in the beginning.

Johnny Dooit next came on the platform with his tool-chest, and in a few minutes built a great flying machine; then put his chest in the machine and the whole thing flew away together—Johnny and all—after he had bid good-bye to those present and thanked the Princess for her hospitality.

The Wizard then announced the last act of all, which was considered really wonderful. He had invented a machine to blow huge soap-bubbles, as big as balloons, and this machine was hidden under the platform so that only the rim of the big clay pipe to produce the bubbles showed above the flooring. The tank of soapsuds, and the air-pumps to inflate the bubbles, were out of sight beneath, so that when the bubbles began to grow upon the floor of the platform it really seemed like magic to the people of Oz, who knew nothing about even the common soap-bubbles that our children blow with a penny clay pipe and a basin of soap-and-water.

The Wizard had invented another thing. Usually, soap-bubbles are frail and burst easily, lasting only a few moments as they float in the air; but the Wizard added a sort of glue to his soapsuds, which made his bubbles tough; and, as the glue dried rapidly when exposed to the air, the Wizard's bubbles were strong enough to float for hours without breaking.

He began by blowing—by means of his machinery and air-pumps—several large bubbles which he allowed to float upward into the sky, where the sunshine fell upon them and gave them iridescent hues that were most beautiful. This aroused much wonder and delight because it was a new amusement to every one present—except perhaps Dorothy and Button-Bright, and even they had never seen such big, strong bubbles before.

The Wizard then blew a bunch of small bubbles and afterward blew a big bubble around them so they were left in the center of it; then he allowed the whole mass of pretty globes to float into the air and disappear in the far distant sky.

"That is really fine!" declared Santa Claus, who loved toys and pretty things. "I think, Mr. Wizard, I shall have you blow a bubble around me; then I can float away home and see the country spread out beneath me as I travel. There isn't a spot on earth that I haven't visited, but I usually go in the night-time, riding behind my swift reindeer. Here is a good chance to observe the country by daylight, while I am riding slowly and at my ease."

"Do you think you will be able to guide the bubble?" asked the Wizard.

"Oh yes; I know enough magic to do that," replied Santa Claus. "You blow the bubble, with me inside of it, and I'll be sure to get home in safety."

"Please send me home in a bubble, too!" begged the Queen of Merryland.

"Very well, madam; you shall try the journey first," politely answered old Santa.

The pretty wax doll bade good-bye to the Princess Ozma and the others and stood on the platform while the Wizard blew a big soap-bubble around her. When completed, he allowed the bubble to float slowly upward, and there could be seen the little Queen of Merryland standing in the middle of it and blowing kisses from her fingers to those below. The bubble took a southerly direction, quickly floating out of sight.

"That's a very nice way to travel," said Princess Fluff. "I'd like to go home in a bubble, too."

So the Wizard blew a big bubble around Princess Fluff, and another around King Bud, her brother, and a third one around Queen Zixi; and soon these three bubbles had mounted into the sky and were floating off in a group in the direction of the kingdom of Noland.

The success of these ventures induced the other guests from foreign lands to undertake bubble journeys, also; so the Wizard put them one by one inside his bubbles, and Santa Claus directed the way they should go, because he knew exactly where everybody lived.

Finally, Button-Bright said: "I want to go home, too."

"Why, so you shall!" cried Santa; "for I'm sure your father and mother will be glad to see you again. Mr. Wizard, please blow a big, fine bubble for Button-Bright to ride in, and I'll agree to send him home to his family as safe as safe can be."

"I'm sorry," said Dorothy with a sigh, for she was fond of her little comrade; "but p'raps it's best for Button-Bright to get home; 'cause his folks must be worrying just dreadful."

She kissed the boy, and Ozma kissed him, too, and all the others waved their hands and said good-bye and wished him a pleasant journey.

"Are you glad to leave us, dear?" asked Dorothy, a little wistfully.

"Don't know," said Button-Bright.

He sat down cross-legged on the platform, with his sailor hat tipped back on his head, and the Wizard blew a beautiful bubble all around him.

A minute later it had mounted into the sky, sailing toward the west, and the last they saw of Button-Bright he was still sitting in the middle of the shining globe and waving his sailor hat at those below.

"Will you ride in a bubble, or shall I send you and Toto home by means of the Magic Belt?" the Princess asked Dorothy.

"Guess I'll use the Belt," replied the little girl. "I'm sort of 'fraid of those bubbles."

"Bow-wow!" said Toto, approvingly. He loved to bark at the

bubbles as they sailed away, but he didn't care to ride in one.

Santa Claus decided to go next. He thanked Ozma for her hospitality and wished her many happy returns of the day. Then the Wizard blew a bubble around his chubby little body and smaller bubbles around each of his Ryls and Knooks.

As the kind and generous friend of children mounted into the air the people all cheered at the top of their voices, for they loved Santa Claus dearly; and the little man heard them through the walls of his bubble and waved his hands in return as he smiled down upon them. The band played bravely while every one watched the bubble until it was completely out of sight.

"How 'bout you, Polly?" Dorothy asked her friend. "Are you 'fraid of bubbles, too?"

"No," answered Polychrome, smiling; "but Santa Claus promised to speak to my father as he passed through the sky. So perhaps I shall get home an easier way."

Indeed, the little maid had scarcely made this speech when a sudden radiance filled the air, and while the people looked on in wonder the end of a gorgeous rainbow slowly settled down upon the platform.

With a glad cry, the Rainbow's Daughter sprang from her seat and danced along the curve of the bow, mounting gradually upward, while the folds of her gauzy gown whirled and floated around her like a cloud and blended with the colors of the rainbow itself.

"Good-bye Ozma! Good-bye Dorothy!" cried a voice they knew belonged to Polychrome; but now the little maiden's form had melted wholly into the rainbow, and their eyes could no longer see her.

Suddenly, the end of the rainbow lifted and its colors slowly faded like mist before a breeze. Dorothy sighed deeply and turned to Ozma.

"I'm sorry to lose Polly," she said; "but I guess she's better off with her father; 'cause even the Land of Oz couldn't be like home to a cloud fairy."

"No indeed," replied the Princess; "but it has been delightful for us to know Polychrome for a little while, and—who knows?—perhaps we may meet the Rainbow's Daughter again, some day."

The entertainment being now ended, all left the pavilion and formed their gay procession back to the Emerald City again. Of Dorothy's recent traveling companions only Toto and the shaggy man remained, and Ozma had decided to allow the latter to live in Oz for a time, at least. If he proved honest and true she promised to let him live there always, and the shaggy man was anxious to earn this reward.

They had a nice quiet dinner together and passed a pleasant evening with the Scarecrow, the Tin Woodman, Tik-tok, and the Yellow Hen for company.

When Dorothy bade them good-night, she kissed them all good-bye at the same time. For Ozma had agreed that while Dorothy slept she and Toto should be transported by means of the Magic Belt to her own little bed in the Kansas farm-house and the little girl laughed as she thought how astonished Uncle Henry and Aunt Em would be when she came down to breakfast with them next morning.

Quite content to have had so pleasant an adventure, and a little tired by all the day's busy scenes, Dorothy clasped Toto in her arms and lay down upon the pretty white bed in her room in Ozma's royal palace.

Presently she was sound asleep.

The Emerald City of Oz

by L. Frank Baum

Author of The Road to Oz, Dorothy and The Wizard in Oz, The Land of Oz, etc.

Author's Note

Perhaps I should admit on the title page that this book is "By L. Frank Baum and his correspondents," for I have used many suggestions conveyed to me in letters from children. Once on a time I really imagined myself "an author of fairy tales," but now I am merely an editor or private secretary for a host of youngsters whose ideas I am requestsed to weave into the thread of my stories.

These ideas are often clever. They are also logical and interesting. So I have used them whenever I could find an opportunity, and it is but just that I acknowledge my indebtedness to my little friends.

My, what imaginations these children have developed! Sometimes I am fairly astounded by their daring and genius. There will be no lack of fairy-tale authors in the future, I am sure. My readers have told me what to do with Dorothy, and Aunt Em and Uncle Henry, and I have obeyed their mandates. They have also given me a variety of subjects to write about in the future: enough, in fact, to keep me busy for some time. I am very proud of this alliance. Children love these stories because children have helped to create them. My readers know what they want and realize that I try to please them. The result is very satisfactory to the publishers, to me, and (I am quite sure) to the children.

I hope, my dears, it will be a long time before we are obliged to dissolve partnership.

L. Frank Baum.
Coronado, 1910

1. How the Nome King Became Angry

The Nome King was in an angry mood, and at such times he was very disagreeable. Every one kept away from him, even his Chief Steward Kaliko.

Therefore the King stormed and raved all by himself, walking up and down in his jewel-studded cavern and getting angrier all the time. Then he remembered that it was no fun being angry unless he had some one to frighten and make miserable, and he rushed to his big gong and made it clatter as loud as he could.

In came the Chief Steward, trying not to show the Nome King how frightened he was.

"Send the Chief Counselor here!" shouted the angry monarch.

Kaliko ran out as fast as his spindle legs could carry his fat, round body, and soon the Chief Counselor entered the cavern. The King scowled and said to him:

"I'm in great trouble over the loss of my Magic Belt. Every little while I want to do something magical, and find I can't because the Belt is gone. That makes me angry, and when I'm angry I can't have a good time. Now, what do you advise?"

"Some people," said the Chief Counselor, "enjoy getting angry."

"But not all the time," declared the King. "To be angry once in a while is really good fun, because it makes others so miserable. But to be angry morning, noon and night, as I am, grows monotonous and prevents my gaining any other pleasure in life. Now what do you advise?"

"Why, if you are angry because you want to do magical things and can't, and if you don't want to get angry at all, my advice is not to want to do magical things."

Hearing this, the King glared at his Counselor with a furious expression and tugged at his own long white whiskers until he pulled them so hard that he yelled with pain.

"You are a fool!" he exclaimed.

"I share that honor with your Majesty," said the Chief Counselor.

The King roared with rage and stamped his foot.

"Ho, there, my guards!" he cried. "Ho" is a royal way of saying, "Come here." So, when the guards had hoed, the King said to them: "Take this Chief Counselor and throw him away."

Then the guards took the Chief Counselor, and bound him with chains to prevent his struggling, and threw him away. And the King paced up and down his cavern more angry than before.

Finally he rushed to his big gong and made it clatter like a fire alarm. Kaliko appeared again, trembling and white with fear.

"Fetch my pipe!" yelled the King.

"Your pipe is already here, your Majesty," replied Kaliko.

"Then get my tobacco!" roared the King.

"The tobacco is in your pipe, your Majesty," returned the Steward.

"Then bring a live coal from the furnace!" commanded the King.

"The tobacco is lighted, and your Majesty is already smoking your pipe," answered the Steward.

"Why, so I am!" said the King, who had forgotten this fact; "but you very rude to remind me of it."

"I am a lowborn, miserable villain," declared the Chief Steward humbly.

The Nome King could think of nothing to say next, so he puffed away at his pipe and paced up and down the room. Finally, he remembered how angry he was, and cried out: "What do you mean, Kaliko, by being so contented when your monarch is unhappy?"

"What makes you unhappy?" asked the Steward.

"I've lost my Magic Belt. A little girl named Dorothy, who was here with Ozma of Oz, stole my Belt and carried it away with her," said the King, grinding his teeth with rage.

"She captured it in a fair fight," Kaliko ventured to say.

"But I want it! I must have it! Half my power is gone with that Belt!" roared the King.

"You will have to go to the Land of Oz to recover it, and you

Majesty can't get to the Land of Oz in any possible way," said the Steward, yawning because he had been on duty ninety-six hours, and was sleepy.

"Why not?" asked the King.

"Because there is a deadly desert all around that fairy country, which no one is able to cross. You know that fact as well as I do, your Majesty. Never mind the lost Belt. You have plenty of power left, for you rule this underground kingdom like a tyrant, and thousands of Nomes obey your commands. I advise you to drink a glass of melted silver, to quiet your nerves, and then go to bed."

The King grabbed a big ruby and threw it at Kaliko's head. The Steward ducked to escape the heavy jewel, which crashed against the door just over his left ear.

"Get out of my sight! Vanish! Go away—and send General Blug here," screamed the Nome King.

Kaliko hastily withdrew, and the Nome King stamped up and down until the General of his armies appeared.

This Nome was known far and wide as a terrible fighter and a cruel, desperate commander. He had fifty thousand Nome soldiers, all well drilled, who feared nothing but their stern master. Yet General Blug was a trifle uneasy when he arrived and saw how angry the Nome King was.

"Ha! So you're here!" cried the King.

"So I am," said the General.

"March your army at once to the Land of Oz, capture and destroy the Emerald City, and bring back to me my Magic Belt!" roared the King.

"You're crazy," calmly remarked the General.

"What's that? What's that? What's that?" And the Nome King danced around on his pointed toes, he was so enraged.

"You don't know what you're talking about," continued the General, seating himself upon a large cut diamond. "I advise you to stand in a corner and count sixty before you speak again. By that time you may be more sensible."

The King looked around for something to throw at General Blug, but as nothing was handy he began to consider that perhaps the man was right and he had been talking foolishly. So he merely threw himself into his glittering throne and tipped his crown over his ear and curled his feet up under him and glared wickedly at Blug.

"In the first place," said the General, "we cannot march across the deadly desert to the Land of Oz. And if we could, the Ruler of that country, Princess Ozma, has certain fairy powers that would render my army helpless. Had you not lost your Magic Belt we might have some chance of defeating Ozma; but the Belt is gone."

"I want it!" screamed the King. "I must have it."

"Well, then, let us try in a sensible way to get it," replied the General. "The Belt was captured by a little girl named Dorothy, who lives in Kansas, in the United States of America."

"But she left it in the Emerald City, with Ozma," declared the King.

"How do you know that?" asked the General.

"One of my spies, who is a Blackbird, flew over the desert to the Land of Oz, and saw the Magic Belt in Ozma's palace," replied the King with a groan.

"Now that gives me an idea," said General Blug, thoughtfully. "There are two ways to get to the Land of Oz without traveling across the sandy desert."

"What are they?" demanded the King, eagerly.

"One way is OVER the desert, through the air; and the other way is UNDER the desert, through the earth."

Hearing this the Nome King uttered a yell of joy and leaped from his throne, to resume his wild walk up and down the cavern.

"That's it, Blug!" he shouted. "That's the idea, General! I'm King of the Under World, and my subjects are all miners. I'll make a secret tunnel under the desert to the Land of Oz—yes! right up to the Emerald City—and you will march your armies there and capture the whole country!"

"Softly, softly, your Majesty. Don't go too fast," warned the General. "My Nomes are good fighters, but they are not strong enough to conquer the Emerald City."

"Are you sure?" asked the King.

"Absolutely certain, your Majesty."

"Then what am I to do?"

"Give up the idea and mind your own business," advised the General. "You have plenty to do trying to rule your underground kingdom."

"But I want the Magic Belt—and I'm going to have it!" roared the Nome King.

"I'd like to see you get it," replied the General, laughing maliciously.

The King was by this time so exasperated that he picked up his scepter, which had a heavy ball, made from a sapphire, at the end of it, and threw it with all his force at General Blug. The sapphire hit the General upon his forehead and knocked him flat upon the ground, where he lay motionless. Then the King rang his gong and told his guards to drag out the General and throw him away; which they did.

This Nome King was named Roquat the Red, and no one loved him. He was a bad man and a powerful monarch, and he had resolved to destroy the Land of Oz and its magnificent Emerald City, to enslave Princess Ozma and little Dorothy and all the Oz people, and recover his Magic Belt. This same Belt had once enabled Roquat the Red to carry out many wicked plans; but that was before Ozma and her people marched to the underground cavern and captured it. The Nome King could not forgive Dorothy or Princess Ozma, and he had determined to be revenged upon them.

But they, for their part, did not know they had so dangerous an enemy. Indeed, Ozma and Dorothy had both almost forgotten that such a person as the Nome King yet lived under the mountains of the Land of Ev—which lay just across the deadly desert to the south of the Land of Oz.

An unsuspected enemy is doubly dangerous.

2. How Uncle Henry Got Into Trouble

Dorothy Gale lived on a farm in Kansas, with her Aunt Em and her Uncle Henry. It was not a big farm, nor a very good one, because sometimes the rain did not come when the crops needed it, and then everything withered and dried up. Once a cyclone had carried away Uncle Henry's house, so that he was obliged to build another; and as he was a poor man he had to mortgage his farm to get the money to pay for the new house. Then his health became bad and he was too feeble to work. The doctor ordered him to take a sea voyage and he went to Australia and took Dorothy with him. That cost a lot of money, too.

Uncle Henry grew poorer every year, and the crops raised on the farm only bought food for the family. Therefore the mortgage could not be paid. At last the banker who had loaned him the money said that if he did not pay on a certain day, his farm would be taken away from him.

This worried Uncle Henry a good deal, for without the farm he would have no way to earn a living. He was a good man, and worked in the field as hard as he could; and Aunt Em did all the housework, with Dorothy's help. Yet they did not seem to get along.

This little girl, Dorothy, was like dozens of little girls you know. She was loving and usually sweet-tempered, and had a round rosy face and earnest eyes. Life was a serious thing to Dorothy, and a wonderful thing, too, for she had encountered more strange adventures in her short life than many other girls of her age.

Aunt Em once said she thought the fairies must have marked Dorothy at her birth, because she had wandered into strange places and had always been protected by some unseen power. As for Uncle Henry, he thought his little niece merely a dreamer, as her dead mother had been, for he could not quite believe all the curious stories Dorothy told them of the Land of Oz, which she had several times visited. He did not think that she tried to deceive her uncle and aunt, but he imagined that she had dreamed all of those astonishing adventures, and that the dreams had been so real to her that she had come to believe them true.

Whatever the explanation might be, it was certain that Dorothy had been absent from her Kansas home for several long periods, always disappearing unexpectedly, yet always coming back safe and sound, with amazing tales of where she had been and the unusual people she had met. Her uncle and aunt listened to her stories eagerly and in spite of their doubts began to feel that the little girl had gained a lot of experience and wisdom that were unaccountable in this age, when fairies are supposed no longer to exist.

Most of Dorothy's stories were about the Land of Oz, with its beautiful Emerald City and a lovely girl Ruler named Ozma, who was the most faithful friend of the little Kansas girl. When Dorothy told about the riches of this fairy country Uncle Henry would sigh, for he knew that a single one of the great emeralds that were so common there would pay all his debts and leave his farm free. But Dorothy never brought any jewels home with her, so their poverty became greater every year.

When the banker told Uncle Henry that he must pay the money in thirty days or leave the farm, the poor man was in despair, as he knew he could not possibly get the money. So he told his wife, Aunt Em, of his trouble, and she first cried a little and then said that they must be brave and do the best they could, and go away somewhere and try to earn an honest living. But they were getting old and feeble and she feared that they could not take care of Dorothy as well as they had formerly done. Probably the little girl would also be obliged to go to work.

They did not tell their niece the sad news for several days, not wishing to make her unhappy; but one morning the little girl found Aunt Em softly crying while Uncle Henry tried to comfort her. Then Dorothy asked them to tell her what was the matter.

"We must give up the farm, my dear," replied her uncle sadly, "and wander away into the world to work for our living."

The girl listened quite seriously, for she had not known before how desperately poor they were.

"We don't mind for ourselves," said her aunt, stroking the little girl's head tenderly; "but we love you as if you were our own child, and we are heart-broken to think that you must also endure poverty, and work for a living before you have grown big and strong."

"What could I do to earn money?" asked Dorothy.

"You might do housework for some one, dear, you are so handy; or perhaps you could be a nurse-maid to little children. I'm sure I don't know exactly what you CAN do to earn money, but if your uncle and I are able to support you we will do it willingly, and send you to school. We fear, though, that we shall have much trouble in earning a living for ourselves. No one wants to employ old people who are broken down in health, as we are."

Dorothy smiled.

"Wouldn't it be funny," she said, "for me to do housework in Kansas, when I'm a Princess in the Land of Oz?"

"A Princess!" they both exclaimed, astonished.

"Yes; Ozma made me a Princess some time ago, and she has often begged me to come and live always in the Emerald City," said the child.

Her uncle and aunt looked at her in amazement. Then the man said: "Do you suppose you could manage to return to your fairyland, my dear?"

"Oh yes," replied Dorothy; "I could do that easily."

"How?" asked Aunt Em.

"Ozma sees me every day at four o'clock, in her Magic Picture. She can see me wherever I am, no matter what I am doing. And at that time, if I make a certain secret sign, she will send for me by means of the Magic Belt, which I once captured from the Nome King. Then, in the wink of an eye, I shall be with Ozma in her palace."

The elder people remained silent for some time after Dorothy had spoken. Finally, Aunt Em said, with another sigh of regret: "If that is the case, Dorothy, perhaps you'd better go and live in the Emerald City. It will break our hearts to lose you from our lives, but you will be so much better off with your fairy friends hat it seems wisest and best for you to go."

"I'm not so sure about that," remarked Uncle Henry, shaking his gray head doubtfully. "These things all seem real to Dorothy, I know; but I'm afraid our little girl won't find her fairyland just what she had dreamed it to be. It would make me very unhappy to think that she was wandering among strangers who might be unkind to her."

Dorothy laughed merrily at this speech, and then she became very sober again, for she could see how all this trouble was worrying her aunt and uncle, and knew that unless she found a way to help them their future lives would be quite miserable and unhappy. She knew that she COULD help them. She had thought of a way already. Yet she did not tell them at once what it was, because she must ask Ozma's consent before she would be able to carry out her plans.

So she only said: "If you will promise not to worry a bit about me, I'll go to the Land of Oz this very afternoon. And I'll make a promise, too; that you shall both see me again before the day comes when you must leave this farm."

"The day isn't far away, now," her uncle sadly replied. "I did not tell you of our trouble until I was obliged to, dear Dorothy, so the evil time is near at hand. But if you are quite sure your fairy friends will give you a home, it will be best for you to go to them, as your aunt says."

That was why Dorothy went to her little room in the attic that afternoon, taking with her a small dog named Toto. The dog had curly black hair and big brown eyes and loved Dorothy very dearly.

The child had kissed her uncle and aunt affectionately before she went upstairs, and now she looked around her little room rather wistfully, gazing at the simple trinkets and worn calico and gingham dresses, as if they were old friends. She was tempted at first to make a bundle of them, yet she knew very well that they would be of no use to her in her future life.

She sat down upon a broken-backed chair—the only one the room contained—and holding Toto in her arms waited patiently until the clock struck four.

Then she made the secret signal that had been agreed upon between her and Ozma.

Uncle Henry and Aunt Em waited downstairs. They were uneasy and a good deal excited, for this is a practical humdrum world, and it seemed to them quite impossible that their little niece could vanish from her home and travel instantly to fairyland.

So they watched the stairs, which seemed to be the only way that Dorothy could get out of the farmhouse, and they watched them a long time. They heard the clock strike four but there was no sound from above.

Half-past four came, and now they were too impatient to wait any longer. Softly, they crept up the stairs to the door of the little girl's room.

"Dorothy! Dorothy!" they called.

There was no answer.

They opened the door and looked in.

The room was empty.

3. How Ozma Granted Dorothy's Request

I suppose you have read so much about the magnificent Emerald City that there is little need for me to describe it here. It is the Capital City of the Land of Oz, which is justly considered the most attractive and delightful fairyland in all the world.

The Emerald City is built all of beautiful marbles in which are set a profusion of emeralds, every one exquisitely cut and of very great size. There are other jewels used in the decorations inside the houses and palaces, such as rubies, diamonds, sapphires, amethysts and turquoises. But in the streets and upon the outside of the buildings only emeralds appear, from which circumstance the place is named the Emerald City of Oz. It has nine thousand, six hundred and fifty-four buildings, in which lived fifty-seven thousand three hundred and eighteen people, up to the time my story opens.

All the surrounding country, extending to the borders of the desert which enclosed it upon every side, was full of pretty and comfortable farmhouses, in which resided those inhabitants of Oz who preferred country to city life.

Altogether there were more than half a million people in the Land of Oz—although some of them, as you will soon learn, were not made of flesh and blood as we are—and every inhabitant of that favored country was happy and prosperous.

No disease of any sort was ever known among the Ozites, and so no one ever died unless he met with an accident that prevented him from living. This happened very seldom, indeed. There were no poor people in the Land of Oz, because there was no such thing as money, and all property of every sort belonged to the Ruler. The people were her children, and she cared for them. Each person was given freely by his neighbors whatever he required for his use, which is as much as any one may reasonably desire. Some tilled the lands and raised great crops of grain, which was divided equally among the entire population, so that all had enough. There were many tailors and dressmakers and shoemakers and the like, who made things that any who desired them might wear. Likewise there were jewelers who made ornaments for the person, which pleased and beautified the people, and these ornaments also were free to those who asked for them. Each man and woman, no matter what he or she produced for the good of the community, was supplied by the neighbors with food and clothing and a house and furniture and ornaments and games. If by chance the supply ever ran short, more was taken from the great storehouses of the Ruler, which were afterward filled up again when there was more of any article than the people needed.

Every one worked half the time and played half the time, and the people enjoyed the work as much as they did the play, because it is good to be occupied and to have something to do. There were no cruel overseers set to watch them, and no one to rebuke them or to find fault with them. So each one was proud to do all he could for his friends and neighbors, and was glad when they would accept the things he produced.

You will know by what I have here told you, that the Land of Oz was a remarkable country. I do not suppose such an arrangement would be practical with us, but Dorothy assures me that it works finely with the Oz people.

Oz being a fairy country, the people were, of course, fairy people; but that does not mean that all of them were very unlike the people of our own world. There were all sorts of queer characters among them, but not a single one who was evil, or who possessed a selfish or violent nature. They were peaceful, kind hearted, loving and merry, and every inhabitant adored the beautiful girl who ruled them and delighted to obey her every command.

In spite of all I have said in a general way, there were some parts of the Land of Oz not quite so pleasant as the farming country and the Emerald City which was its center. Far away in the South Country there lived in the mountains a band of strange people called Hammer-Heads, because they had no arms and used their flat heads to pound any one who came near them. Their necks were like rubber, so that they could shoot out their heads to quite a distance, and afterward draw them back again to their shoulders. The Hammer-Heads were called the "Wild People," but never harmed any but those who disturbed them in the mountains where they lived.

In some of the dense forests there lived great beasts of every sort; yet these were for the most part harmless and even sociable, and conversed agreeably with those who visited their haunts. The Kalidahs—beasts with bodies like bears and heads like tigers—had once been fierce and bloodthirsty, but even they were now nearly all tamed, although at times one or another of them would get cross and disagreeable.

Not so tame were the Fighting Trees, which had a forest of their own. If any one approached them these curious trees would bend down their branches, twine them around the intruders, and hurl them away.

But these unpleasant things existed only in a few remote parts of the Land of Oz. I suppose every country has some drawbacks, so even this almost perfect fairyland could not be quite perfect. Once there had been wicked witches in the land, too; but now these had all been destroyed; so, as I said, only peace and happiness reigned in Oz.

For some time Ozma had ruled over this fair country, and never was Ruler more popular or beloved. She is said to be the most beautiful girl the world has ever known, and her heart and mind are as lovely as her person.

Dorothy Gale had several times visited the Emerald City and experienced adventures in the Land of Oz, so that she and Ozma had now become firm friends. The girl Ruler had even made Dorothy a Princess of Oz, and had often implored her to come to Ozma's stately palace and live there always; but Dorothy had been loyal to her Aunt Em and Uncle Henry, who had cared for her since she was a baby, and she had refused to leave them because she knew they would be lonely without her.

However, Dorothy now realized that things were going to be different with her uncle and aunt from this time forth, so after giving the matter deep thought she decided to ask Ozma to grant her a very great favor.

A few seconds after she had made the secret signal in her little bedchamber, the Kansas girl was seated in a lovely room in Ozma's palace in the Emerald City of Oz. When the first loving kisses and embraces had been exchanged, the fair Ruler inquired: "What is the matter, dear? I know something unpleasant has happened to you, for your face was very sober when I saw it in my Magic Picture. And whenever you signal me to transport you to this safe place, where you are always welcome, I know you are in danger or in trouble."

Dorothy sighed.

"This time, Ozma, it isn't I," she replied. "But it's worse, I guess, for Uncle Henry and Aunt Em are in a heap of trouble, and there seems no way for them to get out of it—anyhow, not while they live in Kansas."

"Tell me about it, Dorothy," said Ozma, with ready sympathy.

"Why, you see Uncle Henry is poor; for the farm in Kansas doesn't 'mount to much, as farms go. So one day Uncle Henry borrowed some money, and wrote a letter saying that if he didn't pay the money back they could take his farm for pay. Course he 'spected to pay by making money from the farm; but he just couldn't. An' so they're going to take the farm, and Uncle Henry and Aunt Em won't have any place to live. They're pretty old to do much hard work, Ozma; so I'll have to work for them unless—"

Ozma had been thoughtful during the story, but now she smiled and pressed her little friend's hand.

"Unless what, dear?" she asked.

Dorothy hesitated, because her request meant so much to them all.

"Well," said she, "I'd like to live here in the Land of Oz, where you've often 'vited me to live. But I can't, you know, unless Uncle Henry and Aunt Em could live here too."

"Of course not," exclaimed the Ruler of Oz, laughing gaily. "So in order to get you, little friend, we must invite your Uncle and Aunt to live in Oz, also."

"Oh, will you, Ozma?" cried Dorothy, clasping her chubby little hands eagerly. "Will you bring them here with the Magic Belt, and give them a nice little farm in the Munchkin Country, or the Winkie Country—or some other place?"

"To be sure," answered Ozma, full of joy at the chance to please her little friend. "I have long been thinking of this very thing, Dorothy dear, and often I have had it in my mind to propose it to you. I am sure your uncle and aunt must be good and worthy people, or you would not love them so much; and for YOU, my friends, Princess, there is always room in the Land of Oz."

Dorothy was delighted, yet not altogether surprised, for she had clung to the hope that Ozma would be kind enough to grant her request. When, indeed, had her powerful and faithful friend refused her anything?

"But you must not call me 'Princess'," she said; "for after this I shall live on the little farm with Uncle Henry and Aunt Em, and princesses ought not to live on farms."

"Princess Dorothy will not," replied Ozma with her sweet smile. "You are going to live in your own rooms in this palace, and be my constant companion."

"But Uncle Henry—" began Dorothy.

"Oh, he is old, and has worked enough in his lifetime," interrupted the girl Ruler; "so we must find a place for your uncle and aunt where they will be comfortable and happy and need not work more than they care to. When shall we transport them here, Dorothy?"

"I promised to go and see them again before they were turned out of the farmhouse," answered Dorothy; "so—perhaps next Saturday—"

"But why wait so long?" asked Ozma. "And why make the journey back to Kansas again? Let us surprise them, and bring them here without any warning."

"I'm not sure that they believe in the Land of Oz," said Dorothy, "though I've told 'em 'bout it lots of times."

"They'll believe when they see it," declared Ozma; "and if they are told they are to make a magical journey to our fairyland, it may make them nervous. I think the best way will be to use the Magic Belt without warning them, and when they have arrived you can explain to them whatever they do not understand."

"Perhaps that's best," decided Dorothy. "There isn't much use in their staying at the farm until they are put out, 'cause it's much nicer here."

"Then to-morrow morning they shall come here," said Princess Ozma. "I will order Jellia Jamb, who is the palace housekeeper, to have rooms all prepared for them, and after breakfast we will get the Magic Belt and by its aid transport your uncle and aunt to the Emerald City."

"Thank you, Ozma!" cried Dorothy, kissing her friend gratefully.

"And now," Ozma proposed, "let us take a walk in the gardens before we dress for dinner. Come, Dorothy dear!"

4. How The Nome King Planned Revenge

The reason most people are bad is because they do not try to be good. Now, the Nome King had never tried to be good, so he was very bad indeed. Having decided to conquer the Land of Oz and to destroy the Emerald City and enslave all its people, King Roquat the Red kept planning ways to do this dreadful thing, and the more he planned the more he believed he would be able to accomplish it.

About the time Dorothy went to Ozma the Nome King called his Chief Steward to him and said: "Kaliko, I think I shall make you the General of my armies."

"I think you won't," replied Kaliko, positively.

"Why not?" inquired the King, reaching for his scepter with the big sapphire.

"Because I'm your Chief Steward and know nothing of warfare," said Kaliko, preparing to dodge if anything were thrown at him. "I manage all the affairs of your kingdom better than you could yourself, and you'll never find another Steward as good as I am. But there are a hundred Nomes better fitted to command your army, and your Generals get thrown away so often that I have no desire to be one of them."

"Ah, there is some truth in your remarks, Kaliko," remarked the King, deciding not to throw the scepter. "Summon my army to assemble in the Great Cavern."

Kaliko bowed and retired, and in a few minutes returned to say that the army was assembled. So the King went out upon a balcony that overlooked the Great Cavern, where fifty thousand Nomes, all armed with swords and pikes, stood marshaled in military array.

When they were not required as soldiers all these Nomes were metal workers and miners, and they had hammered so much at the forges and dug so hard with pick and shovel that they had acquired great muscular strength. They were strangely formed creatures, rather round and not very tall. Their toes were curly and their ears broad and flat.

In time of war every Nome left his forge or mine and became part of the great army of King Roquat. The soldiers wore rock-colored uniforms and were excellently drilled.

The King looked upon this tremendous army, which stood silently arrayed before him, and a cruel smile curled the corners of his mouth, for he saw that his legions were very powerful. Then he addressed them from the balcony, saying: "I have thrown away General Blug, because he did not please me. So I want another General to command this army. Who is next in command?"

"I am," replied Colonel Crinkle, a dapper-looking Nome, as he stepped forward to salute his monarch.

The King looked at him carefully and said: "I want you to march this army through an underground tunnel, which I am going to bore, to the Emerald City of Oz. When you get there I want you to conquer the Oz people, destroy them and their city, and bring all their gold and silver and precious stones back to my cavern. Also you are to recapture my Magic Belt and return it to me. Will you do this, General Crinkle?"

"No, your Majesty," replied the Nome; "for it can't be done."

"Oh indeed!" exclaimed the King. Then he turned to his servants and said: "Please take General Crinkle to the torture chamber. There you will kindly slice him into thin slices. Afterward you may feed him to the seven-headed dogs."

"Anything to oblige your Majesty," replied the servants, politely, and led the condemned man away.

When they had gone, the King addressed the army again.

"Listen!" said he. "The General who is to command my armies must promise to carry out my orders. If he fails he will share the fate of poor Crinkle. Now, then, who will volunteer to lead my hosts to the Emerald City?"

For a time no one moved and all were silent. Then an old Nome with white whiskers so long that they were tied around his waist to prevent their tripping him up, stepped out of the ranks and saluted the King.

"I'd like to ask a few questions, your Majesty," he said.

"Go ahead," replied the King.

"These Oz people are quite good, are they not?"

"As good as apple pie," said the King.

"And they are happy, I suppose?" continued the old Nome.

"Happy as the day is long," said the King.

"And contented and prosperous?" inquired the Nome.

"Very much so," said the King.

"Well, your Majesty," remarked he of the white whiskers, "I think I should like to undertake the job, so I'll be your General. I hate good people; I detest happy people; I'm opposed to any one who is contented and prosperous. That is why I am so fond of your Majesty. Make me your General and I'll promise to conquer and destroy the Oz people. If I fail I'm ready to be sliced thin and fed to the seven-headed dogs."

"Very good! Very good, indeed! That's the way to talk!" cried Roquat the Red, who was greatly pleased. "What is your name, General?"

"I'm called Guph, your Majesty."

"Well, Guph, come with me to my private cave, and we'll talk it over." Then he turned to the army. "Nomes and soldiers," said he, "you are to obey the commands of General Guph until he becomes dog-feed. Any man who fails to obey his new General will be promptly thrown away. You are now dismissed."

Guph went to the King's private cave and sat down upon an amethyst chair and put his feet on the arm of the King's ruby throne. Then he lighted his pipe and threw the live coal he had taken from his pocket upon the King's left foot and puffed the smoke into the King's eyes and made himself comfortable. For he was a wise old Nome, and he knew that the best way to get along with Roquat the Red was to show that he was not afraid of him.

"I'm ready for the talk, your Majesty," he said.

The King coughed and looked at his new General fiercely.

"Do you not tremble to take such liberties with your monarch?" he asked.

"Oh no," replied Guph, calmly, and he blew a wreath of smoke that curled around the King's nose and made him sneeze. "You want to conquer the Emerald City, and I'm the only Nome in all your dominions who can conquer it. So you will be very careful not to hurt me until I have carried out your wishes. After that—"

"Well, what then?" inquired the King.

"Then you will be so grateful to me that you won't care to hurt me," replied the General.

"That is a very good argument," said Roquat. "But suppose you fail?"

"Then it's the slicing machine. I agree to that," announced Guph. "But if you do as I tell you there will be no failure. The trouble with you, Roquat, is that you don't think carefully enough. I do. You would go ahead and march through your tunnel into Oz, and get defeated and driven back. I won't. And the reason I won't is because when I march I'll have all my plans made, and a host of allies to assist my Nomes."

"What do you mean by that?" asked the King.

"I'll explain, King Roquat. You're going to attack a fairy country, and a mighty fairy country, too. They haven't much of an army in Oz, but the Princess who ruled them has a fairy wand; and the little girl Dorothy has your Magic Belt; and at the North of the Emerald City lives a clever sorceress called Glinda the Good, who commands the spirits of the air. Also I have heard that there is a wonderful Wizard in Ozma's palace, who is so skillful that people

used to pay him money in America to see him perform. So you see it will be no easy thing to overcome all this magic."

"We have fifty thousand soldiers!" cried the King proudly.

"Yes; but they are Nomes," remarked Guph, taking a silk handkerchief from the King's pocket and wiping his own pointed shoes with it. "Nomes are immortals, but they are not strong on magic. When you lost your famous Belt the greater part of your own power was gone from you. Against Ozma you and your Nomes would have no show at all."

Roquat's eyes flashed angrily.

"Then away you go to the slicing machine!" he cried.

"Not yet," said the General, filling his pipe from the King's private tobacco pouch.

"What do you propose to do?" asked the monarch.

"I propose to obtain the power we need," answered Guph. "There are a good many evil creatures who have magic powers sufficient to destroy and conquer the Land of Oz. We will get them on our side, band them all together, and then take Ozma and her people by surprise. It's all very simple and easy when you know how. Alone, we should be helpless to injure the Ruler of Oz, but with the aid of the evil powers we can summon we shall easily succeed."

King Roquat was delighted with this idea, for he realized how clever it was.

"Surely, Guph, you are the greatest General I have ever had!" he exclaimed, his eyes sparkling with joy. "You must go at once and make arrangements with the evil powers to assist us, and meantime I'll begin to dig the tunnel."

"I thought you'd agree with me, Roquat," replied the new General. "I'll start this very afternoon to visit the Chief of the Whimsies."

5. How Dorothy Became a Princess

When the people of the Emerald City heard that Dorothy had returned to them every one was eager to see her, for the little girl was a general favorite in the Land of Oz. From time to time some of the folk from the great outside world had found their way into this fairyland, but all except one had been companions of Dorothy and had turned out to be very agreeable people. The exception I speak of was the wonderful Wizard of Oz, a sleight-of-hand performer from Omaha who went up in a balloon and was carried by a current of air to the Emerald City. His queer and puzzling tricks made the people of Oz believe him a great wizard for a time, and he ruled over them until Dorothy arrived on her first visit and showed the Wizard to be a mere humbug. He was a gentle, kind-hearted little man, and Dorothy grew to like him afterward. When, after an absence, the Wizard returned to the Land of Oz, Ozma received him graciously and gave him a home in a part of the palace.

In addition to the Wizard two other personages from the outside world had been allowed to make their home in the Emerald City. The first was a quaint Shaggy Man, whom Ozma had made the Governor of the Royal Storehouses, and the second a Yellow Hen named Billina, who had a fine house in the gardens back of the palace, where she looked after a large family. Both these had been old comrades of Dorothy, so you see the little girl was quite an important personage in Oz, and the people thought she had brought them good luck, and loved her next best to Ozma. During her several visits this little girl had been the means of destroying two wicked witches who oppressed the people, and she had discovered a live scarecrow who was now one of the most popular personages in all the fairy country. With the Scarecrow's help she had rescued Nick Chopper, a Tin Woodman, who had rusted in a lonely forest, and the tin man was now the Emperor of the Country of the Winkies and much beloved because of his kind heart. No wonder the people thought Dorothy had brought them good luck! Yet, strange as it may seem, she had accomplished all these wonders not because she was a fairy or had any magical powers whatever, but because she was a simple, sweet and true little girl who was honest to herself and to all whom she met. In this world in which we live simplicity and kindness are the only magic wands that work wonders, and in the Land of Oz Dorothy found these same qualities had won for her the love and admiration of the people. Indeed, the little girl had made many warm friends in the fairy country, and the only real grief the Ozites had ever experienced was when Dorothy left them and returned to her Kansas home.

Now she received a joyful welcome, although no one except Ozma knew at first that she had finally come to stay for good and all.

That evening Dorothy had many callers, and among them were such important people as Tiktok, a machine man who thought and spoke and moved by clockwork; her old companion the genial Shaggy Man; Jack Pumpkinhead, whose body was brushwood and whose head was a ripe pumpkin with a face carved upon it; the Cowardly Lion and the Hungry Tiger, two great beasts from the forest, who served Princess Ozma, and Professor H. M. Wogglebug, T.E. This wogglebug was a remarkable creature. He had once been a tiny little bug, crawling around in a school-room, but he was discovered and highly magnified so that he could be seen more plainly, and while in this magnified condition he had escaped. He had always remained big, and he dressed like a dandy and was so full of knowledge and information (which are distinct acquirements) that he had been made a Professor and the head of the Royal College.

Dorothy had a nice visit with these old friends, and also talked a long time with the Wizard, who was little and old and withered and dried up, but as merry and active as a child. Afterward, she went to see Billina's fast-growing family of chicks.

Toto, Dorothy's little black dog, also met with a cordial reception. Toto was an especial friend of the Shaggy Man, and he knew every one else. Being the only dog in the Land of Oz, he was highly respected by the people, who believed animals entitled to every consideration if they behaved themselves properly.

Dorothy had four lovely rooms in the palace, which were always reserved for her use and were called "Dorothy's rooms." These consisted of a beautiful sitting room, a dressing room, a dainty bedchamber and a big marble bathroom. And in these rooms were everything that heart could desire, placed there with loving thoughtfulness by Ozma for her little friend's use. The royal dressmakers had the little girl's measure, so they kept the closets in her dressing room filled with lovely dresses of every description and suitable for every occasion. No wonder Dorothy had refrained from bringing with her her old calico and gingham dresses! Here everything that was dear to a little girl's heart was supplied in profusion, and nothing so rich and beautiful could ever have been found in the biggest department stores in America. Of course Dorothy enjoyed all these luxuries, and the only reason she had heretofore preferred to live in Kansas was because her uncle and aunt loved her and needed her with them.

Now, however, all was to be changed, and Dorothy was really more delighted to know that her dear relatives were to share in her good fortune and enjoy the delights of the Land of Oz, than she was to possess such luxury for herself.

Next morning, at Ozma's request, Dorothy dressed herself in a pretty sky-blue gown of rich silk, trimmed with real pearls. The buckles of her shoes were set with pearls, too, and more of these priceless gems were on a lovely coronet which she wore upon her forehead. "For," said her friend Ozma, "from this time forth, my dear, you must assume your rightful rank as a Princess of Oz, and being my chosen companion you must dress in a way befitting the dignity of your position."

Dorothy agreed to this, although she knew that neither gowns nor jewels could make her anything else than the simple, unaffected little girl she had always been.

As soon as they had breakfasted—the girls eating together in Ozma's pretty boudoir—the Ruler of Oz said: "Now, dear friend, we will use the Magic Belt to transport your uncle and aunt from Kansas to the Emerald City. But I think it would be fitting, in receiving such distinguished guests, for us to sit in my Throne Room."

"Oh, they're not very 'stinguished, Ozma," said Dorothy. "They're just plain people, like me."

"Being your friends and relatives, Princess Dorothy, they are certainly distinguished," replied the Ruler, with a smile.

"They—they won't hardly know what to make of all your splendid furniture and things," protested Dorothy, gravely. "It may scare 'em to see your grand Throne Room, an' p'raps we'd better go into the back yard, Ozma, where the cabbages grow an' the chickens are playing. Then it would seem more natural to Uncle Henry and Aunt Em."

"No; they shall first see me in my Throne Room," replied Ozma, decidedly; and when she spoke in that tone Dorothy knew it was not wise to oppose her, for Ozma was accustomed to having her own way.

So together they went to the Throne Room, an immense domed chamber in the center of the palace. Here stood the royal throne, made of solid gold and encrusted with enough precious stones to stock a dozen jewelry stores in our country.

Ozma, who was wearing the Magic Belt, seated herself in the throne, and Dorothy sat at her feet. In the room were assembled many ladies and gentlemen of the court, clothed in rich apparel and wearing fine jewelry. Two immense animals squatted, one on each side of the throne—the Cowardly Lion and the Hungry Tiger. In a balcony high up in the dome an orchestra played sweet music, and beneath the dome two electric fountains sent sprays of colored perfumed water shooting up nearly as high as the arched ceiling.

"Are you ready, Dorothy?" asked the Ruler.

"I am," replied Dorothy; "but I don't know whether Aunt Em and Uncle Henry are ready."

"That won't matter," declared Ozma. "The old life can have very little to interest them, and the sooner they begin the new life here the happier they will be. Here they come, my dear!"

As she spoke, there before the throne appeared Uncle Henry and Aunt Em, who for a moment stood motionless, glaring with white and startled faces at the scene that confronted them. If the ladies and gentlemen present had not been so polite I am sure they would have laughed at the two strangers.

Aunt Em had her calico dress skirt "tucked up," and she wore a faded, blue-checked apron. Her hair was rather straggly and she had on a pair of Uncle Henry's old slippers. In one hand she held a dish-towel and in the other a cracked earthenware plate, which she had been engaged in wiping when so suddenly transported to the Land of Oz.

Uncle Henry, when the summons came, had been out in the barn "doin' chores." He wore a ragged and much soiled straw hat, a checked shirt without any collar and blue overalls tucked into the tops of his old cowhide boots.

"By gum!" gasped Uncle Henry, looking around as if bewildered.

"Well, I swan!" gurgled Aunt Em in a hoarse, frightened voice. Then her eyes fell upon Dorothy, and she said: "D-d-d-don't that look like our little girl—our Dorothy, Henry?"

"Hi, there—look out, Em!" exclaimed the old man, as Aunt Em advanced a step; "take care o' the wild beastses, or you're a goner!"

But now Dorothy sprang forward and embraced and kissed her aunt and uncle affectionately, afterward taking their hands in her own.

"Don't be afraid," she said to them. "You are now in the Land of Oz, where you are to live always, and be comfer'ble an' happy. You'll never have to worry over anything again, 'cause there won't be anything to worry about. And you owe it all to the kindness of my friend Princess Ozma."

Here she led them before the throne and continued:"Your Highness, this is Uncle Henry. And this is Aunt Em. They want to thank you for bringing them here from Kansas."

Aunt Em tried to "slick" her hair, and she hid the dish-towel and dish under her apron while she bowed to the lovely Ozma. Uncle Henry took off his straw hat and held it awkwardly in his hands.

But the Ruler of Oz rose and came from her throne to greet her newly arrived guests, and she smiled as sweetly upon them as if they had been a king and queen.

"You are very welcome here, where I have brought you for Princess Dorothy's sake," she said, graciously, "and I hope you will be quite happy in your new home." Then she turned to her courtiers, who were silently and gravely regarding the scene, and added: "I present to my people our Princess Dorothy's beloved Uncle Henry and Aunt Em, who will hereafter be subjects of our kingdom. It will please me to have you show them every kindness and honor in your power, and to join me in making them happy and contented."

Hearing this, all those assembled bowed low and respectfully to the old farmer and his wife, who bobbed their own heads in return.

"And now," said Ozma to them, "Dorothy will show you the rooms prepared for you. I hope you will like them, and shall expect you to join me at luncheon."

So Dorothy led her relatives away, and as soon as they were out of the Throne Room and alone in the corridor, Aunt Em squeezed Dorothy's hand and said: "Child, child! How in the world did we ever get here so quick? And is it all real? And are we to stay here, as she says? And what does it all mean, anyhow?"

Dorothy laughed.

"Why didn't you tell us what you were goin' to do?" inquired Uncle Henry, reproachfully. "If I'd known about it, I'd 'a put on my Sunday clothes."

"I'll 'splain ever'thing as soon as we get to your rooms," promised Dorothy. "You're in great luck, Uncle Henry and Aunt Em; an' so am I! And oh! I'm so happy to have got you here, at last!"

As he walked by the little girl's side, Uncle Henry stroked his whiskers thoughtfully. "'Pears to me, Dorothy, we won't make bang-up fairies," he remarked.

"An' my back hair looks like a fright!" wailed Aunt Em.

"Never mind," returned the little girl, reassuringly. "You won't have anything to do now but to look pretty, Aunt Em; an' Uncle Henry won't have to work till his back aches, that's certain."

"Sure?" they asked, wonderingly, and in the same breath.

"Course I'm sure," said Dorothy. "You're in the Fairyland of Oz now; an' what's more, you belong to it!"

6. How Guph Visited the Whimsies

The new General of the Nome King's army knew perfectly well that to fail in his plans meant death for him. Yet he was not at all anxious or worried. He hated every one who was good and longed to make all who were happy unhappy. Therefore he had accepted this dangerous position as General quite willingly, feeling sure in his evil mind that he would be able to do a lot of mischief and finally conquer the Land of Oz.

Yet Guph determined to be careful, and to lay his plans well, so as not to fail. He argued that only careless people fail in what they attempt to do.

The mountains underneath which the Nome King's extensive caverns were located lay grouped just north of the Land of Ev, which lay directly across the deadly desert to the east of the Land of Oz. As the mountains were also on the edge of the desert the Nome King found that he had only to tunnel underneath the desert to reach Ozma's dominions. He did not wish his armies to appear above ground in the Country of the Winkies, which was the part of the Land of Oz nearest to King Roquat's own country, as then the people would give the alarm and enable Ozma to fortify the Emerald City and assemble an army. He wanted to take all the Oz people by surprise; so he decided to run the tunnel clear through to the Emerald City, where he and his host could break through the ground without warning and conquer the people before they had time to defend themselves.

Roquat the Red began work at once upon his tunnel, setting a thousand miners at the task and building it high and broad enough for his armies to march through it with ease. The Nome were used to making tunnels, as all the kingdom in which they lived was under ground; so they made rapid progress.

While this work was going on General Guph started out alone to visit the Chief of the Whimsies.

These Whimsies were curious people who lived in a retired country of their own. They had large, strong bodies, but heads so small that they were no bigger than door-knobs. Of course, such tiny heads could not contain any great amount of brains, and the Whimsies were so ashamed of their personal appearance and lack of commonsense that they wore big heads made of pasteboard, which they fastened over their own little heads. On these pasteboard heads they sewed sheep's wool for hair, and the wool was colored many tints—pink, green and lavender being the favorite colors. The faces of these false heads were painted in many ridiculous ways, according to the whims of the owners, and these big, burly creatures looked so whimsical and absurd in their queer masks that they were called "Whimsies." They foolishly imagined that no one would suspect the little heads that were inside the imitation ones, not knowing that it is folly to try to appear otherwise than as nature has made us.

The Chief of the Whimsies had as little wisdom as the others, and had been chosen chief merely because none among them was any wiser or more capable of ruling. The Whimsies were evil spirits and could not be killed. They were hated and feared by every one and were known as terrible fighters because they were so strong and muscular and had not sense enough to know when they were defeated.

General Guph thought the Whimsies would be a great help to the Nomes in the conquest of Oz, for under his leadership they could be induced to fight as long so they could stand up. So he traveled to their country and asked to see the Chief, who lived in a house that had a picture of his grotesque false head painted over the doorway.

The Chief's false head had blue hair, a turned-up nose, and a mouth that stretched half across the face. Big green eyes had been painted upon it, but in the center of the chin were two small holes made in the pasteboard, so that the Chief could see through them with his own tiny eyes; for when the big head was fastened upon his shoulders the eyes in his own natural head were on a level with the false chin.

Said General Guph to the Chief of the Whimsies: "We Nomes are going to conquer the Land of Oz and capture our King's Magic Belt, which the Oz people stole from him. Then we are going to plunder and destroy the whole country. And we want the Whimsies to help us."

"Will there be any fighting?" asked the Chief.

"Plenty," replied Guph.

That must have pleased the Chief, for he got up and danced around the room three times. Then he seated himself again, adjusted his false head, and said: "We have no quarrel with Ozma of Oz."

"But you Whimsies love to fight, and here is a splendid chance to do so," urged Guph.

"Wait till I sing a song," said the Chief. Then he lay back in his chair and sang a foolish song that did not seem to the General to mean anything, although he listened carefully. When he had finished, the Chief Whimsie looked at him through the holes in his chin and asked: "What reward will you give us if we help you?"

The General was prepared for this question, for he had been thinking the matter over on his journey. People often do a good deed without hope of reward, but for an evil deed they always demand payment.

"When we get our Magic Belt," he made reply, "our King, Roquat the Red, will use its power to give every Whimsie a natural head as big and fine as the false head he now wears. Then you will no longer be ashamed because your big strong bodies have such teeny-weeny heads."

"Oh! Will you do that?" asked the Chief, eagerly.

"We surely will," promised the General.

"I'll talk to my people," said the Chief.

So he called a meeting of all the Whimsies and told them of the offer made by the Nomes. The creatures were delighted with the bargain, and at once agreed to fight for the Nome King and help him to conquer Oz.

One Whimsie alone seemed to have a glimmer of sense, for he asked: "Suppose we fail to capture the Magic Belt? What will happen then, and what good will all our fighting do?"

But they threw him into the river for asking foolish questions, and laughed when the water ruined his pasteboard head before he could swim out again.

So the compact was made and General Guph was delighted with his success in gaining such powerful allies.

But there were other people, too, just as important as the Whimsies, whom the clever old Nome had determined to win to his side.

7. How Aunt Em Conquered the Lion

"These are your rooms," said Dorothy, opening a door.

Aunt Em drew back at the sight of the splendid furniture and draperies.

"Ain't there any place to wipe my feet?" she asked.

"You will soon change your slippers for new shoes," replied Dorothy. "Don't be afraid, Aunt Em. Here is where you are to live, so walk right in and make yourself at home."

Aunt Em advanced hesitatingly.

"It beats the Topeka Hotel!" she cried admiringly. "But this place is too grand for us, child. Can't we have some back room in the attic, that's more in our class?"

"No," said Dorothy. "You've got to live here, 'cause Ozma says so. And all the rooms in this palace are just as fine as these, and some are better. It won't do any good to fuss, Aunt Em. You've got to be swell and high-toned in the Land of Oz, whether you want to or not; so you may as well make up your mind to it."

"It's hard luck," replied her aunt, looking around with an awed expression; "but folks can get used to anything, if they try. Eh, Henry?"

"Why, as to that," said Uncle Henry, slowly, "I b'lieve in takin' what's pervided us, an' askin' no questions. I've traveled some, Em, in my time, and you hain't; an' that makes a difference atween us."

Then Dorothy showed them through the rooms. The first was a handsome sitting-room, with windows opening upon the rose gardens. Then came separate bedrooms for Aunt Em and Uncle Henry, with a fine bathroom between them. Aunt Em had a pretty dressing room, besides, and Dorothy opened the closets and showed several exquisite costumes that had been provided for her aunt by the royal dressmakers, who had worked all night to get them ready. Everything that Aunt Em could possibly need was in the drawers and closets, and her dressing-table was covered with engraved gold toilet articles.

Uncle Henry had nine suits of clothes, cut in the popular Munchkin fashion, with knee-breeches, silk stockings, and low shoes with jeweled buckles. The hats to match these costumes had pointed tops and wide brims with small gold bells around the edges. His shirts were of fine linen with frilled bosoms, and his vests were richly embroidered with colored silks.

Uncle Henry decided that he would first take a bath and then dress himself in a blue satin suit that had caught his fancy. He accepted his good fortune with calm composure and refused to have a servant to assist him. But Aunt Em was "all of a flutter," as she said, and it took Dorothy and Jellia Jamb, the housekeeper, and two maids a long time to dress her and do up her hair and get her "rigged like a popinjay," as she quaintly expressed it. She wanted to stop and admire everything that caught her eye, and she sighed continually and declared that such finery was too good for an old country woman, and that she never thought she would have to "put on airs" at her time of life.

Finally she was dressed, and when she went into the sitting-room there was Uncle Henry in his blue satin, walking gravely up and down the room. He had trimmed his beard and mustache and looked very dignified and respectable.

"Tell me, Dorothy," he said; "do all the men here wear duds like these?"

"Yes," she replied; "all 'cept the Scarecrow and the Shaggy Man—and of course the Tin Woodman and Tiktok, who are made of metal. You'll find all the men at Ozma's court dressed just as you are—only perhaps a little finer."

"Henry, you look like a play-actor," announced Aunt Em, looking at her husband critically.

"An' you, Em, look more highfalutin' than a peacock," he replied.

"I guess you're right," she said regretfully; "but we're helpless victims of high-toned royalty."

Dorothy was much amused.

"Come with me," she said, "and I'll show you 'round the palace."

She took them through the beautiful rooms and introduced them to all the people they chanced to meet. Also she showed them her own pretty rooms, which were not far from their own.

"So it's all true," said Aunt Em, wide-eyed with amazement, "and what Dorothy told us of this fairy country was plain facts instead of dreams! But where are all the strange creatures you used to know here?"

"Yes, where's the Scarecrow?" inquired Uncle Henry.

"Why, he's just now away on a visit to the Tin Woodman, who is Emp'ror of the Winkie Country," answered the little girl. "You'll see him when he comes back, and you're sure to like him."

"And where's the Wonderful Wizard?" asked Aunt Em.

"You'll see him at Ozma's luncheon, for he lives here in this palace," was the reply.

"And Jack Pumpkinhead?"

"Oh, he lives a little way out of town, in his own pumpkin field. We'll go there some time and see him, and we'll call on Professor Wogglebug, too. The Shaggy Man will be at the luncheon, I guess, and Tiktok. And now I'll take you out to see Billina, who has a house of her own."

So they went into the back yard, and after walking along winding paths some distance through the beautiful gardens they came to an attractive little house where the Yellow Hen sat on the front porch sunning herself.

"Good morning, my dear Mistress," called Billina, fluttering down to meet them. "I was expecting you to call, for I heard you had come back and brought your uncle and aunt with you."

"We're here for good and all, this time, Billina," cried Dorothy, joyfully. "Uncle Henry and Aunt Em belong to Oz now as much as I do!"

"Then they are very lucky people," declared Billina; "for there couldn't be a nicer place to live. But come, my dear; I must show you all my Dorothys. Nine are living and have grown up to be very respectable hens; but one took cold at Ozma's birthday party and died of the pip, and the other two turned out to be horrid roosters, so I had to change their names from Dorothy to Daniel. They all had the letter 'D' engraved upon their gold lockets, you remember, with your picture inside, and 'D' stands for Daniel as well as for Dorothy."

"Did you call both the roosters Daniel?" asked Uncle Henry.

"Yes, indeed. I've nine Dorothys and two Daniels; and the nine Dorothys have eighty-six sons and daughters and over three hundred grandchildren," said Billina, proudly.

"What names do you give 'em all, dear?" inquired the little girl.

"Oh, they are all Dorothys and Daniels, some being Juniors and some Double-Juniors. Dorothy and Daniel are two good names, and I see no object in hunting for others," declared the Yellow Hen. "But just think, Dorothy, what a big chicken family we've grown to be, and our numbers increase nearly every day! Ozma doesn't know what to do with all the eggs we lay, and we are never eaten or harmed in any way, as chickens are in your country. They give us everything to make us contented and happy, and I, my dear, am the acknowledged Queen and Governor of every chicken in Oz, because I'm the eldest and started the whole colony."

"You ought to be very proud, ma'am," said Uncle Henry, who was astonished to hear a hen talk so sensibly.

"Oh, I am," she replied. "I've the loveliest pearl necklace you ever saw. Come in the house and I'll show it to you. And I've nine leg bracelets and a diamond pin for each wing. But I only wear them on state occasions."

They followed the Yellow Hen into the house, which Aunt Em declared was neat as a pin. They could not sit down, because all Billina's chairs were roosting-poles made of silver; so they had to stand while the hen fussily showed them her treasures.

Then they had to go into the back rooms occupied by Billina's nine Dorothys and two Daniels, who were all plump yellow chickens and greeted the visitors very politely. It was easy to see that they were well bred and that Billina had looked after their education.

In the yards were all the children and grandchildren of these eleven elders and they were of all sizes, from well-grown hens to tiny chickens just out of the shell. About fifty fluffy yellow youngsters were at school, being taught good manners and good grammar by a young hen who wore spectacles. They sang in chorus a patriotic song of the Land of Oz, in honor of their visitors, and Aunt Em was much impressed by these talking chickens.

Dorothy wanted to stay and play with the young chickens for awhile, but Uncle Henry and Aunt Em had not seen the palace grounds and gardens yet and were eager to get better acquainted with the marvelous and delightful land in which they were to live.

"I'll stay here, and you can go for a walk," said Dorothy. "You'll be perfec'ly safe anywhere, and may do whatever you want to. When you get tired, go back to the palace and find your rooms, and I'll come to you before luncheon is ready."

So Uncle Henry and Aunt Em started out alone to explore the grounds, and Dorothy knew that they couldn't get lost, because all the palace grounds were enclosed by a high wall of green marble set with emeralds.

It was a rare treat to these simple folk, who had lived in the country all their lives and known little enjoyment of any sort, to wear beautiful clothes and live in a palace and be treated with respect and consideration by all around them. They were very happy indeed as they strolled up the shady walks and looked upon the gorgeous flowers and shrubs, feeling that their new home was more beautiful than any tongue could describe.

Suddenly, as they turned a corner and walked through a gap in a high hedge, they came face to face with an enormous Lion, which crouched upon the green lawn and seemed surprised by their appearance.

They stopped short, Uncle Henry trembling with horror and Aunt Em too terrified to scream. Next moment the poor woman clasped her husband around the neck and cried:

"Save me, Henry, save me!"

"Can't even save myself, Em," he returned, in a husky voice, "for the animile looks as if it could eat both of us an' lick its chops for more! If I only had a gun—"

"Haven't you, Henry? Haven't you?" she asked anxiously.

"Nary gun, Em. So let's die as brave an' graceful as we can. I knew our luck couldn't last!"

"I won't die. I won't be eaten by a lion!" wailed Aunt Em, glaring upon the huge beast. Then a thought struck her, and she whispered, "Henry, I've heard as savage beastses can be conquered by the human eye. I'll eye that lion out o' countenance an' save our lives."

"Try it, Em," he returned, also in a whisper. "Look at him as you do at me when I'm late to dinner."

Aunt Em turned upon the Lion a determined countenance and a wild dilated eye. She glared at the immense beast steadily, and the Lion, who had been quietly blinking at them, began to appear uneasy and disturbed.

"Is anything the matter, ma'am?" he asked, in a mild voice.

At this speech from the terrible beast Aunt Em and Uncle Henry both were startled, and then Uncle Henry remembered that this must be the Lion they had seen in Ozma's Throne Room.

"Hold on, Em!" he exclaimed. "Quit the eagle eye conquest an' take courage. I guess this is the same Cowardly Lion Dorothy has told us about."

"Oh, is it?" she cried, much relieved.

"When he spoke, I got the idea; and when he looked so 'shamed like, I was sure of it," Uncle Henry continued.

Aunt Em regarded the animal with new interest.

"Are you the Cowardly Lion?" she inquired. "Are you Dorothy's friend?"

"Yes'm," answered the Lion, meekly. "Dorothy and I are old chums and are very fond of each other. I'm the King of Beasts, you know, and the Hungry Tiger and I serve Princess Ozma as her body guards."

"To be sure," said Aunt Em, nodding. "But the King of Beasts shouldn't be cowardly."

"I've heard that said before," remarked the Lion, yawning till he showed two great rows of sharp white teeth; "but that does not keep me from being frightened whenever I go into battle."

"What do you do, run?" asked Uncle Henry.

"No; that would be foolish, for the enemy would run after me," declared the Lion. "So I tremble with fear and pitch in as hard as I can; and so far I have always won my fight."

"Ah, I begin to understand," said Uncle Henry.

"Were you scared when I looked at you just now?" inquired Aunt Em.

"Terribly scared, madam," answered the Lion, "for at first I thought you were going to have a fit. Then I noticed you were trying to overcome me by the power of your eye, and your glance was so fierce and penetrating that I shook with fear."

This greatly pleased the lady, and she said quite cheerfully: "Well, I won't hurt you, so don't be scared any more. I just wanted to see what the human eye was good for."

"The human eye is a fearful weapon," remarked the Lion, scratching his nose softly with his paw to hide a smile. "Had I not known you were Dorothy's friends I might have torn you both into shreds in order to escape your terrible gaze."

Aunt Em shuddered at hearing this, and Uncle Henry said hastily: "I'm glad you knew us. Good morning, Mr. Lion; we'll hope to see you again—by and by—some time in the future."

"Good morning," replied the Lion, squatting down upon the lawn again. "You are likely to see a good deal of me, if you live in the Land of Oz."

8. How the Grand Gallipoot Joined The Nomes

After leaving the Whimsies, Guph continued on his journey and penetrated far into the Northwest. He wanted to get to the Country of the Growleywogs, and in order to do that he must cross the Ripple Land, which was a hard thing to do. For the Ripple Land was a succession of hills and valleys, all very steep and rocky, and they changed places constantly by rippling. While Guph was climbing a hill it sank down under him and became a valley, and while he was descending into a valley it rose up and carried him to the top of a hill. This was very perplexing to the traveler, and a stranger might have thought he could never cross the Ripple Land at all. But Guph knew that if he kept steadily on he would get to the land at last; so he paid no attention to the changing hills and valleys and plodded along as calmly as if walking upon the level ground.

The result of this wise persistence was that the General finally reached firmer soil and, after penetrating a dense forest, came to the Dominion of the Growleywogs.

No sooner had he crossed the border of this domain when two guards seized him and carried him before the Grand Gallipoot of the Growleywogs, who scowled upon him ferociously and asked him why he dared intrude upon his territory.

"I'm the Lord High General of the Invincible Army of the Nomes, and my name is Guph," was the reply. "All the world trembles when that name is mentioned."

The Growleywogs gave a shout of jeering laughter at this, and one of them caught the Nome in his strong arms and tossed him high into the air. Guph was considerably shaken when he fell upon the hard ground, but he appeared to take no notice of the impertinence and composed himself to speak again to the Grand Gallipoot.

"My master, King Roquat the Red, has sent me here to confer with you. He wishes your assistance to conquer the Land of Oz."

Here the General paused, and the Grand Gallipoot scowled upon him more terribly than ever and said: "Go on!"

The voice of the Grand Gallipoot was partly a roar and partly a growl. He mumbled his words badly and Guph had to listen carefully in order to understand him.

These Growleywogs were certainly remarkable creatures. They were of gigantic size, yet were all bone and skin and muscle, there being no meat or fat upon their bodies at all. Their powerful muscles lay just underneath their skins, like bunches of tough rope, and the weakest Growleywog was so strong that he could pick up an elephant and toss it seven miles away.

It seems unfortunate that strong people are usually so disagreeable and overbearing that no one cares for them. In fact, to be different from your fellow creatures is always a misfortune. The Growleywogs knew that they were disliked and avoided by every one, so they had become surly and unsociable even among

themselves. Guph knew that they hated all people, including the Nomes; but he hoped to win them over, nevertheless, and knew that if he succeeded they would afford him very powerful assistance.

"The Land of Oz is ruled by a namby-pamby girl who is disgustingly kind and good," he continued. "Her people are all happy and contented and have no care or worries whatever."

"Go on!" growled the Grand Gallipoot.

"Once the Nome King enslaved the Royal Family of Ev—another goody-goody lot that we detest," said the General. "But Ozma interfered, although it was none of her business, and marched her army against us. With her was a Kansas girl named Dorothy and a Yellow Hen, and they marched directly into the Nome King's cavern. There they liberated our slaves from Ev and stole King Roquat's Magic Belt, which they carried away with them. So now our King is making a tunnel under the deadly desert, so we can march through it to the Emerald City. When we get there we mean to conquer and destroy all the land and recapture the Magic Belt."

Again he paused, and again the Grand Gallipoot growled: "Go on!"

Guph tried to think what to say next, and a happy thought soon occurred to him.

"We want you to help us in this conquest," he announced, "for we need the mighty aid of the Growleywogs in order to make sure that we shall not be defeated. You are the strongest people in all the world, and you hate good and happy creatures as much as we Nomes do. I am sure it will be a real pleasure to you to tear down the beautiful Emerald City, and in return for your valuable assistance we will allow you to bring back to your country ten thousand people of Oz, to be your slaves."

"Twenty thousand!" growled the Grand Gallipoot.

"All right, we promise you twenty thousand," agreed the General.

The Gallipoot made a signal and at once his attendants picked up General Guph and carried him away to a prison, where the jailer amused himself by sticking pins in the round fat body of the old Nome, to see him jump and hear him yell.

But while this was going on the Grand Gallipoot was talking with his counselors, who were the most important officials of the Growleywogs. When he had stated to them the proposition of the Nome King, he said: "My advice is to offer to help them. Then, when we have conquered the Land of Oz, we will take not only our twenty thousand prisoners but all the gold and jewels we want."

"Let us take the Magic Belt, too," suggested one counselor.

"And rob the Nome King and make him our slave," said another.

"That is a good idea," declared the Grand Gallipoot. "I'd like King Roquat for my own slave. He could black my boots and bring me my porridge every morning while I am in bed."

"There is a famous Scarecrow in Oz. I'll take him for my slave," said a counselor.

"I'll take Tiktok, the machine man," said another.

"Give me the Tin Woodman," said a third.

They went on for some time, dividing up the people and the treasure of Oz in advance of the conquest. For they had no doubt at all that they would be able to destroy Ozma's domain. Were they not the strongest people in all the world?

"The deadly desert has kept us out of Oz before," remarked the Grand Gallipoot, "but now that the Nome King is building a tunnel we shall get into the Emerald City very easily. So let us send the little fat General back to his King with our promise to assist him. We will not say that we intend to conquer the Nomes after we have conquered Oz, but we will do so, just the same."

This plan being agreed upon, they all went home to dinner, leaving General Guph still in prison. The Nome had no idea that he had succeeded in his mission, for finding himself in prison he feared the Growleywogs intended to put him to death.

By this time the jailer had tired of sticking pins in the General, and was amusing himself by carefully pulling the Nome's whiskers out by the roots, one at a time. This enjoyment was interrupted by the Grand Gallipoot sending for the prisoner.

"Wait a few hours," begged the jailer. "I haven't pulled out a quarter of his whiskers yet."

"If you keep the Grand Gallipoot waiting, he'll break your back," declared the messenger.

"Perhaps you're right," sighed the jailer. "Take the prisoner away, if you will, but I advise you to kick him at every step he takes. It will be good fun, for he is as soft as a ripe peach."

So Guph was led away to the royal castle, where the Grand Gallipoot told him that the Growleywogs had decided to assist the Nomes in conquering the Land of Oz.

"Whenever you are ready," he added, "send me word and I will march with eighteen thousand of my most powerful warriors to your aid."

Guph was so delighted that he forgot all the smarting caused by the pins and the pulling of whiskers. He did not even complain of the treatment he had received, but thanked the Grand Gallipoot and hurried away upon his journey.

He had now secured the assistance of the Whimsies and the Growleywogs; but his success made him long for still more allies. His own life depended upon his conquering Oz, and he said to himself: "I'll take no chances. I'll be certain of success. Then, when Oz is destroyed, perhaps I shall be a greater man than old Roquat, and I can throw him away and be King of the Nomes myself. Why not? The Whimsies are stronger than the Nomes, and they also are my friends. There are some people still stronger than the Growleywogs, and if I can but induce them to aid me I shall have nothing more to fear."

9. How the Wogglebug Taught Athletics

It did not take Dorothy long to establish herself in her new home, for she knew the people and the manners and customs of the Emerald City just as well as she knew the old Kansas farm.

But Uncle Henry and Aunt Em had some trouble in getting used to the finery and pomp and ceremony of Ozma's palace, and felt uneasy because they were obliged to be "dressed up" all the time. Yet every one was very courteous and kind to them and endeavored to make them happy. Ozma, especially, made much of Dorothy's relatives, for her little friend's sake, and she well knew that the awkwardness and strangeness of their new mode of life would all wear off in time.

The old people were chiefly troubled by the fact that there was no work for them to do.

"Ev'ry day is like Sunday, now," declared Aunt Em, solemnly, "and I can't say I like it. If they'd only let me do up the dishes after meals, or even sweep an' dust my own rooms, I'd be a deal happier. Henry don't know what to do with himself either, and once when he stole out an' fed the chickens Billina scolded him for letting 'em eat between meals. I never knew before what a hardship it is to be rich and have everything you want."

These complaints began to worry Dorothy; so she had a long talk with Ozma upon the subject.

"I see I must find them something to do," said the girlish Ruler of Oz, seriously. "I have been watching your uncle and aunt, and I believe they will be more contented if occupied with some light tasks. While I am considering this matter, Dorothy, you might make a trip with them through the Land of Oz, visiting some of the odd corners and introducing your relatives to some of our curious people."

"Oh, that would be fine!" exclaimed Dorothy, eagerly.

"I will give you an escort befitting your rank as a Princess," continued Ozma; "and you may go to some of the places you have not yet visited yourself, as well as some others that you know. I will mark out a plan of the trip for you and have everything in readiness for you to start to-morrow morning. Take your time, dear, and be gone as long as you wish. By the time you return I shall have found some occupation for Uncle Henry and Aunt Em that will keep them from being restless and dissatisfied."

Dorothy thanked her good friend and kissed the lovely Ruler gratefully. Then she ran to tell the joyful news to her uncle and aunt.

Next morning, after breakfast, everything was found ready for their departure.

The escort included Omby Amby, the Captain General of Ozma's army, which consisted merely of twenty-seven officers besides the Captain General. Once Omby Amby had been a private soldier—the only private in the army—but as there was never any fighting to do Ozma saw no need of a private, so she made Omby Amby the highest officer of them all. He was very tall and slim and wore a gay uniform and a fierce mustache. Yet the mustache was the only fierce thing about Omby Amby, whose nature was as gentle as that of a child.

The wonderful Wizard had asked to join the party, and with him came his friend the Shaggy Man, who was shaggy but not ragged, being dressed in fine silks with satin shags and bobtails. The Shaggy Man had shaggy whiskers and hair, but a sweet disposition and a soft, pleasant voice.

There was an open wagon, with three seats for the passengers, and the wagon was drawn by the famous wooden Sawhorse which had once been brought to life by Ozma by means of a magic powder. The Sawhorse wore wooden shoes to keep his wooden legs from wearing away, and he was strong and swift. As this curious creature was Ozma's own favorite steed, and very popular with all the people of the Emerald City, Dorothy knew that she had been highly favored by being permitted to use the Sawhorse on her journey.

In the front seat of the wagon sat Dorothy and the Wizard. Uncle Henry and Aunt Em sat in the next seat and the Shaggy Man and Omby Amby in the third seat. Of course Toto was with the party, curled up at Dorothy's feet, and just as they were about to start, Billina came fluttering along the path and begged to be taken with them. Dorothy readily agreed, so the Yellow Hen flew up and perched herself upon the dashboard. She wore her pearl necklace and three bracelets upon each leg, in honor of the occasion.

Dorothy kissed Ozma good-bye, and all the people standing around waved their handkerchiefs, and the band in an upper balcony struck up a military march. Then the Wizard clucked to the Sawhorse and said: "Gid-dap!" and the wooden animal pranced away and drew behind him the big red wagon and all the passengers, without any effort at all. A servant threw open a gate of the palace enclosure, that they might pass out; and so, with music and shouts following them, the journey was begun.

"It's almost like a circus," said Aunt Em, proudly. "I can't help feelin' high an' mighty in this kind of a turn-out."

Indeed, as they passed down the street, all the people cheered them lustily, and the Shaggy Man and the Wizard and the Captain General all took off their hats and bowed politely in acknowledgment.

When they came to the great wall of the Emerald City, the gates were opened by the Guardian who always tended them. Over the gateway hung a dull-colored metal magnet shaped like a horse-shoe, placed against a shield of polished gold.

"That," said the Shaggy Man, impressively, "is the wonderful Love Magnet. I brought it to the Emerald City myself, and all who pass beneath this gateway are both loving and beloved."

"It's a fine thing," declared Aunt Em, admiringly. "If we'd had it in Kansas I guess the man who held a mortgage on the farm wouldn't have turned us out."

"Then I'm glad we didn't have it," returned Uncle Henry. "I like Oz better than Kansas, even; an' this little wood Sawhorse beats all the critters I ever saw. He don't have to be curried, or fed, or watered, an' he's strong as an ox. Can he talk, Dorothy?"

"Yes, Uncle," replied the child. "But the Sawhorse never says much. He told me once that he can't talk and think at the same time, so he prefers to think."

"Which is very sensible," declared the Wizard, nodding approvingly. "Which way do we go, Dorothy?"

"Straight ahead into the Quadling Country," she answered. "I've got a letter of interduction to Miss Cuttenclip."

"Oh!" exclaimed the Wizard, much interested. "Are we going there? Then I'm glad I came, for I've always wanted to meet the Cuttenclips."

"Who are they?" inquired Aunt Em.

"Wait till we get there," replied Dorothy, with a laugh; "then you'll see for yourself. I've never seen the Cuttenclips, you know, so I can't 'zactly 'splain 'em to you."

Once free of the Emerald City the Sawhorse dashed away at tremendous speed. Indeed, he went so fast that Aunt Em had hard work to catch her breath, and Uncle Henry held fast to the seat of the red wagon.

"Gently—gently, my boy!" called the Wizard, and at this the Sawhorse slackened his speed.

"What's wrong?" asked the animal, slightly turning his wooden head to look at the party with one eye, which was a knot of wood.

"Why, we wish to admire the scenery, that's all," answered the Wizard.

"Some of your passengers," added the Shaggy Man, "have never been out of the Emerald City before, and the country is all new to them."

"If you go too fast you'll spoil all the fun," said Dorothy. "There's no hurry."

"Very well; it is all the same to me," observed the Sawhorse; and after that he went at a more moderate pace.

Uncle Henry was astonished.

"How can a wooden thing be so intelligent?" he asked.

"Why, I gave him some sawdust brains the last time I fitted his head with new ears," explained the Wizard. "The sawdust was made from hard knots, and now the Sawhorse is able to think out any knotty problem he meets with."

"I see," said Uncle Henry.

"I don't," remarked Aunt Em; but no one paid any attention to this statement.

Before long they came to a stately building that stood upon a green plain with handsome shade trees grouped here and there.

"What is that?" asked Uncle Henry.

"That," replied the Wizard, "is the Royal Athletic College of Oz, which is directed by Professor H. M. Wogglebug, T.E."

"Let's stop and make a call," suggested Dorothy.

So the Sawhorse drew up in front of the great building and they were met at the door by the learned Wogglebug himself. He seemed fully as tall as the Wizard, and was dressed in a red and white checked vest and a blue swallow-tailed coat, and had yellow knee breeches and purple silk stockings upon his slender legs. A tall hat was jauntily set upon his head and he wore spectacles over his big bright eyes.

"Welcome, Dorothy," said the Wogglebug; "and welcome to all your friends. We are indeed pleased to receive you at this great Temple of Learning."

"I thought it was an Athletic College," said the Shaggy Man.

"It is, my dear sir," answered the Wogglebug, proudly. "Here it is that we teach the youth of our great land scientific College Athletics—in all their purity."

"Don't you teach them anything else?" asked Dorothy. "Don't

hey get any reading, writing and 'rithmetic?"

"Oh, yes; of course. They get all those, and more," returned the Professor. "But such things occupy little of their time. Please follow me and I will show you how my scholars are usually occupied. This is a class hour and they are all busy."

They followed him to a big field back of the college building, where several hundred young Ozites were at their classes. In one place they played football, in another baseball. Some played tennis, some golf; some were swimming in a big pool. Upon a river which wound through the grounds several crews in racing boats were rowing with great enthusiasm. Other groups of students played basketball and cricket, while in one place a ring was roped in to permit boxing and wrestling by the energetic youths. All the collegians seemed busy and there was much laughter and shouting.

"This college," said Professor Wogglebug, complacently, "is a great success. Its educational value is undisputed, and we are turning out many great and valuable citizens every year."

"But when do they study?" asked Dorothy.

"Study?" said the Wogglebug, looking perplexed at the question.

"Yes; when do they get their 'rithmetic, and jogerfy, and such things?"

"Oh, they take doses of those every night and morning," was the reply.

"What do you mean by doses?" Dorothy inquired, wonderingly.

"Why, we use the newly invented School Pills, made by your friend the Wizard. These pills we have found to be very effective, and they save a lot of time. Please step this way and I will show you our Laboratory of Learning."

He led them to a room in the building where many large bottles were standing in rows upon shelves.

"These are the Algebra Pills," said the Professor, taking down one of the bottles. "One at night, on retiring, is equal to four hours of study. Here are the Geography Pills—one at night and one in the morning. In this next bottle are the Latin Pills—one three times a day. Then we have the Grammar Pills—one before each meal—and the Spelling Pills, which are taken whenever needed."

"Your scholars must have to take a lot of pills," remarked Dorothy, thoughtfully. "How do they take 'em, in applesauce?"

"No, my dear. They are sugar-coated and are quickly and easily swallowed. I believe the students would rather take the pills than study, and certainly the pills are a more effective method. You see, until these School Pills were invented we wasted a lot of time in study that may now be better employed in practicing athletics."

"Seems to me the pills are a good thing," said Omby Amby, who remembered how it used to make his head ache as a boy to study 'rithmetic.

"They are, sir," declared the Wogglebug, earnestly. "They give us an advantage over all other colleges, because at no loss of time our boys become thoroughly conversant with Greek and Latin, Mathematics and Geography, Grammar and Literature. You see

they are never obliged to interrupt their games to acquire the lesser branches of learning."

"It's a great invention, I'm sure," said Dorothy, looking admiringly at the Wizard, who blushed modestly at this praise.

"We live in an age of progress," announced Professor Wogglebug, pompously. "It is easier to swallow knowledge than to acquire it laboriously from books. Is it not so, my friends?"

"Some folks can swallow anything," said Aunt Em, "but to me this seems too much like taking medicine."

"Young men in college always have to take their medicine, one way or another," observed the Wizard, with a smile; "and, as our Professor says, these School Pills have proved to be a great success. One day while I was making them I happened to drop one of them, and one of Billina's chickens gobbled it up. A few minutes afterward this chick got upon a roost and recited 'The Boy Stood on the Burning Deck' without making a single mistake. Then it recited 'The Charge of the Light Brigade' and afterwards 'Excelsior.' You see, the chicken had eaten an Elocution Pill."

They now bade good-bye to the Professor, and thanking him for his kind reception mounted again into the red wagon and continued their journey.

10. How the Cuttenclips Lived

The travelers had taken no provisions with them because they knew that they would be welcomed wherever they might go in the Land of Oz, and that the people would feed and lodge them with genuine hospitality. So about noon they stopped at a farm-house and were given a delicious luncheon of bread and milk, fruits and wheat cakes with maple syrup. After resting a while and strolling through the orchards with their host—a round, jolly farmer—they got into the wagon and again started the Sawhorse along the pretty, winding road.

There were signposts at all the corners, and finally they came to one which read:

TAKE THIS ROAD TO THE CUTTENCLIPS

There was also a hand pointing in the right direction, so they turned the Sawhorse that way and found it a very good road, but seemingly little traveled.

"I've never seen the Cuttenclips before," remarked Dorothy.

"Nor I," said the Captain General.

"Nor I," said the Wizard.

"Nor I," said Billina.

"I've hardly been out of the Emerald City since I arrived in this country," added the Shaggy Man.

"Why, none of us has been there, then," exclaimed the little girl. "I wonder what the Cuttenclips are like."

"We shall soon find out," said the Wizard, with a sly laugh. "I've heard they are rather flimsy things."

The farm-houses became fewer as they proceeded, and the path was at times so faint that the Sawhorse had hard work to keep in the road. The wagon began to jounce, too; so they were obliged to go slowly.

After a somewhat wearisome journey they came in sight of a high wall, painted blue with pink ornaments. This wall was circular, and seemed to enclose a large space. It was so high that only the tops of the trees could be seen above it.

The path led up to a small door in the wall, which was closed and latched. Upon the door was a sign in gold letters reading as follows:

VISITORS are requested to MOVE SLOWLY and CAREFULLY, and to avoid COUGHING or making any BREEZE or DRAUGHT.

"That's strange," said the Shaggy Man, reading the sign aloud. "Who ARE the Cuttenclips, anyhow?"

"Why, they're paper dolls," answered Dorothy. "Didn't you know that?"

"Paper dolls! Then let's go somewhere else," said Uncle Henry. "We're all too old to play with dolls, Dorothy."

"But these are different," declared the girl. "They're alive."

"Alive!" gasped Aunt Em, in amazement.

"Yes. Let's go in," said Dorothy.

So they all got out of the wagon, since the door in the wall was not big enough for them to drive the Sawhorse and wagon through it.

"You stay here, Toto!" commanded Dorothy, shaking her finger at the little dog. "You're so careless that you might make a breeze if I let you inside."

Toto wagged his tail as if disappointed at being left behind; but he made no effort to follow them. The Wizard unlatched the door, which opened outward, and they all looked eagerly inside.

Just before the entrance was drawn up a line of tiny soldiers, with uniforms brightly painted and paper guns upon their shoulders. They were exactly alike, from one end of the line to the other, and all were cut out of paper and joined together in the centers of their bodies.

As the visitors entered the enclosure the Wizard let the door swing back into place, and at once the line of soldiers tumbled over, fell flat upon their backs, and lay fluttering upon the ground.

"Hi there!" called one of them; "what do you mean by slamming the door and blowing us over?"

"I beg your pardon, I'm sure," said the Wizard, regretfully. "I didn't know you were so delicate."

"We're not delicate!" retorted another soldier, raising his head from the ground. "We are strong and healthy; but we can't stand draughts."

"May I help you up?" asked Dorothy.

"If you please," replied the end soldier. "But do it gently, little girl."

Dorothy carefully stood up the line of soldiers, who first dusted their painted clothes and then saluted the visitors with their paper muskets. From the end it was easy to see that the entire line had been cut out of paper, although from the front the soldiers looked rather solid and imposing.

"I've a letter of introduction from Princess Ozma to Miss Cuttenclip," announced Dorothy.

"Very well," said the end soldier, and blew upon a paper whistle that hung around his neck. At once a paper soldier in a Captain's uniform came out of a paper house near by and approached the group at the entrance. He was not very big, and he walked rather stiffly and uncertainly on his paper legs; but he had a pleasant face, with very red cheeks and very blue eyes, and he bowed so low to the strangers that Dorothy laughed, and the breeze from her mouth nearly blew the Captain over. He wavered and struggled and finally managed to remain upon his feet.

"Take care, Miss!" he said, warningly. "You're breaking the rules, you know, by laughing."

"Oh, I didn't know that," she replied.

"To laugh in this place is nearly as dangerous as to cough," said the Captain. "You'll have to breathe very quietly, I assure you."

"We'll try to," promised the girl. "May we see Miss Cuttenclip, please?"

"You may," promptly returned the Captain. "This is one of her reception days. Be good enough to follow me."

He turned and led the way up a path, and as they followed slowly, because the paper Captain did not move very swiftly, they took the opportunity to gaze around them at this strange paper country.

Beside the path were paper trees, all cut out very neatly and painted a brilliant green color. And back of the trees were rows of cardboard houses, painted in various colors but most of them having green blinds. Some were large and some small, and in the front yards were beds of paper flowers quite natural in appearance. Over some of the porches paper vines were twined, giving them a cozy and shady look.

As the visitors passed along the street a good many paper dolls came to the doors and windows of their houses to look at them curiously. These dolls were nearly all the same height, but were cut into various shapes, some being fat and some lean. The girl dolls wore many beautiful costumes of tissue paper, making them quite fluffy; but their heads and hands were no thicker than the paper of which they were made.

Some of the paper people were on the street, walking along or congregated in groups and talking together; but as soon as they saw the strangers they all fluttered into the houses as fast as they could go, so as to be out of danger.

"Excuse me if I go edgewise," remarked the Captain as they came to a slight hill. "I can get along faster that way and not flutter so much."

"That's all right," said Dorothy. "We don't mind how you go, I'm sure."

At one side of the street was a paper pump, and a paper boy was pumping paper water into a paper pail. The Yellow Hen happened to brush against this boy with her wing, and he flew into the air and fell into a paper tree, where he stuck until the Wizard gently pulled him out. At the same time, the pail went into the air, spilling the paper water, while the paper pump bent nearly double.

"Goodness me!" said the Hen. "If I should flop my wings I believe I'd knock over the whole village!"

"Then don't flop them—please don't!" entreated the Captain. "Miss Cuttenclip would be very much distressed if her village was spoiled."

"Oh, I'll be careful," promised Billina.

"Are not all these paper girls and women named Miss Cuttenclips?" inquired Omby Amby.

"No indeed," answered the Captain, who was walking better since he began to move edgewise. "There is but one Miss Cuttenclip, who is our Queen, because she made us all. These girls are Cuttenclips, to be sure, but their names are Emily and Polly and Sue and Betty and such things. Only the Queen is called Miss Cuttenclip."

"I must say that this place beats anything I ever heard of," observed Aunt Em. "I used to play with paper dolls myself, an' cut 'em out; but I never thought I'd ever see such things alive."

"I don't see as it's any more curious than hearing hens talk," returned Uncle Henry.

"You're likely to see many queer things in the Land of Oz, sir," said the Wizard. "But a fairy country is extremely interesting when you get used to being surprised."

"Here we are!" called the Captain, stopping before a cottage.

This house was made of wood, and was remarkably pretty in design. In the Emerald City it would have been considered a tiny dwelling, indeed; but in the midst of this paper village it seemed immense. Real flowers were in the garden and real trees grew beside it. Upon the front door was a sign reading:

MISS CUTTENCLIP.

Just as they reached the porch the front door opened and a little girl stood before them. She appeared to be about the same age as Dorothy, and smiling upon her visitors she said, sweetly: "You are welcome."

All the party seemed relieved to find that here was a real girl, of flesh and blood. She was very dainty and pretty as she stood there welcoming them. Her hair was a golden blonde and her eyes turquoise blue. She had rosy cheeks and lovely white teeth. Over her simple white lawn dress she wore an apron with pink and white checks, and in one hand she held a pair of scissors.

"May we see Miss Cuttenclip, please?" asked Dorothy.

"I am Miss Cuttenclip," was the reply. "Won't you come in?"

She held the door open while they all entered a pretty sitting-room that was littered with all sorts of paper—some stiff, some thin, and some tissue. The sheets and scraps were of all colors. Upon a table were paints and brushes, while several pair of scissors, of different sizes, were lying about.

"Sit down, please," said Miss Cuttenclip, clearing the paper scraps off some of the chairs. "It is so long since I have had any visitors that I am not properly prepared to receive them. But I'm sure you will pardon my untidy room, for this is my workshop."

"Do you make all the paper dolls?" inquired Dorothy.

"Yes; I cut them out with my scissors, and paint the faces and some of the costumes. It is very pleasant work, and I am happy making my paper village grow."

"But how do the paper dolls happen to be alive?" asked Aunt Em.

"The first dolls I made were not alive," said Miss Cuttenclip. "I used to live near the castle of a great Sorceress named Glinda the Good, and she saw my dolls and said they were very pretty. I told her I thought I would like them better if they were alive, and the next day the Sorceress brought me a lot of magic paper. 'This is live paper,' she said, 'and all the dolls you cut out of it will be alive, and able to think and to talk. When you have used it all up, come to me and I will give you more.'

"Of course I was delighted with this present," continued Miss Cuttenclip, "and at once set to work and made several paper dolls, which, as soon as they were cut out, began to walk around and talk to me. But they were so thin that I found that any breeze would blow them over and scatter them dreadfully; so Glinda found this lonely place for me, where few people ever come. She built the wall to keep any wind from blowing away my people, and told me I could build a paper village here and be its Queen. That is why I came here and settled down to work and started the village you now see. It was many years ago that I built the first houses, and I've kept pretty busy and made my village grow finely; and I need not tell you that I am very happy in my work."

"Many years ago!" exclaimed Aunt Em. "Why, how old are you, child?"

"I never keep track of the years," said Miss Cuttenclip, laughing. "You see, I don't grow up at all, but stay just the same as I was when first I came here. Perhaps I'm older even than you are, madam; but I couldn't say for sure."

They looked at the lovely little girl wonderingly, and the Wizard asked: "What happens to your paper village when it rains?"

"It does not rain here," replied Miss Cuttenclip. "Glinda keeps all the rain storms away; so I never worry about my dolls getting wet. But now, if you will come with me, it will give me pleasure to show you over my paper kingdom. Of course you must go slowly and carefully, and avoid making any breeze."

They left the cottage and followed their guide through the various streets of the village. It was indeed an amazing place, when one considered that it was all made with scissors, and the visitors were not only greatly interested but full of admiration for the skill of little Miss Cuttenclip.

In one place a large group of especially nice paper dolls assembled to greet their Queen, whom it was easy to see they loved early. These dolls marched and danced before the visitors, and then they all waved their paper handkerchiefs and sang in a sweet chorus a song called "The Flag of Our Native Land."

At the conclusion of the song they ran up a handsome paper flag on a tall flagpole, and all of the people of the village gathered around to cheer as loudly as they could—although, of course, their voices were not especially strong.

Miss Cuttenclip was about to make her subjects a speech in reply to this patriotic song, when the Shaggy Man happened to sneeze.

He was a very loud and powerful sneezer at any time, and he had tried so hard to hold in this sneeze that when it suddenly exploded the result was terrible.

The paper dolls were mowed down by dozens, and flew and fluttered in wild confusion in every direction, tumbling this way and that and getting more or less wrinkled and bent.

A wail of terror and grief came from the scattered throng, and Miss Cuttenclip exclaimed:

"Dear me! dear me!" and hurried at once to the rescue of her overturned people.

"Oh, Shaggy Man! How could you?" asked Dorothy, reproachfully.

"I couldn't help it—really I couldn't," protested the Shaggy Man, looking quite ashamed. "And I had no idea it took so little to upset these paper dolls."

"So little!" said Dorothy. "Why, it was 'most as bad as a Kansas cyclone." And then she helped Miss Cuttenclip rescue the paper folk and stand them on their feet again. Two of the cardboard houses had also tumbled over, and the little Queen said she would have to repair them and paste them together before they could be lived in again.

And now, fearing they might do more damage to the flimsy paper people, they decided to go away. But first they thanked Miss Cuttenclip very warmly for her courtesy and kindness to them.

"Any friend of Princess Ozma is always welcome here—unless he sneezes," said the Queen with a rather severe look at the Shaggy Man, who hung his head. "I like to have visitors admire my wonderful village, and I hope you will call again."

Miss Cuttenclip herself led them to the door in the wall, and as they passed along the street the paper dolls peeped at them half fearfully from the doors and windows. Perhaps they will never forget the Shaggy Man's awful sneeze, and I am sure they were all glad to see the meat people go away.

11. How the General Met the First and Foremost

On leaving the Growleywogs General Guph had to recross the Ripple Lands, and he did not find it a pleasant thing to do. Perhaps having his whiskers pulled out one by one and being used as a pin-cushion for the innocent amusement of a good natured jailer had not improved the quality of Guph's temper, for the old Nome raved and raged at the recollection of the wrongs he had suffered, and vowed to take vengeance upon the Growleywogs after he had used them for his purposes and Oz had been conquered. He went on in this furious way until he was half across the Ripple Land. Then he became seasick, and the rest of the way this naughty Nome was almost as miserable as he deserved to be.

But when he reached the plains again and the ground was firm under his feet he began to feel better, and instead of going back home he turned directly west. A squirrel, perched in a tree, saw him take this road and called to him warningly: "Look out!" But

he paid no attention. An eagle paused in its flight through the air to look at him wonderingly and say: "Look out!" But on he went.

No one can say that Guph was not brave, for he had determined to visit those dangerous creatures the Phanfasms, who resided upon the very top of the dread Mountain of Phantastico. The Phanfasms were Erbs, and so dreaded by mortals and immortals alike that no one had been near their mountain home for several thousand years. Yet General Guph hoped to induce them to join in his proposed warfare against the good and happy Oz people.

Guph knew very well that the Phanfasms would be almost as dangerous to the Nomes as they would to the Ozites, but he thought himself so clever that he believed he could manage these strange creatures and make them obey him. And there was no doubt at all that if he could enlist the services of the Phanfasms, their tremendous power, united to the strength of the Growleywogs and the cunning of the Whimsies would doom the Land of Oz to absolute destruction.

So the old Nome climbed the foothills and trudged along the wild mountain paths until he came to a big gully that encircled the Mountain of Phantastico and marked the boundary line of the dominion of the Phanfasms. This gully was about a third of the way up the mountain, and it was filled to the brim with red-hot molten lava in which swam fire-serpents and poisonous salamanders. The heat from this mass and its poisonous smell were both so unbearable that even birds hesitated to fly over the gully, but circled around it. All living things kept away from the mountain.

Now Guph had heard, during his long lifetime, many tales of these dreaded Phanfasms; so he had heard of this barrier of melted lava, and also he had been told that there was a narrow bridge that spanned it in one place. So he walked along the edge until he found the bridge. It was a single arch of gray stone, and lying flat upon the bridge was a scarlet alligator, seemingly fast asleep.

When Guph stumbled over the rocks in approaching the bridge the creature opened its eyes, from which tiny flames shot in all directions, and after looking at the intruder very wickedly the scarlet alligator closed its eyelids again and lay still.

Guph saw there was no room for him to pass the alligator on the narrow bridge, so he called out to it: "Good morning, friend. I don't wish to hurry you, but please tell me if you are coming down, or going up?"

"Neither," snapped the alligator, clicking its cruel jaws together.

The General hesitated.

"Are you likely to stay there long?" he asked.

"A few hundred years or so," said the alligator.

Guph softly rubbed the end of his nose and tried to think what to do.

"Do you know whether the First and Foremost Phanfasm of Phantastico is at home or not?" he presently inquired.

"I expect he is, seeing he is always at home," replied the alligator.

"Ah; who is that coming down the mountain?" asked the Nome, gazing upward.

The alligator turned to look over its shoulder, and at once Guph ran to the bridge and leaped over the sentinel's back before it could turn back again. The scarlet monster made a snap at the Nome's left foot, but missed it by fully an inch.

"Ah ha!" laughed the General, who was now on the mountain path. "I fooled you that time."

"So you did; and perhaps you fooled yourself," retorted the alligator. "Go up the mountain, if you dare, and find out what the First and Foremost will do to you!"

"I will," declared Guph, boldly; and on he went up the path.

At first the scene was wild enough, but gradually it grew more and more awful in appearance. All the rocks had the shapes of frightful beings and even the tree trunks were gnarled and twisted like serpents.

Suddenly there appeared before the Nome a man with the head of an owl. His body was hairy like that of an ape, and his only clothing was a scarlet scarf twisted around his waist. He bore a huge club in his hand and his round owl eyes blinked fiercely upon the intruder.

"What are you doing here?" he demanded, threatening Guph with his club.

"I've come to see the First and Foremost Phanfasm of Phantastico," replied the General, who did not like the way this creature looked at him, but still was not afraid.

"Ah; you shall see him!" the man said, with a sneering laugh. "The First and Foremost shall decide upon the best way to punish you."

"He will not punish me," returned Guph, calmly, "for I have come here to do him and his people a rare favor. Lead on, fellow, and take me directly to your master."

The owl-man raised his club with a threatening gesture.

"If you try to escape," he said, "beware—"

But here the General interrupted him.

"Spare your threats," said he, "and do not be impertinent, or I will have you severely punished. Lead on, and keep silent!"

This Guph was really a clever rascal, and it seems a pity he was so bad, for in a good cause he might have accomplished much. He realized that he had put himself into a dangerous position by coming to this dreadful mountain, but he also knew that if he showed fear he was lost. So he adopted a bold manner as his best defense. The wisdom of this plan was soon evident, for the Phanfasm with the owl's head turned and led the way up the mountain.

At the very top was a level plain upon which were heaps of rock that at first glance seemed solid. But on looking closer Guph discovered that these rock heaps were dwellings, for each had an opening.

Not a person was to be seen outside the rock huts. All was silent.

The owl-man led the way among the groups of dwellings to one standing in the center. It seemed no better and no worse than any of the others. Outside the entrance to this rock heap the guide gave a low wail that sounded like "Lee-ow-ah!"

Suddenly there bounded from the opening another hairy man. This one wore the head of a bear. In his hand he bore a brass hoop. He glared at the stranger in evident surprise.

"Why have you captured this foolish wanderer and brought him here?" he demanded, addressing the owl-man.

"I did not capture him," was the answer. "He passed the scarlet alligator and came here of his own free will and accord."

The First and Foremost looked at the General.

"Have you tired of life, then?" he asked.

"No indeed," answered Guph. "I am a Nome, and the Chief General of King Roquat the Red's great army of Nomes. I come of a long-lived race, and I may say that I expect to live a long time yet. Sit down, you Phanfasms—if you can find a seat in this wild haunt—and listen to what I have to say."

With all his knowledge and bravery General Guph did not know that the steady glare from the bear eyes was reading his inmost thoughts as surely as if they had been put into words. He did not know that these despised rock heaps of the Phanfasms were merely deceptions to his own eyes, nor could he guess that he was standing in the midst of one of the most splendid and luxurious cities ever built by magic power. All that he saw was a barren waste of rock heaps, a hairy man with an owl's head and another with a bear's head. The sorcery of the Phanfasms permitted him to see no more.

Suddenly the First and Foremost swung his brass hoop and caught Guph around the neck with it. The next instant, before the General could think what had happened to him, he was dragged inside the rock hut. Here, his eyes still blinded to realities, he perceived only a dim light, by which the hut seemed as rough and rude inside as it was outside. Yet he had a strange feeling that many bright eyes were fastened upon him and that he stood in a vast and extensive hall.

The First and Foremost now laughed grimly and released his prisoner.

"If you have anything to say that is interesting," he remarked, "speak out, before I strangle you."

So Guph spoke out. He tried not to pay any attention to a strange rustling sound that he heard, as of an unseen multitude drawing near to listen to his words. His eyes could see only the fierce bear-man, and to him he addressed his speech. First he told of his plan to conquer the Land of Oz and plunder the country of its riches and enslave its people, who, being fairies, could not be killed. After relating all this, and telling of the tunnel the Nome King was building, he said he had come to ask the First and Foremost to join the Nomes, with his band of terrible warriors, and help them to defeat the Oz people.

The General spoke very earnestly and impressively, but when he had finished the bear-man began to laugh as if much amused, and his laughter seemed to be echoed by a chorus of merriment from an unseen multitude. Then, for the first time, Guph began to feel a trifle worried.

"Who else has promised to help you?" finally asked the First and Foremost.

"The Whimsies," replied the General.

Again the bear-headed Phanfasm laughed.

"Any others?" he inquired.

"Only the Growleywogs," said Guph.

This answer set the First and Foremost laughing anew.

"What share of the spoils am I to have?" was the next question.

"Anything you like, except King Roquat's Magic Belt," replied Guph.

At this the Phanfasm set up a roar of laughter, which had its echo in the unseen chorus, and the bear-man seemed so amused that he actually rolled upon the ground and shouted with merriment.

"Oh, these blind and foolish Nomes!" he said. "How big they seem to themselves and how small they really are!"

Suddenly he arose and seized Guph's neck with one hairy paw, dragging him out of the hut into the open.

Here he gave a curious wailing cry, and, as if in answer, from all the rocky huts on the mountain-top came flocking a horde of Phanfasms, all with hairy bodies, but wearing heads of various animals, birds and reptiles. All were ferocious and repulsive-looking to the deceived eyes of the Nome, and Guph could not repress a shudder of disgust as he looked upon them.

The First and Foremost slowly raised his arms, and in a twinkling his hairy skin fell from him and he appeared before the astonished Nome as a beautiful woman, clothed in a flowing gown of pink gauze. In her dark hair flowers were entwined, and her face was noble and calm.

At the same instant the entire band of Phanfasms was transformed into a pack of howling wolves, running here and there as they snarled and showed their ugly yellow fangs.

The woman now raised her arms, even as the man-bear had done, and in a twinkling the wolves became crawling lizards, while she herself changed into a huge butterfly.

Guph had only time to cry out in fear and take a step backward to avoid the lizards when another transformation occurred, and all returned instantly to the forms they had originally worn.

Then the First and Foremost, who had resumed his hairy body and bear head, turned to the Nome and asked

"Do you still demand our assistance?"

"More than ever," answered the General, firmly.

"Then tell me: what can you offer the Phanfasms that they have not already?" inquired the First and Foremost.

Guph hesitated. He really did not know what to say. The Nome King's vaunted Magic Belt seemed a poor thing compared to the astonishing magical powers of these people. Gold, jewels and slaves they might secure in any quantity without especial effort. He felt that he was dealing with powers greatly beyond him. There was but one argument that might influence the Phanfasms, who were creatures of evil.

"Permit me to call your attention to the exquisite joy of making the happy unhappy," said he at last. "Consider the pleasure of destroying innocent and harmless people."

"Ah! you have answered me," cried the First and Foremost. "For that reason alone we will aid you. Go home, and tell your bandy-legged king that as soon as his tunnel is finished the Phanfasms will be with him and lead his legions to the conquest of Oz. The deadly desert alone has kept us from destroying Oz long ago, and your underground tunnel is a clever thought. Go home, and prepare for our coming!"

Guph was very glad to be permitted to go with this promise. The owl-man led him back down the mountain path and ordered the scarlet alligator to crawl away and allow the Nome to cross the bridge in safety.

After the visitor had gone a brilliant and gorgeous city appeared upon the mountain top, clearly visible to the eyes of the gaily dressed multitude of Phanfasms that lived there. And the First and Foremost, beautifully arrayed, addressed the others in these words: "It is time we went into the world and brought sorrow and dismay to its people. Too long have we remained for ourselves upon this mountain top, for while we are thus secluded many nations have grown happy and prosperous, and the chief joy of the race of Phanfasms is to destroy happiness. So I think it is lucky that this messenger from the Nomes arrived among us just now, to remind us that the opportunity has come for us to make trouble. We will use King Roquat's tunnel to conquer the Land of Oz. Then we will destroy the Whimsies, the Growleywogs and the Nomes, and afterward go out to ravage and annoy and grieve the whole world."

The multitude of evil Phanfasms eagerly applauded this plan, which they fully approved.

I am told that the Erbs are the most powerful and merciless of all the evil spirits, and the Phanfasms of Phantastico belong to the race of Erbs.

12. How they Matched the Fuddles

Dorothy and her fellow travelers rode away from the Cuttenclip village and followed the indistinct path as far as the sign-post. Here they took the main road again and proceeded pleasantly through the pretty farming country. When evening came they stopped at a dwelling and were joyfully welcomed and given plenty to eat and good beds for the night.

Early next morning, however, they were up and eager to start, and after a good breakfast they bade their host good-bye and climbed into the red wagon, to which the Sawhorse had been hitched all night. Being made of wood, this horse never got tired nor cared to lie down. Dorothy was not quite sure whether he ever slept or not, but it was certain that he never did when anybody was around.

The weather is always beautiful in Oz, and this morning the air was cool and refreshing and the sunshine brilliant and delightful.

In about an hour they came to a place where another road branched off. There was a sign-post here which read:

THIS WAY TO FUDDLECUMJIG

"Oh, here is where we turn," said Dorothy, observing the sign.

"What! Are we going to Fuddlecumjig?" asked the Captain General.

"Yes; Ozma thought we might enjoy the Fuddles. They are said to be very interesting," she replied.

"No one would suspect it from their name," said Aunt Em. "Who are they, anyhow? More paper things?"

"I think not," answered Dorothy, laughing; "but I can't say 'zactly, Aunt Em, what they are. We'll find out when we get there."

"Perhaps the Wizard knows," suggested Uncle Henry.

"No; I've never been there before," said the Wizard. "But I've often heard of Fuddlecumjig and the Fuddles, who are said to be the most peculiar people in all the Land of Oz."

"In what way?" asked the Shaggy Man.

"I don't know, I'm sure," said the Wizard.

Just then, as they rode along the pretty green lane toward Fuddlecumjig, they espied a kangaroo sitting by the roadside. The poor animal had its face covered with both its front paws and was crying so bitterly that the tears coursed down its cheeks in two tiny streams and trickled across the road, where they formed a pool in a small hollow.

The Sawhorse stopped short at this pitiful sight, and Dorothy cried out, with ready sympathy:

"What's the matter, Kangaroo?"

"Boo-hoo! Boo-hoo!" wailed the Kangaroo; "I've lost my mi—mi—mi—Oh, boo-hoo! Boo-hoo!"—

"Poor thing," said the Wizard, "she's lost her mister. It's probably her husband, and he's dead."

"No, no, no!" sobbed the kangaroo. "It—it isn't that. I've lost my mi—mi—Oh, boo, boo-hoo!"

"I know," said the Shaggy Man; "she's lost her mirror."

"No; it's my mi—mi—mi—Boo-hoo! My mi—Oh, Boo-hoo!" and the kangaroo cried harder than ever.

"It must be her mince-pie," suggested Aunt Em.

"Or her milk-toast," proposed Uncle Henry.

"I've lost my mi—mi—mittens!" said the kangaroo, getting it out at last.

"Oh!" cried the Yellow Hen, with a cackle of relief. "Why didn't you say so before?"

"Boo-hoo! I—I—couldn't," answered the kangaroo.

"But, see here," said Dorothy, "you don't need mittens in this warm weather."

"Yes, indeed I do," replied the animal, stopping her sobs and removing her paws from her face to look at the little girl reproachfully. "My hands will get all sunburned and tanned without my mittens, and I've worn them so long that I'll probably catch cold without them."

"Nonsense!" said Dorothy. "I never heard of any kangaroo wearing mittens."

"Didn't you?" asked the animal, as if surprised.

"Never!" repeated the girl. "And you'll probably make yourself sick if you don't stop crying. Where do you live?"

"About two miles beyond Fuddlecumjig," was the answer. "Grandmother Gnit made me the mittens, and she's one of the Fuddles."

"Well, you'd better go home now, and perhaps the old lady will make you another pair," suggested Dorothy. "We're on our way to Fuddlecumjig, and you may hop along beside us."

So they rode on, and the kangaroo hopped beside the red wagon and seemed quickly to have forgotten her loss. By and by the Wizard said to the animal: "Are the Fuddles nice people?"

"Oh, very nice," answered the kangaroo; "that is, when they're properly put together. But they get dreadfully scattered and mixed up, at times, and then you can't do anything with them."

"What do you mean by their getting scattered?" inquired Dorothy.

"Why, they're made in a good many small pieces," explained the kangaroo; "and whenever any stranger comes near them they have a habit of falling apart and scattering themselves around. That's when they get so dreadfully mixed, and it's a hard puzzle to put them together again."

"Who usually puts them together?" asked Omby Amby.

"Any one who is able to match the pieces. I sometimes put Grandmother Gnit together myself, because I know her so well I can tell every piece that belongs to her. Then, when she's all matched, she knits for me, and that's how she made my mittens. But it took a good many days hard knitting, and I had to put Grandmother together a good many times, because every time I came near, she'd scatter herself."

"I should think she would get used to your coming, and not be afraid," said Dorothy.

"It isn't that," replied the kangaroo. "They're not a bit afraid, when they're put together, and usually they're very jolly and pleasant. It's just a habit they have, to scatter themselves, and if they didn't do it they wouldn't be Fuddles."

The travelers thought upon this quite seriously for a time, while the Sawhorse continued to carry them rapidly forward. Then Aunt Em remarked:

"I don't see much use our visitin' these Fuddles. If we find them scattered, all we can do is to sweep 'em up, and then go about our business."

"Oh, I b'lieve we'd better go on," replied Dorothy. "I'm getting hungry, and we must try to get some luncheon at Fuddlecumjig. Perhaps the food won't be scattered as badly as the people."

"You'll find plenty to eat there," declared the kangaroo, hopping along in big bounds because the Sawhorse was going so fast;

"and they have a fine cook, too, if you can manage to put him together. There's the town now—just ahead of us!"

They looked ahead and saw a group of very pretty houses standing in a green field a little apart from the main road.

"Some Munchkins came here a few days ago and matched a lot of people together," said the kangaroo. "I think they are together yet, and if you go softly, without making any noise, perhaps they won't scatter."

"Let's try it," suggested the Wizard.

So they stopped the Sawhorse and got out of the wagon, and, after bidding good bye to the kangaroo, who hopped away home, they entered the field and very cautiously approached the group of houses.

So silently did they move that soon they saw through the windows of the houses, people moving around, while others were passing to and fro in the yards between the buildings. They seemed much like other people from a distance, and apparently they did not notice the little party so quietly approaching.

They had almost reached the nearest house when Toto saw a large beetle crossing the path and barked loudly at it. Instantly a wild clatter was heard from the houses and yards. Dorothy thought it sounded like a sudden hailstorm, and the visitors, knowing that caution was no longer necessary, hurried forward to see what had happened.

After the clatter an intense stillness reigned in the town. The strangers entered the first house they came to, which was also the largest, and found the floor strewn with pieces of the people who lived there. They looked much like fragments of wood neatly painted, and were of all sorts of curious and fantastic shapes, no two pieces being in any way alike.

They picked up some of these pieces and looked at them carefully. On one which Dorothy held was an eye, which looked at her pleasantly but with an interested expression, as if it wondered what she was going to do with it. Quite near by she discovered and picked up a nose, and by matching the two pieces together found that they were part of a face.

"If I could find the mouth," she said, "this Fuddle might be able to talk, and tell us what to do next."

"Then let us find it," replied the Wizard, and so all got down on their hands and knees and began examining the scattered pieces.

"I've found it!" cried the Shaggy Man, and ran to Dorothy with a queer-shaped piece that had a mouth on it. But when they tried to fit it to the eye and nose they found the parts wouldn't match together.

"That mouth belongs to some other person," said Dorothy. "You see we need a curve here and a point there, to make it fit the face."

"Well, it must be here some place," declared the Wizard; "so if we search long enough we shall find it."

Dorothy fitted an ear on next, and the ear had a little patch of red hair above it. So while the others were searching for the mouth she hunted for pieces with red hair, and found several of them which, when matched to the other pieces, formed the top of a man's head. She had also found the other eye and the ear by

the time Omby Amby in a far corner discovered the mouth. When the face was thus completed, all the parts joined together with a nicety that was astonishing.

"Why, it's like a picture puzzle!" exclaimed the little girl. "Let's find the rest of him, and get him all together."

"What's the rest of him like?" asked the Wizard. "Here are some pieces of blue legs and green arms, but I don't know whether they are his or not."

"Look for a white shirt and a white apron," said the head which had been put together, speaking in a rather faint voice. "I'm the cook."

"Oh, thank you," said Dorothy. "It's lucky we started you first, for I'm hungry, and you can be cooking something for us to eat while we match the other folks together."

It was not so very difficult, now that they had a hint as to how the man was dressed, to find the other pieces belonging to him, and as all of them now worked on the cook, trying piece after piece to see if it would fit, they finally had the cook set up complete.

When he was finished he made them a low bow and said: "I will go at once to the kitchen to prepare your dinner. You will find it something of a job to get all the Fuddles together, so I advise you to begin on the Lord High Chigglewitz, whose first name is Larry. He's a bald-headed fat man and is dressed in a blue coat with brass buttons, a pink vest and drab breeches. A piece of his left knee is missing, having been lost years ago when he scattered himself too carelessly. That makes him limp a little, but he gets along very well with half a knee. As he is the chief personage in this town of Fuddlecumjig, he will be able to welcome you and assist you with the others. So it will be best to work on him while I'm getting your dinner."

"We will," said the Wizard; "and thank you very much, Cook, for the suggestion."

Aunt Em was the first to discover a piece of the Lord High Chigglewitz.

"It seems to me like a fool business, this matching folks together," she remarked; "but as we haven't anything to do till dinner's ready, we may as well get rid of some of this rubbish. Here, Henry, get busy and look for Larry's bald head. I've got his pink vest, all right."

They worked with eager interest, and Billina proved a great help to them. The Yellow Hen had sharp eyes and could put her head close to the various pieces that lay scattered around. She would examine the Lord High Chigglewitz and see which piece of him was next needed, and then hunt around until she found it. So before an hour had passed old Larry was standing complete before them.

"I congratulate you, my friends," he said, speaking in a cheerful voice. "You are certainly the cleverest people who ever visited us. I was never matched together so quickly in my life. I'm considered a great puzzle, usually."

"Well," said Dorothy, "there used to be a picture puzzle craze in Kansas, and so I've had some 'sperience matching puzzles. But the pictures were flat, while you are round, and that makes you harder to figure out."

"Thank you, my dear," replied old Larry, greatly pleased. "I feel highly complimented. Were I not a really good puzzle, there would be no object in my scattering myself."

"Why do you do it?" asked Aunt Em, severely. "Why don't you behave yourself, and stay put together?"

The Lord High Chigglewitz seemed annoyed by this speech; but he replied, politely: "Madam, you have perhaps noticed that every person has some peculiarity. Mine is to scatter myself. What your own peculiarity is I will not venture to say; but I shall never find fault with you, whatever you do."

"Now you've got your diploma, Em," said Uncle Henry, with a laugh, "and I'm glad of it. This is a queer country, and we may as well take people as we find them."

"If we did, we'd leave these folks scattered," she returned, and this retort made everybody laugh good-naturedly.

Just then Omby Amby found a hand with a knitting needle in it, and they decided to put Grandmother Gnit together. She proved an easier puzzle than old Larry, and when she was completed they found her a pleasant old lady who welcomed them cordially. Dorothy told her how the kangaroo had lost her mittens, and Grandmother Gnit promised to set to work at once and make the poor animal another pair.

Then the cook came to call them to dinner, and they found an inviting meal prepared for them. The Lord High Chigglewitz sat at the head of the table and Grandmother Gnit at the foot, and the guests had a merry time and thoroughly enjoyed themselves.

After dinner they went out into the yard and matched several other people together, and this work was so interesting that they might have spent the entire day at Fuddlecumjig had not the Wizard suggested that they resume their journey.

"But I don't like to leave all these poor people scattered," said Dorothy, undecided what to do.

"Oh, don't mind us, my dear," returned old Larry. "Every day or so some of the Gillikins, or Munchkins, or Winkies come here to amuse themselves by matching us together, so there will be no harm in leaving these pieces where they are for a time. But I hope you will visit us again, and if you do you will always be welcome, I assure you."

"Don't you ever match each other?" she inquired.

"Never; for we are no puzzles to ourselves, and so there wouldn't be any fun in it."

They now said goodbye to the queer Fuddles and got into their wagon to continue their journey.

"Those are certainly strange people," remarked Aunt Em, thoughtfully, as they drove away from Fuddlecumjig, "but I really can't see what use they are, at all."

"Why, they amused us all for several hours," replied the Wizard. "That is being of use to us, I'm sure."

"I think they're more fun than playing solitaire or mumbletypeg," declared Uncle Henry, soberly. "For my part, I'm glad we visited the Fuddles."

3. How the General Talked to the King

When General Guph returned to the cavern of the Nome King his Majesty asked:

"Well, what luck? Will the Whimsies join us?"

"They will," answered the General. "They will fight for us with all their strength and cunning."

"Good!" exclaimed the King. "What reward did you promise them?"

"Your Majesty is to use the Magic Belt to give each Whimsie a large, fine head, in place of the small one he is now obliged to wear."

"I agree to that," said the King. "This is good news, Guph, and it makes me feel more certain of the conquest of Oz."

"But I have other news for you," announced the General.

"Good or bad?"

"Good, your Majesty."

"Then I will hear it," said the King, with interest.

"The Growleywogs will join us."

"No!" cried the astonished King.

"Yes, indeed," said the General. "I have their promise."

"But what reward do they demand?" inquired the King, suspiciously, for he knew how greedy the Growleywogs were.

"They are to take a few of the Oz people for their slaves," replied Guph. He did not think it necessary to tell Roquat that the Growleywogs demanded twenty thousand slaves. It would be time enough for that when Oz was conquered.

"A very reasonable request, I'm sure," remarked the King. "I must congratulate you, Guph, upon the wonderful success of your journey."

"But that is not all," said the General, proudly.

The King seemed astonished. "Speak out, sir!" he commanded.

"I have seen the First and Foremost Phanfasm of the Mountain of Phantastico, and he will bring his people to assist us."

"What!" cried the King. "The Phanfasms! You don't mean it, Guph!"

"It is true," declared the General, proudly.

The King became thoughtful, and his brows wrinkled.

"I'm afraid, Guph," he said rather anxiously, "that the First and Foremost may prove as dangerous to us as to the Oz people. If he and his terrible band come down from the mountain they may take the notion to conquer the Nomes!"

"Pah! That is a foolish idea," retorted Guph, irritably, but he knew in his heart that the King was right. "The First and Foremost is a particular friend of mine, and will do us no harm. Why, when I was there, he even invited me into his house."

The General neglected to tell the King how he had been jerked into the hut of the First and Foremost by means of the brass hoop. So Roquat the Red looked at his General admiringly and said: "You are a wonderful Nome, Guph. I'm sorry I did not make you my General before. But what reward did the First and Foremost demand?"

"Nothing at all," answered Guph. "Even the Magic Belt itself could not add to his powers of sorcery. All the Phanfasms wish is to destroy the Oz people, who are good and happy. This pleasure will amply repay them for assisting us."

"When will they come?" asked Roquat, half fearfully.

"When the tunnel is completed," said the General.

"We are nearly halfway under the desert now," announced the King; "and that is fast work, because the tunnel has to be drilled through solid rock. But after we have passed the desert it will not take us long to extend the tunnel to the walls of the Emerald City."

"Well, whenever you are ready, we shall be joined by the Whimsies, the Growleywogs and the Phanfasms," said Guph; "so the conquest of Oz is assured without a doubt."

Again, the King seemed thoughtful.

"I'm almost sorry we did not undertake the conquest alone," said he. "All of these allies are dangerous people, and they may demand more than you have promised them. It might have been better to have conquered Oz without any outside assistance."

"We could not do it," said the General, positively.

"Why not, Guph?"

"You know very well. You have had one experience with the Oz people, and they defeated you."

"That was because they rolled eggs at us," replied the King, with a shudder. "My Nomes cannot stand eggs, any more than I can myself. They are poison to all who live underground."

"That is true enough," agreed Guph.

"But we might have taken the Oz people by surprise, and conquered them before they had a chance to get any eggs. Our former defeat was due to the fact that the girl Dorothy had a Yellow Hen with her. I do not know what ever became of that hen, but I believe there are no hens at all in the Land of Oz, and so there could be no eggs there."

"On the contrary," said Guph, "there are now hundreds of chickens in Oz, and they lay heaps of those dangerous eggs. I met a goshawk on my way home, and the bird informed me that he had lately been to Oz to capture and devour some of the young chickens. But they are protected by magic, so the hawk did not get a single one of them."

"That is a very bad report," said the King, nervously. "Very bad, indeed. My Nomes are willing to fight, but they simply can't face hen's eggs—and I don't blame them."

"They won't need to face them," replied Guph. "I'm afraid of eggs myself, and don't propose to take any chances of being poisoned by them. My plan is to send the Whimsies through the tunnel first, and then the Growleywogs and the Phanfasms. By the time we Nomes get there the eggs will all be used up, and we may then pursue and capture the inhabitants at our leisure."

"Perhaps you are right," returned the King, with a dismal sigh. "But I want it distinctly understood that I claim Ozma and Dorothy as my own prisoners. They are rather nice girls, and I do not intend to let any of those dreadful creatures hurt them, or make them their slaves. When I have captured them I will bring them here and transform them into china ornaments to stand on my mantle. They will look very pretty—Dorothy on one end of the mantle and Ozma on the other—and I shall take great care to see they are not broken when the maids dust them."

"Very well, your Majesty. Do what you will with the girls for all I care. Now that our plans are arranged, and we have the three most powerful bands of evil spirits in the world to assist us, let us make haste to get the tunnel finished as soon as possible."

"It will be ready in three days," promised the King, and hurried away to inspect the work and see that the Nomes kept busy.

14. How the Wizard Practiced Sorcery

"Where next?" asked the Wizard when they had left the town of Fuddlecumjig and the Sawhorse had started back along the road.

"Why, Ozma laid out this trip," replied Dorothy, "and she 'vised us to see the Rigmaroles next, and then visit the Tin Woodman."

"That sounds good," said the Wizard. "But what road do we take to get to the Rigmaroles?"

"I don't know, 'zactly," returned the little girl; "but it must be somewhere just southwest from here."

"Then why need we go way back to the crossroads?" asked the Shaggy Man. "We might save a lot of time by branching off here."

"There isn't any path," asserted Uncle Henry.

"Then we'd better go back to the signposts, and make sure of our way," decided Dorothy.

But after they had gone a short distance farther the Sawhorse, who had overheard their conversation, stopped and said: "Here is a path."

Sure enough, a dim path seemed to branch off from the road they were on, and it led across pretty green meadows and past leafy groves, straight toward the southwest.

"That looks like a good path," said Omby Amby. "Why not try it?"

"All right," answered Dorothy. "I'm anxious to see what the Rigmaroles are like, and this path ought to take us there the quickest way."

No one made any objection to this plan, so the Sawhorse turned into the path, which proved to be nearly as good as the one they had taken to get to the Fuddles. As first they passed a few retired farm houses, but soon these scattered dwellings were left behind and only the meadows and the trees were before them. But they rode along in cheerful contentment, and Aunt Em got into an argument with Billina about the proper way to raise chickens.

"I do not care to contradict you," said the Yellow Hen, with dignity, "but I have an idea I know more about chickens than human beings do."

"Pshaw!" replied Aunt Em. "I've raised chickens for nearly forty years, Billina, and I know you've got to starve 'em to make 'em lay lots of eggs, and stuff 'em if you want good broilers."

"Broilers!" exclaimed Billina, in horror. "Broil my chickens!"

"Why, that's what they're for, ain't it?" asked Aunt Em, astonished.

"No, Aunt, not in Oz," said Dorothy. "People do not eat chickens here. You see, Billina was the first hen that was ever seen in this country, and I brought her here myself. Everybody liked her an' respected her, so the Oz people wouldn't any more eat her chickens than they would eat Billina."

"Well, I declare," gasped Aunt Em. "How about the eggs?"

"Oh, if we have more eggs than we want to hatch, we allow people to eat them," said Billina. "Indeed, I am very glad the Oz folks like our eggs, for otherwise they would spoil."

"This certainly is a queer country," sighed Aunt Em.

"Excuse me," called the Sawhorse, "the path has ended and I'd like to know which way to go."

They looked around and sure enough there was no path to be seen.

"Well," said Dorothy, "we're going southwest, and it seems just as easy to follow that direction without a path as with one."

"Certainly," answered the Sawhorse. "It is not hard to draw the wagon over the meadow. I only want to know where to go."

"There's a forest over there across the prairie," said the Wizard, "and it lies in the direction we are going. Make straight for the forest, Sawhorse, and you're bound to go right."

So the wooden animal trotted on again and the meadow grass was so soft under the wheels that it made easy riding. But Dorothy was a little uneasy at losing the path, because now there was nothing to guide them.

No houses were to be seen at all, so they could not ask their way of any farmer; and although the Land of Oz was always beautiful, wherever one might go, this part of the country was strange to all the party.

"Perhaps we're lost," suggested Aunt Em, after they had proceeded quite a way in silence.

"Never mind," said the Shaggy Man; "I've been lost many a time—and so has Dorothy—and we've always been found again."

"But we may get hungry," remarked Omby Amby. "That is the worst of getting lost in a place where there are no houses near."

"We had a good dinner at the Fuddle town," said Uncle Henry, "and that will keep us from starving to death for a long time."

"No one ever starved to death in Oz," declared Dorothy, positively; "but people may get pretty hungry sometimes."

The Wizard said nothing, and he did not seem especially anxious. The Sawhorse was trotting along briskly, yet the forest seemed farther away than they had thought when they first saw it. So it was nearly sundown when they finally came to the trees; but now they found themselves in a most beautiful spot, the wide-spreading trees being covered with flowering vines and having soft mosses underneath them. "This will be a good place to camp," said the Wizard, as the Sawhorse stopped for further instructions.

"Camp!" they all echoed.

"Certainly," asserted the Wizard. "It will be dark before very long and we cannot travel through this forest at night. So let us make a camp here, and have some supper, and sleep until daylight comes again."

They all looked at the little man in astonishment, and Aunt Em said, with a sniff:

"A pretty camp we'll have, I must say! I suppose you intend us to sleep under the wagon."

"And chew grass for our supper," added the Shaggy Man, laughing.

But Dorothy seemed to have no doubts and was quite cheerful

"It's lucky we have the wonderful Wizard with us," she said; "because he can do 'most anything he wants to."

"Oh, yes; I forgot we had a Wizard," said Uncle Henry, looking at the little man curiously.

"I didn't," chirped Billina, contentedly.

The Wizard smiled and climbed out of the wagon, and all the others followed him.

"In order to camp," said he, "the first thing we need is tents. Will some one please lend me a handkerchief?"

The Shaggy Man offered him one, and Aunt Em another. He took them both and laid them carefully upon the grass near to the edge of the forest. Then he laid his own handkerchief down, too, and standing a little back from them he waved his left hand toward the handkerchiefs and said: "Tents of canvas, white as snow, Let me see how fast you grow!"

Then, lo and behold! the handkerchiefs became tiny tents, and as the travelers looked at them the tents grew bigger and bigger until in a few minutes each one was large enough to contain the entire party.

"This," said the Wizard, pointing to the first tent, "is for the accommodation of the ladies. Dorothy, you and your Aunt may step inside and take off your things."

Every one ran to look inside the tent, and they saw two pretty white beds, all ready for Dorothy and Aunt Em, and a silver roost for Billina. Rugs were spread upon the grassy floor and some camp chairs and a table completed the furniture.

"Well, well, well! This beats anything I ever saw or heard of!" exclaimed Aunt Em, and she glanced at the Wizard almost fearfully, as if he might be dangerous because of his great powers.

"Oh, Mr. Wizard! How did you manage to do it?" asked Dorothy.

"It's a trick Glinda the Sorceress taught me, and it is much better magic than I used to practice in Omaha, or when I first came to Oz," he answered. "When the good Glinda found I was to live in the Emerald City always, she promised to help me, because she said the Wizard of Oz ought really to be a clever Wizard, and not a humbug. So we have been much together and I am learning so fast that I expect to be able to accomplish some really wonderful things in time."

"You've done it now!" declared Dorothy. "These tents are just wonderful!"

"But come and see the men's tent," said the Wizard. So they went to the second tent, which had shaggy edges because it has been made from the Shaggy Man's handkerchief, and found that completely furnished also. It contained four neat beds for Uncle Henry, Omby Amby, the Shaggy Man and the Wizard. Also there was a soft rug for Toto to lie upon.

"The third tent," explained the Wizard, "is our dining room and kitchen."

They visited that next, and found a table and dishes in the dining tent, with plenty of those things necessary to use in cooking. The Wizard carried out a big kettle and set it swinging on a crossbar before the tent. While he was doing this Omby Amby and the Shaggy Man brought a supply of twigs from the forest and then they built a fire underneath the kettle.

"Now, Dorothy," said the Wizard, smiling, "I expect you to cook our supper."

"But there is nothing in the kettle," she cried.

"Are you sure?" inquired the Wizard.

"I didn't see anything put in, and I'm almost sure it was empty when you brought it out," she replied.

"Nevertheless," said the little man, winking slyly at Uncle Henry, "you will do well to watch our supper, my dear, and see that it doesn't boil over."

Then the men took some pails and went into the forest to search for a spring of water, and while they were gone Aunt Em said to Dorothy: "I believe the Wizard is fooling us. I saw the kettle myself, and when he hung it over the fire there wasn't a thing in it but air."

"Don't worry," remarked Billina, confidently, as she nestled in the grass before the fire. "You'll find something in the kettle when it's taken off—and it won't be poor, innocent chickens, either."

"Your hen has very bad manners, Dorothy," said Aunt Em, looking somewhat disdainfully at Billina. "It seems too bad she ever learned how to talk."

There might have been another unpleasant quarrel between Aunt Em and Billina had not the men returned just then with their pails filled with clear, sparkling water. The Wizard told Dorothy that she was a good cook and he believed their supper was ready.

So Uncle Henry lifted the kettle from the fire and poured its contents into a big platter which the Wizard held for him. The platter was fairly heaped with a fine stew, smoking hot, with

many kinds of vegetables and dumplings and a rich, delicious gravy.

The Wizard triumphantly placed the platter upon the table in the dining tent and then they all sat down in camp chairs to the feast.

There were several other dishes on the table, all carefully covered, and when the time came to remove these covers they found bread and butter, cakes, cheese, pickles and fruits— including some of the luscious strawberries of Oz.

No one ventured to ask a question as to how these things came there. They contented themselves by eating heartily the good things provided, and Toto and Billina had their full share, you may be sure. After the meal was over, Aunt Em whispered to Dorothy: "That may have been magic food, my dear, and for that reason perhaps it won't be very nourishing; but I'm willing to say it tasted as good as anything I ever et." Then she added, in a louder voice: "Who's going to do the dishes?"

"No one, madam," answered the Wizard. "The dishes have 'done' themselves."

"La sakes!" ejaculated the good lady, holding up her hands in amazement. For, sure enough, when she looked at the dishes they had a moment before left upon the table, she found them all washed and dried and piled up into neat stacks.

15. How Dorothy Happened to Get Lost

It was a beautiful evening, so they drew their camp chairs in a circle before one of the tents and began to tell stories to amuse themselves and pass away the time before they went to bed.

Pretty soon a zebra was seen coming out of the forest, and he trotted straight up to them and said politely: "Good evening, people."

The zebra was a sleek little animal and had a slender head, a stubby mane and a paint-brush tail—very like a donkey's. His neatly shaped white body was covered with regular bars of dark brown, and his hoofs were delicate as those of a deer.

"Good evening, friend Zebra," said Omby Amby, in reply to the creature's greeting. "Can we do anything for you?"

"Yes," answered the zebra. "I should like you to settle a dispute that has long been a bother to me, as to whether there is more water or land in the world."

"Who are you disputing with?" asked the Wizard.

"With a soft-shell crab," said the zebra. "He lives in a pool where I go to drink every day, and he is a very impertinent crab, I assure you. I have told him many times that the land is much greater in extent than the water, but he will not be convinced. Even this very evening, when I told him he was an insignificant creature who lived in a small pool, he asserted that the water was greater and more important than the land. So, seeing your camp, I decided to ask you to settle the dispute for once and all, that I may not be further annoyed by this ignorant crab."

When they had listened to this explanation Dorothy inquired:

"Where is the soft-shell crab?"

"Not far away," replied the zebra. "If you will agree to judge between us I will run and get him."

Run along, then," said the little girl.

So the animal pranced into the forest and soon came trotting back to them. When he drew near they found a soft-shell crab clinging fast to the stiff hair of the zebra's head, where it held on by one claw.

Now then, Mr. Crab," said the zebra, "here are the people I told you about; and they know more than you do, who lives in a pool, and more than I do, who lives in a forest. For they have been travelers all over the world, and know every part of it."

There is more of the world than Oz," declared the crab, in a stubborn voice.

That is true," said Dorothy; "but I used to live in Kansas, in the United States, and I've been to California and to Australia and so has Uncle Henry."

For my part," added the Shaggy Man, "I've been to Mexico and Boston and many other foreign countries."

And I," said the Wizard, "have been to Europe and Ireland."

So you see," continued the zebra, addressing the crab, "here are people of real consequence, who know what they are talking about."

Then they know there's more water in the world than there is land," asserted the crab, in a shrill, petulant voice.

They know you are wrong to make such an absurd statement, and they will probably think you are a lobster instead of a crab," retorted the animal.

At this taunt the crab reached out its other claw and seized the zebra's ear, and the creature gave a cry of pain and began prancing up and down, trying to shake off the crab, which clung fast.

Stop pinching!" cried the zebra. "You promised not to pinch if I would carry you here!"

And you promised to treat me respectfully," said the crab, letting go the ear.

Well, haven't I?" demanded the zebra.

No; you called me a lobster," said the crab.

Ladies and gentlemen," continued the zebra, "please pardon my poor friend, because he is ignorant and stupid, and does not understand. Also the pinch of his claw is very annoying. So pray tell him that the world contains more land than water, and when he has heard your judgment I will carry him back and dump him into his pool, where I hope he will be more modest in the future."

But we cannot tell him that," said Dorothy, gravely, "because it would not be true."

What!" exclaimed the zebra, in astonishment; "do I hear you right?"

The soft-shell crab is correct," declared the Wizard. "There is considerably more water than there is land in the world."

"Impossible!" protested the zebra. "Why, I can run for days upon the land, and find but little water."

"Did you ever see an ocean?" asked Dorothy.

"Never," admitted the zebra. "There is no such thing as an ocean in the Land of Oz."

"Well, there are several oceans in the world," said Dorothy, "and people sail in ships upon these oceans for weeks and weeks, and never see a bit of land at all. And the joggerfys will tell you that all the oceans put together are bigger than all the land put together."

At this the crab began laughing in queer chuckles that reminded Dorothy of the way Billina sometimes cackled.

"NOW will you give up, Mr. Zebra?" it cried, jeeringly; "now will you give up?"

The zebra seemed much humbled.

"Of course I cannot read geographys," he said.

"You could take one of the Wizard's School Pills," suggested Billina, "and that would make you learned and wise without studying."

The crab began laughing again, which so provoked the zebra that he tried to shake the little creature off. This resulted in more ear-pinching, and finally Dorothy told them that if they could not behave they must go back to the forest.

"I'm sorry I asked you to decide this question," said the zebra, crossly. "So long as neither of us could prove we were right we quite enjoyed the dispute; but now I can never drink at that pool again without the soft-shell crab laughing at me. So I must find another drinking place."

"Do! Do, you ignoramus!" shouted the crab, as loudly as his little voice would carry. "Rile some other pool with your clumsy hoofs, and let your betters alone after this!"

Then the zebra trotted back to the forest, bearing the crab with him, and disappeared amid the gloom of the trees. And as it was now getting dark the travelers said good night to one another and went to bed.

Dorothy awoke just as the light was beginning to get strong next morning, and not caring to sleep any later she quietly got out of bed, dressed herself, and left the tent where Aunt Em was yet peacefully slumbering.

Outside she noticed Billina busily pecking around to secure bugs or other food for breakfast, but none of the men in the other tent seemed awake. So the little girl decided to take a walk in the woods and try to discover some path or road that they might follow when they again started upon their journey.

She had reached the edge of the forest when the Yellow Hen came fluttering along and asked where she was going.

"Just to take a walk, Billina; and maybe I'll find some path," said Dorothy.

"Then I'll go along," decided Billina, and scarcely had she spoken when Toto ran up and joined them.

Toto and the Yellow Hen had become quite friendly by this time, although at first they did not get along well together. Billina had been rather suspicious of dogs, and Toto had had an idea that it was every dog's duty to chase a hen on sight. But Dorothy had talked to them and scolded them for not being agreeable to one another until they grew better acquainted and became friends.

I won't say they loved each other dearly, but at least they had stopped quarreling and now managed to get on together very well.

The day was growing lighter every minute and driving the black shadows out of the forest; so Dorothy found it very pleasant walking under the trees. She went some distance in one direction, but not finding a path, presently turned in a different direction. There was no path here, either, although she advanced quite a way into the forest, winding here and there among the trees and peering through the bushes in an endeavor to find some beaten track.

"I think we'd better go back," suggested the Yellow Hen, after a time. "The people will all be up by this time and breakfast will be ready."

"Very well," agreed Dorothy. "Let's see—the camp must be over this way."

She had probably made a mistake about that, for after they had gone far enough to have reached the camp they still found themselves in the thick of the woods. So the little girl stopped short and looked around her, and Toto glanced up into her face with his bright little eyes and wagged his tail as if he knew something was wrong. He couldn't tell much about direction himself, because he had spent his time prowling among the bushes and running here and there; nor had Billina paid much attention to where they were going, being interested in picking bugs from the moss as they passed along. The Yellow Hen now turned one eye up toward the little girl and asked: "Have you forgotten where the camp is, Dorothy?"

"Yes," she admitted; "have you, Billina?"

"I didn't try to remember," returned Billina. "I'd no idea you would get lost, Dorothy."

"It's the thing we don't expect, Billina, that usually happens," observed the girl, thoughtfully. "But it's no use standing here. Let's go in that direction," pointing a finger at random. "It may be we'll get out of the forest over there."

So on they went again, but this way the trees were closer together, and the vines were so tangled that often they tripped Dorothy up.

Suddenly a voice cried sharply: "Halt!"

At first, Dorothy could see nothing, although she looked around very carefully. But Billina exclaimed: "Well, I declare!"

"What is it?" asked the little girl: for Toto began barking at something, and following his gaze she discovered what it was.

A row of spoons had surrounded the three, and these spoons stood straight up on their handles and carried swords and muskets. Their faces were outlined in the polished bowls and they looked very stern and severe.

Dorothy laughed at the queer things.

"Who are you?" she asked.

"We're the Spoon Brigade," said one.

"In the service of his Majesty King Kleaver," said another.

"And you are our prisoners," said a third.

Dorothy sat down on an old stump and looked at them, her eyes twinkling with amusement.

"What would happen," she inquired, "if I should set my dog on your Brigade?"

"He would die," replied one of the spoons, sharply. "One shot from our deadly muskets would kill him, big as he is."

"Don't risk it, Dorothy," advised the Yellow Hen. "Remember this is a fairy country, yet none of us three happens to be a fairy."

Dorothy grew sober at this.

"P'raps you're right, Billina," she answered. "But how funny it is to be captured by a lot of spoons!"

"I do not see anything very funny about it," declared a spoon. "We're the regular military brigade of the kingdom."

"What kingdom?" she asked.

"Utensia," said he.

"I never heard of it before," asserted Dorothy. Then she added thoughtfully, "I don't believe Ozma ever heard of Utensia, either. Tell me, are you not subjects of Ozma of Oz?"

"We have never heard of her," retorted a spoon. "We are subjects of King Kleaver, and obey only his orders, which are to bring all prisoners to him as soon as they are captured. So step lively, my girl, and march with us, or we may be tempted to cut off a few of your toes with our swords."

This threat made Dorothy laugh again. She did not believe she was in any danger; but here was a new and interesting adventure, so she was willing to be taken to Utensia that she might see what King Kleaver's kingdom was like.

16. How Dorothy Visited Utensia

There must have been from six to eight dozen spoons in the Brigade, and they marched away in the shape of a hollow square with Dorothy, Billina and Toto in the center of the square. Before they had gone very far Toto knocked over one of the spoons by wagging his tail, and then the Captain of the Spoons told the little dog to be more careful, or he would be punished. So Toto was careful, and the Spoon Brigade moved along with astonishing swiftness, while Dorothy really had to walk fast to keep up with it.

By and by they left the woods and entered a big clearing, in which was the Kingdom of Utensia.

Standing all around the clearing were a good many cookstoves, ranges and grills, of all sizes and shapes, and besides these there were several kitchen cabinets and cupboards and a few kitchen tables. These things were crowded with utensils of all sorts: frying pans, sauce pans, kettles, forks, knives, basting and soup spoons, nutmeg graters, sifters, colanders, meat saws, flat irons, rolling pins and many other things of a like nature.

When the Spoon Brigade appeared with the prisoners a wild shout arose and many of the utensils hopped off their stoves or their benches and ran crowding around Dorothy and the hen and the dog.

"Stand back!" cried the Captain, sternly, and he led his captives through the curious throng until they came before a big range that stood in the center of the clearing. Beside this range was a butcher block upon which lay a great cleaver with a keen edge. It rested upon the flat of its back, its legs were crossed and it was smoking a long pipe.

"Wake up, your Majesty," said the Captain. "Here are prisoners."

Hearing this, King Kleaver sat up and looked at Dorothy sharply.

"Gristle and fat!" he cried. "Where did this girl come from?"

"I found her in the forest and brought her here a prisoner," replied the Captain.

"Why did you do that?" inquired the King, puffing his pipe lazily.

"To create some excitement," the Captain answered. "It is so quiet here that we are all getting rusty for want of amusement. For my part, I prefer to see stirring times."

"Naturally," returned the cleaver, with a nod. "I have always said, Captain, without a bit of irony, that you are a sterling officer and a solid citizen, bowled and polished to a degree. But what do you expect me to do with these prisoners?"

"That is for you to decide," declared the Captain. "You are the King."

"To be sure; to be sure," muttered the cleaver, musingly. "As you say, we have had dull times since the steel and grindstone eloped and left us. Command my Counselors and the Royal Courtiers to attend me, as well as the High Priest and the Judge. We'll then decide what can be done."

The Captain saluted and retired and Dorothy sat down on an overturned kettle and asked: "Have you anything to eat in your kingdom?"

"Here! Get up! Get off from me!" cried a faint voice, at which his Majesty the cleaver said: "Excuse me, but you're sitting on my friend the Ten-quart Kettle."

Dorothy at once arose, and the kettle turned right side up and looked at her reproachfully.

"I'm a friend of the King, so no one dares sit on me," said he.

"I'd prefer a chair, anyway," she replied.

"Sit on that hearth," commanded the King.

So Dorothy sat on the hearth-shelf of the big range, and the subjects of Utensia began to gather around in a large and inquisitive throng. Toto lay at Dorothy's feet and Billina flew upon the range, which had no fire in it, and perched there as comfortably as she could.

When all the Counselors and Courtiers had assembled—and these seemed to include most of the inhabitants of the kingdom—the King rapped on the block for order and said: "Friends and Fellow Utensils! Our worthy Commander of the Spoon Brigade, Captain Dipp, has captured the three prisoners you see before you and brought them here for—for—I don't know what for. So I ask your advice how to act in this matter, and what fate I should mete out to these captives. Judge Sifter, stand on my right. It is your business to sift this affair to the bottom. High Priest Colender, stand on my left and see that no one testifies falsely in this matter."

As these two officials took their places, Dorothy asked: "Why is the colander the High Priest?"

"He's the holiest thing we have in the kingdom," replied King Kleaver.

"Except me," said a sieve. "I'm the whole thing when it comes to holes."

"What we need," remarked the King, rebukingly, "is a wireless sieve. I must speak to Marconi about it. These old-fashioned sieves talk too much. Now, it is the duty of the King's Counselors to counsel the King at all times of emergency, so I beg you to speak out and advise me what to do with these prisoners."

"I demand that they be killed several times, until they are dead!" shouted a pepperbox, hopping around very excitedly.

"Compose yourself, Mr. Paprica," advised the King. "Your remarks are piquant and highly-seasoned, but you need a scattering of commonsense. It is only necessary to kill a person once to make him dead; but I do not see that it is necessary to kill this little girl at all."

"I don't, either," said Dorothy.

"Pardon me, but you are not expected to advise me in this matter," replied King Kleaver.

"Why not?" asked Dorothy.

"You might be prejudiced in your own favor, and so mislead us," he said. "Now then, good subjects, who speaks next?"

"I'd like to smooth this thing over, in some way," said a flatiron, earnestly. "We are supposed to be useful to mankind, you know."

"But the girl isn't mankind! She's womankind!" yelled a corkscrew.

"What do you know about it?" inquired the King.

"I'm a lawyer," said the corkscrew, proudly. "I am accustomed to appear at the bar."

"But you're crooked," retorted the King, "and that debars you. You may be a corking good lawyer, Mr. Popp, but I must ask you to withdraw your remarks."

"Very well," said the corkscrew, sadly; "I see I haven't any pull at this court."

"Permit me," continued the flatiron, "to press my suit, your Majesty. I do not wish to gloss over any fault the prisoner may have committed, if such a fault exists; but we owe her some consideration, and that's flat!"

"I'd like to hear from Prince Karver," said the King.

At this a stately carvingknife stepped forward and bowed.

"The Captain was wrong to bring this girl here, and she was wrong to come," he said. "But now that the foolish deed is done let us all prove our mettle and have a slashing good time."

"That's it! that's it!" screamed a fat choppingknife. "We'll make mincemeat of the girl and hash of the chicken and sausage of the dog!"

There was a shout of approval at this and the King had to rap again for order.

"Gentlemen, gentlemen!" he said, "your remarks are somewhat cutting and rather disjointed, as might be expected from such acute intellects. But you give me no reasons for your demands."

"See here, Kleaver; you make me tired," said a saucepan, strutting before the King very impudently. "You're about the worst King that ever reigned in Utensia, and that's saying a good deal. Why don't you run things yourself, instead of asking everybody's advice, like the big, clumsy idiot you are?"

The King sighed.

"I wish there wasn't a saucepan in my kingdom," he said. "You fellows are always stewing, over something, and every once in a while you slop over and make a mess of it. Go hang yourself, sir—by the handle—and don't let me hear from you again."

Dorothy was much shocked by the dreadful language the utensils employed, and she thought that they must have had very little proper training. So she said, addressing the King, who seemed very unfit to rule his turbulent subjects: "I wish you'd decide my fate right away. I can't stay here all day, trying to find out what you're going to do with me."

"This thing is becoming a regular broil, and it's time I took part in it," observed a big gridiron, coming forward.

"What I'd like to know," said a can-opener, in a shrill voice, "is why the little girl came to our forest anyhow and why she intruded upon Captain Dipp—who ought to be called Dippy—and who she is, and where she came from, and where she is going, and why and wherefore and therefore and when."

"I'm sorry to see, Sir Jabber," remarked the King to the can-opener, "that you have such a prying disposition. As a matter of fact, all the things you mention are none of our business."

Having said this the King relighted his pipe, which had gone out.

"Tell me, please, what IS our business?" inquired a potato-masher, winking at Dorothy somewhat impertinently. "I'm fond of little girls, myself, and it seems to me she has as much right to wander in the forest as we have."

"Who accuses the little girl, anyway?" inquired a rolling-pin. "What has she done?"

"I don't know," said the King. "What has she done, Captain Dipp?"

"That's the trouble, your Majesty. She hasn't done anything," replied the Captain.

"What do you want me to do?" asked Dorothy.

This question seemed to puzzle them all. Finally, a chafingdish, exclaimed irritably: "If no one can throw any light on this subject you must excuse me if I go out."

At this, a big kitchen fork pricked up its ears and said in a tiny voice: "Let's hear from Judge Sifter."

"That's proper," returned the King.

So Judge Sifter turned around slowly several times and then said: "We have nothing against the girl except the stove-hearth upon which she sits. Therefore I order her instantly discharged."

"Discharged!" cried Dorothy. "Why, I never was discharged in my life, and I don't intend to be. If it's all the same to you, I'll resign."

"It's all the same," declared the King. "You are free—you and your companions—and may go wherever you like."

"Thank you," said the little girl. "But haven't you anything to eat in your kingdom? I'm hungry."

"Go into the woods and pick blackberries," advised the King, lying down upon his back again and preparing to go to sleep. "There isn't a morsel to eat in all Utensia, that I know of."

So Dorothy jumped up and said:

"Come on, Toto and Billina. If we can't find the camp, we may find some blackberries."

The utensils drew back and allowed them to pass without protest, although Captain Dipp marched the Spoon Brigade in close order after them until they had reached the edge of the clearing.

There the spoons halted; but Dorothy and her companions entered the forest again and began searching diligently for a way back to the camp, that they might rejoin their party.

17. How They Came to Bunbury

Wandering through the woods, without knowing where you are going or what adventure you are about to meet next, is not as pleasant as one might think. The woods are always beautiful and impressive, and if you are not worried or hungry you may enjoy them immensely; but Dorothy was worried and hungry that morning, so she paid little attention to the beauties of the forest, and hurried along as fast as she could go. She tried to keep in one direction and not circle around, but she was not at all sure that the direction she had chosen would lead her to the camp.

By and by, to her great joy, she came upon a path. It ran to the right and to the left, being lost in the trees in both directions, and just before her, upon a big oak, were fastened two signs, with arms pointing both ways. One sign read:

TAKE THE OTHER ROAD TO BUNBURY

and the second sign read:

TAKE THE OTHER ROAD TO BUNNYBURY

"Well!" exclaimed Billina, eyeing the signs, "this looks as if we were getting back to civilization again."

"I'm not sure about the civil'zation, dear," replied the little girl; "but it looks as if we might get SOMEWHERE, and that's a big relief, anyhow."

"Which path shall we take?" inquired the Yellow Hen.

Dorothy stared at the signs thoughtfully.

"Bunbury sounds like something to eat," she said. "Let's go there."

"It's all the same to me," replied Billina. She had picked up enough bugs and insects from the moss as she went along to satisfy her own hunger, but the hen knew Dorothy could not eat bugs; nor could Toto.

The path to Bunbury seemed little traveled, but it was distinct enough and ran through the trees in a zigzag course until it finally led them to an open space filled with the queerest houses Dorothy had ever seen. They were all made of crackers laid out in tiny squares, and were of many pretty and ornamental shapes, having balconies and porches with posts of bread-sticks and roofs shingled with wafer-crackers.

There were walks of bread-crusts leading from house to house and forming streets, and the place seemed to have many inhabitants.

When Dorothy, followed by Billina and Toto, entered the place, they found people walking the streets or assembled in groups talking together, or sitting upon the porches and balconies.

And what funny people they were!

Men, women and children were all made of buns and bread. Some were thin and others fat; some were white, some light brown and some very dark of complexion. A few of the buns, which seemed to form the more important class of the people, were neatly frosted. Some had raisins for eyes and currant buttons on their clothes; others had eyes of cloves and legs of stick cinnamon, and many wore hats and bonnets frosted pink and green.

There was something of a commotion in Bunbury when the strangers suddenly appeared among them. Women caught up their children and hurried into their houses, shutting the cracker doors carefully behind them. Some men ran so hastily that they tumbled over one another, while others, more brave, assembled in a group and faced the intruders defiantly.

Dorothy at once realized that she must act with caution in order not to frighten these shy people, who were evidently unused to the presence of strangers. There was a delightful fragrant odor of fresh bread in the town, and this made the little girl more hungry than ever. She told Toto and Billina to stay back while she slowly advanced toward the group that stood silently awaiting her.

"You must 'scuse me for coming unexpected," she said, softly, "but I really didn't know I was coming here until I arrived. I was lost in the woods, you know, and I'm as hungry as anything."

"Hungry!" they murmured, in a horrified chorus.

"Yes; I haven't had anything to eat since last night's supper," she exclaimed. "Are there any eatables in Bunbury?"

They looked at one another undecidedly, and then one portly bun man, who seemed a person of consequence, stepped forward and said: "Little girl, to be frank with you, we are all eatables. Everything in Bunbury is eatable to ravenous human creatures like you. But it is to escape being eaten and destroyed that we have secluded ourselves in this out-of-the-way place, and there is neither right nor justice in your coming here to feed upon us."

Dorothy looked at him longingly.

"You're bread, aren't you?" she asked.

"Yes; bread and butter. The butter is inside me, so it won't melt and run. I do the running myself."

At this joke all the others burst into a chorus of laughter, and Dorothy thought they couldn't be much afraid if they could laugh like that.

"Couldn't I eat something besides people?" she asked. "Couldn't I eat just one house, or a side-walk or something? I wouldn't mind much what it was, you know."

"This is not a public bakery, child," replied the man, sternly. "It's private property."

"I know Mr.—Mr.—"

"My name is C. Bunn, Esquire," said the man. "'C' stands for Cinnamon, and this place is called after my family, which is the most aristocratic in the town."

"Oh, I don't know about that," objected another of the queer people. "The Grahams and the Browns and Whites are all excellent families, and there is none better of their kind. I'm a Boston Brown, myself."

"I admit you are all desirable citizens," said Mr. Bunn rather stiffly; "but the fact remains that our town is called Bunbury."

"'Scuse me," interrupted Dorothy; "but I'm getting hungrier every minute. Now, if you're polite and kind, as I'm sure you ought to be, you'll let me eat SOMETHING. There's so much to eat here that you will never miss it."

Then a big, puffed-up man, of a delicate brown color, stepped forward and said: "I think it would be a shame to send this child away hungry, especially as she agrees to eat whatever we can spare and not touch our people."

"So do I, Pop," replied a Roll who stood near.

"What, then, do you suggest, Mr. Over?" inquired Mr. Bunn.

"Why, I'll let her eat my back fence, if she wants to. It's made of waffles, and they're very crisp and nice."

"She may also eat my wheelbarrow," added a pleasant looking Muffin. "It's made of nabiscos with a zuzu wheel."

"Very good; very good," remarked Mr. Bunn. "That is certainly very kind of you. Go with Pop Over and Mr. Muffin, little girl, and they will feed you."

"Thank you very much," said Dorothy, gratefully. "May I bring my dog Toto, and the Yellow Hen? They're hungry, too."

"Will you make them behave?" asked the Muffin.

"Of course," promised Dorothy.

"Then come along," said Pop Over.

So Dorothy and Billina and Toto walked up the street and the people seemed no longer to be at all afraid of them. Mr. Muffin's house came first, and as his wheelbarrow stood in the front yard the little girl ate that first. It didn't seem very fresh, but she was so hungry that she was not particular. Toto ate some, too, while Billina picked up the crumbs.

While the strangers were engaged in eating, many of the people came and stood in the street curiously watching them. Dorothy noticed six roguish looking brown children standing all in a row, and she asked: "Who are you, little ones?"

"We're the Graham Gems," replied one; "and we're all twins."

"I wonder if your mother could spare one or two of you?" asked Billina, who decided that they were fresh baked; but at this dangerous question the six little gems ran away as fast as they could go.

"You musn't say such things, Billina," said Dorothy, reprovingly. "Now let's go into Pop Over's back yard and get the waffles."

"I sort of hate to let that fence go," remarked Mr. Over, nervously, as they walked toward his house. "The neighbors back of us are Soda Biscuits, and I don't care to mix with them."

"But I'm hungry yet," declared the girl. "That wheelbarrow wasn't very big."

"I've got a shortcake piano, but none of my family can play on it," he said, reflectively. "Suppose you eat that."

"All right," said Dorothy; "I don't mind. Anything to be accommodating."

So Mr. Over led her into the house, where she ate the piano, which was of an excellent flavor.

"Is there anything to drink here?" she asked.

"Yes; I've a milk pump and a water pump; which will you have?" he asked.

"I guess I'll try 'em both," said Dorothy.

So Mr. Over called to his wife, who brought into the yard a pail made of some kind of baked dough, and Dorothy pumped the pail full of cool, sweet milk and drank it eagerly.

The wife of Pop Over was several shades darker than her husband.

"Aren't you overdone?" the little girl asked her.

"No indeed," answered the woman. "I'm neither overdone nor done over; I'm just Mrs. Over, and I'm the President of the Bunbury Breakfast Band."

Dorothy thanked them for their hospitality and went away. At the gate Mr. Cinnamon Bunn met her and said he would show her around the town. "We have some very interesting inhabitants," he remarked, walking stiffly beside her on his stick-cinnamon legs; "and all of us who are in good health are well bred. If you are no longer hungry we will call upon a few of the most important citizens."

Toto and Billina followed behind them, behaving very well, and a little way down the street they came to a handsome residence where Aunt Sally Lunn lived. The old lady was glad to meet the little girl and gave her a slice of white bread and butter which had been used as a door-mat. It was almost fresh and tasted better than anything Dorothy had eaten in the town.

"Where do you get the butter?" she inquired.

"We dig it out of the ground, which, as you may have observed, is all flour and meal," replied Mr. Bunn. "There is a butter mine just at the opposite side of the village. The trees which you see here are all doughleanders and doughderas, and in the season we get quite a crop of dough-nuts off them."

"I should think the flour would blow around and get into your eyes," said Dorothy.

"No," said he; "we are bothered with cracker dust sometimes, but never with flour."

Then he took her to see Johnny Cake, a cheerful old gentleman who lived near by.

"I suppose you've heard of me," said old Johnny, with an air of pride. "I'm a great favorite all over the world."

"Aren't you rather yellow?" asked Dorothy, looking at him critically.

"Maybe, child. But don't think I'm bilious, for I was never in better health in my life," replied the old gentleman. "If anything ailed me, I'd willingly acknowledge the corn."

"Johnny's a trifle stale," said Mr. Bunn, as they went away; "but he's a good mixer and never gets cross-grained. I will now take you to call upon some of my own relatives." They visited the Sugar Bunns, the Currant Bunns and the Spanish Bunns, the latter having a decidedly foreign appearance. Then they saw the French Rolls, who were very polite to them, and made a brief call upon the Parker H. Rolls, who seemed a bit proud and overbearing.

"But they're not as stuck up as the Frosted Jumbles," declared Mr. Bunn, "who are people I really can't abide. I don't like to be suspicious or talk scandal, but sometimes I think the Jumbles have too much baking powder in them."

Just then a dreadful scream was heard, and Dorothy turned hastily around to find a scene of great excitement a little way down the street. The people were crowding around Toto and throwing at him everything they could find at hand. They pelted the little dog with hard-tack, crackers, and even articles of furniture which were hard baked and heavy enough for missiles.

Toto howeled a little as the assortment of bake stuff struck him, but he stood still, with head bowed and tail between his legs until Dorothy ran up and inquired what the matter was.

"Matter!" cried a rye loafer, indignantly, "why the horrid beast has eaten three of our dear Crumpets, and is now devouring a Salt-rising Biscuit!"

"Oh, Toto! How could you?" exclaimed Dorothy, much distressed.

Toto's mouth was full of his salt-rising victim; so he only whined and wagged his tail. But Billina, who had flown to the top of a cracker house to be in a safe place, called out: "Don't blame him, Dorothy; the Crumpets dared him to do it."

"Yes, and you pecked out the eyes of a Raisin Bunn—one of our best citizens!" shouted a bread pudding, shaking its fist at the Yellow Hen.

"What's that! What's that?" wailed Mr. Cinnamon Bunn, who had now joined them. "Oh, what a misfortune—what a terrible misfortune!"

"See here," said Dorothy, determined to defend her pets, "I think we've treated you all pretty well, seeing you're eatables an' reg'lar food for us. I've been kind to you and eaten your old wheelbarrows and pianos and rubbish, an' not said a word. But Toto and Billina can't be 'spected to go hungry when the town's full of good things they like to eat, 'cause they can't understand your stingy ways as I do."

"You must leave here at once!" said Mr. Bunn, sternly.

"Suppose we won't go?" said Dorothy, who was now much provoked.

"Then," said he, "we will put you into the great ovens where we are made, and bake you."

Dorothy gazed around and saw threatening looks upon the faces of all. She had not noticed any ovens in the town, but they might be there, nevertheless, for some of the inhabitants seemed very fresh. So she decided to go, and calling to Toto and Billina to follow her she marched up the street with as much dignity as possible, considering that she was followed by the hoots and cries of the buns and biscuits and other bake stuff.

18. How Ozma Looked into the Magic Picture

Princess Ozma was a very busy little ruler, for she looked carefully after the comfort and welfare of her people and tried to make them happy. If any quarrels arose she decided them justly; if any one needed counsel or advice she was ready and willing to listen to them.

For a day or two after Dorothy and her companions had started on their trip, Ozma was occupied with the affairs of her kingdom. Then she began to think of some manner of occupation for Uncle Henry and Aunt Em that would be light and easy and yet give the old people something to do.

She soon decided to make Uncle Henry the Keeper of the Jewels, for some one really was needed to count and look after the bins and barrels of emeralds, diamonds, rubies and other precious stones that were in the Royal Storehouses. That would keep Uncle Henry busy enough, but it was harder to find something for Aunt Em to do. The palace was full of servants, so there was no detail of housework that Aunt Em could look after.

While Ozma sat in her pretty room engaged in thought she happened to glance at her Magic Picture.

This was one of the most important treasures in all the Land of Oz. It was a large picture, set in a beautiful gold frame, and it hung in a prominent place upon a wall of Ozma's private room.

Usually this picture seemed merely a country scene, but whenever Ozma looked at it and wished to know what any of her friends or acquaintances were doing, the magic of this wonderful picture was straightaway disclosed. For the country scene would gradually fade away and in its place would appear the likeness of the person or persons Ozma might wish to see, surrounded by the actual scenes in which they were then placed. In this way the Princess could view any part of the world she wished, and watch the actions of any one in whom she was interested.

Ozma had often seen Dorothy in her Kansas home by this means, and now, having a little leisure, she expressed a desire to see her little friend again. It was while the travelers were at Fuddlecumjig, and Ozma laughed merrily as she watched in the picture her friends trying to match the pieces of Grandmother Gnit.

"They seem happy and are doubtless having a good time," the girl Ruler said to herself; and then she began to think of the many adventures she herself had encountered with Dorothy.

The image of her friends now faded from the Magic Picture and the old landscape slowly reappeared.

Ozma was thinking of the time when with Dorothy and her army she marched to the Nome King's underground cavern, beyond the Land of Ev, and forced the old monarch to liberate his captives, who belonged to the Royal Family of Ev. That was the time when the Scarecrow nearly frightened the Nome King into fits by throwing one of Billina's eggs at him, and Dorothy had captured King Roquat's Magic Belt and brought it away with her to the Land of Oz.

The pretty Princess smiled at the recollection of this adventure, and then she wondered what had become of the Nome King since then. Merely because she was curious and had nothing better to do, Ozma glanced at the Magic Picture and wished to see in it the King of the Nomes.

Roquat the Red went every day into his tunnel to see how the work was getting along and to hurry his workmen as much as possible. He was there now, and Ozma saw him plainly in the Magic Picture.

She saw the underground tunnel, reaching far underneath the Deadly Desert which separated the Land of Oz from the mountains beneath which the Nome King had his extensive caverns. She saw that the tunnel was being made in the direction of the Emerald City, and knew at once it was being dug so that the army of Nomes could march through it and attack her own beautiful and peaceful country.

"I suppose King Roquat is planning revenge against us," she said, musingly, "and thinks he can surprise us and make us his captives and slaves. How sad it is that any one can have such wicked thoughts! But I must not blame King Roquat too severely, for he is a Nome, and his nature is not so gentle as my own."

Then she dismissed from her mind further thought of the tunnel, for that time, and began to wonder if Aunt Em would not be happy as Royal Mender of the Stockings of the Ruler of Oz. Ozma wore few holes in her stockings; still, they sometimes needed mending. Aunt Em ought to be able to do that very nicely.

Next day, the Princess watched the tunnel again in her Magic Picture, and every day afterward she devoted a few minutes to inspecting the work. It was not especially interesting, but she felt that it was her duty.

Slowly but surely the big, arched hole crept through the rocks underneath the deadly desert, and day by day it drew nearer and nearer to the Emerald City.

19. How Bunnybury Welcomed the Strangers

Dorothy left Bunbury the same way she had entered it and when they were in the forest again she said to Billina: "I never thought that things good to eat could be so dis'gree'ble."

"Often I've eaten things that tasted good but were disagreeable afterward," returned the Yellow Hen. "I think, Dorothy, if eatables are going to act badly, it's better before than after you eat them."

"P'raps you're right," said the little girl, with a sigh. "But what shall we do now?"

"Let us follow the path back to the signpost," suggested Billina. "That will be better than getting lost again."

"Why, we're lost anyhow," declared Dorothy; "but I guess you're right about going back to that signpost, Billina."

They returned along the path to the place where they had first found it, and at once took "the other road" to Bunnybury. This road was a mere narrow strip, worn hard and smooth but not wide enough for Dorothy's feet to tread. Still, it was a guide, and the walking through the forest was not at all difficult.

Before long they reached a high wall of solid white marble, and the path came to an end at this wall.

At first Dorothy thought there was no opening at all in the marble, but on looking closely she discovered a small square door about on a level with her head, and underneath this closed door was a bell-push. Near the bell-push a sign was painted in neat letters upon the marble, and the sign read:

NO ADMITTANCE
EXCEPT ON BUSINESS

This did not discourage Dorothy, however, and she rang the bell.

Pretty soon a bolt was cautiously withdrawn and the marble door swung slowly open. Then she saw it was not really a door, but a window, for several brass bars were placed across it, being set fast in the marble and so close together that the little girl's fingers might barely go between them. Back of the bars appeared the face of a white rabbit—a very sober and sedate face—with an eye-glass held in his left eye and attached to a cord in his button-hole.

"Well! what is it?" asked the rabbit, sharply.

"I'm Dorothy," said the girl, "and I'm lost, and—"

"State your business, please," interrupted the rabbit.

"My business," she replied, "is to find out where I am, and to—"

"No one is allowed in Bunnybury without an order or a letter of introduction from either Ozma of Oz or Glinda the Good," announced the rabbit; "so that settles the matter," and he started to close the window.

"Wait a minute!" cried Dorothy. "I've got a letter from Ozma."

"From the Ruler of Oz?" asked the rabbit, doubtingly.

"Of course. Ozma's my best friend, you know; and I'm a Princess myself," she announced, earnestly.

"Hum—ha! Let me see your letter," returned the rabbit, as if he still doubted her.

So she hunted in her pocket and found the letter Ozma had given her. Then she handed it through the bars to the rabbit, who took it in his paws and opened it. He read it aloud in a pompous voice, as if to let Dorothy and Billina see that he was educated and could read writing. The letter was as follows: "It will please me to have my subjects greet Princess Dorothy, the bearer of this royal missive, with the same courtesy and consideration they would extend to me."

"Ha—hum! It is signed 'Ozma of Oz,'" continued the rabbit, "and is sealed with the Great Seal of the Emerald City. Well, well, well! How strange! How remarkable!"

"What are you going to do about it?" inquired Dorothy, impatiently.

"We must obey the royal mandate," replied the rabbit. "We are subjects of Ozma of Oz, and we live in her country. Also we are under the protection of the great Sorceress Glinda the Good, who made us promise to respect Ozma's commands."

"Then may I come in?" she asked.

"I'll open the door," said the rabbit. He shut the window and disappeared, but a moment afterward a big door in the wall opened and admitted Dorothy to a small room, which seemed to be a part of the wall and built into it.

Here stood the rabbit she had been talking with, and now that she could see all of him, she gazed at the creature in surprise. He was a good sized white rabbit with pink eyes, much like all other white rabbits. But the astonishing thing about him was the manner in which he was dressed. He wore a white satin jacket embroidered with gold, and having diamond buttons. His vest was rose-colored satin, with tourmaline buttons. His trousers were white, to correspond with the jacket, and they were baggy at the knees—like those of a zouave—being tied with knots of rose ribbons. His shoes were of white plush with diamond buckles, and his stockings were rose silk.

The richness and even magnificence of the rabbit's clothing made Dorothy stare at the little creature wonderingly. Toto and Billina had followed her into the room and when he saw them the rabbit ran to a table and sprang upon it nimbly. Then he looked at the three through his monocle and said: "These companions, Princess, cannot enter Bunnybury with you."

"Why not?" asked Dorothy.

"In the first place they would frighten our people, who dislike dogs above all things on earth; and, secondly, the letter of the Royal Ozma does not mention them."

"But they're my friends," persisted Dorothy, "and go wherever I go."

"Not this time," said the rabbit, decidedly. "You, yourself, Princess, are a welcome visitor, since you come so highly recommended; but unless you consent to leave the dog and the hen in this room I cannot permit you to enter the town."

"Never mind us, Dorothy," said Billina. "Go inside and see what the place is like. You can tell us about it afterward, and Toto and I will rest comfortably here until you return."

This seemed the best thing to do, for Dorothy was curious to see how the rabbit people lived and she was aware of the fact that her friends might frighten the timid little creatures. She had not forgotten how Toto and Billina had misbehaved in Bunbury, and perhaps the rabbit was wise to insist on their staying outside the town.

"Very well," she said, "I'll go in alone. I s'pose you're the King of this town, aren't you?"

"No," answered the rabbit, "I'm merely the Keeper of the Wicket, and a person of little importance, although I try to do my duty. I must now inform you, Princess, that before you enter our town you must consent to reduce."

"Reduce what?" asked Dorothy.

"Your size. You must become the size of the rabbits, although you may retain your own form."

"Wouldn't my clothes be too big for me?" she inquired.

"No; they will reduce when your body does."

"Can YOU make me smaller?" asked the girl.

"Easily," returned the rabbit.

"And will you make me big again, when I'm ready to go away?"

"I will," said he.

"All right, then; I'm willing," she announced.

The rabbit jumped from the table and ran—or rather hopped—to the further wall, where he opened a door so tiny that even Toto could scarcely have crawled through it.

"Follow me," he said.

Now, almost any other little girl would have declared that she could not get through so small a door; but Dorothy had already encountered so many fairy adventures that she believed nothing was impossible in the Land of Oz. So she quietly walked toward the door, and at every step she grew smaller and smaller until, by the time the opening was reached, she could pass through it with ease. Indeed, as she stood beside the rabbit, who sat upon his hind legs and used his paws as hands, her head was just about as high as his own.

Then the Keeper of the Wicket passed through and she followed, after which the door swung shut and locked itself with a sharp click.

Dorothy now found herself in a city so strange and beautiful that she gave a gasp of surprise. The high marble wall extended all round the place and shut out all the rest of the world. And here were marble houses of curious forms, most of them resembling overturned kettles but with delicate slender spires and minarets running far up into the sky. The streets were paved with white marble and in front of each house was a lawn of rich green clover. Everything was as neat as wax, the green and white

contrasting prettily together.

But the rabbit people were, after all, the most amazing things Dorothy saw. The streets were full of them, and their costumes were so splendid that the rich dress of the Keeper of the Wicket was commonplace when compared with the others. Silks and satins of delicate hues seemed always used for material, and nearly every costume sparkled with exquisite gems.

But the lady rabbits outshone the gentlemen rabbits in splendor, and the cut of their gowns was really wonderful. They wore bonnets, too, with feathers and jewels in them, and some wheeled baby carriages in which the girl could see wee bunnies. Some were lying asleep while others lay sucking their paws and looking around them with big pink eyes.

As Dorothy was no bigger in size than the grown-up rabbits she had a chance to observe them closely before they noticed her presence. Then they did not seem at all alarmed, although the little girl naturally became the center of attraction and regarded her with great curiosity.

"Make way!" cried the Keeper of the Wicket, in a pompous voice; "make way for Princess Dorothy, who comes from Ozma of Oz."

Hearing this announcement, the throng of rabbits gave place to them on the walks, and as Dorothy passed along they all bowed their heads respectfully.

Walking thus through several handsome streets they came to a square in the center of the City. In this square were some pretty trees and a statue in bronze of Glinda the Good, while beyond it were the portals of the Royal Palace—an extensive and imposing building of white marble covered with a filigree of frosted gold.

20. How Dorothy Lunched With a King

A line of rabbit soldiers was drawn up before the palace entrance, and they wore green and gold uniforms with high shakos upon their heads and held tiny spears in their hands. The Captain had a sword and a white plume in his shako.

"Salute!" called the Keeper of the Wicket. "Salute Princess Dorothy, who comes from Ozma of Oz!"

"Salute!" yelled the Captain, and all the soldiers promptly saluted.

They now entered the great hall of the palace, where they met a gaily dressed attendant, from whom the Keeper of the Wicket inquired if the King were at leisure.

"I think so," was the reply. "I heard his Majesty blubbering and wailing as usual only a few minutes ago. If he doesn't stop acting like a cry-baby I'm going to resign my position here and go to work."

"What's the matter with your King?" asked Dorothy, surprised to hear the rabbit attendant speak so disrespectfully of his monarch.

"Oh, he doesn't want to be King, that's all; and he simply HAS to," was the reply.

"Come!" said the Keeper of the Wicket, sternly; "lead us to his Majesty; and do not air our troubles before strangers, I beg of you."

"Why, if this girl is going to see the King, he'll air his own troubles," returned the attendant.

"That is his royal privilege," declared the Keeper.

So the attendant led them into a room all draped with cloth-of-gold and furnished with satin-covered gold furniture. There was a throne in this room, set on a dais and having a big, cushioned seat, and on this seat reclined the Rabbit King. He was lying on his back, with his paws in the air, and whining very like a puppy-dog.

"Your Majesty! your Majesty! Get up. Here's a visitor," called out the attendant.

The King rolled over and looked at Dorothy with one watery pink eye. Then he sat up and wiped his eyes carefully with a silk handkerchief and put on his jeweled crown, which had fallen off.

"Excuse my grief, fair stranger," he said, in a sad voice. "You behold in me the most miserable monarch in all the world. What time is it, Blinkem?"

"One o'clock, your Majesty," replied the attendant to whom the question was addressed.

"Serve luncheon at once!" commanded the King. "Luncheon for two—that's for my visitor and me—and see that the human has some sort of food she's accustomed to."

"Yes, your Majesty," answered the attendant, and went away.

"Tie my shoe, Bristle," said the King to the Keeper of the Wicket. "Ah me! how unhappy I am!"

"What seems to be worrying your Majesty?" asked Dorothy.

"Why, it's this king business, of course," he returned, while the Keeper tied his shoe. "I didn't want to be King of Bunnybury at all, and the rabbits all knew it. So they elected me—to save themselves from such a dreadful fate, I suppose—and here I am, shut up in a palace, when I might be free and happy."

"Seems to me," said Dorothy, "it's a great thing to be a King."

"Were you ever a King?" inquired the monarch.

"No," she answered, laughing.

"Then you know nothing about it," he said. "I haven't inquired who you are, but it doesn't matter. While we're at luncheon, I'll tell you all my troubles. They're a great deal more interesting than anything you can say about yourself."

"Perhaps they are, to you," replied Dorothy.

"Luncheon is served!" cried Blinkem, throwing open the door, and in came a dozen rabbits in livery, all bearing trays which they placed upon the table, where they arranged the dishes in an orderly manner.

"Now clear out—all of you!" exclaimed the King. "Bristle, you may wait outside, in case I want you."

When they had gone and the King was alone with Dorothy he came down from his throne, tossed his crown into a corner and kicked his ermine robe under the table.

"Sit down," he said, "and try to be happy. It's useless for me to try, because I'm always wretched and miserable. But I'm hungry, and I hope you are."

"I am," said Dorothy. "I've only eaten a wheelbarrow and a piano to-day—oh, yes! and a slice of bread and butter that used to be a door-mat."

"That sounds like a square meal," remarked the King, seating himself opposite her; "but perhaps it wasn't a square piano. Eh?"

Dorothy laughed.

"You don't seem so very unhappy now," she said.

"But I am," protested the King, fresh tears gathering in his eyes. "Even my jokes are miserable. I'm wretched, woeful, afflicted, distressed and dismal as an individual can be. Are you not sorry for me?"

"No," answered Dorothy, honestly, "I can't say I am. Seems to me that for a rabbit you're right in clover. This is the prettiest little city I ever saw."

"Oh, the city is good enough," he admitted. "Glinda, the Good Sorceress, made it for us because she was fond of rabbits. I don't mind the City so much, although I wouldn't live here if I had my choice. It is being King that has absolutely ruined my happiness."

"Why wouldn't you live here by choice?" she asked.

"Because it is all unnatural, my dear. Rabbits are out of place in such luxury. When I was young I lived in a burrow in the forest. I was surrounded by enemies and often had to run for my life. It was hard getting enough to eat, at times, and when I found a bunch of clover I had to listen and look for danger while I ate it. Wolves prowled around the hole in which I lived and sometimes I didn't dare stir out for days at a time. Oh, how happy and contented I was then! I was a real rabbit, as nature made me—wild and free!—and I even enjoyed listening to the startled throbbing of my own heart!"

"I've often thought," said Dorothy, who was busily eating, "that it would be fun to be a rabbit."

"It IS fun—when you're the genuine article," agreed his Majesty. "But look at me now! I live in a marble palace instead of a hole in the ground. I have all I want to eat, without the joy of hunting for it. Every day I must dress in fine clothes and wear that horrible crown till it makes my head ache. Rabbits come to me with all sorts of troubles, when my own troubles are the only ones I care about. When I walk out I can't hop and run; I must strut on my rear legs and wear an ermine robe! And the soldiers salute me and the band plays and the other rabbits laugh and clap their paws and cry out: 'Hail to the King!' Now let me ask you, as a friend and a young lady of good judgment: isn't all this pomp and foolishness enough to make a decent rabbit miserable?"

"Once," said Dorothy, reflectively, "men were wild and unclothed and lived in caves and hunted for food as wild beasts do. But they got civ'lized, in time, and now they'd hate to go back to the old days."

"That is an entirely different case," replied the King. "None of you Humans were civilized in one lifetime. It came to you by degrees. But I have known the forest and the free life, and that is why I resent being civilized all at once, against my will, and being made a King with a crown and an ermine robe. Pah!"

"If you don't like it, why don't you resign?" she asked.

"Impossible!" wailed the Rabbit, wiping his eyes again with his handkerchief. "There's a beastly law in this town that forbids it. When one is elected a King, there's no getting out of it."

"Who made the laws?" inquired Dorothy.

"The same Sorceress who made the town—Glinda the Good. She built the wall, and fixed up the City, and gave us several valuable enchantments, and made the laws. Then she invited all the pink-eyed white rabbits of the forest to come here, after which she left us to our fate."

"What made you 'cept the invitation, and come here?" asked the child.

"I didn't know how dreadful city life was, and I'd no idea I would be elected King," said he, sobbing bitterly. "And—and—now I'm It—with a capital I—and can't escape!"

"I know Glinda," remarked Dorothy, eating for dessert a dish of charlotte russe, "and when I see her again, I'll ask her to put another King in your place."

"Will you? Will you, indeed?" asked the King, joyfully.

"I will if you want me to," she replied.

"Hurroo—huray!" shouted the King; and then he jumped up from the table and danced wildly about the room, waving his napkin like a flag and laughing with glee.

After a time he managed to control his delight and returned to the table.

"When are you likely to see Glinda?" he inquired.

"Oh, p'raps in a few days," said Dorothy.

"And you won't forget to ask her?"

"Of course not."

"Princess," said the Rabbit King, earnestly, "you have relieved me of a great unhappiness, and I am very grateful. Therefore I propose to entertain you, since you are my guest and I am the King, as a slight mark of my appreciation. Come with me to my reception hall."

He then summoned Bristle and said to him: "Assemble all the nobility in the great reception hall, and also tell Blinkem that I want him immediately."

The Keeper of the Wicket bowed and hurried away, and his Majesty turned to Dorothy and continued: "We'll have time for a walk in the gardens before the people get here."

The gardens were back of the palace and were filled with beautiful flowers and fragrant shrubs, with many shade and fruit trees and marble-paved walks running in every direction. As they entered this place Blinkem came running to the King, who gave him several orders in a low voice. Then his Majesty rejoined Dorothy and led her through the gardens, which she admired very much.

"What lovely clothes your Majesty wears!" she said, glancing at the rich blue satin costume, embroidered, with pearls in which the King was dressed.

"Yes," he returned, with an air of pride, "this is one of my favorite suits; but I have a good many that are even more elaborate. We have excellent tailors in Bunnybury, and Glinda supplies all the material. By the way, you might ask the Sorceress, when you see her, to permit me to keep my wardrobe."

"But if you go back to the forest you will not need clothes," she said.

"N—o!" he faltered; "that may be so. But I've dressed up so long that I'm used to it, and I don't imagine I'd care to run around naked again. So perhaps the Good Glinda will let me keep the costumes."

"I'll ask her," agreed Dorothy.

Then they left the gardens and went into a fine, big reception hall, where rich rugs were spread upon the tiled floors and furniture was exquisitely carved and studded with jewels. The King's chair was an especially pretty piece of furniture, being in the shape of a silver lily with one leaf bent over to form the seat. The silver was everywhere thickly encrusted with diamonds and the seat was upholstered in white satin.

"Oh, what a splendid chair!" cried Dorothy, clasping her hands admiringly.

"Isn't it?" answered the King, proudly. "It is my favorite seat, and I think it especially becoming to my complexion. While I think of it, I wish you'd ask Glinda to let me keep this lily chair when I go away."

"It wouldn't look very well in a hole in the ground, would it?" she suggested.

"Maybe not; but I'm used to sitting in it and I'd like to take it with me," he answered. "But here come the ladies and gentlemen of the court; so please sit beside me and be presented."

21. How the King Changed His Mind

Just then a rabbit band of nearly fifty pieces marched in, playing upon golden instruments and dressed in neat uniforms. Following the band came the nobility of Bunnybury, all richly dressed and hopping along on their rear legs. Both the ladies and the gentlemen wore white gloves upon their paws, with their rings on the outside of the gloves, as this seemed to be the fashion here. Some of the lady rabbits carried lorgnettes, while many of the gentlemen rabbits wore monocles in their left eyes.

The courtiers and their ladies paraded past the King, who introduced Princess Dorothy to each couple in a very graceful manner. Then the company seated themselves in chairs and on sofas and looked expectantly at their monarch.

"It is our royal duty, as well as our royal pleasure," he said, "to provide fitting entertainment for our distinguished guest. We will now present the Royal Band of Whiskered Friskers."

As he spoke the musicians, who had arranged themselves in a corner, struck up a dance melody while into the room pranced the Whiskered Friskers. They were eight pretty rabbits dressed only in gauzy purple skirts fastened around their waists with diamond bands. Their whiskers were colored a rich purple, but otherwise they were pure white.

After bowing before the King and Dorothy the Friskers began their pranks, and these were so comical that Dorothy laughed with real enjoyment. They not only danced together, whirling and gyrating around the room, but they leaped over one another, stood upon their heads and hopped and skipped here and there so nimbly that it was hard work to keep track of them. Finally, they all made double somersaults and turned handsprings out of the room.

The nobility enthusiastically applauded, and Dorothy applauded with them.

"They're fine!" she said to the King.

"Yes, the Whiskered Friskers are really very clever," he replied. "I shall hate to part with them when I go away, for they have often amused me when I was very miserable. I wonder if you would ask Glinda—"

"No, it wouldn't do at all," declared Dorothy, positively. "There wouldn't be room in your hole in the ground for so many rabbits, 'spec'ly when you get the lily chair and your clothes there. Don't think of such a thing, your Majesty."

The King sighed. Then he stood up and announced to the company: "We will now hold a military drill by my picked Bodyguard of Royal Pikemen."

Now the band played a march and a company of rabbit soldiers came in. They wore green and gold uniforms and marched very stiffly but in perfect time. Their spears, or pikes, had slender shafts of polished silver with golden heads, and during the drill they handled these weapons with wonderful dexterity.

"I should think you'd feel pretty safe with such a fine Bodyguard," remarked Dorothy.

"I do," said the King. "They protect me from every harm. I suppose Glinda wouldn't—"

"No," interrupted the girl; "I'm sure she wouldn't. It's the King's own Bodyguard, and when you are no longer King you can't have 'em."

The King did not reply, but he looked rather sorrowful for a time.

When the soldiers had marched out he said to the company: "The Royal Jugglers will now appear."

Dorothy had seen many jugglers in her lifetime, but never any so interesting as these. There were six of them, dressed in black satin embroidered with queer symbols in silver—a costume which contrasted strongly with their snow-white fur.

First, they pushed in a big red ball and three of the rabbit jugglers stood upon its top and made it roll. Then two of them caught up a third and tossed him into the air, all vanishing, until only the two were left. Then one of these tossed the other upward and remained alone of all his fellows. This last juggler now touched the red ball, which fell apart, being hollow, and the five rabbits who had disappeared in the air scrambled out of the hollow ball.

Next they all clung together and rolled swiftly upon the floor. When they came to a stop only one fat rabbit juggler was seen,

the others seeming to be inside him. This one leaped lightly into the air and when he came down he exploded and separated into the original six. Then four of them rolled themselves into round balls and the other two tossed them around and played ball with them.

These were but a few of the tricks the rabbit jugglers performed, and they were so skillful that all the nobility and even the King applauded as loudly as did Dorothy.

"I suppose there are no rabbit jugglers in all the world to compare with these," remarked the King. "And since I may not have the Whiskers Friskers or my Bodyguard, you might ask Glinda to let me take away just two or three of these jugglers. Will you?"

"I'll ask her," replied Dorothy, doubtfully.

"Thank you," said the King; "thank you very much. And now you shall listen to the Winsome Waggish Warblers, who have often cheered me in my moments of anguish."

The Winsome Waggish Warblers proved to be a quartette of rabbit singers, two gentlemen and two lady rabbits. The gentlemen Warblers wore full-dress swallow-tailed suits of white satin, with pearls for buttons, while the lady Warblers were gowned in white satin dresses with long trails.

The first song they sang began in this way:
"When a rabbit gets a habit
Of living in a city
And wearing clothes and furbelows
And jewels rare and pretty,
He scorns the Bun who has to run
And burrow in the ground
And pities those whose watchful foes
Are man and gun and hound."

Dorothy looked at the King when she heard this song and noticed that he seemed disturbed and ill at ease.

"I don't like that song," he said to the Warblers. "Give us something jolly and rollicking."

So they sang to a joyous, tinkling melody as follows:
"Bunnies gay
Delight to play
In their fairy town secure;
Ev'ry frisker
Flirts his whisker
At a pink-eyed girl demure.

Ev'ry maid
In silk arrayed
At her partner shyly glances,
Paws are grasped,
Waists are clasped
As they whirl in giddy dances.

Then together
Through the heather
'Neath the moonlight soft they stroll;
Each is very
Blithe and merry,
Gamboling with laughter droll.

Life is fun
To ev'ry one

Guarded by our magic charm
For to dangers
We are strangers,
Safe from any thought of harm."

"You see," said Dorothy to the King, when the song ended, "the rabbits all seem to like Bunnybury except you. And I guess you're the only one that ever has cried or was unhappy and wanted to get back to your muddy hole in the ground."

His Majesty seemed thoughtful, and while the servants passed around glasses of nectar and plates of frosted cakes their King was silent and a bit nervous.

When the refreshments had been enjoyed by all and the servants had retired Dorothy said: "I must go now, for it's getting late and I'm lost. I've got to find the Wizard and Aunt Em and Uncle Henry and all the rest sometime before night comes, if I poss'bly can."

"Won't you stay with us?" asked the King. "You will be very welcome."

"No, thank you," she replied. "I must get back to my friends. And I want to see Glinda just as soon as I can, you know."

So the King dismissed his court and said he would himself walk with Dorothy to the gate. He did not weep nor groan any more, but his long face was quite solemn and his big ears hung dejectedly on each side of it. He still wore his crown and his ermine and walked with a handsome gold-headed cane.

When they arrived at the room in the wall the little girl found Toto and Billina waiting for her very patiently. They had been liberally fed by some of the attendants and were in no hurry to leave such comfortable quarters.

The Keeper of the Wicket was by this time back in his old place, but he kept a safe distance from Toto. Dorothy bade good bye to the King as they stood just inside the wall.

"You've been good to me," she said, "and I thank you ever so much. As soon as poss'ble I'll see Glinda and ask her to put another King in your place and send you back into the wild forest. And I'll ask her to let you keep some of your clothes and the lily chair and one or two jugglers to amuse you. I'm sure she will do it, 'cause she's so kind she doesn't like any one to be unhappy."

"Ahem!" said the King, looking rather downcast. "I don't like to trouble you with my misery; so you needn't see Glinda."

"Oh, yes I will," she replied. "It won't be any trouble at all."

"But, my dear," continued the King, in an embarrassed way, "I've been thinking the subject over carefully, and I find there are a lot of pleasant things here in Bunnybury that I would miss if I went away. So perhaps I'd better stay."

Dorothy laughed. Then she looked grave.

"It won't do for you to be a King and a cry-baby at the same time," she said. "You've been making all the other rabbits unhappy and discontented with your howls about being so miserable. So I guess it's better to have another King."

"Oh, no indeed!" exclaimed the King, earnestly. "If you won't say anything to Glinda I'll promise to be merry and gay all the time, and never cry or wail again."

"Honor bright?" she asked.

"On the royal word of a King I promise it!" he answered.

"All right," said Dorothy. "You'd be a reg'lar lunatic to want to leave Bunnybury for a wild life in the forest, and I'm sure any rabbit outside the city would be glad to take your place."

"Forget it, my dear; forget all my foolishness," pleaded the King, earnestly. "Hereafter I'll try to enjoy myself and do my duty by my subjects."

So then she left him and entered through the little door into the room in the wall, where she grew gradually bigger and bigger until she had resumed her natural size.

The Keeper of the Wicket let them out into the forest and told Dorothy that she had been of great service to Bunnybury because she had brought their dismal King to a realization of the pleasure of ruling so beautiful a city.

"I shall start a petition to have your statue erected beside Glinda's in the public square," said the Keeper. "I hope you will come again, some day, and see it."

"Perhaps I shall," she replied.

Then, followed by Toto and Billina, she walked away from the high marble wall and started back along the narrow path toward the sign-post.

22. How the Wizard Found Dorothy

When they came to the signpost, there, to their joy, were the tents of the Wizard pitched beside the path and the kettle bubbling merrily over the fire. The Shaggy Man and Omby Amby were gathering firewood while Uncle Henry and Aunt Em sat in their camp chairs talking with the Wizard.

They all ran forward to greet Dorothy, as she approached, and Aunt Em exclaimed: "Goodness gracious, child! Where have you been?"

"You've played hookey the whole day," added the Shaggy Man, reproachfully.

"Well, you see, I've been lost," explained the little girl, "and I've tried awful hard to find the way back to you, but just couldn't do it."

"Did you wander in the forest all day?" asked Uncle Henry.

"You must be a'most starved!" said Aunt Em.

"No," said Dorothy, "I'm not hungry. I had a wheelbarrow and a piano for breakfast, and lunched with a King."

"Ah!" exclaimed the Wizard, nodding with a bright smile. "So you've been having adventures again."

"She's stark crazy!" cried Aunt Em. "Whoever heard of eating a wheelbarrow?"

"It wasn't very big," said Dorothy; "and it had a zuzu wheel."

"And I ate the crumbs," said Billina, soberly.

"Sit down and tell us about it," begged the Wizard. "We've hunted for you all day, and at last I noticed your footsteps in this path—and the tracks of Billina. We found the path by accident, and seeing it only led to two places I decided you were at either one or the other of those places. So we made camp and waited for you to return. And now, Dorothy, tell us where you have been—to Bunbury or to Bunnybury?"

"Why, I've been to both," she replied; "but first I went to Utensia, which isn't on any path at all."

She then sat down and related the day's adventures, and you may be sure Aunt Em and Uncle Henry were much astonished at the story.

"But after seeing the Cuttenclips and the Fuddles," remarked her uncle, "we ought not to wonder at anything in this strange country."

"Seems like the only common and ordinary folks here are ourselves," rejoined Aunt Em, diffidently.

"Now that we're together again, and one reunited party," observed the Shaggy Man, "what are we to do next?"

"Have some supper and a night's rest," answered the Wizard promptly, "and then proceed upon our journey."

"Where to?" asked the Captain General.

"We haven't visited the Rigmaroles or the Flutterbudgets yet," said Dorothy. "I'd like to see them—wouldn't you?"

"They don't sound very interesting," objected Aunt Em. "But perhaps they are."

"And then," continued the little Wizard, "we will call upon the Tin Woodman and Jack Pumpkinhead and our old friend the Scarecrow, on our way home."

"That will be nice!" cried Dorothy, eagerly.

"Can't say THEY sound very interesting, either," remarked Aunt Em.

"Why, they're the best friends I have!" asserted the little girl, "and you're sure to like them, Aunt Em, 'cause EVER'body likes them."

By this time twilight was approaching, so they ate the fine supper which the Wizard magically produced from the kettle and then went to bed in the cozy tents.

They were all up bright and early next morning, but Dorothy didn't venture to wander from the camp again for fear of more accidents.

"Do you know where there's a road?" she asked the little man.

"No, my dear," replied the Wizard; "but I'll find one."

After breakfast he waved his hand toward the tents and they became handkerchiefs again, which were at once returned to the pockets of their owners. Then they all climbed into the red wagon and the Sawhorse inquired:

"Which way?"

"Never mind which way," replied the Wizard. "Just go as you please and you're sure to be right. I've enchanted the wheels of the wagon, and they will roll in the right direction, never fear."

As the Sawhorse started away through the trees Dorothy said: "If we had one of those new-fashioned airships we could float away over the top of the forest, and look down and find just the place we want."

"Airship? Pah!" retorted the little man, scornfully. "I hate those things, Dorothy, although they are nothing new to either you or me. I was a balloonist for many years, and once my balloon carried me to the Land of Oz, and once to the Vegetable Kingdom. And once Ozma had a Gump that flew all over this kingdom and had sense enough to go where it was told to—which airships won't do. The house which the cyclone brought to Oz all the way from Kansas, with you and Toto in it—was a real airship at the time; so you see we've got plenty of experience flying with the birds."

"Airships are not so bad, after all," declared Dorothy. "Some day they'll fly all over the world, and perhaps bring people even to the Land of Oz."

"I must speak to Ozma about that," said the Wizard, with a slight frown. "It wouldn't do at all, you know, for the Emerald City to become a way-station on an airship line."

"No," said Dorothy, "I don't s'pose it would. But what can we do to prevent it?"

"I'm working out a magic recipe to fuddle men's brains, so they'll never make an airship that will go where they want it to go," the Wizard confided to her. "That won't keep the things from flying now and then, but it'll keep them from flying to the Land of Oz."

Just then the Sawhorse drew the wagon out of the forest and a beautiful landscape lay spread before the travelers' eyes. Moreover, right before them was a good road that wound away through the hills and valleys.

"Now," said the Wizard, with evident delight, "we are on the right track again, and there is nothing more to worry about."

"It's a foolish thing to take chances in a strange country," observed the Shaggy Man. "Had we kept to the roads we never would have been lost. Roads always lead to some place, else they wouldn't be roads."

"This road," added the Wizard, "leads to Rigmarole Town. I'm sure of that because I enchanted the wagon wheels."

Sure enough, after riding along the road for an hour or two they entered a pretty valley where a village was nestled among the hills. The houses were Munchkin shaped, for they were all domes, with windows wider than they were high, and pretty balconies over the front doors.

Aunt Em was greatly relieved to find this town "neither paper nor patch-work," and the only surprising thing about it was that it was so far distant from all other towns.

As the Sawhorse drew the wagon into the main street the travelers noticed that the place was filled with people, standing in groups and seeming to be engaged in earnest conversation. So occupied with themselves were the inhabitants that they scarcely noticed the strangers at all. So the Wizard stopped a boy and asked: "Is this Rigmarole Town?"

"Sir," replied the boy, "if you have traveled very much you will have noticed that every town differs from every other town in one way or another and so by observing the methods of the people and the way they live as well as the style of their dwelling places it ought not to be a difficult thing to make up your mind without the trouble of asking questions whether the town bears the appearance of the one you intended to visit or whether perhaps having taken a different road from the one you should have taken you have made an error in your way and arrived at some point where—"

"Land sakes!" cried Aunt Em, impatiently; "what's all this rigmarole about?"

"That's it!" said the Wizard, laughing merrily. "It's a rigmarole because the boy is a Rigmarole and we've come to Rigmarole Town."

"Do they all talk like that?" asked Dorothy, wonderingly.

"He might have said 'yes' or 'no' and settled the question," observed Uncle Henry.

"Not here," said Omby Amby. "I don't believe the Rigmaroles know what 'yes' or 'no' means."

While the boy had been talking several other people had approached the wagon and listened intently to his speech. Then they began talking to one another in long, deliberate speeches, where many words were used but little was said. But when the strangers criticized them so frankly one of the women, who had no one else to talk to, began an address to them, saying: "It is the easiest thing in the world for a person to say 'yes' or 'no' when a question is asked for the purpose of gaining information or satisfying the curiosity of the one who has given expression to the inquiry has attracted the attention of an individual who may be competent either from personal experience or the experience of others to answer it with more or less correctness or at least an attempt to satisfy the desire for information on the part of the one who has made the inquiry by—"

"Dear me!" exclaimed Dorothy, interrupting the speech. "I've lost all track of what you are saying."

"Don't let her begin over again, for goodness sake!" cried Aunt Em.

But the woman did not begin again. She did not even stop talking, but went right on as she had begun, the words flowing from her mouth in a stream.

"I'm quite sure that if we waited long enough and listened carefully, some of these people might be able to tell us something, in time," said the Wizard.

"Let's don't wait," returned Dorothy. "I've heard of the Rigmaroles, and wondered what they were like; but now I know, and I'm ready to move on."

"So am I," declared Uncle Henry; "we're wasting time here."

"Why, we're all ready to go," said the Shaggy Man, putting his fingers to his ears to shut out the monotonous babble of those around the wagon.

So the Wizard spoke to the Sawhorse, who trotted nimbly

through the village and soon gained the open country on the other side of it. Dorothy looked back, as they rode away, and noticed that the woman had not yet finished her speech but was talking as glibly as ever, although no one was near to hear her.

"If those people wrote books," Omby Amby remarked with a smile, "it would take a whole library to say the cow jumped over the moon."

"Perhaps some of 'em do write books," asserted the little Wizard. "I've read a few rigmaroles that might have come from this very town."

"Some of the college lecturers and ministers are certainly related to these people," observed the Shaggy Man; "and it seems to me the Land of Oz is a little ahead of the United States in some of its laws. For here, if one can't talk clearly, and straight to the point, they send him to Rigmarole Town; while Uncle Sam lets him roam around wild and free, to torture innocent people."

Dorothy was thoughtful. The Rigmaroles had made a strong impression upon her. She decided that whenever she spoke, after this, she would use only enough words to express what she wanted to say.

23. How They Encountered the Flutterbudgets

They were soon among the pretty hills and valleys again, and the Sawhorse sped up hill and down at a fast and easy pace, the roads being hard and smooth. Mile after mile was speedily covered, and before the ride had grown at all tiresome they sighted another village. The place seemed even larger than Rigmarole Town, but was not so attractive in appearance.

"This must be Flutterbudget Center," declared the Wizard. "You see, it's no trouble at all to find places if you keep to the right road."

"What are the Flutterbudgets like?" inquired Dorothy.

"I do not know, my dear. But Ozma has given them a town all their own, and I've heard that whenever one of the people becomes a Flutterbudget he is sent to this place to live."

"That is true," Omby Amby added; "Flutterbudget Center and Rigmarole Town are called 'the Defensive Settlements of Oz.'"

The village they now approached was not built in a valley, but on top of a hill, and the road they followed wound around the hill, like a corkscrew, ascending the hill easily until it came to the town.

"Look out!" screamed a voice. "Look out, or you'll run over my child!"

They gazed around and saw a woman standing upon the sidewalk nervously wringing her hands as she gazed at them appealingly.

"Where is your child?" asked the Sawhorse.

"In the house," said the woman, bursting into tears; "but if it should happen to be in the road, and you ran over it, those great wheels would crush my darling to jelly. Oh dear! oh dear! Think of my darling child being crushed into jelly by those great wheels!"

"Gid-dap!" said the Wizard sharply, and the Sawhorse started on.

They had not gone far before a man ran out of a house shouting wildly, "Help! Help!"

The Sawhorse stopped short and the Wizard and Uncle Henry and the Shaggy Man and Omby Amby jumped out of the wagon and ran to the poor man's assistance. Dorothy followed them as quickly as she could.

"What's the matter?" asked the Wizard.

"Help! help!" screamed the man; "my wife has cut her finger off and she's bleeding to death!"

Then he turned and rushed back to the house, and all the party went with him. They found a woman in the front dooryard moaning and groaning as if in great pain.

"Be brave, madam!" said the Wizard, consolingly. "You won't die just because you have cut off a finger, you may be sure."

"But I haven't cut off a finger!" she sobbed.

"Then what HAS happened?" asked Dorothy.

"I—I pricked my finger with a needle while I was sewing, and—and the blood came!" she replied. "And now I'll have blood-poisoning, and the doctors will cut off my finger, and that will give me a fever and I shall die!"

"Pshaw!" said Dorothy; "I've pricked my finger many a time, and nothing happened."

"Really?" asked the woman, brightening and wiping her eyes upon her apron.

"Why, it's nothing at all," declared the girl. "You're more scared than hurt."

"Ah, that's because she's a Flutterbudget," said the Wizard, nodding wisely. "I think I know now what these people are like."

"So do I," announced Dorothy.

"Oh, boo-hoo-hoo!" sobbed the woman, giving way to a fresh burst of grief.

"What's wrong now?" asked the Shaggy Man.

"Oh, suppose I had pricked my foot!" she wailed. "Then the doctors would have cut my foot off, and I'd be lamed for life!"

"Surely, ma'am," replied the Wizard, "and if you'd pricked your nose they might cut your head off. But you see you didn't."

"But I might have!" she exclaimed, and began to cry again. So they left her and drove away in their wagon. And her husband came out and began calling "Help!" as he had before; but no one seemed to pay any attention to him.

As the travelers turned into another street they found a man walking excitedly up and down the pavement. He appeared to be in a very nervous condition and the Wizard stopped him to ask: "Is anything wrong, sir?"

"Everything is wrong," answered the man, dismally. "I can't sleep."

"Why not?" inquired Omby Amby.

"If I go to sleep I'll have to shut my eyes," he explained; "and if I shut my eyes they may grow together, and then I'd be blind for life!"

"Did you ever hear of any one's eyes growing together?" asked Dorothy.

"No," said the man, "I never did. But it would be a dreadful thing, wouldn't it? And the thought of it makes me so nervous I'm afraid to go to sleep."

"There's no help for this case," declared the Wizard; and they went on.

At the next street corner a woman rushed up to them crying:

"Save my baby! Oh, good, kind people, save my baby!"

"Is it in danger?" asked Dorothy, noticing that the child was clasped in her arms and seemed sleeping peacefully.

"Yes, indeed," said the woman, nervously. "If I should go into the house and throw my child out of the window, it would roll way down to the bottom of the hill; and then if there were a lot of tigers and bears down there, they would tear my darling babe to pieces and eat it up!"

"Are there any tigers and bears in this neighborhood?" the Wizard asked.

"I've never heard of any," admitted the woman, "but if there were—"

"Have you any idea of throwing your baby out of the window?" questioned the little man.

"None at all," she said; "but if—"

"All your troubles are due to those 'ifs'," declared the Wizard. "If you were not a Flutterbudget you wouldn't worry."

"There's another 'if'," replied the woman. "Are you a Flutterbudget, too?"

"I will be, if I stay here long," exclaimed the Wizard, nervously.

"Another 'if'!" cried the woman.

But the Wizard did not stop to argue with her. He made the Sawhorse canter all the way down the hill, and only breathed easily when they were miles away from the village.

After they had ridden in silence for a while Dorothy turned to the little man and asked: "Do 'ifs' really make Flutterbudgets?"

"I think the 'ifs' help," he answered seriously. "Foolish fears, and worries over nothing, with a mixture of nerves and ifs, will soon make a Flutterbudget of anyone."

Then there was another long silence, for all the travelers were thinking over this statement, and nearly all decided it must be true.

The country they were now passing through was everywhere tinted purple, the prevailing color of the Gillikin Country; but as the Sawhorse ascended a hill they found that upon the other side everything was of a rich yellow hue.

"Aha!" cried the Captain General; "here is the Country of the Winkies. We are just crossing the boundary line."

"Then we may be able to lunch with the Tin Woodman," announced the Wizard, joyfully.

"Must we lunch on tin?" asked Aunt Em.

"Oh, no;" replied Dorothy. "Nick Chopper knows how to feed meat people, and he will give us plenty of good things to eat, never fear. I've been to his castle before."

"Is Nick Chopper the Tin Woodman's name?" asked Uncle Henry.

"Yes; that's one of his names," answered the little girl; "and another of his names is 'Emp'ror of the Winkies.' He's the King of this country, you know, but Ozma rules over all the countries of Oz."

"Does the Tin Woodman keep any Flutterbudgets or Rigmaroles at his castle?" inquired Aunt Em, uneasily.

"No indeed," said Dorothy, positively. "He lives in a new tin castle, all full of lovely things."

"I should think it would rust," said Uncle Henry.

"He has thousands of Winkies to keep it polished for him," explained the Wizard. "His people love to do anything in their power for their beloved Emperor, so there isn't a particle of rust on all the big castle."

"I suppose they polish their Emperor, too," said Aunt Em.

"Why, some time ago he had himself nickel-plated," the Wizard answered; "so he only needs rubbing up once in a while. He's the brightest man in all the world, is dear Nick Chopper; and the kindest-hearted."

"I helped find him," said Dorothy, reflectively. "Once the Scarecrow and I found the Tin Woodman in the woods, and he was just rusted still, that time, an' no mistake. But we oiled his joints an' got 'em good and slippery, and after that he went with us to visit the Wizard at the Em'rald City."

"Was that the time the Wizard scared you?" asked Aunt Em.

"He didn't treat us well, at first," acknowledged Dorothy; "for he made us go away and destroy the Wicked Witch. But after we found out he was only a humbug wizard we were not afraid of him."

The Wizard sighed and looked a little ashamed.

"When we try to deceive people we always make mistakes," he said. "But I'm getting to be a real wizard now, and Glinda the Good's magic, that I am trying to practice, can never harm any one."

"You were always a good man," declared Dorothy, "even when you were a bad wizard."

"He's a good wizard now," asserted Aunt Em, looking at the little man admiringly. "The way he made those tents grow out of

handkerchiefs was just wonderful! And didn't he enchant the wagon wheels so they'd find the road?"

"All the people of Oz," said the Captain General, "are very proud of their Wizard. He once made some soap-bubbles that astonished the world."

The Wizard blushed at this praise, yet it pleased him. He no longer looked sad, but seemed to have recovered his usual good humor.

The country through which they now rode was thickly dotted with farmhouses, and yellow grain waved in all the fields. Many of the Winkies could be seen working on their farms and the wild and unsettled parts of Oz were by this time left far behind.

These Winkies appeared to be happy, light-hearted folk, and all removed their caps and bowed low when the red wagon with its load of travelers passed by.

It was not long before they saw something glittering in the sunshine far ahead.

"See!" cried Dorothy; "that's the Tin Castle, Aunt Em!"

And the Sawhorse, knowing his passengers were eager to arrive, broke into a swift trot that soon brought them to their destination.

24. How the Tin Woodman Told the Sad News

The Tin Woodman received Princess Dorothy's party with much grace and cordiality, yet the little girl decided that something must be worrying with her old friend, because he was not so merry as usual.

But at first she said nothing about this, for Uncle Henry and Aunt Em were fairly bubbling over with admiration for the beautiful tin castle and its polished tin owner. So her suspicion that something unpleasant had happened was for a time forgotten.

"Where is the Scarecrow?" she asked, when they had all been ushered into the big tin drawing-room of the castle, the Sawhorse being led around to the tin stable in the rear.

"Why, our old friend has just moved into his new mansion," explained the Tin Woodman. "It has been a long time in building, although my Winkies and many other people from all parts of the country have been busily working upon it. At last, however, it is completed, and the Scarecrow took possession of his new home just two days ago."

"I hadn't heard that he wanted a home of his own," said Dorothy. "Why doesn't he live with Ozma in the Emerald City? He used to, you know; and I thought he was happy there."

"It seems," said the Tin Woodman, "that our dear Scarecrow cannot be contented with city life, however beautiful his surroundings might be. Originally he was a farmer, for he passed his early life in a cornfield, where he was supposed to frighten away the crows."

"I know," said Dorothy, nodding. "I found him, and lifted him down from his pole."

"So now, after a long residence in the Emerald City, his tastes have turned to farm life again," continued the Tin Man. "He feels that he cannot be happy without a farm of his own, so Ozma gave him some land and every one helped him build his mansion, and now he is settled there for good."

"Who designed his house?" asked the Shaggy Man.

"I believe it was Jack Pumpkinhead, who is also a farmer," was the reply.

They were now invited to enter the tin dining room, where luncheon was served.

Aunt Em found, to her satisfaction, that Dorothy's promise was more than fulfilled; for, although the Tin Woodman had no appetite of his own, he respected the appetites of his guests and saw that they were bountifully fed.

They passed the afternoon in wandering through the beautiful gardens and grounds of the palace. The walks were all paved with sheets of tin, brightly polished, and there were tin fountains and tin statues here and there among the trees. The flowers were mostly natural flowers and grew in the regular way; but their host showed them one flower bed which was his especial pride.

"You see, all common flowers fade and die in time," he explained, "and so there are seasons when the pretty blooms are scarce. Therefore I decided to make one tin flower bed all of tin flowers, and my workmen have created them with rare skill. Here you see tin camelias, tin marigolds, tin carnations, tin poppies and tin hollyhocks growing as naturally as if they were real."

Indeed, they were a pretty sight, and glistened under the sunlight like spun silver. "Isn't this tin hollyhock going to seed?" asked the Wizard, bending over the flowers.

"Why, I believe it is!" exclaimed the Tin Woodman, as if surprised. "I hadn't noticed that before. But I shall plant the tin seeds and raise another bed of tin hollyhocks."

In one corner of the gardens Nick Chopper had established a fish-pond in which they saw swimming and disporting themselves many pretty tin fishes.

"Would they bite on hooks?" asked Aunt Em, curiously.

The Tin Woodman seemed hurt at this question.

"Madam," said he, "do you suppose I would allow anyone to catch my beautiful fishes, even if they were foolish enough to bite on hooks? No, indeed! Every created thing is safe from harm in my domain, and I would as soon think of killing my little friend Dorothy as killing one of my tin fishes."

"The Emperor is very kind-hearted, ma'am," explained the Wizard. "If a fly happens to light upon his tin body he doesn't rudely brush it off, as some people might do; he asks it politely to find some other resting place."

"What does the fly do then?" enquired Aunt Em.

"Usually it begs his pardon and goes away," said the Wizard, gravely. "Flies like to be treated politely as well as other creatures, and here in Oz they understand what we say to them, and behave very nicely."

"Well," said Aunt Em, "the flies in Kansas, where I came from, don't understand anything but a swat. You have to smash 'em to

make 'em behave; and it's the same way with 'skeeters. Do you have 'skeeters in Oz?"

"We have some very large mosquitoes here, which sing as beautifully as song birds," replied the Tin Woodman. "But they never bite or annoy our people, because they are well fed and taken care of. The reason they bite people in your country is because they are hungry—poor things!"

"Yes," agreed Aunt Em; "they're hungry, all right. An' they ain't very particular who they feed on. I'm glad you've got the 'skeeters educated in Oz."

That evening after dinner they were entertained by the Emperor's Tin Cornet Band, which played for them several sweet melodies. Also the Wizard did a few sleight-of-hand tricks to amuse the company; after which they all retired to their cozy tin bedrooms and slept soundly until morning.

After breakfast Dorothy said to the Tin Woodman: "If you'll tell us which way to go we'll visit the Scarecrow on our way home."

"I will go with you, and show you the way," replied the Emperor, "for I must journey to-day to the Emerald City."

He looked so anxious, as he said this, that the little girl asked, "There isn't anything wrong with Ozma, is there?"

"Not yet," said he; "but I'm afraid the time has come when I must tell you some very bad news, little friend."

"Oh, what is it?" cried Dorothy.

"Do you remember the Nome King?" asked the Tin Woodman.

"I remember him very well," she replied.

"The Nome King has not a kind heart," said the Emperor, sadly, "and he has been harboring wicked thoughts of revenge, because we once defeated him and liberated his slaves and you took away his Magic Belt. So he has ordered his Nomes to dig a long tunnel underneath the deadly desert, so that he may march his host right into the Emerald City. When he gets there he intends to destroy our beautiful country."

Dorothy was much surprised to hear this.

"How did Ozma find out about the tunnel?" she asked.

"She saw it in her Magic Picture."

"Of course," said Dorothy; "I might have known that. And what is she going to do?"

"I cannot tell," was the reply.

"Pooh!" cried the Yellow Hen. "We're not afraid of the Nomes. If we roll a few of our eggs down the tunnel they'll run away back home as fast as they can go."

"Why, that's true enough!" exclaimed Dorothy. "The Scarecrow once conquered all the Nome King's army with some of Billina's eggs."

"But you do not understand all of the dreadful plot," continued the Tin Woodman. "The Nome King is clever, and he knows his Nomes would run from eggs; so he has bargained with many terrible creatures to help him. These evil spirits are not afraid of eggs or anything else, and they are very powerful. So the Nome King will send them through the tunnel first, to conquer and destroy, and then the Nomes will follow after to get their share of the plunder and slaves."

They were all startled to hear this, and every face wore a troubled look.

"Is the tunnel all ready?" asked Dorothy.

"Ozma sent me word yesterday that the tunnel was all completed except for a thin crust of earth at the end. When our enemies break through this crust, they will be in the gardens of the royal palace, in the heart of the Emerald City. I offered to arm all my Winkies and march to Ozma's assistance; but she said no."

"I wonder why?" asked Dorothy.

"She answered that all the inhabitants of Oz, gathered together, were not powerful enough to fight and overcome the evil forces of the Nome King. Therefore she refuses to fight at all."

"But they will capture and enslave us, and plunder and ruin all our lovely land!" exclaimed the Wizard, greatly disturbed by this statement.

"I fear they will," said the Tin Woodman, sorrowfully. "And I also fear that those who are not fairies, such as the Wizard, and Dorothy, and her uncle and aunt, as well as Toto and Billina, will be speedily put to death by the conquerors."

"What can be done?" asked Dorothy, shuddering a little at the prospect of this awful fate.

"Nothing can be done!" gloomily replied the Emperor of the Winkies. "But since Ozma refuses my army I will go myself to the Emerald City. The least I may do is to perish beside my beloved Ruler."

25. How the Scarecrow Displayed His Wisdom

This amazing news had saddened every heart and all were now anxious to return to the Emerald City and share Ozma's fate. So they started without loss of time, and as the road led past the Scarecrow's new mansion they determined to make a brief halt there and confer with him.

"The Scarecrow is probably the wisest man in all Oz," remarked the Tin Woodman, when they had started upon their journey. "His brains are plentiful and of excellent quality, and often he has told me things I might never have thought of myself. I must say I rely a great deal upon the Scarecrow's brains in this emergency."

The Tin Woodman rode on the front seat of the wagon, where Dorothy sat between him and the Wizard.

"Has the Scarecrow heard of Ozma's trouble?" asked the Captain General.

"I do not know, sir," was the reply.

"When I was a private," said Omby Amby, "I was an excellent army, as I fully proved in our war against the Nomes. But now there is not a single private left in our army, since Ozma made me the Captain General, so there is no one to fight and defend our lovely Ruler."

"True," said the Wizard. "The present army is composed only of officers, and the business of an officer is to order his men to fight. Since there are no men there can be no fighting."

"Poor Ozma!" whispered Dorothy, with tears in her sweet eyes. "It's dreadful to think of all her lovely fairy country being destroyed. I wonder if we couldn't manage to escape and get back to Kansas by means of the Magic Belt? And we might take Ozma with us and all work hard to get money for her, so she wouldn't be so VERY lonely and unhappy about the loss of her fairyland."

"Do you think there would be any work for ME in Kansas?" asked the Tin Woodman.

"If you are hollow, they might use you in a canning factory," suggested Uncle Henry. "But I can't see the use of your working for a living. You never eat or sleep or need a new suit of clothes."

"I was not thinking of myself," replied the Emperor, with dignity. "I merely wondered if I could not help to support Dorothy and Ozma."

As they indulged in these sad plans for the future they journeyed in sight of the Scarecrow's new mansion, and even though filled with care and worry over the impending fate of Oz, Dorothy couldn't help a feeling of wonder at the sight she saw.

The Scarecrow's new house was shaped like an immense ear of corn. The rows of kernels were made of solid gold, and the green upon which the ear stood upright was a mass of sparkling emeralds. Upon the very top of the structure was perched a figure representing the Scarecrow himself, and upon his extended arms, as well as upon his head, were several crows carved out of ebony and having ruby eyes. You may imagine how big this ear of corn was when I tell you that a single gold kernel formed a window, swinging outward upon hinges, while a row of four kernels opened to make the front entrance. Inside there were five stories, each story being a single room.

The gardens around the mansion consisted of cornfields, and Dorothy acknowledged that the place was in all respects a very appropriate home for her good friend the Scarecrow.

"He would have been very happy here, I'm sure," she said, "if only the Nome King had left us alone. But if Oz is destroyed of course this place will be destroyed too."

"Yes," replied the Tin Woodman, "and also my beautiful tin castle, that has been my joy and pride."

"Jack Pumpkinhead's house will go too," remarked the Wizard, "as well as Professor Wogglebug's Athletic College, and Ozma's royal palace, and all our other handsome buildings."

"Yes, Oz will indeed become a desert when the Nome King gets through with it," sighed Omby Amby.

The Scarecrow came out to meet them and gave them all a hearty welcome.

"I hear you have decided always to live in the Land of Oz, after this," he said to Dorothy; "and that will delight my heart, for I have greatly disliked our frequent partings. But why are you all so downcast?"

"Have you heard the news?" asked the Tin Woodman.

"No news to make me sad," replied the Scarecrow.

Then Nick Chopper told his friend of the Nome King's tunnel, and how the evil creatures of the North had allied themselves with the underground monarch for the purpose of conquering and destroying Oz. "Well," said the Scarecrow, "it certainly looks bad for Ozma, and all of us. But I believe it is wrong to worry over anything before it happens. It is surely time enough to be sad when our country is despoiled and our people made slaves. So let us not deprive ourselves of the few happy hours remaining to us."

"Ah! that is real wisdom," declared the Shaggy Man, approvingly. "After we become really unhappy we shall regret these few hours that are left to us, unless we enjoy them to the utmost."

"Nevertheless," said the Scarecrow, "I shall go with you to the Emerald City and offer Ozma my services."

"She says we can do nothing to oppose our enemies," announced the Tin Woodman.

"And doubtless she is right, sir," answered the Scarecrow. "Still, she will appreciate our sympathy, and it is the duty of Ozma's friends to stand by her side when the final disaster occurs."

He then led them into his queer mansion and showed them the beautiful rooms in all the five stories. The lower room was a grand reception hall, with a hand-organ in one corner. This instrument the Scarecrow, when alone, could turn to amuse himself, as he was very fond of music. The walls were hung with white silk, upon which flocks of black crows were embroidered in black diamonds. Some of the chairs were made in the shape of big crows and upholstered with cushions of corn-colored silk.

The second story contained a fine banquet room, where the Scarecrow might entertain his guests, and the three stories above that were bed-chambers exquisitely furnished and decorated.

"From these rooms," said the Scarecrow, proudly, "one may obtain fine views of the surrounding cornfields. The corn I grow is always husky, and I call the ears my regiments, because they have so many kernels. Of course I cannot ride my cobs, but I really don't care shucks about that. Taken altogether, my farm will stack up with any in the neighborhood."

The visitors partook of some light refreshment and then hurried away to resume the road to the Emerald City. The Scarecrow found a seat in the wagon between Omby Amby and the Shaggy Man, and his weight did not add much to the load because he was stuffed with straw.

"You will notice I have one oat-field on my property," he remarked, as they drove away. "Oat-straw is, I have found, the best of all straws to re-stuff myself with when my interior gets musty or out of shape."

"Are you able to re-stuff yourself without help?" asked Aunt Em. "I should think that after the straw was taken out of you there wouldn't be anything left but your clothes."

"You are almost correct, madam," he answered. "My servants do the stuffing, under my direction. For my head, in which are my excellent brains, is a bag tied at the bottom. My face is neatly painted upon one side of the bag, as you may see. My head does not need re-stuffing, as my body does, for all that it requires is to have the face touched up with fresh paint occasionally."

It was not far from the Scarecrow's mansion to the farm of Jack Pumpkinhead, and when they arrived there both Uncle Henry and Aunt Em were much impressed. The farm was one vast pumpkin field, and some of the pumpkins were of enormous size. In one of them, which had been neatly hollowed out, Jack himself lived, and he declared that it was a very comfortable residence. The reason he grew so many pumpkins was in order that he might change his head as often as it became wrinkled or threatened to spoil.

The pumpkin-headed man welcomed his visitors joyfully and offered them several delicious pumpkin pies to eat.

"I don't indulge in pumpkin pies myself, for two reasons," he said. "One reason is that were I to eat pumpkins I would become a cannibal, and the other reason is that I never eat, not being hollow inside."

"Very good reasons," agreed the Scarecrow.

They told Jack Pumpkinhead of the dreadful news about the Nome King, and he decided to go with them to the Emerald City and help comfort Ozma.

"I had expected to live here in ease and comfort for many centuries," said Jack, dolefully; "but of course if the Nome King destroys everything in Oz I shall be destroyed too. Really, it seems too bad, doesn't it?"

They were soon on their journey again, and so swiftly did the Sawhorse draw the wagon over the smooth roads that before twilight fell they had reached the royal palace in the Emerald City, and were at their journey's end.

26. How Ozma Refused to Fight for Her Kingdom

Ozma was in her rose garden picking a bouquet when the party arrived, and she greeted all her old and new friends as smilingly and sweetly as ever.

Dorothy's eyes were full of tears as she kissed the lovely Ruler of Oz, and she whispered to her:

"Oh, Ozma, Ozma! I'm SO sorry!"

Ozma seemed surprised.

"Sorry for what, Dorothy?" she asked.

"For all your trouble about the Nome King," was the reply.

Ozma laughed with genuine amusement.

"Why, that has not troubled me a bit, dear Princess," she replied. Then, looking around at the sad faces of her friends, she added: "Have you all been worrying about this tunnel?"

"We have!" they exclaimed in a chorus.

"Well, perhaps it is more serious than I imagined," admitted the fair Ruler; "but I haven't given the matter much thought. After dinner we will all meet together and talk it over."

So they went to their rooms and prepared for dinner, and Dorothy dressed herself in her prettiest gown and put on her coronet, for she thought that this might be the last time she would ever appear as a Princess of Oz.

The Scarecrow, the Tin Woodman and Jack Pumpkinhead all sat at the dinner table, although none of them was made so he could eat. Usually they served to enliven the meal with their merry talk, but to-night all seemed strangely silent and uneasy.

As soon as the dinner was finished Ozma led the company to her own private room in which hung the Magic Picture. When they had seated themselves the Scarecrow was the first to speak.

"Is the Nome King's tunnel finished, Ozma?" he asked.

"It was completed to-day," she replied. "They have built it right under my palace grounds, and it ends in front of the Forbidden Fountain. Nothing but a crust of earth remains to separate our enemies from us, and when they march here, they will easily break through this crust and rush upon us."

"Who will assist the Nome King?" inquired the Scarecrow.

"The Whimsies, the Growleywogs and the Phanfasms," she replied. "I watched to-day in my Magic Picture the messengers whom the Nome King sent to all these people to summon them to assemble in his great caverns."

"Let us see what they are doing now," suggested the Tin Woodman.

So Ozma wished to see the Nome King's cavern, and at once the landscape faded from the Magic Picture and was replaced by the scene then being enacted in the jeweled cavern of King Roquat.

A wild and startling scene it was which the Oz people beheld.

Before the Nome King stood the Chief of the Whimsies and the Grand Gallipoot of the Growleywogs, surrounded by their most skillful generals. Very fierce and powerful they looked, so that even the Nome King and General Guph, who stood beside his master, seemed a bit fearful in the presence of their allies.

Now a still more formidable creature entered the cavern. It was the First and Foremost of the Phanfasms and he proudly sat down in King Roquat's own throne and demanded the right to lead his forces through the tunnel in advance of all the others. The First and Foremost now appeared to all eyes in his hairy skin and the bear's head. What his real form was even Roquat did not know.

Through the arches leading into the vast series of caverns that lay beyond the throne room of King Roquat could be seen ranks upon ranks of the invaders—thousands of Phanfasms, Growleywogs and Whimsies standing in serried lines, while behind them were massed the thousands upon thousands of General Guph's own army of Nomes.

"Listen!" whispered Ozma. "I think we can hear what they are saying."

So they kept still and listened.

"Is all ready?" demanded the First and Foremost, haughtily.

"The tunnel is finally completed," replied General Guph.

"How long will it take us to march to the Emerald City?" asked the Grand Gallipoot of the Growleywogs.

"If we start at midnight," replied the Nome King, "we shall arrive at the Emerald City by daybreak. Then, while all the Oz people are sleeping, we will capture them and make them our slaves. After that we will destroy the city itself and march through the Land of Oz, burning and devastating as we go."

"Good!" cried the First and Foremost. "When we get through with Oz it will be a desert wilderness. Ozma shall be my slave."

"She shall be MY slave!" shouted the Grand Gallipoot, angrily.

"We'll decide that by and by," said King Roquat hastily. "Don't let us quarrel now, friends. First let us conquer Oz, and then we will divide the spoils of war in a satisfactory manner."

The First and Foremost smiled wickedly; but he only said: "I and my Phanfasms go first, for nothing on earth can oppose our power."

They all agreed to that, knowing the Phanfasms to be the mightiest of the combined forces. King Roquat now invited them to attend a banquet he had prepared, where they might occupy themselves in eating and drinking until midnight arrived.

As they had now seen and heard all of the plot against them that they cared to, Ozma allowed her Magic Picture to fade away. Then she turned to her friends and said: "Our enemies will be here sooner than I expected. What do you advise me to do?"

"It is now too late to assemble our people," said the Tin Woodman, despondently. "If you had allowed me to arm and drill my Winkies, we might have put up a good fight and destroyed many of our enemies before we were conquered."

"The Munchkins are good fighters, too," said Omby Amby; "and so are the Gillikins."

"But I do not wish to fight," declared Ozma, firmly. "No one has the right to destroy any living creatures, however evil they may be, or to hurt them or make them unhappy. I will not fight, even to save my kingdom."

"The Nome King is not so particular," remarked the Scarecrow. "He intends to destroy us all and ruin our beautiful country."

"Because the Nome King intends to do evil is no excuse for my doing the same," replied Ozma.

"Self-preservation is the first law of nature," quoted the Shaggy Man.

"True," she said, readily. "I would like to discover a plan to save ourselves without fighting."

That seemed a hopeless task to them, but realizing that Ozma was determined not to fight, they tried to think of some means that might promise escape.

"Couldn't we bribe our enemies, by giving them a lot of emeralds and gold?" asked Jack Pumpkinhead.

"No, because they believe they are able to take everything we have," replied the Ruler.

"I have thought of something," said Dorothy.

"What is it, dear?" asked Ozma.

"Let us use the Magic Belt to wish all of us in Kansas. We will put some emeralds in our pockets, and can sell them in Topeka for enough to pay off the mortgage on Uncle Henry's farm. Then we can all live together and be happy."

"A clever idea!" exclaimed the Scarecrow.

"Kansas is a very good country. I've been there," said the Shaggy Man.

"That seems to me an excellent plan," approved the Tin Woodman.

"No!" said Ozma, decidedly. "Never will I desert my people and leave them to so cruel a fate. I will use the Magic Belt to send the rest of you to Kansas, if you wish, but if my beloved country must be destroyed and my people enslaved I will remain and share their fate."

"Quite right," asserted the Scarecrow, sighing. "I will remain with you."

"And so will I," declared the Tin Woodman and the Shaggy Man and Jack Pumpkinhead, in turn. Tiktok, the machine man, also said he intended to stand by Ozma. "For," said he, "I should be of no use at all in Kan-sas."

"For my part," announced Dorothy, gravely, "if the Ruler of Oz must not desert her people, a Princess of Oz has no right to run away, either. I'm willing to become a slave with the rest of you; so all we can do with the Magic Belt is to use it to send Uncle Henry and Aunt Em back to Kansas."

"I've been a slave all my life," Aunt Em replied, with considerable cheerfulness, "and so has Henry. I guess we won't go back to Kansas, anyway. I'd rather take my chances with the rest of you."

Ozma smiled upon them all gratefully.

"There is no need to despair just yet," she said. "I'll get up early to-morrow morning and be at the Forbidden Fountain when the fierce warriors break through the crust of the earth. I will speak to them pleasantly and perhaps they won't be so very bad, after all."

"Why do they call it the Forbidden Fountain?" asked Dorothy, thoughtfully.

"Don't you know, dear?" returned Ozma, surprised.

"No," said Dorothy. "Of course I've seen the fountain in the palace grounds, ever since I first came to Oz; and I've read the sign which says: 'All Persons are Forbidden to Drink at this Fountain.' But I never knew WHY they were forbidden. The water seems clear and sparkling and it bubbles up in a golden basin all the time."

"That water," declared Ozma, gravely, "is the most dangerous thing in all the Land of Oz. It is the Water of Oblivion."

"What does that mean?" asked Dorothy.

"Whoever drinks at the Forbidden Fountain at once forgets everything he has ever known," Ozma asserted.

"It wouldn't be a bad way to forget our troubles," suggested Uncle Henry.

"That is true; but you would forget everything else, and become as ignorant as a baby," returned Ozma.

"Does it make one crazy?" asked Dorothy.

"No; it only makes one forget," replied the girl Ruler. "It is said that once—long, long ago—a wicked King ruled Oz, and made himself and all his people very miserable and unhappy. So Glinda, the Good Sorceress, placed this fountain here, and the King drank of its water and forgot all his wickedness. His mind became innocent and vacant, and when he learned the things of life again they were all good things. But the people remembered how wicked their King had been, and were still afraid of him. Therefore, he made them all drink of the Water of Oblivion and forget everything they had known, so that they became as simple and innocent as their King. After that, they all grew wise together, and their wisdom was good, so that peace and happiness reigned in the land. But for fear some one might drink of the water again, and in an instant forget all he had learned, the King put that sign upon the fountain, where it has remained for many centuries up to this very day."

They had all listened intently to Ozma's story, and when she finished speaking there was a long period of silence while all thought upon the curious magical power of the Water of Oblivion.

Finally the Scarecrow's painted face took on a broad smile that stretched the cloth as far as it would go.

"How thankful I am," he said, "that I have such an excellent assortment of brains!"

"I gave you the best brains I ever mixed," declared the Wizard, with an air of pride.

"You did, indeed!" agreed the Scarecrow, "and they work so splendidly that they have found a way to save Oz—to save us all!"

"I'm glad to hear that," said the Wizard. "We never needed saving more than we do just now."

"Do you mean to say you can save us from those awful Phanfasms, and Growleywogs and Whimsies?" asked Dorothy eagerly.

"I'm sure of it, my dear," asserted the Scarecrow, still smiling genially.

"Tell us how!" cried the Tin Woodman.

"Not now," said the Scarecrow. "You may all go to bed, and advise you to forget your worries just as completely as if you had drunk of the Water of Oblivion in the Forbidden Fountain. I'm going to stay here and tell my plan to Ozma alone, but if you will all be at the Forbidden Fountain at daybreak, you'll see how easily we will save the kingdom when our enemies break through the crust of earth and come from the tunnel."

So they went away and let the Scarecrow and Ozma alone; but Dorothy could not sleep a wink all night.

"He is only a Scarecrow," she said to herself, "and I'm not sure that his mixed brains are as clever as he thinks they are."

But she knew that if the Scarecrow's plan failed they were all lost; so she tried to have faith in him.

27. How the Fierce Warriors Invaded Oz

The Nome King and his terrible allies sat at the banquet table until midnight. There was much quarreling between the Growleywogs and Phanfasms, and one of the wee-headed Whimsies got angry at General Guph and choked him until he nearly stopped breathing. Yet no one was seriously hurt, and the Nome King felt much relieved when the clock struck twelve and they all sprang up and seized their weapons.

"Aha!" shouted the First and Foremost. "Now to conquer the Land of Oz!"

He marshaled his Phanfasms in battle array and at his word of command they marched into the tunnel and began the long journey through it to the Emerald City. The First and Foremost intended to take all the treasures of Oz for himself; to kill all who could be killed and enslave the rest; to destroy and lay waste the whole country, and afterward to conquer and enslave the Nomes, the Growleywogs and the Whimsies. And he knew his power was sufficient to enable him to do all these things easily.

Next marched into the tunnel the army of gigantic Growleywogs, with their Grand Gallipoot at their head. They were dreadful beings, indeed, and longed to get to Oz that they might begin to pilfer and destroy. The Grand Gallipoot was a little afraid of the First and Foremost, but had a cunning plan to murder or destroy that powerful being and secure the wealth of Oz for himself. Mighty little of the plunder would the Nome King get, thought the Grand Gallipoot.

The Chief of the Whimsies now marched his false-headed forces into the tunnel. In his wicked little head was a plot to destroy both the First and Foremost and the Grand Gallipoot. He intended to let them conquer Oz, since they insisted on going first; but he would afterward treacherously destroy them, as well as King Roquat, and keep all the slaves and treasure of Ozma's kingdom for himself.

After all his dangerous allies had marched into the tunnel the Nome King and General Guph started to follow them, at the head of fifty thousand Nomes, all fully armed.

"Guph," said the King, "those creatures ahead of us mean mischief. They intend to get everything for themselves and leave us nothing."

"I know," replied the General; "but they are not as clever as they think they are. When you get the Magic Belt you must at once wish the Whimsies and Growleywogs and Phanfasms all back into their own countries—and the Belt will surely take them there."

"Good!" cried the King. "An excellent plan, Guph. I'll do it. While they are conquering Oz I'll get the Magic Belt, and then only the Nomes will remain to ravage the country."

So you see there was only one thing that all were agreed upon— that Oz should be destroyed.

On, on, on the vast ranks of invaders marched, filling the tunnel from side to side. With a steady tramp, tramp, they advanced, every step taking them nearer to the beautiful Emerald City.

"Nothing can save the Land of Oz!" thought the First and Foremost, scowling until his bear face was as black as the tunnel.

"The Emerald City is as good as destroyed already!" muttered the Grand Gallipoot, shaking his war club fiercely.

"In a few hours Oz will be a desert!" said the Chief of the Whimsies, with an evil laugh.

"My dear Guph," remarked the Nome King to his General, "at last my vengeance upon Ozma of Oz and her people is about to be accomplished."

"You are right!" declared the General. "Ozma is surely lost."

And now the First and Foremost, who was in advance and nearing the Emerald City, began to cough and to sneeze.

"This tunnel is terribly dusty," he growled, angrily. "I'll punish that Nome King for not having it swept clean. My throat and eyes are getting full of dust and I'm as thirsty as a fish!"

The Grand Gallipoot was coughing too, and his throat was parched and dry.

"What a dusty place!" he cried. "I'll be glad when we reach Oz, where we can get a drink."

"Who has any water?" asked the Whimsie Chief, gasping and choking. But none of his followers carried a drop of water, so he hastened on to get through the dusty tunnel to the Land of Oz.

"Where did all this dust come from?" demanded General Guph, trying hard to swallow but finding his throat so dry he couldn't.

"I don't know," answered the Nome King. "I've been in the tunnel every day while it was being built, but I never noticed any dust before."

"Let's hurry!" cried the General. "I'd give half the gold in Oz for a drink of water."

The dust grew thicker and thicker, and the throats and eyes and noses of the invaders were filled with it. But not one halted or turned back. They hurried forward more fierce and vengeful than ever.

28. How They Drank at the Forbidden Fountain

The Scarecrow had no need to sleep; neither had the Tin Woodman or Tiktok or Jack Pumpkinhead. So they all wandered out into the palace grounds and stood beside the sparkling water of the Forbidden Fountain until daybreak. During this time they indulged in occasional conversation.

"Nothing could make me forget what I know," remarked the Scarecrow, gazing into the fountain, "for I cannot drink the Water of Oblivion or water of any kind. And I am glad that this is so, for I consider my wisdom unexcelled."

"You are cer-tain-ly ve-ry wise," agreed Tiktok. "For my part, I can on-ly think by ma-chin-er-y, so I do not pre-tend to know as much as you do."

"My tin brains are very bright, but that is all I claim for them," said Nick Chopper, modestly. "Yet I do not aspire to being very wise, for I have noticed that the happiest people are those who do not let their brains oppress them."

"Mine never worry me," Jack Pumpkinhead acknowledged. "There are many seeds of thought in my head, but they do not sprout easily. I am glad that it is so, for if I occupied my days in thinking I should have no time for anything else."

In this cheery mood they passed the hours until the first golden streaks of dawn appeared in the sky. Then Ozma joined them, as fresh and lovely as ever and robed in one of her prettiest gowns.

"Our enemies have not yet arrived," said the Scarecrow, after greeting affectionately the sweet and girlish Ruler.

"They will soon be here," she said, "for I have just glanced at my Magic Picture, and have seen them coughing and choking with the dust in the tunnel."

"Oh, is there dust in the tunnel?" asked the Tin Woodman.

"Yes; Ozma placed it there by means of the Magic Belt," explained the Scarecrow, with one of his broad smiles.

Then Dorothy came to them, Uncle Henry and Aunt Em following close after her. The little girl's eyes were heavy because she had had a sleepless and anxious night. Toto walked by her side, but the little dog's spirits were very much subdued. Billina, who was always up by daybreak, was not long in joining the group by the fountain.

The Wizard and the Shaggy Man next arrived, and soon after appeared Omby Amby, dressed in his best uniform.

"There lies the tunnel," said Ozma, pointing to a part of the ground just before the Forbidden Fountain, "and in a few moments the dreadful invaders will break through the earth and swarm over the land. Let us all stand on the other side of the Fountain and watch to see what happens."

At once they followed her suggestion and moved around the fountain of the Water of Oblivion. There they stood silent and expectant until the earth beyond gave way with a sudden crash and up leaped the powerful form of the First and Foremost, followed by all his grim warriors.

As the leader sprang forward his gleaming eyes caught the play of the fountain and he rushed toward it and drank eagerly of the sparkling water. Many of the other Phanfasms drank, too, in order to clear their dry and dusty throats. Then they stood around and looked at one another with simple, wondering smiles.

The First and Foremost saw Ozma and her companions beyond the fountain, but instead of making an effort to capture her he merely stared at her in pleased admiration of her beauty—for he had forgotten where he was and why he had come there.

But now the Grand Gallipoot arrived, rushing from the tunnel with a hoarse cry of mingled rage and thirst. He too saw the fountain and hastened to drink of its forbidden waters. The other Growleywogs were not slow to follow suit, and even before they had finished drinking the Chief of the Whimsies and his people came to push them away, while they one and all cast off their false heads that they might slake their thirst at the fountain.

When the Nome King and General Guph arrived they both made a dash to drink, but the General was so mad with thirst that he knocked his King over, and while Roquat lay sprawling upon the ground the General drank heartily of the Water of Oblivion.

This rude act of his General made the Nome King so angry that for a moment he forgot he was thirsty and rose to his feet to glare upon the group of terrible warriors he had brought here to assist him. He saw Ozma and her people, too, and yelled out: "Why don't you capture them? Why don't you conquer Oz, you idiots? Why do you stand there like a lot of dummies?"

But the great warriors had become like little children. They had forgotten all their enmity against Ozma and against Oz. They had even forgotten who they themselves were, or why they were in this strange and beautiful country. As for the Nome King, they did not recognize him, and wondered who he was.

The sun came up and sent its flood of silver rays to light the faces of the invaders. The frowns and scowls and evil looks were all gone. Even the most monstrous of the creatures there assembled smiled innocently and seemed light-hearted and content merely to be alive.

Not so with Roquat, the Nome King. He had not drunk from the Forbidden Fountain and all his former rage against Ozma and Dorothy now inflamed him as fiercely as ever. The sight of General Guph babbling like a happy child and playing with his hands in the cool waters of the fountain astonished and maddened Red Roquat. Seeing that his terrible allies and his own General refused to act, the Nome King turned to order his great army of Nomes to advance from the tunnel and seize the helpless Oz people.

But the Scarecrow suspected what was in the King's mind and spoke a word to the Tin Woodman. Together they ran at Roquat and grabbing him up tossed him into the great basin of the fountain.

The Nome King's body was round as a ball, and it bobbed up and down in the Water of Oblivion while he spluttered and screamed with fear lest he should drown. And when he cried out, his mouth filled with water, which ran down his throat, so that straightway he forgot all he had formerly known just as completely as had all the other invaders.

Ozma and Dorothy could not refrain from laughing to see their dreaded enemies become as harmless as babies. There was no danger now that Oz would be destroyed. The only question remaining to solve was how to get rid of this horde of intruders.

The Shaggy Man kindly pulled the Nome King out of the fountain and set him upon his thin legs. Roquat was dripping wet, but he chattered and laughed and wanted to drink more of the water. No thought of injuring any person was now in his mind.

Before he left the tunnel he had commanded his fifty thousand Nomes to remain there until he ordered them to advance, as he wished to give his allies time to conquer Oz before he appeared with his own army. Ozma did not wish all these Nomes to overrun her land, so she advanced to King Roquat and taking his hand in her own said gently: "Who are you? What is your name?"

"I don't know," he replied, smiling at her. "Who are you, my dear?"

"My name is Ozma," she said; "and your name is Roquat."

"Oh, is it?" he replied, seeming pleased.

"Yes; you are King of the Nomes," she said.

"Ah; I wonder what the Nomes are!" returned the King, as if puzzled.

"They are underground elves, and that tunnel over there is full of them," she answered. "You have a beautiful cavern at the other end of the tunnel, so you must go to your Nomes and say: 'March home!' Then follow after them and in time you will reach the pretty cavern where you live."

The Nome King was much pleased to learn this, for he had forgotten he had a cavern. So he went to the tunnel and said to his army: 'March home!' At once the Nomes turned and marched back through the tunnel, and the King followed after them, laughing with delight to find his orders so readily obeyed.

The Wizard went to General Guph, who was trying to count his fingers, and told him to follow the Nome King, who was his master. Guph meekly obeyed, and so all the Nomes quitted the Land of Oz forever.

But there were still the Phanfasms and Whimsies and Growleywogs standing around in groups, and they were so many that they filled the gardens and trampled upon the flowers and grass because they did not know that the tender plants would be injured by their clumsy feet. But in all other respects they were perfectly harmless and played together like children or gazed with pleasure upon the pretty sights of the royal gardens.

After counseling with the Scarecrow Ozma sent Omby Amby to the palace for the Magic Belt, and when the Captain General returned with it the Ruler of Oz at once clasped the precious Belt around her waist.

"I wish all these strange people—the Whimsies and the Growleywogs and the Phanfasms—safe back in their own homes!" she said.

It all happened in a twinkling, for of course the wish was no sooner spoken than it was granted.

All the hosts of the invaders were gone, and only the trampled grass showed that they had ever been in the Land of Oz.

29. How Glinda Worked a Magic Spell

"That was better than fighting," said Ozma, when all our friends were assembled in the palace after the exciting events of the morning; and each and every one agreed with her.

"No one was hurt," said the Wizard, delightedly.

"And no one hurt us," added Aunt Em.

"But, best of all," said Dorothy, "the wicked people have all forgotten their wickedness, and will not wish to hurt any one after this."

"True, Princess," declared the Shaggy Man. "It seems to me that to have reformed all those evil characters is more important than to have saved Oz."

"Nevertheless," remarked the Scarecrow, "I am glad Oz is saved. I can now go back to my new mansion and live happily."

"And I am glad and grateful that my pumpkin farm is saved," said Jack.

"For my part," added the Tin Woodman, "I cannot express my joy that my lovely tin castle is not to be demolished by wicked enemies."

"Still," said Tiktok, "o-ther en-e-mies may come to Oz some day."

"Why do you allow your clock-work brains to interrupt our joy?" asked Omby Amby, frowning at the machine man.

"I say what I am wound up to say," answered Tiktok.

"And you are right," declared Ozma. "I myself have been thinking of this very idea, and it seems to me there are entirely too many ways for people to get to the Land of Oz. We used to think the deadly desert that surrounds us was enough protection; but that is no longer the case. The Wizard and Dorothy have both come here through the air, and I am told the earth people have invented airships that can fly anywhere they wish to go."

"Why, sometimes they do, and sometimes they don't," asserted Dorothy.

"But in time the airships may cause us trouble," continued Ozma, "for if the earth folk learn how to manage them we would be overrun with visitors who would ruin our lovely, secluded fairyland."

"That is true enough," agreed the Wizard.

"Also the desert fails to protect us in other ways," Ozma went on, thoughtfully. "Johnny Dooit once made a sand-boat that sailed across it, and the Nome King made a tunnel under it. So I believe something ought to be done to cut us off from the rest of the world entirely, so that no one in the future will ever be able to intrude upon us."

"How will you do that?" asked the Scarecrow.

"I do not know; but in some way I am sure it can be accomplished. To-morrow I will make a journey to the castle of Glinda the Good, and ask her advice."

"May I go with you?" asked Dorothy, eagerly.

"Of course, my dear Princess; and I also invite any of our friends here who would like to undertake the journey."

They all declared they wished to accompany their girl Ruler, for this was indeed an important mission, since the future of the Land of Oz to a great extent depended upon it. So Ozma gave orders to her servants to prepare for the journey on the morrow.

That day she watched her Magic Picture, and when it showed her that all the Nomes had returned through the tunnel to their underground caverns, Ozma used the Magic Belt to close up the tunnel, so that the earth underneath the desert sands became as solid as it was before the Nomes began to dig.

Early the following morning a gay cavalcade set out to visit the famous Sorceress, Glinda the Good. Ozma and Dorothy rode in a chariot drawn by the Cowardly Lion and the Hungry Tiger, while the Sawhorse drew the red wagon in which rode the rest of the party.

With hearts light and free from care they traveled merrily along through the lovely and fascinating Land of Oz, and in good season reached the stately castle in which resided the Sorceress.

Glinda knew that they were coming.

"I have been reading about you in my Magic Book," she said, as she greeted them in her gracious way.

"What is your Magic Book like?" inquired Aunt Em, curiously.

"It is a record of everything that happens," replied the Sorceress. "As soon as an event takes place, anywhere in the world, it is immediately found printed in my Magic Book. So when I read its pages I am well informed."

"Did it tell you how our enemies drank the Water of 'Blivion?" asked Dorothy.

"Yes, my dear; it told all about it. And also it told me you were all coming to my castle, and why."

"Then," said Ozma, "I suppose you know what is in my mind, and that I am seeking a way to prevent any one in the future from discovering the Land of Oz."

"Yes; I know that. And while you were on your journey I have thought of a way to accomplish your desire. For it seems to me unwise to allow too many outside people to come here. Dorothy, with her uncle and aunt, has now returned to Oz to live always, and there is no reason why we should leave any way open for others to travel uninvited to our fairyland. Let us make it impossible for any one ever to communicate with us in any way, after this. Then we may live peacefully and contentedly."

"Your advice is wise," returned Ozma. "I thank you, Glinda, for your promise to assist me."

"But how can you do it?" asked Dorothy. "How can you keep every one from ever finding Oz?"

"By making our country invisible to all eyes but our own," replied the Sorceress, smiling. "I have a magic charm powerful enough to accomplish that wonderful feat, and now that we have been warned of our danger by the Nome King's invasion, I believe we must not hesitate to separate ourselves forever from all the rest of the world."

"I agree with you," said the Ruler of Oz.

"Won't it make any difference to us?" asked Dorothy, doubtfully.

"No, my dear," Glinda answered, assuringly. "We shall still be able to see each other and everything in the Land of Oz. It won't affect us at all; but those who fly through the air over our country will look down and see nothing at all. Those who come to the edge of the desert, or try to cross it, will catch no glimpse of Oz, or know in what direction it lies. No one will try to tunnel to us again because we cannot be seen and therefore cannot be found. In other words, the Land of Oz will entirely disappear from the knowledge of the rest of the world."

"That's all right," said Dorothy, cheerfully. "You may make Oz invis'ble as soon as you please, for all I care."

"It is already invisible," Glinda stated. "I knew Ozma's wishes, and performed the Magic Spell before you arrived."

Ozma seized the hand of the Sorceress and pressed it gratefully.

"Thank you!" she said.

30. How the Story of Oz Came to an End

The writer of these Oz stories has received a little note from Princess Dorothy of Oz which, for a time, has made him feel rather disconcerted. The note was written on a broad, white feather from a stork's wing, and it said: "You will never hear anything more about Oz, because we are now cut off forever from all the rest of the world. but Toto and I will always love you and all the other children who love us. Dorothy Gale."

This seemed to me too bad, at first, for Oz is a very interesting fairyland. Still, we have no right to feel grieved, for we have had enough of the history of the Land of Oz to fill six story books, and from its quaint people and their strange adventures we have been able to learn many useful and amusing things.

So good luck to little Dorothy and her companions. May they live long in their invisible country and be very happy!

The Patchwork Girl Of Oz

by L. Frank Baum

Affectionately Dedicated to my young friend Sumner Hamilton Britton of Chicago

Prologue

Through the kindness of Dorothy Gale of Kansas, afterward Princess Dorothy of Oz, a humble writer in the United States of America was once appointed Royal Historian of Oz, with the privilege of writing the chronicle of that wonderful fairyland. But after making six books about the adventures of those interesting but queer people who live in the Land of Oz, the Historian learned with sorrow that by an edict of the Supreme Ruler, Ozma of Oz, her country would thereafter be rendered invisible to all who lived outside its borders and that all communication with Oz would, in the future, be cut off.

The children who had learned to look for the books about Oz and who loved the stories about the gay and happy people inhabiting that favored country, were as sorry as their Historian that there would be no more books of Oz stories. They wrote many letters asking if the Historian did not know of some adventures to write about that had happened before the Land of Oz was shut out from all the rest of the world. But he did not know of any. Finally one of the children inquired why we couldn't hear from Princess Dorothy by wireless telegraph, which would enable her to communicate to the Historian whatever happened in the far-off Land of Oz without his seeing her, or even knowing just where Oz is.

That seemed a good idea; so the Historian rigged up a high tower in his back yard, and took lessons in wireless telegraphy until he understood it, and then began to call "Princess Dorothy of Oz" by sending messages into the air.

Now, it wasn't likely that Dorothy would be looking for wireless messages or would heed the call; but one thing the Historian was sure of, and that was that the powerful Sorceress, Glinda, would know what he was doing and that he desired to communicate with Dorothy. For Glinda has a big book in which is recorded every event that takes place anywhere in the world, just the moment that it happens, and so of course the book would tell her about the wireless message.

And that was the way Dorothy heard that the Historian wanted to speak with her, and there was a Shaggy Man in the Land of Oz who knew how to telegraph a wireless reply. The result was that the Historian begged so hard to be told the latest news of Oz, so that he could write it down for the children to read, that Dorothy asked permission of Ozma and Ozma graciously consented.

That is why, after two long years of waiting, another Oz story is now presented to the children of America. This would not have been possible had not some clever man invented the "wireless" and an equally clever child suggested the idea of reaching the mysterious Land of Oz by its means.

L. Frank Baum,
"Ozcot" at Hollywood in California

1. Ojo and Unc Nunkie

"Where's the butter, Unc Nunkie?" asked Ojo.

Unc looked out of the window and stroked his long beard. Then he turned to the Munchkin boy and shook his head.

"Isn't," said he.

"Isn't any butter? That's too bad, Unc. Where's the jam then?" inquired Ojo, standing on a stool so he could look through all the shelves of the cupboard. But Unc Nunkie shook his head again.

"Gone," he said.

"No jam, either? And no cake—no jelly—no apples—nothing but bread?"

"All," said Unc, again stroking his beard as he gazed from the window.

The little boy brought the stool and sat beside his uncle, munching the dry bread slowly and seeming in deep thought.

"Nothing grows in our yard but the bread tree," he mused, "and there are only two more loaves on that tree; and they're not ripe yet. Tell me, Unc; why are we so poor?"

The old Munchkin turned and looked at Ojo. He had kindly eyes, but he hadn't smiled or laughed in so long that the boy had forgotten that Unc Nunkie could look any other way than solemn. And Unc never spoke any more words than he was obliged to, so his little nephew, who lived alone with him, had learned to understand a great deal from one word.

"Why are we so poor, Unc?" repeated the boy.

"Not," said the old Munchkin.

"I think we are," declared Ojo. "What have we got?"

"House," said Unc Nunkie.

"I know; but everyone in the Land of Oz has a place to live. What else, Unc?"

"Bread."

"I'm eating the last loaf that's ripe. There; I've put aside your share, Unc. It's on the table, so you can eat it when you get hungry. But when that is gone, what shall we eat, Unc?"

The old man shifted in his chair but merely shook his head.

"Of course," said Ojo, who was obliged to talk because his uncle would not, "no one starves in the Land of Oz, either. There is plenty for everyone, you know; only, if it isn't just where you happen to be, you must go where it is."

The aged Munchkin wriggled again and stared at his small nephew as if disturbed by his argument.

"By to-morrow morning," the boy went on, "we must go where there is something to eat, or we shall grow very hungry and become very unhappy."

"Where?" asked Unc.

"Where shall we go? I don't know, I'm sure," replied Ojo. "But you must know, Unc. You must have traveled, in your time, because you're so old. I don't remember it, because ever since I could remember anything we've lived right here in this lonesome, round house, with a little garden back of it and the thick woods all around. All I've ever seen of the great Land of Oz,

Unc dear, is the view of that mountain over at the south, where they say the Hammerheads live—who won't let anybody go by them—and that mountain at the north, where they say nobody lives."

"One," declared Unc, correcting him.

"Oh, yes; one family lives there, I've heard. That's the Crooked Magician, who is named Dr. Pipt, and his wife Margolotte. One year you told me about them; I think it took you a whole year, Unc, to say as much as I've just said about the Crooked Magician and his wife. They live high up on the mountain, and the good Munchkin Country, where the fruits and flowers grow, is just the other side. It's funny you and I should live here all alone, in the middle of the forest, isn't it?"

"Yes," said Unc.

"Then let's go away and visit the Munchkin Country and its jolly, good-natured people. I'd love to get a sight of something besides woods, Unc Nunkie."

"Too little," said Unc.

"Why, I'm not so little as I used to be," answered the boy earnestly. "I think I can walk as far and as fast through the woods as you can, Unc. And now that nothing grows in our back yard that is good to eat, we must go where there is food."

Unc Nunkie made no reply for a time. Then he shut down the window and turned his chair to face the room, for the sun was sinking behind the tree-tops and it was growing cool.

By and by Ojo lighted the fire and the logs blazed freely in the broad fireplace. The two sat in the firelight a long time—the old, white-bearded Munchkin and the little boy. Both were thinking. When it grew quite dark outside, Ojo said: "Eat your bread, Unc, and then we will go to bed."

But Unc Nunkie did not eat the bread; neither did he go directly to bed. Long after his little nephew was sound asleep in the corner of the room the old man sat by the fire, thinking.

2. The Crooked Magician

Just at dawn next morning Unc Nunkie laid his hand tenderly on Ojo's head and awakened him.

"Come," he said.

Ojo dressed. He wore blue silk stockings, blue knee pants with gold buckles, a blue ruffled waist and a jacket of bright blue braided with gold. His shoes were of blue leather and turned up at the toes, which were pointed. His hat had a peaked crown and a flat brim, and around the brim was a row of tiny golden bells that tinkled when he moved. This was the native costume of those who inhabited the Munchkin Country of the Land of Oz, so Unc Nunkie's dress was much like that of his nephew. Instead of shoes, the old man wore boots with turnover tops and his blue coat had wide cuffs of gold braid.

The boy noticed that his uncle had not eaten the bread, and supposed the old man had not been hungry. Ojo was hungry, though; so he divided the piece of bread upon the table and ate his half for breakfast, washing it down with fresh, cool water from the brook. Unc put the other piece of bread in his jacket pocket, after which he again said, as he walked out through the doorway: "Come."

Ojo was well pleased. He was dreadfully tired of living all alone in the woods and wanted to travel and see people. For a long time he had wished to explore the beautiful Land of Oz in which they lived. When they were outside, Unc simply latched the door and started up the path. No one would disturb their little house, even if anyone came so far into the thick forest while they were gone.

At the foot of the mountain that separated the Country of the Munchkins from the Country of the Gillikins, the path divided. One way led to the left and the other to the right—straight up the mountain. Unc Nunkie took this right-hand path and Ojo followed without asking why. He knew it would take them to the house of the Crooked Magician, whom he had never seen but who was their nearest neighbor.

All the morning they trudged up the mountain path and at noon Unc and Ojo sat on a fallen tree-trunk and ate the last of the bread which the old Munchkin had placed in his pocket. Then they started on again and two hours later came in sight of the house of Dr. Pipt.

It was a big house, round, as were all the Munchkin houses, and painted blue, which is the distinctive color of the Munchkin Country of Oz. There was a pretty garden around the house, where blue trees and blue flowers grew in abundance and in one place were beds of blue cabbages, blue carrots and blue lettuce, all of which were delicious to eat. In Dr. Pipt's garden grew bun-trees, cake-trees, cream-puff bushes, blue buttercups which yielded excellent blue butter and a row of chocolate-caramel plants. Paths of blue gravel divided the vegetable and flower beds and a wider path led up to the front door. The place was in a clearing on the mountain, but a little way off was the grim forest, which completely surrounded it.

Unc knocked at the door of the house and a chubby, pleasant-faced woman, dressed all in blue, opened it and greeted the visitors with a smile.

"Ah," said Ojo; "you must be Dame Margolotte, the good wife of Dr. Pipt."

"I am, my dear, and all strangers are welcome to my home."

"May we see the famous Magician, Madam?"

"He is very busy just now," she said, shaking her head doubtfully. "But come in and let me give you something to eat, for you must have traveled far in order to get our lonely place."

"We have," replied Ojo, as he and Unc entered the house. "We have come from a far lonelier place than this."

"A lonelier place! And in the Munchkin Country?" she exclaimed. "Then it must be somewhere in the Blue Forest."

"It is, good Dame Margolotte."

"Dear me!" she said, looking at the man, "you must be Unc Nunkie, known as the Silent One." Then she looked at the boy. "And you must be Ojo the Unlucky," she added.

"Yes," said Unc.

"I never knew I was called the Unlucky," said Ojo, soberly; "but it is really a good name for me."

"Well," remarked the woman, as she bustled around the room and set the table and brought food from the cupboard, "you were unlucky to live all alone in that dismal forest, which is much worse than the forest around here; but perhaps your luck will change, now you are away from it. If, during your travels, you can manage to lose that 'Un' at the beginning of your name 'Unlucky,' you will then become Ojo the Lucky, which will be a great improvement."

"How can I lose that 'Un,' Dame Margolotte?"

"I do not know how, but you must keep the matter in mind and perhaps the chance will come to you," she replied.

Ojo had never eaten such a fine meal in all his life. There was a savory stew, smoking hot, a dish of blue peas, a bowl of sweet milk of a delicate blue tint and a blue pudding with blue plums in it. When the visitors had eaten heartily of this fare the woman said to them: "Do you wish to see Dr. Pipt on business or for pleasure?"

Unc shook his head.

"We are traveling," replied Ojo, "and we stopped at your house just to rest and refresh ourselves. I do not think Unc Nunkie cares very much to see the famous Crooked Magician; but for my part I am curious to look at such a great man."

The woman seemed thoughtful.

"I remember that Unc Nunkie and my husband used to be friends, many years ago," she said, "so perhaps they will be glad to meet again. The Magician is very busy, as I said, but if you will promise not to disturb him you may come into his workshop and watch him prepare a wonderful charm."

"Thank you," replied the boy, much pleased. "I would like to do that."

She led the way to a great domed hall at the back of the house, which was the Magician's workshop. There was a row of windows extending nearly around the sides of the circular room, which rendered the place very light, and there was a back door in addition to the one leading to the front part of the house. Before the row of windows a broad seat was built and there were some chairs and benches in the room besides. At one end stood a great fireplace, in which a blue log was blazing with a blue flame, and over the fire hung four kettles in a row, all bubbling and steaming at a great rate. The Magician was stirring all four of these kettles at the same time, two with his hands and two with his feet, to the latter, wooden ladles being strapped, for this man was so very crooked that his legs were as handy as his arms.

Unc Nunkie came forward to greet his old friend, but not being able to shake either his hands or his feet, which were all occupied in stirring, he patted the Magician's bald head and asked: "What?"

"Ah, it's the Silent One," remarked Dr. Pipt, without looking up, and he wants to know what I'm making. Well, when it is quite finished this compound will be the wonderful Powder of Life, which no one knows how to make but myself. Whenever it is sprinkled on anything, that thing will at once come to life, no matter what it is. It takes me several years to make this magic Powder, but at this moment I am pleased to say it is nearly done. You see, I am making it for my good wife Margolotte, who wants to use some of it for a purpose of her own. Sit down and make yourself comfortable, Unc Nunkie, and after I've finished my task I will talk to you."

"You must know," said Margolottte, when they were all seated together on the broad window-seat, "that my husband foolishly gave away all the Powder of Life he first made to old Mombi the Witch, who used to live in the Country of the Gillikins, to the north of here. Mombi gave to Dr. Pipt a Powder of Perpetual Youth in exchange for his Powder of Life, but she cheated him wickedly, for the Powder of Youth was no good and could work no magic at all."

"Perhaps the Powder of Life couldn't either," said Ojo.

"Yes; it is perfection," she declared. "The first lot we tested on our Glass Cat, which not only began to live but has lived ever since. She's somewhere around the house now."

"A Glass Cat!" exclaimed Ojo, astonished.

"Yes; she makes a very pleasant companion, but admires herself a little more than is considered modest, and she positively refuses to catch mice," explained Margolotte. "My husband made the cat some pink brains, but they proved to be too high-bred and particular for a cat, so she thinks it is undignified in her to catch mice. Also she has a pretty blood-red heart, but it is made of stone—a ruby, I think—and so is rather hard and unfeeling. I think the next Glass Cat the Magician makes will have neither brains nor heart, for then it will not object to catching mice and may prove of some use to us."

"What did old Mombi the Witch do with the Powder of Life your husband gave her?" asked the boy.

"She brought Jack Pumpkinhead to life, for one thing," was the reply. "I suppose you've heard of Jack Pumpkinhead. He is now living near the Emerald City and is a great favorite with the Princess Ozma, who rules all the Land of Oz."

"No; I've never heard of him," remarked Ojo. "I'm afraid I don't know much about the Land of Oz. You see, I've lived all my life with Unc Nunkie, the Silent One, and there was no one to tell me anything."

"That is one reason you are Ojo the Unlucky," said the woman, in a sympathetic tone. "The more one knows, the luckier he is, for knowledge is the greatest gift in life."

"But tell me, please, what you intend to do with this new lot of the Powder of Life, which Dr. Pipt is making. He said his wife wanted it for some especial purpose."

"So I do," she answered. "I want it to bring my Patchwork Girl to life."

"Oh! A Patchwork Girl? What is that?" Ojo asked, for this seemed even more strange and unusual than a Glass Cat.

"I think I must show you my Patchwork Girl," said Margolotte, laughing at the boy's astonishment, "for she is rather difficult to explain. But first I will tell you that for many years I have longed for a servant to help me with the housework and to cook the meals and wash the dishes. No servant will come here because the place is so lonely and out-of-the-way, so my clever husband, the Crooked Magician, proposed that I make a girl out of some sort of material and he would make her live by sprinkling over her the Powder of Life. This seemed an excellent suggestion and at once Dr. Pipt set to work to make a new batch of his magic powder. He has been at it a long, long while, and so I have had plenty of time to make the girl. Yet that task was not so easy as you may suppose. At first I couldn't think what to make her of, but finally in searching through a chest I came across an old patchwork quilt, which my grandmother once made when she was young."

"What is a patchwork quilt?" asked Ojo.

"A bed-quilt made of patches of different kinds and colors of cloth, all neatly sewed together. The patches are of all shapes and sizes, so a patchwork quilt is a very pretty and gorgeous thing to look at. Sometimes it is called a 'crazy-quilt,' because the patches and colors are so mixed up. We never have used my grandmother's many-colored patchwork quilt, handsome as it is, for we Munchkins do not care for any color other than blue, so it has been packed away in the chest for about a hundred years. When I found it, I said to myself that it would do nicely for my servant girl, for when she was brought to life she would not be proud nor haughty, as the Glass Cat is, for such a dreadful mixture of colors would discourage her from trying to be as dignified as the blue Munchkins are."

"Is blue the only respectable color, then?" inquired Ojo.

"Yes, for a Munchkin. All our country is blue, you know. But in other parts of Oz the people favor different colors. At the Emerald City, where our Princess Ozma lives, green is the popular color. But all Munchkins prefer blue to anything else and when my housework girl is brought to life she will find herself to be of so many unpopular colors that she'll never dare be rebellious or impudent, as servants are sometimes liable to be when they are made the same way their mistresses are."

Unc Nunkie nodded approval.

"Good i-dea," he said; and that was a long speech for Unc Nunkie because it was two words.

"So I cut up the quilt," continued Margolotte, "and made from it a very well-shaped girl, which I stuffed with cotton-wadding. I will show you what a good job I did," and she went to a tall cupboard and threw open the doors.

Then back she came, lugging in her arms the Patchwork Girl, which she set upon the bench and propped up so that the figure would not tumble over.

3. The Patchwork Girl

Ojo examined this curious contrivance with wonder. The Patchwork Girl was taller than he, when she stood upright, and her body was plump and rounded because it had been so neatly stuffed with cotton. Margolotte had first made the girl's form from the patchwork quilt and then she had dressed it with a patchwork skirt and an apron with pockets in it— using the same gay material throughout. Upon the feet she had sewn a pair of red leather shoes with pointed toes. All the fingers and thumbs of the girl's hands had been carefully formed and stuffed and stitched at the edges, with gold plates at the ends to serve as finger-nails.

"She will have to work, when she comes to life," said Marglotte.

The head of the Patchwork Girl was the most curious part of her. While she waited for her husband to finish making his Powder of Life the woman had found ample time to complete the head as her fancy dictated, and she realized that a good servant's head must be properly constructed. The hair was of brown yarn and

hung down on her neck in several neat braids. Her eyes were two silver suspender-buttons cut from a pair of the Magician's old trousers, and they were sewed on with black threads, which formed the pupils of the eyes. Margolotte had puzzled over the ears for some time, for these were important if the servant was to hear distinctly, but finally she had made them out of thin plates of gold and attached them in place by means of stitches through tiny holes bored in the metal. Gold is the most common metal in the Land of Oz and is used for many purposes because it is soft and pliable.

The woman had cut a slit for the Patchwork Girl's mouth and sewn two rows of white pearls in it for teeth, using a strip of scarlet plush for a tongue. This mouth Ojo considered very artistic and lifelike, and Margolotte was pleased when the boy praised it. There were almost too many patches on the face of the girl for her to be considered strictly beautiful, for one cheek was yellow and the other red, her chin blue, her forehead purple and the center, where her nose had been formed and padded, a bright yellow.

"You ought to have had her face all pink," suggested the boy.

"I suppose so; but I had no pink cloth," replied the woman. "Still I cannot see as it matters much, for I wish my Patchwork Girl to be useful rather than ornamental. If I get tired looking at her patched face I can whitewash it."

"Has she any brains?" asked Ojo.

"No; I forgot all about the brains!" exclaimed the woman. "I am glad you reminded me of them, for it is not too late to supply them, by any means. Until she is brought to life I can do anything I please with this girl. But I must be careful not to give her too much brains, and those she has must be such as are fitted to the station she is to occupy in life. In other words, her brains mustn't be very good."

"Wrong," said Unc Nunkie.

"No; I am sure I am right about that," returned the woman.

"He means," explained Ojo, "that unless your servant has good brains she won't know how to obey you properly, nor do the things you ask her to do."

"Well, that may be true," agreed Margolotte; "but, on the contrary, a servant with too much brains is sure to become independent and high-and-mighty and feel above her work. This is a very delicate task, as I said, and I must take care to give the girl just the right quantity of the right sort of brains. I want her to know just enough, but not too much."

With this she went to another cupboard which was filled with shelves. All the shelves were lined with blue glass bottles, neatly labeled by the Magician to show what they contained. One whole shelf was marked: "Brain Furniture," and the bottles on this shelf were labeled as follows: "Obedience," "Cleverness," "Judgment," "Courage," "Ingenuity," "Amiability," "Learning," "Truth," "Poesy," "Self Reliance."

"Let me see," said Margolotte; "of those qualities she must have 'Obedience' first of all," and she took down the bottle bearing that label and poured from it upon a dish several grains of the contents. "'Amiability' is also good and 'Truth.'" She poured into the dish a quantity from each of these bottles. "I think that will do," she continued, "for the other qualities are not needed in a servant."

Unc Nunkie, who with Ojo stood beside her, touched the bottle marked "Cleverness."

"Little," said he.

"A little 'Cleverness'? Well, perhaps you are right, sir," said she, and was about to take down the bottle when the Crooked Magician suddenly called to her excitedly from the fireplace.

"Quick, Margolotte! Come and help me."

She ran to her husband's side at once and helped him lift the four kettles from the fire. Their contents had all boiled away, leaving in the bottom of each kettle a few grains of fine white powder. Very carefully the Magician removed this powder, placing it all together in a golden dish, where he mixed it with a golden spoon. When the mixture was complete there was scarcely a handful, all told.

"That," said Dr. Pipt, in a pleased and triumphant tone, "is the wonderful Powder of Life, which I alone in the world know how to make. It has taken me nearly six years to prepare these precious grains of dust, but the little heap on that dish is worth the price of a kingdom and many a king would give all he has to possess it. When it has become cooled I will place it in a small bottle; but meantime I must watch it carefully, lest a gust of wind blow it away or scatter it."

Unc Nunkie, Margolotte and the Magician all stood looking at the marvelous Powder, but Ojo was more interested just then in the Patchwork Girl's brains. Thinking it both unfair and unkind to deprive her of any good qualities that were handy, the boy took down every bottle on the shelf and poured some of the contents in Margolotte's dish. No one saw him do this, for all were looking at the Powder of Life; but soon the woman remembered what she had been doing, and came back to the cupboard.

"Let's see," she remarked; "I was about to give my girl a little 'Cleverness,' which is the Doctor's substitute for 'Intelligence'—a quality he has not yet learned how to manufacture." Taking down the bottle of "Cleverness" she added some of the powder to the heap on the dish. Ojo became a bit uneasy at this, for he had already put quite a lot of the "Cleverness" powder in the dish; but he dared not interfere and so he comforted himself with the thought that one cannot have too much cleverness.

Margolotte now carried the dish of brains to the bench. Ripping the seam of the patch on the girl's forehead, she placed the powder within the head and then sewed up the seam as neatly and securely as before.

"My girl is all ready for your Powder of Life, my dear," she said to her husband. But the Magician replied: "This powder must not be used before to-morrow morning; but I think it is now cool enough to be bottled."

He selected a small gold bottle with a pepper-box top, so that the powder might be sprinkled on any object through the small holes. Very carefully he placed the Powder of Life in the gold bottle and then locked it up in a drawer of his cabinet.

"At last," said he, rubbing his hands together gleefully, "I have ample leisure for a good talk with my old friend Unc Nunkie. So let us sit down cosily and enjoy ourselves. After stirring those four kettles for six years I am glad to have a little rest."

"You will have to do most of the talking," said Ojo, "for Unc is called the Silent One and uses few words."

"I know; but that renders your uncle a most agreeable companion and gossip," declared Dr. Pipt. "Most people talk too much, so it is a relief to find one who talks too little."

Ojo looked at the Magician with much awe and curiosity.

"Don't you find it very annoying to be so crooked?" he asked.

"No; I am quite proud of my person," was the reply. "I suppose I am the only Crooked Magician in all the world. Some others are accused of being crooked, but I am the only genuine."

He was really very crooked and Ojo wondered how he managed to do so many things with such a twisted body. When he sat down upon a crooked chair that had been made to fit him, one knee was under his chin and the other near the small of his back; but he was a cheerful man and his face bore a pleasant and agreeable expression.

"I am not allowed to perform magic, except for my own amusement," he told his visitors, as he lighted a pipe with a crooked stem and began to smoke. "Too many people were working magic in the Land of Oz, and so our lovely Princess Ozma put a stop to it. I think she was quite right. There were several wicked Witches who caused a lot of trouble; but now they are all out of business and only the great Sorceress, Glinda the Good, is permitted to practice her arts, which never harm anybody. The Wizard of Oz, who used to be a humbug and knew no magic at all, has been taking lessons of Glinda, and I'm told he is getting to be a pretty good Wizard; but he is merely the assistant of the great Sorceress. I've the right to make a servant girl for my wife, you know, or a Glass Cat to catch our mice—which she refuses to do—but I am forbidden to work magic for others, or to use it as a profession."

"Magic must be a very interesting study," said Ojo.

"It truly is," asserted the Magician. "In my time I've performed some magical feats that were worthy of the skill of Glinda the Good. For instance, there's the Powder of Life, and my Liquid of Petrifaction, which is contained in that bottle on the shelf yonder—over the window."

"What does the Liquid of Petrifaction do?" inquired the boy.

"Turns everything it touches to solid marble. It's an invention of my own, and I find it very useful. Once two of those dreadful Kalidahs, with bodies like bears and heads like tigers, came here from the forest to attack us; but I sprinkled some of that Liquid on them and instantly they turned to marble. I now use them as ornamental statuary in my garden. This table looks to you like wood, and once it really was wood; but I sprinkled a few drops of the Liquid of Petrifaction on it and now it is marble. It will never break nor wear out."

"Fine!" said Unc Nunkie, wagging his head and stroking his long gray beard.

"Dear me; what a chatterbox you're getting to be, Unc," remarked the Magician, who was pleased with the compliment. But just then there came a scratching at the back door and a shrill voice cried: "Let me in! Hurry up, can't you? Let me in!"

Margolotte got up and went to the door.

"Ask like a good cat, then," she said.

"Mee-ee-ow-w-w! There; does that suit your royal highness?" asked the voice, in scornful accents.

"Yes; that's proper cat talk," declared the woman, and opened the door.

At once a cat entered, came to the center of the room and stopped short at the sight of strangers. Ojo and Unc Nunkie both stared at it with wide open eyes, for surely no such curious creature had ever existed before—even in the Land of Oz.

4. The Glass Cat

The cat was made of glass, so clear and transparent that you could see through it as easily as through a window. In the top of its head, however, was a mass of delicate pink balls which looked like jewels, and it had a heart made of a blood-red ruby. The eyes were two large emeralds, but aside from these colors all the rest of the animal was clear glass, and it had a spun-glass tail that was really beautiful.

"Well, Doc Pipt, do you mean to introduce us, or not?" demanded the cat, in a tone of annoyance. "Seems to me you are forgetting your manners."

"Excuse me," returned the Magician. "This is Unc Nunkie, the descendant of the former kings of the Munchkins, before this country became a part of the Land of Oz."

"He needs a haircut," observed the cat, washing its face.

"True," replied Unc, with a low chuckle of amusement.

"But he has lived alone in the heart of the forest for many years," the Magician explained; "and, although that is a barbarous country, there are no barbers there."

"Who is the dwarf?" asked the cat.

"That is not a dwarf, but a boy," answered the Magician. "You have never seen a boy before. He is now small because he is young. With more years he will grow big and become as tall as Unc Nunkie."

"Oh. Is that magic?" the glass animal inquired.

"Yes; but it is Nature's magic, which is more wonderful than any art known to man. For instance, my magic made you, and made you live; and it was a poor job because you are useless and a bother to me; but I can't make you grow. You will always be the same size—and the same saucy, inconsiderate Glass Cat, with pink brains and a hard ruby heart."

"No one can regret more than I the fact that you made me," asserted the cat, crouching upon the floor and slowly swaying its spun-glass tail from side to side. "Your world is a very uninteresting place. I've wandered through your gardens and in the forest until I'm tired of it all, and when I come into the house the conversation of your fat wife and of yourself bores me dreadfully."

"That is because I gave you different brains from those we ourselves possess—and much too good for a cat," returned Dr. Pipt.

"Can't you take 'em out, then, and replace 'em with pebbles, so that I won't feel above my station in life?" asked the cat, pleadingly.

"Perhaps so. I'll try it, after I've brought the Patchwork Girl to life," he said.

The cat walked up to the bench on which the Patchwork Girl reclined and looked at her attentively.

"Are you going to make that dreadful thing live?" she asked.

The Magician nodded.

"It is intended to be my wife's servant maid," he said. "When she is alive she will do all our work and mind the house. But you are not to order her around, Bungle, as you do us. You must treat the Patchwork Girl respectfully."

"I won't. I couldn't respect such a bundle of scraps under any circumstances."

"If you don't, there will be more scraps than you will like," cried Margolotte, angrily.

"Why didn't you make her pretty to look at?" asked the cat. "You made me pretty—very pretty, indeed—and I love to watch my pink brains roll around when they're working, and to see my precious red heart beat." She went to a long mirror, as she said this, and stood before it, looking at herself with an air of much pride. "But that poor patched thing will hate herself, when she's once alive," continued the cat. "If I were you I'd use her for a mop, and make another servant that is prettier."

"You have a perverted taste," snapped Margolotte, much annoyed at this frank criticism. "I think the Patchwork Girl is beautiful, considering what she's made of. Even the rainbow hasn't as many colors, and you must admit that the rainbow is a pretty thing."

The Glass Cat yawned and stretched herself upon the floor.

"Have your own way," she said. "I'm sorry for the Patchwork Girl, that's all."

Ojo and Unc Nunkie slept that night in the Magician's house, and the boy was glad to stay because he was anxious to see the Patchwork Girl brought to life. The Glass Cat was also a wonderful creature to little Ojo, who had never seen or known anything of magic before, although he had lived in the Fairyland of Oz ever since he was born. Back there in the woods nothing unusual ever happened. Unc Nunkie, who might have been King of the Munchkins, had not his people united with all the other countries of Oz in acknowledging Ozma as their sole ruler, had retired into this forgotten forest nook with his baby nephew and they had lived all alone there. Only that the neglected garden had failed to grow food for them, they would always have lived in the solitary Blue Forest; but now they had started out to mingle with other people, and the first place they came to proved so interesting that Ojo could scarcely sleep a wink all night.

Margolotte was an excellent cook and gave them a fine breakfast. While they were all engaged in eating, the good woman said:

"This is the last meal I shall have to cook for some time, for right after breakfast Dr. Pipt has promised to bring my new servant to life. I shall let her wash the breakfast dishes and sweep and dust the house. What a relief it will be!"

"It will, indeed, relieve you of much drudgery," said the Magician. "By the way, Margolotte, I thought I saw you getting some brains from the cupboard, while I was busy with my kettles. What qualities have you given your new servant?"

"Only those that an humble servant requires," she answered. "I do not wish her to feel above her station, as the Glass Cat does. That would make her discontented and unhappy, for of course she must always be a servant."

Ojo was somewhat disturbed as he listened to this, and the boy began to fear he had done wrong in adding all those different qualities of brains to the lot Margolotte had prepared for the servant. But it was too late now for regret, since all the brains were securely sewn up inside the Patchwork Girl's head. He might have confessed what he had done and thus allowed Margolotte and her husband to change the brains; but he was afraid of incurring their anger. He believed that Unc had seen him add to the brains, and Unc had not said a word against it; but then, Unc never did say anything unless it was absolutely necessary.

As soon as breakfast was over they all went into the Magician's big workshop, where the Glass Cat was lying before the mirror and the Patchwork Girl lay limp and lifeless upon the bench.

"Now, then," said Dr. Pipt, in a brisk tone, "we shall perform one of the greatest feats of magic possible to man, even in this marvelous Land of Oz. In no other country could it be done at all. I think we ought to have a little music while the Patchwork Girl comes to life. It is pleasant to reflect that the first sounds her golden ears will hear will be delicious music."

As he spoke he went to a phonograph, which screwed fast to a small table, and wound up the spring of the instrument and adjusted the big gold horn.

"The music my servant will usually hear," remarked Margolotte, "will be my orders to do her work. But I see no harm in allowing her to listen to this unseen band while she wakens to her first realization of life. My orders will beat the band, afterward."

The phonograph was now playing a stirring march tune and the Magician unlocked his cabinet and took out the gold bottle containing the Powder of Life.

They all bent over the bench on which the Patchwork Girl reclined. Unc Nunkie and Margolotte stood behind, near the windows, Ojo at one side and the Magician in front, where he would have freedom to sprinkle the powder. The Glass Cat came near, too, curious to watch the important scene.

"All ready?" asked Dr. Pipt.

"All is ready," answered his wife.

So the Magician leaned over and shook from the bottle some grains of the wonderful Powder, and they fell directly on the Patchwork Girl's head and arms.

5. A Terrible Accident

"It will take a few minutes for this powder to do its work," remarked the Magician, sprinkling the body up and down with much care.

But suddenly the Patchwork Girl threw up one arm, which knocked the bottle of powder from the crooked man's hand and sent it flying across the room. Unc Nunkie and Margolotte were so startled that they both leaped backward and bumped together, and Unc's head joggled the shelf above them and upset the bottle containing the Liquid of Petrifaction.

The Magician uttered such a wild cry that Ojo jumped away and the Patchwork Girl sprang after him and clasped her stuffed arms around him in terror. The Glass Cat snarled and hid under the table, and so it was that when the powerful Liquid of Petrifaction was spilled it fell only upon the wife of the Magician and the uncle of Ojo. With these two the charm worked promptly. They stood motionless and stiff as marble statues, in exactly the positions they were in when the Liquid struck them.

Ojo pushed the Patchwork Girl away and ran to Unc Nunkie, filled with a terrible fear for the only friend and protector he had ever known. When he grasped Unc's hand it was cold and hard. Even the long gray beard was solid marble. The Crooked Magician was dancing around the room in a frenzy of despair, calling upon his wife to forgive him, to speak to him, to come to life again!

The Patchwork Girl, quickly recovering from her fright, now came nearer and looked from one to another of the people with deep interest. Then she looked at herself and laughed. Noticing the mirror, she stood before it and examined her extraordinary features with amazement—her button eyes, pearl bead teeth and puffy nose. Then, addressing her reflection in the glass, she exclaimed:
"Whee, but there's a gaudy dame!
Makes a paint-box blush with shame.
Razzle-dazzle, fizzle-fazzle!
Howdy-do, Miss What's-your-name?"

She bowed, and the reflection bowed. Then she laughed again, long and merrily, and the Glass Cat crept out from under the table and said: "I don't blame you for laughing at yourself. Aren't you horrid?"

"Horrid?" she replied. "Why, I'm thoroughly delightful. I'm an Original, if you please, and therefore incomparable. Of all the comic, absurd, rare and amusing creatures the world contains, I must be the supreme freak. Who but poor Margolotte could have managed to invent such an unreasonable being as I? But I'm glad—I'm awfully glad!—that I'm just what I am, and nothing else."

"Be quiet, will you?" cried the frantic Magician; "be quiet and let me think! If I don't think I shall go mad."

"Think ahead," said the Patchwork Girl, seating herself in a chair. "Think all you want to. I don't mind."

"Gee! but I'm tired playing that tune," called the phonograph, speaking through its horn in a brazen, scratchy voice. "If you don't mind, Pipt, old boy, I'll cut it out and take a rest."

The Magician looked gloomily at the music-machine.

"What dreadful luck!" he wailed, despondently. "The Powder of Life must have fallen on the phonograph."

He went up to it and found that the gold bottle that contained the precious powder had dropped upon the stand and scattered its life-giving grains over the machine. The phonograph was very much alive, and began dancing a jig with the legs of the table to which it was attached, and this dance so annoyed Dr. Pipt that he kicked the thing into a corner and pushed a bench against it, "to hold it quiet.

"You were bad enough before," said the Magician, resentfully; "but a live phonograph is enough to drive every sane person in the Land of Oz stark crazy."

"No insults, please," answered the phonograph in a surly tone. "You did it, my boy; don't blame me."

"You've bungled everything, Dr. Pipt," added the Glass Cat, contemptuously.

"Except me," said the Patchwork Girl, jumping up to whirl merrily around the room.

"I think," said Ojo, almost ready to cry through grief over Unc Nunkie's sad fate, "it must all be my fault, in some way. I'm called Ojo the Unlucky, you know."

"That's nonsense, kiddie," retorted the Patchwork Girl cheerfully. "No one can be unlucky who has the intelligence to direct his own actions. The unlucky ones are those who beg for a chance to think, like poor Dr. Pipt here. What's the row about, anyway, Mr. Magic-maker?"

"The Liquid of Petrifaction has accidentally fallen upon my dear wife and Unc Nunkie and turned them into marble," he sadly replied.

"Well, why don't you sprinkle some of that powder on them and bring them to life again?" asked the Patchwork Girl.

The Magician gave a jump.

"Why, I hadn't thought of that!" he joyfully cried, and grabbed up the golden bottle, with which he ran to Margolotte.

Said the Patchwork Girl:
"Higgledy, piggledy, dee—
What fools magicians be!
His head's so thick
He can't think quick,
So he takes advice from me."

Standing upon the bench, for he was so crooked he could not reach the top of his wife's head in any other way, Dr. Pipt began shaking the bottle. But not a grain of powder came out. He pulled off the cover, glanced within, and then threw the bottle from him with a wail of despair.

"Gone—gone! Every bit gone," he cried. "Wasted on that miserable phonograph when it might have saved my dear wife!"

Then the Magician bowed his head on his crooked arms and began to cry.

Ojo was sorry for him. He went up to the sorrowful man and said softly: "You can make more Powder of Life, Dr. Pipt."

"Yes; but it will take me six years—six long, weary years of stirring four kettles with both feet and both hands," was the agonized reply. "Six years! while poor Margolotte stands watching me as a marble image."

"Can't anything else be done?" asked the Patchwork Girl.

The Magician shook his head. Then he seemed to remember something and looked up.

"There is one other compound that would destroy the magic spell of the Liquid of Petrifaction and restore my wife and Unc Nunkie to life," said he. "It may be hard to find the things I need to make this magic compound, but if they were found I could do in an instant what will otherwise take six long, weary years of stirring kettles with both hands and both feet."

"All right; let's find the things, then," suggested the Patchwork Girl. "That seems a lot more sensible than those stirring times with the kettles."

"That's the idea, Scraps," said the Glass Cat, approvingly. "I'm glad to find you have decent brains. Mine are exceptionally good. You can see 'em work; they're pink."

"Scraps?" repeated the girl. "Did you call me 'Scraps'? Is that my name?"

"I—I believe my poor wife had intended to name you 'Angeline,'" said the Magician.

"But I like 'Scraps' best," she replied with a laugh. "It fits me better, for my patchwork is all scraps, and nothing else. Thank you for naming me, Miss Cat. Have you any name of your own?"

"I have a foolish name that Margolotte once gave me, but which is quite undignified for one of my importance," answered the cat. "She called me 'Bungle.'"

"Yes," sighed the Magician; "you were a sad bungle, taken all in all. I was wrong to make you as I did, for a more useless, conceited and brittle thing never before existed."

"I'm not so brittle as you think," retorted the cat. "I've been alive a good many years, for Dr. Pipt experimented on me with the first magic Powder of Life he ever made, and so far I've never broken or cracked or chipped any part of me."

"You seem to have a chip on your shoulder," laughed the Patchwork Girl, and the cat went to the mirror to see.

"Tell me," pleaded Ojo, speaking to the Crooked Magician, "what must we find to make the compound that will save Unc Nunkie?"

"First," was the reply, "I must have a six-leaved clover. That can only be found in the green country around the Emerald City, and six-leaved clovers are very scarce, even there."

"I'll find it for you," promised Ojo.

"The next thing," continued the Magician, "is the left wing of a yellow butterfly. That color can only be found in the yellow country of the Winkies, West of the Emerald City."

"I'll find it," declared Ojo. "Is that all?"

"Oh, no; I'll get my Book of Recipes and see what comes next."

Saying this, the Magician unlocked a drawer of his cabinet and drew out a small book covered with blue leather. Looking through the pages he found the recipe he wanted and said: "I must have a gill of water from a dark well."

"What kind of a well is that, sir?" asked the boy.

"One where the light of day never penetrates. The water must be put in a gold bottle and brought to me without any light ever reaching it."

"I'll get the water from the dark well," said Ojo.

"Then I must have three hairs from the tip of a Woozy's tail, and a drop of oil from a live man's body."

Ojo looked grave at this.

"What is a Woozy, please?" he inquired.

"Some sort of an animal. I've never seen one, so I can't describe it," replied the Magician.

"If I can find a Woozy, I'll get the hairs from its tail," said Ojo. "But is there ever any oil in a man's body?"

The Magician looked in the book again, to make sure.

"That's what the recipe calls for," he replied, "and of course we must get everything that is called for, or the charm won't work. The book doesn't say 'blood'; it says 'oil,' and there must be oil somewhere in a live man's body or the book wouldn't ask for it."

"All right," returned Ojo, trying not to feel discouraged; "I'll try to find it."

The Magician looked at the little Munchkin boy in a doubtful way and said: "All this will mean a long journey for you; perhaps several long journeys; for you must search through several of the different countries of Oz in order to get the things I need."

"I know it, sir; but I must do my best to save Unc Nunkie."

"And also my poor wife Margolotte. If you save one you will save the other, for both stand there together and the same compound will restore them both to life. Do the best you can, Ojo, and while you are gone I shall begin the six years job of making a new batch of the Powder of Life. Then, if you should unluckily fail to secure any one of the things needed, I will have lost no time. But if you succeed you must return here as quickly as you can, and that will save me much tiresome stirring of four kettles with both feet and both hands."

"I will start on my journey at once, sir," said the boy.

"And I will go with you," declared the Patchwork Girl.

"No, no!" exclaimed the Magician. "You have no right to leave this house. You are only a servant and have not been discharged."

Scraps, who had been dancing up and down the room, stopped and looked at him.

"What is a servant?" she asked.

"One who serves. A—a sort of slave," he explained.

"Very well," said the Patchwork Girl, "I'm going to serve you and your wife by helping Ojo find the things you need. You need a lot, you know, such as are not easily found."

"It is true," sighed Dr. Pipt. "I am well aware that Ojo has undertaken a serious task."

Scraps laughed, and resuming her dance she said:
"Here's a job for a boy of brains:

A drop of oil from a live man's veins;
A six-leaved clover; three nice hairs
From a Woozy's tail, the book declares
Are needed for the magic spell,
And water from a pitch-dark well.

The yellow wing of a butterfly
To find must Ojo also try,
And if he gets them without harm,
Doc Pipt will make the magic charm;
But if he doesn't get 'em, Unc
Will always stand a marble chunk."

The Magician looked at her thoughtfully.

"Poor Margolotte must have given you some of the quality of poesy, by mistake," he said. "And, if that is true, I didn't make a very good article when I prepared it, or else you got an overdose or an underdose. However, I believe I shall let you go with Ojo, for my poor wife will not need your services until she is restored to life. Also I think you may be able to help the boy, for your head seems to contain some thoughts I did not expect to find in it. But be very careful of yourself, for you're a souvenir of my dear Margolotte. Try not to get ripped, or your stuffing may fall out. One of your eyes seems loose, and you may have to sew it on tighter. If you talk too much you'll wear out your scarlet plush tongue, which ought to have been hemmed on the edges. And remember you belong to me and must return here as soon as your mission is accomplished."

"I'm going with Scraps and Ojo," announced the Glass Cat.

"You can't," said the Magician.

"Why not?"

"You'd get broken in no time, and you couldn't be a bit of use to the boy and the Patchwork Girl."

"I beg to differ with you," returned the cat, in a haughty tone. "Three heads are better than two, and my pink brains are beautiful. You can see 'em work."

"Well, go along," said the Magician, irritably. "You're only an annoyance, anyhow, and I'm glad to get rid of you."

"Thank you for nothing, then," answered the cat, stiffly.

Dr. Pipt took a small basket from a cupboard and packed several things in it. Then he handed it to Ojo.

"Here is some food and a bundle of charms," he said. "It is all I can give you, but I am sure you will find friends on your journey who will assist you in your search. Take care of the Patchwork Girl and bring her safely back, for she ought to prove useful to my wife. As for the Glass Cat— properly named Bungle—if she bothers you I now give you my permission to break her in two, for she is not respectful and does not obey me. I made a mistake in giving her the pink brains, you see."

Then Ojo went to Unc Nunkie and kissed the old man's marble face very tenderly.

"I'm going to try to save you, Unc," he said, just as if the marble image could hear him; and then he shook the crooked hand of the Crooked Magician, who was already busy hanging the four kettles in the fireplace, and picking up his basket left the house.

The Patchwork Girl followed him, and after them came the Glass Cat.

6. The Journey

Ojo had never traveled before and so he only knew that the path down the mountainside led into the open Munchkin Country, where large numbers of people dwelt. Scraps was quite new and not supposed to know anything of the Land of Oz, while the Glass Cat admitted she had never wandered very far away from the Magician's house. There was only one path before them, at the beginning, so they could not miss their way, and for a time they walked through the thick forest in silent thought, each one impressed with the importance of the adventure they had undertaken.

Suddenly the Patchwork Girl laughed. It was funny to see her laugh, because her cheeks wrinkled up, her nose tipped, her silver button eyes twinkled and her mouth curled at the corners in a comical way.

"Has something pleased you?" asked Ojo, who was feeling solemn and joyless through thinking upon his uncle's sad fate.

"Yes," she answered. "Your world pleases me, for it's a queer world, and life in it is queerer still. Here am I, made from an old bedquilt and intended to be a slave to Margolotte, rendered free as air by an accident that none of you could foresee. I am enjoying life and seeing the world, while the woman who made me is standing helpless as a block of wood. If that isn't funny enough to laugh at, I don't know what is."

"You're not seeing much of the world yet, my poor, innocent Scraps," remarked the Cat. "The world doesn't consist wholly of the trees that are on all sides of us."

"But they're part of it; and aren't they pretty trees?" returned Scraps, bobbing her head until her brown yarn curls fluttered in the breeze. "Growing between them I can see lovely ferns and wild-flowers, and soft green mosses. If the rest of your world is half as beautiful I shall be glad I'm alive."

"I don't know what the rest of the world is like, I'm sure," said the cat; "but I mean to find out."

"I have never been out of the forest," Ojo added; "but to me the trees are gloomy and sad and the wild-flowers seem lonesome. It must be nicer where there are no trees and there is room for lots of people to live together."

"I wonder if any of the people we shall meet will be as splendid as I am," said the Patchwork Girl. "All I have seen, so far, have pale, colorless skins and clothes as blue as the country they live in, while I am of many gorgeous colors— face and body and clothes. That is why I am bright and contented, Ojo, while you are blue and sad."

"I think I made a mistake in giving you so many sorts of brains," observed the boy. "Perhaps, as the Magician said, you have an overdose, and they may not agree with you."

"What had you to do with my brains?" asked Scraps.

"A lot," replied Ojo. "Old Margolotte meant to give you only a few—just enough to keep you going—but when she wasn't looking I added a good many more, of the best kinds I could find in the Magician's cupboard."

"Thanks," said the girl, dancing along the path ahead of Ojo and then dancing back to his side. "If a few brains are good, many brains must be better."

"But they ought to be evenly balanced," said the boy, "and I had no time to be careful. From the way you're acting, I guess the dose was badly mixed."

"Scraps hasn't enough brains to hurt her, so don't worry," remarked the cat, which was trotting along in a very dainty and graceful manner. "The only brains worth considering are mine, which are pink. You can see 'em work."

After walking a long time they came to a little brook that trickled across the path, and here Ojo sat down to rest and eat something from his basket. He found that the Magician had given him part of a loaf of bread and a slice of cheese. He broke off some of the bread and was surprised to find the loaf just as large as it was before. It was the same way with the cheese: however much he broke off from the slice, it remained exactly the same size.

"Ah," said he, nodding wisely; "that's magic. Dr. Pipt has enchanted the bread and the cheese, so it will last me all through my journey, however much I eat."

"Why do you put those things into your mouth?" asked Scraps, gazing at him in astonishment. "Do you need more stuffing? Then why don't you use cotton, such as I am stuffed with?"

"I don't need that kind," said Ojo.

"But a mouth is to talk with, isn't it?"

"It is also to eat with," replied the boy. "If I didn't put food into my mouth, and eat it, I would get hungry and starve.

"Ah, I didn't know that," she said. "Give me some."

Ojo handed her a bit of the bread and she put it in her mouth.

"What next?" she asked, scarcely able to speak.

"Chew it and swallow it," said the boy.

Scraps tried that. Her pearl teeth were unable to chew the bread and beyond her mouth there was no opening. Being unable to swallow she threw away the bread and laughed.

"I must get hungry and starve, for I can't eat," she said.

"Neither can I," announced the cat; "but I'm not fool enough to try. Can't you understand that you and I are superior people and not made like these poor humans?"

"Why should I understand that, or anything else?" asked the girl. "Don't bother my head by asking conundrums, I beg of you. Just let me discover myself in my own way."

With this she began amusing herself by leaping across the brook and back again.

"Be careful, or you'll fall in the water," warned Ojo.

"Never mind."

"You'd better. If you get wet you'll be soggy and can't walk. Your colors might run, too," he said.

"Don't my colors run whenever I run?" she asked.

"Not in the way I mean. If they get wet, the reds and greens and yellows and purples of your patches might run into each other and become just a blur—no color at all, you know."

"Then," said the Patchwork Girl, "I'll be careful, for if I spoiled my splendid colors I would cease to be beautiful."

"Pah!" sneered the Glass Cat, "such colors are not beautiful; they're ugly, and in bad taste. Please notice that my body has no color at all. I'm transparent, except for my exquisite red heart and my lovely pink brains—you can see 'em work."

"Shoo—shoo—shoo!" cried Scraps, dancing around and laughing. "And your horrid green eyes, Miss Bungle! You can't see your eyes, but we can, and I notice you're very proud of what little color you have. Shoo, Miss Bungle, shoo—shoo—shoo! If you were all colors and many colors, as I am, you'd be too stuck up for anything." She leaped over the cat and back again, and the startled Bungle crept close to a tree to escape her. This made Scraps laugh more heartily than ever, and she said:
"Whoop-te-doodle-doo!
The cat has lost her shoe.
Her tootsie's bare, but she don't care,
So what's the odds to you?"

"Dear me, Ojo," said the cat; "don't you think the creature is a little bit crazy?"

"It may be," he answered, with a puzzled look.

"If she continues her insults I'll scratch off her suspender-button eyes," declared the cat.

"Don't quarrel, please," pleaded the boy, rising to resume the journey. "Let us be good comrades and as happy and cheerful as possible, for we are likely to meet with plenty of trouble on our way."

It was nearly sundown when they came to the edge of the forest and saw spread out before them a delightful landscape. There were broad blue fields stretching for miles over the valley, which was dotted everywhere with pretty, blue domed houses, none of which, however, was very near to the place where they stood. Just at the point where the path left the forest stood a tiny house covered with leaves from the trees, and before this stood a Munchkin man with an axe in his hand. He seemed very much surprised when Ojo and Scraps and the Glass Cat came out of the woods, but as the Patchwork Girl approached nearer he sat down upon a bench and laughed so hard that he could not speak for a long time.

This man was a woodchopper and lived all alone in the little house. He had bushy blue whiskers and merry blue eyes and his blue clothes were quite old and worn.

"Mercy me!" exclaimed the woodchopper, when at last he could stop laughing. "Who would think such a funny harlequin lived in the Land of Oz? Where did you come from, Crazy-quilt?"

"Do you mean me?" asked the Patchwork Girl.

"Of course," he replied.

"You misjudge my ancestry. I'm not a crazy-quilt; I'm patchwork," she said.

"There's no difference," he replied, beginning to laugh again. "When my old grandmother sews such things together she calls it a crazy-quilt; but I never thought such a jumble could come to life."

"It was the Magic Powder that did it," explained Ojo.

"Oh, then you have come from the Crooked Magician on the mountain. I might have known it, for—Well, I declare! here's a glass cat. But the Magician will get in trouble for this; it's against the law for anyone to work magic except Glinda the Good and the royal Wizard of Oz. If you people—or things—or glass spectacles—or crazy-quilts—or whatever you are, go near the Emerald City, you'll be arrested."

"We're going there, anyhow," declared Scraps, sitting upon the bench and swinging her stuffed legs.
"If any of us takes a rest,
We'll be arrested sure,
And get no restitution
'Cause the rest we must endure."

"I see," said the woodchopper, nodding; "you're as crazy as the crazy-quilt you're made of."

"She really is crazy," remarked the Glass Cat. "But that isn't to be wondered at when you remember how many different things she's made of. For my part, I'm made of pure glass—except my jewel heart and my pretty pink brains. Did you notice my brains, stranger? You can see 'em work."

"So I can," replied the woodchopper; "but I can't see that they accomplish much. A glass cat is a useless sort of thing, but a Patchwork Girl is really useful. She makes me laugh, and laughter is the best thing in life. There was once a woodchopper, a friend of mine, who was made all of tin, and I used to laugh every time I saw him."

"A tin woodchopper?" said Ojo. "That is strange."

"My friend wasn't always tin," said the man, "but he was careless with his axe, and used to chop himself very badly. Whenever he lost an arm or a leg he had it replaced with tin; so after a while he was all tin."

"And could he chop wood then?" asked the boy.

"He could if he didn't rust his tin joints. But one day he met Dorothy in the forest and went with her to the Emerald City, where he made his fortune. He is now one of the favorites of Princess Ozma, and she has made him the Emperor of the Winkies—the Country where all is yellow."

"Who is Dorothy?" inquired the Patchwork Girl.

"A little maid who used to live in Kansas, but is now a Princess of Oz. She's Ozma's best friend, they say, and lives with her in the royal palace."

"Is Dorothy made of tin?" inquired Ojo.

"Is she patchwork, like me?" inquired Scraps.

"No," said the man; "Dorothy is flesh, just as I am. I know of only one tin person, and that is Nick Chopper, the Tin Woodman; and there will never be but one Patchwork Girl, for any magician that sees you will refuse to make another one like you."

"I suppose we shall see the Tin Woodman, for we are going to the Country of the Winkies," said the boy.

"What for?" asked the woodchopper.

"To get the left wing of a yellow butterfly."

"It is a long journey," declared the man, "and you will go through lonely parts of Oz and cross rivers and traverse dark forests before you get there."

"Suits me all right," said Scraps. "I'll get a chance to see the country."

"You're crazy, girl. Better crawl into a rag-bag and hide there; or give yourself to some little girl to play with. Those who travel are likely to meet trouble; that's why I stay at home."

The woodchopper then invited them all to stay the night at his little hut, but they were anxious to get on and so left him and continued along the path, which was broader, now, and more distinct.

They expected to reach some other house before it grew dark, but the twilight was brief and Ojo soon began to fear they had made a mistake in leaving the woodchopper.

"I can scarcely see the path," he said at last. "Can you see it, Scraps?"

"No," replied the Patchwork Girl, who was holding fast to the boy's arm so he could guide her.

"I can see," declared the Glass Cat. "My eyes are better than yours, and my pink brains—"

"Never mind your pink brains, please," said Ojo hastily; "just run ahead and show us the way. Wait a minute and I'll tie a string to you; for then you can lead us."

He got a string from his pocket and tied it around the cat's neck, and after that the creature guided them along the path. They had proceeded in this way for about an hour when a twinkling blue light appeared ahead of them.

"Good! there's a house at last," cried Ojo. "When we reach it the good people will surely welcome us and give us a night's lodging." But however far they walked the light seemed to get no nearer, so by and by the cat stopped short, saying: "I think the light is traveling, too, and we shall never be able to catch up with it. But here is a house by the roadside, so why go farther?"

"Where is the house, Bungle?"

"Just here beside us, Scraps."

Ojo was now able to see a small house near the pathway. It was dark and silent, but the boy was tired and wanted to rest, so he went up to the door and knocked.

"Who is there?" cried a voice from within.

"I am Ojo the Unlucky, and with me are Miss Scraps Patchwork and the Glass Cat," he replied.

"What do you want?" asked the Voice.

"A place to sleep," said Ojo.

"Come in, then; but don't make any noise, and you must go directly to bed," returned the Voice.

Ojo unlatched the door and entered. It was very dark inside and he could see nothing at all. But the cat exclaimed: "Why, there's no one here!"

"There must be," said the boy. "Some one spoke to me."

"I can see everything in the room," replied the cat, "and no one is present but ourselves. But here are three beds, all made up, so we may as well go to sleep."

"What is sleep?" inquired the Patchwork Girl.

"It's what you do when you go to bed," said Ojo.

"But why do you go to bed?" persisted the Patchwork Girl.

"Here, here! You are making altogether too much noise," cried the Voice they had heard before. "Keep quiet, strangers, and go to bed."

The cat, which could see in the dark, looked sharply around for the owner of the Voice, but could discover no one, although the Voice had seemed close beside them. She arched her back a little and seemed afraid. Then she whispered to Ojo: "Come!" and led him to a bed.

With his hands the boy felt of the bed and found it was big and soft, with feather pillows and plenty of blankets. So he took off his shoes and hat and crept into the bed. Then the cat led Scraps to another bed and the Patchwork Girl was puzzled to know what to do with it.

"Lie down and keep quiet," whispered the cat, warningly.

"Can't I sing?" asked Scraps.

"No."

"Can't I whistle?" asked Scraps.

"No."

"Can't I dance till morning, if I want to?" asked Scraps.

"You must keep quiet," said the cat, in a soft voice.

"I don't want to," replied the Patchwork Girl, speaking as loudly as usual. "What right have you to order me around? If I want to talk, or yell, or whistle—"

Before she could say anything more an unseen hand seized her firmly and threw her out of the door, which closed behind her with a sharp slam. She found herself bumping and rolling in the road and when she got up and tried to open the door of the house again she found it locked.

"What has happened to Scraps?" asked Ojo.

"Never mind. Let's go to sleep, or something will happen to us, answered the Glass Cat.

So Ojo snuggled down in his bed and fell asleep, and he was so tired that he never wakened until broad daylight.

7. The Troublesome Phonograph

When the boy opened his eyes next morning he looked carefully around the room. These small Munchkin houses seldom had more than one room in them. That in which Ojo now found himself had three beds, set all in a row on one side of it. The Glass Cat lay asleep on one bed, Ojo was in the second, and the third was neatly made up and smoothed for the day. On the other side of the room was a round table on which breakfast was already placed, smoking hot. Only one chair was drawn up to the table, where a place was set for one person. No one seemed to be in the room except the boy and Bungle.

Ojo got up and put on his shoes. Finding a toilet stand at the head of his bed he washed his face and hands and brushed his hair. Then he went to the table and said: "I wonder if this is my breakfast?"

"Eat it!" commanded a Voice at his side, so near that Ojo jumped. But no person could he see.

He was hungry, and the breakfast looked good; so he sat down and ate all he wanted. Then, rising, he took his hat and wakened the Glass Cat.

"Come on, Bungle," said he; "we must go."

He cast another glance about the room and, speaking to the air, he said: "Whoever lives here has been kind to me, and I'm much obliged."

There was no answer, so he took his basket and went out the door, the cat following him. In the middle of the path sat the Patchwork Girl, playing with pebbles she had picked up.

"Oh, there you are!" she exclaimed cheerfully. "I thought you were never coming out. It has been daylight a long time."

"What did you do all night?" asked the boy.

"Sat here and watched the stars and the moon," she replied. "They're interesting. I never saw them before, you know."

"Of course not," said Ojo.

"You were crazy to act so badly and get thrown outdoors," remarked Bungle, as they renewed their journey.

"That's all right," said Scraps. "If I hadn't been thrown out I wouldn't have seen the stars, nor the big gray wolf."

"What wolf?" inquired Ojo.

"The one that came to the door of the house three times during the night."

"I don't see why that should be," said the boy, thoughtfully; "there was plenty to eat in that house, for I had a fine breakfast, and I slept in a nice bed."

"Don't you feel tired?" asked the Patchwork Girl, noticing that the boy yawned.

"Why, yes; I'm as tired as I was last night; and yet I slept very well."

"And aren't you hungry?"

"It's strange," replied Ojo. "I had a good breakfast, and yet I think I'll now eat some of my crackers and cheese."

Scraps danced up and down the path. Then she sang:
"Kizzle-kazzle-kore;
The wolf is at the door,
There's nothing to eat but a bone without meat,
And a bill from the grocery store."

"What does that mean?" asked Ojo.

"Don't ask me," replied Scraps. "I say what comes into my head, but of course I know nothing of a grocery store or bones without meat or— very much else."

"No," said the cat; "she's stark, staring, raving crazy, and her brains can't be pink, for they don't work properly."

"Bother the brains!" cried Scraps. "Who cares for 'em, anyhow? Have you noticed how beautiful my patches are in this sunlight?"

Just then they heard a sound as of footsteps pattering along the path behind them and all three turned to see what was coming. To their astonishment they beheld a small round table running as fast as its four spindle legs could carry it, and to the top was screwed fast a phonograph with a big gold horn.

"Hold on!" shouted the phonograph. "Wait for me!"

"Goodness me; it's that music thing which the Crooked Magician scattered the Powder of Life over," said Ojo.

"So it is," returned Bungle, in a grumpy tone of voice; and then, as the phonograph overtook them, the Glass Cat added sternly: "What are you doing here, anyhow?"

"I've run away," said the music thing. "After you left, old Dr. Pipt and I had a dreadful quarrel and he threatened to smash me to pieces if I didn't keep quiet. Of course I wouldn't do that, because a talking-machine is supposed to talk and make a noise—and sometimes music. So I slipped out of the house while the Magician was stirring his four kettles and I've been running after you all night. Now that I've found such pleasant company, I can talk and play tunes all I want to."

Ojo was greatly annoyed by this unwelcome addition to their party. At first he did not know what to say to the newcomer, but a little thought decided him not to make friends.

"We are traveling on important business," he declared, "and you'll excuse me if I say we can't be bothered."

"How very impolite!" exclaimed the phonograph.

"I'm sorry; but it's true," said the boy. "You'll have to go somewhere else."

"This is very unkind treatment, I must say," whined the phonograph, in an injured tone. "Everyone seems to hate me, and yet I was intended to amuse people."

"It isn't you we hate, especially," observed the Glass Cat; "it's your dreadful music. When I lived in the same room with you I was much annoyed by your squeaky horn. It growls and grumbles and clicks and scratches so it spoils the music, and your machinery rumbles so that the racket drowns every tune you attempt."

"That isn't my fault; it's the fault of my records. I must admit that I haven't a clear record," answered the machine.

"Just the same, you'll have to go away," said Ojo.

"Wait a minute," cried Scraps. "This music thing interests me. I remember to have heard music when I first came to life, and I would like to hear it again. What is your name, my poor abused phonograph?"

"Victor Columbia Edison," it answered.

"Well, I shall call you 'Vic' for short," said the Patchwork Girl. "Go ahead and play something."

"It'll drive you crazy," warned the cat.

"I'm crazy now, according to your statement. Loosen up and reel out the music, Vic."

"The only record I have with me," explained the phonograph, "is one the Magician attached just before we had our quarrel. It's a highly classical composition."

"A what?" inquired Scraps.

"It is classical music, and is considered the best and most puzzling ever manufactured. You're supposed to like it, whether you do or not, and if you don't, the proper thing is to look as if you did. Understand?"

"Not in the least," said Scraps.

"Then, listen!"

At once the machine began to play and in a few minutes Ojo put his hands to his ears to shut out the sounds and the cat snarled and Scraps began to laugh.

"Cut it out, Vic," she said. "That's enough."

But the phonograph continued playing the dreary tune, so Ojo seized the crank, jerked it free and threw it into the road. However, the moment the crank struck the ground it bounded back to the machine again and began winding it up. And still the music played.

"Let's run!" cried Scraps, and they all started and ran down the path as fast as they could go. But the phonograph was right behind them and could run and play at the same time. It called out, reproachfully: "What's the matter? Don't you love classical music?"

"No, Vic," said Scraps, halting. "We will passical the classical and preserve what joy we have left. I haven't any nerves, thank goodness, but your music makes my cotton shrink."

"Then turn over my record. There's a rag-time tune on the other side," said the machine.

"What's rag-time?"

"The opposite of classical."

"All right," said Scraps, and turned over the record.

The phonograph now began to play a jerky jumble of sounds which proved so bewildering that after a moment Scraps stuffed

her patchwork apron into the gold horn and cried: "Stop—stop! That's the other extreme. It's extremely bad!"

Muffled as it was, the phonograph played on.

"If you don't shut off that music I'll smash your record," threatened Ojo.

The music stopped, at that, and the machine turned its horn from one to another and said with great indignation: "What's the matter now? Is it possible you can't appreciate rag-time?"

"Scraps ought to, being rags herself," said the cat; "but I simply can't stand it; it makes my whiskers curl."

"It is, indeed, dreadful!" exclaimed Ojo, with a shudder.

"It's enough to drive a crazy lady mad," murmured the Patchwork Girl. "I'll tell you what, Vic," she added as she smoothed out her apron and put it on again, "for some reason or other you've missed your guess. You're not a concert; you're a nuisance."

"Music hath charms to soothe the savage breast," asserted the phonograph sadly.

"Then we're not savages. I advise you to go home and beg the Magician's pardon."

"Never! He'd smash me."

"That's what we shall do, if you stay here," Ojo declared.

"Run along, Vic, and bother some one else," advised Scraps. "Find some one who is real wicked, and stay with him till he repents. In that way you can do some good in the world."

The music thing turned silently away and trotted down a side path, toward a distant Munchkin village.

"Is that the way we go?" asked Bungle anxiously.

"No," said Ojo; "I think we shall keep straight ahead, for this path is the widest and best. When we come to some house we will inquire the way to the Emerald City."

8. The Foolish Owl and the Wise Donkey

On they went, and half an hour's steady walking brought them to a house somewhat better than the two they had already passed. It stood close to the roadside and over the door was a sign that read: "Miss Foolish Owl and Mr. Wise Donkey: Public Advisers."

When Ojo read this sign aloud Scraps said laughingly: "Well, here is a place to get all the advice we want, maybe more than we need. Let's go in."

The boy knocked at the door.

"Come in!" called a deep bass voice.

So they opened the door and entered the house, where a little light-brown donkey, dressed in a blue apron and a blue cap, was engaged in dusting the furniture with a blue cloth. On a shelf over the window sat a great blue owl with a blue sunbonnet on her head, blinking her big round eyes at the visitors.

"Good morning," said the donkey, in his deep voice, which

seemed bigger than he was. "Did you come to us for advice?"

"Why, we came, anyhow," replied Scraps, "and now we are here we may as well have some advice. It's free, isn't it?"

"Certainly," said the donkey. "Advice doesn't cost anything—unless you follow it. Permit me to say, by the way, that you are the queerest lot of travelers that ever came to my shop. Judging you merely by appearances, I think you'd better talk to the Foolish Owl yonder."

They turned to look at the bird, which fluttered its wings and stared back at them with its big eyes.

"Hoot-ti-toot-ti-toot!" cried the owl.
"Fiddle-cum-foo,
Howdy-do?
Riddle-cum, tiddle-cum,
Too-ra-la-loo!"

"That beats your poetry, Scraps," said Ojo.

"It's just nonsense!" declared the Glass Cat.

"But it's good advice for the foolish," said the donkey, admiringly. "Listen to my partner, and you can't go wrong."

Said the owl in a grumbling voice:
"Patchwork Girl has come to life;
No one's sweetheart, no one's wife;
Lacking sense and loving fun,
She'll be snubbed by everyone."

"Quite a compliment! Quite a compliment, I declare," exclaimed the donkey, turning to look at Scraps. "You are certainly a wonder, my dear, and I fancy you'd make a splendid pincushion. If you belonged to me, I'd wear smoked glasses when I looked at you."

"Why?" asked the Patchwork Girl.

"Because you are so gay and gaudy."

"It is my beauty that dazzles you," she asserted. "You Munchkin people all strut around in your stupid blue color, while I—"

"You are wrong in calling me a Munchkin," interrupted the donkey, "for I was born in the Land of Mo and came to visit the Land of Oz on the day it was shut off from all the rest of the world. So here I am obliged to stay, and I confess it is a very pleasant country to live in."

"Hoot-ti-toot!" cried the owl;
"Ojo's searching for a charm,
'Cause Unc Nunkie's come to harm.
Charms are scarce; they're hard to get;
Ojo's got a job, you bet!"

"Is the owl so very foolish?" asked the boy.

"Extremely so," replied the donkey. "Notice what vulgar expressions she uses. But I admire the owl for the reason that she is positively foolish. Owls are supposed to be so very wise, generally, that a foolish one is unusual, and you perhaps know that anything or anyone unusual is sure to be interesting to the wise."

The owl flapped its wings again, muttering these words:

"It's hard to be a glassy cat—
No cat can be more hard than that;
She's so transparent, every act
Is clear to us, and that's a fact."

"Have you noticed my pink brains?" inquired Bungle, proudly. "You can see 'em work."

"Not in the daytime," said the donkey. "She can't see very well by day, poor thing. But her advice is excellent. I advise you all to follow it."

"The owl hasn't given us any advice, as yet," the boy declared.

"No? Then what do you call all those sweet poems?"

"Just foolishness," replied Ojo. "Scraps does the same thing."

"Foolishness! Of course! To be sure! The Foolish Owl must be foolish or she wouldn't be the Foolish Owl. You are very complimentary to my partner, indeed," asserted the donkey, rubbing his front hoofs together as if highly pleased.

"The sign says that you are wise," remarked Scraps to the donkey. "I wish you would prove it."

"With great pleasure," returned the beast. "Put me to the test, my dear Patches, and I'll prove my wisdom in the wink of an eye."

"What is the best way to get to the Emerald City?" asked Ojo.

"Walk," said the donkey.

"I know; but what road shall I take?" was the boy's next question.

"The road of yellow bricks, of course. It leads directly to the Emerald City."

"And how shall we find the road of yellow bricks?"

"By keeping along the path you have been following. You'll come to the yellow bricks pretty soon, and you'll know them when you see them because they're the only yellow things in the blue country."

"Thank you," said the boy. "At last you have told me something."

"Is that the extent of your wisdom?" asked Scraps.

"No," replied the donkey; "I know many other things, but they wouldn't interest you. So I'll give you a last word of advice: move on, for the sooner you do that the sooner you'll get to the Emerald City of Oz."

"Hoot-ti-toot-ti-toot-ti-too!" screeched the owl;
"Off you go! fast or slow,
Where you're going you don't know.
Patches, Bungle, Muchkin lad,
Facing fortunes good and bad,
Meeting dangers grave and sad,
Sometimes worried, sometimes glad—
Where you're going you don't know,
Nor do I, but off you go!"

"Sounds like a hint, to me," said the Patchwork Girl.

"Then let's take it and go," replied Ojo.

They said good-bye to the Wise Donkey and the Foolish Owl and at once resumed their journey.

9. They Meet the Woozy

"There seem to be very few houses around here, after all," remarked Ojo, after they had walked for a time in silence.

"Never mind," said Scraps; "we are not looking for houses, but rather the road of yellow bricks. Won't it be funny to run across something yellow in this dismal blue country?"

"There are worse colors than yellow in this country," asserted the Glass Cat, in a spiteful tone.

"Oh; do you mean the pink pebbles you call your brains, and your red heart and green eyes?" asked the Patchwork Girl.

"No; I mean you, if you must know it," growled the cat.

"You're jealous!" laughed Scraps. "You'd give your whiskers for a lovely variegated complexion like mine."

"I wouldn't!" retorted the cat. "I've the clearest complexion in the world, and I don't employ a beauty-doctor, either."

"I see you don't," said Scraps.

"Please don't quarrel," begged Ojo. "This is an important journey, and quarreling makes me discouraged. To be brave, one must be cheerful, so I hope you will be as good-tempered as possible."

They had traveled some distance when suddenly they faced a high fence which barred any further progress straight ahead. It ran directly across the road and enclosed a small forest of tall trees, set close together. When the group of adventurers peered through the bars of the fence they thought this forest looked more gloomy and forbidding than any they had ever seen before.

They soon discovered that the path they had been following now made a bend and passed around the enclosure, but what made Ojo stop and look thoughtful was a sign painted on the fence which read:

BEWARE OF THE WOOZY!

"That means," he said, "that there's a Woozy inside that fence, and the Woozy must be a dangerous animal or they wouldn't tell people to beware of it."

"Let's keep out, then," replied Scraps. "That path is outside the fence, and Mr. Woozy may have all his little forest to himself, for all we care."

"But one of our errands is to find a Woozy," Ojo explained. "The Magician wants me to get three hairs from the end of a Woozy's tail."

"Let's go on and find some other Woozy," suggested the cat. "This one is ugly and dangerous, or they wouldn't cage him up. Maybe we shall find another that is tame and gentle."

"Perhaps there isn't any other, at all," answered Ojo. "The sign doesn't say: 'Beware a Woozy'; it says: 'Beware the Woozy,' which may mean there's only one in all the Land of Oz."

"Then," said Scraps, "suppose we go in and find him? Very likely if we ask him politely to let us pull three hairs out of the tip of his tail he won't hurt us."

"It would hurt him, I'm sure, and that would make him cross," said the cat.

"You needn't worry, Bungle," remarked the Patchwork Girl; "for if there is danger you can climb a tree. Ojo and I are not afraid, are we, Ojo?"

"I am, a little," the boy admitted; "but this danger must be faced if we intend to save poor Unc Nunkie. How shall we get over the fence?"

"Climb," answered Scraps, and at once she began climbing up the rows of bars. Ojo followed and found it more easy than he had expected. When they got to the top of the fence they began to get down on the other side and soon were in the forest. The Glass Cat, being small, crept between the lower bars and joined them.

Here there was no path of any sort, so they entered the woods, the boy leading the way, and wandered through the trees until they were nearly in the center of the forest. They now came upon a clear space in which stood a rocky cave.

So far they had met no living creature, but when Ojo saw the cave he knew it must be the den of the Woozy.

It is hard to face any savage beast without a sinking of the heart, but still more terrifying is it to face an unknown beast, which you have never seen even a picture of. So there is little wonder that the pulses of the Munchkin boy beat fast as he and his companions stood facing the cave. The opening was perfectly square, and about big enough to admit a goat.

"I guess the Woozy is asleep," said Scraps. "Shall I throw in a stone, to waken him?"

"No; please don't," answered Ojo, his voice trembling a little. "I'm in no hurry."

But he had not long to wait, for the Woozy heard the sound of voices and came trotting out of his cave. As this is the only Woozy that has ever lived, either in the Land of Oz or out of it, I must describe it to you.

The creature was all squares and flat surfaces and edges. Its head was an exact square, like one of the building-blocks a child plays with; therefore it had no ears, but heard sounds through two openings in the upper corners. Its nose, being in the center of a square surface, was flat, while the mouth was formed by the opening of the lower edge of the block. The body of the Woozy was much larger than its head, but was likewise block-shaped—being twice as long as it was wide and high. The tail was square and stubby and perfectly straight, and the four legs were made in the same way, each being four-sided. The animal was covered with a thick, smooth skin and had no hair at all except at the extreme end of its tail, where there grew exactly three stiff, stubby hairs. The beast was dark blue in color and his face was not fierce nor ferocious in expression, but rather good-humored and droll.

Seeing the strangers, the Woozy folded his hind legs as if they had been hinged and sat down to look his visitors over.

"Well, well," he exclaimed; "what a queer lot you are! At first I thought some of those miserable Munchkin farmers had come to annoy me, but I am relieved to find you in their stead. It is plain to me that you are a remarkable group—as remarkable in your way as I am in mine—and so you are welcome to my domain. Nice place, isn't it? But lonesome—dreadfully lonesome."

"Why did they shut you up here?" asked Scraps, who was regarding the queer, square creature with much curiosity.

"Because I eat up all the honey-bees which the Munchkin farmers who live around here keep to make them honey."

"Are you fond of eating honey-bees?" inquired the boy.

"Very. They are really delicious. But the farmers did not like to lose their bees and so they tried to destroy me. Of course they couldn't do that."

"Why not?"

"My skin is so thick and tough that nothing can get through it to hurt me. So, finding they could not destroy me, they drove me into this forest and built a fence around me. Unkind, wasn't it?"

"But what do you eat now?" asked Ojo.

"Nothing at all. I've tried the leaves from the trees and the mosses and creeping vines, but they don't seem to suit my taste. So, there being no honey-bees here, I've eaten nothing for years."

"You must be awfully hungry," said the boy. "I've got some bread and cheese in my basket. Would you like that kind of food?"

"Give me a nibble and I will try it; then I can tell you better whether it is grateful to my appetite," returned the Woozy.

So the boy opened his basket and broke a piece off the loaf of bread. He tossed it toward the Woozy, who cleverly caught it in his mouth and ate it in a twinkling.

"That's rather good," declared the animal. "Any more?"

"Try some cheese," said Ojo, and threw down a piece.

The Woozy ate that, too, and smacked its long, thin lips.

"That's mighty good!" it exclaimed. "Any more?"

"Plenty," replied Ojo. So he sat down on a Stump and fed the Woozy bread and cheese for a long time; for, no matter how much the boy broke off, the loaf and the slice remained just as big.

"That'll do," said the Woozy, at last; "I'm quite full. I hope the strange food won't give me indigestion."

"I hope not," said Ojo. "It's what I eat."

"Well, I must say I'm much obliged, and I'm glad you came," announced the beast. "Is there anything I can do in return for your kindness?"

"Yes," said Ojo earnestly, "you have it in your power to do me a great favor, if you will."

"What is it?" asked the Woozy. "Name the favor and I will grant it."

"I—I want three hairs from the tip of your tail," said Ojo, with some hesitation.

"Three hairs! Why, that's all I have—on my tail or anywhere else," exclaimed the beast.

"I know; but I want them very much."

"They are my sole ornaments, my prettiest feature," said the Woozy, uneasily. "If I give up those three hairs I—I'm just a blockhead."

"Yet I must have them," insisted the boy, firmly, and he then told the Woozy all about the accident to Unc Nunkie and Margolotte, and how the three hairs were to be a part of the magic charm that would restore them to life. The beast listened with attention and when Ojo had finished the recital it said, with a sigh: "I always keep my word, for I pride myself on being square. So you may have the three hairs, and welcome. I think, under such circumstances, it would be selfish in me to refuse you."

"Thank you! Thank you very much," cried the boy, joyfully. "May I pull out the hairs now?"

"Any time you like," answered the Woozy.

So Ojo went up to the queer creature and taking hold of one of the hairs began to pull. He pulled harder. He pulled with all his might; but the hair remained fast.

"What's the trouble?" asked the Woozy, which Ojo had dragged here and there all around the clearing in his endeavor to pull out the hair.

"It won't come," said the boy, panting.

"I was afraid of that," declared the beast. "You'll have to pull harder."

"I'll help you," exclaimed Scraps, coming to the boy's side. "You pull the hair, and I'll pull you, and together we ought to get it out easily."

"Wait a jiffy," called the Woozy, and then it went to a tree and hugged it with its front paws, so that its body couldn't be dragged around by the pull. "All ready, now. Go ahead!"

Ojo grasped the hair with both hands and pulled with all his strength, while Scraps seized the boy around his waist and added her strength to his. But the hair wouldn't budge. Instead, it slipped out of Ojo's hands and he and Scraps both rolled upon the ground in a heap and never stopped until they bumped against the rocky cave.

"Give it up," advised the Glass Cat, as the boy arose and assisted the Patchwork Girl to her feet. "A dozen strong men couldn't pull out those hairs. I believe they're clinched on the under side of the Woozy's thick skin."

"Then what shall I do?" asked the boy, despairingly. "If on our return I fail to take these three hairs to the Crooked Magician, the other things I have come to seek will be of no use at all, and we cannot restore Unc Nunkie and Margolotte to life."

"They're goners, I guess," said the Patchwork Girl.

"Never mind," added the cat. "I can't see that old Unc and Margolotte are worth all this trouble, anyhow."

But Ojo did not feel that way. He was so disheartened that he sat down upon a stump and began to cry.

The Woozy looked at the boy thoughtfully.

"Why don't you take me with you?" asked the beast. "Then, when at last you get to the Magician's house, he can surely find some way to pull out those three hairs."

Ojo was overjoyed at this suggestion.

"That's it!" he cried, wiping away the tears and springing to his feet with a smile. "If I take the three hairs to the Magician, it won't matter if they are still in your body."

"It can't matter in the least," agreed the Woozy.

"Come on, then," said the boy, picking up his basket; "let us start at once. I have several other things to find, you know."

But the Glass Cat gave a little laugh and inquired in her scornful way: "How do you intend to get the beast out of this forest?"

That puzzled them all for a time.

"Let us go to the fence, and then we may find a way," suggested Scraps. So they walked through the forest to the fence, reaching it at a point exactly opposite that where they had entered the enclosure.

"How did you get in?" asked the Woozy.

"We climbed over," answered Ojo.

"I can't do that," said the beast. "I'm a very swift runner, for I can overtake a honey-bee as it flies; and I can jump very high, which is the reason they made such a tall fence to keep me in. But I can't climb at all, and I'm too big to squeeze between the bars of the fence."

Ojo tried to think what to do.

"Can you dig?" he asked.

"No," answered the Woozy, "for I have no claws. My feet are quite flat on the bottom of them. Nor can I gnaw away the boards, as I have no teeth."

"You're not such a terrible creature, after all," remarked Scraps.

"You haven't heard me growl, or you wouldn't say that," declared the Woozy. "When I growl, the sound echoes like thunder all through the valleys and woodlands, and children tremble with fear, and women cover their heads with their aprons, and big men run and hide. I suppose there is nothing in the world so terrible to listen to as the growl of a Woozy."

"Please don't growl, then," begged Ojo, earnestly.

"There is no danger of my growling, for I am not angry. Only when angry do I utter my fearful, ear-splitting, soul-shuddering growl. Also, when I am angry, my eyes flash fire, whether I growl or not."

"Real fire?" asked Ojo.

"Of course, real fire. Do you suppose they'd flash imitation fire?" inquired the Woozy, in an injured tone.

"In that case, I've solved the riddle," cried Scraps, dancing with glee. "Those fence-boards are made of wood, and if the Woozy stands close to the fence and lets his eyes flash fire, they might set fire to the fence and burn it up. Then he could walk away with us easily, being free."

"Ah, I have never thought of that plan, or I would have been free long ago," said the Woozy. "But I cannot flash fire from my eyes unless I am very angry."

"Can't you get angry 'bout something, please?" asked Ojo.

"I'll try. You just say 'Krizzle-Kroo' to me."

"Will that make you angry?" inquired the boy.

"Terribly angry."

"What does it mean?" asked Scraps.

"I don't know; that's what makes me so angry," replied the Woozy.

He then stood close to the fence, with his head near one of the boards, and Scraps called out "Krizzle-Kroo!" Then Ojo said "Krizzle-Kroo!" and the Glass Cat said "Krizzle-Kroo!" The Woozy began to tremble with anger and small sparks darted from his eyes. Seeing this, they all cried "Krizzle-Kroo!" together, and that made the beast's eyes flash fire so fiercely that the fence-board caught the sparks and began to smoke. Then it burst into flame, and the Woozy stepped back and said triumphantly: "Aha! That did the business, all right. It was a happy thought for you to yell all together, for that made me as angry as I have ever been. Fine sparks, weren't they?"

"Reg'lar fireworks," replied Scraps, admiringly.

In a few moments the board had burned to a distance of several feet, leaving an opening big enough for them all to pass through. Ojo broke some branches from a tree and with them whipped the fire until it was extinguished.

"We don't want to burn the whole fence down," said he, "for the flames would attract the attention of the Munchkin farmers, who would then come and capture the Woozy again. I guess they'll be rather surprised when they find he's escaped."

"So they will," declared the Woozy, chuckling gleefully. "When they find I'm gone the farmers will be badly scared, for they'll expect me to eat up their honey-bees, as I did before."

"That reminds me," said the boy, "that you must promise not to eat honey-bees while you are in our company."

"None at all?"

"Not a bee. You would get us all into trouble, and we can't afford to have any more trouble than is necessary. I'll feed you all the bread and cheese you want, and that must satisfy you."

"All right; I'll promise," said the Woozy, cheerfully. "And when I promise anything you can depend on it, 'cause I'm square."

"I don't see what difference that makes," observed the Patchwork Girl, as they found the path and continued their journey. "The shape doesn't make a thing honest, does it?"

"Of course it does," returned the Woozy, very decidedly. "No one could trust that Crooked Magician, for instance, just because he is crooked; but a square Woozy couldn't do anything crooked if he wanted to."

"I am neither square nor crooked," said Scraps, looking down at her plump body.

"No; you're round, so you're liable to do anything," asserted the Woozy. "Do not blame me, Miss Gorgeous, if I regard you with suspicion. Many a satin ribbon has a cotton back."

Scraps didn't understand this, but she had an uneasy misgiving that she had a cotton back herself. It would settle down, at times, and make her squat and dumpy, and then she had to roll herself in the road until her body stretched out again.

10. Shaggy Man to the Rescue

They had not gone very far before Bungle, who had run on ahead, came bounding back to say that the road of yellow bricks was just before them. At once they hurried forward to see what this famous road looked like.

It was a broad road, but not straight, for it wandered over hill and dale and picked out the easiest places to go. All its length and breadth was paved with smooth bricks of a bright yellow color, so it was smooth and level except in a few places where the bricks had crumbled or been removed, leaving holes that might cause the unwary to stumble.

"I wonder," said Ojo, looking up and down the road, "which way to go."

"Where are you bound for?" asked the Woozy.

"The Emerald City," he replied.

"Then go west," said the Woozy. "I know this road pretty well, for I've chased many a honey-bee over it."

"Have you ever been to the Emerald City?" asked Scraps.

"No. I am very shy by nature, as you may have noticed, so I haven't mingled much in society."

"Are you afraid of men?" inquired the Patchwork Girl.

"Me? With my heart-rending growl—my horrible, shudderful growl? I should say not. I am not afraid of anything," declared the Woozy.

"I wish I could say the same," sighed Ojo. "I don't think we need be afraid when we get to the Emerald City, for Unc Nunkie has told me that Ozma, our girl Ruler, is very lovely and kind, and tries to help everyone who is in trouble. But they say there are many dangers lurking on the road to the great Fairy City, and so we must be very careful."

"I hope nothing will break me," said the Glass Cat, in a nervous voice. "I'm a little brittle, you know, and can't stand many hard knocks."

"If anything should fade the colors of my lovely patches it would break my heart," said the Patchwork Girl.

"I'm not sure you have a heart," Ojo reminded her.

"Then it would break my cotton," persisted Scraps. "Do you think they are all fast colors, Ojo?" she asked anxiously.

"They seem fast enough when you run," he replied; and then, looking ahead of them, he exclaimed: "Oh, what lovely trees!"

They were certainly pretty to look upon and the travelers hurried forward to observe them more closely.

"Why, they are not trees at all," said Scraps; "they are just monstrous plants."

That is what they really were: masses of great broad leaves which rose from the ground far into the air, until they towered twice as high as the top of the Patchwork Girl's head, who was a little taller than Ojo. The plants formed rows on both sides of the road and from each plant rose a dozen or more of the big broad leaves, which swayed continually from side to side, although no wind was blowing. But the most curious thing about the swaying leaves was their color. They seemed to have a general groundwork of blue, but here and there other colors glinted at times through the blue—gorgeous yellows, turning to pink, purple, orange and scarlet, mingled with more sober browns and grays—each appearing as a blotch or stripe anywhere on a leaf and then disappearing, to be replaced by some other color of a different shape. The changeful coloring of the great leaves was very beautiful, but it was bewildering, as well, and the novelty of the scene drew our travelers close to the line of plants, where they stood watching them with rapt interest.

Suddenly a leaf bent lower than usual and touched the Patchwork Girl. Swiftly it enveloped her in its embrace, covering her completely in its thick folds, and then it swayed back upon its stem.

"Why, she's gone!" gasped Ojo, in amazement, and listening carefully he thought he could hear the muffled screams of Scraps coming from the center of the folded leaf. But, before he could think what he ought to do to save her, another leaf bent down and captured the Glass Cat, rolling around the little creature until she was completely hidden, and then straightening up again upon its stem.

"Look out," cried the Woozy. "Run! Run fast, or you are lost."

Ojo turned and saw the Woozy running swiftly up the road. But the last leaf of the row of plants seized the beast even as he ran and instantly he disappeared from sight.

The boy had no chance to escape. Half a dozen of the great leaves were bending toward him from different directions and as he stood hesitating one of them clutched him in its embrace. In a flash he was in the dark. Then he felt himself gently lifted until he was swaying in the air, with the folds of the leaf hugging him on all sides.

At first he struggled hard to escape, crying out in anger: "Let me go! Let me go!" But neither struggles nor protests had any effect whatever. The leaf held him firmly and he was a prisoner.

Then Ojo quieted himself and tried to think. Despair fell upon him when he remembered that all his little party had been captured, even as he was, and there was none to save them.

"I might have expected it," he sobbed, miserably. "I'm Ojo the Unlucky, and something dreadful was sure to happen to me."

He pushed against the leaf that held him and found it to be soft, but thick and firm. It was like a great bandage all around him and he found it difficult to move his body or limbs in order to change their position.

The minutes passed and became hours. Ojo wondered how long one could live in such a condition and if the leaf would gradually sap his strength and even his life, in order to feed itself. The little Munchkin boy had never heard of any person dying in the Land of Oz, but he knew one could suffer a great deal of pain. His greatest fear at this time was that he would always remain imprisoned in the beautiful leaf and never see the light of day again.

No sound came to him through the leaf; all around was intense silence. Ojo wondered if Scraps had stopped screaming, or if the folds of the leaf prevented his hearing her. By and by he thought he heard a whistle, as of some one whistling a tune. Yes; it really must be some one whistling, he decided, for he could follow the strains of a pretty Munchkin melody that Unc Nunkie used to sing to him. The sounds were low and sweet and, although they reached Ojo's ears very faintly, they were clear and harmonious.

Could the leaf whistle, Ojo wondered? Nearer and nearer came the sounds and then they seemed to be just the other side of the leaf that was hugging him.

Suddenly the whole leaf toppled and fell, carrying the boy with it, and while he sprawled at full length the folds slowly relaxed and set him free. He scrambled quickly to his feet and found that a strange man was standing before him—a man so curious in appearance that the boy stared with round eyes.

He was a big man, with shaggy whiskers, shaggy eyebrows, shaggy hair—but kindly blue eyes that were gentle as those of a cow. On his head was a green velvet hat with a jeweled band, which was all shaggy around the brim. Rich but shaggy laces were at his throat; a coat with shaggy edges was decorated with diamond buttons; the velvet breeches had jeweled buckles at the knees and shags all around the bottoms. On his breast hung a medallion bearing a picture of Princess Dorothy of Oz, and in his hand, as he stood looking at Ojo, was a sharp knife shaped like a dagger.

"Oh!" exclaimed Ojo, greatly astonished at the sight of this stranger; and then he added: "Who has saved me, sir?"

"Can't you see?" replied the other, with a smile; "I'm the Shaggy Man."

"Yes; I can see that," said the boy, nodding. "Was it you who rescued me from the leaf?"

"None other, you may be sure. But take care, or I shall have to rescue you again."

Ojo gave a jump, for he saw several broad leaves leaning toward him; but the Shaggy Man began to whistle again, and at the sound the leaves all straightened up on their stems and kept still.

The man now took Ojo's arm and led him up the road, past the last of the great plants, and not till he was safely beyond their reach did he cease his whistling.

"You see, the music charms 'em," said he. "Singing or whistling—it doesn't matter which— makes 'em behave, and nothing else will. I always whistle as I go by 'em and so they always let me alone. To-day as I went by, whistling, I saw a leaf curled and knew there must be something inside it. I cut down the leaf with

my knife and—out you popped. Lucky I passed by, wasn't it?"

"You were very kind," said Ojo, "and I thank you. Will you please rescue my companions, also?"

"What companions?" asked the Shaggy Man.

"The leaves grabbed them all," said the boy. "There's a Patchwork Girl and—"

"A what?"

"A girl made of patchwork, you know. She's alive and her name is Scraps. And there's a Glass Cat—"

"Glass?" asked the Shaggy Man.

"All glass."

"And alive?"

"Yes," said Ojo; "she has pink brains. And there's a Woozy—"

"What's a Woozy?" inquired the Shaggy Man.

"Why, I—I—can't describe it," answered the boy, greatly perplexed. "But it's a queer animal with three hairs on the tip of its tail that won't come out and—"

"What won't come out?" asked the Shaggy Man; "the tail?"

"The hairs won't come out. But you'll see the Woozy, if you'll please rescue it, and then you'll know just what it is."

"Of course," said the Shaggy Man, nodding his shaggy head. And then he walked back among the plants, still whistling, and found the three leaves which were curled around Ojo's traveling companions. The first leaf he cut down released Scraps, and on seeing her the Shaggy Man threw back his shaggy head, opened wide his mouth and laughed so shaggily and yet so merrily that Scraps liked him at once. Then he took off his hat and made her a low bow, saying: "My dear, you're a wonder. I must introduce you to my friend the Scarecrow."

When he cut down the second leaf he rescued the Glass Cat, and Bungle was so frightened that she scampered away like a streak and soon had joined Ojo, when she sat beside him panting and trembling. The last plant of all the row had captured the Woozy and a big bunch in the center of the curled leaf showed plainly where he was. With his sharp knife the Shaggy Man sliced off the stem of the leaf and as it fell and unfolded out trotted the Woozy and escaped beyond the reach of any more of the dangerous plants.

11. A Good Friend

Soon the entire party was gathered on the road of yellow bricks, quite beyond the reach of the beautiful but treacherous plants. The Shaggy Man, staring first at one and then at the other, seemed greatly pleased and interested.

"I've seen queer things since I came to the Land of Oz," said he, "but never anything queerer than this band of adventurers. Let us sit down a while, and have a talk and get acquainted."

"Haven't you always lived in the Land of Oz?" asked the Munchkin boy.

"No; I used to live in the big, outside world. But I came here once with Dorothy, and Ozma let me stay."

"How do you like Oz?" asked Scraps. "Isn't the country and the climate grand?"

"It's the finest country in all the world, even if it is a fairyland. and I'm happy every minute I live in it," said the Shaggy Man. "But tell me something about yourselves."

So Ojo related the story of his visit to the house of the Crooked Magician, and how he met there the Glass Cat, and how the Patchwork Girl was brought to life and of the terrible accident to Unc Nunkie and Margolotte. Then he told how he had set out to find the five different things which the Magician needed to make a charm that would restore the marble figures to life, one requirement being three hairs from a Woozy's tail.

"We found the Woozy," explained the boy, "and he agreed to give us the three hairs; but we couldn't pull them out. So we had to bring the Woozy along with us."

"I see," returned the Shaggy Man, who had listened with interest to the story. "But perhaps I, who am big and strong, can pull those three hairs from the Woozy's tail."

"Try it, if you like," said the Woozy.

So the Shaggy Man tried it, but pull as hard as he could he failed to get the hairs out of the Woozy's tail. So he sat down again and wiped his shaggy face with a shaggy silk handkerchief and said: "It doesn't matter. If you can keep the Woozy until you get the rest of the things you need, you can take the beast and his three hairs to the Crooked Magician and let him find a way to extract 'em. What are the other things you are to find?"

"One," said Ojo, "is a six-leaved clover."

"You ought to find that in the fields around the Emerald City," said the Shaggy Man. "There is a Law against picking six-leaved clovers, but I think I can get Ozma to let you have one."

"Thank you," replied Ojo. "The next thing is the left wing of a yellow butterfly."

"For that you must go to the Winkie Country," the Shaggy Man declared. "I've never noticed any butterflies there, but that is the yellow country of Oz and it's ruled by a good friend of mine, the Tin Woodman."

"Oh, I've heard of him!" exclaimed Ojo. "He must be a wonderful man."

"So he is, and his heart is wonderfully kind. I'm sure the Tin Woodman will do all in his power to help you to save your Unc Nunkie and poor Margolotte."

"The next thing I must find," said the Munchkin boy, "is a gill of water from a dark well."

"Indeed! Well, that is more difficult," said the Shaggy Man, scratching his left ear in a puzzled way. "I've never heard of a dark well; have you?"

"No," said Ojo.

"Do you know where one may be found?" inquired the Shaggy Man.

"I can't imagine," said Ojo.

"Then we must ask the Scarecrow."

"The Scarecrow! But surely, sir, a scarecrow can't know anything."

"Most scarecrows don't, I admit," answered the Shaggy Man. "But this Scarecrow of whom I speak is very intelligent. He claims to possess the best brains in all Oz."

"Better than mine?" asked Scraps.

"Better than mine?" echoed the Glass Cat. "Mine are pink, and you can see 'em work."

"Well, you can't see the Scarecrow's brains work, but they do a lot of clever thinking," asserted the Shaggy Man. "If anyone knows where a dark well is, it's my friend the Scarecrow."

"Where does he live?" inquired Ojo.

"He has a splendid castle in the Winkie Country, near to the palace of his friend the Tin Woodman, and he is often to be found in the Emerald City, where he visits Dorothy at the royal palace."

"Then we will ask him about the dark well," said Ojo.

"But what else does this Crooked Magician want?" asked the Shaggy Man.

"A drop of oil from a live man's body."

"Oh; but there isn't such a thing."

"That is what I thought," replied Ojo; "but the Crooked Magician said it wouldn't be called for by the recipe if it couldn't be found, and therefore I must search until I find it."

"I wish you good luck," said the Shaggy Man, shaking his head doubtfully; "but I imagine you'll have a hard job getting a drop of oil from a live man's body. There's blood in a body, but no oil."

"There's cotton in mine," said Scraps, dancing a little jig.

"I don't doubt it," returned the Shaggy Man admiringly. "You're a regular comforter and as sweet as patchwork can be. All you lack is dignity."

"I hate dignity," cried Scraps, kicking a pebble high in the air and then trying to catch it as it fell. "Half the fools and all the wise folks are dignified, and I'm neither the one nor the other."

"She's just crazy," explained the Glass Cat.

The Shaggy Man laughed.

"She's delightful, in her way," he said. "I'm sure Dorothy will be pleased with her, and the Scarecrow will dote on her. Did you say you were traveling toward the Emerald City?"

"Yes," replied Ojo. "I thought that the best place to go, at first, because the six-leaved clover may be found there."

"I'll go with you," said the Shaggy Man, "and show you the way."

"Thank you," exclaimed Ojo. "I hope it won't put you out any."

"No," said the other, "I wasn't going anywhere in particular. I've been a rover all my life, and although Ozma has given me a suite of beautiful rooms in her palace I still get the wandering fever once in a while and start out to roam the country over. I've been away from the Emerald City several weeks, this time, and now that I've met you and your friends I'm sure it will interest me to accompany you to the great city of Oz and introduce you to my friends."

"That will be very nice," said the boy, gratefully.

"I hope your friends are not dignified," observed Scraps.

"Some are, and some are not," he answered; "but I never criticise my friends. If they are really true friends, they may be anything they like, for all of me."

"There's some sense in that," said Scraps, nodding her queer head in approval. "Come on, and let's get to the Emerald City as soon as possible." With this she ran up the path, skipping and dancing, and then turned to await them.

"It is quite a distance from here to the Emerald City," remarked the Shaggy Man, "so we shall not get there to-day, nor to-morrow. Therefore let us take the jaunt in an easy manner. I'm an old traveler and have found that I never gain anything by being in a hurry. 'Take it easy' is my motto. If you can't take it easy, take it as easy as you can."

After walking some distance over the road of yellow bricks Ojo said he was hungry and would stop to eat some bread and cheese. He offered a portion of the food to the Shaggy Man, who thanked him but refused it.

"When I start out on my travels," said he, "I carry along enough square meals to last me several weeks. Think I'll indulge in one now, as long as we're stopping anyway."

Saying this, he took a bottle from his pocket and shook from it a tablet about the size of one of Ojo's finger-nails.

"That," announced the Shaggy Man, "is a square meal, in condensed form. Invention of the great Professor Woggle-Bug, of the Royal College of Athletics. It contains soup, fish, roast meat, salad, apple-dumplings, ice cream and chocolate-drops, all boiled down to this small size, so it can be conveniently carried and swallowed when you are hungry and need a square meal."

"I'm square," said the Woozy. "Give me one, please."

So the Shaggy Man gave the Woozy a tablet from his bottle and the beast ate it in a twinkling.

"You have now had a six course dinner," declared the Shaggy Man.

"Pshaw!" said the Woozy, ungratefully, "I want to taste something. There's no fun in that sort of eating."

"One should only eat to sustain life," replied the Shaggy Man, "and that tablet is equal to a peck of other food."

"I don't care for it. I want something I can chew and taste," grumbled the Woozy.

"You are quite wrong, my poor beast," said the Shaggy Man in a tone of pity. "Think how tired your jaws would get chewing a square meal like this, if it were not condensed to the size of a small tablet—which you can swallow in a jiffy."

"Chewing isn't tiresome; it's fun, maintained the Woozy. "I always chew the honey-bees when I catch them. Give me some bread and cheese, Ojo."

"No, no! You've already eaten a big dinner!" protested the Shaggy Man.

"May be," answered the Woozy; "but I guess I'll fool myself by munching some bread and cheese. I may not be hungry, having eaten all those things you gave me, but I consider this eating business a matter of taste, and I like to realize what's going into me."

Ojo gave the beast what he wanted, but the Shaggy Man shook his shaggy head reproachfully and said there was no animal so obstinate or hard to convince as a Woozy.

At this moment a patter of footsteps was heard, and looking up they saw the live phonograph standing before them. It seemed to have passed through many adventures since Ojo and his comrades last saw the machine, for the varnish of its wooden case was all marred and dented and scratched in a way that gave it an aged and disreputable appearance.

"Dear me!" exclaimed Ojo, staring hard. "What has happened to you?"

"Nothing much," replied the phonograph in a sad and depressed voice. "I've had enough things thrown at me, since I left you, to stock a department store and furnish half a dozen bargain-counters."

"Are you so broken up that you can't play?" asked Scraps.

"No; I still am able to grind out delicious music. Just now I've a record on tap that is really superb," said the phonograph, growing more cheerful.

"That is too bad," remarked Ojo. "We've no objection to you as a machine, you know; but as a music-maker we hate you."

"Then why was I ever invented?" demanded the machine, in a tone of indignant protest.

They looked at one another inquiringly, but no one could answer such a puzzling question. Finally the Shaggy Man said: "I'd like to hear the phonograph play."

Ojo sighed. "We've been very happy since we met you, sir," he said.

"I know. But a little misery, at times, makes one appreciate happiness more. Tell me, Phony, what is this record like, which you say you have on tap?"

"It's a popular song, sir. In all civilized lands the common people have gone wild over it."

"Makes civilized folks wild folks, eh? Then it's dangerous."

"Wild with joy, I mean," explained the phonograph. "Listen. This song will prove a rare treat to you, I know. It made the author rich—for an author. It is called 'My Lulu.'"

Then the phonograph began to play. A strain of odd, jerky sounds was followed by these words, sung by a man through his nose with great vigor of expression:

"Ah wants mah Lulu, mah Lulu;
Ah wants mah loo-loo, loo-loo, loo-loo, Lu!
Ah loves mah Lulu, mah Lulu,
There ain't nobody else loves loo-loo, Lu!"

"Here—shut that off!" cried the Shaggy Man, springing to his feet. "What do you mean by such impertinence?"

"It's the latest popular song," declared the phonograph, speaking in a sulky tone of voice.

"A popular song?"

"Yes. One that the feeble-minded can remember the words of and those ignorant of music can whistle or sing. That makes a popular song popular, and the time is coming when it will take the place of all other songs."

"That time won't come to us, just yet," said the Shaggy Man, sternly: "I'm something of a singer myself, and I don't intend to be throttled by any Lulus like your one. I shall take you all apart, Mr. Phony, and scatter your pieces far and wide over the country, as a matter of kindness to the people you might meet if allowed to run around loose. Having performed this painful duty I shall—"

But before he could say more the phonograph turned and dashed up the road as fast as its four table-legs could carry it, and soon it had entirely disappeared from their view.

The Shaggy Man sat down again and seemed well pleased. "Some one else will save me the trouble of scattering that phonograph," said he; "for it is not possible that such a music-maker can last long in the Land of Oz. When you are rested, friends, let us go on our way."

During the afternoon the travelers found themselves in a lonely and uninhabited part of the country. Even the fields were no longer cultivated and the country began to resemble a wilderness. The road of yellow bricks seemed to have been neglected and became uneven and more difficult to walk upon. Scrubby under-brush grew on either side of the way, while huge rocks were scattered around in abundance.

But this did not deter Ojo and his friends from trudging on, and they beguiled the journey with jokes and cheerful conversation. Toward evening they reached a crystal spring which gushed from a tall rock by the roadside and near this spring stood a deserted cabin. Said the Shaggy Man, halting here: "We may as well pass the night here, where there is shelter for our heads and good water to drink. Road beyond here is pretty bad; worst we shall have to travel; so let's wait until morning before we tackle it."

They agreed to this and Ojo found some brushwood in the cabin and made a fire on the hearth. The fire delighted Scraps, who danced before it until Ojo warned her she might set fire to herself and burn up. After that the Patchwork Girl kept at a respectful distance from the darting flames, but the Woozy lay down before the fire like a big dog and seemed to enjoy its warmth.

For supper the Shaggy Man ate one of his tablets, but Ojo stuck to his bread and cheese as the most satisfying food. He also gave a portion to the Woozy.

When darkness came on and they sat in a circle on the cabin floor, facing the firelight—there being no furniture of any sort in the place—Ojo said to the Shaggy Man: "Won't you tell us a story?"

"I'm not good at stories," was the reply; "but I sing like a bird."

"Raven, or crow?" asked the Glass Cat.

"Like a song bird. I'll prove it. I'll sing a song I composed myself. Don't tell anyone I'm a poet; they might want me to write a book. Don't tell 'em I can sing, or they'd want me to make records for that awful phonograph. Haven't time to be a public benefactor, so I'll just sing you this little song for your own amusement."

They were glad enough to be entertained, and listened with interest while the Shaggy Man chanted the following verses to a tune that was not unpleasant:

"I'll sing a song of Ozland, where wondrous creatures dwell
And fruits and flowers and shady bowers abound in every dell,
Where magic is a science and where no one shows surprise
If some amazing thing takes place before his very eyes.

Our Ruler's a bewitching girl whom fairies love to please;
She's always kept her magic sceptre to enforce decrees
To make her people happy, for her heart is kind and true
And to aid the needy and distressed is what she longs to do.

And then there's Princess Dorothy, as sweet as any rose,
A lass from Kansas, where they don't grow fairies, I suppose;
And there's the brainy Scarecrow, with a body stuffed with straw,
Who utters words of wisdom rare that fill us all with awe.

I'll not forget Nick Chopper, the Woodman made of Tin,
Whose tender heart thinks killing time is quite a dreadful sin,
Nor old Professor Woggle-Bug, who's highly magnified
And looks so big to everyone that he is filled with pride.

Jack Pumpkinhead's a dear old chum who might be called a chump,
But won renown by riding round upon a magic Gump;
The Sawhorse is a splendid steed and though he's made of wood
He does as many thrilling stunts as any meat horse could.

And now I'll introduce a beast that ev'ryone adores—
The Cowardly Lion shakes with fear 'most ev'ry time he roars,
And yet he does the bravest things that any lion might,
Because he knows that cowardice is not considered right.

There's Tik-Tok—he's a clockwork man and quite a funny sight—
He talks and walks mechanically, when he's wound up tight;
And we've a Hungry Tiger who would babies love to eat
But never does because we feed him other kinds of meat.

It's hard to name all of the freaks this noble Land's acquired;
'Twould make my song so very long that you would soon be tired;
But give attention while I mention one wise Yellow Hen
And Nine fine Tiny Piglets living in a golden pen.

Just search the whole world over—sail the seas from coast to coast—
No other nation in creation queerer folk can boast;
And now our rare museum will include a Cat of Glass,
A Woozy, and—last but not least—a crazy Patchwork Lass."

Ojo was so pleased with this song that he applauded the singer by clapping his hands, and Scraps followed suit by clapping her padded fingers together, although they made no noise. The cat pounded on the floor with her glass paws—gently, so as not to break them—and the Woozy, which had been asleep, woke up to ask what the row was about.

"I seldom sing in public, for fear they might want me to start an opera company," remarked the Shaggy Man, who was pleased to know his effort was appreciated. "Voice, just now, is a little out of training; rusty, perhaps."

"Tell me," said the Patchwork Girl earnestly, "do all those queer people you mention really live in the Land of Oz?"

"Every one of 'em. I even forgot one thing: Dorothy's Pink Kitten."

"For goodness sake!" exclaimed Bungle, sitting up and looking interested. "A Pink Kitten? How absurd! Is it glass?"

"No; just ordinary kitten."

"Then it can't amount to much. I have pink brains, and you can see 'em work."

"Dorothy's kitten is all pink—brains and all— except blue eyes. Name's Eureka. Great favorite at the royal palace," said the Shaggy Man, yawning.

The Glass Cat seemed annoyed.

"Do you think a pink kitten—common meat—is as pretty as I am?" she asked.

"Can't say. Tastes differ, you know," replied the Shaggy Man, yawning again. "But here's a pointer that may be of service to you: make friends with Eureka and you'll be solid at the palace."

"I'm solid now; solid glass."

"You don't understand," rejoined the Shaggy Man, sleepily. "Anyhow, make friends with the Pink Kitten and you'll be all right. If the Pink Kitten despises you, look out for breakers."

"Would anyone at the royal palace break a Glass Cat?"

"Might. You never can tell. Advise you to purr soft and look humble—if you can. And now I'm going to bed."

Bungle considered the Shaggy Man's advice so carefully that her pink brains were busy long after the others of the party were fast asleep.

12. The Giant Porcupine

Next morning they started out bright and early to follow the road of yellow bricks toward the Emerald City. The little Munchkin boy was beginning to feel tired from the long walk, and he had a great many things to think of and consider besides the events of the journey. At the wonderful Emerald City, which he would presently reach, were so many strange and curious people that he was half afraid of meeting them and wondered if they would prove friendly and kind. Above all else, he could not drive from his mind the important errand on which he had come, and he was determined to devote every energy to finding the things that were necessary to prepare the magic recipe. He believed that until dear Unc Nunkie was restored to life he could feel no joy in anything, and often he wished that Unc could be with him, to see all the astonishing things Ojo was seeing. But alas Unc Nunkie

was now a marble statue in the house of the Crooked Magician and Ojo must not falter in his efforts to save him.

The country through which they were passing was still rocky and deserted, with here and there a bush or a tree to break the dreary landscape. Ojo noticed one tree, especially, because it had such long, silky leaves and was so beautiful in shape. As he approached it he studied the tree earnestly, wondering if any fruit grew on it or if it bore pretty flowers.

Suddenly he became aware that he had been looking at that tree a long time—at least for five minutes—and it had remained in the same position, although the boy had continued to walk steadily on. So he stopped short, and when he stopped, the tree and all the landscape, as well as his companions, moved on before him and left him far behind.

Ojo uttered such a cry of astonishment that it aroused the Shaggy Man, who also halted. The others then stopped, too, and walked back to the boy.

"What's wrong?" asked the Shaggy Man.

"Why, we're not moving forward a bit, no matter how fast we walk," declared Ojo. "Now that we have stopped, we are moving backward! Can't you see? Just notice that rock."

Scraps looked down at her feet and said: "The yellow bricks are not moving."

"But the whole road is," answered Ojo.

"True; quite true," agreed the Shaggy Man. "I know all about the tricks of this road, but I have been thinking of something else and didn't realize where we were."

"It will carry us back to where we started from," predicted Ojo, beginning to be nervous.

"No," replied the Shaggy Man; "it won't do that, for I know a trick to beat this tricky road. I've traveled this way before, you know. Turn around, all of you, and walk backward."

"What good will that do?" asked the cat.

"You'll find out, if you obey me," said the Shaggy Man.

So they all turned their backs to the direction in which they wished to go and began walking backward. In an instant Ojo noticed they were gaining ground and as they proceeded in this curious way they soon passed the tree which had first attracted his attention to their difficulty.

"How long must we keep this up, Shags?" asked Scraps, who was constantly tripping and tumbling down, only to get up again with a laugh at her mishap.

"Just a little way farther," replied the Shaggy Man.

A few minutes later he called to them to turn about quickly and step forward, and as they obeyed the order they found themselves treading solid ground.

"That task is well over," observed the Shaggy Man. "It's a little tiresome to walk backward, but that is the only way to pass this part of the road, which has a trick of sliding back and carrying with it anyone who is walking upon it."

With new courage and energy they now trudged forward and after a time came to a place where the road cut through a low hill, leaving high banks on either side of it. They were traveling along this cut, talking together, when the Shaggy Man seized Scraps with one arm and Ojo with another and shouted: "Stop!"

"What's wrong now?" asked the Patchwork Girl.

"See there!" answered the Shaggy Man, pointing with his finger.

Directly in the center of the road lay a motionless object that bristled all over with sharp quills, which resembled arrows. The body was as big as a ten-bushel-basket, but the projecting quills made it appear to be four times bigger.

"Well, what of it?" asked Scraps.

"That is Chiss, who causes a lot of trouble along this road," was the reply.

"Chiss! What is Chiss?   .

"I think it is merely an overgrown porcupine, but here in Oz they consider Chiss an evil spirit. He's different from a reg'lar porcupine, because he can throw his quills in any direction, which an American porcupine cannot do. That's what makes old Chiss so dangerous. If we get too near, he'll fire those quills at us and hurt us badly."

"Then we will be foolish to get too near," said Scraps.

"I'm not afraid," declared the Woozy. "The Chiss is cowardly, I'm sure, and if it ever heard my awful, terrible, frightful growl, it would be scared stiff."

"Oh; can you growl?" asked the Shaggy Man.

"That is the only ferocious thing about me," asserted the Woozy with evident pride. "My growl makes an earthquake blush and the thunder ashamed of itself. If I growled at that creature you call Chiss, it would immediately think the world had cracked in two and bumped against the sun and moon, and that would cause the monster to run as far and as fast as its legs could carry it."

"In that case," said the Shaggy Man, "you are now able to do us all a great favor. Please growl."

"But you forget," returned the Woozy; "my tremendous growl would also frighten you, and if you happen to have heart disease you might expire."

"True; but we must take that risk," decided the Shaggy Man, bravely. "Being warned of what is to occur we must try to bear the terrific noise of your growl; but Chiss won't expect it, and it will scare him away."

The Woozy hesitated.

"I'm fond of you all, and I hate to shock you," it said.

"Never mind," said Ojo.

"You may be made deaf."

"If so, we will forgive you."

"Very well, then," said the Woozy in a determined voice, and advanced a few steps toward the giant porcupine. Pausing to look back, it asked: "All ready?"

"All ready!" they answered.

"Then cover up your ears and brace yourselves firmly. Now, then—look out!"

The Woozy turned toward Chiss, opened wide its mouth and said: "Quee-ee-ee-eek."

"Go ahead and growl," said Scraps.

"Why, I—I did growl!" retorted the Woozy, who seemed much astonished.

"What, that little squeak?" she cried.

"It is the most awful growl that ever was heard, on land or sea, in caverns or in the sky," protested the Woozy. "I wonder you stood the shock so well. Didn't you feel the ground tremble? I suppose Chiss is now quite dead with fright."

The Shaggy Man laughed merrily.

"Poor Wooz!" said he; "your growl wouldn't scare a fly."

The Woozy seemed to be humiliated and surprised. It hung its head a moment, as if in shame or sorrow, but then it said with renewed confidence: "Anyhow, my eyes can flash fire; and good fire, too; good enough to set fire to a fence!"

"That is true," declared Scraps; "I saw it done myself. But your ferocious growl isn't as loud as the tick of a beetle—or one of Ojo's snores when he's fast asleep."

"Perhaps," said the Woozy, humbly, "I have been mistaken about my growl. It has always sounded very fearful to me, but that may have been because it was so close to my ears."

"Never mind," Ojo said soothingly; "it is a great talent to be able to flash fire from your eyes. No one else can do that."

As they stood hesitating what to do Chiss stirred and suddenly a shower of quills came flying toward them, almost filling the air, they were so many. Scraps realized in an instant that they had gone too near to Chiss for safety, so she sprang in front of Ojo and shielded him from the darts, which stuck their points into her own body until she resembled one of those targets they shoot arrows at in archery games. The Shaggy Man dropped flat on his face to avoid the shower, but one quill struck him in the leg and went far in. As for the Glass Cat, the quills rattled off her body without making even a scratch, and the skin of the Woozy was so thick and tough that he was not hurt at all.

When the attack was over they all ran to the Shaggy Man, who was moaning and groaning, and Scraps promptly pulled the quill out of his leg. Then up he jumped and ran over to Chiss, putting his foot on the monster's neck and holding it a prisoner. The body of the great porcupine was now as smooth as leather, except for the holes where the quills had been, for it had shot every single quill in that one wicked shower.

"Let me go!" it shouted angrily. "How dare you put your foot on Chiss?"

"I'm going to do worse than that, old boy," replied the Shaggy Man. "You have annoyed travelers on this road long enough, and now I shall put an end to you."

"You can't!" returned Chiss. "Nothing can kill me, as you know perfectly well."

"Perhaps that is true," said the Shaggy Man in a tone of disappointment. "Seems to me I've been told before that you can't be killed. But if I let you go, what will you do?"

"Pick up my quills again," said Chiss in a sulky voice.

"And then shoot them at more travelers? No; that won't do. You must promise me to stop throwing quills at people."

"I won't promise anything of the sort," declared Chiss.

"Why not?"

"Because it is my nature to throw quills, and every animal must do what Nature intends it to do. It isn't fair for you to blame me. If it were wrong for me to throw quills, then I wouldn't be made with quills to throw. The proper thing for you to do is to keep out of my way."

"Why, there's some sense in that argument," admitted the Shaggy Man, thoughtfully; "but people who are strangers, and don't know you are here, won't be able to keep out of your way."

"Tell you what," said Scraps, who was trying to pull the quills out of her own body, "let's gather up all the quills and take them away with us; then old Chiss won't have any left to throw at people."

"Ah, that's a clever idea. You and Ojo must gather up the quills while I hold Chiss a prisoner; for, if I let him go, he will get some of his quills and be able to throw them again."

So Scraps and Ojo picked up all the quills and tied them in a bundle so they might easily be carried. After this the Shaggy Man released Chiss and let him go, knowing that he was harmless to injure anyone.

"It's the meanest trick I ever heard of," muttered the porcupine gloomily. "How would you like it, Shaggy Man, if I took all your shags away from you?"

"If I threw my shags and hurt people, you would be welcome to capture them," was the reply.

Then they walked on and left Chiss standing in the road sullen and disconsolate. The Shaggy Man limped as he walked, for his wound still hurt him, and Scraps was much annoyed because the quills had left a number of small holes in her patches.

When they came to a flat stone by the roadside the Shaggy Man sat down to rest, and then Ojo opened his basket and took out the bundle of charms the Crooked Magician had given him.

"I am Ojo the Unlucky," he said, "or we would never have met that dreadful porcupine. But I will see if I can find anything among these charms which will cure your leg."

Soon he discovered that one of the charms was labelled: "For flesh wounds," and this the boy separated from the others. It was only a bit of dried root, taken from some unknown shrub, but the boy rubbed it upon the wound made by the quill and in a few moments the place was healed entirely and the Shaggy Man's leg was as good as ever.

"Rub it on the holes in my patches," suggested Scraps, and Ojo tried it, but without any effect.

"The charm you need is a needle and thread," said the Shaggy Man. "But do not worry, my dear; those holes do not look badly, at all."

"They'll let in the air, and I don't want people to think I'm airy, or that I've been stuck up," said the Patchwork Girl.

"You were certainly stuck up until we pulled out those quills," observed Ojo, with a laugh.

So now they went on again and coming presently to a pond of muddy water they tied a heavy stone to the bundle of quills and sunk it to the bottom of the pond, to avoid carrying it farther.

13. Scraps and the Scarecrow

From here on the country improved and the desert places began to give way to fertile spots; still no houses were yet to be seen near the road. There were some hills, with valleys between them, and on reaching the top of one of these hills the travelers found before them a high wall, running to the right and the left as far as their eyes could reach. Immediately in front of them, where the wall crossed the roadway, stood a gate having stout iron bars that extended from top to bottom. They found, on coming nearer, that this gate was locked with a great padlock, rusty through lack of use.

"Well," said Scraps, "I guess we'll stop here."

"It's a good guess," replied Ojo. "Our way is barred by this great wall and gate. It looks as if no one had passed through in many years."

"Looks are deceiving," declared the Shaggy Man, laughing at their disappointed faces, "and this barrier is the most deceiving thing in all Oz."

"It prevents our going any farther, anyhow," said Scraps. "There is no one to mind the gate and let people through, and we've no key to the padlock."

"True," replied Ojo, going a little nearer to peep through the bars of the gate. "What shall we do, Shaggy Man? If we had wings we might fly over the wall, but we cannot climb it and unless we get to the Emerald City I won't be able to find the things to restore Unc Nunkie to life."

"All very true," answered the Shaggy Man, quietly; "but I know this gate, having passed through it many times."

"How?" they all eagerly inquired.

"I'll show you how," said he. He stood Ojo in the middle of the road and placed Scraps just behind him, with her padded hands on his shoulders. After the Patchwork Girl came the Woozy, who held a part of her skirt in his mouth. Then, last of all, was the Glass Cat, holding fast to the Woozy's tail with her glass jaws.

"Now," said the Shaggy Man, "you must all shut your eyes tight, and keep them shut until I tell you to open them."

"I can't," objected Scraps. "My eyes are buttons, and they won't shut."

So the Shaggy Man tied his red handkerchief over the Patchwork Girl's eyes and examined all the others to make sure they had their eyes fast shut and could see nothing.

"What's the game, anyhow—blind-man's-buff?" asked Scraps.

"Keep quiet!" commanded the Shaggy Man, sternly. "All ready? Then follow me."

He took Ojo's hand and led him forward over the road of yellow bricks, toward the gate. Holding fast to one another they all followed in a row, expecting every minute to bump against the iron bars. The Shaggy Man also had his eyes closed, but marched straight ahead, nevertheless, and after he had taken one hundred steps, by actual count, he stopped and said: "Now you may open your eyes."

They did so, and to their astonishment found the wall and the gateway far behind them, while in front the former Blue Country of the Munchkins had given way to green fields, with pretty farm-houses scattered among them.

"That wall," explained the Shaggy Man, "is what is called an optical illusion. It is quite real while you have your eyes open, but if you are not looking at it the barrier doesn't exist at all. It's the same way with many other evils in life; they seem to exist, and yet it's all seeming and not true. You will notice that the wall—or what we thought was a wall—separates the Munchkin Country from the green country that surrounds the Emerald City, which lies exactly in the center of Oz. There are two roads of yellow bricks through the Munchkin Country, but the one we followed is the best of the two. Dorothy once traveled the other way, and met with more dangers than we did. But all our troubles are over for the present, as another day's journey will bring us to the great Emerald City."

They were delighted to know this, and proceeded with new courage. In a couple of hours they stopped at a farmhouse, where the people were very hospitable and invited them to dinner. The farm folk regarded Scraps with much curiosity but no great astonishment, for they were accustomed to seeing extraordinary people in the Land of Oz.

The woman of this house got her needle and thread and sewed up the holes made by the porcupine quills in the Patchwork Girl's body, after which Scraps was assured she looked as beautiful as ever.

"You ought to have a hat to wear," remarked the woman, "for that would keep the sun from fading the colors of your face. I have some patches and scraps put away, and if you will wait two or three days I'll make you a lovely hat that will match the rest of you."

"Never mind the hat," said Scraps, shaking her yarn braids; "it's a kind offer, but we can't stop. I can't see that my colors have faded a particle, as yet; can you?"

"Not much," replied the woman. "You are still very gorgeous, in spite of your long journey."

The children of the house wanted to keep the Glass Cat to play with, so Bungle was offered a good home if she would remain; but the cat was too much interested in Ojo's adventures and refused to stop.

"Children are rough playmates," she remarked to the Shaggy Man, "and although this home is more pleasant than that of the Crooked Magician I fear I would soon be smashed to pieces by the boys and girls."

After they had rested themselves they renewed their journey, finding the road now smooth and pleasant to walk upon and the country growing more beautiful the nearer they drew to the Emerald City.

By and by Ojo began to walk on the green grass, looking carefully around him.

"What are you trying to find?" asked Scraps.

"A six-leaved clover," said he.

"Don't do that!" exclaimed the Shaggy Man, earnestly. "It's against the Law to pick a six-leaved clover. You must wait until you get Ozma's consent."

"She wouldn't know it," declared the boy.

"Ozma knows many things," said the Shaggy Man. "In her room is a Magic Picture that shows any scene in the Land of Oz where strangers or travelers happen to be. She may be watching the picture of us even now, and noticing everything that we do."

"Does she always watch the Magic Picture?" asked Ojo.

"Not always, for she has many other things to do; but, as I said, she may be watching us this very minute."

"I don't care," said Ojo, in an obstinate tone of voice; "Ozma's only a girl."

The Shaggy Man looked at him in surprise.

"You ought to care for Ozma," said he, "if you expect to save your uncle. For, if you displease our powerful Ruler, your journey will surely prove a failure; whereas, if you make a friend of Ozma, she will gladly assist you. As for her being a girl, that is another reason why you should obey her laws, if you are courteous and polite. Everyone in Oz loves Ozma and hates her enemies, for she is as just as she is powerful."

Ojo sulked a while, but finally returned to the road and kept away from the green clover. The boy was moody and bad tempered for an hour or two afterward, because he could really see no harm in picking a six-leaved clover, if he found one, and in spite of what the Shaggy Man had said he considered Ozma's law to be unjust.

They presently came to a beautiful grove of tall and stately trees, through which the road wound in sharp curves—first one way and then another. As they were walking through this grove they heard some one in the distance singing, and the sounds grew nearer and nearer until they could distinguish the words, although the bend in the road still hid the singer. The song was something like this:
"Here's to the hale old bale of straw
That's cut from the waving grain,
The sweetest sight man ever saw
In forest, dell or plain.

It fills me with a crunkling joy
A straw-stack to behold,
For then I pad this lucky boy
With strands of yellow gold."

"Ah!" exclaimed the Shaggy Man; "here comes my friend the Scarecrow."

"What, a live Scarecrow?" asked Ojo.

"Yes; the one I told you of. He's a splendid fellow, and very intelligent. You'll like him, I'm sure."

Just then the famous Scarecrow of Oz came around the bend in the road, riding astride a wooden Sawhorse which was so small that its rider's legs nearly touched the ground.

The Scarecrow wore the blue dress of the Munchkins, in which country he was made, and on his head was set a peaked hat with a flat brim trimmed with tinkling bells. A rope was tied around his waist to hold him in shape, for he was stuffed with straw in every part of him except the top of his head, where at one time the Wizard of Oz had placed sawdust, mixed with needles and pins, to sharpen his wits. The head itself was merely a bag of cloth, fastened to the body at the neck, and on the front of this bag was painted the face—ears, eyes, nose and mouth.

The Scarecrow's face was very interesting, for it bore a comical and yet winning expression, although one eye was a bit larger than the other and ears were not mates. The Munchkin farmer who had made the Scarecrow had neglected to sew him together with close stitches and therefore some of the straw with which he was stuffed was inclined to stick out between the seams. His hands consisted of padded white gloves, with the fingers long and rather limp, and on his feet he wore Munchkin boots of blue leather with broad turns at the tops of them.

The Sawhorse was almost as curious as its rider. It had been rudely made, in the beginning, to saw logs upon, so that its body was a short length of a log, and its legs were stout branches fitted into four holes made in the body. The tail was formed by a small branch that had been left on the log, while the head was a gnarled bump on one end of the body. Two knots of wood formed the eyes, and the mouth was a gash chopped in the log. When the Sawhorse first came to life it had no ears at all, and so could not hear; but the boy who then owned him had whittled two ears out of bark and stuck them in the head, after which the Sawhorse heard very distinctly.

This queer wooden horse was a great favorite with Princess Ozma, who had caused the bottoms of its legs to be shod with plates of gold, so the wood would not wear away. Its saddle was made of cloth-of-gold richly encrusted with precious gems. It had never worn a bridle.

As the Scarecrow came in sight of the party of travelers, he reined in his wooden steed and dismounted, greeting the Shaggy Man with a smiling nod. Then he turned to stare at the Patchwork Girl in wonder, while she in turn stared at him.

"Shags," he whispered, drawing the Shaggy Man aside, "pat me into shape, there's a good fellow!"

While his friend punched and patted the Scarecrow's body, to smooth out the humps, Scraps turned to Ojo and whispered: "Roll me out, please; I've sagged down dreadfully from walking so much and men like to see a stately figure."

She then fell upon the ground and the boy rolled her back and forth like a rolling-pin, until the cotton had filled all the spaces in her patchwork covering and the body had lengthened to its fullest extent. Scraps and the Scarecrow both finished their hasty toilets at the same time, and again they faced each other.

"Allow me, Miss Patchwork," said the Shaggy Man, "to present my friend, the Right Royal Scarecrow of Oz. Scarecrow, this is Miss Scraps Patches; Scraps, this is the Scarecrow. Scarecrow—Scraps; Scraps—Scarecrow."

They both bowed with much dignity.

"Forgive me for staring so rudely," said the Scarecrow, "but you are the most beautiful sight my eyes have ever beheld."

"That is a high compliment from one who is himself so beautiful," murmured Scraps, casting down her suspender-button eyes by lowering her head. "But, tell me, good sir, are you not a trifle lumpy?"

"Yes, of course; that's my straw, you know. It bunches up sometimes, in spite of all my efforts to keep it even. Doesn't your straw ever bunch?"

"Oh, I'm stuffed with cotton," said Scraps. "It never bunches, but it's inclined to pack down and make me sag."

"But cotton is a high-grade stuffing. I may say it is even more stylish, not to say aristocratic, than straw," said the Scarecrow politely. "Still, it is but proper that one so entrancingly lovely should have the best stuffing there is going. I— er—I'm so glad I've met you, Miss Scraps! Introduce us again, Shaggy."

"Once is enough," replied the Shaggy Man, laughing at his friend's enthusiasm.

"Then tell me where you found her, and—Dear me, what a queer cat! What are you made of—gelatine?"

"Pure glass," answered the cat, proud to have attracted the Scarecrow's attention. "I am much more beautiful than the Patchwork Girl. I'm transparent, and Scraps isn't; I've pink brains— you can see 'em work; and I've a ruby heart, finely polished, while Scraps hasn't any heart at all."

"No more have I," said the Scarecrow, shaking hands with Scraps, as if to congratulate her on the fact. "I've a friend, the Tin Woodman, who has a heart, but I find I get along pretty well without one. And so—Well, well! here's a little Munchkin boy too. Shake hands, my little man. How are you?"

Ojo placed his hand in the flabby stuffed glove that served the Scarecrow for a hand, and the Scarecrow pressed it so cordially that the straw in his glove crackled.

Meantime, the Woozy had approached the Sawhorse and begun to sniff at it. The Sawhorse resented this familiarity and with a sudden kick pounded the Woozy squarely on its head with one gold-shod foot.

"Take that, you monster!" it cried angrily.

The Woozy never even winked. "To be sure," he said; "I'll take anything I have to. But don't make me angry, you wooden beast, or my eyes will flash fire and burn you up."

The Sawhorse rolled its knot eyes wickedly and kicked again, but the Woozy trotted away and said to the Scarecrow: "What a sweet disposition that creature has! I advise you to chop it up for kindling-wood and use me to ride upon. My back is flat and you can't fall off."

"I think the trouble is that you haven't been properly introduced," said the Scarecrow, regarding the Woozy with much wonder, for he had never seen such a queer animal before.

"The Sawhorse is the favorite steed of Princess Ozma, the Ruler of the Land of Oz, and he lives in a stable decorated with pearls and emeralds, at the rear of the royal palace. He is swift as the wind, untiring, and is kind to his friends. All the people of Oz respect the Sawhorse highly, and when I visit Ozma she sometimes allows me to ride him—as I am doing to-day. Now you know what an important personage the Sawhorse is, and if some one—perhaps yourself—will tell me your name, your rank and station, and your history, it will give me pleasure to relate them to the Sawhorse. This will lead to mutual respect and friendship."

The Woozy was somewhat abashed by this speech and did not know how to reply. But Ojo said: "This square beast is called the Woozy, and he isn't of much importance except that he has three hairs growing on the tip of his tail."

The Scarecrow looked and saw that this was true.

"But," said he, in a puzzled way, "what makes those three hairs important? The Shaggy Man has thousands of hairs, but no one has ever accused him of being important."

So Ojo related the sad story of Unc Nunkie's transformation into a marble statue, and told how he had set out to find the things the Crooked Magician wanted, in order to make a charm that would restore his uncle to life. One of the requirements was three hairs from a Woozy's tail, but not being able to pull out the hairs they had been obliged to take the Woozy with them.

The Scarecrow looked grave as he listened and he shook his head several times, as if in disapproval.

"We must see Ozma about this matter," he said. "That Crooked Magician is breaking the Law by practicing magic without a license, and I'm not sure Ozma will allow him to restore your uncle to life."

"Already I have warned the boy of that," declared the Shaggy Man.

At this Ojo began to cry. "I want my Unc Nunkie!" he exclaimed. "I know how he can be restored to life, and I'm going to do it— Ozma or no Ozma! What right has this girl Ruler to keep my Unc Nunkie a statue forever?"

"Don't worry about that just now," advised the Scarecrow. "Go on to the Emerald City, and when you reach it have the Shaggy Man take you to see Dorothy. Tell her your story and I'm sure she will help you. Dorothy is Ozma's best friend, and if you can win her to your side your uncle is pretty safe to live again." Then he turned to the Woozy and said: "I'm afraid you are not important enough to be introduced to the Sawhorse, after all."

"I'm a better beast than he is," retorted the Woozy, indignantly. "My eyes can flash fire, and his can't."

"Is this true?" inquired the Scarecrow, turning to the Munchkin boy.

"Yes," said Ojo, and told how the Woozy had set fire to the fence.

"Have you any other accomplishments?" asked the Scarecrow.

"I have a most terrible growl—that is, sometimes," said the Woozy, as Scraps laughed merrily and the Shaggy Man smiled. But the Patchwork Girl's laugh made the Scarecrow forget all about the Woozy. He said to her: "What an admirable young lady you are, and what jolly good company! We must be better acquainted, for never before have I met a girl with such exquisite coloring or such natural, artless manners."

"No wonder they call you the Wise Scarecrow," replied Scraps.

"When you arrive at the Emerald City I will see you again," continued the Scarecrow. "Just now I am going to call upon an old friend—an ordinary young lady named Jinjur—who has promised to repaint my left ear for me. You may have noticed that the paint on my left ear has peeled off and faded, which affects my hearing on that side. Jinjur always fixes me up when I get weather- worn."

"When do you expect to return to the Emerald City?" asked the Shaggy Man.

"I'll be there this evening, for I'm anxious to have a long talk with Miss Scraps. How is it, Sawhorse; are you equal to a swift run?"

"Anything that suits you suits me," returned the wooden horse.

So the Scarecrow mounted to the jeweled saddle and waved his hat, when the Sawhorse darted away so swiftly that they were out of sight in an instant.

14. Ojo Breaks the Law

"What a queer man," remarked the Munchkin boy, when the party had resumed its journey.

"And so nice and polite," added Scraps, bobbing her head. "I think he is the handsomest man I've seen since I came to life."

"Handsome is as handsome does," quoted the Shaggy Man; "but we must admit that no living scarecrow is handsomer. The chief merit of my friend is that he is a great thinker, and in Oz it is considered good policy to follow his advice."

"I didn't notice any brains in his head," observed the Glass Cat.

"You can't see 'em work, but they're there, all right," declared the Shaggy Man. "I hadn't much confidence in his brains myself, when first I came to Oz, for a humbug Wizard gave them to him; but I was soon convinced that the Scarecrow is really wise; and, unless his brains make him so, such wisdom is unaccountable."

"Is the Wizard of Oz a humbug?" asked Ojo.

"Not now. He was once, but he has reformed and now assists Glinda the Good, who is the Royal Sorceress of Oz and the only one licensed to practice magic or sorcery. Glinda has taught our old Wizard a good many clever things, so he is no longer a humbug."

They walked a little while in silence and then Ojo said: "If Ozma forbids the Crooked Magician to restore Unc Nunkie to life, what shall I do?"

The Shaggy Man shook his head.

"In that case you can't do anything," he said. "But don't be discouraged yet. We will go to Princess Dorothy and tell her your troubles, and then we will let her talk to Ozma. Dorothy has the kindest little heart in the world, and she has been through so many troubles herself that she is sure to sympathize with you."

"Is Dorothy the little girl who came here from Kansas?" asked the boy.

"Yes. In Kansas she was Dorothy Gale. I used to know her there, and she brought me to the Land of Oz. But now Ozma has made her a Princess, and Dorothy's Aunt Em and Uncle Henry are here, too." Here the Shaggy Man uttered a long sigh, and then he continued: "It's a queer country, this Land of Oz; but I like it, nevertheless."

"What is queer about it?" asked Scraps.

"You, for instance," said he.

"Did you see no girls as beautiful as I am in your own country?" she inquired.

"None with the same gorgeous, variegated beauty," he confessed. "In America a girl stuffed with cotton wouldn't be alive, nor would anyone think of making a girl out of a patchwork quilt."

"What a queer country America must be!" she exclaimed in great surprise. "The Scarecrow, whom you say is wise, told me I am the most beautiful creature he has ever seen."

"I know; and perhaps you are—from a scarecrow point of view," replied the Shaggy Man; but why he smiled as he said it Scraps could not imagine.

As they drew nearer to the Emerald City the travelers were filled with admiration for the splendid scenery they beheld. Handsome houses stood on both sides of the road and each had a green lawn before it as well as a pretty flower garden.

"In another hour," said the Shaggy Man, "we shall come in sight of the walls of the Royal City."

He was walking ahead, with Scraps, and behind them came the Woozy and the Glass Cat. Ojo had lagged behind, for in spite of the warnings he had received the boy's eyes were fastened on the clover that bordered the road of yellow bricks and he was eager to discover if such a thing as a six-leaved clover really existed.

Suddenly he stopped short and bent over to examine the ground more closely. Yes; here at last was a clover with six spreading leaves. He counted them carefully, to make sure. In an instant his heart leaped with joy, for this was one of the important things he had come for—one of the things that would restore dear Unc Nunkie to life.

He glanced ahead and saw that none of his companions was looking back. Neither were any other people about, for it was midway between two houses. The temptation was too strong to be resisted.

"I might search for weeks and weeks, and never find another six-leaved clover," he told himself, and quickly plucking the stem from the plant he placed the prized clover in his basket, covering it with the other things he carried there. Then, trying to look as if nothing had happened, he hurried forward and overtook his comrades.

The Emerald City, which is the most splendid as well as the most beautiful city in any fairyland, is surrounded by a high, thick wall of green marble, polished smooth and set with glistening emeralds. There are four gates, one facing the Munchkin Country, one facing the Country of the Winkies, one facing the Country of the Quadlings and one facing the Country of the Gillikins. The Emerald City lies directly in the center of these four important countries of Oz. The gates had bars of pure gold, and on either side of each gateway were built high towers, from which floated gay banners. Other towers were set at distances along the walls, which were broad enough for four people to walk abreast upon.

This enclosure, all green and gold and glittering with precious gems, was indeed a wonderful sight to greet our travelers, who first observed it from the top of a little hill; but beyond the wall was the vast city it surrounded, and hundreds of jeweled spires, domes and minarets, flaunting flags and banners, reared their crests far above the towers of the gateways. In the center of the city our friends could see the tops of many magnificent trees, some nearly as tall as the spires of the buildings, and the Shaggy Man told them that these trees were in the royal gardens of Princess Ozma.

They stood a long time on the hilltop, feasting their eyes on the splendor of the Emerald City.

"Whee!" exclaimed Scraps, clasping her padded hands in ecstacy, "that'll do for me to live in, all right. No more of the Munchkin Country for these patches—and no more of the Crooked Magician!"

"Why, you belong to Dr. Pipt," replied Ojo, looking at her in amazement. "You were made for a servant, Scraps, so you are personal property and not your own mistress."

"Bother Dr. Pipt! If he wants me, let him come here and get me. I'll not go back to his den of my own accord; that's certain. Only one place in the Land of Oz is fit to live in, and that's the Emerald City. It's lovely! It's almost as beautiful as I am, Ojo."

"In this country," remarked the Shaggy Man, "people live wherever our Ruler tells them to. It wouldn't do to have everyone live in the Emerald City, you know, for some must plow the land and raise grains and fruits and vegetables, while others chop wood in the forests, or fish in the rivers, or herd the sheep and the cattle."

"Poor things!" said Scraps.

"I'm not sure they are not happier than the city people," replied the Shaggy Man. "There's a freedom and independence in country life that not even the Emerald City can give one. I know that lots of the city people would like to get back to the land. The Scarecrow lives in the country, and so do the Tin Woodman and Jack Pumpkinhead; yet all three would be welcome to live in Ozma's palace if they cared to. Too much splendor becomes tiresome, you know. But, if we're to reach the Emerald City before sundown, we must hurry, for it is yet a long way off."

The entrancing sight of the city had put new energy into them all and they hurried forward with lighter steps than before. There was much to interest them along the roadway, for the houses were now set more closely together and they met a good many people who were coming or going from one place or another. All these seemed happy-faced, pleasant people, who nodded graciously to the strangers as they passed, and exchanged words of greeting.

At last they reached the great gateway, just as the sun was setting and adding its red glow to the glitter of the emeralds on the green walls and spires. Somewhere inside the city a band could be heard playing sweet music; a soft, subdued hum, as of many voices, reached their ears; from the neighboring yards came the low mooing of cows waiting to be milked.

They were almost at the gate when the golden bars slid back and a tall soldier stepped out and faced them. Ojo thought he had never seen so tall a man before. The soldier wore a handsome green and gold uniform, with a tall hat in which was a waving plume, and he had a belt thickly encrusted with jewels. But the most peculiar thing about him was his long green beard, which fell far below his waist and perhaps made him seem taller than he really was.

"Halt!" said the Soldier with the Green Whiskers, not in a stern voice but rather in a friendly tone.

They halted before he spoke and stood looking at him.

"Good evening, Colonel," said the Shaggy Man. "What's the news since I left? Anything important?"

"Billina has hatched out thirteen new chickens," replied the Soldier with the Green Whiskers, "and they're the cutest little fluffy yellow balls you ever saw. The Yellow Hen is mighty proud of those children, I can tell you."

"She has a right to be," agreed the Shaggy Man. "Let me see; that's about seven thousand chicks she has hatched out; isn't it, General?"

"That, at least," was the reply. "You will have to visit Billina and congratulate her."

"It will give me pleasure to do that," said the Shaggy Man. "But you will observe that I have brought some strangers home with me. I am going to take them to see Dorothy."

"One moment, please," said the soldier, barring their way as they started to enter the gate. "I am on duty, and I have orders to execute. Is anyone in your party named Ojo the Unlucky?"

"Why, that's me!" cried Ojo, astonished at hearing his name on the lips of a stranger.

The Soldier with the Green Whiskers nodded. "I thought so," said he, "and I am sorry to announce that it is my painful duty to arrest you."

"Arrest me!" exclaimed the boy. "What for?"

"I haven't looked to see," answered the soldier. Then he drew a paper from his breast pocket and glanced at it. "Oh, yes; you are to be arrested for willfully breaking one of the Laws of Oz."

"Breaking a law!" said Scraps. "Nonsense, Soldier; you're joking."

"Not this time," returned the soldier, with a sigh. "My dear child—what are you, a rummage sale or a guess-me-quick?—in me you behold the Body-Guard of our gracious Ruler, Princess Ozma, as well as the Royal Army of Oz and the Police Force of the Emerald City."

"And only one man!" exclaimed the Patchwork Girl.

"Only one, and plenty enough. In my official positions I've had nothing to do for a good many years—so long that I began to fear I was absolutely useless—until to-day. An hour ago I was called to the presence of her Highness, Ozma of Oz, and told to arrest a boy named Ojo the Unlucky, who was journeying from the Munchkin Country to the Emerald City and would arrive in a short time. This command so astonished me that I nearly fainted, for it is the first time anyone has merited arrest since I can remember. You are rightly named Ojo the Unlucky, my poor boy, since you have broken a Law of Oz."

"But you are wrong," said Scraps. "Ozma is wrong—you are all wrong—for Ojo has broken no Law."

"Then he will soon be free again," replied the Soldier with the Green Whiskers. "Anyone accused of crime is given a fair trial by our Ruler and has every chance to prove his innocence. But just now Ozma's orders must be obeyed."

With this he took from his pocket a pair of handcuffs made of gold and set with rubies and diamonds, and these he snapped over Ojo's wrists.

15. Ozma's Prisoner

The boy was so bewildered by this calamity that he made no resistance at all. He knew very well he was guilty, but it surprised him that Ozma also knew it. He wondered how she had found out so soon that he had picked the six-leaved clover. He handed his basket to Scraps and said: "Keep that, until I get out of prison. If I never get out, take it to the Crooked Magician, to whom it belongs."

The Shaggy Man had been gazing earnestly in the boy's face, uncertain whether to defend him or not; but something he read in Ojo's expression made him draw back and refuse to interfere to save him. The Shaggy Man was greatly surprised and grieved, but he knew that Ozma never made mistakes and so Ojo must really have broken the Law of Oz.

The Soldier with the Green Whiskers now led them all through the gate and into a little room built in the wall. Here sat a jolly little man, richly dressed in green and having around his neck a heavy gold chain to which a number of great golden keys were attached. This was the Guardian of the Gate and at the moment they entered his room he was playing a tune upon a mouth-organ.

"Listen!" he said, holding up his hand for silence. "I've just composed a tune called 'The Speckled Alligator.' It's in patch-time, which is much superior to rag-time, and I've composed it in honor of the Patchwork Girl, who has just arrived."

"How did you know I had arrived?" asked Scraps, much interested.

"It's my business to know who's coming, for I'm the Guardian of the Gate. Keep quiet while I play you 'The Speckled Alligator.'"

It wasn't a very bad tune, nor a very good one, but all listened respectfully while he shut his eyes and swayed his head from side to side and blew the notes from the little instrument. When it was all over the Soldier with the Green Whiskers said: "Guardian, I have here a prisoner."

"Good gracious! A prisoner?" cried the little man, jumping up from his chair. "Which one? Not the Shaggy Man?"

"No; this boy."

"Ah; I hope his fault is as small as himself," said the Guardian of the Gate. "But what can he have done, and what made him do it?"

"Can't say," replied the soldier. "All I know is that he has broken the Law."

"But no one ever does that!"

"Then he must be innocent, and soon will be released. I hope you are right, Guardian. Just now I am ordered to take him to prison. Get me a prisoner's robe from your Official Wardrobe."

The Guardian unlocked a closet and took from it a white robe, which the soldier threw over Ojo. It covered him from head to foot, but had two holes just in front of his eyes, so he could see where to go. In this attire the boy presented a very quaint appearance.

As the Guardian unlocked a gate leading from his room into the streets of the Emerald City, the Shaggy Man said to Scraps: "I think I shall take you directly to Dorothy, as the Scarecrow advised, and the Glass Cat and the Woozy may come with us. Ojo must go to prison with the Soldier with the Green Whiskers, but he will be well treated and you need not worry about him."

"What will they do with him?" asked Scraps.

"That I cannot tell. Since I came to the Land of Oz no one has ever been arrested or imprisoned— until Ojo broke the Law."

"Seems to me that girl Ruler of yours is making a big fuss over nothing," remarked Scraps, tossing her yarn hair out of her eyes with a jerk of her patched head. "I don't know what Ojo has done, but it couldn't be anything very bad, for you and I were with him all the time."

The Shaggy Man made no reply to this speech and presently the Patchwork Girl forgot all about Ojo in her admiration of the wonderful city she had entered.

They soon separated from the Munchkin boy, who was led by the Soldier with the Green Whiskers down a side street toward the prison. Ojo felt very miserable and greatly ashamed of himself, but he was beginning to grow angry because he was treated in such a disgraceful manner. Instead of entering the splendid Emerald City as a respectable traveler who was entitled to a welcome and to hospitality, he was being brought in as a criminal, handcuffed and in a robe that told all he met of his deep disgrace.

Ojo was by nature gentle and affectionate and if he had disobeyed the Law of Oz it was to restore his dear Unc Nunkie to life. His fault was more thoughtless than wicked, but that did not alter the fact that he had committed a fault. At first he had felt sorrow and remorse, but the more he thought about the unjust treatment he had received—unjust merely because he considered it so—the more he resented his arrest, blaming Ozma for making foolish laws and then punishing folks who broke them. Only a six-leaved clover! A tiny green plant growing neglected and trampled under foot. What harm could there be in picking it? Ojo began to think Ozma must be a very bad and oppressive Ruler for such a lovely fairyland as Oz. The Shaggy Man said the people loved her; but how could they?

The little Munchkin boy was so busy thinking these things— which many guilty prisoners have thought before him—that he scarcely noticed all the splendor of the city streets through which they passed. Whenever they met any of the happy, smiling people, the boy turned his head away in shame, although none knew who was beneath the robe.

By and by they reached a house built just beside the great city wall, but in a quiet, retired place. It was a pretty house, neatly painted and with many windows. Before it was a garden filled with blooming flowers. The Soldier with the Green Whiskers led Ojo up the gravel path to the front door, on which he knocked.

A woman opened the door and, seeing Ojo in his white robe, exclaimed: "Goodness me! A prisoner at last. But what a small one, Soldier."

"The size doesn't matter, Tollydiggle, my dear. The fact remains that he is a prisoner," said the soldier. "And, this being the prison, and you the jailer, it is my duty to place the prisoner in your charge."

"True. Come in, then, and I'll give you a receipt for him."

They entered the house and passed through a hall to a large circular room, where the woman pulled the robe off from Ojo and looked at him with kindly interest. The boy, on his part, was gazing around him in amazement, for never had he dreamed of such a magnificent apartment as this in which he stood. The roof of the dome was of colored glass, worked into beautiful designs. The walls were paneled with plates of gold decorated with gems of great size and many colors, and upon the tiled floor were soft rugs delightful to walk upon. The furniture was framed in gold and upholstered in satin brocade and it consisted of easy chairs, divans and stools in great variety. Also there were several tables with mirror tops and cabinets filled with rare and curious things. In one place a case filled with books stood against the wall, and elsewhere Ojo saw a cupboard containing all sorts of games.

"May I stay here a little while before I go to prison?" asked the boy, pleadingly.

"Why, this is your prison," replied Tollydiggle, "and in me behold your jailor. Take off those handcuffs, Soldier, for it is impossible for anyone to escape from this house."

"I know that very well," replied the soldier and at once unlocked the handcuffs and released the prisoner.

The woman touched a button on the wall and lighted a big chandelier that hung suspended from the ceiling, for it was growing dark outside. Then she seated herself at a desk and asked: "What name?"

"Ojo the Unlucky," answered the Soldier with the Green Whiskers.

"Unlucky? Ah, that accounts for it," said she. "What crime?"

"Breaking a Law of Oz."

"All right. There's your receipt, Soldier; and now I'm responsible for the prisoner. I'm glad of it, for this is the first time I've ever had anything to do, in my official capacity," remarked the jailer in a pleased tone.

"It's the same with me, Tollydiggle," laughed the soldier. "But my task is finished and I must go and report to Ozma that I've done my duty like a faithful Police Force, a loyal Army and an honest Body-Guard—as I hope I am."

Saying this, he nodded farewell to Tollydiggle and Ojo and went away.

"Now, then," said the woman briskly, "I must get you some supper, for you are doubtless hungry. What would you prefer: planked whitefish, omelet with jelly or mutton-chops with gravy?"

Ojo thought about it. Then he said: "I'll take the chops, if you please."

"Very well; amuse yourself while I'm gone; I won't be long," and then she went out by a door and left the prisoner alone.

Ojo was much astonished, for not only was this unlike any prison he had ever heard of, but he was being treated more as a guest than a criminal. There were many windows and they had no locks. There were three doors to the room and none were bolted. He cautiously opened one of the doors and found it led into a hallway. But he had no intention of trying to escape. If his jailor was willing to trust him in this way he would not betray her trust, and moreover a hot supper was being prepared for him and his prison was very pleasant and comfortable. So he took a book from the case and sat down in a big chair to look at the pictures.

This amused him until the woman came in with a large tray and spread a cloth on one of the tables. Then she arranged his supper, which proved the most varied and delicious meal Ojo had ever eaten in his life.

Tollydiggle sat near him while he ate, sewing on some fancy work she held in her lap. When he had finished she cleared the table and then read to him a story from one of the books.

"Is this really a prison?" he asked, when she had finished reading.

"Indeed it is," she replied. "It is the only prison in the Land of Oz."

"And am I a prisoner?"

"Bless the child! Of course."

"Then why is the prison so fine, and why are you so kind to me?" he earnestly asked.

Tollydiggle seemed surprised by the question, but she presently answered: "We consider a prisoner unfortunate. He is unfortunate in two ways—because he has done something wrong and because he is deprived of his liberty. Therefore we should treat him kindly, because of his misfortune, for otherwise he would become hard and bitter and would not be sorry he had done wrong. Ozma thinks that one who has committed a fault did so because he was not strong and brave; therefore she puts him in prison to make him strong and brave. When that is accomplished he is no longer a prisoner, but a good and loyal citizen and everyone is glad that he is now strong enough to resist doing wrong. You see, it is kindness that makes one strong and brave; and so we are kind to our prisoners."

Ojo thought this over very carefully. "I had an idea," said he, "that prisoners were always treated harshly, to punish them."

"That would be dreadful!" cried Tollydiggle. "Isn't one punished enough in knowing he has done wrong? Don't you wish, Ojo, with all your heart, that you had not been disobedient and broken a Law of Oz?"

"I—I hate to be different from other people," he admitted.

"Yes; one likes to be respected as highly as his neighbors are," said the woman. "When you are tried and found guilty, you will be obliged to make amends, in some way. I don't know just what Ozma will do to you, because this is the first time one of us has broken a Law; but you may be sure she will be just and merciful. Here in the Emerald City people are too happy and contented ever to do wrong; but perhaps you came from some faraway corner of our land, and having no love for Ozma carelessly broke one of her Laws."

"Yes," said Ojo, "I've lived all my life in the heart of a lonely forest, where I saw no one but dear Unc Nunkie."

"I thought so," said Tollydiggle. "But now we have talked enough, so let us play a game until bedtime."

16. Princess Dorothy

Dorothy Gale was sitting in one of her rooms in the royal palace, while curled up at her feet was a little black dog with a shaggy coat and very bright eyes. She wore a plain white frock, without any jewels or other ornaments except an emerald-green hair-ribbon, for Dorothy was a simple little girl and had not been in the least spoiled by the magnificence surrounding her. Once the child had lived on the Kansas prairies, but she seemed marked for adventure, for she had made several trips to the Land of Oz before she came to live there for good. Her very best friend was the beautiful Ozma of Oz, who loved Dorothy so well that she kept her in her own palace, so as to be near her. The girl's Uncle Henry and Aunt Em—the only relatives she had in the world—had also been brought here by Ozma and given a pleasant home. Dorothy knew almost everybody in Oz, and it was she who had discovered the Scarecrow, the Tin Woodman and the Cowardly Lion, as well as Tik-Tok the Clockwork Man. Her life was very pleasant now, and although she had been made a Princess of Oz by her friend Ozma she did not care much to be a Princess and remained as sweet as when she had been plain Dorothy Gale of Kansas.

Dorothy was reading in a book this evening when Jellia Jamb, the favorite servant-maid of the palace, came to say that the Shaggy Man wanted to see her.

"All right," said Dorothy; "tell him to come right up."

"But he has some queer creatures with him—some of the queerest I've ever laid eyes on," reported Jellia.

"Never mind; let 'em all come up," replied Dorothy.

But when the door opened to admit not only the Shaggy Man, but Scraps, the Woozy and the Glass Cat, Dorothy jumped up and looked at her strange visitors in amazement. The Patchwork Girl was the most curious of all and Dorothy was uncertain at first whether Scraps was really alive or only a dream or a nightmare. Toto, her dog, slowly uncurled himself and going to the Patchwork Girl sniffed at her inquiringly; but soon he lay down again, as if to say he had no interest in such an irregular creation.

"You're a new one to me," Dorothy said reflectively, addressing the Patchwork Girl. "I can't imagine where you've come from."

"Who, me?" asked Scraps, looking around the pretty room

instead of at the girl. "Oh, I came from a bed-quilt, I guess. That's what they say, anyhow. Some call it a crazy-quilt and some a patchwork quilt. But my name is Scraps—and now you know all about me."

"Not quite all," returned Dorothy with a smile. "I wish you'd tell me how you came to be alive."

"That's an easy job," said Scraps, sitting upon a big upholstered chair and making the springs bounce her up and down. "Margolotte wanted a slave, so she made me out of an old bed-quilt she didn't use. Cotton stuffing, suspender-button eyes, red velvet tongue, pearl beads for teeth. The Crooked Magician made a Powder of Life, sprinkled me with it and—here I am. Perhaps you've noticed my different colors. A very refined and educated gentleman named the Scarecrow, whom I met, told me I am the most beautiful creature in all Oz, and I believe it."

"Oh! Have you met our Scarecrow, then?" asked Dorothy, a little puzzled to understand the brief history related.

"Yes; isn't he jolly?"

"The Scarecrow has many good qualities," replied Dorothy. "But I'm sorry to hear all this 'bout the Crooked Magician. Ozma'll be mad as hops when she hears he's been doing magic again. She told him not to."

"He only practices magic for the benefit of his own family," explained Bungle, who was keeping at a respectful distance from the little black dog.

"Dear me," said Dorothy; "I hadn't noticed you before. Are you glass, or what?"

"I'm glass, and transparent, too, which is more than can be said of some folks," answered the cat. "Also I have some lovely pink brains; you can see 'em work."

"Oh; is that so? Come over here and let me see."

The Glass Cat hesitated, eyeing the dog.

"Send that beast away and I will," she said.

"Beast! Why, that's my dog Toto, an' he's the kindest dog in all the world. Toto knows a good many things, too; 'most as much as I do, I guess."

"Why doesn't he say anything?" asked Bungle.

"He can't talk, not being a fairy dog," explained Dorothy. "He's just a common United States dog; but that's a good deal; and I understand him, and he understands me, just as well as if he could talk."

Toto, at this, got up and rubbed his head softly against Dorothy's hand, which she held out to him, and he looked up into her face as if he had understood every word she had said.

"This cat, Toto," she said to him, "is made of glass, so you mustn't bother it, or chase it, any more than you do my Pink Kitten. It's prob'ly brittle and might break if it bumped against anything."

"Woof!" said Toto, and that meant he understood.

The Glass Cat was so proud of her pink brains that she ventured

to come close to Dorothy, in order that the girl might "see 'em work." This was really interesting, but when Dorothy patted the cat she found the glass cold and hard and unresponsive, so she decided at once that Bungle would never do for a pet.

"What do you know about the Crooked Magician who lives on the mountain?" asked Dorothy.

"He made me," replied the cat; "so I know all about him. The Patchwork Girl is new—three or four days old—but I've lived with Dr. Pipt for years; and, though I don't much care for him, I will say that he has always refused to work magic for any of the people who come to his house. He thinks there's no harm in doing magic things for his own family, and he made me out of glass because the meat cats drink too much milk. He also made Scraps come to life so she could do the housework for his wife Margolotte."

"Then why did you both leave him?" asked Dorothy.

"I think you'd better let me explain that," interrupted the Shaggy Man, and then he told Dorothy all of Ojo's story and how Unc Nunkie and Margolotte had accidentally been turned to marble by the Liquid of Petrifaction. Then he related how the boy had started out in search of the things needed to make the magic charm, which would restore the unfortunates to life, and how he had found the Woozy and taken him along because he could not pull the three hairs out of its tail. Dorothy listened to all this with much interest, and thought that so far Ojo had acted very well. But when the Shaggy Man told her of the Munchkin boy's arrest by the Soldier with the Green Whiskers, because he was accused of wilfully breaking a Law of Oz, the little girl was greatly shocked.

"What do you s'pose he's done?" she asked.

"I fear he has picked a six-leaved clover," answered the Shaggy Man, sadly. "I did not see him do it, and I warned him that to do so was against the Law; but perhaps that is what he did, nevertheless."

"I'm sorry 'bout that," said Dorothy gravely, "for now there will be no one to help his poor uncle and Margolotte 'cept this Patchwork Girl, the Woozy and the Glass Cat."

"Don't mention it," said Scraps. "That's no affair of mine. Margolotte and Unc Nunkie are perfect strangers to me, for the moment I came to life they came to marble."

"I see," remarked Dorothy with a sigh of regret; "the woman forgot to give you a heart."

"I'm glad she did," retorted the Patchwork Girl. "A heart must be a great annoyance to one. It makes a person feel sad or sorry or devoted or sympathetic—all of which sensations interfere with one's happiness."

"I have a heart," murmured the Glass Cat. "It's made of a ruby; but I don't imagine I shall let it bother me about helping Unc Nunkie and Margolotte."

"That's a pretty hard heart of yours," said Dorothy. "And the Woozy, of course—"

"Why, as for me," observed the Woozy, who was reclining on the floor with his legs doubled under him, so that he looked much like a square box, "I have never seen those unfortunate people you are speaking of, and yet I am sorry for them, having at times been unfortunate myself. When I was shut up in that forest I longed for some one to help me, and by and by Ojo came and did help me. So I'm willing to help his uncle. I'm only a stupid beast, Dorothy, but I can't help that, and if you'll tell me what to do to help Ojo and his uncle, I'll gladly do it."

Dorothy walked over and patted the Woozy on his square head.

"You're not pretty," she said, "but I like you. What are you able to do; anything 'special?"

"I can make my eyes flash fire—real fire—when I'm angry. When anyone says: 'Krizzle-Kroo' to me I get angry, and then my eyes flash fire."

"I don't see as fireworks could help Ojo's uncle," remarked Dorothy. "Can you do anything else?"

"I—I thought I had a very terrifying growl," said the Woozy, with hesitation; "but perhaps I was mistaken."

"Yes," said the Shaggy Man, "you were certainly wrong about that." Then he turned to Dorothy and added: "What will become of the Munchkin boy?"

"I don't know," she said, shaking her head thoughtfully. "Ozma will see him 'bout it, of course, and then she'll punish him. But now, I don't know, 'cause no one ever has been punished in Oz since I knew anything about the place. Too bad, Shaggy Man, isn't it?"

While they were talking Scraps had been roaming around the room and looking at all the pretty things it contained. She had carried Ojo's basket in her hand, until now, when she decided to see what was inside it. She found the bread and cheese, which she had no use for, and the bundle of charms, which were curious but quite a mystery to her. Then, turning these over, she came upon the six-leaved clover which the boy had plucked.

Scraps was quick-witted, and although she had no heart she recognized the fact that Ojo was her first friend. She knew at once that because the boy had taken the clover he had been imprisoned, and she understood that Ojo had given her the basket so they would not find the clover in his possession and have proof of his crime. So, turning her head to see that no one noticed her, she took the clover from the basket and dropped it into a golden vase that stood on Dorothy's table. Then she came forward and said to Dorothy: "I wouldn't care to help Ojo's uncle, but I will help Ojo. He did not break the Law—no one can prove he did—and that green-whiskered soldier had no right to arrest him."

"Ozma ordered the boy's arrest," said Dorothy, "and of course she knew what she was doing. But if you can prove Ojo is innocent they will set him free at once."

"They'll have to prove him guilty, won't they?" asked Scraps.

"I s'pose so."

"Well, they can't do that," declared the Patchwork Girl.

As it was nearly time for Dorothy to dine with Ozma, which she did every evening, she rang for a servant and ordered the Woozy taken to a nice room and given plenty of such food as he liked best.

"That's honey-bees," said the Woozy.

"You can't eat honey-bees, but you'll be given something just as nice," Dorothy told him. Then she had the Glass Cat taken to another room for the night and the Patchwork Girl she kept in one of her own rooms, for she was much interested in the strange creature and wanted to talk with her again and try to understand her better.

17. Ozma and Her Friends

The Shaggy Man had a room of his own in the royal palace, so there he went to change his shaggy suit of clothes for another just as shaggy but not so dusty from travel. He selected a costume of pea-green and pink satin and velvet, with embroidered shags on all the edges and iridescent pearls for ornaments. Then he bathed in an alabaster pool and brushed his shaggy hair and whiskers the wrong way to make them still more shaggy. This accomplished, and arrayed in his splendid shaggy garments, he went to Ozma's banquet hall and found the Scarecrow, the Wizard and Dorothy already assembled there. The Scarecrow had made a quick trip and returned to the Emerald City with his left ear freshly painted.

A moment later, while they all stood in waiting, a servant threw open a door, the orchestra struck up a tune and Ozma of Oz entered.

Much has been told and written concerning the beauty of person and character of this sweet girl Ruler of the Land of Oz—the richest, the happiest and most delightful fairyland of which we have any knowledge. Yet with all her queenly qualities Ozma was a real girl and enjoyed the things in life that other real girls enjoy. When she sat on her splendid emerald throne in the great Throne Room of her palace and made laws and settled disputes and tried to keep all her subjects happy and contented, she was as dignified and demure as any queen might be; but when she had thrown aside her jeweled robe of state and her sceptre, and had retired to her private apartments, the girl— joyous, light-hearted and free—replaced the sedate Ruler.

In the banquet hall to-night were gathered only old and trusted friends, so here Ozma was herself—a mere girl. She greeted Dorothy with a kiss, the Shaggy Man with a smile, the little old Wizard with a friendly handshake and then she pressed the Scarecrow's stuffed arm and cried merrily: "What a lovely left ear! Why, it's a hundred times better than the old one."

"I'm glad you like it," replied the Scarecrow, well pleased. "Jinjur did a neat job, didn't she? And my hearing is now perfect. Isn't it wonderful what a little paint will do, if it's properly applied?"

"It really is wonderful," she agreed, as they all took their seats; "but the Sawhorse must have made his legs twinkle to have carried you so far in one day. I didn't expect you back before to-morrow, at the earliest."

"Well," said the Scarecrow, "I met a charming girl on the road and wanted to see more of her, so I hurried back."

Ozma laughed.

"I know," she returned; "it's the Patchwork Girl. She is certainly bewildering, if not strictly beautiful."

"Have you seen her, then?" the straw man eagerly asked.

"Only in my Magic Picture, which shows me all scenes of interest in the Land of Oz."

"I fear the picture didn't do her justice," said the Scarecrow.

"It seemed to me that nothing could be more gorgeous," declared Ozma. "Whoever made that patchwork quilt, from which Scraps was formed, must have selected the gayest and brightest bits of cloth that ever were woven."

"I am glad you like her," said the Scarecrow in a satisfied tone. Although the straw man did not eat, not being made so he could, he often dined with Ozma and her companions, merely for the pleasure of talking with them. He sat at the table and had a napkin and plate, but the servants knew better than to offer him food. After a little while he asked: "Where is the Patchwork Girl now?"

"In my room," replied Dorothy. "I've taken a fancy to her; she's so queer and—and—uncommon."

"She's half crazy, I think," added the Shaggy Man.

"But she is so beautiful!" exclaimed the Scarecrow, as if that fact disarmed all criticism. They all laughed at his enthusiasm, but the Scarecrow was quite serious. Seeing that he was interested in Scraps they forbore to say anything against her. The little band of friends Ozma had gathered around her was so quaintly assorted that much care must be exercised to avoid hurting their feelings or making any one of them unhappy. It was this considerate kindness that held them close friends and enabled them to enjoy one another's society.

Another thing they avoided was conversing on unpleasant subjects, and for that reason Ojo and his troubles were not mentioned during the dinner. The Shaggy Man, however, related his adventures with the monstrous plants which had seized and enfolded the travelers, and told how he had robbed Chiss, the giant porcupine, of the quills which it was accustomed to throw at people. Both Dorothy and Ozma were pleased with this exploit and thought it served Chiss right.

Then they talked of the Woozy, which was the most remarkable animal any of them had ever before seen—except, perhaps, the live Sawhorse. Ozma had never known that her dominions contained such a thing as a Woozy, there being but one in existence and this being confined in his forest for many years. Dorothy said she believed the Woozy was a good beast, honest and faithful; but she added that she did not care much for the Glass Cat.

"Still," said the Shaggy Man, "the Glass Cat is very pretty and if she were not so conceited over her pink brains no one would object to her as a companion."

The Wizard had been eating silently until now, when he looked up and remarked: "That Powder of Life which is made by the Crooked Magician is really a wonderful thing. But Dr. Pipt does not know its true value and he uses it in the most foolish ways."

"I must see about that," said Ozma, gravely. Then she smiled again and continued in a lighter tone: "It was Dr. Pipt's famous Powder of Life that enabled me to become the Ruler of Oz."

"I've never heard that story," said the Shaggy Man, looking at Ozma questioningly.

"Well, when I was a baby girl I was stolen by an old Witch named Mombi and transformed into a boy," began the girl Ruler. "I did not know who I was and when I grew big enough to work, the Witch made me wait upon her and carry wood for the fire and hoe in the garden. One day she came back from a journey bringing some of the Powder of Life, which Dr. Pipt had given her. I had made a pumpkin-headed man and set it up in her path to frighten her, for I was fond of fun and hated the Witch. But she knew what the figure was and to test her Powder of Life she sprinkled some of it on the man I had made. It came to life and is now our dear friend Jack Pumpkinhead. That night I ran away with Jack to escape punishment, and I took old Mombi's Powder of Life with me. During our journey we came upon a wooden Sawhorse standing by the road and I used the magic powder to bring it to life. The Sawhorse has been with me ever since. When I got to the Emerald City the good Sorceress, Glinda, knew who I was and restored me to my proper person, when I became the rightful Ruler of this land. So you see had not old Mombi brought home the Powder of Life I might never have run away from her and become Ozma of Oz, nor would we have had Jack Pumpkinhead and the Sawhorse to comfort and amuse us."

That story interested the Shaggy Man very much, as well as the others, who had often heard it before. The dinner being now concluded, they all went to Ozma's drawing-room, where they passed a pleasant evening before it came time to retire.

18. Ojo is Forgiven

The next morning the Soldier with the Green Whiskers went to the prison and took Ojo away to the royal palace, where he was summoned to appear before the girl Ruler for judgment. Again the soldier put upon the boy the jeweled handcuffs and white prisoner's robe with the peaked top and holes for the eyes. Ojo was so ashamed, both of his disgrace and the fault he had committed, that he was glad to be covered up in this way, so that people could not see him or know who he was. He followed the Soldier with the Green Whiskers very willingly, anxious that his fate might be decided as soon as possible.

The inhabitants of the Emerald City were polite people and never jeered at the unfortunate; but it was so long since they had seen a prisoner that they cast many curious looks toward the boy and many of them hurried away to the royal palace to be present during the trial.

When Ojo was escorted into the great Throne Room of the palace he found hundreds of people assembled there. In the magnificent emerald throne, which sparkled with countless jewels, sat Ozma of Oz in her Robe of State, which was embroidered with emeralds and pearls. On her right, but a little lower, was Dorothy, and on her left the Scarecrow. Still lower but nearly in front of Ozma, sat the wonderful Wizard of Oz and on a small table beside him was the golden vase from Dorothy's room, into which Scraps had dropped the stolen clover.

At Ozma's feet crouched two enormous beasts, each the largest and most powerful of its kind. Although these beasts were quite free, no one present was alarmed by them; for the Cowardly Lion and the Hungry Tiger were well known and respected in the Emerald City and they always guarded the Ruler when she held high court in the Throne Room. There was still another beast present, but this one Dorothy held in her arms, for it was her constant companion, the little dog Toto. Toto knew the Cowardly Lion and the Hungry Tiger and often played and romped with them, for they were good friends.

Seated on ivory chairs before Ozma, with a clear space between them and the throne, were many of the nobility of the Emerald City, lords and ladies in beautiful costumes, and officials of the kingdom in the royal uniforms of Oz. Behind these courtiers were others of less importance, filling the great hall to the very doors.

At the same moment that the Soldier with the Green Whiskers arrived with Ojo, the Shaggy Man entered from a side door, escorting the Patchwork Girl, the Woozy and the Glass Cat. All these came to the vacant space before the throne and stood facing the Ruler.

"Hullo, Ojo," said Scraps; "how are you?"

"All right," he replied; but the scene awed the boy and his voice trembled a little with fear. Nothing could awe the Patchwork Girl, and although the Woozy was somewhat uneasy in these splendid surroundings the Glass Cat was delighted with the sumptuousness of the court and the impressiveness of the occasion—pretty big words but quite expressive.

At a sign from Ozma the soldier removed Ojo's white robe and the boy stood face to face with the girl who was to decide his punishment. He saw at a glance how lovely and sweet she was, and his heart gave a bound of joy, for he hoped she would be merciful.

Ozma sat looking at the prisoner a long time. Then she said gently: "One of the Laws of Oz forbids anyone to pick a six-leaved clover. You are accused of having broken this Law, even after you had been warned not to do so."

Ojo hung his head and while he hesitated how to reply the Patchwork Girl stepped forward and spoke for him.

"All this fuss is about nothing at all," she said, facing Ozma unabashed. "You can't prove he picked the six-leaved clover, so you've no right to accuse him of it. Search him, if you like, but you won't find the clover; look in his basket and you'll find it's not there. He hasn't got it, so I demand that you set this poor Munchkin boy free."

The people of Oz listened to this defiance in amazement and wondered at the queer Patchwork Girl who dared talk so boldly to their Ruler. But Ozma sat silent and motionless and it was the little Wizard who answered Scraps.

"So the clover hasn't been picked, eh?" he said. "I think it has. I think the boy hid it in his basket, and then gave the basket to you. I also think you dropped the clover into this vase, which stood in Princess Dorothy's room, hoping to get rid of it so it would not prove the boy guilty. You're a stranger here, Miss Patches, and so you don't know that nothing can be hidden from our powerful Ruler's Magic Picture—nor from the watchful eyes of the humble Wizard of Oz. Look, all of you!" With these words he waved his hands toward the vase on the table, which Scraps now noticed for the first time.

From the mouth of the vase a plant sprouted, slowly growing before their eyes until it became a beautiful bush, and on the topmost branch appeared the six-leaved clover which Ojo had unfortunately picked.

The Patchwork Girl looked at the clover and said: "Oh, so you've found it. Very well; prove he picked it, if you can."

Ozma turned to Ojo.

"Did you pick the six-leaved clover?" she asked.

"Yes," he replied. "I knew it was against the Law, but I wanted to save Unc Nunkie and I was afraid if I asked your consent to pick it you would refuse me."

"What caused you to think that?" asked the Ruler.

"Why, it seemed to me a foolish law, unjust and unreasonable. Even now I can see no harm in picking a six-leaved clover. And I—I had not seen the Emerald City, then, nor you, and I thought a girl who would make such a silly Law would not be likely to help anyone in trouble."

Ozma regarded him musingly, her chin resting upon her hand; but she was not angry. On the contrary she smiled a little at her thoughts and then grew sober again.

"I suppose a good many laws seem foolish to those people who do not understand them," she said; "but no law is ever made without some purpose, and that purpose is usually to protect all the people and guard their welfare. As you are a stranger, I will explain this Law which to you seems so foolish. Years ago there were many Witches and Magicians in the Land of Oz, and one of the things they often used in making their magic charms and transformations was a six-leaved clover. These Witches and Magicians caused so much trouble among my people, often using their powers for evil rather than good, that I decided to forbid anyone to practice magic or sorcery except Glinda the Good and her assistant, the Wizard of Oz, both of whom I can trust to use their arts only to benefit my people and to make them happier. Since I issued that Law the Land of Oz has been far more peaceful and quiet; but I learned that some of the Witches and Magicians were still practicing magic on the sly and using the six-leaved clovers to make their potions and charms. Therefore I made another Law forbidding anyone from plucking a six-leaved clover or from gathering other plants and herbs which the Witches boil in their kettles to work magic with. That has almost put an end to wicked sorcery in our land, so you see the Law was not a foolish one, but wise and just; and, in any event, it is wrong to disobey a Law."

Ojo knew she was right and felt greatly mortified to realize he had acted and spoken so ridiculously. But he raised his head and looked Ozma in the face, saying: "I am sorry I have acted wrongly and broken your Law. I did it to save Unc Nunkie, and thought I would not be found out. But I am guilty of this act and whatever punishment you think I deserve I will suffer willingly."

Ozma smiled more brightly, then, and nodded graciously.

"You are forgiven," she said. "For, although you have committed a serious fault, you are now penitent and I think you have been punished enough. Soldier, release Ojo the Lucky and—"

"I beg your pardon; I'm Ojo the Unlucky," said the boy.

"At this moment you are lucky," said she. "Release him, Soldier, and let him go free."

The people were glad to hear Ozma's decree and murmured their approval. As the royal audience was now over, they began to leave the Throne Room and soon there were none remaining except Ojo and his friends and Ozma and her favorites.

The girl Ruler now asked Ojo to sit down and tell her all his story, which he did, beginning at the time he had left his home in the forest and ending with his arrival at the Emerald City and his arrest. Ozma listened attentively and was thoughtful for some moments after the boy had finished speaking. Then she said: "The Crooked Magician was wrong to make the Glass Cat and the

Patchwork Girl, for it was against the Law. And if he had not unlawfully kept the bottle of Liquid of Petrifaction standing on his shelf, the accident to his wife Margolotte and to Unc Nunkie could not have occurred. I can understand, however, that Ojo, who loves his uncle, will be unhappy unless he can save him. Also I feel it is wrong to leave those two victims standing as marble statues, when they ought to be alive. So I propose we allow Dr. Pipt to make the magic charm which will save them, and that we assist Ojo to find the things he is seeking. What do you think, Wizard?"

"That is perhaps the best thing to do," replied the Wizard. "But after the Crooked Magician has restored those poor people to life you must take away his magic powers."

"I will," promised Ozma.

"Now tell me, please, what magic things must you find?" continued the Wizard, addressing Ojo.

"The three hairs from the Woozy's tail I have," said the boy. "That is, I have the Woozy, and the hairs are in his tail. The six-leaved clover I—I—"

"You may take it and keep it," said Ozma. "That will not be breaking the Law, for it is already picked, and the crime of picking it is forgiven."

"Thank you!" cried Ojo gratefully. Then he continued: "The next thing I must find is a gill of water from a dark well."

The Wizard shook his head. "That," said he, "will be a hard task, but if you travel far enough you may discover it."

"I am willing to travel for years, if it will save Unc Nunkie," declared Ojo, earnestly.

"Then you'd better begin your journey at once," advised the Wizard.

Dorothy had been listening with interest to this conversation. Now she turned to Ozma and asked: "May I go with Ojo, to help him?"

"Would you like to?" returned Ozma.

"Yes. I know Oz pretty well, but Ojo doesn't know it at all. I'm sorry for his uncle and poor Margolotte and I'd like to help save them. May I go?"

"If you wish to," replied Ozma.

"If Dorothy goes, then I must go to take care of her," said the Scarecrow, decidedly. "A dark well can only be discovered in some out-of-the-way place, and there may be dangers there."

"You have my permission to accompany Dorothy," said Ozma. "And while you are gone I will take care of the Patchwork Girl."

"I'll take care of myself," announced Scraps, "for I'm going with the Scarecrow and Dorothy. I promised Ojo to help him find the things he wants and I'll stick to my promise."

"Very well," replied Ozma. "But I see no need for Ojo to take the Glass Cat and the Woozy."

"I prefer to remain here," said the cat. "I've nearly been nicked half a dozen times, already, and if they're going into dangers it's

best for me to keep away from them."

"Let Jellia Jamb keep her till Ojo returns," suggested Dorothy. "We won't need to take the Woozy, either, but he ought to be saved because of the three hairs in his tail."

"Better take me along," said the Woozy. "My eyes can flash fire, you know, and I can growl—a little."

"I'm sure you'll be safer here," Ozma decided, and the Woozy made no further objection to the plan.

After consulting together they decided that Ojo and his party should leave the very next day to search for the gill of water from a dark well, so they now separated to make preparations for the journey.

Ozma gave the Munchkin boy a room in the palace for that night and the afternoon he passed with Dorothy—getting acquainted, as she said—and receiving advice from the Shaggy Man as to where they must go. The Shaggy Man had wandered in many parts of Oz, and so had Dorothy, for that matter, yet neither of them knew where a dark well was to be found.

"If such a thing is anywhere in the settled parts of Oz," said Dorothy, "we'd prob'ly have heard of it long ago. If it's in the wild parts of the country, no one there would need a dark well. P'raps there isn't such a thing."

"Oh, there must be!" returned Ojo, positively; "or else the recipe of Dr. Pipt wouldn't call for it."

"That's true," agreed Dorothy; "and, if it's anywhere in the Land of Oz, we're bound to find it."

"Well, we're bound to search for it, anyhow," said the Scarecrow. "As for finding it, we must trust to luck."

"Don't do that," begged Ojo, earnestly. "I'm called Ojo the Unlucky, you know."

19. Trouble with the Tottenhots

A day's journey from the Emerald City brought the little band of adventurers to the home of Jack Pumpkinhead, which was a house formed from the shell of an immense pumpkin. Jack had made it himself and was very proud of it. There was a door, and several windows, and through the top was stuck a stovepipe that led from a small stove inside. The door was reached by a flight of three steps and there was a good floor on which was arranged some furniture that was quite comfortable.

It is certain that Jack Pumpkinhead might have had a much finer house to live in had he wanted it, for Ozma loved the stupid fellow, who had been her earliest companion; but Jack preferred his pumpkin house, as it matched himself very well, and in this he was not so stupid, after all.

The body of this remarkable person was made of wood, branches of trees of various sizes having been used for the purpose. This wooden framework was covered by a red shirt—with white spots in it—blue trousers, a yellow vest, a jacket of green-and-gold and stout leather shoes. The neck was a sharpened stick on which the pumpkin head was set, and the eyes, ears, nose and mouth were carved on the skin of the pumpkin, very like a child's jack-o'-lantern.

The house of this interesting creation stood in the center of a vast pumpkin-field, where the vines grew in profusion and bore pumpkins of extraordinary size as well as those which were smaller. Some of the pumpkins now ripening on the vines were almost as large as Jack's house, and he told Dorothy he intended to add another pumpkin to his mansion.

The travelers were cordially welcomed to this quaint domicile and invited to pass the night there, which they had planned to do. The Patchwork Girl was greatly interested in Jack and examined him admiringly.

"You are quite handsome," she said; "but not as really beautiful as the Scarecrow."

Jack turned, at this, to examine the Scarecrow critically, and his old friend slyly winked one painted eye at him.

"There is no accounting for tastes," remarked the Pumpkinhead, with a sigh. "An old crow once told me I was very fascinating, but of course the bird might have been mistaken. Yet I have noticed that the crows usually avoid the Scarecrow, who is a very honest fellow, in his way, but stuffed. I am not stuffed, you will observe; my body is good solid hickory."

"I adore stuffing," said the Patchwork Girl.

"Well, as for that, my head is stuffed with pumpkin-seeds," declared Jack. "I use them for brains, and when they are fresh I am intellectual. Just now, I regret to say, my seeds are rattling a bit, so I must soon get another head."

"Oh; do you change your head?" asked Ojo.

"To be sure. Pumpkins are not permanent, more's the pity, and in time they spoil. That is why I grow such a great field of pumpkins—that I may select a new head whenever necessary."

"Who carves the faces on them?" inquired the boy.

"I do that myself. I lift off my old head, place it on a table before me, and use the face for a pattern to go by. Sometimes the faces I carve are better than others—more expressive and cheerful, you know—but I think they average very well."

Before she had started on the journey Dorothy had packed a knapsack with the things she might need, and this knapsack the Scarecrow carried strapped to his back. The little girl wore a plain gingham dress and a checked sunbonnet, as she knew they were best fitted for travel. Ojo also had brought along his basket, to which Ozma had added a bottle of "Square Meal Tablets" and some fruit. But Jack Pumpkinhead grew a lot of things in his garden besides pumpkins, so he cooked for them a fine vegetable soup and gave Dorothy, Ojo and Toto, the only ones who found it necessary to eat, a pumpkin pie and some green cheese. For beds they must use the sweet dried grasses which Jack had strewn along one side of the room, but that satisfied Dorothy and Ojo very well. Toto, of course, slept beside his little mistress.

The Scarecrow, Scraps and the Pumpkinhead were tireless and had no need to sleep, so they sat up and talked together all night; but they stayed outside the house, under the bright stars, and talked in low tones so as not to disturb the sleepers. During the conversation the Scarecrow explained their quest for a dark well, and asked Jack's advice where to find it.

The Pumpkinhead considered the matter gravely.

"That is going to be a difficult task," said he, "and if I were you

I'd take any ordinary well and enclose it, so as to make it dark."

"I fear that wouldn't do," replied the Scarecrow. "The well must be naturally dark, and the water must never have seen the light of day, for otherwise the magic charm might not work at all."

"How much of the water do you need?" asked Jack.

"A gill."

"How much is a gill?"

"Why—a gill is a gill, of course," answered the Scarecrow, who did not wish to display his ignorance.

"I know!" cried Scraps. "Jack and Jill went up the hill to fetch—"

"No, no; that's wrong," interrupted the Scarecrow. "There are two kinds of gills, I think; one is a girl, and the other is—"

"A gillyflower," said Jack.

"No; a measure."

"How big a measure?"

"Well, I'll ask Dorothy."

So next morning they asked Dorothy, and she said: "I don't just know how much a gill is, but I've brought along a gold flask that holds a pint. That's more than a gill, I'm sure, and the Crooked Magician may measure it to suit himself. But the thing that's bothering us most, Jack, is to find the well."

Jack gazed around the landscape, for he was standing in the doorway of his house.

"This is a flat country, so you won't find any dark wells here," said he. "You must go into the mountains, where rocks and caverns are."

"And where is that?" asked Ojo.

"In the Quadling Country, which lies south of here," replied the Scarecrow. "I've known all along that we must go to the mountains."

"So have I," said Dorothy.

"But—goodness me!—the Quadling Country is full of dangers," declared Jack. "I've never been there myself, but—"

"I have," said the Scarecrow. "I've faced the dreadful Hammerheads, which have no arms and butt you like a goat; and I've faced the Fighting Trees, which bend down their branches to pound and whip you, and had many other adventures there."

"It's a wild country," remarked Dorothy, soberly, "and if we go there we're sure to have troubles of our own. But I guess we'll have to go, if we want that gill of water from the dark well."

So they said good-bye to the Pumpkinhead and resumed their travels, heading now directly toward the South Country, where mountains and rocks and caverns and forests of great trees abounded. This part of the Land of Oz, while it belonged to Ozma and owed her allegiance, was so wild and secluded that many queer peoples hid in its jungles and lived in their own way, without even a knowledge that they had a Ruler in the Emerald

City. If they were left alone, these creatures never troubled the inhabitants of the rest of Oz, but those who invaded their domains encountered many dangers from them.

It was a two days journey from Jack Pumkinhead's house to the edge of the Quadling Country, for neither Dorothy nor Ojo could walk very fast and they often stopped by the wayside to rest. The first night they slept on the broad fields, among the buttercups and daisies, and the Scarecrow covered the children with a gauze blanket taken from his knapsack, so they would not be chilled by the night air. Toward evening of the second day they reached a sandy plain where walking was difficult; but some distance before them they saw a group of palm trees, with many curious black dots under them; so they trudged bravely on to reach that place by dark and spend the night under the shelter of the trees.

The black dots grew larger as they advanced and although the light was dim Dorothy thought they looked like big kettles turned upside down. Just beyond this place a jumble of huge, jagged rocks lay scattered, rising to the mountains behind them.

Our travelers preferred to attempt to climb these rocks by daylight, and they realized that for a time this would be their last night on the plains.

Twilight had fallen by the time they came to the trees, beneath which were the black, circular objects they had marked from a distance. Dozens of them were scattered around and Dorothy bent near to one, which was about as tall as she was, to examine it more closely. As she did so the top flew open and out popped a creature, rising its length into the air and then plumping down upon the ground just beside the little girl. Another and another popped out of the circular, pot-like dwelling, while from all the other black objects came popping more creatures—very like jumping-jacks when their boxes are unhooked—until fully a hundred stood gathered around our little group of travelers.

By this time Dorothy had discovered they were people, tiny and curiously formed, but still people. Their hair stood straight up, like wires, and was brilliant scarlet in color. Their bodies were bare except for skins fastened around their waists and they wore bracelets on their ankles and wrists, and necklaces, and great pendant earrings.

Toto crouched beside his mistress and wailed as if he did not like these strange creatures a bit. Scraps began to mutter something about "hoppity, poppity, jumpity, dump!" but no one paid any attention to her. Ojo kept close to the Scarecrow and the Scarecrow kept close to Dorothy; but the little girl turned to the queer creatures and asked: "Who are you?"

They answered this question all together, in a sort of chanting chorus, the words being as follows:
"We're the jolly Tottenhots;
We do not like the day,
But in the night 'tis our delight
To gambol, skip and play.

We hate the sun and from it run,
The moon is cool and clear,
So on this spot each Tottenhot
Waits for it to appear.

We're ev'ry one chock full of fun,
And full of mischief, too;
But if you're gay and with us play
We'll do no harm to you."

"Glad to meet you, Tottenhots," said the Scarecrow solemnly "But you mustn't expect us to play with you all night, for we've traveled all day and some of us are tired."

"And we never gamble," added the Patchwork Girl. "It's against the Law."

These remarks were greeted with shouts of laughter by the impish creatures and one seized the Scarecrow's arm and was astonished to find the straw man whirl around so easily. So the Tottenhot raised the Scarecrow high in the air and tossed him over the heads of the crowd. Some one caught him and tossed him back, and so with shouts of glee they continued throwing the Scarecrow here and there, as if he had been a basket-ball.

Presently another imp seized Scraps and began to throw her about, in the same way. They found her a little heavier than the Scarecrow but still light enough to be tossed like a sofa-cushion and they were enjoying the sport immensely when Dorothy angry and indignant at the treatment her friends were receiving rushed among the Tottenhots and began slapping and pushing them until she had rescued the Scarecrow and the Patchwork Girl and held them close on either side of her. Perhaps she would not have accomplished this victory so easily had not Toto helped her, barking and snapping at the bare legs of the imps until they were glad to flee from his attack. As for Ojo, some of the creatures had attempted to toss him, also, but finding his body too heavy they threw him to the ground and a row of the imps sat on him and held him from assisting Dorothy in her battle.

The little folks were much surprised at being attacked by the girl and the dog, and one or two who had been slapped hardest began to cry. Then suddenly they gave a shout, all together, and disappeared in a flash into their various houses, the tops of which closed with a series of pops that sounded like a bunch of firecrackers being exploded.

The adventurers now found themselves alone, and Dorothy asked anxiously: "Is anybody hurt?"

"Not me," answered the Scarecrow. "They have given my straw a good shaking up and taken all the lumps out of it. I am now in splendid condition and am really obliged to the Tottenhots for their kind treatment."

"I feel much the same way," said Scraps. "My cotton stuffing had sagged a good deal with the day's walking and they've loosened it up until I feel as plump as a sausage. But the play was a little rough and I'd had quite enough of it when you interfered."

"Six of them sat on me," said Ojo, "but as they are so little they didn't hurt me much."

Just then the roof of the house in front of them opened and a Tottenhot stuck his head out, very cautiously, and looked at the strangers.

"Can't you take a joke?" he asked, reproachfully; "haven't you any fun in you at all?"

"If I had such a quality," replied the Scarecrow, "your people would have knocked it out of me. But I don't bear grudges. I forgive you."

"So do I," added Scraps. "That is, if you behave yourselves after this."

"It was just a little rough-house, that's all," said the Tottenhot

"But the question is not if we will behave, but if you will behave? We can't be shut up here all night, because this is our time to play; nor do we care to come out and be chewed up by a savage beast or slapped by an angry girl. That slapping hurts like sixty; some of my folks are crying about it. So here's the proposition: you let us alone and we'll let you alone."

"You began it," declared Dorothy.

"Well, you ended it, so we won't argue the matter. May we come out again? Or are you still cruel and slappy?"

"Tell you what we'll do," said Dorothy. "We're all tired and want to sleep until morning. If you'll let us get into your house, and stay there until daylight, you can play outside all you want to."

"That's a bargain!" cried the Tottenhot eagerly, and he gave a queer whistle that brought his people popping out of their houses on all sides. When the house before them was vacant, Dorothy and Ojo leaned over the hole and looked in, but could see nothing because it was so dark. But if the Tottenhots slept there all day the children thought they could sleep there at night, so Ojo lowered himself down and found it was not very deep.

"There's a soft cushion all over," said he. "Come on in."

Dorothy handed Toto to the boy and then climbed in herself. After her came Scraps and the Scarecrow, who did not wish to sleep but preferred to keep out of the way of the mischievous Tottenhots.

There seemed no furniture in the round den, but soft cushions were strewn about the floor and these they found made very comfortable beds. They did not close the hole in the roof but left it open to admit air. It also admitted the shouts and ceaseless laughter of the impish Tottenhots as they played outside, but Dorothy and Ojo, being weary from their journey, were soon fast asleep.

Toto kept an eye open, however, and uttered low, threatening growls whenever the racket made by the creatures outside became too boisterous; and the Scarecrow and the Patchwork Girl sat leaning against the wall and talked in whispers all night long. No one disturbed the travelers until daylight, when in popped the Tottenhot who owned the place and invited them to vacate his premises.

20. The Captive Yoop

As they were preparing to leave, Dorothy asked: "Can you tell us where there is a dark well?"

"Never heard of such a thing," said the Tottenhot. "We live our lives in the dark, mostly, and sleep in the daytime; but we've never seen a dark well, or anything like one."

"Does anyone live on those mountains beyond here?" asked the Scarecrow.

"Lots of people. But you'd better not visit them. We never go there," was the reply.

"What are the people like?" Dorothy inquired.

"Can't say. We've been told to keep away from the mountain paths, and so we obey. This sandy desert is good enough for us, and we're not disturbed here," declared the Tottenhot.

So they left the man snuggling down to sleep in his dusky dwelling, and went out into the sunshine, taking the path that led toward the rocky places. They soon found it hard climbing, for the rocks were uneven and full of sharp points and edges, and now there was no path at all. Clambering here and there among the boulders they kept steadily on, gradually rising higher and higher until finally they came to a great rift in a part of the mountain, where the rock seemed to have split in two and left high walls on either side.

"S'pose we go this way," suggested Dorothy; "it's much easier walking than to climb over the hills."

"How about that sign?" asked Ojo.

"What sign?" she inquired.

The Munchkin boy pointed to some words painted on the wall of rock beside them, which Dorothy had not noticed. The words read:

LOOK OUT FOR YOOP.

The girl eyed this sign a moment and turned to the Scarecrow, asking: "Who is Yoop; or what is Yoop?"

The straw man shook his head. Then looked at Toto and the dog said "Woof!"

"Only way to find out is to go on," said Scraps.

This being quite true, they went on. As they proceeded, the walls of rock on either side grew higher and higher. Presently they came upon another sign which read:

BEWARE THE CAPTIVE YOOP.

"Why, as for that," remarked Dorothy, "if Yoop is a captive there's no need to beware of him. Whatever Yoop happens to be, I'd much rather have him a captive than running around loose."

"So had I," agreed the Scarecrow, with a nod of his painted head.

"Still," said Scraps, reflectively:
"Yoop-te-hoop-te-loop-te-goop!
Who put noodles in the soup?
We may beware but we don't care,
And dare go where we scare the Yoop."

"Dear me! Aren't you feeling a little queer, just now?" Dorothy asked the Patchwork Girl.

"Not queer, but crazy," said Ojo. "When she says those things I'm sure her brains get mixed somehow and work the wrong way."

"I don't see why we are told to beware the Yoop unless he is dangerous," observed the Scarecrow in a puzzled tone.

"Never mind; we'll find out all about him when we get to where he is," replied the little girl.

The narrow canyon turned and twisted this way and that, and the rift was so small that they were able to touch both walls at the same time by stretching out their arms. Toto had run on ahead, frisking playfully, when suddenly he uttered a sharp bark of fear and came running back to them with his tail between his legs, as dogs do when they are frightened.

"Ah," said the Scarecrow, who was leading the way, "we must be near Yoop."

Just then, as he rounded a sharp turn, the Straw man stopped so suddenly that all the others bumped against him.

"What is it?" asked Dorothy, standing on tip-toes to look over his shoulder. But then she saw what it was and cried "Oh!" in a tone of astonishment.

In one of the rock walls—that at their left— was hollowed a great cavern, in front of which was a row of thick iron bars, the tops and bottoms being firmly fixed in the solid rock. Over this cavern was a big sign, which Dorothy read with much curiosity, speaking the words aloud that all might know what they said: "MISTER YOOP—HIS CAVE.

The Largest Untamed Giant in Captivity. Height, 21 Feet.— (And yet he has but 2 feet.) Weight, 1640 Pounds.— (But he waits all the time.) Age, 400 Years 'and Up' (as they say in the Department Store advertisements). Temper, Fierce and Ferocious.— (Except when asleep.) Appetite, Ravenous.— (Prefers Meat People and Orange Marmalade.)

STRANGERS APPROACHING THIS CAVE DO SO AT THEIR OWN PERIL!

P.S.—Don't feed the Giant yourself."

"Very well," said Ojo, with a sigh; "let's go back."

"It's a long way back," declared Dorothy.

"So it is," remarked the Scarecrow, "and it means a tedious climb over those sharp rocks if we can't use this passage. I think it will be best to run by the Giant's cave as fast as we can go. Mister Yoop seems to be asleep just now."

But the Giant wasn't asleep. He suddenly appeared at the front of his cavern, seized the iron bars in his great hairy hands and shook them until they rattled in their sockets. Yoop was so tall that our friends had to tip their heads way back to look into his face, and they noticed he was dressed all in pink velvet, with silver buttons and braid. The Giant's boots were of pink leather and had tassels on them and his hat was decorated with an enormous pink ostrich feather, carefully curled.

"Yo-ho!" he said in a deep bass voice; "I smell dinner."

"I think you are mistaken," replied the Scarecrow. "There is no orange marmalade around here."

"Ah, but I eat other things," asserted Mister Yoop. "That is, I eat them when I can get them. But this is a lonely place, and no good meat has passed by my cave for many years; so I'm hungry."

"Haven't you eaten anything in many years?" asked Dorothy.

"Nothing except six ants and a monkey. I thought the monkey would taste like meat people, but the flavor was different. I hope you will taste better, for you seem plump and tender."

"Oh, I'm not going to be eaten," said Dorothy.

"Why not?"

"I shall keep out of your way," she answered.

"How heartless!" wailed the Giant, shaking the bars again. "Consider how many years it is since I've eaten a single plump little girl! They tell me meat is going up, but if I can manage to catch you I'm sure it will soon be going down. And I'll catch you if I can."

With this the Giant pushed his big arms, which looked like tree-trunks (except that tree- trunks don't wear pink velvet) between the iron bars, and the arms were so long that they touched the opposite wall of the rock passage. Then he extended them as far as he could reach toward our travelers and found he could almost touch the Scarecrow—but not quite.

"Come a little nearer, please," begged the Giant.

"I'm a Scarecrow."

"A Scarecrow? Ugh! I don't care a straw for a scarecrow. Who is that bright-colored delicacy behind you?"

"Me?" asked Scraps. "I'm a Patchwork Girl, and I'm stuffed with cotton."

"Dear me," sighed the Giant in a disapointed tone; "that reduces my dinner from four to two— and the dog. I'll save the dog for dessert."

Toto growled, keeping a good distance away.

"Back up," said the Scarecrow to those behind him. "Let us go back a little way and talk this over."

So they turned and went around the bend in the passage, where they were out of sight of the cave and Mister Yoop could not hear them.

"My idea," began the Scarecrow, when they had halted, "is to make a dash past the cave, going on a run."

"He'd grab us," said Dorothy.

"Well, he can't grab but one at a time, and I'll go first. As soon as he grabs me the rest of you can slip past him, out of his reach, and he will soon let me go because I am not fit to eat."

They decided to try this plan and Dorothy took Toto in her arms, so as to protect him. She followed just after the Scarecrow. Then came Ojo, with Scraps the last of the four. Their hearts beat a little faster than usual as they again approached the Giant's cave, this time moving swiftly forward.

It turned out about the way the Scarecrow had planned. Mister Yoop was quite astonished to see them come flying toward him, and thrusting his arms between the bars he seized the Scarecrow in a firm grip. In the next instant he realized, from the way the straw crunched between his fingers, that he had captured the non-eatable man, but during that instant of delay Dorothy and Ojo had slipped by the Giant and were out of reach. Uttering a howl of rage the monster threw the Scarecrow after them with one hand and grabbed Scraps with the other.

The poor Scarecrow went whirling through the air and so cleverly was he aimed that he struck Ojo's back and sent the boy tumbling head over heels, and he tripped Dorothy and sent her, also, sprawling upon the ground. Toto flew out of the little girl's arms and landed some distance ahead, and all were so dazed that it was a moment before they could scramble to their feet again. When they did so they turned to look toward the Giant's cave, and at that moment the ferocious Mister Yoop threw the Patchwork Girl at them.

Down went all three again, in a heap, with Scraps on top. The Giant roared so terribly that for a time they were afraid he had broken loose; but he hadn't. So they sat in the road and looked at one another in a rather bewildered way, and then began to feel glad.

"We did it!" exclaimed the Scarecrow, with satisfaction. "And now we are free to go on our way."

"Mister Yoop is very impolite," declared Scraps. "He jarred me terribly. It's lucky my stitches are so fine and strong, for otherwise such harsh treatment might rip me up the back."

"Allow me to apologize for the Giant," said the Scarecrow, raising the Patchwork Girl to her feet and dusting her skirt with his stuffed hands. "Mister Yoop is a perfect stranger to me, but I fear, from the rude manner in which he has acted, that he is no gentleman."

Dorothy and Ojo laughed at this statement and Toto barked as if he understood the joke, after which they all felt better and resumed the journey in high spirits.

"Of course," said the little girl, when they had walked a way along the passage, "it was lucky for us the Giant was caged; for, if he had happened to be loose, he—he—"

"Perhaps, in that case, he wouldn't be hungry any more," said Ojo gravely.

21. Hip Hopper the Champion

They must have had good courage to climb all those rocks, for after getting out of the canyon they encountered more rock hills to be surmounted. Toto could jump from one rock to another quite easily, but the others had to creep and climb with care, so that after a whole day of such work Dorothy and Ojo found themselves very tired.

As they gazed upward at the great mass of tumbled rocks that covered the steep incline, Dorothy gave a little groan and said: "That's going to be a ter'ble hard climb, Scarecrow. I wish we could find the dark well without so much trouble."

"Suppose," said Ojo, "you wait here and let me do the climbing, for it's on my account we're searching for the dark well. Then, if I don't find anything, I'll come back and join you."

"No," replied the little girl, shaking her head positively, "we'll all go together, for that way we can help each other. If you went alone, something might happen to you, Ojo."

So they began the climb and found it indeed difficult, for a way. But presently, in creeping over the big crags, they found a path at their feet which wound in and out among the masses of rock and was quite smooth and easy to walk upon. As the path gradually ascended the mountain, although in a roundabout way, they decided to follow it.

"This must be the road to the Country of the Hoppers," said the Scarecrow.

"Who are the Hoppers?" asked Dorothy.

"Some people Jack Pumpkinhead told me about," he replied.

"I didn't hear him," replied the girl.

"No; you were asleep," explained the Scarecrow. "But he told Scraps and me that the Hoppers and the Horners live on this mountain."

"He said in the mountain," declared Scraps; "but of course he meant on it."

"Didn't he say what the Hoppers and Horners were like?" inquired Dorothy.

"No; he only said they were two separate nations, and that the Horners were the most important."

"Well, if we go to their country we'll find out all about 'em," said the girl. "But I've never heard Ozma mention those people, so they can't be very important."

"Is this mountain in the Land of Oz?" asked Scraps.

"Course it is," answered Dorothy. "It's in the South Country of the Quadlings. When one comes to the edge of Oz, in any direction, there is nothing more to be seen at all. Once you could see sandy desert all around Oz; but now it's diff'rent, and no other people can see us, any more than we can see them."

"If the mountain is under Ozma's rule, why doesn't she know about the Hoppers and the Horners?" Ojo asked.

"Why, it's a fairyland," explained Dorothy, "and lots of queer people live in places so tucked away that those in the Emerald City never even hear of 'em. In the middle of the country it's diff'rent, but when you get around the edges you're sure to run into strange little corners that surprise you. I know, for I've traveled in Oz a good deal, and so has the Scarecrow."

"Yes," admitted the straw man, "I've been considerable of a traveler, in my time, and I like to explore strange places. I find I learn much more by traveling than by staying at home."

During this conversation they had been walking up the steep pathway and now found themselves well up on the mountain. They could see nothing around them, for the rocks beside their path were higher than their heads. Nor could they see far in front of them, because the path was so crooked. But suddenly they stopped, because the path ended and there was no place to go. Ahead was a big rock lying against the side of the mountain, and this blocked the way completely.

"There wouldn't be a path, though, if it didn't go somewhere," said the Scarecrow, wrinkling his forehead in deep thought.

"This is somewhere, isn't it?" asked the Patchwork Girl, laughing at the bewildered looks of the others.
"The path is locked, the way is blocked,
Yet here we've innocently flocked;
And now we're here it's rather queer
There's no front door that can be knocked."

"Please don't, Scraps," said Ojo. "You make me nervous."

"Well," said Dorothy, "I'm glad of a little rest, for that's a drea'ful steep path."

As she spoke she leaned against the edge of the big rock that stood in their way. To her surprise it slowly swung backward and showed behind it a dark hole that looked like the mouth of a tunnel.

"Why, here's where the path goes to!" she exclaimed.

"So it is," answered the Scarecrow. "But the question is, do we want to go where the path does?"

"It's underground; right inside the mountain," said Ojo, peering into the dark hole. "Perhaps there's a well there; and, if there is, it's sure to be a dark one."

"Why, that's true enough!" cried Dorothy with eagerness. "Let's go in, Scarecrow; 'cause, if others have gone, we're pretty safe to go, too."

Toto looked in and barked, but he did not venture to enter until the Scarecrow had bravely gone first. Scraps followed closely after the straw man and then Ojo and Dorothy timidly stepped inside the tunnel. As soon as all of them had passed the big rock, it slowly turned and filled up the opening again; but now they were no longer in the dark, for a soft, rosy light enabled them to see around them quite distinctly.

It was only a passage, wide enough for two of them to walk abreast—with Toto in between them—and it had a high, arched roof. They could not see where the light which flooded the place so pleasantly came from, for there were no lamps anywhere visible. The passage ran straight for a little way and then made a bend to the right and another sharp turn to the left, after which it went straight again. But there were no side passages, so they could not lose their way.

After proceeding some distance, Toto, who had gone on ahead, began to bark loudly. They ran around a bend to see what was the matter and found a man sitting on the floor of the passage and leaning his back against the wall. He had probably been asleep before Toto's barks aroused him, for he was now rubbing his eyes and staring at the little dog with all his might.

There was something about this man that Toto objected to, and when he slowly rose to his foot they saw what it was. He had but one leg, set just below the middle of his round, fat body; but it was a stout leg and had a broad, flat foot at the bottom of it, on which the man seemed to stand very well. He had never had but this one leg, which looked something like a pedestal, and when Toto ran up and made a grab at the man's ankle he hopped first one way and then another in a very active manner, looking so frightened that Scraps laughed aloud.

Toto was usually a well behaved dog, but this time he was angry and snapped at the man's leg again and again. This filled the poor fellow with fear, and in hopping out of Toto's reach he suddenly lost his balance and tumbled heel over head upon the floor. When he sat up he kicked Toto on the nose and made the dog howl angrily, but Dorothy now ran forward and caught Toto's collar, holding him back.

"Do you surrender?" she asked the man.

"Who? Me?" asked the Hopper.

"Yes; you," said the little girl.

"Am I captured?" he inquired.

"Of course. My dog has captured you," she said.

"Well," replied the man, "if I'm captured I must surrender, fo it's the proper thing to do. I like to do everything proper, for i saves one a lot of trouble."

"It does, indeed," said Dorothy. "Please tell us who you are."

"I'm Hip Hopper—Hip Hopper, the Champion."

"Champion what?" she asked in surprise.

"Champion wrestler. I'm a very strong man, and that ferociou animal which you are so kindly holding is the first living thing that has ever conquered me."

"And you are a Hopper?" she continued.

"Yes. My people live in a great city not far from here. Would yo like to visit it?"

"I'm not sure," she said with hesitation. "Have you any dar wells in your city?"

"I think not. We have wells, you know, but they're all we lighted, and a well lighted well cannot well be a dark well. Bu there may be such a thing as a very dark well in the Horne Country, which is a black spot on the face of the earth."

"Where is the Horner Country?" Ojo inquired.

"The other side of the mountain. There's a fence between th Hopper Country and the Horner Country, and a gate in th fence; but you can't pass through just now, because we are at wa with the Horners."

"That's too bad," said the Scarecrow. "What seems to be th trouble?"

"Why, one of them made a very insulting remark about m people. He said we were lacking in understanding, because w had only one leg to a person. I can't see that legs have anythin to do with understanding things. The Horners each have tw legs, just as you have. That's one leg too many, it seems to me."

"No," declared Dorothy, "it's just the right number."

"You don't need them," argued the Hopper, obstinately. "You'v only one head, and one body, and one nose and mouth. Two leg are quite unnecessary, and they spoil one's shape."

"But how can you walk, with only one leg?" asked Ojo.

"Walk! Who wants to walk?" exclaimed the man. "Walking is terribly awkward way to travel. I hop, and so do all my people It's so much more graceful and agreeable than walking."

"I don't agree with you," said the Scarecrow. "But tell me, i there any way to get to the Horner Country without goin through the city of the Hoppers?"

"Yes; there is another path from the rocky lowlands, outside th mountain, that leads straight to the entrance of the Horne Country. But it's a long way around, so you'd better come wit me. Perhaps they will allow you to go through the gate; but w expect to conquer them this afternoon, if we get time, and the you may go and come as you please."

They thought it best to take the Hopper's advice, and asked hir to lead the way. This he did in a series of hops, and he moved s swiftly in this strange manner that those with two legs had to run to keep up with him.

22. The Joking Horners

It was not long before they left the passage and came to a great cave, so high that it must have reached nearly to the top of the mountain within which it lay. It was a magnificent cave, illumined by the soft, invisible light, so that everything in it could be plainly seen. The walls were of polished marble, white with veins of delicate colors running through it, and the roof was arched and fantastic and beautiful.

Built beneath this vast dome was a pretty village—not very large, for there seemed not more than fifty houses altogether—and the dwellings were of marble and artistically designed. No grass nor flowers nor trees grew in this cave, so the yards surrounding the houses carved in designs both were smooth and bare and had low walls around them to mark their boundaries.

In the streets and the yards of the houses were many people all having one leg growing below their bodies and all hopping here and there whenever they moved. Even the children stood firmly upon their single legs and never lost their balance.

"All hail, Champion!" cried a man in the first group of Hoppers they met; "whom have you captured?"

"No one," replied the Champion in a gloomy voice; "these strangers have captured me."

"Then," said another, "we will rescue you, and capture them, for we are greater in number."

"No," answered the Champion, "I can't allow it. I've surrendered, and it isn't polite to capture those you've surrendered to."

"Never mind that," said Dorothy. "We will give you your liberty and set you free."

"Really?" asked the Champion in joyous tones.

"Yes," said the little girl; "your people may need you to help conquer the Horners."

At this all the Hoppers looked downcast and sad. Several more had joined the group by this time and quite a crowd of curious men, women and children surrounded the strangers.

"This war with our neighbors is a terrible thing," remarked one of the women. "Some one is almost sure to get hurt."

"Why do you say that, madam?" inquired the Scarecrow.

"Because the horns of our enemies are sharp, and in battle they will try to stick those horns into our warriors," she replied.

"How many horns do the Horners have?" asked Dorothy.

"Each has one horn in the center of his forehead," was the answer.

"Oh, then they're unicorns," declared the Scarecrow.

"No; they're Horners. We never go to war with them if we can help it, on account of their dangerous horns; but this insult was so great and so unprovoked that our brave men decided to fight, in order to be revenged," said the woman.

"What weapons do you fight with?" the Scarecrow asked.

"We have no weapons," explained the Champion. "Whenever we fight the Horners, our plan is to push them back, for our arms are longer than theirs."

"Then you are better armed," said Scraps.

"Yes; but they have those terrible horns, and unless we are careful they prick us with the points," returned the Champion with a shudder. "That makes a war with them dangerous, and a dangerous war cannot be a pleasant one."

"I see very clearly," remarked the Scarecrow, "that you are going to have trouble in conquering those Horners—unless we help you."

"Oh!" cried the Hoppers in a chorus; "can you help us? Please do! We will be greatly obliged! It would please us very much!" and by these exclamations the Scarecrow knew that his speech had met with favor.

"How far is it to the Horner Country?" he asked.

"Why, it's just the other side of the fence," they answered, and the Champion added:

"Come with me, please, and I'll show you the Horners."

So they followed the Champion and several others through the streets and just beyond the village came to a very high picket fence, built all of marble, which seemed to divide the great cave into two equal parts.

But the part inhabited by the Horners was in no way as grand in appearance as that of the Hoppers. Instead of being marble, the walls and roof were of dull gray rock and the square houses were plainly made of the same material. But in extent the city was much larger than that of the Hoppers and the streets were thronged with numerous people who busied themselves in various ways.

Looking through the open pickets of the fence our friends watched the Horners, who did not know they were being watched by strangers, and found them very unusual in appearance. They were little folks in size and had bodies round as balls and short legs and arms. Their heads were round, too, and they had long, pointed ears and a horn set in the center of the forehead. The horns did not seem very terrible, for they were not more than six inches long; but they were ivory white and sharp pointed, and no wonder the Hoppers feared them.

The skins of the Horners were light brown, but they wore snow-white robes and were bare-footed. Dorothy thought the most striking thing about them was their hair, which grew in three distinct colors on each and every head—red, yellow and green. The red was at the bottom and sometimes hung over their eyes; then came a broad circle of yellow and the green was at the top and formed a brush-shaped top-knot.

None of the Horners was yet aware of the presence of strangers, who watched the little brown people for a time and then went to the big gate in the center of the dividing fence. It was locked on both sides and over the latch was a sign reading:

WAR IS DECLARED

"Can't we go through?" asked Dorothy.

"Not now," answered the Champion.

"I think," said the Scarecrow, "that if I could talk with those Horners they would apologize to you, and then there would be no need to fight."

"Can't you talk from this side?" asked the Champion.

"Not so well," replied the Scarecrow. "Do you suppose you could throw me over that fence? It is high, but I am very light."

"We can try it," said the Hopper. "I am perhaps the strongest man in my country, so I'll undertake to do the throwing. But I won't promise you will land on your feet."

"No matter about that," returned the Scarecrow. "Just toss me over and I'll be satisfied."

So the Champion picked up the Scarecrow and balanced him a moment, to see how much he weighed, and then with all his strength tossed him high into the air.

Perhaps if the Scarecrow had been a trifle heavier he would have been easier to throw and would have gone a greater distance; but, as it was, instead of going over the fence he landed just on top of it, and one of the sharp pickets caught him in the middle of his back and held him fast prisoner. Had he been face downward the Scarecrow might have managed to free himself, but lying on his back on the picket his hands waved in the air of the Horner Country while his feet kicked the air of the Hopper Country; so there he was.

"Are you hurt?" called the Patchwork Girl anxiously.

"Course not," said Dorothy. "But if he wiggles that way he may tear his clothes. How can we get him down, Mr. Champion?"

The Champion shook his head.

"I don't know," he confessed. "If he could scare Horners as well as he does crows, it might be a good idea to leave him there."

"This is terrible," said Ojo, almost ready to cry. "I s'pose it's because I am Ojo the Unlucky that everyone who tries to help me gets into trouble."

"You are lucky to have anyone to help you," declared Dorothy. "But don't worry. We'll rescue the Scarecrow somehow."

"I know how," announced Scraps. "Here, Mr. Champion; just throw me up to the Scarecrow. I'm nearly as light as he is, and when I'm on top the fence I'll pull our friend off the picket and toss him down to you."

"All right," said the Champion, and he picked up the Patchwork Girl and threw her in the same manner he had the Scarecrow. He must have used more strength this time, however, for Scraps sailed far over the top of the fence and, without being able to grab the Scarecrow at all, tumbled to the ground in the Horner Country, where her stuffed body knocked over two men and a woman and made a crowd that had collected there run like rabbits to get away from her.

Seeing the next moment that she was harmless, the people slowly returned and gathered around the Patchwork Girl, regarding her with astonishment. One of them wore a jeweled star in his hair, just above his horn, and this seemed a person of importance. He spoke for the rest of his people, who treated him with great respect.

"Who are you, Unknown Being?" he asked.

"Scraps," she said, rising to her feet and patting her cotton wadding smooth where it had bunched up.

"And where did you come from?" he continued.

"Over the fence. Don't be silly. There's no other place I could have come from," she replied.

He looked at her thoughtfully.

"You are not a Hopper," said he, "for you have two legs. They're not very well shaped, but they are two in number. And that strange creature on top the fence—why doesn't he stop kicking?—must be your brother, or father, or son, for he also has two legs."

"You must have been to visit the Wise Donkey," said Scraps, laughing so merrily that the crowd smiled with her, in sympathy. "But that reminds me, Captain—or King—"

"I am Chief of the Horners, and my name is Jak."

"Of course; Little Jack Horner; I might have known it. But the reason I volplaned over the fence was so I could have a talk with you about the Hoppers."

"What about the Hoppers?" asked the Chief, frowning.

"You've insulted them, and you'd better beg their pardon," said Scraps. "If you don't, they'll probably hop over here and conquer you."

"We're not afraid—as long as the gate is locked," declared the Chief. "And we didn't insult them at all. One of us made a joke that the stupid Hoppers couldn't see."

The Chief smiled as he said this and the smile made his face look quite jolly.

"What was the joke?" asked Scraps.

"A Horner said they have less understanding than we, because they've only one leg. Ha, ha! You see the point, don't you? If you stand on your legs, and your legs are under you, then—ha, ha, ha!— then your legs are your under-standing. Hee, hee, hee! Ho, ho! My, but that's a fine joke. And the stupid Hoppers couldn't see it! They couldn't see that with only one leg they must have less under-standing than we who have two legs. Ha, ha, ha! Hee, hee! Ho, ho!" The Chief wiped the tears of laughter from his eyes with the bottom hem of his white robe, and all the other Horners wiped their eyes on their robes, for they had laughed just as heartily as their Chief at the absurd joke.

"Then," said Scraps, "their understanding of the understanding you meant led to the misunderstanding."

"Exactly; and so there's no need for us to apologize," returned the Chief.

"No need for an apology, perhaps, but much need for an explanation," said Scraps decidedly. "You don't want war, do you?"

'Not if we can help it," admitted Jak Horner. "The question is, who's going to explain the joke to the Horners? You know it spoils any joke to be obliged to explain it, and this is the best joke I ever heard."

"Who made the joke?" asked Scraps.

'Diksey Horner. He is working in the mines, just now, but he'll be home before long. Suppose we wait and talk with him about it? Maybe he'll be willing to explain his joke to the Hoppers."

'All right," said Scraps. "I'll wait, if Diksey isn't too long."

'No, he's short; he's shorter than I am. Ha, ha, ha! Say! that's a better joke than Diksey's. He won't be too long, because he's short. Hee, hee, ho!"

The other Horners who were standing by roared with laughter and seemed to like their Chief's joke as much as he did. Scraps thought it was odd that they could be so easily amused, but decided there could be little harm in people who laughed so merrily.

23. Peace Is Declared

'Come with me to my dwelling and I'll introduce you to my daughters," said the Chief. "We're bringing them up according to a book of rules that was written by one of our leading old bachelors, and everyone says they're a remarkable lot of girls."

So Scraps accompanied him along the street to a house that seemed on the outside exceptionally grimy and dingy. The streets of this city were not paved nor had any attempt been made to beautify the houses or their surroundings, and having noticed this condition Scraps was astonished when the Chief ushered her into his home.

Here was nothing grimy or faded, indeed. On the contrary, the room was of dazzling brilliance and beauty, for it was lined throughout with an exquisite metal that resembled translucent frosted silver. The surface of this metal was highly ornamented in raised designs representing men, animals, flowers and trees, and from the metal itself was radiated the soft light which flooded the room. All the furniture was made of the same glorious metal, and Scraps asked what it was.

That's radium," answered the Chief. "We Horners spend all our time digging radium from the mines under this mountain, and we use it to decorate our homes and make them pretty and cosy. It is a medicine, too, and no one can ever be sick who lives near radium."

'Have you plenty of it?" asked the Patchwork Girl.

More than we can use. All the houses in this city are decorated with it, just the same as mine is."

Why don't you use it on your streets, then, and the outside of your houses, to make them as pretty as they are within?" she inquired.

'Outside? Who cares for the outside of anything?" asked the Chief. "We Horners don't live on the outside of our homes; we live inside. Many people are like those stupid Hoppers, who love to make an outside show. I suppose you strangers thought their city more beautiful than ours, because you judged from appearances and they have handsome marble houses and marble streets; but if you entered one of their stiff dwellings you would find it bare and uncomfortable, as all their show is on the outside. They have an idea that what is not seen by others is not important, but with us the rooms we live in are our chief delight and care, and we pay no attention to outside show."

"Seems to me," said Scraps, musingly, "it would be better to make it all pretty—inside and out."

"Seems? Why, you're all seams, my girl!" said the Chief; and then he laughed heartily at his latest joke and a chorus of small voices echoed the chorus with "tee-hee-hee! ha, ha!"

Scraps turned around and found a row of girls seated in radium chairs ranged along one wall of the room. There were nineteen of them, by actual count, and they were of all sizes from a tiny child to one almost a grown woman. All were neatly dressed in spotless white robes and had brown skins, horns on their foreheads and three-colored hair.

"These," said the Chief, "are my sweet daughters. My dears, I introduce to you Miss Scraps Patchwork, a lady who is traveling in foreign parts to increase her store of wisdom."

The nineteen Horner girls all arose and made a polite curtsey, after which they resumed their seats and rearranged their robes properly.

"Why do they sit so still, and all in a row?" asked Scraps.

"Because it is ladylike and proper," replied the Chief.

"But some are just children, poor things! Don't they ever run around and play and laugh, and have a good time?"

"No, indeed," said the Chief. "That would he improper in young ladies, as well as in those who will sometime become young ladies. My daughters are being brought up according to the rules and regulations laid down by a leading bachelor who has given the subject much study and is himself a man of taste and culture. Politeness is his great hobby, and he claims that if a child is allowed to do an impolite thing one cannot expect the grown person to do anything better."

"Is it impolite to romp and shout and be jolly?" asked Scraps.

"Well, sometimes it is, and sometimes it isn't," replied the Horner, after considering the question. "By curbing such inclinations in my daughters we keep on the safe side. Once in a while I make a good joke, as you have heard, and then I permit my daughters to laugh decorously; but they are never allowed to make a joke themselves."

"That old bachelor who made the rules ought to be skinned alive!" declared Scraps, and would have said more on the subject had not the door opened to admit a little Horner man whom the Chief introduced as Diksey.

"What's up, Chief?" asked Diksey, winking nineteen times at the nineteen girls, who demurely cast down their eyes because their father was looking.

The Chief told the man that his joke had not been understood by the dull Hoppers, who had become so angry that they had declared war. So the only way to avoid a terrible battle was to explain the joke so they could understand it.

"All right," replied Diksey, who seemed a good-natured man; "I'll go at once to the fence and explain. I don't want any war with the Hoppers, for wars between nations always cause hard feelings."

So the Chief and Diksey and Scraps left the house and went back to the marble picket fence. The Scarecrow was still stuck on the top of his picket but had now ceased to struggle. On the other side of the fence were Dorothy and Ojo, looking between the pickets; and there, also, were the Champion and many other Hoppers.

Diksey went close to the fence and said: "My good Hoppers, I wish to explain that what I said about you was a joke. You have but one leg each, and we have two legs each. Our legs are under us, whether one or two, and we stand on them. So, when I said you had less understanding than we, I did not mean that you had less understanding, you understand, but that you had less standundering, so to speak. Do you understand that?"

The Hoppers thought it over carefully. Then one said: "That is clear enough; but where does the joke come in?'"

Dorothy laughed, for she couldn't help it, although all the others were solemn enough.

"I'll tell you where the joke comes in," she said, and took the Hoppers away to a distance, where the Horners could not hear them. "You know," she then explained, "those neighbors of yours are not very bright, poor things, and what they think is a joke isn't a joke at all—it's true, don't you see?"

"True that we have less understanding?" asked the Champion.

"Yes; it's true because you don't understand such a poor joke; if you did, you'd be no wiser than they are."

"Ah, yes; of course," they answered, looking very wise.

"So I'll tell you what to do," continued Dorothy. "Laugh at their poor joke and tell 'em it's pretty good for a Horner. Then they won't dare say you have less understanding, because you understand as much as they do."

The Hoppers looked at one another questioningly and blinked their eyes and tried to think what it all meant; but they couldn't figure it out.

"What do you think, Champion?" asked one of them.

"I think it is dangerous to think of this thing any more than we can help," he replied. "Let us do as this girl says and laugh with the Horners, so as to make them believe we see the joke. Then there will be peace again and no need to fight."

They readily agreed to this and returned to the fence laughing as loud and as hard as they could, although they didn't feel like laughing a bit. The Horners were much surprised.

"That's a fine joke—for a Horner—and we are much pleased with it," said the Champion, speaking between the pickets. "But please don't do it again."

"I won't," promised Diksey. "If I think of another such joke I'll try to forget it."

"Good!" cried the Chief Horner. "The war is over and peace is declared."

There was much joyful shouting on both sides of the fence and the gate was unlocked and thrown wide open, so that Scraps was able to rejoin her friends.

"What about the Scarecrow?" she asked Dorothy.

"We must get him down, somehow or other," was the reply.

"Perhaps the Horners can find a way," suggested Ojo. So they all went through the gate and Dorothy asked the Chief Horner how they could get the Scarecrow off the fence. The Chief didn't know how, but Diksey said: "A ladder's the thing."

"Have you one?" asked Dorothy.

"To be sure. We use ladders in our mines," said he. Then he ran away to get the ladder, and while he was gone the Horners gathered around and welcomed the strangers to their country, for through them a great war had been avoided.

In a little while Diksey came back with a tall ladder which he placed against the fence. Ojo at once climbed to the top of the ladder and Dorothy went about halfway up and Scraps stood at the foot of it. Toto ran around it and barked. Then Ojo pulled the Scarecrow away from the picket and passed him down to Dorothy, who in turn lowered him to the Patchwork Girl.

As soon as he was on his feet and standing on solid ground the Scarecrow said: "Much obliged. I feel much better. I'm not stuck on that picket any more."

The Horners began to laugh, thinking this was a joke, but the Scarecrow shook himself and patted his straw a little and said to Dorothy: "Is there much of a hole in my back?"

The little girl examined him carefully.

"There's quite a hole," she said. "But I've got a needle and thread in the knapsack and I'll sew you up again."

"Do so," he begged earnestly, and again the Hoppers laughed, to the Scarecrow's great annoyance.

While Dorothy was sewing up the hole in the straw man's back Scraps examined the other parts of him.

"One of his legs is ripped, too!" she exclaimed.

"Oho!" cried little Diksey; "that's bad. Give him the needle and thread and let him mend his ways."

"Ha, ha, ha!" laughed the Chief, and the other Horners at once roared with laughter.

"What's funny?" inquired the Scarecrow sternly.

"Don't you see?" asked Diksey, who had laughed even harder than the others. "That's a joke. It's by odds the best joke I ever made. You walk with your legs, and so that's the way you walk, and your legs are the ways. See? So, when you mend your legs you mend your ways. Ho, ho, ho! hee, hee! I'd no idea I could make such a fine joke!"

"Just wonderful!" echoed the Chief. "How do you manage to do it, Diksey?"

"I don't know," said Diksey modestly. "Perhaps it's the radium, but I rather think it's my splendid intellect."

"If you don't quit it," the Scarecrow told him, "there'll be a worse war than the one you've escaped from."

Ojo had been deep in thought, and now he asked the Chief: "Is there a dark well in any part of your country?"

"A dark well? None that ever I heard of," was the answer.

"Oh, yes," said Diksey, who overheard the boy's question. "There's a very dark well down in my radium mine."

"Is there any water in it?" Ojo eagerly asked.

"Can't say; I've never looked to see. But we can find out."

So, as soon as the Scarecrow was mended, they decided to go with Diksey to the mine. When Dorothy had patted the straw man into shape again he declared he felt as good as new and equal to further adventures.

"Still," said he, "I prefer not to do picket duty again. High life doesn't seem to agree with my constitution." And then they hurried away to escape the laughter of the Horners, who thought this was another joke.

24. Ojo Finds the Dark Well

They now followed Diksey to the farther end of the great cave, beyond the Horner city, where there were several round, dark holes leading into the ground in a slanting direction. Diksey went to one of these holes and said: "Here is the mine in which lies the dark well you are seeking. Follow me and step carefully and I'll lead you to the place."

He went in first and after him came Ojo, and then Dorothy, with the Scarecrow behind her. The Patchwork Girl entered last of all, for Toto kept close beside his little mistress.

A few steps beyond the mouth of the opening it was pitch dark. "You won't lose your way, though," said the Horner, "for there's only one way to go. The mine's mine and I know every step of the way. How's that for a joke, eh? The mine's mine." Then he chuckled gleefully as they followed him silently down the steep slant. The hole was just big enough to permit them to walk upright, although the Scarecrow, being much the taller of the party, often had to bend his head to keep from hitting the top.

The floor of the tunnel was difficult to walk upon because it had been worn smooth as glass, and pretty soon Scraps, who was some distance behind the others, slipped and fell head foremost. At once she began to slide downward, so swiftly that when she came to the Scarecrow she knocked him off his feet and sent him tumbling against Dorothy, who tripped up Ojo. The boy fell against the Horner, so that all went tumbling down the slide in a regular mix-up, unable to see where they were going because of the darkness.

Fortunately, when they reached the bottom the Scarecrow and Scraps were in front, and the others bumped against them, so that no one was hurt. They found themselves in a vast cave which was dimly lighted by the tiny grains of radium that lay scattered among the loose rocks.

"Now," said Diksey, when they had all regained their feet, "I will show you where the dark well is. This is a big place, but if we hold fast to each other we won't get lost."

They took hold of hands and the Horner led them into a dark corner, where he halted.

"Be careful," said he warningly. "The well is at your feet."

"All right," replied Ojo, and kneeling down he felt in the well with his hand and found that it contained a quantity of water. "Where's the gold flask, Dorothy?" he asked, and the little girl handed him the flask, which she had brought with her.

Ojo knelt again and by feeling carefully in the dark managed to fill the flask with the unseen water that was in the well. Then he screwed the top of the flask firmly in place and put the precious water in his pocket.

"All right!" he said again, in a glad voice; "now we can go back."

They returned to the mouth of the tunnel and began to creep cautiously up the incline. This time they made Scraps stay behind, for fear she would slip again; but they all managed to get up in safety and the Munchkin boy was very happy when he stood in the Horner city and realized that the water from the dark well, which he and his friends had traveled so far to secure, was safe in his jacket pocket.

25. They Bribe the Lazy Quadling

"Now," said Dorothy, as they stood on the mountain path, having left behind them the cave in which dwelt the Hoppers and the Horners, "I think we must find a road into the Country of the Winkies, for there is where Ojo wants to go next."

"Is there such a road?" asked the Scarecrow.

"I don't know," she replied. "I s'pose we can go back the way we came, to Jack Pumpkinhead's house, and then turn into the Winkie Country; but that seems like running 'round a haystack, doesn't it?"

"Yes," said the Scarecrow. "What is the next thing Ojo must get?"

"A yellow butterfly," answered the boy.

"That means the Winkie Country, all right, for it's the yellow country of Oz," remarked Dorothy. "I think, Scarecrow, we ought to take him to the Tin Woodman, for he's the Emp'ror of the Winkies and will help us to find what Ojo wants."

"Of course," replied the Scarecrow, brightening at the suggestion. "The Tin Woodman will do anything we ask him, for he's one of my dearest friends. I believe we can take a crosscut into his country and so get to his castle a day sooner than if we travel back the way we came."

"I think so, too," said the girl; "and that means we must keep to the left."

They were obliged to go down the mountain before they found any path that led in the direction they wanted to go, but among the tumbled rocks at the foot of the mountain was a faint trail which they decided to follow. Two or three hours walk along this trail brought them to a clear, level country, where there were a few farms and some scattered houses. But they knew they were still in the Country of the Quadlings, because everything had a bright red color. Not that the trees and grasses were red, but the fences and houses were painted that color and all the wild-flowers that bloomed by the wayside had red blossoms. This part of the Quadling Country seemed peaceful and prosperous, if rather lonely, and the road was more distinct and easier to follow.

But just as they were congratulating themselves upon the progress they had made they came upon a broad river which swept along between high banks, and here the road ended and there was no bridge of any sort to allow them to cross.

"This is queer," mused Dorothy, looking at the water reflectively. "Why should there be any road, if the river stops everyone walking along it?"

"Wow!" said Toto, gazing earnestly into her face.

"That's the best answer you'll get," declared the Scarecrow, with his comical smile, "for no one knows any more than Toto about this road."

Said Scraps:
"Ev'ry time I see a river,
I have chills that make me shiver,
For I never can forget
All the water's very wet.

If my patches get a soak
It will be a sorry joke;
So to swim I'll never try
Till I find the water dry."

"Try to control yourself, Scraps," said Ojo; "you're getting crazy again. No one intends to swim that river."

"No," decided Dorothy, "we couldn't swim it if we tried. It's too big a river, and the water moves awful fast."

"There ought to be a ferryman with a boat," said the Scarecrow; "but I don't see any."

"Couldn't we make a raft?" suggested Ojo.

"There's nothing to make one of," answered Dorothy.

"Wow!" said Toto again, and Dorothy saw he was looking along the bank of the river.

"Why, he sees a house over there!" cried the little girl. "I wonder we didn't notice it ourselves. Let's go and ask the people how to get 'cross the river."

A quarter of a mile along the bank stood a small, round house, painted bright red, and as it was on their side of the river they hurried toward it. A chubby little man, dressed all in red, came out to greet them, and with him were two children, also in red costumes. The man's eyes were big and staring as he examined the Scarecrow and the Patchwork Girl, and the children shyly hid behind him and peeked timidly at Toto.

"Do you live here, my good man?" asked the Scarecrow.

"I think I do, Most Mighty Magician," replied the Quadling, bowing low; "but whether I'm awake or dreaming I can't be positive, so I'm not sure where I live. If you'll kindly pinch me I'll find out all about it!"

"You're awake," said Dorothy, "and this is no magician, but just the Scarecrow."

"But he's alive," protested the man, "and he oughtn't to be, you know. And that other dreadful person—the girl who is all

patches—seems to be alive, too."

"Very much so," declared Scraps, making a face at him. "But that isn't your affair, you know."

"I've a right to be surprised, haven't I?" asked the man meekly.

"I'm not sure; but anyhow you've no right to say I'm dreadful. The Scarecrow, who is a gentleman of great wisdom, thinks I'm beautiful," retorted Scraps.

"Never mind all that," said Dorothy. "Tell us, good Quadling, how we can get across the river."

"I don't know," replied the Quadling.

"Don't you ever cross it?" asked the girl.

"Never."

"Don't travelers cross it?"

"Not to my knowledge," said he.

They were much surprised to hear this, and the man added: "It's a pretty big river, and the current is strong. I know a man who lives on the opposite bank, for I've seen him there a good many years; but we've never spoken because neither of us has ever crossed over."

"That's queer," said the Scarecrow. "Don't you own a boat?"

The man shook his head.

"Nor a raft?"

"Where does this river go to?" asked Dorothy.

"That way," answered the man, pointing with one hand, "it goes into the Country of the Winkies, which is ruled by the Tin Emperor, who must be a mighty magician because he's all made of tin, and yet he's alive. And that way," pointing with the other hand, "the river runs between two mountains where dangerous people dwell."

The Scarecrow looked at the water before them.

"The current flows toward the Winkie Country," said he; "and so, if we had a boat, or a raft, the river would float us there more quickly and more easily than we could walk."

"That is true," agreed Dorothy; and then they all looked thoughtful and wondered what could be done.

"Why can't the man make us a raft?" asked Ojo.

"Will you?" inquired Dorothy, turning to the Quadling.

The chubby man shook his head.

"I'm too lazy," he said. "My wife says I'm the laziest man in all Oz, and she is a truthful woman. I hate work of any kind, and making a raft is hard work."

"I'll give you my em'rald ring," promised the girl.

"No; I don't care for emeralds. If it were a ruby, which is the color I like best, I might work a little while."

"I've got some Square Meal Tablets," said the Scarecrow. "Each one is the same as a dish of soup, a fried fish, a mutton pot-pie, lobster salad, charlotte russe and lemon jelly—all made into one little tablet that you can swallow without trouble."

"Without trouble!" exclaimed the Quadling, much interested; "then those tablets would be fine for a lazy man. It's such hard work to chew when you eat."

"I'll give you six of those tablets if you'll help us make a raft," promised the Scarecrow. "They're a combination of food which people who eat are very fond of. I never eat, you know, being straw; but some of my friends eat regularly. What do you say to my offer, Quadling?"

"I'll do it," decided the man. "I'll help, and you can do most of the work. But my wife has gone fishing for red eels to-day, so some of you will have to mind the children."

Scraps promised to do that, and the children were not so shy when the Patchwork Girl sat down to play with them. They grew to like Toto, too, and the little dog allowed them to pat him on his head, which gave the little ones much joy.

There were a number of fallen trees near the house and the Quadling got his axe and chopped them into logs of equal length. He took his wife's clothesline to bind these logs together, so that they would form a raft, and Ojo found some strips of wood and nailed them along the tops of the logs, to render them more firm. The Scarecrow and Dorothy helped roll the logs together and carry the strips of wood, but it took so long to make the raft that evening came just as it was finished, and with evening the Quadling's wife returned from her fishing.

The woman proved to be cross and bad-tempered, perhaps because she had only caught one red eel during all the day. When she found that her husband had used her clothesline, and the logs she had wanted for firewood, and the boards she had intended to mend the shed with, and a lot of gold nails, she became very angry. Scraps wanted to shake the woman, to make her behave, but Dorothy talked to her in a gentle tone and told the Quadling's wife she was a Princess of Oz and a friend of Ozma and that when she got back to the Emerald City she would send them a lot of things to repay them for the raft, including a new clothesline. This promise pleased the woman and she soon became more pleasant, saying they could stay the night at her house and begin their voyage on the river next morning.

This they did, spending a pleasant evening with the Quadling family and being entertained with such hospitality as the poor people were able to offer them. The man groaned a good deal and said he had overworked himself by chopping the logs, but the Scarecrow gave him two more tablets than he had promised, which seemed to comfort the lazy fellow.

26. The Trick River

Next morning they pushed the raft into the water and all got aboard. The Quadling man had to hold the log craft fast while they took their places, and the flow of the river was so powerful that it nearly tore the raft from his hands. As soon as they were all seated upon the logs he let go and away it floated and the adventurers had begun their voyage toward the Winkie Country.

The little house of the Quadlings was out of sight almost before they had cried their good-byes, and the Scarecrow said in a pleased voice: "It won't take us long to get to the Winkie Country, at this rate."

They had floated several miles down the stream and were enjoying the ride when suddenly the raft slowed up, stopped short, and then began to float back the way it had come.

"Why, what's wrong?" asked Dorothy, in astonishment; but they were all just as bewildered as she was and at first no one could answer the question. Soon, however, they realized the truth: that the current of the river had reversed and the water was now flowing in the opposite direction— toward the mountains.

They began to recognize the scenes they had passed, and by and by they came in sight of the little house of the Quadlings again. The man was standing on the river bank and he called to them: "How do you do? Glad to see you again. I forgot to tell you that the river changes its direction every little while. Sometimes it flows one way, and sometimes the other."

They had no time to answer him, for the raft was swept past the house and a long distance on the other side of it.

"We're going just the way we don't want to go," said Dorothy, "and I guess the best thing we can do is to get to land before we're carried any farther."

But they could not get to land. They had no oars, nor even a pole to guide the raft with. The logs which bore them floated in the middle of the stream and were held fast in that position by the strong current.

So they sat still and waited and, even while they were wondering what could be done, the raft slowed down, stopped, and began drifting the other way—in the direction it had first followed. After a time they repassed the Quadling house and the man was still standing on the bank. He cried out to them: "Good day! Glad to see you again. I expect I shall see you a good many times, as you go by, unless you happen to swim ashore."

By that time they had left him behind and were headed once more straight toward the Winkie Country.

"This is pretty hard luck," said Ojo in a discouraged voice. "The Trick River keeps changing, it seems, and here we must float back and forward forever, unless we manage in some way to get ashore."

"Can you swim?" asked Dorothy.

"No; I'm Ojo the Unlucky."

"Neither can I. Toto can swim a little, but that won't help us to get to shore."

"I don't know whether I could swim, or not," remarked Scraps; "but if I tried it I'd surely ruin my lovely patches."

"My straw would get soggy in the water and I would sink," said the Scarecrow.

So there seemed no way out of their dilemma and being helpless they simply sat still. Ojo, who was on the front of the raft, looked over into the water and thought he saw some large fishes swimming about. He found a loose end of the clothesline which fastened the logs together, and taking a gold nail from his pocket he bent it nearly double, to form a hook, and tied it to the end of the line. Having baited the hook with some bread which he broke from his loaf, he dropped the line into the water and almost instantly it was seized by a great fish.

They knew it was a great fish, because it pulled so hard on the line that it dragged the raft forward even faster than the current of the river had carried it. The fish was frightened, and it was a strong swimmer. As the other end of the clothesline was bound around the logs he could not get it away, and as he had greedily swallowed the gold hook at the first bite he could not get rid of that, either.

When they reached the place where the current had before changed, the fish was still swimming ahead in its wild attempt to escape. The raft slowed down, yet it did not stop, because the fish would not let it. It continued to move in the same direction it had been going. As the current reversed and rushed backward on its course it failed to drag the raft with it. Slowly, inch by inch, they floated on, and the fish tugged and tugged and kept them going.

"I hope he won't give up," said Ojo anxiously. "If the fish can hold out until the current changes again, we'll be all right."

The fish did not give up, but held the raft bravely on its course, till at last the water in the river shifted again and floated them the way they wanted to go. But now the captive fish found its strength failing. Seeking a refuge, it began to drag the raft toward the shore. As they did not wish to land in this place the boy cut the rope with his pocket-knife and set the fish free, just in time to prevent the raft from grounding.

The next time the river backed up the Scarecrow managed to seize the branch of a tree that overhung the water and they all assisted him to hold fast and prevent the raft from being carried backward. While they waited here, Ojo spied a long broken branch lying upon the bank, so he leaped ashore and got it. When he had stripped off the side shoots he believed he could use the branch as a pole, to guide the raft in case of emergency.

They clung to the tree until they found the water flowing the right way, when they let go and permitted the raft to resume its voyage. In spite of these pauses they were really making good progress toward the Winkie Country and having found a way to conquer the adverse current their spirits rose considerably. They could see little of the country through which they were passing, because of the high banks, and they met with no boats or other craft upon the surface of the river.

Once more the trick river reversed its current, but this time the Scarecrow was on guard and used the pole to push the raft toward a big rock which lay in the water. He believed the rock would prevent their floating backward with the current, and so it did. They clung to this anchorage until the water resumed its proper direction, when they allowed the raft to drift on.

Floating around a bend they saw ahead a high bank of water, extending across the entire river, and toward this they were being irresistibly carried. There being no way to arrest the progress of the raft they clung fast to the logs and let the river sweep them on. Swiftly the raft climbed the bank of water and slid down on the other side, plunging its edge deep into the water and drenching them all with spray.

As again the raft righted and drifted on, Dorothy and Ojo laughed at the ducking they had received; but Scraps was much dismayed and the Scarecrow took out his handkerchief and wiped the water off the Patchwork Girl's patches as well as he was able to. The sun soon dried her and the colors of her patches proved good, for they did not run together nor did they fade.

After passing the wall of water the current did not change or flow backward any more but continued to sweep them steadily forward. The banks of the river grew lower, too, permitting them to see more of the country, and presently they discovered yellow buttercups and dandelions growing amongst the grass, from which evidence they knew they had reached the Winkie Country.

"Don't you think we ought to land?" Dorothy asked the Scarecrow.

"Pretty soon," he replied. "The Tin Woodman's castle is in the southern part of the Winkie Country, and so it can't be a great way from here."

Fearing they might drift too far, Dorothy and Ojo now stood up and raised the Scarecrow in their arms, as high as they could, thus allowing him a good view of the country. For a time he saw nothing he recognized, but finally he cried: "There it is! There it is!"

"What?" asked Dorothy.

"The Tin Woodman's tin castle. I can see its turrets glittering in the sun. It's quite a way off, but we'd better land as quickly as we can."

They let him down and began to urge the raft toward the shore by means of the pole. It obeyed very well, for the current was more sluggish now, and soon they had reached the bank and landed safely.

The Winkie Country was really beautiful, and across the fields they could see afar the silvery sheen of the tin castle. With light hearts they hurried toward it, being fully rested by their long ride on the river.

By and by they began to cross an immense field of splendid yellow lilies, the delicate fragrance of which was very delightful.

"How beautiful they are!" cried Dorothy, stopping to admire the perfection of these exquisite flowers.

"Yes," said the Scarecrow, reflectively, "but we must be careful not to crush or injure any of these lilies."

"Why not?" asked Ojo.

"The Tin Woodman is very kind-hearted," was the reply, "and he hates to see any living thing hurt in any way."

"Are flowers alive?" asked Scraps.

"Yes, of course. And these flowers belong to the Tin Woodman. So, in order not to offend him, we must not tread on a single blossom."

"Once," said Dorothy, "the Tin Woodman stepped on a beetle and killed the little creature. That made him very unhappy and he cried until his tears rusted his joints, so he couldn't move 'em."

"What did he do then?" asked Ojo.

"Put oil on them, until the joints worked smooth again."

"Oh!" exclaimed the boy, as if a great discovery had flashed across his mind. But he did not tell anybody what the discovery was and kept the idea to himself.

It was a long walk, but a pleasant one, and they did not mind it a bit. Late in the afternoon they drew near to the wonderful tin castle of the Emperor of the Winkies, and Ojo and Scraps, who had never seen it before, were filled with amazement.

Tin abounded in the Winkie Country and the Winkies were said to be the most skillful tinsmiths in all the world. So the Tin Woodman had employed them in building his magnificent castle, which was all of tin, from the ground to the tallest turret, and so brightly polished that it glittered in the sun's rays more gorgeously than silver. Around the grounds of the castle ran a tin wall, with tin gates; but the gates stood wide open because the Emperor had no enemies to disturb him.

When they entered the spacious grounds our travelers found more to admire. Tin fountains sent sprays of clear water far into the air and there were many beds of tin flowers, all as perfectly formed as any natural flowers might be. There were tin trees, too, and here and there shady bowers of tin, with tin benches and chairs to sit upon. Also, on the sides of the pathway leading up to the front door of the castle, were rows of tin statuary, very cleverly executed. Among these Ojo recognized statues of Dorothy, Toto, the Scarecrow, the Wizard, the Shaggy Man, Jack Pumpkinhead and Ozma, all standing upon neat pedestals of tin.

Toto was well acquainted with the residence of the Tin Woodman and, being assured a joyful welcome, he ran ahead and barked so loudly at the front door that the Tin Woodman heard him and came out in person to see if it were really his old friend Toto. Next moment the tin man had clasped the Scarecrow in a warm embrace and then turned to hug Dorothy. But now his eye was arrested by the strange sight of the Patchwork Girl, and he gazed upon her in mingled wonder and admiration.

27. The Tin Woodman Objects

The Tin Woodman was one of the most important personages in all Oz. Though Emperor of the Winkies, he owed allegiance to Ozma, who ruled all the land, and the girl and the tin man were warm personal friends. He was something of a dandy and kept his tin body brilliantly polished and his tin joints well oiled. Also he was very courteous in manner and so kind and gentle that everyone loved him. The Emperor greeted Ojo and Scraps with cordial hospitality and ushered the entire party into his handsome tin parlor, where all the furniture and pictures were made of tin. The walls were paneled with tin and from the tin ceiling hung tin chandeliers.

The Tin Woodman wanted to know, first of all, where Dorothy had found the Patchwork Girl, so between them the visitors told the story of how Scraps was made, as well as the accident to Margolotte and Unc Nunkie and how Ojo had set out upon a journey to procure the things needed for the Crooked Magician's magic charm. Then Dorothy told of their adventures in the Quadling Country and how at last they succeeded in getting the water from a dark well.

While the little girl was relating these adventures the Tin Woodman sat in an easy chair listening with intense interest, while the others sat grouped around him. Ojo, however, had kept his eyes fixed upon the body of the tin Emperor, and now he noticed that under the joint of his left knee a tiny drop of oil was forming. He watched this drop of oil with a fast-beating heart, and feeling in his pocket brought out a tiny vial of crystal, which he held secreted in his hand.

Presently the Tin Woodman changed his position, and at once Ojo, to the astonishment of all, dropped to the floor and held his crystal vial under the Emperor's knee joint. Just then the drop of oil fell, and the boy caught it in his bottle and immediately corked it tight. Then, with a red face and embarrassed manner, he rose to confront the others.

"What in the world were you doing?" asked the Tin Woodman.

"I caught a drop of oil that fell from your knee-joint," confessed Ojo.

"A drop of oil!" exclaimed the Tin Woodman. "Dear me, how careless my valet must have been in oiling me this morning. I'm afraid I shall have to scold the fellow, for I can't be dropping oil wherever I go."

"Never mind," said Dorothy. "Ojo seems glad to have the oil, for some reason."

"Yes," declared the Munchkin boy, "I am glad. For one of the things the Crooked Magician sent me to get was a drop of oil from a live man's body. I had no idea, at first, that there was such a thing; but it's now safe in the little crystal vial."

"You are very welcome to it, indeed," said the Tin Woodman. "Have you now secured all the things you were in search of?"

"Not quite all," answered Ojo. "There were five things I had to get, and I have found four of them. I have the three hairs in the tip of a Woozy's tail, a six-leaved clover, a gill of water from a dark well and a drop of oil from a live man's body. The last thing is the easiest of all to get, and I'm sure that my dear Unc Nunkie—and good Margolotte, as well—will soon be restored to life."

The Munchkin boy said this with much pride and pleasure.

"Good!" exclaimed the Tin Woodman; "I congratulate you. But what is the fifth and last thing you need, in order to complete the magic charm?"

"The left wing of a yellow butterfly," said Ojo. "In this yellow country, and with your kind assistance, that ought to be very easy to find."

The Tin Woodman stared at him in amazement.

"Surely you are joking!" he said.

"No," replied Ojo, much surprised; "I am in earnest."

"But do you think for a moment that I would permit you, or anyone else, to pull the left wing from a yellow butterfly?" demanded the Tin Woodman sternly.

"Why not, sir?"

"Why not? You ask me why not? It would be cruel—one of the most cruel and heartless deeds I ever heard of," asserted the Tin Woodman. "The butterflies are among the prettiest of all created things, and they are very sensitive to pain. To tear a wing from one would cause it exquisite torture and it would soon die in great agony. I would not permit such a wicked deed under any circumstances!"

Ojo was astounded at hearing this. Dorothy, too, looked grave and disconcerted, but she knew in her heart that the Tin Woodman was right. The Scarecrow nodded his head in approval of his friend's speech, so it was evident that he agreed with the Emperor's decision. Scraps looked from one to another in perplexity.

"Who cares for a butterfly?" she asked.

"Don't you?" inquired the Tin Woodman.

"Not the snap of a finger, for I have no heart," said the Patchwork Girl. "But I want to help Ojo, who is my friend, to rescue the uncle whom he loves, and I'd kill a dozen useless butterflies to enable him to do that."

The Tin Woodman sighed regretfully.

"You have kind instincts," he said, "and with a heart you would indeed be a fine creature. I cannot blame you for your heartless remark, as you cannot understand the feelings of those who possess hearts. I, for instance, have a very neat and responsive heart which the wonderful Wizard of Oz once gave me, and so I shall never—never— never permit a poor yellow butterfly to be tortured by anyone."

"The yellow country of the Winkies," said Ojo sadly, "is the only place in Oz where a yellow butterfly can be found."

"I'm glad of that," said the Tin Woodman. "As I rule the Winkie Country, I can protect my butterflies."

"Unless I get the wing—just one left wing—" said Ojo miserably, "I can't save Unc Nunkie."

"Then he must remain a marble statue forever," declared the Tin Emperor, firmly.

Ojo wiped his eyes, for he could not hold back the tears.

"I'll tell you what to do," said Scraps. "We'll take a whole yellow butterfly, alive and well, to the Crooked Magician, and let him pull the left wing off."

"No, you won't," said the Tin Woodman. "You can't have one of my dear little butterflies to treat in that way."

"Then what in the world shall we do?" asked Dorothy.

They all became silent and thoughtful. No one spoke for a long time. Then the Tin Woodman suddenly roused himself and said:

"We must all go back to the Emerald City and ask Ozma's advice. She's a wise little girl, our Ruler, and she may find a way to help Ojo save his Unc Nunkie."

So the following morning the party started on the journey to the Emerald City, which they reached in due time without any important adventure. It was a sad journey for Ojo, for without the wing of the yellow butterfly he saw no way to save Unc Nunkie—unless he waited six years for the Crooked Magician to make a new lot of the Powder of Life. The boy was utterly discouraged, and as he walked along he groaned aloud.

"Is anything hurting you?" inquired the Tin Woodman in a kindly tone, for the Emperor was with the party.

"I'm Ojo the Unlucky," replied the boy. "I might have known I would fail in anything I tried to do."

"Why are you Ojo the Unlucky?" asked the tin man.

"Because I was born on a Friday."

"Friday is not unlucky," declared the Emperor. "It's just one of seven days. Do you suppose all the world becomes unlucky one-seventh of the time?"

"It was the thirteenth day of the month," said Ojo.

"Thirteen! Ah, that is indeed a lucky number," replied the Tin Woodman. "All my good luck seems to happen on the thirteenth. I suppose most people never notice the good luck that comes to them with the number 13, and yet if the least bit of bad luck falls on that day, they blame it to the number, and not to the proper cause."

"Thirteen's my lucky number, too," remarked the Scarecrow.

"And mine," said Scraps. "I've just thirteen patches on my head."

"But," continued Ojo, "I'm left-handed."

"Many of our greatest men are that way," asserted the Emperor. "To be left-handed is usually to be two-handed; the right-handed people are usually one-handed."

"And I've a wart under my right arm," said Ojo.

"How lucky!" cried the Tin Woodman. "If it were on the end of your nose it might be unlucky, but under your arm it is luckily out of the way."

"For all those reasons," said the Munchkin boy, "I have been called Ojo the Unlucky."

"Then we must turn over a new leaf and call you henceforth Ojo the Lucky," declared the tin man. "Every reason you have given is absurd. But I have noticed that those who continually dread ill luck and fear it will overtake them, have no time to take advantage of any good fortune that comes their way. Make up your mind to be Ojo the Lucky."

"How can I?" asked the boy, "when all my attempts to save my dear uncle have failed?"

"Never give up, Ojo," advised Dorothy. "No one ever knows what's going to happen next."

Ojo did not reply, but he was so dejected that even their arrival at the Emerald City failed to interest him.

The people joyfully cheered the appearance of the Tin Woodman, the Scarecrow and Dorothy, who were all three general favorites, and on entering the royal palace word came to them from Ozma that she would at once grant them an audience.

Dorothy told the girl Ruler how successful they had been in their quest until they came to the item of the yellow butterfly, which the Tin Woodman positively refused to sacrifice to the magic potion.

"He is quite right," said Ozma, who did not seem a bit surprised. "Had Ojo told me that one of the things he sought was the wing of a yellow butterfly I would have informed him, before he started out, that he could never secure it. Then you would have been saved the troubles and annoyances of your long journey."

"I didn't mind the journey at all," said Dorothy; "it was fun."

"As it has turned out," remarked Ojo, "I can never get the things the Crooked Magician sent me for; and so, unless I wait the six years for him to make the Powder of Life, Unc Nunkie cannot be saved."

Ozma smiled.

"Dr. Pipt will make no more Powder of Life, I promise you," said she. "I have sent for him and had him brought to this palace, where he now is, and his four kettles have been destroyed and his book of recipes burned up. I have also had brought here the marble statues of your uncle and of Margolotte, which are standing in the next room."

They were all greatly astonished at this announcement.

"Oh, let me see Unc Nunkie! Let me see him at once, please!" cried Ojo eagerly.

"Wait a moment," replied Ozma, "for I have something more to say. Nothing that happens in the Land of Oz escapes the notice of our wise Sorceress, Glinda the Good. She knew all about the magic-making of Dr. Pipt, and how he had brought the Glass Cat and the Patchwork Girl to life, and the accident to Unc Nunkie and Margolotte, and of Ojo's quest and his journey with Dorothy. Glinda also knew that Ojo would fail to find all the things he sought, so she sent for our Wizard and instructed him what to do. Something is going to happen in this palace, presently, and that 'something' will, I am sure, please you all. And now," continued the girl Ruler, rising from her chair, "you may follow me into the next room."

28. The Wonderful Wizard of Oz

When Ojo entered the room he ran quickly to the statue of Unc Nunkie and kissed the marble face affectionately.

"I did my best, Unc," he said, with a sob, "but it was no use!"

Then he drew back and looked around the room, and the sight of the assembled company quite amazed him.

Aside from the marble statues of Unc Nunkie and Margolotte, the Glass Cat was there, curled up on a rug; and the Woozy was there, sitting on its square hind legs and looking on the scene with solemn interest; and there was the Shaggy Man, in a suit of shaggy pea-green satin, and at a table sat the little Wizard, looking quite important and as if he knew much more than he cared to tell.

Last of all, Dr. Pipt was there, and the Crooked Magician sat humped up in a chair, seeming very dejected but keeping his eyes fixed on the lifeless form of his wife Margolotte, whom he fondly loved but whom he now feared was lost to him forever.

Ozma took a chair which Jellia Jamb wheeled forward for the Ruler, and back of her stood the Scarecrow, the Tin Woodman and Dorothy, as well as the Cowardly Lion and the Hungry Tiger. The Wizard now arose and made a low bow to Ozma and another less deferent bow to the assembled company.

Ladies and gentlemen and beasts," he said, "I beg to announce that our Gracious Ruler has permitted me to obey the commands of the great Sorceress, Glinda the Good, whose humble Assistant am proud to be. We have discovered that the Crooked Magician has been indulging in his magical arts contrary to Law, and therefore, by Royal Edict, I hereby deprive him of all power to work magic in the future. He is no longer a crooked magician, but a simple Munchkin; he is no longer even crooked, but a man like other men."

As he pronounced these words the Wizard waved his hand toward Dr. Pipt and instantly every crooked limb straightened out and became perfect. The former magician, with a cry of joy, sprang to his feet, looked at himself in wonder, and then fell back in his chair and watched the Wizard with fascinated interest.

"The Glass Cat, which Dr. Pipt lawlessly made," continued the Wizard, "is a pretty cat, but its pink brains made it so conceited that it was a disagreeable companion to everyone. So the other day I took away the pink brains and replaced them with transparent ones, and now the Glass Cat is so modest and well behaved that Ozma has decided to keep her in the palace as a pet."

"I thank you," said the cat, in a soft voice.

"The Woozy has proved himself a good Woozy and a faithful friend," the Wizard went on, "so we will send him to the Royal Menagerie, where he will have good care and plenty to eat all his life."

"Much obliged," said the Woozy. "That beats being fenced up in a lonely forest and starved."

"As for the Patchwork Girl," resumed the Wizard, "she is so remarkable in appearance, and so clever and good tempered, that our Gracious Ruler intends to preserve her carefully, as one of the curiosities of the curious Land of Oz. Scraps may live in the palace, or wherever she pleases, and be nobody's servant but her own."

"That's all right," said Scraps.

"We have all been interested in Ojo," the little Wizard continued, "because his love for his unfortunate uncle has led him bravely to face all sorts of dangers, in order that he might rescue him. The Munchkin boy has a loyal and generous heart and has done his best to restore Unc Nunkie to life. He has failed, but there are others more powerful than the Crooked Magician, and there are more ways than Dr. Pipt knew of to destroy the charm of the Liquid of Petrifaction. Glinda the Good has told me of one way, and you shall now learn how great is the knowledge and power of our peerless Sorceress."

As he said this the Wizard advanced to the statue of Margolote and made a magic pass, at the same time muttering a magic word that none could hear distinctly. At once the woman moved, turned her head wonderingly this way and that, to note all who stood before her, and seeing Dr. Pipt, ran forward and threw herself into her husband's outstretched arms.

Then the Wizard made the magic pass and spoke the magic word before the statue of Unc Nunkie. The old Munchkin immediately came to life and with a low bow to the Wizard said: "Thanks."

But now Ojo rushed up and threw his arms joyfully about his uncle, and the old man hugged his little nephew tenderly and stroked his hair and wiped away the boy's tears with a handkerchief, for Ojo was crying from pure happiness.

Ozma came forward to congratulate them.

"I have given to you, my dear Ojo and Unc Nunkie, a nice house just outside the walls of the Emerald City," she said, "and there you shall make your future home and be under my protection."

"Didn't I say you were Ojo the Lucky?" asked the Tin Woodman, as everyone crowded around to shake Ojo's hand.

"Yes; and it is true!" replied Ojo, gratefully.

Little Wizard Stories of Oz
by L. Frank Baum

The Cowardly Lion And The Hungry Tiger

In the splendid palace of the Emerald City, which is in the center of the fairy Land of Oz, is a great Throne Room, where Princess Ozma, the Ruler, for an hour each day sits in a throne of glistening emeralds and listens to all the troubles of her people, which they are sure to tell her about. Around Ozma's throne, on such occasions, are grouped all the important personages of Oz, such as the Scarecrow, Jack Pumpkinhead, Tiktok the Clockwork Man, the Tin Woodman, the Wizard of Oz, the Shaggy Man and other famous fairy people. Little Dorothy usually has a seat at Ozma's feet, and crouched on either side the throne are two enormous beasts known as the Hungry Tiger and the Cowardly Lion.

These two beasts are Ozma's chief guardians, but as everyone loves the beautiful girl Princess there has never been any disturbance in the great Throne Room, or anything for the guardians to do but look fierce and solemn and keep quiet until the Royal Audience is over and the people go away to their homes.

Of course no one would dare be naughty while the huge Lion and Tiger crouched beside the throne; but the fact is, the people of Oz are very seldom naughty. So Ozma's big guards are more ornamental than useful, and no one realizes that better than the beasts themselves.

One day, after everybody had left the Throne Room except the Cowardly Lion and the hungry Tiger, the Lion yawned and said to his friend: "I'm getting tired of this job. No one is afraid of us and no one pays any attention to us."

"That is true," replied the big Tiger, purring softly. "We might as well be in the thick jungles where we were born, as trying to protect Ozma when she needs no protection. And I'm dreadfully hungry all the time."

"You have enough to eat, I'm sure," said the Lion, swaying his tail slowly back and forth.

"Enough, perhaps; but not the kind of food I long for," answered the Tiger. "What I'm hungry for is fat babies. I have a great desire to eat a few fat babies. Then, perhaps, the people of Oz would fear me and I'd become more important."

"True," agreed the Lion. "It would stir up quite a rumpus if you ate but one fat baby. As for myself, my claws are sharp as needles and strong as crowbars, while my teeth are powerful enough to tear a person to pieces in a few seconds. If I should spring upon a man and make chop suey of him, there would be wild excitement in the Emerald City and the people would fall upon their knees and beg me for mercy. That, in my opinion, would render me of considerable importance."

"After you had torn the person to pieces, what would you do next?" asked the Tiger sleepily.

"Then I would roar so loudly it would shake the earth and stalk away to the jungle to hide myself, before anyone could attack me or kill me for what I had done."

"I see," nodded the Tiger. "You are really cowardly."

"To be sure. That is why I am named the Cowardly Lion. That is why I have always been so tame and peaceable. But I'm awfully tired of being tame," added the Lion, with a sigh, "and it would be fun to raise a row and show people what a terrible beast I really am."

The Tiger remained silent for several minutes, thinking deeply as he slowly washed his face with his left paw. Then he said: "I'm getting old, and it would please me to eat at least one fat baby before I die. Suppose we surprise these people of Oz and prove our power. What do you say? We will walk out of here just as usual and the first baby we meet I'll eat in a jiffy, and the first man or woman you meet you will tear to pieces. Then we will both run out of the city gates and gallop across the country and hide in the jungle before anyone can stop us."

"All right; I'm game," said the Lion, yawning again so that he showed two rows of dreadfully sharp teeth.

The tiger got up and stretched his great, sleek body.

"Come on," he said. The Lion stood up and proved he was the larger of the two, for he was almost as big as a small horse.

Out of the palace they walked, and met no one. They passed through the beautiful grounds, passed through the beautiful grounds, past fountains and beds of lovely flowers, and met no one. Then they unlatched a gate and entered a street of the city, and met no one.

"I wonder how a fat baby will taste," remarked the Tiger, as they stalked majestically along side by side.

"I imagine it will taste like nutmegs," said the Lion.

"No," said the Tiger, "I've an idea it will taste like gumdrops."

They turned a corner, but met no one, for the people of the emerald City were accustomed to take their naps at this hour of the afternoon.

"I wonder how many pieces I ought to tear a person into," said the Lion, in a thoughtful voice.

"Sixty would be about right," suggested the Tiger.

"Would that hurt any more than to tear one into a dozen pieces?" inquired the Lion, with a little shudder.

"Who cares whether it hurts or not?" growled the Tiger.

The Lion did not reply. They entered a side street, but met no one.

Suddenly they heard a child crying.

"Aha!" exclaimed the Tiger. "There is my meat."

He rushed around a corner, the Lion following, and came upon a nice fat baby sitting in the middle of the street and crying as if in great distress.

"What's the matter?" asked the Tiger, crouching before the baby.

"I—I—I-lost my m-m-mamma!" wailed the baby.

"Why, you poor little thing," said the great beast, softly stroking the child's head with its paw. "Don't cry, my dear; for mamma can't be far away and I'll help you to find her."

"Go on," said the Lion, who stood by.

"Go on where?" asked the Tiger, looking up.

"Go on and eat your fat baby."

"Why, you dreadful creature!" said the tiger reproachfully; "would you want me to eat a poor little lost baby, that doesn't know where its mother is?" And the beast gathered the little one into its strong, hairy arms and tried to comfort it by rocking it gently back and forth.

The Lion growled low in his throat and seemed very much disappointed; but at that moment a scream reached their ears and a woman came bounding out of a house and into the street. Seeing her baby in the embrace of the monster Tiger the woman screamed again and rushed forward to rescue it, but in her haste she caught her foot in her skirt and tumbled head over heels and heels over head, stopping with such a bump that she saw many stars in the heavens, although it was broad daylight. And there she lay, in a helpless manner, all tangled up and unable to stir.

With one bound and a roar like thunder the huge Lion was beside her. With his strong jaws he grasped her dress and raised her into an upright position.

"Poor thing! Are you hurt?" he gently asked.

Gasping for breath the woman struggled to free herself and tried to walk, but she limped badly and tumbled down again.

"My baby!" she said pleadingly.

"The baby is all right; don't worry," replied the Lion; and then he added; "Keep quiet, now, and I'll carry you back to your house, and the Hungry Tiger will carry your baby."

The tiger, who had approached the place with the child in its arms, asked in astonishment: "Aren't you going to tear her into sixty pieces?"

"No, nor into six pieces," answered the Lion indignantly. "I'm not such a brute as to destroy a poor woman who has hurt herself trying to save her lost baby. If you are so ferocious and cruel and bloodthirsty, you may leave me and go away, for I do not care to associate with you."

"That's all right," answered the Tiger. "I'm not cruel — not in the least — I'm only hungry. But I thought you were cruel."

"Thank heaven I'm respectable," said the Lion, with dignity. He then raised the woman and with much gentleness carried her into her house, where he laid her upon a sofa. The Tiger followed with the baby, which he safely deposited beside its mother. The little one liked the Hungry Tiger and grasping the enormous beast by both ears the baby kissed the beast's nose to show he was grateful and happy.

"Thank you very much," said the woman. "I've often heard what good beasts you are, in spite of your power to do mischief to mankind, and now I know that the stories are true. I do not think either of you have ever had an evil thought."

The Hungry Tiger and the Cowardly Lion hung their heads and did not look into each other's eyes, for both were shamed and humbled. They crept away and stalked back through the streets until they again entered the palace grounds, where they retreated to the pretty, comfortable rooms they occupied at the back of the palace. There they silently crouched in their usual corners to think over their adventure.

After a while the Tiger said sleepily: "I don't believe fat babies taste like gumdrops. I'm quite sure they have the flavor of raspberry tarts. My, how hungry I am for fat babies!"

The Lion grunted disdainfully.

"You're a humbug," said he.

"Am I?" retorted the Tiger, with a sneer. "Tell me, then, into how many pieces you usually tear your victims, my bold Lion?"

The Lion impatiently thumped the floor with his tail.

"To tear anyone into pieces would soil my claws and blunt my teeth,' he said. "I'm glad I didn't muss myself up this afternoon by hurting that poor mother."

The Tiger looked at him steadily and then yawned a wide, wide yawn.

"You're a coward," he remarked.

"Well," said the Lion, "it's better to be a coward than to do wrong."

"To be sure," answered the other. "And that reminds me that I nearly lost my own reputation. For, had I eaten that fat baby, I would not now be the Hungry Tiger. It's better to go hungry, seems to me, than to be cruel to a little child."

And then they dropped their heads on their paws and went to sleep.

* * * * *

Little Dorothy And Toto

Dorothy was a little Kansas girl who once accidentally found the beautiful Land of Oz and was invited to live there always. Toto was Dorothy's small black dog, with fuzzy, curly hair and bright black eyes. Together, when they tired of the grandeur of the Emerald City of Oz, they would wander out into the country and all through the land, peering into queer nooks and corners and having a good time in their own simple way. There was a little Wizard living in Oz who was a faithful friend of Dorothy and did not approve of her traveling alone in this way, but the girl always laughed at the little man's fears for her and said she was not afraid of anything that might happen.

One day, while on such a journey, Dorothy and Toto found themselves among the wild wooded hills at the southeast of Oz — a place usually avoided by travelers because so many magical things abounded there. And, as they entered a forest path, the little girl noticed a sign tacked to a tree, which said: "Look out for Crinklink."

Toto could not talk, as many of the animals of Oz can, for he was just a common Kansas dog; but he looked at the sign so seriously that Dorothy almost believed he could read it, and she knew quite well that Toto understood every word she said to him.

"Never mind Crinklink," said she. "I don't believe anything in Oz will try to hurt us, Toto, and if I get into trouble you must take care of me."

"Bow-wow!" said Toto, and Dorothy knew that meant a promise.

The path was narrow and wound here and there between the trees, but they could not lose their way, because thick vines and creepers shut them in on both sides. They had walked a long time when, suddenly turning a curve of the pathway, they came upon a lake of black water, so big and so deep that they were forced to stop.

"Well, Toto," said Dorothy, looking at the lake, "we must turn back, I guess, for there is neither a bridge nor a boat to take us across the black water."

"Here's the ferryman, though," cried a tiny voice beside them, and the girl gave a start and looked down at her feet, where a man no taller than three inches sat at the edge of the path with his legs dangling over the lake.

"Oh!" said Dorothy; "I didn't see you before."

Toto growled fiercely and made his ears stand up straight, but the little man did not seem in the least afraid of the dog. He merely repeated: "I'm the ferryman, and it's my business to carry people across the lake."

Dorothy couldn't help feeling surprised, for she could have picked the little man up with one hand, and the lake was big and broad. Looking at the ferryman more closely she saw that he had small eyes, a big nose, and a sharp chin. His hair was blue and his clothes scarlet, and Dorothy noticed that every button on his jacket was the head of some animal. The top button was a bear's head and the next button a wolf's head; the next was a cat's head and the next a weasel's head, while the last button of all was the head of a field-mouse. When Dorothy looked into the eyes of these animals' heads, they all nodded and said in a chorus: "Don't believe all you hear, little girl!"

"Silence!" said the small ferryman, slapping each button head in turn, but not hard enough to hurt them. Then he turned to Dorothy and asked: "Do you wish to cross over the lake?"

"Why, I'd like to," she answered, hesitating; "but I can't see how you will manage to carry us, without any boat."

"If you can't see, you mustn't see," he answered with a laugh. "All you need do is shut your eyes, say the word, and — over you go!"

Dorothy wanted to get across, in order that she might continue her journey.

"All right," she said, closing her eyes; "I'm ready."

Instantly she was seized in a pair of strong arms — arms so big and powerful that she was startled and cried out in fear.

"Silence!" roared a great voice, and the girl opened her eyes to find that the tiny man had suddenly grown to a giant and was holding both her and Toto in a tight embrace while in one step he spanned the lake and reached the other shore.

Dorothy became frightened, then, especially as the giant did not stop but continued tramping in great steps over the wooded hills, crushing bushes and trees beneath his broad feet. She struggled in vain to free herself, while Toto whined and trembled beside her, for the little dog was frightened, too.

"Stop!" screamed the girl. "Let me down!" But the giant paid no attention. "Who are you, and where are you taking me?" she continued; but the giant said not a word. Close to Dorothy's ear, however, a voice answered her, saying: "This is the terrible Crinklink, and he has you in his power."

Dorothy managed to twist her head around and found it was the second button on the jacket — the wolf's head — which had spoken to her.

"What will Crinklink do with me?" she asked anxiously.

"No one knows. You must wait and see," replied the wolf.

"Some of his captives he whips," squeaked the weasel's head.

"Some he transforms into bugs and other things," growled the bear's head.

"Some he enchants, so that they become doorknobs," sighed the cat's head.

"Some he makes his slaves — even as we are — and that is the most dreadful fate of all," added the field-mouse. "As long as Crinklink exists we shall remain buttons, but as there are no more buttonholes on his jacket he will probably make you a slave."

Dorothy began to wish she had not met Crinklink. Meanwhile, the giant took such big steps that he soon reached the heart of the hills, where, perched upon the highest peak, stood a little castle. Before this castle he paused to set down Dorothy and Toto, for Crinklink was at present far too large to enter his own doorway. So he made himself grow smaller, until he was about the size of an ordinary man. Then he said to Dorothy, in stern, commanding tones: "Enter, girl!"

Dorothy obeyed and entered the castle, with Toto at her heels. She found the place to be merely one big room. There was a table and chair of ordinary size near the center, and at one side a wee bed that seemed scarcely big enough for a doll. Everywhere else were dishes — dishes — dished! They were all soiled, and were piled upon the floor, in all the corners and upon every shelf. Evidently Crinklink had not washed a dish for years, but had cast them aside as he used them.

Dorothy's captor sat down in the chair and frowned at her. "You are young and strong, and will make a good dishwasher," said he.

"Do you mean me to wash all those dishes?" she asked, feeling both indignant and fearful, for such a task would take weeks to accomplish.

"That's just what I mean," he retorted. "I need clean dishes, for all I have are soiled, and you're going to make 'em clean or get trounced. So get to work and be careful not to break anything. If you smash a dish, the penalty is one lash from my dreadful cat-o'-nine-tails for every piece the dish breaks into," and here Crinklink displayed a terrible whip that made the little girl shudder.

Dorothy knew how to wash dishes, but she remembered that often she carelessly broke one. In this case, however, a good deal depended on being careful, so she handled the dishes very cautiously.

While she worked, Toto sat by the hearth and growled low at Crinklink, and Crinklink sat in his chair and growled at Dorothy because she moved so slowly. He expected her to break a dish any minute, but as the hours passed away and this did not happen Crinklink began to grow sleepy. It was tiresome watching the girl wash dishes and often he glanced longingly at the tiny bed. Now he began to yawn, and he yawned and yawned until finally he said: "I'm going to take a nap. But the buttons on my jacket will be wide awake and whenever you break a dish the crash will waken me. As I'm rather sleepy I hope you won't interrupt my nap by breaking anything for a long time."

Then Crinklink made himself grow smaller and smaller until he was three inches high and of a size to fit the tiny bed. At once he lay down and fell fast asleep.

Dorothy came close to the buttons and whispered: "Would you really warn Crinklink if I tried to escape?"

"You can't escape," growled the bear. "Crinklink would become a giant, and soon overtake you."

"But you might kill him while he sleeps," suggested the cat, in a soft voice.

"Oh!" cried Dorothy, drawing back; "I couldn't poss'bly kill anything — even to save my life."

But Toto had heard this conversation and was not so particular about killing monsters. Also the little dog knew he must try to save his mistress. In an instant he sprang upon the wee bed and was about to seize the sleeping Crinklink in his jaws when Dorothy heard a loud crash and a heap of dishes fell from the table to the floor. Then the girl saw Toto and the little man rolling on the floor together, like a fuzzy ball, and when the ball stopped rolling, behold! There was Toto wagging his tail joyfully and there sat the little Wizard of Oz, laughing merrily at the expression of surprise on Dorothy's face.

"Yes, my dear, it's me," said he, "and I've been playing tricks on you — for your own good. I wanted to prove to you that it is really dangerous for a little girl to wander alone in a fairy country; so I took the form of Crinklink to teach you a lesson. There isn't any Crinklink, to be sure; but if there had been you'd be severely whipped for breaking all those dishes."

The Wizard now rose, took off the coat with the button heads, and spread it on the floor wrong side up. At once there crept from beneath it a bear, a wolf, a cat, a weasel, and a field-mouse, who all rushed from the room and escaped into the mountains.

"Come on, toto," said Dorothy; "let's go back to the Emerald City. You've given me a good scare, wizard," she added, with dignity, "and p'raps I'll forgive you, by'n'by; but just now I'm mad to think how easily you fooled me."

* * * * *

Tiktok And The Nome King

The Nome King was unpleasantly angry. He had carelessly bitten his tongue at breakfast and it still hurt; so he roared and raved and stamped around in his underground palace in a way that rendered him very disagreeable.

It so happened that on this unfortunate day Tiktok, the Clockwork Man, visited the Nome King to ask a favor. Tiktok lived in the Land of Oz, and although he was an active and important person, he was made entirely of metal. Machinery within him, something like the works of a clock, made him move; other machinery made him talk; still other machinery made him think.

Although so cleverly constructed, the Clockwork Man was far from perfect. Three separate keys wound up his motion machinery, his speech works, and his thoughts. One or more of these contrivances was likely to run down at a critical moment leaving poor Tiktok helpless. Also some of his parts were wearing out, through much use, and just now his thought machinery needed repair. The skillful little Wizard of Oz had tinkered with Tiktok's thoughts without being able to get them properly regulated, so he had advised the Clockwork Man to go to the Nome King and secure a new set of springs, which would render his thoughts more elastic and responsive.

"Be careful what you say to the Nome King," warned the wizard "He has a bad temper and the least little thing makes him angry."

Tiktok promised, and the Wizard wound his machinery and set him walking in the direction of the Nome King's dominions, just across the desert from the Land of Oz. He ran down just as he reached the entrance to the underground palace, and there Kaliko, the Nome King's Chief Steward, found him and wound him up again.

"I want to see the King," said Tiktok, in his jerky voice.

"Well," remarked Kaliko, "it may be safe for a cast-iron person like you to face his Majesty this morning, but you must announce yourself, for should I show my face inside the jewel studded cavern where the King is now raving, I'd soon look like a dish of mashed potatoes, and be of no further use to anyone."

"I'm not a-fraid," said Tiktok.

"Then walk in and make yourself at home," answered Kaliko and threw open the door of the Kings's cavern.

Tiktok promptly walked in and faced the astonished Nome King to whom he said: "good morn-ing. I want two new steel springs for my thought-works and a new cog-wheel for my speech-pro-du-cer. How a-bout it, your Maj-es-ty?"

The Nome King growled a menacing growl and his eyes were red with rage.

"How dare you enter my presence?" he shouted.

"I dare an-y-thing," said Tiktok. "I'm not a-fraid of a fat Nome."

This was true, yet an unwise speech. Had Tiktok's thoughts been in good working order he would have said something else. The angry Nome King quickly caught up his heavy mace and hurled it straight at Tiktok. When it struck the metal man's breast, the force of the blow burst the bolts which held the plates of his body together and they clattered to the floor in a score of pieces Hundreds and hundreds of wheels, pins, cogs and springs filled the air like a cloud and then rattled like hail upon the floor.

Where Tiktok had stood was now only a scrap-heap and the Nome King was so amazed by the terrible effects of his blow that he stared in wonder.

His Majesty's anger quickly cooled. He remembered that the Clockwork Man was a favorite subject of the powerful Princess Ozma of Oz, who would be sure to resent Tiktok's ruin.

"Too bad! too bad!" he muttered, regretfully. "I'm really sorry I made junk of the fellow. I didn't know he'd break."

"You'd better be," remarked Kaliko, who now ventured to enter the room. "You'll have a war on your hands when Ozma hears of this, and the chances are you will lose your throne and your kingdom."

The Nome King turned pale, for he loved to rule the Nomes and did not know of any other way to earn a living in case Ozma fought and conquered him.

"Do — do you think Ozma will be angry?" he asked anxiously.

"I'm sure of it," said Kaliko. "And she has the right to be. You've made scrap-iron of her favorite."

The King groaned.

"Sweep him up and throw the rubbish into the black pit," he commanded; and then he shut himself up in his private den and for days would see no one, because he was so ashamed of his unreasoning anger and so feared the results of his rash act.

Kaliko swept up the pieces, but he did not throw them into the black pit. Being a clever and skillful mechanic he determined to fit the pieces together again.

No man ever faced a greater puzzle; but it was interesting work and Kaliko succeeded. When he found a spring or wheel worn or imperfect, he made a new one.

Within two weeks, by working steadily night and day, the Chief Steward completed his task and put the three sets of clockwork and the last rivet into Tiktok's body. He then would up the motion machinery, and the Clockwork Man walked up and down the room as naturally as ever. Then Kaliko wound up the thought works and the speech regulator and said to Tiktok: "How do you feel now?"

"Fine," said the Clockwork Man. "You have done a ve-ry good job, Kal-i-ko, and saved me from de-struc-tion. Much o-bliged."

"Don't mention it," replied the Chief Steward. "I quite enjoyed the work."

Just then the Nome King's gong sounded, and Kaliko rushed away through the jewel-studded cavern and into the den where the King had hidden, leaving the doors ajar.

"Kaliko," said the King, in a meek voice. "I've been shut up here long enough to repent bitterly the destruction of Tiktok. Of course Ozma will have revenge, and send an army to fight us, but we must take our medicine. One thing comforts me: Tiktok wasn't really a live person; he was only a machine man, and so it wasn't very wicked to stop his clockworks. I couldn't sleep nights, at first, for worry; but there's no more harm in smashing a machine man than in breaking a wax doll. Don't you think so?"

"I am too humble to think in the presence of your Majesty," said Kaliko.

"Then get me something to eat," commanded the King, "for I'm nearly starved. Two roasted goats, a barrel of cakes and nine mince pies will do me until dinnertime."

Kaliko bowed and hurried away to the royal kitchen, forgetting

Tiktok, who was wandering around in the outer cavern. Suddenly the Nome King looked up and saw the Clockwork Man standing before him, and at the sight the monarch's eyes grew big and round and he fell a-trembling in every limb.

"Away, grim Shadow!" he cried. "You're not here, you know; you're only a hash of cogwheels and springs, lying at the bottom of the black pit. Vanish, thou Vision of the demolished Tiktok, and leave me in peace — for I have bitterly repented!"

"Then beg my pardon," said Tiktok in a gruff voice, for Kaliko had forgotten to oil the speech works.

But the sound of a voice coming from what he thought a mere vision was too much for the Nome King's shaken nerves. He gave a yell of fear and rushed from the room. Tiktok followed, so the King bolted through the corridors on a swift run and bumped against Kaliko, who was returning with a tray of things to eat. The sound of the breaking dishes, as they struck the floor, added to the King's terror and he yelled again and dashed into a great cavern where a thousand Nomes were at work hammering metal.

"Look out! Here comes a phantom clockwork man!" screamed the terrified monarch, and every Nome dropped his tools and made a rush from the cavern, knocking over their King in their mad flight and recklessly trampling upon his prostrate fat body. So, when Tiktok came into the cavern, there was only the Nome King left, and he was rolling upon the rocky floor and howling for mercy, with his eyes fast shut so that he could not see what he was sure was a dreadful phantom that was coming straight toward him.

"It occurs to me," said Tiktok calmly, "that your Maj-es-ty is acting like a baby. I am not a phan-tom. A phan-tom is unreal, while I am the real thing.

The King rolled over, sat up and opened his eyes.

"Didn't I smash you to pieces?" he asked in trembling tones.

"Yes," said Tiktok.

"Then you are nothing but a junk-heap, and this form in which you now appear cannot be real."

"It is, though," declared Tiktok. "Kal-i-ko picked up my piec-es and put me to-geth-er a-gain. I'm as good as new, and perhaps bet-ter."

"That is true, your Majesty," added Kaliko, who now made his appearance, "and I hope you will forgive me for mending Tiktok. He was quite broken up, after you smashed him, and I found it almost as hard a job to match his pieces as to pick turnips from gooseberry bushes. But I did it," he added proudly.

"You are forgiven," announced the Nome King, rising to his feet and drawing a long breath. "I will raise your wages one specto a year and Tiktok shall return to the Land of Oz loaded with jewels for the Princess Ozma."

"That is all right," said Tiktok. "But what I want to know is, why did you hit me with your mace?"

"Because I was angry," admitted the King. "When I am angry I always do something that I am sorry for afterward. So I have firmly resolved never to get angry again; unless — unless —"

"Unless what, your Majesty?" inquired Kaliko.

"Unless something annoys me," said the Nome King. And then he went to his treasure-chamber to get the jewels for Princess Ozma of Oz.

* * * * *

Ozma And The Little Wizard

Once upon a time there lived in the beautiful emerald City, which lies in the center of the fairy Land of Oz, a lovely girl called Princess Ozma, who was ruler of all that country. And among those who served this girlish Ruler and lived in a cozy suite of rooms in her splendid palace, was a little, withered old man known as the Wizard of Oz.

This little Wizard could do a good many queer things in magic; but he was a kind man, with merry, twinkling eyes and a sweet smile; so, instead of fearing him because of his magic, everybody loved him.

Now, Ozma was very anxious that all her people who inhabited the pleasant Land of Oz should be happy and contented, and therefore she decided one morning to make a journey to all parts of the country, that she might discover if anything was amiss, or anyone discontented, or if there was any wrong that ought to be righted. She asked the little Wizard to accompany her and he was glad to go.

"Shall I take my bag of magic tools with me?" he asked.

"Of course," said Ozma. "We may need a lot of magic before we return, for we are going into strange corners of the land, where we may meet with unknown creatures and dangerous adventures."

So the wizard took his bag of magic tools and the two left the Emerald City and wandered over the country for many days, at last reaching a place far up in the mountains which neither of them had ever visited before. Stopping one morning at a cottage, built beside the rocky path which led into a pretty valley beyond, Ozma asked a man: "Are you happy? Have you any complaint to make of your lot?"

And the man replied: "We are happy except for three mischievous Imps that live in yonder valley and often come here to annoy us. If your Highness would only drive away those Imps, I and my family would be very happy and very grateful to you."

"Who are these bad Imps?" inquired the girl Ruler.

"One is named Olite, and one Udent and one Ertinent, and they have no respect for anyone or anything. If strangers pass through the valley, the Imps jeer at them and make horrid faces and call names, and often they push travelers out of the path or throw stones at them. Whenever Imp Olite or Imp Udent or Imp Ertinent comes here to bother us, I and my family run into the house and lock all the doors and windows, and we dare not venture out again until the Imps have gone away."

Princess Ozma was grieved to hear this report and the little Wizard shook his head gravely and said the naughty imps deserved to be punished. They told the good man they would see what could be done to protect him and at once entered the valley to seek the dwelling place of the three mischievous creatures.

Before long they came upon three caves, hollowed from the rocks, and in front of each cave squatted a queer little dwarf.

Ozma and the Wizard paused to examine them and found them well-shaped, strong and lively. They had big round ears, flat noses and wide grinning mouths, and their jet-black hair came to points on top of their heads, much resembling horns. Their clothing fitted snugly to their bodies and limbs and the Imps were so small in size that at first Ozma did not consider them at all dangerous. But one of them suddenly reached out a hand and caught the dress of the Princess, jerking it so sharply that she nearly fell down, and a moment later another Imp pushed the little Wizard so hard that he bumped against Ozma and both unexpectedly sat down upon the ground.

At this the Imps laughed boisterously and began running around in a circle and kicking dust upon the Royal Princess, who cried in a sharp voice: "Wizard, do your duty!"

The Wizard promptly obeyed. Without rising from the ground he opened his bag, got the tools he required and muttered a magic spell.

Instantly the three Imps became three bushes — of a thorny, stubby kind — with their roots in the ground. As the bushes were at first motionless, perhaps through surprise at their sudden transformation, the Wizard and the Princess found time to rise from the ground and brush the dust off their pretty clothes.

Then Ozma turned to the bushes and said: "The unhappy lot you now endure, my poor Imps, is due entirely to your naughty actions. You can no longer annoy harmless travelers and you must remain ugly bushes, covered with sharp thorns, until you repent of your bad ways and promise to be good Imps."

"They can't help being good now, your Highness," said the Wizard, who was much pleased with his work, "and the safest plan will be to allow them always to remain bushes."

But something must have been wrong with the Wizard's magic, or the creatures had magic of their own, for no sooner were the words spoken than the bushes began to move. First they only waved their branches at the girl and little man, but pretty soon they began to slide over the ground, their roots dragging through the earth, and one pushed itself against the Wizard and pricked him so sharply with its thorns that he cried out: "Ouch!" and started to run away.

Ozma followed, for the other bushes were trying to stick their thorns into her legs and one actually got so near her that it tore a great rent in her beautiful dress. The girl Princess could run, however, and she followed the fleeing Wizard until he tumbled head first over a log and rolled upon the ground. Then she sprang behind a tree and shouted: "Quick! Transform them into something else."

The Wizard heard, but he was much confused by his fall. Grabbing from his bag the first magical tool he could find he transformed the bushes into three white pigs. That astonished the Imps. In the shape of pigs — fat, roly-poly and cute — they scampered off a little distance and sat down to think about their new condition.

Ozma drew a long breath and coming from behind the tree she said: "That is much better, Wiz, for such pigs as these must be quite harmless. No one need now fear the mischievous Imps."

"I intended to transform them into mice," replied the Wizard, "but in my excitement I worked the wrong magic. However, unless the horrid creatures behave themselves hereafter, they are liable to be killed and eaten. They would make good chops, sausages or roasts."

But the Imps were now angry and had no intention of behaving. As Ozma and the little Wizard turned to resume their journey, the three pigs rushed forward, dashed between their legs, and tripped them up, so that both lost their balance and toppled over, clinging to one another. As the Wizard tried to get up he was tripped again and fell across the back of the third pig, which carried him on a run far down the valley until it dumped the little man in the river. Ozma had been sprawled upon the ground but found she was not hurt, so she picked herself up and ran to the assistance of the Wizard, reaching him just as he was crawling out of the river, grasping for breath and dripping with water. The girl could not help laughing at his woeful appearance. But he had no sooner wiped the wet from his eyes than one of the impish pigs tripped him again and sent him into the river for a second bath. The pigs tried to trip Ozma, too, but she ran around a stump and so managed to keep out of their way. So the Wizard scrambled out of the water again and picked up a sharp stick to defend himself. Then he mumbled a magic mutter which instantly dried his clothes, after which he hurried to assist Ozma. The pigs were afraid of the sharp stick and kept away from it.

"This won't do," said the Princess. "We have accomplished nothing, for the pig Imps would annoy travelers as much as the real Imps. Transform them into something else, Wiz."

The Wizard took time to think. Then he transformed the white pigs into blue doves.

"Doves," said he, "are the most harmless things in the world."

But scarcely had he spoken when the doves flew at them and tried to peck out their eyes. When they endeavored to shield their eyes with their hands, two of the doves bit the Wizard's fingers and another caught the pretty pink ear of the Princess in its bill and gave it such a cruel tweak that she cried out in pain and threw her skirt over her head.

"These birds are worse than pigs, Wizard," she called to her companion. "Nothing is harmless that is animated by impudent anger or impertinent mischief. You must transform the Imps into something that is not alive."

The Wizard was pretty busy, just then, driving off the birds, but he managed to open his bag of magic and find a charm which instantly transformed the doves into three buttons. As they fell to the ground he picked them up and smiled with satisfaction. The tin button was Imp Olite, the brass button was Imp Udent and the lead button was Imp Ertinent. These buttons the Wizard placed in a little box which he put in his jacket pocket.

"Now," said he, "the Imps cannot annoy travelers, for we shall carry them back with us to the Emerald City."

"But we dare not use the buttons," said Ozma, smiling once more now that the danger was over.

"Why not?" asked the Wizard. "I intend to sew them upon my coat and watch them carefully. The spirits of the Imps are still in the buttons, and after a time they will repent and be sorry for their naughtiness. Then they will decide to be very good in the future. When they feel that way, the tin button will turn silver and the brass to gold, while the lead button will become aluminum. I shall then restore them to their proper forms, changing their names to pretty names instead of the ugly one they used to bear. Thereafter the three Imps will become good citizens of the Land of Oz and I think you will find they will

prove faithful subjects of our beloved Princess Ozma."

"Ah, that is magic well worthwhile," exclaimed Ozma, well pleased. "There is no doubt, my friend, but that you are a very clever Wizard."

* * * * *

Jack Pumpkinhead And The Sawhorse

In a room of the Royal Palace of the Emerald City of Oz hangs a Magic Picture, in which are shown all the important scenes that transpire in those fairy dominions. The scenes shift constantly, and by watching them, Ozma, the girl Ruler, is able to discover events taking place in any part of her kingdom.

One day she saw in her Magic Picture that a little girl and a little boy had wandered together into a great, gloomy forest at the far west of Oz and had become hopelessly lost. Their friends were seeking them in the wrong direction and unless Ozma came to their rescue the little ones would never be found in time to save them from starving.

So the Princess sent a message to Jack Pumpkinhead and asked him to come to the palace. This personage, one of the queerest of the queer inhabitants of Oz, was an old friend and companion of Ozma. His form was made of rough sticks fitted together and dressed in ordinary clothes. His head was a pumpkin with a face carved upon it, and was set on top a sharp stake which formed his neck.

Jack was active, good-natured and a general favorite; but his pumpkin head was likely to spoil with age, so in order to secure a good supply of heads he grew a big field of pumpkins and lived in the middle of it, his house being a huge pumpkin hollowed out. Whenever he needed a new head he picked a pumpkin, carved a face on it and stuck it upon the stake of his neck, throwing away the old head as of no further use.

The day Ozma sent for him Jack was in prime condition and was glad to be of service in rescuing the lost children. Ozma made him a map, showing just where the forest was and how to get to it and the paths he must take to reach the little ones. Then she said: "You'd better ride the Sawhorse, for he is swift and intelligent and will help you accomplish your task."

"All right," answered Jack, and went to the royal stable to tell the Sawhorse to be ready for the trip.

This remarkable animal was not unlike Jack Pumpkinhead in form, although so different in shape. Its body was a log with four sticks stuck into it for legs. A branch at one end of the log served as a tail, while in the other end was chopped a gash that formed a mouth. Above this were two small knots that did nicely for eyes. The Sawhorse was the favorite steed of Ozma and to prevent its wooden legs from wearing out she had them shod with plates of gold.

Jack said "Good morning" to the Sawhorse and placed upon the creature's back a saddle of purple leather, studded with jewels.

"Where now?" asked the horse, blinking its knot eyes at Jack.

"We're going to rescue two babes in the wood," was the reply. Then he climbed into the saddle and the wooden animal pranced out of the stable, through the streets of the Emerald City and out upon the highway leading to the western forest where the children were lost.

Small though he was, the Sawhorse was swift and untiring. By nightfall they were in the far west and quite close to the forest they sought. They passed the night standing quietly by the roadside. They needed no food, for their wooden bodies never became hungry; nor did they sleep, because they never tired. At daybreak they continued their journey and soon reached the forest.

Jack now examined the map Ozma had given him and found the right path to take, which the Sawhorse obediently followed. Underneath the trees all was silent and gloomy and Jack beguiled the way by whistling gayly as the Sawhorse trotted along.

The paths branched so many times and in so many different ways that the Pumpkinhead was often obliged to consult Ozma's map, and finally the Sawhorse became suspicious.

"Are you sure you are right?" it asked.

"Of course," answered Jack. "Even a Pumpkinhead whose brains are seeds can follow so clear a map as this. Every path is plainly marked, and here is a cross where the children are."

Finally they reached a place, in the very heart of the forest, where they came upon the lost boy and girl. But they found the two children bound fast to the trunk of a big tree, at the foot of which they were sitting.

When the rescuers arrived, the little girl was sobbing bitterly and the boy was trying to comfort her, though he was probably frightened as much as she.

"Cheer up, my dears," said Jack, getting out of the saddle. "I have come to take you back to your parents. But why are you bound to that tree?"

"Because," cried a small, sharp voice, "they are thieves and robbers. That's why!"

"Dear me!" said Jack, looking around to see who had spoken. The voice seemed to come from above.

A big grey squirrel was sitting upon a low branch of the tree. Upon the squirrel's head was a circle of gold, with a diamond set in the center of it. He was running up and down the limbs and chattering excitedly.

"These children," continued the squirrel, angrily, "robbed our storehouse of all the nuts we had saved up for winter. Therefore, being King of all the Squirrels in this forest, I ordered them arrested and put in prison, as you now see them. They had no right to steal our provisions and we are going to punish them."

"We were hungry," said the boy, pleadingly, "and we found a hollow tree full of nuts, and ate them to keep alive. We didn't want to starve when there was food right in front of us."

"Quite right," remarked Jack, nodding his pumpkin head. "I don't blame you one bit under the circumstances. Not a bit."

Then he began to untie the ropes that bound the children to the tree.

"Stop that!" cried the King Squirrel, chattering and whisking about. "You mustn't release our prisoners. You have no right to."

But Jack paid no attention to the protest. His wooden fingers were awkward and it took him some time to untie the ropes. When at last he succeeded, the tree was full of squirrels, called together by their King, and they were furious at losing their prisoners. From the tree they began to hurl nuts at Pumpkinhead, who laughed at them as he helped the two children to their feet.

Now, at the top of this tree was a big dead limb, and so many squirrels gathered upon it that suddenly it broke away and fell to the ground. Poor Jack was standing directly under it and when the limb struck him it smashed his pumpkin head into a pulpy mass and sent Jack's wooden form tumbling, to stop with a bump against a tree a dozen feet away.

He sat up, a moment afterward, but when he felt for his head it was gone. He could not see; neither could he speak. It was perhaps the greatest misfortune that could have happened to Jack Pumpkinhead, and the squirrels were delighted. They danced around in the tree in great glee as they saw Jack's plight.

The boy and girl were indeed free, but their protector was ruined. The Sawhorse was there, however, and in his way he was wise. He had seen the accident and knew that the smashed pumpkin would never again serve Jack as a head. So he said to the children, who were frightened at this accident to their new-found friend: "Pick up the Pumpkinhead's body and set it on my saddle. Then mount behind it and hold on. We must get out of this forest as soon as we can, or the squirrels may capture you again. I must guess at the right path, for Jack's map is no longer of any use to him since that limb destroyed his head."

The two children lifted Jack's body, which was not at all heavy, and placed it upon the saddle. Then they climbed up behind it and the Sawhorse immediately turned and trotted back along the path he had come, bearing all three with ease. However, when the path began to branch into many paths, all following different directions, the wooden animal became puzzled and soon was wandering aimlessly about, without any hope of finding the right way. Toward evening they came upon a fine fruit tree, which furnished the children a supper, and at night the little ones lay upon a bed of leaves while the Sawhorse stood watch, with the limp, headless form of poor Jack Pumpkinhead lying helpless across the saddle.

Now, Ozma had seen in her Magic Picture all that had happened in the forest, so she sent the little wizard, mounted upon the Cowardly Lion, to save the unfortunates. The Lion knew the forest well and when he reached it he bounded straight through the tangled paths to where the Sawhorse was wandering, with Jack and the two children on his back.

The wizard was grieved at the sight of the headless Jack, but believed he could save him. He first led the Sawhorse out of the forest and restored the boy and girl to the arms of their anxious friends, and then he sent the Lion back to Ozma to tell her what had happened.

The Wizard now mounted the Sawhorse and supported Jack's form on the long ride to the pumpkin field. When they arrived at Jack's house the Wizard selected a fine pumpkin — not too ripe — and very neatly carved a face on it. Then he stuck the pumpkin solidly on Jack's neck and asked him: "Well, old friend, how do you feel?"

"Fine!" replied Jack, and shook the hand of the little Wizard gratefully. "You have really saved my life, for without your assistance I could not have found my way home to get a new head. But I'm all right, now, and I shall be very careful not to get this beautiful head smashed." And he shook the Wizard's hand again.

"Are the brains in the new head any better than the old ones?" inquired the Sawhorse, who had watched Jack's restoration.

"Why, these seeds are quite tender," replied the Wizard, "so they will give our friend tender thoughts. But, to speak truly, my dear Sawhorse, Jack Pumpkinhead, with all his good qualities, will never be noted for his wisdom."

* * * * *

The Scarecrow And The Tin Woodman

There lived in the Land of Oz two queerly made men who were the best of friends. They were so much happier when together that they were seldom apart; yet they liked to separate, once in a while, that they might enjoy the pleasure of meeting again.

One was Scarecrow. That means he was a suit of blue Munchkin clothes, stuffed with straw, on top of which was fastened a round cloth head, filled with bran to hold it in shape. On the head were painted two eyes, two ears, a nose and a mouth. The Scarecrow had never been much of a success in scaring crows, but he prided himself on being a superior man, because he could feel no pain, was never tired and did not have to eat or drink. His brains were sharp, for the Wizard of Oz had put pins and needles in the Scarecrow's brains.

The other man was made all of tin, his arms and legs and head being cleverly jointed so that he could move them freely. He was known as the Tin Woodman, having at one time been a woodchopper, and everyone loved him because the Wizard had given him an excellent heart of red plush.

The Tin Woodman lived in a magnificent tin castle, built on his country estate in the Winkie Land, not far from the Emerald City of Oz. It had pretty tin furniture and was surrounded by lovely gardens in which were many tin trees and beds of tin flowers. The palace of the Scarecrow was not far distant, on the banks of a river, and this palace was in the shape of an immense ear of corn.

One morning the tin Woodman went to visit his friend the Scarecrow, and as they had nothing better to do they decided to take a boat ride on the river. So they got into the Scarecrow's boat, which was formed from a big corncob, hollowed out and pointed at both ends and decorated around the edges with brilliant jewels. The sail was of purple silk and glittered gayly in the sunshine.

There was a good breeze that day, so the boat glided swiftly over the water. By and by they came to a smaller river that flowed from out a deep forest, and the Tin Woodman proposed they sail up this stream, as it would be cool and shady beneath the trees of the forest. So the Scarecrow, who was steering, turned the boat up the stream and the friends continued talking together of old times and the wonderful adventures they had met with while traveling with Dorothy, the little Kansas girl. They became so much interested in this talk that they forgot to notice that the boat was now sailing through the forest, or that the stream was growing more narrow and crooked.

Suddenly the Scarecrow glanced up and saw a big rock just ahead of them.

"Look out!" he cried; but the warning came too late.

The Tin Woodman sprang to his feet just as the boat bumped into the rock, and the jar made him lose his balance. He toppled and fell overboard and being made of tin he sank to the bottom of the water in an instant and lay there at full length, face up.

Immediately the Scarecrow threw out the anchor, so as to hold the boat in that place, and then he leaned over the side and through the clear water looked at his friend sorrowfully.

"Dear me!" he exclaimed; "what a misfortune!"

"It is, indeed," replied the Tin Woodman, speaking in muffled tones because so much water covered him. "I cannot drown, of course, but I must lie here until you find a way to get me out. Meantime, the water is soaking into all my joints and I shall become badly rusted before I am rescued."

"Very true,' agreed the Scarecrow; "but be patient, my friend, and I'll dive down and get you. My straw will not rust, and is easily replaced, if damaged, so I'm not afraid of water."

The Scarecrow now took off his hat and made a dive from the boat into the water; but he was so light in weight that he barely dented the surface of the stream, nor could he reach the Tin Woodman with this outstretched straw arms. So he floated to the boat and climbed into it, saying the while: "Do not despair, my friend. We have an extra anchor aboard, and I will tie it around my waist, to make me sink, and dive again."

"Don't do that!" called the tin man. "That would anchor you also to the bottom, where I am. And we'd both be helpless."

"True enough," sighed the Scarecrow, wiping his wet face with a handkerchief; and then he gave a cry of astonishment, for he found he had wiped off one painted eye and now had but one eye to see with.

"How dreadful!" said the poor Scarecrow. "That eye must have been painted in watercolor, instead of oil. I must be careful not to wipe off the other eye, for then I could not see to help you at all."

A shriek of elfish laughter greeted this speech and looking up the Scarecrow found the trees full of black crows, who seemed much amused by the straw man's one-eyed countenance. He knew the crows well, however, and they had usually been friendly to him because he had never deceived them into thinking he was a meat man — the sort of man they really feared.

"Don't laugh," said he; "you may lose an eye yourselves some day."

"We couldn't look as funny as you, if we did," replied one old crow, the king of them. "But what had gone wrong with you?"

"The Tin Woodman, my dear friend and companion, had fallen overboard and is now on the bottom of the river," said Scarecrow. "I'm trying to get him out again, but I fear I shall not succeed."

"Why, it's easy enough," declared the old crow. "Tie a string to him and all of my crows will fly down, take hold of the string, and pull him up out of the water. There are hundreds of us here, so our united strength could lift much more than that."

"But I can't tie a string to him," replied the Scarecrow. "My straw is so light that I am unable to dive through the water. I've tried it, and knocked one eye out."

"Can't you fish for him?"

"Ah, that is a good idea," said the Scarecrow. "I'll make the attempt."

He found a fishline in the boat, with a stout hook at the end of it. No bait was needed, so the Scarecrow dropped the hook into the water till it touched the Woodman.

"Hook it into a joint," advised the crow, who was now perched upon a branch that stuck far out and bent down over the water.

The Scarecrow tried to do this, but having only one eye he could not see the joints very clearly.

"Hurry up, please," begged the Tin Woodman; "you've no idea how damp it is down here."

"Can't you help?" asked the crow.

"How?" inquired the tin man.

"Catch the line and hook it around your neck."

The Tin Woodman made the attempt and after several trials wound the line around his neck and hooked it securely.

"Good!" cried the King Crow, a mischievous old fellow. "Now, then, we'll all grab the line and pull you out."

At once the air was filled with black crows, each of whom seized the cord with beak or talons. The Scarecrow watched them with much interest and forgot that he had tied the other end of the line around his own waist, so he would not lose it while fishing for his friend.

"All together for the good caws!" shrieked the King Crow, and with a great flapping of wings the birds rose into the air.

The Scarecrow clapped his stuffed hands in glee as he saw his friend drawn from the water into the air; but the next moment the straw man was himself in the air, his stuffed legs kicking wildly; for the crows had flown straight up through the trees. On one end of the line dangled the Tin Woodman, hung by the neck, and on the other dangled the Scarecrow, hung by the waist and clinging fast to the spare anchor of the boat, which he had seized hoping to save himself.

"Hi, there — be careful!" shouted the Scarecrow to the crows. "Don't take us so high. Land us on the river bank."

But the crows were bent on mischief. They thought it a good joke to bother the two, now that they held them captive.

"Here's where the crows scare the Scarecrow!" chuckled the naughty King Crow, and at his command the birds flew over the forest to where a tall dead tree stood higher than all the other trees. At the very top was a crotch, formed by two dead limbs and into the crotch the crows dropped the center of the line. Then, letting go their hold, they flew away, chattering with laughter, and left the two friends suspended high in the air — one on each side of the tree.

Now the Tin Woodman was much heavier than the Scarecrow, but the reason they balanced so nicely was because the straw man still clung fast to the iron anchor. There they hung, not ten feet apart, yet unable to reach the bare tree-trunk.

"For goodness sake don't drop that anchor," said the Tin Woodman anxiously.

"Why not?" inquired the Scarecrow.

"If you did I'd tumble to the ground, where my tin would be badly dented by the fall. Also you would shoot into the air and alight somewhere among the tree-tops."

"Then," said the Scarecrow, earnestly, "I shall hold fast to the anchor."

For a time they both dangled in silence, the breeze swaying them gently to and fro. Finally the tin man said: "Here is an emergency, friend, where only brains can help us. We must think of some way to escape."

"I'll do the thinking," replied the Scarecrow. "My brains are the sharpest."

He thought so long that the tin man grew tired and tried to change his position, but found his joints had already rusted so badly that he could not move them. And his oilcan was back in the boat.

"Do you suppose your brains are rusted, friend Scarecrow?" he asked in a weak voice, for his jaws would scarcely move.

"No, indeed. Ah, here's an idea at last!"

And with this the Scarecrow clapped his hands to his head, forgetting the anchor, which tumbled to the ground. The result was astonishing; for, just as the tin man had said, the light Scarecrow flew into the air, sailing over the top of the tree and landed in a bramble-bush, while the tin man fell plump to the ground, and landing on a bed of dry leaves was not dented at all. The Tin Woodman's joints were so rusted, however, that he was unable to move, while the thorns held the Scarecrow a fast prisoner.

While they were in this sad plight the sound of hoofs was heard and along the forest path rode the little Wizard of Oz, seated on a wooden Sawhorse. He smiled when he saw the one-eyed head of the Scarecrow sticking out of the bramble-bush, but he helped the poor straw man out of his prison.

"Thank you, dear Wiz," said the grateful Scarecrow. "Now we must get the oil-can and rescue the Tin woodman."

Together they ran to the river bank, but the boat was floating in midstream and the Wizard was obliged to mumble some magic words to draw it to the bank, so the Scarecrow could get the oil-can. Then back they flew to the tin man, and while the Scarecrow carefully oiled each joint the little Wizard moved the joints gently back and forth until they worked freely. After an hour of this labor the Tin Woodman was again on his feet, and although still a little stiff he managed to walk to the boat.

The wizard and the Sawhorse also got aboard the corncob craft and together they returned to the Scarecrow's palace. But the Tin Woodman was very careful not to stand up in the boat again.

Tik-Tok of Oz

by L. Frank Baum

To Louis F. Gottschalk, whose sweet and dainty melodies breathe the true spirit of fairyland, this book is affectionately dedicated.

To My Readers

The very marked success of my last year's fairy book, "The Patchwork Girl of Oz," convinces me that my readers like the Oz stories "best of all," as one little girl wrote me. So here, my dears, is a new Oz story in which is introduced Ann Soforth, the Queen of Oogaboo, whom Tik-Tok assisted in conquering our old acquaintance, the Nome King. It also tells of Betsy Bobbin and how, after many adventures, she finally reached the marvelous Land of Oz.

There is a play called "The Tik-Tok Man of Oz," but it is not like this story of "Tik-Tok of Oz," although some of the adventures recorded in this book, as well as those in several other Oz books, are included in the play. Those who have seen the play and those who have read the other Oz books will find in this story a lot of strange characters and adventures that they have never heard of before.

In the letters I receive from children there has been an urgent appeal for me to write a story that will take Trot and Cap'n Bill to the Land of Oz, where they will meet Dorothy and Ozma. Also they think Button-Bright ought to get acquainted with Ojo the Lucky. As you know, I am obliged to talk these matters over with Dorothy by means of the "wireless," for that is the only way I can communicate with the Land of Oz. When I asked her about this idea, she replied: "Why, haven't you heard?" I said "No." "Well," came the message over the wireless, "I'll tell you all about it, by and by, and then you can make a book of that story for the children to read."

So, if Dorothy keeps her word and I am permitted to write another Oz book, you will probably discover how all these characters came together in the famous Emerald City. Meantime, I want to tell all my little friends—whose numbers are increasing by many thousands every year—that I am very grateful for the favor they have shown my books and for the delightful little letters I am constantly receiving. I am almost sure that I have as many friends among the children of America as any story writer alive; and this, of course, makes me very proud and happy.

L. Frank Baum.

"Ozcot" at Hollywood in California, 1914.

1. Ann's Army

"I won't!" cried Ann; "I won't sweep the floor. It is beneath my dignity."

"Some one must sweep it," replied Ann's younger sister, Salye; "else we shall soon be wading in dust. And you are the eldest, and the head of the family."

"I'm Queen of Oogaboo," said Ann, proudly. "But," she added with a sigh, "my kingdom is the smallest and the poorest in all the Land of Oz."

This was quite true. Away up in the mountains, in a far corner of the beautiful fairyland of Oz, lies a small valley which is named Oogaboo, and in this valley lived a few people who were usually happy and contented and never cared to wander over the mountain pass into the more settled parts of the land. They knew that all of Oz, including their own territory, was ruled by a beautiful Princess named Ozma, who lived in the splendid Emerald City; yet the simple folk of Oogaboo never visited Ozma. They had a royal family of their own—not especially to rule over them, but just as a matter of pride. Ozma permitted the various parts of her country to have their Kings and Queens and Emperors and the like, but all were ruled over by the lovely girl Queen of the Emerald City.

The King of Oogaboo used to be a man named Jol Jemkiph Soforth, who for many years did all the drudgery of deciding disputes and telling his people when to plant cabbages and pickle onions. But the King's wife had a sharp tongue and small respect for the King, her husband; therefore one night King Jol crept over the pass into the Land of Oz and disappeared from Oogaboo for good and all. The Queen waited a few years for him to return and then started in search of him, leaving her eldest daughter, Ann Soforth, to act as Queen.

Now, Ann had not forgotten when her birthday came, for that meant a party and feasting and dancing, but she had quite forgotten how many years the birthdays marked. In a land where people live always, this is not considered a cause for regret, so we may justly say that Queen Ann of Oogaboo was old enough to make jelly—and let it go at that.

But she didn't make jelly, or do any more of the housework than she could help. She was an ambitious woman and constantly resented the fact that her kingdom was so tiny and her people so stupid and unenterprising. Often she wondered what had become of her father and mother, out beyond the pass, in the wonderful Land of Oz, and the fact that they did not return to Oogaboo led Ann to suspect that they had found a better place to live. So, when Salye refused to sweep the floor of the living room in the palace, and Ann would not sweep it, either, she said to her sister: "I'm going away. This absurd Kingdom of Oogaboo tires me."

"Go, if you want to," answered Salye; "but you are very foolish to leave this place."

"Why?" asked Ann.

"Because in the Land of Oz, which is Ozma's country, you will be a nobody, while here you are a Queen."

"Oh, yes! Queen over eighteen men, twenty-seven women and forty-four children!" returned Ann bitterly.

"Well, there are certainly more people than that in the great Land of Oz," laughed Salye. "Why don't you raise an army and conquer them, and be Queen of all Oz?" she asked, trying to taunt Ann and so to anger her. Then she made a face at her sister and went into the back yard to swing in the hammock.

Her jeering words, however, had given Queen Ann an idea. She reflected that Oz was reported to be a peaceful country and Ozma a mere girl who ruled with gentleness to all and was obeyed because her people loved her. Even in Oogaboo the story was told that Ozma's sole army consisted of twenty-seven fine officers, who wore beautiful uniforms but carried no weapons, because there was no one to fight. Once there had been a private soldier, besides the officers, but Ozma had made him a Captain-General and taken away his gun for fear it might accidentally hurt some one.

The more Ann thought about the matter the more she was convinced it would be easy to conquer the Land of Oz and set herself up as Ruler in Ozma's place, if she but had an Army to do it with. Afterward she could go out into the world and conquer other lands, and then perhaps she could find a way to the moon, and conquer that. She had a warlike spirit that preferred trouble to idleness.

It all depended on an Army, Ann decided. She carefully counted in her mind all the men of her kingdom. Yes; there were exactly eighteen of them, all told. That would not make a very big Army, but by surprising Ozma's unarmed officers her men might easily subdue them. "Gentle people are always afraid of those that bluster," Ann told herself. "I don't wish to shed any blood, for that would shock my nerves and I might faint; but if we threaten and flash our weapons I am sure the people of Oz will fall upon their knees before me and surrender."

This argument, which she repeated to herself more than once, finally determined the Queen of Oogaboo to undertake the audacious venture.

"Whatever happens," she reflected, "can make me no more unhappy than my staying shut up in this miserable valley and sweeping floors and quarreling with Sister Salye; so I will venture all, and win what I may."

That very day she started out to organize her Army.

The first man she came to was Jo Apple, so called because he had an apple orchard.

"Jo," said Ann, "I am going to conquer the world, and I want you to join my Army."

"Don't ask me to do such a fool thing, for I must politely refuse Your Majesty," said Jo Apple."

"I have no intention of asking you. I shall command you, as Queen of Oogaboo, to join," said Ann.

"In that case, I suppose I must obey," the man remarked, in a sad voice. "But I pray you to consider that I am a very important citizen, and for that reason am entitled to an office of high rank."

"You shall be a General," promised Ann.

"With gold epaulets and a sword?" he asked.

"Of course," said the Queen.

Then she went to the next man, whose name was Jo Bunn, as he owned an orchard where graham-buns and wheat-buns, in great variety, both hot and cold, grew on the trees.

"Jo," said Ann, "I am going to conquer the world, and I command you to join my Army."

"Impossible!" he exclaimed. "The bun crop has to be picked."

"Let your wife and children do the picking," said Ann.

"But I'm a man of great importance, Your Majesty," he protested.

"For that reason you shall be one of my Generals, and wear a cocked hat with gold braid, and curl your mustaches and clank a long sword," she promised.

So he consented, although sorely against his will, and the Queen walked on to the next cottage. Here lived Jo Cone, so called because the trees in his orchard bore crops of excellent ice-cream cones.

"Jo," said Ann, "I am going to conquer the world, and you must join my Army."

"Excuse me, please," said Jo Cone. "I am a bad fighter. My good wife conquered me years ago, for she can fight better than I. Take her, Your Majesty, instead of me, and I'll bless you for the favor."

"This must be an army of men—fierce, ferocious warriors," declared Ann, looking sternly upon the mild little man.

"And you will leave my wife here in Oogaboo?" he asked.

"Yes; and make you a General."

"I'll go," said Jo Cone, and Ann went on to the cottage of Jo Clock, who had an orchard of clock-trees. This man at first insisted that he would not join the army, but Queen Ann's promise to make him a General finally won his consent.

"How many Generals are there in your army?" he asked.

"Four, so far," replied Ann.

"And how big will the army be?" was his next question.

"I intend to make every one of the eighteen men in Oogaboo join it," she said.

"Then four Generals are enough," announced Jo Clock. "I advise you to make the rest of them Colonels."

Ann tried to follow his advice. The next four men she visited— who were Jo Plum, Jo Egg, Jo Banjo and Jo Cheese, named after the trees in their orchards—she made Colonels of her Army; but the fifth one, Jo Nails, said Colonels and Generals were getting to be altogether too common in the Army of Oogaboo and he preferred to be a Major. So Jo Nails, Jo Cake, Jo Ham and Jo Stockings were all four made Majors, while the next four—Jo Sandwich, Jo Padlocks, Jo Sundae and Jo Buttons—were appointed Captains of the Army.

But now Queen Ann was in a quandary. There remained but two other men in all Oogaboo, and if she made these two Lieutenants, while there were four Captains, four Majors, four Colonels and four Generals, there was likely to be jealousy in her army, and perhaps mutiny and desertions.

One of these men, however, was Jo Candy, and he would not go at all. No promises could tempt him, nor could threats move him. He said he must remain at home to harvest his crop of jackson-balls, lemon-drops, bonbons and chocolate-creams. Also he had large fields of crackerjack and buttered pop corn to be mowed and threshed, and he was determined not to disappoint the children of Oogaboo by going away to conquer the world and so let the candy crop spoil.

Finding Jo Candy so obstinate, Queen Ann let him have his own way and continued her journey to the house of the eighteenth and last man in Oogaboo, who was a young fellow named Jo Files. This Files had twelve trees which bore steel files of various sorts; but also he had nine book-trees, on which grew a choice selection of story-books. In case you have never seen books growing upon trees, I will explain that those in Jo Files' orchard were enclosed in broad green husks which, when fully ripe, turned to a deep red color. Then the books were picked and husked and were ready to read. If they were picked too soon, the stories were found to be confused and uninteresting and the spelling bad. However, if allowed to ripen perfectly, the stories were fine reading and the spelling and grammar excellent.

Files freely gave his books to all who wanted them, but the people of Oogaboo cared little for books and so he had to read most of them himself, before they spoiled. For, as you probably know, as soon as the books were read the words disappeared and the leaves withered and faded—which is the worst fault of all books which grow upon trees.

When Queen Ann spoke to this young man Files, who was both intelligent and ambitious, he said he thought it would be great fun to conquer the world. But he called her attention to the fact that he was far superior to the other men of her army. Therefore, he would not be one of her Generals or Colonels or Majors or Captains, but claimed the honor of being sole Private.

Ann did not like this idea at all.

"I hate to have a Private Soldier in my army," she said; "they're so common. I am told that Princess Ozma once had a private soldier, but she made him her Captain-General, which is good evidence that the private was unnecessary."

"Ozma's army doesn't fight," returned Files; "but your army must fight like fury in order to conquer the world. I have read in my books that it is always the private soldiers who do the fighting, for no officer is ever brave enough to face the foe. Also, it stands to reason that your officers must have some one to command and to issue their orders to; therefore I'll be the one. I long to slash and slay the enemy and become a hero. Then, when we return to Oogaboo, I'll take all the marbles away from the children and melt them up and make a marble statue of myself for all to look upon and admire."

Ann was much pleased with Private Files. He seemed indeed to be such a warrior as she needed in her enterprise, and her hopes of success took a sudden bound when Files told her he knew where a gun-tree grew and would go there at once and pick the ripest and biggest musket the tree bore.

2. Out of Oogaboo

Three days later the Grand Army of Oogaboo assembled in the square in front of the royal palace. The sixteen officers were attired in gorgeous uniforms and carried sharp, glittering swords. The Private had picked his gun and, although it was not a very big weapon, Files tried to look fierce and succeeded so well that all his commanding officers were secretly afraid of him.

The women were there, protesting that Queen Ann Soforth had no right to take their husbands and fathers from them; but Ann commanded them to keep silent, and that was the hardest order to obey they had ever received.

The Queen appeared before her Army dressed in an imposing uniform of green, covered with gold braid. She wore a green soldier-cap with a purple plume in it and looked so royal and dignified that everyone in Oogaboo except the Army was glad she was going. The Army was sorry she was not going alone.

"Form ranks!" she cried in her shrill voice.

Salye leaned out of the palace window and laughed.

"I believe your Army can run better than it can fight," she observed.

"Of course," replied General Bunn, proudly. "We're not looking for trouble, you know, but for plunder. The more plunder and the less fighting we get, the better we shall like our work."

"For my part," said Files, "I prefer war and carnage to anything. The only way to become a hero is to conquer, and the story-books all say that the easiest way to conquer is to fight."

"That's the idea, my brave man!" agreed Ann. "To fight is to conquer and to conquer is to secure plunder and to secure plunder is to become a hero. With such noble determination to back me, the world is mine! Good-bye, Salye. When we return we shall be rich and famous. Come, Generals; let us march."

At this the Generals straightened up and threw out their chests. Then they swung their glittering swords in rapid circles and cried to the Colonels: "For-ward March!"

Then the Colonels shouted to the Majors: "For-ward March!" and the Majors yelled to the Captains: "For-ward March!" and the Captains screamed to the Private: "For-ward March!"

So Files shouldered his gun and began to march, and all the officers followed after him. Queen Ann came last of all, rejoicing in her noble army and wondering why she had not decided long ago to conquer the world.

In this order the procession marched out of Oogaboo and took the narrow mountain pass which led into the lovely Fairyland of Oz.

3. Magic Mystifies the Marchers

Princess Ozma was all unaware that the Army of Oogaboo, led by their ambitious Queen, was determined to conquer her Kingdom. The beautiful girl Ruler of Oz was busy with the welfare of her subjects and had no time to think of Ann Soforth and her disloyal plans. But there was one who constantly guarded the peace and happiness of the Land of Oz and this was the Official Sorceress of the Kingdom, Glinda the Good.

In her magnificent castle, which stands far north of the Emerald City where Ozma holds her court, Glinda owns a wonderful magic Record Book, in which is printed every event that takes place anywhere, just as soon as it happens.

The smallest things and the biggest things are all recorded in this book. If a child stamps its foot in anger, Glinda reads about it; if a city burns down, Glinda finds the fact noted in her book.

The Sorceress always reads her Record Book every day, and so it was she knew that Ann Soforth, Queen of Oogaboo, had foolishly assembled an army of sixteen officers and one private soldier, with which she intended to invade and conquer the Land of Oz.

There was no danger but that Ozma, supported by the magic arts of Glinda the Good and the powerful Wizard of Oz—both her firm friends—could easily defeat a far more imposing army than Ann's; but it would be a shame to have the peace of Oz interrupted by any sort of quarreling or fighting. So Glinda did not even mention the matter to Ozma, or to anyone else. She merely went into a great chamber of her castle, known as the Magic Room, where she performed a magical ceremony which caused the mountain pass that led from Oogaboo to make several turns and twists. The result was that when Ann and her army came to the end of the pass they were not in the Land of Oz at all, but in an adjoining territory that was quite distinct from Ozma's domain and separated from Oz by an invisible barrier.

As the Oogaboo people emerged into this country, the pass they had traversed disappeared behind them and it was not likely they would ever find their way back into the valley of Oogaboo. They were greatly puzzled, indeed, by their surroundings and did not know which way to go. None of them had ever visited Oz, so it took them some time to discover they were not in Oz at all, but in an unknown country.

"Never mind," said Ann, trying to conceal her disappointment; "we have started out to conquer the world, and here is part of it. In time, as we pursue our victorious journey, we will doubtless come to Oz; but, until we get there, we may as well conquer whatever land we find ourselves in."

"Have we conquered this place, Your Majesty?" anxiously inquired Major Cake.

"Most certainly," said Ann. "We have met no people, as yet, but when we do, we will inform them that they are our slaves."

"And afterward we will plunder them of all their possessions," added General Apple.

"They may not possess anything," objected Private Files; "but I hope they will fight us, just the same. A peaceful conquest wouldn't be any fun at all."

"Don't worry," said the Queen. "We can fight, whether our foes do or not; and perhaps we would find it more comfortable to have the enemy surrender promptly."

It was a barren country and not very pleasant to travel in. Moreover, there was little for them to eat, and as the officers became hungry they became fretful. Many would have deserted had they been able to find their way home, but as the Oogaboo people were now hopelessly lost in a strange country they considered it more safe to keep together than to separate.

Queen Ann's temper, never very agreeable, became sharp and irritable as she and her army tramped over the rocky roads without encountering either people or plunder. She scolded her officers until they became surly, and a few of them were disloyal enough to ask her to hold her tongue. Others began to reproach her for leading them into difficulties and in the space of three unhappy days every man was mourning for his orchard in the pretty valley of Oogaboo.

Files, however, proved a different sort. The more difficulties he encountered the more cheerful he became, and the sighs of the officers were answered by the merry whistle of the Private. His pleasant disposition did much to encourage Queen Ann and before long she consulted the Private Soldier more often than she did his superiors.

It was on the third day of their pilgrimage that they encountered their first adventure. Toward evening the sky was suddenly darkened and Major Nails exclaimed: "A fog is coming toward us."

"I do not think it is a fog," replied Files, looking with interest at the approaching cloud. "It seems to me more like the breath of a Rak."

"What is a Rak?" asked Ann, looking about fearfully.

"A terrible beast with a horrible appetite," answered the soldier, growing a little paler than usual. "I have never seen a Rak, to be sure, but I have read of them in the story-books that grew in my orchard, and if this is indeed one of those fearful monsters, we are not likely to conquer the world."

Hearing this, the officers became quite worried and gathered closer about their soldier.

"What is the thing like?" asked one.

"The only picture of a Rak that I ever saw in a book was rather blurred," said Files, "because the book was not quite ripe when it was picked. But the creature can fly in the air and run like a deer and swim like a fish. Inside its body is a glowing furnace of fire, and the Rak breathes in air and breathes out smoke, which darkens the sky for miles around, wherever it goes. It is bigger than a hundred men and feeds on any living thing."

The officers now began to groan and to tremble, but Files tried to cheer them, saying: "It may not be a Rak, after all, that we see approaching us, and you must not forget that we people of Oogaboo, which is part of the fairyland of Oz, cannot be killed."

"Nevertheless," said Captain Buttons, "if the Rak catches us, and chews us up into small pieces, and swallows us—what will happen then?"

"Then each small piece will still be alive," declared Files.

"I cannot see how that would help us," wailed Colonel Banjo. "A hamburger steak is a hamburger steak, whether it is alive or not!"

"I tell you, this may not be a Rak," persisted Files. "We will know, when the cloud gets nearer, whether it is the breath of a Rak or not. If it has no smell at all, it is probably a fog; but if it has an odor of salt and pepper, it is a Rak and we must prepare for a desperate fight."

They all eyed the dark cloud fearfully. Before long it reached the frightened group and began to envelop them. Every nose sniffed the cloud— and every one detected in it the odor of salt and pepper.

"The Rak!" shouted Private Files, and with a howl of despair the sixteen officers fell to the ground, writhing and moaning in anguish. Queen Ann sat down upon a rock and faced the cloud more bravely, although her heart was beating fast. As for Files, he calmly loaded his gun and stood ready to fight the foe, as a soldier should.

They were now in absolute darkness, for the cloud which covered the sky and the setting sun was black as ink. Then through the gloom appeared two round, glowing balls of red, and Files at once decided these must be the monster's eyes.

He raised his gun, took aim and fired.

There were several bullets in the gun, all gathered from an excellent bullet-tree in Oogaboo, and they were big and hard. They flew toward the monster and struck it, and with a wild, weird cry the Rak came fluttering down and its huge body fell plump upon the forms of the sixteen officers, who thereupon screamed louder than before.

"Badness me!" moaned the Rak. "See what you've done with that dangerous gun of yours!"

"I can't see," replied Files, "for the cloud formed by your breath darkens my sight!"

"Don't tell me it was an accident," continued the Rak, reproachfully, as it still flapped its wings in a helpless manner. "Don't claim you didn't know the gun was loaded, I beg of you!"

"I don't intend to," replied Files. "Did the bullets hurt you very badly?"

"One has broken my jaw, so that I can't open my mouth. You will notice that my voice sounds rather harsh and husky, because I have to talk with my teeth set close together. Another bullet broke my left wing, so that I can't fly; and still another broke my right leg, so that I can't walk. It was the most careless shot I ever heard of!"

"Can't you manage to lift your body off from my commanding officers?" inquired Files. "From their cries I'm afraid your great weight is crushing them."

"I hope it is," growled the Rak. "I want to crush them, if possible, for I have a bad disposition. If only I could open my mouth, I'd eat all of you, although my appetite is poorly this warm weather."

With this the Rak began to roll its immense body sidewise, so as to crush the officers more easily; but in doing this it rolled completely off from them and the entire sixteen scrambled to their feet and made off as fast as they could run.

Private Files could not see them go but he knew from the sound of their voices that they had escaped, so he ceased to worry about them.

"Pardon me if I now bid you good-bye," he said to the Rak. "The parting is caused by our desire to continue our journey. If you die, do not blame me, for I was obliged to shoot you as a matter of self-protection."

"I shall not die," answered the monster, "for I bear a charmed life. But I beg you not to leave me!"

"Why not?" asked Files.

"Because my broken jaw will heal in about an hour, and then I shall be able to eat you. My wing will heal in a day and my leg will heal in a week, when I shall be as well as ever. Having shot me, and so caused me all this annoyance, it is only fair and just that you remain here and allow me to eat you as soon as I can open my jaws."

"I beg to differ with you," returned the soldier firmly. "I have made an engagement with Queen Ann of Oogaboo to help her conquer the world, and I cannot break my word for the sake of being eaten by a Rak."

"Oh; that's different," said the monster. "If you've an engagement, don't let me detain you."

So Files felt around in the dark and grasped the hand of the trembling Queen, whom he led away from the flapping, sighing Rak. They stumbled over the stones for a way but presently began to see dimly the path ahead of them, as they got farther and farther away from the dreadful spot where the wounded monster lay. By and by they reached a little hill and could see the last rays of the sun flooding a pretty valley beyond, for now they had passed beyond the cloudy breath of the Rak. Here were huddled the sixteen officers, still frightened and panting from their run. They had halted only because it was impossible for them to run any farther.

Queen Ann gave them a severe scolding for their cowardice, at the same time praising Files for his courage.

"We are wiser than he, however," muttered General Clock, "for by running away we are now able to assist Your Majesty in conquering the world; whereas, had Files been eaten by the Rak, he would have deserted your Army."

After a brief rest they descended into the valley, and as soon as they were out of sight of the Rak the spirits of the entire party rose quickly. Just at dusk they came to a brook, on the banks of which Queen Ann commanded them to make camp for the night.

Each officer carried in his pocket a tiny white tent. This, when placed upon the ground, quickly grew in size until it was large enough to permit the owner to enter it and sleep within its canvas walls. Files was obliged to carry a knapsack, in which was not only his own tent but an elaborate pavilion for Queen Ann, besides a bed and chair and a magic table. This table, when set upon the ground in Ann's pavilion, became of large size, and in a drawer of the table was contained the Queen's supply of extra clothing, her manicure and toilet articles and other necessary things. The royal bed was the only one in the camp, the officers and private sleeping in hammocks attached to their tent poles.

There was also in the knapsack a flag bearing the royal emblem of Oogaboo, and this flag Files flew upon its staff every night, to show that the country they were in had been conquered by the Queen of Oogaboo. So far, no one but themselves had seen the flag, but Ann was pleased to see it flutter in the breeze and considered herself already a famous conqueror.

4. Betsy Braves the Billows

The waves dashed and the lightning flashed and the thunder rolled and the ship struck a rock. Betsy Bobbin was running across the deck and the shock sent her flying through the air until she fell with a splash into the dark blue water. The same shock caught Hank, a thin little, sad-faced mule, and tumbled him also into the sea, far from the ship's side.

When Betsy came up, gasping for breath because the wet plunge had surprised her, she reached out in the dark and grabbed a bunch of hair. At first she thought it was the end of a rope, but presently she heard a dismal "Hee-haw!" and knew she was holding fast to the end of Hank's tail.

Suddenly the sea was lighted up by a vivid glare. The ship, now in the far distance, caught fire, blew up and sank beneath the waves.

Betsy shuddered at the sight, but just then her eye caught a mass of wreckage floating near her and she let go the mule's tail and seized the rude raft, pulling herself up so that she rode upon it in safety. Hank also saw the raft and swam to it, but he was so clumsy he never would have been able to climb upon it had not Betsy helped him to get aboard.

They had to crowd close together, for their support was only a hatch-cover torn from the ship's deck; but it floated them fairly well and both the girl and the mule knew it would keep them from drowning.

The storm was not over, by any means, when the ship went down. Blinding bolts of lightning shot from cloud to cloud and the clamor of deep thunderclaps echoed far over the sea. The waves tossed the little raft here and there as a child tosses a rubber ball and Betsy had a solemn feeling that for hundreds of watery miles in every direction there was no living thing besides herself and the small donkey.

Perhaps Hank had the same thought, for he gently rubbed his nose against the frightened girl and said "Hee-haw!" in his softest voice, as if to comfort her.

"You'll protect me, Hank dear, won't you?" she cried helplessly, and the mule said "Hee-haw!" again, in tones that meant a promise.

On board the ship, during the days that preceded the wreck, when the sea was calm, Betsy and Hank had become good friends; so, while the girl might have preferred a more powerful protector in this dreadful emergency, she felt that the mule would do all in a mule's power to guard her safety.

All night they floated, and when the storm had worn itself out and passed away with a few distant growls, and the waves had grown smaller and easier to ride, Betsy stretched herself out on the wet raft and fell asleep.

Hank did not sleep a wink. Perhaps he felt it his duty to guard Betsy. Anyhow, he crouched on the raft beside the tired sleeping girl and watched patiently until the first light of dawn swept over the sea.

The light wakened Betsy Bobbin. She sat up, rubbed her eyes and stared across the water.

"Oh, Hank; there's land ahead!" she exclaimed.

"Hee-haw!" answered Hank in his plaintive voice.

The raft was floating swiftly toward a very beautiful country and as they drew near Betsy could see banks of lovely flowers showing brightly between leafy trees. But no people were to be seen at all.

5. The Roses Repulse the Refugees

Gently the raft grated on the sandy beach. Then Betsy easily waded ashore, the mule following closely behind her. The sun was now shining and the air was warm and laden with the fragrance of roses.

"I'd like some breakfast, Hank," remarked the girl, feeling more cheerful now that she was on dry land; "but we can't eat the flowers, although they do smell mighty good."

"Hee-haw!" replied Hank and trotted up a little pathway to the top of the bank.

Betsy followed and from the eminence looked around her. A little way off stood a splendid big greenhouse, its thousands of crystal panes glittering in the sunlight.

"There ought to be people somewhere 'round," observed Betsy thoughtfully; "gardeners, or somebody. Let's go and see, Hank. I'm getting hungrier ev'ry minute."

So they walked toward the great greenhouse and came to its entrance without meeting with anyone at all. A door stood ajar so Hank went in first, thinking if there was any danger he could back out and warn his companion. But Betsy was close at his heels and the moment she entered was lost in amazement at the wonderful sight she saw.

The greenhouse was filled with magnificent rosebushes, all growing in big pots. On the central stem of each bush bloomed a splendid Rose, gorgeously colored and deliciously fragrant, and in the center of each Rose was the face of a lovely girl.

As Betsy and Hank entered, the heads of the Roses were drooping and their eyelids were closed in slumber; but the mule was so amazed that he uttered a loud "Hee-haw!" and at the sound of his harsh voice the rose leaves fluttered, the Roses raised their heads and a hundred startled eyes were instantly fixed upon the intruders.

"I—I beg your pardon!" stammered Betsy, blushing and confused.

"O-o-o-h!" cried the Roses, in a sort of sighing chorus; and one of them added: "What a horrid noise!"

"Why, that was only Hank," said Betsy, and as if to prove the truth of her words the mule uttered another loud "Hee-haw!"

At this all the Roses turned on their stems as far as they were able and trembled as if some one were shaking their bushes. A dainty Moss Rose gasped: "Dear me! How dreadfully dreadful!"

"It isn't dreadful at all," said Betsy, somewhat indignant. "When you get used to Hank's voice it will put you to sleep."

The Roses now looked at the mule less fearfully and one of them asked: "Is that savage beast named Hank?"

"Yes; Hank's my comrade, faithful and true," answered the girl twining her arms around the little mule's neck and hugging him tight. "Aren't you, Hank?"

Hank could only say in reply: "Hee-haw!" and at his bray the Roses shivered again.

"Please go away!" begged one. "Can't you see you're frightening us out of a week's growth?"

"Go away!" echoed Betsy. "Why, we've no place to go. We've just been wrecked."

"Wrecked?" asked the Roses in a surprised chorus.

"Yes; we were on a big ship and the storm came and wrecked it," explained the girl. "But Hank and I caught hold of a raft and floated ashore to this place, and—we're tired and hungry. What country is this, please?"

"This is the Rose Kingdom," replied the Moss Rose, haughtily, "and it is devoted to the culture of the rarest and fairest Roses grown."

"I believe it," said Betsy, admiring the pretty blossoms.

"But only Roses are allowed here," continued a delicate Tea Rose, bending her brows in a frown; "therefore you must go away before the Royal Gardener finds you and casts you back into the sea."

"Oh! Is there a Royal Gardener, then?" inquired Betsy.

"To be sure."

"And is he a Rose, also?"

"Of course not; he's a man—a wonderful man," was the reply.

"Well, I'm not afraid of a man," declared the girl, much relieved, and even as she spoke the Royal Gardener popped into the greenhouse—a spading fork in one hand and a watering pot in the other.

He was a funny little man, dressed in a rose-colored costume, with ribbons at his knees and elbows, and a bunch of ribbons in his hair. His eyes were small and twinkling, his nose sharp and his face puckered and deeply lined.

"O-ho!" he exclaimed, astonished to find strangers in his greenhouse, and when Hank gave a loud bray the Gardener threw the watering pot over the mule's head and danced around with his fork, in such agitation that presently he fell over the handle of the implement and sprawled at full length upon the ground.

Betsy laughed and pulled the watering pot off from Hank's head. The little mule was angry at the treatment he had received and backed toward the Gardener threateningly.

"Look out for his heels!" called Betsy warningly and the Gardener scrambled to his feet and hastily hid behind the Roses.

"You are breaking the Law!" he shouted, sticking out his head to glare at the girl and the mule.

"What Law?" asked Betsy.

"The Law of the Rose Kingdom. No strangers are allowed in these domains."

"Not when they're shipwrecked?" she inquired.

"The Law doesn't except shipwrecks," replied the Royal Gardener, and he was about to say more when suddenly there was a crash of glass and a man came tumbling through the roof of the greenhouse and fell plump to the ground.

6. Shaggy Seeks his Stray Brother

This sudden arrival was a queer looking man, dressed all in garments so shaggy that Betsy at first thought he must be some animal. But the stranger ended his fall in a sitting position and then the girl saw it was really a man. He held an apple in his hand, which he had evidently been eating when he fell, and so little was he jarred or flustered by the accident that he continued to munch this apple as he calmly looked around him.

"Good gracious!" exclaimed Betsy, approaching him. "Who are you, and where did you come from?"

"Me? Oh, I'm Shaggy Man," said he, taking another bite of the apple. "Just dropped in for a short call. Excuse my seeming haste."

"Why, I s'pose you couldn't help the haste," said Betsy.

"No. I climbed an apple tree, outside; branch gave way and—

here I am."

As he spoke the Shaggy Man finished his apple, gave the core to Hank—who ate it greedily —and then stood up to bow politely to Betsy and the Roses.

The Royal Gardener had been frightened nearly into fits by the crash of glass and the fall of the shaggy stranger into the bower of Roses, but now he peeped out from behind a bush and cried in his squeaky voice: "You're breaking the Law! You're breaking the Law!"

Shaggy stared at him solemnly.

"Is the glass the Law in this country?" he asked.

"Breaking the glass is breaking the Law," squeaked the Gardener, angrily. "Also, to intrude in any part of the Rose Kingdom is breaking the Law."

"How do you know?" asked Shaggy.

"Why, it's printed in a book," said the Gardener, coming forward and taking a small book from his pocket. "Page thirteen. Here it is: 'If any stranger enters the Rose Kingdom he shall at once be condemned by the Ruler and put to death.' So you see, strangers," he continued triumphantly, "it's death for you all and your time has come!"

But just here Hank interposed. He had been stealthily backing toward the Royal Gardener, whom he disliked, and now the mule's heels shot out and struck the little man in the middle. He doubled up like the letter "U" and flew out of the door so swiftly—never touching the ground —that he was gone before Betsy had time to wink.

But the mule's attack frightened the girl.

"Come," she whispered, approaching the Shaggy Man and taking his hand; "let's go somewhere else. They'll surely kill us if we stay here!"

"Don't worry, my dear," replied Shaggy, patting the child's head. "I'm not afraid of anything, so long as I have the Love Magnet."

"The Love Magnet! Why, what is that?" asked Betsy.

"It's a charming little enchantment that wins the heart of everyone who looks upon it," was the reply. "The Love Magnet used to hang over the gateway to the Emerald City, in the Land of Oz; but when I started on this journey our beloved Ruler, Ozma of Oz, allowed me to take it with me."

"Oh!" cried Betsy, staring hard at him; "are you really from the wonderful Land of Oz?"

"Yes. Ever been there, my dear?"

"No; but I've heard about it. And do you know Princess Ozma?"

"Very well indeed."

"And—and Princess Dorothy?"

"Dorothy's an old chum of mine," declared Shaggy.

"Dear me!" exclaimed Betsy. "And why did you ever leave such a beautiful land as Oz?"

"On an errand," said Shaggy, looking sad and solemn. "I'm trying to find my dear little brother."

"Oh! Is he lost?" questioned Betsy, feeling very sorry for the poor man.

"Been lost these ten years," replied Shaggy, taking out a handkerchief and wiping a tear from his eye. "I didn't know it until lately, when I saw it recorded in the magic Record Book of the Sorceress Glinda, in the Land of Oz. So now I'm trying to find him."

"Where was he lost?" asked the girl sympathetically.

"Back in Colorado, where I used to live before I went to Oz. Brother was a miner, and dug gold out of a mine. One day he went into his mine and never came out. They searched for him, but he was not there. Disappeared entirely," Shaggy ended miserably.

"For goodness sake! What do you s'pose became of him?" she asked.

"There is only one explanation," replied Shaggy, taking another apple from his pocket and eating it to relieve his misery. "The Nome King probably got him."

"The Nome King! Who is he?"

"Why, he's sometimes called the Metal Monarch, and his name is Ruggedo. Lives in some underground cavern. Claims to own all the metals hidden in the earth. Don't ask me why."

"Why?"

"'Cause I don't know. But this Ruggedo gets wild with anger if anyone digs gold out of the earth, and my private opinion is that he captured brother and carried him off to his underground kingdom. No—don't ask me why. I see you're dying to ask me why. But I don't know."

"But—dear me!—in that case you will never find your lost brother!" exclaimed the girl.

"Maybe not; but it's my duty to try," answered Shaggy. "I've wandered so far without finding him, but that only proves he is not where I've been looking. What I seek now is the hidden passage to the underground cavern of the terrible Metal Monarch."

"Well," said Betsy doubtfully, "it strikes me that if you ever manage to get there the Metal Monarch will make you, too, his prisoner."

"Nonsense!" answered Shaggy, carelessly. "You mustn't forget the Love Magnet."

"What about it?" she asked.

"When the fierce Metal Monarch sees the Love Magnet, he will love me dearly and do anything I ask."

"It must be wonderful," said Betsy, with awe.

"It is," the man assured her. "Shall I show it to you?"

"Oh, do!" she cried; so Shaggy searched in his shaggy pocket and drew out a small silver magnet, shaped like a horseshoe.

The moment Betsy saw it she began to like the Shaggy Man better than before. Hank also saw the Magnet and crept up to Shaggy to rub his head lovingly against the man's knee.

But they were interrupted by the Royal Gardener, who stuck his head into the greenhouse and shouted angrily: "You are all condemned to death! Your only chance to escape is to leave here instantly."

This startled little Betsy, but the Shaggy Man merely waved the Magnet toward the Gardener, who, seeing it, rushed forward and threw himself at Shaggy's feet, murmuring in honeyed words: "Oh, you lovely, lovely man! How fond I am of you! Every shag and bobtail that decorates you is dear to me—all I have is yours! But for goodness' sake get out of here before you die the death."

"I'm not going to die," declared Shaggy Man.

"You must. It's the Law," exclaimed the Gardener, beginning to weep real tears. "It breaks my heart to tell you this bad news, but the Law says that all strangers must be condemned by the Ruler to die the death."

"No Ruler has condemned us yet," said Betsy.

"Of course not," added Shaggy. "We haven't even seen the Ruler of the Rose Kingdom."

"Well, to tell the truth," said the Gardener, in a perplexed tone of voice, "we haven't any real Ruler, just now. You see, all our Rulers grow on bushes in the Royal Gardens, and the last one we had got mildewed and withered before his time. So we had to plant him, and at this time there is no one growing on the Royal Bushes who is ripe enough to pick."

"How do you know?" asked Betsy.

"Why, I'm the Royal Gardener. Plenty of royalties are growing, I admit; but just now they are all green. Until one ripens, I am supposed to rule the Rose Kingdom myself, and see that its Laws are obeyed. Therefore, much as I love you, Shaggy, I must put you to death."

"Wait a minute," pleaded Betsy. "I'd like to see those Royal Gardens before I die."

"So would I," added Shaggy Man. "Take us there, Gardener."

"Oh, I can't do that," objected the Gardener. But Shaggy again showed him the Love Magnet and after one glance at it the Gardener could no longer resist.

He led Shaggy, Betsy and Hank to the end of the great greenhouse and carefully unlocked a small door. Passing through this they came into the splendid Royal Garden of the Rose Kingdom.

It was all surrounded by a tall hedge and within the enclosure grew several enormous rosebushes having thick green leaves of the texture of velvet. Upon these bushes grew the members of the Royal Family of the Rose Kingdom—men, women and children in all stages of maturity. They all seemed to have a light green hue, as if unripe or not fully developed, their flesh and clothing being alike green. They stood perfectly lifeless upon their branches, which swayed softly in the breeze, and their wide open eyes stared straight ahead, unseeing and unintelligent.

While examining these curious growing people, Betsy passed behind a big central bush and at once uttered an exclamation of surprise and pleasure. For there, blooming in perfect color and shape, stood a Royal Princess, whose beauty was amazing.

"Why, she's ripe!" cried Betsy, pushing aside some of the broad leaves to observe her more clearly.

"Well, perhaps so," admitted the Gardener, who had come to the girl's side; "but she's a girl, and so we can't use her for a Ruler."

"No, indeed!" came a chorus of soft voices, and looking around Betsy discovered that all the Roses had followed them from the greenhouse and were now grouped before the entrance.

"You see," explained the Gardener, "the subjects of Rose Kingdom don't want a girl Ruler. They want a King."

"A King! We want a King!" repeated the chorus of Roses.

"Isn't she Royal?" inquired Shaggy, admiring the lovely Princess.

"Of course, for she grows on a Royal Bush. This Princess is named Ozga, as she is a distant cousin of Ozma of Oz; and, were she but a man, we would joyfully hail her as our Ruler."

The Gardener then turned away to talk with his Roses and Betsy whispered to her companion: "Let's pick her, Shaggy."

"All right," said he. "If she's royal, she has the right to rule this Kingdom, and if we pick her she will surely protect us and prevent our being hurt, or driven away."

So Betsy and Shaggy each took an arm of the beautiful Rose Princess and a little twist of her feet set her free of the branch upon which she grew. Very gracefully she stepped down from the bush to the ground, where she bowed low to Betsy and Shaggy and said in a delightfully sweet voice: "I thank you."

But at the sound of these words the Gardener and the Roses turned and discovered that the Princess had been picked, and was now alive. Over every face flashed an expression of resentment and anger, and one of the Roses cried aloud.

"Audacious mortals! What have you done?"

"Picked a Princess for you, that's all," replied Betsy, cheerfully.

"But we won't have her! We want a King!" exclaimed a Jacque Rose, and another added with a voice of scorn: "No girl shall rule over us!"

The newly-picked Princess looked from one to another of her rebellious subjects in astonishment. A grieved look came over her exquisite features.

"Have I no welcome here, pretty subjects?" she asked gently. "Have I not come from my Royal Bush to be your Ruler?"

"You were picked by mortals, without our consent," replied the Moss Rose, coldly; "so we refuse to allow you to rule us."

"Turn her out, Gardener, with the others!" cried the Tea Rose.

"Just a second, please!" called Shaggy, taking the Love Magnet from his pocket. "I guess this will win their love, Princess. Here—take it in your hand and let the roses see it."

Princess Ozga took the Magnet and held it poised before the eyes of her subjects; but the Roses regarded it with calm disdain.

"Why, what's the matter?" demanded Shaggy in surprise. "The Magnet never failed to work before!"

"I know," said Betsy, nodding her head wisely. "These Roses have no hearts."

"That's it," agreed the Gardener. "They're pretty, and sweet, and alive; but still they are Roses. Their stems have thorns, but no hearts."

The Princess sighed and handed the Magnet to the Shaggy Man.

"What shall I do?" she asked sorrowfully.

"Turn her out, Gardener, with the others!" commanded the Roses. "We will have no Ruler until a man-rose—a King—is ripe enough to pick."

"Very well," said the Gardener meekly. "You must excuse me, my dear Shaggy, for opposing your wishes, but you and the others, including Ozga, must get out of Rose Kingdom immediately, if not before."

"Don't you love me, Gardy?" asked Shaggy, carelessly displaying the Magnet.

"I do. I dote on thee!" answered the Gardener earnestly; "but no true man will neglect his duty for the sake of love. My duty is to drive you out, so—out you go!"

With this he seized a garden fork and began jabbing it at the strangers, in order to force them to leave. Hank the mule was not afraid of the fork and when he got his heels near to the Gardener the man fell back to avoid a kick.

But now the Roses crowded around the outcasts and it was soon discovered that beneath their draperies of green leaves were many sharp thorns which were more dangerous than Hank's heels. Neither Betsy nor Ozga nor Shaggy nor the mule cared to brave those thorns and when they pressed away from them they found themselves slowly driven through the garden door into the greenhouse. From there they were forced out at the entrance and so through the territory of the flower-strewn Rose Kingdom, which was not of very great extent.

The Rose Princess was sobbing bitterly; Betsy was indignant and angry; Hank uttered defiant "Hee-haws" and the Shaggy Man whistled softly to himself.

The boundary of the Rose Kingdom was a deep gulf, but there was a drawbridge in one place and this the Royal Gardener let down until the outcasts had passed over it. Then he drew it up again and returned with his Roses to the greenhouse, leaving the four queerly assorted comrades to wander into the bleak and unknown country that lay beyond.

"I don't mind, much," remarked Shaggy, as he led the way over the stony, barren ground. "I've got to search for my long-lost little brother, anyhow, so it won't matter where I go."

"Hank and I will help you find your brother," said Betsy in her most cheerful voice. "I'm so far away from home now that I don't s'pose I'll ever find my way back; and, to tell the truth, it's more fun traveling around and having adventures than sticking at home. Don't you think so, Hank?"

"Hee-haw!" said Hank, and the Shaggy Man thanked them both.

"For my part," said Princess Ozga of Roseland, with a gentle sigh, "I must remain forever exiled from my Kingdom. So I, too, will be glad to help the Shaggy Man find his lost brother."

"That's very kind of you, ma'am," said Shaggy. "But unless I can find the underground cavern of Ruggedo, the Metal Monarch, I shall never find poor brother."

(This King was formerly named "Roquat," but after he drank of the "Waters of Oblivion" he forgot his own name and had to take another.)

"Doesn't anyone know where it is?" inquired Betsy.

"Some one must know, of course," was Shaggy's reply. "But we are not the ones. The only way to succeed is for us to keep going until we find a person who can direct us to Ruggedo's cavern."

"We may find it ourselves, without any help," suggested Betsy. "Who knows?"

"No one knows that, except the person who's writing this story," said Shaggy. "But we won't find anything—not even supper—unless we travel on. Here's a path. Let's take it and see where it leads to."

7. Polychrome's Pitiful Plight

The Rain King got too much water in his basin and spilled some over the brim. That made it rain in a certain part of the country—a real hard shower, for a time—and sent the Rainbow scampering to the place to show the gorgeous colors of his glorious bow as soon as the mist of rain had passed and the sky was clear.

The coming of the Rainbow is always a joyous event to earth folk, yet few have ever seen it close by. Usually the Rainbow is so far distant that you can observe its splendid hues but dimly, and that is why we seldom catch sight of the dancing Daughters of the Rainbow.

In the barren country where the rain had just fallen there appeared to be no human beings at all; but the Rainbow appeared, just the same, and dancing gayly upon its arch were the Rainbow's Daughters, led by the fairylike Polychrome, who is so dainty and beautiful that no girl has ever quite equalled her in loveliness.

Polychrome was in a merry mood and danced down the arch of the bow to the ground, daring her sisters to follow her. Laughing and gleeful, they also touched the ground with their twinkling feet; but all the Daughters of the Rainbow knew that this was a dangerous pastime, so they quickly climbed upon their bow again.

All but Polychrome. Though the sweetest and merriest of them all, she was likewise the most reckless. Moreover, it was an unusual sensation to pat the cold, damp earth with her rosy toes. Before she realized it the bow had lifted and disappeared in the billowy blue sky, and here was Polychrome standing helpless upon a rock, her gauzy draperies floating about her like brilliant cobwebs and not a soul—fairy or mortal—to help her regain her lost bow!

"Dear me!" she exclaimed, a frown passing across her pretty face, "I'm caught again. This is the second time my carelessness has left me on earth while my sisters returned to our Sky Palaces. The first time I enjoyed some pleasant adventures, but this is a lonely, forsaken country and I shall be very unhappy until my Rainbow comes again and I can climb aboard. Let me think what is best to be done."

She crouched low upon the flat rock, drew her draperies about her and bowed her head.

It was in this position that Betsy Bobbin spied Polychrome as she came along the stony path, followed by Hank, the Princess and Shaggy. At once the girl ran up to the radiant Daughter of the Rainbow and exclaimed: "Oh, what a lovely, lovely creature!"

Polychrome raised her golden head. There were tears in her blue eyes.

"I'm the most miserable girl in the whole world!" she sobbed.

The others gathered around her.

"Tell us your troubles, pretty one," urged the Princess.

"I—I've lost my bow!" wailed Polychrome.

"Take me, my dear," said Shaggy Man in a sympathetic tone, thinking she meant "beau" instead of "bow."

"I don't want you!" cried Polychrome, stamping her foot imperiously; "I want my Rainbow."

"Oh; that's different," said Shaggy. "But try to forget it. When I was young I used to cry for the Rainbow myself, but I couldn't have it. Looks as if you couldn't have it, either; so please don't cry."

Polychrome looked at him reproachfully.

"I don't like you," she said.

"No?" replied Shaggy, drawing the Love Magnet from his pocket; "not a little bit?—just a wee speck of a like?"

"Yes, yes!" said Polychrome, clasping her hands in ecstasy as she gazed at the enchanted talisman; "I love you, Shaggy Man!"

"Of course you do," said he calmly; "but I don't take any credit for it. It's the Love Magnet's powerful charm. But you seem quite alone and friendless, little Rainbow. Don't you want to join our party until you find your father and sisters again?"

"Where are you going?" she asked.

"We don't just know that," said Betsy, taking her hand; "but we're trying to find Shaggy's long-lost brother, who has been captured by the terrible Metal Monarch. Won't you come with us, and help us?"

Polychrome looked from one to another of the queer party of travelers and a bewitching smile suddenly lighted her face.

"A donkey, a mortal maid, a Rose Princess and a Shaggy Man!" she exclaimed. "Surely you need help, if you intend to face Ruggedo."

"Do you know him, then?" inquired Betsy.

"No, indeed. Ruggedo's caverns are beneath the earth's surface, where no Rainbow can ever penetrate. But I've heard of the Metal Monarch. He is also called the Nome King, you know, and he has made trouble for a good many people —mortals and fairies—in his time," said Polychrome.

"Do you fear him, then?" asked the Princess, anxiously.

"No one can harm a Daughter of the Rainbow," said Polychrome proudly. "I'm a sky fairy."

"Then," said Betsy, quickly, "you will be able to tell us the way to Ruggedo's cavern."

"No," returned Polychrome, shaking her head, "that is one thing I cannot do. But I will gladly go with you and help you search for the place."

This promise delighted all the wanderers and after the Shaggy Man had found the path again they began moving along it in a more happy mood. The Rainbow's Daughter danced lightly over the rocky trail, no longer sad, but with her beautiful features wreathed in smiles. Shaggy came next, walking steadily and now and then supporting the Rose Princess, who followed him. Betsy and Hank brought up the rear, and if she tired with walking the girl got upon Hank's back and let the stout little donkey carry her for a while.

At nightfall they came to some trees that grew beside a tiny brook and here they made camp and rested until morning. Then away they tramped, finding berries and fruits here and there which satisfied the hunger of Betsy, Shaggy and Hank, so that they were well content with their lot.

It surprised Betsy to see the Rose Princess partake of their food, for she considered her a fairy; but when she mentioned this to Polychrome, the Rainbow's Daughter explained that when Ozga was driven out of her Rose Kingdom she ceased to be a fairy and would never again be more than a mere mortal. Polychrome, however, was a fairy wherever she happened to be, and if she sipped a few dewdrops by moonlight for refreshment no one ever saw her do it.

As they continued their wandering journey, direction meant very little to them, for they were hopelessly lost in this strange country. Shaggy said it would be best to go toward the mountains, as the natural entrance to Ruggedo's underground cavern was likely to be hidden in some rocky, deserted place; but mountains seemed all around them except in the one direction that they had come from, which led to the Rose Kingdom and the sea. Therefore it mattered little which way they traveled.

By and by they espied a faint trail that looked like a path and after following this for some time they reached a crossroads. Here were many paths, leading in various directions, and there was a signpost so old that there were now no words upon the sign. At one side was an old well, with a chain windlass for drawing water, yet there was no house or other building anywhere in sight.

While the party halted, puzzled which way to proceed, the mule approached the well and tried to look into it.

"He's thirsty," said Betsy.

"It's a dry well," remarked Shaggy. "Probably there has been no water in it for many years. But, come; let us decide which way to travel."

No one seemed able to decide that. They sat down in a group and tried to consider which road might be the best to take. Hank, however, could not keep away from the well and finally he reared up on his hind legs, got his head over the edge and uttered a loud "Hee-haw!" Betsy watched her animal friend curiously.

"I wonder if he sees anything down there?" she said.

At this, Shaggy rose and went over to the well to investigate, and Betsy went with him. The Princess and Polychrome, who had become fast friends, linked arms and sauntered down one of the roads, to find an easy path.

"Really," said Shaggy, "there does seem to be something at the bottom of this old well."

"Can't we pull it up, and see what it is?" asked the girl.

There was no bucket at the end of the windlass chain, but there was a big hook that at one time was used to hold a bucket. Shaggy let down this hook, dragged it around on the bottom and then pulled it up. An old hoopskirt came with it, and Betsy laughed and threw it away. The thing frightened Hank, who had never seen a hoopskirt before, and he kept a good distance away from it.

Several other objects the Shaggy Man captured with the hook and drew up, but none of these was important.

"This well seems to have been the dump for all the old rubbish in the country," he said, letting down the hook once more. "I guess I've captured everything now. No—the hook has caught again. Help me, Betsy! Whatever this thing is, it's heavy."

She ran up and helped him turn the windlass and after much effort a confused mass of copper came in sight.

"Good gracious!" exclaimed Shaggy. "Here is a surprise, indeed!"

"What is it?" inquired Betsy, clinging to the windlass and panting for breath.

For answer the Shaggy Man grasped the bundle of copper and dumped it upon the ground, free of the well. Then he turned it over with his foot, spread it out, and to Betsy's astonishment the thing proved to be a copper man.

"Just as I thought," said Shaggy, looking hard at the object. "But unless there are two copper men in the world this is the most astonishing thing I ever came across."

At this moment the Rainbow's Daughter and the Rose Princess approached them, and Polychrome said: "What have you found, Shaggy One?"

"Either an old friend, or a stranger," he replied.

"Oh, here's a sign on his back!" cried Betsy, who had knelt down to examine the man. "Dear me; how funny! Listen to this."

Then she read the following words, engraved upon the copper plates of the man's body:

> SMITH & TINKER'S
> Patent Double-Action,
> Extra-Responsive,
> Thought-Creating,
> Perfect-Talking
> MECHANICAL MAN
> Fitted with our Special Clockwork Attachment.
> Thinks, Speaks, Acts, and Does Everything but Live.

"Isn't he wonderful!" exclaimed the Princess.

"Yes; but here's more," said Betsy, reading from another engraved plate:

> DIRECTIONS FOR USING:
> For THINKING:—Wind the Clockwork Man under his left arm, (marked No. 1).
> For SPEAKING:—Wind the Clockwork Man under his right arm, (marked No. 2).
> For WALKING and ACTION:—Wind Clockwork Man in the middle of his back, (marked No. 3).
> N.B. This Mechanism is guaranteed to work perfectly for a thousand years.

"If he's guaranteed for a thousand years," said Polychrome, "he ought to work yet."

"Of course," replied Shaggy. "Let's wind him up."

In order to do this they were obliged to set the copper man upon his feet, in an upright position, and this was no easy task. He was inclined to topple over, and had to be propped again and again. The girls assisted Shaggy, and at last Tik-Tok seemed to be balanced and stood alone upon his broad feet.

"Yes," said Shaggy, looking at the copper man carefully, "this must be, indeed, my old friend Tik-Tok, whom I left ticking merrily in the Land of Oz. But how he came to this lonely place, and got into that old well, is surely a mystery."

"If we wind him, perhaps he will tell us," suggested Betsy. "Here's the key, hanging to a hook on his back. What part of him shall I wind up first?"

"His thoughts, of course," said Polychrome, "for it requires thought to speak or move intelligently."

So Betsy wound him under his left arm, and at once little flashes of light began to show in the top of his head, which was proof that he had begun to think.

"Now, then," said Shaggy, "wind up his phonograph."

"What's that?" she asked.

"Why, his talking-machine. His thoughts may be interesting, but they don't tell us anything."

So Betsy wound the copper man under his right arm, and then from the interior of his copper body came in jerky tones the words: "Ma-ny thanks!"

"Hurrah!" cried Shaggy, joyfully, and he slapped Tik-Tok upon the back in such a hearty manner that the copper man lost his balance and tumbled to the ground in a heap. But the clockwork that enabled him to speak had been wound up and he kept saying: "Pick-me-up! Pick-me-up! Pick-me-up!" until they had again raised him and balanced him upon his feet, when he added

politely: "Ma-ny thanks!"

"He won't be self-supporting until we wind up his action," remarked Shaggy; so Betsy wound it, as tight as she could—for the key turned rather hard—and then Tik-Tok lifted his feet, marched around in a circle and ended by stopping before the group and making them all a low bow.

"How in the world did you happen to be in that well, when I left you safe in Oz?" inquired Shaggy.

"It is a long sto-ry," replied Tik-Tok, "but I'll tell it in a few words. Af-ter you had gone in search of your broth-er, Oz-ma saw you wan-der-ing in strange lands when-ev-er she looked in her mag-ic pic-ture, and she also saw your broth-er in the Nome King's cavern; so she sent me to tell you where to find your broth-er and told me to help you if I could. The Sor-cer-ess, Glin-da the Good, trans-port-ed me to this place in the wink of an eye; but here I met the Nome King him-self—old Rug-ge-do, who is called in these parts the Met-al Mon-arch. Rug-ge-do knew what I had come for, and he was so an-gry that he threw me down the well. Af-ter my works ran down I was help-less un-til you came a-long and pulled me out a-gain. Ma-ny thanks."

"This is, indeed, good news," said Shaggy. "I suspected that my brother was the prisoner of Ruggedo; but now I know it. Tell us, Tik-Tok, how shall we get to the Nome King's underground cavern?"

"The best way is to walk," said Tik-Tok. "We might crawl, or jump, or roll o-ver and o-ver until we get there; but the best way is to walk."

"I know; but which road shall we take?"

"My ma-chin-er-y is-n't made to tell that," replied Tik-Tok.

"There is more than one entrance to the underground cavern," said Polychrome; "but old Ruggedo has cleverly concealed every opening, so that earth dwellers can not intrude in his domain. If we find our way underground at all, it will be by chance."

"Then," said Betsy, "let us select any road, haphazard, and see where it leads us."

"That seems sensible," declared the Princess. "It may require a lot of time for us to find Ruggedo, but we have more time than anything else."

"If you keep me wound up," said Tik-Tok, "I will last a thou-sand years."

"Then the only question to decide is which way to go," added Shaggy, looking first at one road and then at another.

But while they stood hesitating, a peculiar sound reached their ears—a sound like the tramping of many feet.

"What's coming?" cried Betsy; and then she ran to the left-hand road and glanced along the path. "Why, it's an army!" she exclaimed. "What shall we do, hide or run?"

"Stand still," commanded Shaggy. "I'm not afraid of an army. If they prove to be friendly, they can help us; if they are enemies, I'll show them the Love Magnet."

8. Tik-Tok Tackles a Tough Task

While Shaggy and his companions stood huddled in a group at one side, the Army of Oogaboo was approaching along the pathway, the tramp of their feet being now and then accompanied by a dismal groan as one of the officers stepped on a sharp stone or knocked his funnybone against his neighbor's sword-handle.

Then out from among the trees marched Private Files, bearing the banner of Oogaboo, which fluttered from a long pole. This pole he stuck in the ground just in front of the well and then he cried in a loud voice: "I hereby conquer this territory in the name of Queen Ann Soforth of Oogaboo, and all the inhabitants of the land I proclaim her slaves!"

Some of the officers now stuck their heads out of the bushes and asked: "Is the coast clear, Private Files?"

"There is no coast here," was the reply, "but all's well."

"I hope there's water in it," said General Cone, mustering courage to advance to the well; but just then he caught a glimpse of Tik-Tok and Shaggy and at once fell upon his knees, trembling and frightened and cried out:

"Mercy, kind enemies! Mercy! Spare us, and we will be your slaves forever!"

The other officers, who had now advanced into the clearing, likewise fell upon their knees and begged for mercy.

Files turned around and, seeing the strangers for the first time, examined them with much curiosity. Then, discovering that three of the party were girls, he lifted his cap and made a polite bow.

"What's all this?" demanded a harsh voice, as Queen Ann reached the place and beheld her kneeling army.

"Permit us to introduce ourselves," replied Shaggy, stepping forward. "This is Tik-Tok, the Clockwork Man—who works better than some meat people. And here is Princess Ozga of Roseland, just now unfortunately exiled from her Kingdom of Roses. I next present Polychrome, a sky fairy, who lost her Bow by an accident and can't find her way home. The small girl here is Betsy Bobbin, from some unknown earthly paradise called Oklahoma, and with her you see Mr. Hank, a mule with a long tail and a short temper."

"Puh!" said Ann, scornfully; "a pretty lot of vagabonds you are, indeed; all lost or strayed, I suppose, and not worth a Queen's plundering. I'm sorry I've conquered you."

"But you haven't conquered us yet," called Betsy indignantly.

"No," agreed Files, "that is a fact. But if my officers will kindly command me to conquer you, I will do so at once, after which we can stop arguing and converse more at our ease."

The officers had by this time risen from their knees and brushed the dust from their trousers. To them the enemy did not look very fierce, so the Generals and Colonels and Majors and Captains gained courage to face them and began strutting in their most haughty manner.

"You must understand," said Ann, "that I am the Queen of Oogaboo, and this is my invincible Army. We are busy conquering the world, and since you seem to be a part of the world, and are obstructing our journey, it is necessary for us to conquer you—unworthy though you may be of such high honor."

"That's all right," replied Shaggy. "Conquer us as often as you like. We don't mind."

"But we won't be anybody's slaves," added Betsy, positively.

"We'll see about that," retorted the Queen, angrily. "Advance, Private Files, and bind the enemy hand and foot!"

But Private Files looked at pretty Betsy and fascinating Polychrome and the beautiful Rose Princess and shook his head.

"It would be impolite, and I won't do it," he asserted.

"You must!" cried Ann. "It is your duty to obey orders."

"I haven't received any orders from my officers," objected the Private.

But the Generals now shouted: "Forward, and bind the prisoners!" and the Colonels and Majors and Captains repeated the command, yelling it as loud as they could.

All this noise annoyed Hank, who had been eyeing the Army of Oogaboo with strong disfavor. The mule now dashed forward and began backing upon the officers and kicking fierce and dangerous heels at them. The attack was so sudden that the officers scattered like dust in a whirlwind, dropping their swords as they ran and trying to seek refuge behind the trees and bushes.

Betsy laughed joyously at the comical rout of the "noble army," and Polychrome danced with glee. But Ann was furious at this ignoble defeat of her gallant forces by one small mule.

"Private Files, I command you to do your duty!" she cried again, and then she herself ducked to escape the mule's heels—for Hank made no distinction in favor of a lady who was an open enemy. Betsy grabbed her champion by the forelock, however, and so held him fast, and when the officers saw that the mule was restrained from further attacks they crept fearfully back and picked up their discarded swords.

"Private Files, seize and bind these prisoners!" screamed the Queen.

"No," said Files, throwing down his gun and removing the knapsack which was strapped to his back, "I resign my position as the Army of Oogaboo. I enlisted to fight the enemy and become a hero, but if you want some one to bind harmless girls you will have to hire another Private."

Then he walked over to the others and shook hands with Shaggy and Tik-Tok.

"Treason!" shrieked Ann, and all the officers echoed her cry.

"Nonsense," said Files. "I've the right to resign if I want to."

"Indeed you haven't!" retorted the Queen. "If you resign it will break up my Army, and then I cannot conquer the world." She now turned to the officers and said: "I must ask you to do me a favor. I know it is undignified in officers to fight, but unless you immediately capture Private Files and force him to obey my orders there will be no plunder for any of us. Also it is likely you will all suffer the pangs of hunger, and when we meet a powerful foe you are liable to be captured and made slaves."

The prospect of this awful fate so frightened the officers that they drew their swords and rushed upon Files, who stood beside Shaggy, in a truly ferocious manner. The next instant, however, they halted and again fell upon their knees; for there, before them, was the glistening Love Magnet, held in the hand of the smiling Shaggy Man, and the sight of this magic talisman at once won the heart of every Oogabooite. Even Ann saw the Love Magnet, and forgetting all enmity and anger threw herself upon Shaggy and embraced him lovingly.

Quite disconcerted by this unexpected effect of the Magnet, Shaggy disengaged himself from the Queen's encircling arms and quickly hid the talisman in his pocket. The adventurers from Oogaboo were now his firm friends, and there was no more talk about conquering and binding any of his party.

"If you insist on conquering anyone," said Shaggy, "you may march with me to the underground Kingdom of Ruggedo. To conquer the world, as you have set out to do, you must conquer everyone under its surface as well as those upon its surface, and no one in all the world needs conquering so much as Ruggedo."

"Who is he?" asked Ann.

"The Metal Monarch, King of the Nomes."

"Is he rich?" inquired Major Stockings in an anxious voice.

"Of course," answered Shaggy. "He owns all the metal that lies underground—gold, silver, copper, brass and tin. He has an idea he also owns all the metals above ground, for he says all metal was once a part of his kingdom. So, by conquering the Metal Monarch, you will win all the riches in the world."

"Ah!" exclaimed General Apple, heaving a deep sigh, "that would be plunder worth our while. Let's conquer him, Your Majesty."

The Queen looked reproachfully at Files, who was sitting next to the lovely Princess and whispering in her ear.

"Alas," said Ann, "I have no longer an Army. I have plenty of brave officers, indeed, but no private soldier for them to command. Therefore I cannot conquer Ruggedo and win all his wealth."

"Why don't you make one of your officers the Private?" asked Shaggy; but at once every officer began to protest and the Queen of Oogaboo shook her head as she replied: "That is impossible. A private soldier must be a terrible fighter, and my officers are unable to fight. They are exceptionally brave in commanding others to fight, but could not themselves meet the enemy and conquer."

"Very true, Your Majesty," said Colonel Plum, eagerly. "There are many kinds of bravery and one cannot be expected to possess them all. I myself am brave as a lion in all ways until it comes to fighting, but then my nature revolts. Fighting is unkind and liable to be injurious to others; so, being a gentleman, I never fight."

"Nor I!" shouted each of the other officers.

"You see," said Ann, "how helpless I am. Had not Private Files proved himself a traitor and a deserter, I would gladly have conquered this Ruggedo; but an Army without a private soldier is like a bee without a stinger."

"I am not a traitor, Your Majesty," protested Files. "I resigned in a proper manner, not liking the job. But there are plenty of people to take my place. Why not make Shaggy Man the private soldier?"

"He might be killed," said Ann, looking tenderly at Shaggy, "for he is mortal, and able to die. If anything happened to him, it would break my heart."

"It would hurt me worse than that," declared Shaggy. "You must admit, Your Majesty, that I am commander of this expedition, for it is my brother we are seeking, rather than plunder. But my companions would like the assistance of your Army, and if you help us to conquer Ruggedo and to rescue my brother from captivity we will allow you to keep all the gold and jewels and other plunder you may find."

This prospect was so tempting that the officers began whispering together and presently Colonel Cheese said: "Your Majesty, by combining our brains we have just evolved a most brilliant idea. We will make the Clockwork Man the private soldier!"

"Who? Me?" asked Tik-Tok. "Not for a sin-gle sec-ond! I can-not fight, and you must not for-get that it was Rug-ge-do who threw me in the well."

"At that time you had no gun," said Polychrome. "But if you join the Army of Oogaboo you will carry the gun that Mr. Files used."

"A sol-dier must be a-ble to run as well as to fight," protested Tik-Tok, "and if my works run down, as they of-ten do, I could nei-ther run nor fight."

"I'll keep you wound up, Tik-Tok," promised Betsy.

"Why, it isn't a bad idea," said Shaggy. "Tik-Tok will make an ideal soldier, for nothing can injure him except a sledge hammer. And, since a private soldier seems to be necessary to this Army, Tik-Tok is the only one of our party fitted to undertake the job."

"What must I do?" asked Tik-Tok.

"Obey orders," replied Ann. "When the officers command you to do anything, you must do it; that is all."

"And that's enough, too," said Files.

"Do I get a salary?" inquired Tik-Tok.

"You get your share of the plunder," answered the Queen.

"Yes," remarked Files, "one-half of the plunder goes to Queen Ann, the other half is divided among the officers, and the Private gets the rest."

"That will be sat-is-fac-tor-y," said Tik-Tok, picking up the gun and examining it wonderingly, for he had never before seen such a weapon.

Then Ann strapped the knapsack to Tik-Tok's copper back and said: "Now we are ready to march to Ruggedo's Kingdom and conquer it. Officers, give the command to march."

"Fall—in!" yelled the Generals, drawing their swords.

"Fall—in!" cried the Colonels, drawing their swords.

"Fall—in!" shouted the Majors, drawing their swords.

"Fall—in!" bawled the Captains, drawing their swords.

Tik-Tok looked at them and then around him in surprise.

"Fall in what? The well?" he asked.

"No," said Queen Ann, "you must fall in marching order."

"Can-not I march without fall-ing in-to it?" asked the Clockwork Man.

"Shoulder your gun and stand ready to march," advised Files; so Tik-Tok held the gun straight and stood still.

"What next?" he asked.

The Queen turned to Shaggy.

"Which road leads to the Metal Monarch's cavern?"

"We don't know, Your Majesty," was the reply.

"But this is absurd!" said Ann with a frown. "If we can't get to Ruggedo, it is certain that we can't conquer him."

"You are right," admitted Shaggy; "but I did not say we could not get to him. We have only to discover the way, and that was the matter we were considering when you and your magnificent Army arrived here."

"Well, then, get busy and discover it," snapped the Queen.

That was no easy task. They all stood looking from one road to another in perplexity. The paths radiated from the little clearing like the rays of the midday sun, and each path seemed like all the others.

Files and the Rose Princess, who had by this time become good friends, advanced a little way along one of the roads and found that it was bordered by pretty wild flowers.

"Why don't you ask the flowers to tell you the way?" he said to his companion.

"The flowers?" returned the Princess, surprised at the question.

"Of course," said Files. "The field-flowers must be second-cousins to a Rose Princess, and I believe if you ask them they will tell you."

She looked more closely at the flowers. There were hundreds of white daisies, golden buttercups, bluebells and daffodils growing by the roadside, and each flower-head was firmly set upon its slender but stout stem. There were even a few wild roses scattered here and there and perhaps it was the sight of these that gave the Princess courage to ask the important question.

She dropped to her knees, facing the flowers, and extended both her arms pleadingly toward them.

"Tell me, pretty cousins," she said in her sweet, gentle voice, "which way will lead us to the Kingdom of Ruggedo, the Nome King?"

At once all the stems bent gracefully to the right and the flower heads nodded once—twice— thrice in that direction.

"That's it!" cried Files joyfully. "Now we know the way."

Ozga rose to her feet and looked wonderingly at the field-flowers, which had now resumed their upright position.

"Was it the wind, do you think?" she asked in a low whisper.

"No, indeed," replied Files. "There is not a breath of wind stirring. But these lovely blossoms are indeed your cousins and answered your question at once, as I knew they would."

9. Ruggedo's Rage is Rash and Reckless

The way taken by the adventurers led up hill and down dale and wound here and there in a fashion that seemed aimless. But always it drew nearer to a range of low mountains and Files said more than once that he was certain the entrance to Ruggedo's cavern would be found among these rugged hills.

In this he was quite correct. Far underneath the nearest mountain was a gorgeous chamber hollowed from the solid rock, the walls and roof of which glittered with thousands of magnificent jewels. Here, on a throne of virgin gold, sat the famous Nome King, dressed in splendid robes and wearing a superb crown cut from a single blood-red ruby.

Ruggedo, the Monarch of all the Metals and Precious Stones of the Underground World, was a round little man with a flowing white beard, a red face, bright eyes and a scowl that covered all his forehead. One would think, to look at him, that he ought to be jolly; one might think, considering his enormous wealth, that he ought to be happy; but this was not the case. The Metal Monarch was surly and cross because mortals had dug so much treasure out of the earth and kept it above ground, where all the power of Ruggedo and his nomes was unable to recover it. He hated not only the mortals but also the fairies who live upon the earth or above it, and instead of being content with the riches he still possessed he was unhappy because he did not own all the gold and jewels in the world.

Ruggedo had been nodding, half asleep, in his chair when suddenly he sat upright, uttered a roar of rage and began pounding upon a huge gong that stood beside him.

The sound filled the vast cavern and penetrated to many caverns beyond, where countless thousands of nomes were working at their unending tasks, hammering out gold and silver and other metals, or melting ores in great furnaces, or polishing glittering gems. The nomes trembled at the sound of the King's gong and whispered fearfully to one another that something unpleasant was sure to happen; but none dared pause in his task.

The heavy curtains of cloth-of-gold were pushed aside and Kaliko, the King's High Chamberlain, entered the royal presence.

"What's up, Your Majesty?" he asked, with a wide yawn, for he had just wakened.

"Up?" roared Ruggedo, stamping his foot viciously. "Those foolish mortals are up, that's what! And they want to come down."

"Down here?" inquired Kaliko.

"Yes!"

"How do you know?" continued the Chamberlain, yawning again.

"I feel it in my bones," said Ruggedo. "I can always feel it when those hateful earth-crawlers draw near to my Kingdom. I am positive, Kaliko, that mortals are this very minute on their way here to annoy me—and I hate mortals more than I do catnip tea!"

"Well, what's to be done?" demanded the nome.

"Look through your spyglass, and see where the invaders are," commanded the King.

So Kaliko went to a tube in the wall of rock and put his eye to it. The tube ran from the cavern up to the side of the mountain and turned several curves and corners, but as it was a magic spyglass Kaliko was able to see through it just as easily as if it had been straight.

"Ho—hum," said he. "I see 'em, Your Majesty."

"What do they look like?" inquired the Monarch.

"That's a hard question to answer, for a queerer assortment of creatures I never yet beheld," replied the nome. "However, such a collection of curiosities may prove dangerous. There's a copper man, worked by machinery—"

"Bah! that's only Tik-Tok," said Ruggedo. "I'm not afraid of him. Why, only the other day I met the fellow and threw him down a well."

"Then some one must have pulled him out again," said Kaliko. "And there's a little girl—"

"Dorothy?" asked Ruggedo, jumping up in fear.

"No; some other girl. In fact, there are several girls, of various sizes; but Dorothy is not with them, nor is Ozma."

"That's good!" exclaimed the King, sighing in relief.

Kaliko still had his eye to the spyglass.

"I see," said he, "an army of men from Oogaboo. They are all officers and carry swords. And there is a Shaggy Man—who seems very harmless—and a little donkey with big ears."

"Pooh!" cried Ruggedo, snapping his fingers in scorn. "I've no fear of such a mob as that. A dozen of my nomes can destroy them all in a jiffy."

"I'm not so sure of that," said Kaliko. "The people of Oogaboo are hard to destroy, and I believe the Rose Princess is a fairy. As for Polychrome, you know very well that the Rainbow's Daughter cannot be injured by a nome."

"Polychrome! Is she among them?" asked the King.

"Yes; I have just recognized her."

"Then these people are coming here on no peaceful errand," declared Ruggedo, scowling fiercely. "In fact, no one ever comes here on a peaceful errand. I hate everybody, and everybody hates me!"

"Very true," said Kaliko.

"I must in some way prevent these people from reaching my dominions. Where are they now?"

"Just now they are crossing the Rubber Country, Your Majesty."

"Good! Are your magnetic rubber wires in working order?"

"I think so," replied Kaliko. "Is it your Royal Will that we have some fun with these invaders?"

"It is," answered Ruggedo. "I want to teach them a lesson they will never forget."

Now, Shaggy had no idea that he was in a Rubber Country, nor had any of his companions. They noticed that everything around them was of a dull gray color and that the path upon which they walked was soft and springy, yet they had no suspicion that the rocks and trees were rubber and even the path they trod was made of rubber.

Presently they came to a brook where sparkling water dashed through a deep channel and rushed away between high rocks far down the mountain-side. Across the brook were stepping-stones, so placed that travelers might easily leap from one to another and in that manner cross the water to the farther bank.

Tik-Tok was marching ahead, followed by his officers and Queen Ann. After them came Betsy Bobbin and Hank, Polychrome and Shaggy, and last of all the Rose Princess with Files. The Clockwork Man saw the stream and the stepping stones and, without making a pause, placed his foot upon the first stone.

The result was astonishing. First he sank down in the soft rubber, which then rebounded and sent Tik-Tok soaring high in the air, where he turned a succession of flip-flops and alighted upon a rubber rock far in the rear of the party.

General Apple did not see Tik-Tok bound, so quickly had he disappeared; therefore he also stepped upon the stone (which you will guess was connected with Kaliko's magnetic rubber wire) and instantly shot upward like an arrow. General Cone came next and met with a like fate, but the others now noticed that something was wrong and with one accord they halted the column and looked back along the path.

There was Tik-Tok, still bounding from one rubber rock to another, each time rising a less distance from the ground. And there was General Apple, bounding away in another direction, his three-cornered hat jammed over his eyes and his long sword thumping him upon the arms and head as it swung this way and that. And there, also, appeared General Cone, who had struck a rubber rock headforemost and was so crumpled up that his round body looked more like a bouncing-ball than the form of a man.

Betsy laughed merrily at the strange sight and Polychrome echoed her laughter. But Ozga was grave and wondering, while Queen Ann became angry at seeing the chief officers of the Army of Oogaboo bounding around in so undignified a manner. She shouted to them to stop, but they were unable to obey, even though they would have been glad to do so. Finally, however, they all ceased bounding and managed to get upon their feet and rejoin the Army.

"Why did you do that?" demanded Ann, who seemed greatly provoked.

"Don't ask them why," said Shaggy earnestly. "I knew you would ask them why, but you ought not to do it. The reason is plain.

Those stones are rubber; therefore they are not stones. Those rocks around us are rubber, and therefore they are not rocks. Even this path is not a path; it's rubber. Unless we are very careful, your Majesty, we are all likely to get the bounce, just as your poor officers and Tik-Tok did."

"Then let's be careful," remarked Files, who was full of wisdom; but Polychrome wanted to test the quality of the rubber, so she began dancing. Every step sent her higher and higher into the air, so that she resembled a big butterfly fluttering lightly. Presently she made a great bound and bounded way across the stream, landing lightly and steadily on the other side.

"There is no rubber over here," she called to them. "Suppose you all try to bound over the stream, without touching the stepping-stones."

Ann and her officers were reluctant to undertake such a risky adventure, but Betsy at once grasped the value of the suggestion and began jumping up and down until she found herself bounding almost as high as Polychrome had done. Then she suddenly leaned forward and the next bound took her easily across the brook, where she alighted by the side of the Rainbow's Daughter.

"Come on, Hank!" called the girl, and the donkey tried to obey. He managed to bound pretty high but when he tried to bound across the stream he misjudged the distance and fell with a splash into the middle of the water.

"Hee-haw!" he wailed, struggling toward the far bank. Betsy rushed forward to help him out, but when the mule stood safely beside her she was amazed to find he was not wet at all.

"It's dry water," said Polychrome, dipping her hand into the stream and showing how the water fell from it and left it perfectly dry.

"In that case," returned Betsy, "they can all walk through the water."

She called to Ozga and Shaggy to wade across, assuring them the water was shallow and would not wet them. At once they followed her advice, avoiding the rubber stepping stones, and made the crossing with ease. This encouraged the entire party to wade through the dry water, and in a few minutes all had assembled on the bank and renewed their journey along the path that led to the Nome King's dominions.

When Kaliko again looked through his magic spyglass he exclaimed: "Bad luck, Your Majesty! All the invaders have passed the Rubber Country and now are fast approaching the entrance to your caverns."

Ruggedo raved and stormed at the news and his anger was so great that several times, as he strode up and down his jeweled cavern, he paused to kick Kaliko upon his shins, which were so sensitive that the poor nome howled with pain. Finally the King said: "There's no help for it; we must drop these audacious invaders down the Hollow Tube."

Kaliko gave a jump, at this, and looked at his master wonderingly.

"If you do that, Your Majesty," he said, "you will make Tititi-Hoochoo very angry."

"Never mind that," retorted Ruggedo. "Tititi-Hoochoo lives on the other side of the world, so what do I care for his anger?"

Kaliko shuddered and uttered a little groan.

"Remember his terrible powers," he pleaded, "and remember that he warned you, the last time you slid people through the Hollow Tube, that if you did it again he would take vengeance upon you."

The Metal Monarch walked up and down in silence, thinking deeply.

"Of two dangers," said he, "it is wise to choose the least. What do you suppose these invaders want?"

"Let the Long-Eared Hearer listen to them," suggested Kaliko.

"Call him here at once!" commanded Ruggedo eagerly.

So in a few minutes there entered the cavern a nome with enormous ears, who bowed low before the King.

"Strangers are approaching," said Ruggedo, "and I wish to know their errand. Listen carefully to their talk and tell me why they are coming here, and what for."

The nome bowed again and spread out his great ears, swaying them gently up and down and back and forth. For half an hour he stood silent, in an attitude of listening, while both the King and Kaliko grew impatient at the delay. At last the Long-Eared Hearer spoke: "Shaggy Man is coming here to rescue his brother from captivity," said he.

"Ha, the Ugly One!" exclaimed Ruggedo. "Well, Shaggy Man may have his ugly brother, for all I care. He's too lazy to work and is always getting in my way. Where is the Ugly One now, Kaliko?"

"The last time Your Majesty stumbled over the prisoner you commanded me to send him to the Metal Forest, which I did. I suppose he is still there."

"Very good. The invaders will have a hard time finding the Metal Forest," said the King, with a grin of malicious delight, "for half the time I can't find it myself. Yet I created the forest and made every tree, out of gold and silver, so as to keep the precious metals in a safe place and out of the reach of mortals. But tell me, Hearer, do the strangers want anything else?"

"Yes, indeed they do!" returned the nome. "The Army of Oogaboo is determined to capture all the rich metals and rare jewels in your kingdom, and the officers and their Queen have arranged to divide the spoils and carry them away."

When he heard this Ruggedo uttered a bellow of rage and began dancing up and down, rolling his eyes, clicking his teeth together and swinging his arms furiously. Then, in an ecstasy of anger he seized the long ears of the Hearer and pulled and twisted them cruelly; but Kaliko grabbed up the King's sceptre and rapped him over the knuckles with it, so that Ruggedo let go the ears and began to chase his Royal Chamberlain around the throne.

The Hearer took advantage of this opportunity to slip away from the cavern and escape, and after the King had tired himself out chasing Kaliko he threw himself into his throne and panted for breath, while he glared wickedly at his defiant subject.

"You'd better save your strength to fight the enemy," suggested Kaliko. "There will be a terrible battle when the Army of

Oogaboo gets here."

"The Army won't get here," said the King, still coughing and panting. "I'll drop 'em down the Hollow Tube—every man Jack and every girl Jill of 'em!"

"And defy Tititi-Hoochoo?" asked Kaliko.

"Yes. Go at once to my Chief Magician and order him to turn the path toward the Hollow Tube, and to make the tip of the Tube invisible, so they'll all fall into it."

Kaliko went away shaking his head, for he thought Ruggedo was making a great mistake. He found the Magician and had the path twisted so that it led directly to the opening of the Hollow Tube, and this opening he made invisible.

Having obeyed the orders of his master, the Royal Chamberlain went to his private room and began to write letters of recommendation of himself, stating that he was an honest man, a good servant and a small eater.

"Pretty soon," he said to himself, "I shall have to look for another job, for it is certain that Ruggedo has ruined himself by this reckless defiance of the mighty Tititi-Hoochoo. And in seeking a job nothing is so effective as a letter of recommendation."

10. A Terrible Tumble Through a Tube

I suppose that Polychrome, and perhaps Queen Ann and her Army, might have been able to dispel the enchantment of Ruggedo's Chief Magician had they known that danger lay in their pathway; for the Rainbow's Daughter was a fairy and as Oogaboo is a part of the Land of Oz its inhabitants cannot easily be deceived by such common magic as the Nome King could command. But no one suspected any especial danger until after they had entered Ruggedo's cavern, and so they were journeying along in quite a contented manner when Tik-Tok, who marched ahead, suddenly disappeared.

The officers thought he must have turned a corner, so they kept on their way and all of them likewise disappeared—one after another. Queen Ann was rather surprised at this, and in hastening forward to learn the reason she also vanished from sight.

Betsy Bobbin had tired her feet by walking, so she was now riding upon the back of the stout little mule, facing backward and talking to Shaggy and Polychrome, who were just behind. Suddenly Hank pitched forward and began falling and Betsy would have tumbled over his head had she not grabbed the mule's shaggy neck with both arms and held on for dear life.

All around was darkness, and they were not falling directly downward but seemed to be sliding along a steep incline. Hank's hoofs were resting upon some smooth substance over which he slid with the swiftness of the wind. Once Betsy's heels flew up and struck a similar substance overhead. They were, indeed, descending the "Hollow Tube" that led to the other side of the world.

"Stop, Hank—stop!" cried the girl; but Hank only uttered a plaintive "Hee-haw!" for it was impossible for him to obey.

After several minutes had passed and no harm had befallen them, Betsy gained courage. She could see nothing at all, nor could she hear anything except the rush of air past her ears as they plunged downward along the Tube. Whether she and Hank were alone, or the others were with them, she could not tell. But had some one been able to take a flash-light photograph of the Tube at that time a most curious picture would have resulted. There was Tik-Tok, flat upon his back and sliding headforemost down the incline. And there were the Officers of the Army of Oogaboo, all tangled up in a confused crowd, flapping their arms and trying to shield their faces from the clanking swords, which swung back and forth during the swift journey and pommeled everyone within their reach. Now followed Queen Ann, who had struck the Tube in a sitting position and went flying along with a dash and abandon that thoroughly bewildered the poor lady who had no idea what had happened to her. Then, a little distance away, but unseen by the others in the inky darkness, slid Betsy and Hank, while behind them were Shaggy and Polychrome and finally Files and the Princess.

When first they tumbled into the Tube all were too dazed to think clearly, but the trip was a long one, because the cavity led straight through the earth to a place just opposite the Nome King's dominions, and long before the adventurers got to the end they had begun to recover their wits.

"This is awful, Hank!" cried Betsy in a loud voice, and Queen Ann heard her and called out: "Are you safe, Betsy?"

"Mercy, no!" answered the little girl. "How could anyone be safe when she's going about sixty miles a minute?" Then, after a pause, she added: "But where do you s'pose we're going to, Your Maj'sty?"

"Don't ask her that, please don't!" said Shaggy, who was not too far away to overhear them. "And please don't ask me why either."

"Why?" said Betsy.

"No one can tell where we are going until we get there," replied Shaggy, and then he yelled "Ouch!" for Polychrome had overtaken him and was now sitting on his head.

The Rainbow's Daughter laughed merrily, and so infectious was this joyous laugh that Betsy echoed it and Hank said "Hee haw!" in a mild and sympathetic tone of voice.

"I'd like to know where and when we'll arrive, just the same," exclaimed the little girl.

"Be patient and you'll find out, my dear," said Polychrome. "But isn't this an odd experience? Here am I, whose home is in the skies, making a journey through the center of the earth—where I never expected to be!"

"How do you know we're in the center of the earth?" asked Betsy, her voice trembling a little through nervousness.

"Why, we can't be anywhere else," replied Polychrome. "I have often heard of this passage, which was once built by a Magician who was a great traveler. He thought it would save him the bother of going around the earth's surface, but he tumbled through the Tube so fast that he shot out at the other end and hit a star in the sky, which at once exploded."

"The star exploded?" asked Betsy wonderingly.

"Yes; the Magician hit it so hard."

"And what became of the Magician?" inquired the girl.

"No one knows that," answered Polychrome. "But I don't think it matters much."

"It matters a good deal, if we also hit the stars when we come out," said Queen Ann, with a moan.

"Don't worry," advised Polychrome. "I believe the Magician was going the other way, and probably he went much faster than we are going."

"It's fast enough to suit me," remarked Shaggy, gently removing Polychrome's heel from his left eye. "Couldn't you manage to fall all by yourself, my dear?"

"I'll try," laughed the Rainbow's Daughter.

All this time they were swiftly falling through the Tube, and it was not so easy for them to talk as you may imagine when you read their words. But although they were so helpless and altogether in the dark as to their fate, the fact that they were able to converse at all cheered them, considerably.

Files and Ozga were also conversing as they clung tightly to one another, and the young fellow bravely strove to reassure the Princess, although he was terribly frightened, both on her account and on his own.

An hour, under such trying circumstances, is a very long time, and for more than an hour they continued their fearful journey. Then, just as they began to fear the Tube would never end, Tik-Tok popped out into broad daylight and, after making a graceful circle in the air, fell with a splash into a great marble fountain.

Out came the officers, in quick succession, tumbling heels over head and striking the ground in many undignified attitudes.

"For the love of sassafras!" exclaimed a Peculiar Person who was hoeing pink violets in a garden. "What can all this mean?"

For answer, Queen Ann sailed up from the Tube, took a ride through the air as high as the treetops, and alighted squarely on top of the Peculiar Person's head, smashing a jeweled crown over his eyes and tumbling him to the ground.

The mule was heavier and had Betsy clinging to his back, so he did not go so high up. Fortunately for his little rider he struck the ground upon his four feet. Betsy was jarred a trifle but not hurt and when she looked around her she saw the Queen and the Peculiar Person struggling together upon the ground, where the man was trying to choke Ann and she had both hands in his bushy hair and was pulling with all her might. Some of the officers, when they got upon their feet, hastened to separate the combatants and sought to restrain the Peculiar Person so that he could not attack their Queen again.

By this time, Shaggy, Polychrome, Ozga and Files had all arrived and were curiously examining the strange country in which they found themselves and which they knew to be exactly on the opposite side of the world from the place where they had fallen into the Tube. It was a lovely place, indeed, and seemed to be the garden of some great Prince, for through the vistas of trees and shrubbery could be seen the towers of an immense castle. But as yet the only inhabitant to greet them was the Peculiar Person just mentioned, who had shaken off the grasp of the officers without effort and was now trying to pull the battered crown from off his eyes.

Shaggy, who was always polite, helped him to do this and when the man was free and could see again he looked at his visitors with evident amazement.

"Well, well, well!" he exclaimed. "Where did you come from and how did you get here?"

Betsy tried to answer him, for Queen Ann was surly and silent.

"I can't say, exac'ly where we came from, cause I don't know the name of the place," said the girl, "but the way we got here was through the Hollow Tube."

"Don't call it a 'hollow' Tube, please," exclaimed the Peculiar Person in an irritated tone of voice. "If it's a tube, it's sure to be hollow."

"Why?" asked Betsy.

"Because all tubes are made that way. But this Tube is private property and everyone is forbidden to fall into it."

"We didn't do it on purpose," explained Betsy, and Polychrome added: "I am quite sure that Ruggedo, the Nome King, pushed us down that Tube."

"Ha! Ruggedo! Did you say Ruggedo?" cried the man, becoming much excited.

"That is what she said," replied Shaggy, "and I believe she is right. We were on our way to conquer the Nome King when suddenly we fell into the Tube."

"Then you are enemies of Ruggedo?" inquired the peculiar Person.

"Not exac'ly enemies," said Betsy, a little puzzled by the question, "'cause we don't know him at all; but we started out to conquer him, which isn't as friendly as it might be."

"True," agreed the man. He looked thoughtfully from one to another of them for a while and then he turned his head over his shoulder and said: "Never mind the fire and pincers, my good brothers. It will be best to take these strangers to the Private Citizen."

"Very well, Tubekins," responded a Voice, deep and powerful, that seemed to come out of the air, for the speaker was invisible.

All our friends gave a jump, at this. Even Polychrome was so startled that her gauze draperies fluttered like a banner in a breeze. Shaggy shook his head and sighed; Queen Ann looked very unhappy; the officers clung to each other, trembling violently.

But soon they gained courage to look more closely at the Peculiar Person. As he was a type of all the inhabitants of this extraordinary land whom they afterward met, I will try to tell you what he looked like.

His face was beautiful, but lacked expression. His eyes were large and blue in color and his teeth finely formed and white as snow. His hair was black and bushy and seemed inclined to curl at the ends. So far no one could find any fault with his appearance. He wore a robe of scarlet, which did not cover his arms and extended no lower than his bare knees. On the bosom of the robe was embroidered a terrible dragon's head, as horrible to look at as the man was beautiful. His arms and legs were left bare and the skin of one arm was bright yellow and the skin of the other arm a vivid green. He had one blue leg and one pink one, while both his feet—which showed through the open sandals he wore—were jet black.

Betsy could not decide whether these gorgeous colors were dyes or the natural tints of the skin, but while she was thinking it over the man who had been called "Tubekins" said: "Follow me to the Residence—all of you!"

But just then a Voice exclaimed: "Here's another of them, Tubekins, lying in the water of the fountain."

"Gracious!" cried Betsy; "it must be Tik-Tok, and he'll drown."

"Water is a bad thing for his clockworks, anyway," agreed Shaggy, as with one accord they all started for the fountain. But before they could reach it, invisible hands raised Tik-Tok from the marble basin and set him upon his feet beside it, water dripping from every joint of his copper body.

"Ma—ny tha—tha—tha—thanks!" he said; and then his copper jaws clicked together and he could say no more. He next made an attempt to walk but after several awkward trials found he could not move his joints.

Peals of jeering laughter from persons unseen greeted Tik-Tok's failure, and the new arrivals in this strange land found it very uncomfortable to realize that there were many creatures around them who were invisible, yet could be heard plainly.

"Shall I wind him up?" asked Betsy, feeling very sorry for Tik-Tok.

"I think his machinery is wound; but he needs oiling," replied Shaggy.

At once an oil-can appeared before him, held on a level with his eyes by some unseen hand. Shaggy took the can and tried to oil Tik-Tok's joints. As if to assist him, a strong current of warm air was directed against the copper man which quickly dried him. Soon he was able to say "Ma-ny thanks!" quite smoothly and his joints worked fairly well.

"Come!" commanded Tubekins, and turning his back upon them he walked up the path toward the castle.

"Shall we go?" asked Queen Ann, uncertainly; but just then she received a shove that almost pitched her forward on her head; so she decided to go. The officers who hesitated received several energetic kicks, but could not see who delivered them; therefore they also decided—very wisely—to go. The others followed willingly enough, for unless they ventured upon another terrible journey through the Tube they must make the best of the unknown country they were in, and the best seemed to be to obey orders.

11. The Famous Fellowship of Fairies

After a short walk through very beautiful gardens they came to the castle and followed Tubekins through the entrance and into a great domed chamber, where he commanded them to be seated.

From the crown which he wore, Betsy had thought this man must be the King of the country they were in, yet after he had seated all the strangers upon benches that were ranged in a semicircle before a high throne, Tubekins bowed humbly before the vacant throne and in a flash became invisible and disappeared.

The hall was an immense place, but there seemed to be no one in it beside themselves. Presently, however, they heard a low cough near them, and here and there was the faint rustling of a robe and a slight patter as of footsteps. Then suddenly there rang out the clear tone of a bell and at the sound all was changed.

Gazing around the hall in bewilderment they saw that it was filled with hundreds of men and women, all with beautiful faces and staring blue eyes and all wearing scarlet robes and jeweled crowns upon their heads. In fact, these people seemed exact duplicates of Tubekins and it was difficult to find any mark by which to tell them apart.

"My! what a lot of Kings and Queens!" whispered Betsy to Polychrome, who sat beside her and appeared much interested in the scene but not a bit worried.

"It is certainly a strange sight," was Polychrome's reply; "but I cannot see how there can be more than one King, or Queen, in any one country, for were these all rulers, no one could tell who was Master."

One of the Kings who stood near and overheard this remark turned to her and said: "One who is Master of himself is always a King, if only to himself. In this favored land all Kings and Queens are equal, and it is our privilege to bow before one supreme Ruler—the Private Citizen."

"Who's he?" inquired Betsy.

As if to answer her, the clear tones of the bell again rang out and instantly there appeared seated in the throne the man who was lord and master of all these royal ones. This fact was evident when with one accord they fell upon their knees and touched their foreheads to the floor.

The Private Citizen was not unlike the others, except that his eyes were black instead of blue and in the centers of the black irises glowed red sparks that seemed like coals of fire. But his features were very beautiful and dignified and his manner composed and stately. Instead of the prevalent scarlet robe, he wore one of white, and the same dragon's head that decorated the others was embroidered upon its bosom.

"What charge lies against these people, Tubekins?" he asked in quiet, even tones.

"They came through the forbidden Tube, O Mighty Citizen," was the reply.

"You see, it was this way," said Betsy. "We were marching to the Nome King, to conquer him and set Shaggy's brother free, when on a sudden—"

"Who are you?" demanded the Private Citizen sternly.

"Me? Oh, I'm Betsy Bobbin, and—"

"Who is the leader of this party?" asked the Citizen.

"Sir, I am Queen Ann of Oogaboo, and—"

"Then keep quiet," said the Citizen. "Who is the leader?"

No one answered for a moment. Then General Bunn stood up.

"Sit down!" commanded the Citizen. "I can see that sixteen of you are merely officers, and of no account."

"But we have an Army," said General Clock, blusteringly, for he didn't like to be told he was of no account.

"Where is your Army?" asked the Citizen.

"It's me," said Tik-Tok, his voice sounding a little rusty. "I'm the on-ly Pri-vate Sol-dier in the par-ty."

Hearing this, the Citizen rose and bowed respectfully to the Clockwork Man.

"Pardon me for not realizing your importance before," said he. "Will you oblige me by taking a seat beside me on my throne?"

Tik-Tok rose and walked over to the throne, all the Kings and Queens making way for him. Then with clanking steps he mounted the platform and sat on the broad seat beside the Citizen.

Ann was greatly provoked at this mark of favor shown to the humble Clockwork Man, but Shaggy seemed much pleased that his old friend's importance had been recognized by the ruler of this remarkable country. The Citizen now began to question Tik-Tok, who told in his mechanical voice about Shaggy's quest of his lost brother, and how Ozma of Oz had sent the Clockwork Man to assist him, and how they had fallen in with Queen Ann and her people from Oogaboo. Also he told how Betsy and Hank and Polychrome and the Rose Princess had happened to join their party.

"And you intended to conquer Ruggedo, the Metal Monarch and King of the Nomes?" asked the Citizen.

"Yes. That seemed the on-ly thing for us to do," was Tik-Tok's reply. "But he was too cle-ver for us. When we got close to his cav-ern he made our path lead to the Tube, and made the op-en-ing in- vis-i-ble, so that we all fell in-to it be-fore we knew it was here. It was an eas-y way to get rid of us and now Rug-gedo is safe and we are far a- way in a strange land."

The Citizen was silent a moment and seemed to be thinking. Then he said: "Most noble Private Soldier, I must inform you that by the laws of our country anyone who comes through the Forbidden Tube must be tortured for nine days and ten nights and then thrown back into the Tube. But it is wise to disregard laws when they conflict with justice, and it seems that you and your followers did not disobey our laws willingly, being forced into the Tube by Ruggedo. Therefore the Nome King is alone to blame, and he alone must be punished."

"That suits me," said Tik-Tok. "But Rug-ge-do is on the o-ther side of the world where he is a-way out of your reach."

The Citizen drew himself up proudly.

"Do you imagine anything in the world or upon it can be out of the reach of the Great Jinjin?" he asked.

"Oh! Are you, then, the Great Jinjin?" inquired Tik-Tok.

"I am."

"Then your name is Ti-ti-ti-Hoo-choo?"

"It is."

Queen Ann gave a scream and began to tremble. Shaggy was so disturbed that he took out a handkerchief and wiped the perspiration from his brow. Polychrome looked sober and uneasy for the first time, while Files put his arms around the Rose Princess as if to protect her. As for the officers, the name of the great Jinjin set them moaning and weeping at a great rate and every one fell upon his knees before the throne, begging for mercy. Betsy was worried at seeing her companions so disturbed, but did not know what it was all about. Only Tik-Tok was unmoved at the discovery.

"Then," said he, "if you are Ti-ti-ti-Hoo-choo, and think Rug-ge-do is to blame, I am sure that some-thing queer will hap-pen to the King of the Nomes."

"I wonder what 'twill be," said Betsy.

The Private Citizen—otherwise known as Tititi-Hoochoo, the Great Jinjin—looked at the little girl steadily.

"I will presently decide what is to happen to Ruggedo," said he in a hard, stern voice. Then, turning to the throng of Kings and Queens, he continued: "Tik-Tok has spoken truly, for his machinery will not allow him to lie, nor will it allow his thoughts to think falsely. Therefore these people are not our enemies and must be treated with consideration and justice. Take them to your palaces and entertain them as guests until to-morrow, when I command that they be brought again to my Residence. By then I shall have formed my plans."

No sooner had Tititi-Hoochoo spoken than he disappeared from sight. Immediately after, most of the Kings and Queens likewise disappeared. But several of them remained visible and approached the strangers with great respect. One of the lovely Queens said to Betsy: "I trust you will honor me by being my guest. I am Erma, Queen of Light."

"May Hank come with me?" asked the girl.

"The King of Animals will care for your mule," was the reply. "But do not fear for him, for he will be treated royally. All of your party will be reunited on the morrow."

"I—I'd like to have some one with me," said Betsy, pleadingly.

Queen Erma looked around and smiled upon Polychrome.

"Will the Rainbow's Daughter be an agreeable companion?" she asked.

"Oh, yes!" exclaimed the girl.

So Polychrome and Betsy became guests of the Queen of Light, while other beautiful Kings and Queens took charge of the others of the party.

The two girls followed Erma out of the hall and through the gardens of the Residence to a village of pretty dwellings. None of these was so large or imposing as the castle of the Private Citizen, but all were handsome enough to be called palaces—as, in fact, they really were.

12. The Lovely Lady of Light

The palace of the Queen of Light stood on a little eminence and was a mass of crystal windows, surmounted by a vast crystal dome. When they entered the portals Erma was greeted by six lovely maidens, evidently of high degree, who at once aroused

Betsy's admiration. Each bore a wand in her hand, tipped with an emblem of light, and their costumes were also emblematic of the lights they represented. Erma introduced them to her guests and each made a graceful and courteous acknowledgment.

First was Sunlight, radiantly beautiful and very fair; the second was Moonlight, a soft, dreamy damsel with nut-brown hair; next came Starlight, equally lovely but inclined to be retiring and shy. These three were dressed in shimmering robes of silvery white. The fourth was Daylight, a brilliant damsel with laughing eyes and frank manners, who wore a variety of colors. Then came Firelight, clothed in a fleecy flame-colored robe that wavered around her shapely form in a very attractive manner. The sixth maiden, Electra, was the most beautiful of all, and Betsy thought from the first that both Sunlight and Daylight regarded Electra with envy and were a little jealous of her.

But all were cordial in their greetings to the strangers and seemed to regard the Queen of Light with much affection, for they fluttered around her in a flashing, radiant group as she led the way to her regal drawing-room.

This apartment was richly and cosily furnished, the upholstery being of many tints, and both Betsy and Polychrome enjoyed resting themselves upon the downy divans after their strenuous adventures of the day.

The Queen sat down to chat with her guests, who noticed that Daylight was the only maiden now seated beside Erma. The others had retired to another part of the room, where they sat modestly with entwined arms and did not intrude themselves at all.

The Queen told the strangers all about this beautiful land, which is one of the chief residences of fairies who minister to the needs of mankind. So many important fairies lived there that, to avoid rivalry, they had elected as their Ruler the only important personage in the country who had no duties to mankind to perform and was, in effect, a Private Citizen. This Ruler, or Jinjin, as was his title, bore the name of Tititi-Hoochoo, and the most singular thing about him was that he had no heart. But instead of this he possessed a high degree of Reason and Justice and while he showed no mercy in his judgments he never punished unjustly or without reason. To wrong-doers Tititi-Hoochoo was as terrible as he was heartless, but those who were innocent of evil had nothing to fear from him.

All the Kings and Queens of this fairyland paid reverence to Jinjin, for as they expected to be obeyed by others they were willing to obey the one in authority over them.

The inhabitants of the Land of Oz had heard many tales of this fearfully just Jinjin, whose punishments were always equal to the faults committed. Polychrome also knew of him, although this was the first time she had ever seen him face to face. But to Betsy the story was all new, and she was greatly interested in Tititi-Hoochoo, whom she no longer feared.

Time sped swiftly during their talk and suddenly Betsy noticed that Moonlight was sitting beside the Queen of Light, instead of Daylight.

"But tell me, please," she pleaded, "why do you all wear a dragon's head embroidered on your gowns?"

Erma's pleasant face became grave as she answered: "The Dragon, as you must know, was the first living creature ever made; therefore the Dragon is the oldest and wisest of living things. By good fortune the Original Dragon, who still lives, is a resident of this land and supplies us with wisdom whenever we are in need of it. He is old as the world and remembers everything that has happened since the world was created."

"Did he ever have any children?" inquired the girl.

"Yes, many of them. Some wandered into other lands, where men, not understanding them, made war upon them; but many still reside in this country. None, however, is as wise as the Original Dragon, for whom we have great respect. As he was the first resident here, we wear the emblem of the dragon's head to show that we are the favored people who alone have the right to inhabit this fairyland, which in beauty almost equals the Fairyland of Oz, and in power quite surpasses it."

"I understand about the dragon, now," said Polychrome nodding her lovely head. Betsy did not quite understand, but she was at present interested in observing the changing lights. As Daylight had given way to Moonlight, so now Starlight sat at the right hand of Erma the Queen, and with her coming a spirit of peace and content seemed to fill the room. Polychrome, being herself a fairy, had many questions to ask about the various Kings and Queens who lived in this far-away, secluded place, and before Erma had finished answering them a rosy glow filled the room and Firelight took her place beside the Queen.

Betsy liked Firelight, but to gaze upon her warm and glowing features made the little girl sleepy, and presently she began to nod. Thereupon Erma rose and took Betsy's hand gently in her own.

"Come," said she; "the feast time has arrived and the feast is spread."

"That's nice," exclaimed the small mortal. "Now that I think of it I'm awful hungry. But p'raps I can't eat your fairy food."

The Queen smiled and led her to a doorway. As she pushed aside a heavy drapery a flood of silvery light greeted them, and Betsy saw before her a splendid banquet hall, with a table spread with snowy linen and crystal and silver. At one side was a broad throne-like seat for Erma and beside her now sat the brilliant maid Electra. Polychrome was placed on the Queen's right hand and Betsy upon her left. The other five messengers of light now waited upon them, and each person was supplied with just the food she liked best. Polychrome found her dish of dewdrops, all fresh and sparkling, while Betsy was so lavishly served that she decided she had never in her life eaten a dinner half so good.

"I s'pose," she said to the Queen, "that Miss Electra is the youngest of all these girls."

"Why do you suppose that?" inquired Erma, with a smile.

"'Cause electric'ty is the newest light we know of. Didn't Mr Edison discover it?"

"Perhaps he was the first mortal to discover it," replied the Queen. "But electricity was a part of the world from its creation, and therefore my Electra is as old as Daylight or Moonlight, and equally beneficent to mortals and fairies alike."

Betsy was thoughtful for a time. Then she remarked, as she looked at the six messengers of light: "We couldn't very well do without any of 'em; could we?"

Erma laughed softly. "I couldn't, I'm sure," she replied, "and think mortals would miss any one of my maidens, as well. Daylight cannot take the place of Sunlight, which gives us strength and energy. Moonlight is of value when Daylight, worn out with her long watch, retires to rest. If the moon in its course is hidden behind the earth's rim, and my sweet Moonlight cannot cheer us, Starlight takes her place, for the skies always lend her power. Without Firelight we should miss much of our warmth and comfort, as well as much cheer when the walls of houses encompass us. But always, when other lights forsake us, our glorious Electra is ready to flood us with bright rays. As Queen of Light, I love all my maidens, for I know them to be faithful and true."

"I love 'em too!" declared Betsy. "But sometimes, when I'm real sleepy, I can get along without any light at all."

"Are you sleepy now?" inquired Erma, for the feast had ended.

"A little," admitted the girl.

So Electra showed her to a pretty chamber where there was a soft, white bed, and waited patiently until Betsy had undressed and put on a shimmery silken nightrobe that lay beside her pillow. Then the light-maid bade her good night and opened the door.

When she closed it after her Betsy was in darkness. In six winks the little girl was fast asleep.

13. The Jinjin's Just Judgment

All the adventurers were reunited next morning when they were brought from various palaces to the Residence of Tititi-Hoochoo and ushered into the great Hall of State.

As before, no one was visible except our friends and their escorts until the first bell sounded. Then in a flash the room was seen to be filled with the beautiful Kings and Queens of the land. The second bell marked the appearance in the throne of the mighty Jinjin, whose handsome countenance was as composed and expressionless as ever.

All bowed low to the Ruler. Their voices softly murmured: "We greet the Private Citizen, mightiest of Rulers, whose word is Law and whose Law is just."

Tititi-Hoochoo bowed in acknowledgment. Then, looking around the brilliant assemblage, and at the little group of adventurers before him, he said:

"An unusual thing has happened. Inhabitants of other lands than ours, who are different from ourselves in many ways, have been thrust upon us through the Forbidden Tube, which one of our people foolishly made years ago and was properly punished for his folly. But these strangers had no desire to come here and were wickedly thrust into the Tube by a cruel King on the other side of the world, named Ruggedo. This King is an immortal, but he is not good. His magic powers hurt mankind more than they benefit them. Because he had unjustly kept the Shaggy Man's brother a prisoner, this little band of honest people, consisting of both mortals and immortals, determined to conquer Ruggedo and to punish him. Fearing they might succeed in this, the Nome King misled them so that they fell into the Tube.

"Now, this same Ruggedo has been warned by me, many times, that if ever he used this Forbidden Tube in any way he would be severely punished. I find, by referring to the Fairy Records, that this King's servant, a nome named Kaliko, begged his master not to do such a wrong act as to drop these people into the Tube and send them tumbling into our country. But Ruggedo defied me and my orders.

"Therefore these strangers are innocent of any wrong. It is only Ruggedo who deserves punishment, and I will punish him." He paused a moment and then continued in the same cold, merciless voice: "These strangers must return through the Tube to their own side of the world; but I will make their fall more easy and pleasant than it was before. Also I shall send with them an Instrument of Vengeance, who in my name will drive Ruggedo from his underground caverns, take away his magic powers and make him a homeless wanderer on the face of the earth—a place he detests."

There was a little murmur of horror from the Kings and Queens at the severity of this punishment, but no one uttered a protest, for all realized that the sentence was just.

"In selecting my Instrument of Vengeance," went on Tititi-Hoochoo, "I have realized that this will be an unpleasant mission. Therefore no one of us who is blameless should be forced to undertake it. In this wonderful land it is seldom one is guilty of wrong, even in the slightest degree, and on examining the Records I found no King or Queen had erred. Nor had any among their followers or servants done any wrong. But finally I came to the Dragon Family, which we highly respect, and then it was that I discovered the error of Quox.

"Quox, as you well know, is a young dragon who has not yet acquired the wisdom of his race. Because of this lack, he has been disrespectful toward his most ancient ancestor, the Original Dragon, telling him once to mind his own business and again saying that the Ancient One had grown foolish with age. We are aware that dragons are not the same as fairies and cannot be altogether guided by our laws, yet such disrespect as Quox has shown should not be unnoticed by us. Therefore I have selected Quox as my royal Instrument of Vengeance and he shall go through the Tube with these people and inflict upon Ruggedo the punishment I have decreed."

All had listened quietly to this speech and now the Kings and Queens bowed gravely to signify their approval of the Jinjin's judgment.

Tititi-Hoochoo turned to Tubekins.

"I command you," said he, "to escort these strangers to the Tube and see that they all enter it."

The King of the Tube, who had first discovered our friends and brought them to the Private Citizen, stepped forward and bowed. As he did so, the Jinjin and all the Kings and Queens suddenly disappeared and only Tubekins remained visible.

"All right," said Betsy, with a sigh; "I don't mind going back so very much, 'cause the Jinjin promised to make it easy for us."

Indeed, Queen Ann and her officers were the only ones who looked solemn and seemed to fear the return journey. One thing that bothered Ann was her failure to conquer this land of Tititi-Hoochoo. As they followed their guide through the gardens to the mouth of the Tube she said to Shaggy: "How can I conquer the world, if I go away and leave this rich country unconquered?"

"You can't," he replied. "Don't ask me why, please, for if you don't know I can't inform you."

"Why not?" said Ann; but Shaggy paid no attention to the question.

This end of the Tube had a silver rim and around it was a gold railing to which was attached a sign that read.

IF YOU ARE OUT, STAY THERE.
IF YOU ARE IN, DON'T COME OUT.

On a little silver plate just inside the Tube was engraved the words:

> Burrowed and built by Hiergargo the Magician,
> In the Year of the World 1 9 6 2 5 4 7 8
> For his own exclusive uses.

"He was some builder, I must say," remarked Betsy, when she had read the inscription; "but if he had known about that star I guess he'd have spent his time playing solitaire."

"Well, what are we waiting for?" inquired Shaggy, who was impatient to start.

"Quox," replied Tubekins. "But I think I hear him coming."

"Is the young dragon invisible?" asked Ann, who had never seen a live dragon and was a little fearful of meeting one.

"No, indeed," replied the King of the Tube. "You'll see him in a minute; but before you part company I'm sure you'll wish he was invisible."

"Is he dangerous, then?" questioned Files.

"Not at all. But Quox tires me dreadfully," said Tubekins, "and I prefer his room to his company.

At that instant a scraping sound was heard, drawing nearer and nearer until from between two big bushes appeared a huge dragon, who approached the party, nodded his head and said: "Good morning."

Had Quox been at all bashful I am sure he would have felt uncomfortable at the astonished stare of every eye in the group— except Tubekins, of course, who was not astonished because he had seen Quox so often.

Betsy had thought a "young" dragon must be a small dragon, yet here was one so enormous that the girl decided he must be full grown, if not overgrown. His body was a lovely sky-blue in color and it was thickly set with glittering silver scales, each one as big as a serving-tray. Around his neck was a pink ribbon with a bow just under his left ear, and below the ribbon appeared a chain of pearls to which was attached a golden locket about as large around as the end of a bass drum. This locket was set with many large and beautiful jewels.

The head and face of Quox were not especially ugly, when you consider that he was a dragon; but his eyes were so large that it took him a long time to wink and his teeth seemed very sharp and terrible when they showed, which they did whenever the beast smiled. Also his nostrils were quite large and wide, and those who stood near him were liable to smell brimstone— especially when he breathed out fire, as it is the nature of dragons to do. To the end of his long tail was attached a big electric light.

Perhaps the most singular thing about the dragon's appearance at this time was the fact that he had a row of seats attached to his back, one seat for each member of the party. These seats were double, with curved backs, so that two could sit in them, and there were twelve of these double seats, all strapped firmly around the dragon's thick body and placed one behind the other, in a row that extended from his shoulders nearly to his tail.

"Aha!" exclaimed Tubekins; "I see that Tititi-Hoochoo has transformed Quox into a carryall."

"I'm glad of that," said Betsy. "I hope, Mr. Dragon, you won't mind our riding on your back."

"Not a bit," replied Quox. "I'm in disgrace just now, you know, and the only way to redeem my good name is to obey the orders of the Jinjin. If he makes me a beast of burden, it is only a part of my punishment, and I must bear it like a dragon. I don't blame you people at all, and I hope you'll enjoy the ride. Hop on, please. All aboard for the other side of the world!"

Silently they took their places. Hank sat in the front seat with Betsy, so that he could rest his front hoofs upon the dragon's head. Behind them were Shaggy and Polychrome, then Files and the Princess, and Queen Ann and Tik-Tok. The officers rode in the rear seats. When all had mounted to their places the dragon looked very like one of those sightseeing wagons so common in big cities— only he had legs instead of wheels.

"All ready?" asked Quox, and when they said they were he crawled to the mouth of the Tube and put his head in.

"Good-bye, and good luck to you!" called Tubekins; but no one thought to reply, because just then the dragon slid his great body into the Tube and the journey to the other side of the world had begun.

At first they went so fast that they could scarcely catch their breaths, but presently Quox slowed up and said with a sort of cackling laugh: "My scales! but that is some tumble. I think I shall take it easy and fall slower, or I'm likely to get dizzy. Is it very far to the other side of the world?"

"Haven't you ever been through this Tube before?" inquired Shaggy.

"Never. Nor has anyone else in our country; at least, not since I was born."

"How long ago was that?" asked Betsy.

"That I was born? Oh, not very long ago. I'm only a mere child. If I had not been sent on this journey, I would have celebrated my three thousand and fifty-sixth birthday next Thursday. Mother was going to make me a birthday cake with three thousand and fifty-six candles on it; but now, of course, there will be no celebration, for I fear I shall not get home in time for it."

"Three thousand and fifty-six years!" cried Betsy. "Why, I had no idea anything could live that long!"

"My respected Ancestor, whom I would call a stupid old humbug if I had not reformed, is so old that I am a mere baby compared with him," said Quox. "He dates from the beginning of the world, and insists on telling us stories of things that happened fifty thousand years ago, which are of no interest at all to youngsters like me. In fact, Grandpa isn't up to date. He lives altogether in the past, so I can't see any good reason for his being alive to-day.... Are you people able to see your way, or shall I turn on more light?"

"Oh, we can see very nicely, thank you; only there's nothing to see but ourselves," answered Betsy.

This was true. The dragon's big eyes were like headlights on an automobile and illuminated the Tube far ahead of them. Also he curled his tail upward so that the electric light on the end of it enabled them to see one another quite clearly. But the Tube itself was only dark metal, smooth as glass but exactly the same from one of its ends to the other. Therefore there was no scenery of interest to beguile the journey.

They were now falling so gently that the trip was proving entirely comfortable, as the Jinjin had promised it would be; but this meant a longer journey and the only way they could make time pass was to engage in conversation. The dragon seemed a willing and persistent talker and he was of so much interest to them that they encouraged him to chatter. His voice was a little gruff but not unpleasant when one became used to it.

"My only fear," said he presently, "is that this constant sliding over the surface of the Tube will dull my claws. You see, this hole isn't straight down, but on a steep slant, and so instead of tumbling freely through the air I must skate along the Tube. Fortunately, there is a file in my tool-kit, and if my claws get dull they can be sharpened again."

"Why do you want sharp claws?" asked Betsy.

"They are my natural weapons, and you must not forget that I have been sent to conquer Ruggedo."

"Oh, you needn't mind about that," remarked Queen Ann, in her most haughty manner; "for when we get to Ruggedo I and my invincible Army can conquer him without your assistance."

"Very good," returned the dragon, cheerfully. "That will save me a lot of bother—if you succeed. But I think I shall file my claws, just the same."

He gave a long sigh, as he said this, and a sheet of flame, several feet in length, shot from his mouth. Betsy shuddered and Hank said "Hee-haw!" while some of the officers screamed in terror. But the dragon did not notice that he had done anything unusual.

"Is there fire inside of you?" asked Shaggy.

"Of course," answered Quox. "What sort of a dragon would I be if my fire went out?"

"What keeps it going?" Betsy inquired.

"I've no idea. I only know it's there," said Quox. "The fire keeps me alive and enables me to move; also to think and speak."

"Ah! You are ver-y much like my-self," said Tik-Tok. "The on-ly dif-fer-ence is that I move by clock-work, while you move by fire."

"I don't see a particle of likeness between us, I must confess," retorted Quox, gruffly. "You are not a live thing; you're a dummy."

"But I can do things, you must ad-mit," said Tik-Tok.

"Yes, when you are wound up," sneered the dragon. "But if you run down, you are helpless."

"What would happen to you, Quox, if you ran out of gasoline?" inquired Shaggy, who did not like this attack upon his friend.

"I don't use gasoline."

"Well, suppose you ran out of fire."

"What's the use of supposing that?" asked Quox. "My great-great-great-grandfather has lived since the world began, and he has never once run out of fire to keep him going. But I will confide to you that as he gets older he shows more smoke and less fire. As for Tik-Tok, he's well enough in his way, but he's merely copper. And the Metal Monarch knows copper through and through. I wouldn't be surprised if Ruggedo melted Tik-Tok in one of his furnaces and made copper pennies of him."

"In that case, I would still keep going," remarked Tik-Tok, calmly.

"Pennies do," said Betsy regretfully.

"This is all nonsense," said the Queen, with irritation. "Tik-Tok is my great Army—all but the officers—and I believe he will be able to conquer Ruggedo with ease. What do you think, Polychrome?"

"You might let him try," answered the Rainbow's Daughter, with her sweet ringing laugh, that sounded like the tinkling of tiny bells. "And if Tik-Tok fails, you have still the big fire-breathing dragon to fall back on."

"Ah!" said the dragon, another sheet of flame gushing from his mouth and nostrils; "it's a wise little girl, this Polychrome. Anyone would know she is a fairy."

14. The Long-Eared Hearer Learns by Listening

During this time Ruggedo, the Metal Monarch and King of the Nomes, was trying to amuse himself in his splendid jeweled cavern. It was hard work for Ruggedo to find amusement to-day, for all the nomes were behaving well and there was no one to scold or to punish. The King had thrown his sceptre at Kaliko six times, without hitting him once. Not that Kaliko had done anything wrong. On the contrary, he had obeyed the King in every way but one: he would not stand still, when commanded to do so, and let the heavy sceptre strike him.

We can hardly blame Kaliko for this, and even the cruel Ruggedo forgave him; for he knew very well that if he mashed his Royal Chamberlain he could never find another so intelligent and obedient. Kaliko could make the nomes work when their King could not, for the nomes hated Ruggedo and there were so many thousands of the quaint little underground people that they could easily have rebelled and defied the King had they dared to do so. Sometimes, when Ruggedo abused them worse than usual, they grew sullen and threw down their hammers and picks. Then, however hard the King scolded or whipped them, they would not work until Kaliko came and begged them to. For Kaliko was one of themselves and was as much abused by the King as any nome in the vast series of caverns.

But to-day all the little people were working industriously at their tasks and Ruggedo, having nothing to do, was greatly bored. He sent for the Long-Eared Hearer and asked him to listen carefully and report what was going on in the big world.

"It seems," said the Hearer, after listening for awhile, "that the women in America have clubs."

"Are there spikes in them?" asked Ruggedo, yawning.

"I cannot hear any spikes, Your Majesty," was the reply.

"Then their clubs are not as good as my sceptre. What else do you hear?'

"There's a war.

"Bah! there's always a war. What else?"

For a time the Hearer was silent, bending forward and spreading out his big ears to catch the slightest sound. Then suddenly he said: "Here is an interesting thing, Your Majesty. These people are arguing as to who shall conquer the Metal Monarch, seize his treasure and drive him from his dominions."

"What people?" demanded Ruggedo, sitting up straight in his throne.

"The ones you threw down the Hollow Tube."

"Where are they now?"

"In the same Tube, and coming back this way," said the Hearer.

Ruggedo got out of his throne and began to pace up and down the cavern.

"I wonder what can be done to stop them," he mused.

"Well," said the Hearer, "if you could turn the Tube upside down, they would be falling the other way, Your Majesty."

Ruggedo glared at him wickedly, for it was impossible to turn the Tube upside down and he believed the Hearer was slyly poking fun at him. Presently he asked: "How far away are those people now?"

"About nine thousand three hundred and six miles, seventeen furlongs, eight feet and four inches—as nearly as I can judge from the sound of their voices," replied the Hearer.

"Aha! Then it will be some time before they arrive," said Ruggedo, "and when they get here I shall be ready to receive them."

He rushed to his gong and pounded upon it so fiercely that Kaliko came bounding into the cavern with one shoe off and one shoe on, for he was just dressing himself after a swim in the hot bubbling lake of the Underground Kingdom.

"Kaliko, those invaders whom we threw down the Tube are coming back again!" he exclaimed.

"I thought they would," said the Royal Chamberlain, pulling on the other shoe. "Tititi-Hoochoo would not allow them to remain in his kingdom, of course, and so I've been expecting them back for some time. That was a very foolish action of yours, Rug."

"What, to throw them down the Tube?"

"Yes. Tititi-Hoochoo has forbidden us to throw even rubbish into the Tube."

"Pooh! what do I care for the Jinjin?" asked Ruggedo scornfully.

"He never leaves his own kingdom, which is on the other side of the world."

"True; but he might send some one through the Tube to punish you," suggested Kaliko.

"I'd like to see him do it! Who could conquer my thousands of nomes?"

"Why, they've been conquered before, if I remember aright," answered Kaliko with a grin. "Once I saw you running from a little girl named Dorothy, and her friends, as if you were really afraid."

"Well, I was afraid, that time," admitted the Nome King, with deep sigh, "for Dorothy had a Yellow Hen that laid eggs!"

The King shuddered as he said "eggs," and Kaliko also shuddered, and so did the Long-Eared Hearer; for eggs are the only things that the nomes greatly dread. The reason for this is that eggs belong on the earth's surface, where birds and fowl of all sorts live, and there is something about a hen's egg, especially, that fills a nome with horror. If by chance the inside of an egg touches one of these underground people, he withers up and blows away and that is the end of him—unless he manages quickly to speak a magical word which only a few of the nomes know. Therefore Ruggedo and his followers had very good cause to shudder at the mere mention of eggs.

"But Dorothy," said the King, "is not with this band of invaders nor is the Yellow Hen. As for Tititi-Hoochoo, he has no means of knowing that we are afraid of eggs."

"You mustn't be too sure of that," Kaliko warned him. "Tititi-Hoochoo knows a great many things, being a fairy, and his powers are far superior to any we can boast."

Ruggedo shrugged impatiently and turned to the Hearer.

"Listen," said he, "and tell me if you hear any eggs coming through the Tube."

The Long-Eared one listened and then shook his head. But Kaliko laughed at the King.

"No one can hear an egg, Your Majesty," said he. "The only way to discover the truth is to look through the Magic Spyglass."

"That's it!" cried the King. "Why didn't I think of it before? Look at once, Kaliko!"

So Kaliko went to the Spyglass and by uttering a mumbled charm he caused the other end of it to twist around, so that it pointed down the opening of the Tube. Then he put his eye to the glass and was able to gaze along all the turns and windings of the Magic Spyglass and then deep into the Tube, to where our friends were at that time falling.

"Dear me!" he exclaimed. "Here comes a dragon."

"A big one?" asked Ruggedo.

"A monster. He has an electric light on the end of his tail, so I can see him very plainly. And the other people are all riding upon his back."

"How about the eggs?" inquired the King.

Kaliko looked again.

"I can see no eggs at all," said he; "but I imagine that the dragon is as dangerous as eggs. Probably Tititi-Hoochoo has sent him here to punish you for dropping those strangers into the Forbidden Tube. I warned you not to do it, Your Majesty."

This news made the Nome King anxious. For a few minutes he paced up and down, stroking his long beard and thinking with all his might. After this he turned to Kaliko and said: "All the harm a dragon can do is to scratch with his claws and bite with his teeth."

"That is not all, but it's quite enough," returned Kaliko earnestly. "On the other hand, no one can hurt a dragon, because he's the toughest creature alive. One flap of his huge tail could smash a hundred nomes to pancakes, and with teeth and claws he could tear even you or me into small bits, so that it would be almost impossible to put us together again. Once, a few hundred years ago, while wandering through some deserted caverns, I came upon a small piece of a nome lying on the rocky floor. I asked the piece of nome what had happened to it. Fortunately the mouth was a part of this piece—the mouth and the left eye—so it was able to tell me that a fierce dragon was the cause. It had attacked the poor nome and scattered him in every direction, and as there was no friend near to collect his pieces and put him together, they had been separated for a great many years. So you see, Your Majesty, it is not in good taste to sneer at a dragon."

The King had listened attentively to Kaliko. Said he: "It will only be necessary to chain this dragon which Tititi-Hoochoo has sent here, in order to prevent his reaching us with his claws and teeth."

"He also breathes flames," Kaliko reminded him.

"My nomes are not afraid of fire, nor am I," said Ruggedo.

"Well, how about the Army of Oogaboo?"

"Sixteen cowardly officers and Tik-Tok! Why, I could defeat them single-handed; but I won't try to. I'll summon my army of nomes to drive the invaders out of my territory, and if we catch any of them I intend to stick needles into them until they hop with pain."

"I hope you won't hurt any of the girls," said Kaliko.

"I'll hurt 'em all!" roared the angry Metal Monarch. "And that braying Mule I'll make into hoof-soup, and feed it to my nomes, that it may add to their strength."

"Why not be good to the strangers and release your prisoner, the Shaggy Man's brother?" suggested Kaliko.

"Never!"

"It may save you a lot of annoyance. And you don't want the Ugly One."

"I don't want him; that's true. But I won't allow anybody to order me around. I'm King of the Nomes and I'm the Metal Monarch, and I shall do as I please and what I please and when I please!"

With this speech Ruggedo threw his sceptre at Kaliko's head, aiming it so well that the Royal Chamberlain had to fall flat upon the floor in order to escape it. But the Hearer did not see the sceptre coming and it swept past his head so closely that it broke off the tip of one of his long ears. He gave a dreadful yell that quite startled Ruggedo, and the King was sorry for the accident because those long ears of the Hearer were really valuable to him.

So the Nome King forgot to be angry with Kaliko and ordered his Chamberlain to summon General Guph and the army of nomes and have them properly armed. They were then to march to the mouth of the Tube, where they could seize the travelers as soon as they appeared.

15. The Dragon Defies Danger

Although the journey through the Tube was longer, this time, than before, it was so much more comfortable that none of our friends minded it at all. They talked together most of the time and as they found the dragon good-natured and fond of the sound of his own voice they soon became well acquainted with him and accepted him as a companion.

"You see," said Shaggy, in his frank way, "Quox is on our side, and therefore the dragon is a good fellow. If he happened to be an enemy, instead of a friend, I am sure I should dislike him very much, for his breath smells of brimstone, he is very conceited and he is so strong and fierce that he would prove a dangerous foe."

"Yes, indeed," returned Quox, who had listened to this speech with pleasure; "I suppose I am about as terrible as any living thing. I am glad you find me conceited, for that proves I know my good qualities. As for my breath smelling of brimstone, I really can't help it, and I once met a man whose breath smelled of onions, which I consider far worse."

"I don't," said Betsy; "I love onions."

"And I love brimstone," declared the dragon, "so don't let us quarrel over one another's peculiarities."

Saying this, he breathed a long breath and shot a flame fifty feet from his mouth. The brimstone made Betsy cough, but she remembered about the onions and said nothing.

They had no idea how far they had gone through the center of the earth, nor when to expect the trip to end. At one time the little girl remarked: "I wonder when we'll reach the bottom of this hole. And isn't it funny, Shaggy Man, that what is the bottom to us now, was the top when we fell the other way?"

"What puzzles me," said Files, "is that we are able to fall both ways."

"That," announced Tik-Tok, "is be-cause the world is round."

"Exactly," responded Shaggy. "The machinery in your head is in fine working order, Tik-Tok. You know, Betsy, that there is such a thing as the Attraction of Gravitation, which draws everything toward the center of the earth. That is why we fall out of bed, and why everything clings to the surface of the earth."

"Then why doesn't everyone go on down to the center of the earth?" inquired the little girl.

"I was afraid you were going to ask me that," replied Shaggy in a sad tone. "The reason, my dear, is that the earth is so solid that other solid things can't get through it. But when there's a hole, as there is in this case, we drop right down to the center of the world."

"Why don't we stop there?" asked Betsy.

"Because we go so fast that we acquire speed enough to carry us right up to the other end."

"I don't understand that, and it makes my head ache to try to figure it out," she said after some thought. "One thing draws us to the center and another thing pushes us away from it. But—"

"Don't ask me why, please," interrupted the Shaggy Man. "If you can't understand it, let it go at that."

"Do you understand it?" she inquired.

"All the magic isn't in fairyland," he said gravely. "There's lots of magic in all Nature, and you may see it as well in the United States, where you and I once lived, as you can here."

"I never did," she replied.

"Because you were so used to it all that you didn't realize it was magic. Is anything more wonderful than to see a flower grow and blossom, or to get light out of the electricity in the air? The cows that manufacture milk for us must have machinery fully as remarkable as that in Tik-Tok's copper body, and perhaps you've noticed that—"

And then, before Shaggy could finish his speech, the strong light of day suddenly broke upon them, grew brighter, and completely enveloped them. The dragon's claws no longer scraped against the metal Tube, for he shot into the open air a hundred feet or more and sailed so far away from the slanting hole that when he landed it was on the peak of a mountain and just over the entrance to the many underground caverns of the Nome King.

Some of the officers tumbled off their seats when Quox struck the ground, but most of the dragon's passengers only felt a slight jar. All were glad to be on solid earth again and they at once dismounted and began to look about them. Queerly enough, as soon as they had left the dragon, the seats that were strapped to the monster's back disappeared, and this probably happened because there was no further use for them and because Quox looked far more dignified in just his silver scales. Of course he still wore the forty yards of ribbon around his neck, as well as the great locket, but these only made him look "dressed up," as Betsy remarked.

Now the army of nomes had gathered thickly around the mouth of the Tube, in order to be ready to capture the band of invaders as soon as they popped out. There were, indeed, hundreds of nomes assembled, and they were led by Guph, their most famous General. But they did not expect the dragon to fly so high, and he shot out of the Tube so suddenly that it took them by surprise. When the nomes had rubbed the astonishment out of their eyes and regained their wits, they discovered the dragon quietly seated on the mountainside far above their heads, while the other strangers were standing in a group and calmly looking down upon them.

General Guph was very angry at the escape, which was no one's fault but his own.

"Come down here and be captured!" he shouted, waving his sword at them.

"Come up here and capture us—if you dare!" replied Queen Ann, who was winding up the clockwork of her Private Soldier, so he

could fight more briskly.

Guph's first answer was a roar of rage at the defiance; then he turned and issued a command to his nomes. These were all armed with sharp spears and with one accord they raised these spears and threw them straight at their foes, so that they rushed through the air in a perfect cloud of flying weapons.

Some damage might have been done had not the dragon quickly crawled before the others, his body being so big that it shielded every one of them, including Hank. The spears rattled against the silver scales of Quox and then fell harmlessly to the ground. They were magic spears, of course, and all straightway bounded back into the hands of those who had thrown them, but even Guph could see that it was useless to repeat the attack.

It was now Queen Ann's turn to attack, so the Generals yelled "For—ward march!" and the Colonels and Majors and Captains repeated the command and the valiant Army of Oogaboo, which seemed to be composed mainly of Tik-Tok, marched forward in single column toward the nomes, while Betsy and Polychrome cheered and Hank gave a loud "Hee-haw!" and Shaggy shouted "Hooray!" and Queen Ann screamed: "At 'em, Tik-Tok—at 'em!"

The nomes did not await the Clockwork Man's attack but in a twinkling disappeared into the underground caverns. They made a great mistake in being so hasty, for Tik-Tok had not taken a dozen steps before he stubbed his copper toe on a rock and fell flat to the ground, where he cried: "Pick me up! Pick me up! Pick me up!" until Shaggy and Files ran forward and raised him to his feet again.

The dragon chuckled softly to himself as he scratched his left ear with his hind claw, but no one was paying much attention to Quox just then.

It was evident to Ann and her officers that there could be no fighting unless the enemy was present, and in order to find the enemy they must boldly enter the underground Kingdom of the nomes. So bold a step demanded a council of war.

"Don't you think I'd better drop in on Ruggedo and obey the orders of the Jinjin?" asked Quox.

"By no means!" returned Queen Ann. "We have already put the army of nomes to flight and all that yet remains is to force our way into those caverns, and conquer the Nome King and all his people."

"That seems to me something of a job," said the dragon, closing his eyes sleepily. "But go ahead, if you like, and I'll wait here for you. Don't be in any hurry on my account. To one who lives thousands of years the delay of a few days means nothing at all, and I shall probably sleep until the time comes for me to act."

Ann was provoked at this speech.

"You may as well go back to Tititi-Hoochoo now," she said, "for the Nome King is as good as conquered already."

But Quox shook his head. "No," said he; "I'll wait."

16. The Naughty Nome

Shaggy Man had said nothing during the conversation between Queen Ann and Quox, for the simple reason that he did not consider the matter worth an argument. Safe within his pocket reposed the Love Magnet, which had never failed to win every heart. The nomes, he knew, were not like the heartless Roses and therefore could be won to his side as soon as he exhibited the magic talisman.

Shaggy's chief anxiety had been to reach Ruggedo's Kingdom and now that the entrance lay before him he was confident he would be able to rescue his lost brother. Let Ann and the dragon quarrel as to who should conquer the nomes, if they liked; Shaggy would let them try, and if they failed he had the means of conquest in his own pocket.

But Ann was positive she could not fail, for she thought her Army could do anything. So she called the officers together and told them how to act, and she also instructed Tik-Tok what to do and what to say.

"Please do not shoot your gun except as a last resort," she added, "for I do not wish to be cruel or to shed any blood—unless it is absolutely necessary."

"All right," replied Tik-Tok; "but I do not think Rug-ge-do would bleed if I filled him full of holes and put him in a ci-der press."

Then the officers fell in line, the four Generals abreast and then the four Colonels and the four Majors and the four Captains. They drew their glittering swords and commanded Tik-Tok to march, which he did. Twice he fell down, being tripped by the rough rocks, but when he struck the smooth path he got along better. Into the gloomy mouth of the cavern entrance he stepped without hesitation, and after him proudly pranced the officers and Queen Ann. The others held back a little, waiting to see what would happen.

Of course the Nome King knew they were coming and was prepared to receive them. Just within the rocky passage that led to the jeweled throne-room was a deep pit, which was usually covered. Ruggedo had ordered the cover removed and it now stood open, scarcely visible in the gloom.

The pit was so large around that it nearly filled the passage and there was barely room for one to walk around it by pressing close to the rock walls. This Tik-Tok did, for his copper eyes saw the pit clearly and he avoided it; but the officers marched straight into the hole and tumbled in a heap on the bottom. An instant later Queen Ann also walked into the pit, for she had her chin in the air and was careless where she placed her feet. Then one of the nomes pulled a lever which replaced the cover on the pit and made the officers of Oogaboo and their Queen fast prisoners.

As for Tik-Tok, he kept straight on to the cavern where Ruggedo sat in his throne and there he faced the Nome King and said: "I here-by con-quer you in the name of Queen Ann So-forth of Oo-ga-boo, whose Ar-my I am, and I de-clare that you are her pris-on-er!"

Ruggedo laughed at him.

"Where is this famous Queen?" he asked.

"She'll be here in a min-ute," said Tik-Tok. "Per-haps she stopped to tie her shoe-string."

"Now, see here, Tik-Tok," began the Nome King, in a stern voice, "I've had enough of this nonsense. Your Queen and her officers are all prisoners, having fallen into my power, so perhaps you'll tell me what you mean to do."

"My or-ders were to con-quer you," replied Tik-Tok, "and my

ma-chin-er-y has done the best it knows how to car-ry out those or-ders."

Ruggedo pounded on his gong and Kaliko appeared, followed closely by General Guph.

"Take this copper man into the shops and set him to work hammering gold," commanded the King. "Being run by machinery he ought to be a steady worker. He ought never to have been made, but since he exists I shall hereafter put him to good use."

"If you try to cap-ture me," said Tik-Tok, "I shall fight."

"Don't do that!" exclaimed General Guph, earnestly, "for it will be useless to resist and you might hurt some one."

But Tik-Tok raised his gun and took aim and not knowing what damage the gun might do the nomes were afraid to face it.

While he was thus defying the Nome King and his high officials, Betsy Bobbin rode calmly into the royal cavern, seated upon the back of Hank the mule. The little girl had grown tired of waiting for "something to happen" and so had come to see if Ruggedo had been conquered.

"Nails and nuggets!" roared the King; "how dare you bring that beast here and enter my presence unannounced?"

"There wasn't anybody to announce me," replied Betsy. "I guess your folks were all busy. Are you conquered yet?"

"No!" shouted the King, almost beside himself with rage.

"Then please give me something to eat, for I'm awful hungry," said the girl. "You see, this conquering business is a good deal like waiting for a circus parade; it takes a long time to get around and don't amount to much anyhow."

The nomes were so much astonished at this speech that for a time they could only glare at her silently, not finding words to reply. The King finally recovered the use of his tongue and said: "Earth-crawler! this insolence to my majesty shall be your death-warrant. You are an ordinary mortal, and to stop a mortal from living is so easy a thing to do that I will not keep you waiting half so long as you did for my conquest."

"I'd rather you wouldn't stop me from living," remarked Betsy, getting off Hank's back and standing beside him. "And it would be a pretty cheap King who killed a visitor while she was hungry. If you'll give me something to eat, I'll talk this killing business over with you afterward; only, I warn you now that I don't approve of it, and never will."

Her coolness and lack of fear impressed the Nome King, although he bore an intense hatred toward all mortals.

"What do you wish to eat?" he asked gruffly.

"Oh, a ham-sandwich would do, or perhaps a couple of hard-boiled eggs—"

"Eggs!" shrieked the three nomes who were present, shuddering till their teeth chattered.

"What's the matter?" asked Betsy wonderingly. "Are eggs as high here as they are at home?"

"Guph," said the King in an agitated voice, turning to his General, "let us destroy this rash mortal at once! Seize her and take her to the Slimy Cave and lock her in."

Guph glanced at Tik-Tok, whose gun was still pointed, but just then Kaliko stole softly behind the copper man and kicked his knee-joints so that they suddenly bent forward and tumbled Tik-Tok to the floor, his gun falling from his grasp.

Then Guph, seeing Tik-Tok helpless, made a grab at Betsy. At the same time Hank's heels shot out and caught the General just where his belt was buckled. He rose into the air swift as a cannon-ball, struck the Nome King fairly and flattened his Majesty against the wall of rock on the opposite side of the cavern. Together they fell to the floor in a dazed and crumpled condition, seeing which Kaliko whispered to Betsy: "Come with me—quick!—and I will save you."

She looked into Kaliko's face inquiringly and thought he seemed honest and good-natured, so she decided to follow him. He led her and the mule through several passages and into a small cavern very nicely and comfortably furnished.

"This is my own room," said he, "but you are quite welcome to use it. Wait here a minute and I'll get you something to eat."

When Kaliko returned he brought a tray containing some broiled mushrooms, a loaf of mineral bread and some petroleum-butter. The butter Betsy could not eat, but the bread was good and the mushrooms delicious.

"Here's the door key," said Kaliko, "and you'd better lock yourself in."

"Won't you let Polychrome and the Rose Princess come here, too?" she asked.

"I'll see. Where are they?"

"I don't know. I left them outside," said Betsy.

"Well, if you hear three raps on the door, open it," said Kaliko; "but don't let anyone in unless they give the three raps."

"All right," promised Betsy, and when Kaliko left the cosy cavern she closed and locked the door.

In the meantime Ann and her officers, finding themselves prisoners in the pit, had shouted and screamed until they were tired out, but no one had come to their assistance. It was very dark and damp in the pit and they could not climb out because the walls were higher than their heads and the cover was on. The Queen was first angry and then annoyed and then discouraged; but the officers were only afraid. Every one of the poor fellows heartily wished he was back in Oogaboo caring for his orchard, and some were so unhappy that they began to reproach Ann for causing them all this trouble and danger.

Finally the Queen sat down on the bottom of the pit and leaned her back against the wall. By good luck her sharp elbow touched a secret spring in the wall and a big flat rock swung inward. Ann fell over backward, but the next instant she jumped up and cried to the others:

"A passage! A passage! Follow me, my brave men, and we may yet escape."

Then she began to crawl through the passage, which was as dark and dank as the pit, and the officers followed her in single file. They crawled, and they crawled, and they kept on crawling, for the passage was not big enough to allow them to stand upright. It turned this way and twisted that, sometimes like a corkscrew and sometimes zigzag, but seldom ran for long in a straight line.

"It will never end—never!" moaned the officers, who were rubbing all the skin off their knees on the rough rocks.

"It must end," retorted Ann courageously, "or it never would have been made. We don't know where it will lead us to, but any place is better than that loathsome pit."

So she crawled on, and the officers crawled on, and while they were crawling through this awful underground passage Polychrome and Shaggy and Files and the Rose Princess, who were standing outside the entrance to Ruggedo's domains, were wondering what had become of them.

17. A Tragic Transformation

"Don't let us worry," said Shaggy to his companions, "for it may take the Queen some time to conquer the Metal Monarch, as Tik Tok has to do everything in his slow, mechanical way."

"Do you suppose they are likely to fail?" asked the Rose Princess.

"I do, indeed," replied Shaggy. "This Nome King is really a powerful fellow and has a legion of nomes to assist him, whereas our bold Queen commands a Clockwork Man and a band of faint-hearted officers."

"She ought to have let Quox do the conquering," said Polychrome, dancing lightly upon a point of rock and fluttering her beautiful draperies. "But perhaps the dragon was wise to let her go first, for when she fails to conquer Ruggedo she may become more modest in her ambitions."

"Where is the dragon now?" inquired Ozga.

"Up there on the rocks," replied Files. "Look, my dear; you may see him from here. He said he would take a little nap while we were mixing up with Ruggedo, and he added that after we had gotten into trouble he would wake up and conquer the Nome King in a jiffy, as his master the Jinjin has ordered him to do."

"Quox means well," said Shaggy, "but I do not think we shall need his services; for just as soon as I am satisfied that Queen Ann and her army have failed to conquer Ruggedo, I shall enter the caverns and show the King my Love Magnet. That he cannot resist; therefore the conquest will be made with ease."

This speech of Shaggy Man's was overheard by the Long-Eared Hearer, who was at that moment standing by Ruggedo's side. For when the King and Guph had recovered from Hank's kick and had picked themselves up, their first act was to turn Tik-Tok on his back and put a heavy diamond on top of him, so that he could not get up again. Then they carefully put his gun in a corner of the cavern and the King sent Guph to fetch the Long Eared Hearer.

The Hearer was still angry at Ruggedo for breaking his ear, but he acknowledged the Nome King to be his master and was ready to obey his commands. Therefore he repeated Shaggy's speech to the King, who at once realized that his Kingdom was in grave danger. For Ruggedo knew of the Love Magnet and its power and was horrified at the thought that Shaggy might show him the magic talisman and turn all the hatred in his heart into love

Ruggedo was proud of his hatred and abhorred love of any sort.

"Really," said he, "I'd rather be conquered and lose my wealth and my Kingdom than gaze at that awful Love Magnet. What can I do to prevent the Shaggy Man from taking it out of his pocket?"

Kaliko returned to the cavern in time to overhear this question, and being a loyal nome and eager to serve his King, he answered by saying: "If we can manage to bind the Shaggy Man's arms, tight to his body, he could not get the Love Magnet out of his pocket."

"True!" cried the King in delight at this easy solution of the problem. "Get at once a dozen nomes, with ropes, and place them in the passage where they can seize and bind Shaggy as soon as he enters."

This Kaliko did, and meanwhile the watchers outside the entrance were growing more and more uneasy about their friends.

"I don't worry so much about the Oogaboo people," said Polychrome, who had grown sober with waiting, and perhaps a little nervous, "for they could not be killed, even though Ruggedo might cause them much suffering and perhaps destroy them utterly. But we should not have allowed Betsy and Hank to go alone into the caverns. The little girl is mortal and possesses no magic powers whatever, so if Ruggedo captures her she will be wholly at his mercy."

"That is indeed true," replied Shaggy. "I wouldn't like to have anything happen to dear little Betsy, so I believe I'll go in right away and put an end to all this worry."

"We may as well go with you," asserted Files, "for by means of the Love Magnet, you can soon bring the Nome King to reason."

So it was decided to wait no longer. Shaggy walked through the entrance first, and after him came the others. They had no thought of danger to themselves, and Shaggy, who was going along with his hands thrust into his pockets, was much surprised when a rope shot out from the darkness and twined around his body, pinning down his arms so securely that he could not even withdraw his hands from the pockets. Then appeared several grinning nomes, who speedily tied knots in the ropes and then led the prisoner along the passage to the cavern. No attention was paid to the others, but Files and the Princess followed on after Shaggy, determined not to desert their friend and hoping that an opportunity might arise to rescue him.

As for Polychrome, as soon as she saw that trouble had overtaken Shaggy she turned and ran lightly back through the passage and out of the entrance. Then she easily leaped from rock to rock until she paused beside the great dragon, who lay fast asleep.

"Wake up, Quox!" she cried. "It is time for you to act."

But Quox did not wake up. He lay as one in a trance, absolutely motionless, with his enormous eyes tight closed. The eyelids had big silver scales on them, like all the rest of his body.

Polychrome might have thought Quox was dead had she not known that dragons do not die easily or had she not observed his huge body swelling as he breathed. She picked up a piece of rock and pounded against his eyelids with it, saying: "Wake up, Quox—wake up!"

But he would not waken.

"Dear me, how unfortunate!" sighed the lovely Rainbow's Daughter. "I wonder what is the best and surest way to waken a dragon. All our friends may be captured and destroyed while this great beast lies asleep."

She walked around Quox two or three times, trying to discover some tender place on his body where a thump or a punch might he felt; but he lay extended along the rocks with his chin flat upon the ground and his legs drawn underneath his body, and all that one could see was his thick sky-blue skin—thicker than that of a rhinoceros—and his silver scales.

Then, despairing at last of wakening the beast, and worried over the fate of her friends, Polychrome again ran down to the entrance and hurried along the passage into the Nome King's cavern.

Here she found Ruggedo lolling in his throne and smoking a long pipe. Beside him stood General Guph and Kaliko, and ranged before the King were the Rose Princess, Files and the Shaggy Man. Tik-Tok still lay upon the floor, weighted down by the big diamond.

Ruggedo was now in a more contented frame of mind. One by one he had met the invaders and easily captured them. The dreaded Love Magnet was indeed in Shaggy's pocket, only a few feet away from the King, but Shaggy was powerless to show it and unless Ruggedo's eyes beheld the talisman it could not affect him. As for Betsy Bobbin and her mule, he believed Kaliko had placed them in the Slimy Cave, while Ann and her officers he thought safely imprisoned in the pit. Ruggedo had no fear of Files or Ozga, but to be on the safe side he had ordered golden handcuffs placed upon their wrists. These did not cause them any great annoyance but prevented them from making an attack, had they been inclined to do so.

The Nome King, thinking himself wholly master of the situation, was laughing and jeering at his prisoners when Polychrome, exquisitely beautiful and dancing like a ray of light, entered the cavern.

"Oho!" cried the King; "a Rainbow under ground, eh?" and then he stared hard at Polychrome, and still harder, and then he sat up and pulled the wrinkles out of his robe and arranged his whiskers. "On my word," said he, "you are a very captivating creature; moreover, I perceive you are a fairy."

"I am Polychrome, the Rainbow's Daughter," she said proudly.

"Well," replied Ruggedo, "I like you. The others I hate. I hate everybody—but you! Wouldn't you like to live always in this beautiful cavern, Polychrome? See! the jewels that stud the walls have every tint and color of your Rainbow—and they are not so elusive. I'll have fresh dewdrops gathered for your feasting every day and you shall be Queen of all my nomes and pull Kaliko's nose whenever you like."

"No, thank you," laughed Polychrome. "My home is in the sky, and I'm only on a visit to this solid, sordid earth. But tell me, Ruggedo, why my friends have been wound with cords and bound with chains?"

"They threatened me," answered Ruggedo. "The fools did not know how powerful I am."

"Then, since they are now helpless, why not release them and send them back to the earth's surface?"

"Because I hate 'em and mean to make 'em suffer for their invasion. But I'll make a bargain with you, sweet Polly. Remain here and live with me and I'll set all these people free. You shall be my daughter or my wife or my aunt or grandmother—whichever you like—only stay here to brighten my gloomy kingdom and make me happy!"

Polychrome looked at him wonderingly. Then she turned to Shaggy and asked: "Are you sure he hasn't seen the Love Magnet?"

"I'm positive," answered Shaggy. "But you seem to be something of a Love Magnet yourself, Polychrome."

She laughed again and said to Ruggedo: "Not even to rescue my friends would I live in your kingdom. Nor could I endure for long the society of such a wicked monster as you."

"You forget," retorted the King, scowling darkly, "that you also are in my power."

"Not so, Ruggedo. The Rainbow's Daughter is beyond the reach of your spite or malice."

"Seize her!" suddenly shouted the King, and General Guph sprang forward to obey. Polychrome stood quite still, yet when Guph attempted to clutch her his hands met in air, and now the Rainbow's Daughter was in another part of the room, as smiling and composed as before.

Several times Guph endeavored to capture her and Ruggedo even came down from his throne to assist his General; but never could they lay hands upon the lovely sky fairy, who flitted here and there with the swiftness of light and constantly defied them with her merry laughter as she evaded their efforts.

So after a time they abandoned the chase and Ruggedo returned to his throne and wiped the perspiration from his face with a finely-woven handkerchief of cloth-of-gold.

"Well," said Polychrome, "what do you intend to do now?"

"I'm going to have some fun, to repay me for all my bother," replied the Nome King. Then he said to Kaliko: "Summon the executioners."

Kaliko at once withdrew and presently returned with a score of nomes, all of whom were nearly as evil looking as their hated master. They bore great golden pincers, and prods of silver, and clamps and chains and various wicked-looking instruments, all made of precious metals and set with diamonds and rubies.

"Now, Pang," said Ruggedo, addressing the leader of the executioners, "fetch the Army of Oogaboo and their Queen from the pit and torture them here in my presence—as well as in the presence of their friends. It will be great sport."

"I hear Your Majesty, and I obey Your Majesty," answered Pang, and went with his nomes into the passage. In a few minutes he returned and bowed to Ruggedo.

"They're all gone," said he.

"Gone!" exclaimed the Nome King. "Gone where?"

"They left no address, Your Majesty; but they are not in the pit."

"Picks and puddles!" roared the King; "who took the cover off?"

"No one," said Pang. "The cover was there, but the prisoners were not under it."

"In that case," snarled the King, trying to control his disappointment, "go to the Slimy Cave and fetch hither the girl and the donkey. And while we are torturing them Kaliko must take a hundred nomes and search for the escaped prisoners—the Queen of Oogaboo and her officers. If he does not find them, I will torture Kaliko."

Kaliko went away looking sad and disturbed, for he knew the King was cruel and unjust enough to carry out this threat. Pang and the executioners also went away, in another direction, but when they came back Betsy Bobbin was not with them, nor was Hank.

"There is no one in the Slimy Cave, Your Majesty," reported Pang.

"Jumping jellycakes!" screamed the King. "Another escape? Are you sure you found the right cave?"

"There is but one Slimy Cave, and there is no one in it," returned Pang positively.

Ruggedo was beginning to be alarmed as well as angry. However, these disappointments but made him the more vindictive and he cast an evil look at the other prisoners and said: "Never mind the girl and the donkey. Here are four, at least, who cannot escape my vengeance. Let me see; I believe I'll change my mind about Tik-Tok. Have the gold crucible heated to a white, seething heat, and then we'll dump the copper man into it and melt him up."

"But, Your Majesty," protested Kaliko, who had returned to the room after sending a hundred nomes to search for the Oogaboo people, "you must remember that Tik-Tok is a very curious and interesting machine. It would be a shame to deprive the world of such a clever contrivance."

"Say another word, and you'll go into the furnace with him!" roared the King. "I'm getting tired of you, Kaliko, and the first thing you know I'll turn you into a potato and make Saratoga-chips of you! The next to consider," he added more mildly, "is the Shaggy Man. As he owns the Love Magnet, I think I'll transform him into a dove, and then we can practice shooting at him with Tik- Tok's gun. Now, this is a very interesting ceremony and I beg you all to watch me closely and see that I've nothing up my sleeve."

He came out of his throne to stand before the Shaggy Man, and then he waved his hands, palms downward, in seven semicircles over his victim's head, saying in a low but clear tone of voice the magic wugwa:

"Adi, edi, idi, odi, udi, oo-i-oo! Idu, ido, idi, ide, ida, woo!"

The effect of this well-known sorcery was instantaneous. Instead of the Shaggy Man, a pretty dove lay fluttering upon the floor, its wings confined by tiny cords wound around them. Ruggedo gave an order to Pang, who cut the cords with a pair of scissors. Being freed, the dove quickly flew upward and alighted on the shoulder of the Rose Princess, who stroked it tenderly.

"Very good! Very good!" cried Ruggedo, rubbing his hands gleefully together. "One enemy is out of my way, and now for the others."

(Perhaps my readers should be warned not to attempt the above transformation; for, although the exact magical formula has been described, it is unlawful in all civilized countries for anyone to transform a person into a dove by muttering the words Ruggedo used. There were no laws to prevent the Nome King from performing this transformation, but if it should be attempted in any other country, and the magic worked, the magician would be severely punished.)

When Polychrome saw Shaggy Man transformed into a dove and realized that Ruggedo was about do something as dreadful to the Princess and Files, and that Tik-Tok would soon be melted in a crucible, she turned and ran from the cavern, through the passage and back to the place where Quox lay asleep.

18. A Clever Conquest

The great dragon still had his eyes closed and was even snoring in a manner that resembled distant thunder; but Polychrome was now desperate, because any further delay meant the destruction of her friends. She seized the pearl necklace, to which was attached the great locket, and jerked it with all her strength.

The result was encouraging. Quox stopped snoring and his eyelids flickered. So Polychrome jerked again—and again—till slowly the great lids raised and the dragon looked at her steadily. Said he, in a sleepy tone: "What's the matter, little Rainbow?"

"Come quick!" exclaimed Polychrome. "Ruggedo has captured all our friends and is about to destroy them."

"Well, well," said Quox, "I suspected that would happen. Step a little out of my path, my dear, and I'll make a rush for the Nome King's cavern."

She fell back a few steps and Quox raised himself on his stout legs, whisked his long tail and in an instant had slid down the rocks and made a dive through the entrance.

Along the passage he swept, nearly filling it with his immense body, and now he poked his head into the jeweled cavern of Ruggedo.

But the King had long since made arrangements to capture the dragon, whenever he might appear. No sooner did Quox stick his head into the room than a thick chain fell from above and encircled his neck. Then the ends of the chain were drawn tight—for in an adjoining cavern a thousand nomes were pulling on them—and so the dragon could advance no further toward the King. He could not use his teeth or his claws and as his body was still in the passage he had not even room to strike his foes with his terrible tail.

Ruggedo was delighted with the success of his stratagem. He had just transformed the Rose Princess into a fiddle and was about to transform Files into a fiddle bow, when the dragon appeared to interrupt him. So he called out: "Welcome, my dear Quox, to my royal entertainment. Since you are here, you shall witness some very neat magic, and after I have finished with Files and Tik-Tok I mean to transform you into a tiny lizard—one of the chameleon sort—and you shall live in my cavern and amuse me."

"Pardon me for contradicting Your Majesty," returned Quox in a quiet voice, "but I don't believe you'll perform any more magic."

"Eh? Why not?" asked the King in surprise.

"There's a reason," said Quox. "Do you see this ribbon around my neck?"

"Yes; and I'm astonished that a dignified dragon should wear such a silly thing."

"Do you see it plainly?" persisted the dragon, with a little chuckle of amusement.

"I do," declared Ruggedo.

"Then you no longer possess any magical powers, and are as helpless as a clam," asserted Quox. "My great master, Tititi-Hoochoo, the Jinjin, enchanted this ribbon in such a way that whenever Your Majesty looked upon it all knowledge of magic would desert you instantly, nor will any magical formula you can remember ever perform your bidding."

"Pooh! I don't believe a word of it!" cried Ruggedo, half frightened, nevertheless. Then he turned toward Files and tried to transform him into a fiddle bow. But he could not remember the right words or the right pass of the hands and after several trials he finally gave up the attempt.

By this time the Nome King was so alarmed that he was secretly shaking in his shoes.

"I told you not to anger Tititi-Hoochoo," grumbled Kaliko, "and now you see the result of your disobedience."

Ruggedo promptly threw his sceptre at his Royal Chamberlain, who dodged it with his usual cleverness, and then he said with an attempt to swagger: "Never mind; I don't need magic to enable me to destroy these invaders; fire and the sword will do the business and I am still King of the Nomes and lord and master of my Underground Kingdom!"

"Again I beg to differ with Your Majesty," said Quox. "The Great Jinjin commands you to depart instantly from this Kingdom and seek the earth's surface, where you will wander for all time to come, without a home or country, without a friend or follower, and without any more riches than you can carry with you in your pockets. The Great Jinjin is so generous that he will allow you to fill your pockets with jewels or gold, but you must take nothing more."

Ruggedo now stared at the dragon in amazement.

"Does Tititi-Hoochoo condemn me to such a fate?" he asked in a hoarse voice.

"He does," said Quox.

"And just for throwing a few strangers down the Forbidden Tube?"

"Just for that," repeated Quox in a stern, gruff voice.

"Well, I won't do it. And your crazy old Jinjin can't make me do it, either!" declared Ruggedo. "I intend to remain here, King of the Nomes, until the end of the world, and I defy your Tititi-Hoochoo and all his fairies—as well as his clumsy messenger, whom I have been obliged to chain up!"

The dragon smiled again, but it was not the sort of smile that made Ruggedo feel very happy. Instead, there was something so cold and merciless in the dragon's expression that the condemned Nome King trembled and was sick at heart.

There was little comfort for Ruggedo in the fact that the dragon was now chained, although he had boasted of it. He glared at the immense head of Quox as if fascinated and there was fear in the old King's eyes as he watched his enemy's movements.

For the dragon was now moving; not abruptly, but as if he had something to do and was about to do it. Very deliberately he raised one claw, touched the catch of the great jeweled locket that was suspended around his neck, and at once it opened wide.

Nothing much happened at first; half a dozen hen's eggs rolled out upon the floor and then the locket closed with a sharp click. But the effect upon the nomes of this simple thing was astounding. General Guph, Kaliko, Pang and his band of executioners were all standing close to the door that led to the vast series of underground caverns which constituted the dominions of the nomes, and as soon as they saw the eggs they raised a chorus of frantic screams and rushed through the door, slamming it in Ruggedo's face and placing a heavy bronze bar across it.

Ruggedo, dancing with terror and uttering loud cries, now leaped upon the seat of his throne to escape the eggs, which had rolled steadily toward him. Perhaps these eggs, sent by the wise and crafty Tititi-Hoochoo, were in some way enchanted, for they all rolled directly after Ruggedo and when they reached the throne where he had taken refuge they began rolling up the legs to the seat.

This was too much for the King to bear. His horror of eggs was real and absolute and he made a leap from the throne to the center of the room and then ran to a far corner.

The eggs followed, rolling slowly but steadily in his direction. Ruggedo threw his sceptre at them, and then his ruby crown, and then he drew off his heavy golden sandals and hurled these at the advancing eggs. But the eggs dodged every missile and continued to draw nearer. The King stood trembling, his eyes staring in terror, until they were but half a yard distant; then with an agile leap he jumped clear over them and made a rush for the passage that led to the outer entrance.

Of course the dragon was in his way, being chained in the passage with his head in the cavern, but when he saw the King making toward him he crouched as low as he could and dropped his chin to the floor, leaving a small space between his body and the roof of the passage.

Ruggedo did not hesitate an instant. Impelled by fear, he leaped to the dragon's nose and then scrambled to his back, where he succeeded in squeezing himself through the opening. After the head was passed there was more room and he slid along the dragon's scales to his tail and then ran as fast as his legs would carry him to the entrance. Not pausing here, so great was his fright, the King dashed on down the mountain path, but before he had gone very far he stumbled and fell.

When he picked himself up he observed that no one was following him, and while he recovered his breath he happened to think of the decree of the Jinjin—that he should be driven from his Kingdom and made a wanderer on the face of the earth. Well, here he was, driven from his cavern in truth; driven by those dreadful eggs; but he would go back and defy them; he would not submit to losing his precious Kingdom and his tyrannical powers, all because Tititi-Hoochoo had said he must.

So, although still afraid, Ruggedo nerved himself to creep back along the path to the entrance, and when he arrived there he saw the six eggs lying in a row just before the arched opening.

At first he paused a safe distance away to consider the case, for the eggs were now motionless. While he was wondering what could be done, he remembered there was a magical charm which would destroy eggs and render them harmless to nomes. There were nine passes to be made and six verses of incantation to be recited; but Ruggedo knew them all. Now that he had ample time to be exact, he carefully went through the entire ceremony.

But nothing happened. The eggs did not disappear, as he had expected; so he repeated the charm a second time. When that also failed, he remembered, with a moan of despair, that his magic power had been taken away from him and in the future he could do no more than any common mortal.

And there were the eggs, forever barring him from the Kingdom which he had ruled so long with absolute sway! He threw rocks at them, but could not hit a single egg. He raved and scolded and tore his hair and beard, and danced in helpless passion, but that did nothing to avert the just judgment of the Jinjin, which Ruggedo's own evil deeds had brought upon him.

From this time on he was an outcast—a wanderer upon the face of the earth—and he had even forgotten to fill his pockets with gold and jewels before he fled from his former Kingdom!

19. King Kaliko

After the King had made good his escape Files said to the dragon, in a sad voice:

"Alas! why did you not come before? Because you were sleeping instead of conquering, the lovely Rose Princess has become a fiddle without a bow, while poor Shaggy sits there a cooing dove!"

"Don't worry," replied Quox. "Tititi-Hoochoo knows his business, and I have my orders from the Great Jinjin himself. Bring the fiddle here and touch it lightly to my pink ribbon."

Files obeyed and at the moment of contact with the ribbon the Nome King's charm was broken and the Rose Princess herself stood before them as sweet and smiling as ever.

The dove, perched on the back of the throne, had seen and heard all this, so without being told what to do it flew straight to the dragon and alighted on the ribbon. Next instant Shaggy was himself again and Quox said to him grumblingly: "Please get off my left toe, Shaggy Man, and be more particular where you step."

"I beg your pardon!" replied Shaggy, very glad to resume his natural form. Then he ran to lift the heavy diamond off Tik-Tok's chest and to assist the Clockwork Man to his feet.

"Ma-ny thanks!" said Tik-Tok. "Where is the wicked King who want-ed to melt me in a cru-ci-ble?"

"He has gone, and gone for good," answered Polychrome, who had managed to squeeze into the room beside the dragon and had witnessed the occurrences with much interest. "But I wonder where Betsy Bobbin and Hank can be, and if any harm has befallen them."

"We must search the cavern until we find them," declared Shaggy; but when he went to the door leading to the other caverns he found it shut and barred.

"I've a pretty strong push in my forehead," said Quox, "and I believe I can break down that door, even though it's made of solid gold."

"But you are a prisoner, and the chains that hold you are fastened in some other room, so that we cannot release you," Files said anxiously.

"Oh, never mind that," returned the dragon. "I have remained a prisoner only because I wished to be one," and with this he stepped forward and burst the stout chains as easily as if they had been threads.

But when he tried to push in the heavy metal door, even his mighty strength failed, and after several attempts he gave it up and squatted himself in a corner to think of a better way.

"I'll o-pen the door," asserted Tik-Tok, and going to the King's big gong he pounded upon it until the noise was almost deafening.

Kaliko, in the next cavern, was wondering what had happened to Ruggedo and if he had escaped the eggs and outwitted the dragon. But when he heard the sound of the gong, which had so often called him into the King's presence, he decided that Ruggedo had been victorious; so he took away the bar, threw open the door and entered the royal cavern.

Great was his astonishment to find the King gone and the enchantments removed from the Princess and Shaggy. But the eggs were also gone and so Kaliko advanced to the dragon, whom he knew to be Tititi-Hoochoo's messenger, and bowed humbly before the beast.

"What is your will?" he inquired.

"Where is Betsy?" demanded the dragon.

"Safe in my own private room," said Kaliko.

"Go and get her!" commanded Quox.

So Kaliko went to Betsy's room and gave three raps upon the door. The little girl had been asleep, but she heard the raps and opened the door.

"You may come out now," said Kaliko. "The King has fled in disgrace and your friends are asking for you."

So Betsy and Hank returned with the Royal Chamberlain to the throne cavern, where she was received with great joy by her friends. They told her what had happened to Ruggedo and she told them how kind Kaliko had been to her. Quox did not have much to say until the conversation was ended, but then he turned to Kaliko and asked: "Do you suppose you could rule your nomes better than Ruggedo has done?"

"Me?" stammered the Chamberlain, greatly surprised by the question. "Well, I couldn't be a worse King, I'm sure."

"Would the nomes obey you?" inquired the dragon.

"Of course," said Kaliko. "They like me better than ever they did Ruggedo."

"Then hereafter you shall be the Metal Monarch, King of the Nomes, and Tititi-Hoochoo expects you to rule your Kingdom wisely and well," said Quox.

"Hooray!" cried Betsy; "I'm glad of that. King Kaliko, I salute Your Majesty and wish you joy in your gloomy old Kingdom!"

"We all wish him joy," said Polychrome; and then the others made haste to congratulate the new King.

"Will you release my dear brother?" asked Shaggy.

"The Ugly One? Very willingly," replied Kaliko. "I begged Ruggedo long ago to send him away, but he would not do so. I also offered to help your brother to escape, but he would not go."

"He's so conscientious!" said Shaggy, highly pleased. "All of our family have noble natures. But is my dear brother well?" he added anxiously.

"He eats and sleeps very steadily," replied the new King.

"I hope he doesn't work too hard," said Shaggy.

"He doesn't work at all. In fact, there is nothing he can do in these dominions as well as our nomes, whose numbers are so great that it worries us to keep them all busy. So your brother has only to amuse himself."

"Why, it's more like visiting, than being a prisoner," asserted Betsy.

"Not exactly," returned Kaliko. "A prisoner cannot go where or when he pleases, and is not his own master."

"Where is my brother now?" inquired Shaggy.

"In the Metal Forest."

"Where is that?"

"The Metal Forest is in the Great Domed Cavern, the largest in all our dominions," replied Kaliko. "It is almost like being out of doors, it is so big, and Ruggedo made the wonderful forest to amuse himself, as well as to tire out his hard-working nomes. All the trees are gold and silver and the ground is strewn with precious stones, so it is a sort of treasury."

"Let us go there at once and rescue my dear brother," pleaded Shaggy earnestly.

Kaliko hesitated.

"I don't believe I can find the way," said he. "Ruggedo made three secret passages to the Metal Forest, but he changes the location of these passages every week, so that no one can get to the Metal Forest without his permission. However, if we look sharp, we may be able to discover one of these secret ways."

"That reminds me to ask what has become of Queen Ann and the Officers of Oogaboo," said Files.

"I'm sure I can't say," replied Kaliko.

"Do you suppose Ruggedo destroyed them?"

"Oh, no; I'm quite sure he didn't. They fell into the big pit in the passage, and we put the cover on to keep them there; but when the executioners went to look for them they had all disappeared from the pit and we could find no trace of them."

"That's funny," remarked Betsy thoughtfully. "I don't believe Ann knew any magic, or she'd have worked it before. But to disappear like that seems like magic; now, doesn't it?"

They agreed that it did, but no one could explain the mystery.

"However," said Shaggy, "they are gone, that is certain, so we cannot help them or be helped by them. And the important thing just now is to rescue my dear brother from captivity."

"Why do they call him the Ugly One?" asked Betsy.

"I do not know," confessed Shaggy. "I can not remember his looks very well, it is so long since I have seen him; but all of our family are noted for their handsome faces."

Betsy laughed and Shaggy seemed rather hurt; but Polychrome relieved his embarrassment by saying softly: "One can be ugly in looks, but lovely in disposition."

"Our first task," said Shaggy, a little comforted by this remark, "is to find one of those secret passages to the Metal Forest."

"True," agreed Kaliko. "So I think I will assemble the chief nomes of my kingdom in this throne room and tell them that I am their new King. Then I can ask them to assist us in searching for the secret passages.

"That's a good idea," said the dragon, who seemed to be getting sleepy again.

Kaliko went to the big gong and pounded on it just as Ruggedo used to do; but no one answered the summons.

"Of course not," said he, jumping up from the throne, where he had seated himself. "That is my call, and I am still the Royal Chamberlain, and will be until I appoint another in my place."

So he ran out of the room and found Guph and told him to answer the summons of the King's gong. Having returned to the royal cavern, Kaliko first pounded the gong and then sat in the throne, wearing Ruggedo's discarded ruby crown and holding in his hand the sceptre which Ruggedo had so often thrown at his head.

When Guph entered he was amazed.

"Better get out of that throne before old Ruggedo comes back," he said warningly.

"He isn't coming back, and I am now the King of the Nomes, in his stead," announced Kaliko.

"All of which is quite true," asserted the dragon, and all of those who stood around the throne bowed respectfully to the new King.

Seeing this, Guph also bowed, for he was glad to be rid of such a hard master as Ruggedo. Then Kaliko, in quite a kingly way, informed Guph that he was appointed the Royal Chamberlain, and promised not to throw the sceptre at his head unless he deserved it.

All this being pleasantly arranged, the new Chamberlain went away to tell the news to all the nomes of the underground Kingdom, every one of whom would be delighted with the change in Kings.

20. Quox Quietly Quits

When the chief nomes assembled before their new King they joyfully saluted him and promised to obey his commands. But, when Kaliko questioned them, none knew the way to the Metal Forest, although all had assisted in its making. So the King instructed them to search carefully for one of the passages and to bring him the news as soon as they had found it.

Meantime Quox had managed to back out of the rocky corridor and so regain the open air and his old station on the mountain-side, and there he lay upon the rocks, sound asleep, until the next day. The others of the party were all given as good rooms as the caverns of the nomes afforded, for King Kaliko felt that he was indebted to them for his promotion and was anxious to be as hospitable as he could.

Much wonderment had been caused by the absolute disappearance of the sixteen officers of Oogaboo and their Queen. Not a nome had seen them, nor were they discovered during the search for the passages leading to the Metal Forest. Perhaps no one was unhappy over their loss, but all were curious to know what had become of them.

On the next day, when our friends went to visit the dragon, Quox said to them: "I must now bid you good-bye, for my mission here is finished and I must depart for the other side of the world, where I belong."

"Will you go through the Tube again?" asked Betsy.

"To be sure. But it will be a lonely trip this time, with no one to talk to, and I cannot invite any of you to go with me. Therefore, as soon as I slide into the hole I shall go to sleep, and when I pop out at the other end I will wake up at home."

They thanked the dragon for befriending them and wished him a pleasant journey. Also they sent their thanks to the great Jinjin, whose just condemnation of Ruggedo had served their interests so well. Then Quox yawned and stretched himself and ambled over to the Tube, into which he slid headforemost and disappeared.

They really felt as if they had lost a friend, for the dragon had been both kind and sociable during their brief acquaintance with him; but they knew it was his duty to return to his own country. So they went back to the caverns to renew the search for the hidden passages that led to the forest, but for three days all efforts to find them proved in vain.

It was Polychrome's custom to go every day to the mountain and watch for her father, the Rainbow, for she was growing tired with wandering upon the earth and longed to rejoin her sisters in their sky palaces. And on the third day, while she sat motionless upon a point of rock, whom should she see slyly creeping up the mountain but Ruggedo!

The former King looked very forlorn. His clothes were soiled and torn and he had no sandals upon his feet or hat upon his head. Having left his crown and sceptre behind when he fled, the old nome no longer seemed kingly, but more like a beggarman.

Several times had Ruggedo crept up to the mouth of the caverns, only to find the six eggs still on guard. He knew quite well that he must accept his fate and become a homeless wanderer, but his chief regret now was that he had neglected to fill his pockets with gold and jewels. He was aware that a wanderer with wealth at his command would fare much better than one who was a pauper, so he still loitered around the caverns wherein he knew so much treasure was stored, hoping for a chance to fill his pockets.

That was how he came to recollect the Metal Forest.

"Aha!" said he to himself, "I alone know the way to that Forest, and once there I can fill my pockets with the finest jewels in all the world."

He glanced at his pockets and was grieved to find them so small. Perhaps they might be enlarged, so that they would hold more. He knew of a poor woman who lived in a cottage at the foot of the mountain, so he went to her and begged her to sew pockets all over his robe, paying her with the gift of a diamond ring which he had worn upon his finger. The woman was delighted to possess so valuable a ring and she sewed as many pockets on Ruggedo's robe as she possibly could.

Then he returned up the mountain and, after gazing cautiously around to make sure he was not observed, he touched a spring in a rock and it swung slowly backward, disclosing a broad passageway. This he entered, swinging the rock in place behind him.

However, Ruggedo had failed to look as carefully as he might have done, for Polychrome was seated only a little distance off and her clear eyes marked exactly the manner in which Ruggedo had released the hidden spring. So she rose and hurried into the cavern, where she told Kaliko and her friends of her discovery.

"I've no doubt that that is a way to the Metal Forest," exclaimed Shaggy. "Come, let us follow Ruggedo at once and rescue my poor brother!"

They agreed to this and King Kaliko called together a band of nomes to assist them by carrying torches to light their way.

"The Metal Forest has a brilliant light of its own," said he, "but the passage across the valley is likely to be dark."

Polychrome easily found the rock and touched the spring, so in less than an hour after Ruggedo had entered they were all in the passage and following swiftly after the former King.

"He means to rob the Forest, I'm sure," said Kaliko; "but he will find he is no longer of any account in this Kingdom and I will have my nomes throw him out."

"Then please throw him as hard as you can," said Betsy, "for he deserves it. I don't mind an honest, out-an'-out enemy, who fights square; but changing girls into fiddles and ordering 'em put into Slimy Caves is mean and tricky, and Ruggedo doesn't deserve any sympathy. But you'll have to let him take as much treasure as he can get in his pockets, Kaliko."

"Yes, the Jinjin said so; but we won't miss it much. There is more treasure in the Metal Forest than a million nomes could carry in their pockets."

It was not difficult to walk through this passage, especially when the torches lighted the way, so they made good progress. But it proved to be a long distance and Betsy had tired herself with walking and was seated upon the back of the mule when the passage made a sharp turn and a wonderful and glorious light burst upon them. The next moment they were all standing upon the edge of the marvelous Metal Forest.

It lay under another mountain and occupied a great domed cavern, the roof of which was higher than a church steeple. In this space the industrious nomes had built, during many years of labor, the most beautiful forest in the world. The trees—trunks, branches and leaves—were all of solid gold, while the bushes and underbrush were formed of filigree silver, virgin pure. The trees towered as high as natural live oaks do and were of exquisite workmanship.

On the ground were thickly strewn precious gems of every hue and size, while here and there among the trees were paths pebbled with cut diamonds of the clearest water. Taken all together, more treasure was gathered in this Metal Forest than is contained in all the rest of the world—if we except the land of Oz, where perhaps its value is equalled in the famous Emerald City.

Our friends were so amazed at the sight that for a while they stood gazing in silent wonder. Then Shaggy exclaimed, "My brother! My dear lost brother! Is he indeed a prisoner in this place?"

"Yes," replied Kaliko. "The Ugly One has been here for two or three years, to my positive knowledge."

"But what could he find to eat?" inquired Betsy. "It's an awfully swell place to live in, but one can't breakfast on rubies and di'monds, or even gold."

"One doesn't need to, my dear," Kaliko assured her. "The Metal Forest does not fill all of this great cavern, by any means. Beyond these gold and silver trees are other trees of the real sort, which bear foods very nice to eat. Let us walk in that direction, for I am quite sure we will find Shaggy's brother in that part of the cavern, rather than in this."

So they began to tramp over the diamond-pebbled paths, and at every step they were more and more bewildered by the wondrous beauty of the golden trees with their glittering foliage.

Suddenly they heard a scream. Jewels scattered in every direction as some one hidden among the bushes scampered away before them. Then a loud voice cried: "Halt!" and there was the sound of a struggle.

21. A Bashful Brother

With fast beating hearts they all rushed forward and, beyond a group of stately metal trees, came full upon a most astonishing scene.

There was Ruggedo in the hands of the officers of Oogaboo, a dozen of whom were clinging to the old nome and holding him fast in spite of his efforts to escape. There also was Queen Ann, looking grimly upon the scene of strife; but when she observed her former companions approaching she turned away in a shamefaced manner.

For Ann and her officers were indeed a sight to behold. Her Majesty's clothing, once so rich and gorgeous, was now worn and torn into shreds by her long crawl through the tunnel, which, by the way, had led her directly into the Metal Forest. It was, indeed, one of the three secret passages, and by far the most difficult of the three. Ann had not only torn her pretty skirt and jacket, but her crown had become bent and battered and even her shoes were so cut and slashed that they were ready to fall from her feet.

The officers had fared somewhat worse than their leader, for holes were worn in the knees of their trousers, while sharp points of rock in the roof and sides of the tunnel had made rags of every inch of their once brilliant uniforms. A more tattered and woeful army never came out of a battle, than these harmless victims of the rocky passage. But it had seemed their only means of escape from the cruel Nome King; so they had crawled on, regardless of their sufferings.

When they reached the Metal Forest their eyes beheld more plunder than they had ever dreamed of; yet they were prisoners in this huge dome and could not escape with the riches heaped about them. Perhaps a more unhappy and homesick lot of "conquerors" never existed than this band from Oogaboo.

After several days of wandering in their marvelous prison they were frightened by the discovery that Ruggedo had come among them. Rendered desperate by their sad condition, the officers exhibited courage for the first time since they left home and, ignorant of the fact that Ruggedo was no longer King of the nomes, they threw themselves upon him and had just succeeded in capturing him when their fellow adventurers reached the spot.

"Goodness gracious!" cried Betsy. "What has happened to you all?"

Ann came forward to greet them, sorrowful and indignant.

"We were obliged to escape from the pit through a small tunnel, which was lined with sharp and jagged rocks," said she, "and not only was our clothing torn to rags but our flesh is so bruised and sore that we are stiff and lame in every joint. To add to our troubles we find we are still prisoners; but now that we have succeeded in capturing the wicked Metal Monarch we shall force him to grant us our liberty."

"Ruggedo is no longer Metal Monarch, or King of the nomes," Files informed her. "He has been deposed and cast out of his kingdom by Quox; but here is the new King, whose name is Kaliko, and I am pleased to assure Your Majesty that he is our friend."

"Glad to meet Your Majesty, I'm sure," said Kaliko, bowing as courteously as if the Queen still wore splendid raiment.

The officers, having heard this explanation, now set Ruggedo free; but, as he had no place to go, he stood by and faced his former servant, who was now King in his place, in a humble and pleading manner.

"What are you doing here?" asked Kaliko sternly.

"Why, I was promised as much treasure as I could carry in my pockets," replied Ruggedo; "so I came here to get it, not wishing to disturb Your Majesty."

"You were commanded to leave the country of the nomes forever!" declared Kaliko.

"I know; and I'll go as soon as I have filled my pockets," said Ruggedo, meekly.

"Then fill them, and be gone," returned the new King.

Ruggedo obeyed. Stooping down, he began gathering up jewels by the handful and stuffing them into his many pockets. They were heavy things, these diamonds and rubies and emeralds and amethysts and the like, so before long Ruggedo was staggering with the weight he bore, while the pockets were not yet filled. When he could no longer stoop over without falling, Betsy and Polychrome and the Rose Princess came to his assistance, picking up the finest gems and tucking them into his pockets.

At last these were all filled and Ruggedo presented a comical sight, for surely no man ever before had so many pockets, or any at all filled with such a choice collection of precious stones. He neglected to thank the young ladies for their kindness, but gave them a surly nod of farewell and staggered down the path by the way he had come. They let him depart in silence, for with all he had taken, the masses of jewels upon the ground seemed scarcely to have been disturbed, so numerous were they. Also they hoped they had seen the last of the degraded King.

"I'm awful glad he's gone," said Betsy, sighing deeply. "If he doesn't get reckless and spend his wealth foolishly, he's got enough to start a bank when he gets to Oklahoma."

"But my brother—my dear brother! Where is he?" inquired Shaggy anxiously. "Have you seen him, Queen Ann?"

"What does your brother look like?" asked the Queen.

Shaggy hesitated to reply, but Betsy said: "He's called the Ugly One. Perhaps you'll know him by that."

"The only person we have seen in this cavern," said Ann, "has run away from us whenever we approached him. He hides over yonder, among the trees that are not gold, and we have never been able to catch sight of his face. So I can not tell whether he is ugly or not."

"That must be my dear brother!" exclaimed Shaggy.

"Yes, it must be," assented Kaliko. "No one else inhabits this splendid dome, so there can be no mistake."

"But why does he hide among those green trees, instead of enjoying all these glittery golden ones?" asked Betsy.

"Because he finds food among the natural trees," replied Kaliko "and I remember that he has built a little house there, to sleep in As for these glittery golden trees, I will admit they are very pretty at first sight. One cannot fail to admire them, as well as the rich jewels scattered beneath them; but if one has to look at them always, they become pretty tame."

"I believe that is true," declared Shaggy. "My dear brother is very wise to prefer real trees to the imitation ones. But come; let us go there and find him."

Shaggy started for the green grove at once, and the others followed him, being curious to witness the final rescue of his long-sought, long-lost brother.

Not far from the edge of the grove they came upon a small hut cleverly made of twigs and golden branches woven together. As they approached the place they caught a glimpse of a form that darted into the hut and slammed the door tight shut after him.

Shaggy Man ran to the door and cried aloud: "Brother! Brother!"

"Who calls," demanded a sad, hollow voice from within.

"It is Shaggy—your own loving brother—who has been searching for you a long time and has now come to rescue you."

"Too late!" replied the gloomy voice. "No one can rescue me now."

"Oh, but you are mistaken about that," said Shaggy. "There is a new King of the nomes, named Kaliko, in Ruggedo's place, and he has promised you shall go free."

"Free! I dare not go free!" said the Ugly One, in a voice of despair.

"Why not, Brother?" asked Shaggy, anxiously.

"Do you know what they have done to me?" came the answer through the closed door.

"No. Tell me, Brother, what have they done?"

"When Ruggedo first captured me I was very handsome. Don't you remember, Shaggy?"

"Not very well, Brother; you were so young when I left home. But I remember that mother thought you were beautiful."

"She was right! I am sure she was right," wailed the prisoner. "But Ruggedo wanted to injure me—to make me ugly in the eyes of all the world—so he performed a wicked enchantment. I went to bed beautiful—or you might say very modest I will merely claim that I was good-looking—and I wakened the next morning the homeliest man in all the world! I am so repulsive that when I look in a mirror I frighten myself."

"Poor Brother!" said Shaggy softly, and all the others were silent from sympathy.

"I was so ashamed of my looks," continued the voice of Shaggy's brother, "that I tried to hide; but the cruel King Ruggedo forced me to appear before all the legion of nomes, to whom he said: 'Behold the Ugly One!' But when the nomes saw my face they all fell to laughing and jeering, which prevented them from working at their tasks. Seeing this, Ruggedo became angry and pushed me into a tunnel, closing the rock entrance so that I could not get out. I followed the length of the tunnel until I reached this huge dome, where the marvelous Metal Forest stands, and here I have remained ever since."

"Poor Brother!" repeated Shaggy. "But I beg you now to come forth and face us, who are your friends. None here will laugh or jeer, however unhandsome you may be."

"No, indeed," they all added pleadingly.

But the Ugly One refused the invitation.

"I cannot," said he; "indeed, I cannot face strangers, ugly as I am."

Shaggy Man turned to the group surrounding him.

"What shall I do?" he asked in sorrowful tones. "I cannot leave my dear brother here, and he refuses to come out of that house and face us."

"I'll tell you," replied Betsy. "Let him put on a mask."

"The very idea I was seeking!" exclaimed Shaggy joyfully; and

then he called out: "Brother, put a mask over your face, and then none of us can see what your features are like."

"I have no mask," answered the Ugly One.

"Look here," said Betsy; "he can use my handkerchief."

Shaggy looked at the little square of cloth and shook his head.

"It isn't big enough," he objected; "I'm sure it isn't big enough to hide a man's face. But he can use mine."

Saying this he took from his pocket his own handkerchief and went to the door of the hut.

"Here, my Brother," he called, "take this handkerchief and make a mask of it. I will also pass you my knife, so that you may cut holes for the eyes, and then you must tie it over your face."

The door slowly opened, just far enough for the Ugly One to thrust out his hand and take the handkerchief and the knife. Then it closed again.

"Don't forget a hole for your nose," cried Betsy. "You must breathe, you know."

For a time there was silence. Queen Ann and her army sat down upon the ground to rest. Betsy sat on Hank's back. Polychrome danced lightly up and down the jeweled paths while Files and the Princess wandered through the groves arm in arm. Tik-Tok, who never tired, stood motionless.

By and by a noise sounded from within the hut.

"Are you ready?" asked Shaggy.

"Yes, Brother," came the reply and the door was thrown open to allow the Ugly One to step forth.

Betsy might have laughed aloud had she not remembered how sensitive to ridicule Shaggy's brother was, for the handkerchief with which he had masked his features was a red one covered with big white polka dots. In this two holes had been cut—in front of the eyes—while two smaller ones before the nostrils allowed the man to breathe freely. The cloth was then tightly drawn over the Ugly One's face and knotted at the back of his neck.

He was dressed in clothes that had once been good, but now were sadly worn and frayed. His silk stockings had holes in them, and his shoes were stub-toed and needed blackening. "But what can you expect," whispered Betsy, "when the poor man has been a prisoner for so many years?"

Shaggy had darted forward, and embraced his newly found brother with both his arms. The brother also embraced Shaggy, who then led him forward and introduced him to all the assembled company.

"This is the new Nome King," he said when he came to Kaliko. "He is our friend, and has granted you your freedom."

"That is a kindly deed," replied Ugly in a sad voice, "but I dread to go back to the world in this direful condition. Unless I remain forever masked, my dreadful face would curdle all the milk and stop all the clocks."

"Can't the enchantment be broken in some way?" inquired Betsy.

Shaggy looked anxiously at Kaliko, who shook his head.

"I am sure I can't break the enchantment," he said. "Ruggedo was fond of magic, and learned a good many enchantments that we nomes know nothing of."

"Perhaps Ruggedo himself might break his own enchantment," suggested Ann; "but unfortunately we have allowed the old King to escape."

"Never mind, my dear Brother," said Shaggy consolingly; "I am very happy to have found you again, although I may never see your face. So let us make the most of this joyful reunion."

The Ugly One was affected to tears by this tender speech, and the tears began to wet the red handkerchief; so Shaggy gently wiped them away with his coat sleeve.

22. Kindly Kisses

"Won't you be dreadful sorry to leave this lovely place?" Betsy asked the Ugly One.

"No, indeed," said he. "Jewels and gold are cold and heartless things, and I am sure I would presently have died of loneliness had I not found the natural forest at the edge of the artificial one. Anyhow, without these real trees I should soon have starved to death."

Betsy looked around at the quaint trees.

"I don't just understand that," she admitted. "What could you find to eat here."

"The best food in the world," Ugly answered. "Do you see that grove at your left?" he added, pointing it out; "well, such trees as those do not grow in your country, or in any other place but this cavern. I have named them 'Hotel Trees,' because they bear a certain kind of table d'hote fruit called 'Three-Course Nuts.' "

"That's funny!" said Betsy. "What are the 'Three-Course Nuts' like?"

"Something like coconuts, to look at," explained the Ugly One. "All you have to do is to pick one of them and then sit down and eat your dinner. You first unscrew the top part and find a cupfull of good soup. After you've eaten that, you unscrew the middle part and find a hollow filled with meat and potatoes, vegetables and a fine salad. Eat that, and unscrew the next section, and you come to the dessert in the bottom of the nut. That is, pie and cake, cheese and crackers, and nuts and raisins. The Three-Course Nuts are not all exactly alike in flavor or in contents, but they are all good and in each one may be found a complete three-course dinner."

"But how about breakfasts?" inquired Betsy.

"Why, there are Breakfast Trees for that, which grow over there at the right. They bear nuts, like the others, only the nuts contain coffee or chocolate, instead of soup; oatmeal instead of meat-and-potatoes, and fruits instead of dessert. Sad as has been my life in this wonderful prison, I must admit that no one could live more luxuriously in the best hotel in the world than I have lived here; but I will be glad to get into the open air again and see the good old sun and the silvery moon and the soft green grass and the flowers that are kissed by the morning dew. Ah, how much more lovely are those blessed things than the glitter of gems or the cold gleam of gold!"

"Of course," said Betsy. "I once knew a little boy who wanted to catch the measles, because all the little boys in his neighborhood but him had 'em, and he was really unhappy 'cause he couldn't catch 'em, try as he would. So I'm pretty certain that the things we want, and can't have, are not good for us. Isn't that true, Shaggy?"

"Not always, my dear," he gravely replied. "If we didn't want anything, we would never get anything, good or bad. I think our longings are natural, and if we act as nature prompts us we can't go far wrong."

"For my part," said Queen Ann, "I think the world would be a dreary place without the gold and jewels."

"All things are good in their way," said Shaggy; "but we may have too much of any good thing. And I have noticed that the value of anything depends upon how scarce it is, and how difficult it is to obtain."

"Pardon me for interrupting you," said King Kaliko, coming to their side, "but now that we have rescued Shaggy's brother I would like to return to my royal cavern. Being the King of the Nomes, it is my duty to look after my restless subjects and see that they behave themselves."

So they all turned and began walking through the Metal Forest to the other side of the great domed cave, where they had first entered it. Shaggy and his brother walked side by side and both seemed rejoiced that they were together after their long separation. Betsy didn't dare look at the polka dot handkerchief, for fear she would laugh aloud; so she walked behind the two brothers and led Hank by holding fast to his left ear.

When at last they reached the place where the passage led to the outer world, Queen Ann said, in a hesitating way that was unusual with her: "I have not conquered this Nome Country, nor do I expect to do so; but I would like to gather a few of these pretty jewels before I leave this place."

"Help yourself, ma'am," said King Kaliko, and at once the officers of the Army took advantage of his royal permission and began filling their pockets, while Ann tied a lot of diamonds in a big handkerchief.

This accomplished, they all entered the passage, the nomes going first to light the way with their torches. They had not proceeded far when Betsy exclaimed: "Why, there are jewels here, too!"

All eyes were turned upon the ground and they found a regular trail of jewels strewn along the rock floor.

"This is queer!" said Kaliko, much surprised. "I must send some of my nomes to gather up these gems and replace them in the Metal Forest, where they belong. I wonder how they came to be here?"

All the way along the passage they found this trail of jewels, but when they neared the end the mystery was explained. For there, squatted upon the floor with his back to the rock wall, sat old Ruggedo, puffing and blowing as if he was all tired out. Then they realized it was he who had scattered the jewels, from his many pockets, which one by one had burst with the weight of their contents as he had stumbled along the passage.

"But I don't mind," said Ruggedo, with a deep sigh. "I now

realize that I could not have carried such a weighty load very far, even had I managed to escape from this passage with it. The woman who sewed the pockets on my robe used poor thread, for which I shall thank her."

"Have you any jewels left?" inquired Betsy.

He glanced into some of the remaining pockets.

"A few," said he, "but they will be sufficient to supply my wants, and I no longer have any desire to be rich. If some of you will kindly help me to rise, I'll get out of here and leave you, for I know you all despise me and prefer my room to my company."

Shaggy and Kaliko raised the old King to his feet, when he was confronted by Shaggy's brother, whom he now noticed for the first time. The queer and unexpected appearance of the Ugly One so startled Ruggedo that he gave a wild cry and began to tremble, as if he had seen a ghost.

"Wh—wh—who is this?" he faltered.

"I am that helpless prisoner whom your cruel magic transformed from a handsome man into an ugly one!" answered Shaggy's brother, in a voice of stern reproach.

"Really, Ruggedo," said Betsy, "you ought to be ashamed of that mean trick."

"I am, my dear," admitted Ruggedo, who was now as meek and humble as formerly he had been cruel and vindictive.

"Then," returned the girl, "you'd better do some more magic and give the poor man his own face again."

"I wish I could," answered the old King; "but you must remember that Tititi-Hoochoo has deprived me of all my magic powers. However, I never took the trouble to learn just how to break the charm I cast over Shaggy's brother, for I intended he should always remain ugly."

"Every charm," remarked pretty Polychrome, "has its antidote; and, if you knew this charm of ugliness, Ruggedo, you must have known how to dispel it."

He shook his head.

"If I did, I—I've forgotten," he stammered regretfully.

"Try to think!" pleaded Shaggy, anxiously. "Please try to think!"

Ruggedo ruffled his hair with both hands, sighed, slapped his chest, rubbed his ear, and stared stupidly around the group.

"I've a faint recollection that there was one thing that would break the charm," said he; "but misfortune has so addled my brain that I can't remember what it was."

"See here, Ruggedo," said Betsy, sharply, "we've treated you pretty well, so far, but we won't stand for any nonsense, and if you know what's good for yourself you'll think of that charm!"

"Why?" he demanded, turning to look wonderingly at the little girl.

"Because it means so much to Shaggy's brother. He's dreadfully ashamed of himself, the way he is now, and you're to blame for it. Fact is, Ruggedo, you've done so much wickedness in your life

that it won't hurt you to do a kind act now."

Ruggedo blinked at her, and sighed again, and then tried very hard to think.

"I seem to remember, dimly," said he, "that a certain kind of a kiss will break the charm of ugliness."

"What kind of a kiss?"

"What kind? Why, it was—it was—it was either the kiss of a Mortal Maid; or—or—the kiss of a Mortal Maid who had once been a Fairy; or—or the kiss of one who is still a Fairy. I can't remember which. But of course no maid, mortal or fairy, would ever consent to kiss a person so ugly—so dreadfully, fearfully, terribly ugly—as Shaggy's brother."

"I'm not so sure of that," said Betsy, with admirable courage; "I'm a Mortal Maid, and if it is my kiss that will break this awful charm, I— I'll do it!"

"Oh, you really couldn't," protested Ugly. "I would be obliged to remove my mask, and when you saw my face, nothing could induce you to kiss me, generous as you are."

"Well, as for that," said the little girl, "I needn't see your face at all. Here's my plan: You stay in this dark passage, and we'll send away the nomes with their torches. Then you'll take off the handkerchief, and I—I'll kiss you."

"This is awfully kind of you, Betsy!" said Shaggy, gratefully.

"Well, it surely won't kill me," she replied; "and, if it makes you and your brother happy, I'm willing to take some chances."

So Kaliko ordered the torch-bearers to leave the passage, which they did by going through the rock opening. Queen Ann and her army also went out; but the others were so interested in Betsy's experiment that they remained grouped at the mouth of the passageway. When the big rock swung into place, closing tight the opening, they were left in total darkness.

"Now, then," called Betsy in a cheerful voice, "have you got that handkerchief off your face, Ugly?"

"Yes," he replied.

"Well, where are you, then?" she asked, reaching out her arms.

"Here," said he.

"You'll have to stoop down, you know."

He found her hands and clasping them in his own stooped until his face was near to that of the little girl. The others heard a clear, smacking kiss, and then Betsy exclaimed: "There! I've done it, and it didn't hurt a bit!"

"Tell me, dear brother; is the charm broken?" asked Shaggy.

"I do not know," was the reply. "It may be, or it may not be. I cannot tell."

"Has anyone a match?" inquired Betsy.

"I have several," said Shaggy.

"Then let Ruggedo strike one of them and look at your brother's face, while we all turn our backs. Ruggedo made your brother ugly, so I guess he can stand the horror of looking at him, if the charm isn't broken."

Agreeing to this, Ruggedo took the match and lighted it. He gave one look and then blew out the match.

"Ugly as ever!" he said with a shudder. "So it wasn't the kiss of a Mortal Maid, after all."

"Let me try," proposed the Rose Princess, in her sweet voice. "I am a Mortal Maid who was once a Fairy. Perhaps my kiss will break the charm."

Files did not wholly approve of this, but he was too generous to interfere. So the Rose Princess felt her way through the darkness to Shaggy's brother and kissed him.

Ruggedo struck another match, while they all turned away.

"No," announced the former King; "that didn't break the charm, either. It must be the kiss of a Fairy that is required—or else my memory has failed me altogether."

"Polly," said Betsy, pleadingly, "won't you try?"

"Of course I will!" answered Polychrome, with a merry laugh. "I've never kissed a mortal man in all the thousands of years I have existed, but I'll do it to please our faithful Shaggy Man, whose unselfish affection for his ugly brother deserves to be rewarded."

Even as Polychrome was speaking she tripped lightly to the side of the Ugly One and quickly touched his cheek with her lips.

"Oh, thank you—thank you!" he fervently cried. "I've changed, this time, I know. I can feel it! I'm different. Shaggy—dear Shaggy—I am myself again!"

Files, who was near the opening, touched the spring that released the big rock and it suddenly swung backward and let in a flood of daylight.

Everyone stood motionless, staring hard at Shaggy's brother, who, no longer masked by the polka-dot handkerchief, met their gaze with a glad smile.

"Well," said Shaggy Man, breaking the silence at last and drawing a long, deep breath of satisfaction, "you are no longer the Ugly One, my dear brother; but, to be entirely frank with you, the face that belongs to you is no more handsome than it ought to be."

"I think he's rather good looking," remarked Betsy, gazing at the man critically.

"In comparison with what he was," said King Kaliko, "he is really beautiful. You, who never beheld his ugliness, may not understand that; but it was my misfortune to look at the Ugly One many times, and I say again that, in comparison with what he was, the man is now beautiful."

"All right," returned Betsy, briskly, "we'll take your word for it, Kaliko. And now let us get out of this tunnel and into the world again."

23. Ruggedo Reforms

It did not take them long to regain the royal cavern of the Nome King, where Kaliko ordered served to them the nicest refreshments the place afforded.

Ruggedo had come trailing along after the rest of the party and while no one paid any attention to the old King they did not offer any objection to his presence or command him to leave them. He looked fearfully to see if the eggs were still guarding the entrance, but they had now disappeared; so he crept into the cavern after the others and humbly squatted down in a corner of the room.

There Betsy discovered him. All of the little girl's companions were now so happy at the success of Shaggy's quest for his brother, and the laughter and merriment seemed so general, that Betsy's heart softened toward the friendless old man who had once been their bitter enemy, and she carried to him some of the food and drink. Ruggedo's eyes filled with tears at this unexpected kindness. He took the child's hand in his own and pressed it gratefully.

"Look here, Kaliko," said Betsy, addressing the new King, "what's the use of being hard on Ruggedo? All his magic power is gone, so he can't do any more harm, and I'm sure he's sorry he acted so badly to everybody."

"Are you?" asked Kaliko, looking down at his former master.

"I am," said Ruggedo. "The girl speaks truly. I'm sorry and I'm harmless. I don't want to wander through the wide world, on top of the ground, for I'm a nome. No nome can ever be happy any place but underground."

"That being the case," said Kaliko, "I will let you stay here as long as you behave yourself; but, if you try to act badly again, I shall drive you out, as Tititi-Hoochoo has commanded, and you'll have to wander."

"Never fear. I'll behave," promised Ruggedo. "It is hard work being a King, and harder still to be a good King. But now that I am a common nome I am sure I can lead a blameless life."

They were all pleased to hear this and to know that Ruggedo had really reformed.

"I hope he'll keep his word," whispered Betsy to Shaggy; "but if he gets bad again we will be far away from the Nome Kingdom and Kaliko will have to 'tend to the old nome himself."

Polychrome had been a little restless during the last hour or two. The lovely Daughter of the Rainbow knew that she had now done all in her power to assist her earth friends, and so she began to long for her sky home.

"I think," she said, after listening intently, "that it is beginning to rain. The Rain King is my uncle, you know, and perhaps he has read my thoughts and is going to help me. Anyway I must take a look at the sky and make sure."

So she jumped up and ran through the passage to the outer entrance, and they all followed after her and grouped themselves on a ledge of the mountain-side. Sure enough, dark clouds had filled the sky and a slow, drizzling rain had set in.

"It can't last for long," said Shaggy, looking upward, "and when it stops we shall lose the sweet little fairy we have learned to love. Alas," he continued, after a moment, "the clouds are already breaking in the west, and—see!—isn't that the Rainbow coming?

Betsy didn't look at the sky; she looked at Polychrome, whose happy, smiling face surely foretold the coming of her father to take her to the Cloud Palaces. A moment later a gleam of sunshine flooded the mountain and a gorgeous Rainbow appeared.

With a cry of gladness Polychrome sprang upon a point of rock and held out her arms. Straightway the Rainbow descended until its end was at her very feet, when with a graceful leap she sprang upon it and was at once clasped in the arms of her radiant sisters, the Daughters of the Rainbow. But Polychrome released herself to lean over the edge of the glowing arch and nod, and smile and throw a dozen kisses to her late comrades.

"Good-bye!" she called, and they all shouted "Good-bye!" in return and waved their hands to their pretty friend.

Slowly the magnificent bow lifted and melted into the sky, until the eyes of the earnest watchers saw only fleecy clouds flitting across the blue.

"I'm dreadful sorry to see Polychrome go," said Betsy, who felt like crying; "but I s'pose she'll be a good deal happier with her sisters in the sky palaces."

"To be sure," returned Shaggy, nodding gravely. "It's her home, you know, and those poor wanderers who, like ourselves, have no home, can realize what that means to her."

"Once," said Betsy, "I, too, had a home. Now, I've only—only—dear old Hank!"

She twined her arms around her shaggy friend who was not human, and he said: "Hee-haw!" in a tone that showed he understood her mood. And the shaggy friend who was human stroked the child's head tenderly and said: "You're wrong about that, Betsy, dear. I will never desert you."

"Nor I!" exclaimed Shaggy's brother, in earnest tones.

The little girl looked up at them gratefully, and her eyes smiled through their tears.

"All right," she said. "It's raining again, so let's go back into the cavern."

Rather soberly, for all loved Polychrome and would miss her, they reentered the dominions of the Nome King.

24. Dorothy is Delighted

"Well," said Queen Ann, when all were again seated in Kaliko's royal cavern, "I wonder what we shall do next. If I could find my way back to Oogaboo I'd take my army home at once, for I'm sick and tired of these dreadful hardships."

"Don't you want to conquer the world?" asked Betsy.

"No; I've changed my mind about that," admitted the Queen. "The world is too big for one person to conquer and I was happier with my own people in Oogaboo. I wish—Oh, how earnestly I wish—that I was back there this minute!"

"So do I!" yelled every officer in a fervent tone.

Now, it is time for the reader to know that in the far-away Land of Oz the lovely Ruler, Ozma, had been following the adventures of her Shaggy Man, and Tik-Tok, and all the others they had met. Day by day Ozma, with the wonderful Wizard of Oz seated beside her, had gazed upon a Magic Picture in a radium frame, which occupied one side of the Ruler's cosy boudoir in the palace of the Emerald City. The singular thing about this Magic Picture was that it showed whatever scene Ozma wished to see, with the figures all in motion, just as it was taking place. So Ozma and the Wizard had watched every action of the adventurers from the time Shaggy had met shipwrecked Betsy and Hank in the Rose Kingdom, at which time the Rose Princess, a distant cousin of Ozma, had been exiled by her heartless subjects.

When Ann and her people so earnestly wished to return to Oogaboo, Ozma was sorry for them and remembered that Oogaboo was a corner of the Land of Oz. She turned to her attendant and asked: "Can not your magic take these unhappy people to their old home, Wizard?"

"It can, Your Highness," replied the little Wizard.

"I think the poor Queen has suffered enough in her misguided effort to conquer the world," said Ozma, smiling at the absurdity of the undertaking, "so no doubt she will hereafter be contented in her own little Kingdom. Please send her there, Wizard, and with her the officers and Files."

"How about the Rose Princess?" asked the Wizard.

"Send her to Oogaboo with Files," answered Ozma. "They have become such good friends that I am sure it would make them unhappy to separate them."

"Very well," said the Wizard, and without any fuss or mystery whatever he performed a magical rite that was simple and effective. Therefore those seated in the Nome King's cavern were both startled and amazed when all the people of Oogaboo suddenly disappeared from the room, and with them the Rose Princess. At first they could not understand it at all; but presently Shaggy suspected the truth, and believing that Ozma was now taking an interest in the party he drew from his pocket a tiny instrument which he placed against his ear.

Ozma, observing this action in her Magic Picture, at once caught up a similar instrument from a table beside her and held it to her own ear. The two instruments recorded the same delicate vibrations of sound and formed a wireless telephone, an invention of the Wizard. Those separated by any distance were thus enabled to converse together with perfect ease and without any wire connection.

"Do you hear me, Shaggy Man?" asked Ozma.

"Yes, Your Highness," he replied.

"I have sent the people of Oogaboo back to their own little valley," announced the Ruler of Oz; "so do not worry over their disappearance."

"That was very kind of you," said Shaggy. "But Your Highness must permit me to report that my own mission here is now ended. I have found my lost brother, and he is now beside me, freed from the enchantment of ugliness which Ruggedo cast upon him. Tik-Tok has served me and my comrades faithfully, as you requested him to do, and I hope you will now transport the Clockwork Man back to your fairyland of Oz."

"I will do that," replied Ozma. "But how about yourself, Shaggy?"

"I have been very happy in Oz," he said, "but my duty to others forces me to exile myself from that delightful land. I must take care of my new-found brother, for one thing, and I have a new comrade in a dear little girl named Betsy Bobbin, who has no home to go to, and no other friends but me and a small donkey named Hank. I have promised Betsy never to desert her as long as she needs a friend, and so I must give up the delights of the Land of Oz forever."

He said this with a sigh of regret, and Ozma made no reply but laid the tiny instrument on her table, thus cutting off all further communication with the Shaggy Man. But the lovely Ruler of Oz still watched her magic picture, with a thoughtful expression upon her face, and the little Wizard of Oz watched Ozma and smiled softly to himself.

In the cavern of the Nome King Shaggy replaced the wireless telephone in his pocket and turning to Betsy said in as cheerful a voice as he could muster: "Well, little comrade, what shall we do next?"

"I don't know, I'm sure," she answered with a puzzled face. "I'm kind of sorry our adventures are over, for I enjoyed them, and now that Queen Ann and her people are gone, and Polychrome is gone, and—dear me!—where's Tik-Tok, Shaggy?"

"He also has disappeared," said Shaggy, looking around the cavern and nodding wisely. "By this time he is in Ozma's palace in the Land of Oz, which is his home."

"Isn't it your home, too?" asked Betsy.

"It used to be, my dear; but now my home is wherever you and my brother are. We are wanderers, you know, but if we stick together I am sure we shall have a good time."

"Then," said the girl, "let us get out of this stuffy, underground cavern and go in search of new adventures. I'm sure it has stopped raining."

"I'm ready," said Shaggy, and then they bade good-bye to King Kaliko, and thanked him for his assistance, and went out to the mouth of the passage.

The sky was now clear and a brilliant blue in color; the sun shone brightly and even this rugged, rocky country seemed delightful after their confinement underground. There were but four of them now—Betsy and Hank, and Shaggy and his brother—and the little party made their way down the mountain and followed a faint path that led toward the southwest.

During this time Ozma had been holding a conference with the Wizard, and later with Tik-Tok, whom the magic of the Wizard had quickly transported to Ozma's palace. Tik-Tok had only words of praise for Betsy Bobbin, "who," he said, "is al-most as nice as Dor-o-thy her-self."

"Let us send for Dorothy," said Ozma, and summoning her favorite maid, who was named Jellia Jamb, she asked her to request Princess Dorothy to attend her at once. So a few moments later Dorothy entered Ozma's room and greeted her and the Wizard and Tik-Tok with the same gentle smile and simple manner that had won for the little girl the love of everyone she met.

"Did you want to see me, Ozma?" she asked.

"Yes, dear. I am puzzled how to act, and I want your advice."

"I don't b'lieve it's worth much," replied Dorothy, "but I'll do the best I can. What is it all about, Ozma?"

"You all know," said the girl Ruler, addressing her three friends, "what a serious thing it is to admit any mortals into this fairyland of Oz. It is true I have invited several mortals to make their home here, and all of them have proved true and loyal subjects. Indeed, no one of you three was a native of Oz. Dorothy and the Wizard came here from the United States, and Tik-Tok came from the Land of Ev. But of course he is not a mortal. Shaggy is another American, and he is the cause of all my worry, for our dear Shaggy will not return here and desert the new friends he has found in his recent adventures, because he believes they need his services."

"Shaggy Man was always kind-hearted," remarked Dorothy. "But who are these new friends he has found?"

"One is his brother, who for many years has been a prisoner of the Nome King, our old enemy Ruggedo. This brother seems a kindly, honest fellow, but he has done nothing to entitle him to a home in the Land of Oz."

"Who else?" asked Dorothy.

"I have told you about Betsy Bobbin, the little girl who was shipwrecked—in much the same way you once were—and has since been following the Shaggy Man in his search for his lost brother. You remember her, do you not?"

"Oh, yes!" exclaimed Dorothy. "I've often watched her and Hank in the Magic Picture, you know. She's a dear little girl, and old Hank is a darling! Where are they now?"

"Look and see," replied Ozma with a smile at her friend's enthusiasm.

Dorothy turned to the Picture, which showed Betsy and Hank, with Shaggy and his brother, trudging along the rocky paths of a barren country.

"Seems to me," she said, musingly, "that they're a good way from any place to sleep, or any nice things to eat."

"You are right," said Tik-Tok. "I have been in that coun-try, and it is a wil-der-ness."

"It is the country of the nomes," explained the Wizard, "who are so mischievous that no one cares to live near them. I'm afraid Shaggy and his friends will endure many hardships before they get out of that rocky place, unless—"

He turned to Ozma and smiled.

"Unless I ask you to transport them all here?" she asked.

"Yes, your Highness."

"Could your magic do that?" inquired Dorothy.

"I think so," said the Wizard.

"Well," said Dorothy, "as far as Betsy and Hank are concerned, I'd like to have them here in Oz. It would be such fun to have a girl playmate of my own age, you see. And Hank is such a dear little mule!"

Ozma laughed at the wistful expression in the girl's eyes, and then she drew Dorothy to her and kissed her.

"Am I not your friend and playmate?" she asked.

Dorothy flushed.

"You know how dearly I love you, Ozma!" she cried. "But you're so busy ruling all this Land of Oz that we can't always be together."

"I know, dear. My first duty is to my subjects, and I think it would be a delight to us all to have Betsy with us. There's a pretty suite of rooms just opposite your own where she can live, and I'll build a golden stall for Hank in the stable where the Sawhorse lives. Then we'll introduce the mule to the Cowardly Lion and the Hungry Tiger, and I'm sure they will soon become firm friends. But I cannot very well admit Betsy and Hank into Oz unless I also admit Shaggy's brother."

"And, unless you admit Shaggy's brother, you will keep out poor Shaggy, whom we are all very fond of," said the Wizard.

"Well, why not ad-mit him?" demanded Tik-Tok.

"The Land of Oz is not a refuge for all mortals in distress," explained Ozma. "I do not wish to be unkind to Shaggy Man, but his brother has no claim on me."

"The Land of Oz isn't crowded," suggested Dorothy.

"Then you advise me to admit Shaggy's brother?" inquired Ozma.

"Well, we can't afford to lose our Shaggy Man, can we?"

"No, indeed!" returned Ozma. "What do you say, Wizard?"

"I'm getting my magic ready to transport them all."

"And you, Tik-Tok?"

"Shag-gy's broth-er is a good fel-low, and we can't spare Shag-gy."

"So, then; the question is settled," decided Ozma. "Perform your magic, Wizard!"

He did so, placing a silver plate upon a small standard and pouring upon the plate a small quantity of pink powder which was contained in a crystal vial. Then he muttered a rather difficult incantation which the sorceress Glinda the Good had taught him, and it all ended in a puff of perfumed smoke from the silver plate. This smoke was so pungent that it made both Ozma and Dorothy rub their eyes for a moment.

"You must pardon these disagreeable fumes," said the Wizard. "I assure you the smoke is a very necessary part of my wizardry."

"Look!" cried Dorothy, pointing to the Magic Picture; "they're gone! All of them are gone."

Indeed, the picture now showed the same rocky landscape as before, but the three people and the mule had disappeared from it.

"They are gone," said the Wizard, polishing the silver plate and wrapping it in a fine cloth, "because they are here."

At that moment Jellia Jamb entered the room.

"Your Highness," she said to Ozma, "the Shaggy Man and another man are in the waiting room and ask to pay their respects to you. Shaggy is crying like a baby, but he says they are tears of joy."

"Send them here at once, Jellia!" commanded Ozma.

"Also," continued the maid, "a girl and a small-sized mule have mysteriously arrived, but they don't seem to know where they are or how they came here. Shall I send them here, too?"

"Oh, no!" exclaimed Dorothy, eagerly jumping up from her chair; "I'll go to meet Betsy myself, for she'll feel awful strange in this big palace."

And she ran down the stairs two at a time to greet her new friend, Betsy Bobbin.

25. The Land of Love

"Well, is 'hee-haw' all you are able to say?" inquired the Sawhorse, as he examined Hank with his knot eyes and slowly wagged the branch that served him for a tail.

They were in a beautiful stable in the rear of Ozma's palace, where the wooden Sawhorse—very much alive—lived in a gold-paneled stall, and where there were rooms for the Cowardly Lion and the Hungry Tiger, which were filled with soft cushions for them to lie upon and golden troughs for them to eat from.

Beside the stall of the Sawhorse had been placed another for Hank, the mule. This was not quite so beautiful as the other, for the Sawhorse was Ozma's favorite steed; but Hank had a supply of cushions for a bed (which the Sawhorse did not need because he never slept) and all this luxury was so strange to the little mule that he could only stand still and regard his surroundings and his queer companions with wonder and amazement.

The Cowardly Lion, looking very dignified, was stretched out upon the marble floor of the stable, eyeing Hank with a calm and critical gaze, while near by crouched the huge Hungry Tiger, who seemed equally interested in the new animal that had just arrived. The Sawhorse, standing stiffly before Hank, repeated his question: "Is 'hee-haw' all you are able to say?"

Hank moved his ears in an embarrassed manner.

"I have never said anything else, until now," he replied; and then he began to tremble with fright to hear himself talk.

"I can well understand that," remarked the Lion, wagging his great head with a swaying motion. "Strange things happen in this Land of Oz, as they do everywhere else. I believe you came here from the cold, civilized, outside world, did you not?"

"I did," replied Hank. "One minute I was outside of Oz—and the next minute I was inside! That was enough to give me a nervous shock, as you may guess; but to find myself able to talk, as Betsy does, is a marvel that staggers me."

"That is because you are in the Land of Oz," said the Sawhorse. "All animals talk, in this favored country, and you must admit it is more sociable than to bray your dreadful 'hee-haw,' which nobody can understand."

"Mules understand it very well," declared Hank.

"Oh, indeed! Then there must be other mules in your outside world," said the Tiger, yawning sleepily.

"There are a great many in America," said Hank. "Are you the only Tiger in Oz?"

"No," acknowledged the Tiger, "I have many relatives living in the Jungle Country; but I am the only Tiger living in the Emerald City."

"There are other Lions, too," said the Sawhorse; "but I am the only horse, of any description, in this favored Land."

"That is why this Land is favored," said the Tiger. "You must understand, friend Hank, that the Sawhorse puts on airs because he is shod with plates of gold, and because our beloved Ruler, Ozma of Oz, likes to ride upon his back."

"Betsy rides upon my back," declared Hank proudly.

"Who is Betsy?"

"The dearest, sweetest girl in all the world!"

The Sawhorse gave an angry snort and stamped his golden feet. The Tiger crouched and growled. Slowly the great Lion rose to his feet, his mane bristling.

"Friend Hank," said he, "either you are mistaken in judgment or you are willfully trying to deceive us. The dearest, sweetest girl in the world is our Dorothy, and I will fight anyone—animal or human— who dares to deny it!"

"So will I!" snarled the Tiger, showing two rows of enormous white teeth.

"You are all wrong!" asserted the Sawhorse in a voice of scorn. "No girl living can compare with my mistress, Ozma of Oz!"

Hank slowly turned around until his heels were toward the others. Then he said stubbornly: "I am not mistaken in my statement, nor will I admit there can be a sweeter girl alive than Betsy Bobbin. If you want to fight, come on—I'm ready for you!"

While they hesitated, eyeing Hank's heels doubtfully, a merry peal of laughter startled the animals and turning their heads they beheld three lovely girls standing just within the richly carved entrance to the stable. In the center was Ozma, her arms encircling the waists of Dorothy and Betsy, who stood on either side of her. Ozma was nearly half a head taller than the two other girls, who were almost of one size. Unobserved, they had listened to the talk of the animals, which was a very strange experience indeed to little Betsy Bobbin.

"You foolish beasts!" exclaimed the Ruler of Oz, in a gentle but chiding voice. "Why should you fight to defend us, who are all three loving friends and in no sense rivals? Answer me!" she continued, as they bowed their heads sheepishly.

"I have the right to express my opinion, your Highness," pleaded the Lion.

"And so have the others," replied Ozma. "I am glad you and the Hungry Tiger love Dorothy best, for she was your first friend and companion. Also I am pleased that my Sawhorse loves me best, for together we have endured both joy and sorrow. Hank has

proved his faith and loyalty by defending his own little mistress; and so you are all right in one way, but wrong in another. Our Land of Oz is a Land of Love, and here friendship outranks every other quality. Unless you can all be friends, you cannot retain our love."

They accepted this rebuke very meekly.

"All right," said the Sawhorse, quite cheerfully; "shake hoofs, friend Mule."

Hank touched his hoof to that of the wooden horse.

"Let us be friends and rub noses," said the Tiger. So Hank modestly rubbed noses with the big beast.

The Lion merely nodded and said, as he crouched before the mule: "Any friend of a friend of our beloved Ruler is a friend of the Cowardly Lion. That seems to cover your case. If ever you need help or advice, friend Hank, call on me."

"Why, this is as it should be," said Ozma, highly pleased to see them so fully reconciled. Then she turned to her companions: "Come, my dears, let us resume our walk."

As they turned away Betsy said wonderingly: "Do all the animals in Oz talk as we do?"

"Almost all," answered Dorothy. "There's a Yellow Hen here, and she can talk, and so can her chickens; and there's a Pink Kitten upstairs in my room who talks very nicely; but I've a little fuzzy black dog, named Toto, who has been with me in Oz a long time and he's never said a single word but 'Bow-wow!'"

"Do you know why?" asked Ozma.

"Why, he's a Kansas dog; so I s'pose he's different from these fairy animals," replied Dorothy.

"Hank isn't a fairy animal, any more than Toto," said Ozma, "yet as soon as he came under the spell of our fairyland he found he could talk. It was the same way with Billina, the Yellow Hen whom you brought here at one time. The same spell has affected Toto, I assure you; but he's a wise little dog and while he knows everything that is said to him he prefers not to talk."

"Goodness me!" exclaimed Dorothy. "I never s'pected Toto was fooling me all this time." Then she drew a small silver whistle from her pocket and blew a shrill note upon it. A moment later there was a sound of scurrying footsteps, and a shaggy black dog came running up the path.

Dorothy knelt down before him and shaking her finger just above his nose she said: "Toto, haven't I always been good to you?"

Toto looked up at her with his bright black eyes and wagged his tail.

"Bow-wow!" he said, and Betsy knew at once that meant yes, as well as Dorothy and Ozma knew it, for there was no mistaking the tone of Toto's voice.

"That's a dog answer," said Dorothy. "How would you like it, Toto, if I said nothing to you but 'bow-wow'?"

Toto's tail was wagging furiously now, but otherwise he was silent.

"Really, Dorothy," said Betsy, "he can talk with his bark and his tail just as well as we can. Don't you understand such dog language?"

"Of course I do," replied Dorothy. "But Toto's got to be more sociable. See here, sir!" she continued, addressing the dog, "I've just learned, for the first time, that you can say words—if you want to. Don't you want to, Toto?"

"Woof!" said Toto, and that meant "no."

"Not just one word, Toto, to prove you're as any other animal in Oz?"

"Woof!"

"Just one word, Toto—and then you may run away."

He looked at her steadily a moment.

"All right. Here I go!" he said, and darted away as swift as an arrow.

Dorothy clapped her hands in delight, while Betsy and Ozma both laughed heartily at her pleasure and the success of her experiment. Arm in arm they sauntered away through the beautiful gardens of the palace, where magnificent flowers bloomed in abundance and fountains shot their silvery sprays far into the air. And by and by, as they turned a corner, they came upon Shaggy Man and his brother, who were seated together upon a golden bench.

The two arose to bow respectfully as the Ruler of Oz approached them.

"How are you enjoying our Land of Oz?" Ozma asked the stranger.

"I am very happy here, Your Highness," replied Shaggy's brother. "Also I am very grateful to you for permitting me to live in this delightful place."

"You must thank Shaggy for that," said Ozma. "Being his brother, I have made you welcome here."

"When you know Brother better," said Shaggy earnestly, "you will be glad he has become one of your loyal subjects. I am just getting acquainted with him myself and I find much in his character to admire."

Leaving the brothers, Ozma and the girls continued their walk. Presently Betsy exclaimed: "Shaggy's brother can't ever be as happy in Oz as I am. Do you know, Dorothy, I didn't believe any girl could ever have such a good time— anywhere—as I'm having now?"

"I know," answered Dorothy. "I've felt that way myself, lots of times."

"I wish," continued Betsy, dreamily, "that every little girl in the world could live in the Land of Oz; and every little boy, too!"

Ozma laughed at this.

"It is quite fortunate for us, Betsy, that your wish cannot be granted," said she, "for all that army of girls and boys would crowd us so that we would have to move away."

"Yes," agreed Betsy, after a little thought, "I guess that's true."

The Scarecrow Of Oz
by L. Frank Baum

Dedicated to "The Uplifters" of Los Angeles, California, in grateful appreciation of the pleasure I have derived from association with them, and in recognition of their sincere endeavor to uplift humanity through kindness, consideration and good-fellowship. They are big men—all of them—and all with the generous hearts of little children. L. Frank Baum

Twixt You And Me

The Army of Children which besieged the Post Office, conquered the Postmen and delivered to me its imperious Commands, insisted that Trot and Cap'n Bill be admitted to the Land of Oz, where Trot could enjoy the society of Dorothy, Betsy Bobbin and Ozma, while the one-legged sailor-man might become a comrade of the Tin Woodman, the Shaggy Man, Tik-Tok and all the other quaint people who inhabit this wonderful fairyland.

It was no easy task to obey this order and land Trot and Cap'n Bill safely in Oz, as you will discover by reading this book. Indeed, it required the best efforts of our dear old friend, the Scarecrow, to save them from a dreadful fate on the journey; but the story leaves them happily located in Ozma's splendid palace and Dorothy has promised me that Button-Bright and the three girls are sure to encounter, in the near future, some marvelous adventures in the Land of Oz, which I hope to be permitted to relate to you in the next Oz Book.

Meantime, I am deeply grateful to my little readers for their continued enthusiasm over the Oz stories, as evinced in the many letters they send me, all of which are lovingly cherished. It takes more and more Oz Books every year to satisfy the demands of old and new readers, and there have been formed many "Oz Reading Societies," where the Oz Books owned by different members are read aloud. All this is very gratifying to me and encourages me to write more stories. When the children have had enough of them, I hope they will let me know, and then I'll try to write something different.

L. Frank Baum, "Royal Historian of Oz."
"Ozcot" at Hollywood in California, 1915.

1. The Great Whirlpool

"Seems to me," said Cap'n Bill, as he sat beside Trot under the big acacia tree, looking out over the blue ocean, "seems to me, Trot, as how the more we know, the more we find we don't know."

"I can't quite make that out, Cap'n Bill," answered the little girl in a serious voice, after a moment's thought, during which her eyes followed those of the old sailor-man across the glassy surface of the sea. "Seems to me that all we learn is jus' so much gained."

"I know; it looks that way at first sight," said the sailor, nodding his head; "but those as knows the least have a habit of thinkin' they know all there is to know, while them as knows the most admits what a turr'ble big world this is. It's the knowing ones that realize one lifetime ain't long enough to git more'n a few dips o' the oars of knowledge."

Trot didn't answer. She was a very little girl, with big, solemn eyes and an earnest, simple manner. Cap'n Bill had been her faithful companion for years and had taught her almost everything she knew.

He was a wonderful man, this Cap'n Bill. Not so very old, although his hair was grizzled — what there was of it. Most of his head was bald as an egg and as shiny as oilcloth, and this made his big ears stick out in a funny way. His eyes had a gentle look and were pale blue in color, and his round face was rugged and bronzed. Cap'n Bill's left leg was missing, from the knee down, and that was why the sailor no longer sailed the seas. The wooden leg he wore was good enough to stump around with on land, or even to take Trot out for a row or a sail on the ocean, but when it came to "runnin' up aloft" or performing active duties on shipboard, the old sailor was not equal to the task. The loss of his leg had ruined his career and the old sailor found comfort in devoting himself to the education and companionship of the little girl.

The accident to Cap'n Bill's leg bad happened at about the time Trot was born, and ever since that he had lived with Trot's mother as "a star boarder," having enough money saved up to pay for his weekly "keep." He loved the baby and often held her on his lap; her first ride was on Cap'n Bill's shoulders, for she had no baby-carriage; and when she began to toddle around, the child and the sailor became close comrades and enjoyed many strange adventures together. It is said the fairies had been present at Trot's birth and had marked her forehead with their invisible mystic signs, so that she was able to see and do many wonderful things.

The acacia tree was on top of a high bluff, but a path ran down the bank in a zigzag way to the water's edge, where Cap'n Bill's boat was moored to a rock by means of a stout cable. It had been a hot, sultry afternoon, with scarcely a breath of air stirring, so Cap'n Bill and Trot had been quietly sitting beneath the shade of the tree, waiting for the sun to get low enough for them to take a row.

They had decided to visit one of the great caves which the waves had washed out of the rocky coast during many years of steady effort. The caves were a source of continual delight to both the girl and the sailor, who loved to explore their awesome depths.

"I b'lieve, Cap'n," remarked Trot, at last, "that it's time for us to start."

The old man cast a shrewd glance at the sky, the sea and the motionless boat. Then he shook his head.

"Mebbe it's time, Trot," he answered, "but I don't jes' like the looks o' things this afternoon."

"What's wrong?" she asked wonderingly.

"Can't say as to that. Things is too quiet to suit me, that's all. No breeze, not a ripple a-top the water, nary a gull a-flyin' anywhere, an' the end o' the hottest day o' the year. I ain't no weather-prophet, Trot, but any sailor would know the signs is ominous."

"There's nothing wrong that I can see," said Trot.

"If there was a cloud in the sky even as big as my thumb, we might worry about it; but — look, Cap'n! — the sky is as clear as can be."

He looked again and nodded.

"P'r'aps we can make the cave, all right," he agreed, not wishing to disappoint her. "It's only a little way out, an' we'll be on the watch; so come along, Trot."

Together they descended the winding path to the beach. It was no trouble for the girl to keep her footing on the steep way, but Cap'n Bill, because of his wooden leg, had to hold on to rocks and roots now and then to save himself from tumbling. On a level path he was as spry as anyone, but to climb up hill or down required some care.

They reached the boat safely and while Trot was untying the rope Cap'n Bill reached into a crevice of the rock and drew out several tallow candles and a box of wax matches, which he thrust into the capacious pockets of his "sou'wester." This sou'wester was a short coat of oilskin which the old sailor wore on all occasions — when he wore a coat at all — and the pockets always contained a variety of objects, useful and ornamental, which made even Trot wonder where they all came from and why Cap'n Bill should treasure them. The jackknives — a big one and a little one — the bits of cord, the fishhooks, the nails: these were handy to have on certain occasions. But bits of shell, and tin boxes with unknown contents, buttons, pincers, bottles of curious stones and the like, seemed quite unnecessary to carry around. That was Cap'n Bill's business, however, and now that he added the candles and the matches to his collection Trot made no comment, for she knew these last were to light their way through the caves. The sailor always rowed the boat, for he handled the oars with strength and skill. Trot sat in the stern and steered. The place where they embarked was a little bight or circular bay, and the boat cut across a much larger bay toward a distant headland where the caves were located, right at the water's edge. They were nearly a mile from shore and about halfway across the bay when Trot suddenly sat up straight and exclaimed: "What's that, Cap'n?"

He stopped rowing and turned half around to look.

"That, Trot," he slowly replied, "looks to me mighty like a whirlpool."

"What makes it, Cap'n?"

"A whirl in the air makes the whirl in the water. I was afraid as we'd meet with trouble, Trot. Things didn't look right. The air was too still."

"It's coming closer," said the girl.

The old man grabbed the oars and began rowing with all his strength.

"Tain't comin' closer to us, Trot," he gasped; "it's we that are comin' closer to the whirlpool. The thing is drawin' us to it like a magnet!"

Trot's sun-bronzed face was a little paler as she grasped the tiller firmly and tried to steer the boat away; but she said not a word to indicate fear.

The swirl of the water as they came nearer made a roaring sound that was fearful to listen to. So fierce and powerful was the whirlpool that it drew the surface of the sea into the form of a great basin, slanting downward toward the center, where a big hole had been made in the ocean — a hole with walls of water that were kept in place by the rapid whirling of the air.

The boat in which Trot and Cap'n Bill were riding was just on the outer edge of this saucer-like slant, and the old sailor knew very well that unless he could quickly force the little craft away from the rushing current they would soon be drawn into the great black hole that yawned in the middle. So he exerted all his might and pulled as he had never pulled before. He pulled so hard that the left oar snapped in two and sent Cap'n Bill sprawling upon the bottom of the boat.

He scrambled up quickly enough and glanced over the side. Then he looked at Trot, who sat quite still, with a serious, far-away look in her sweet eyes. The boat was now speeding swiftly of its own accord, following the line of the circular basin round and round and gradually drawing nearer to the great hole in the center. Any further effort to escape the whirlpool was useless, and realizing this fact Cap'n Bill turned toward Trot and put an arm around her, as if to shield her from the awful fate before them. He did not try to speak, because the roar of the waters would have drowned the sound of his voice.

These two faithful comrades had faced dangers before, but nothing to equal that which now faced them. Yet Cap'n Bill, noting the look in Trot's eyes and remembering how often she had been protected by unseen powers, did not quite give way to despair.

The great hole in the dark water — now growing nearer and nearer — looked very terrifying; but they were both brave enough to face it and await the result of the adventure.

2. The Cavern Under the Sea

The circles were so much smaller at the bottom of the basin, and the boat moved so much more swiftly, that Trot was beginning to get dizzy with the motion, when suddenly the boat made a leap and dived headlong into the murky depths of the hole. Whirling like tops, but still clinging together, the sailor and the girl were separated from their boat and plunged down — down — down — into the farthermost recesses of the great ocean.

At first their fall was swift as an arrow, but presently they seemed to be going more moderately and Trot was almost sure that unseen arms were about her, supporting her and protecting her. She could see nothing, because the water filled her eyes and blurred her vision, but she clung fast to Cap'n Bill's sou'wester, while other arms clung fast to her, and so they gradually sank down and down until a full stop was made, when they began to ascend again.

But it seemed to Trot that they were not rising straight to the surface from where they had come. The water was no longer whirling them and they seemed to be drawn in a slanting direction through still, cool ocean depths. And then — in much quicker time than I have told it — up they popped to the surface and were cast at full length upon a sandy beach, where they lay choking and gasping for breath and wondering what had happened to them.

Trot was the first to recover. Disengaging herself from Cap'n Bill's wet embrace and sitting up, she rubbed the water from her eyes and then looked around her. A soft, bluish-green glow lighted the place, which seemed to be a sort of cavern, for above and on either side of her were rugged rocks. They had been cast upon a beach of clear sand, which slanted upward from the pool of water at their feet — a pool which doubtless led into the big ocean that fed it. Above the reach of the waves of the pool were more rocks, and still more and more, into the dim windings and recesses of which the glowing light from the water did not penetrate.

The place looked grim and lonely, but Trot was thankful that she was still alive and had suffered no severe injury during her trying adventure under water. At her side Cap'n Bill was sputtering and coughing, trying to get rid of the water he had swallowed. Both of them were soaked through, yet the cavern was warm and comfortable and a wetting did not dismay the little girl in the least.

She crawled up the slant of sand and gathered in her hand a bunch of dried seaweed, with which she mopped the face of Cap'n Bill and cleared the water from his eyes and ears. Presently the old man sat up and stared at her intently. Then he nodded his bald head three times and said in a gurgling voice: "Mighty good, Trot; mighty good! We didn't reach Davy Jones's locker that time, did we? Though why we didn't, an' why we're here, is more'n I kin make out."

"Take it easy, Cap'n," she replied. "We're safe enough, I guess, at least for the time being."

He squeezed the water out of the bottoms of his loose trousers and felt of his wooden leg and arms and head, and finding he had brought all of his person with him he gathered courage to examine closely their surroundings.

"Where d'ye think we are, Trot?." he presently asked.

"Can't say, Cap'n. P'r'aps in one of our caves."

He shook his head. "No," said he, "I don't think that, at all. The distance we came up didn't seem half as far as the distance we went down; an' you'll notice there ain't any outside entrance to this cavern whatever. It's a reg'lar dome over this pool o' water, and unless there's some passage at the back, up yonder, we're fast pris'ners."

Trot looked thoughtfully over her shoulder.

"When we're rested," she said, "we will crawl up there and see if there's a way to get out."

Cap'n Bill reached in the pocket of his oilskin coat and took out his pipe. It was still dry, for he kept it in an oilskin pouch with his tobacco. His matches were in a tight tin box, so in a few moments the old sailor was smoking contentedly. Trot knew it helped him to think when he was in any difficulty. Also, the pipe did much to restore the old sailor's composure, after his long ducking and his terrible fright — a fright that was more on Trot's account than his own.

The sand was dry where they sat, and soaked up the water that dripped from their clothing. When Trot had squeezed the wet out of her hair she began to feel much like her old self again. By and by they got upon their feet and crept up the incline to the scattered boulders above. Some of these were of huge size, but by passing between some and around others, they were able to reach the extreme rear of the cavern.

"Yes," said Trot, with interest, "here's a round hole."

"And it's black as night inside it," remarked Cap'n Bill.

Just the same," answered the girl, "we ought to explore it, and see where it goes, 'cause it's the only poss'ble way we can get out of this place."

Cap'n Bill eyed the hole doubtfully

"It may be a way out o' here, Trot," he said, "but it may be a way into a far worse place than this. I'm not sure but our best plan is to stay right here."

Trot wasn't sure, either, when she thought of it in that light After awhile she made her way back to the sands again, and Cap'n Bill followed her. As they sat down, the child looked thoughtfully at the sailor's bulging pockets.

"How much food have we got, Cap'n?" she asked.

"Half a dozen ship's biscuits an' a hunk o' cheese," he replied "Want some now, Trot?"

She shook her head, saying: "That ought to keep us alive 'bout three days if we're careful of it."

"Longer'n that, Trot," said Cap'n Bill, but his voice was a little troubled and unsteady.

"But if we stay here we're bound to starve in time," continued the girl, "while if we go into the dark hole —"

"Some things are more hard to face than starvation," said the sailor-man, gravely. "We don't know what's inside that dark hole: Trot, nor where it might lead us to."

"There's a way to find that out," she persisted.

Instead of replying, Cap'n Bill began searching in his pockets. He soon drew out a little package of fish-hooks and a long line. Trot watched him join them together. Then he crept a little way up the slope and turned over a big rock. Two or three small crabs began scurrying away over the sands and the old sailor caught them and put one on his hook and the others in his pocket Coming back to the pool he swung the hook over his shoulder and circled it around his head and cast it nearly into the center of the water, where he allowed it to sink gradually, paying out the line as far as it would go. When the end was reached, he began drawing it in again, until the crab bait was floating on the surface.

Trot watched him cast the line a second time, and a third. She decided that either there were no fishes in the pool or they would not bite the crab bait. But Cap'n Bill was an old fisherman and not easily discouraged. When the crab got away he put another on the hook. When the crabs were all gone he climbed up the rocks and found some more.

Meantime Trot tired of watching him and lay down upon the sands, where she fell fast asleep. During the next two hours her clothing dried completely, as did that of the old sailor. They were both so used to salt water that there was no danger of taking cold.

Finally the little girl was wakened by a splash beside her and a grunt of satisfaction from Cap'n Bill. She opened her eyes to find that the Cap'n had landed a silver-scaled fish weighing about two pounds. This cheered her considerably and she hurried to scrape together a heap of seaweed, while Cap'n Bill cut up the fish with his jackknife and got it ready for cooking.

They had cooked fish with seaweed before. Cap'n Bill wrapped his fish in some of the weed and dipped it in the water to dampen it. Then he lighted a match and set fire to Trot's heap which speedily burned down to a glowing bed of ashes. Then they laid the wrapped fish on the ashes, covered it with more seaweed, and allowed this to catch fire and burn to embers. After feeding the fire with seaweed for some time, the sailor finally decided that their supper was ready, so he scattered the ashe and drew out the bits of fish, still encased in their smoking wrappings.

When these wrappings were removed, the fish was found thoroughly cooked and both Trot and Cap'n Bill ate of it freely. It had a slight flavor of seaweed and would have been better with a sprinkling of salt.

The soft glow which until now had lighted the cavern, began to grow dim, but there was a great quantity of seaweed in the place, so after they had eaten their fish they kept the fire alive for a time by giving it a handful of fuel now and then.

From an inner pocket the sailor drew a small flask of battered metal and unscrewing the cap handed it to Trot. She took but one swallow of the water although she wanted more, and she noticed that Cap'n Bill merely wet his lips with it.

"S'pose," said she, staring at the glowing seaweed fire and speaking slowly, "that we can catch all the fish we need; how 'bout the drinking-water, Cap'n?"

He moved uneasily but did not reply. Both of them were thinking about the dark hole, but while Trot had little fear of it the old man could not overcome his dislike to enter the place. He knew that Trot was right, though. To remain in the cavern, where they now were, could only result in slow but sure death.

It was nighttime up on the earth's surface, so the little girl became drowsy and soon fell asleep. After a time the old sailor slumbered on the sands beside her. It was very still and nothing disturbed them for hours. When at last they awoke the cavern was light again.

They had divided one of the biscuits and were munching it for breakfast when they were startled by a sudden splash in the pool. Looking toward it they saw emerging from the water the most curious creature either of them had ever beheld. It wasn't a fish, Trot decided, nor was it a beast. It had wings, though, and queer wings they were: shaped like an inverted chopping-bowl and covered with tough skin instead of feathers. It had four legs — much like the legs of a stork, only double the number — and its head was shaped a good deal like that of a poll parrot, with a beak that curved downward in front and upward at the edges, and was half bill and half mouth. But to call it a bird was out of the question, because it had no feathers whatever except a crest of wavy plumes of a scarlet color on the very top of its head. The strange creature must have weighed as much as Cap'n Bill, and as it floundered and struggled to get out of the water to the sandy beach it was so big and unusual that both Trot and her companion stared at it in wonder — in wonder that was not unmixed with fear.

3. The Ork

The eyes that regarded them, as the creature stood dripping before them, were bright and mild in expression, and the queer addition to their party made no attempt to attack them and seemed quite as surprised by the meeting as they were.

"I wonder," whispered Trot, "what it is."

"Who, me?" exclaimed the creature in a shrill, high- pitched voice. "Why, I'm an Ork."

"Oh!" said the girl. "But what is an Ork?"

"I am," he repeated, a little proudly, as he shook the water from his funny wings; "and if ever an Ork was glad to be out of the

water and on dry land again, you can be mighty sure that I'm that especial, individual Ork!"

"Have you been in the water long?" inquired Cap'n Bill, thinking it only polite to show an interest in the strange creature.

"Why, this last ducking was about ten minutes, I believe, and that's about nine minutes and sixty seconds too long for comfort," was the reply. "But last night I was in an awful pickle, I assure you. The whirlpool caught me, and —"

"Oh, were you in the whirlpool, too?" asked Trot eagerly

He gave her a glance that was somewhat reproachful.

"I believe I was mentioning the fact, young lady, when your desire to talk interrupted me," said the Ork. "I am not usually careless in my actions, but that whirlpool was so busy yesterday that I thought I'd see what mischief it was up to. So I flew a little too near it and the suction of the air drew me down into the depths of the ocean. Water and I are natural enemies, and it would have conquered me this time had not a bevy of pretty mermaids come to my assistance and dragged me away from the whirling water and far up into a cavern, where they deserted me."

"Why, that's about the same thing that happened to us," cried Trot. "Was your cavern like this one?"

"I haven't examined this one yet," answered the Ork; "but if they happen to be alike I shudder at our fate, for the other one was a prison, with no outlet except by means of the water. I stayed there all night, however, and this morning I plunged into the pool, as far down as I could go, and then swam as hard and as far as I could. The rocks scraped my back, now and then, and I barely escaped the clutches of an ugly sea-monster; but by and by I came to the surface to catch my breath, and found myself here. That's the whole story, and as I see you have something to eat I entreat you to give me a share of it. The truth is, I'm half starved."

With these words the Ork squatted down beside them. Very reluctantly Cap'n Bill drew another biscuit from his pocket and held it out. The Ork promptly seized it in one of its front claws and began to nibble the biscuit in much the same manner a parrot might have done.

"We haven't much grub," said the sailor-man, "but we're willin' to share it with a comrade in distress."

"That's right," returned the Ork, cocking its head sidewise in a cheerful manner, and then for a few minutes there was silence while they all ate of the biscuits. After a while Trot said: "I've never seen or heard of an Ork before. Are there many of you?"

"We are rather few and exclusive, I believe," was the reply. "In the country where I was born we are the absolute rulers of all living things, from ants to elephants."

"What country is that?" asked Cap'n Bill.

"Orkland."

"Where does it lie?"

"I don't know, exactly. You see, I have a restless nature, for some reason, while all the rest of my race are quiet and contented Orks and seldom stray far from home. From childhood days I loved to fly long distances away, although father often warned me that I would get into trouble by so doing.

"'It's a big world, Flipper, my son,' he would say, 'and I've heard that in parts of it live queer two-legged creatures called Men, who war upon all other living things and would have little respect for even an Ork.'

"This naturally aroused my curiosity and after I had completed my education and left school I decided to fly out into the world and try to get a glimpse of the creatures called Men. So I left home without saying good-bye, an act I shall always regret. Adventures were many, I found. I sighted men several times, but have never before been so close to them as now. Also I had to fight my way through the air, for I met gigantic birds, with fluffy feathers all over them, which attacked me fiercely. Besides, it kept me busy escaping from floating airships. In my rambling I had lost all track of distance or direction, so that when I wanted to go home I had no idea where my country was located. I've now been trying to find it for several months and it was during one of my flights over the ocean that I met the whirlpool and became its victim."

Trot and Cap'n Bill listened to this recital with much interest, and from the friendly tone and harmless appearance of the Ork they judged he was not likely to prove so disagreeable a companion as at first they had feared he might be.

The Ork sat upon its haunches much as a cat does, but used the finger-like claws of its front legs almost as cleverly as if they were hands. Perhaps the most curious thing about the creature was its tail, or what ought to have been its tail. This queer arrangement of skin, bones and muscle was shaped like the propellers used on boats and airships, having fan-like surfaces and being pivoted to its body. Cap'n Bill knew something of mechanics, and observing the propeller-like tail of the Ork he said: "I s'pose you're a pretty swift flyer?"

"Yes, indeed; the Orks are admitted to be Kings of the Air."

"Your wings don't seem to amount to much," remarked Trot.

"Well, they are not very big," admitted the Ork, waving the four hollow skins gently to and fro, "but they serve to support my body in the air while I speed along by means of my tail. Still, taken altogether, I'm very handsomely formed, don't you think?"

Trot did not like to reply, but Cap'n Bill nodded gravely. "For an Ork," said he, "you're a wonder. I've never seen one afore, but I can imagine you're as good as any."

That seemed to please the creature and it began walking around the cavern, making its way easily up the slope. while it was gone, Trot and Cap'n Bill each took another sip from the water-flask, to wash down their breakfast.

"Why, here's a hole — an exit — an outlet!" exclaimed the Ork from above.

"We know," said Trot. "We found it last night."

"Well, then, let's be off," continued the Ork, after sticking its head into the black hole and sniffing once or twice. "The air seems fresh and sweet, and it can't lead us to any worse place than this."

The girl and the sailor-man got up and climbed to the side of the Ork.

"We'd about decided to explore this hole before you came," explained Cap'n Bill; "but it's a dangerous place to navigate in the dark, so wait till I light a candle."

"What is a candle?" inquired the Ork.

"You'll see in a minute," said Trot.

The old sailor drew one of the candles from his right-side pocket and the tin matchbox from his left-side pocket. When he lighted the match the Ork gave a startled jump and eyed the flame suspiciously; but Cap'n Bill proceeded to light the candle and the action interested the Ork very much.

"Light," it said, somewhat nervously, "is valuable in a hole of this sort. The candle is not dangerous, I hope?"

"Sometimes it burns your fingers," answered Trot, "but that's about the worst it can do — 'cept to blow out when you don't want it to."

Cap'n Bill shielded the flame with his hand and crept into the hole. It wasn't any too big for a grown man, but after he had crawled a few feet it grew larger. Trot came close behind him and then the Ork followed.

"Seems like a reg'lar tunnel," muttered the sailor-man, who was creeping along awkwardly because of his wooden leg. The rocks, too, hurt his knees.

For nearly half an hour the three moved slowly along the tunnel, which made many twists and turns and sometimes slanted downward and sometimes upward. Finally Cap'n Bill stopped short, with an exclamation of disappointment, and held the flickering candle far ahead to light the scene.

"What's wrong?" demanded Trot, who could see nothing because the sailor's form completely filled the hole.

"Why, we've come to the end of our travels, I guess," he replied.

"Is the hole blocked?" inquired the Ork.

"No; it's wuss nor that," replied Cap'n Bill sadly. "I'm on the edge of a precipice. Wait a minute an' I'll move along and let you see for yourselves. Be careful, Trot, not to fall."

Then he crept forward a little and moved to one side, holding the candle so that the girl could see to follow him. The Ork came next and now all three knelt on a narrow ledge of rock which dropped straight away and left a huge black space which the tiny flame of the candle could not illuminate.

"H-m!" said the Ork, peering over the edge; "this doesn't look very promising, I'll admit. But let me take your candle, and I'll fly down and see what's below us."

"Aren't you afraid?" asked Trot.

"Certainly I'm afraid," responded the Ork. "But if we intend to escape we can't stay on this shelf forever. So, as I notice you poor creatures cannot fly, it is my duty to explore the place for you."

Cap'n Bill handed the Ork the candle, which had now burned to about half its length. The Ork took it in one claw rather cautiously and then tipped its body forward and slipped over the edge. They heard a queer buzzing sound, as the tail revolved, and a brisk flapping of the peculiar wings, but they were more interested just then in following with their eyes the tiny speck of light which marked the location of the candle. This light first made a great circle, then dropped slowly downward and suddenly was extinguished, leaving everything before them black as ink.

"Hi, there! How did that happen?" cried the Ork.

"It blew out, I guess," shouted Cap'n Bill. "Fetch it here."

"I can't see where you are," said the Ork.

So Cap'n Bill got out another candle and lighted it, and its flame enabled the Ork to fly back to them. It alighted on the edge and held out the bit of candle.

"What made it stop burning?" asked the creature.

"The wind," said Trot. "You must be more careful, this time."

"What's the place like?" inquired Cap'n Bill.

"I don't know, yet; but there must be a bottom to it, so I'll try to find it."

With this the Ork started out again and this time sank downward more slowly. Down, down, down it went, till the candle was a mere spark, and then it headed away to the left and Trot and Cap'n Bill lost all sight of it.

In a few minutes, however, they saw the spark of light again, and as the sailor still held the second lighted candle the Ork made straight toward them. It was only a few yards distant when suddenly it dropped the candle with a cry of pain and next moment alighted, fluttering wildly, upon the rocky ledge.

"What's the matter?" asked Trot.

"It bit me!" wailed the Ork. "I don't like your candles. The thing began to disappear slowly as soon as I took it in my claw, and it grew smaller and smaller until just now it turned and bit me — a most unfriendly thing to do. Oh — oh! Ouch, what a bite!"

"That's the nature of candles, I'm sorry to say," explained Cap'n Bill, with a grin. "You have to handle 'em mighty keerful. But tell us, what did you find down there?"

"I found a way to continue our journey," said the Ork, nursing tenderly the claw which had been burned. "Just below us is a great lake of black water, which looked so cold and wicked that it made me shudder; but away at the left there's a big tunnel, which we can easily walk through. I don't know where it leads to, of course, but we must follow it and find out."

"Why, we can't get to it," protested the little girl. "We can't fly, as you do, you must remember."

"No, that's true," replied the Ork musingly. "Your bodies are built very poorly, it seems to me, since all you can do is crawl upon the earth's surface. But you may ride upon my back, and in that way I can promise you a safe journey to the tunnel."

"Are you strong enough to carry us?" asked Cap'n Bill, doubtfully.

"Yes, indeed; I'm strong enough to carry a dozen of you, if you could find a place to sit," was the reply; "but there's only room between my wings for one at a time, so I'll have to make two trips."

"All right; I'll go first," decided Cap'n Bill.

He lit another candle for Trot to hold while they were gone and to light the Ork on his return to her, and then the old sailor got upon the Ork's back, where he sat with his wooden leg sticking straight out sidewise.

"If you start to fall, clasp your arms around my neck," advised the creature.

"If I start to fall, it's good night an' pleasant dreams," said Cap'n Bill.

"All ready?" asked the Ork.

"Start the buzz-tail," said Cap'n Bill, with a tremble in his voice. But the Ork flew away so gently that the old man never even tottered in his seat. Trot watched the light of Cap'n Bill's candle till it disappeared in the far distance. She didn't like to be left alone on this dangerous ledge, with a lake of black water hundreds of feet below her; but she was a brave little girl and waited patiently for the return of the Ork. It came even sooner than she had expected and the creature said to her: "Your friend is safe in the tunnel. Now, then, get aboard and I'll carry you to him in a jiffy."

I'm sure not many little girls would have cared to take that awful ride through the huge black cavern on the back of a skinny Ork. Trot didn't care for it, herself, but it just had to be done and so she did it as courageously as possible. Her heart beat fast and she was so nervous she could scarcely hold the candle in her fingers as the Ork sped swiftly through the darkness.

It seemed like a long ride to her, yet in reality the Ork covered the distance in a wonderfully brief period of time and soon Trot stood safely beside Cap'n Bill on the level floor of a big arched tunnel. The sailor-man was very glad to greet his little comrade again and both were grateful to the Ork for his assistance.

"I dunno where this tunnel leads to," remarked Cap'n Bill, "but it surely looks more promisin' than that other hole we crept through."

"When the Ork is rested," said Trot, "we'll travel on and see what happens."

"Rested!" cried the Ork, as scornfully as his shrill voice would allow. "That bit of flying didn't tire me at all. I'm used to flying days at a time, without ever once stopping."

"Then let's move on," proposed Cap'n Bill. He still held in his hand one lighted candle, so Trot blew out the other flame and placed her candle in the sailor's big pocket. She knew it was not wise to burn two candles at once.

The tunnel was straight and smooth and very easy to walk through, so they made good progress. Trot thought that the tunnel began about two miles from the cavern where they had been cast by the whirlpool, but now it was impossible to guess the miles traveled, for they walked steadily for hours and hours without any change in their surroundings.

Finally Cap'n Bill stopped to rest.

"There's somethin' queer about this 'ere tunnel, I'm certain," he declared, wagging his head dolefully. "Here's three candles gone a'ready, an' only three more left us, yet the tunnel's the same as it was when we started. An' how long it's goin' to keep up, no one knows."

"Couldn't we walk without a light?" asked Trot. "The way seems safe enough."

"It does right now," was the reply, "but we can't tell when we are likely to come to another gulf, or somethin' jes' as dangerous. In that case we'd be killed afore we knew it."

"Suppose I go ahead?" suggested the Ork. "I don't fear a fall, you know, and if anything happens I'll call out and warn you."

"That's a good idea," declared Trot, and Cap'n Bill thought so, too. So the Ork started off ahead, quite in the dark, and hand in band the two followed him.

When they had walked in this way for a good long time the Ork halted and demanded food. Cap'n Bill had not mentioned food because there was so little left — only three biscuits and a lump of cheese about as big as his two fingers — but he gave the Ork half of a biscuit, sighing as he did so. The creature didn't care for the cheese, so the sailor divided it between himself and Trot. They lighted a candle and sat down in the tunnel while they ate.

"My feet hurt me," grumbled the Ork. "I'm not used to walking and this rocky passage is so uneven and lumpy that it hurts me to walk upon it."

"Can't you fly along?" asked Trot.

"No; the roof is too low," said the Ork.

After the meal they resumed their journey, which Trot began to fear would never end. When Cap'n Bill noticed how tired the little girl was, he paused and lighted a match and looked at his big silver watch.

"Why, it's night!" he exclaimed. "We've tramped all day, an' still we're in this awful passage, which mebbe goes straight through the middle of the world, an' mebbe is a circle — in which case we can keep walkin' till doomsday. Not knowin' what's before us so well as we know what's behind us, I propose we make a stop, now, an' try to sleep till mornin'."

"That will suit me," asserted the Ork, with a groan. "My feet are hurting me dreadfully and for the last few miles I've been limping with pain."

"My foot hurts, too," said the sailor, looking for a smooth place on the rocky floor to sit down.

"Your foot!" cried the Ork. "why, you've only one to hurt you, while I have four. So I suffer four times as much as you possibly can. Here; hold the candle while I look at the bottoms of my claws. I declare," he said, examining them by the flickering light, "there are bunches of pain all over them!"

"P'r'aps," said Trot, who was very glad to sit down beside her companions, "you've got corns."

"Corns? Nonsense! Orks never have corns," protested the creature, rubbing its sore feet tenderly.

"Then mebbe they're - they're - What do you call 'em, Cap'n Bill? Something 'bout the Pilgrim's Progress, you know."

"Bunions," said Cap'n Bill.

"Oh, yes; mebbe you've got bunions."

"It is possible," moaned the Ork. "But whatever they are, another day of such walking on them would drive me crazy."

"I'm sure they'll feel better by mornin'," said Cap'n Bill encouragingly. "Go to sleep an' try to forget your sore feet."

The Ork cast a reproachful look at the sailor-man, who didn't see it. Then the creature asked plaintively: "Do we eat now, or do we starve?"

"There's only half a biscuit left for you," answered Cap'n Bill. "No one knows how long we'll have to stay in this dark tunnel, where there's nothing whatever to eat; so I advise you to save that morsel o' food till later."

"Give it me now!" demanded the Ork. "If I'm going to starve, I'll do it all at once — not by degrees."

Cap'n Bill produced the biscuit and the creature ate it in a trice. Trot was rather hungry and whispered to Cap'n Bill that she'd take part of her share; but the old man secretly broke his own half-biscuit in two, saving Trot's share for a time of greater need.

He was beginning to be worried over the little girl's plight and long after she was asleep and the Ork was snoring in a rather disagreeable manner, Cap'n Bill sat with his back to a rock and smoked his pipe and tried to think of some way to escape from this seemingly endless tunnel. But after a time he also slept, for hobbling on a wooden leg all day was tiresome, and there in the dark slumbered the three adventurers for many hours, until the Ork roused itself and kicked the old sailor with one foot.

"It must be another day," said he.

4. Daylight at Last

Cap'n Bill rubbed his eyes, lit a match and consulted his watch.

"Nine o'clock. Yes, I guess it's another day, sure enough. Shall we go on?" he asked.

"Of course," replied the Ork. "Unless this tunnel is different from everything else in the world, and has no end, we'll find a way out of it sooner or later."

The sailor gently wakened Trot. She felt much rested by her long sleep and sprang to her feet eagerly.

"Let's start, Cap'n," was all she said.

They resumed the journey and had only taken a few steps when the Ork cried "Wow!" and made a great fluttering of its wings and whirling of its tail. The others, who were following a short distance behind, stopped abruptly.

"What's the matter?" asked Cap'n Bill.

"Give us a light," was the reply. "I think we've come to the end of the tunnel." Then, while Cap'n Bill lighted a candle, the creature added: "If that is true, we needn't have wakened so soon, for we were almost at the end of this place when we went to sleep."

The sailor-man and Trot came forward with a light. A wall of rock really faced the tunnel, but now they saw that the opening made a sharp turn to the left. So they followed on, by a narrower passage, and then made another sharp turn this time to the right.

"Blow out the light, Cap'n," said the Ork, in a pleased voice. "We've struck daylight."

Daylight at last! A shaft of mellow light fell almost at their feet as Trot and the sailor turned the corner of the passage, but it came from above, and raising their eyes they found they were at the bottom of a deep, rocky well, with the top far, far above their heads. And here the passage ended.

For a while they gazed in silence, at least two of them being filled with dismay at the sight. But the Ork merely whistled softly and said cheerfully: "That was the toughest journey I ever had the misfortune to undertake, and I'm glad it's over. Yet, unless I can manage to fly to the top of this pit, we are entombed here forever."

"Do you think there is room enough for you to fly in?" asked the little girl anxiously; and Cap'n Bill added:

"It's a straight-up shaft, so I don't see how you'll ever manage it."

"Were I an ordinary bird — one of those horrid feathered things — I wouldn't even make the attempt to fly out," said the Ork. "But my mechanical propeller tail can accomplish wonders, and whenever you're ready I'll show you a trick that is worth while."

"Oh!" exclaimed Trot; "do you intend to take us up, too?"

"Why not?"

"I thought," said Cap'n Bill, "as you'd go first, an' then send somebody to help us by lettin' down a rope."

"Ropes are dangerous," replied the Ork, "and I might not be able to find one to reach all this distance. Besides, it stands to reason that if I can get out myself I can also carry you two with me."

"Well, I'm not afraid," said Trot, who longed to be on the earth's surface again.

"S'pose we fall?" suggested Cap'n Bill, doubtfully.

"Why, in that case we would all fall together," returned the Ork. "Get aboard, little girl; sit across my shoulders and put both your arms around my neck."

Trot obeyed and when she was seated on the Ork, Cap'n Bill inquired:

"How 'bout me, Mr. Ork?"

"Why, I think you'd best grab hold of my rear legs and let me carry you up in that manner," was the reply.

Cap'n Bill looked way up at the top of the well, and then he looked at the Ork's slender, skinny legs and heaved a deep sigh.

"It's goin' to be some dangle, I guess; but if you don't waste too much time on the way up, I may be able to hang on," said he.

"All ready, then!" cried the Ork, and at once his whirling tail began to revolve. Trot felt herself rising into the air; when the creature's legs left the ground Cap'n Bill grasped two of them

firmly and held on for dear life. The Ork's body was tipped straight upward, and Trot had to embrace the neck very tightly to keep from sliding off. Even in this position the Ork had trouble in escaping the rough sides of the well. Several times it exclaimed "Wow!" as it bumped its back, or a wing hit against some jagged projection; but the tail kept whirling with remarkable swiftness and the daylight grew brighter and brighter. It was, indeed, a long journey from the bottom to the top, yet almost before Trot realized they had come so far, they popped out of the hole into the clear air and sunshine and a moment later the Ork alighted gently upon the ground.

The release was so sudden that even with the creature's care for its passengers Cap'n Bill struck the earth with a shock that sent him rolling heel over head; but by the time Trot had slid down from her seat the old sailor-man was sitting up and looking around him with much satisfaction.

"It's sort o' pretty here," said he.

"Earth is a beautiful place!" cried Trot.

"I wonder where on earth we are?" pondered the Ork, turning first one bright eye and then the other to this side and that. Trees there were, in plenty, and shrubs and flowers and green turf. But there were no houses; there were no paths; there was no sign of civilization whatever.

"Just before I settled down on the ground I thought I caught a view of the ocean," said the Ork. "Let's see if I was right." Then he flew to a little hill, near by, and Trot and Cap'n Bill followed him more slowly. When they stood on the top of the hill they could see the blue waves of the ocean in front of them, to the right of them, and at the left of them. Behind the hill was a forest that shut out the view.

"I hope it ain't an island, Trot," said Cap'n Bill gravely.

"If it is, I s'pose we're prisoners," she replied.

"Ezzackly so, Trot."

"But, 'even so, it's better than those terr'ble underground tunnels and caverns," declared the girl.

"You are right, little one," agreed the Ork. "Anything above ground is better than the best that lies under ground. So let's not quarrel with our fate but be thankful we've escaped."

"We are, indeed!" she replied. "But I wonder if we can find something to eat in this place?"

"Let's explore an' find out," proposed Cap'n Bill. "Those trees over at the left look like cherry-trees."

On the way to them the explorers had to walk through a tangle of vines and Cap'n Bill, who went first, stumbled and pitched forward on his face.

"Why, it's a melon!" cried Trot delightedly, as she saw what had caused the sailor to fall.

Cap'n Bill rose to his foot, for he was not at all hurt, and examined the melon. Then he took his big jackknife from his pocket and cut the melon open. It was quite ripe and looked delicious; but the old man tasted it before he permitted Trot to eat any. Deciding it was good he gave her a big slice and then offered the Ork some. The creature looked at the fruit somewhat disdainfully, at first, but once he had tasted its flavor he ate of it as heartily as did the others. Among the vines they discovered many other melons, and Trot said gratefully: "Well, there's no danger of our starving, even if this is an island."

"Melons," remarked Cap'n Bill, "are both food an' water. We couldn't have struck anything better."

Farther on they came to the cherry trees, where they obtained some of the fruit, and at the edge of the little forest were wild plums. The forest itself consisted entirely of nut trees — walnuts, filberts, almonds and chestnuts — so there would be plenty of wholesome food for them while they remained there.

Cap'n Bill and Trot decided to walk through the forest, to discover what was on the other side of it, but the Ork's feet were still so sore and "lumpy" from walking on the rocks that the creature said he preferred to fly over the tree-tops and meet them on the other side. The forest was not large, so by walking briskly for fifteen minutes they reached its farthest edge and saw before them the shore of the ocean.

"It's an island, all right," said Trot, with a sigh.

"Yes, and a pretty island, too," said Cap'n Bill, trying to conceal his disappointment on Trot's account. "I guess, partner, if the wuss comes to the wuss, I could build a raft — or even a boat — from those trees, so's we could sail away in it."

The little girl brightened at this suggestion. "I don't see the Ork anywhere," she remarked, looking around. Then her eyes lighted upon something and she exclaimed: "Oh, Cap'n Bill! Isn't that a house, over there to the left?"

Cap'n Bill, looking closely, saw a shed-like structure built at one edge of the forest.

"Seems like it, Trot. Not that I'd call it much of a house, but it's a buildin', all right. Let's go over an' see if it's occypied."

5. The Little Old Man of the Island

A few steps brought them to the shed, which was merely a roof of boughs built over a square space, with some branches of trees fastened to the sides to keep off the wind. The front was quite open and faced the sea, and as our friends came nearer they observed a little man, with a long pointed beard, sitting motionless on a stool and staring thoughtfully out over the water.

"Get out of the way, please," he called in a fretful voice. "Can't you see you are obstructing my view?"

"Good morning," said Cap'n Bill, politely.

"It isn't a good morning!" snapped the little man. "I've seen plenty of mornings better than this. Do you call it a good morning when I'm pestered with such a crowd as you?"

Trot was astonished to hear such words from a stranger whom they had greeted quite properly, and Cap'n Bill grew red at the little man's rudeness. But the sailor said, in a quiet tone of voice: "Are you the only one as lives on this 'ere island?"

"Your grammar's bad," was the reply. "But this is my own exclusive island, and I'll thank you to get off it as soon as possible."

"We'd like to do that," said Trot, and then she and Cap'n Bill turned away and walked down to the shore, to see if any other land was in sight.

The little man rose and followed them, although both were now too provoked to pay any attention to him.

Nothin' in sight, partner," reported Cap'n Bill, shading his eyes with his hand; "so we'll have to stay here for a time, anyhow. It isn't a bad place, Trot, by any means."

"That's all you know about it!" broke in the little man. "The trees are altogether too green and the rocks are harder than they ought to be. I find the sand very grainy and the water dreadfully wet. Every breeze makes a draught and the sun shines in the daytime, when there's no need of it, and disappears just as soon as it begins to get dark. If you remain here you'll find the island very unsatisfactory."

Trot turned to look at him, and her sweet face was grave and curious.

"I wonder who you are," she said.

"My name is Pessim," said he, with an air of pride. "I'm called the Observer,"

"Oh. What do you observe?" asked the little girl.

"Everything I see," was the reply, in a more surly tone. Then Pessim drew back with a startled exclamation and looked at some footprints in the sand. "Why, good gracious me!" he cried in distress.

"What's the matter now?" asked Cap'n Bill.

"Someone has pushed the earth in! Don't you see it?

"It isn't pushed in far enough to hurt anything," said Trot, examining the footprints.

"Everything hurts that isn't right," insisted the man. "If the earth were pushed in a mile, it would be a great calamity, wouldn't it?"

"I s'pose so," admitted the little girl.

"Well, here it is pushed in a full inch! That's a twelfth of a foot, or a little more than a millionth part of a mile. Therefore it is one-millionth part of a calamity — Oh, dear! How dreadful!" said Pessim in a wailing voice.

"Try to forget it, sir," advised Cap'n Bill, soothingly. "It's beginning to rain. Let's get under your shed and keep dry."

"Raining! Is it really raining?" asked Pessim, beginning to weep.

"It is," answered Cap'n Bill, as the drops began to descend, "and I don't see any way to stop it — although I'm some observer myself."

"No; we can't stop it, I fear," said the man. "Are you very busy just now?"

"I won't be after I get to the shed," replied the sailor-man.

"Then do me a favor, please," begged Pessim, walking briskly along behind them, for they were hastening to the shed.

'Depends on what it is," said Cap'n Bill.

'I wish you would take my umbrella down to the shore and hold it over the poor fishes till it stops raining. I'm afraid they'll get wet," said Pessim.

Trot laughed, but Cap'n Bill thought the little man was poking fun at him and so he scowled upon Pessim in a way that showed he was angry.

They reached the shed before getting very wet, although the rain was now coming down in big drops. The roof of the shed protected them and while they stood watching the rainstorm something buzzed in and circled around Pessim's head. At once the Observer began beating it away with his hands, crying out: 'A bumblebee! A bumblebee! The queerest bumblebee I ever saw!"

Cap'n Bill and Trot both looked at it and the little girl said in surprise: "Dear me! It's a wee little Ork!"

'That's what it is, sure enough," exclaimed Cap'n Bill.

Really, it wasn't much bigger than a big bumblebee, and when it came toward Trot she allowed it to alight on her shoulder.

'It's me, all right," said a very small voice in her ear; "but I'm in an awful pickle, just the same!"

'What, are you our Ork, then?" demanded the girl, much amazed.

'No, I'm my own Ork. But I'm the only Ork you know," replied the tiny creature.

'What's happened to you?" asked the sailor, putting his head close to Trot's shoulder in order to hear the reply better. Pessim also put his head close, and the Ork said: "You will remember that when I left you I started to fly over the trees, and just as I got to this side of the forest I saw a bush that was loaded down with the most luscious fruit you can imagine. The fruit was about the size of a gooseberry and of a lovely lavender color. So I swooped down and picked off one in my bill and ate it. At once I began to grow small. I could feel myself shrinking, shrinking away, and it frightened me terribly, so that I lighted on the ground to think over what was happening. In a few seconds I had shrunk to the size you now see me; but there I remained, getting no smaller, indeed, but no larger. It is certainly a dreadful affliction! After I had recovered somewhat from the shock I began to search for you. It is not so easy to find one's way when a creature is so small, but fortunately I spied you here in this shed and came to you at once."

Cap'n Bill and Trot were much astonished at this story and felt grieved for the poor Ork, but the little man Pessim seemed to think it a good joke. He began laughing when he heard the story and laughed until he choked, after which he lay down on the ground and rolled and laughed again, while the tears of merriment coursed down his wrinkled cheeks.

Oh, dear! Oh, dear!" he finally gasped, sitting up and wiping his eyes. "This is too rich! It's almost too joyful to be true."

I don't see anything funny about it," remarked Trot indignantly.

You would if you'd had my experience," said Pessim, getting upon his feet and gradually resuming his solemn and dissatisfied expression of countenance.

"The same thing happened to me."

"Oh, did it? And how did you happen to come to this island?" asked the girl.

"I didn't come; the neighbors brought me," replied the little man, with a frown at the recollection. "They said I was quarrelsome and fault-finding and blamed me because I told them all the things that went wrong, or never were right, and because I told them how things ought to be. So they brought me here and left me all alone, saying that if I quarreled with myself, no one else would be made unhappy. Absurd, wasn't it?"

"Seems to me," said Cap'n Bill, "those neighbors did the proper thing."

"Well," resumed Pessim, "when I found myself King of this island I was obliged to live upon fruits, and I found many fruits growing here that I had never seen before. I tasted several and found them good and wholesome. But one day I ate a lavender berry — as the Ork did — and immediately I grew so small that I was scarcely two inches high. It was a very unpleasant condition and like the Ork I became frightened. I could not walk very well nor very far, for every lump of earth in my way seemed a mountain, every blade of grass a tree and every grain of sand a rocky boulder. For several days I stumbled around in an agony of fear. Once a tree toad nearly gobbled me up, and if I ran out from the shelter of the bushes the gulls and cormorants swooped down upon me. Finally I decided to eat another berry and become nothing at all, since life, to one as small as I was, had become a dreary nightmare.

"At last I found a small tree that I thought bore the same fruit as that I had eaten. The berry was dark purple instead of light lavender, but otherwise it was quite similar. Being unable to climb the tree, I was obliged to wait underneath it until a sharp breeze arose and shook the limbs so that a berry fell. Instantly I seized it and taking a last view of the world — as I then thought — I ate the berry in a twinkling. Then, to my surprise, I began to grow big again, until I became of my former stature, and so I have since remained. Needless to say, I have never eaten again of the lavender fruit, nor do any of the beasts or birds that live upon this island eat it."

They had all three listened eagerly to this amazing tale, and when it was finished the Ork exclaimed: "Do you think, then, that the deep purple berry is the antidote for the lavender one?"

"I'm sure of it," answered Pessim.

"Then lead me to the tree at once!" begged the Ork, "for this tiny form I now have terrifies me greatly."

Pessim examined the Ork closely.

"You are ugly enough as you are," said he. "Were you any larger you might be dangerous."

"Oh, no," Trot assured him; "the Ork has been our good friend. Please take us to the tree."

Then Pessim consented, although rather reluctantly. He led them to the right, which was the east side of the island, and in a few minutes brought them near to the edge of the grove which faced the shore of the ocean. Here stood a small tree bearing berries of a deep purple color. The fruit looked very enticing and Cap'n Bill reached up and selected one that seemed especially plump and ripe.

The Ork had remained perched upon Trot's shoulder but now it flew down to the ground. It was so difficult for Cap'n Bill to kneel down, with his wooden leg, that the little girl took the berry from him and held it close to the Ork's head.

"It's too big to go into my mouth," said the little creature, looking at the fruit sidewise.

"You'll have to make sev'ral mouthfuls of it, I guess," said Trot; and that is what the Ork did. He pecked at the soft, ripe fruit with his bill and ate it up very quickly, because it was good.

Even before he had finished the berry they could see the Ork begin to grow. In a few minutes he had regained his natural size and was strutting before them, quite delighted with his transformation.

"Well, well! What do you think of me now?" he asked proudly.

"You are very skinny and remarkably ugly," declared Pessim.

"You are a poor judge of Orks," was the reply. "Anyone can see that I'm much handsomer than those dreadful things called birds, which are all fluff and feathers."

"Their feathers make soft beds," asserted Pessim. "And my skin would make excellent drumheads," retorted the Ork. "Nevertheless, a plucked bird or a skinned Ork would be of no value to himself, so we needn't brag of our usefulness after we are dead. But for the sake of argument, friend Pessim, I'd like to know what good you would be, were you not alive?"

"Never mind that," said Cap'n Bill. "He isn't much good as he is."

"I am King of this Island, allow me to say, and you're intruding on my property," declared the little man, scowling upon them. "If you don't like me —and I'm sure you don't, for no one else does — why don't you go away and leave me to myself?"

"Well, the Ork can fly, but we can't," explained Trot, in answer. "We don't want to stay here a bit, but I don't see how we can get away."

"You can go back into the hole you came from."

Cap'n Bill shook his head; Trot shuddered at the thought; the Ork laughed aloud.

"You may be King here," the creature said to Pessim, "but we intend to run this island to suit ourselves, for we are three and you are one, and the balance of power lies with us."

The little man made no reply to this, although as they walked back to the shed his face wore its fiercest scowl. Cap'n Bill gathered a lot of leaves and, assisted by Trot, prepared two nice beds in opposite corners of the shed. Pessim slept in a hammock which he swung between two trees.

They required no dishes, as all their food consisted of fruits and nuts picked from the trees; they made no fire, for the weather was warm and there was nothing to cook; the shed had no furniture other than the rude stool which the little man was accustomed to sit upon. He called it his "throne" and they let him keep it.

So they lived upon the island for three days, and rested and ate

to their hearts' content. Still, they were not at all happy in this life because of Pessim. He continually found fault with them, and all that they did, and all their surroundings. He could see nothing good or admirable in all the world and Trot soon came to understand why the little man's former neighbors had brought him to this island and left him there, all alone, so he could not annoy anyone. It was their misfortune that they had been led to this place by their adventures, for often they would have preferred the company of a wild beast to that of Pessim.

On the fourth day a happy thought came to the Ork. They had all been racking their brains for a possible way to leave the island, and discussing this or that method, without finding a plan that was practical. Cap'n Bill had said he could make a raft of the trees, big enough to float them all, but he had no tools except those two pocketknives and it was not possible to chop down trees with such small blades.

"And s'pose we got afloat on the ocean," said Trot, "where would we drift to, and how long would it take us to get there?"

Cap'n Bill was forced to admit he didn't know. The Ork could fly away from the island any time it wished to, but the queer creature was loyal to his new friends and refused to leave them in such a lonely, forsaken place.

It was when Trot urged him to go, on this fourth morning, that the Ork had his happy thought.

"I will go," said he, "if you two will agree to ride upon my back."

"We are too heavy; you might drop us," objected Cap'n Bill.

"Yes, you are rather heavy for a long journey," acknowledged the Ork, "but you might eat of those lavender berries and become so small that I could carry you with ease."

This quaint suggestion startled Trot and she looked gravely at the speaker while she considered it, but Cap'n Bill gave a scornful snort and asked: "What would become of us afterward? We wouldn't be much good if we were some two or three inches high. No, Mr. Ork, I'd rather stay here, as I am, than be a hop-o'-my-thumb somewhere else."

"Why couldn't you take some of the dark purple berries along with you, to eat after we had reached our destination?" inquired the Ork. "Then you could grow big again whenever you pleased."

Trot clapped her hands with delight.

"That's it!" she exclaimed. "Let's do it, Cap'n Bill."

The old sailor did not like the idea at first, but he thought it over carefully and the more he thought the better it seemed.

"How could you manage to carry us, if we were so small?" he asked.

"I could put you in a paper bag, and tie the bag around my neck."

"But we haven't a paper bag," objected Trot.

The Ork looked at her.

"There's your sunbonnet," it said presently, "which is hollow in the middle and has two strings that you could tie around my neck."

Trot took off her sunbonnet and regarded it critically. Yes, it might easily hold both her and Cap'n Bill, after they had eaten the lavender berries and been reduced in size. She tied the strings around the Ork's neck and the sunbonnet made a bag in which two tiny people might ride without danger of falling out. So she said: "I b'lieve we'll do it that way, Cap'n."

Cap'n Bill groaned but could make no logical objection except that the plan seemed to him quite dangerous — and dangerous in more ways than one.

"I think so, myself," said Trot soberly. "But nobody can stay alive without getting into danger sometimes, and danger doesn't mean getting hurt, Cap'n; it only means we might get hurt. So I guess we'll have to take the risk."

"Let's go and find the berries," said the Ork.

They said nothing to Pessim, who was sitting on his stool and scowling dismally as he stared at the ocean, but started at once to seek the trees that bore the magic fruits. The Ork remembered very well where the lavender berries grew and led his companions quickly to the spot.

Cap'n Bill gathered two berries and placed them carefully in his pocket. Then they went around to the east side of the island and found the tree that bore the dark purple berries.

"I guess I'll take four of these," said the sailor-man, so in case one doesn't make us grow big we can eat another."

"Better take six," advised the Ork. "It's well to be on the safe side, and I'm sure these trees grow nowhere else in all the world."

So Cap'n Bill gathered six of the purple berries and with their precious fruit they returned to the shed to big good-bye to Pessim. Perhaps they would not have granted the surly little man this courtesy had they not wished to use him to tie the sunbonnet around the Ork's neck.

When Pessim learned they were about to leave him he at first looked greatly pleased, but he suddenly recollected that nothing ought to please him and so began to grumble about being left alone.

"We knew it wouldn't suit you," remarked Cap'n Bill. "It didn't suit you to have us here, and it won't suit you to have us go away."

"That is quite true," admitted Pessim. "I haven't been suited since I can remember; so it doesn't matter to me in the least whether you go or stay."

He was interested in their experiment, however, and willingly agreed to assist, although he prophesied they would fall out of the sunbonnet on their way and be either drowned in the ocean or crushed upon some rocky shore. This uncheerful prospect did not daunt Trot, but it made Cap'n Bill quite nervous.

"I will eat my berry first," said Trot, as she placed her sunbonnet on the ground, in such manner that they could get into it.

Then she ate the lavender berry and in a few seconds became so small that Cap'n Bill picked her up gently with his thumb and one finger and placed her in the middle of the sunbonnet. Then he placed beside her the six purple berries — each one being about as big as the tiny Trot's head — and all preparations being now made the old sailor ate his lavender berry and became very

small — wooden leg and all!

Cap'n Bill stumbled sadly in trying to climb over the edge of the sunbonnet and pitched in beside Trot headfirst, which caused the unhappy Pessim to laugh with glee. Then the King of the Island picked up the sunbonnet — so rudely that he shook its occupants like peas in a pod — and tied it, by means of its strings, securely around the Ork's neck.

"I hope, Trot, you sewed those strings on tight," said Cap'n Bill anxiously.

"Why, we are not very heavy, you know," she replied, "so I think the stitches will hold. But be careful and not crush the berries, Cap'n."

"One is jammed already," he said, looking at them.

"All ready?" asked the Ork.

"Yes!" they cried together, and Pessim came close to the sunbonnet and called out to them: "You'll be smashed or drowned, I'm sure you will! But farewell, and good riddance to you."

The Ork was provoked by this unkind speech, so he turned his tail toward the little man and made it revolve so fast that the rush of air tumbled Pessim over backward and he rolled several times upon the ground before he could stop himself and sit up. By that time the Ork was high in the air and speeding swiftly over the ocean.

6. The Flight of the Midgets

Cap'n Bill and Trot rode very comfortably in the sunbonnet. The motion was quite steady, for they weighed so little that the Ork flew without effort. Yet they were both somewhat nervous about their future fate and could not help wishing they were safe on land and their natural size again.

"You're terr'ble small, Trot," remarked Cap'n Bill, looking at his companion.

"Same to you, Cap'n," she said with a laugh; "but as long as we have the purple berries we needn't worry about our size."

"In a circus," mused the old man, "we'd be curiosities. But in a sunbonnet — high up in the air — sailin' over a big, unknown ocean — they ain't no word in any booktionary to describe us."

"Why, we're midgets, that's all," said the little girl. The Ork flew silently for a long time. The slight swaying of the sunbonnet made Cap'n Bill drowsy, and he began to doze. Trot, however, was wide awake, and after enduring the monotonous journey as long as she was able she called out: "Don't you see land anywhere, Mr. Ork?"

"Not yet," he answered. "This is a big ocean and I've no idea in which direction the nearest land to that island lies; but if I keep flying in a straight line I'm sure to reach some place some time."

That seemed reasonable, so the little people in the sunbonnet remained as patient as possible; that is, Cap'n Bill dozed and Trot tried to remember her geography lessons so she could figure out what land they were likely to arrive at.

For hours and hours the Ork flew steadily, keeping to the straight line and searching with his eyes the horizon of the ocean for land. Cap'n Bill was fast asleep and snoring and Trot had laid her head on his shoulder to rest it when suddenly the Ork exclaimed: "There! I've caught a glimpse of land, at last."

At this announcement they roused themselves. Cap'n Bill stood up and tried to peek over the edge of the sunbonnet.

"What does it look like?" he inquired.

"Looks like another island," said the Ork; "but I can judge it better in a minute or two."

"I don't care much for islands, since we visited that other one," declared Trot.

Soon the Ork made another announcement.

"It is surely an island, and a little one, too," said he. "But I won't stop, because I see a much bigger land straight ahead of it."

"That's right," approved Cap'n Bill. "The bigger the land, the better it will suit us."

"It's almost a continent," continued the Ork after a brief silence, during which he did not decrease the speed of his flight. "I wonder if it can be Orkland, the place I have been seeking so long?"

"I hope not," whispered Trot to Cap'n Bill — so softly that the Ork could not hear her — "for I shouldn't like to be in a country where only Orks live. This one Ork isn't a bad companion, but a lot of him wouldn't be much fun."

After a few more minutes of flying the Ork called out in a sad voice: "No! this is not my country. It's a place I have never seen before, although I have wandered far and wide. It seems to be all mountains and deserts and green valleys and queer cities and lakes and rivers —mixed up in a very puzzling way."

"Most countries are like that," commented Cap'n Bill. "Are you going to land?"

"Pretty soon," was the reply. "There is a mountain peak just ahead of me. What do you say to our landing on that?"

"All right," agreed the sailor-man, for both he and Trot were getting tired of riding in the sunbonnet and longed to set foot on solid ground again.

So in a few minutes the Ork slowed down his speed and then came to a stop so easily that they were scarcely jarred at all. Then the creature squatted down until the sunbonnet rested on the ground, and began trying to unfasten with its claws the knotted strings.

This proved a very clumsy task, because the strings were tied at the back of the Ork's neck, just where his claws would not easily reach. After much fumbling he said: "I'm afraid I can't let you out, and there is no one near to help me."

This was at first discouraging, but after a little thought Cap'n Bill said: "If you don't mind, Trot, I can cut a slit in your sunbonnet with my knife."

"Do," she replied. "The slit won't matter, 'cause I can sew it up again afterward, when I am big."

So Cap'n Bill got out his knife, which was just as small, in

proportion, as he was, and after considerable trouble managed to cut a long slit in the sunbonnet. First he squeezed through the opening himself and then helped Trot to get out.

When they stood on firm ground again their first act was to begin eating the dark purple berries which they had brought with them. Two of these Trot had guarded carefully during the long journey, by holding them in her lap, for their safety meant much to the tiny people.

"I'm not very hungry," said the little girl as she handed a berry to Cap'n Bill, "but hunger doesn't count, in this case. It's like taking medicine to make you well, so we must manage to eat 'em, somehow or other."

But the berries proved quite pleasant to taste and as Cap'n Bill and Trot nibbled at their edges their forms began to grow in size — slowly but steadily. The bigger they grew the easier it was for them to eat the berries, which of course became smaller to them, and by the time the fruit was eaten our friends had regained their natural size.

The little girl was greatly relieved when she found herself as large as she had ever been, and Cap'n Bill shared her satisfaction; for, although they had seen the effect of the berries on the Ork, they had not been sure the magic fruit would have the same effect on human beings, or that the magic would work in any other country than that in which the berries grew.

"What shall we do with the other four berries?" asked Trot, as she picked up her sunbonnet, marveling that she had ever been small. enough to ride in it. "They're no good to us now, are they, Cap'n?"

"I'm not sure as to that," he replied. "If they were eaten by one who had never eaten the lavender berries, they might have no effect at all; but then, contrary-wise, they might. One of 'em has got badly jammed, so I'll throw it away, but the other three I b'lieve I'll carry with me. They're magic things, you know, and may come handy to us some time."

He now searched in his big pockets and drew out a small wooden box with a sliding cover. The sailor had kept an assortment of nails, of various sizes, in this box, but those he now dumped loosely into his pocket and in the box placed the three sound purple berries.

When this important matter was attended to they found time to look about them and see what sort of place the Ork had landed them in.

7. The Bumpy Man

The mountain on which they had alighted was not a barren waste, but had on its sides patches of green grass, some bushes, a few slender trees and here and there masses of tumbled rocks. The sides of the slope seemed rather steep, but with care one could climb up or down them with ease and safety. The view from where they now stood showed pleasant valleys and fertile hills lying below the heights. Trot thought she saw some houses of queer shapes scattered about the lower landscape, and there were moving dots that might be people or animals, yet were too far away for her to see them clearly.

Not far from the place where they stood was the top of the mountain, which seemed to be flat, so the Ork proposed to his companions that he would fly up and see what was there.

"That's a good idea," said Trot, "'cause it's getting toward evening and we'll have to find a place to sleep."

The Ork had not been gone more than a few minutes when they saw him appear on the edge of the top which was nearest them.

"Come on up!" he called.

So Trot and Cap'n Bill began to ascend the steep slope and it did not take them long to reach the place where the Ork awaited them.

Their first view of the mountain top pleased them very much. It was a level space of wider extent than they had guessed and upon it grew grass of a brilliant green color. In the very center stood a house built of stone and very neatly constructed. No one was in sight, but smoke was coming from the chimney, so with one accord all three began walking toward the house.

"I wonder," said Trot, "in what country we are, and if it's very far from my home in California." "Can't say as to that, partner," answered Cap'n Bill, "but I'm mighty certain we've come a long way since we struck that whirlpool."

"Yes," she agreed, with a sigh, "it must be miles and miles!"

"Distance means nothing," said the Ork. "I have flown pretty much all over the world, trying to find my home, and it is astonishing how many little countries there are, hidden away in the cracks and corners of this big globe of Earth. If one travels, he may find some new country at every turn, and a good many of them have never yet been put upon the maps."

"P'raps this is one of them," suggested Trot.

They reached the house after a brisk walk and Cap'n Bill knocked upon the door. It was at once opened by a rugged looking man who had "bumps all over him," as Trot afterward declared. There were bumps on his head, bumps on his body and bumps on his arms and legs and hands. Even his fingers had bumps on the ends of them. For dress he wore an old gray suit of fantastic design, which fitted him very badly because of the bumps it covered but could not conceal.

But the Bumpy Man's eyes were kind and twinkling in expression and as soon as he saw his visitors he bowed low and said in a rather bumpy voice:

"Happy day! Come in and shut the door, for it grows cool when the sun goes down. Winter is now upon us."

"Why, it isn't cold a bit, outside," said Trot, "so it can't be winter yet."

"You will change your mind about that in a little while," declared the Bumpy Man. "My bumps always tell me the state of the weather, and they feel just now as if a snowstorm was coming this way. But make yourselves at home, strangers. Supper is nearly ready and there is food enough for all."

Inside the house there was but one large room, simply but comfortably furnished. It had benches, a table and a fireplace, all made of stone. On the hearth a pot was bubbling and steaming, and Trot thought it had a rather nice smell. The visitors seated themselves upon the benches — except the Ork. which squatted by the fireplace — and the Bumpy Man began stirring the kettle briskly.

"May I ask what country this is, sir?" inquired Cap'n Bill.

"Goodness me — fruit-cake and apple-sauce! —don't you know where you are?" asked the Bumpy Man, as he stopped stirring and looked at the speaker in surprise.

"No," admitted Cap'n Bill. "We've just arrived."

"Lost your way?" questioned the Bumpy Man.

"Not exactly," said Cap'n Bill. "We didn't have any way to lose."

"Ah!" said the Bumpy Man, nodding his bumpy head. "This," he announced, in a solemn, impressive voice, "is the famous Land of Mo."

"Oh!" exclaimed the sailor and the girl, both in one breath. But, never having heard of the Land of Mo, they were no wiser than before.

"I thought that would startle you," remarked the Bumpy Man, well pleased, as he resumed his stirring. The Ork watched him a while in silence and then asked: "Who may you be?"

"Me?" answered the Bumpy Man. "Haven't you heard of me? Gingerbread and lemon-juice! I'm known, far and wide, as the Mountain Ear."

They all received this information in silence at first, for they were trying to think what he could mean. Finally Trot mustered up courage to ask: "What is a Mountain Ear, please?"

For answer the man turned around and faced them, waving the spoon with which he had been stirring the kettle, as he recited the following verses in a singsong tone of voice:
"Here's a mountain, hard of hearing,
That's sad-hearted and needs cheering,
So my duty is to listen to all sounds that Nature makes,

So the hill won't get uneasy —
Get to coughing, or get sneezy —
For this monster bump, when frightened, is quite liable to quakes.

You can hear a bell that's ringing;
I can feel some people's singing;
But a mountain isn't sensible of what goes on, and so

When I hear a blizzard blowing
Or it's raining hard, or snowing,
I tell it to the mountain and the mountain seems to know.

Thus I benefit all people
While I'm living on this steeple,
For I keep the mountain steady so my neighbors all may thrive.

With my list'ning and my shouting
I prevent this mount from spouting,
And that makes me so important that I'm glad that I'm alive."

When he had finished these lines of verse the Bumpy Man turned again to resume his stirring. The Ork laughed softly and Cap'n Bill whistled to himself and Trot made up her mind that the Mountain Ear must be a little crazy. But the Bumpy Man seemed satisfied that he had explained his position fully and presently he placed four stone plates upon the table and then lifted the kettle from the fire and poured some of its contents on each of the plates. Cap'n Bill and Trot at once approached the table, for they were hungry, but when she examined her plate the little girl exclaimed: "Why, it's molasses candy!"

"To be sure," returned the Bumpy Man, with a pleasant smile. "Eat it quick, while it's hot, for it cools very quickly this winter weather."

With this he seized a stone spoon and began putting the hot molasses candy into his mouth, while the others watched him in astonishment.

"Doesn't it burn you?" asked the girl.

"No indeed," said he. "Why don't you eat? Aren't you hungry?"

"Yes," she replied, "I am hungry. But we usually eat our candy when it is cold and hard. We always pull molasses candy before we eat it."

"Ha, ha, ha!" laughed the Mountain Ear. "What a funny idea! Where in the world did you come from?"

"California," she said.

"California! Pooh! there isn't any such place. I've heard of every place in the Land of Mo, but I never before heard of California."

"It isn't in the Land of Mo," she explained.

"Then it isn't worth talking about," declared the Bumpy Man, helping himself again from the steaming kettle, for he had been eating all the time he talked.

"For my part," sighed Cap'n Bill, "I'd like a decent square meal, once more, just by way of variety. In the last place there was nothing but fruit to eat, and here it's worse, for there's nothing but candy."

"Molasses candy isn't so bad," said Trot. "Mine's nearly cool enough to pull, already. Wait a bit, Cap'n, and you can eat it."

A little later she was able to gather the candy from the stone plate and begin to work it back and forth with her hands. The Mountain Ear was greatly amazed at this and watched her closely. It was really good candy and pulled beautifully, so that Trot was soon ready to cut it into chunks for eating.

Cap'n Bill condescended to eat one or two pieces and the Ork ate several, but the Bumpy Man refused to try it. Trot finished the plate of candy herself and then asked for a drink of water.

"Water?" said the Mountain Ear wonderingly. "What is that?"

"Something to drink. Don't you have water in Mo?"

"None that ever I heard of," said he. "But I can give you some fresh lemonade. I caught it in a jar the last time it rained, which was only day before yesterday."

"Oh, does it rain lemonade here?" she inquired.

"Always; and it is very refreshing and healthful."

With this he brought from a cupboard a stone jar and a dipper, and the girl found it very nice lemonade, indeed. Cap'n Bill liked it, too; but the Ork would not touch it.

"If there is no water in this country, I cannot stay here for long," the creature declared. "Water means life to man and beast and bird."

"There must be water in lemonade," said Trot.

"Yes," answered the Ork, "I suppose so; but there are other things in it, too, and they spoil the good water."

The day's adventures had made our wanderers tired, so the Bumpy Man brought them some blankets in which they rolled themselves and then lay down before the fire, which their host kept alive with fuel all through the night. Trot wakened several times and found the Mountain Ear always alert and listening intently for the slightest sound. But the little girl could hear no sound at all except the snores of Cap'n Bill.

8. Button-Bright is Lost and Found Again

"Wake up — wake up!" called the voice of the Bumpy Man. "Didn't I tell you winter was coming? I could hear it coming with my left ear, and the proof is that it is now snowing hard outside."

"Is it?" said Trot, rubbing her eyes and creeping out of her blanket. "Where I live, in California, I have never seen snow except far away on the tops of high mountains."

"Well, this is the top of a high mountain," returned the bumpy one, "and for that reason we get our heaviest snowfalls right here."

The little girl went to the window and looked out. The air was filled with falling white flakes, so large in size and so queer in form that she was puzzled.

"Are you certain this is snow?" she asked.

"To be sure. I must get my snow-shovel and turn out to shovel a path. Would you like to come with me?"

"Yes," she said, and followed the Bumpy Man out when he opened the door. Then she exclaimed: "Why, it isn't cold a bit!"

"Of course not," replied the man. "It was cold last night, before the snowstorm; but snow, when it falls, is always crisp and warm."

Trot gathered a handful of it.

"Why, it's popcorn?" she cried.

"Certainly; all snow is popcorn. What did you expect it to be?"

"Popcorn is not snow in my country."

"Well, it is the only snow we have in the Land of Mo, so you may as well make the best of it," said he, a little impatiently. "I'm not responsible for the absurd things that happen in your country, and when you're in Mo you must do as the Momen do. Eat some of our snow, and you will find it is good. The only fault I find with our snow is that we get too much of it at times."

With this the Bumpy Man set to work shoveling a path and he was so quick and industrious that he piled up the popcorn in great banks on either side of the trail that led to the mountain top from the plains below. While he worked, Trot ate popcorn and found it crisp and slightly warm, as well as nicely salted and buttered. Presently Cap'n Bill came out of the house and joined her.

"What's this?" he asked.

"Mo snow," said she. "But it isn't real snow, although it falls from the sky. It's popcorn."

Cap'n Bill tasted it; then he sat down in the path and began to eat. The Ork came out and pecked away with its bill as fast as it could. They all liked popcorn and they all were hungry this morning.

Meantime the flakes of "Mo snow" came down so fast that the number of them almost darkened the air. The Bumpy Man was now shoveling quite a distance down the mountain- side, while the path behind him rapidly filled up with fresh-fallen popcorn. Suddenly Trot heard him call out: "Goodness gracious — mince pie and pancakes! — here is some one buried in the snow."

She ran toward him at once and the others followed, wading through the corn and crunching it underneath their feet. The Mo snow was pretty deep where the Bumpy Man was shoveling and from beneath a great bank of it he had uncovered a pair of feet.

"Dear me! Someone has been lost in the storm," said Cap'n Bill. "I hope he is still alive. Let's pull him out and see."

He took hold of one foot and the Bumpy Man took hold of the other. Then they both pulled and out from the heap of popcorn came a little boy. He was dressed in a brown velvet jacket and knickerbockers, with brown stockings, buckled shoes and a blue shirt-waist that had frills down its front. When drawn from the heap the boy was chewing a mouthful of popcorn and both his hands were full of it. So at first he couldn't speak to his rescuers but lay quite still and eyed them calmly until he had swallowed his mouthful. Then he said: "Get my cap," and stuffed more popcorn into his mouth.

While the Bumpy Man began shoveling into the corn-bank to find the boy's cap, Trot was laughing joyfully and Cap'n Bill had a broad grin on his face. The Ork looked from one to another and asked: "Who is this stranger?"

"Why, it's Button-Bright, of course," answered Trot. "If anyone ever finds a lost boy, he can make up his mind it's Button-Bright. But how he ever came to be lost in this far-away country is more'n I can make out."

"Where does he belong?" inquired the Ork.

"His home used to be in Philadelphia, I think; but I'm quite sure Button-Bright doesn't belong anywhere."

"That's right," said the boy, nodding his head as he swallowed the second mouthful.

"Everyone belongs somewhere," remarked the Ork.

"Not me," insisted Button-Bright. "I'm half way round the world from Philadelphia, and I've lost my Magic Umbrella, that used to carry me anywhere. Stands to reason that if I can't get back I haven't any home. But I don't care much. This is a pretty good country, Trot. I've had lots of fun here."

By this time the Mountain Ear had secured the boy's cap and was listening to the conversation with much interest.

"It seems you know this poor, snow-covered cast-away," he said.

"Yes, indeed," answered Trot. "We made a journey together to Sky Island, once, and were good friends."

"Well, then I'm glad I saved his life," said the Bumpy Man.

"Much obliged, Mr. Knobs," said Button-Bright, sitting up and staring at him, "but I don't believe you've saved anything except some popcorn that I might have eaten had you not disturbed me. It was nice and warm in that bank of popcorn, and there was plenty to eat. What made you dig me out? And what makes you so bumpy everywhere?"

"As for the bumps," replied the man, looking at himself with much pride, "I was born with them and I suspect they were a gift from the fairies. They make me look rugged and big, like the mountain I serve."

"All right," said Button-Bright and began eating popcorn again.

It had stopped snowing, now, and great flocks of birds were gathering around the mountain-side, eating the popcorn with much eagerness and scarcely noticing the people at all. There were birds of every size and color, most of them having gorgeous feathers and plumes.

"Just look at them!" exclaimed the Ork scornfully. "Aren't they dreadful creatures, all covered with feathers?"

"I think they're beautiful," said Trot, and this made the Ork so indignant that he went back into the house and sulked.

Button-Bright reached out his hand and caught a big bird by the leg. At once it rose into the air and it was so strong that it nearly carried the little boy with it. He let go the leg in a hurry and the bird flew down again and began to eat of the popcorn, not being frightened in the least.

This gave Cap'n Bill an idea. He felt in his pocket and drew out several pieces of stout string. Moving very quietly, so as to not alarm the birds, he crept up to several of the biggest ones and tied cords around their legs, thus making them prisoners. The birds were so intent on their eating that they did not notice what had happened to them, and when about twenty had been captured in this manner Cap'n Bill tied the ends of all the strings together and fastened them to a huge stone, so they could not escape.

The Bumpy Man watched the old sailor's actions with much curiosity.

"The birds will be quiet until they've eaten up all the snow," he said, "but then they will want to fly away to their homes. Tell me, sir, what will the poor things do when they find they can't fly?"

"It may worry 'em a little," replied Cap'n Bill, "but they're not going to be hurt if they take it easy and behave themselves."

Our friends had all made a good breakfast of the delicious popcorn and now they walked toward the house again. Button-Bright walked beside Trot and held her hand in his, because they were old friends and he liked the little girl very much. The boy was not so old as Trot, and small as she was he was half a head shorter in height. The most remarkable thing about Button-Bright was that he was always quiet and composed, whatever happened, and nothing was ever able to astonish him. Trot liked him because he was not rude and never tried to plague her. Cap'n Bill liked him because he had found the boy cheerful and brave at all times, and willing to do anything he was asked to do.

When they came to the house Trot sniffed the air and asked "Don't I smell perfume?"

"I think you do," said the Bumpy Man. "You smell violets, and that proves there is a breeze springing up from the south. All our winds and breezes are perfumed and for that reason we are glad to have them blow in our direction. The south breeze always has a violet odor; the north breeze has the fragrance of wild roses; the east breeze is perfumed with lilies-of-the-valley and the west wind with lilac blossoms. So we need no weathervane to tell us which way the wind is blowing. We have only to smell the perfume and it informs us at once."

Inside the house they found the Ork, and Button-Bright regarded the strange, birdlike creature with curious interest. After examining it closely for a time he asked: "Which way does your tail whirl?"

"Either way," said the Ork.

Button-Bright put out his hand and tried to spin it.

"Don't do that!" exclaimed the Ork.

"Why not?" inquired the boy.

"Because it happens to be my tail, and I reserve the right to whirl it myself," explained the Ork.

"Let's go out and fly somewhere," proposed Button-Bright. "I want to see how the tail works."

"Not now," said the Ork. "I appreciate your interest in me, which I fully deserve; but I only fly when I am going somewhere, and if I got started I might not stop."

"That reminds me," remarked Cap'n Bill, "to ask you, friend Ork, how we are going to get away from here?"

"Get away!" exclaimed the Bumpy Man. "Why don't you stay here? You won't find any nicer place than Mo."

"Have you been anywhere else, sir?"

"No; I can't say that I have," admitted the Mountain Ear.

"Then permit me to say you're no judge," declared Cap'n Bill. "But you haven't answered my question, friend Ork. How are we to get away from this mountain?"

The Ork reflected a while before he answered.

"I might carry one of you — the boy or the girl —upon my back," said he, "but three big people are more than I can manage, although I have carried two of you for a short distance. You ought not to have eaten those purple berries so soon."

"P'r'aps we did make a mistake," Cap'n Bill acknowledged.

"Or we might have brought some of those lavender berries with us, instead of so many purple ones," suggested Trot regretfully.

Cap'n Bill made no reply to this statement, which showed he did not fully agree with the little girl; but he fell into deep thought, with wrinkled brows, and finally he said: "If those purple berries would make anything grow bigger, whether it'd eaten the lavender ones or not, I could find a way out of our troubles."

They did not understand this speech and looked at the old sailor as if expecting him to explain what he meant. But just then a chorus of shrill cries rose from outside.

"Here! Let me go — let me go!" the voices seemed to say. "Why are we insulted in this way? Mountain Ear, come and help us!"

Trot ran to the window and looked out.

"It's the birds you caught, Cap'n," she said. "I didn't know they could talk."

"Oh, yes; all the birds in Mo are educated to talk," said the Bumpy Man. Then he looked at Cap'n Bill uneasily and added: "Won't you let the poor things go?"

"I'll see," replied the sailor, and walked out to where the birds were fluttering and complaining because the strings would not allow them to fly away.

"Listen to me!" he cried, and at once they became still. "We three people who are strangers in your land want to go to some other country, and we want three of you birds to carry us there. We know we are asking a great favor, but it's the only way we can think of — excep' walkin', an' I'm not much good at that because I've a wooden leg. Besides, Trot an' Button-Bright are too small to undertake a long and tiresome journey. Now, tell me: Which three of you birds will consent to carry us?"

The birds looked at one another as if greatly astonished. Then one of them replied: "You must be crazy, old man. Not one of us is big enough to fly with even the smallest of your party."

"I'll fix the matter of size," promised Cap'n Bill. "If three of you will agree to carry us, I'll make you big an' strong enough to do it, so it won't worry you a bit."

The birds considered this gravely. Living in a magic country, they had no doubt but that the strange one-legged man could do what he said. After a little, one of them asked: "If you make us big, would we stay big always?"

"I think so," replied Cap'n Bill.

They chattered a while among themselves and then the bird that had first spoken said: "I'll go, for one."

"So will I," said another; and after a pause a third said: "I'll go, too."

Perhaps more would have volunteered, for it seemed that for some reason they all longed to be bigger than they were; but three were enough for Cap'n Bill's purpose and so he promptly released all the others, who immediately flew away.

The three that remained were cousins, and all were of the same brilliant plumage and in size about as large as eagles. When Trot questioned them she found they were quite young, having only abandoned their nests a few weeks before. They were strong young birds, with clear, brave eyes, and the little girl decided they were the most beautiful of all the feathered creatures she had ever seen.

Cap'n Bill now took from his pocket the wooden box with the sliding cover and removed the three purple berries, which were still in good condition.

"Eat these," he said, and gave one to each of the birds. They obeyed, finding the fruit very pleasant to taste. In a few seconds they began to grow in size and grew so fast that Trot feared they would never stop. But they finally did stop growing, and then they were much larger than the Ork, and nearly the size of full-grown ostriches.

Cap'n Bill was much pleased by this result.

"You can carry us now, all right," said he.

The birds strutted around with pride, highly pleased with their immense size.

"I don't see, though," said Trot doubtfully, "how we're going to ride on their backs without falling off."

"We're not going to ride on their backs," answered Cap'n Bill. "I'm going to make swings for us to ride in."

He then asked the Bumpy Man for some rope, but the man had no rope. He had, however, an old suit of gray clothes which he gladly presented to Cap'n Bill, who cut the cloth into strips and twisted it so that it was almost as strong as rope. With this material he attached to each bird a swing that dangled below its feet, and Button-Bright made a trial flight in one of them to prove that it was safe and comfortable. When all this had been arranged one of the birds asked: "Where do you wish us to take you?"

"Why, just follow the Ork," said Cap'n Bill. "He will be our leader, and wherever the Ork flies you are to fly, and wherever the Ork lands you are to land. Is that satisfactory?"

The birds declared it was quite satisfactory, so Cap'n Bill took counsel with the Ork.

"On our way here," said that peculiar creature, "I noticed a broad, sandy desert at the left of me, on which was no living thing."

"Then we'd better keep away from it," replied the sailor.

"Not so," insisted the Ork. "I have found, on my travels, that the most pleasant countries often lie in the midst of deserts; so I think it would be wise for us to fly over this desert and discover what lies beyond it. For in the direction we came from lies the ocean, as we well know, and beyond here is this strange Land of Mo, which we do not care to explore. On one side, as we can see from this mountain, is a broad expanse of plain, and on the other the desert. For my part, I vote for the desert."

"What do you say, Trot?" inquired Cap'n Bill.

"It's all the same to me," she replied.

No one thought of asking Button-Bright's opinion, so it was decided to fly over the desert. They bade good-bye to the Bumpy Man and thanked him for his kindness and hospitality. Then they seated themselves in the swings — one for each bird — and told the Ork to start away and they would follow.

The whirl of the Ork's tail astonished the birds at first, but after he had gone a short distance they rose in the air, carrying their passengers easily, and flew with strong, regular strokes of their great wings in the wake of their leader.

9. The Kingdom of Jinxland

Trot rode with more comfort than she had expected, although the swing swayed so much that she had to hold on tight with both hands. Cap'n Bill's bird followed the Ork, and Trot came next, with Button-Bright trailing behind her. It was quite an imposing procession, but unfortunately there was no one to see it, for the Ork had headed straight for the great sandy desert and in a few minutes after starting they were flying high over the broad waste, where no living thing could exist.

The little girl thought this would be a bad place for the birds to lose strength, or for the cloth ropes to give way; but although she could not help feeling a trifle nervous and fidgety she had confidence in the huge and brilliantly plumaged bird that bore her, as well as in Cap'n Bill's knowledge of how to twist and fasten a rope so it would hold.

That was a remarkably big desert. There was nothing to relieve the monotony of view and every minute seemed an hour and every hour a day. Disagreeable fumes and gases rose from the sands, which would have been deadly to the travelers had they not been so high in the air. As it was, Trot was beginning to feel sick, when a breath of fresher air filled her nostrils and on looking ahead she saw a great cloud of pink-tinted mist. Even while she wondered what it could be, the Ork plunged boldly into the mist and the other birds followed. She could see nothing for a time, nor could the bird which carried her see where the Ork had gone, but it kept flying as sturdily as ever and in a few moments the mist was passed and the girl saw a most beautiful landscape spread out below her, extending as far as her eye could reach.

She saw bits of forest, verdure clothed hills, fields of waving grain, fountains, rivers and lakes; and throughout the scene were scattered groups of pretty houses and a few grand castles and palaces.

Over all this delightful landscape — which from Trot's high perch seemed like a magnificent painted picture — was a rosy glow such as we sometimes see in the west at sunset. In this case, however, it was not in the west only, but everywhere.

No wonder the Ork paused to circle slowly over this lovely country. The other birds followed his action, all eyeing the place with equal delight. Then, as with one accord, the four formed a group and slowly sailed downward. This brought them to that part of the newly-discovered land which bordered on the desert's edge; but it was just as pretty here as anywhere, so the Ork and the birds alighted and the three passengers at once got out of their swings.

"Oh, Cap'n Bill, isn't this fine an' dandy?" exclaimed Trot rapturously. "How lucky we were to discover this beautiful country!"

"The country seems rather high class, I'll admit, Trot," replied the old sailor-man, looking around him, "but we don't know, as yet, what its people are like."

"No one could live in such a country without being happy and good — I'm sure of that," she said earnestly. "Don't you think so, Button-Bright?"

"I'm not thinking, just now," answered the little boy. "It tires me to think, and I never seem to gain anything by it. When we see the people who live here we will know what they are like, and no 'mount of thinking will make them any different."

"That's true enough," said the Ork. "But now I want to make a proposal. While you are getting acquainted with this new country, which looks as if it contains everything to make one happy, I would like to fly along — all by myself — and see if I can find my home on the other side of the great desert. If I do, I will stay there, of course. But if I fail to find Orkland I will return to you in a week, to see if I can do anything more to assist you."

They were sorry to lose their queer companion, but could offer no objection to the plan; so the Ork bade them good-bye and rising swiftly in the air, he flew over the country and was soon lost to view in the distance.

The three birds which had carried our friends now begged permission to return by the way they had come, to their own homes, saying they were anxious to show their families how big they had become. So Cap'n Bill and Trot and Button-Bright all thanked them gratefully for their assistance and soon the birds began their long flight toward the Land of Mo. Being now left to themselves in this strange land, the three comrades selected a pretty pathway and began walking along it. They believed this path would lead them to a splendid castle which they espied in the distance, the turrets of which towered far above the tops of the trees which surrounded it. It did not seem very far away, so they sauntered on slowly, admiring the beautiful ferns and flowers that lined the pathway and listening to the singing of the birds and the soft chirping of the grasshoppers.

Presently the path wound over a little hill. In a valley that lay beyond the hill was a tiny cottage surrounded by flower beds and fruit trees. On the shady porch of the cottage they saw, as they approached, a pleasant faced woman sitting amidst a group of children, to whom she was telling stories. The children quickly discovered the strangers and ran toward them with exclamations of astonishment, so that Trot and her friends became the center of a curious group, all chattering excitedly. Cap'n Bill's wooden leg seemed to arouse the wonder of the children, as they could not understand why he had not two meat legs. This attention seemed to please the old sailor, who patted the heads of the children kindly and then, raising his hat to the woman, he inquired: "Can you tell us, madam, just what country this is?"

She stared hard at all three of the strangers as she replied briefly: "Jinxland."

"Oh!" exclaimed Cap'n Bill, with a puzzled look. "And where is Jinxland, please?"

"In the Quadling Country," said she.

"What!" cried Trot, in sudden excitement. "Do you mean to say this is the Quadling Country of the Land of Oz?"

"To be sure I do," the woman answered. "Every bit of land that is surrounded by the great desert is the Land of Oz, as you ought to know as well as I do; but I'm sorry to say that Jinxland is separated from the rest of the Quadling Country by that row of high mountains you see yonder, which have such steep sides that no one can cross them. So we live here all by ourselves, and are ruled by our own King, instead of by Ozma of Oz."

"I've been to the Land of Oz before," said Button-Bright, "but I've never been here."

"Did you ever hear of Jinxland before?" asked Trot.

"No," said Button-Bright.

"It is on the Map of Oz, though," asserted the woman, "and it's a fine country, I assure you. If only," she added, and then paused to look around her with a frightened expression. "If only —" here she stopped again, as if not daring to go on with her speech.

"If only what, ma'am?" asked Cap'n Bill.

The woman sent the children into the house. Then she came closer to the strangers and whispered: "If only we had a different King, we would be very happy and contented."

"What's the matter with your King?" asked Trot, curiously. But the woman seemed frightened to have said so much. She retreated to her porch, merely saying: "The King punishes severely any treason on the part of his subjects."

"What's treason?" asked Button-Bright.

"In this case," replied Cap'n Bill, "treason seems to consist of knockin' the King; but I guess we know his disposition now as well as if the lady had said more."

"I wonder," said Trot, going up to the woman, "if you could spare us something to eat. We haven't had anything but popcorn and lemonade for a long time."

"Bless your heart! Of course I can spare you some food," the woman answered, and entering her cottage she soon returned with a tray loaded with sandwiches, cakes and cheese. One of the children drew a bucket of clear, cold water from a spring and the three wanderers ate heartily and enjoyed the good things immensely.

When Button-Bright could eat no more he filled the pockets of his jacket with cakes and cheese, and not even the children objected to this. Indeed they all seemed pleased to see the strangers eat, so Cap'n Bill decided that no matter what the King of Jinxland was like, the people would prove friendly and hospitable.

"Whose castle is that, yonder, ma'am?" he asked, waving his hand toward the towers that rose above the trees.

"It belongs to his Majesty, King Krewl." she said.

"Oh, indeed; and does he live there?"

"When he is not out hunting with his fierce courtiers and war captains," she replied.

"Is he hunting now?" Trot inquired.

"I do not know, my dear. The less we know about the King's actions the safer we are."

It was evident the woman did not like to talk about King Krewl and so, having finished their meal, they said good-bye and continued along the pathway.

"Don't you think we'd better keep away from that King's castle Cap'n?" asked Trot.

"Well," said he, "King Krewl would find out, sooner or later, that we are in his country, so we may as well face the music now. Perhaps he isn't quite so bad as that woman thinks he is. Kings aren't always popular with their people, you know, even if they do the best they know how."

"Ozma is pop'lar," said Button-Bright.

"Ozma is diff'rent from any other Ruler, from all I've heard," remarked Trot musingly, as she walked beside the boy. "And, after all, we are really in the Land of Oz, where Ozma rules ev'ry King and ev'rybody else. I never heard of anybody getting hurt in her dominions, did you, Button-Bright?"

"Not when she knows about it," he replied. "But those birds landed us in just the wrong place, seems to me. They might have carried us right on, over that row of mountains, to the Em'rald City."

"True enough," said Cap'n Bill; "but they didn't, an' so we must make the best of Jinxland. Let's try not to be afraid."

"Oh, I'm not very scared," said Button-Bright, pausing to look at a pink rabbit that popped its head out of a hole in the field near by.

"Nor am I," added Trot. "Really, Cap'n, I'm so glad to be anywhere at all in the wonderful fairyland of Oz that I think I'm the luckiest girl in all the world. Dorothy lives in the Em'rald City, you know, and so does the Scarecrow and the Tin Woodman and Tik-Tok and the Shaggy Man — and all the rest of 'em that we've heard so much about — not to mention Ozma, who must be the sweetest and loveliest girl in all the world!"

"Take your time, Trot," advised Button-Bright. "You don't have to say it all in one breath, you know. And you haven't mentioned half of the curious people in the Em'rald City."

"That 'ere Em'rald City," said Cap'n Bill impressively, "happens to be on the other side o' those mountains, that we're told no one is able to cross. I don't want to discourage of you, Trot, but we're a'most as much separated from your Ozma an' Dorothy as we were when we lived in Californy."

There was so much truth in this statement that they all walked on in silence for some time. Finally they reached the grove of stately trees that bordered the grounds of the King's castle. They had gone halfway through it when the sound of sobbing, as of someone in bitter distress, reached their ears and caused them to halt abruptly.

10. Pon, the Gardener's Boy

It was Button-Bright who first discovered, lying on his face beneath a broad spreading tree near the pathway, a young man whose body shook with the force of his sobs. He was dressed in a long brown smock and had sandals on his feet, betokening one in humble life. His head was bare and showed a shock of brown, curly hair. Button-Bright looked down on the young man and said: "Who cares, anyhow?"

"I do!" cried the young man, interrupting his sobs to roll over, face upward, that he might see who had spoken. "I care, for my heart is broken!"

"Can't you get another one?" asked the little boy.

"I don't want another!" wailed the young man.

By this time Trot and Cap'n Bill arrived at the spot and the girl leaned over and said in a sympathetic voice:

"Tell us your troubles and perhaps we may help you."

The youth sat up, then, and bowed politely. Afterward he got upon his feet, but still kept wringing his hands as he tried to choke down his sobs. Trot thought he was very brave to control such awful agony so well.

"My name is Pon," he began. "I'm the gardener's boy."

"Then the gardener of the King is your father, I suppose," said Trot.

"Not my father, but my master," was the reply

"I do the work and the gardener gives the orders. And it was not my fault, in the least, that the Princess Gloria fell in love with me."

"Did she, really?" asked the little girl.

"I don't see why," remarked Button-Bright, staring at the youth.

"And who may the Princess Gloria be?" inquired Cap'n Bill.

"She is the niece of King Krewl, who is her guardian. The Princess lives in the castle and is the loveliest and sweetest maiden in all Jinxland. She is fond of flowers and used to walk in the gardens with her attendants. At such times, if I was working at my tasks, I used to cast down my eyes as Gloria passed me; but one day I glanced up and found her gazing at me with a very tender look in her eyes. The next day she dismissed her attendants and, coming to my side, began to talk with me. She said I had touched her heart as no other young man had ever done. I kissed her hand. Just then the King came around a bend in the walk. He struck me with his fist and kicked me with his foot. Then he seized the arm of the Princess and rudely dragged her into the castle."

"Wasn't he awful!" gasped Trot indignantly.

"He is a very abrupt King," said Pon, "so it was the least I could expect. Up to that time I had not thought of loving Princess Gloria, but realizing it would be impolite not to return her love, I did so. We met at evening, now and then, and she told me the King wanted her to marry a rich courtier named Googly-Goo, who is old enough to be Gloria's father. She has refused Googly-Goo thirty-nine times, but he still persists and has brought many rich presents to bribe the King. On that account King Krewl has commanded his niece to marry the old man, but the Princess has assured me, time and again, that she will wed only me. This morning we happened to meet in the grape arbor and as I was respectfully saluting the cheek of the Princess, two of the King's guards seized me and beat me terribly before the very eyes of Gloria, whom the King himself held back so she could not interfere."

"Why, this King must be a monster!" cried Trot.

"He is far worse than that," said Pon, mournfully.

"But, see here," interrupted Cap'n Bill, who had listened carefully to Pon. "This King may not be so much to blame, after all. Kings are proud folks, because they're so high an' mighty, an' it isn't reasonable for a royal Princess to marry a common gardener's boy."

"It isn't right," declared Button-Bright. "A Princess should marry a Prince."

"I'm not a common gardener's boy," protested Pon. "If I had my rights I would be the King instead of Krewl. As it is, I'm a Prince, and as royal as any man in Jinxland."

"How does that come?" asked Cap'n Bill.

"My father used to be the King and Krewl was his Prime Minister. But one day while out hunting, King Phearse — that was my father's name — had a quarrel with Krewl and tapped him gently on the nose with the knuckles of his closed hand. This so provoked the wicked Krewl that he tripped my father backward, so that he fell into a deep pond. At once Krewl threw in a mass of heavy stones, which so weighted down my poor father that his body could not rise again to the surface. It is impossible to kill anyone in this land, as perhaps you know, but when my father was pressed down into the mud at the bottom of the deep pool and the stones held him so he could never escape, he was of no more use to himself or the world than if he had died. Knowing this, Krewl proclaimed himself King, taking possession of the royal castle and driving all my father's people out. I was a small boy, then, but when I grew up I became a gardener. I have served King Krewl without his knowing that I am the son of the same King Phearse whom he so cruelly made away with."

"My, but that's a terr'bly exciting story!" said Trot, drawing a long breath. "But tell us, Pon, who was Gloria's father?"

"Oh, he was the King before my father," replied Pon. "Father was Prime Minister for King Kynd, who was Gloria's father. She was only a baby when King Kynd fell into the Great Gulf that lies just this side of the mountains — the same mountains that separate Jinxland from the rest of the Land of Oz. It is said the Great Gulf has no bottom; but, however that may be, King Kynd has never been seen again and my father became King in his place."

"Seems to me," said Trot, "that if Gloria had her rights she would be Queen of Jinxland."

"Well, her father was a King," admitted Pon, "and so was my father; so we are of equal rank, although she's a great lady and I'm a humble gardener's boy. I can't see why we should not marry if we want to except that King Krewl won't let us."

"It's a sort of mixed-up mess, taken altogether," remarked Cap'n Bill. "But we are on our way to visit King Krewl, and if we get a chance, young man, we'll put in a good word for you."

"Do, please!" begged Pon.

"Was it the flogging you got that broke your heart?" inquired Button-Bright.

"Why, it helped to break it, of course," said Pon.

"I'd get it fixed up, if I were you," advised the boy, tossing a pebble at a chipmunk in a tree. "You ought to give Gloria just as good a heart as she gives you."

"That's common sense," agreed Cap'n Bill. So they left the gardener's boy standing beside the path, and resumed their journey toward the castle.

11. The Wicked King and Googly-Goo

When our friends approached the great doorway of the castle they found it guarded by several soldiers dressed in splendid uniforms. They were armed with swords and lances. Cap'n Bill walked straight up to them and asked: "Does the King happen to be at home?"

"His Magnificent and Glorious Majesty, King Krewl, is at present inhabiting his Royal Castle," was the stiff reply.

"Then I guess we'll go in an' say how-d'ye-do," continued Cap'n Bill, attempting to enter the doorway. But a soldier barred his way with a lance.

"Who are you, what are your names, and where do you come from?" demanded the soldier.

"You wouldn't know if we told you," returned the sailor, "seein' as we're strangers in a strange land."

"Oh, if you are strangers you will be permitted to enter," said the soldier, lowering his lance. "His Majesty is very fond of strangers."

"Do many strangers come here?" asked Trot.

"You are the first that ever came to our country," said the man. "But his Majesty has often said that if strangers ever arrived in Jinxland he would see that they had a very exciting time."

Cap'n Bill scratched his chin thoughtfully. He wasn't very favorably impressed by this last remark. But he decided that as there was no way of escape from Jinxland it would be wise to confront the King boldly and try to win his favor. So they entered the castle, escorted by one of the soldiers.

It was certainly a fine castle, with many large rooms, all beautifully furnished. The passages were winding and handsomely decorated, and after following several of these the soldier led them into an open court that occupied the very center of the huge building. It was surrounded on every side by high turreted walls, and contained beds of flowers, fountains and walks of many colored marbles which were matched together in quaint designs. In an open space near the middle of the court they saw a group of courtiers and their ladies, who surrounded a lean man who wore upon his head a jeweled crown. His face was hard and sullen and through the slits of his half-closed eyelids the eyes glowed like coals of fire. He was dressed in brilliant satins and velvets and was seated in a golden throne-chair.

This personage was King Krewl, and as soon as Cap'n Bill saw him the old sailor knew at once that he was not going to like the King of Jinxland.

"Hello! who's here?" said his Majesty, with a deep scowl.

"Strangers, Sire," answered the soldier, bowing so low that his forehead touched the marble tiles.

"Strangers, eh? Well, well; what an unexpected visit! Advance, strangers, and give an account of yourselves."

The King's voice was as harsh as his features. Trot shuddered a little but Cap'n Bill calmly replied: "There ain't much for us to say, 'cept as we've arrived to look over your country an' see how we like it. Judgin' from the way you speak, you don't know who we are, or you'd be jumpin' up to shake hands an' offer us seats. Kings usually treat us pretty well, in the great big Outside World where we come from, but in this little kingdom — which don't amount to much, anyhow — folks don't seem to 'a' got much culchure."

The King listened with amazement to this bold speech, first with a frown and then gazing at the two children and the old sailor with evident curiosity. The courtiers were dumb with fear, for no one had ever dared speak in such a manner to their self-willed, cruel King before. His Majesty, however, was somewhat frightened, for cruel people are always cowards, and he feared these mysterious strangers might possess magic powers that would destroy him unless he treated them well. So he commanded his people to give the new arrivals seats, and they obeyed with trembling haste.

After being seated, Cap'n Bill lighted his pipe and began puffing smoke from it, a sight so strange to them that it filled them all with wonder. Presently the King asked: "How did you penetrate to this hidden country? Did you cross the desert or the mountains?"

"Desert," answered Cap'n Bill, as if the task were too easy to be worth talking about.

"Indeed! No one has ever been able to do that before," said the King.

"Well, it's easy enough, if you know how," asserted Cap'n Bill, so carelessly that it greatly impressed his hearers. The King shifted in his throne uneasily. He was more afraid of these strangers than before.

"Do you intend to stay long in Jinxland?" was his next anxious question.

"Depends on how we like it," said Cap'n Bill. "Just now I might suggest to your Majesty to order some rooms got ready for us in your dinky little castle here. And a royal banquet, with some fried onions an' pickled tripe, would set easy on our stomicks an' make us a bit happier than we are now."

"Your wishes shall be attended to," said King Krewl, but his eyes flashed from between their slits in a wicked way that made Trot hope the food wouldn't be poisoned. At the King's command several of his attendants hastened away to give the proper orders to the castle servants and no sooner were they gone than a skinny old man entered the courtyard and bowed before the King.

This disagreeable person was dressed in rich velvets, with many furbelows and laces. He was covered with golden chains, finely wrought rings and jeweled ornaments. He walked with mincing steps and glared at all the courtiers as if he considered himself far superior to any or all of them.

"Well, well, your Majesty; what news — what news?" he demanded, in a shrill, cracked voice.

The King gave him a surly look.

"No news, Lord Googly-Goo, except that strangers have arrived," he said.

Googly-Goo cast a contemptuous glance at Cap'n Bill and a disdainful one at Trot and Button-Bright. Then he said: "Strangers do not interest me, your Majesty. But the Princess Gloria is very interesting — very interesting, indeed! What does she say, Sire? Will she marry me?"

"Ask her," retorted the King.

"I have, many times; and every time she has refused."

"Well?" said the King harshly.

"Well," said Googly-Goo in a jaunty tone, "a bird that can sing, and won't sing, must be made to sing."

"Huh!" sneered the King. "That's easy, with a bird; but a girl is harder to manage."

"Still," persisted Googly-Goo, "we must overcome difficulties. The chief trouble is that Gloria fancies she loves that miserable gardener's boy, Pon. Suppose we throw Pon into the Great Gulf, your Majesty?"

"It would do you no good," returned the King. "She would still love him."

"Too bad, too bad!" sighed Googly-Goo. "I have laid aside more than a bushel of precious gems —each worth a king's ransom — to present to your Majesty on the day I wed Gloria."

The King's eyes sparkled, for he loved wealth above everything; but the next moment he frowned deeply again.

"It won't help us to kill Pon," he muttered. "What we must do is kill Gloria's love for Pon."

"That is better, if you can find a way to do it," agreed Googly-Goo. "Everything would come right if you could kill Gloria's love for that gardener's boy. Really, Sire, now that I come to think of it, there must be fully a bushel and a half of those jewels!"

Just then a messenger entered the court to say that the banquet was prepared for the strangers. So Cap'n Bill, Trot and Button-Bright entered the castle and were taken to a room where a fine feast was spread upon the table.

"I don't like that Lord Googly-Goo," remarked Trot as she was busily eating.

"Nor I," said Cap'n Bill. "But from the talk we heard I guess the gardener's boy won't get the Princess."

"Perhaps not," returned the girl; "but I hope old Googly doesn't get her, either."

"The King means to sell her for all those jewels," observed Button-Bright, his mouth half full of cake and jam.

"Poor Princess!" sighed Trot. "I'm sorry for her, although I've never seen her. But if she says no to Googly-Goo, and means it, what can they do?"

"Don't let us worry about a strange Princess," advised Cap'n Bill. "I've a notion we're not too safe, ourselves, with this cruel King."

The two children felt the same way and all three were rather solemn during the remainder of the meal.

When they had eaten, the servants escorted them to their rooms. Cap'n Bill's room was way to one end of the castle, very high up, and Trot's room was at the opposite end, rather low down. As for Button-Bright, they placed him in the middle, so that all were as far apart as they could possibly be. They didn't like this arrangement very well, but all the rooms were handsomely furnished and being guests of the King they dared not complain.

After the strangers had left the courtyard the King and Googly-Goo had a long talk together, and the King said: "I cannot force

Gloria to marry you just now, because those strangers may interfere. I suspect that the wooden-legged man possesses great magical powers, or he would never have been able to carry himself and those children across the deadly desert."

"I don't like him; he looks dangerous," answered Googly-Goo. "But perhaps you are mistaken about his being a wizard. Why don't you test his powers?"

"How?" asked the King.

"Send for the Wicked Witch. She will tell you in a moment whether that wooden-legged person is a common man or a magician."

"Ha! that's a good idea," cried the King. "Why didn't I think of the Wicked Witch before? But the woman demands rich rewards for her services."

"Never mind; I will pay her," promised the wealthy Googly-Goo.

So a servant was dispatched to summon the Wicked Witch, who lived but a few leagues from King Krewl's castle. While they awaited her, the withered old courtier proposed that they pay a visit to Princess Gloria and see if she was not now in a more complaisant mood. So the two started away together and searched the castle over without finding Gloria.

At last Googly-Goo suggested she might be in the rear garden, which was a large park filled with bushes and trees and surrounded by a high wall. And what was their anger, when they turned a corner of the path, to find in a quiet nook the beautiful Princess, and kneeling before her, Pon, the gardener's boy! With a roar of rage the King dashed forward; but Pon had scaled the wall by means of a ladder, which still stood in its place, and when he saw the King coming he ran up the ladder and made good his escape. But this left Gloria confronted by her angry guardian, the King, and by old Googly-Goo, who was trembling with a fury he could not express in words.

Seizing the Princess by her arm the King dragged her back to the castle. Pushing her into a room on the lower floor he locked the door upon the unhappy girl. And at that moment the arrival of the Wicked Witch was announced.

Hearing this, the King smiled, as a tiger smiles, showing his teeth. And Googly-Goo smiled, as a serpent smiles, for he had no teeth except a couple of fangs. And having frightened each other with these smiles the two dreadful men went away to the Royal Council Chamber to meet the Wicked Witch.

12. The Wooden-Legged Grass-Hopper

Now it so happened that Trot, from the window of her room, had witnessed the meeting of the lovers in the garden and had seen the King come and drag Gloria away. The little girl's heart went out in sympathy for the poor Princess, who seemed to her to be one of the sweetest and loveliest young ladies she had ever seen, so she crept along the passages and from a hidden niche saw Gloria locked in her room.

The key was still in the lock, so when the King had gone away, followed by Googly-Goo, Trot stole up to the door, turned the key and entered. The Princess lay prone upon a couch, sobbing bitterly. Trot went up to her and smoothed her hair and tried to comfort her.

"Don't cry," she said. "I've unlocked the door, so you can go away

any time you want to."

"It isn't that," sobbed the Princess. "I am unhappy because they will not let me love Pon, the gardener's boy!"

"Well, never mind; Pon isn't any great shakes, anyhow, seems to me," said Trot soothingly. "There are lots of other people you can love."

Gloria rolled over on the couch and looked at the little girl reproachfully.

"Pon has won my heart, and I can't help loving him," she explained. Then with sudden indignation she added: "But I'll never love Googly-Goo — never, as long as I live!"

"I should say not!" replied Trot. "Pon may not be much good, but old Googly is very, very bad. Hunt around, and I'm sure you'll find someone worth your love. You're very pretty, you know, and almost anyone ought to love you."

"You don't understand, my dear," said Gloria, as she wiped the tears from her eyes with a dainty lace handkerchief bordered with pearls. "When you are older you will realize that a young lady cannot decide whom she will love, or choose the most worthy. Her heart alone decides for her, and whomsoever her heart selects, she must love, whether he amounts to much or not."

Trot was a little puzzled by this speech, which seemed to her unreasonable; but she made no reply and presently Gloria's grief softened and she began to question the little girl about herself and her adventures. Trot told her how they had happened to come to Jinxland, and all about Cap'n Bill and the Ork and Pessim and the Bumpy Man.

While they were thus conversing together, getting more and more friendly as they became better acquainted, in the Council Chamber the King and Googly-Goo were talking with the Wicked Witch.

This evil creature was old and ugly. She had lost one eye and wore a black patch over it, so the people of Jinxland had named her "Blinkie." Of course witches are forbidden to exist in the Land of Oz, but Jinxland was so far removed from the center of Ozma's dominions, and so absolutely cut off from it by the steep mountains and the bottomless gulf, that the laws of Oz were not obeyed very well in that country. So there were several witches in Jinxland who were the terror of the people, but King Krewl favored them and permitted them to exercise their evil sorcery.

Blinkie was the leader of all the other witches and therefore the most hated and feared. The King used her witchcraft at times to assist him in carrying out his cruelties and revenge, but he was always obliged to pay Blinkie large sums of money or heaps of precious jewels before she would undertake an enchantment. This made him hate the old woman almost as much as his subjects did, but to-day Lord Googly-Goo had agreed to pay the witch's price, so the King greeted her with gracious favor.

"Can you destroy the love of Princess Gloria for the gardener's boy?" inquired his Majesty.

The Wicked Witch thought about it before she replied: "That's a hard question to answer. I can do lots of clever magic, but love is a stubborn thing to conquer. When you think you've killed it, it is liable to bob up again as strong as ever. I believe love and cats have nine lives. In other words, killing love is a hard job, even for a skillful witch, but I believe I can do something that will answer your purpose just as well."

"What is that?" asked the King.

"I can freeze the girl's heart. I've got a special incantation for that, and when Gloria's heart is thoroughly frozen she can no longer love Pon."

"Just the thing!" exclaimed Googly-Goo, and the King was likewise much pleased.

They bargained a long time as to the price, but finally the old courtier agreed to pay the Wicked Witch's demands. It was arranged that they should take Gloria to Blinkie's house the next day, to have her heart frozen.

Then King Krewl mentioned to the old hag the strangers who had that day arrived in Jinxland, and said to her: "I think the two children — the boy and the girl — are unable to harm me, but I have a suspicion that the wooden-legged man is a powerful wizard."

The witch's face wore a troubled look when she heard this.

"If you are right," she said, "this wizard might spoil my incantation and interfere with me in other ways. So it will be best for me to meet this stranger at once and match my magic against his, to decide which is the stronger."

"All right," said the King. "Come with me and I will lead you to the man's room."

Googly-Goo did not accompany them, as he was obliged to go home to get the money and jewels he had promised to pay old Blinkie, so the other two climbed several flights of stairs and went through many passages until they came to the room occupied by Cap'n Bill.

The sailor-man, finding his bed soft and inviting, and being tired with the adventures he had experienced, had decided to take a nap. When the Wicked Witch and the King softly opened his door and entered, Cap'n Bill was snoring with such vigor that he did not hear them at all.

Blinkie approached the bed and with her one eye anxiously stared at the sleeping stranger.

"Ah," she said in a soft whisper, "I believe you are right, King Krewl. The man looks to me like a very powerful wizard. But by good luck I have caught him asleep, so I shall transform him before he wakes up, giving him such a form that he will be unable to oppose me."

"Careful!" cautioned the King, also speaking low. "If he discovers what you are doing he may destroy you, and that would annoy me because I need you to attend to Gloria."

But the Wicked Witch realized as well as he did that she must be careful. She carried over her arm a black bag, from which she now drew several packets carefully wrapped in paper. Three of these she selected, replacing the others in the bag. Two of the packets she mixed together. and then she cautiously opened the third.

"Better stand back, your Majesty," she advised, "for if this powder falls on you you might be transformed yourself."

The King hastily retreated to the end of the room. As Blinkie mixed the third powder with the others she waved her hands over it, mumbled a few words, and then backed away as quickly as she could.

Cap'n Bill was slumbering peacefully, all unconscious of what was going on. Puff! A great cloud of smoke rolled over the bed and completely hid him from view. When the smoke rolled away, both Blinkie and the King saw that the body of the stranger had quite disappeared, while in his place, crouching in the middle of the bed, was a little gray grasshopper.

One curious thing about this grasshopper was that the last joint of its left leg was made of wood. Another curious thing — considering it was a grasshopper — was that it began talking, crying out in a tiny but sharp voice: "Here — you people! What do you mean by treating me so? Put me back where I belong, at once, or you'll be sorry!"

The cruel King turned pale at hearing the grasshopper's threats, but the Wicked Witch merely laughed in derision. Then she raised her stick and aimed a vicious blow at the grasshopper, but before the stick struck the bed the tiny hopper made a marvelous jump — marvelous, indeed, when we consider that it had a wooden leg. It rose in the air and sailed across the room and passed right through the open window, where it disappeared from their view.

"Good!" shouted the King. "We are well rid of this desperate wizard." And then they both laughed heartily at the success of the incantation, and went away to complete their horrid plans.

After Trot had visited a time with Princess Gloria, the little girl went to Button-Bright's room but did not find him there. Then she went to Cap'n Bill's room, but he was not there because the witch and the King had been there before her. So she made her way downstairs and questioned the servants. They said they had seen the little boy go out into the garden, some time ago, but the old man with the wooden leg they had not seen at all.

Therefore Trot, not knowing what else to do, rambled through the great gardens, seeking for Button-Bright or Cap'n Bill and not finding either of them. This part of the garden, which lay before the castle, was not walled in, but extended to the roadway, and the paths were open to the edge of the forest; so, after two hours of vain search for her friends, the little girl returned to the castle.

But at the doorway a soldier stopped her.

"I live here," said Trot, "so it's all right to let me in. The King has given me a room."

"Well, he has taken it back again," was the soldier's reply. "His Majesty's orders are to turn you away if you attempt to enter. I am also ordered to forbid the boy, your companion, to again enter the King's castle."

"How 'bout Cap'n Bill?" she inquired.

"Why, it seems he has mysteriously disappeared," replied the soldier, shaking his head ominously. "Where he has gone to, I can't make out, but I can assure you he is no longer in this castle. I'm sorry, little girl, to disappoint you. Don't blame me; I must obey my master's orders."

Now, all her life Trot had been accustomed to depend on Cap'n Bill, so when this good friend was suddenly taken from her she felt very miserable and forlorn indeed. She was brave enough not to cry before the soldier, or even to let him see her grief and anxiety, but after she was turned away from the castle she sought a quiet bench in the garden and for a time sobbed as if her heart would break.

It was Button-Bright who found her, at last, just as the sun had set and the shades of evening were falling. He also had been turned away from the King's castle, when he tried to enter it, and in the park he came across Trot.

"Never mind," said the boy. "We can find a place to sleep."

"I want Cap'n Bill," wailed the girl.

"Well, so do I," was the reply. "But we haven't got him. Where do you s'pose he is, Trot?"

"I don't s'pose anything. He's gone, an' that's all I know 'bout it."

Button-Bright sat on the bench beside her and thrust his hands in the pockets of his knickerbockers. Then he reflected somewhat gravely for him.

"Cap'n Bill isn't around here," he said, letting his eyes wander over the dim garden, "so we must go somewhere else if we want to find him. Besides, it's fast getting dark, and if we want to find a place to sleep we must get busy while we can see where to go."

He rose from the bench as he said this and Trot also jumped up, drying her eyes on her apron. Then she walked beside him out of the grounds of the King's castle. They did not go by the main path, but passed through an opening in a hedge and found themselves in a small but well-worn roadway. Following this for some distance, along a winding way, they came upon no house or building that would afford them refuge for the night. It became so dark that they could scarcely see their way, and finally Trot stopped and suggested that they camp under a tree.

"All right," said Button-Bright, "I've often found that leaves make a good warm blanket. But — look there, Trot! — isn't that a light flashing over yonder?"

"It certainly is, Button-Bright. Let's go over and see if it's a house. Whoever lives there couldn't treat us worse than the King did."

To reach the light they had to leave the road, so they stumbled over hillocks and brushwood, hand in hand, keeping the tiny speck of light always in sight.

They were rather forlorn little waifs, outcasts in a strange country and forsaken by their only friend and guardian, Cap'n Bill. So they were very glad when finally they reached a small cottage and, looking in through its one window, saw Pon, the gardener's boy, sitting by a fire of twigs.

As Trot opened the door and walked boldly in, Pon sprang up to greet them. They told him of Cap'n Bill's disappearance and how they had been turned out of the King's castle. As they finished the story Pon shook his head sadly.

"King Krewl is plotting mischief, I fear," said he, "for to-day he sent for old Blinkie, the Wicked Witch, and with my own eyes I saw her come from the castle and hobble away toward her hut. She had been with the King and Googly-Goo, and I was afraid they were going to work some enchantment on Gloria so she would no longer love me. But perhaps the witch was only called

to the castle to enchant your friend, Cap'n Bill."

"Could she do that?" asked Trot, horrified by the suggestion.

"I suppose so, for old Blinkie can do a lot of wicked magical things."

"What sort of an enchantment could she put on Cap'n Bill?"

"I don't know. But he has disappeared, so I'm pretty certain she has done something dreadful to him. But don't worry. If it has happened, it can't be helped, and if it hasn't happened we may be able to find him in the morning."

With this Pon went to the cupboard and brought food for them. Trot was far too worried to eat, but Button-Bright made a good supper from the simple food and then lay down before the fire and went to sleep. The little girl and the gardener's boy, however, sat for a long time staring into the fire, busy with their thoughts. But at last Trot, too, became sleepy and Pon gently covered her with the one blanket he possessed. Then he threw more wood on the fire and laid himself down before it, next to Button-Bright. Soon all three were fast asleep. They were in a good deal of trouble; but they were young, and sleep was good to them because for a time it made them forget.

13. Glinda the Good and the Scarecrow of Oz

That country south of the Emerald City, in the Land of Oz, is known as the Quadling Country, and in the very southernmost part of it stands a splendid palace in which lives Glinda the Good.

Glinda is the Royal Sorceress of Oz. She has wonderful magical powers and uses them only to benefit the subjects of Ozma's kingdom. Even the famous Wizard of Oz pays tribute to her, for Glinda taught him all the real magic he knows, and she is his superior in all sorts of sorcery Everyone loves Glinda, from the dainty and exquisite Ruler, Ozma, down to the humblest inhabitant of Oz, for she is always kindly and helpful and willing to listen to their troubles, however busy she may be. No one knows her age, but all can see how beautiful and stately she is. Her hair is like red gold and finer than the finest silken strands. Her eyes are blue as the sky and always frank and smiling. Her cheeks are the envy of peach-blows and her mouth is enticing as a rosebud. Glinda is tall and wears splendid gowns that trail behind her as she walks. She wears no jewels, for her beauty would shame them.

For attendants Glinda has half a hundred of the loveliest girls in Oz. They are gathered from all over Oz, from among the Winkies, the Munchkins, the Gillikins and the Quadlings, as well as from Ozma's magnificent Emerald City, and it is considered a great favor to be allowed to serve the Royal Sorceress.

Among the many wonderful things in Glinda's palace is the Great Book of Records. In this book is inscribed everything that takes place in all the world, just the instant it happens; so that by referring to its pages Glinda knows what is taking place far and near, in every country that exists. In this way she learns when and where she can help any in distress or danger, and although her duties are confined to assisting those who inhabit the Land of Oz, she is always interested in what takes place in the unprotected outside world.

So it was that on a certain evening Glinda sat in her library, surrounded by a bevy of her maids, who were engaged in spinning, weaving and embroidery, when an attendant announced the arrival at the palace of the Scarecrow.

This personage was one of the most famous and popular in all the Land of Oz. His body was merely a suit of Munchkin clothes stuffed with straw, but his head was a round sack filled with bran, with which the Wizard of Oz had mixed some magic brains of a very superior sort. The eyes, nose and mouth of the Scarecrow were painted upon the front of the sack, as were his ears, and since this quaint being had been endowed with life, the expression of his face was very interesting, if somewhat comical.

The Scarecrow was good all through, even to his brains, and while he was naturally awkward in his movements and lacked the neat symmetry of other people, his disposition was so kind and considerate and he was so obliging and honest, that all who knew him loved him, and there were few people in Oz who had not met our Scarecrow and made his acquaintance. He lived part of the time in Ozma's palace at the Emerald City, part of the time in his own corncob castle in the Winkie Country, and part of the time he traveled over all Oz, visiting with the people and playing with the children, whom he dearly loved.

It was on one of his wandering journeys that the Scarecrow had arrived at Glinda's palace, and the Sorceress at once made him welcome. As he sat beside her, talking of his adventures, he asked: "What's new in the way of news?"

Glinda opened her Great Book of Records and read some of the last pages.

Here is an item quite curious and interesting," she announced, an accent of surprise in her voice. "Three people from the big Outside World have arrived in Jinxland."

Where is Jinxland?" inquired the Scarecrow.

Very near here, a little to the east of us," she said. "In fact, Jinxland is a little slice taken off the Quadling Country, but separated from it by a range of high mountains, at the foot of which lies a wide, deep gulf that is supposed to be impassable."

Then Jinxland is really a part of the Land of Oz," said he.

Yes," returned Glinda, "but Oz people know nothing of it, except what is recorded here in my book."

What does the Book say about it?" asked the Scarecrow.

It is ruled by a wicked man called King Krewl, although he has no right to the title. Most of the people are good, but they are very timid and live in constant fear of their fierce ruler. There are also several Wicked Witches who keep the inhabitants of Jinxland in a state of terror."

Do those witches have any magical powers?" inquired the Scarecrow.

Yes, they seem to understand witchcraft in its most evil form, for one of them has just transformed a respectable and honest old sailor — one of the strangers who arrived there — into a grasshopper. This same witch, Blinkie by name, is also planning to freeze the heart of a beautiful Jinxland girl named Princess Gloria."

Why, that's a dreadful thing to do!" exclaimed the Scarecrow.

Glinda's face was very grave. She read in her book how Trot and Button-Bright were turned out of the King's castle, and how they found refuge in the hut of Pon, the gardener's boy

"I'm afraid those helpless earth people will endure much suffering in Jinxland, even if the wicked King and the witches permit them to live," said the good Sorceress, thoughtfully. "I wish I might help them."

"Can I do anything?" asked the Scarecrow, anxiously. "If so, tell me what to do, and I'll do it."

For a few moments Glinda did not reply, but sat musing over the records. Then she said: "I am going to send you to Jinxland, to protect Trot and Button-Bright and Cap'n Bill."

"All right," answered the Scarecrow in a cheerful voice. "I know Button-Bright already, for he has been in the Land of Oz before. You remember he went away from the Land of Oz in one of our Wizard's big bubbles."

"Yes," said Glinda, "I remember that." Then she carefully instructed the Scarecrow what to do and gave him certain magical things which he placed in the pockets of his ragged Munchkin coat.

"As you have no need to sleep," said she, "you may as well start at once."

"The night is the same as day to me," he replied, "except that I cannot see my way so well in the dark."

"I will furnish a light to guide you," promised the Sorceress.

So the Scarecrow bade her good-bye and at once started on his journey. By morning he had reached the mountains that separated the Quadling Country from Jinxland. The sides of these mountains were too steep to climb, but the Scarecrow took a small rope from his pocket and tossed one end upward, into the air. The rope unwound itself for hundreds of feet, until it caught upon a peak of rock at the very top of a mountain, for it was a magic rope furnished him by Glinda. The Scarecrow climbed the rope and, after pulling it up, let it down on the other side of the mountain range. When he descended the rope on this side he found himself in Jinxland, but at his feet yawned the Great Gulf, which must be crossed before he could proceed any farther.

The Scarecrow knelt down and examined the ground carefully, and in a moment he discovered a fuzzy brown spider that had rolled itself into a ball. So he took two tiny pills from his pocket and laid them beside the spider, which unrolled itself and quickly ate up the pills. Then the Scarecrow said in a voice of command: "Spin!" and the spider obeyed instantly.

In a few moments the little creature had spun two slender but strong strands that reached way across the gulf, one being five or six feet above the other. When these were completed the Scarecrow started across the tiny bridge, walking upon one strand as a person walks upon a rope, and holding to the upper strand with his hands to prevent him from losing his balance and toppling over into the gulf. The tiny threads held him safely, thanks to the strength given them by the magic pills.

Presently he was safe across and standing on the plains of Jinxland. Far away he could see the towers of the King's castle and toward this he at once began to walk.

14. The Frozen Heart

In the hut of Pon, the gardener's boy, Button-Bright was the first to waken in the morning. Leaving his companions still asleep, he went out into the fresh morning air and saw some blackberries growing on bushes in a field not far away. Going to the bushes he found the berries ripe and sweet, so he began eating them. More bushes were scattered over the fields, so the boy wandered on, from bush to bush, without paying any heed to where he was wandering. Then a butterfly fluttered by. He gave chase to it and followed it a long way. When finally he paused to look around him, Button-Bright could see no sign of Pon's house, nor had he the slightest idea in which direction it lay.

"Well, I'm lost again," he remarked to himself. "But never mind; I've been lost lots of times. Someone is sure to find me."

Trot was a little worried about Button-Bright when she awoke and found him gone. Knowing how careless he was, she believed that he had strayed away, but felt that he would come back in time, because he had a habit of not staying lost. Pon got the little girl some food for her breakfast and then together they went out of the hut and stood in the sunshine.

Pon's house was some distance off the road, but they could see it from where they stood and both gave a start of surprise when they discovered two soldiers walking along the roadway and escorting Princess Gloria between them. The poor girl had her hands bound together, to prevent her from struggling, and the soldiers rudely dragged her forward when her steps seemed to lag.

Behind this group came King Krewl, wearing his jeweled crown and swinging in his hand a slender golden staff with a ball of clustered gems at one end.

"Where are they going?" asked Trot. "To the house of the Wicked Witch, I fear," Pon replied. "Come, let us follow them, for I am sure they intend to harm my dear Gloria."

"Won't they see us?" she asked timidly.

"We won't let them. I know a short cut through the trees to Blinkie's house," said he.

So they hurried away through the trees and reached the house of the witch ahead of the King and his soldiers. Hiding themselves in the shrubbery, they watched the approach of poor Gloria and her escort, all of whom passed so near to them that Pon could have put out a hand and touched his sweetheart, had he dared to.

Blinkie's house had eight sides, with a door and a window in each side. Smoke was coming out of the chimney and as the guards brought Gloria to one of the doors it was opened by the old witch in person. She chuckled with evil glee and rubbed her skinny hands together to show the delight with which she greeted her victim, for Blinkie was pleased to be able to perform her wicked rites on one so fair and sweet as the Princess.

Gloria struggled to resist when they bade her enter the house, so the soldiers forced her through the doorway and even the King gave her a shove as he followed close behind. Pon was so incensed at the cruelty shown Gloria that he forgot all caution and rushed forward to enter the house also; but one of the soldiers prevented him, pushing the gardener's boy away with violence and slamming the door in his face.

"Never mind," said Trot soothingly, as Pon rose from where he had fallen. "You couldn't do much to help the poor Princess if

you were inside. How unfortunate it is that you are in love with her!"

"True," he answered sadly, "it is indeed my misfortune. If I did not love her, it would be none of my business what the King did to his niece Gloria; but the unlucky circumstance of my loving her makes it my duty to defend her."

"I don't see how you can, duty or no duty," observed Trot.

"No; I am powerless, for they are stronger than I. But we might peek in through the window and see what they are doing."

Trot was somewhat curious, too, so they crept up to one of the windows and looked in, and it so happened that those inside the witch's house were so busy they did not notice that Pon and Trot were watching them.

Gloria had been tied to a stout post in the center of the room and the King was giving the Wicked Witch a quantity of money and jewels, which Googly-Goo had provided in payment. When this had been done the King said to her: "Are you perfectly sure you can freeze this maiden's heart, so that she will no longer love that low gardener's boy?"

"Sure as witchcraft, your Majesty," the creature replied.

"Then get to work," said the King. "There may be some unpleasant features about the ceremony that would annoy me, so I'll bid you good day and leave you to carry out your contract. One word, however: If you fail, I shall burn you at the stake!" Then he beckoned to his soldiers to follow him, and throwing wide the door of the house walked out.

This action was so sudden that King Krewl almost caught Trot and Pon eavesdropping, but they managed to run around the house before he saw them. Away he marched, up the road followed by his men, heartlessly leaving Gloria to the mercies of old Blinkie.

When they again crept up to the window, Trot and Pon saw Blinkie gloating over her victim. Although nearly fainting from fear, the proud Princess gazed with haughty defiance into the face of the wicked creature; but she was bound so tightly to the post that she could do no more to express her loathing.

Pretty soon Blinkie went to a kettle that was swinging by a chain over the fire and tossed into it several magical compounds. The kettle gave three flashes, and at every flash another witch appeared in the room.

These hags were very ugly but when one-eyed Blinkie whispered her orders to them they grinned with joy as they began dancing around Gloria. First one and then another cast something into the kettle, when to the astonishment of the watchers at the window all three of the old women were instantly transformed into maidens of exquisite beauty, dressed in the daintiest costumes imaginable. Only their eyes could not be disguised, and an evil glare still shone in their depths. But if the eyes were cast down or hidden, one could not help but admire these beautiful creatures, even with the knowledge that they were mere illusions of witchcraft.

Trot certainly admired them, for she had never seen anything so dainty and bewitching, but her attention was quickly drawn to their deeds instead of their persons, and then horror replaced admiration. Into the kettle old Blinkie poured another mess from a big brass bottle she took from a chest, and this made the kettle begin to bubble and smoke violently. One by one the beautiful witches approached to stir the contents of the kettle and to mutter a magic charm. Their movements were graceful and rhythmic and the Wicked Witch who had called them to her aid watched them with an evil grin upon her wrinkled face.

Finally the incantation was complete. The kettle ceased bubbling and together the witches lifted it from the fire. Then Blinkie brought a wooden ladle and filled it from the contents of the kettle. Going with the spoon to Princess Gloria she cried:
"Love no more! Magic art
Now will freeze your mortal heart!"

With this she dashed the contents of the ladle full upon Gloria's breast.

Trot saw the body of the Princess become transparent, so that her beating heart showed plainly. But now the heart turned from a vivid red to gray, and then to white. A layer of frost formed about it and tiny icicles clung to its surface. Then slowly the body of the girl became visible again and the heart was hidden from view. Gloria seemed to have fainted, but now she recovered and, opening her beautiful eyes, stared coldly and without emotion at the group of witches confronting her.

Blinkie and the others knew by that one cold look that their charm had been successful. They burst into a chorus of wild laughter and the three beautiful ones began dancing again, while Blinkie unbound the Princess and set her free.

Trot rubbed her eyes to prove that she was wide awake and seeing clearly, for her astonishment was great when the three lovely maidens turned into ugly, crooked hags again, leaning on broomsticks and canes. They jeered at Gloria, but the Princess regarded them with cold disdain. Being now free, she walked to a door, opened it and passed out. And the witches let her go.

Trot and Pon had been so intent upon this scene that in their eagerness they had pressed quite hard against the window. Just as Gloria went out of the house the window- sash broke loose from its fastenings and fell with a crash into the room. The witches uttered a chorus of screams and then, seeing that their magical incantation had been observed, they rushed for the open window with uplifted broomsticks and canes. But Pon was off like the wind, and Trot followed at his heels. Fear lent them strength to run, to leap across ditches, to speed up the hills and to vault the low fences as a deer would.

The band of witches had dashed through the window in pursuit; but Blinkie was so old, and the others so crooked and awkward, that they soon realized they would be unable to overtake the fugitives. So the three who had been summoned by the Wicked Witch put their canes or broomsticks between their legs and flew away through the air, quickly disappearing against the blue sky. Blinkie, however, was so enraged at Pon and Trot that she hobbled on in the direction they had taken, fully determined to catch them, in time, and to punish them terribly for spying upon her witchcraft.

When Pon and Trot had run so far that they were confident they had made good their escape, they sat down near the edge of a forest to get their breath again, for both were panting hard from their exertions. Trot was the first to recover speech, and she said to her companion: "My! wasn't it terr'ble?"

"The most terrible thing I ever saw," Pon agreed.

"And they froze Gloria's heart; so now she can't love you any more."

"Well, they froze her heart, to be sure," admitted Pon, "but I'm in hopes I can melt it with my love."

Where do you s'pose Gloria is?" asked the girl, after a pause.

"She left the witch's house just before we did. Perhaps she has gone back to the King's castle," he said.

"I'm pretty sure she started off in a diff'rent direction," declared Trot. "I looked over my shoulder, as I ran, to see how close the witches were, and I'm sure I saw Gloria walking slowly away toward the north."

"Then let us circle around that way," proposed Pon, "and perhaps we shall meet her."

Trot agreed to this and they left the grove and began to circle around toward the north, thus drawing nearer and nearer to old Blinkie's house again. The Wicked Witch did not suspect this change of direction, so when she came to the grove she passed through it and continued on.

Pon and Trot had reached a place less than half a mile from the witch's house when they saw Gloria walking toward them. The Princess moved with great dignity and with no show of haste whatever, holding her head high and looking neither to right nor left.

Pon rushed forward, holding out his arms as if to embrace her and calling her sweet names. But Gloria gazed upon him coldly and repelled him with a haughty gesture. At this the poor gardener's boy sank upon his knees and hid his face in his arms, weeping bitter tears; but the Princess was not at all moved by his distress. Passing him by, she drew her skirts aside, as if unwilling they should touch him, and then she walked up the path a way and hesitated, as if uncertain where to go next.

Trot was grieved by Pon's sobs and indignant because Gloria treated him so badly. But she remembered why.

"I guess your heart is frozen, all right," she said to the Princess. Gloria nodded gravely, in reply, and then turned her back upon the little girl. "Can't you like even me?" asked Trot, half pleadingly.

"No," said Gloria.

"Your voice sounds like a refrig'rator," sighed the little girl. "I'm awful sorry for you, 'cause you were sweet an' nice to me before this happened. You can't help it, of course; but it's a dreadful thing, jus' the same."

"My heart is frozen to all mortal loves," announced Gloria, calmly. "I do not love even myself."

"That's too bad," said Trot, "for, if you can't love anybody, you can't expect anybody to love you."

"I do!" cried Pon. "I shall always love her."

"Well, you're just a gardener's boy," replied Trot, "and I didn't think you 'mounted to much, from the first. I can love the old Princess Gloria, with a warm heart an' nice manners, but this one gives me the shivers."

"It's her icy heart, that's all," said Pon.

"That's enough," insisted Trot. "Seeing her heart isn't big enough to skate on, I can't see that she's of any use to anyone. For my part, I'm goin' to try to find Button-Bright an' Cap'n Bill."

"I will go with you," decided Pon. "It is evident that Gloria no longer loves me and that her heart is frozen too stiff for me to melt it with my own love; therefore I may as well help you to find your friends."

As Trot started off, Pon cast one more imploring look at the Princess, who returned it with a chilly stare. So he followed after the little girl.

As for the Princess, she hesitated a moment and then turned in the same direction the others had taken, but going far more slowly. Soon she heard footsteps pattering behind her, and up came Googly-Goo. a little out of breath with running.

"Stop, Gloria!" he cried. "I have come to take you back to my mansion, where we are to be married."

She looked at him wonderingly a moment, then tossed her head disdainfully and walked on. But Googly-Goo kept beside her.

"What does this mean?" he demanded. "Haven't you discovered that you no longer love that gardener's boy, who stood in my way?"

"Yes; I have discovered it," she replied. "My heart is frozen to all mortal loves. I cannot love you, or Pon, or the cruel King my uncle, or even myself. Go your way, Googly-Goo, for I will wed no one at all."

He stopped in dismay when he heard this, but in another minute he exclaimed angrily: "You must wed me, Princess Gloria, whether you want to or not! I paid to have your heart frozen; I also paid the King to permit our marriage. If you now refuse me it will mean that I have been robbed — robbed — robbed of my precious money and jewels!"

He almost wept with despair, but she laughed a cold, bitter laugh and passed on. Googly-Goo caught at her arm, as if to restrain her, but she whirled and dealt him a blow that sent him reeling into a ditch beside the path. Here he lay for a long time, half covered by muddy water, dazed with surprise.

Finally the old courtier arose, dripping, and climbed from the ditch. The Princess had gone; so, muttering threats of vengeance upon her, upon the King and upon Blinkie, old Googly-Goo hobbled back to his mansion to have the mud removed from his costly velvet clothes.

15. Trot Meets the Scarecrow

Trot and Pon covered many leagues of ground, searching through forests, in fields and in many of the little villages of Jinxland, but could find no trace of either Cap'n Bill or Button-Bright. Finally they paused beside a cornfield and sat upon a stile to rest. Pon took some apples from his pocket and gave one to Trot. Then he began eating another himself, for this was their time for luncheon. When his apple was finished Pon tossed the core into the field.

"Tchuk-tchuk!" said a strange voice. "what do you mean by hitting me in the eye with an apple-core?"

Then rose up the form of the Scarecrow, who had hidden himself in the cornfield while he examined Pon and Trot and decided whether they were worthy to be helped.

"Excuse me," said Pon. "I didn't know you were there."

"How did you happen to be there, anyhow?" asked Trot.

The Scarecrow came forward with awkward steps and stood beside them.

"Ah, you are the gardener's boy," he said to Pon. Then he turned to Trot. "And you are the little girl who came to Jinxland riding on a big bird, and who has had the misfortune to lose her friend, Cap'n Bill, and her chum, Button-Bright."

"Why, how did you know all that?" she inquired.

"I know a lot of things," replied the Scarecrow, winking at her comically. "My brains are the Carefully-Assorted, Double-Distilled, High-Efficiency sort that the Wizard of Oz makes. He admits, himself, that my brains are the best he ever manufactured."

"I think I've heard of you," said Trot slowly, as she looked the Scarecrow over with much interest; "but you used to live in the Land of Oz."

"Oh, I do now," he replied cheerfully. "I've just come over the mountains from the Quadling Country to see if I can be of any help to you."

"Who, me?" asked Pon.

"No, the strangers from the big world. It seems they need looking after."

"I'm doing that myself," said Pon, a little ungraciously. "If you will pardon me for saying so, I don't see how a Scarecrow with painted eyes can look after anyone."

"If you don't see that, you are more blind than the Scarecrow," asserted Trot. "He's a fairy man, Pon, and comes from the fairyland of Oz, so he can do 'most anything. I hope," she added, turning to the Scarecrow, "you can find Cap'n Bill for me."

"I will try, anyhow," he promised. "But who is that old woman who is running toward us and shaking her stick at us?"

Trot and Pon turned around and both uttered an exclamation of fear. The next instant they took to their heels and ran fast up the path. For it was old Blinkie, the Wicked Witch, who had at last traced them to this place. Her anger was so great that she was determined not to abandon the chase of Pon and Trot until she had caught and punished them. The Scarecrow understood at once that the old woman meant harm to his new friends, so as she drew near he stepped before her. His appearance was so sudden and unexpected that Blinkie ran into him and toppled him over, but she tripped on his straw body and went rolling in the path beside him.

The Scarecrow sat up and said: "I beg your pardon!" but she whacked him with her stick and knocked him flat again. Then, furious with rage, the old witch sprang upon her victim and began pulling the straw out of his body. The poor Scarecrow was helpless to resist and in a few moments all that was left of him was an empty suit of clothes and a heap of straw beside it. Fortunately, Blinkie did not harm his head, for it rolled into a little hollow and escaped her notice. Fearing that Pon and Trot would escape her, she quickly resumed the chase and disappeared over the brow of a hill, following the direction in which she had seen them go.

Only a short time elapsed before a gray grasshopper with a wooden leg came hopping along and lit directly on the upturned face of the Scarecrow's head.

"Pardon me, but you are resting yourself upon my nose," remarked the Scarecrow

"Oh! are you alive?" asked the grasshopper.

"That is a question I have never been able to decide," said the Scarecrow's head. "When my body is properly stuffed I have animation and can move around as well as any live person. The brains in the head you are now occupying as a throne, are of very superior quality and do a lot of very clever thinking. But whether that is being alive, or not, I cannot prove to you; for one who lives is liable to death, while I am only liable to destruction."

"Seems to me," said the grasshopper, rubbing his nose with his front legs, "that in your case it doesn't matter — unless you're destroyed already."

"I am not; all I need is re-stuffing," declared the Scarecrow; "and if Pon and Trot escape the witch, and come back here, I am sure they will do me that favor."

"Tell me! Are Trot and Pon around here?" inquired the grasshopper, its small voice trembling with excitement.

The Scarecrow did not answer at once, for both his eyes were staring straight upward at a beautiful face that was slightly bent over his head. It was, indeed, Princess Gloria, who had wandered to this spot, very much surprised when she heard the Scarecrow's head talk and the tiny gray grasshopper answer it.

"This," said the Scarecrow, still staring at her, "must be the Princess who loves Pon, the gardener's boy."

"Oh, indeed!" exclaimed the grasshopper — who of course was Cap'n Bill — as he examined the young lady curiously.

"No," said Gloria frigidly, "I do not love Pon, or anyone else, for the Wicked Witch has frozen my heart."

"What a shame!" cried the Scarecrow. "One so lovely should be able to love. But would you mind, my dear, stuffing that straw into my body again?"

The dainty Princess glanced at the straw and at the well-worn blue Munchkin clothes and shrank back in disdain. But she was spared from refusing the Scarecrow's request by the appearance of Trot and Pon, who had hidden in some bushes just over the brow of the hill and waited until old Blinkie had passed them by. Their hiding place was on the same side as the witch's blind eye, and she rushed on in the chase of the girl and the youth without being aware that they had tricked her.

Trot was shocked at the Scarecrow's sad condition and at once began putting the straw back into his body. Pon, at sight of Gloria, again appealed to her to take pity on him, but the frozen-hearted Princess turned coldly away and with a sigh the gardener's boy began to assist Trot.

Neither of them at first noticed the small grasshopper, which at their appearance had skipped off the Scarecrow's nose and was now clinging to a wisp of grass beside the path, where he was not likely to be stepped upon. Not until the Scarecrow had been neatly restuffed and set upon his feet again — when he bowed to his restorers and expressed his thanks — did the grasshopper move from his perch. Then he leaped lightly into the path and called out: "Trot — Trot! Look at me. I'm Cap'n Bill! See what the Wicked Witch has done to me."

The voice was small, to be sure, but it reached Trot's ears and startled her greatly. She looked intently at the grasshopper, her eyes wide with fear at first; then she knelt down and, noticing the wooden leg, she began to weep sorrowfully.

"Oh, Cap'n Bill — dear Cap'n Bill! What a cruel thing to do!" she sobbed.

"Don't cry, Trot," begged the grasshopper. "It didn't hurt any, and it doesn't hurt now. But it's mighty inconvenient an' humiliatin', to say the least."

"I wish," said the girl indignantly, while trying hard to restrain her tears, "that I was big 'nough an' strong 'nough to give that horrid witch a good beating. She ought to be turned into a toad for doing this to you, Cap'n Bill!"

"Never mind," urged the Scarecrow, in a comforting voice, "such a transformation doesn't last always, and as a general thing there's some way to break the enchantment. I'm sure Glinda could do it, in a jiffy."

"Who is Glinda?" inquired Cap'n Bill.

Then the Scarecrow told them all about Glinda, not forgetting to mention her beauty and goodness and her wonderful powers of magic. He also explained how the Royal Sorceress had sent him to Jinxland especially to help the strangers, whom she knew to be in danger because of the wiles of the cruel King and the Wicked Witch.

16. Pon Summons the King to Surrender

Gloria had drawn near to the group to listen to their talk, and it seemed to interest her in spite of her frigid manner. They knew, of course, that the poor Princess could not help being cold and reserved, so they tried not to blame her.

"I ought to have come here a little sooner," said the Scarecrow, regretfully; "but Glinda sent me as soon as she discovered you were here and were likely to get into trouble. And now that we are all together — except Button-Bright, over whom it is useless to worry — I propose we hold a council of war, to decide what is best to be done."

That seemed a wise thing to do, so they all sat down upon the grass, including Gloria, and the grasshopper perched upon Trot's shoulder and allowed her to stroke him gently with her hand.

"In the first place," began the Scarecrow, "this King Krewl is a usurper and has no right to rule this Kingdom of Jinxland."

"That is true," said Pon, eagerly. "My father was King before him, and I —"

"You are a gardener's boy," interrupted the Scarecrow. "Your father had no right to rule, either, for the rightful King of this land was the father of Princess Gloria, and only she is entitled to sit upon the throne of Jinxland."

"Good!" exclaimed Trot. "But what'll we do with King Krewl? I s'pose he won't give up the throne unless he has to."

"No, of course not," said the Scarecrow. "Therefore it will be our duty to make him give up the throne."

"How?" asked Trot.

"Give me time to think," was the reply. "That's what my brains are for. I don't know whether you people ever think, or not, but my brains are the best that the Wizard of Oz ever turned out, and if I give them plenty of time to work, the result usually surprises me."

"Take your time, then," suggested Trot. "There's no hurry."

"Thank you," said the straw man, and sat perfectly still for half an hour. During this interval the grasshopper whispered in Trot's ear, to which he was very close, and Trot whispered back to the grasshopper sitting upon her shoulder. Pon cast loving glances at Gloria, who paid not the slightest heed to them.

Finally the Scarecrow laughed aloud.

"Brains working?" inquired Trot.

"Yes. They seem in fine order to-day. We will conquer King Krewl and put Gloria upon his throne as Queen of Jinxland."

"Fine!" cried the little girl, clapping her hands together gleefully. "But how?"

"Leave the how to me," said the Scarecrow proudly. "As a conqueror I'm a wonder. We will, first of all, write a message to send to King Krewl, asking him to surrender. If he refuses, then we will make him surrender."

"Why ask him. when we know he'll refuse?" inquired Pon.

"Why, we must be polite, whatever we do," explained the Scarecrow. "It would be very rude to conquer a King without proper notice."

They found it difficult to write a message without paper, pen and ink, none of which was at hand; so it was decided to send Pon as a messenger, with instructions to ask the King, politely but firmly, to surrender.

Pon was not anxious to be the messenger. Indeed, he hinted that it might prove a dangerous mission. But the Scarecrow was now the acknowledged head of the Army of Conquest, and he would listen to no refusal. So off Pon started for the King's castle, and the others accompanied him as far as his hut, where they had decided to await the gardener's boy's return.

I think it was because Pon had known the Scarecrow such a short time that he lacked confidence in the straw man's wisdom. It was easy to say: "We will conquer King Krewl," but when Pon drew near to the great castle he began to doubt the ability of a straw-stuffed man, a girl, a grasshopper and a frozen-hearted Princess to do it. As for himself, he had never thought of defying the King before.

That was why the gardener's boy was not very bold when he entered the castle and passed through to the enclosed court where the King was just then seated, with his favorite courtiers around him. None prevented Pon's entrance, because he was known to be the gardener's boy, but when the King saw him he began to frown fiercely. He considered Pon to be to blame for all his trouble with Princess Gloria, who since her heart had been frozen had escaped to some unknown place, instead of returning to the castle to wed Goqgly-Goo, as she had been expected to do. So the King bared his teeth angrily as he demanded: "What have you done with Princess Gloria?"

"Nothing, your Majesty! I have done nothing at all," answered Pon in a faltering voice. "She does not love me any more and even refuses to speak to me."

"Then why are you here, you rascal?" roared the King.

Pon looked first one way and then another, but saw no means of escape; so he plucked up courage.

"I am here to summon your Majesty to surrender."

"What!" shouted the King. "Surrender? Surrender to whom?"

Pon's heart sank to his boots.

"To the Scarecrow," he replied.

Some of the courtiers began to titter, but King Krewl was greatly annoyed. He sprang up and began to beat poor Pon with the golden staff he carried. Pon howled lustily and would have run away had not two of the soldiers held him until his Majesty was exhausted with punishing the boy. Then they let him go and he left the castle and returned along the road, sobbing at every step because his body was so sore and aching.

"Well," said the Scarecrow, "did the King surrender?"

"No; but he gave me a good drubbing!" sobbed poor Pon.

Trot was very sorry for Pon, but Gloria did not seem affected in any way by her lover's anguish. The grasshopper leaped to the Scarecrow's shoulder and asked him what he was going to do next.

"Conquer," was the reply. "But I will go alone, this time, for beatings cannot hurt me at all; nor can lance thrusts — or sword cuts — or arrow pricks."

"Why is that?" inquired Trot.

"Because I have no nerves, such as you meat people possess. Even grasshoppers have nerves, but straw doesn't; so whatever they do — except just one thing — they cannot injure me. Therefore I expect to conquer King Krewl with ease."

"What is that one thing you excepted?" asked Trot.

"They will never think of it, so never mind. And now, if you will kindly excuse me for a time, I'll go over to the castle and do my conquering."

"You have no weapons," Pon reminded him.

"True," said the Scarecrow. "But if I carried weapons I might injure someone — perhaps seriously — and that would make me unhappy. I will just borrow that riding- whip, which I see in the corner of your hut, if you don't mind. It isn't exactly proper to walk with a riding-whip, but I trust you will excuse the inconsistency."

Pon handed him the whip and the Scarecrow bowed to all the

party and left the hut, proceeding leisurely along the way to the King's castle.

17. The Ork Rescues Button-Bright

I must now tell you what had become of Button-Bright since he wandered away in the morning and got lost. This small boy, as perhaps you have discovered, was almost as destitute of nerves as the Scarecrow. Nothing ever astonished him much; nothing ever worried him or made him unhappy. Good fortune or bad fortune he accepted with a quiet smile, never complaining, whatever happened. This was one reason why Button-Bright was a favorite with all who knew him — and perhaps it was the reason why he so often got into difficulties, or found himself lost.

To-day, as he wandered here and there, over hill and down dale, he missed Trot and Cap'n Bill, of whom he was fond, but nevertheless he was not unhappy. The birds sang merrily and the wildflowers were beautiful and the breeze had a fragrance of new-mown hay.

"The only bad thing about this country is its King," he reflected; "but the country isn't to blame for that."

A prairie-dog stuck its round head out of a mound of earth and looked at the boy with bright eyes.

"Walk around my house, please," it said, "and then you won't harm it or disturb the babies."

"All right," answered Button-Bright, and took care not to step on the mound. He went on, whistling merrily, until a petulant voice cried: "Oh, stop it! Please stop that noise. It gets on my nerves."

Button-Bright saw an old gray owl sitting in the crotch of a tree, and he replied with a laugh: "All right, old Fussy," and stopped whistling until he had passed out of the owl's hearing. At noon he came to a farmhouse where an aged couple lived. They gave him a good dinner and treated him kindly, but the man was deaf and the woman was dumb, so they could answer no questions to guide him on the way to Pon's house. When he left them he was just as much lost as he had been before.

Every grove of trees he saw from a distance he visited, for he remembered that the King's castle was near a grove of trees and Pon's hut was near the King's castle; but always he met with disappointment. Finally, passing through one of these groves, he came out into the open and found himself face to face with the Ork.

"Hello!" said Button-Bright. "Where did you come from?"

"From Orkland," was the reply. "I've found my own country, at last, and it is not far from here, either. I would have come back to you sooner, to see how you are getting along, had not my family and friends welcomed my return so royally that a great celebration was held in my honor. So I couldn't very well leave Orkland again until the excitement was over."

"Can you find your way back home again?" asked the boy.

"Yes, easily; for now I know exactly where it is. But where are Trot and Cap'n Bill?"

Button-Bright related to the Ork their adventures since it had left them in Jinxland, telling of Trot's fear that the King had done something wicked to Cap'n Bill, and of Pon's love for Gloria, and how Trot and Button-Bright had been turned out of the King's castle. That was all the news that the boy had, but it made the Ork anxious for the safety of his friends.

"We must go to them at once, for they may need us," he said.

"I don't know where to go," confessed Button-Bright. "I'm lost."

"Well, I can take you back to the hut of the gardener's boy," promised the Ork, "for when I fly high in the air I can look down and easily spy the King's castle. That was how I happened to spy you, just entering the grove; so I flew down and waited until you came out."

"How can you carry me?" asked the boy.

"You'll have to sit straddle my shoulders and put your arms around my neck. Do you think you can keep from falling off?"

"I'll try," said Button-Bright. So the Ork squatted down and the boy took his seat and held on tight. Then the skinny creature's tail began whirling and up they went, far above all the tree-tops.

After the Ork had circled around once or twice, its sharp eyes located the towers of the castle and away it flew, straight toward the place. As it hovered in the air, near by the castle, Button-Bright pointed out Pon's hut, so they landed just before it and Trot came running out to greet them.

Gloria was introduced to the Ork, who was surprised to find Cap'n Bill transformed into a grasshopper.

"How do you like it?" asked the creature.

"Why, it worries me good deal," answered Cap'n Bill, perched upon Trot's shoulder. "I'm always afraid o' bein' stepped on, and I don't like the flavor of grass an' can't seem to get used to it. It's my nature to eat grass, you know, but I begin to suspect it's an acquired taste."

"Can you give molasses?" asked the Ork.

"I guess I'm not that kind of a grasshopper," replied Cap'n Bill. "But I can't say what I might do if I was squeezed — which I hope I won't be."

"Well," said the Ork, "it's a great pity, and I'd like to meet that cruel King and his Wicked Witch and punish them both severely. You're awfully small, Cap'n Bill, but I think I would recognize you anywhere by your wooden leg."

Then the Ork and Button-Bright were told all about Gloria's frozen heart and how the Scarecrow had come from the Land of Oz to help them. The Ork seemed rather disturbed when it learned that the Scarecrow had gone alone to conquer King Krewl.

"I'm afraid he'll make a fizzle of it," said the skinny creature, "and there's no telling what that terrible King might do to the poor Scarecrow, who seems like a very interesting person. So I believe I'll take a hand in this conquest myself."

"How?" asked Trot.

"Wait and see," was the reply. "But, first of all, I must fly home again — back to my own country — so if you'll forgive my leaving you so soon, I'll be off at once. Stand away from my tail, please, so that the wind from it, when it revolves, won't knock you over."

They gave the creature plenty of room and away it went like a flash and soon disappeared in the sky.

"I wonder," said Button-Bright, looking solemnly after the Ork, "whether he'll ever come back again."

"Of course he will!" returned Trot. "The Ork's a pretty good fellow, and we can depend on him. An' mark my words, Button-Bright, whenever our Ork does come back, there's one cruel King in Jinxland that'll wish he hadn't."

18. The Scarecrow Meets an Enemy

The Scarecrow was not a bit afraid of King Krewl. Indeed, he rather enjoyed the prospect of conquering the evil King and putting Gloria on the throne of Jinxland in his place. So he advanced boldly to the royal castle and demanded admittance.

Seeing that he was a stranger, the soldiers allowed him to enter. He made his way straight to the throne room, where at that time his Majesty was settling the disputes among his subjects.

"Who are you?" demanded the King.

"I'm the Scarecrow of Oz, and I command you to surrender yourself my prisoner."

"Why should I do that? " inquired the King, much astonished at the straw man's audacity.

"Because I've decided you are too cruel a King to rule so beautiful a country. You must remember that Jinxland is a part of Oz, and therefore you owe allegiance to Ozma of Oz, whose friend and servant I am."

Now, when he heard this, King Krewl was much disturbed in mind, for he knew the Scarecrow spoke the truth. But no one had ever before come to Jinxland from the Land of Oz and the King did not intend to be put out of his throne if he could help it. Therefore he gave a harsh, wicked laugh of derision and said: "I'm busy, now. Stand out of my way, Scarecrow, and I'll talk with you by and by."

But the Scarecrow turned to the assembled courtiers and people and called in a loud voice: "I hereby declare, in the name of Ozma of Oz, that this man is no longer ruler of Jinxland. From this moment Princess Gloria is your rightful Queen, and I ask all of you to be loyal to her and to obey her commands."

The people looked fearfully at the King, whom they all hated in their hearts, but likewise feared. Krewl was now in a terrible rage and he raised his golden sceptre and struck the Scarecrow so heavy a blow that he fell to the floor.

But he was up again, in an instant, and with Pon's riding-whip he switched the King so hard that the wicked monarch roared with pain as much as with rage, calling on his soldiers to capture the Scarecrow.

They tried to do that, and thrust their lances and swords into the straw body, but without doing any damage except to make holes in the Scarecrow's clothes. However, they were many against one and finally old Googly-Goo brought a rope which he wound around the Scarecrow, binding his legs together and his arms to his sides, and after that the fight was over.

The King stormed and danced around in a dreadful fury, for he had never been so switched since he was a boy — and perhaps

not then. He ordered the Scarecrow thrust into the castle prison, which was no task at all because one man could carry him easily, bound. as he was.

Even after the prisoner was removed the King could not control his anger. He tried to figure out some way to be revenged upon the straw man, but could think of nothing that could hurt him. At last, when the terrified people and the frightened courtiers had all slunk away, old Googly-Goo approached the king with a malicious grin upon his face.

"I'll tell you what to do," said he. "Build a big bonfire and burn the Scarecrow up, and that will be the end of him."

The King was so delighted with this suggestion that he hugged old Googly-Goo in his joy.

"Of course!" he cried. "The very thing. Why did I not think of it myself?"

So he summoned his soldiers and retainers and bade them prepare a great bonfire in an open space in the castle park. Also he sent word to all his people to assemble and witness the destruction of the Scarecrow who had dared to defy his power. Before long a vast throng gathered in the park and the servants had heaped up enough fuel to make a fire that might be seen for miles away — even in the daytime.

When all was prepared, the King had his throne brought out for him to sit upon and enjoy the spectacle, and then he sent his soldiers to fetch the Scarecrow.

Now the one thing in all the world that the straw man really feared was fire. He knew he would burn very easily and that his ashes wouldn't amount to much afterward. It wouldn't hurt him to be destroyed in such a manner, but he realized that many people in the Land of Oz, and especially Dorothy and the Royal Ozma, would feel sad if they learned that their old friend the Scarecrow was no longer in existence.

In spite of this, the straw man was brave and faced his fiery fate like a hero. When they marched him out before the concourse of people he turned to the King with great calmness and said: "This wicked deed will cost you your throne, as well as much suffering, for my friends will avenge my destruction."

"Your friends are not here, nor will they know what I have done to you, when you are gone and cannot tell them," answered the King in a scornful voice.

Then he ordered the Scarecrow bound to a stout stake that he had had driven into the ground, and the materials for the fire were heaped all around him. When this had been done, the King's brass band struck up a lively tune and old Googly-Goo came forward with a lighted match and set fire to the pile.

At once the flames shot up and crept closer and closer toward the Scarecrow. The King and all his people were so intent upon this terrible spectacle that none of them noticed how the sky grew suddenly dark. Perhaps they thought that the loud buzzing sound — like the noise of a dozen moving railway trains — came from the blazing fagots; that the rush of wind was merely a breeze. But suddenly down swept a flock of Orks, half a hundred of them at the least, and the powerful currents of air caused by their revolving tails sent the bonfire scattering in every direction, so that not one burning brand ever touched the Scarecrow.

But that was not the only effect of this sudden tornado. King

Krewl was blown out of his throne and went tumbling heels over head until he landed with a bump against the stone wall of his own castle, and before he could rise a big Ork sat upon him and held him pressed flat to the ground. Old Googly-Goo shot up into the air like a rocket and landed on a tree, where he hung by the middle on a high limb, kicking the air with his feet and clawing the air with his hands, and howling for mercy like the coward he was.

The people pressed back until they were jammed close together, while all the soldiers were knocked over and sent sprawling to the earth. The excitement was great for a few minutes, and every frightened inhabitant of Jinxland looked with awe and amazement at the great Orks whose descent had served to rescue the Scarecrow and conquer King Krewl at one and the same time.

The Ork, who was the leader of the band, soon had the Scarecrow free of his bonds. Then he said: "Well, we were just in time to save you, which is better than being a minute too late. You are now the master here, and we are determined to see your orders obeyed."

With this the Ork picked up Krewl's golden crown, which had fallen off his head, and placed it upon the head of the Scarecrow, who in his awkward way then shuffled over to the throne and sat down in it.

Seeing this, a rousing cheer broke from the crowd of people, who tossed their hats and waved their handkerchiefs and hailed the Scarecrow as their King. The soldiers joined the people in the cheering, for now they fully realized that their hated master was conquered and it would be wise to show their good will to the conqueror. Some of them bound Krewl with ropes and dragged him forward, dumping his body on the ground before the Scarecrow's throne. Googly-Goo struggled until he finally slid off the limb of the tree and came tumbling to the ground. He then tried to sneak away and escape, but the soldiers seized and bound him beside Krewl.

"The tables are turned," said the Scarecrow, swelling out his chest until the straw within it crackled pleasantly, for he was highly pleased; "but it was you and your people who did it, friend Ork, and from this time you may count me your humble servant."

19. The Conquest of the Witch

Now as soon as the conquest of King Krewl had taken place, one of the Orks had been dispatched to Pon's house with the joyful news. At once Gloria and Pon and Trot and Button-Bright hastened toward the castle. They were somewhat surprised by the sight that met their eyes, for there was the Scarecrow, crowned King, and all the people kneeling humbly before him. So they likewise bowed low to the new ruler and then stood beside the throne. Cap'n Bill, as the gray grasshopper, was still perched upon Trot's shoulder, but now he hopped to the shoulder of the Scarecrow and whispered into the painted ear: "I thought Gloria was to be Queen of Jinxland."

The Scarecrow shook his head.

"Not yet," he answered. "No Queen with a frozen heart is fit to rule any country." Then he turned to his new friend, the Ork, who was strutting about, very proud of what he had done, and said: "Do you suppose you, or your followers, could find old Blinkie the Witch?"

"Where is she?" asked the Ork.

"Somewhere in Jinxland, I'm sure."

"Then," said the Ork, "we shall certainly be able to find her."

"It will give me great pleasure," declared the Scarecrow. "When you have found her, bring her here to me. and I will then decide what to do with her."

The Ork called his followers together and spoke a few words to them in a low tone. A moment after they rose into the air — so suddenly that the Scarecrow, who was very light in weight, was blown quite out of his throne and into the arms of Pon, who replaced him carefully upon his seat. There was an eddy of dust and ashes, too, and the grasshopper only saved himself from being whirled into the crowd of people by jumping into a tree, from where a series of hops soon brought him back to Trot's shoulder again. The Orks were quite out of sight by this time, so the Scarecrow made a speech to the people and presented Gloria to them, whom they knew well already and were fond of. But not all of them knew of her frozen heart, and when the Scarecrow related the story of the Wicked Witch's misdeeds, which had been encouraged and paid for by Krewl and Googly-Goo, the people were very indignant.

Meantime the fifty Orks had scattered all over Jinx land, which is not a very big country, and their sharp eyes were peering into every valley and grove and gully. Finally one of them spied a pair of heels sticking out from underneath some bushes, and with a shrill whistle to warn his comrades that the witch was found the Ork flew down and dragged old Blinkie from her hiding-place. Then two or three of the Orks seized the clothing of the wicked woman in their strong claws and, lifting her high in the air, where she struggled and screamed to no avail, they flew with her straight to the royal castle and set her down before the throne of the Scarecrow.

"Good!" exclaimed the straw man, nodding his stuffed head with satisfaction. "Now we can proceed to business. Mistress Witch, I am obliged to request, gently but firmly, that you undo all the wrongs you have done by means of your witchcraft."

"Pah!" cried old Blinkie in a scornful voice. "I defy you all! By my magic powers I can turn you all into pigs, rooting in the mud, and I'll do it if you are not careful."

"I think you are mistaken about that," said the Scarecrow, and rising from his throne he walked with wobbling steps to the side of the Wicked Witch. "Before I left the Land of Oz, Glinda the Royal Sorceress gave me a box, which I was not to open except in an emergency. But I feel pretty sure that this occasion is an emergency; don't you, Trot?" he asked, turning toward the little girl.

"Why, we've got to do something," replied Trot seriously. "Things seem in an awful muddle here, jus' now, and they'll be worse if we don't stop this witch from doing more harm to people."

"That is my idea, exactly," said the Scarecrow, and taking a small box from his pocket he opened the cover and tossed the contents toward Blinkie.

The old woman shrank back, pale and trembling, as a fine white dust settled all about her. Under its influence she seemed to the eyes of all observers to shrivel and grow smaller.

"Oh, dear - oh, dear!" she wailed, wringing her hands in fear. "Haven't you the antidote, Scarecrow? Didn't the great Sorceress give you another box?"

"She did," answered the Scarecrow.

"Then give it me — quick!" pleaded the witch. "Give it me — and I'll do anything you ask me to!"

"You will do what I ask first," declared the Scarecrow, firmly.

The witch was shriveling and growing smaller every moment.

"Be quick, then!" she cried. "Tell me what I must do and let me do it, or it will be too late."

"You made Trot's friend, Cap'n Bill, a grasshopper. I command you to give him back his proper form again," said the Scarecrow.

"Where is he? Where's the grasshopper? Quick — quick!" she screamed.

Cap'n Bill, who had been deeply interested in this conversation, gave a great leap from Trot's shoulder and landed on that of the Scarecrow. Blinkie saw him alight and at once began to make magic passes and to mumble magic incantations. She was in a desperate hurry, knowing that she had no time to waste, and the grasshopper was so suddenly transformed into the old sailor-man, Cap'n Bill, that he had no opportunity to jump off the Scarecrow's shoulder; so his great weight bore the stuffed Scarecrow to the ground. No harm was done, however, and the straw man got up and brushed the dust from his clothes while Trot delightedly embraced Cap'n Bill.

"The other box! Quick! Give me the other box," begged Blinkie, who had now shrunk to half her former size.

"Not yet," said the Scarecrow. "You must first melt Princess Gloria's frozen heart."

"I can't; it's an awful job to do that! I can't," asserted the witch, in an agony of fear — for still she was growing smaller.

"You must!" declared the Scarecrow, firmly.

The witch cast a shrewd look at him and saw that he meant it; so she began dancing around Gloria in a frantic manner. The Princess looked coldly on, as if not at all interested in the proceedings, while Blinkie tore a handful of hair from her own head and ripped a strip of cloth from the bottom of her gown. Then the witch sank upon her knees, took a purple powder from her black bag and sprinkled it over the hair and cloth.

"I hate to do it — I hate to do it!" she wailed, "for there is no more of this magic compound in all the world. But I must sacrifice it to save my own life. A match! Give me a match, quick!" and panting from lack of breath she gazed imploringly from one to another.

Cap'n Bill was the only one who had a match, but he lost no time in handing it to Blinkie, who quickly set fire to the hair and the cloth and the purple powder. At once a purple cloud enveloped Gloria, and this gradually turned to a rosy pink color —brilliant and quite transparent. Through the rosy cloud they could all see the beautiful Princess, standing proud and erect. Then her heart became visible, at first frosted with ice but slowly growing brighter and warmer until all the frost had disappeared and it was beating as softly and regularly as any other heart. And now

the cloud dispersed and disclosed Gloria, her face suffused with joy, smiling tenderly upon the friends who were grouped about her.

Poor Pon stepped forward — timidly, fearing a repulse, but with pleading eyes and arms fondly outstretched toward his former sweetheart — and the Princess saw him and her sweet face lighted with a radiant smile. Without an instant's hesitation she threw herself into Pon's arms and this reunion of two loving hearts was so affecting that the people turned away and lowered their eyes so as not to mar the sacred joy of the faithful lovers.

But Blinkie's small voice was shouting to the Scarecrow for help.

"The antidote!" she screamed. "Give me the other box — quick!"

The Scarecrow looked at the witch with his quaint, painted eyes and saw that she was now no taller than his knee. So he took from his pocket the second box and scattered its contents on Blinkie. She ceased to grow any smaller, but she could never regain her former size, and this the wicked old woman well knew.

She did not know, however, that the second powder had destroyed all her power to work magic, and seeking to be revenged upon the Scarecrow and his friends she at once began to mumble a charm so terrible in its effect that it would have destroyed half the population of Jinxland — had it worked. But it did not work at all, to the amazement of old Blinkie. And by this time the Scarecrow noticed what the little witch was trying to do and said to her:

"Go home, Blinkie, and behave yourself. You are no longer a witch, but an ordinary old woman, and since you are powerless to do more evil I advise you to try to do some good in the world. Believe me, it is more fun to accomplish a good act than an evil one, as you will discover when once you have tried it."

But Blinkie was at that moment filled with grief and chagrin at losing her magic powers. She started away toward her home, sobbing and bewailing her fate, and not one who saw her go was at all sorry for her.

20. Queen Gloria

Next morning the Scarecrow called upon all the courtiers and the people to assemble in the throne room of the castle, where there was room enough for all that were able to attend. They found the straw man seated upon the velvet cushions of the throne, with the King's glittering crown still upon his stuffed head. On one side of the throne, in a lower chair, sat Gloria, looking radiantly beautiful and fresh as a new-blown rose. On the other side sat Pon, the gardener's boy, still dressed in his old smock frock and looking sad and solemn; for Pon could not make himself believe that so splendid a Princess would condescend to love him when she had come to her own and was seated upon a throne. Trot and Cap'n Bill sat at the feet of the Scarecrow and were much interested in the proceedings. Button-Bright had lost himself before breakfast, but came into the throne room before the ceremonies were over. Back of the throne stood a row of the great Orks, with their leader in the center, and the entrance to the palace was guarded by more Orks, who were regarded with wonder and awe.

When all were assembled, the Scarecrow stood up and made a speech. He told how Gloria's father, the good King Kynd, who had once ruled them and been loved by everyone, had been destroyed by King Phearce, the father of Pon, and how King

Phearce had been destroyed by King Krewl. This last King had been a bad ruler, as they knew very well, and the Scarecrow declared that the only one in all Jinxland who had the right to sit upon the throne was Princess Gloria, the daughter of King Kynd.

"But," he added, "it is not for me, a stranger, to say who shall rule you. You must decide for yourselves, or you will not be content. So choose now who shall be your future ruler."

And they all shouted: "The Scarecrow! The Scarecrow shall rule us!"

Which proved that the stuffed man had made himself very popular by his conquest of King Krewl, and the people thought they would like him for their King. But the Scarecrow shook his head so vigorously that it became loose, and Trot had to pin it firmly to his body again.

"No," said he, "I belong in the Land of Oz, where I am the humble servant of the lovely girl who rules us all — the royal Ozma. You must choose one of your own inhabitants to rule over Jinxland. Who shall it be?"

They hesitated for a moment, and some few cried: "Pon!" but many more shouted: "Gloria!"

So the Scarecrow took Gloria's hand and led her to the throne, where he first seated her and then took the glittering crown off his own head and placed it upon that of the young lady, where it nestled prettily amongst her soft curls. The people cheered and shouted then, kneeling before their new Queen; but Gloria leaned down and took Pon's hand in both her own and raised him to the seat beside her.

"You shall have both a King and a Queen to care for you and to protect you, my dear subjects," she said in a sweet voice, while her face glowed with happiness; "for Pon was a King's son before he became a gardener's boy, and because I love him he is to be my Royal Consort."

That pleased them all, especially Pon, who realized that this was the most important moment of his life. Trot and Button-Bright and Cap'n Will all congratulated him on winning the beautiful Gloria; but the Ork sneezed twice and said that in his opinion the young lady might have done better.

Then the Scarecrow ordered the guards to bring in the wicked Krewl, King no longer, and when he appeared, loaded with chains and dressed in fustian, the people hissed him and drew back as he passed so their garments would not touch him.

Krewl was not haughty or overbearing any more; on the contrary he seemed very meek and in great fear of the fate his conquerors had in store for him. But Gloria and Pon were too happy to be revengeful and so they offered to appoint Krewl to the position of gardener's boy at the castle, Pon having resigned to become King. But they said he must promise to reform his wicked ways and to do his duty faithfully, and he must change his name from Krewl to Grewl. All this the man eagerly promised to do, and so when Pon retired to a room in the castle to put on princely raiment, the old brown smock he had formerly worn was given to Grewl, who then went out into the garden to water the roses.

The remainder of that famous day, which was long remembered in Jinxland, was given over to feasting and merrymaking. In the evening there was a grand dance in the courtyard, where the brass band played a new piece of music called the "Ork Trot" which was dedicated to "Our Glorious Gloria, the Queen."

While the Queen and Pon were leading this dance, and all the Jinxland people were having a good time, the strangers were gathered in a group in the park outside the castle. Cap'n Bill, Trot, Button-Bright and the Scarecrow were there, and so was their old friend the Ork; but of all the great flock of Orks which had assisted in the conquest but three remained in Jinxland, besides their leader, the others having returned to their own country as soon as Gloria was crowned Queen. To the young Ork who had accompanied them in their adventures Cap'n Bill said: "You've surely been a friend in need, and we're mighty grateful to you for helping us. I might have been a grasshopper yet if it hadn't been for you, an' I might remark that bein' a grasshopper isn't much fun."

"If it hadn't been for you, friend Ork," said the Scarecrow, "I fear I could not have conquered King Krewl."

"No," agreed Trot, "you'd have been just a heap of ashes by this time."

And I might have been lost yet," added Button-Bright. "Much obliged, Mr. Ork."

"Oh, that's all right," replied the Ork. "Friends must stand together, you know, or they wouldn't be friends. But now I must leave you and be off to my own country, where there's going to be a surprise party on my uncle, and I've promised to attend it."

"Dear me," said the Scarecrow, regretfully. "That is very unfortunate."

"Why so?" asked the Ork.

"I hoped you would consent to carry us over those mountains, into the Land of Oz. My mission here is now finished and I want to get back to the Emerald City."

"How did you cross the mountains before?" inquired the Ork.

"I scaled the cliffs by means of a rope, and crossed the Great Gulf on a strand of spider web. Of course I can return in the same manner, but it would be a hard journey — and perhaps an impossible one — for Trot and Button-Bright and Cap'n Bill. So I thought that if you had the time you and your people would carry us over the mountains and land us all safely on the other side, in the Land of Oz."

The Ork thoughtfully considered the matter for a while. Then he said: "I mustn't break my promise to be present at the surprise party; but, tell me, could you go to Oz to-night?"

"What, now?" exclaimed Trot.

"It is a fine moonlight night," said the Ork, "and I've found in my experience that there's no time so good as right away. The fact is," he explained, "it's a long journey to Orkland and I and my cousins here are all rather tired by our day's work. But if you will start now, and be content to allow us to carry you over the mountains and dump you on the other side, just say the word and — off we go!"

Cap'n Bill and Trot looked at one another questioningly. The little girl was eager to visit the famous fairyland of Oz and the old sailor had endured such hardships in Jinxland that he would be glad to be out of it.

"It's rather impolite of us not to say good-bye to the new King and Queen," remarked the Scarecrow, "but I'm sure they're too happy to miss us, and I assure you it will be much easier to fly on the backs of the Orks over those steep mountains than to climb them as I did."

"All right; let's go!" Trot decided. "But where's Button-Bright?"

Just at this important moment Button-Bright was lost again, and they all scattered in search of him. He had been standing beside them just a few minutes before, but his friends had an exciting hunt for him before they finally discovered the boy seated among the members of the band, beating the end of the bass drum with the bone of a turkey-leg that he had taken from the table in the banquet room.

"Hello, Trot," he said, looking up at the little girl when she found him. "This is the first chance I ever had to pound a drum with a reg'lar drum stick. And I ate all the meat off the bone myself."

"Come quick. We're going to the Land of Oz."

"Oh, what's the hurry?" said Button-Bright; but she seized his arm and dragged him away to the park, where the others were waiting.

Trot climbed upon the back of her old friend, the Ork leader, and the others took their seats on the backs of his three cousins. As soon as all were placed and clinging to the skinny necks of the creatures, the revolving tails began to whirl and up rose the four monster Orks and sailed away toward the mountains. They were so high in the air that when they passed the crest of the highest peak it seemed far below them. No sooner were they well across the barrier than the Orks swooped downward and landed their passengers upon the ground.

"Here we are, safe in the Land of Oz!" cried the Scarecrow joyfully.

"Oh, are we?" asked Trot, looking around her curiously.

She could see the shadows of stately trees and the outlines of rolling hills; beneath her feet was soft turf, but otherwise the subdued light of the moon disclosed nothing clearly.

"Seems jus' like any other country," was Cap'n Bill's comment.

"But it isn't," the Scarecrow assured him. "You are now within the borders of the most glorious fairyland in all the world. This part of it is just a corner of the Quadling Country, and the least interesting portion of it. It's not very thickly settled, around here, I'll admit, but —"

He was interrupted by a sudden whir and a rush of air as the four Orks mounted into the sky.

"Good night!" called the shrill voices of the strange creatures, and although Trot shouted "Good night!" as loudly as she could, the little girl was almost ready to cry because the Orks had not waited to be properly thanked for all their kindness to her and to Cap'n Bill.

But the Orks were gone, and thanks for good deeds do not amount to much except to prove one's politeness.

"Well, friends," said the Scarecrow, "we mustn't stay here in the meadows all night, so let us find a pleasant place to sleep. Not that it matters to me, in the least, for I never sleep; but I know that meat people like to shut their eyes and lie still during the dark hours."

"I'm pretty tired," admitted Trot, yawning as she followed the straw man along a tiny path, "so, if you don't find a house handy, Cap'n Bill and I will sleep under the trees, or even on this soft grass."

But a house was not very far off, although when the Scarecrow stumbled upon it there was no light in it whatever. Cap'n Bill knocked on the door several times, and there being no response the Scarecrow boldly lifted the latch and walked in, followed by the others. And no sooner had they entered than a soft light filled the room. Trot couldn't tell where it came from, for no lamp of any sort was visible, but she did not waste much time on this problem, because directly in the center of the room stood a table set for three, with lots of good food on it and several of the dishes smoking hot.

The little girl and Button-Bright both uttered exclamations of pleasure, but they looked in vain for any cook stove or fireplace, or for any person who might have prepared for them this delicious feast.

"It's fairyland," muttered the boy, tossing his cap in a corner and seating himself at the table. "This supper smells 'most as good as that turkey-leg I had in Jinxland. Please pass the muffins, Cap'n Bill."

Trot thought it was strange that no people but themselves were in the house, but on the wall opposite the door was a gold frame bearing in big letters the word:

WELCOME

So she had no further hesitation in eating of the food so mysteriously prepared for them.

"But there are only places for three!" she exclaimed.

"Three are quite enough," said the Scarecrow. "I never eat, because I am stuffed full already, and I like my nice clean straw better than I do food."

Trot and the sailor-man were hungry and made a hearty meal, for not since they had left home had they tasted such good food. It was surprising that Button-Bright could eat so soon after his feast in Jinxland, but the boy always ate whenever there was an opportunity. "If I don't eat now," he said, "the next time I'm hungry I'll wish I had."

"Really, Cap'n," remarked Trot, when she found a dish of ice-cream appear beside her plate, "I b'lieve this is fairyland, sure enough."

"There's no doubt of it, Trot," he answered gravely

"I've been here before," said Button-Bright, "so I know."

After supper they discovered three tiny bedrooms adjoining the big living room of the house, and in each room was a comfortable white bed with downy pillows. You may be sure that the tired mortals were not long in bidding the Scarecrow good night and creeping into their beds, where they slept soundly until morning.

For the first time since they set eyes on the terrible whirlpool, Trot and Cap'n Bill were free from anxiety and care. Button-Bright never worried about anything. The Scarecrow, not being able to sleep, looked out of the window and tried to count the stars.

21. Dorothy, Betsy and Ozma

I suppose many of my readers have read descriptions of the beautiful and magnificent Emerald City of Oz, so I need not describe it here, except to state that never has any city in any fairyland ever equalled this one in stately splendor. It lies almost exactly in the center of the Land of Oz, and in the center of the Emerald City rises the wall of glistening emeralds that surrounds the palace of Ozma. The palace is almost a city in itself and is inhabited by many of the Ruler's especial friends and those who have won her confidence and favor. As for Ozma herself, there are no words in any dictionary I can find that are fitted to describe this young girl's beauty of mind and person. Merely to see her is to love her for her charming face and manners; to know her is to love her for her tender sympathy, her generous nature, her truth and honor. Born of a long line of Fairy Queens, Ozma is as nearly perfect as any fairy may be, and she is noted for her wisdom as well as for her other qualities. Her happy subjects adore their girl Ruler and each one considers her a comrade and protector.

At the time of which I write, Ozma's best friend and most constant companion was a little Kansas girl named Dorothy, a mortal who had come to the Land of Oz in a very curious manner and had been offered a home in Ozma's palace. Furthermore, Dorothy had been made a Princess of Oz, and was as much at home in the royal palace as was the gentle Ruler. She knew almost every part of the great country and almost all of its numerous inhabitants. Next to Ozma she was loved better than anyone in all Oz, for Dorothy was simple and sweet, seldom became angry and had such a friendly, chummy way that she made friends where-ever she wandered. It was she who first brought the Scarecrow and the Tin Woodman and the Cowardly Lion to the Emerald City. Dorothy had also introduced to Ozma the Shaggy Man and the Hungry Tiger, as well as Billina the Yellow Hen, Eureka the Pink Kitten, and many other delightful characters and creatures. Coming as she did from our world, Dorothy was much like many other girls we know; so there were times when she was not so wise as she might have been, and other times when she was obstinate and got herself into trouble. But life in a fairy-land had taught the little girl to accept all sorts of surprising things as matters-of-course, for while Dorothy was no fairy — but just as mortal as we are — she had seen more wonders than most mortals ever do.

Another little girl from our outside world also lived in Ozma's palace. This was Betsy Bobbin, whose strange adventures had brought her to the Emerald City, where Ozma had cordially welcomed her. Betsy was a shy little thing and could never get used to the marvels that surrounded her, but she and Dorothy were firm friends and thought themselves very fortunate in being together in this delightful country.

One day Dorothy and Betsy were visiting Ozma in the girl Ruler's private apartment, and among the things that especially interested them was Ozma's Magic Picture, set in a handsome frame and hung upon the wall of the room. This picture was a magic one because it constantly changed its scenes and showed events and adventures happening in all parts of the world. Thus it was really a "moving picture" of life, and if the one who stood before it wished to know what any absent person was doing, the picture instantly showed that person, with his or her surroundings.

The two girls were not wishing to see anyone in particular, on this occasion, but merely enjoyed watching the shifting scenes, some of which were exceedingly curious and remarkable. Suddenly Dorothy exclaimed: "Why, there's Button-Bright!" and this drew Ozma also to look at the picture, for she and Dorothy knew the boy well.

"Who is Button-Bright?" asked Betsy, who had never met him.

"Why, he's the little boy who is just getting off the back of that strange flying creature," exclaimed Dorothy. Then she turned to Ozma and asked: "What is that thing, Ozma? A bird? I've never seen anything like it before."

"It is an Ork," answered Ozma, for they were watching the scene where the Ork and the three big birds were first landing their passengers in Jinxland after the long flight across the desert. "I wonder," added the girl Ruler, musingly, "why those strangers dare venture into that unfortunate country, which is ruled by a wicked King."

"That girl, and the one-legged man, seem to be mortals from the outside world," said Dorothy

"The man isn't one-legged," corrected Betsy; "he has one wooden leg."

"It's almost as bad," declared Dorothy, watching Cap'n Bill stump around.

"They are three mortal adventurers," said Ozma, "and they seem worthy and honest. But I fear they will be treated badly in Jinxland, and if they meet with any misfortune there it will reflect upon me, for Jinxland is a part of my dominions."

"Can't we help them in any way?" inquired Dorothy. "That seems like a nice little girl. I'd be sorry if anything happened to her."

"Let us watch the picture for awhile," suggested Ozma, and so they all drew chairs before the Magic Picture and followed the adventures of Trot and Cap'n Bill and Button-Bright. Presently the scene shifted and showed their friend the Scarecrow crossing the mountains into Jinxland, and that somewhat relieved Ozma's anxiety, for she knew at once that Glinda the Good had sent the Scarecrow to protect the strangers.

The adventures in Jinxland proved very interesting to the three girls in Ozma's palace, who during the succeeding days spent much of their time in watching the picture. It was like a story to them.

"That girl's a reg'lar trump!" exclaimed Dorothy, referring to Trot, and Ozma answered: "She's a dear little thing, and I'm sure nothing very bad will happen to her. The old sailor is a fine character, too, for he has never once grumbled over being a grasshopper, as so many would have done."

When the Scarecrow was so nearly burned up the girls all shivered a little, and they clapped their hands in joy when the flock of Orks came and saved him.

So it was that when all the exciting adventures in Jinxland were over and the four Orks had begun their flight across the mountains to carry the mortals into the Land of Oz, Ozma called the Wizard to her and asked him to prepare a place for the strangers to sleep.

The famous Wizard of Oz was a quaint little man who inhabited the royal palace and attended to all the magical things that Ozma wanted done. He was not as powerful as Glinda, to be sure, but he could do a great many wonderful things. He proved this by placing a house in the uninhabited part of the Quadling Country where the Orks landed Cap'n Bill and Trot and Button-Bright, and fitting it with all the comforts I have described in the last chapter.

Next morning Dorothy said to Ozma: "Oughtn't we to go meet the strangers, so we can show them the way to the Emerald City? I'm sure that little girl will feel shy in this beautiful land, and I know if 'twas me I'd like somebody to give me a welcome."

Ozma smiled at her little friend and answered: "You and Betsy may go to meet them, if you wish, but I can not leave my palace just now, as I am to have a conference with Jack Pumpkinhead and Professor Wogglebug on important matters. You may take the Sawhorse and the Red Wagon, and if you start soon you will be able to meet the Scarecrow and the strangers at Glinda's palace."

"Oh, thank you!" cried Dorothy, and went away to tell Betsy and to make preparations for the journey.

22. The Waterfall

Glinda's castle was a long way from the mountains, but the Scarecrow began the journey cheerfully, since time was of no great importance in the Land of Oz and he had recently made the trip and knew the way. It never mattered much to Button-Bright where he was or what he was doing; the boy was content in being alive and having good companions to share his wanderings. As for Trot and Cap'n Bill, they now found themselves so comfortable and free from danger, in this fine fairyland, and they were so awed and amazed by the adventures they were encountering, that the journey to Glinda's castle was more like a pleasure trip than a hardship, so many wonderful things were there to see.

Button-Bright had been in Oz before, but never in this part of it, so the Scarecrow was the only one who knew the paths and could lead them. They had eaten a hearty breakfast, which they found already prepared for them and awaiting them on the table when they arose from their refreshing sleep, so they left the magic house in a contented mood and with hearts lighter and more happy than they had known for many a day. As they marched along through the fields, the sun shone brightly and the breeze was laden with delicious fragrance, for it carried with it the breath of millions of wildflowers.

At noon, when they stopped to rest by the bank of a pretty river, Trot said with a long-drawn breath that was much like a sigh: "I wish we'd brought with us some of the food that was left from our breakfast, for I'm getting hungry again."

Scarcely had she spoken when a table rose up before them, as if from the ground itself, and it was loaded with fruits and nuts and cakes and many other good things to eat. The little girl's eyes opened wide at this display of magic, and Cap'n Bill was not sure that the things were actually there and fit to eat until he had taken them in his hand and tasted them. But the Scarecrow said with a laugh: "Someone is looking after your welfare, that is certain, and from the looks of this table I suspect my friend the Wizard has taken us in his charge. I've known him to do things like this before, and if we are in the Wizard's care you need not worry about your future."

"Who's worrying?" inquired Button-Bright, already at the table and busily eating.

The Scarecrow looked around the place while the others were feasting, and finding many things unfamiliar to him he shook his head and remarked: "I must have taken the wrong path, back in that last valley, for on my way to Jinxland I remember that I passed around the foot of this river, where there was a great waterfall."

"Did the river make a bend, after the waterfall?" asked Cap'n Bill.

"No, the river disappeared. Only a pool of whirling water showed what had become of the river; but I suppose it is under ground, somewhere, and will come to the surface again in another part of the country."

"Well," suggested Trot, as she finished her luncheon, "as there is no way to cross this river, I s'pose we'll have to find that waterfall, and go around it."

"Exactly," replied the Scarecrow; so they soon renewed their journey, following the river for a long time until the roar of the waterfall sounded in their ears. By and by they came to the waterfall itself, a sheet of silver dropping far, far down into a tiny lake which seemed to have no outlet. From the top of the fall, where they stood, the banks gradually sloped away, so that the descent by land was quite easy, while the river could do nothing but glide over an edge of rock and tumble straight down to the depths below.

"You see," said the Scarecrow, leaning over the brink, "this is called by our Oz people the Great Waterfall, because it is certainly the highest one in all the land; but I think — Help!"

He had lost his balance and pitched headforemost into the river. They saw a flash of straw and blue clothes, and the painted face looking upward in surprise. The next moment the Scarecrow was swept over the waterfall and plunged into the basin below.

The accident had happened so suddenly that for a moment they were all too horrified to speak or move.

"Quick! We must go to help him or he will be drowned," Trot exclaimed.

Even while speaking she began to descend the bank to the pool below, and Cap'n Bill followed as swiftly as his wooden leg would let him. Button-Bright came more slowly, calling to the girl: "He can't drown, Trot; he's a Scarecrow."

But she wasn't sure a Scarecrow couldn't drown and never relaxed her speed until she stood on the edge of the pool, with the spray dashing in her face. Cap'n Bill, puffing and panting, had just voice enough to ask, as he reached her side: "See him, Trot?"

"Not a speck of him. Oh, Cap'n, what do you s'pose has become of him?"

"I s'pose," replied the sailor, "that he's in that water, more or less far down, and I'm 'fraid it'll make his straw pretty soggy. But as fer his bein' drowned, I agree with Button-Bright that it can't be done."

There was small comfort in this assurance and Trot stood for some time searching with her eyes the bubbling water, in the hope that the Scarecrow would finally come to the surface. Presently she heard Button-Bright calling: "Come here, Trot!" and looking around she saw that the boy had crept over the we rocks to the edge of the waterfall and seemed to be peering behind it. Making her way toward him, she asked: "What do you see?"

"A cave," he answered. "Let's go in. P'r'aps we'll find the Scarecrow there."

She was a little doubtful of that, but the cave interested her, and so did it Cap'n Bill. There was just space enough at the edge of the sheet of water for them to crowd in behind it, but after that dangerous entrance they found room enough to walk upright and after a time they came to an opening in the wall of rock. Approaching this opening, they gazed within it and found a series of steps, cut so that they might easily descend into the cavern.

Trot turned to look inquiringly at her companions. The falling water made such din and roaring that her voice could not be heard. Cap'n Bill nodded his head, but before he could enter the cave, Button-Bright was before him, clambering down the steps without a particle of fear. So the others followed the boy.

The first steps were wet with spray, and slippery, but the remainder were quite dry. A rosy light seemed to come from the interior of the cave, and this lighted their way. After the steps there was a short tunnel, high enough for them to walk erect in. and then they reached the cave itself and paused in wonder and admiration.

They stood on the edge of a vast cavern, the walls and domed roof of which were lined with countless rubies, exquisitely cut and flashing sparkling rays from one to another. This caused a radiant light that permitted the entire cavern to be distinctly seen, and the effect was so marvelous that Trot drew in her breath with a sort of a gasp, and stood quite still in wonder.

But the walls and roof of the cavern were merely a setting for a more wonderful scene. In the center was a bubbling caldron of water, for here the river rose again, splashing and dashing till its spray rose high in the air, where it took the ruby color of the jewels and seemed like a seething mass of flame. And while they gazed into the tumbling, tossing water, the body of the Scarecrow suddenly rose in the center, struggling and kicking, and the next instant wholly disappeared from view.

"My, but he's wet!" exclaimed Button-Bright; but none of the others heard him.

Trot and Cap'n Bill discovered that a broad ledge — covered, like the walls, with glittering rubies — ran all around the cavern; so they followed this gorgeous path to the rear and found where the water made its final dive underground, before it disappeared entirely. Where it plunged into this dim abyss the river was black and dreary looking, and they stood gazing in awe until just beside them the body of the Scarecrow again popped up from the water.

23. The Land of Oz

The straw man's appearance on the water was so sudden that it startled Trot, but Cap'n Bill had the presence of mind to stick his wooden leg out over the water and the Scarecrow made a desperate clutch and grabbed the leg with both hands. He managed to hold on until Trot and Button-Bright knelt down and seized his clothing, but the children would have been powerless to drag the soaked Scarecrow ashore had not Cap'n Bill now assisted them. When they laid him on the ledge of rubies he was the most useless looking Scarecrow you can

imagine — his straw sodden and dripping with water, his clothing wet and crumpled, while even the sack upon which his face was painted had become so wrinkled that the old jolly expression of their stuffed friend's features was entirely gone. But he could still speak, and when Trot bent down her ear she heard him say: "Get me out of here as soon as you can."

That seemed a wise thing to do, so Cap'n Bill lifted his head and shoulders, and Trot and Button-Bright each took a leg; among them they partly carried and partly dragged the damp Scarecrow out of the Ruby Cavern, along the tunnel, and up the flight of rock steps. It was somewhat difficult to get him past the edge of the waterfall, but they succeeded, after much effort, and a few minutes later laid their poor comrade on a grassy bank where the sun shone upon him freely and he was beyond the reach of the spray.

Cap'n Bill now knelt down and examined the straw that the Scarecrow was stuffed with.

"I don't believe it'll be of much use to him, any more," said he, "for it's full of polliwogs an' fish eggs, an' the water has took all the crinkle out o' the straw an ruined it. I guess, Trot, that the best thing for us to do is to empty out all his body an' carry his head an' clothes along the road till we come to a field or a house where we can get some fresh straw."

"Yes, Cap'n," she agreed, "there's nothing else to be done. But how shall we ever find the road to Glinda's palace, without the Scarecrow to guide us?"

"That's easy," said the Scarecrow, speaking in a rather feeble but distinct voice. "If Cap'n Bill will carry my head on his shoulders, eyes front, I can tell him which way to go."

So they followed that plan and emptied all the old, wet straw out of the Scarecrow's body. Then the sailor-man wrung out the clothes and laid them in the sun till they were quite dry. Trot took charge of the head and pressed the wrinkles out of the face as it dried, so that after a while the Scarecrow's expression became natural again, and as jolly as before.

This work consumed some time, but when it was completed they again started upon their journey, Button-Bright carrying the boots and hat, Trot the bundle of clothes, and Cap'n Bill the head. The Scarecrow, having regained his composure and being now in a good humor, despite his recent mishaps, beguiled their way with stories of the Land of Oz.

It was not until the next morning, however, that they found straw with which to restuff the Scarecrow. That evening they came to the same little house they had slept in before, only now it was magically transferred to a new place. The same bountiful supper as before was found smoking hot upon the table and the same cosy beds were ready for them to sleep in.

They rose early and after breakfast went out of doors, and there, lying just beside the house, was a heap of clean, crisp straw. Ozma had noticed the Scarecrow's accident in her Magic Picture and had notified the Wizard to provide the straw, for she knew the adventurers were not likely to find straw in the country through which they were now traveling.

They lost no time in stuffing the Scarecrow anew, and he was greatly delighted at being able to walk around again and to assume the leadership of the little party.

"Really," said Trot, "I think you're better than you were before, for you are fresh and sweet all through and rustle beautifully when you move."

"Thank you, my dear," he replied gratefully. "I always feel like a new man when I'm freshly stuffed. No one likes to get musty, you know, and even good straw may be spoiled by age."

"It was water that spoiled you, the last time," remarked Button-Bright, "which proves that too much bathing is as bad as too little. But, after all, Scarecrow, water is not as dangerous for you as fire."

"All things are good in moderation," declared the Scarecrow. "But now, let us hurry on, or we shall not reach Glinda's palace by nightfall."

24. The Royal Reception

At about four o'clock of that same day the Red Wagon drew up at the entrance to Glinda's palace and Dorothy and Betsy jumped out. Ozma's Red Wagon was almost a chariot, being inlaid with rubies and pearls, and it was drawn by Ozma's favorite steed, the wooden Sawhorse.

"Shall I unharness you," asked Dorothy, "so you can come in and visit?"

"No," replied the Sawhorse. "I'll just stand here and think. Take your time. Thinking doesn't seem to bore me at all."

"What will you think of?" inquired Betsy.

"Of the acorn that grew the tree from which I was made."

So they left the wooden animal and went in to see Glinda, who welcomed the little girls in her most cordial manner.

"I knew you were on your way," said the good Sorceress when they were seated in her library, "for I learned from my Record Book that you intended to meet Trot and Button-Bright on their arrival here."

"Is the strange little girl named Trot?" asked Dorothy.

"Yes; and her companion, the old sailor, is named Cap'n Bill. I think we shall like them very much, for they are just the kind of people to enjoy and appreciate our fairyland and I do not see any way, at present, for them to return again to the outside world."

"Well, there's room enough here for them, I'm sure," said Dorothy. "Betsy and I are already eager to welcome Trot. It will keep us busy for a year, at least, showing her all the wonderful things in Oz."

Glinda smiled.

"I have lived here many years," said she, "and I have not seen all the wonders of Oz yet."

Meantime the travelers were drawing near to the palace, and when they first caught sight of its towers Trot realized that it was far more grand and imposing than was the King's castle in Jinxland. The nearer they came, the more beautiful the palace appeared, and when finally the Scarecrow led them up the great marble steps, even Button-Bright was filled with awe.

"I don't see any soldiers to guard the place," said the little girl.

"There is no need to guard Glinda's palace," replied the Scarecrow. "We have no wicked people in Oz, that we know of, and even if there were any, Glinda's magic would be powerful enough to protect her."

Button-Bright was now standing on the top steps of the entrance, and he suddenly exclaimed: "Why, there's the Sawhorse and the Red Wagon! Hip, hooray!" and next moment he was rushing down to throw his arms around the neck of the wooden horse, which good-naturedly permitted this familiarity when it recognized in the boy an old friend.

Button-Bright's shout had been heard inside the palace, so now Dorothy and Betsy came running out to embrace their beloved friend, the Scarecrow, and to welcome Trot and Cap'n Bill to the Land of Oz.

"We've been watching you for a long time, in Ozma's Magic Picture," said Dorothy, "and Ozma has sent us to invite you to her own palace in the Em'rald City. I don't know if you realize how lucky you are to get that invitation, but you'll understand it better after you've seen the royal palace and the Em'rald City."

Glinda now appeared in person to lead all the party into her Azure Reception Room. Trot was a little afraid of the stately Sorceress, but gained courage by holding fast to the hands of Betsy and Dorothy. Cap'n Bill had no one to help him feel at ease, so the old sailor sat stiffly on the edge of his chair and said: "Yes, ma'am," or "No, ma'am," when he was spoken to, and was greatly embarrassed by so much splendor.

The Scarecrow had lived so much in palaces that he felt quite at home, and he chatted to Glinda and the Oz girls in a merry, light-hearted way. He told all about his adventures in Jinxland, and at the Great Waterfall, and on the journey hither — most of which his hearers knew already — and then he asked Dorothy and Betsy what had happened in the Emerald City since he had left there.

They all passed the evening and the night at Glinda's palace, and the Sorceress was so gracious to Cap'n Bill that the old man by degrees regained his self-possession and began to enjoy himself. Trot had already come to the conclusion that in Dorothy and Betsy she had found two delightful comrades, and Button-Bright was just as much at home here as he had been in the fields of Jinxland or when he was buried in the popcorn snow of the Land of Mo.

The next morning they arose bright and early and after breakfast bade good-bye to the kind Sorceress, whom Trot and Cap'n Bill thanked earnestly for sending the Scarecrow to Jinxland to rescue them. Then they all climbed into the Red Wagon.

There was room for all on the broad seats, and when all had taken their places — Dorothy, Trot and Betsy on the rear seat and Cap'n Bill, Button-Bright and the Scarecrow in front — they called "Gid-dap!" to the Sawhorse and the wooden steed moved briskly away, pulling the Red Wagon with ease.

It was now that the strangers began to perceive the real beauties of the Land of Oz, for they were passing through a more thickly settled part of the country and the population grew more dense as they drew nearer to the Emerald City. Everyone they met had a cheery word or a smile for the Scarecrow, Dorothy and Betsy Bobbin, and some of them remembered Button-Bright and welcomed him back to their country.

It was a happy party, indeed, that journeyed in the Red Wagon to the Emerald City, and Trot already began to hope that Ozma would permit her and Cap'n Bill to live always in the Land of Oz.

When they reached the great city they were more amazed than ever, both by the concourse of people in their quaint and picturesque costumes, and by the splendor of the city itself. But the magnificence of the Royal Palace quite took their breath away, until Ozma received them in her own pretty apartment and by her charming manners and assuring smiles made them feel they were no longer strangers.

Trot was given a lovely little room next to that of Dorothy, while Cap'n Bill had the cosiest sort of a room next to Trot's and overlooking the gardens. And that evening Ozma gave a grand banquet and reception in honor of the new arrivals. While Trot had read of many of the people she then met, Cap'n Bill was less familiar with them and many of the unusual characters introduced to him that evening caused the old sailor to open his eyes wide in astonishment.

He had thought the live Scarecrow about as curious as anyone could be, but now he met the Tin Woodman, who was all made of tin, even to his heart, and carried a gleaming axe over his shoulder wherever he went. Then there was Jack Pumpkinhead, whose head was a real pumpkin with the face carved upon it; and Professor Wogglebug, who had the shape of an enormous bug but was dressed in neat fitting garments. The Professor was an interesting talker and had very polite manners, but his face was so comical that it made Cap'n Bill smile to look at it. A great friend of Dorothy and Ozma seemed to be a machine man called Tik-Tok, who ran down several times during the evening and had to be wound up again by someone before he could move or speak.

At the reception appeared the Shaggy Man and his brother, both very popular in Oz, as well as Dorothy's Uncle Henry and Aunt Em, two happy old people who lived in a pretty cottage near the palace.

But what perhaps seemed most surprising to both Trot and Cap'n Bill was the number of peculiar animals admitted into Ozma's parlors, where they not only conducted themselves quite properly but were able to talk as well as anyone.

There was the Cowardly Lion, an immense beast with a beautiful mane; and the Hungry Tiger, who smiled continually; and Eureka the Pink Kitten, who lay curled upon a cushion and had rather supercilious manners; and the wooden Sawhorse; and nine tiny piglets that belonged to the Wizard; and a mule named Hank, who belonged to Betsy Bobbin. A fuzzy little terrier dog, named Toto, lay at Dorothy's feet but seldom took part in the conversation, although he listened to every word that was said. But the most wonderful of all to Trot was a square beast with a grinning smile, that squatted in a corner of the room and wagged his square head at everyone in quite a jolly way. Betsy told Trot that this unique beast was called the Woozy, and there was no other like him in all the world.

Cap'n Bill and Trot had both looked around expectantly for the Wizard of Oz, but the evening was far advanced before the famous little man entered the room. But he went up to the strangers at once and said: "I know you, but you don't know me; so let's get acquainted."

And they did get acquainted, in a very short time, and before the evening was over Trot felt that she knew every person and animal present at the reception, and that they were all her good friends.

Suddenly they looked around for Button-Bright, but he was nowhere to be found.

"Dear me!" cried Trot. "He's lost again."

"Never mind, my dear," said Ozma, with her charming smile, "no one can go far astray in the Land of Oz, and if Button-Bright isn't lost occasionally, he isn't happy."

Rinkitink In Oz
by L. Frank Baum

Wherein is recorded the Perilous Quest of Prince Inga of Pingaree and King Rinkitink in the Magical Isles that lie beyond the Borderland of Oz, By L. Frank Baum, "Royal Historian of Oz"

Introducing this Story

Here is a story with a boy hero, and a boy of whom you have never before heard. There are girls in the story, too, including our old friend Dorothy, and some of the characters wander a good way from the Land of Oz before they all assemble in the Emerald City to take part in Ozma's banquet. Indeed, I think you will find this story quite different from the other histories of Oz, but I hope you will not like it the less on that account.

If I am permitted to write another Oz book it will tell of some thrilling adventures encountered by Dorothy, Betsy Bobbin, Trot and the Patchwork Girl right in the Land of Oz, and how they discovered some amazing creatures that never could have existed outside a fairy-land. I have an idea that about the time you are reading this story of Rinkitink I shall be writing that story of Adventures in Oz.

Don't fail to write me often and give me your advice and suggestions, which I always appreciate. I get a good many letters from my readers, but every one is a joy to me and I answer them as soon as I can find time to do so.

L. Frank Baum, "Royal Historian of Oz"
"Ozcot" at Hollywood in California, 1916.

1. The Prince of Pingaree

If you have a map of the Land of Oz handy, you will find that the great Nonestic Ocean washes the shores of the Kingdom of Rinkitink, between which and the Land of Oz lies a strip of the country of the Nome King and a Sandy Desert. The Kingdom of Rinkitink isn't very big and lies close to the ocean, all the houses and the King's palace being built near the shore. The people live much upon the water, boating and fishing, and the wealth of Rinkitink is gained from trading along the coast and with the islands nearest it.

Four days' journey by boat to the north of Rinkitink is the Island of Pingaree, and as our story begins here I must tell you something about this island. At the north end of Pingaree, where it is widest, the land is a mile from shore to shore, but at the south end it is scarcely half a mile broad; thus, although Pingaree is four miles long, from north to south, it cannot be called a very big island. It is exceedingly pretty, however, and to the gulls who approach it from the sea it must resemble a huge green wedge lying upon the waters, for its grass and trees give it the color of an emerald.

The grass came to the edge of the sloping shores; the beautiful trees occupied all the central portion of Pingaree, forming a continuous grove where the branches met high overhead and there was just space beneath them for the cosy houses of the inhabitants. These houses were scattered everywhere throughout the island, so that there was no town or city, unless the whole island might be called a city. The canopy of leaves, high overhead, formed a shelter from sun and rain, and the dwellers in the grove could all look past the straight tree-trunks and across the grassy slopes to the purple waters of the Nonestic Ocean.

At the big end of the island, at the north, stood the royal palace of King Kitticut, the lord and ruler of Pingaree. It was a beautiful palace, built entirely of snow-white marble and capped by domes of burnished gold, for the King was exceedingly wealthy. All along the coast of Pingaree were found the largest and finest pearls in the whole world.

These pearls grew within the shells of big oysters, and the people raked the oysters from their watery beds, sought out the milky pearls and carried them dutifully to their King. Therefore, once every year His Majesty was able to send six of his boats, with sixty rowers and many sacks of the valuable pearls, to the Kingdom of Rinkitink, where there was a city called Gilgad, in which King Rinkitink's palace stood on a rocky headland and served, with its high towers, as a lighthouse to guide sailors to the harbor. In Gilgad the pearls from Pingaree were purchased by the King's treasurer, and the boats went back to the island laden with stores of rich merchandise and such supplies of food as the people and the royal family of Pingaree needed.

The Pingaree people never visited any other land but that of Rinkitink, and so there were few other lands that knew there was such an island. To the southwest was an island called the Isle of Phreex, where the inhabitants had no use for pearls. And far north of Pingaree — six days' journey by boat, it was said — were twin islands named Regos and Coregos, inhabited by a fierce and warlike people.

Many years before this story really begins, ten big boatloads of those fierce warriors of Regos and Coregos visited Pingaree landing suddenly upon the north end of the island. There they began to plunder and conquer, as was their custom, but the people of Pingaree, although neither so big nor so strong as their foes, were able to defeat them and drive them all back to the sea where a great storm overtook the raiders from Regos and Coregos and destroyed them and their boats, not a single warrior returning to his own country.

This defeat of the enemy seemed the more wonderful because the pearl-fishers of Pingaree were mild and peaceful in disposition and seldom quarreled even among themselves. Their only weapons were their oyster rakes; yet the fact remains that they drove their fierce enemies from Regos and Coregos from their shores.

King Kitticut was only a boy when this remarkable battle was fought, and now his hair was gray; but he remembered the day well and, during the years that followed, his one constant fear was of another invasion of his enemies. He feared they might send a more numerous army to his island, both for conquest and revenge, in which case there could be little hope of successfully opposing them.

This anxiety on the part of King Kitticut led him to keep a sharp lookout for strange boats, one of his men patrolling the beach constantly, but he was too wise to allow any fear to make him or his subjects unhappy. He was a good King and lived very contentedly in his fine palace, with his fair Queen Garee and their one child, Prince Inga.

The wealth of Pingaree increased year by year; and the happiness of the people increased, too. Perhaps there was no place, outside the Land of Oz, where contentment and peace were more manifest than on this pretty island, hidden in the besom of the Nonestic Ocean. Had these conditions remained undisturbed, there would have been no need to speak of Pingaree in this story.

Prince Inga, the heir to all the riches and the kingship of Pingaree, grew up surrounded by every luxury; but he was a manly little fellow, although somewhat too grave and thoughtful, and he could never bear to be idle a single minute. He knew where the finest oysters lay hidden along the coast and was as successful in finding pearls as any of the men of the island, although he was so slight and small. He had a little boat of his own and a rake for dragging up the oysters and he was very proud indeed when he could carry a big white pearl to his father.

There was no school upon the island, as the people of Pingaree were far removed from the state of civilization that gives our modern children such advantages as schools and learned professors, but the King owned several manuscript books, the pages being made of sheepskin. Being a man of intelligence, he was able to teach his son something of reading, writing and arithmetic.

When studying his lessons Prince Inga used to go into the grove near his father's palace and climb into the branches of a tall tree, where he had built a platform with a comfortable seat to rest upon, all hidden by the canopy of leaves. There, with no one to disturb him, he would pore over the sheepskin on which were written the queer characters of the Pingarese language.

King Kitticut was very proud of his little son, as well he might be, and he soon felt a high respect for Inga's judgment and thought that he was worthy to be taken into the confidence of his father in many matters of state. He taught the boy the needs of the people and how to rule them justly, for some day he knew that Inga would be King in his place. One day he called his son to his side and said to him: "Our island now seems peaceful enough, Inga, and we are happy and prosperous, but I cannot forget those terrible people of Regos and Coregos. My constant fear is that they will send a fleet of boats to search for those of their race whom we defeated many years ago, and whom the sea afterwards destroyed. If the warriors come in great numbers we may be unable to oppose them, for my people are little trained to fighting at best; they surely would cause us much injury and suffering."

"Are we, then, less powerful than in my grandfather's day?" asked Prince Inga.

The King shook his head thoughtfully.

"It is not that," said he. "That you may fully understand that marvelous battle, I must confide to, you a great secret. I have in my possession three Magic Talismans, which I have ever guarded with utmost care, keeping the knowledge of their existence from anyone else. But, lest I should die, and the secret be lost, I have decided to tell you what these talismans are and where they are hidden. Come with me, my son.

He led the way through the rooms of the palace until they came to the great banquet hall. There, stopping in the center of the room, he stooped down and touched a hidden spring in the tiled floor. At once one of the tiles sank downward and the King reached within the cavity and drew out a silken bag.

This bag he proceeded to open, showing Inga that it contained three great pearls, each one as big around as a marble. One had a blue tint and one was of a delicate rose color, but the third was pure white.

"These three pearls," said the King, speaking in a solemn, impressive voice, "are the most wonderful the world has ever known. They were gifts to one of my ancestors from the Mermaid Queen, a powerful fairy whom he once had the good fortune to rescue from her enemies. In gratitude for this favor she presented him with these pearls. Each of the three possesses an astonishing power, and whoever is their owner may count himself a fortunate man. This one having the blue tint will give to the person who carries it a strength so great that no power can resist him. The one with the pink glow will protect its owner from all dangers that may threaten him, no matter from what source they may come. The third pearl — this one of pure white — can speak, and its words are always wise and helpful."

"What is this, my father!" exclaimed the Prince, amazed; "do you tell me that a pearl can speak? It sounds impossible."

"Your doubt is due to your ignorance of fairy powers," returned the King, gravely. "Listen, my son, and you will know that I speak the truth."

He held the white pearl to Inga's ear and the Prince heard a small voice say distinctly: "Your father is right. Never question the truth of what you fail to understand, for the world is filled with wonders."

"I crave your pardon, dear father," said the Prince, "for clearly I heard the pearl speak, and its words were full of wisdom."

"The powers of the other pearls are even greater," resumed the King. "Were I poor in all else, these gems would make me richer than any other monarch the world holds."

"I believe that," replied Inga, looking at the beautiful pearls with much awe. "But tell me, my father, why do you fear the warriors of Regos and Coregos when these marvelous powers are yours?"

"The powers are mine only while I have the pearls upon my person," answered King Kitticut, "and I dare not carry them constantly for fear they might be lost. Therefore, I keep them safely hidden in this recess. My only danger lies in the chance that my watchmen might fail to discover the approach of our enemies and allow the warrior invaders to seize me before I could secure the pearls. I should, in that case, be quite powerless to resist. My father owned the magic pearls at the time of the Great Fight, of which you have so often heard, and the pink pearl protected him from harm, while the blue pearl enabled him and his people to drive away the enemy. Often have I suspected that the destroying storm was caused by the fairy mermaids, but that is a matter of which I have no proof."

"I have often wondered how we managed to win that battle," remarked Inga thoughtfully. "But the pearls will assist us in case the warriors come again, will they not?"

"They are as powerful as ever," declared the King. "Really, my son, I have little to fear from any foe. But lest I die and the secret be lost to the next King, I have now given it into your keeping. Remember that these pearls are the rightful heritage of all Kings of Pingaree. If at any time I should be taken from you, Inga, guard this treasure well and do not forget where it is hidden."

"I shall not forget," said Inga.

Then the King returned the pearls to their hiding place and the boy went to his own room to ponder upon the wonderful secret his father had that day confided to his care.

2. The Coming of King Rinkitink

A few days after this, on a bright and sunny morning when the breeze blew soft and sweet from the ocean and the trees waved their leaf-laden branches, the Royal Watchman, whose duty it was to patrol the shore, came running to the King with news that a strange boat was approaching the island.

At first the King was sore afraid and made a step toward the hidden pearls, but the next moment he reflected that one boat, even if filled with enemies, would be powerless to injure him, so he curbed his fear and went down to the beach to discover who the strangers might be. Many of the men of Pingaree assembled there also, and Prince Inga followed his father. Arriving at the water's edge, they all stood gazing eagerly at the oncoming boat.

It was quite a big boat, they observed, and covered with a canopy of purple silk, embroidered with gold. It was rowed by twenty men, ten on each side. As it came nearer, Inga could see that in the stern, seated upon a high, cushioned chair of state, was a little man who was so very fat that he was nearly as broad as he was high. This man was dressed in a loose silken robe of purple that fell in folds to his feet, while upon his head was a cap of white velvet curiously worked with golden threads and having a circle of diamonds sewn around the band. At the opposite end of the boat stood an oddly shaped cage, and several large boxes of sandalwood were piled near the center of the craft.

As the boat approached the shore the fat little man got upon his feet and bowed several times in the direction of those who had assembled to greet him, and as he bowed he flourished his white cap in an energetic manner. His face was round as an apple and nearly as rosy. When he stopped bowing he smiled in such a sweet and happy way that Inga thought he must be a very jolly fellow.

The prow of the boat grounded on the beach, stopping its speed so suddenly that the little man was caught unawares and nearly toppled headlong into the sea. But he managed to catch hold of the chair with one hand and the hair of one of his rowers with the other, and so steadied himself. Then, again waving his jeweled cap around his head, he cried in a merry voice: "Well, here I am at last!"

"So I perceive," responded King Kitticut, bowing with much dignity.

The fat man glanced at all the sober faces before him and burst into a rollicking laugh. Perhaps I should say it was half laughter and half a chuckle of merriment, for the sounds he emitted were quaint and droll and tempted every hearer to laugh with him.

"Heh, heh — ho, ho, ho!" he roared. "Didn't expect me, I see. Keek-eek-eek-eek! This is funny — it's really funny. Didn't know I was coming, did you? Hoo, hoo, hoo, hoo! This is certainly amusing. But I'm here, just the same."

"Hush up!" said a deep, growling voice. "You're making yourself ridiculous."

Everyone looked to see where this voice came from; but none could guess who had uttered the words of rebuke. The rowers of the boat were all solemn and silent and certainly no one on the shore had spoken. But the little man did not seem astonished in the least, or even annoyed.

King Kitticut now addressed the stranger, saying courteously: "You are welcome to the Kingdom of Pingaree. Perhaps you will deign to come ashore and at your convenience inform us whom we have the honor of receiving as a guest."

"Thanks; I will," returned the little fat man, waddling from his place in the boat and stepping, with some difficulty, upon the sandy beach. "I am King Rinkitink, of the City of Gilgad in the Kingdom of Rinkitink, and I have come to Pingaree to see for myself the monarch who sends to my city so many beautiful pearls. I have long wished to visit this island; and so, as I said before, here I am!"

"I am pleased to welcome you," said King Kitticut. "But why has Your Majesty so few attendants? Is it not dangerous for the King of a great country to make distant journeys in one frail boat, and with but twenty men?"

"Oh, I suppose so," answered King Rinkitink, with a laugh. "But what else could I do? My subjects would not allow me to go anywhere at all, if they knew it. So I just ran away."

"Ran away!" exclaimed King Kitticut in surprise.

"Funny, isn't it? Heh, heh, heh — woo, hoo!" laughed Rinkitink, and this is as near as I can spell with letters the jolly sounds of his laughter. "Fancy a King running away from his own ple — hoo, hoo — keek, eek, eek, eek! But I had to, don't you see!"

"Why?" asked the other King.

"They're afraid I'll get into mischief. They don't trust me. Keek-eek-eek — Oh, dear me! Don't trust their own King. Funny, isn't it?"

"No harm can come to you on this island," said Kitticut, pretending not to notice the odd ways of his guest. "And, whenever it pleases you to return to your own country, I will send with you a fitting escort of my own people. In the meantime, pray accompany me to my palace, where everything shall be done to make you comfortable and happy."

"Much obliged," answered Rinkitink, tipping his white cap over his left ear and heartily shaking the hand of his brother monarch. "I'm sure you can make me comfortable if you've plenty to eat. And as for being happy — ha, ha, ha, ha! — why, that's my trouble. I'm too happy. But stop! I've brought you some presents in those boxes. Please order your men to carry them up to the palace."

"Certainly," answered King Kitticut, well pleased, and at once he gave his men the proper orders.

"And, by the way," continued the fat little King, "let them also take my goat from his cage."

"A goat!" exclaimed the King of Pingaree.

"Exactly; my goat Bilbil. I always ride him wherever I go, for I'm not at all fond of walking, being a trifle stout — eh, Kitticut? — a trifle stout! Hoo, hoo, hoo-keek, eek!"

The Pingaree people started to lift the big cage out of the boat, but just then a gruff voice cried: "Be careful, you villains!" and as the words seemed to come from the goat's mouth the men were so astonished that they dropped the cage upon the sand with a sudden jar.

"There! I told you so!" cried the voice angrily. "You've rubbed the skin off my left knee. Why on earth didn't you handle me gently?"

"There, there, Bilbil," said King Rinkitink soothingly; "don't scold, my boy. Remember that these are strangers, and we their guests." Then he turned to Kitticut and remarked: "You have no talking goats on your island, I suppose."

"We have no goats at all," replied the King; "nor have we any animals, of any sort, who are able to talk."

"I wish my animal couldn't talk, either," said Rinkitink, winking comically at Inga and then looking toward the cage. "He is very cross at times, and indulges in language that is not respectful. I thought, at first, it would be fine to have a talking goat, with whom I could converse as I rode about my city on his back; but — keek-eek-eek-eek! — the rascal treats me as if I were a chimney sweep instead of a King. Heh, heh, heh, keek, eek! A chimney sweep-hoo, hoo, hoo! — and me a King! Funny, isn't it?" This last was addressed to Prince Inga, whom he chucked familiarly under the chin, to the boy's great embarrassment.

"Why do you not ride a horse?" asked King Kitticut.

"I can't climb upon his back, being rather stout; that's why. Kee, kee, keek, eek! — rather stout — hoo, hoo, hoo!" He paused to wipe the tears of merriment from his eyes and then added: "But I can get on and off Bilbil's back with ease."

He now opened the cage and the goat deliberately walked out and looked about him in a sulky manner. One of the rowers brought from the boat a saddle made of red velvet and beautifully embroidered with silver thistles, which he fastened upon the goat's back. The fat King put his leg over the saddle and seated himself comfortably, saying: "Lead on, my noble host, and we will follow."

"What! Up that steep hill?" cried the goat. "Get off my back at once, Rinkitink, or I won't budge a step.

"But-consider, Bilbil," remonstrated the King. "How am I to get up that hill unless I ride?"

"Walk!" growled Bilbil.

"But I'm too fat. Really, Bilbil, I'm surprised at you. Haven't I brought you all this distance so you may see something of the world and enjoy life? And now you are so ungrateful as to refuse to carry me! Turn about is fair play, my boy. The boat carried you to this shore, because you can't swim, and now you must carry me up the hill, because I can't climb. Eh, Bilbil, isn't that reasonable?"

"Well, well, well," said the goat, surlily, "keep quiet and I'll carry you. But you make me very tired, Rinkitink, with your ceaseless chatter."

After making this protest Bilbil began walking up the hill, carrying the fat King upon his back with no difficulty whatever.

Prince Inga and his father and all the men of Pingaree were much astonished to overhear this dispute between King Rinkitink and his goat; but they were too polite to make critical remarks in the presence of their guests. King Kitticut walked beside the goat and the Prince followed after, the men coming last with the boxes of sandalwood.

When they neared the palace, the Queen and her maidens came out to meet them and the royal guest was escorted in state to the splendid throne room of the palace. Here the boxes were opened and King Rinkitink displayed all the beautiful silks and laces and jewelry with which they were filled. Every one of the courtiers and ladies received a handsome present, and the King and Queen had many rich gifts and Inga not a few. Thus the time passed pleasantly until the Chamberlain announced that dinner was served.

Bilbil the goat declared that he preferred eating of the sweet, rich grass that grew abundantly in the palace grounds, and Rinkitink said that the beast could never bear being shut up in a stable; so they removed the saddle from his back and allowed him to wander wherever he pleased.

During the dinner Inga divided his attention between admiring the pretty gifts he had received and listening to the jolly sayings of the fat King, who laughed when he was not eating and ate when he was not laughing and seemed to enjoy himself immensely.

"For four days I have lived in that narrow boat," said he, "with no other amusement than to watch the rowers and quarrel with Bilbil; so I am very glad to be on land again with such friendly and agreeable people."

"You do us great honor," said King Kitticut, with a polite bow.

"Not at all — not at all, my brother. This Pingaree must be a wonderful island, for its pearls are the admiration of all the world; nor will I deny the fact that my kingdom would be a poor one without the riches and glory it derives from the trade in your pearls. So I have wished for many years to come here to see you, but my people said: 'No! Stay at home and behave yourself, or we'll know the reason why.'"

"Will they not miss Your Majesty from your palace at Gilgad?" inquired Kitticut.

"I think not," answered Rinkitink. "You see, one of my clever subjects has written a parchment entitled 'How to be Good,' and I believed it would benefit me to study it, as I consider the accomplishment of being good one of the fine arts. I had just scolded severely my Lord High Chancellor for coming to breakfast without combing his eyebrows, and was so sad and regretful at having hurt the poor man's feelings that I decided to shut myself up in my own room and study the scroll until I knew how to be good — hee, heek, keek, eek, eek! —to be good! Clever idea, that, wasn't it? Mighty clever! And I issued a decree that no one should enter my room, under pain of my royal displeasure, until I was ready to come out. They're awfully afraid of my royal displeasure, although not a bit afraid of me. Then I put the parchment in my pocket and escaped through the back door to my boat — and here I am. Oo, hoo-hoo, keek-eek! Imagine the fuss there would be in Gilgad if my subjects knew where I am this very minute!"

"I would like to see that parchment," said the solemn-eyed Prince Inga, "for if it indeed teaches one to be good it must be worth its weight in pearls."

"Oh, it's a fine essay," said Rinkitink, "and beautifully written with a goosequill. Listen to this: You'll enjoy it — tee, hee, hee! — enjoy it."

He took from his pocket a scroll of parchment tied with a black ribbon, and having carefully unrolled it, he proceeded to read as follows: "'A Good Man is One who is Never Bad.' How's that, eh? Fine thought, what? 'Therefore, in order to be Good, you must avoid those Things which are Evil.' Oh, hoo-hoo-hoo! — how clever! When I get back I shall make the man who wrote that a royal hippolorum, for, beyond question, he is the wisest man in my kingdom — as he has often told me himself."

With this, Rinkitink lay back in his chair and chuckled his queer chuckle until he coughed, and coughed until he choked and choked until he sneezed. And he wrinkled his face in such a jolly, droll way that few could keep from laughing with him, and even the good Queen was forced to titter behind her fan.

When Rinkitink had recovered from his fit of laughter and had wiped his eyes upon a fine lace handkerchief, Prince Inga said to him: "The parchment speaks truly."

"Yes, it is true beyond doubt," answered Rinkitink, "and if I could persuade Bilbil to read it he would be a much better goat than he is now. Here is another selection: 'To avoid saying Unpleasant Things, always Speak Agreeably.' That would hit Bilbil, to a dot. And here is one that applies to you, my Prince: 'Good Children are seldom punished, for the reason that they deserve no punishment.' Now, I think that is neatly put, and shows the author to be a deep thinker. But the advice that has impressed me the most is in the following paragraph: 'You may not find it as Pleasant to be Good as it is to be Bad, but Other People will find it more Pleasant.' Haw-hoo-ho! keek-eek! 'Other people will find it more pleasant!' — hee, hee, heek, keek! — 'more pleasant.' Dear me — dear me! Therein lies a noble incentive to be good, and whenever I get time I'm surely going to try it."

Then he wiped his eyes again with the lace handkerchief and, suddenly remembering his dinner, seized his knife and fork and began eating.

3. The Warriors from the North

King Rinkitink was so much pleased with the Island of Pingaree that he continued his stay day after day and week after week, eating good dinners, talking with King Kitticut and sleeping. Once in a while he would read from his scroll. "For," said he, "whenever I return home, my subjects will be anxious to know if I have learned 'How to be Good,' and I must not disappoint them."

The twenty rowers lived on the small end of the island, with the pearl fishers, and seemed not to care whether they ever returned to the Kingdom of Rinkitink or not. Bilbil the goat wandered over the grassy slopes, or among the trees, and passed his days exactly as he pleased. His master seldom cared to ride him. Bilbil was a rare curiosity to the islanders, but since there was little pleasure in talking with the goat they kept away from him. This pleased the creature, who seemed well satisfied to be left to his own devices.

Once Prince Inga, wishing to be courteous, walked up to the goat and said: "Good morning, Bilbil."

"It isn't a good morning," answered Bilbil grumpily. "It is cloudy and damp, and looks like rain."

"I hope you are contented in our kingdom," continued the boy, politely ignoring the other's harsh words.

"I'm not," said Bilbil. "I'm never contented; so it doesn't matter to me whether I'm in your kingdom or in some other kingdom. Go away — will you?"

"Certainly," answered the Prince, and after this rebuff he did not again try to make friends with Bilbil.

Now that the King, his father, was so much occupied with his royal guest, Inga was often left to amuse himself, for a boy could not be allowed to take part in the conversation of two great monarchs. He devoted himself to his studies, therefore, and day after day he climbed into the branches of his favorite tree and sat for hours in his "tree-top rest," reading his father's precious manuscripts and thinking upon what he read.

You must not think that Inga was a molly-coddle or a prig, because he was so solemn and studious. Being a King's son and heir to a throne, he could not play with the other boys of Pingaree, and he lived so much in the society of the King and Queen, and was so surrounded by the pomp and dignity of a court, that he missed all the jolly times boys usually have. I have no doubt that had he been able to live as other boys do, he would have been much like other boys; as it was, he was subdued by his surroundings, and more grave and thoughtful than one of his years should be.

Inga was in his tree one morning when, without warning, a great fog enveloped the Island of Pingaree. The boy could scarcely see the tree next to that in which he sat, but the leaves above him prevented the dampness from wetting him, so he curled himself up in his seat and fell fast asleep.

All that forenoon the fog continued. King Kitticut, who sat in his palace talking with his merry visitor, ordered the candles lighted, that they might be able to see one another. The good Queen, Inga's mother, found it was too dark to work at her embroidery, so she called her maidens together and told them wonderful stories of bygone days, in order to pass away the dreary hours.

But soon after noon the weather changed. The dense fog rolled away like a heavy cloud and suddenly the sun shot his bright rays over the island.

"Very good!" exclaimed King Kitticut. "We shall have a pleasant afternoon, I am sure," and he blew out the candles.

Then he stood a moment motionless, as if turned to stone, for a terrible cry from without the palace reached his ears — a cry so full of fear and horror that the King's heart almost stopped beating. Immediately there was a scurrying of feet as every one in the palace, filled with dismay, rushed outside to see what had happened. Even fat little Rinkitink sprang from his chair and followed his host and the others through the arched vestibule.

After many years the worst fears of King Kitticut were realized.

Landing upon the beach, which was but a few steps from the palace itself, were hundreds of boats, every one filled with a throng of fierce warriors. They sprang upon the land with wild shouts of defiance and rushed to the King's palace, waving aloft their swords and spears and battleaxes.

King Kitticut, so completely surprised that he was bewildered, gazed at the approaching host with terror and grief.

"They are the men of Regos and Coregos!" he groaned. "We are indeed, lost!"

Then he bethought himself, for the first time, of his wonderful pearls. Turning quickly, he ran back into the palace and hastened to the hall where the treasures were hidden. But the leader of the warriors had seen the King enter the palace and bounded after him, thinking he meant to escape. Just as the King had stooped to press the secret spring in the tiles, the warrior seized him from the rear and threw him backward upon the floor, at the same time shouting to his men to fetch ropes and bind the prisoner. This they did very quickly and King Kitticut soon found himself helplessly bound and in the power of his enemies. In this sad condition he was lifted by the warriors and carried outside, when the good King looked upon a sorry sight.

The Queen and her maidens, the officers and servants of the royal household and all who had inhabited this end of the Island of Pingaree had been seized by the invaders and bound with ropes. At once they began carrying their victims to the boats, tossing them in as unceremoniously as if they had been bales of merchandise.

The King looked around for his son Inga, but failed to find the boy among the prisoners. Nor was the fat King, Rinkitink, to be seen anywhere about.

The warriors were swarming over the palace like bees in a hive, seeking anyone who might be in hiding, and after the search had been prolonged for some time the leader asked impatiently: "Do you find anyone else?"

"No," his men told him. "We have captured them all."

"Then," commanded the leader, "remove everything of value from the palace and tear down its walls and towers, so that not one stone remains upon another!"

While the warriors were busy with this task we will return to the boy Prince, who, when the fog lifted and the sun came out, wakened from his sleep and began to climb down from his perch in the tree. But the terrifying cries of the people, mingled with the shouts of the rude warriors, caused him to pause and listen eagerly.

Then he climbed rapidly up the tree, far above his platform, to the topmost swaying branches. This tree, which Inga called his own, was somewhat taller than the other trees that surrounded it, and when he had reached the top he pressed aside the leaves and saw a great fleet of boats upon the shore — strange boats, with banners that he had never seen before. Turning to look upon his father's palace, he found it surrounded by a horde of enemies. Then Inga knew the truth: that tile island had been invaded by the barbaric warriors from the north. He grew so faint from the terror of it all that he might have fallen had he not wound his arms around a limb and clung fast until the dizzy feeling passed away. Then with his sash he bound himself to the limb and again ventured to look out through the leaves.

The warriors were now engaged in carrying King Kitticut and Queen Garee and all their other captives down to the boats, where they were thrown in and chained one to another. It was a dreadful sight for the Prince to witness, but he sat very still, concealed from the sight of anyone below by the bower of leafy branches around him. Inga knew very well that he could do nothing to help his beloved parents, and that if he came down he would only be forced to share their cruel fate.

Now a procession of the Northmen passed between the boats and the palace, bearing the rich furniture, splendid draperies and rare ornaments of which the royal palace had been robbed, together with such food and other plunder as they could lay their hands upon. After this, the men of Regos and Coregos threw ropes around the marble domes and towers and hundreds of warriors tugged at these ropes until the domes and towers toppled and fell in ruins upon the ground. Then the walls themselves were torn down, till little remained of the beautiful palace but a vast heap of white marble blocks tumbled and scattered upon the ground.

Prince Inga wept bitter tears of grief as he watched the ruin of his home; yet he was powerless to avert the destruction. When the palace had been demolished, some of the warriors entered their boats and rowed along the coast of the island, while the others marched in a great body down the length of the island itself. They were so numerous that they formed a line stretching from shore to shore and they destroyed every house they came to and took every inhabitant prisoner.

The pearl fishers who lived at the lower end of the island tried to escape in their boats, but they were soon overtaken and made prisoners, like the others. Nor was there any attempt to resist the foe, for the sharp spears and pikes and swords of the invaders terrified the hearts of the defenseless people of Pingaree, whose sole weapons were their oyster rakes.

When night fell the whole of the Island of Pingaree had been conquered by the men of the North, and all its people were slaves of the conquerors. Next morning the men of Regos and Coregos, being capable of no further mischief, departed from the scene of their triumph, carrying their prisoners with them and taking also every boat to be found upon the island. Many of the boats they had filled with rich plunder, with pearls and silks and velvets, with silver and gold ornaments and all the treasure that had made Pingaree famed as one of the richest kingdoms in the world. And the hundreds of slaves they had captured would be set to work in the mines of Regos and the grain fields of Coregos.

So complete was the victory of the Northmen that it is no wonder the warriors sang songs of triumph as they hastened back to their homes. Great rewards were awaiting them when they showed the haughty King of Regos and the terrible Queen of Coregos the results of their ocean raid and conquest.

4. The Deserted Island

All through that terrible night Prince Inga remained hidden in his tree. In the morning he watched the great fleet of boats depart for their own country, carrying his parents and his countrymen with them, as well as everything of value the Island of Pingaree had contained.

Sad, indeed, were the boy's thoughts when the last of the boats had become a mere speck in the distance, but Inga did not dare leave his perch of safety until all of the craft of the invaders had disappeared beyond the horizon. Then he came down, very slowly and carefully, for he was weak from hunger and the long and weary watch, as he had been in the tree for twenty-four hours without food.

The sun shone upon the beautiful green isle as brilliantly as if no ruthless invader had passed and laid it in ruins. The birds still chirped among the trees and the butterflies darted from flower to flower as happily as when the land was filled with a prosperous and contented people.

Inga feared that only he was left of all his nation. Perhaps he might be obliged to pass his life there alone. He would not starve, for the sea would give him oysters and fish, and the trees fruit; yet the life that confronted him was far from enticing.

The boy's first act was to walk over to where the palace had stood and search the ruins until he found some scraps of food that had been overlooked by the enemy. He sat upon a block of marble and ate of this, and tears filled his eyes as he gazed upon the desolation around him. But Inga tried to bear up bravely, and having satisfied his hunger he walked over to the well, intending to draw a bucket of drinking water.

Fortunately, this well had been overlooked by the invaders and the bucket was still fastened to the chain that wound around a stout wooden windlass. Inga took hold of the crank and began letting the bucket down into the well, when suddenly he was startled by a muffled voice crying out: "Be careful, up there!"

The sound and the words seemed to indicate that the voice came from the bottom of the well, so Inga looked down. Nothing could be seen, on account of the darkness.

"Who are you?" he shouted.

"It's I — Rinkitink," came the answer, and the depths of the well echoed: "Tink-i-tink-i-tink!" in a ghostly manner.

"Are you in the well?" asked the boy, greatly surprised.

"Yes, and nearly drowned. I fell in while running from those terrible warriors, and I've been standing in this damp hole ever since, with my head just above the water. It's lucky the well was no deeper, for had my head been under water, instead of above it — hoo, hoo, hoo, keek, eek! — under instead of over, you know — why, then I wouldn't be talking to you now! Ha, hoo, hee!" And the well dismally echoed: "Ha, hoo, hee!" which you must imagine was a laugh half merry and half sad.

"I'm awfully sorry," cried the boy, in answer. "I wonder you have the heart to laugh at all. But how am I to get you out?"

"I've been considering that all night," said Rinkitink, "and I believe the best plan will be for you to let down the bucket to me, and I'll hold fast to it while you wind up the chain and so draw me to the top."

"I will try to do that," replied Inga, and he let the bucket down very carefully until he heard the King call out:

"I've got it! Now pull me up — slowly, my boy, slowly — so I won't rub against the rough sides."

Inga began winding up the chain, but King Rinkitink was so fat that he was very heavy and by the time the boy had managed to pull him halfway up the well his strength was gone. He clung to the crank as long as possible, but suddenly it slipped from his grasp and the next minute he heard Rinkitink fall "plump!" into the water again.

"That's too bad!" called Inga, in real distress; "but you were so heavy I couldn't help it."

"Dear me!" gasped the King, from the darkness below, as he spluttered and coughed to get the water out of his mouth. "Why didn't you tell me you were going to let go?"

"I hadn't time," said Inga, sorrowfully.

"Well, I'm not suffering from thirst," declared the King, "for there's enough water inside me to float all the boats of Regos and Coregos or at least it feels that way. But never mind! So long as I'm not actually drowned, what does it matter?"

"What shall we do next?" asked the boy anxiously.

"Call someone to help you," was the reply.

"There is no one on the island but myself," said the boy; "— excepting you," he added, as an afterthought.

"I'm not on it — more's the pity! — but in it," responded Rinkitink. "Are the warriors all gone?"

"Yes," said Inga, "and they have taken my father and mother, and all our people, to be their slaves," he added, trying in vain to repress a sob.

"So — so!" said Rinkitink softly; and then he paused a moment, as if in thought. Finally he said: "There are worse things than slavery, but I never imagined a well could be one of them. Tell me, Inga, could you let down some food to me? I'm nearly starved, and if you could manage to send me down some food I'd be well fed — hoo, hoo, heek, keek, eek! — well fed. Do you see the joke, Inga?"

"Do not ask me to enjoy a joke just now, Your Majesty," begged Inga in a sad voice; "but if you will be patient I will try to find something for you to eat."

He ran back to the ruins of the palace and began searching for bits of food with which to satisfy the hunger of the King, when to his surprise he observed the goat, Bilbil, wandering among the marble blocks.

"What!" cried Inga. "Didn't the warriors get you, either?"

"If they had," calmly replied Bilbil, "I shouldn't be here."

"But how did you escape?" asked the boy.

"Easily enough. I kept my mouth shut and stayed away from the rascals," said the goat. "I knew that the soldiers would not care for a skinny old beast like me, for to the eye of a stranger I seem good for nothing. Had they known I could talk, and that my head contained more wisdom than a hundred of their own noddles, I might not have escaped so easily."

"Perhaps you are right," said the boy.

"I suppose they got the old man?" carelessly remarked Bilbil.

"What old man?"

"Rinkitink."

"Oh, no! His Majesty is at the bottom of the well," said Inga, "and I don't know how to get him out again."

"Then let him stay there," suggested the goat.

"That would be cruel. I am sure, Bilbil, that you are fond of the good King, your master, and do not mean what you say. Together, let us find some way to save poor King Rinkitink. He is a very jolly companion, and has a heart exceedingly kind and gentle."

"Oh, well; the old boy isn't so bad, taken altogether," admitted Bilbil, speaking in a more friendly tone. "But his bad jokes and fat laughter tire me dreadfully, at times."

Prince Inga now ran back to the well, the goat following more leisurely.

"Here's Bilbil!" shouted the boy to the King. "The enemy didn't get him, it seems."

"That's lucky for the enemy," said Rinkitink. "But it's lucky for me, too, for perhaps the beast can assist me out of this hole. If you can let a rope down the well, I am sure that you and Bilbil, pulling together, will be able to drag me to the earth's surface."

"Be patient and we will make the attempt," replied Inga encouragingly, and he ran to search the ruins for a rope. Presently he found one that had been used by the warriors in toppling over the towers, which in their haste they had neglected to remove, and with some difficulty he untied the knots and carried the rope to the mouth of the well.

Bilbil had lain down to sleep and the refrain of a merry song came in muffled tones from the well, proving that Rinkitink was making a patient endeavor to amuse himself.

"I've found a rope!" Inga called down to him; and then the boy proceeded to make a loop in one end of the rope, for the King to put his arms through, and the other end he placed over the drum of the windlass. He now aroused Bilbil and fastened the rope firmly around the goat's shoulders.

"Are you ready?" asked the boy, leaning over the well.

"I am," replied the King.

"And I am not," growled the goat, "for I have not yet had my nap out. Old Rinki will be safe enough in the well until I've slept an hour or two longer."

"But it is damp in the well," protested the boy, "and King Rinkitink may catch the rheumatism, so that he will have to ride upon your back wherever he goes."

Hearing this, Bilbil jumped up at once.

"Let's get him out," he said earnestly.

"Hold fast!" shouted Inga to the King. Then he seized the rope and helped Bilbil to pull. They soon found the task more difficult than they had supposed. Once or twice the King's weight threatened to drag both the boy and the goat into the well, to keep Rinkitink company. But they pulled sturdily, being aware of this danger, and at last the King popped out of the hole and fell sprawling full length upon the ground.

For a time he lay panting and breathing hard to get his breath back, while Inga and Bilbil were likewise worn out from their long strain at the rope; so the three rested quietly upon the grass and looked at one another in silence.

Finally Bilbil said to the King: "I'm surprised at you. Why were you so foolish as to fall down that well? Don't you know it's a dangerous thing to do? You might have broken your neck in the fall, or been drowned in the water."

"Bilbil," replied the King solemnly, "you're a goat. Do you imagine I fell down the well on purpose?"

"I imagine nothing," retorted Bilbil. "I only know you were there."

"There? Heh-heh-heek-keek-eek! To be sure I was there," laughed Rinkitink. "There in a dark hole, where there was no light; there in a watery well, where the wetness soaked me through and through — keek-eek-eek-eek! — through and through!"

"How did it happen?" inquired Inga.

"I was running away from the enemy," explained the King, "and I was carelessly looking over my shoulder at the same time, to see if they were chasing me. So I did not see the well, but stepped into it and found myself tumbling down to the bottom. I struck the water very neatly and began struggling to keep myself from drowning, but presently I found that when I stood upon my feet on the bottom of the well, that my chin was just above the water. So I stood still and yelled for help; but no one heard me."

"If the warriors had heard you," said Bilbil, "they would have pulled you out and carried you away to be a slave. Then you would have been obliged to work for a living, and that would be a new experience."

"Work!" exclaimed Rinkitink. "Me work? Hoo, hoo, heek-keek-eek! How absurd! I'm so stout — not to say chubby — not to say fat — that I can hardly walk, and I couldn't earn my salt at hard work. So I'm glad the enemy did not find me, Bilbil. How many others escaped?"

"That I do not know," replied the boy, "for I have not yet had time to visit the other parts of the island. When you have rested and satisfied your royal hunger, it might be well for us to look around and see what the thieving warriors of Regos and Coregos have left us."

"An excellent idea," declared Rinkitink. "I am somewhat feeble from my long confinement in the well, but I can ride upon Bilbil's back and we may as well start at once."

Hearing this, Bilbil cast a surly glance at his master but said nothing, since it was really the goat's business to carry King Rinkitink wherever he desired to go.

They first searched the ruins of the palace, and where the kitchen had once been they found a small quantity of food that had been half hidden by a block of marble. This they carefully placed in a sack to preserve it for future use, the little fat King having first eaten as much as he cared for. This consumed some time, for Rinkitink had been exceedingly hungry and liked to eat in a leisurely manner. When he had finished the meal he straddled Bilbil's back and set out to explore the island, Prince Inga walking by his side.

They found on every hand ruin and desolation. The houses of the people had been pilfered of all valuables and then torn down or burned. Not a boat had been left upon the shore, nor was there a single person, man or woman or child, remaining upon the island, save themselves. The only inhabitants of Pingaree now consisted of a fat little King, a boy and a goat.

Even Rinkitink, merry hearted as he was, found it hard to laugh in the face of this mighty disaster. Even the goat, contrary to its usual habit, refrained from saying anything disagreeable. As for the poor boy whose home was now a wilderness, the tears came often to his eyes as he marked the ruin of his dearly loved island.

When, at nightfall, they reached the lower end of Pingaree and found it swept as bare as the rest, Inga's grief was almost more than he could bear. Everything had been swept from him — parents, home and country — in so brief a time that his bewilderment was equal to his sorrow.

Since no house remained standing, in which they might sleep, the three wanderers crept beneath the overhanging branches of a cassa tree and curled themselves up as comfortably as possible. So tired and exhausted were they by the day's anxieties and griefs that their troubles soon faded into the mists of dreamland. Beast and King and boy slumbered peacefully together until wakened by the singing of the birds which greeted the dawn of a new day.

5. The Three Pearls

When King Rinkitink and Prince Inga had bathed themselves in the sea and eaten a simple breakfast, they began wondering what they could do to improve their condition.

"The poor people of Gilgad," said Rinkitink cheerfully, "are little likely ever again to behold their King in the flesh, for my boat and my rowers are gone with everything else. Let us face the fact that we are imprisoned for life upon this island, and that our lives will be short unless we can secure more to eat than is in this small sack."

"I'll not starve, for I can eat grass," remarked the goat in a pleasant tone — or a tone as pleasant as Bilbil could assume.

"True, quite true," said the King. Then he seemed thoughtful for a moment and turning to Inga he asked: "Do you think, Prince, that if the worst comes, we could eat Bilbil?"

The goat gave a groan and cast a reproachful look at his master as he said: "Monster! Would you, indeed, eat your old friend and servant?"

"Not if I can help it, Bilbil," answered the King pleasantly. "You would make a remarkably tough morsel, and my teeth are not as good as they once were.

While this talk was in progress Inga suddenly remembered the three pearls which his father had hidden under the tiled floor of the banquet hall. Without doubt King Kitticut had been so suddenly surprised by the invaders that he had found no opportunity to get the pearls, for otherwise the fierce warriors would have been defeated and driven out of Pingaree. So they must still be in their hiding place, and Inga believed they would prove of great assistance to him and his comrades in this hour of need. But the palace was a mass of ruins; perhaps he would be unable now to find the place where the pearls were hidden.

He said nothing of this to Rinkitink, remembering that his father had charged him to preserve the secret of the pearls and of their magic powers. Nevertheless, the thought of securing the wonderful treasures of his ancestors gave the boy new hope.

He stood up and said to the King: "Let us return to the other end of Pingaree. It is more pleasant than here in spite of the desolation of my father's palace. And there, if anywhere, we shall discover a way out of our difficulties."

This suggestion met with Rinkitink's approval and the little party at once started upon the return journey. As there was no occasion to delay upon the way, they reached the big end of the island about the middle of the day and at once began searching the ruins of the palace.

They found, to their satisfaction, that one room at the bottom of a tower was still habitable, although the roof was broken in and the place was somewhat littered with stones. The King was, as he said, too fat to do any hard work, so he sat down on a block of marble and watched Inga clear the room of its rubbish. This done, the boy hunted through the ruins until he discovered a stool and an armchair that had not been broken beyond use Some bedding and a mattress were also found, so that by nightfall the little room had been made quite comfortable

The following morning, while Rinkitink was still sound asleep and Bilbil was busily cropping the dewy grass that edged the shore, Prince Inga began to search the tumbled heaps of marble for the place where the royal banquet hall had been. After climbing over the ruins for a time he reached a flat place which he recognized, by means of the tiled flooring and the broken furniture scattered about, to be the great hall he was seeking. But in the center of the floor, directly over the spot where the pearls were hidden, lay several large and heavy blocks of marble, which had been torn from the dismantled walls.

This unfortunate discovery for a time discouraged the boy, who realized how helpless he was to remove such vast obstacles; but it was so important to secure the pearls that he dared not give way to despair until every human effort had been made, so he sat him down to think over the matter with great care.

Meantime Rinkitink had risen from his bed and walked out upon the lawn, where he found Bilbil reclining at ease upon the greensward.

"Where is Inga?" asked Rinkitink, rubbing his eyes with his knuckles because their vision was blurred with too much sleep.

"Don't ask me," said the goat, chewing with much satisfaction a cud of sweet grasses.

"Bilbil," said the King, squatting down beside the goat and resting his fat chin upon his hands and his elbows on his knees "allow me to confide to you the fact that I am bored, and need amusement. My good friend Kitticut has been kidnapped by the barbarians and taken from me, so there is no one to converse with me intelligently. I am the King and you are the goat Suppose you tell me a story."

"Suppose I don't," said Bilbil, with a scowl, for a goat's face is very expressive.

"If you refuse, I shall be more unhappy than ever, and I know your disposition is too sweet to permit that. Tell me a story Bilbil."

The goat looked at him with an expression of scorn. Said he "One would think you are but four years old, Rinkitink! But there — I will do as you command. Listen carefully, and the story may do you some good — although I doubt if you understand the moral."

"I am sure the story will do me good," declared the King, whose eyes were twinkling.

"Once on a time," began the goat.

"When was that, Bilbil?" asked the King gently.

"Don't interrupt; it is impolite. Once on a time there was a King with a hollow inside his head, where most people have their brains, and —"

"Is this a true story, Bilbil?"

"And the King with a hollow head could chatter words, which had no sense, and laugh in a brainless manner at senseless things. That part of the story is true enough, Rinkitink."

"Then proceed with the tale, sweet Bilbil. Yet it is hard to believe that any King could be brainless — unless, indeed, he proved it by owning a talking goat."

Bilbil glared at him a full minute in silence. Then he resumed his story: "This empty-headed man was a King by accident, having been born to that high station. Also the King was empty-headed by the same chance, being born without brains."

"Poor fellow!" quoth the King. "Did he own a talking goat?"

"He did," answered Bilbil.

"Then he was wrong to have been born at all. Cheek-eek-eek-eek, oo, hoo!" chuckled Rinkitink, his fat body shaking with merriment. "But it's hard to prevent oneself from being born; there's no chance for protest, eh, Bilbil?"

"Who is telling this story, I'd like to know," demanded the goat, with anger.

"Ask someone with brains, my boy; I'm sure I can't tell," replied the King, bursting into one of his merry fits of laughter.

Bilbil rose to his hoofs and walked away in a dignified manner, leaving Rinkitink chuckling anew at the sour expression of the animal's face.

"Oh, Bilbil, you'll be the death of me, some day — I'm sure you will!" gasped the King, taking out his lace handkerchief to wipe his eyes; for, as he often did, he had laughed till the tears came.

Bilbil was deeply vexed and would not even turn his head to look at his master. To escape from Rinkitink he wandered among the ruins of the palace, where he came upon Prince Inga.

"Good morning, Bilbil," said the boy. "I was just going to find you, that I might consult you upon an important matter. If you will kindly turn back with me I am sure your good judgment will be of great assistance."

The angry goat was quite mollified by the respectful tone in which he was addressed, but he immediately asked: "Are you also going to consult that empty-headed King over yonder?"

"I am sorry to hear you speak of your kind master in such a way," said the boy gravely. "All men are deserving of respect, being the highest of living creatures, and Kings deserve respect more than others, for they are set to rule over many people."

"Nevertheless," said Bilbil with conviction, "Rinkitink's head is certainly empty of brains."

"That I am unwilling to believe," insisted Inga. "But anyway his heart is kind and gentle and that is better than being wise. He is merry in spite of misfortunes that would cause others to weep and he never speaks harsh words that wound the feelings of his friends."

"Still," growled Bilbil, "he is —"

"Let us forget everything but his good nature, which puts new heart into us when we are sad," advised the boy."

"But he is —"

"Come with me, please," interrupted Inga, "for the matter of which I wish to speak is very important."

Bilbil followed him, although the boy still heard the goat muttering that the King had no brains. Rinkitink, seeing them turn into the ruins, also followed, and upon joining them asked for his breakfast.

Inga opened the sack of food and while he and the King ate of it the boy said: "If I could find a way to remove some of the blocks of marble which have fallen in the banquet hall, I think I could find means for us to escape from this barren island."

"Then," mumbled Rinkitink, with his mouth full, "let us move the blocks of marble."

"But how?" inquired Prince Inga. "They are very heavy."

"Ah, how, indeed?" returned the King, smacking his lips contentedly. "That is a serious question. But — I have it! Let us see what my famous parchment says about it." He wiped his fingers upon a napkin and then, taking the scroll from a pocket inside his embroidered blouse, he unrolled it and read the following words: 'Never step on another man's toes.'

The goat gave a snort of contempt; Inga was silent; the King looked from one to the other inquiringly.

"That's the idea, exactly!" declared Rinkitink.

"To be sure," said Bilbil scornfully, "it tells us exactly how to move the blocks of marble."

"Oh, does it?" responded the King, and then for a moment he rubbed the top of his bald head in a perplexed manner. The next moment he burst into a peal of joyous laughter. The goat looked at Inga and sighed.

"What did I tell you?" asked the creature. "Was I right, or was I wrong?"

"This scroll," said Rinkitink, "is indeed a masterpiece. Its advice is of tremendous value. 'Never step on another man's toes.' Let us think this over. The inference is that we should step upon our own toes, which were given us for that purpose. Therefore, if I stepped upon another man's toes, I would be the other man. Hoo, hoo, hoo! — the other man — hee, hee, heek- keek-eek! Funny, isn't it?"

"Didn't I say —" began Bilbil.

"No matter what you said, my boy," roared the King. "No fool could have figured that out as nicely as I did."

"We have still to decide how to remove the blocks of marble," suggested Inga anxiously.

"Fasten a rope to them, and pull," said Bilbil. "Don't pay any more attention to Rinkitink, for he is no wiser than the man who wrote that brainless scroll. Just get the rope, and we'll fasten Rinkitink to one end of it for a weight and I'll help you pull."

"Thank you, Bilbil," replied the boy. "I'll get the rope at once.

Bilbil found it difficult to climb over the ruins to the floor of the banquet hall, but there are few places a goat cannot get to when it makes the attempt, so Bilbil succeeded at last, and even fat little Rinkitink finally joined them, though much out of breath.

Inga fastened one end of the rope around a block of marble and then made a loop at the other end to go over Bilbil's head. When all was ready the boy seized the rope and helped the goat to pull; yet, strain as they might, the huge block would not stir from its place. Seeing this, King Rinkitink came forward and lent his assistance, the weight of his body forcing the heavy marble to slide several feet from where it had lain.

But it was hard work and all were obliged to take a long rest before undertaking the removal of the next block.

"Admit, Bilbil," said the King, "that I am of some use in the world."

"Your weight was of considerable help," acknowledged the goat, "but if your head were as well filled as your stomach the task would be still easier."

When Inga went to fasten the rope a second time he was rejoiced to discover that by moving one more block of marble he could uncover the tile with the secret spring. So the three pulled with renewed energy and to their joy the block moved and rolled upon its side, leaving Inga free to remove the treasure when he pleased.

But the boy had no intention of allowing Bilbil and the King to share the secret of the royal treasures of Pingaree; so, although both the goat and its master demanded to know why the marble blocks had been moved, and how it would benefit them, Inga begged them to wait until the next morning, when he hoped to be able to satisfy them that their hard work had not been in vain.

Having little confidence in this promise of a mere boy, the goat grumbled and the King laughed; but Inga paid no heed to their ridicule and set himself to work rigging up a fishing rod, with line and hook. During the afternoon he waded out to some rocks near the shore and fished patiently until he had captured enough yellow perch for their supper and breakfast.

"Ah," said Rinkitink, looking at the fine catch when Inga returned to the shore; "these will taste delicious when they are cooked; but do you know how to cook them?"

"No," was the reply. I have often caught fish, but never cooked them. Perhaps Your Majesty understands cooking."

"Cooking and majesty are two different things," laughed the little King. "I could not cook a fish to save me from starvation."

"For my part," said Bilbil, "I never eat fish, but I can tell you how to cook them, for I have often watched the palace cooks at their work." And so, with the goat's assistance, the boy and the King managed to prepare the fish and cook them, after which they were eaten with good appetite.

That night, after Rinkitink and Bilbil were both fast asleep, Inga stole quietly through the moonlight to the desolate banquet hall. There, kneeling down, he touched the secret spring as his father had instructed him to do and to his joy the tile sank downward and disclosed the opening. You may imagine how the boy's heart throbbed with excitement as he slowly thrust his hand into the cavity and felt around to see if the precious pearls were still there. In a moment his fingers touched the silken bag and, without pausing to close the recess, he pressed the treasure against his breast and ran out into the moonlight to examine it. When he reached a bright place he started to open the bag, but he observed Bilbil lying asleep upon the grass near by. So, trembling with the fear of discovery, he ran to another place, and

when he paused he heard Rinkitink snoring lustily. Again he fled and made his way to the seashore, where he squatted under a bank and began to untie the cords that fastened the mouth of the bag. But now another fear assailed him.

"If the pearls should slip from my hand," he thought, "and roll into the water, they might be lost to me forever. I must find some safer place."

Here and there he wandered, still clasping the silken bag in both hands, and finally he went to the grove and climbed into the tall tree where he had made his platform and seat. But here it was pitch dark, so he found he must wait patiently until morning before he dared touch the pearls. During those hours of waiting he had time for reflection and reproached himself for being so frightened by the possession of his father's treasures.

"These pearls have belonged to our family for generations," he mused, "yet no one has ever lost them. If I use ordinary care I am sure I need have no fears for their safety."

When the dawn came and he could see plainly, Inga opened the bag and took out the Blue Pearl. There was no possibility of his being observed by others, so he took time to examine it wonderingly, saying to himself: "This will give me strength."

Taking off his right shoe he placed the Blue Pearl within it, far up in the pointed toe. Then he tore a piece from his handkerchief and stuffed it into the shoe to hold the pearl in place. Inga's shoes were long and pointed, as were all the shoes worn in Pingaree, and the points curled upward, so that there was quite a vacant space beyond the place where the boy's toes reached when the shoe was upon his foot.

After he had put on the Shoe and laced it up he opened the bag and took out the Pink Pearl. "This will protect me from danger," said Inga, and removing the shoe from his left foot he carefully placed the pearl in the hollow toe. This, also, he secured in place by means of a strip torn from his handkerchief.

Having put on the second shoe and laced it up, the boy drew from the silken bag the third pearl — that which was pure white — and holding it to his ear he asked, "Will you advise me what to do, in this my hour of misfortune?"

Clearly the small voice of the pearl made answer: "I advise you to go to the Islands of Regos and Coregos, where you may liberate your parents from slavery."

"How could I do that?" exclaimed Prince Inga, amazed at receiving such advice.

"To-night," spoke the voice of the pearl, "there will be a storm, and in the morning a boat will strand upon the shore. Take this boat and row to Regos and Coregos."

"How can I, a weak boy, pull the boat so far?" he inquired, doubting the possibility.

"The Blue Pearl will give you strength," was the reply.

"But I may be shipwrecked and drowned, before ever I reach Regos and Coregos," protested the boy.

"The Pink Pearl will protect you from harm," murmured the voice, soft and low but very distinct.

"Then I shall act as you advise me," declared Inga, speaking firmly because this promise gave him courage, and as he removed the pearl from his ear it whispered: "The wise and fearless are sure to win success."

Restoring the White Pearl to the depths of the silken bag, Inga fastened it securely around his neck and buttoned his waist above it to hide the treasure from all prying eyes. Then he slowly climbed down from the tree and returned to the room where King Rinkitink still slept.

The goat was browsing upon the grass but looked cross and surly. When the boy said good morning as he passed, Bilbil made no response whatever. As Inga entered the room the King awoke and asked: "What is that mysterious secret of yours? I've been dreaming about it, and I haven't got my breath yet from tugging at those heavy blocks. Tell me the secret."

"A secret told is no longer a secret," replied Inga, with a laugh. "Besides, this is a family secret, which it is proper I should keep to myself. But I may tell you one thing, at least: We are going to leave this island to-morrow morning."

The King seemed puzzled by this statement.

"I'm not much of a swimmer," said he, "and, though I'm fat enough to float upon the surface of the water, I'd only bob around and get nowhere at all."

"We shall not swim, but ride comfortably in a boat," promised Inga.

"There isn't a boat on this island!" declared Rinkitink, looking upon the boy with wonder.

"True," said Inga. "But one will come to us in the morning." He spoke positively, for he had perfect faith in the promise of the White Pearl; but Rinkitink, knowing nothing of the three marvelous jewels, began to fear that the little Prince had lost his mind through grief and misfortune.

For this reason the King did not question the boy further but tried to cheer him by telling him witty stories. He laughed at all the stories himself, in his merry, rollicking way, and Inga joined freely in the laughter because his heart had been lightened by the prospect of rescuing his dear parents. Not since the fierce warriors had descended upon Pingaree had the boy been so hopeful and happy.

With Rinkitink riding upon Bilbil's back, the three made a tour of the island and found in the central part some bushes and trees bearing ripe fruit. They gathered this freely, for — aside from the fish which Inga caught — it was the only food they now had, and the less they had, the bigger Rinkitink's appetite seemed to grow.

"I am never more happy," said he with a sigh, "than when I am eating."

Toward evening the sky became overcast and soon a great storm began to rage. Prince Inga and King Rinkitink took refuge within the shelter of the room they had fitted up and there Bilbil joined them. The goat and the King were somewhat disturbed by the violence of the storm, but Inga did not mind it, being pleased at this evidence that the White Pearl might be relied upon.

All night the wind shrieked around the island; thunder rolled, lightning flashed and rain came down in torrents. But with morning the storm abated and when the sun arose no sign of the tempest remained save a few fallen trees.

6. The Magic Boat

Prince Inga was up with the sun and, accompanied by Bilbil, began walking along the shore in search of the boat which the White Pearl had promised him. Never for an instant did he doubt that he would find it and before he had walked any great distance a dark object at the water's edge caught his eye.

"It is the boat, Bilbil!" he cried joyfully, and running down to it he found it was, indeed, a large and roomy boat. Although stranded upon the beach, it was in perfect order and had suffered in no way from the storm.

Inga stood for some moments gazing upon the handsome craft and wondering where it could have come from. Certainly it was unlike any boat he had ever seen. On the outside it was painted a lustrous black, without any other color to relieve it; but all the inside of the boat was lined with pure silver, polished so highly that the surface resembled a mirror and glinted brilliantly in the rays of the sun. The seats had white velvet cushions upon them and the cushions were splendidly embroidered with threads of gold. At one end, beneath the broad seat, was a small barrel with silver hoops, which the boy found was filled with fresh, sweet water. A great chest of sandalwood, bound and ornamented with silver, stood in the other end of the boat. Inga raised the lid and discovered the chest filled with sea-biscuits, cakes, tinned meats and ripe, juicy melons; enough good and wholesome food to last the party a long time.

Lying upon the bottom of the boat were two shining oars, and overhead, but rolled back now, was a canopy of silver cloth to ward off the heat of the sun.

It is no wonder the boy was delighted with the appearance of this beautiful boat; but on reflection he feared it was too large for him to row any great distance. Unless, indeed, the Blue Pearl gave him unusual strength.

While he was considering this matter, King Rinkitink came waddling up to him and said: "Well, well, well, my Prince, your words have come true! Here is the boat, for a certainty, yet how it came here — and how you knew it would come to us — are puzzles that mystify me. I do not question our good fortune, however, and my heart is bubbling with joy, for in this boat I will return at once to my City of Gilgad, from which I have remained absent altogether too long a time."

"I do not wish to go to Gilgad," said Inga.

"That is too bad, my friend, for you would be very welcome. But you may remain upon this island, if you wish," continued Rinkitink, "and when I get home I will send some of my people to rescue you."

"It is my boat, Your Majesty," said Inga quietly.

"May be, may be," was the careless answer, "but I am King of a great country, while you are a boy Prince without any kingdom to speak of. Therefore, being of greater importance than you, it is just and right that I take, your boat and return to my own country in it."

"I am sorry to differ from Your Majesty's views," said Inga, "but instead of going to Gilgad I consider it of greater importance that we go to the islands of Regos and Coregos."

"Hey? What!" cried the astounded King. "To Regos and Coregos!

To become slaves of the barbarians, like the King, your father? No, no, my boy! Your Uncle Rinki may have an empty noddle, as Bilbil claims, but he is far too wise to put his head in the lion's mouth. It's no fun to be a slave."

"The people of Regos and Coregos will not enslave us," declared Inga. "On the contrary, it is my intention to set free my dear parents, as well as all my people, and to bring them back again to Pingaree."

"Cheek-eek-eek-eek-eek! How funny!" chuckled Rinkitink, winking at the goat, which scowled in return. "Your audacity takes my breath away, Inga, but the adventure has its charm, I must, confess. Were I not so fat, I'd agree to your plan at once, and could probably conquer that horde of fierce warriors without any assistance at all — any at all — eh, Bilbil? But I grieve to say that I am fat, and not in good fighting trim. As for your determination to do what I admit I can't do, Inga, I fear you forget that you are only a boy, and rather small at that."

"No, I do not forget that," was Inga's reply.

"Then please consider that you and I and Bilbil are not strong enough, as an army, to conquer a powerful nation of skilled warriors. We could attempt it, of course, but you are too young to die, while I am too old. Come with me to my City of Gilgad, where you will be greatly honored. I'll have my professors teach you how to be good. Eh? What do you say?"

Inga was a little embarrassed how to reply to these arguments, which he knew King Rinkitink considered were wise; so, after a period of thought, he said: "I will make a bargain with Your Majesty, for I do not wish to fail in respect to so worthy a man and so great a King as yourself. This boat is mine, as I have said, and in my father's absence you have become my guest; therefore I claim that I am entitled to some consideration, as well as you."

"No doubt of it," agreed Rinkitink. "What is the bargain you propose, Inga?"

"Let us both get into the boat, and you shall first try to row us to Gilgad. If you succeed, I will accompany you right willingly; but should you fail, I will then row the boat to Regos, and you must come with me without further protest."

"A fair and just bargain!" cried the King, highly pleased. "Yet, although I am a man of mighty deeds, I do not relish the prospect of rowing so big a boat all the way to Gilgad. But I will do my best and abide by the result."

The matter being thus peaceably settled, they prepared to embark. A further supply of fruits was placed in the boat and Inga also raked up a quantity of the delicious oysters that abounded on the coast of Pingaree but which he had before been unable to reach for lack of a boat. This was done at the suggestion of the ever-hungry Rinkitink, and when the oysters had been stowed in their shells behind the water barrel and a plentiful supply of grass brought aboard for Bilbil, they decided they were ready to start on their voyage.

It proved no easy task to get Bilbil into the boat, for he was a remarkably clumsy goat and once, when Rinkitink gave him a push, he tumbled into the water and nearly drowned before they could get him out again. But there was no thought of leaving the quaint animal behind. His power of speech made him seem almost human in the eyes of the boy, and the fat King was so accustomed to his surly companion that nothing could have induced him to part with him. Finally Bilbil fell sprawling into the bottom of the boat, and Inga helped him to get to the front end, where there was enough space for him to lie down.

Rinkitink now took his seat in the silver-lined craft and the boy came last, pushing off the boat as he sprang aboard, so that it floated freely upon the water.

"Well, here we go for Gilgad!" exclaimed the King, picking up the oars and placing them in the row-locks. Then he began to row as hard as he could, singing at the same time an odd sort of a song that ran like this:
"The way to Gilgad isn't bad
For a stout old King and a brave young lad,
For a cross old goat with a dripping coat,
And a silver boat in which to float.
So our hearts are merry, light and glad
As we speed away to fair Gilgad!"

"Don't, Rinkitink; please don't! It makes me seasick," growled Bilbil.

Rinkitink stopped rowing, for by this time he was all out of breath and his round face was covered with big drops of perspiration. And when he looked over his shoulder he found to his dismay that the boat had scarcely moved a foot from its former position.

Inga said nothing and appeared not to notice the King's failure. So now Rinkitink, with a serious look on his fat, red face, took off his purple robe and rolled up the sleeves of his tunic and tried again.

However, he succeeded no better than before and when he heard Bilbil give a gruff laugh and saw a smile upon the boy Prince's face, Rinkitink suddenly dropped the oars and began shouting with laughter at his own defeat. As he wiped his brow with a yellow silk handkerchief he sang in a merry voice:
"A sailor bold am I, I hold,
But boldness will not row a boat.
So I confess I'm in distress
And just as useless as the goat."

"Please leave me out of your verses," said Bilbil with a snort of anger.

"When I make a fool of myself, Bilbil, I'm a goat," replied Rinkitink.

"Not so," insisted Bilbil. "Nothing could make you a member of my superior race."

"Superior? Why, Bilbil, a goat is but a beast, while I am a King!"

"I claim that superiority lies in intelligence," said the goat.

Rinkitink paid no attention to this remark, but turning to Inga he said: "We may as well get back to the shore, for the boat is too heavy to row to Gilgad or anywhere else. Indeed, it will be hard for us to reach land again."

"Let me take the oars," suggested Inga. "You must not forget our bargain."

"No, indeed," answered Rinkitink. "If you can row us to Regos or to any other place, I will go with you without protest."

So the King took Inga's place at the stern of the boat and the boy grasped the oars and commenced to row. And now, to the great wonder of Rinkitink — and even to Inga's surprise — the oars became light as feathers as soon as the Prince took hold of them. In an instant the boat began to glide rapidly through the water and, seeing this, the boy turned its prow toward the north. He did not know exactly where Regos and Coregos were located, but he did know that the islands lay to the north of Pingaree, so he decided to trust to luck and the guidance of the pearls to carry him to them.

Gradually the Island of Pingaree became smaller to their view as the boat sped onward, until at the end of an hour they had lost sight of it altogether and were wholly surrounded by the purple waters of the Nonestic Ocean.

Prince Inga did not tire from the labor of rowing; indeed, it seemed to him no labor at all. Once he stopped long enough to place the poles of the canopy in the holes that had been made for them, in the edges of the boat, and to spread the canopy of silver over the poles, for Rinkitink had complained of the sun's heat. But the canopy shut out the hot rays and rendered the interior of the boat cool and pleasant.

"This is a glorious ride!" cried Rinkitink, as he lay back in the shade. "I find it a decided relief to be away from that dismal island of Pingaree.

"It may be a relief for a short time," said Bilbil, "but you are going to the land of your enemies, who will probably stick your fat body full of spears and arrows."

"Oh, I hope not!" exclaimed Inga, distressed at the thought.

"Never mind," said the King calmly, "a man can die but once, you know, and when the enemy kills me I shall beg him to kill Bilbil, also, that we may remain together in death as in life."

"They may be cannibals, in which case they will roast and eat us," suggested Bilbil, who wished to terrify his master.

"Who knows?" answered Rinkitink, with a shudder. "But cheer up, Bilbil; they may not kill us after all, or even capture us; so let us not borrow trouble. Do not look so cross, my sprightly quadruped, and I will sing to amuse you."

"Your song would make me more cross than ever," grumbled the goat.

"Quite impossible, dear Bilbil. You couldn't be more surly if you tried. So here is a famous song for you."

While the boy rowed steadily on and the boat rushed fast over the water, the jolly King, who never could be sad or serious for many minutes at a time, lay back on his embroidered cushions and sang as follows:
"A merry maiden went to sea —
Sing too-ral-oo-ral-i-do!

She sat upon the Captain's knee
And looked around the sea to see
What she could see, but she couldn't see me —
Sing too-ral-oo-ral-i-do!

"How do you like that, Bilbil?"

"I don't like it," complained the goat. "It reminds me of the alligator that tried to whistle."

"Did he succeed, Bilbil?" asked the King.

"He whistled as well as you sing."

"Ha, ha, ha, ha, heek, keek, eek!" chuckled the King. "He must have whistled most exquisitely, eh, my friend?"

"I am not your friend," returned the goat, wagging his ears in a surly manner.

"I am yours, however," was the King's cheery reply; "and to prove it I'll sing you another verse."

"Don't, I beg of you!"

But the King sang as follows:
"The wind blew off the maiden's shoe —
Sing too-ral-oo-ral-i-do!

And the shoe flew high to the sky so blue
And the maiden knew 'twas a new shoe, too;
But she couldn't pursue the shoe, 'tis true-
Sing too-ral-oo-ral-i-do!

Isn't that sweet, my pretty goat?"

"Sweet, do you ask?" retorted Bilbil. "I consider it as sweet as candy made from mustard and vinegar."

"But not as sweet as your disposition, I admit. Ah, Bilbil, your temper would put honey itself to shame."

"Do not quarrel, I beg of you," pleaded Inga. "Are we not sad enough already?"

"But this is a jolly quarrel," said the King, "and it is the way Bilbil and I often amuse ourselves. Listen, now, to the last verse of all:
"The maid who shied her shoe now cried —
Sing too-ral-oo-ral-i-do!

Her tears were fried for the Captain's bride
Who ate with pride her sobs, beside,
And gently sighed 'I'm satisfied' —
Sing to-ral-oo-ral-i-do!"

"Worse and worse!" grumbled Bilbil, with much scorn. "I am glad that is the last verse, for another of the same kind might cause me to faint."

"I fear you have no ear for music," said the King.

"I have heard no music, as yet," declared the goat. "You must have a strong imagination, King Rinkitink, if you consider your songs music. Do you remember the story of the bear that hired out for a nursemaid?"

"I do not recall it just now," said Rinkitink, with a wink at Inga.

"Well, the bear tried to sing a lullaby to put the baby to sleep."

"And then?" said the King.

"The bear was highly pleased with its own voice, but the baby was nearly frightened to death."

"Heh, heb, heh, heh, whoo, hoo, hoo! You are a merry rogue, Bilbil," laughed the King; "a merry rogue in spite of your gloomy features. However, if I have not amused you, I have at least pleased myself, for I am exceedingly fond of a good song. So let us say no more about it."

All this time the boy Prince was rowing. the boat. He was not in the least tired, for the oars he held seemed to move of their own accord. He paid little heed to the conversation of Rinkitink and the goat, but busied his thoughts with plans of what he should do when he reached the islands of Regos and Coregos and confronted his enemies. When the others finally became silent, Inga inquired.

"Can you fight, King Rinkitink?"

"I have never tried," was the answer. "In time of danger I have found it much easier to run away than to face the foe."

"But could you fight?" asked the boy.

"I might try, if there was no chance to escape by running. Have you a proper weapon for me to fight with?"

"I have no weapon at all," confessed Inga.

"Then let us use argument and persuasion instead of fighting. For instance, if we could persuade the warriors of Regos to lie down, and let me step on them, they would be crushed with ease.

Prince Inga had expected little support from the King, so he was not discouraged by this answer. After all, he reflected, a conquest by battle would be out of the question, yet the White Pearl would not have advised him to go to Regos and Coregos had the mission been a hopeless one. It seemed to him, on further reflection, that he must rely upon circumstances to determine his actions when he reached the islands of the barbarians.

By this time Inga felt perfect confidence in the Magic Pearls. It was the White Pearl that had given him the boat, and the Blue Pearl that had given him strength to row it. He believed that the Pink Pearl would protect him from any danger that might arise; so his anxiety was not for himself, but for his companions. King Rinkitink and the goat had no magic to protect them, so Inga resolved to do all in his power to keep them from harm.

For three days and three nights the boat with the silver lining sped swiftly over the ocean. On the morning of the fourth day, so quickly had they traveled, Inga saw before him the shores of the two great islands of Regos and Coregos.

"The pearls have guided me aright!" he whispered to himself. "Now, if I am wise, and cautious, and brave, I believe I shall be able to rescue my father and mother and my people."

7. The Twin Islands

The Island of Regos was ten miles wide and forty miles long and it was ruled by a big and powerful King named Gos. Near to the shores were green and fertile fields, but farther back from the sea were rugged hills and mountains, so rocky that nothing would grow there. But in these mountains were mines of gold and silver, which the slaves of the King were forced to work, being confined in dark underground passages for that purpose. In the course of time huge caverns had been hollowed out by the slaves, in which they lived and slept, never seeing the light of day. Cruel overseers with whips stood over these poor people, who had been captured in many countries by the raiding parties of King Cos, and the overseers were quite willing to lash the slaves with their whips if they faltered a moment in their work.

Between the green shores and the mountains were forests of thick, tangled trees, between which narrow paths had been cut to lead up to the caves of the mines. It was on the level green meadows, not far from the ocean, that the great City of Regos had been built, wherein was located the palace of the King. This city was inhabited by thousands of the fierce warriors of Gos, who frequently took to their boats and spread over the sea to the neighboring islands to conquer and pillage, as they had done in Pingaree. When they were not absent on one of these expeditions, the City of Regos swarmed with them and so became a dangerous place for any peaceful person to live in, for the warriors were as lawless as their King.

The Island of Coregos lay close beside the Island of Regos; so close, indeed, that one might have thrown a stone from one shore to another. But Coregos was only half the size of Regos and instead of being mountainous it was a rich and pleasant country, covered with fields of grain. The fields of Coregos furnished food for the warriors and citizens of both countries, while the mines of Regos made them all rich.

Coregos was ruled by Queen Cor, who was wedded to King Gos; but so stern and cruel was the nature of this Queen that the people could not decide which of their sovereigns they dreaded most.

Queen Cor lived in her own City of Coregos, which lay on that side of her island facing Regos, and her slaves, who were mostly women, were made to plow the land and to plant and harvest grain.

From Regos to Coregos stretched a bridge of boats, set close together, with planks laid across their edges for people to walk upon. In this way it was easy to pass from one island to the other and in times of danger the bridge could be quickly removed.

The native inhabitants of Regos and Coregos consisted of the warriors, who did nothing but fight and ravage, and the trembling servants who waited on them. King Gos and Queen Cor were at war with all the rest of the world. Other islanders hated and feared them, for their slaves were badly treated and absolutely no mercy was shown to the weak or ill.

When the boats that had gone to Pingaree returned loaded with rich plunder and a host of captives, there was much rejoicing in Regos and Coregos and the King and Queen gave a fine feast to the warriors who had accomplished so great a conquest. This feast was set for the warriors in the grounds of King Gos's palace, while with them in the great throne room all the captains and leaders of the fighting men were assembled with King Gos and Queen Cor, who had come from her island to attend the ceremony. Then all the goods that had been stolen from the King of Pingaree were divided according to rank, the King and Queen taking half, the captains a quarter, and the rest being divided amongst the warriors.

The day following the feast King Gos sent King Kitticut and all the men of Pingaree to work in his mines under the mountains, having first chained them together so they could not escape. The gentle Queen of Pingaree and all her women, together with the captured children, were given to Queen Cor, who set them to work in her grain fields.

Then the rulers and warriors of these dreadful islands thought they had done forever with Pingaree. Despoiled of all its wealth, its houses torn down, its boats captured and all its people enslaved, what likelihood was there that they might ever again hear of the desolated island? So the people of Regos and Coregos were surprised and puzzled when one morning they observed approaching their shores from the direction of the south a black boat containing a boy, a fat man and a goat. The warriors asked one another who these could be, and where they had come from? No one ever came to those islands of their own accord, that was certain.

Prince Inga guided his boat to the south end of the Island of Regos, which was the landing place nearest to the city, and when the warriors saw this action they went down to the shore to meet him, being led by a big captain named Buzzub.

"Those people surely mean us no good," said Rinkitink uneasily to the boy. "Without doubt they intend to capture us and make us their slaves."

"Do not fear, sir," answered Inga, in a calm voice. "Stay quietly in the boat with Bilbil until I have spoken with these men."

He stopped the boat a dozen feet from the shore, and standing up in his place made a grave bow to the multitude confronting him. Said the big Captain Buzzub in a gruff voice: "Well, little one, who may you be? And how dare you come, uninvited and all alone, to the Island of Regos?"

"I am Inga, Prince of Pingaree," returned the boy, "and I have come here to free my parents and my people, whom you have wrongfully enslaved."

When they heard this bold speech a mighty laugh arose from the band of warriors, and when it had subsided the captain said:

"You love to jest, my baby Prince, and the joke is fairly good. But why did you willingly thrust your head into the lion's mouth? When you were free, why did you not stay free? We did not know we had left a single person in Pingaree! But since you managed to escape us then, it is really kind of you to come here of your own free will, to be our slave. Who is the funny fat person with you?"

"It is His Majesty, King Rinkitink, of the great City of Gilgad. He has accompanied me to see that you render full restitution for all you have stolen from Pingaree."

"Better yet!" laughed Buzzub. "He will make a fine slave for Queen Cor, who loves to tickle fat men, and see them jump."

King Rinkitink was filled with horror when he heard this, but the Prince answered as boldly as before, saying: "We are not to be frightened by bluster, believe me; nor are we so weak as you imagine. We have magic powers so great and terrible that no host of warriors can possibly withstand us, and therefore I call upon you to surrender your city and your island to us, before we rush you with our mighty powers."

The boy spoke very gravely and earnestly, but his words only roused another shout of laughter. So while the men of Regos were laughing Inga drove the boat we'll up onto the sandy beach and leaped out. He also helped Rinkitink out, and when the goat had unaided sprung to the sands, the King got upon Bilbil's back, trembling a little internally, but striving to look as brave as possible.

There was a bunch of coarse hair between the goat's ears, and this Inga clutched firmly in his left hand. The boy knew the Pink Pearl would protect not only himself, but all whom he touched, from any harm, and as Rinkitink was astride the goat and Inga had his hand upon the animal, the three could not be injured by anything the warriors could do. But Captain Buzzub did not

know this, and the little group of three seemed so weak and ridiculous that he believed their capture would be easy. So he turned to his men and with a wave of his hand said: "Seize the intruders!"

Instantly two or three of the warriors stepped forward to obey, but to their amazement they could not reach any of the three; their hands were arrested as if by an invisible wall of iron. Without paying any attention to these attempts at capture, Inga advanced slowly and the goat kept pace with him. And when Rinkitink saw that he was safe from harm he gave one of his big, merry laughs, and it startled the warriors and made them nervous. Captain Buzzub's eyes grew big with surprise as the three steadily advanced and forced his men backward; nor was he free from terror himself at the magic that protected these strange visitors. As for the warriors, they presently became terror-stricken and fled in a panic up the slope toward the city, and Buzzub was obliged to chase after them and shout threats of punishment before he could halt them and form them into a line of battle.

All the men of Regos bore spears and bows-and-arrows, and some of the officers had swords and battle-axes; so Buzzub ordered them to stand their ground and shoot and slay the strangers as they approached. This they tried to do. Inga being in advance, the warriors sent a flight of sharp arrows straight at the boy's breast, while others cast their long spears at him.

It seemed to Rinkitink that the little Prince must surely perish as he stood facing this hail of murderous missiles; but the power of the Pink Pearl did not desert him, and when the arrows and spears had reached to within an inch of his body they bounded back again and fell harmlessly at his feet. Nor were Rinkitink or Bilbil injured in the least, although they stood close beside Inga.

Buzzub stood for a moment looking upon the boy in silent wonder. Then, recovering himself, he shouted in a loud voice: "Once again! All together, my men. No one shall ever defy our might and live!"

Again a flight of arrows and spears sped toward the three, and since many more of the warriors of Regos had by this time joined their fellows, the air was for a moment darkened by the deadly shafts. But again all fell harmless before the power of the Pink Pearl, and Bilbil, who had been growing very angry at the attempts to injure him and his party, suddenly made a bolt forward, casting off Inga's hold, and butted into the line of warriors, who were standing amazed at their failure to conquer.

Taken by surprise at the goat's attack, a dozen big warriors tumbled in a heap, yelling with fear, and their comrades, not knowing what had happened but imagining that their foes were attacking them, turned about and ran to the city as hard as they could go. Bilbil, still angry, had just time to catch the big captain as he turned to follow his men, and Buzzub first sprawled headlong upon the ground, then rolled over two or three times, and finally jumped up and ran yelling after his defeated warriors. This butting on the part of the goat was very hard upon King Rinkitink, who nearly fell off Bilbil's back at the shock of encounter; but the little fat King wound his arms around the goat's neck and shut his eyes and clung on with all his might. It was not until he heard Inga say triumphantly, "We have won the fight without striking a blow!" that Rinkitink dared open his eyes again. Then he saw the warriors rushing into the City of Regos and barring the heavy gates, and he was very much relieved at the sight.

"Without striking a blow!" said Bilbil indignantly. "That is not quite true, Prince Inga. You did not fight, I admit, but I struck a couple of times to good purpose, and I claim to have conquered the cowardly warriors unaided."

"You and I together, Bilbil," said Rinkitink mildly. "But the next time you make a charge, please warn me in time, so that I may dismount and give you all the credit for the attack."

There being no one now to oppose their advance, the three walked to the gates of the city, which had been closed against them. The gates were of iron and heavily barred, and upon the top of the high walls of the city a host of the warriors now appeared armed with arrows and spears and other weapons. For Buzzub had gone straight to the palace of King Cos and reported his defeat, relating the powerful magic of the boy, the fat King and the goat, and had asked what to do next.

The big captain still trembled with fear, but King Gos did not believe in magic, and called Buzzub a coward and a weakling. At once the King took command of his men personally, and he ordered the walls manned with warriors and instructed them to shoot to kill if any of the three strangers approached the gates.

Of course, neither Rinkitink nor Bilbil knew how they had been protected from harm and so at first they were inclined to resent the boy's command that the three must always keep together and touch one another at all times. But when Inga explained that his magic would not otherwise save them from injury, they agreed to obey, for they had now seen enough to convince them that the Prince was really protected by some invisible power.

As they came before the gates another shower of arrows and spears descended upon them, and as before not a single missile touched their bodies. King Gos, who was upon the wall, was greatly amazed and somewhat worried, but he depended upon the strength of his gates and commanded his men to continue shooting until all their weapons were gone.

Inga let them shoot as much as they wished, while he stood before the great gates and examined them carefully.

"Perhaps Bilbil can batter down the gates, suggested Rinkitink.

"No," replied the goat; "my head is hard, but not harder than iron."

"Then," returned the King, "let us stay outside; especially as we can't get in."

But Inga was not at all sure they could not get in. The gates opened inward, and three heavy bars were held in place by means of stout staples riveted to the sheets of steel. The boy had been told that the power of the Blue Pearl would enable him to accomplish any feat of strength, and he believed that this was true.

The warriors, under the direction of King Gos, continued to hurl arrows and darts and spears and axes and huge stones upon the invaders, all without avail. The ground below was thickly covered with weapons, yet not one of the three before the gates had been injured in the slightest manner. When everything had been cast that was available and not a single weapon of any sort remained at hand, the amazed warriors saw the boy put his shoulder against the gates and burst asunder the huge staples that held the bars in place. A thousand of their men could not have accomplished this feat, yet the small, slight boy did it with seeming ease. The gates burst open, and Inga advanced into the city street and called upon King Gos to surrender.

But Gos was now as badly frightened as were his warriors. He and his men were accustomed to war and pillage and they had carried terror into many countries, but here was a small boy, a fat man and a goat who could not be injured by all his skill in warfare, his numerous army and thousands of death-dealing weapons. Moreover, they not only defied King Gos's entire army but they had broken in the huge gates of the city — as easily as if they had been made of paper — and such an exhibition of enormous strength made the wicked King fear for his life. Like all bullies and marauders, Gos was a coward at heart, and now a panic seized him and he turned and fled before the calm advance of Prince Inga of Pingaree. The warriors were like their master, and having thrown all their weapons over the wall and being helpless to oppose the strangers, they all swarmed after Gos who abandoned his city and crossed the bridge of boats to the Island of Coregos. There was a desperate struggle among these cowardly warriors to get over the bridge, and many were pushed into the water and obliged to swim; but finally every fighting man of Regos had gained the shore of Coregos and then they tore away the bridge of boats and drew them up on their own side, hoping the stretch of open water would prevent the magic invaders from following them.

The humble citizens and serving people of Regos, who had been terrified and abused by the rough warriors all their lives, were not only greatly astonished by this sudden conquest of their masters but greatly delighted. As the King and his army fled to Coregos, the people embraced one another and danced for very joy, and then they turned to see what the conquerors of Regos were like.

8. Rinkitink Makes a Great Mistake

The fat King rode his goat through the streets of the conquered city and the boy Prince walked proudly beside him, while all the people bent their heads humbly to their new masters, whom they were prepared to serve in the same manner they had King Gos.

Not a warrior remained in all Regos to oppose the triumphant three; the bridge of boats had been destroyed; Inga and his companions were free from danger — for a time, at least.

The jolly little King appreciated this fact and rejoiced that he had escaped all injury during the battle. How it had all happened he could not tell, nor even guess, but he was content in being safe and free to take possession of the enemy's city. So, as they passed through the lines of respectful civilians on their way to the palace, the King tipped his crown back on his bald head and folded his arms and sang in his best voice the following lines:
"Oh, here comes the army of King Rinkitink!
It isn't a big one, perhaps you may think,
But it scattered the warriors quicker than wink —

Rink-i-tink, tink-i-tink, tink!

Our Bilbil's a hero and so is his King;
Our foemen have vanished like birds on the wing;
I guess that as fighters we're quite the real thing —

Rink-i-tink, tink-i-tink, tink!"

"Why don't you give a little credit to Inga?" inquired the goat. "If I remember aright, he did a little of the conquering himself."

"So he did," responded the King, "and that's the reason I'm sounding our own praise, Bilbil. Those who do the least, often shout the loudest and so get the most glory. Inga did so much that there is danger of his becoming more important than we are, and so we'd best say nothing about him."

When they reached the palace, which was an immense building, furnished throughout in regal splendor, Inga took formal possession and ordered the majordomo to show them the finest rooms the building contained. There were many pleasant apartments, but Rinkitink proposed to Inga that they share one of the largest bedrooms together.

"For," said he, "we are not sure that old Gos will not return and try to recapture his city, and you must remember that I have no magic to protect me. In any danger, were I alone, I might be easily killed or captured, while if you are by my side you can save me from injury."

The boy realized the wisdom of this plan, and selected a fine big bedroom on the second floor of the palace, in which he ordered two golden beds placed and prepared for King Rinkitink and himself. Bilbil was given a suite of rooms on the other side of the palace, where servants brought the goat fresh-cut grass to eat and made him a soft bed to lie upon.

That evening the boy Prince and the fat King dined in great state in the lofty-domed dining hall of the palace, where forty servants waited upon them. The royal chef, anxious to win the favor of the conquerors of Regos, prepared his finest and most savory dishes for them, which Rinkitink ate with much appetite and found so delicious that he ordered the royal chef brought into the banquet hall and presented him with a gilt button which the King cut from his own jacket.

"You are welcome to it," said he to the chef, "because I have eaten so much that I cannot use that lower button at all."

Rinkitink was mightily pleased to live in a comfortable palace again and to dine at a well spread table. His joy grew every moment, so that he came in time to be as merry and cheery as before Pingaree was despoiled. And, although he had been much frightened during Inga's defiance of the army of King Gos, he now began to turn the matter into a joke.

"Why, my boy," said he, "you whipped the big black-bearded King exactly as if he were a schoolboy, even though you used no warlike weapon at all upon him. He was cowed through fear of your magic, and that reminds me to demand from you an explanation. How did you do it, Inga? And where did the wonderful magic come from?"

Perhaps it would have been wise for the Prince to have explained about the magic pearls, but at that moment he was not inclined to do so. Instead, he replied: "Be patient, Your Majesty. The secret is not my own, so please do not ask me to divulge it. Is it not enough, for the present, that the magic saved you from death to-day?"

"Do not think me ungrateful," answered the King earnestly. "A million spears fell on me from the wall, and several stones as big as mountains, yet none of them hurt me!"

"The stones were not as big as mountains, sire," said the Prince with a smile. "They were, indeed, no larger than your head."

"Are you sure about that?" asked Rinkitink.

"Quite sure, Your Majesty."

"How deceptive those things are!" sighed the King. "This argument reminds me of the story of Tom Tick, which my father used to tell."

"I have never heard that story," Inga answered.

"Well, as he told it, it ran like this:
"When Tom walked out, the sky to spy,
A naughty gnat flew in his eye;
But Tom knew not it was a gnat —
He thought, at first, it was a cat.

And then, it felt so very big,
He thought it surely was a pig
Till, standing still to hear it grunt,
He cried: 'Why, it's an elephunt!'

But — when the gnat flew out again
And Tom was free from all his pain,
He said: 'There flew into my eye
A leetle, teenty-tiny fly.'"

"Indeed," said Inga, laughing, "the gnat was much like your stones that seemed as big as mountains."

After their dinner they inspected the palace, which was filled with valuable goods stolen by King Gos from many nations. But the day's events had tired them and they retired early to their big sleeping apartment.

"In the morning," said the boy to Rinkitink, as he was undressing for bed, "I shall begin the search for my father and mother and the people of Pingaree. And, when they are found and rescued, we will all go home again, and be as happy as we were before."

They carefully bolted the door of their room, that no one might enter, and then got into their beds, where Rinkitink fell asleep in an instant. The boy lay awake for a while thinking over the day's adventures, but presently he fell sound asleep also, and so weary was he that nothing disturbed his slumber until he awakened next morning with a ray of sunshine in his eyes, which had crept into the room through the open window by King Rinkitink's bed.

Resolving to begin the search for his parents without any unnecessary delay, Inga at once got out of bed and began to dress himself, while Rinkitink, in the other bed, was still sleeping peacefully. But when the boy had put on both his stockings and began looking for his shoes, he could find but one of them. The left shoe, that containing the Pink Pearl, was missing.

Filled with anxiety at this discovery, Inga searched through the entire room, looking underneath the beds and divans and chairs and behind the draperies and in the corners and every other possible place a shoe might be. He tried the door, and found it still bolted; so, with growing uneasiness, the boy was forced to admit that the precious shoe was not in the room.

With a throbbing heart he aroused his companion.

"King Rinkitink," said he, "do you know what has become of my left shoe?"

"Your shoe!" exclaimed the King, giving a wide yawn and rubbing his eyes to get the sleep out of them. "Have you lost a shoe?"

"Yes," said Inga. "I have searched everywhere in the room, and cannot find it."

"But why bother me about such a small thing?" inquired Rinkitink. "A shoe is only a shoe, and you can easily get another one. But, stay! Perhaps it was your shoe which I threw at the cat last night."

"The cat!" cried Inga. "What do you mean?"

"Why, in the night," explained Rinkitink, sitting up and beginning to dress himself, "I was wakened by the mewing of a cat that sat upon a wall of the palace, just outside my window. As the noise disturbed me, I reached out in the dark and caught up something and threw it at the cat, to frighten the creature away. I did not know what it was that I threw, and I was too sleepy to care; but probably it was your shoe, since it is now missing."

"Then," said the boy, in a despairing tone of voice, "your carelessness has ruined me, as well as yourself, King Rinkitink, for in that shoe was concealed the magic power which protected us from danger."

The King's face became very serious when he heard this and he uttered a low whistle of surprise and regret.

"Why on earth did you not warn me of this?" he demanded. "And why did you keep such a precious power in an old shoe? And why didn't you put the shoe under a pillow? You were very wrong, my lad, in not confiding to me, your faithful friend, the secret, for in that case the shoe would not now be lost."

To all this Inga had no answer. He sat on the side of his bed, with hanging head, utterly disconsolate, and seeing this, Rinkitink had pity for his sorrow.

"Come!" cried the King; "let us go out at once and look for the shoe which I threw at the cat. It must even now be lying in the yard of the palace."

This suggestion roused the boy to action. He at once threw open the door and in his stocking feet rushed down the staircase, closely followed by Rinkitink. But although they looked on both sides of the palace wall and in every possible crack and corner where a shoe might lodge, they failed to find it.

After a half hour's careful search the boy said sorrowfully: "Someone must have passed by, as we slept, and taken the precious shoe, not knowing its value. To us, King Rinkitink, this will be a dreadful misfortune, for we are surrounded by dangers from which we have now no protection. Luckily I have the other shoe left, within which is the magic power that gives me strength; so all is not lost."

Then he told Rinkitink, in a few words, the secret of the wonderful pearls, and how he had recovered them from the ruins and hidden them in his shoes, and how they had enabled him to drive King Gos and his men from Regos and to capture the city. The King was much astonished, and when the story was concluded he said to Inga: "What did you do with the other shoe?"

"Why, I left it in our bedroom," replied the boy.

"Then I advise you to get it at once," continued Rinkitink, "for we can ill afford to lose the second shoe, as well as the one I threw at the cat."

"You are right!" cried Inga, and they hastened back to their bedchamber.

On entering the room they found an old woman sweeping and raising a great deal of dust.

"Where is my shoe?" asked the Prince, anxiously.

The old woman stopped sweeping and looked at him in a stupid way, for she was not very intelligent.

"Do you mean the one odd shoe that was lying on the floor when I came in?" she finally asked.

"Yes — yes!" answered the boy. "Where is it? Tell me where it is!"

"Why, I threw it on the dust-heap, outside the back gate," said she, "for, it being but a single shoe, with no mate, it can be of no use to anyone."

"Show us the way to the dust-heap — at once!" commanded the boy, sternly, for he was greatly frightened by this new misfortune which threatened him.

The old woman hobbled away and they followed her, constantly urging her to hasten; but when they reached the dust-heap no shoe was to be seen.

"This is terrible!" wailed the young Prince, ready to weep at his loss. "We are now absolutely ruined, and at the mercy of our enemies. Nor shall I be able to liberate my dear father and mother."

"Well," replied Rinkitink, leaning against an old barrel and looking quite solemn, "the thing is certainly unlucky, any way we look at it. I suppose someone has passed along here and, seeing the shoe upon the dust-heap, has carried it away. But no one could know the magic power the shoe contains and so will not use it against us. I believe, Inga, we must now depend upon our wits to get us out of the scrape we are in.

With saddened hearts they returned to the palace, and entering a small room where no one could observe them or overhear them, the boy took the White Pearl from its silken bag and held it to his ear, asking: "What shall I do now?"

"Tell no one of your loss," answered the Voice of the Pearl. "If your enemies do not know that you are powerless, they will fear you as much as ever. Keep your secret, be patient, and fear not!"

Inga heeded this advice and also warned Rinkitink to say nothing to anyone of the loss of the shoes and the powers they contained. He sent for the shoemaker of King Gos, who soon brought him a new pair of red leather shoes that fitted him quite well. When these had been put upon his feet, the Prince, accompanied by the King, started to walk through the city.

Wherever they went the people bowed low to the conqueror, although a few, remembering Inga's terrible strength, ran away in fear and trembling. They had been used to severe masters and did not yet know how they would be treated by King Gos's successor. There being no occasion for the boy to exercise the powers he had displayed the previous day, his present helplessness was not suspected by any of the citizens of Regos, who still considered him a wonderful magician.

Inga did not dare to fight his way to the mines, at present, nor could he try to conquer the Island of Coregos, where his mother was enslaved; so he set about the regulation of the City of Regos, and having established himself with great state in the royal palace he began to govern the people by kindness, having consideration for the most humble.

The King of Regos and his followers sent spies across to the island they had abandoned in their flight, and these spies returned with the news that the terrible boy conqueror was still occupying the city. Therefore none of them ventured to go back to Regos but continued to live upon the neighboring island of Coregos, where they passed the days in fear and trembling and sought to plot and plan ways how they might overcome the Prince of Pingaree and the fat King of Gilgad.

9. A Present for Zella

Now it so happened that on the morning of that same day when the Prince of Pingaree suffered the loss of his priceless shoes, there chanced to pass along the road that wound beside the royal palace a poor charcoal-burner named Nikobob, who was about to return to his home in the forest.

Nikobob carried an ax and a bundle of torches over his shoulder and he walked with his eyes to the ground, being deep in thought as to the strange manner in which the powerful King Gos and his city had been conquered by a boy Prince who had come from Pingaree.

Suddenly the charcoal-burner espied a shoe lying upon the ground, just beyond the high wall of the palace and directly in his path. He picked it up and, seeing it was a pretty shoe, although much too small for his own foot, he put it in his pocket.

Soon after, on turning a corner of the wall, Nikobob came to a dust-heap where, lying amidst a mass of rubbish, was another shoe — the mate to the one he had before found. This also he placed in his pocket, saying to himself: "I have now a fine pair of shoes for my daughter Zella, who will be much pleased to find I have brought her a present from the city."

And while the charcoal-burner turned into the forest and trudged along the path toward his home, Inga and Rinkitink were still searching for the missing shoes. Of course, they could not know that Nikobob had found them, nor did the honest man think he had taken anything more than a pair of cast-off shoes which nobody wanted.

Nikobob had several miles to travel through the forest before he could reach the little log cabin where his wife, as well as his little daughter Zella, awaited his return, but he was used to long walks and tramped along the path whistling cheerfully to beguile the time.

Few people, as I said before, ever passed through the dark and tangled forests of Regos, except to go to the mines in the mountain beyond, for many dangerous creatures lurked in the wild jungles, and King Gos never knew, when he sent a messenger to the mines, whether he would reach there safely or not.

The charcoal-burner, however, knew the wild forest well, and especially this part of it lying between the city and his home. It was the favorite haunt of the ferocious beast Choggenmugger, dreaded by every dweller in the Island of Regos. Choggenmugger was so old that everyone thought it must have been there since the world was made, and each year of its life the huge scales that covered its body grew thicker and harder and its jaws grew wider and its teeth grew sharper and its appetite grew more keen than ever.

In former ages there had been many dragons in Regos, but Choggenmugger was so fond of dragons that he had eaten all of them long ago. There had also been great serpents and crocodiles in the forest marshes, but all had gone to feed the hunger of Choggenmugger. The people of Regos knew well there was no use opposing the Great Beast, so when one unfortunately met with it he gave himself up for lost.

All this Nikobob knew well, but fortune had always favored him in his journey through the forest, and although he had at times met many savage beasts and fought them with his sharp ax, he had never to this day encountered the terrible Choggenmugger. Indeed, he was not thinking of the Great Beast at all as he walked along, but suddenly he heard a crashing of broken trees and felt a trembling of the earth and saw the immense jaws of Choggenmugger opening before him. Then Nikobob gave himself up for lost and his heart almost ceased to beat.

He believed there was no way of escape. No one ever dared oppose Choggenmugger. But Nikobob hated to die without showing the monster, in some way, that he was eaten only under protest. So he raised his ax and brought it down upon the red, protruding tongue of the monster — and cut it clean off!

For a moment the charcoal-burner scarcely believed what his eyes saw, for he knew nothing of the pearls he carried in his pocket or the magic power they lent his arm. His success, however, encouraged him to strike again, and this time the huge scaly jaw of Choggenmugger was severed in twain and the beast howled in terrified rage.

Nikobob took off his coat, to give himself more freedom of action, and then he earnestly renewed the attack. But now the ax seemed blunted by the hard scales and made no impression upon them whatever. The creature advanced with glaring, wicked eyes, and Nikobob seized his coat under his arm and turned to flee.

That was foolish, for Choggenmugger could run like the wind. In a moment it overtook the charcoal-burner and snapped its four rows of sharp teeth together. But they did not touch Nikobob, because he still held the coat in his grasp, close to his body, and in the coat pocket were Inga's shoes, and in the points of the shoes were the magic pearls. Finding himself uninjured, Nikobob put on his coat, again seized his ax, and in a short time had chopped Choggenmugger into many small pieces — a task that proved not only easy but very agreeable.

"I must be the strongest man in all the world!" thought the charcoal-burner, as he proudly resumed his way, "for Choggenmugger has been the terror of Regos since the world began, and I alone have been able to destroy the beast. Yet it is singular that never before did I discover how powerful a man I am."

He met no further adventure and at midday reached a little clearing in the forest where stood his humble cabin.

"Great news! I have great news for you," he shouted, as his wife and little daughter came to greet him. "King Gos has been conquered by a boy Prince from the far island of Pingaree, and I have this day — unaided — destroyed Choggenmugger by the might of my strong arm."

This was, indeed, great news. They brought Nikobob into the house and set him in an easy chair and made him tell everything he knew about the Prince of Pingaree and the fat King of Gilgad, as well as the details of his wonderful fight with mighty Choggenmugger.

"And now, my daughter," said the charcoalburner, when all his news had been related for at least the third time, "here is a pretty present I have brought you from the city."

With this he drew the shoes from the pocket of his coat and handed them to Zella, who gave him a dozen kisses in payment and was much pleased with her gift. The little girl had never worn shoes before, for her parents were too poor to buy her such luxuries, so now the possession of these, which were not much worn, filled the child's heart with joy. She admired the red leather and the graceful curl of the pointed toes. When she tried them on her feet, they fitted as well as if made for her.

All the afternoon, as she helped her mother with the housework, Zella thought of her pretty shoes. They seemed more important to her than the coming to Regos of the conquering Prince of Pingaree, or even the death of Choggenmugger.

When Zella and her mother were not working in the cabin, cooking or sewing, they often searched the neighboring forest for honey which the wild bees cleverly hid in hollow trees. The day after Nikobob's return, as they were starting out after honey, Zella decided to put on her new shoes, as they would keep the twigs that covered the ground from hurting her feet. She was used to the twigs, of course, but what is the use of having nice, comfortable shoes, if you do not wear them?

So she danced along, very happily, followed by her mother, and presently they came to a tree in which was a deep hollow. Zella thrust her hand and arm into the space and found that the tree was full of honey, so she began to dig it out with a wooden paddle. Her mother, who held the pail, suddenly cried in warning: "Look out, Zella; the bees are coming!" and then the good woman ran fast toward the house to escape.

Zella, however, had no more than time to turn her head when a thick swarm of bees surrounded her, angry because they had caught her stealing their honey and intent on stinging the girl as a punishment. She knew her danger and expected to be badly injured by the multitude of stinging bees, but to her surprise the little creatures were unable to fly close enough to her to stick their dart-like stingers into her flesh. They swarmed about her in a dark cloud, and their angry buzzing was terrible to hear, yet the little girl remained unharmed.

When she realized this, Zella was no longer afraid but continued to ladle out the honey until she had secured all that was in the tree. Then she returned to the cabin, where her mother was weeping and bemoaning the fate of her darling child, and the good woman was greatly astonished to find Zella had escaped injury.

Again they went to the woods to search for honey, and although the mother always ran away whenever the bees came near them, Zella paid no attention to the creatures but kept at her work, so that before supper time came the pails were again filled to overflowing with delicious honey.

"With such good fortune as we have had this day," said her mother, "we shall soon gather enough honey for you to carry to Queen Cor." For it seems the wicked Queen was very fond of honey and it had been Zella's custom to go, once every year, to the City of Coregos, to carry the Queen a supply of sweet honey for her table. Usually she had but one pail.

"But now," said Zella, "I shall be able to carry two pailsful to the Queen, who will, I am sure, give me a good price for it."

"True," answered her mother, "and, as the boy Prince may take it into his head to conquer Coregos, as well as Regos, I think it best for you to start on your journey to Queen Cor tomorrow morning. Do you not agree with me, Nikobob?" she added turning to her husband, the charcoal-burner, who was eating his supper.

"I agree with you," he replied. "If Zella must go to the City of Coregos, she may as well start to-morrow morning."

10. The Cunning of Queen Cor

You may be sure the Queen of Coregos was not well pleased to have King Gos and all his warriors living in her city after they had fled from their own. They were savage natured and quarrelsome men at all times, and their tempers had not improved since their conquest by the Prince of Pingaree. Moreover, they were eating up Queen Cor's provisions and crowding the houses of her own people, who grumbled and complained until their Queen was heartily tired.

"Shame on you!" she said to her husband, King Gos, "to be driven out of your city by a boy, a roly-poly King and a billy goat. Why do you not go back and fight them?"

"No human can fight against the powers of magic," returned the King in a surly voice. "That boy is either a fairy or under the protection of fairies. We escaped with our lives only because we were quick to run away; but, should we return to Regos, the same terrible power that burst open the city gates would crush us all to atoms."

"Bah! you are a coward," cried the Queen, tauntingly.

"I am not a coward," said the big King. "I have killed in battle scores of my enemies; by the might of my sword and my good right arm I have conquered many nations; all my life people have feared me. But no one would dare face the tremendous power of the Prince of Pingaree, boy though he is. It would not be courage it would be folly, to attempt it."

"Then meet his power with cunning," suggested the Queen. "Take my advice, and steal over to Regos at night, when it is dark, and capture or destroy the boy while he sleeps."

"No weapon can touch his body," was the answer. "He bears a charmed life and cannot be injured."

"Does the fat King possess magic powers, or the goat?" inquired Cor.

"I think not," said Gos. "We could not injure them, indeed, any more than we could the boy, but they did not seem to have any unusual strength, although the goat's head is harder than a battering-ram."

"Well," mused the Queen, "there is surely some way to conquer that slight boy. If you are afraid to undertake the job, I shall go myself. By some stratagem I shall manage to make him my prisoner. He will not dare to defy a Queen, and no magic can stand against a woman's cunning."

"Go ahead, if you like," replied the King, with an evil grin, "and if you are hung up by the thumbs or cast into a dungeon, it will serve you right for thinking you can succeed where a skilled warrior dares not make the attempt."

"I'm not afraid," answered the Queen. "It is only soldiers and bullies who are cowards."

In spite of this assertion, Queen Cor was not so brave as she was cunning. For several days she thought over this plan and that, and tried to decide which was most likely to succeed. She had never seen the boy Prince but had heard so many tales of him from the defeated warriors, and especially from Captain Buzzub, that she had learned to respect his power.

Spurred on by the knowledge that she would never get rid of her unwelcome guests until Prince Inga was overcome and Regos regained for King Gos, the Queen of Coregos finally decided to trust to luck and her native wit to defeat a simple-minded boy, however powerful he might be. Inga could not suspect what she was going to do, because she did not know herself. She intended to act boldly and trust to chance to win.

It is evident that had the cunning Queen known that Inga had lost all his magic, she would not have devoted so much time to the simple matter of capturing him, but like all others she was impressed by the marvelous exhibition of power he had shown in capturing Regos, and had no reason to believe the boy was less powerful now.

One morning Queen Cor boldly entered a boat, and, taking four men with her as an escort and bodyguard, was rowed across the narrow channel to Regos. Prince Inga was sitting in the palace playing checkers with King Rinkitink when a servant came to him, saying that Queen Cor had arrived and desired an audience with him.

With many misgivings lest the wicked Queen discover that he had now lost his magic powers, the boy ordered her to be admitted, and she soon entered the room and bowed low before him, in mock respect.

Cor was a big woman, almost as tall as King Gos. She had flashing black eyes and the dark complexion you see on gypsies. Her temper, when irritated, was something dreadful, and her face wore an evil expression which she tried to cover by smiling sweetly — often when she meant the most mischief.

"I have come," said she in a low voice, "to render homage to the noble Prince of Pingaree. I am told that Your Highness is the strongest person in the world, and invincible in battle, and therefore I wish you to become my friend, rather than my enemy."

Now Inga did not know how to reply to this speech. He disliked the appearance of the woman and was afraid of her and he was unused to deception and did not know how to mask his real feelings. So he took time to think over his answer, which he finally made in these words: "I have no quarrel with Your Majesty, and my only reason for coming here is to liberate my father and mother, and my people, whom you and your husband have made your slaves, and to recover the goods King Gos has plundered from the Island of Pingaree. This I hope soon to accomplish, and if you really wish to be my friend, you can assist me greatly."

While he was speaking Queen Cor had been studying the boy's face stealthily, from the corners of her eyes, and she said to herself: "He is so small and innocent that I believe I can capture him alone, and with ease. He does not seem very terrible and I suspect that King Gos and his warriors were frightened at nothing."

Then, aloud, she said to Inga: "I wish to invite you, mighty Prince, and your friend, the great King of Gilgad, to visit my poor palace at Coregos, where all my people shall do you honor. Will you come?"

"At present," replied Inga, uneasily, "I must refuse your kind invitation."

"There will be feasting, and dancing girls, and games and fireworks," said the Queen, speaking as if eager to entice him and at each word coming a step nearer to where he stood.

"I could not enjoy them while my poor parents are slaves," said the boy, sadly.

"Are you sure of that?" asked Queen Cor, and by that time she was close beside Inga. Suddenly she leaned forward and threw both of her long arms around Inga's body, holding him in a grasp that was like a vise.

Now Rinkitink sprang forward to rescue his friend, but Cor kicked out viciously with her foot and struck the King squarely on his stomach — a very tender place to be kicked, especially if one is fat. Then, still hugging Inga tightly, the Queen called aloud: "I've got him! Bring in the ropes."

Instantly the four men she had brought with her sprang into the room and bound the boy hand and foot. Next they seized Rinkitink, who was still rubbing his stomach, and bound him likewise.

With a laugh of wicked triumph, Queen Cor now led her captives down to the boat and returned with them to Coregos.

Great was the astonishment of King Gos and his warriors when they saw that the mighty Prince of Pingaree, who had put them all to flight, had been captured by a woman. Cowards as they were, they now crowded around the boy and jeered at him, and some of them would have struck him had not the Queen cried out: "Hands off! He is my prisoner, remember, not yours."

"Well, Cor, what are you going to do with him?" inquired King Gos.

"I shall make him my slave, that he may amuse my idle hours. For he is a pretty boy, and gentle, although he did frighten all of you big warriors so terribly."

The King scowled at this speech, not liking to be ridiculed, but he said nothing more. He and his men returned that same day to Regos, after restoring the bridge of boats. And they held a wild carnival of rejoicing, both in the King's palace and in the city, although the poor people of Regos who were not warriors were all sorry that the kind young Prince who had been captured by his enemies and could rule them no longer.

When her unwelcome guests had all gone back to Regos and the Queen was alone in her palace, she ordered Inga and Rinkitink brought before her and their bonds removed. They came sadly enough, knowing they were in serious straits and at the mercy of a cruel mistress. Inga had taken counsel of the White Pearl, which had advised him to bear up bravely under his misfortune, promising a change for the better very soon. With this promise to comfort him, Inga faced the Queen with a dignified bearing that indicated both pride and courage.

"Well, youngster," said she, in a cheerful tone because she was pleased with her success, "you played a clever trick on my poor husband and frightened him badly, but for that prank I am inclined to forgive you. Hereafter I intend you to be my page, which means that you must fetch and carry for me at my will. And let me advise you to obey my every whim without question or delay, for when I am angry I become ugly, and when I am ugly someone is sure to feel the lash. Do you understand me?"

Inga bowed, but made no answer. Then she turned to Rinkitink and said: "As for you, I cannot decide how to make you useful to me, as you are altogether too fat and awkward to work in the fields. It may be, however, that I can use you as a pincushion."

"What!" cried Rinkitink in horror, "would you stick pins into the King of Gilgad?"

"Why not?" returned Queen Cor. "You are as fat as a pincushion, as you must yourself admit, and whenever I needed a pin I could call you to me." Then she laughed at his frightened look and asked: "By the way, are you ticklish?"

This was the question Rinkitink had been dreading. He gave a moan of despair and shook his head.

"I should love to tickle the bottom of your feet with a feather," continued the cruel woman. "Please take off your shoes."

"Oh, your Majesty!" pleaded poor Rinkitink, "I beg you to allow me to amuse you in some other way. I can dance, or I can sing you a song."

"Well," she answered, shaking with laughter, "you may sing a song — if it be a merry one. But you do not seem in a merry mood."

"I feel merry — indeed, Your Majesty, I do!" protested Rinkitink, anxious to escape the tickling. But even as he professed to "feel merry" his round, red face wore an expression of horror and anxiety that was realty comical.

"Sing, then!" commanded Queen Cor, who was greatly amused.

Rinkitink gave a sigh of relief and after clearing his throat and trying to repress his sobs he began to sing this song-gently, at first, but finally roaring it out at the top of his voice:
"Oh! There was a Baby Tiger lived in a men-ag-er-ie —
Fizzy-fezzy-fuzzy — they wouldn't set him free;
And ev'rybody thought that he was gentle as could be —
Fizzy-fezzy-fuzzy — Ba-by Ti-ger!

Oh! They patted him upon his head and shook him by the paw -
Fizzy-fezzy-fuzzy — he had a bone to gnaw;
But soon he grew the biggest Tiger that you ever saw —
Fizzy-fezzy-fuzzy — what a Ti-ger!

Oh! One day they came to pet the brute and he began to fight —
Fizzy-fezzy-fuzzy — how he did scratch and bite!
He broke the cage and in a rage he darted out of sight —
Fizzy-fezzy-fuzzy was a Ti-ger!"

"And is there a moral to the song?" asked Queen Cor, when King Rinkitink had finished his song with great spirit.

"If there is," replied Rinkitink, "it is a warning not to fool with tigers."

The little Prince could not help smiling at this shrewd answer, but Queen Cor frowned and gave the King a sharp look.

"Oh," said she; "I think I know the difference between a tiger and a lapdog. But I'll bear the warning in mind, just the same."

For, after all her success in capturing them, she was a little afraid of these people who had once displayed such extraordinary powers.

11. Zella Goes to Coregos

The forest in which Nikobob lived with his wife and daughter stood between the mountains and the City of Regos, and a well-beaten path wound among the trees, leading from the city to the mines. This path was used by the King's messengers, and captured prisoners were also sent by this way from Regos to work in the underground caverns.

Nikobob had built his cabin more than a mile away from this path, that he might not be molested by the wild and lawless soldiers of King Gos, but the family of the charcoal-burner was surrounded by many creatures scarcely less dangerous to encounter, and often in the night they could hear savage animals growling and prowling about the cabin. Because Nikobob minded his own business and never hunted the wild creatures to injure them, the beasts had come to regard him as one of the natural dwellers in the forest and did not molest him or his family. Still Zella and her mother seldom wandered far from home, except on such errands as carrying honey to Coregos, and at these times Nikobob cautioned them to be very careful.

So when Zella set out on her journey to Queen Cor, with the two pails of honey in her hands, she was undertaking a dangerous adventure and there was no certainty that she would return safely to her loving parents. But they were poor, and Queen Cor's money, which they expected to receive for the honey, would enable them to purchase many things that were needed; so it was deemed best that Zella should go. She was a brave little girl and poor people are often obliged to take chances that rich ones are spared.

A passing woodchopper had brought news to Nikobob's cabin that Queen Cor had made a prisoner of the conquering Prince of Pingaree and that Gos and his warriors were again back in their city of Regos; but these struggles and conquests were matters which, however interesting, did not concern the poor charcoal-burner or his family. They were more anxious over the report that the warriors had become more reckless than ever before, and delighted in annoying all the common people; so Zella was told to keep away from the beaten path as much as possible, that she might not encounter any of the King's soldiers.

"When it is necessary to choose between the warriors and the wild beasts," said Nikobob, "the beasts will be found the more merciful."

The little girl had put on her best attire for the journey and her mother threw a blue silk shawl over her head and shoulders. Upon her feet were the pretty red shoes her father had brought her from Regos. Thus prepared, she kissed her parents good-bye and started out with a light heart, carrying the pails of honey in either hand.

It was necessary for Zella to cross the path that led from the mines to the city, but once on the other side she was not likely to meet with anyone, for she had resolved to cut through the forest and so reach the bridge of boats without entering the City of Regos, where she might be interrupted. For an hour or two she found the walking easy enough, but then the forest, which in this part was unknown to her, became badly tangled. The trees were thicker and creeping vines intertwined between them. She had to turn this way and that to get through at all, and finally she came to a place where a network of vines and branches effectually barred her farther progress.

Zella was dismayed, at first, when she encountered this obstacle, but setting down her pails she made an endeavor to push the branches aside. At her touch they parted as if by magic, breaking asunder like dried twigs, and she found she could pass freely. At another place a great log had fallen across her way, but the little girl lifted it easily and cast it aside, although six ordinary men could scarcely have moved it.

The child was somewhat worried at this evidence of a strength she had heretofore been ignorant that she possessed. In order to satisfy herself that it was no delusion, she tested her new-found power in many ways, finding that nothing was too big nor too heavy for her to lift. And, naturally enough, the girl gained courage from these experiments and became confident that she could protect herself in any emergency. When, presently, a wild boar ran toward her, grunting horribly and threatening her with its great tusks, she did not climb a tree to escape, as she had always done before on meeting such creatures, but stood still and faced the boar. When it had come quite close and Zella saw that it could not injure her — a fact that astonished both the beast and the girl — she suddenly reached down and seizing it by one ear threw the great beast far off amongst the trees, where it fell headlong to the earth, grunting louder than ever with surprise and fear.

The girl laughed merrily at this incident and, picking up her pails, resumed her journey through the forest. It is not recorded whether the wild boar told his adventure to the other beasts or they had happened to witness his defeat, but certain it is that Zella was not again molested. A brown bear watched her pass without making any movement in her direction and a great puma — a beast much dreaded by all men — crept out of her path as she approached, and disappeared among the trees.

Thus everything favored the girl's journey and she made such good speed that by noon she emerged from the forest's edge and found she was quite near to the bridge of boats that led to Coregos. This she crossed safely and without meeting any of the rude warriors she so greatly feared, and five minutes later the laughter of the charcoal-burner was seeking admittance at the back door of Queen Cor's palace.

12. The Excitement of Bilbil the Goat

Our story must now return to one of our characters whom we have been forced to neglect. The temper of Bilbil the goat was not sweet under any circumstances, and whenever he had a grievance he was inclined to be quite grumpy. So, when his master settled down in the palace of King Gos for a quiet life with the boy Prince, and passed his time in playing checkers and eating and otherwise enjoying himself, he had no use whatever for Bilbil, and shut the goat in an upstairs room to prevent his wandering through the city and quarreling with the citizens. But this Bilbil did not like at all. He became very cross and disagreeable at being left alone and he did not speak nicely to the servants who came to bring him food; therefore those people decided not to wait upon him any more, resenting his conversation and not liking to be scolded by a lean, scraggly goat, even though it belonged to a conqueror. The servants kept away from the room and Bilbil grew more hungry and more angry every hour. He tried to eat the rugs and ornaments, but found them not at all nourishing. There was no grass to be had unless he escaped from the palace.

When Queen Cor came to capture Inga and Rinkitink, both the prisoners were so filled with despair at their own misfortune that they gave no thought whatever to the goat, who was left in his room. Nor did Bilbil know anything of the changed fortunes of his comrades until he heard shouts and boisterous laughter in the courtyard below. Looking out of a window, with the intention of rebuking those who dared thus to disturb him, Bilbil saw the courtyard quite filled with warriors and knew from this that the palace had in some way again fallen into the hands of the enemy.

Now, although Bilbil was often exceedingly disagreeable to King Rinkitink, as well as to the Prince, and sometimes used harsh words in addressing them, he was intelligent enough to know them to be his friends, and to know that King Gos and his people were his foes. In sudden anger, provoked by the sight of the warriors and the knowledge that he was in the power of the dangerous men of Regos, Bilbil butted his head against the door of his room and burst it open. Then he ran to the head of the staircase and saw King Gos coming up the stairs followed by a long line of his chief captains and warriors.

The goat lowered his head, trembling with rage and excitement, and just as the King reached the top stair the animal dashed forward and butted His Majesty so fiercely that the big and powerful King, who did not expect an attack, doubled up and tumbled backward. His great weight knocked over the man just behind him and he in turn struck the next warrior and upset him, so that in an instant the whole line of Bilbil's foes was tumbling heels over head to the bottom of the stairs, where they piled up in a heap, struggling and shouting and in the mixup hitting one another with their fists, until every man of them was bruised and sore.

Finally King Gos scrambled out of the heap and rushed up the stairs again, very angry indeed. Bilbil was ready for him and a second time butted the King down the stairs; but now the goat also lost his balance and followed the King, landing full upon the confused heap of soldiers. Then he kicked out so viciously with his heels that he soon freed himself and dashed out of the doorway of the palace.

"Stop him!" cried King Gos, running after.

But the goat was now so wild and excited that it was not safe for anyone to stand in his way. None of the men were armed and when one or two tried to head off the goat, Bilbil sent them sprawling upon the ground. Most of the warriors, however, were wise enough not to attempt to interfere with his flight.

Coursing down the street, Bilbil found himself approaching the bridge of boats and without pausing to think where it might lead him he crossed over and proceeded on his way. A few moments later a great stone building blocked his path. It was the palace of Queen Cor, and seeing the gates of the courtyard standing wide open, Bilbil rushed through them without slackening his speed.

13. Zella Saves the Prince

The wicked Queen of Coregos was in a very bad humor this morning, for one of her slave drivers had come from the fields to say that a number of slaves had rebelled and would not work.

"Bring them here to me!" she cried savagely. "A good whipping may make them change their minds."

So the slave driver went to fetch the rebellious ones and Queen Cor sat down to eat her breakfast, an ugly look on her face.

Prince Inga had been ordered to stand behind his new mistress with a big fan of peacock's feathers, but he was so unused to such service that he awkwardly brushed her ear with the fan. At once she flew into a terrible rage and slapped the Prince twice with her hand-blows that tingled, too, for her hand was big and hard and she was not inclined to be gentle. Inga took the blows without shrinking or uttering a cry, although they stung his pride far more than his body. But King Rinkitink, who was acting as the queen's butler and had just brought in her coffee, was so startled at seeing the young Prince punished that he tipped over the urn and the hot coffee streamed across the lap of the Queen's best morning gown.

Cor sprang from her seat with a scream of anger and poor Rinkitink would doubtless have been given a terrible beating had not the slave driver returned at this moment and attracted the woman's attention. The overseer had brought with him all of the women slaves from Pingaree, who had been loaded down with chains and were so weak and ill they could scarcely walk, much less work in the fields.

Prince Inga's eyes were dimmed with sorrowful tears when he discovered how his poor people had been abused, but his own plight was so helpless that he was unable to aid them. Fortunately the boy's mother, Queen Garee, was not among these slaves, for Queen Cor had placed her in the royal dairy to make butter.

"Why do you refuse to work?" demanded Cor in a harsh voice, as the slaves from Pingaree stood before her, trembling and with downcast eyes.

"Because we lack strength to perform the tasks your overseers demand," answered one of the women.

"Then you shall be whipped until your strength returns!" exclaimed the Queen, and turning to Inga, she commanded: "Get me the whip with the seven lashes."

As the boy left the room, wondering how he might manage to save the unhappy women from their undeserved punishment, he met a girl entering by the back way, who asked: "Can you tell me where to find Her Majesty, Queen Cor?"

"She is in the chamber with the red dome, where green dragons are painted upon the walls," replied Inga; "but she is in an angry and ungracious mood to-day. Why do you wish to see her?"

"I have honey to sell," answered the girl, who was Zella, just come from the forest. "The Queen is very fond of my honey."

"You may go to her, if you so desire," said the boy, "but take care not to anger the cruel Queen, or she may do you a mischief."

"Why should she harm me, who brings her the honey she so dearly loves?" inquired the child innocently. "But I thank you for your warning; and I will try not to anger the Queen."

As Zella started to go, Inga's eyes suddenly fell upon her shoes and instantly he recognized them as his own. For only in Pingaree were shoes shaped in this manner: high at the heel and pointed at the toes.

"Stop!" he cried in an excited voice, and the girl obeyed, wonderingly. "Tell me," he continued, more gently, "where did you get those shoes?"

"My father brought them to me from Regos," she answered.

"From Regos!"

"Yes. Are they not pretty?" asked Zella, looking down at her feet to admire them. "One of them my father found by the palace wall, and the other on an ash-heap. So he brought them to me and they fit me perfectly."

By this time Inga was trembling with eager joy, which of course the girl could not understand.

"What is your name, little maid?" he asked.

"I am called Zella, and my father is Nikobob, the charcoal burner."

"Zella is a pretty name. I am Inga, Prince of Pingaree," said he, "and the shoes you are now wearing, Zella, belong to me. They were not cast away, as your father supposed, but were lost. Will you let me have them again?"

Zella's eyes filled with tears.

"Must I give up my pretty shoes, then?" she asked. "They are the only ones I have ever owned."

Inga was sorry for the poor child, but he knew how important it was that he regain possession of the Magic Pearls. So he said pleadingly: "Please let me have them, Zella. See! I will exchange for them the shoes I now have on, which are newer and prettier than the others."

The girl hesitated. She wanted to please the boy Prince, yet she hated to exchange the shoes which her father had brought her as a present.

"If you will give me the shoes," continued the boy, anxiously, "I will promise to make you and your father and mother rich and prosperous. Indeed, I will promise to grant any favors you may ask of me," and he sat down upon the floor and drew off the shoes he was wearing and held them toward the girl.

"I'll see if they will fit me," said Zella, taking off her left shoe — the one that contained the Pink Pearl — and beginning to put on one of Inga's.

Just then Queen Cor, angry at being made to wait for her whip with the seven lashes, rushed into the room to find Inga. Seeing the boy sitting upon the floor beside Zella, the woman sprang toward him to beat him with her clenched fists; but Inga had now slipped on the shoe and the Queen's blows could not reach his body.

Then Cor espied the whip lying beside Inga and snatching it up she tried to lash him with it — all to no avail.

While Zella sat horrified by this scene, the Prince, who realized he had no time to waste, reached out and pulled the right shoe from the girl's foot, quickly placing it upon his own. Then he stood up and, facing the furious but astonished Queen, said to her in a quiet voice:

"Madam, please give me that whip."

"I won't!" answered Cor. "I'm going to lash those Pingaree women with it."

The boy seized hold of the whip and with irresistible strength drew it from the Queen's hand. But she drew from her bosom a sharp dagger and with the swiftness of lightning aimed a blow at Inga's heart. He merely stood still and smiled, for the blade rebounded and fell clattering to the floor.

Then, at last, Queen Cor understood the magic power that had terrified her husband but which she had ridiculed in her ignorance, not believing in it. She did not know that Inga's power had been lost, and found again, but she realized the boy was no common foe and that unless she could still manage to outwit him her reign in the Island of Coregos was ended. To gain time, she went back to the red-domed chamber and seated herself in her throne, before which were grouped the weeping slaves from Pingaree.

Inga had taken Zella's hand and assisted her to put on the shoes he had given her in exchange for his own. She found them quite comfortable and did not know she had lost anything by the transfer.

"Come with me," then said the boy Prince, and led her into the presence of Queen Cor, who was giving Rinkitink a scolding. To the overseer Inga said.

"Give me the keys which unlock these chains, that I may set these poor women at liberty."

"Don't you do it!" screamed Queen Cor.

"If you interfere, madam," said the boy, "I will put you into a dungeon."

By this Rinkitink knew that Inga had recovered his Magic Pearls and the little fat King was so overjoyed that he danced and capered all around the room. But the Queen was alarmed at the threat and the slave driver, fearing the conqueror of Regos, tremblingly gave up the keys.

Inga quickly removed all the shackles from the women of his country and comforted them, telling them they should work no more but would soon be restored to their homes in Pingaree. Then he commanded the slave driver to go and get all the children who had been made slaves, and to bring them to their mothers. The man obeyed and left at once to perform his errand, while Queen Cor, growing more and more uneasy, suddenly sprang from her throne and before Inga could stop her had rushed through the room and out into the courtyard of the palace, meaning to make her escape. Rinkitink followed her, running as fast as he could go.

It was at this moment that Bilbil, in his mad dash from Regos, turned in at the gates of the courtyard, and as he was coming one way and Queen Cor was going the other they bumped into each other with great force. The woman sailed through the air, over Bilbil's head, and landed on the ground outside the gates, where her crown rolled into a ditch and she picked herself up, half dazed, and continued her flight. Bilbil was also somewhat dazed by the unexpected encounter, but he continued his rush rather blindly and so struck poor Rinkitink, who was chasing after Queen Cor. They rolled over one another a few times and then Rinkitink sat up and Bilbil sat up and they looked at each other in amazement.

"Bilbil," said the King, "I'm astonished at you!"

"Your Majesty," said Bilbil, "I expected kinder treatment at your hands."

"You interrupted me," said Rinkitink.

"There was plenty of room without your taking my path," declared the goat.

And then Inga came running out and said. "Where is the Queen?"

"Gone," replied Rinkitink, "but she cannot go far, as this is an island. However, I have found Bilbil, and our party is again reunited. You have recovered your magic powers, and again we are masters of the situation. So let us be thankful."

Saying this, the good little King got upon his feet and limped back into the throne room to help comfort the women.

Presently the children of Pingaree, who had been gathered together by the overseer, were brought in and restored to their mothers, and there was great rejoicing among them, you may be sure.

"But where is Queen Garee, my dear mother?" questioned Inga; but the women did not know and it was some time before the overseer remembered that one of the slaves from Pingaree had been placed in the royal dairy. Perhaps this was the woman the boy was seeking.

Inga at once commanded him to lead the way to the butter house, but when they arrived there Queen Garee was nowhere in the place, although the boy found a silk scarf which he recognized as one that his mother used to wear. Then they began a search throughout the island of Coregos, but could not find Inga's mother anywhere.

When they returned to the palace of Queen Cor, Rinkitink discovered that the bridge of boats had again been removed, separating them from Regos, and from this they suspected that Queen Cor had fled to her husband's island and had taken Queen Garee with her. Inga was much perplexed what to do and returned with his friends to the palace to talk the matter over.

Zella was now crying because she had not sold her honey and was unable to return to her parents on the island of Regos, but the boy prince comforted her and promised she should be protected until she could be restored to her home. Rinkitink found Queen Cor's purse, which she had had no time to take with her, and gave Zella several gold pieces for the honey. Then Inga ordered the palace servants to prepare a feast for all the women and children of Pingaree and to prepare for them beds in the great palace, which was large enough to accommodate them all.

Then the boy and the goat and Rinkitink and Zella went into a private room to consider what should be done next.

14. The Escape

"Our fault," said Rinkitink, "is that we conquer only one of these twin islands at a time. When we conquered Regos, our foes all came to Coregos, and now that we have conquered Coregos, the Queen has fled to Regos. And each time they removed the bridge of boats, so that we could not follow them."

"What has become of our own boat, in which we came from Pingaree?" asked Bilbil.

"We left it on the shore of Regos," replied the Prince, "but I wonder if we could not get it again."

"Why don't you ask the White Pearl?" suggested Rinkitink.

"That is a good idea," returned the boy, and at once he drew the White Pearl from its silken bag and held it to his ear. Then he asked: "How may I regain our boat?"

The Voice of the Pearl replied: "Go to the south end of the Island of Coregos, and clap your hands three times and the boat will come to you.

"Very good!" cried Inga, and then he turned to his companions and said: "We shall be able to get our boat whenever we please; but what then shall we do?"

"Take me home in it!" pleaded Zella.

"Come with me to my City of Gilgad," said the King, "where you will be very welcome to remain forever."

"No," answered Inga, "I must rescue my father and mother, as well as my people. Already I have the women and children of Pingaree, but the men are with my father in the mines of Regos, and my dear mother has been taken away by Queen Cor. Not until all are rescued will I consent to leave these islands."

"Quite right!" exclaimed Bilbil.

"On second thought," said Rinkitink, "I agree with you. If you are careful to sleep in your shoes, and never take them off again, I believe you will be able to perform the task you have undertaken."

They counseled together for a long time as to their mode of action and it was finally considered best to make the attempt to liberate King Kitticut first of all, and with him the men from Pingaree. This would give them an army to assist them and afterward they could march to Regos and compel Queen Cor to give up the Queen of Pingaree. Zella told them that they could go in their boat along the shore of Regos to a point opposite the mines, thus avoiding any conflict with the warriors of King Gos.

This being considered the best course to pursue, they resolved to start on the following morning, as night was even now approaching. The servants being all busy in caring for the women and children, Zella undertook to get a dinner for Inga and Rinkitink and herself and soon prepared a fine meal in the palace kitchen, for she was a good little cook and had often helped her mother. The dinner was served in a small room overlooking the gardens and Rinkitink thought the best part of it was the sweet honey, which he spread upon the biscuits that Zella had made. As for Bilbil, he wandered through the palace grounds and found some grass that made him a good dinner.

During the evening Inga talked with the women and cheered them, promising soon to reunite them with their husbands who were working in the mines and to send them back to their own island of Pingaree.

Next morning the boy rose bright and early and found that Zella had already prepared a nice breakfast. And after the meal they went to the most southern point of the island, which was not very far away, Rinkitink riding upon Bilbil's back and Inga and Zella following behind them, hand in hand.

When they reached the water's edge the boy advanced and clapped his hands together three times, as the White Pearl had told him to do. And in a few moments they saw in the distance the black boat with the silver lining, coming swiftly toward them from the sea. Presently it grounded on the beach and they all got into it.

Zella was delighted with the boat, which was the most beautiful she had ever seen, and the marvel of its coming to them through the water without anyone to row it, made her a little afraid of the fairy craft. But Inga picked up the oars and began to row and at once the boat shot swiftly in the direction of Regos. They rounded the point of that island where the city was built and noticed that the shore was lined with warriors who had discovered their boat but seemed undecided whether to pursue it or not. This was probably because they had received no commands what to do, or perhaps they had learned to fear the magic powers of these adventurers from Pingaree and were unwilling to attack them unless their King ordered them to.

The coast on the western side of the Island of Regos was very uneven and Zella, who knew fairly well the location of the mines from the inland forest path, was puzzled to decide which mountain they now viewed from the sea was the one where the entrance to the underground caverns was located. First she thought it was this peak, and then she guessed it was that; so considerable time was lost through her uncertainty.

They finally decided to land and explore the country, to see where they were, so Inga ran the boat into a little rocky cove where they all disembarked. For an hour they searched for the path without finding any trace of it and now Zella believed they had gone too far to the north and must return to another mountain that was nearer to the city.

Once again they entered the boat and followed the winding coast south until they thought they had reached the right place. By this time, however, it was growing dark, for the entire day had been spent in the search for the entrance to the mines, and Zella warned them that it would be safer to spend the night in the boat than on the land, where wild beasts were sure to disturb them. None of them realized at this time how fatal this day of search had been to their plans and perhaps if Inga had realized what was going on he would have landed and fought all the wild beasts in the forest rather than quietly remain in the boat until morning.

However, knowing nothing of the cunning plans of Queen Cor and King Gos, they anchored their boat in a little bay and cheerfully ate their dinner, finding plenty of food and drink in the boat's lockers. In the evening the stars came out in the sky and tipped the waves around their boat with silver. All around them was delightfully still save for the occasional snarl of a beast on the neighboring shore.

They talked together quietly of their adventures and their future plans and Zella told them her simple history and how hard her poor father was obliged to work, burning charcoal to sell for enough money to support his wife and child. Nikobob might be the humblest man in all Regos, but Zella declared he was a good man, and honest, and it was not his fault that his country was ruled by so wicked a King.

Then Rinkitink, to amuse them, offered to sing a song, and although Bilbil protested in his gruff way, claiming that his master's voice was cracked and disagreeable, the little King was encouraged by the others to sing his song, which he did.

"A red-headed man named Ned was dead;
Sing fiddle-cum-faddle-cum-fi-do!
In battle he had lost his head;

Sing fiddle-cum-faddle-cum-fi-do!
'Alas, poor Ned,' to him I said,
'How did you lose your head so red?'
Sing fiddle-cum-faddle-cum-fi-do!

Said Ned: 'I for my country bled,'
Sing fiddle-cum-faddle-cum-fi-do!
'Instead of dying safe in bed',
Sing fiddle-cum-faddle-cum-fi-do!
'If I had only fled, instead,
I then had been a head ahead.'
Sing fiddle-cum-faddle-cum-fi-do!

I said to Ned —"

"Do stop, Your Majesty!" pleaded Bilbil. "You're making my head ache."

"But the song isn't finished," replied Rinkitink, "and as for your head aching, think of poor Ned, who hadn't any head at all!"

"I can think of nothing but your dismal singing," retorted Bilbil. "Why didn't you choose a cheerful subject, instead of telling how a man who was dead lost his red head? Really, Rinkitink, I'm surprised at you.

"I know a splendid song about a live man, said the King.

"Then don't sing it," begged Bilbil.

Zella was both astonished and grieved by the disrespectful words of the goat, for she had quite enjoyed Rinkitink's singing and had been taught a proper respect for Kings and those high in authority. But as it was now getting late they decided to go to sleep, that they might rise early the following morning, so they all reclined upon the bottom of the big boat and covered themselves with blankets which they found stored underneath the seats for just such occasions. They were not long in falling asleep and did not waken until daybreak.

After a hurried breakfast, for Inga was eager to liberate his father, the boy rowed the boat ashore and they all landed and began searching for the path. Zella found it within the next half hour and declared they must be very close to the entrance to the mines; so they followed the path toward the north, Inga going first, and then Zella following him, while Rinkitink brought up the rear riding upon Bilbil's back.

Before long they saw a great wall of rock towering before them, in which was a low arched entrance, and on either side of this entrance stood a guard, armed with a sword and a spear. The guards of the mines were not so fierce as the warriors of King Gos, their duty being to make the slaves work at their tasks and guard them from escaping; but they were as cruel as their cruel master wished them to be, and as cowardly as they were cruel.

Inga walked up to the two men at the entrance and said: "Does this opening lead to the mines of King Gos?"

"It does," replied one of the guards, "but no one is allowed to pass out who once goes in."

"Nevertheless," said the boy, we intend to go in and we shall come out whenever it pleases us to do so. I am the Prince of Pingaree, and I have come to liberate my people, whom King Gos has enslaved."

Now when the two guards heard this speech they looked at one another and laughed, and one of them said: "The King was right, for he said the boy was likely to come here and that he would try to set his people free. Also the King commanded that we must keep the little Prince in the mines, and set him to work, together with his companions."

"Then let us obey the King," replied the other man.

Inga was surprised at hearing this, and asked: "When did King Gos give you this order?"

"His Majesty was here in person last night," replied the man, "and went away again but an hour ago. He suspected you were coming here and told us to capture you if we could."

This report made the boy very anxious, not for himself but for his father, for he feared the King was up to some mischief. So he hastened to enter the mines and the guards did nothing to oppose him or his companions, their orders being to allow him to go in but not to come out.

The little group of adventurers passed through a long rocky corridor and reached a low, wide cavern where they found a dozen guards and a hundred slaves, the latter being hard at work with picks and shovels digging for gold, while the guards stood over them with long whips.

Inga found many of the men from Pingaree among these slaves, but King Kitticut was not in this cavern; so they passed through it and entered another corridor that led to a second cavern. Here also hundreds of men were working, but the boy did not find his father amongst them, and so went on to a third cavern.

The corridors all slanted downward, so that the farther they went the lower into the earth they descended, and now they found the air hot and close and difficult to breathe. Flaming torches were stuck into the walls to give light to the workers, and these added to the oppressive heat.

The third and lowest cavern was the last in the mines, and here were many scores of slaves and many guards to keep them at work. So far, none of the guards had paid any attention to Inga's party, but allowed them to proceed as they would, and while the slaves cast curious glances at the boy and girl and man and goat, they dared say nothing. But now the boy walked up to some of the men of Pingaree and asked news of his father, telling them not to fear the guards as he would protect them from the whips.

Then he Teamed that King Kitticut had indeed been working in this very cavern until the evening before, when King Gos had come and taken him away — still loaded with chains.

"Seems to me," said King Rinkitink, when he heard this report, "that Gos has carried your father away to Regos, to prevent us from rescuing him. He may hide poor Kitticut in a dungeon, where we cannot find him."

"Perhaps you are right," answered the boy, "but I am determined to find him, wherever he may be."

Inga spoke firmly and with courage, but he was greatly disappointed to find that King Gos had been before him at the mines and had taken his father away. However, he tried not to feel disheartened, believing he would succeed in the end, in spite of all opposition. Turning to the guards, he said: "Remove the chains from these slaves and set them free."

The guards laughed at this order, and one of them brought

forward a handful of chains, saying: "His Majesty has commanded us to make you, also, a slave, for you are never to leave these caverns again."

Then he attempted to place the chains on Inga, but the boy indignantly seized them and broke them apart as easily as if they had been cotton cords. When a dozen or more of the guards made a dash to capture him, the Prince swung the end of the chain like a whip and drove them into a corner, where they cowered and begged for mercy.

Stories of the marvelous strength of the boy Prince had already spread to the mines of Regos, and although King Gos had told them that Inga had been deprived of all his magic power, the guards now saw this was not true, so they deemed it wise not to attempt to oppose him.

The chains of the slaves had all been riveted fast to their ankles and wrists, but Inga broke the bonds of steel with his hands and set the poor men free — not only those from Pingaree but all who had been captured in the many wars and raids of King Gos. They were very grateful, as you may suppose, and agreed to support Prince Inga in whatever action he commanded.

He led them to the middle cavern, where all the guards and overseers fled in terror at his approach, and soon he had broken apart the chains of the slaves who had been working in that part of the mines. Then they approached the first cavern and liberated all there.

The slaves had been treated so cruelly by the servants of King Gos that they were eager to pursue and slay them, in revenge; but Inga held them back and formed them into companies, each company having its own leader. Then he called the leaders together and instructed them to march in good order along the path to the City of Regos, where he would meet them and tell them what to do next.

They readily agreed to obey him, and, arming themselves with iron bars and pick-axes which they brought from the mines, the slaves began their march to the city.

Zella at first wished to be left behind, that she might make her way to her home, but neither Rinkitink nor Inga thought it was safe for her to wander alone through the forest, so they induced her to return with them to the city.

The boy beached his boat this time at the same place as when he first landed at Regos, and while many of the warriors stood on the shore and before the walls of the city, not one of them attempted to interfere with the boy in any way. Indeed, they seemed uneasy and anxious, and when Inga met Captain Buzzub the boy asked if anything had happened in his absence.

"A great deal has happened," replied Buzzub. "Our King and Queen have run away and left us, and we don't know what to do."

"Run away!" exclaimed Inga. "Where did they go to?"

"Who knows?" said the man, shaking his head despondently. "They departed together a few hours ago, in a boat with forty rowers, and they took with them the King and Queen of Pingaree!"

15. The Flight of the Rulers

Now it seems that when Queen Cor fled from her island to Regos, she had wit enough, although greatly frightened, to make a stop at the royal dairy, which was near to the bridge, and to drag poor Queen Garee from the butter-house and across to Regos with her. The warriors of King Gos had never before seen the terrible Queen Cor frightened, and therefore when she came running across the bridge of boats, dragging the Queen of Pingaree after her by one arm, the woman's great fright had the effect of terrifying the waiting warriors.

"Quick!" cried Cor. "Destroy the bridge, or we are lost."

While the men were tearing away the bridge of boats the Queen ran up to the palace of Gos, where she met her husband.

"That boy is a wizard!" she gasped. "There is no standing against him."

"Oh, have you discovered his magic at last?" replied Gos, laughing in her face. "Who, now, is the coward?"

"Don't laugh!" cried Queen Cor. "It is no laughing matter. Both our islands are as good as conquered, this very minute. What shall we do, Gos?"

"Come in," he said, growing serious, "and let us talk it over."

So they went into a room of the palace and talked long and earnestly.

"The boy intends to liberate his father and mother, and all the people of Pingaree, and to take them back to their island," said Cor. "He may also destroy our palaces and make us his slaves. I can see but one way, Gos, to prevent him from doing all this, and whatever else he pleases to do."

"What way is that?" asked King Gos.

"We must take the boy's parents away from here as quickly as possible. I have with me the Queen of Pingaree, and you can run up to the mines and get the King. Then we will carry them away in a boat and hide them where the boy cannot find them, with all his magic. We will use the King and Queen of Pingaree as hostages, and send word to the boy wizard that if he does not go away from our islands and allow us to rule them undisturbed, in our own way, we will put his father and mother to death. Also we will say that as long as we are let alone his parents will be safe, although still safely hidden. I believe, Gos, that in this way we can compel Prince Inga to obey us, for he seems very fond of his parents."

"It isn't a bad idea," said Gos, reflectively; "but where can we hide the King and Queen, so that the boy cannot find them?"

"In the country of the Nome King, on the mainland away at the south," she replied. "The nomes are our friends, and they possess magic powers that will enable them to protect the prisoners from discovery. If we can manage to get the King and Queen of Pingaree to the Nome Kingdom before the boy knows what we are doing, I am sure our plot will succeed."

Gos gave the plan considerable thought in the next five minutes, and the more he thought about it the more clever and reasonable it seemed. So he agreed to do as Queen Cor suggested and at once hurried away to the mines, where he arrived before Prince Inga did. The next morning he carried King Kitticut back to Regos.

While Gos was gone, Queen Cor busied herself in preparing a

large and swift boat for the journey. She placed in it several bags of gold and jewels with which to bribe the nomes, and selected forty of the strongest oarsmen in Regos to row the boat. The instant King Gos returned with his royal prisoner all was ready for departure. They quickly entered the boat with their two important captives and without a word of explanation to any of their people they commanded the oarsmen to start, and were soon out of sight upon the broad expanse of the Nonestic Ocean.

Inga arrived at the city some hours later and was much distressed when he learned that his father and mother had been spirited away from the islands.

"I shall follow them, of course," said the boy to Rinkitink, "and if I cannot overtake them on the ocean I will search the world over until I find them. But before I leave here I must arrange to send our people back to Pingaree."

16. Nikobob Refuses a Crown

Almost the first persons that Zella saw when she landed from the silver-lined boat at Regos were her father and mother. Nikobob and his wife had been greatly worried when their little daughter failed to return from Coregos, so they had set out to discover what had become of her. When they reached the City of Regos, that very morning, they were astonished to hear news of all the strange events that had taken place; still, they found comfort when told that Zella had been seen in the boat of Prince Inga, which had gone to the north. Then, while they wondered what this could mean, the silver-lined boat appeared again, with their daughter in it, and they ran down to the shore to give her a welcome and many joyful kisses.

Inga invited the good people to the palace of King Gos, where he conferred with them, as well as with Rinkitink and Bilbil.

"Now that the King and Queen of Regos and Coregos have run away," he said, "there is no one to rule these islands. So it is my duty to appoint a new ruler, and as Nikobob, Zella's father, is an honest and worthy man, I shall make him the King of the Twin Islands."

"Me?" cried Nikobob, astounded by this speech. "I beg Your Highness, on my bended knees, not to do so cruel a thing as to make me King!"

"Why not?" inquired Rinkitink. "I'm a King, and I know how it feels. I assure you, good Nikobob, that I quite enjoy my high rank, although a jeweled crown is rather heavy to wear in hot weather."

"With you, noble sir, it is different," said Nikobob, "for you are far from your kingdom and its trials and worries and may do as you please. But to remain in Regos, as King over these fierce and unruly warriors, would be to live in constant anxiety and peril, and the chances are that they would murder me within a month. As I have done no harm to anyone and have tried to be a good and upright man, I do not think that I should be condemned to such a dreadful fate."

"Very well," replied Inga, "we will say no more about your being King. I merely wanted to make you rich and prosperous, as I had promised Zella."

"Please forget that promise," pleaded the charcoal-burner, earnestly; "I have been safe from molestation for many years, because I was poor and possessed nothing that anyone else could envy. But if you make me rich and prosperous I shall at once become the prey of thieves and marauders and probably will lose my life in the attempt to protect my fortune."

Inga looked at the man in surprise.

"What, then, can I do to please you?" he inquired.

"Nothing more than to allow me to go home to my poor cabin," said Nikobob.

"Perhaps," remarked King Rinkitink, "the charcoal- burner has more wisdom concealed in that hard head of his than we gave him credit for. But let us use that wisdom, for the present, to counsel us what to do in this emergency."

"What you call my wisdom," said Nikobob, "is merely common sense. I have noticed that some men become rich, and are scorned by some and robbed by others. Other men become famous, and are mocked at and derided by their fellows. But the poor and humble man who lives unnoticed and unknown escapes all these troubles and is the only one who can appreciate the joy of living."

"If I had a hand, instead of a cloven hoof, I'd like to shake hands with you, Nikobob," said Bilbil the goat. "But the poor man must not have a cruel master, or he is undone."

During the council they found, indeed, that the advice of the charcoal-burner was both shrewd and sensible, and they profited much by his words.

Inga gave Captain Buzzub the command of the warriors and made him promise to keep his men quiet and orderly — if he could. Then the boy allowed all of King Gos's former slaves, except those who came from Pingaree, to choose what boats they required and to stock them with provisions and row away to their own countries. When these had departed, with grateful thanks and many blessings showered upon the boy Prince who had set them free, Inga made preparations to send his own people home, where they were told to rebuild their houses and then erect a new royal palace. They were then to await patiently the coming of King Kitticut or Prince Inga.

"My greatest worry," said the boy to his friends, "is to know whom to appoint to take charge of this work of restoring Pingaree to its former condition. My men are all pearl fishers, and although willing and honest, have no talent for directing others how to work."

While the preparations for departure were being made, Nikobob offered to direct the men of Pingaree, and did so in a very capable manner. As the island had been despoiled of all its valuable furniture and draperies and rich cloths and paintings and statuary and the like, as well as gold and silver and ornaments, Inga thought it no more than just that they be replaced by the spoilers. So he directed his people to search through the storehouses of King Gos and to regain all their goods and chattels that could be found. Also he instructed them to take as much else as they required to make their new homes comfortable, so that many boats were loaded full of goods that would enable the people to restore Pingaree to its former state of comfort.

For his father's new palace the boy plundered the palaces of both Queen Cor and King Gos, sending enough wares away with his people to make King Kitticut's new residence as handsomely fitted and furnished as had been the one which the ruthless invaders from Regos had destroyed.

It was a great fleet of boats that set out one bright, sunny morning on the voyage to Pingaree, carrying all the men, women and children and all the goods for refitting their homes. As he saw the fleet depart, Prince Inga felt that he had already successfully accomplished a part of his mission, but he vowed he would never return to Pingaree in person until he could take his father and mother there with him; unless, indeed, King Gos wickedly destroyed his beloved parents, in which case Inga would become the King of Pingaree and it would be his duty to go to his people and rule over them.

It was while the last of the boats were preparing to sail for Pingaree that Nikobob, who had been of great service in getting them ready, came to Inga in a thoughtful mood and said: "Your Highness, my wife and my daughter Zella have been urging me to leave Regos and settle down in your island, in a new home. From what your people have told me, Pingaree is a better place to live than Regos, and there are no cruel warriors or savage beasts there to keep one in constant fear for the safety of those he loves. Therefore, I have come to ask to go with my family in one of the boats."

Inga was much pleased with this proposal and not only granted Nikobob permission to go to Pingaree to live, but instructed him to take with him sufficient goods to furnish his new home in a comfortable manner. In addition to this, he appointed Nikobob general manager of the buildings and of the pearl fisheries, until his father or he himself arrived, and the people approved this order because they liked Nikobob and knew him to be just and honest.

Soon as the last boat of the great flotilla had disappeared from the view of those left at Regos, Inga and Rinkitink prepared to leave the island themselves. The boy was anxious to overtake the boat of King Gos, if possible, and Rinkitink had no desire to remain in Regos.

Buzzub and the warriors stood silently on the shore and watched the black boat with its silver lining depart, and I am sure they were as glad to be rid of their unwelcome visitors as Inga and Rinkitink and Bilbil were to leave.

The boy asked the White Pearl what direction the boat of King Gos had taken and then he followed after it, rowing hard and steadily for eight days without becoming at all weary. But, although the black boat moved very swiftly, it failed to overtake the barge which was rowed by Queen Cor's forty picked oarsmen.

17. The Nome King

The Kingdom of the Nomes does not border on the Nonestic Ocean, from which it is separated by the Kingdom of Rinkitink and the Country of the Wheelers, which is a part of the Land of Ev. Rinkitink's country is separated from the country of the Nomes by a row of high and steep mountains, from which it extends to the sea. The Country of the Wheelers is a sandy waste that is open on one side to the Nonestic Ocean and on the other side has no barrier to separate it from the Nome Country, therefore it was on the coast of the Wheelers that King Cos landed — in a spot quite deserted by any of the curious inhabitants of that country.

The Nome Country is very large in extent, and is only separated from the Land of Oz, on its eastern borders, by a Deadly Desert that can not be crossed by mortals, unless they are aided by the fairies or by magic.

The nomes are a numerous and mischievous people, living in underground caverns of wide extent, connected one with another by arches and passages. The word "nome" means "one who knows," and these people are so called because they know where all the gold and silver and precious stones are hidden in the earth — a knowledge that no other living creatures share with them. The nomes are busy people, constantly digging up gold in one place and taking it to another place, where they secretly bury it, and perhaps this is the reason they alone know where to find it. The nomes were ruled, at the time of which I write, by a King named Kaliko.

King Gos had expected to be pursued by Inga in his magic boat, so he made all the haste possible, urging his forty rowers to their best efforts night and day. To his joy he was not overtaken but landed on the sandy beach of the Wheelers on the morning of the eighth day.

The forty rowers were left with the boat, while Queen Cor and King Cos, with their royal prisoners, who were still chained, began the journey to the Nome King.

It was not long before they passed the sands and reached the rocky country belonging to the nomes, but they were still a long way from the entrance to the underground caverns in which lived the Nome King. There was a dim path, winding between stones and boulders, over which the walking was quite difficult, especially as the path led up hills that were small mountains, and then down steep and abrupt slopes where any misstep might mean a broken leg. Therefore it was the second day of their journey before they climbed halfway up a rugged mountain and found themselves at the entrance of the Nome King's caverns.

On their arrival, the entrance seemed free and unguarded, but Gos and Cor had been there before, and they were too wise to attempt to enter without announcing themselves, for the passage to the caves was full of traps and pitfalls. So King Gos stood still and shouted, and in an instant they were surrounded by a group of crooked nomes, who seemed to have sprung from the ground.

One of these had very long ears and was called The Long-Eared Hearer. He said: "I heard you coming early this morning."

Another had eyes that looked in different directions at the same time and were curiously bright and penetrating. He could look over a hill or around a corner and was called The Lookout. Said he: "I saw you coming yesterday."

"Then," said King Gos, "perhaps King Kaliko is expecting us."

"It is true," replied another nome, who wore a gold collar around his neck and carried a bunch of golden keys. "The mighty Nome King expects you, and bids you follow me to his presence."

With this he led the way into the caverns and Gos and Cor followed, dragging their weary prisoners with them, for poor King Kitticut and his gentle Queen had been obliged to carry, all through the tedious journey, the bags of gold and jewels which were to bribe the Nome King to accept them as slaves.

Through several long passages the guide led them and at last they entered a small cavern which was beautifully decorated and set with rare jewels that flashed from every part of the wall, floor and ceiling. This was a waiting-room for visitors, and there their guide left them while he went to inform King Kaliko of their arrival.

Before long they were ushered into a great domed chamber, cut from the solid rock and so magnificent that all of them — the King and Queen of Pingaree and the King and Queen of Regos and Coregos — drew long breaths of astonishment and opened their eyes as wide as they could.

In an ivory throne sat a little round man who had a pointed beard and hair that rose to a tall curl on top of his head. He was dressed in silken robes, richly embroidered, which had large buttons of cut rubies. On his head was a diamond crown and in his hand he held a golden sceptre with a big jeweled ball at one end of it. This was Kaliko, the King and ruler of all the nomes. He nodded pleasantly enough to his visitors and said in a cheery voice: "Well, Your Majesties, what can I do for you?"

"It is my desire," answered King Gos, respectfully, "to place in your care two prisoners, whom you now see before you. They must be carefully guarded, to prevent them from escaping, for they have the cunning of foxes and are not to be trusted. In return for the favor I am asking you to grant, I have brought Your Majesty valuable presents of gold and precious gems."

He then commanded Kitticut and Garee to lay before the Nome King the bags of gold and jewels, and they obeyed, being helpless.

"Very good," said King Kaliko, nodding approval, for like all the nomes he loved treasures of gold and jewels. "But who are the prisoners you have brought here, and why do you place them in my charge instead of guarding them, yourself? They seem gentle enough, I'm sure."

"The prisoners," returned King Gos, "are the King and Queen of Pingaree, a small island north of here. They are very evil people and came to our islands of Regos and Coregos to conquer them and slay our poor people. Also they intended to plunder us of all our riches, but by good fortune we were able to defeat and capture them. However, they have a son who is a terrible wizard and who by magic art is trying to find this awful King and Queen of Pingaree, and to set them free, that they may continue their wicked deeds. Therefore, as we have no magic to defend ourselves with, we have brought the prisoners to you for safe keeping."

"Your Majesty," spoke up King Kitticut, addressing the Nome King with great indignation, "do not believe this tale, I implore you. It is all a lie!"

"I know it," said Kaliko. "I consider it a clever lie, though, because it is woven without a thread of truth. However, that is none of my business. The fact remains that my good friend King Gos wishes to put you in my underground caverns, so that you will be unable to escape. And why should I not please him in this little matter? Gos is a mighty King and a great warrior, while your island of Pingaree is desolated and your people scattered. In my heart, King Kitticut, I sympathize with you, but as a matter of business policy we powerful Kings must stand together and trample the weaker ones under our feet."

King Kitticut was surprised to find the King of the nomes so candid and so well informed, and he tried to argue that he and his gentle wife did not deserve their cruel fate and that it would be wiser for Kaliko to side with them than with the evil King of Regos. But Kaliko only shook his head and smiled, saying: "The fact that you are a prisoner, my poor Kitticut, is evidence that you are weaker than King Cos, and I prefer to deal with the strong. By the way," he added, turning to the King of Regos, "have these prisoners any connection with the Land of Oz?"

"Why do you ask?" said Gos.

"Because I dare not offend the Oz people," was the reply. "I am very powerful, as you know, but Ozma of Oz is far more powerful than I; therefore, if this King and Queen of Pingaree happened to be under Ozma's protection, I would have nothing to do with them."

"I assure Your Majesty that the prisoners have nothing to do with the Oz people," Gos hastened to say. And Kitticut, being questioned, admitted that this was true.

"But how about that wizard you mentioned?" asked the Nome King.

"Oh, he is merely a boy; but he is very ferocious and obstinate and he is assisted by a little fat sorcerer called Rinkitink and a talking goat."

"Oho! A talking goat, do you say? That certainly sounds like magic; and it also sounds like the Land of Oz, where all the animals talk," said Kaliko, with a doubtful expression.

But King Gos assured him the talking goat had never been to Oz.

"As for Rinkitink, whom you call a sorcerer," continued the Nome King, "he is a neighbor of mine, you must know, but as we are cut off from each other by high mountains beneath which a powerful river runs, I have never yet met King Rinkitink. But I have heard of him, and from all reports he is a jolly rogue, and perfectly harmless. However, in spite of your false statements and misrepresentations, I will earn the treasure you have brought me, by keeping your prisoners safe in my caverns."

"Make them work," advised Queen Cor. "They are rather delicate, and to make them work will make them suffer delightfully."

"I'll do as I please about that," said the Nome King sternly. "Be content that I agree to keep them safe."

The bargain being thus made and concluded, Kaliko first examined the gold and jewels and then sent it away to his royal storehouse, which was well filled with like treasure. Next the captives were sent away in charge of the nome with the golden collar and keys, whose name was Klik, and he escorted them to a small cavern and gave them a good supper.

"I shall lock your door," said Klik, "so there is no need of your wearing those heavy chains any longer." He therefore removed the chains and left King Kitticut and his Queen alone. This was the first time since the Northmen had carried them away from Pingaree that the good King and Queen had been alone together and free of all bonds, and as they embraced lovingly and mingled their tears over their sad fate they were also grateful that they had passed from the control of the heartless King Gos into the more considerate care of King Kaliko. They were still captives but they believed they would be happier in the underground caverns of the nomes than in Regos and Coregos.

Meantime, in the King's royal cavern a great feast had been spread. King Gos and Queen Cor, having triumphed in their plot, were so well pleased that they held high revelry with the jolly Nome King until a late hour that night. And the next morning, having cautioned Kaliko not to release the prisoners under any consideration without their orders, the King and Queen of Regos and Coregos left the caverns of the nomes to return to the shore of the ocean where they had left their boat.

18. Inga Parts with his Pink Pearl

The White Pearl guided Inga truly in his pursuit of the boat of King Gos, but the boy had been so delayed in sending his people home to Pingaree that it was a full day after Gos and Cor landed on the shore of the Wheeler Country that Inga's boat arrived at the same place.

There he found the forty rowers guarding the barge of Queen Cor, and although they would not or could not tell the boy where the King and Queen had taken his father and mother, the White Pearl advised him to follow the path to the country and the caverns of the nomes.

Rinkitink didn't like to undertake the rocky and mountainous journey, even with Bilbil to carry him, but he would not desert Inga, even though his own kingdom lay just beyond a range of mountains which could be seen towering southwest of them. So the King bravely mounted the goat, who always grumbled but always obeyed his master, and the three set off at once for the caverns of the nomes.

They traveled just as slowly as Queen Cor and King Gos had done, so when they were about halfway they discovered the King and Queen coming back to their boat. The fact that Gos and Cor were now alone proved that they had left Inga's father and mother behind them; so, at the suggestion of Rinkitink, the three hid behind a high rock until the King of Regos and the Queen of Coregos, who had not observed them, had passed them by. Then they continued their journey, glad that they had not again been forced to fight or quarrel with their wicked enemies.

"We might have asked them, however, what they had done with your poor parents," said Rinkitink.

"Never mind," answered Inga. "I am sure the White Pearl will guide us aright."

For a time they proceeded in silence and then Rinkitink began to chuckle with laughter in the pleasant way he was wont to do before his misfortunes came upon him.

"What amuses Your Majesty?" inquired the boy.

"The thought of how surprised my dear subjects would be if they realized how near to them I am, and yet how far away. I have always wanted to visit the Nome Country, which is full of mystery and magic and all sorts of adventures, but my devoted subjects forbade me to think of such a thing, fearing I would get hurt or enchanted."

"Are you afraid, now that you are here?" asked Inga.

"A little, but not much, for they say the new Nome King is not as wicked as the old King used to be. Still, we are undertaking a dangerous journey and I think you ought to protect me by lending me one of your pearls."

Inga thought this over and it seemed a reasonable request.

"Which pearl would you like to have?" asked the boy.

"Well, let us see," returned Rinkitink; "you may need strength to liberate your captive parents, so you must keep the Blue Pearl. And you will need the advice of the White Pearl, so you had best keep that also. But in case we should be separated I would have nothing to protect me from harm, so you ought to lend me the Pink Pearl."

"Very well," agreed Inga, and sitting down upon a rock he removed his right shoe and after withdrawing the cloth from the pointed toe took out the Pink Pearl — the one which protected from any harm the person who carried it.

"Where can you put it, to keep it safely?" he asked.

"In my vest pocket," replied the King. "The pocket has a flap to it and I can pin it down in such a way that the pearl cannot get out and become lost. As for robbery, no one with evil intent can touch my person while I have the pearl."

So Inga gave Rinkitink the Pink Pearl and the little King placed it in the pocket of his red-and-green brocaded velvet vest, pinning the flap of the pocket down tightly.

They now resumed their journey and finally reached the entrance to the Nome King's caverns. Placing the White Pearl to his ear, Inga asked: "What shall I do now?" and the Voice of the Pearl replied: "Clap your hands together four times and call aloud the word 'Klik.' Then allow yourselves to be conducted to the Nome King, who is now holding your father and mother captive."

Inga followed these instructions and when Klik appeared in answer to his summons the boy requested an audience of the Nome King. So Klik led them into the presence of King Kaliko who was suffering from a severe headache, due to his revelry the night before, and therefore was unusually cross and grumpy.

"I know what you've come for," said he, before Inga could speak "You want to get the captives from Regos away from me; but you can't do it, so you'd best go away again."

"The captives are my father and mother, and I intend to liberate them," said the boy firmly.

The King stared hard at Inga, wondering at his audacity. Then he turned to look at King Rinkitink and said: "I suppose you are the King of Gilgad, which is in the Kingdom of Rinkitink."

"You've guessed it the first time," replied Rinkitink.

"How round and fat you are!" exclaimed Kaliko.

"I was just thinking how fat and round you are," said Rinkitink "Really, King Kaliko, we ought to be friends, we're so much alike in everything but disposition and intelligence."

Then he began to chuckle, while Kaliko stared hard at him, no knowing whether to accept his speech as a compliment or not And now the nome's eyes wandered to Bilbil, and he asked:

"Is that your talking goat?"

Bilbil met the Nome King's glowering look with a gaze equall surly and defiant, while Rinkitink answered: "It is, You Majesty."

"Can he really talk?" asked Kaliko, curiously.

"He can. But the best thing he does is to scold. Talk to Hi Majesty, Bilbil."

But Bilbil remained silent and would not speak.

"Do you always ride upon his back?" continued Kaliko, questioning Rinkitink.

"Yes," was the answer, "because it is difficult for a fat man to walk far, as perhaps you know from experience.

"That is true," said Kaliko. "Get off the goat's back and let me ride him a while, to see how I like it. Perhaps I'll take him away from you, to ride through my caverns."

Rinkitink chuckled softly as he heard this, but at once got off Bilbil's back and let Kaliko get on. The Nome King was a little awkward, but when he was firmly astride the saddle he called in a loud voice: "Giddap!"

When Bilbil paid no attention to the command and refused to stir, Kaliko kicked his heels viciously against the goat's body, and then Bilbil made a sudden start. He ran swiftly across the great cavern, until he had almost reached the opposite wall, when he stopped so abruptly that King Kaliko sailed over his head and bumped against the jeweled wall. He bumped so hard that the points of his crown were all mashed out of shape and his head was driven far into the diamond-studded band of the crown, so that it covered one eye and a part of his nose. Perhaps this saved Kaliko's head from being cracked against the rock wall, but it was hard on the crown.

Bilbil was highly pleased at the success of his feat and Rinkitink laughed merrily at the Nome King's comical appearance; but Kaliko was muttering and growling as he picked himself up and struggled to pull the battered crown from his head, and it was evident that he was not in the least amused. Indeed, Inga could see that the King was very angry, and the boy knew that the incident was likely to turn Kaliko against the entire party.

The Nome King sent Klik for another crown and ordered his workmen to repair the one that was damaged. While he waited for the new crown he sat regarding his visitors with a scowling face, and this made Inga more uneasy than ever. Finally, when the new crown was placed upon his head, King Kaliko said: "Follow me, strangers!" and led the way to a small door at one end of the cavern.

Inga and Rinkitink followed him through the doorway and found themselves standing on a balcony that overlooked an enormous domed cave — so extensive that it seemed miles to the other side of it. All around this circular cave, which was brilliantly lighted from an unknown source, were arches connected with other caverns.

Kaliko took a gold whistle from his pocket and blew a shrill note that echoed through every part of the cave. Instantly nomes began to pour in through the side arches in great numbers, until the immense space was packed with them as far as the eye could reach. All were armed with glittering weapons of polished silver and gold, and Inga was amazed that any King could command so great an army.

They began marching and countermarching in very orderly array until another blast of the gold whistle sent them scurrying away as quickly as they had appeared. And as soon as the great cave was again empty Kaliko returned with his visitors to his own royal chamber, where he once more seated himself upon his ivory throne.

"I have shown you," said he to Inga, "a part of my bodyguard. The royal armies, of which this is only a part, are as numerous as the sands of the ocean, and live in many thousands of my underground caverns. You have come here thinking to force me to give up the captives of King Gos and Queen Cor, and I wanted to convince you that my power is too mighty for anyone to oppose. I am told that you are a wizard, and depend upon magic to aid you; but you must know that the nomes are not mortals, and understand magic pretty well themselves, so if we are obliged to fight magic with magic the chances are that we are a hundred times more powerful than you can be. Think this over carefully, my boy, and try to realize that you are in my power. I do not believe you can force me to liberate King Kitticut and Queen Garee, and I know that you cannot coax me to do so, for I have given my promise to King Gos. Therefore, as I do not wish to hurt you, I ask you to go away peaceably and let me alone."

"Forgive me if I do not agree with you, King Kaliko," answered the boy. "However difficult and dangerous my task may be, I cannot leave your dominions until every effort to release my parents has failed and left me completely discouraged."

"Very well," said the King, evidently displeased. "I have warned you, and now if evil overtakes you it is your own fault. I've a headache to-day, so I cannot entertain you properly, according to your rank; but Klik will attend you to my guest chambers and to-morrow I will talk with you again."

This seemed a fair and courteous way to treat one's declared enemies, so they politely expressed the wish that Kaliko's headache would be better, and followed their guide, Klik, down a well-lighted passage and through several archways until they finally reached three nicely furnished bedchambers which were cut from solid gray rock and well lighted and aired by some mysterious method known to the nomes.

The first of these rooms was given King Rinkitink, the second was Inga's and the third was assigned to Bilbil the goat. There was a swinging rock door between the third and second rooms and another between the second and first, which also had a door that opened upon the passage. Rinkitink's room was the largest, so it was here that an excellent dinner was spread by some of the nome servants, who, in spite of their crooked shapes, proved to be well trained and competent.

"You are not prisoners, you know," said Klik; neither are you welcome guests, having declared your purpose to oppose our mighty King and all his hosts. But we bear you no ill will, and you are to be well fed and cared for as long as you remain in our caverns. Eat hearty, sleep tight, and pleasant dreams to you."

Saying this, he left them alone and at once Rinkitink and Inga began to counsel together as to the best means to liberate King Kitticut and Queen Garee. The White Pearl's advice was rather unsatisfactory to the boy, just now, for all that the Voice said in answer to his questions was: "Be patient, brave and determined."

Rinkitink suggested that they try to discover in what part of the series of underground caverns Inga's parents had been confined, as that knowledge was necessary before they could take any action; so together they started out, leaving Bilbil asleep in his room, and made their way unopposed through many corridors and caverns. In some places were great furnaces, where gold dust was being melted into bricks. In other rooms workmen were fashioning the gold into various articles and ornaments. In one cavern immense wheels revolved which polished precious gems, and they found many caverns used as storerooms, where treasure of every sort was piled high. Also they came to the barracks of the army and the great kitchens.

There were nomes everywhere — countless thousands of them —

but none paid the slightest heed to the visitors from the earth's surface. Yet, although Inga and Rinkitink walked until they were weary, they were unable to locate the place where the boy's father and mother had been confined, and when they tried to return to their own rooms they found that they had hopelessly lost themselves amid the labyrinth of passages. However, Klik presently came to them, laughing at their discomfiture, and led them back to their bedchambers.

Before they went to sleep they carefully barred the door from Rinkitink's room to the corridor, but the doors that connected the three rooms one with another were left wide open.

In the night Inga was awakened by a soft grating sound that filled him with anxiety because he could not account for it. It was dark in his room, the light having disappeared as soon as he got into bed, but he managed to feel his way to the door that led to Rinkitink's room and found it tightly closed and immovable. Then he made his way to the opposite door, leading to Bilbil's room, to discover that also had been closed and fastened.

The boy had a curious sensation that all of his room — the walls, floor and ceiling — was slowly whirling as if on a pivot, and it was such an uncomfortable feeling that he got into bed again, not knowing what else to do. And as the grating noise had ceased and the room now seemed stationary, he soon fell asleep again.

When the boy wakened, after many hours, he found the room again light. So he dressed himself and discovered that a small table, containing a breakfast that was smoking hot, had suddenly appeared in the center of his room. He tried the two doors, but finding that he could not open them he ate some breakfast, thoughtfully wondering who had locked him in and why he had been made a prisoner. Then he again went to the door which he thought led to Rinkitink's chamber and to his surprise the latch lifted easily and the door swung open.

Before him was a rude corridor hewn in the rock and dimly lighted. It did not look inviting, so Inga closed the door, puzzled to know what had become of Rinkitink's room and the King, and went to the opposite door. Opening this, he found a solid wall of rock confronting him, which effectually prevented his escape in that direction.

The boy now realized that King Kaliko had tricked him, and while professing to receive him as a guest had plotted to separate him from his comrades. One way had been left, however, by which he might escape and he decided to see where it led to.

So, going to the first door, he opened it and ventured slowly into the dimly lighted corridor. When he had advanced a few steps he heard the door of his room slam shut behind him. He ran back at once, but the door of rock fitted so closely into the wall that he found it impossible to open it again. That did not matter so much, however, for the room was a prison and the only way of escape seemed ahead of him.

Along the corridor he crept until, turning a corner, he found himself in a large domed cavern that was empty and deserted. Here also was a dim light that permitted him to see another corridor at the opposite side; so he crossed the rocky floor of the cavern and entered a second corridor. This one twisted and turned in every direction but was not very long, so soon the boy reached a second cavern, not so large as the first. This he found vacant also, but it had another corridor leading out of it, so Inga entered that. It was straight and short and beyond was a third cavern, which differed little from the others except that it had a strong iron grating at one side of it.

All three of these caverns had been roughly hewn from the rock and it seemed they had never been put to use, as had all the other caverns of the nomes he had visited. Standing in the third cavern, Inga saw what he thought was still another corridor at its farther side, so he walked toward it. This opening was dark, and that fact, and the solemn silence all around him, made him hesitate for a while to enter it. Upon reflection, however, he realized that unless he explored the place to the very end he could not hope to escape from it, so he boldly entered the dark corridor and felt his way cautiously as he moved forward.

Scarcely had he taken two paces when a crash resounded back of him and a heavy sheet of steel closed the opening into the cavern from which he had just come. He paused a moment, but it still seemed best to proceed, and as Inga advanced in the dark, holding his hands outstretched before him to feel his way, handcuffs fell upon his wrists and locked themselves with a sharp click, and an instant later he found he was chained to a stout iron post set firmly in the rock floor.

The chains were long enough to permit him to move a yard or so in any direction and by feeling the walls he found he was in a small circular room that had no outlet except the passage by which he had entered, and that was now closed by the door of steel. This was the end of the series of caverns and corridors.

It was now that the horror of his situation occurred to the boy with full force. But he resolved not to submit to his fate without a struggle, and realizing that he possessed the Blue Pearl, which gave him marvelous strength, he quickly broke the chains and set himself free of the handcuffs. Next he twisted the steel door from its hinges, and creeping along the short passage, found himself in the third cave.

But now the dim light, which had before guided him, had vanished; yet on peering into the gloom of the cave he saw what appeared to be two round disks of flame, which cast a subdued glow over the floor and walls. By this dull glow he made out the form of an enormous man, seated in the center of the cave, and he saw that the iron grating had been removed, permitting the man to enter.

The giant was unclothed and its limbs were thickly covered with coarse red hair. The round disks of flame were its two eyes and when it opened its mouth to yawn Inga saw that its jaws were wide enough to crush a dozen men between the great rows of teeth.

Presently the giant looked up and perceived the boy crouching at the other side of the cavern, so he called out in a hoarse, rude voice: "Come hither, my pretty one. We will wrestle together, you and I, and if you succeed in throwing me I will let you pass through my cave."

The boy made no reply to the challenge. He realized he was in dire peril and regretted that he had lent the Pink Pearl to King Rinkitink. But it was now too late for vain regrets, although he feared that even his great strength would avail him little against this hairy monster. For his arms were not long enough to span a fourth of the giant's huge body, while the monster's powerful limbs would be likely to crush out Inga's life before he could gain the mastery.

Therefore the Prince resolved to employ other means to combat this foe, who had doubtless been placed there to bar his return. Retreating through the passage he reached the room where he had been chained and wrenched the iron post from its socket. It was a foot thick and four feet long, and being of solid iron was so heavy that three ordinary men would have found it hard to lift.

Returning to the cavern, the boy swung the great bar above his head and dashed it with mighty force full at the giant. The end of the bar struck the monster upon its forehead, and with a single groan it fell full length upon the floor and lay still.

When the giant fell, the glow from its eyes faded away, and all was dark. Cautiously, for Inga was not sure the giant was dead, the boy felt his way toward the opening that led to the middle cavern. The entrance was narrow and the darkness was intense, but, feeling braver now, the boy stepped boldly forward. Instantly the floor began to sink beneath him and in great alarm he turned and made a leap that enabled him to grasp the rocky sides of the wall and regain a footing in the passage through which he had just come.

Scarcely had he obtained this place of refuge when a mighty crash resounded throughout the cavern and the sound of a rushing torrent came from far below. Inga felt in his pocket and found several matches, one of which he lighted and held before him. While it flickered he saw that the entire floor of the cavern had fallen away, and knew that had he not instantly regained his footing in the passage he would have plunged into the abyss that lay beneath him.

By the light of another match he saw the opening at the other side of the cave and the thought came to him that possibly he might leap across the gulf. Of course, this could never be accomplished without the marvelous strength lent him by the Blue Pearl, but Inga had the feeling that one powerful spring might carry him over the chasm into safety. He could not stay where he was, that was certain, so he resolved to make the attempt.

He took a long run through the first cave and the short corridor; then, exerting all his strength, he launched himself over the black gulf of the second cave. Swiftly he flew and, although his heart stood still with fear, only a few seconds elapsed before his feet touched the ledge of the opposite passageway and he knew he had safely accomplished the wonderful feat.

Only pausing to draw one long breath of relief, Inga quickly traversed the crooked corridor that led to the last cavern of the three. But when he came in sight of it he paused abruptly, his eyes nearly blinded by a glare of strong light which burst upon them. Covering his face with his hands, Inga retreated behind a projecting corner of rock and by gradually getting his eyes used to the light he was finally able to gaze without blinking upon the strange glare that had so quickly changed the condition of the cavern. When he had passed through this vault it had been entirely empty. Now the flat floor of rock was covered everywhere with a bed of glowing coals, which shot up little tongues of red and white flames. Indeed, the entire cave was one monster furnace and the heat that came from it was fearful.

Inga's heart sank within him as he realized the terrible obstacle placed by the cunning Nome King between him and the safety of the other caverns. There was no turning back, for it would be impossible for him again to leap over the gulf of the second cave, the corridor at this side being so crooked that he could get no run before he jumped. Neither could he leap over the glowing coals of the cavern that faced him, for it was much larger than the middle cavern. In this dilemma he feared his great strength would avail him nothing and he bitterly reproached himself for parting with the Pink Pearl, which would have preserved him from injury.

However, it was not in the nature of Prince Inga to despair for long, his past adventures having taught him confidence and courage, sharpened his wits and given him the genius of invention. He sat down and thought earnestly on the means of escape from his danger and at last a clever idea came to his mind. This is the way to get ideas: never to let adverse circumstances discourage you, but to believe there is a way out of every difficulty, which may be found by earnest thought.

There were many points and projections of rock in the walls of the crooked corridor in which Inga stood and some of these rocks had become cracked and loosened, although still clinging to their places. The boy picked out one large piece, and, exerting all his strength, tore it away from the wall. He then carried it to the cavern and tossed it upon the burning coals, about ten feet away from the end of the passage. Then he returned for another fragment of rock, and wrenching it free from its place, he threw it ten feet beyond the first one, toward the opposite side of the cave. The boy continued this work until he had made a series of stepping-stones reaching straight across the cavern to the dark passageway beyond, which he hoped would lead him back to safety if not to liberty.

When his work had been completed, Inga did not long hesitate to take advantage of his stepping-stones, for he knew his best chance of escape lay in his crossing the bed of coals before the rocks became so heated that they would burn his feet. So he leaped to the first rock and from there began jumping from one to the other in quick succession. A withering wave of heat at once enveloped him, and for a time he feared he would suffocate before he could cross the cavern; but he held his breath, to keep the hot air from his lungs, and maintained his leaps with desperate resolve.

Then, before he realized it, his feet were pressing the cooler rocks of the passage beyond and he rolled helpless upon the floor, gasping for breath. His skin was so red that it resembled the shell of a boiled lobster, but his swift motion had prevented his being burned, and his shoes had thick soles, which saved his feet.

After resting a few minutes, the boy felt strong enough to go on. He went to the end of the passage and found that the rock door by which he had left his room was still closed, so he returned to about the middle of the corridor and was thinking what he should do next, when suddenly the solid rock before him began to move and an opening appeared through which shone a brilliant light. Shielding his eyes, which were somewhat dazzled, Inga sprang through the opening and found himself in one of the Nome King's inhabited caverns, where before him stood King Kaliko, with a broad grin upon his features, and Klik, the King's chamberlain, who looked surprised, and King Rinkitink seated astride Bilbil the goat, both of whom seemed pleased that Inga had rejoined them.

19. Rinkitink Chuckles

We will now relate what happened to Rinkitink and Bilbil that morning, while Inga was undergoing his trying experience in escaping the fearful dangers of the three caverns.

The King of Gilgad wakened to find the door of Inga's room fast shut and locked, but he had no trouble in opening his own door into the corridor, for it seems that the boy's room, which was the middle one, whirled around on a pivot, while the adjoining rooms occupied by Bilbil and Rinkitink remained stationary. The little King also found a breakfast magically served in his room, and while he was eating it, Klik came to him and stated that His Majesty, King Kaliko, desired his presence in the royal cavern.

So Rinkitink, having first made sure that the Pink Pearl was still in his vest pocket, willingly followed Klik, who ran on some distance ahead. But no sooner had Rinkitink set foot in the passage than a great rock, weighing at least a ton, became dislodged and dropped from the roof directly over his head. Of course, it could not harm him, protected as he was by the Pink Pearl, and it bounded aside and crashed upon the floor, where it was shattered by its own weight.

"How careless!" exclaimed the little King, and waddled after Klik, who seemed amazed at his escape.

Presently another rock above Rinkitink plunged downward, and then another, but none touched his body. Klik seemed much perplexed at these continued escapes and certainly Kaliko was surprised when Rinkitink, safe and sound, entered the royal cavern.

"Good morning," said the King of Gilgad. "Your rocks are getting loose, Kaliko, and you'd better have them glued in place before they hurt someone." Then he began to chuckle: "Hoo, hoo, hoo-hee, hee-heek, keek, eek!" and Kaliko sat and frowned because he realized that the little fat King was poking fun at him.

"I asked Your Majesty to come here," said the Nome King, "to show you a curious skein of golden thread which my workmen have made. If it pleases you, I will make you a present of it."

With this he held out a small skein of glittering gold twine, which was really pretty and curious. Rinkitink took it in his hand and at once the golden thread began to unwind — so swiftly that the eye could not follow its motion. And, as it unwound, it coiled itself around Rinkitink's body, at the same time weaving itself into a net, until it had enveloped the little King from head to foot and placed him in a prison of gold.

"Aha!" cried Kaliko; "this magic worked all right, it seems."

"Oh, did it?" replied Rinkitink, and stepping forward he walked right through the golden net, which fell to the floor in a tangled mass

Kaliko rubbed his chin thoughtfully and stared hard at Rinkitink.

"I understand a good bit of magic," said, he, "but Your Majesty has a sort of magic that greatly puzzles me, because it is unlike anything of the sort that I ever met with before."

"Now, see here, Kaliko," said Rinkitink; "if you are trying to harm me or my companions, give it up, for you will never succeed. We're harm-proof, so to speak, and you are merely wasting your time trying to injure us."

"You may be right, and I hope I am not so impolite as to argue with a guest," returned the Nome King. "But you will pardon me if I am not yet satisfied that you are stronger than my famous magic. However, I beg you to believe that I bear you no ill will, King Rinkitink; but it is my duty to destroy you, if possible, because you and that insignificant boy Prince have openly threatened to take away my captives and have positively refused to go back to the earth's surface and let me alone. I'm very tender-hearted, as a matter of fact, and I like you immensely, and would enjoy having you as a friend, but —" Here he pressed a button on the arm of his throne chair and the section of the floor where Rinkitink stood suddenly opened and disclosed a black pit beneath, which was a part of the terrible Bottomless Gulf.

But Rinkitink did not fall into the pit; his body remained suspended in the air until he put out his foot and stepped to the solid floor, when the opening suddenly closed again.

"I appreciate Your Majesty's friendship," remarked Rinkitink, as calmly as if nothing had happened, "but I am getting tired with standing. Will you kindly send for my goat, Bilbil, that I may sit upon his back to rest?"

"Indeed I will!" promised Kaliko. "I have not yet completed my test of your magic, and as I owe that goat a slight grudge for bumping my head and smashing my second-best crown, I will be glad to discover if the beast can also escape my delightful little sorceries."

So Klik was sent to fetch Bilbil and presently returned with the goat, which was very cross this morning because it had not slept well in the underground caverns.

Rinkitink lost no time in getting upon the red velvet saddle which the goat constantly wore, for he feared the Nome King would try to destroy Bilbil and knew that as long as his body touched that of the goat the Pink Pearl would protect them both whereas, if Bilbil stood alone, there was no magic to save him.

Bilbil glared wickedly at King Kaliko, who moved uneasily in his ivory throne. Then the Nome King whispered a moment in the ear of Klik, who nodded and left the room.

"Please make yourselves at home here for a few minutes, while I attend to an errand," said the Nome King, getting up from the throne. "I shall return pretty soon, when I hope to find you pieceful — ha, ha, ha! — that's a joke you can't appreciate now but will later. Be pieceful — that's the idea. Ho, ho, ho! How funny." Then he waddled from the cavern, closing the door behind him.

"Well, why didn't you laugh when Kaliko laughed?" demanded the goat, when they were left alone in the cavern.

"Because he means mischief of some sort," replied Rinkitink "and we'll laugh after the danger is over, Bilbil. There's an old adage that says: 'He laughs best who laughs last,' and the only way to laugh last is to give the other fellow a chance. Where did that knife come from, I wonder."

For a long, sharp knife suddenly appeared in the air near them twisting and turning from side to side and darting here and there in a dangerous manner, without any support whatever. Then another knife became visible — and another and another — until all the space in the royal cavern seemed filled with them. Their sharp points and edges darted toward Rinkitink and Bilbil perpetually and nothing could have saved them from being cut to pieces except the protecting power of the Pink Pearl. As it was not a knife touched them and even Bilbil gave a gruff laugh at the failure of Kaliko's clever magic.

The goat wandered here and there in the cavern, carrying Rinkitink upon his back, and neither of them paid the slightest heed to the knives, although the glitter of the hundreds of polished blades was rather trying to their eyes. Perhaps for ten minutes the knives darted about them in bewildering fury; then they disappeared as suddenly as they had appeared.

Kaliko cautiously stuck his head through the doorway and found the goat chewing the embroidery of his royal cloak, which he had left lying over the throne, while Rinkitink was reading his manuscript on "How to be Good" and chuckling over its advice. The Nome King seemed greatly disappointed as he came in and resumed his seat on the throne. Said Rinkitink with a chuckle: "We've really had a peaceful time, Kaliko, although not the pieceful time you expected. Forgive me if I indulge in a laugh — hoo, hoo, hoo-hee, heek-keek-eek! And now, tell me; aren't you getting tired of trying to injure us?"

"Eh — heh," said the Nome King. "I see now that your magic can protect you from all my arts. But is the boy Inga as, well protected as Your Majesty and the goat?'

"Why do you ask?" inquired Rinkitink, uneasy at the question because he remembered he had not seen the little Prince of Pingaree that morning.

"Because," said Kaliko, "the boy has been undergoing trials far greater and more dangerous than any you have encountered, and it has been hundreds of years since anyone has been able to escape alive from the perils of my Three Trick Caverns."

King Rinkitink was much alarmed at hearing this, for although he knew that Inga possessed the Blue Pearl, that would only give to him marvelous strength, and perhaps strength alone would not enable him to escape from danger. But he would not let Kaliko see the fear he felt for Inga's safety, so he said in a careless way: "You're a mighty poor magician, Kaliko, and I'll give you my crown if Inga hasn't escaped any danger you have threatened him with."

"Your whole crown is not worth one of the valuable diamonds in my crown," answered the Nome King, "but I'll take it. Let us go at once, therefore, and see what has become of the boy Prince, for if he is not destroyed by this time I will admit he cannot be injured by any of the magic arts which I have at my command."

He left the room, accompanied by Klik, who had now rejoined his master, and by Rinkitink riding upon Bilbil. After traversing several of the huge caverns they entered one that was somewhat more bright and cheerful than the others, where the Nome King paused before a wall of rock. Then Klik pressed a secret spring and a section of the wall opened and disclosed the corridor where Prince Inga stood facing them.

"Tarts and tadpoles!" cried Kaliko in surprise. "The boy is still alive!"

20. Dorothy to the Rescue

One day when Princess Dorothy of Oz was visiting Glinda the Good, who is Ozma's Royal Sorceress, she was looking through Glinda's Great Book of Records — wherein is inscribed all important events that happen in every part of the world — when she came upon the record of the destruction of Pingaree, the capture of King Kitticut and Queen Garee and all their people, and the curious escape of Inga, the boy Prince, and of King Rinkitink and the talking goat. Turning over some of the following pages, Dorothy read how Inga had found the Magic Pearls and was rowing the silver-lined boat to Regos to try to rescue his parents.

The little girl was much interested to know how well Inga succeeded, but she returned to the palace of Ozma at the Emerald City of Oz the next day and other events made her forget the boy Prince of Pingaree for a time. However, she was one day idly looking at Ozma's Magic Picture, which shows any scene you may wish to see, when the girl thought of Inga and commanded the Magic Picture to show what the boy was doing at that moment.

It was the time when Inga and Rinkitink had followed the King of Regos and Queen of Coregos to the Nome King's country and she saw them hiding behind the rock as Cor and Gos passed them by after having placed the King and Queen of Pingaree in the keeping of the Nome King. From that time Dorothy followed, by means of the Magic Picture, the adventures of Inga and his friend in the Nome King's caverns, and the danger and helplessness of the poor boy aroused the little girl's pity and indignation.

So she went to Ozma and told the lovely girl Ruler of Oz all about Inga and Rinkitink.

"I think Kaliko is treating them dreadfully mean," declared Dorothy, "and I wish you'd let me go to the Nome Country and help them out of their troubles."

"Go, my dear, if you wish to," replied Ozma, "but I think it would be best for you to take the Wizard with you."

"Oh, I'm not afraid of the nomes," said Dorothy, "but I'll be glad to take the Wizard, for company. And may we use your Magic Carpet, Ozma?"

"Of course. Put the Magic Carpet in the Red Wagon and have the Sawhorse take you and the Wizard to the edge of the desert. While you are gone, Dorothy, I'll watch you in the Magic Picture, and if any danger threatens you I'll see you are not harmed."

Dorothy thanked the Ruler of Oz and kissed her good-bye, for she was determined to start at once. She found the Wizard of Oz, who was planting shoetrees in the garden, and when she told him Inga's story he willingly agreed to accompany the little girl to the Nome King's caverns. They had both been there before and had conquered the nomes with ease, so they were not at all afraid.

The Wizard, who was a cheery little man with a bald head and a winning smile, harnessed the Wooden Sawhorse to the Red Wagon and loaded on Ozma's Magic Carpet. Then he and Dorothy climbed to the seat and the Sawhorse started off and carried them swiftly through the beautiful Land of Oz to the edge of the Deadly Desert that separated their fairyland from the Nome Country.

Even Dorothy and the clever Wizard would not have dared to cross this desert without the aid of the Magic Carpet, for it would have quickly destroyed them; but when the roll of carpet had been placed upon the edge of the sands, leaving just enough lying flat for them to stand upon, the carpet straightway began to unroll before them and as they walked on it continued to unroll, until they had safely passed over the stretch of Deadly Desert and were on the border of the Nome King's dominions.

This journey had been accomplished in a few minutes, although such a distance would have required several days travel had they not been walking on the Magic Carpet. On arriving they at once walked toward the entrance to the caverns of the nomes.

The Wizard carried a little black bag containing his tools of wizardry, while Dorothy carried over her arm a covered basket in which she had placed a dozen eggs, with which to conquer the nomes if she had any trouble with them.

Eggs may seem to you to be a queer weapon with which to fight, but the little girl well knew their value. The nomes are immortal; that is, they do not perish, as mortals do, unless they happen to come in contact with an egg. If an egg touches them — either the outer shell or the inside of the egg — the nomes lose their charm of perpetual life and thereafter are liable to die through accident or old age, just as all humans are.

For this reason the sight of an egg fills a nome with terror and he will do anything to prevent an egg from touching him, even for an instant. So, when Dorothy took her basket of eggs with her, she knew that she was more powerfully armed than if she had a regiment of soldiers at her back.

21. The Wizard Finds an Enchantment

After Kaliko had failed in his attempts to destroy his guests, as has been related, the Nome King did nothing more to injure them but treated them in a friendly manner. He refused, however, to permit Inga to see or to speak with his father and mother, or even to know in what part of the underground caverns they were confined.

"You are able to protect your lives and persons, I freely admit," said Kaliko; "but I firmly believe you have no power, either of magic or otherwise, to take from me the captives I have agreed to keep for King Gos."

Inga would not agree to this. He determined not to leave the caverns until he had liberated his father and mother, although he did not then know how that could be accomplished. As for Rinkitink, the jolly King was well fed and had a good bed to sleep upon, so he was not worrying about anything and seemed in no hurry to go away.

Kaliko and Rinkitink were engaged in pitching a game with solid gold quoits, on the floor of the royal chamber, and Inga and Bilbil were watching them, when Klik came running in, his hair standing on end with excitement, and cried out that the Wizard of Oz and Dorothy were approaching.

Kaliko turned pale on hearing this unwelcome news and, abandoning his game, went to sit in his ivory throne and try to think what had brought these fearful visitors to his domain.

"Who is Dorothy?" asked Inga.

"She is a little girl who once lived in Kansas," replied Klik, with a shudder, "but she now lives in Ozma's palace at the Emerald City and is a Princess of Oz — which means that she is a terrible foe to deal with."

"Doesn't she like the nomes?" inquired the boy.

"It isn't that," said King Kaliko, with a groan, "but she insists on the nomes being goody-goody, which is contrary to their natures. Dorothy gets angry if I do the least thing that is wicked, and tries to make me stop it, and that naturally makes me downhearted. I can't imagine why she has come here just now, for I've been behaving very well lately. As for that Wizard of Oz, he's chock-full of magic that I can't overcome, for he learned it from Glinda, who is the most powerful sorceress in the world. Woe is me! Why didn't Dorothy and the Wizard stay in Oz, where they belong?"

Inga and Rinkitink listened to this with much joy, for at once the idea came to them both to plead with Dorothy to help them. Even Bilbil pricked up his ears when he heard the Wizard of Oz mentioned, and the goat seemed much less surly, and more thoughtful than usual.

A few minutes later a nome came to say that Dorothy and the Wizard had arrived and demanded admittance, so Klik was sent to usher them into the royal presence of the Nome King.

As soon as she came in the little girl ran up to the boy Prince and seized both his hands.

"Oh, Inga!" she exclaimed, "I'm so glad to find you alive and well."

Inga was astonished at so warm a greeting. Making a low bow he said: "I don't think we have met before, Princess."

"No, indeed," replied Dorothy, "but I know all about you and I've come to help you and King Rinkitink out of your troubles." Then she turned to the Nome King and continued: "You ought to be ashamed of yourself, King Kaliko, to treat an honest Prince and an honest King so badly."

"I haven't done anything to them," whined Kaliko, trembling as her eyes flashed upon him.

"No; but you tried to, an' that's just as bad, if not worse," said Dorothy, who was very indignant. "And now I want you to send for the King and Queen of Pingaree and have them brought here immejitly!"

"I won't," said Kaliko.

"Yes, you will!" cried Dorothy, stamping her foot at him. "I won't have those poor people made unhappy any longer, or separated from their little boy. Why, it's dreadful, Kaliko, an' I'm su'prised at you. You must be more wicked than I thought you were."

"I can't do it, Dorothy," said the Nome King, almost weeping with despair. "I promised King Gos I'd keep them captives. You wouldn't ask me to break my promise, would you?"

"King Gos was a robber and an outlaw," she said, "and p'r'aps you don't know that a storm at sea wrecked his boat, while he was going back to Regos, and that he and Queen Cor were both drowned."

"Dear me!" exclaimed Kaliko. "Is that so?"

"I saw it in Glinda's Record Book," said Dorothy. "So now you trot out the King and Queen of Pingaree as quick as you can."

"No," persisted the contrary Nome King, shaking his head. "I won't do it. Ask me anything else and I'll try to please you, but I can't allow these friendly enemies to triumph over me.

"In that case," said Dorothy, beginning to remove the cover from her basket, "I'll show you some eggs."

"Eggs!" screamed the Nome King in horror. "Have you eggs in that basket?"

"A dozen of 'em," replied Dorothy.

"Then keep them there — I beg — I implore you! — and I'll do anything you say," pleaded Kaliko, his teeth chattering so that he could hardly speak.

"Send for the King and Queen of Pingaree," said Dorothy.

'Go, Klik," commanded the Nome King, and Klik ran away in great haste, for he was almost as much frightened as his master.

It was an affecting scene when the unfortunate King and Queen of Pingaree entered the chamber and with sobs and tears of joy embraced their brave and adventurous son. All the others stood silent until greetings and kisses had been exchanged and Inga had told his parents in a few words of his vain struggles to rescue them and how Princess Dorothy had finally come to his assistance.

Then King Kitticut shook the hands of his friend King Rinkitink and thanked him for so loyally supporting his son Inga, and Queen Garee kissed little Dorothy's forehead and blessed her for restoring her husband and herself to freedom.

The Wizard had been standing near Bilbil the goat and now he was surprised to hear the animal say: "Joyful reunion, isn't it? But it makes me tired to see grown people cry like children."

"Oho!" exclaimed the Wizard. "How does it happen, Mr. Goat, that you, who have never been to the Land of Oz, are able to talk?"

"That's my business," returned Bilbil in a surly tone.

The Wizard stooped down and gazed fixedly into the animal's eyes. Then he said, with a pitying sigh: "I see; you are under an enchantment. Indeed, I believe you to be Prince Bobo of Boboland."

Bilbil made no reply but dropped his head as if ashamed.

"This is a great discovery," said the Wizard, addressing Dorothy and the others of the party. "A good many years ago a cruel magician transformed the gallant Prince of Boboland into a talking goat, and this goat, being ashamed of his condition, ran away and was never after seen in Boboland, which is a country far to the south of here but bordering on the Deadly Desert, opposite the Land of Oz. I heard of this story long ago and know that a diligent search has been made for the enchanted Prince, without result. But I am well assured that, in the animal you call Bilbil, I have discovered the unhappy Prince of Boboland."

"Dear me, Bilbil," said Rinkitink, "why have you never told me this?"

"What would be the use?" asked Bilbil in a low voice and still refusing to look up.

"The use?" repeated Rinkitink, puzzled.

"Yes, that's the trouble," said the Wizard. "It is one of the most powerful enchantments ever accomplished, and the magician is now dead and the secret of the anti-charm lost. Even I, with all my skill, cannot restore Prince Bobo to his proper form. But I think Glinda might be able to do so and if you will all return with Dorothy and me to the Land of Oz, where Ozma will make you welcome, I will ask Glinda to try to break this enchantment."

This was willingly agreed to, for they all welcomed the chance to visit the famous Land of Oz. So they bade good-bye to King Kaliko, whom Dorothy warned not to be wicked any more if he could help it, and the entire party returned over the Magic Carpet to the Land of Oz. They filled the Red Wagon, which was still waiting for them, pretty full; but the Sawhorse didn't mind that and with wonderful speed carried them safely to the Emerald City.

22. Ozma's Banquet

Ozma had seen in her Magic Picture the liberation of Inga's parents and the departure of the entire party for the Emerald City, so with her usual hospitality she ordered a splendid banquet prepared and invited all her quaint friends who were then in the Emerald City to be present that evening to meet the strangers who were to become her guests.

Glinda, also, in her wonderful Record Book had learned of the events that had taken place in the caverns of the Nome King and she became especially interested in the enchantment of the Prince of Boboland. So she hastily prepared several of her most powerful charms and then summoned her flock of sixteen white storks, which swiftly bore her to Ozma's palace. She arrived there before the Red Wagon did and was warmly greeted by the girl Ruler.

Realizing that the costume of Queen Garee of Pingaree must have become sadly worn and frayed, owing to her hardships and adventures, Ozma ordered a royal outfit prepared for the good Queen and had it laid in her chamber ready for her to put on as soon as she arrived, so she would not be shamed at the banquet. New costumes were also provided for King Kitticut and King Rinkitink and Prince Inga, all cut and made and embellished in the elaborate and becoming style then prevalent in the Land of Oz, and as soon as the party arrived at the palace Ozma's guests were escorted by her servants to their rooms, that they might bathe and dress themselves.

Glinda the Sorceress and the Wizard of Oz took charge of Bilbil the goat and went to a private room where they were not likely to be interrupted. Glinda first questioned Bilbil long and earnestly about the manner of his enchantment and the ceremony that had been used by the magician who enchanted him. At first Bilbil protested that he did not want to be restored to his natural shape, saying that he had been forever disgraced in the eyes of his people and of the entire world by being obliged to exist as a scrawny, scraggly goat. But Glinda pointed out that any person who incurred the enmity of a wicked magician was liable to suffer a similar fate, and assured him that his misfortune would make him better beloved by his subjects when he returned to them freed from his dire enchantment.

Bilbil was finally convinced of the truth of this assertion and agreed to submit to the experiments of Glinda and the Wizard, who knew they had a hard task before them and were not at all sure they could succeed. We know that Glinda is the most complete mistress of magic who has ever existed, and she was wise enough to guess that the clever but evil magician who had enchanted Prince Bobo had used a spell that would puzzle any ordinary wizard or sorcerer to break; therefore she had given the matter much shrewd thought and hoped she had conceived a plan that would succeed. But because she was not positive of success she would have no one present at the incantation except her assistant, the Wizard of Oz.

First she transformed Bilbil the goat into a lamb, and this was done quite easily. Next she transformed the lamb into an ostrich, giving it two legs and feet instead of four. Then she tried to transform the ostrich into the original Prince Bobo, but this incantation was an utter failure. Glinda was not discouraged, however, but by a powerful spell transformed the ostrich into a tottenhot. Then the tottenhot was transformed into a mifket, which was a great step in advance and, finally, Glinda transformed the mifket into a handsome young man, tall and shapely, who fell on his knees before the great Sorceress and gratefully kissed her hand, admitting that he had now recovered his proper shape and was indeed Prince Bobo of Boboland.

This process of magic, successful though it was in the end, had required so much time that the banquet was now awaiting their presence. Bobo was already dressed in princely raiment and although he seemed very much humbled by his recent lowly condition, they finally persuaded him to join the festivities.

When Rinkitink saw that his goat had now become a Prince, he did not know whether to be sorry or glad, for he felt that he would miss the companionship of the quarrelsome animal he had so long been accustomed to ride upon, while at the same time he rejoiced that poor Bilbil had come to his own again.

Prince Bobo humbly begged Rinkitink's forgiveness for having been so disagreeable to him, at times, saying that the nature of a goat had influenced him and the surly disposition he had shown was a part of his enchantment. But the jolly King assured the Prince that he had really enjoyed Bilbil's grumpy speeches and forgave him readily. Indeed, they all discovered the young Prince Bobo to be an exceedingly courteous and pleasant person, although he was somewhat reserved and dignified.

Ah, but it was a great feast that Ozma served in her gorgeous banquet hall that night and everyone was as happy as could be. The Shaggy Man was there, and so was Jack Pumpkinhead and the Tin Woodman and Cap'n Bill. Beside Princess Dorothy sat Tiny Trot and Betsy Bobbin, and the three little girls were almost as sweet to look upon as was Ozma, who sat at the head of her table and outshone all her guests in loveliness.

King Rinkitink was delighted with the quaint people of Oz and laughed and joked with the tin man and the pumpkin-headed man and found Cap'n Bill a very agreeable companion. But what amused the jolly King most were the animal guests, which Ozma always invited to her banquets and seated at a table by themselves, where they talked and chatted together as people do but were served the sort of food their natures required. The Hungry Tiger and Cowardly Lion and the Glass Cat were much admired by Rinkitink, but when he met a mule named Hank, which Betsy Bobbin had brought to Oz, the King found the creature so comical that he laughed and chuckled until his friends thought he would choke. Then while the banquet was still in progress, Rinkitink composed and sang a song to the mule and they all joined in the chorus, which was something like this:
"It's very queer how big an ear
Is worn by Mr. Donkey;
And yet I fear he could not hear
If it were on a monkey.

'Tis thick and strong and broad and long
And also very hairy;
It's quite becoming to our Hank
But might disgrace a fairy!"

This song was received with so much enthusiasm that Rinkitink was prevailed upon to sing another. They gave him a little time to compose the rhyme, which he declared would be better if he could devote a month or two to its composition, but the sentiment he expressed was so admirable that no one criticized the song or the manner in which the jolly little King sang it.

Dorothy wrote down the words on a piece of paper, and here they are:
"We're merry comrades all, to-night,
Because we've won a gallant fight
And conquered all our foes.

We're not afraid of anything,
So let us gayly laugh and sing
Until we seek repose.

We've all our grateful hearts can wish;
King Gos has gone to feed the fish,
Queen Cor has gone, as well;
King Kitticut has found his own,
Prince Bobo soon will have a throne
Relieved of magic spell.

So let's forget the horrid strife
That fell upon our peaceful life
And caused distress and pain;
For very soon across the sea
We'll all be sailing merrily
To Pingaree again."

23. The Pearl Kingdom

It was unfortunate that the famous Scarecrow - the most popular person in all Oz, next to Ozma — was absent at the time of the banquet, for he happened just then to be making one of his trips through the country; but the Scarecrow had a chance later to meet Rinkitink and Inga and the King and Queen of Pingaree and Prince Bobo, for the party remained several weeks at the Emerald City, where they were royally entertained, and where both the gentle Queen Garee and the noble King Kitticut recovered much of their good spirits and composure and tried to forget their dreadful experiences.

At last, however, the King and Queen desired to return to their own Pingaree, as they longed to be with their people again and see how well they had rebuilt their homes. Inga also was anxious to return, although he had been very happy in Oz, and King Rinkitink, who was happy anywhere except at Gilgad, decided to go with his former friends to Pingaree. As for prince Bobo, he had become so greatly attached to King Rinkitink that he was loth to leave him.

On a certain day they all bade good-bye to Ozma and Dorothy and Glinda and the Wizard and all their good friends in Oz, and were driven in the Red Wagon to the edge of the Deadly Desert which they crossed safely on the Magic Carpet. They then made their way across the Nome Kingdom and the Wheeler Country where no one molested them, to the shores of the Nonestic Ocean. There they found the boat with the silver lining still lying undisturbed on the beach.

There were no important adventures during the trip and on their arrival at the pearl kingdom they were amazed at the beautiful appearance of the island they had left in ruins. All the houses of the people had been rebuilt and were prettier than before, with green lawns before them and flower gardens in the back yards. The marble towers of King Kitticut's new palace were very striking and impressive, while the palace itself proved far more magnificent than it had been before the warriors from Regos destroyed it.

Nikobob had been very active and skillful in directing all this work, and he had also built a pretty cottage for himself, not far from the King's palace, and there Inga found Zella, who was living very happy and contented in her new home. Not only had Nikobob accomplished all this in a comparatively brief space of time, but he had started the pearl fisheries again and when King Kitticut returned to Pingaree he found a quantity of fine pearl already in the royal treasury.

So pleased was Kitticut with the good judgment, industry and honesty of the former charcoal-burner of Regos, that he made Nikobob his Lord High Chamberlain and put him in charge of the pearl fisheries and all the business matters of the island kingdom.

They all settled down very comfortably in the new palace and the Queen gathered her maids about her once more and set them to work embroidering new draperies for the royal throne. Inga placed the three Magic Pearls in their silken bag and again deposited them in the secret cavity under the tiled flooring of the banquet hall, where they could be quickly secured if danger ever threatened the now prosperous island.

King Rinkitink occupied a royal guest chamber built especially for his use and seemed in no hurry to leave his friends in Pingaree. The fat little King had to walk wherever he went and so missed Bilbil more and more; but he seldom walked far and he was so fond of Prince Bobo that he never regretted Bilbil's disenchantment.

Indeed, the jolly monarch was welcome to remain forever in Pingaree, if he wished to, for his merry disposition set smiles on the faces of all his friends and made everyone near him as jolly as he was himself. When King Kitticut was not too busy with affairs of state he loved to join his guest and listen to his brother monarch's songs and stories. For he found Rinkitink to be, with all his careless disposition, a shrewd philosopher, and in talking over their adventures one day the King of Gilgad said: "The beauty of life is its sudden changes. No one knows what is going to happen next, and so we are constantly being surprised and entertained. The many ups and downs should not discourage us, for if we are down, we know that a change is coming and we will go up again; while those who are up are almost certain to go down. My grandfather had a song which well expresses this and if you will listen I will sing it."

"Of course I will listen to your song," returned Kitticut, "for it would be impolite not to."

So Rinkitink sang his grandfather's song:
"A mighty King once ruled the land —
But now he's baking pies.
A pauper, on the other hand,
Is ruling, strong and wise.

A tiger once in jungles raged —
But now he's in a zoo;
A lion, captive-born and caged,
Now roams the forest through.

A man once slapped a poor boy's pate
And made him weep and wail.
The boy became a magistrate
And put the man in jail.

A sunny day succeeds the night;
It's summer — then it snows!
Right oft goes wrong and wrong comes right,
As ev'ry wise man knows."

24. The Captive King

One morning, just as the royal party was finishing breakfast, a servant came running to say that a great fleet of boats was approaching the island from the south. King Kitticut sprang up at once, in great alarm, for he had much cause to fear strange boats. The others quickly followed him to the shore to see what invasion might be coming upon them.

Inga was there with the first, and Nikobob and Zella soon joined the watchers. And presently, while all were gazing eagerly at the approaching fleet, King Rinkitink suddenly cried out: "Get your pearls, Prince Inga — get them quick!"

"Are these our enemies, then?" asked the boy, looking with surprise upon the fat little King, who had begun to tremble violently.

"They are my people of Gilgad!" answered Rinkitink, wiping a tear from his eye. "I recognize my royal standards flying from the boats. So, please, dear Inga, get out your pearls to protect me!"

"What can you fear at the hands of your own subjects?" asked Kitticut, astonished.

But before his frightened guest could answer the question Prince Bobo, who was standing beside his friend, gave an amused laugh and said: "You are caught at last, dear Rinkitink. Your people will take you home again and oblige you to reign as King."

Rinkitink groaned aloud and clasped his hands together with a gesture of despair, an attitude so comical that the others could scarcely forbear laughing.

But now the boats were landing upon the beach. They were fifty in number, beautifully decorated and upholstered and rowed by men clad in the gay uniforms of the King of Gilgad. One splended boat had a throne of gold in the center, over which was draped the King's royal robe of purple velvet, embroidered with gold buttercups.

Rinkitink shuddered when he saw this throne; but now a tall man, handsomely dressed, approached and knelt upon the grass before his King, while all the other occupants of the boats shouted joyfully and waved their plumed hats in the air.

"Thanks to our good fortune," said the man who kneeled, "we have found Your Majesty at last!"

"Pinkerbloo," answered Rinkitink sternly, "I must have you hanged, for thus finding me against my will."

"You think so now, Your Majesty, but you will never do it," returned Pinkerbloo, rising and kissing the King's hand.

"Why won't I?" asked Rinkitink.

"Because you are much too tender-hearted, Your Majesty."

"It may be — it may be," agreed Rinkitink, sadly. "It is one of my greatest failings. But what chance brought you here, my Lord Pinkerbloo?"

"We have searched for you everywhere, sire, and all the people of Gilgad have been in despair since you so mysteriously disappeared. We could not appoint a new King, because we did not know but that you still lived; so we set out to find you, dead or alive. After visiting many islands of the Nonestic Ocean we at last thought of Pingaree, from where come the precious pearls; and now our faithful quest has been rewarded."

"And what now?" asked Rinkitink.

"Now, Your Majesty, you must come home with us, like a good and dutiful King, and rule over your people," declared the man in a firm voice.

"I will not."

"But you must — begging Your Majesty's pardon for the contradiction."

"Kitticut," cried poor Rinkitink, "you must save me from being captured by these, my subjects. What! must I return to Gilgad and be forced to reign in splendid state when I much prefer to eat and sleep and sing in my own quiet way? They will make me sit in a throne three hours a day and listen to dry and tedious affairs of state; and I must stand up for hours at the court receptions, till I get corns on my heels; and forever must I listen to tiresome speeches and endless petitions and complaints!"

"But someone must do this, Your Majesty," said Pinkerbloo respectfully, "and since you were born to be our King you cannot escape your duty."

"'Tis a horrid fate!" moaned Rinkitink. "I would die willingly, rather than be a King — if it did not hurt so terribly to die."

"You will find it much more comfortable to reign than to die, although I fully appreciate Your Majesty's difficult position and am truly sorry for you," said Pinkerbloo.

King Kitticut had listened to this conversation thoughtfully, so now he said to his friend: "The man is right, dear Rinkitink. It is your duty to reign, since fate has made you a King, and I see no honorable escape for you. I shall grieve to lose your companionship, but I feel the separation cannot be avoided."

Rinkitink sighed.

"Then," said he, turning to Lord Pinkerbloo, "in three days I will depart with you for Gilgad; but during those three days I propose to feast and make merry with my good friend King Kitticut."

Then all the people of Gilgad shouted with delight and eagerly scrambled ashore to take their part in the festival.

Those three days were long remembered in Pingaree, for never — before nor since — has such feasting and jollity been known upon that island. Rinkitink made the most of his time and everyone laughed and sang with him by day and by night.

Then, at last, the hour of parting arrived and the King of Gilgad and Ruler of the Dominion of Rinkitink was escorted by a grand procession to his boat and seated upon his golden throne. The rowers of the fifty boats paused, with their glittering oars pointed into the air like gigantic uplifted sabres, while the people of Pingaree — men, women and children — stood upon the shore shouting a royal farewell to the jolly King.

Then came a sudden hush, while Rinkitink stood up and, with a bow to those assembled to witness his departure, sang the following song, which he had just composed for the occasion.

"Farewell, dear Isle of Pingaree —
The fairest land in all the sea!
No living mortals, kings or churls,
Would scorn to wear thy precious pearls.

King Kitticut, 'tis with regret
I'm forced to say farewell; and yet
Abroad no longer can I roam
When fifty boats would drag me home.

Good-bye, my Prince of Pingaree;
A noble King some time you'll be
And long and wisely may you reign
And never face a foe again!"

They cheered him from the shore; they cheered him from the boats; and then all the oars of the fifty boats swept downward with a single motion and dipped their blades into the purple-hued waters of the Nonestic Ocean.

As the boats shot swiftly over the ripples of the sea Rinkitink turned to Prince Bobo, who had decided not to desert his former master and his present friend, and asked anxiously: "How did you like that song, Bilbil — I mean Bobo? Is it a masterpiece, do you think?"

And Bobo replied with a smile: "Like all your songs, dear Rinkitink, the sentiment far excels the poetry."

The Lost Princess Of Oz

by L. Frank Baum

This Book is Dedicated To My Granddaughter, Ozma Baum.

To My Readers

Some of my youthful readers are developing wonderful imaginations. This pleases me. Imagination has brought mankind through the Dark Ages to its present state of civilization. Imagination led Columbus to discover America. Imagination led Franklin to discover electricity. Imagination has given us the steam engine, the telephone, the talking-machine and the automobile, for these things had to be dreamed of before they became realities. So I believe that dreams — day dreams, you know, with your eyes wide open and your brain-machinery whizzing — are likely to lead to the betterment of the world. The imaginative child will become the imaginative man or woman most apt to create, to invent, and therefore to foster civilization. A prominent educator tells me that fairy tales are of untold value in developing imagination in the young. I believe it.

Among the letters I receive from children are many containing suggestions of "what to write about in the next Oz Book." Some of the ideas advanced are mighty interesting, while others are so extravagant to be seriously considered — even in a fairy tale. Yet I like them all, and I must admit that the main idea in "The Lost Princess of Oz" was suggested to me by a sweet little girl of eleven who called to see me and to talk about the Land of Oz. She said: "I s'pose if Ozma ever got lost, or stolen, ev'rybody in Oz would be dreadful sorry."

That was all, but quite enough foundation to build this present story on. If you happen to like the story, give credit to my little friend's clever hint.

L. Frank Baum, "Royal Historian of Oz"

A Terrible Loss

There could be no doubt of the fact: Princess Ozma, the lovely girl ruler of the Fairyland of Oz, was lost. She had completely disappeared. Not one of her subjects—not even her closest friends—knew what had become of her. It was Dorothy who first discovered it. Dorothy was a little Kansas girl who had come to the Land of Oz to live and had been given a delightful suite of rooms in Ozma's royal palace just because Ozma loved Dorothy and wanted her to live as near her as possible so the two girls might be much together.

Dorothy was not the only girl from the outside world who had been welcomed to Oz and lived in the royal palace. There was another named Betsy Bobbin, whose adventures had led her to seek refuge with Ozma, and still another named Trot, who had been invited, together with her faithful companion Cap'n Bill, to make her home in this wonderful fairyland. The three girls all had rooms in the palace and were great chums; but Dorothy was the dearest friend of their gracious Ruler and only she at any hour dared to seek Ozma in her royal apartments. For Dorothy had lived in Oz much longer than the other girls and had been made a Princess of the realm.

Betsy was a year older than Dorothy and Trot was a year younger, yet the three were near enough of an age to become great playmates and to have nice times together. It was while the three were talking together one morning in Dorothy's room that Betsy proposed they make a journey into the Munchkin Country, which was one of the four great countries of the Land of Oz ruled by Ozma. "I've never been there yet," said Betsy Bobbin, "but the Scarecrow once told me it is the prettiest country in all Oz."

"I'd like to go, too," added Trot.

"All right," said Dorothy. "I'll go and ask Ozma. Perhaps she will let us take the Sawhorse and the Red Wagon, which would be much nicer for us than having to walk all the way. This Land of Oz is a pretty big place when you get to all the edges of it."

So she jumped up and went along the halls of the splendid palace until she came to the royal suite, which filled all the front of the second floor. In a little waiting room sat Ozma's maid, Jellia Jamb, who was busily sewing. "Is Ozma up yet?" inquired Dorothy.

"I don't know, my dear," replied Jellia. "I haven't heard a word from her this morning. She hasn't even called for her bath or her breakfast, and it is far past her usual time for them."

"That's strange!" exclaimed the little girl.

"Yes," agreed the maid, "but of course no harm could have happened to her. No one can die or be killed in the Land of Oz, and Ozma is herself a powerful fairy, and she has no enemies so far as we know. Therefore I am not at all worried about her, though I must admit her silence is unusual."

"Perhaps," said Dorothy thoughtfully, "she has overslept. Or she may be reading or working out some new sort of magic to do good to her people."

"Any of these things may be true," replied Jellia Jamb, "so I haven't dared disturb our royal mistress. You, however, are a privileged character, Princess, and I am sure that Ozma wouldn't mind at all if you went in to see her."

"Of course not," said Dorothy, and opening the door of the outer chamber, she went in. All was still here. She walked into another room, which was Ozma's boudoir, and then, pushing back a heavy drapery richly broidered with threads of pure gold, the girl entered the sleeping-room of the fairy Ruler of Oz. The bed of ivory and gold was vacant; the room was vacant; not a trace of Ozma was to be found. Very much surprised, yet still with no fear that anything had happened to her friend, Dorothy returned through the boudoir to the other rooms of the suite. the bath, the wardrobe, and even into the great throne room, which adjoined the royal suite, but in none of these places could she find Ozma.

So she returned to the anteroom where she had left the maid, Jellia Jamb, and said, "She isn't in her rooms now, so she must have gone out."

"I don't understand how she could do that without my seeing her," replied Jellia, "unless she made herself invisible."

"She isn't there, anyhow," declared Dorothy.

"Then let us go find her," suggested the maid, who appeared to be a little uneasy. So they went into the corridors, and there Dorothy almost stumbled over a queer girl who was dancing lightly along the passage.

"Stop a minute, Scraps!" she called, "Have you seen Ozma this morning?"

"Not I!" replied the queer girl, dancing nearer. "I lost both my eyes in a tussle with the Woozy last night, for the creature scraped 'em both off my face with his square paws. So I put the eyes in my pocket, and this morning Button-Bright led me to Aunt Em, who sewed 'em on again. So I've seen nothing at all today, except during the last five minutes. So of course I haven't seen Ozma."

"Very well, Scraps," said Dorothy, looking curiously at the eyes, which were merely two round, black buttons sewed upon the girl's face.

There were other things about Scraps that would have seemed curious to one seeing her for the first time. She was commonly called "the Patchwork Girl" because her body and limbs were made from a gay-colored patchwork quilt which had been cut into shape and stuffed with cotton. Her head was a round ball stuffed in the same manner and fastened to her shoulders. For hair, she had a mass of brown yarn, and to make a nose for her a part of the cloth had been pulled out into the shape of a knob and tied with a string to hold it in place. Her mouth had been carefully made by cutting a slit in the proper place and lining it with red silk, adding two rows of pearls for teeth and a bit of red flannel for a tongue.

In spite of this queer make-up, the Patchwork Girl was magically alive and had proved herself not the least jolly and agreeable of the many quaint characters who inhabit the astonishing Fairyland of Oz. Indeed, Scraps was a general favorite, although she was rather flighty and erratic and did and said many things that surprised her friends. She was seldom still, but loved to dance, to turn handsprings and somersaults, to climb trees and to indulge in many other active sports.

"I'm going to search for Ozma," remarked Dorothy, "for she isn't in her rooms, and I want to ask her a question."

"I'll go with you," said Scraps, "for my eyes are brighter than yours, and they can see farther."

"I'm not sure of that," returned Dorothy. "But come along, if you like."

Together they searched all through the great palace and even to the farthest limits of the palace grounds, which were quite extensive, but nowhere could they find a trace of Ozma. When Dorothy returned to where Betsy and Trot awaited her, the little girl's face was rather solemn and troubled, for never before had Ozma gone away without telling her friends where she was going, or without an escort that befitted her royal state. She was gone, however, and none had seen her go. Dorothy had met and questioned the Scarecrow, Tik-Tok, the Shaggy Man, Button-Bright, Cap'n Bill, and even the wise and powerful Wizard of Oz, but not one of them had seen Ozma since she parted with her friends the evening before and had gone to her own rooms.

"She didn't say anything las' night about going anywhere," observed little Trot.

"No, and that's the strange part of it," replied Dorothy. "Usually Ozma lets us know of everything she does."

"Why not look in the Magic Picture?" suggested Betsy Bobbin. "That will tell us where she is in just one second."

"Of course!" cried Dorothy. "Why didn't I think of that before?" And at once the three girls hurried away to Ozma's boudoir, where the Magic Picture always hung. This wonderful Magic Picture was one of the royal Ozma's greatest treasures. There was a large gold frame in the center of which was a bluish-gray canvas on which various scenes constantly appeared and disappeared. If one who stood before it wished to see what any person anywhere in the world was doing, it was only necessary to make the wish and the scene in the Magic Picture would shift to the scene where that person was and show exactly what he or she was then engaged in doing. So the girls knew it would be easy for them to wish to see Ozma, and from the picture they could quickly learn where she was.

Dorothy advanced to the place where the picture was usually protected by thick satin curtains and pulled the draperies aside. Then she stared in amazement, while her two friends uttered exclamations of disappointment.

The Magic Picture was gone. Only a blank space on the wall behind the curtains showed where it had formerly hung.

2. The Troubles Of Glinda The Good

That same morning there was great excitement in the castle of the powerful Sorceress of Oz, Glinda the Good. This castle, situated in the Quadling Country, far south of the Emerald City where Ozma ruled, was a splendid structure of exquisite marble and silver grilles. Here the Sorceress lived, surrounded by a bevy of the most beautiful maidens of Oz, gathered from all the four countries of that fairyland as well as from the magnificent Emerald City itself, which stood in the place where the four countries cornered. It was considered a great honor to be allowed to serve the good Sorceress, whose arts of magic were used only to benefit the Oz people. Glinda was Ozma's most valued servant, for her knowledge of sorcery was wonderful, and she could accomplish almost anything that her mistress, the lovely girl Ruler of Oz, wished her to.

Of all the magical things which surrounded Glinda in her castle there was none more marvelous than her Great Book of Records. On the pages of this Record Book were constantly being inscribed, day by day and hour by hour, all the important events that happened anywhere in the known world, and they were inscribed in the book at exactly the moment the event happened. Every adventure in the Land of Oz and in the big outside world, and even in places that you and I have never heard of, were recorded accurately in the Great Book, which never made a mistake and stated only the exact truth. For that reason, nothing could be concealed from Glinda the Good, who had only to look at the pages of the Great Book of Records to know everything that had taken place. That was one reason she was such a great Sorceress, for the records made her wiser than any other living person.

This wonderful book was placed upon a big gold table that stood in the middle of Glinda's drawing room. The legs of the table, which were incrusted with precious gems, were firmly fastened to the tiled floor, and the book itself was chained to the table and locked with six stout golden padlocks, the keys to which Glinda carried on a chain that was secured around her own neck. The pages of the Great Book were larger in size than those of an American newspaper, and although they were exceedingly thin there were so many of them that they made an enormous, bulky volume. With its gold cover and gold clasps, the book was so heavy that three men could scarcely have lifted it. Yet this morning when Glinda entered her drawing room after breakfast the good Sorceress was amazed to discover that her Great Book of Records had mysteriously disappeared.

Advancing to the table, she found the chains had been cut with some sharp instrument, and this must have been done while all in the castle slept. Glinda was shocked and grieved. Who could have done this wicked, bold thing? And who could wish to deprive her of her Great Book of Records?

The Sorceress was thoughtful for a time, considering the consequences of her loss. Then she went to her Room of Magic to prepare a charm that would tell her who had stolen the Record Book. But when she unlocked her cupboard and threw open the doors, all of her magical instruments and rare chemical compounds had been removed from the shelves. The Sorceress has now both angry and alarmed. She sat down in a chair and tried to think how this extraordinary robbery could have taken place. It was evident that the thief was some person of very great power, or the theft could not have been accomplished without her knowledge. But who, in all the Land of Oz, was powerful and skillful enough to do this awful thing? And who, having the power, could also have an object in defying the wisest and most talented Sorceress the world has ever known?

Glinda thought over the perplexing matter for a full hour, at the end of which time she was still puzzled how to explain it. But although her instruments and chemicals were gone, her KNOWLEDGE of magic had not been stolen, by any means, since no thief, however skillful, can rob one of knowledge, and that is why knowledge is the best and safest treasure to acquire. Glinda believed that when she had time to gather more magical herbs and elixirs and to manufacture more magical instruments, she would be able to discover who the robber was and what had become of her precious Book of Records.

"Whoever has done this," she said to her maidens, "is a very foolish person, for in time he is sure to be found out and will then be severely punished."

She now made a list of the things she needed and dispatched messengers to every part of Oz with instructions to obtain them and bring them to her as soon as possible. And one of her messengers met the little Wizard of Oz, who was seated on the back of the famous live Sawhorse and was clinging to its neck with both his arms, for the Sawhorse was speeding to Glinda's castle with the velocity of the wind, bearing the news that Royal Ozma, Ruler of all the great Land of Oz, had suddenly disappeared and no one in the Emerald City knew what had become of her.

"Also," said the Wizard as he stood before the astonished Sorceress, "Ozma's Magic Picture is gone, so we cannot consult it to discover where she is. So I came to you for assistance as soon as we realized our loss. Let us look in the Great Book of Records."

"Alas," returned the Sorceress sorrowfully, "we cannot do that, for the Great Book of Records has also disappeared!"

3. Of Cayke The Cookie Cook

One more important theft was reported in the Land of Oz that eventful morning, but it took place so far from either the Emerald City or the castle of Glinda the Good that none of those persons we have mentioned learned of the robbery until long afterward.

In the far southwestern corner of the Winkie Country is a broad tableland that can be reached only by climbing a steep hill, whichever side one approaches it. On the hillside surrounding this tableland are no paths at all, but there are quantities of bramble bushes with sharp prickers on them, which prevent any of the Oz people who live down below from climbing up to see what is on top. But on top live the Yips, and although the space they occupy is not great in extent, the wee country is all their own. The Yips had never—up to the time this story begins—left their broad tableland to go down into the Land of Oz, nor had the Oz people ever climbed up to the country of the Yips.

Living all alone as they did, the Yips had queer ways and notions of their own and did not resemble any other people of the Land of Oz. Their houses were scattered all over the flat surface; not like a city, grouped together, but set wherever their owners' fancy dictated, with fields here, trees there, and odd little paths connecting the houses one with another. It was here, on the morning when Ozma so strangely disappeared from the Emerald City, that Cayke the Cookie Cook discovered that her diamond-studded gold dishpan had been stolen, and she raised such a hue and cry over her loss and wailed and shrieked so loudly that many of the Yips gathered around her house to inquire what was the matter.

It was a serious thing in any part of the Land of Oz to accuse one of stealing, so when the Yips heard Cayke the Cookie Cook declare that her jeweled dishpan had been stolen, they were both humiliated and disturbed and forced Cayke to go with them to the Frogman to see what could be done about it. I do not suppose you have ever before heard of the Frogman, for like all other dwellers on that tableland, he had never been away from it, nor had anyone come up there to see him. The Frogman was in truth descended from the common frogs of Oz, and when he was first born he lived in a pool in the Winkie Country and was much like any other frog. Being of an adventurous nature, however, he soon hopped out of his pool and began to travel, when a big bird came along and seized him in its beak and started to fly away with him to its nest. When high in the air, the frog wriggled so frantically that he got loose and fell down, down, down into a small hidden pool on the tableland of the Yips. Now that pool, it seems, was unknown to the Yips because it was surrounded by thick bushes and was not near to any dwelling, and it proved to be an enchanted pool, for the frog grew very fast and very big, feeding on the magic skosh which is found nowhere else on earth except in that one pool. And the skosh not only made the frog very big so that when he stood on his hind legs he was as tall as any Yip in the country, but it made him unusually intelligent, so that he soon knew more than the Yips did and was able to reason and to argue very well indeed.

No one could expect a frog with these talents to remain in a hidden pool, so he finally got out of it and mingled with the people of the tableland, who were amazed at his appearance and greatly impressed by his learning. They had never seen a frog before, and the frog had never seen a Yip before, but as there were plenty of Yips and only one frog, the frog became the most important. He did not hop any more, but stood upright on his hind legs and dressed himself in fine clothes and sat in chairs and did all the things that people do, so he soon came to be called the Frogman, and that is the only name he has ever had. After some years had passed, the people came to regard the Frogman as their adviser in all matters that puzzled them. They brought all their difficulties to him, and when he did not know anything, he pretended to know it, which seemed to answer just as well. Indeed, the Yips thought the Frogman was much wiser than he really was, and he allowed them to think so, being very proud of his position of authority.

There was another pool on the tableland which was not enchanted but contained good, clear water and was located close to the dwellings. Here the people built the Frogman a house of his own, close to the edge of the pool so that he could take a bath or a swim whenever he wished. He usually swam in the pool in the early morning before anyone else was up, and during the day he dressed himself in his beautiful clothes and sat in his house and received the visits of all the Yips who came to him to ask his advice. The Frogman's usual costume consisted of knee-breeches made of yellow satin plush, with trimmings of gold braid and jeweled knee-buckles; a white satin vest with silver buttons in which were set solitaire rubies; a swallow-tailed coat of bright yellow; green stockings and red leather shoes turned up at the toes and having diamond buckles. He wore, when he walked out, a purple silk hat and carried a gold-headed cane. Over his eyes he wore great spectacles with gold rims, not because his eyes were bad, but because the spectacles made him look wise, and so distinguished and gorgeous was his appearance that all the Yips were very proud of him.

There was no King or Queen in the Yip Country, so the simple inhabitants naturally came to look upon the Frogman as their leader as well as their counselor in all times of emergency. In his heart the big frog knew he was no wiser than the Yips, but for a frog to know as much as a person was quite remarkable, and the Frogman was shrewd enough to make the people believe he was far more wise than he really was. They never suspected he was a humbug, but listened to his words with great respect and did just what he advised them to do.

Now when Cayke the Cookie Cook raised such an outcry over the theft of her diamond-studded dishpan, the first thought of the people was to take her to the Frogman and inform him of the loss, thinking that of course he would tell her where to find it. He listened to the story with his big eyes wide open behind his spectacles, and said in his deep, croaking voice, "If the dishpan is stolen, somebody must have taken it."

"But who?"asked Cayke anxiously. "Who is the thief?"

"The one who took the dishpan, of course," replied the Frogman, and hearing this all the Yips nodded their heads gravely and said to one another, "It is absolutely true!"

"But I want my dishpan!" cried Cayke.

"No one can blame you for that wish," remarked the Frogman.

"Then tell me where I may find it," she urged.

The look the Frogman gave her was a very wise look, and he rose from his chair and strutted up and down the room with his hands under his coattails in a very pompous and imposing manner. This was the first time so difficult a matter had been brought to him, and he wanted time to think. It would never do to let them suspect his ignorance, and so he thought very, very hard how best to answer the woman without betraying himself. "I beg to inform you," said he, "that nothing in the Yip Country has ever been stolen before."

"We know that already," answered Cayke the Cookie Cook impatiently.

"Therefore," continued the Frogman, "this theft becomes a very important matter."

"Well, where is my dishpan?" demanded the woman.

"It is lost, but it must be found. Unfortunately, we have no policemen or detectives to unravel the mystery, so we must employ other means to regain the lost article. Cayke must first write a Proclamation and tack it to the door of her house, and the Proclamation must read that whoever stole the jeweled dishpan must return it at once."

"But suppose no one returns it," suggested Cayke.

"Then," said the Frogman, "that very fact will be proof that no one has stolen it."

Cayke was not satisfied, but the other Yips seemed to approve the plan highly. They all advised her to do as the Frogman had told her to, so she posted the sign on her door and waited patiently for someone to return the dishpan—which no one ever did. Again she went, accompanied by a group of her neighbors, to the Frogman, who by this time had given the matter considerable thought. Said he to Cayke, "I am now convinced that no Yip has taken your dishpan, and since it is gone from the Yip Country, I suspect that some stranger came from the world down below us in the darkness of night when all of us were asleep and took away your treasure. There can be no other explanation of its disappearance. So if you wish to recover that golden, diamond-studded dishpan, you must go into the lower world after it."

This was indeed a startling proposition. Cayke and her friends went to the edge of the flat tableland and looked down the steep hillside to the plains below. It was so far to the bottom of the hill that nothing there could be seen very distinctly, and it seemed to the Yips very venturesome, if not dangerous, to go so far from home into an unknown land. However, Cayke wanted her dishpan very badly, so she turned to her friends and asked, "Who will go with me?"

No one answered the question, but after a period of silence one of the Yips said, "We know what is here on the top of this flat hill, and it seems to us a very pleasant place, but what is down below we do not know. The chances are it is not so pleasant, so we had best stay where we are."

"It may be a far better country than this is," suggested the Cookie Cook.

"Maybe, maybe," responded another Yip, "but why take chances? Contentment with one's lot is true wisdom. Perhaps in some other country there are better cookies than you cook, but as we have always eaten your cookies and liked them—except when they are burned on the bottom—we do not long for any better ones."

Cayke might have agreed to this argument had she not been so anxious to find her precious dishpan, but now she exclaimed impatiently, "You are cowards, all of you! If none of you are willing to explore with me the great world beyond this small hill, I will surely go alone."

"That is a wise resolve," declared the Yips, much relieved. "It is your dishpan that is lost, not ours. And if you are willing to risk your life and liberty to regain it, no one can deny you the privilege."

While they were thus conversing, the Frogman joined them and looked down at the plain with his big eyes and seemed unusually thoughtful. In fact, the Frogman was thinking that he'd like to see more of the world. Here in the Yip Country he had become the most important creature of them all, and his importance was getting to be a little tame. It would be nice to have other people defer to him and ask his advice, and there seemed no reason so far as he could see why his fame should not spread throughout all Oz. He knew nothing of the rest of the world, but it was reasonable to believe that there were more people beyond the mountain where he now lived than there were Yips, and if he went among them he could surprise them with his display of wisdom and make them bow down to him as the Yips did. In other words, the Frogman was ambitious to become still greater than he was, which was impossible if he always remained upon this mountain. He wanted others to see his gorgeous clothes and listen to his solemn sayings, and here was an excuse for him to get away from the Yip Country. So he said to Cayke the Cookie Cook, "I will go with you, my good woman," which greatly pleased Cayke because she felt the Frogman could be of much assistance to her in her search.

But now, since the mighty Frogman had decided to undertake the journey, several of the Yips who were young and daring at once made up their minds to go along, so the next morning after breakfast the Frogman and Cayke the Cookie Cook and nine of the Yips started to slide down the side of the mountain. The bramble bushes and cactus plants were very prickly and uncomfortable to the touch, so the Frogman quickly commanded the Yips to go first and break a path, so that when he followed them he would not tear his splendid clothes. Cayke, too, was wearing her best dress and was likewise afraid of the thorns and prickers, so she kept behind the Frogman.

They made rather slow progress and night overtook them before they were halfway down the mountainside, so they found a cave in which they sought shelter until morning. Cayke had brought along a basket full of her famous cookies, so they all had plenty to eat. On the second day the Yips began to wish they had not embarked on this adventure. They grumbled a good deal at having to cut away the thorns to make the path for the Frogman and the Cookie Cook, for their own clothing suffered many tears, while Cayke and the Frogman traveled safely and in comfort.

"If it is true that anyone came to our country to steal your diamond dishpan," said one of the Yips to Cayke, "it must have been a bird, for no person in the form of a man, woman or child could have climbed through these bushes and back again."

"And, allowing he could have done so," said another Yip, "the diamond-studded gold dishpan would not have repaid him for his troubles and his tribulations."

"For my part," remarked a third Yip, "I would rather go back home and dig and polish some more diamonds and mine some more gold and make you another dishpan than be scratched from head to heel by these dreadful bushes. Even now, if my mother saw me, she would not know I am her son."

Cayke paid no heed to these mutterings, nor did the Frogman. Although their journey was slow, it was being made easy for them by the Yips, so they had nothing to complain of and no desire to turn back. Quite near to the bottom of the great hill they came upon a great gulf, the sides of which were as smooth as glass. The gulf extended a long distance—as far as they could see in either direction—and although it was not very wide, it was far too wide for the Yips to leap across it. And should they fall into it, it was likely they might never get out again. "Here our journey ends," said the Yips. "We must go back again."

Cayke the Cookie Cook began to weep.

"I shall never find my pretty dishpan again, and my heart will be broken!" she sobbed.

The Frogman went to the edge of the gulf and with his eye carefully measured the distance to the other side. "Being a frog," said he, "I can leap, as all frogs do, and being so big and strong, I am sure I can leap across this gulf with ease. But the rest of you,

not being frogs, must return the way you came."

"We will do that with pleasure," cried the Yips, and at once they turned and began to climb up the steep mountain, feeling they had had quite enough of this unsatisfactory adventure. Cayke the Cookie Cook did not go with them, however. She sat on a rock and wept and wailed and was very miserable.

"Well," said the Frogman to her, "I will now bid you goodbye. If I find your diamond-decorated gold dishpan, I will promise to see that it is safely returned to you."

"But I prefer to find it myself!" she said. "See here, Frogman, why can't you carry me across the gulf when you leap it? You are big and strong, while I am small and thin."

The Frogman gravely thought over this suggestion. It was a fact that Cayke the Cookie Cook was not a heavy person. Perhaps he could leap the gulf with her on his back. "If you are willing to risk a fall," said he, "I will make the attempt."

At once she sprang up and grabbed him around his neck with both her arms. That is, she grabbed him where his neck ought to be, for the Frogman had no neck at all. Then he squatted down, as frogs do when they leap, and with his powerful rear legs he made a tremendous jump. Over the gulf they sailed, with the Cookie Cook on his back, and he had leaped so hard—to make sure of not falling in—that he sailed over a lot of bramble bushes that grew on the other side and landed in a clear space which was so far beyond the gulf that when they looked back they could not see it at all.

Cayke now got off the Frogman's back and he stood erect again and carefully brushed the dust from his velvet coat and rearranged his white satin necktie.

"I had no idea I could leap so far," he said wonderingly. "Leaping is one more accomplishment I can now add to the long list of deeds I am able to perform."

"You are certainly fine at leap-frog," said the Cookie Cook admiringly, "but, as you say, you are wonderful in many ways. If we meet with any people down here, I am sure they will consider you the greatest and grandest of all living creatures."

"Yes," he replied, "I shall probably astonish strangers, because they have never before had the pleasure of seeing me. Also, they will marvel at my great learning. Every time I open my mouth, Cayke, I am liable to say something important."

"That is true," she agreed, "and it is fortunate your mouth is so very wide and opens so far, for otherwise all the wisdom might not be able to get out of it." "Perhaps nature made it wide for that very reason," said the Frogman. "But come, let us now go on, for it is getting late and we must find some sort of shelter before night overtakes us."

4. Among The Winkies

The settled parts of the Winkie Country are full of happy and contented people who are ruled by a tin Emperor named Nick Chopper, who in turn is a subject of the beautiful girl Ruler, Ozma of Oz. But not all of the Winkie Country is fully settled. At the east, which part lies nearest the Emerald City, there are beautiful farmhouses and roads, but as you travel west, you first come to a branch of the Winkie River, beyond which there is a rough country where few people live, and some of these are quite unknown to the rest of the world. After passing through this rude section of territory, which no one ever visits, you would come to still another branch of the Winkie River, after crossing which you would find another well-settled part of the Winkie Country extending westward quite to the Deadly Desert that surrounds all the Land of Oz and separates that favored fairyland from the more common outside world. The Winkies who live in this west section have many tin mines, from which metal they make a great deal of rich jewelry and other articles, all of which are highly esteemed in the Land of Oz because tin is so bright and pretty and there is not so much of it as there is of gold and silver.

Not all the Winkies are miners, however, for some till the fields and grow grains for food, and it was at one of these far-west Winkie farms that the Frogman and Cayke the Cookie Cook first arrived after they had descended from the mountain of the Yips. "Goodness me!" cried Nellary the Winkie wife when she saw the strange couple approaching her house. "I have seen many queer creatures in the Land of Oz, but none more queer than this giant frog who dresses like a man and walks on his hind legs. Come here, Wiljon," she called to her husband, who was eating his breakfast, "and take a look at this astonishing freak."

Wiljon the Winkie came to the door and looked out. He was still standing in the doorway when the Frogman approached and said with a haughty croak, "Tell me, my good man, have you seen a diamond-studded gold dishpan?"

"No, nor have I seen a copper-plated lobster," replied Wiljon in an equally haughty tone.

The Frogman stared at him and said, "Do not be insolent, fellow!"

"No," added Cayke the Cookie Cook hastily, "you must be very polite to the great Frogman, for he is the wisest creature in all the world."

"Who says that?" inquired Wiljon.

"He says so himself," replied Cayke, and the Frogman nodded and strutted up and down, twirling his gold-headed cane very gracefully.

"Does the Scarecrow admit that this overgrown frog is the wisest creature in the world?" asked Wiljon.

"I do not know who the Scarecrow is," answered Cayke the Cookie Cook.

"Well, he lives at the Emerald City, and he is supposed to have the finest brains in all Oz. The Wizard gave them to him, you know."

"Mine grew in my head," said the Frogman pompously, "so I think they must be better than any wizard brains. I am so wise that sometimes my wisdom makes my head ache. I know so much that often I have to forget part of it, since no one creature, however great, is able to contain so much knowledge."

"It must be dreadful to be stuffed full of wisdom," remarked Wiljon reflectively and eyeing the Frogman with a doubtful look. "It is my good fortune to know very little."

"I hope, however, you know where my jeweled dishpan is," said the Cookie Cook anxiously.

"I do not know even that," returned the Winkie. "We have trouble

enough in keeping track of our own dishpans without meddling with the dishpans of strangers."

Finding him so ignorant, the Frogman proposed that they walk on and seek Cayke's dishpan elsewhere. Wiljon the Winkie did not seem greatly impressed by the great Frogman, which seemed to that personage as strange as it was disappointing. But others in this unknown land might prove more respectful.

"I'd like to meet that Wizard of Oz," remarked Cayke as they walked along a path. "If he could give a Scarecrow brains, he might be able to find my dishpan."

"Poof!" grunted the Frogman scornfully. "I am greater than any wizard. Depend on ME. If your dishpan is anywhere in the world, I am sure to find it."

"If you do not, my heart will be broken," declared the Cookie Cook in a sorrowful voice.

For a while the Frogman walked on in silence. Then he asked, "Why do you attach so much importance to a dishpan?"

"It is the greatest treasure I possess," replied the woman. "It belonged to my mother and to all my grandmothers since the beginning of time. It is, I believe, the very oldest thing in all the Yip Country—or was while it was there—and," she added, dropping her voice to an awed whisper, "it has magic powers!"

"In what way?" inquired the Frogman, seeming to be surprised at this statement.

"Whoever has owned that dishpan has been a good cook, for one thing. No one else is able to make such good cookies as I have cooked, as you and all the Yips know. Yet the very morning after my dishpan was stolen, I tried to make a batch of cookies and they burned up in the oven! I made another batch that proved too tough to eat, and I was so ashamed of them that I buried them in the ground. Even the third batch of cookies, which I brought with me in my basket, were pretty poor stuff and no better than any woman could make who does not own my diamond-studded gold dishpan. In fact, my good Frogman, Cayke the Cookie Cook will never be able to cook good cookies again until her magic dishpan is restored to her."

"In that case," said the Frogman with a sigh, "I suppose we must manage to find it."

5. Ozma's Friends Are Perplexed

"Really," said Dorothy, looking solemn, "this is very s'prising. We can't even find a shadow of Ozma anywhere in the Em'rald City and wherever she's gone, she's taken her Magic Picture with her." She was standing in the courtyard of the palace with Betsy and Trot, while Scraps, the Patchwork Girl, danced around the group, her hair flying in the wind.

"P'raps," said Scraps, still dancing, "someone has stolen Ozma."

"Oh, they'd never dare do that!" exclaimed tiny Trot.

"And stolen the Magic Picture, too, so the thing can't tell where she is," added the Patchwork Girl.

"That's nonsense," said Dorothy. "Why, ev'ryone loves Ozma. There isn't a person in the Land of Oz who would steal a single thing she owns."

"Huh!" replied the Patchwork Girl. "You don't know ev'ry person in the Land of Oz."

"Why don't I?"

"It's a big country," said Scraps. "There are cracks and corners in it that even Ozma doesn't know of."

"The Patchwork Girl's just daffy," declared Betsy.

"No, she's right about that," replied Dorothy thoughtfully. "There are lots of queer people in this fairyland who never come near Ozma or the Em'rald City. I've seen some of 'em myself, girls. But I haven't seen all, of course, and there MIGHT be some wicked persons left in Oz yet, though I think the wicked witches have all been destroyed."

Just then the Wooden Sawhorse dashed into the courtyard with the Wizard of Oz on his back. "Have you found Ozma?"cried the Wizard when the Sawhorse stopped beside them.

"Not yet," said Dorothy. "Doesn't Glinda the Good know where she is?"

"No. Glinda's Book of Records and all her magic instruments are gone. Someone must have stolen them."

"Goodness me!"exclaimed Dorothy in alarm. "This is the biggest steal I ever heard of. Who do you think did it, Wizard?"

"I've no idea," he answered. "But I have come to get my own bag of magic tools and carry them to Glinda. She is so much more powerful than I that she may be able to discover the truth by means of my magic quicker and better than I could myself."

"Hurry, then," said Dorothy, "for we've all gotten terr'bly worried."

The Wizard rushed away to his rooms but presently came back with a long, sad face. "It's gone!" he said.

"What's gone?" asked Scraps.

"My black bag of magic tools. Someone must have stolen it!"

They looked at one another in amazement.

"This thing is getting desperate," continued the Wizard. "All the magic that belongs to Ozma or to Glinda or to me has been stolen."

"Do you suppose Ozma could have taken them, herself, for some purpose?" asked Betsy.

"No indeed," declared the Wizard. "I suspect some enemy has stolen Ozma and for fear we would follow and recapture her has taken all our magic away from us."

"How dreadful!" cried Dorothy. "The idea of anyone wanting to injure our dear Ozma! Can't we do ANYthing to find her, Wizard?"

"I'll ask Glinda. I must go straight back to her and tell her that my magic tools have also disappeared. The good Sorceress will be greatly shocked, I know."

With this, he jumped upon the back of the Sawhorse again, and the quaint steed, which never tired, dashed away at full speed.

The three girls were very much disturbed in mind. Even the Patchwork Girl seemed to realize that a great calamity had overtaken them all. Ozma was a fairy of considerable power, and all the creatures in Oz as well as the three mortal girls from the outside world looked upon her as their protector and friend. The idea of their beautiful girl Ruler's being overpowered by an enemy and dragged from her splendid palace a captive was too astonishing for them to comprehend at first. Yet what other explanation of the mystery could there be?

"Ozma wouldn't go away willingly, without letting us know about it," asserted Dorothy, "and she wouldn't steal Glinda's Great Book of Records or the Wizard's magic, 'cause she could get them any time just by asking for 'em. I'm sure some wicked person has done all this."

"Someone in the Land of Oz?" asked Trot.

"Of course. No one could get across the Deadly Desert, you know, and no one but an Oz person could know about the Magic Picture and the Book of Records and the Wizard's magic or where they were kept, and so be able to steal the whole outfit before we could stop 'em. It MUST be someone who lives in the Land of Oz."

"But who—who—who?" asked Scraps. "That's the question. Who?"

"If we knew," replied Dorothy severely, "we wouldn't be standing here doing nothing."

Just then two boys entered the courtyard and approached the group of girls. One boy was dressed in the fantastic Munchkin costume—a blue jacket and knickerbockers, blue leather shoes and a blue hat with a high peak and tiny silver bells dangling from its rim—and this was Ojo the Lucky, who had once come from the Munchkin Country of Oz and now lived in the Emerald City. The other boy was an American from Philadelphia and had lately found his way to Oz in the company of Trot and Cap'n Bill. His name was Button-Bright; that is, everyone called him by that name and knew no other. Button-Bright was not quite as big as the Munchkin boy, but he wore the same kind of clothes, only they were of different colors. As the two came up to the girls, arm in arm, Button-Bright remarked, "Hello, Dorothy. They say Ozma is lost."

"WHO says so?" she asked.

"Ev'rybody's talking about it in the City," he replied.

"I wonder how the people found it out," Dorothy asked.

"I know," said Ojo. "Jellia Jamb told them. She has been asking everywhere if anyone has seen Ozma."

"That's too bad," observed Dorothy, frowning.

"Why?" asked Button-Bright.

"There wasn't any use making all our people unhappy till we were dead certain that Ozma can't be found."

"Pshaw," said Button-Bright, "it's nothing to get lost. I've been lost lots of times."

"That's true," admitted Trot, who knew that the boy had a habit of getting lost and then finding himself again, "but it's diff'rent with Ozma. She's the Ruler of all this big fairyland, and we're 'fraid that the reason she's lost is because somebody has stolen her away."

"Only wicked people steal," said Ojo. "Do you know of any wicked people in Oz, Dorothy?"

"No," she replied.

"They're here, though," cried Scraps, dancing up to them and then circling around the group. "Ozma's stolen; someone in Oz stole her; only wicked people steal; so someone in Oz is wicked!"

There was no denying the truth of this statement. The faces of all of them were now solemn and sorrowful. "One thing is sure," said Button-Bright after a time, "if Ozma has been stolen, someone ought to find her and punish the thief."

"There may be a lot of thieves," suggested Trot gravely, "and in this fairy country they don't seem to have any soldiers or policemen."

"There is one soldier," claimed Dorothy.

"He has green whiskers and a gun and is a Major-General, but no one is afraid of either his gun or his whiskers, 'cause he's so tender-hearted that he wouldn't hurt a fly."

"Well, a soldier is a soldier," said Betsy, "and perhaps he'd hurt a wicked thief if he wouldn't hurt a fly. Where is he?"

"He went fishing about two months ago and hasn't come back yet," explained Button-Bright.

"Then I can't see that he will be of much use to us in this trouble," sighed little Trot. "But p'raps Ozma, who is a fairy, can get away from the thieves without any help from anyone."

"She MIGHT be able to," answered Dorothy reflectively, "but if she had the power to do that, it isn't likely she'd have let herself be stolen. So the thieves must have been even more powerful in magic than our Ozma."

There was no denying this argument, and although they talked the matter over all the rest of that day, they were unable to decide how Ozma had been stolen against her will or who had committed the dreadful deed. Toward evening the Wizard came back, riding slowly upon the Sawhorse because he felt discouraged and perplexed. Glinda came later in her aerial chariot drawn by twenty milk-white swans, and she also seemed worried and unhappy. More of Ozma's friends joined them, and that evening they all had a big talk together. "I think," said Dorothy, "we ought to start out right away in search of our dear Ozma. It seems cruel for us to live comf'tably in her palace while she is a pris'ner in the power of some wicked enemy."

"Yes," agreed Glinda the Sorceress, "someone ought to search for her. I cannot go myself, because I must work hard in order to create some new instruments of sorcery by means of which I may rescue our fair Ruler. But if you can find her in the meantime and let me know who has stolen her, it will enable me to rescue her much more quickly."

"Then we'll start tomorrow morning," decided Dorothy. "Betsy and Trot and I won't waste another minute."

"I'm not sure you girls will make good detectives," remarked the Wizard, "but I'll go with you to protect you from harm and to give you my advice. All my wizardry, alas, is stolen, so I am now

really no more a wizard than any of you, but I will try to protect you from any enemies you may meet."

"What harm could happen to us in Oz?" inquired Trot.

"What harm happened to Ozma?" returned the Wizard.

"If there is an Evil Power abroad in our fairyland, which is able to steal not only Ozma and her Magic Picture, but Glinda's Book of Records and all her magic, and my black bag containing all my tricks of wizardry, then that Evil Power may yet cause us considerable injury. Ozma is a fairy, and so is Glinda, so no power can kill or destroy them, but you girls are all mortals and so are Button-Bright and I, so we must watch out for ourselves."

"Nothing can kill me," said Ojo the Munchkin boy.

"That is true," replied the Sorceress, "and I think it may be well to divide the searchers into several parties, that they may cover all the land of Oz more quickly. So I will send Ojo and Unc Nunkie and Dr. Pipt into the Munchkin Country, which they are well acquainted with; and I will send the Scarecrow and the Tin Woodman into the Quadling Country, for they are fearless and brave and never tire; and to the Gillikin Country, where many dangers lurk, I will send the Shaggy Man and his brother, with Tik-Tok and Jack Pumpkinhead. Dorothy may make up her own party and travel into the Winkie Country. All of you must inquire everywhere for Ozma and try to discover where she is hidden."

They thought this a very wise plan and adopted it without question. In Ozma's absence, Glinda the Good was the most important person in Oz, and all were glad to serve under her direction.

6. The Search Party

Next morning as soon as the sun was up, Glinda flew back to her castle, stopping on the way to instruct the Scarecrow and the Tin Woodman, who were at that time staying at the college of Professor H. M. Wogglebug, T.E., and taking a course of his Patent Educational Pills.

On hearing of Ozma's loss, they started at once for the Quadling Country to search for her. As soon as Glinda had left the Emerald City, Tik-Tok and the Shaggy Man and Jack Pumpkinhead, who had been present at the conference, began their journey into the Gillikin Country, and an hour later Ojo and Unc Nunkie joined Dr. Pipt and together they traveled toward the Munchkin Country. When all these searchers were gone, Dorothy and the Wizard completed their own preparations.

The Wizard hitched the Sawhorse to the Red Wagon, which would seat four very comfortably. He wanted Dorothy, Betsy, Trot and the Patchwork Girl to ride in the wagon, but Scraps came up to them mounted upon the Woozy, and the Woozy said he would like to join the party. Now this Woozy was a most peculiar animal, having a square head, square body, square legs and square tail. His skin was very tough and hard, resembling leather, and while his movements were somewhat clumsy, the beast could travel with remarkable swiftness. His square eyes were mild and gentle in expression, and he was not especially foolish. The Woozy and the Patchwork Girl were great friends, and so the Wizard agreed to let the Woozy go with them.

Another great beast now appeared and asked to go along. This was none other than the famous Cowardly Lion, one of the most interesting creatures in all Oz. No lion that roamed the jungles or plains could compare in size or intelligence with this Cowardly

Lion, who—like all animals living in Oz—could talk and who talked with more shrewdness and wisdom than many of the people did. He said he was cowardly because he always trembled when he faced danger, but he had faced danger many times and never refused to fight when it was necessary. This Lion was a great favorite with Ozma and always guarded her throne on state occasions. He was also an old companion and friend of the Princess Dorothy, so the girl was delighted to have him join the party.

"I'm so nervous over our dear Ozma," said the Cowardly Lion in his deep, rumbling voice, "that it would make me unhappy to remain behind while you are trying to find her. But do not get into any danger, I beg of you, for danger frightens me terribly."

"We'll not get into danger if we can poss'bly help it," promised Dorothy, "but we shall do anything to find Ozma, danger or no danger."

The addition of the Woozy and the Cowardly Lion to the party gave Betsy Bobbin an idea, and she ran to the marble stables at the rear of the palace and brought out her mule, Hank by name. Perhaps no mule you ever saw was so lean and bony and altogether plain looking as this Hank, but Betsy loved him dearly because he was faithful and steady and not nearly so stupid as most mules are considered to be. Betsy had a saddle for Hank, and he declared she would ride on his back, an arrangement approved by the Wizard because it left only four of the party to ride on the seats of the Red Wagon—Dorothy and Button-Bright and Trot and himself.

An old sailor man who had one wooden leg came to see them off and suggested that they put a supply of food and blankets in the Red Wagon inasmuch as they were uncertain how long they would be gone. This sailor man was called Cap'n Bill. He was a former friend and comrade of Trot and had encountered many adventures in company with the little girl. I think he was sorry he could not go with her on this trip, but Glinda the Sorceress had asked Cap'n Bill to remain in the Emerald City and take charge of the royal palace while everyone else was away, and the one-legged sailor had agreed to do so.

They loaded the back end of the Red Wagon with everything they thought they might need, and then they formed a procession and marched from the palace through the Emerald City to the great gates of the wall that surrounded this beautiful capital of the Land of Oz. Crowds of citizens lined the streets to see them pass and to cheer them and wish them success, for all were grieved over Ozma's loss and anxious that she be found again. First came the Cowardly Lion, then the Patchwork Girl riding upon the Woozy, then Betsy Bobbin on her mule Hank, and finally the Sawhorse drawing the Red Wagon, in which were seated the Wizard and Dorothy and Button-Bright and Trot. No one was obliged to drive the Sawhorse, so there were no reins to his harness; one had only to tell him which way to go, fast or slow, and he understood perfectly.

It was about this time that a shaggy little black dog who had been lying asleep in Dorothy's room in the palace woke up and discovered he was lonesome. Everything seemed very still throughout the great building, and Toto—that was the little dog's name—missed the customary chatter of the three girls. He never paid much attention to what was going on around him, and although he could speak, he seldom said anything, so the little dog did not know about Ozma's loss or that everyone had gone in search of her. But he liked to be with people, and especially with his own mistress, Dorothy, and having yawned and stretched himself and found the door of the room ajar, he

trotted out into the corridor and went down the stately marble stairs to the hall of the palace, where he met Jellia Jamb.

"Where's Dorothy?" asked Toto.

"She's gone to the Winkie Country," answered the maid.

"When?"

"A little while ago," replied Jellia.

Toto turned and trotted out into the palace garden and down the long driveway until he came to the streets of the Emerald City. Here he paused to listen, and hearing sounds of cheering, he ran swiftly along until he came in sight of the Red Wagon and the Woozy and the Lion and the Mule and all the others. Being a wise little dog, he decided not to show himself to Dorothy just then, lest he be sent back home, but he never lost sight of the party of travelers, all of whom were so eager to get ahead that they never thought to look behind them. When they came to the gates in the city wall, the Guardian of the Gates came out to throw wide the golden portals and let them pass through.

"Did any strange person come in or out of the city on the night before last when Ozma was stolen?" asked Dorothy.

"No indeed, Princess," answered the Guardian of the Gates.

"Of course not," said the Wizard. "Anyone clever enough to steal all the things we have lost would not mind the barrier of a wall like this in the least. I think the thief must have flown through the air, for otherwise he could not have stolen from Ozma's royal palace and Glinda's faraway castle in the same night. Moreover, as there are no airships in Oz and no way for airships from the outside world to get into this country, I believe the thief must have flown from place to place by means of magic arts which neither Glinda nor I understand."

On they went, and before the gates closed behind them, Toto managed to dodge through them. The country surrounding the Emerald City was thickly settled, and for a while our friends rode over nicely paved roads which wound through a fertile country dotted with beautiful houses, all built in the quaint Oz fashion. In the course of a few hours, however, they had left the tilled fields and entered the Country of the Winkies, which occupies a quarter of all the territory in the Land of Oz but is not so well known as many other parts of Ozma's fairyland. Long before night the travelers had crossed the Winkie River near to the Scarecrow's Tower (which was now vacant) and had entered the Rolling Prairie where few people live. They asked everyone they met for news of Ozma, but none in this district had seen her or even knew that she had been stolen. And by nightfall they had passed all the farmhouses and were obliged to stop and ask for shelter at the hut of a lonely shepherd. When they halted, Toto was not far behind. The little dog halted, too, and stealing softly around the party, he hid himself behind the hut.

The shepherd was a kindly old man and treated the travelers with much courtesy. He slept out of doors that night, giving up his hut to the three girls, who made their beds on the floor with the blankets they had brought in the Red Wagon. The Wizard and Button-Bright also slept out of doors, and so did the Cowardly Lion and Hank the Mule. But Scraps and the Sawhorse did not sleep at all, and the Woozy could stay awake for a month at a time if he wished to, so these three sat in a little group by themselves and talked together all through the night.

In the darkness, the Cowardly Lion felt a shaggy little form nestling beside his own, and he said sleepily, "Where did you come from, Toto?"

"From home," said the dog. "If you roll over, roll the other way so you won't smash me."

"Does Dorothy know you are here?" asked the Lion.

"I believe not," admitted Toto, and he added a little anxiously, "Do you think, friend Lion, we are now far enough from the Emerald City for me to risk showing myself, or will Dorothy send me back because I wasn't invited?"

"Only Dorothy can answer that question," said the Lion. "For my part, Toto, I consider this affair none of my business, so you must act as you think best." Then the huge beast went to sleep again, and Toto snuggled closer to the warm, hairy body and also slept. He was a wise little dog in his way, and didn't intend to worry when there was something much better to do.

In the morning the Wizard built a fire, over which the girls cooked a very good breakfast. Suddenly Dorothy discovered Toto sitting quietly before the fire, and the little girl exclaimed, "Goodness me, Toto! Where did YOU come from?"

"From the place you cruelly left me," replied the dog in a reproachful tone.

"I forgot all about you," admitted Dorothy, "and if I hadn't, I'd prob'ly left you with Jellia Jamb, seeing this isn't a pleasure trip but stric'ly business. But now that you're here, Toto, I s'pose you'll have to stay with us, unless you'd rather go back again. We may get ourselves into trouble before we're done, Toto."

"Never mind that," said Toto, wagging his tail. "I'm hungry, Dorothy."

"Breakfas'll soon be ready, and then you shall have your share," promised his little mistress, who was really glad to have her dog with her. She and Toto had traveled together before, and she knew he was a good and faithful comrade.

When the food was cooked and served, the girls invited the old shepherd to join them in the morning meal. He willingly consented, and while they ate he said to them, "You are now about to pass through a very dangerous country, unless you turn to the north or to the south to escape its perils."

"In that case," said the Cowardly Lion, "let us turn, by all means, for I dread to face dangers of any sort."

"What's the matter with the country ahead of us?" inquired Dorothy.

"Beyond this Rolling Prairie," explained the shepherd, "are the Merry-Go-Round Mountains, set close together and surrounded by deep gulfs so that no one is able to get past them. Beyond the Merry-Go-Round Mountains it is said the Thistle-Eaters and the Herkus live."

"What are they like?" demanded Dorothy.

"No one knows, for no one has ever passed the Merry-Go-Round Mountains," was the reply, "but it is said that the Thistle-Eaters hitch dragons to their chariots and that the Herkus are waited upon by giants whom they have conquered and made their slaves."

"Who says all that?" asked Betsy.

"It is common report," declared the shepherd. "Everyone believes it."

"I don't see how they know," remarked little Trot, "if no one has been there."

"Perhaps the birds who fly over that country brought the news," suggested Betsy.

"If you escaped those dangers," continued the shepherd, "you might encounter others still more serious before you came to the next branch of the Winkie River. It is true that beyond that river there lies a fine country inhabited by good people, and if you reached there, you would have no further trouble. It is between here and the west branch of the Winkie River that all dangers lie, for that is the unknown territory that is inhabited by terrible, lawless people."

"It may be, and it may not be," said the Wizard. "We shall know when we get there."

"Well," persisted the shepherd, "in a fairy country such as ours, every undiscovered place is likely to harbor wicked creatures. If they were not wicked, they would discover themselves and by coming among us submit to Ozma's rule and be good and considerate, as are all the Oz people whom we know."

"That argument," stated the little Wizard, "convinces me that it is our duty to go straight to those unknown places, however dangerous they may be, for it is surely some cruel and wicked person who has stolen our Ozma, and we know it would be folly to search among good people for the culprit. Ozma may not be hidden in the secret places of the Winkie Country, it is true, but it is our duty to travel to every spot, however dangerous, where our beloved Ruler is likely to be imprisoned."

"You're right about that," said Button-Bright approvingly. "Dangers don't hurt us. Only things that happen ever hurt anyone, and a danger is a thing that might happen and might not happen, and sometimes don't amount to shucks. I vote we go ahead and take our chances."

They were all of the same opinion, so they packed up and said goodbye to the friendly shepherd and proceeded on their way.

7. The Merry-Go-Round Mountains

The Rolling Prairie was not difficult to travel over, although it was all uphill and downhill, so for a while they made good progress. Not even a shepherd was to be met with now, and the farther they advanced the more dreary the landscape became. At noon they stopped for a "picnic luncheon," as Betsy called it, and then they again resumed their journey. All the animals were swift and tireless, and even the Cowardly Lion and the Mule found they could keep up with the pace of the Woozy and the Sawhorse.

It was the middle of the afternoon when first they came in sight of a cluster of low mountains. These were cone-shaped, rising from broad bases to sharp peaks at the tops. From a distance the mountains appeared indistinct and seemed rather small—more like hills than mountains—but as the travelers drew nearer, they noted a most unusual circumstance: the hills were all whirling around, some in one direction and some the opposite way.

"I guess these are the Merry-Go-Round Mountains, all right,

said Dorothy.

"They must be," said the Wizard.

"They go 'round, sure enough," agreed Trot, "but they don't seem very merry."

There were several rows of these mountains, extending both to the right and to the left for miles and miles. How many rows there might be none could tell, but between the first row of peaks could be seen other peaks, all steadily whirling around one way or another. Continuing to ride nearer, our friends watched these hills attentively, until at last, coming close up, they discovered there was a deep but narrow gulf around the edge of each mountain, and that the mountains were set so close together that the outer gulf was continuous and barred farther advance. At the edge of the gulf they all dismounted and peered over into its depths. There was no telling where the bottom was, if indeed there was any bottom at all. From where they stood it seemed as if the mountains had been set in one great hole in the ground, just close enough together so they would not touch, and that each mountain was supported by a rocky column beneath its base which extended far down in the black pit below. From the land side it seemed impossible to get across the gulf or, succeeding in that, to gain a foothold on any of the whirling mountains.

"This ditch is too wide to jump across," remarked Button-Bright.

"P'raps the Lion could do it," suggested Dorothy.

"What, jump from here to that whirling hill?" cried the Lion indignantly. "I should say not! Even if I landed there and could hold on, what good would it do? There's another spinning mountain beyond it, and perhaps still another beyond that. I don't believe any living creature could jump from one mountain to another when both are whirling like tops and in different directions."

"I propose we turn back," said the Wooden Sawhorse with a yawn of his chopped-out mouth as he stared with his knot eyes at the Merry-Go-Round Mountains.

"I agree with you," said the Woozy, wagging his square head.

"We should have taken the shepherd's advice," added Hank the Mule.

The others of the party, however they might be puzzled by the serious problem that confronted them, would not allow themselves to despair. "If we once get over these mountains," said Button-Bright, "we could probably get along all right."

"True enough," agreed Dorothy. "So we must find some way, of course, to get past these whirligig hills. But how?"

"I wish the Ork was with us," sighed Trot.

"But the Ork isn't here," said the Wizard, "and we must depend upon ourselves to conquer this difficulty. Unfortunately, all my magic has been stolen, otherwise I am sure I could easily get over the mountains."

"Unfortunately," observed the Woozy, "none of us has wings. And we're in a magic country without any magic."

"What is that around your waist, Dorothy?" asked the Wizard.

"That? Oh, that's just the Magic Belt I once captured from the Nome King," she replied.

"A Magic Belt! Why, that's fine. I'm sure a Magic Belt would take you over these hills."

"It might if I knew how to work it," said the little girl. "Ozma knows a lot of its magic, but I've never found out about it. All I know is that while I am wearing it, nothing can hurt me."

"Try wishing yourself across and see if it will obey you," suggested the Wizard.

"But what good would that do?" asked Dorothy. "If I got across, it wouldn't help the rest of you, and I couldn't go alone among all those giants and dragons while you stayed here."

"True enough," agreed the Wizard sadly. And then, after looking around the group, he inquired, "What is that on your finger, Trot?"

"A ring. The Mermaids gave it to me," she explained, "and if ever I'm in trouble when I'm on the water, I can call the Mermaids and they'll come and help me. But the Mermaids can't help me on the land, you know, 'cause they swim, and—and—they haven't any legs."

"True enough," repeated the Wizard, more sadly.

There was a big, broad, spreading tree near the edge of the gulf, and as the sun was hot above them, they all gathered under the shade of the tree to study the problem of what to do next. "If we had a long rope," said Betsy, "we could fasten it to this tree and let the other end of it down into the gulf and all slide down it."

"Well, what then?" asked the Wizard.

"Then, if we could manage to throw the rope up the other side," explained the girl, "we could all climb it and be on the other side of the gulf."

"There are too many 'ifs' in that suggestion," remarked the little Wizard. "And you must remember that the other side is nothing but spinning mountains, so we couldn't possibly fasten a rope to them, even if we had one."

"That rope idea isn't half bad, though," said the Patchwork Girl, who had been dancing dangerously near to the edge of the gulf.

"What do you mean?" asked Dorothy.

The Patchwork Girl suddenly stood still and cast her button eyes around the group. "Ha, I have it!" she exclaimed. "Unharness the Sawhorse, somebody. My fingers are too clumsy."

"Shall we?" asked Button-Bright doubtfully, turning to the others.

"Well, Scraps has a lot of brains, even if she IS stuffed with cotton," asserted the Wizard. "If her brains can help us out of this trouble, we ought to use them."

So he began unharnessing the Sawhorse, and Button-Bright and Dorothy helped him. When they had removed the harness, the Patchwork Girl told them to take it all apart and buckle the straps together, end to end. And after they had done this, they found they had one very long strap that was stronger than any rope. "It would reach across the gulf easily," said the Lion, who with the other animals had sat on his haunches and watched this proceeding. "But I don't see how it could be fastened to one of those dizzy mountains."

Scraps had no such notion as that in her baggy head. She told them to fasten one end of the strap to a stout limb of the tree, pointing to one which extended quite to the edge of the gulf. Button-Bright did that, climbing the tree and then crawling out upon the limb until he was nearly over the gulf. There he managed to fasten the strap, which reached to the ground below, and then he slid down it and was caught by the Wizard, who feared he might fall into the chasm. Scraps was delighted. She seized the lower end of the strap, and telling them all to get out of her way, she went back as far as the strap would reach and then made a sudden run toward the gulf. Over the edge she swung, clinging to the strap until it had gone as far as its length permitted, when she let go and sailed gracefully through the air until she alighted upon the mountain just in front of them.

Almost instantly, as the great cone continued to whirl, she was sent flying against the next mountain in the rear, and that one had only turned halfway around when Scraps was sent flying to the next mountain behind it. Then her patchwork form disappeared from view entirely, and the amazed watchers under the tree wondered what had become of her. "She's gone, and she can't get back," said the Woozy.

"My, how she bounded from one mountain to another!" exclaimed the Lion.

"That was because they whirl so fast," the Wizard explained. "Scraps had nothing to hold on to, and so of course she was tossed from one hill to another. I'm afraid we shall never see the poor Patchwork Girl again."

"I shall see her," declared the Woozy. "Scraps is an old friend of mine, and if there are really Thistle-Eaters and Giants on the other side of those tops, she will need someone to protect her. So here I go!" He seized the dangling strap firmly in his square mouth, and in the same way that Scraps had done swung himself over the gulf. He let go the strap at the right moment and fell upon the first whirling mountain. Then he bounded to the next one back of it—not on his feet, but "all mixed up," as Trot said—and then he shot across to another mountain, disappearing from view just as the Patchwork Girl had done.

"It seems to work, all right," remarked Button-Bright. "I guess I'll try it."

"Wait a minute," urged the Wizard. "Before any more of us make this desperate leap into the beyond, we must decide whether all will go or if some of us will remain behind."

"Do you s'pose it hurt them much to bump against those mountains?" asked Trot.

"I don't s'pose anything could hurt Scraps or the Woozy," said Dorothy, "and nothing can hurt ME, because I wear the Magic Belt. So as I'm anxious to find Ozma, I mean to swing myself across too."

"I'll take my chances," decided Button-Bright.

"I'm sure it will hurt dreadfully, and I'm afraid to do it," said the Lion, who was already trembling, "but I shall do it if Dorothy does."

"Well, that will leave Betsy and the Mule and Trot," said the

Wizard, "for of course I shall go that I may look after Dorothy. Do you two girls think you can find your way back home again?" he asked, addressing Trot and Betsy.

"I'm not afraid. Not much, that is," said Trot. "It looks risky, I know, but I'm sure I can stand it if the others can."

"If it wasn't for leaving Hank," began Betsy in a hesitating voice.

But the Mule interrupted her by saying, "Go ahead if you want to, and I'll come after you. A mule is as brave as a lion any day."

"Braver," said the Lion, "for I'm a coward, friend Hank, and you are not. But of course the Sawhorse—"

"Oh, nothing ever hurts ME," asserted the Sawhorse calmly. "There's never been any question about my going. I can't take the Red Wagon, though."

"No, we must leave the wagon," said the wizard, "and also we must leave our food and blankets, I fear. But if we can defy these Merry-Go-Round Mountains to stop us, we won't mind the sacrifice of some of our comforts."

"No one knows where we're going to land!" remarked the Lion in a voice that sounded as if he were going to cry.

"We may not land at all," replied Hank, "but the best way to find out what will happen to us is to swing across as Scraps and the Woozy have done."

"I think I shall go last," said the Wizard, "so who wants to go first?"

"I'll go," decided Dorothy.

"No, it's my turn first," said Button-Bright. "Watch me!"

Even as he spoke, the boy seized the strap, and after making a run swung himself across the gulf. Away he went, bumping from hill to hill until he disappeared. They listened intently, but the boy uttered no cry until he had been gone some moments, when they heard a faint Hullo-a!" as if called from a great distance. The sound gave them courage, however, and Dorothy picked up Toto and held him fast under one arm while with the other hand she seized the strap and bravely followed after Button-Bright.

When she struck the first whirling mountain, she fell upon it quite softly, but before she had time to think, she flew through the air and lit with a jar on the side of the next mountain. Again she flew and alighted, and again and still again, until after five successive bumps she fell sprawling upon a green meadow and was so dazed and bewildered by her bumpy journey across the Merry-Go-Round Mountains that she lay quite still for a time to collect her thoughts. Toto had escaped from her arms just as she fell, and he now sat beside her panting with excitement. Then Dorothy realized that someone was helping her to her feet, and here was Button-Bright on one side of her and Scraps on the other, both seeming to be unhurt. The next object her eyes fell upon was the Woozy, squatting upon his square back end and looking at her reflectively, while Toto barked joyously to find his mistress unhurt after her whirlwind trip.

"Good!"said the Woozy. "Here's another and a dog, both safe and sound. But my word, Dorothy, you flew some! If you could have seen yourself, you'd have been absolutely astonished."

"They say 'Time flies,'" laughed Button-Bright, "but Time never made a quicker journey than that."

Just then, as Dorothy turned around to look at the whirling mountains, she was in time to see tiny Trot come flying from the nearest hill to fall upon the soft grass not a yard away from where she stood. Trot was so dizzy she couldn't stand at first, but she wasn't at all hurt, and presently Betsy came flying to them and would have bumped into the others had they not retreated in time to avoid her. Then, in quick succession, came the Lion, Hank and the Sawhorse, bounding from mountain to mountain to fall safely upon the greensward. Only the Wizard was now left behind, and they waited so long for him that Dorothy began to be worried.

But suddenly he came flying from the nearest mountain and tumbled heels over head beside them. Then they saw that he had wound two of their blankets around his body to keep the bumps from hurting him and had fastened the blankets with some of the spare straps from the harness of the Sawhorse.

8. The Mysterious City

There they sat upon the grass, their heads still swimming from their dizzy flights, and looked at one another in silent bewilderment. But presently, when assured that no one was injured, they grew more calm and collected, and the Lion said with a sigh of relief, "Who would have thought those Merry-Go-Round Mountains were made of rubber?"

"Are they really rubber?" asked Trot.

"They must be," replied the Lion, "for otherwise we would not have bounded so swiftly from one to another without getting hurt."

"That is all guesswork," declared the Wizard, unwinding the blankets from his body, "for none of us stayed long enough on the mountains to discover what they are made of. But where are we?"

"That's guesswork," said Scraps. "The shepherd said the Thistle-Eaters live this side of the mountains and are waited on by giants."

"Oh no," said Dorothy, "it's the Herkus who have giant slaves, and the Thistle-Eaters hitch dragons to their chariots."

"How could they do that?" asked the Woozy. "Dragons have long tails, which would get in the way of the chariot wheels."

"And if the Herkus have conquered the giants," said Trot, "they must be at least twice the size of giants. P'raps the Herkus are the biggest people in all the world!"

"Perhaps they are," assented the Wizard in a thoughtful tone of voice. "And perhaps the shepherd didn't know what he was talking about. Let us travel on toward the west and discover for ourselves what the people of this country are like."

It seemed a pleasant enough country, and it was quite still and peaceful when they turned their eyes away from the silently whirling mountains. There were trees here and there and green bushes, while throughout the thick grass were scattered brilliantly colored flowers. About a mile away was a low hill that hid from them all the country beyond it, so they realized they could not tell much about the country until they had crossed the hill. The Red Wagon having been left behind, it was now necessary to make other arrangements for traveling. The Lion told Dorothy she could ride upon his back as she had often done before, and the Woozy said he could easily carry both Trot and the Patchwork Girl. Betsy still had her mule, Hank, and Button-Bright and the Wizard could sit together upon the long, thin back of the Sawhorse, but they took care to soften their seat with a pad of blankets before they started. Thus mounted, the adventurers started for the hill, which was reached after a brief journey.

As they mounted the crest and gazed beyond the hill, they discovered not far away a walled city, from the towers and spires of which gay banners were flying. It was not a very big city, indeed, but its walls were very high and thick, and it appeared that the people who lived there must have feared attack by a powerful enemy, else they would not have surrounded their dwellings with so strong a barrier. There was no path leading from the mountains to the city, and this proved that the people seldom or never visited the whirling hills, but our friends found the grass soft and agreeable to travel over, and with the city before them they could not well lose their way. When they drew nearer to the walls, the breeze carried to their ears the sound of music—dim at first, but growing louder as they advanced.

"That doesn't seem like a very terr'ble place," remarked Dorothy.

"Well, it LOOKS all right," replied Trot from her seat on the Woozy, "but looks can't always be trusted."

"MY looks can," said Scraps. "I LOOK patchwork, and I AM patchwork, and no one but a blind owl could ever doubt that I'm the Patchwork Girl." Saying which, she turned a somersault off the Woozy and, alighting on her feet, began wildly dancing about.

"Are owls ever blind?" asked Trot.

"Always, in the daytime," said Button-Bright. "But Scraps can see with her button eyes both day and night. Isn't it queer?"

"It's queer that buttons can see at all," answered Trot. "But good gracious! What's become of the city?"

"I was going to ask that myself," said Dorothy. "It's gone!"

The animals came to a sudden halt, for the city had really disappeared, walls and all, and before them lay the clear, unbroken sweep of the country. "Dear me!" exclaimed the Wizard. "This is rather disagreeable. It is annoying to travel almost to a place and then find it is not there."

"Where can it be, then?" asked Dorothy. "It cert'nly was there a minute ago."

"I can hear the music yet," declared Button-Bright, and when they all listened, the strains of music could plainly be heard.

"Oh! There's the city over at the left," called Scraps, and turning their eyes, they saw the walls and towers and fluttering banners far to the left of them.

"We must have lost our way," suggested Dorothy.

"Nonsense," said the Lion. "I, and all the other animals, have been tramping straight toward the city ever since we first saw it."

"Then how does it happen—"

"Never mind," interrupted the Wizard, "we are no farther from it than we were before. It is in a different direction, that's all, so let us hurry and get there before it again escapes us."

So on they went directly toward the city, which seemed only a couple of miles distant. But when they had traveled less than a mile, it suddenly disappeared again. Once more they paused, somewhat discouraged, but in a moment the button eyes of Scraps again discovered the city, only this time it was just behind them in the direction from which they had come. "Goodness gracious!" cried Dorothy. "There's surely something wrong with that city. Do you s'pose it's on wheels, Wizard?"

"It may not be a city at all," he replied, looking toward it with a speculative glance.

"What COULD it be, then?"

"Just an illusion."

"What's that?" asked Trot.

"Something you think you see and don't see."

"I can't believe that," said Button-Bright. "If we only saw it, we might be mistaken, but if we can see it and hear it, too, it must be there."

"Where?" asked the Patchwork Girl.

"Somewhere near us," he insisted.

We will have to go back, I suppose," said the Woozy with a sigh.

So back they turned and headed for the walled city until it disappeared again, only to reappear at the right of them. They were constantly getting nearer to it, however, so they kept their faces turned toward it as it flitted here and there to all points of the compass. Presently the Lion, who was leading the procession, halted abruptly and cried out, "Ouch!"

"What's the matter?" asked Dorothy.

"Ouch — Ouch!" repeated the Lion, and leaped backward so suddenly that Dorothy nearly tumbled from his back. At the same time Hank the Mule yelled "Ouch!""Ouch! Ouch!" repeated the Lion and leaped backward so suddenly that Dorothy nearly tumbled from his back. At the same time, Hank the Mule yelled "Ouch!" almost as loudly as the Lion had done, and he also pranced backward a few paces.

"It's the thistles," said Betsy. "They prick their legs."

Hearing this, all looked down, and sure enough the ground was thick with thistles, which covered the plain from the point where they stood way up to the walls of the mysterious city. No pathways through them could be seen at all; here the soft grass ended and the growth of thistles began. "They're the prickliest thistles I ever felt," grumbled the Lion. "My legs smart yet from their stings, though I jumped out of them as quickly as I could."

"Here is a new difficulty," remarked the Wizard in a grieved tone. "The city has stopped hopping around, it is true, but how are we to get to it over this mass of prickers?"

"They can't hurt ME," said the thick-skinned Woozy, advancing fearlessly and trampling among the thistles.

"Nor me," said the Wooden Sawhorse.

"But the Lion and the Mule cannot stand the prickers," asserted Dorothy, "and we can't leave them behind."

"Must we all go back?" asked Trot.

"Course not!" replied Button-Bright scornfully. "Always when there's trouble, there's a way out of it if you can find it."

"I wish the Scarecrow was here," said Scraps, standing on her head on the Woozy's square back. "His splendid brains would soon show us how to conquer this field of thistles."

"What's the matter with YOUR brains?" asked the boy.

"Nothing," she said, making a flip-flop into the thistles and dancing among them without feeling their sharp points. "I could tell you in half a minute how to get over the thistles if I wanted to."

"Tell us, Scraps!" begged Dorothy.

"I don't want to wear my brains out with overwork," replied the Patchwork Girl.

"Don't you love Ozma? And don't you want to find her?" asked Betsy reproachfully.

"Yes indeed," said Scraps, walking on her hands as an acrobat does at the circus.

"Well, we can't find Ozma unless we get past these thistles," declared Dorothy.

Scraps danced around them two or three times without reply. Then she said, "Don't look at me, you stupid folks. Look at those blankets."

The Wizard's face brightened at once.

"Why didn't we think of those blankets before?"

"Because you haven't magic brains," laughed Scraps. "Such brains as you have are of the common sort that grow in your heads, like weeds in a garden. I'm sorry for you people who have to be born in order to be alive."

But the Wizard was not listening to her. He quickly removed the blankets from the back of the Sawhorse and spread one of them upon the thistles, just next the grass. The thick cloth rendered the prickers harmless, so the Wizard walked over this first blanket and spread the second one farther on, in the direction of the phantom city. "These blankets," said he, "are for the Lion and the Mule to walk upon. The Sawhorse and the Woozy can walk on the thistles."

So the Lion and the Mule walked over the first blanket and stood upon the second one until the Wizard had picked up the one they had passed over and spread it in front of them, when they advanced to that one and waited while the one behind them was again spread in front. "This is slow work," said the Wizard, "but it will get us to the city after a while."

"The city is a good half mile away yet," announced Button-Bright.

"And this is awful hard work for the Wizard," added Trot.

"Why couldn't the Lion ride on the Woozy's back?" asked Dorothy."it's a big, flat back, and the Woozy's mighty strong. Perhaps the Lion wouldn't fall off."

"You may try it if you like," said the Woozy to the Lion. "I can take you to the city in a jiffy and then come back for Hank."

"I'm—I'm afraid," said the Cowardly Lion. He was twice as big as the Woozy.

"Try it," pleaded Dorothy.

"And take a tumble among the thistles?" asked the Lion reproachfully.

But when the Woozy came close to him, the big beast suddenly bounded upon its back and managed to balance himself there, although forced to hold his four legs so close together that he was in danger of toppling over. The great weight of the monster Lion did not seem to affect the Woozy, who called to his rider, "Hold on tight!" and ran swiftly over the thistles toward the city. The others stood on the blanket and watched the strange sight anxiously. Of course, the Lion couldn't "hold on tight" because there was nothing to hold to, and he swayed from side to side as if likely to fall off any moment. Still, he managed to stick to the Woozy's back until they were close to the walls of the city, when he leaped to the ground. Next moment the Woozy came dashing back at full speed.

"There's a little strip of ground next the wall where there are no thistles," he told them when he had reached the adventurers once more. "Now then, friend Hank, see if you can ride as well as the Lion did."

"Take the others first," proposed the Mule. So the Sawhorse and the Woozy made a couple of trips over the thistles to the city walls and carried all the people in safety, Dorothy holding little Toto in her arms. The travelers then sat in a group on a little hillock just outside the wall and looked at the great blocks of gray stone and waited for the Woozy to bring Hank to them. The Mule was very awkward, and his legs trembled so badly that more than once they thought he would tumble off, but finally he reached them in safety, and the entire party was now reunited. More than that, they had reached the city that had eluded them for so long and in so strange a manner.

"The gates must be around the other side," said the Wizard. "Let us follow the curve of the wall until we reach an opening in it."

"Which way?" asked Dorothy.

"We must guess that," he replied. "Suppose we go to the left. One direction is as good as another." They formed in marching order and went around the city wall to the left. It wasn't a big city, as I have said, but to go way around it outside the high wall was quite a walk, as they became aware. But around it our adventurers went without finding any sign of a gateway or other opening. When they had returned to the little mound from which they had started, they dismounted from the animals and again seated themselves on the grassy mound.

"It's mighty queer, isn't it?" asked Button-Bright.

"There must be SOME way for the people to get out and in," declared Dorothy. "Do you s'pose they have flying machines, Wizard?"

"No," he replied, "for in that case they would be flying all over the Land of Oz, and we know they have not done that. Flying machines are unknown here. I think it more likely that the people use ladders to get over the walls."

"It would be an awful climb over that high stone wall," said Betsy.

"Stone, is it?" Scraps, who was again dancing wildly around, for she never tired and could never keep still for long.

"Course it's stone," answered Betsy scornfully. "Can't you see?"

"Yes," said Scraps, going closer. "I can SEE the wall, but I can't FEEL it." And then, with her arms outstretched, she did a very queer thing. She walked right into the wall and disappeared.

"For goodness sake!" Dorothy, amazed, as indeed they all were.

9. The High Coco-Lorum Of Thi

And now the Patchwork Girl came dancing out of the wall again. "Come on!" she called. "It isn't there. There isn't any wall at all."

"What? No wall?" exclaimed the Wizard.

"Nothing like it," said Scraps. "It's a make-believe. You see it, but it isn't. Come on into the city; we've been wasting our time." With this, she danced into the wall again and once more disappeared. Button-Bright, who was rather venture-some, dashed away after her and also became invisible to them. The others followed more cautiously, stretching out their hands to feel the wall and finding, to their astonishment, that they could feel nothing because nothing opposed them. They walked on a few steps and found themselves in the streets of a very beautiful city. Behind them they again saw the wall, grim and forbidding as ever, but now they knew it was merely an illusion prepared to keep strangers from entering the city.

But the wall was soon forgotten, for in front of them were a number of quaint people who stared at them in amazement as if wondering where they had come from. Our friends forgot their good manners for a time and returned the stares with interest, for so remarkable a people had never before been discovered in all the remarkable Land of Oz. Their heads were shaped like diamonds, and their bodies like hearts. All the hair they had was a little bunch at the tip top of their diamond-shaped heads, and their eyes were very large and round, and their noses and mouths very small. Their clothing was tight fitting and of brilliant colors, being handsomely embroidered in quaint designs with gold or silver threads; but on their feet they wore sandals with no stockings whatever. The expression of their faces was pleasant enough, although they now showed surprise at the appearance of strangers so unlike themselves, and our friends thought they seemed quite harmless.

"I beg your pardon," said the Wizard, speaking for his party, "for intruding upon you uninvited, but we are traveling on important business and find it necessary to visit your city. Will you kindly tell us by what name your city is called?"

They looked at one another uncertainly, each expecting some other to answer. Finally, a short one whose heart-shaped body was very broad replied, "We have no occasion to call our city anything. It is where we live, that is all."

"But by what name do others call your city?"asked the Wizard.

"We know of no others except yourselves," said the man. And

then he inquired, "Were you born with those queer forms you have, or has some cruel magician transformed you to them from your natural shapes?"

"These are our natural shapes," declared the Wizard, "and we consider them very good shapes, too."

The group of inhabitants was constantly being enlarged by others who joined it. All were evidently startled and uneasy at the arrival of strangers. "Have you a King?"asked Dorothy, who knew it was better to speak with someone in authority.

But the man shook his diamond-like head. "What is a King?" he asked.

"Isn't there anyone who rules over you?"inquired the Wizard.

"No," was the reply, "each of us rules himself, or at least tries to do so. It is not an easy thing to do, as you probably know."

The Wizard reflected.

"If you have disputes among you," said he after a little thought, "who settles them?"

"The High Coco-Lorum," they answered in a chorus.

"And who is he?"

"The judge who enforces the laws," said the man who had first spoken.

"Then he is the principal person here?"continued the Wizard.

"Well, I would not say that," returned the man in a puzzled way. "The High Coco-Lorum is a public servant. However, he represents the laws, which we must all obey."

"I think," said the Wizard, "we ought to see your High Coco-Lorum and talk with him. Our mission here requires us to consult one high in authority, and the High Coco-Lorum ought to be high, whatever else he is."

The inhabitants seemed to consider this proposition reasonable, for they nodded their diamond-shaped heads in approval. So the broad one who had been their spokesman said, "Follow me," and turning led the way along one of the streets. The entire party followed him, the natives falling in behind. The dwellings they passed were quite nicely planned and seemed comfortable and convenient. After leading them a few blocks, their conductor stopped before a house which was neither better nor worse than the others. The doorway was shaped to admit the strangely formed bodies of these people, being narrow at the top, broad in the middle and tapering at the bottom. The windows were made in much the same way, giving the house a most peculiar appearance. When their guide opened the gate, a music box concealed in the gatepost began to play, and the sound attracted the attention of the High Coco-Lorum, who appeared at an open window and inquired, "What has happened now?"

But in the same moment his eyes fell upon the strangers and he hastened to open the door and admit them—all but the animals, which were left outside with the throng of natives that had now gathered. For a small city there seemed to be a large number of inhabitants, but they did not try to enter the house and contented themselves with staring curiously at the strange animals. Toto followed Dorothy.

Our friends entered a large room at the front of the house, where the High Coco-Lorum asked them to be seated. "I hope your mission here is a peaceful one," he said, looking a little worried, "for the Thists are not very good fighters and object to being conquered."

"Are your people called Thists?" asked Dorothy.

"Yes. I thought you knew that. And we call our city Thi."

"Oh!"

"We are Thists because we eat thistles, you know," continued the High Coco-Lorum.

"Do you really eat those prickly things?"inquired Button-Bright wonderingly.

"Why not?" replied the other. "The sharp points of the thistles cannot hurt us, because all our insides are gold-lined."

"Gold-lined!"

"To be sure. Our throats and stomachs are lined with solid gold, and we find the thistles nourishing and good to eat. As a matter of fact, there is nothing else in our country that is fit for food. All around the City of Thi grow countless thistles, and all we need do is to go and gather them. If we wanted anything else to eat, we would have to plant it, and grow it, and harvest it, and that would be a lot of trouble and make us work, which is an occupation we detest."

"But tell me, please," said the Wizard, "how does it happen that your city jumps around so, from one part of the country to another?"

"The city doesn't jump. It doesn't move at all," declared the High Coco-Lorum. "However, I will admit that the land that surrounds it has a trick of turning this way or that, and so if one is standing upon the plain and facing north, he is likely to find himself suddenly facing west or east or south. But once you reach the thistle fields, you are on solid ground."

"Ah, I begin to understand," said the Wizard, nodding his head. "But I have another question to ask: How does it happen that the Thists have no King to rule over them?"

"Hush!"whispered the High Coco-Lorum, looking uneasily around to make sure they were not overheard. "In reality, I am the King, but the people don't know it. They think they rule themselves, but the fact is I have everything my own way. No one else knows anything about our laws, and so I make the laws to suit myself. If any oppose me or question my acts, I tell them it's the law and that settles it. If I called myself King, however, and wore a crown and lived in royal style, the people would not like me and might do me harm. As the High Coco-Lorum of Thi, I am considered a very agreeable person."

"It seems a very clever arrangement," said the Wizard. "And now, as you are the principal person in Thi, I beg you to tell us if the Royal Ozma is a captive in your city."

"No," answered the diamond-headed man. "We have no captives. No strangers but yourselves are here, and we have never before heard of the Royal Ozma."

"She rules over all of Oz," said Dorothy, "and so she rules your city and you, because you are in the Winkie Country, which is a part of the Land of Oz."

"It may be," returned the High Coco-Lorum, "for we do not study geography and have never inquired whether we live in the Land of Oz or not. And any Ruler who rules us from a distance and unknown to us is welcome to the job. But what has happened to your Royal Ozma?"

"Someone has stolen her," said the Wizard. "Do you happen to have any talented magician among your people, one who is especially clever, you know?"

"No, none especially clever. We do some magic, of course, but it is all of the ordinary kind. I do not think any of us has yet aspired to stealing Rulers, either by magic or otherwise."

"Then we've come a long way for nothing!"exclaimed Trot regretfully.

"But we are going farther than this," asserted the Patchwork Girl, bending her stuffed body backward until her yarn hair touched the floor and then walking around on her hands with her feet in the air.

The High Coco-Lorum watched Scraps admiringly.

"You may go farther on, of course," said he, "but I advise you not to. The Herkus live back of us, beyond the thistles and the twisting lands, and they are not very nice people to meet, I assure you."

"Are they giants?" asked Betsy.

"They are worse than that," was the reply. "They have giants for their slaves and they are so much stronger than giants that the poor slaves dare not rebel for fear of being torn to pieces."

"How do you know?" asked Scraps.

"Everyone says so," answered the High Coco-Lorum.

"Have you seen the Herkus yourself?"inquired Dorothy.

"No, but what everyone says must be true, otherwise what would be the use of their saying it?"

"We were told before we got here that you people hitch dragons to your chariots," said the little girl.

"So we do," declared the High Coco-Lorum. "And that reminds me that I ought to entertain you as strangers and my guests by taking you for a ride around our splendid City of Thi." He touched a button, and a band began to play. At least, they heard the music of a band, but couldn't tell where it came from. "That tune is the order to my charioteer to bring around my dragon-chariot," said the High Coco-Lorum. "Every time I give an order, it is in music, which is a much more pleasant way to address servants than in cold, stern words."

"Does this dragon of yours bite?" asked Button-Bright.

"Mercy no! Do you think I'd risk the safety of my innocent people by using a biting dragon to draw my chariot? I'm proud to say that my dragon is harmless, unless his steering gear breaks, and he was manufactured at the famous dragon factory in this City of Thi. Here he comes, and you may examine him for yourselves."

They heard a low rumble and a shrill squeaking sound, and going out to the front of the house, they saw coming around the corner a car drawn by a gorgeous jeweled dragon, which moved its head to right and left and flashed its eyes like headlights of an automobile and uttered a growling noise as it slowly moved toward them. When it stopped before the High Coco-Lorum's house, Toto barked sharply at the sprawling beast, but even tiny Trot could see that the dragon was not alive. Its scales were of gold, and each one was set with sparkling jewels, while it walked in such a stiff, regular manner that it could be nothing else than a machine. The chariot that trailed behind it was likewise of gold and jewels, and when they entered it, they found there were no seats. Everyone was supposed to stand up while riding. The charioteer was a little, diamond-headed fellow who straddled the neck of the dragon and moved the levers that made it go.

"This," said the High Coco-Lorum pompously, "is a wonderful invention. We are all very proud of our auto-dragons, many of which are in use by our wealthy inhabitants. Start the thing going, charioteer!"

The charioteer did not move.

"You forgot to order him in music," suggested Dorothy.

"Ah, so I did."

He touched a button and a music box in the dragon's head began to play a tune. At once the little charioteer pulled over a lever, and the dragon began to move, very slowly and groaning dismally as it drew the clumsy chariot after it. Toto trotted between the wheels. The Sawhorse, the Mule, the Lion and the Woozy followed after and had no trouble in keeping up with the machine. Indeed, they had to go slow to keep from running into it. When the wheels turned, another music box concealed somewhere under the chariot played a lively march tune which was in striking contrast with the dragging movement of the strange vehicle, and Button-Bright decided that the music he had heard when they first sighted this city was nothing else than a chariot plodding its weary way through the streets.

All the travelers from the Emerald City thought this ride the most uninteresting and dreary they had ever experienced, but the High Coco-Lorum seemed to think it was grand. He pointed out the different buildings and parks and fountains in much the same way that the conductor does on an American "sightseeing wagon" does, and being guests they were obliged to submit to the ordeal. But they became a little worried when their host told them he had ordered a banquet prepared for them in the City Hall. "What are we going to eat?"asked Button-Bright suspiciously.

"Thistles," was the reply. "Fine, fresh thistles, gathered this very day."

Scraps laughed, for she never ate anything, but Dorothy said in a protesting voice, "OUR insides are not lined with gold, you know."

"How sad!"exclaimed the High Coco-Lorum, and then he added as an afterthought, "but we can have the thistles boiled, if you prefer."

"I'm 'fraid they wouldn't taste good even then," said little Trot. "Haven't you anything else to eat?"

The High Coco-Lorum shook his diamond-shaped head.

"Nothing that I know of," said he. "But why should we have anything else when we have so many thistles? However, if you can't eat what we eat, don't eat anything. We shall not be offended, and the banquet will be just as merry and delightful."

Knowing his companions were all hungry, the Wizard said, "I trust you will excuse us from the banquet, sir, which will be merry enough without us, although it is given in our honor. For, as Ozma is not in your city, we must leave here at once and seek her elsewhere."

"Sure we must!" Dorothy, and she whispered to Betsy and Trot, "I'd rather starve somewhere else than in this city, and who knows, we may run across somebody who eats reg'lar food and will give us some."

So when the ride was finished, in spite of the protests of the High Coco-Lorum, they insisted on continuing their journey. "It will soon be dark," he objected.

"We don't mind the darkness," replied the Wizard.

"Some wandering Herku may get you."

"Do you think the Herkus would hurt us?"asked Dorothy.

"I cannot say, not having had the honor of their acquaintance. But they are said to be so strong that if they had any other place to stand upon they could lift the world."

"All of them together?"asked Button-Bright wonderingly.

"Any one of them could do it," said the High Coco-Lorum.

"Have you heard of any magicians being among them?" asked the Wizard, knowing that only a magician could have stolen Ozma in the way she had been stolen.

"I am told it is quite a magical country," declared the High Coco-Lorum, "and magic is usually performed by magicians. But I have never heard that they have any invention or sorcery to equal our wonderful auto-dragons."

They thanked him for his courtesy, and mounting their own animals rode to the farther side of the city and right through the Wall of Illusion out into the open country. "I'm glad we got away so easily," said Betsy. "I didn't like those queer-shaped people."

"Nor did I," agreed Dorothy. "It seems dreadful to be lined with sheets of pure gold and have nothing to eat but thistles."

"They seemed happy and contented, though," remarked the Wizard, "and those who are contented have nothing to regret and nothing more to wish for."

10. Toto Loses Something

For a while the travelers were constantly losing their direction, for beyond the thistle fields they again found themselves upon the turning-lands, which swung them around one way and then another. But by keeping the City of Thi constantly behind them, the adventurers finally passed the treacherous turning-lands and came upon a stony country where no grass grew at all. There were plenty of bushes, however, and although it was now almost dark, the girls discovered some delicious yellow berries growing upon the bushes, one taste of which set them all to picking as many as they could find. The berries relieved their pangs of hunger for a time, and as it now became too dark to see anything, they camped where they were.

The three girls lay down upon one of the blankets—all in a row—and the Wizard covered them with the other blanket and tucked them in. Button-Bright crawled under the shelter of some bushes and was asleep

The Wizard sat down with his back to a big stone and looked at the stars in the sky and thought gravely upon the dangerous adventure they had undertaken, wondering if they would ever be able to find their beloved Ozma again. The animals lay in a group by themselves, a little distance from the others. "I've lost my growl!" said Toto, who had been very silent and sober all that day. "What do you suppose has become of it?"

"If you had asked me to keep track of your growl, I might be able to tell you," remarked the Lion sleepily. "But frankly, Toto, I supposed you were taking care of it yourself."

"It's an awful thing to lose one's growl," said Toto, wagging his tail disconsolately. "What if you lost your roar, Lion? Wouldn't you feel terrible?"

"My roar,"replied the Lion, "is the fiercest thing about me. I depend on it to frighten my enemies so badly that they won't dare to fight me."

"Once," said the Mule, "I lost my bray so that I couldn't call to Betsy to let her know I was hungry. That was before I could talk you know, for I had not yet come into the Land of Oz, and I found it was certainly very uncomfortable not to be able to make a noise."

"You make enough noise now," declared Toto. "But none of you have answered my question: Where is my growl?"

"You may search ME," said the Woozy. "I don't care for such things, myself."

"You snore terribly," asserted Toto.

"It may be," said the Woozy. "What one does when asleep one is not accountable for. I wish you would wake me up sometime when I'm snoring and let me hear the sound. Then I can judge whether it is terrible or delightful."

"It isn't pleasant, I assure you," said the Lion, yawning.

"To me it seems wholly unnecessary," declared Hank the Mule.

"You ought to break yourself of the habit," said the Sawhorse. "You never hear me snore, because I never sleep. I don't even whinny as those puffy meat horses do. I wish that whoever stole Toto's growl had taken the Mule's bray and the Lion's roar and the Woozy's snore at the same time."

"Do you think, then, that my growl was stolen?"

"You have never lost it before, have you?" inquired inquired the Sawhorse.

"Only once, when I had a sore throat from barking too long at the moon."

"Is your throat sore now?" asked the Woozy.

"No," replied the dog.

"I can't understand," said Hank, "why dogs bark at the moon. They can't scare the moon, and the moon doesn't pay any attention to the bark. So why do dogs do it?"

"Were you ever a dog?" asked Toto.

"No indeed," replied Hank. "I am thankful to say I was created a mule—the most beautiful of all beasts—and have always remained one."

The Woozy sat upon his square haunches to examine Hank with care. "Beauty," he said, "must be a matter of taste. I don't say your judgment is bad, friend Hank, or that you are so vulgar as to be conceited. But if you admire big, waggy ears and a tail like a paintbrush and hoofs big enough for an elephant and a long neck and a body so skinny that one can count the ribs with one eye shut—if that's your idea of beauty, Hank, then either you or I must be much mistaken."

"You're full of edges," sneered the Mule. "If I were square as you are, I suppose you'd think me lovely."

"Outwardly, dear Hank, I would," replied the Woozy. "But to be really lovely, one must be beautiful without and within."

The Mule couldn't deny this statement, so he gave a disgusted grunt and rolled over so that his back was toward the Woozy. But the Lion, regarding the two calmly with his great, yellow eyes, said to the dog, "My dear Toto, our friends have taught us a lesson in humility. If the Woozy and the Mule are indeed beautiful creatures as they seem to think, you and I must be decidedly ugly."

"Not to ourselves," protested Toto, who was a shrewd little dog. "You and I, Lion, are fine specimens of our own races. I am a fine dog, and you are a fine lion. Only in point of comparison, one with another, can we be properly judged, so I will leave it to the poor old Sawhorse to decide which is the most beautiful animal among us all. The Sawhorse is wood, so he won't be prejudiced and will speak the truth."

"I surely will," responded the Sawhorse, wagging his ears, which were chips set in his wooden head. "Are you all agreed to accept my judgment?"

"We are!" they declared, each one hopeful.

"Then," said the Sawhorse, "I must point out to you the fact that you are all meat creatures, who tire unless they sleep and starve unless they eat and suffer from thirst unless they drink. Such animals must be very imperfect, and imperfect creatures cannot be beautiful. Now, I am made of wood."

"You surely have a wooden head," said the Mule.

"Yes, and a wooden body and wooden legs, which are as swift as the wind and as tireless. I've heard Dorothy say that 'handsome is as handsome does,' and I surely perform my duties in a handsome manner. Therefore, if you wish my honest judgment, I will confess that among us all I am the most beautiful."

The Mule snorted, and the Woozy laughed; Toto had lost his growl and could only look scornfully at the Sawhorse, who stood in his place unmoved. But the Lion stretched himself and yawned, saying quietly, "Were we all like the Sawhorse, we would all be Sawhorses, which would be too many of the kind. Were we all like Hank, we would be a herd of mules; if like Toto, we would be a pack of dogs; should we all become the shape of

the Woozy, he would no longer be remarkable for his unusual appearance. Finally, were you all like me, I would consider you so common that I would not care to associate with you. To be individual, my friends, to be different from others, is the only way to become distinguished from the common herd. Let us be glad, therefore, that we differ from one another in form and in disposition. Variety is the spice of life, and we are various enough to enjoy one another's society; so let us be content."

"There is some truth in that speech," remarked Toto reflectively. "But how about my lost growl?"

"The growl is of importance only to you," responded the Lion, "so it is your business to worry over the loss, not ours. If you love us, do not afflict your burdens on us; be unhappy all by yourself."

"If the same person stole my growl who stole Ozma," said the little dog, "I hope we shall find him very soon and punish him as he deserves. He must be the most cruel person in all the world, for to prevent a dog from growling when it is his nature to growl is just as wicked, in my opinion, as stealing all the magic in Oz."

11. Button-Bright Loses Himself

The Patchwork Girl, who never slept and who could see very well in the dark, had wandered among the rocks and bushes all night long, with the result that she was able to tell some good news the next morning. "Over the crest of the hill before us," she said, "is a big grove of trees of many kinds on which all sorts of fruits grow. If you will go there, you will find a nice breakfast awaiting you." This made them eager to start, so as soon as the blankets were folded and strapped to the back of the Sawhorse, they all took their places on the animals and set out for the big grove Scraps had told them of.

As soon as they got over the brow of the hill, they discovered it to be a really immense orchard, extending for miles to the right and left of them. As their way led straight through the trees, they hurried forward as fast as possible. The first trees they came to bore quinces, which they did not like. Then there were rows of citron trees and then crab apples and afterward limes and lemons. But beyond these they found a grove of big, golden oranges, juicy and sweet, and the fruit hung low on the branches so they could pluck it easily.

They helped themselves freely and all ate oranges as they continued on their way. Then, a little farther along, they came to some trees bearing fine, red apples, which they also feasted on, and the Wizard stopped here long enough to tie a lot of the apples in one end of a blanket.

"We do not know what will happen to us after we leave this delightful orchard," he said, "so I think it wise to carry a supply of apples with us. We can't starve as long as we have apples, you know."

Scraps wasn't riding the Woozy just now. She loved to climb the trees and swing herself by the branches from one tree to another. Some of the choicest fruit was gathered by the Patchwork Girl from the very highest limbs and tossed down to the others. Suddenly, Trot asked, "Where's Button-Bright?" and when the others looked for him, they found the boy had disappeared.

"Dear me!" cried Dorothy. "I guess he's lost again, and that will mean our waiting here until we can find him."

"It's a good place to wait," suggested Betsy, who had found a plum tree and was eating some of its fruit.

"How can you wait here and find Button-Bright at one and the same time?" inquired the Patchwork Girl, hanging by her toes on a limb just over the heads of the three mortal girls.

"Perhaps he'll come back here," answered Dorothy.

"If he tries that, he'll prob'ly lose his way," said Trot. "I've known him to do that lots of times. It's losing his way that gets him lost."

"Very true," said the Wizard. "So all the rest of you must stay here while I go look for the boy."

"Won't YOU get lost, too?" asked Betsy.

"I hope not, my dear."

"Let ME go," said Scraps, dropping lightly to the ground. "I can't get lost, and I'm more likely to find Button-Bright than any of you." Without waiting for permission, she darted away through the trees and soon disappeared from their view.

"Dorothy," said Toto, squatting beside his little mistress, "I've lost my growl."

"How did that happen?" she asked.

"I don't know," replied Toto. "Yesterday morning the Woozy nearly stepped on me, and I tried to growl at him and found I couldn't growl a bit."

"Can you bark?" inquired Dorothy.

"Oh, yes indeed."

"Then never mind the growl," said she.

"But what will I do when I get home to the Glass Cat and the Pink Kitten?" asked the little dog in an anxious tone.

"They won't mind if you can't growl at them, I'm sure," said Dorothy. "I'm sorry for you, of course, Toto, for it's just those things we can't do that we want to do most of all; but before we get back, you may find your growl again."

"Do you think the person who stole Ozma stole my growl?"

Dorothy smiled.

"Perhaps, Toto."

"Then he's a scoundrel!" cried the little dog.

"Anyone who would steal Ozma is as bad as bad can be," agreed Dorothy, "and when we remember that our dear friend, the lovely Ruler of Oz, is lost, we ought not to worry over just a growl."

Toto was not entirely satisfied with this remark, for the more he thought upon his lost growl, the more important his misfortune became. When no one was looking, he went away among the trees and tried his best to growl—even a little bit—but could not manage to do so. All he could do was bark, and a bark cannot take the place of a growl, so he sadly returned to the others.

Now Button-Bright had no idea that he was lost at first. He had merely wandered from tree to tree seeking the finest fruit until he discovered he was alone in the great orchard. But that didn't worry him just then, and seeing some apricot trees farther on, he went to them. Then he discovered some cherry trees; just beyond these were some tangerines. "We've found 'most ev'ry kind of fruit but peaches," he said to himself, "so I guess there are peaches here, too, if I can find the trees."

He searched here and there, paying no attention to his way, until he found that the trees surrounding him bore only nuts. He put some walnuts in his pockets and kept on searching, and at last— right among the nut trees—he came upon one solitary peach tree. It was a graceful, beautiful tree, but although it was thickly leaved, it bore no fruit except one large, splendid peach, rosy-cheeked and fuzzy and just right to eat.

In his heart he doubted this statement, for this was a solitary peach tree, while all the other fruits grew upon many trees set close to one another; but that one luscious bite made him unable to resist eating the rest of it, and soon the peach was all gone except the pit. Button-Bright was about to throw this peach pit away when he noticed that it was of pure gold. Of course, this surprised him, but so many things in the Land of Oz were surprising that he did not give much thought to the golden peach pit. He put it in his pocket, however, to show to the girls, and five minutes afterward had forgotten all about it.

For now he realized that he was far separated from his companions, and knowing that this would worry them and delay their journey, he began to shout as loud as he could. His voice did not penetrate very far among all those trees, and after shouting a dozen times and getting no answer, he sat down on the ground and said, "Well, I'm lost again. It's too bad, but I don't see how it can be helped."

As he leaned his back against a tree, he looked up and saw a Bluefinch fly down from the sky and alight upon a branch just before him. The bird looked and looked at him. First it looked with one bright eye and then turned its head and looked at him with the other eye. Then, fluttering its wings a little, it said, "Oho! So you've eaten the enchanted peach, have you?"

"Was it enchanted?" asked Button-Bright.

"Of course," replied the Bluefinch."Ugu the Shoemaker did that."

"But why? And how was it enchanted? And what will happen to one who eats it?" questioned the boy.

"Ask Ugu the Shoemaker. He knows," said the bird, preening its feathers with its bill.

"And who is Ugu the Shoemaker?"

"The one who enchanted the peach and placed it here—in the exact center of the Great Orchard—so no one would ever find it. We birds didn't dare to eat it; we are too wise for that. But you are Button-Bright from the Emerald City, and you, YOU, YOU ate the enchanted peach! You must explain to Ugu the Shoemaker why you did that."

And then, before the boy could ask any more questions, the bird flew away and left him alone.

Button-Bright was not much worried to find that the peach he had eaten was enchanted. It certainly had tasted very good, and his stomach didn't ache a bit. So again he began to reflect upon the best way to rejoin his friends. "Whichever direction I follow is likely to be the wrong one," he said to himself, "so I'd better stay just where I am and let THEM find ME—if they can."

A White Rabbit came hopping through the orchard and paused a little way off to look at him. "Don't be afraid," said Button-Bright. "I won't hurt you."

"Oh, I'm not afraid for myself," returned the White Rabbit. "It's you I'm worried about."

"Yes, I'm lost,' said the boy.

"I fear you are, indeed," answered the Rabbit. "Why on earth did you eat the enchanted peach?"

The boy looked at the excited little animal thoughtfully. "There were two reasons," he explained. "One reason was that I like peaches, and the other reason was that I didn't know it was enchanted."

"That won't save you from Ugu the Shoemaker," declared the White Rabbit, and it scurried away before the boy could ask any more questions.

"Rabbits and birds," he thought, "are timid creatures and seem afraid of this shoemaker, whoever he may be. If there was another peach half as good as that other, I'd eat it in spite of a dozen enchantments or a hundred shoemakers!"

Just then, Scraps came dancing along and saw him sitting at the foot of the tree. "Oh, here you are!" she said. "Up to your old tricks, eh? Don't you know it's impolite to get lost and keep everybody waiting for you? Come along, and I'll lead you back to Dorothy and the others."

Button-Bright rose slowly to accompany her.

"That wasn't much of a loss," he said cheerfully. "I haven't been gone half a day, so there's no harm done."

Dorothy, however, when the boy rejoined the party, gave him a good scolding. "When we're doing such an important thing as searching for Ozma," said she, "it's naughty for you to wander away and keep us from getting on. S'pose she's a pris'ner in a dungeon cell! Do you want to keep our dear Ozma there any longer than we can help?"

"If she's in a dungeon cell, how are you going to get her out?" inquired the boy.

"Never you mind. We'll leave that to the Wizard. He's sure to find a way."

The Wizard said nothing, for he realized that without his magic tools he could do no more than any other person. But there was no use reminding his companions of that fact; it might discourage them. "The important thing just now," he remarked, "is to find Ozma, and as our party is again happily reunited, I propose we move on."

As they came to the edge of the Great Orchard, the sun was setting and they knew it would soon be dark. So it was decided to camp under the trees, as another broad plain was before them. The Wizard spread the blankets on a bed of soft leaves, and presently all of them except Scraps and the Sawhorse were fast asleep. Toto snuggled close to his friend the Lion, and the Woozy snored so loudly that the Patchwork Girl covered his square head with her apron to deaden the sound.

12. Czarover of Herku

Trot wakened just as the sun rose, and slipping out of the blankets, went to the edge of the Great Orchard and looked across the plain. Something glittered in the far distance. "That looks like another city," she said half aloud.

"And another city it is," declared Scraps, who had crept to Trot's side unheard, for her stuffed feet made no sound. "The Sawhorse and I made a journey in the dark while you were all asleep, and we found over there a bigger city than Thi. There's a wall around it, too, but it has gates and plenty of pathways."

"Did you get in?" asked Trot.

"No, for the gates were locked and the wall was a real wall. So we came back here again. It isn't far to the city. We can reach it in two hours after you've had your breakfasts."

Trot went back, and finding the other girls now awake, told them what Scraps had said. So they hurriedly ate some fruit—there were plenty of plums and fijoas in this part of the orchard—and then they mounted the animals and set out upon the journey to the strange city. Hank the Mule had breakfasted on grass, and the Lion had stolen away and found a breakfast to his liking; he never told what it was, but Dorothy hoped the little rabbits and the field mice had kept out of his way. She warned Toto not to chase birds and gave the dog some apple, with which he was quite content. The Woozy was as fond of fruit as of any other food except honey, and the Sawhorse never ate at all.

Except for their worry over Ozma, they were all in good spirits as they proceeded swiftly over the plain. Toto still worried over his lost growl, but like a wise little dog kept his worry to himself. Before long, the city grew nearer and they could examine it with interest.

In outward appearance the place was more imposing than Thi, and it was a square city, with a square, four-sided wall around it, and on each side was a square gate of burnished copper. Everything about the city looked solid and substantial; there were no banners flying, and the towers that rose above the city wall seemed bare of any ornament whatever.

A path led from the fruit orchard directly to one of the city gates, showing that the inhabitants preferred fruit to thistles. Our friends followed this path to the gate, which they found fast shut. But the Wizard advanced and pounded upon it with his fist, saying in a loud voice, "Open!"

At once there rose above the great wall a row of immense heads, all of which looked down at them as if to see who was intruding. The size of these heads was astonishing, and our friends at once realized that they belonged to giants who were standing within the city. All had thick, bushy hair and whiskers, on some the hair being white and on others black or red or yellow, while the hair of a few was just turning gray, showing that the giants were of all ages. However fierce the heads might seem, the eyes were mild in expression, as if the creatures had been long subdued, and their faces expressed patience rather than ferocity.

"What's wanted?" asked one old giant in a low, grumbling voice.

"We are strangers, and we wish to enter the city," replied the Wizard.

"Do you come in war or peace?" asked another.

"In peace, of course," retorted the Wizard, and he added impatiently, "Do we look like an army of conquest?"

"No," said the first giant who had spoken, "you look like innocent tramps; but you never can tell by appearances. Wait here until we report to our masters. No one can enter here without the permission of Vig, the Czarover."

"Who's that?" inquired Dorothy.

But the heads had all bobbed down and disappeared behind the walls, so there was no answer. They waited a long time before the gate rolled back with a rumbling sound, and a loud voice cried, "Enter!" But they lost no time in taking advantage of the invitation.

On either side of the broad street that led into the city from the gate stood a row of huge giants, twenty of them on a side and all standing so close together that their elbows touched. They wore uniforms of blue and yellow and were armed with clubs as big around as treetrunks. Each giant had around his neck a broad band of gold, riveted on, to show he was a slave.

As our friends entered riding upon the Lion, the Woozy, the Sawhorse and the Mule, the giants half turned and walked in two files on either side of them, as if escorting them on their way. It looked to Dorothy as if all her party had been made prisoners, for even mounted on their animals their heads scarcely reached to the knees of the marching giants. The girls and Button-Bright were anxious to know what sort of a city they had entered, and what the people were like who had made these powerful creatures their slaves. Through the legs of the giants as they walked, Dorothy could see rows of houses on each side of the street and throngs of people standing on the sidewalks, but the people were of ordinary size and the only remarkable thing about them was the fact that they were dreadfully lean and thin. Between their skin and their bones there seemed to be little or no flesh, and they were mostly stoop-shouldered and weary looking, even to the little children.

More and more, Dorothy wondered how and why the great giants had ever submitted to become slaves of such skinny, languid masters, but there was no chance to question anyone until they arrived at a big palace located in the heart of the city. Here the giants formed lines to the entrance and stood still while our friends rode into the courtyard of the palace. Then the gates closed behind them, and before them was a skinny little man who bowed low and said in a sad voice, "If you will be so obliging as to dismount, it will give me pleasure to lead you into the presence of the World's Most Mighty Ruler, Vig the Czarover."

"I don't believe it!" said Dorothy indignantly.

"What don't you believe?" asked the man.

"I don't believe your Czarover can hold a candle to our Ozma."

"He wouldn't hold a candle under any circumstances, or to any living person," replied the man very seriously, "for he has slaves to do such things and the Mighty Vig is too dignified to do anything that others can do for him. He even obliges a slave to sneeze for him, if ever he catches cold. However, if you dare to face our powerful ruler, follow me."

"We dare anything," said the Wizard, "so go ahead."

Through several marble corridors having lofty ceilings they passed, finding each corridor and doorway guarded by servants.

But these servants of the palace were of the people and not giants, and they were so thin that they almost resembled skeletons. Finally, they entered a great circular room with a high domed ceiling, where the Czarover sat on a throne cut from a solid block of white marble and decorated with purple silk hangings and gold tassels.

The ruler of these people was combing his eyebrows when our friends entered the throne room and stood before him, but he put the comb in his pocket and examined the strangers with evident curiosity. Then he said, "Dear me, what a surprise! You have really shocked me. For no outsider has ever before come to our City of Herku, and I cannot imagine why you have ventured to do so."

"We are looking for Ozma, the Supreme Ruler of the Land of Oz," replied the Wizard.

"Do you see her anywhere around here?" asked the Czarover.

"Not yet, Your Majesty, but perhaps you may tell us where she is."

"No, I have my hands full keeping track of my own people. I find them hard to manage because they are so tremendously strong."

"They don't look very strong," said Dorothy. "It seems as if a good wind would blow 'em way out of the city if it wasn't for the wall."

"Just so, just so," admitted the Czarover. "They really look that way, don't they? But you must never trust to appearances, which have a way of fooling one. Perhaps you noticed that I prevented you from meeting any of my people. I protected you with my giants while you were on the way from the gates to my palace so that not a Herku got near you."

"Are your people so dangerous, then?" asked the Wizard.

"To strangers, yes. But only because they are so friendly. For if they shake hands with you, they are likely to break your arms or crush your fingers to a jelly."

"Why?" asked Button-Bright.

"Because we are the strongest people in all the world."

"Pshaw!" exclaimed the boy. "That's bragging. You prob'ly don't know how strong other people are. Why, once I knew a man in Philadelphi' who could bend iron bars with just his hands!"

"But mercy me, it's no trick to bend iron bars," said His Majesty. "Tell me, could this man crush a block of stone with his bare hands?"

"No one could do that," declared the boy.

"If I had a block of stone, I'd show you," said the Czarover, looking around the room. "Ah, here is my throne. The back is too high, anyhow, so I'll just break off a piece of that." He rose to his feet and tottered in an uncertain way around the throne. Then he took hold of the back and broke off a piece of marble over a foot thick. "This," said he, coming back to his seat, "is very solid marble and much harder than ordinary stone. Yet I can crumble it easily with my fingers, a proof that I am very strong."

Even as he spoke, he began breaking off chunks of marble and crumbling them as one would a bit of earth. The Wizard was so astonished that he took a piece in his own hands and tested it, finding it very hard indeed.

Just then one of the giant servants entered and exclaimed, "Oh, Your Majesty, the cook has burned the soup! What shall we do?"

"How dare you interrupt me?", asked the Czarover, and grasping the immense giant by one of his legs, he raised him in the air and threw him headfirst out of an open window. "Now, tell me," he said, turning to Button-Bright, "could your man in Philadelphia crumble marble in his fingers?"

"I guess not," said Button-Bright, much impressed by the skinny monarch's strength.

"What makes you so strong?" inquired Dorothy.

"It's the zosozo," he explained, "which is an invention of my own. I and all my people eat zosozo, and it gives us tremendous strength. Would you like to eat some?"

"No thank you," replied the girl. "I—I don't want to get so thin."

"Well, of course one can't have strength and flesh at the same time," said the Czarover. "Zosozo is pure energy, and it's the only compound of its sort in existence. I never allow our giants to have it, you know, or they would soon become our masters, since they are bigger that we; so I keep all the stuff locked up in my private laboratory. Once a year I feed a teaspoonful of it to each of my people—men, women and children—so every one of them is nearly as strong as I am. Wouldn't YOU like a dose, sir?" he asked, turning to the Wizard.

"Well," said the Wizard, "if you would give me a little zosozo in a bottle, I'd like to take it with me on my travels. It might come in handy on occasion."

"To be sure. I'll give you enough for six doses," promised the Czarover. "But don't take more than a teaspoonful at a time. Once Ugu the Shoemaker took two teaspoonsful, and it made him so strong that when he leaned against the city wall, he pushed it over, and we had to build it up again."

"Who is Ugu the Shoemaker?"

Button-Bright curiously, for he now remembered that the bird and the rabbit had claimed Ugu the Shoemaker had enchanted the peach he had eaten.

"Why, Ugu is a great magician who used to live here. But he's gone away now," replied the Czarover.

"Where has he gone?" asked the Wizard quickly.

"I am told he lives in a wickerwork castle in the mountains to the west of here. You see, Ugu became such a powerful magician that he didn't care to live in our city any longer for fear we would discover some of his secrets. So he went to the mountains and built him a splendid wicker castle which is so strong that even I and my people could not batter it down, and there he lives all by himself."

"This is good news," declared the Wizard, "for I think this is just the magician we are searching for. But why is he called Ugu the Shoemaker?"

"Once he was a very common citizen here and made shoes for a living," replied the monarch of Herku. "But he was descended from the greatest wizard and sorcerer who ever lived in this or in any other country, and one day Ugu the Shoemaker discovered all the magical books and recipes of his famous great-grandfather, which had been hidden away in the attic of his house. So he began to study the papers and books and to practice magic, and in time he became so skillful that, as I said, he scorned our city and built a solitary castle for himself."

"Do you think" asked Dorothy anxiously, "that Ugu the Shoemaker would be wicked enough to steal our Ozma of Oz?"

"And the Magic Picture?" asked Trot.

"And the Great Book of Records of Glinda the Good?" asked Betsy.

"And my own magic tools?" asked the Wizard.

"Well," replied the Czarover, "I won't say that Ugu is wicked, exactly, but he is very ambitious to become the most powerful magician in the world, and so I suppose he would not be too proud to steal any magic things that belonged to anybody else—if he could manage to do so."

"But how about Ozma? Why would he wish to steal HER?"questioned Dorothy.

"Don't ask me, my dear. Ugu doesn't tell me why he does things, I assure you."

Then we must go and ask him ourselves," declared the little girl.

"I wouldn't do that if I were you," advised the Czarover, looking first at the three girls and then at the boy and the little Wizard and finally at the stuffed Patchwork Girl. "If Ugu has really stolen your Ozma, he will probably keep her a prisoner, in spite of all your threats or entreaties. And with all his magical knowledge he would be a dangerous person to attack. Therefore, if you are wise, you will go home again and find a new Ruler for the Emerald City and the Land of Oz. But perhaps it isn't Ugu the Shoemaker who has stolen your Ozma."

"The only way to settle that question," replied the Wizard, "is to go to Ugu's castle and see if Ozma is there. If she is, we will report the matter to the great Sorceress Glinda the Good, and I'm pretty sure she will find a way to rescue our darling ruler from the Shoemaker."

"Well, do as you please," said the Czarover, "but if you are all transformed into hummingbirds or caterpillars, don't blame me for not warning you."

They stayed the rest of that day in the City of Herku and were fed at the royal table of the Czarover and given sleeping rooms in his palace. The strong monarch treated them very nicely and gave the Wizard a little golden vial of zosozo to use if ever he or any of his

Even at the last, the Czarover tried to persuade them not to go near Ugu the Shoemaker, but they were resolved on the venture, and the next morning bade the friendly monarch a cordial goodbye and, mounting upon their animals, left the Herkus and the City of Herku and headed for the mountains that lay to the west.

13. Truth Pond

It seems a long time since we have heard anything of the

Frogman and Cayke the Cookie Cook, who had left the Yip Country in search of the diamond-studded dishpan which had been mysteriously stolen the same night that Ozma had disappeared from the Emerald City. But you must remember that while the Frogman and the Cookie Cook were preparing to descend from their mountaintop, and even while on their way to the farmhouse of Wiljon the Winkie, Dorothy and the Wizard and their friends were encountering the adventures we have just related.

So it was that on the very morning when the travelers from the Emerald City bade farewell to the Czarover of the City of Herku, Cayke and the Frogman awoke in a grove in which they had passed the night sleeping on beds of leaves. There were plenty of farmhouses in the neighborhood, but no one seemed to welcome the puffy, haughty Frogman or the little dried-up Cookie Cook, and so they slept comfortably enough underneath the trees of the grove. The Frogman wakened first on this morning, and after going to the tree where Cayke slept and finding her still wrapped in slumber, he decided to take a little walk and seek some breakfast. Coming to the edge of the grove, he observed half a mile away a pretty yellow house that was surrounded by a yellow picket fence, so he walked toward this house and on entering the yard found a Winkie woman picking up sticks with which to build a fire to cook her morning meal.

"For goodness sake!" she exclaimed on seeing the Frogman. "What are you doing out of your frog-pond?"

"I am traveling in search of a jeweled gold dishpan, my good woman," he replied with an air of great dignity.

"You won't find it here, then," said she."Our dishpans are tin, and they're good enough for anybody. So go back to your pond and leave me alone." She spoke rather crossly and with a lack of respect that greatly annoyed the Frogman.

"Allow me to tell you, madam," said he, "that although I am a frog, I am the Greatest and Wisest Frog in all the world. I may add that I possess much more wisdom than any Winkie—man or woman—in this land. Wherever I go, people fall on their knees before me and render homage to the Great Frogman! No one else knows so much as I; no one else is so grand, so magnificent!"

"If you know so much," she retorted, "why don't you know where your dishpan is instead of chasing around the country after it?"

"Presently," he answered, "I am going where it is, but just now I am traveling and have had no breakfast. Therefore I honor you by asking you for something to eat."

"Oho! The Great Frogman is hungry as any tramp, is he? Then pick up these sticks and help me to build the fire," said the woman contemptuously.

"Me! The Great Frogman pick up sticks?" he exclaimed in horror. "In the Yip Country where I am more honored and powerful than any King could be, people weep with joy when I ask them to feed me."

"Then that's the place to go for your breakfast," declared the woman.

"I fear you do not realize my importance," urged the Frogman. "Exceeding wisdom renders me superior to menial duties."

"It's a great wonder to me," remarked the woman, carrying her sticks to the house, "that your wisdom doesn't inform you that you'll get no breakfast here." And she went in and slammed the door behind her.

The Frogman felt he had been insulted, so he gave a loud croak of indignation and turned away. After going a short distance, he came upon a faint path which led across a meadow in the direction of a grove of pretty trees, and thinking this circle of evergreens must surround a house where perhaps he would be kindly received, he decided to follow the path. And by and by he came to the trees, which were set close together, and pushing aside some branches he found no house inside the circle, but instead a very beautiful pond of clear water.

Now the Frogman, although he was so big and well educated and now aped the ways and customs of human beings, was still a frog. As he gazed at this solitary, deserted pond, his love for water returned to him with irresistible force. "If I cannot get a breakfast, I may at least have a fine swim," said he, and pushing his way between the trees, he reached the bank. There he took off his fine clothing, laying his shiny purple hat and his gold-headed cane beside it. A moment later, he sprang with one leap into the water and dived to the very bottom of the pond.

The water was deliciously cool and grateful to his thick, rough skin, and the Frogman swam around the pond several times before he stopped to rest. Then he floated upon the surface and examined the pond with The bottom and sides were all lined with glossy tiles of a light pink color; just one place in the bottom where the water bubbled up from a hidden spring had been left free. On the banks, the green grass grew to the edge of the pink tiling. And now, as the Frogman examined the place, he found that on one side of the pool, just above the water line, had been set a golden plate on which some words were deeply engraved. He swam toward this plate, and on reaching it read the following inscription:

> This is
> THE TRUTH POND
> Whoever bathes in this
> water must always afterward tell
> THE TRUTH

This statement startled the Frogman. It even worried him, so that he leaped upon the bank and hurriedly began to dress himself. "A great misfortune has befallen me," he told himself, "for hereafter I cannot tell people I am wise, since it is not the truth. The truth is that my boasted wisdom is all a sham, assumed by me to deceive people and make them defer to me. In truth, no living creature can know much more than his fellows, for one may know one thing, and another know another thing, so that wisdom is evenly scattered throughout the world. But—ah me!—what a terrible fate will now be mine. Even Cayke the Cookie Cook will soon discover that my knowledge is no greater than her own, for having bathed in the enchanted water of the Truth Pond, I can no longer deceive her or tell a lie."

More humbled than he had been for many years, the Frogman went back to the grove where he had left Cayke and found the woman now awake and washing her face in a tiny brook. "Where has Your Honor been?" she asked.

"To a farmhouse to ask for something to eat," said he, "but the woman refused me."

"How dreadful!" she exclaimed. "But never mind, there are other houses where the people will be glad to feed the Wisest Creature in all the World."

"Do you mean yourself?" he asked.

"No, I mean you."

The Frogman felt strongly impelled to tell the truth, but struggled hard against it. His reason told him there was no use in letting Cayke know he was not wise, for then she would lose much respect for him, but each time he opened his mouth to speak, he realized he was about to tell the truth and shut it again as quickly as possible. He tried to talk about something else, but the words necessary to undeceive the woman would force themselves to his lips in spite of all his struggles. Finally, knowing that he must either remain dumb or let the truth prevail, he gave a low groan of despair and said, "Cayke, I am NOT the Wisest Creature in all the World; I am not wise at all."

"Oh, you must be!" she protested. "You told me so yourself, only last evening."

"Then last evening I failed to tell you the truth," he admitted, looking very shamefaced for a frog. "I am sorry I told you this lie, my good Cayke, but if you must know the truth, the whole truth and nothing but the truth, I am not really as wise as you are."

The Cookie Cook was greatly shocked to hear this, for it shattered one of her most pleasing illusions. She looked at the gorgeously dressed Frogman in amazement. "What has caused you to change your mind so suddenly?" she inquired.

"I have bathed in the Truth Pond," he said, "and whoever bathes in that water is ever afterward obliged to tell the truth."

"You were foolish to do that," declared the woman. "It is often very embarrassing to tell the truth. I'm glad I didn't bathe in that dreadful water!"

The Frogman looked at his companion thoughtfully. "Cayke," said he, "I want you to go to the Truth Pond and take a bath in its water. For if we are to travel together and encounter unknown adventures, it would not be fair that I alone must always tell you the truth, while you could tell me whatever you pleased. If we both dip in the enchanted water, there will be no chance in the future of our deceiving one another."

"No," she asserted, shaking her head positively, "I won't do it, Your Honor. For if I told you the truth, I'm sure you wouldn't like me. No Truth Pond for me. I'll be just as I am, an honest woman who can say what she wants to without hurting anyone's feelings."

With this decision the Frogman was forced to be content, although he was sorry the Cookie Cook would not listen to his advice.

4. The Unhappy Ferryman

Leaving the grove where they had slept, the Frogman and the Cookie Cook turned to the east to seek another house, and after a short walk came to one where the people received them very politely. The children stared rather hard at the big, pompous Frogman, but the woman of the house, when Cayke asked for something to eat, at once brought them food and said they were welcome to it. "Few people in need of help pass this way," she remarked, "for the Winkies are all prosperous and love to stay in their own homes. But perhaps you are not a Winkie," she added.

"No," said Cayke, "I am a Yip, and my home is on a high mountain at the southeast of your country."

"And the Frogman, is he also a Yip?"

"I do not know what he is, other than a very remarkable and highly educated creature," replied the Cookie Cook. "But he has lived many years among the Yips, who have found him so wise and intelligent that they always go to him for advice."

"May I ask why you have left your home and where you are going?" said the Winkie woman.

Then Cayke told her of the diamond-studded gold dishpan and how it had been mysteriously stolen from her house, after which she had discovered that she could no longer cook good cookies. So she had resolved to search until she found her dishpan again, because a Cookie cook who cannot cook good cookies is not of much use. The Frogman, who had wanted to see more of the world, had accompanied her to assist in the search. When the woman had listened to this story, she asked, "Then you have no idea as yet who has stolen your dishpan?"

"I only know it must have been some mischievous fairy, or a magician, or some such powerful person, because none other could have climbed the steep mountain to the Yip Country. And who else could have carried away my beautiful magic dishpan without being seen?"

The woman thought about this during the time that Cayke and the Frogman ate their breakfast. When they had finished, she said, "Where are you going next?"

"We have not decided," answered the Cookie cook.

"Our plan," explained the Frogman in his important way, "is to travel from place to place until we learn where the thief is located and then to force him to return the dishpan to its proper owner."

"The plan is all right," agreed the woman, "but it may take you a long time before you succeed, your method being sort of haphazard and indefinite. However, I advise you to travel toward the east."

"Why?" asked the Frogman.

"Because if you went west, you would soon come to the desert, and also because in this part of the Winkie Country no one steals, so your time here would be wasted. But toward the east, beyond the river, live many strange people whose honesty I would not vouch for. Moreover, if you journey far enough east and cross the river for a second time, you will come to the Emerald City, where there is much magic and sorcery. The Emerald City is ruled by a dear little girl called Ozma, who also rules the Emperor of the Winkies and all the Land of Oz. So, as Ozma is a fairy, she may be able to tell you just who has taken your precious dishpan. Provided, of course, you do not find it before you reach her."

"This seems to be to be excellent advice," said the Frogman, and Cayke agreed with him.

"The most sensible thing for you to do," continued the woman, "would be to return to your home and use another dishpan, learn to cook cookies as other people cook cookies, without the aid of magic. But if you cannot be happy without the magic dishpan you have lost, you are likely to learn more about it in the Emerald City than at any other place in Oz."

They thanked the good woman, and on leaving her house faced the east and continued in that direction all the way. Toward evening they came to the west branch of the Winkie River and there, on the riverbank, found a ferryman who lived all alone in a little yellow house. This ferryman was a Winkie with a very small head and a very large body. He was sitting in his doorway as the travelers approached him and did not even turn his head to look at them.

"Good evening," said the Frogman.

The ferryman made no reply.

"We would like some supper and the privilege of sleeping in your house until morning," continued the Frogman. "At daybreak, we would like some breakfast, and then we would like to have you row us across the river."

The ferryman neither moved nor spoke. He sat in his doorway and looked straight ahead. "I think he must be deaf and dumb," Cayke whispered to her companion. Then she stood directly in front of the ferryman, and putting her mouth close to his ear, she yelled as loudly as she could, "Good evening!"

The ferryman scowled.

"Why do you yell at me, woman?" he asked.

"Can you hear what I say?" asked in her ordinary tone of voice.

"Of course," replied the man.

"Then why didn't you answer the Frogman?"

"Because," said the ferryman, "I don't understand the frog language."

"He speaks the same words that I do and in the same way," declared Cayke.

"Perhaps," replied the ferryman, "but to me his voice sounded like a frog's croak. I know that in the Land of Oz animals can speak our language, and so can the birds and bugs and fishes; but in MY ears, they sound merely like growls and chirps and croaks."

"Why is that?" asked the Cookie Cook in surprise.

"Once, many years ago, I cut the tail off a fox which had taunted me, and I stole some birds' eggs from a nest to make an omelet with, and also I pulled a fish from the river and left it lying on the bank to gasp for lack of water until it died. I don't know why I did those wicked things, but I did them. So the Emperor of the Winkies—who is the Tin Woodman and has a very tender tin heart—punished me by denying me any communication with beasts, birds or fishes. I cannot understand them when they speak to me, although I know that other people can do so, nor can the creatures understand a word I say to them. Every time I meet one of them, I am reminded of my former cruelty, and it makes me very unhappy."

"Really," said Cayke, "I'm sorry for you, although the Tin Woodman is not to blame for punishing you."

"What is he mumbling about?" asked the Frogman.

"He is talking to me, but you don't understand him," she replied. And then she told him of the ferryman's punishment and afterward explained to the ferryman that they wanted to stay all night with him and be fed. He gave them some fruit and bread, which was the only sort of food he had, and he allowed Cayke to sleep in a room of his cottage. But the Frogman he refused to admit to his house, saying that the frog's presence made him miserable and unhappy. At no time would he look directly at the Frogman, or even toward him, fearing he would shed tears if he did so; so the big frog slept on the river bank where he could hear little frogs croaking in the river all the night through. But that did not keep him awake; it merely soothed him to slumber, for he realized how much superior he was to them.

Just as the sun was rising on a new day, the ferryman rowed the two travelers across the river—keeping his back to the Frogman all the way—and then Cayke thanked him and bade him goodbye and the ferryman rowed home again.

On this side of the river, there were no paths at all, so it was evident they had reached a part of the country little frequented by travelers. There was a marsh at the south of them, sandhills at the north, and a growth of scrubby underbrush leading toward a forest at the east. So the east was really the least difficult way to go, and that direction was the one they had determined to follow.

Now the Frogman, although he wore green patent-leather shoes with ruby buttons, had very large and flat feet, and when he tramped through the scrub, his weight crushed down the underbrush and made a path for Cayke to follow him. Therefore they soon reached the forest, where the tall trees were set far apart but were so leafy that they shaded all the spaces between them with their branches. "There are no bushes here," said Cayke, much pleased, "so we can now travel faster and with more comfort."

15. The Big Lavender Bear

It was a pleasant place to wander, and the two travelers were proceeding at a brisk pace when suddenly a voice shouted, "Halt!"

They looked around in surprise, seeing at first no one at all. Then from behind a tree there stepped a brown, fuzzy bear whose head came about as high as Cayke's waist—and Cayke was a small woman. The bear was chubby as well as fuzzy; his body was even puffy, while his legs and arms seemed jointed at the knees and elbows and fastened to his body by pins or rivets. His ears were round in shape and stuck out in a comical way, while his round black eyes were bright and sparkling as beads. Over his shoulder the little brown bear bore a gun with a tin barrel. The barrel had a cork in the end of it, and a string was attached to the cork and to the handle of the gun. Both the Frogman and Cayke gazed hard at this curious gun, standing silent for some time. But finally the Frogman recovered from his surprise and remarked, "It seems to me that you are stuffed with sawdust and ought not to be alive."

"That's all you know about it," answered the little Brown Bear in a squeaky voice. "I am stuffed with a very good quality of curled hair, and my skin is the best plush that was ever made. As for my being alive, that is my own affair and cannot concern you at all except that it gives me the privilege to say you are my prisoners."

"Prisoners! Why do you speak such nonsense?" the Frogman angrily. "Do you think we are afraid of a toy bear with a toy gun?"

"You ought to be," was the confident reply, "for I am merely the sentry guarding the way to Bear Center, which is a cit containing hundreds of my race, who are ruled by a very powerful sorcerer known as the Lavender Bear. He ought to be a purple color, you know, seeing he is a King, but he's only light lavender, which is, of course, second cousin to royal purple. So unless you come with me peaceably as my prisoners, I shall fire my gun and bring a hundred bears of all sizes and colors to capture you."

"Why do you wish to capture us?" inquired the Frogman, who had listened to his speech with much astonishment.

"I don't wish to, as a matter of fact," replied the little Brown Bear, "but it is my duty to, because you are now trespassing on the domain of His Majesty, the King of Bear Center. Also, I will admit that things are rather quiet in our city just now, and the excitement of your capture, followed by your trial and execution, should afford us much entertainment."

"We defy you!" said the Frogman.

"Oh no, don't do that," pleaded Cayke, speaking to her companion. "He says his King is a sorcerer, so perhaps it is he or one of his bears who ventured to steal my jeweled dishpan. Let us go to the City of the Bears and discover if my dishpan is there."

"I must now register one more charge against you," remarked the little Brown Bear with evident satisfaction. "You have just accused us of stealing, and that is such a dreadful thing to say that I am quite sure our noble King will command you to be executed."

"But how could you execute us?" inquired the Cookie Cook.

"I've no idea. But our King is a wonderful inventor, and there is no doubt he can find a proper way to destroy you. So tell me, are you going to struggle, or will you go peaceably to meet your doom?"

It was all so ridiculous that Cayke laughed aloud, and even the Frogman's wide mouth curled in a smile. Neither was a bit afraid to go to the Bear City, and it seemed to both that there was a possibility they might discover the missing dishpan. So the Frogman said, "Lead the way, little Bear, and we will follow without a struggle."

"That's very sensible of you, very sensible indeed," declared the Brown Bear. "So for-ward, MARCH!" And with the command he turned around and began to waddle along a path that led between the trees.

Cayke and the Frogman, as they followed their conductor, could scarce forbear laughing at his stiff, awkward manner of walking, and although he moved his stuffy legs fast, his steps were so short that they had to go slowly in order not to run into him. But after a time they reached a large, circular space in the center of the forest, which was clear of any stumps or underbrush. The ground was covered by a soft, gray moss, pleasant to tread upon. All the trees surrounding this space seemed to be hollow and had round holes in their trunks, set a little way above the ground, but otherwise there was nothing unusual about the place and nothing, in the opinion of the prisoners, to indicate a settlement. But the little Brown Bear said in a proud and impressive voice (although it still squeaked), "This is the wonderful city known to fame as Bear Center!"

"But there are no houses, there are no bears living here at all!" exclaimed Cayke.

"Oh indeed!" retorted their captor, and raising his gun he pulled the trigger. The cork flew out of the tin barrel with a loud "pop!" and at once from every hole in every tree within view of the clearing appeared the head of a bear. They were of many colors and of many sizes, but all were made in the same manner as the bear who had met and captured them.

At first a chorus of growls arose, and then a sharp voice cried, "What has happened, Corporal Waddle?"

"Captives, Your Majesty!" answered the Brown Bear. "Intruders upon our domain and slanderers of our good name."

"Ah, that's important," answered the voice.

Then from out the hollow trees tumbled a whole regiment of stuffed bears, some carrying tin swords, some popguns and others long spears with gay ribbons tied to the handles. There were hundreds of them, altogether, and they quietly formed a circle around the Frogman and the Cookie Cook, but kept at a distance and left a large space for the prisoners to stand in. Presently, this circle parted, and into the center of it stalked a huge toy bear of a lovely lavender color. He walked upon his hind legs, as did all the others, and on his head he wore a tin crown set with diamonds and amethysts, while in one paw he carried a short wand of some glittering metal that resembled silver but wasn't.

"His Majesty the King!" Corporal Waddle, and all the bears bowed low. Some bowed so low that they lost their balance and toppled over, but they soon scrambled up again, and the Lavender King squatted on his haunches before the prisoners and gazed at them steadily with his bright, pink eyes.

16. The Little Pink Bear

"One Person and one Freak," said the big Lavender Bear when he had carefully examined the strangers.

"I am sorry to hear you call poor Cayke the Cookie Cook a Freak," remonstrated the Frogman.

"She is the Person," asserted the King. "Unless I am mistaken, it is you who are the Freak."

The Frogman was silent, for he could not truthfully deny it.

"Why have you dared intrude in my forest?" demanded demanded the Bear King.

"We didn't know it was your forest," said Cayke, "and we are on our way to the far east, where the Emerald City is."

"Ah, it's a long way from here to the Emerald City," remarked the King. "It is so far away, indeed, that no bear among us has even been there. But what errand requires you to travel such a distance?"

"Someone has stolen my diamond-studded gold dishpan," explained Cayke, "and as I cannot be happy without it, I have decided to search the world over until I find it again. The Frogman, who is very learned and wonderfully wise, has come with me to give me his assistance. Isn't it kind of him?"

The King looked at the Frogman.

"What makes you so wonderfully wise?" he asked.

"I'm not," was the candid reply."The Cookie Cook and some others in the Yip Country think because I am a big frog and talk and act like a man that I must be very wise. I have learned more than a frog usually knows, it is true, but I am not yet so wise as I hope to become at some future time."

The King nodded, and when he did so, something squeaked in his chest. "Did Your Majesty speak?" asked Cayke.

"Not just then," answered the Lavender Bear, seeming to be somewhat embarrassed. "I am so built, you must know, that when anything pushes against my chest, as my chin accidentally did just then, I make that silly noise. In this city it isn't considered good manners to notice. But I like your Frogman. He is honest and truthful, which is more than can be said of many others. As for your late lamented dishpan, I'll show it to you."

With this he waved three times the metal wand which he held in his paw, and instantly there appeared upon the ground midway between the King and Cayke a big, round pan made of beaten gold. Around the top edge was a row of small diamonds; around the center of the pan was another row of larger diamonds; and at the bottom was a row of exceedingly large and brilliant diamonds. In fact, they all sparkled magnificently, and the pan was so big and broad that it took a lot of diamonds to go around it three times.

Cayke stared so hard that her eyes seemed about to pop out of her head. "O-o-o-h!" she exclaimed, drawing a deep breath of delight.

"Is this your dishpan?" inquired the King.

"It is, it is!" cried the Cookie Cook, and rushing forward, she fell on her knees and threw her arms around the precious pan. But her arms came together without meeting any resistance at all. Cayke tried to seize the edge, but found nothing to grasp. The pan was surely there, she thought, for she could see it plainly; but it was not solid; she could not feel it at all. With a moan of astonishment and despair, she raised her head to look at the Bear King, who was watching her actions curiously. Then she turned to the pan again, only to find it had completely disappeared.

"Poor creature!" murmured the King pityingly. "You must have thought, for the moment, that you had actually recovered your dishpan. But what you saw was merely the image of it, conjured up by means of my magic. It is a pretty dishpan, indeed, though rather big and awkward to handle. I hope you will some day find it."

Cayke was grievously disappointed. She began to cry, wiping her eyes on her apron. The King turned to the throng of toy bears surrounding him and asked, "Has any of you ever seen this golden dishpan before?"

"No," they answered in a chorus.

The King seemed to reflect. Presently he inquired, "Where is the Little Pink Bear?"

"At home, Your Majesty," was the reply.

"Fetch him here," commanded the King.

Several of the bears waddled over to one of the trees and pulled from its hollow a tiny pink bear, smaller than any of the others.

A big, white bear carried the pink one in his arms and set it down beside the King, arranging the joints of its legs so that it would stand upright.

This Pink Bear seemed lifeless until the King turned a crank which protruded from its side, when the little creature turned its head stiffly from side to side and said in a small, shrill voice, "Hurrah for the King of Bear Center!"

"Very good," said the big Lavender Bear. "He seems to be working very well today. Tell me, my Pink Pinkerton, what has become of this lady's jeweled dishpan?"

"U-u-u," said the Pink Bear, and then stopped short.

The King turned the crank again.

"U-g-u the Shoemaker has it," said the Pink Bear.

"Who is Ugu the Shoemaker?" demanded the King, again turning the crank.

"A magician who lives on a mountain in a wickerwork castle," was the reply.

"Where is the mountain?" was the next question.

"Nineteen miles and three furlongs from Bear Center to the northeast."

"And is the dishpan still at the castle of Ugu the Shoemaker?" asked the King.

"It is."

The King turned to Cayke.

"You may rely on this information," said he. "The Pink Bear can tell us anything we wish to know, and his words are always words of truth."

"Is he alive?" asked the Frogman, much interested in the Pink Bear.

"Something animates him when you turn his crank," replied the King. "I do not know if it is life or what it is or how it happens that the Little Pink Bear can answer correctly every question put to him. We discovered his talent a long time ago, and whenever we wish to know anything—which is not very often—we ask the Pink Bear. There is no doubt whatever, madam, that Ugu the Magician has your dishpan, and if you dare to go to him, you may be able to recover it. But of that I am not certain."

"Can't the Pink Bear tell?" asked Cayke anxiously.

"No, for that is in the future. He can tell anything that HAS happened, but nothing that is going to happen. Don't ask me why, for I don't know."

"Well," said the Cookie Cook after a little thought, "I mean to go to this magician, anyhow, and tell him I want my dishpan. I wish I knew what Ugu the Shoemaker is like."

"Then I'll show him to you," promised the King. "But do not be frightened. It won't be Ugu, remember, but only his image." With this, he waved his metal wand, and in the circle suddenly appeared a thin little man, very old and skinny, who was seated on a wicker stool before a wicker table. On the table lay a Great

Book with gold clasps. The Book was open, and the man was reading in it. He wore great spectacles which were fastened before his eyes by means of a ribbon that passed around his head and was tied in a bow at the neck. His hair was very thin and white; his skin, which clung fast to his bones, was brown and seared with furrows; he had a big, fat nose and little eyes set close together.

On no account was Ugu the Shoemaker a pleasant person to gaze at. As his image appeared before the, all were silent and intent until Corporal Waddle, the Brown Bear, became nervous and pulled the trigger of his gun. Instantly, the cork flew out of the tin barrel with a loud "pop!" that made them all jump. And at this sound, the image of the magician vanished. "So THAT'S the thief, is it?" said Cayke in an angry voice. "I should think he'd be ashamed of himself for stealing a poor woman's diamond dishpan! But I mean to face him in his wicker castle and force him to return my property."

To me," said the Bear King reflectively, "he looked like a dangerous person. I hope he won't be so unkind as to argue the matter with you."

The Frogman was much disturbed by the vision of Ugu the Shoemaker, and Cayke's determination to go to the magician filled her companion with misgivings. But he would not break his pledged word to assist the Cookie Cook, and after breathing a deep sigh of resignation, he asked the King, "Will Your Majesty lend us this Pink Bear who answers questions that we may take him with us on our journey? He would be very useful to us, and we will promise to bring him safely back to you."

The King did not reply at once. He seemed to be thinking.

PLEASE let us take the Pink Bear," begged Cayke. "I'm sure he would be a great help to us."

The Pink Bear," said the King, "is the best bit of magic I possess, and there is not another like him in the world. I do not care to let him out of my sight, nor do I wish to disappoint you; so I believe I will make the journey in your company and carry my Pink Bear with me. He can walk when you wind the other side of him, but so slowly and awkwardly that he would delay you. But if I go along, I can carry him in my arms, so I will join your party. Whenever you are ready to start, let me know."

But Your Majesty!" exclaimed Corporal Waddle in protest, "I hope you do not intend to let these prisoners escape without punishment."

Of what crime do you accuse them?" inquired the King.

Why, they trespassed on your domain, for one thing," said the Brown Bear.

We didn't know it was private property, Your Majesty," said the Cookie Cook. "And they asked if any of us had stolen the dishpan!" continued Corporal Waddle indignantly. "That is the same thing as calling us thieves and robbers and bandits and brigands, is it not?"

Every person has the right to ask questions," said the Frogman.

But the Corporal is quite correct," declared the Lavender Bear. "I condemn you both to death, the execution to take place ten years from this hour."

But we belong in the Land of Oz, where no one ever dies," Cayke

reminded him.

"Very true," said the King. "I condemn you to death merely as a matter of form. It sounds quite terrible, and in ten years we shall have forgotten all about it. Are you ready to start for the wicker castle of Ugu the Shoemaker?"

"Quite ready, Your Majesty."

"But who will rule in your place while you are gone?" asked a big Yellow Bear.

"I myself will rule while I am gone," was the reply. "A King isn't required to stay at home forever, and if he takes a notion to travel, whose business is it but his own? All I ask is that you bears behave yourselves while I am away. If any of you is naughty, I'll send him to some girl or boy in America to play with."

This dreadful threat made all the toy bears look solemn. They assured the King in a chorus of growls that they would be good. Then the big Lavender Bear picked up the little Pink Bear, and after tucking it carefully under one arm, he said, "Goodbye till I come back!" and waddled along the path that led through the forest. The Frogman and Cayke the Cookie Cook also said goodbye to the bears and then followed after the King, much to the regret of the little Brown Bear, who pulled the trigger of his gun and popped the cork as a parting salute.

17. The Meeting

While the Frogman and his party were advancing from the west, Dorothy and her party were advancing from the east, and so it happened that on the following night they all camped at a little hill that was only a few miles from the wicker castle of Ugu the Shoemaker. But the two parties did not see one another that night, for one camped on one side of the hill while the other camped on the opposite side. But the next morning, the Frogman thought he would climb the hill and see what was on top of it, and at the same time Scraps, the Patchwork Girl, also decided to climb the hill to find if the wicker castle was visible from its top. So she stuck her head over an edge just as the Frogman's head appeared over another edge, and both, being surprised, kept still while they took a good look at one another.

Scraps recovered from her astonishment first, and bounding upward, she turned a somersault and landed sitting down and facing the big Frogman, who slowly advanced and sat opposite her. "Well met, Stranger!" cried the Patchwork Girl with a whoop of laughter. "You are quite the funniest individual I have seen in all my travels."

"Do you suppose I can be any funnier than you?" asked the Frogman, gazing at her in wonder.

"I'm not funny to myself, you know," returned Scraps. "I wish I were. And perhaps you are so used to your own absurd shape that you do not laugh whenever you see your reflection in a pool or in a mirror."

"No," said the Frogman gravely, "I do not. I used to be proud of my great size and vain of my culture and education, but since I bathed in the Truth Pond, I sometimes think it is not right that I should be different from all other frogs."

"Right or wrong," said the Patchwork Girl, "to be different is to be distinguished. Now in my case, I'm just like all other Patchwork Girls because I'm the only one there is. But tell me, where did you come from?"

"The Yip Country," said he.

"Is that in the Land of Oz?"

"Of course," replied the Frogman.

"And do you know that your Ruler, Ozma of Oz, has been stolen?"

"I was not aware that I had a Ruler, so of course I couldn't know that she was stolen."

"Well, you have. All the people of Oz," explained Scraps, "are ruled by Ozma, whether they know it or not. And she has been stolen. Aren't you angry? Aren't you indignant? Your Ruler, whom you didn't know you had, has positively been stolen!"

"That is queer," remarked the Frogman thoughtfully. "Stealing is a thing practically unknown in Oz, yet this Ozma has been taken, and a friend of mine has also had her dishpan stolen. With her I have traveled all the way from the Yip Country in order to recover it."

"I don't see any connection between a Royal Ruler of Oz and a dishpan!" declared Scraps.

"They've both been stolen, haven't they?"

"True. But why can't your friend wash her dishes in another dishpan?" asked Scraps.

"Why can't you use another Royal Ruler? I suppose you prefer the one who is lost, and my friend wants her own dishpan, which is made of gold and studded with diamonds and has magic powers."

"Magic, eh?" exclaimed Scraps. "THERE is a link that connects the two steals, anyhow, for it seems that all the magic in the Land of Oz was stolen at the same time, whether it was in the Emerald City of in Glinda's castle or in the Yip Country. Seems mighty strange and mysterious, doesn't it?"

"It used to seem that way to me," admitted the Frogman, "but we have now discovered who took our dishpan. It was Ugu the Shoemaker."

"Ugu? Good gracious! That's the same magician we think has stolen Ozma. We are now on our way to the castle of this Shoemaker."

"So are we," said the Frogman.

"Then follow me, quick! And let me introduce you to Dorothy and the other girls and to the Wizard of Oz and all the rest of us."

She sprang up and seized his coatsleeve, dragging him off the hilltop and down the other side from that whence he had come. And at the foot of the hill, the Frogman was astonished to find the three girls and the Wizard and Button-Bright, who were surrounded by a wooden Sawhorse, a lean Mule, a square Woozy, and a Cowardly Lion. A little black dog ran up and smelled at the Frogman, but couldn't growl at him.

"I've discovered another party that has been robbed," shouted Scraps as she joined them. "This is their leader, and they're all going to Ugu's castle to fight the wicked Shoemaker!"

They regarded the Frogman with much curiosity and interest, and finding all eyes fixed upon him, the newcomer arranged his necktie and smoothed his beautiful vest and swung his gold-headed cane like a regular dandy. The big spectacles over his eyes quite altered his froglike countenance and gave him a learned and impressive look. Used as she was to seeing strange creatures in the Land of Oz, Dorothy was amazed at discovering the Frogman. So were all her companions. Toto wanted to growl at him, but couldn't, and he didn't dare bark. The Sawhorse snorted rather contemptuously, but the Lion whispered to the wooden steed, "Bear with this strange creature, my friend, and remember he is no more extraordinary than you are. Indeed, it is more natural for a frog to be big than for a Sawhorse to be alive."

On being questioned, the Frogman told them the whole story of the loss of Cayke's highly prized dishpan and their adventures in search of it. When he came to tell of the Lavender Bear King and of the Little Pink Bear who could tell anything you wanted to know, his hearers became eager to see such interesting animals. "It will be best," said the Wizard, "to unite our two parties and share our fortunes together, for we are all bound on the same errand, and as one band we may more easily defy this shoemaker magician than if separate. Let us be allies."

"I will ask my friends about that," replied the Frogman, and he climbed over the hill to find Cayke and the toy bears. The Patchwork Girl accompanied him, and when they came upon the Cookie Cook and the Lavender Bear and the Pink Bear, it was hard to tell which of the lot was the most surprised.

"Mercy me!" cried Cayke, addressing the Patchwork Girl "However did you come alive?"

Scraps stared at the bears.

"Mercy me!" she echoed, "You are stuffed, as I am, with cotton and you appear to be living. That makes me feel ashamed, for I have prided myself on being the only live cotton-stuffed person in Oz."

"Perhaps you are," returned the Lavender Bear, "for I am stuffed with extra-quality curled hair, and so is the Little Pink Bear."

"You have relieved my mind of a great anxiety," declared the Patchwork Girl, now speaking more cheerfully. "The Scarecrow is stuffed with straw and you with hair, so I am still the Original and Only Cotton-Stuffed!"

"I hope I am too polite to criticize cotton as compared with curled hair," said the King, "especially as you seem satisfied with it."

Then the Frogman told of his interview with the party from the Emerald City and added that the Wizard of Oz had invited the bears and Cayke and himself to travel in company with them to the castle of Ugu the Shoemaker. Cayke was much pleased, but the Bear King looked solemn. He set the Little Pink Bear on his lap and turned the crank in its side and asked, "Is it safe for us to associate with those people from the Emerald City?"

And the Pink Bear at once replied, "Safe for you and safe for me Perhaps no others safe will be."

"That 'perhaps' need not worry us," said the King, "so let us join the others and offer them our protection."

Even the Lavender Bear was astonished, however, when on

climbing over the hill he found on the other side the group of queer animals and the people from the Emerald City. The bears and Cayke were received very cordially, although Button-Bright was cross when they wouldn't let him play with the Little Pink Bear. The three girls greatly admired the toy bears, and especially the pink one, which they longed to hold.

"You see," explained the Lavender King in denying them this privilege, "he's a very valuable bear, because his magic is a correct guide on all occasions, and especially if one is in difficulties. It was the Pink Bear who told us that Ugu the Shoemaker had stolen the Cookie Cook's dishpan."

"And the King's magic is just as wonderful," added Cayke, "because it showed us the Magician himself."

"What did he look like?" inquired Dorothy.

"He was dreadful!"

"He was sitting at a table and examining an immense Book which had three golden clasps," remarked the King.

"Why, that must have been Glinda's Great Book of Records!" exclaimed Dorothy. "If it is, it proves that Ugu the Shoemaker stole Ozma, and with her all the magic in the Emerald City."

"And my dishpan," said Cayke.

And the Wizard added, "It also proves that he is following our adventures in the Book of Records, and therefore knows that we are seeking him and that we are determined to find him and reach Ozma at all hazards."

"If we can," added the Woozy, but everybody frowned at him.

The Wizard's statement was so true that the faces around him were very serious until the Patchwork Girl broke into a peal of laughter. "Wouldn't it be a rich joke if he made prisoners of us, too?" she said.

"No one but a crazy Patchwork Girl would consider that a joke," grumbled Button-Bright.

And then the Lavender Bear King asked, "Would you like to see this magical shoemaker?"

"Wouldn't he know it?" Dorothy inquired.

"No, I think not."

Then the King waved his metal wand and before them appeared a room in the wicker castle of Ugu. On the wall of the room hung Ozma's Magic Picture, and seated before it was the Magician. They could see the Picture as well as he could, because it faced them, and in the Picture was the hillside where they were now sitting, all their forms being reproduced in miniature. And curiously enough, within the scene of the Picture was the scene they were now beholding, so they knew that the Magician at this moment watching them in the Picture, and also that he saw himself and the room he was in become visible to the people on the hillside. Therefore he knew very well that they were watching him while he was watching them.

In proof of this, Ugu sprang from his seat and turned a scowling face in their direction; but now he could not see the travelers who were seeking him, although they could still see him. His actions were so distinct, indeed, that it seemed he was actually before them. "It is only a ghost," said the Bear King. "It isn't real at all except that it shows us Ugu just as he looks and tells us truly just what he is doing."

"I don't see anything of my lost growl, though," said Toto as if to himself.

Then the vision faded away, and they could see nothing but the grass and trees and bushes around them.

18. The Conference

"Now then," said the Wizard, "let us talk this matter over and decide what to do when we get to Ugu's wicker castle. There can be no doubt that the Shoemaker is a powerful Magician, and his powers have been increased a hundredfold since he secured the Great Book of Records, the Magic Picture, all of Glinda's recipes for sorcery, and my own black bag, which was full of tools of wizardry. The man who could rob us of those things and the man with all their powers at his command is one who may prove somewhat difficult to conquer, therefore we should plan our actions well before we venture too near to his castle."

"I didn't see Ozma in the Magic Picture," said Trot. "What do you suppose Ugu has done with her?"

"Couldn't the Little Pink Bear tell us what he did with Ozma?" asked Button-Bright.

"To be sure," replied the Lavender King. "I'll ask him." So he turned the crank in the Little Pink Bear's side and inquired, "Did Ugu the Shoemaker steal Ozma of Oz?"

"Yes," answered the Little Pink Bear.

"Then what did he do with her?" asked the King.

"Shut her up in a dark place," answered the Little Pink Bear.

"Oh, that must be a dungeon cell!" cried Dorothy, horrified. "How dreadful!"

"Well, we must get her out of it," said the Wizard. "That is what we came for, and of course we must rescue Ozma. But how?"

Each one looked at some other one for an answer, and all shook their heads in a grave and dismal manner. All but Scraps, who danced around them gleefully. "You're afraid," said the Patchwork Girl, "because so many things can hurt your meat bodies. Why don't you give it up and go home? How can you fight a great magician when you have nothing to fight with?"

Dorothy looked at her reflectively.

"Scraps," said she, "you know that Ugu couldn't hurt you a bit, whatever he did, nor could he hurt ME, 'cause I wear the Gnome King's Magic Belt. S'pose just we two go on together and leave the others here to wait for us."

"No, no!" said the Wizard positively. "That won't do at all. Ozma is more powerful than either of you, yet she could not defeat the wicked Ugu, who has shut her up in a dungeon. We must go to the Shoemaker in one mighty band, for only in union is there strength."

"That is excellent advice," said the Lavender Bear approvingly.

"But what can we do when we get to Ugu?" inquired the Cookie

Cook anxiously.

"Do not expect a prompt answer to that important question," replied the Wizard, "for we must first plan our line of conduct. Ugu knows, of course, that we are after him, for he has seen our approach in the Magic Picture, and he has read of all we have done up to the present moment in the Great Book of Records. Therefore we cannot expect to take him by surprise."

"Don't you suppose Ugu would listen to reason?" asked Betsy. "If we explained to him how wicked he has been, don't you think he'd let poor Ozma go?"

"And give me back my dishpan?" added the Cookie Cook eagerly.

"Yes, yes, won't he say he's sorry and get on his knees and beg our pardon?" cried Scraps, turning a flip-flop to show her scorn of the suggestion. "When Ugu the Shoemaker does that, please knock at the front door and let me know."

The Wizard sighed and rubbed his bald head with a puzzled air. "I'm quite sure Ugu will not be polite to us," said he, "so we must conquer this cruel magician by force, much as we dislike to be rude to anyone. But none of you has yet suggested a way to do that. Couldn't the Little Pink Bear tell us how?" he asked, turning to the Bear King.

"No, for that is something that is GOING to happen," replied the Lavender Bear. "He can only tell us what already HAS happened."

Again, they were grave and thoughtful. But after a time, Betsy said in a hesitating voice, "Hank is a great fighter. Perhaps HE could conquer the magician."

The Mule turned his head to look reproachfully at his old friend, the young girl. "Who can fight against magic?" he asked.

"The Cowardly Lion could," said Dorothy.

The Lion, who was lying with his front legs spread out, his chin on his paws, raised his shaggy head. "I can fight when I'm not afraid," said he calmly, "but the mere mention of a fight sets me to trembling."

"Ugu's magic couldn't hurt the Sawhorse," suggested tiny Trot.

"And the Sawhorse couldn't hurt the Magician," declared that wooden animal.

"For my part," said Toto, "I am helpless, having lost my growl."

"Then," said Cayke the Cookie Cook, "we must depend upon the Frogman. His marvelous wisdom will surely inform him how to conquer the wicked Magician and restore to me my dishpan."

All eyes were now turned questioningly upon the Frogman. Finding himself the center of observation, he swung his gold-headed cane, adjusted his big spectacles, and after swelling out his chest, sighed and said in a modest tone of voice, "Respect for truth obliges me to confess that Cayke is mistaken in regard to my superior wisdom. I am not very wise. Neither have I had any practical experience in conquering magicians. But let us consider this case. What is Ugu, and what is a magician? Ugu is a renegade shoemaker, and a magician is an ordinary man who, having learned how to do magical tricks, considers himself above his fellows. In this case, the Shoemaker has been naughty enough to steal a lot of magical tools and things that did not

belong to him, and he is more wicked to steal than to be a magician. Yet with all the arts at his command, Ugu is still a man, and surely there are ways in which a man may be conquered. How, do you say, how? Allow me to state that I don't know. In my judgment, we cannot decide how best to act until we get to Ugu's castle. So let us go to it and take a look at it. After that, we may discover an idea that will guide us to victory."

"That may not be a wise speech, but it sounds good," said Dorothy approvingly. "Ugu the Shoemaker is not only a common man, but he's a wicked man and a cruel man and deserves to be conquered. We musn't have any mercy on him till Ozma is set free. So let's go to his castle as the Frogman says and see what the place looks like."

No one offered any objection to this plan, and so it was adopted. They broke camp and were about to start on the journey to Ugu's castle when they discovered that Button-Bright was lost again. The girls and the Wizard shouted his name, and the Lion roared and the Donkey brayed and the Frogman croaked and the Big Lavender Bear growled (to the envy of Toto, who couldn't growl but barked his loudest), yet none of them could make Button-Bright hear. So after vainly searching for the boy a full hour, they formed a procession and proceeded in the direction of the wicker castle of Ugu the Shoemaker.

"Button-Bright's always getting lost," said Dorothy. "And if he wasn't always getting found again, I'd prob'ly worry. He may have gone ahead of us, and he may have gone back, but wherever he is, we'll find him sometime and somewhere, I'm almost sure."

19. Ugu the Shoemaker

A curious thing about Ugu the Shoemaker was that he didn't suspect in the least that he was wicked. He wanted to be powerful and great, and he hoped to make himself master of all the Land of Oz that he might compel everyone in that fairy country to obey him. His ambition blinded him to the rights of others, and he imagined anyone else would act just as he did if anyone else happened to be as clever as himself.

When he inhabited his little shoemaking shop in the City of Herku, he had been discontented, for a shoemaker is not looked upon with high respect, and Ugu knew that his ancestors had been famous magicians for many centuries past and therefore his family was above the ordinary. Even his father practiced magic when Ugu was a boy, but his father had wandered away from Herku and had never come back again. So when Ugu grew up, he was forced to make shoes for a living, knowing nothing of the magic of his forefathers. But one day, in searching through the attic of his house, he discovered all the books of magical recipes and many magical instruments which had formerly been in use in his family. From that day, he stopped making shoes and began to study magic. Finally, he aspired to become the greatest magician in Oz, and for days and weeks and months he thought on a plan to render all the other sorcerers and wizards, as well as those with fairy powers, helpless to oppose him.

From the books of his ancestors, he learned the following facts:

(1) That Ozma of Oz was the fairy ruler of the Emerald City and the Land of Oz and that she could not be destroyed by any magic ever devised. Also, by means of her Magic Picture she would be able to discover anyone who approached her royal palace with the idea of conquering it.

(2) That Glinda the Good was the most powerful Sorceress in Oz, among her other magical possessions being the Great Book of

Records, which told her all that happened anywhere in the world. This Book of Records was very dangerous to Ugu's plans, and Glinda was in the service of Ozma and would use her arts of sorcery to protect the girl Ruler.

(3) That the Wizard of Oz, who lived in Ozma's palace, had been taught much powerful magic by Glinda and had a bag of magic tools with which he might be able to conquer the Shoemaker.

(4) That there existed in Oz—in the Yip Country—a jeweled dishpan made of gold, which dishpan would grow large enough for a man to sit inside it. Then, when he grasped both the golden handles, the dishpan would transport him in an instant to any place he wished to go within the borders of the Land of Oz.

No one now living except Ugu knew of the powers of the Magic Dishpan, so after long study, the shoemaker decided that if he could manage to secure the dishpan, he could by its means rob Ozma and Glinda and the Wizard of Oz of all their magic, thus becoming himself the most powerful person in all the land. His first act was to go away from the City of Herku and build for himself the Wicker Castle in the hills. Here he carried his books and instruments of magic, and here for a full year he diligently practiced all the magical arts learned from his ancestors. At the end of that time, he could do a good many wonderful things.

Then, when all his preparations were made, he set out for the Yip Country, and climbing the steep mountain at night he entered the house of Cayke the Cookie Cook and stole her diamond-studded gold dishpan while all the Yips were asleep, Taking his prize outside, he set the pan upon the ground and uttered the required magic word. Instantly, the dishpan grew as large as a big washtub, and Ugu seated himself in it and grasped the two handles. Then he wished himself in the great drawing room of Glinda the Good.

He was there in a flash. First he took the Great Book of Records and put it in the dishpan. Then he went to Glinda's laboratory and took all her rare chemical compounds and her instruments of sorcery, placing these also in the dishpan, which he caused to grow large enough to hold them. Next he seated himself amongst the treasures he had stolen and wished himself in the room in Ozma's palace which the Wizard occupied and where he kept his bag of magic tools. This bag Ugu added to his plunder and then wished himself in the apartments of Ozma.

Here he first took the Magic Picture from the wall and then seized all the other magical things which Ozma possessed. Having placed these in the dishpan, he was about to climb in himself when he looked up and saw Ozma standing beside him. Her fairy instinct had warned her that danger was threatening her, so the beautiful girl Ruler rose from her couch and leaving her bedchamber at once confronted the thief.

Ugu had to think quickly, for he realized that if he permitted Ozma to rouse the inmates of her palace, all his plans and his present successes were likely to come to naught. So he threw a scarf over the girl's head so she could not scream, and pushed her into the dishpan and tied her fast so she could not move. Then he climbed in beside her and wished himself in his own wicker castle. The Magic Dishpan was there in an instant, with all its contents, and Ugu rubbed his hands together in triumphant joy as he realized that he now possessed all the important magic in the Land of Oz and could force all the inhabitants of that fairyland to do as he willed.

So quickly had his journey been accomplished that before daylight the robber magician had locked Ozma in a room, making her a prisoner, and had unpacked and arranged all his stolen goods. The next day he placed the Book of Records on his table and hung the Magic Picture on his wall and put away in his cupboards and drawers all the elixirs and magic compounds he had stolen. The magical instruments he polished and arranged, and this was fascinating work and made him very happy.

By turns the imprisoned Ruler wept and scolded the Shoemaker, haughtily threatening him with dire punishment for the wicked deeds he had done. Ugu became somewhat afraid of his fairy prisoner, in spite of the fact that he believed he had robbed her of all her powers; so he performed an enchantment that quickly disposed of her and placed her out of his sight and hearing. After that, being occupied with other things, he soon forgot her.

But now, when he looked into the Magic Picture and read the Great Book of Records, the Shoemaker learned that his wickedness was not to go unchallenged. Two important expeditions had set out to find him and force him to give up his stolen property. One was the party headed by the Wizard and Dorothy, while the other consisted of Cayke and the Frogman. Others were also searching, but not in the right places. These two groups, however, were headed straight for the wicker castle, and so Ugu began to plan how best to meet them and to defeat their efforts to conquer him.

20. More Surprises

All that first day after the union of the two parties, our friends marched steadily toward the wicker castle of Ugu the Shoemaker. When night came, they camped in a little grove and passed a pleasant evening together, although some of them were worried because Button-Bright was still lost.

"Perhaps," said Toto as the animals lay grouped together for the night, "this Shoemaker who stole my growl and who stole Ozma has also stolen Button-Bright."

"How do you know that the Shoemaker stole your growl?" demanded the Woozy.

"He has stolen about everything else of value in Oz, hasn't he?" replied the dog.

"He has stolen everything he wants, perhaps," agreed the Lion, "but what could anyone want with your growl?"

"Well," said the dog, wagging his tail slowly, "my recollection is that it was a wonderful growl, soft and low and—and—"

"And ragged at the edges," said the Sawhorse.

"So," continued Toto, "if that magician hadn't any growl of his own, he might have wanted mine and stolen it."

"And if he has, he will soon wish he hadn't," remarked the Mule. "Also, if he has stolen Button-Bright, he will be sorry."

"Don't you like Button-Bright, then?" asked the Lion in surprise.

"It isn't a question of liking him," replied the Mule. "It's a question of watching him and looking after him. Any boy who causes his friends so much worry isn't worth having around. I never get lost."

"If you did," said Toto, "no one would worry a bit. I think Button-Bright is a very lucky boy because he always gets found."

"See here," said the Lion, "this chatter is keeping us all awake, and tomorrow is likely to be a busy day. Go to sleep and forget your quarrels."

"Friend Lion," retorted the dog, "if I hadn't lost my growl, you would hear it now. I have as much right to talk as you have to sleep."

The Lion sighed.

"If only you had lost your voice when you lost your growl," said he, "you would be a more agreeable companion."

But they quieted down after that, and soon the entire camp was wrapped in slumber. Next morning they made an early start, but had hardly proceeded on their way an hour when, on climbing a slight elevation, they beheld in the distance a low mountain on top of which stood Ugu's wicker castle. It was a good-sized building and rather pretty because the sides, roofs and domes were all of wicker, closely woven as it is in fine baskets.

"I wonder if it is strong?"said Dorothy musingly as she eyed the queer castle.

"I suppose it is, since a magician built it," answered the Wizard. "With magic to protect it, even a paper castle might be as strong as if made of stone. This Ugu must be a man of ideas, because he does things in a different way from other people."

"Yes. No one else would steal our dear Ozma," sighed tiny Trot.

"I wonder if Ozma is there?" said Betsy, indicating the castle with a nod of her head.

"Where else could she be?" asked Scraps.

"Suppose we ask the Pink Bear," suggested Dorothy.

That seemed a good idea, so they halted the procession, and the Bear King held the little Pink Bear on his lap and turned the crank in its side and asked, "Where is Ozma of Oz?"

And the little Pink Bear answered, "She is in a hole in the ground a half mile away at your left."

"Good gracious!" cried Dorothy.

"Then she is not in Ugu's castle at all."

"It is lucky we asked that question," said the Wizard, "for if we can find Ozma and rescue her, there will be no need for us to fight that wicked and dangerous magician."

"Indeed!" said Cayke. "Then what about my dishpan?"

The Wizard looked puzzled at her tone of remonstrance, so she added, "Didn't you people from the Emerald City promise that we would all stick together, and that you would help me to get my dishpan if I would help you to get your Ozma? And didn't I bring to you the little Pink Bear, which has told you where Ozma is hidden?"

"She's right," said Dorothy to the Wizard.

"We must do as we agreed."

"Well, first of all, let us go and rescue Ozma," proposed the Wizard. "Then our beloved Ruler may be able to advise us how to conquer Ugu the Shoemaker." So they turned to the left and marched for half a mile until they came to a small but deep hole in the ground. At once, all rushed to the brim to peer into the hole, but instead of finding there Princess Ozma of Oz, all that they saw was Button-Bright, who was lying asleep on the bottom.

Their cries soon wakened the boy, who sat up and rubbed his eyes. When he recognized his friends, he smiled sweetly, saying "Found again!"

"Where is Ozma?" inquired Dorothy anxiously.

"I don't know," answered Button-Bright from the depths of the hole. "I got lost yesterday, as you may remember, and in the night while I was wandering around in the moonlight trying to find my way back to you, I suddenly fell into this hole."

"And wasn't Ozma in it then?"

"There was no one in it but me, and I was sorry it wasn't entirely empty. The sides are so steep I can't climb out, so there was nothing to be done but sleep until someone found me. Thank you for coming. If you'll please let down a rope, I'll empty this hole in a hurry."

"How strange!" said Dorothy, greatly disappointed.

"It's evident the Pink Bear didn't tell the truth."

"He never makes a mistake," declared the Lavender Bear King in a tone that showed his feelings were hurt. And then he turned the crank of the little Pink Bear again and asked, "Is this the hole that Ozma of Oz is in?"

"Yes," answered the Pink Bear.

"That settles it," said the King positively. "Your Ozma is in this hole in the ground."

"Don't be silly," returned Dorothy impatiently. "Even your bead eyes can see there is no one in the hole but Button-Bright."

"Perhaps Button-Bright is Ozma," suggested the King.

"And perhaps he isn't! Ozma is a girl, and Button-Bright is a boy."

"Your Pink Bear must be out of order," said the Wizard, "for, this time at least, his machinery has caused him to make an untrue statement."

The Bear King was so angry at this remark that he turned away holding the Pink Bear in his paws, and refused to discuss the matter in any further way.

"At any rate," said the Frogman, "the Pink Bear has led us to your boy friend and so enabled you to rescue him."

Scraps was leaning so far over the hole trying to find Ozma in it that suddenly she lost her balance and pitched in head foremost. She fell upon Button-Bright and tumbled him over, but he was not hurt by her soft, stuffed body and only laughed at the mishap. The Wizard buckled some straps together and let one end of them down into the hole, and soon both Scraps and the boy had climbed up and were standing safely beside the others. They looked once more for Ozma, but the hole was now absolutely vacant. It was a round hole, so from the top they could plainly see every part of it. Before they left the place, Dorothy went to the Bear King and said, "I'm sorry we couldn't believe what the little Pink Bear said, 'cause we don't want to make you feel bad by doubting him. There must be a mistake, somewhere, and we prob'ly don't understand just what the little Pink Bear said. Will you let me ask him one more question?"

The Lavender Bear King was a good-natured bear, considering how he was made and stuffed and jointed, so he accepted Dorothy's apology and turned the crank and allowed the little girl to question his wee Pink Bear.

"Is Ozma REALLY in this hole?" asked Dorothy.

"No," said the little Pink Bear.

This surprised everybody. Even the Bear King was now puzzled by the contradictory statements of his oracle.

"Where IS she?" asked the King.

"Here, among you," answered the little Pink Bear.

"Well," said Dorothy, "this beats me entirely! I guess the little Pink Bear has gone crazy."

"Perhaps," called Scraps, who was rapidly turning "cartwheels" all around the perplexed group, "Ozma is invisible."

"Of course!" cried Betsy. That would account for it."

"Well, I've noticed that people can speak, even when they've been made invisible," said the Wizard. And then he looked all around him and said in a solemn voice, "Ozma, are you here?"

There was no reply. Dorothy asked the question, too, and so did Button-Bright and Trot and Betsy, but none received any reply at all.

"It's strange, it's terrible strange!" muttered Cayke the Cookie Cook. "I was sure that the little Pink Bear always tells the truth."

"I still believe in his honesty," said the Frogman, and this tribute so pleased the Bear King that he gave these last speakers grateful looks, but still gazed sourly on the others.

"Come to think of it," remarked the Wizard, "Ozma couldn't be invisible, for she is a fairy, and fairies cannot be made invisible against their will. Of course, she could be imprisoned by the magician or enchanted or transformed, in spite of her fairy powers, but Ugu could not render her invisible by any magic at his command."

"I wonder if she's been transformed into Button-Bright?" said Dorothy nervously. Then she looked steadily at the boy and asked, "Are you Ozma? Tell me truly!"

Button-Bright laughed.

"You're getting rattled, Dorothy," he replied. "Nothing ever enchants ME. If I were Ozma, do you think I'd have tumbled into that hole?"

"Anyhow," said the Wizard, "Ozma would never try to deceive her friends or prevent them from recognizing her in whatever form she happened to be. The puzzle is still a puzzle, so let us go on to the wicker castle and question the magician himself. Since it was he who stole our Ozma, Ugu is the one who must tell us where to find her."

21. Magic Against Magic

The Wizard's advice was good, so again they started in the direction of the low mountain on the crest of which the wicker castle had been built. They had been gradually advancing uphill, so now the elevation seemed to them more like a round knoll than a mountaintop. However, the sides of the knoll were sloping and covered with green grass, so there was a stiff climb before them yet. Undaunted, they plodded on and had almost reached the knoll when they suddenly observed that it was surrounded by a circle of flame. At first, the flames barely rose above the ground, but presently they grew higher and higher until a circle of flaming tongues of fire taller than any of their heads quite surrounded the hill on which the wicker castle stood. When they approached the flames, the heat was so intense that it drove them back again.

"This will never do for me!" exclaimed the Patchwork Girl. "I catch fire very easily."

"It won't do for me either," grumbled the Sawhorse, prancing to the rear.

"I also strongly object to fire," said the Bear King, following the Sawhorse to a safe distance and hugging the little Pink Bear with his paws.

"I suppose the foolish Shoemaker imagines these blazes will stop us," remarked the Wizard with a smile of scorn for Ugu. "But I am able to inform you that this is merely a simple magic trick which the robber stole from Glinda the Good, and by good fortune I know how to destroy these flames as well as how to produce them. Will some one of you kindly give me a match?"

You may be sure the girls carried no matches, nor did the Frogman or any of the animals. But Button-Bright, after searching carefully through his pockets, which contained all sorts of useful and useless things, finally produced a match and handed it to the Wizard, who tied it to the end of a branch which he tore from a small tree growing near them. Then the little Wizard carefully lighted the match, and running forward thrust it into the nearest flame. Instantly, the circle of fire began to die away, and soon vanished completely leaving the way clear for them to proceed.

"That was funny!" laughed Button-Bright.

"Yes," agreed the Wizard, "it seems odd that a little match could destroy such a great circle of fire, but when Glinda invented this trick, she believed no one would ever think of a match being a remedy for fire. I suppose even Ugu doesn't know how we managed to quench the flames of his barrier, for only Glinda and I know the secret. Glinda's Book of Magic which Ugu stole told how to make the flames, but not how to put them out."

They now formed in marching order and proceeded to advance up the slope of the hill, but had not gone far when before them rose a wall of steel, the surface of which was thickly covered with sharp, gleaming points resembling daggers. The wall completely surrounded the wicker castle, and its sharp points prevented anyone from climbing it. Even the Patchwork Girl might be ripped to pieces if she dared attempt it. "Ah!" exclaimed the Wizard cheerfully, "Ugu is now using one of my own tricks against me. But this is more serious than the Barrier of Fire, because the only way to destroy the wall is to get on the other side of it."

"How can that be done?" asked Dorothy.

The Wizard looked thoughtfully around his little party, and his face grew troubled. "It's a pretty high wall," he sadly remarked. "I'm pretty sure the Cowardly Lion could not leap over it."

"I'm sure of that, too!" said the Lion with a shudder of fear. "If I foolishly tried such a leap, I would be caught on those dreadful spikes."

"I think I could do it, sir," said the Frogman with a bow to the Wizard. "It is an uphill jump as well as being a high jump, but I'm considered something of a jumper by my friends in the Yip Country, and I believe a good, strong leap will carry me to the other side."

"I'm sure it would," agreed the Cookie Cook.

"Leaping, you know, is a froglike accomplishment," continued the Frogman modestly, "but please tell me what I am to do when I reach the other side of the wall."

"You're a brave creature," said the Wizard admiringly. "Has anyone a pin?"

Betsy had one, which she gave him. "All you need do," said the Wizard to the Frogman, giving him the pin, "is to stick this into the other side of the wall."

"But the wall is of steel!" exclaimed the big frog.

"I know. At least, it SEEMS to be steel, but do as I tell you. Stick the pin into the wall, and it will disappear."

The Frogman took off his handsome coat and carefully folded it and laid it on the grass. Then he removed his hat and laid it together with his gold-headed cane beside the coat. He then went back a way and made three powerful leaps in rapid succession. The first two leaps took him to the wall, and the third leap carried him well over it, to the amazement of all. For a short time, he disappeared from their view, but when he had obeyed the Wizard's injunction and had thrust the pin into the wall, the huge barrier vanished and showed them the form of the Frogman, who now went to where his coat lay and put it on again.

"We thank you very much," said the delighted Wizard. "That was the most wonderful leap I ever saw, and it has saved us from defeat by our enemy. Let us now hurry on to the castle before Ugu the Shoemaker thinks up some other means to stop us."

"We must have surprised him so far," declared Dorothy.

"Yes indeed. The fellow knows a lot of magic—all of our tricks and some of his own," replied the Wizard. "So if he is half as clever as he ought to be, we shall have trouble with him yet."

He had scarcely spoken these words when out from the gates of the wicker castle marched a regiment of soldiers, clad in gay uniforms and all bearing long, pointed spears and sharp battle axes. These soldiers were girls, and the uniforms were short skirts of yellow and black satin, golden shoes, bands of gold across their foreheads and necklaces of glittering jewels. Their jackets were scarlet, braided with silver cords. There were hundreds of these girl-soldiers, and they were more terrible than beautiful, being strong and fierce in appearance. They formed a circle all around the castle and faced outward, their spears pointed toward the invaders, and their battle axes held over their

shoulders, ready to strike. Of course, our friends halted at once, for they had not expected this dreadful array of soldiery. The Wizard seemed puzzled, and his companions exchanged discouraged looks.

"I'd no idea Ugu had such an army as that," said Dorothy. "The castle doesn't look big enough to hold them all."

"It isn't," declared the Wizard.

"But they all marched out of it."

"They seemed to, but I don't believe it is a real army at all. If Ugu the Shoemaker had so many people living with him, I'm sure the Czarover of Herku would have mentioned the fact to us."

"They're only girls!" laughed Scraps.

"Girls are the fiercest soldiers of all," declared the Frogman. "They are more brave than men, and they have better nerves. That is probably why the magician uses them for soldiers and has sent them to oppose us."

No one argued this statement, for all were staring hard at the line of soldiers, which now, having taken a defiant position, remained motionless.

"Here is a trick of magic new to me," admitted the Wizard after a time. "I do not believe the army is real, but the spears may be sharp enough to prick us, nevertheless, so we must be cautious. Let us take time to consider how to meet this difficulty."

While they were thinking it over, Scraps danced closer to the line of girl soldiers. Her button eyes sometimes saw more than did the natural eyes of her comrades, and so after staring hard at the magician's army, she boldly advanced and danced right through the threatening line! On the other side, she waved her stuffed arms and called out, "Come on, folks. The spears can't hurt you."

"Ah!" said the Wizard gaily. "An optical illusion, as I thought. Let us all follow the Patchwork Girl."

The three little girls were somewhat nervous in attempting to brave the spears and battle axes, but after the others had safely passed the line, they ventured to follow. And when all had passed through the ranks of the girl army, the army itself magically disappeared from view.

All this time our friends had been getting farther up the hill and nearer to the wicker castle. Now, continuing their advance, they expected something else to oppose their way, but to their astonishment nothing happened, and presently they arrived at the wicker gates, which stood wide open, and boldly entered the domain of Ugu the Shoemaker.

22. In the Wicker Castle

No sooner were the Wizard of Oz and his followers well within the castle entrance when the big gates swung to with a clang and heavy bars dropped across them. They looked at one another uneasily, but no one cared to speak of the incident. If they were indeed prisoners in the wicker castle, it was evident they must find a way to escape, but their first duty was to attend to the errand on which they had come and seek the Royal Ozma, whom they believed to be a prisoner of the magician, and rescue her.

They found they had entered a square courtyard, from which an entrance led into the main building of the castle. No person had appeared to greet them so far, although a gaudy peacock perched upon the wall cackled with laughter and said in its sharp, shrill voice, "Poor fools! Poor fools!"

"I hope the peacock is mistaken," remarked the Frogman, but no one else paid any attention to the bird. They were a little awed by the stillness and loneliness of the place. As they entered the doors of the castle, which stood invitingly open, these also closed behind them and huge bolts shot into place. The animals had all accompanied the party into the castle because they felt it would be dangerous for them to separate. They were forced to follow a zigzag passage, turning this way and that, until finally they entered a great central hall, circular in form and with a high dome from which was suspended an enormous chandelier.

The Wizard went first, and Dorothy, Betsy and Trot followed him, Toto keeping at the heels of his little mistress. Then came the Lion, the Woozy and the Sawhorse, then Cayke the Cookie Cook and Button-Bright, then the Lavender Bear carrying the Pink Bear, and finally the Frogman and the Patchwork Girl, with Hank the Mule tagging behind. So it was the Wizard who caught the first glimpse of the big, domed hall, but the others quickly followed and gathered in a wondering group just within the entrance.

Upon a raised platform at one side was a heavy table on which lay Glinda's Great Book of Records, but the platform was firmly fastened to the floor and the table was fastened to the platform and the Book was chained fast to the table, just as it had been when it was kept in Glinda's palace. On the wall over the table hung Ozma's Magic Picture. On a row of shelves at the opposite side of the hall stood all the chemicals and essences of magic and all the magical instruments that had been stolen from Glinda and Ozma and the Wizard, with glass doors covering the shelves so that no one could get at them.

And in a far corner sat Ugu the Shoemaker, his feet lazily extended, his skinny hands clasped behind his head. He was leaning back at his ease and calmly smoking a long pipe. Around the magician was a sort of cage, seemingly made of golden bars set wide apart, and at his feet, also within the cage, reposed the long-sought diamond-studded dishpan of Cayke the Cookie Cook. Princess Ozma of Oz was nowhere to be seen.

"Well, well," said Ugu when the invaders had stood in silence for a moment, staring about them. "This visit is an unexpected pleasure, I assure you. I knew you were coming, and I know why you are here. You are not welcome, for I cannot use any of you to my advantage, but as you have insisted on coming, I hope you will make the afternoon call as brief as possible. It won't take long to transact your business with me. You will ask me for Ozma, and my reply will be that you may find her—if you can."

"Sir," answered the Wizard in a tone of rebuke, "you are a very wicked and cruel person. I suppose you imagine, because you have stolen this poor woman's dishpan and all the best magic in Oz, that you are more powerful than we are and will be able to triumph over us."

"Yes," said Ugu the Shoemaker, slowly filling his pipe with fresh tobacco from a silver bowl that stood beside him, "that is exactly what I imagine. It will do you no good to demand from me the girl who was formerly the Ruler of Oz, because I will not tell you where I have hidden her, and you can't guess in a thousand years. Neither will I restore to you any of the magic I have captured. I am not so foolish. But bear this in mind: I mean to be the Ruler of Oz myself, hereafter, so I advise you to be careful how you address your future Monarch."

"Ozma is still Ruler of Oz, wherever you may have hidden her," declared the Wizard. "And bear this in mind, miserable Shoemaker: we intend to find her and to rescue her in time, but our first duty and pleasure will be to conquer you and then punish you for your misdeeds."

"Very well, go ahead and conquer," said Ugu. "I'd really like to see how you can do it."

Now although the little Wizard had spoken so boldly, he had at the moment no idea how they might conquer the magician. He had that morning given the Frogman, at his request, a dose of zosozo from his bottle, and the Frogman had promised to fight a good fight if it was necessary, but the Wizard knew that strength alone could not avail against magical arts. The toy Bear King seemed to have some pretty good magic, however, and the Wizard depended to an extent on that. But something ought to be done right away, and the Wizard didn't know what it was.

While he considered this perplexing question and the others stood looking at him as their leader, a queer thing happened. The floor of the great circular hall on which they were standing suddenly began to tip. Instead of being flat and level, it became a slant, and the slant grew steeper and steeper until none of the party could manage to stand upon it. Presently they all slid down to the wall, which was now under them, and then it became evident that the whole vast room was slowly turning upside down! Only Ugu the Shoemaker, kept in place by the bars of his golden cage, remained in his former position, and the wicked magician seemed to enjoy the surprise of his victims immensely.

First they all slid down to the wall back of them, but as the room continued to turn over, they next slid down the wall and found themselves at the bottom of the great dome, bumping against the big chandelier which, like everything else, was now upside down. The turning movement now stopped, and the room became stationary. Looking far up, they saw Ugu suspended in his cage at the very top, which had once been the floor.

"Ah," said he, grinning down at them, "the way to conquer is to act, and he who acts promptly is sure to win. This makes a very good prison, from which I am sure you cannot escape. Please amuse yourselves in any way you like, but I must beg you to excuse me, as I have business in another part of my castle."

Saying this, he opened a trap door in the floor of his cage (which was now over his head) and climbed through it and disappeared from their view. The diamond dishpan still remained in the cage, but the bars kept it from falling down on their heads.

"Well, I declare," said the Patchwork Girl, seizing one of the bars of the chandelier and swinging from it, "we must peg one for the Shoemaker, for he has trapped us very cleverly."

"Get off my foot, please," said the Lion to the Sawhorse.

"And oblige me, Mr. Mule," remarked the Woozy, "by taking your tail out of my left eye."

"It's rather crowded down here," explained Dorothy, "because the dome is rounding and we have all slid into the middle of it. But let us keep as quiet as possible until we can think what's best to be done."

"Dear, dear!" wailed Cayke, "I wish I had my darling dishpan," and she held her arms longingly toward it.

"I wish I had the magic on those shelves up there," sighed the Wizard.

"Don't you s'pose we could get to it?" asked Trot anxiously.

"We'd have to fly," laughed the Patchwork Girl.

But the Wizard took the suggestion seriously, and so did the Frogman. They talked it over and soon planned an attempt to reach the shelves where the magical instruments were. First the Frogman lay against the rounding dome and braced his foot on the stem of the chandelier; then the Wizard climbed over him and lay on the dome with his feet on the Frogman's shoulders; the Cookie Cook came next; then Button-Bright climbed to the woman's shoulders; then Dorothy climbed up and Betsy and Trot, and finally the Patchwork Girl, and all their lengths made a long line that reached far up the dome, but not far enough for Scraps to touch the shelves.

"Wait a minute. Perhaps I can reach the magic," called the Bear King, and began scrambling up the bodies of the others. But when he came to the Cookie Cook, his soft paws tickled her side so that she squirmed and upset the whole line. Down they came, tumbling in a heap against the animals, and although no one was much hurt, it was a bad mix-up, and the Frogman, who was at the bottom, almost lost his temper before he could get on his feet again.

Cayke positively refused to try what she called "the pyramid act" again, and as the Wizard was now convinced they could not reach the magic tools in that manner, the attempt was abandoned. "But SOMETHING must be done," said the Wizard, and then he turned to the Lavender Bear and asked, "Cannot Your Majesty's magic help us to escape from here?"

"My magic powers are limited," was the reply. "When I was stuffed, the fairies stood by and slyly dropped some magic into my stuffing. Therefore I can do any of the magic that's inside me, but nothing else. You, however, are a wizard, and a wizard should be able to do anything."

"Your Majesty forgets that my tools of magic have been stolen," said the Wizard sadly, "and a wizard without tools is as helpless as a carpenter without a hammer or saw."

"Don't give up," pleaded Button-Bright, "because if we can't get out of this queer prison, we'll all starve to death."

"Not I!" laughed the Patchwork Girl, now standing on top of the chandelier at the place that was meant to be the bottom of it.

"Don't talk of such dreadful things," said Trot, shuddering. "We came here to capture the Shoemaker, didn't we?"

"Yes, and to save Ozma," said Betsy.

"And here we are, captured ourselves, and my darling dishpan up there in plain sight!" wailed the Cookie Cook, wiping her eyes on the tail of the Frogman's coat.

"Hush!" called the Lion with a low, deep growl. "Give the Wizard time to think."

"He has plenty of time," said Scraps. "What he needs is the Scarecrow's brains."

After all, it was little Dorothy who came to their rescue, and her ability to save them was almost as much a surprise to the girl as it was to her friends. Dorothy had been secretly testing the powers of her Magic Belt, which she had once captured from the Nome King, and experimenting with it in various ways ever since she had started on this eventful journey. At different times she had stolen away from the others of her party and in solitude had tried to find out what the Magic Belt could do and what it could not do. There were a lot of things it could not do, she discovered but she learned some things about the Belt which even her girl friends did not suspect she knew.

For one thing, she had remembered that when the Nome King owned it, the Magic Belt used to perform transformations, and by thinking hard she had finally recalled the way in which such transformations had been accomplished. Better than this however, was the discovery that the Magic Belt would grant its wearer one wish a day. All she need do was close her right eye and wiggle her left toe and then draw a long breath and make her wish. Yesterday she had wished in secret for a box of caramels and instantly found the box beside her. Today she had saved her daily wish in case she might need it in an emergency, and the time had now come when she must use the wish to enable her to escape with her friends from the prison in which Ugu had caught them.

So without telling anyone what she intended to do—for she had only used the wish once and could not be certain how powerful the Magic Belt might be—Dorothy closed her right eye and wiggled her left big toe and drew a long breath and wished with all her might. The next moment the room began to revolve again as slowly as before, and by degrees they all slid to the side wall and down the wall to the floor—all but Scraps, who was so astonished that she still clung to the chandelier. When the big hall was in its proper position again and the others stood firmly upon the floor of it, they looked far up the dome and saw the Patchwork girl swinging from the chandelier.

"Good gracious!" cried Dorothy. "How ever will you get down?"

"Won't the room keep turning?" asked Scraps.

"I hope not. I believe it has stopped for good," said Princess Dorothy.

"Then stand from under, so you won't get hurt!" shouted the PatchworkGirl, and as soon as they had obeyed this request, she let go the chandelier and came tumbling down heels over head and twisting and turning in a very exciting manner. Plump! She fell on the tiled floor, and they ran to her and rolled her and patted her into shape again.

23. The Defiance of Ugu The Shoemaker

The delay caused by Scraps had prevented anyone from running to the shelves to secure the magic instruments so badly needed Even Cayke neglected to get her diamond-studded dishpan because she was watching the Patchwork Girl. And now the magician had opened his trap door and appeared in his golden cage again, frowning angrily because his prisoners had been able to turn their upside-down prison right side up. "Which of you has dared defy my magic?" he shouted in a terrible voice.

"It was I," answered Dorothy calmly.

"Then I shall destroy you, for you are only an Earth girl and no fairy," he said, and began to mumble some magic words.

Dorothy now realized that Ugu must be treated as an enemy, so she advanced toward the corner in which he sat, saying as she went, "I am not afraid of you, Mr. Shoemaker, and I think you'll be sorry, pretty soon, that you're such a bad man. You can't destroy me, and I won't destroy you, but I'm going to punish you for your wickedness."

Ugu laughed, a laugh that was not nice to hear, and then he waved his hand. Dorothy was halfway across the room when suddenly a wall of glass rose before her and stopped her progress. Through the glass she could see the magician sneering at her because she was a weak little girl, and this provoked her. Although the glass wall obliged her to halt, she instantly pressed both hands to her Magic Belt and cried in a loud voice, "Ugu the Shoemaker, by the magic virtues of the Magic Belt, I command you to become a dove!"

The magician instantly realized he was being enchanted, for he could feel his form changing. He struggled desperately against the enchantment, mumbling magic words and making magic passes with his hands. And in one way he succeeded in defeating Dorothy's purpose, for while his form soon changed to that of a gray dove, the dove was of an enormous size, bigger even than Ugu had been as a man, and this feat he had been able to accomplish before his powers of magic wholly deserted him.

And the dove was not gentle, as doves usually are, for Ugu was terribly enraged at the little girl's success. His books had told him nothing of the Nome King's Magic Belt, the Country of the Nomes being outside the Land of Oz. He knew, however, that he was likely to be conquered unless he made a fierce fight, so he spread his wings and rose in the air and flew directly toward Dorothy. The Wall of Glass had disappeared the instant Ugu became transformed.

Dorothy had meant to command the Belt to transform the magician into a Dove of Peace, but in her excitement she forgot to say more than "dove," and now not Ugu was not a Dove of Peace by any means, but rather a spiteful Dove of War. His size made his sharp beak and claws very dangerous, but Dorothy was not afraid when he came darting toward her with his talons outstretched and his sword-like beak open. She knew the Magic Belt would protect its wearer from harm.

But the Frogman did not know that fact and became alarmed at the little girl's seeming danger. So he gave a sudden leap and leaped full upon the back of the great dove. Then began a desperate struggle. The dove was as strong as Ugu had been, and in size it was considerably bigger than the Frogman. But the Frogman had eaten the zosozo, and it had made him fully as strong as Ugu the Dove. At the first leap he bore the dove to the floor, but the giant bird got free and began to bite and claw the Frogman, beating him down with its great wings whenever he attempted to rise. The thick, tough skin of the big frog was not easily damaged, but Dorothy feared for her champion, and by again using the transformation power of the Magic Belt, she made the dove grow small until it was no larger than a canary bird. Ugu had not lost his knowledge of magic when he lost his shape as a man, and he now realized it was hopeless to oppose the power of the Magic Belt and knew that his only hope of escape lay in instant action. So he quickly flew into the golden jeweled dishpan he had stolen from Cayke the Cookie Cook, and as birds can talk as well as beasts or men in the Fairyland of Oz, he muttered the magic word that was required and wished himself in the Country of the Quadlings, which was as far away from the wicker castle as he believed he could get.

Our friends did not know, of course, what Ugu was about to do. They saw the dishpan tremble an instant and then disappear, the dove disappearing with it, and although they waited expectantly for some minutes for the magician's return, Ugu did not come back again. "Seems to me," said the Wizard in a cheerful voice, "that we have conquered the wicked magician more quickly than we expected to."

"Don't say 'we.' Dorothy did it!" cried the Patchwork Girl, turning three somersaults in succession and then walking around on her hands. "Hurrah for Dorothy!"

"I thought you said you did not know how to use the magic of the Nome King's Belt," said the Wizard to Dorothy.

"I didn't know at that time," she replied, "but afterward I remembered how the Nome King once used the Magic Belt to enchant people and transform 'em into ornaments and all sorts of things, so I tried some enchantments in secret, and after a while I transformed the Sawhorse into a potato masher and back again, and the Cowardly Lion into a pussycat and back again, and then I knew the thing would work all right."

"When did you perform those enchantments?" asked the Wizard, much surprised.

"One night when all the rest of you were asleep but Scraps, and she had gone chasing moonbeams."

"Well," remarked the Wizard, "your discovery has certainly saved us a lot of trouble, and we must all thank the Frogman, too, for making such a good fight. The dove's shape had Ugu's evil disposition inside it, and that made the monster bird dangerous."

The Frogman was looking sad because the bird's talons had torn his pretty clothes, but he bowed with much dignity at this well-deserved praise. Cayke, however, had squatted on the floor and was sobbing bitterly. "My precious dishpan is gone!" she wailed. "Gone, just as I had found it again!"

"Never mind," said Trot, trying to comfort her, "it's sure to be SOMEWHERE, so we'll cert'nly run across it some day."

"Yes indeed," added Betsy, "now that we have Ozma's Magic Picture, we can tell just where the Dove went with your dishpan." They all approached the Magic Picture, and Dorothy wished it to show the enchanted form of Ugu the Shoemaker, wherever it might be. At once there appeared in the frame of the Picture a scene in the far Quadling Country, where the Dove was perched disconsolately on the limb of a tree and the jeweled dishpan lay on the ground just underneath the limb.

"But where is the place? How far or how near?" asked Cayke anxiously.

"The Book of Records will tell us that," answered the Wizard. So they looked in the Great Book and read the following: *Ugu the Magician, being transformed into a dove by Princess Dorothy of Oz, has used the magic of the golden dishpan to carry him instantly to the northeast corner of the Quadling Country.*

"Don't worry, Cayke, for the Scarecrow and the Tin Woodman are in that part of the country looking for Ozma, and they'll surely find your dishpan."

"Good gracious!" exclaimed Button-Bright. "We've forgot all about Ozma. Let's find out where the magician hid her."

Back to the Magic Picture they trooped, but when they wished to see Ozma wherever she might be hidden, only a round black spot appeared in the center of the canvas. "I don't see how THAT can be Ozma!" said Dorothy, much puzzled.

"It seems to be the best the Magic Picture can do, however," said the Wizard, no less surprised. "If it's an enchantment, looks as if the magician had transformed Ozma into a chunk of pitch."

24. The Little Pink Bear Speaks Truly

For several minutes they all stood staring at the black spot on the canvas of the Magic Picture, wondering what it could mean. "P'r'aps we'd better ask the little Pink Bear about Ozma," suggested Trot.

"Pshaw!" said Button-Bright. "HE don't know anything."

"He never makes a mistake," declared the King.

"He did once, surely," said Betsy. "But perhaps he wouldn't make a mistake again."

"He won't have the chance," grumbled the Bear King.

"We might hear what he has to say," said Dorothy. "It won't do any harm to ask the Pink Bear where Ozma is."

"I will not have him questioned," declared the King in a surly voice. "I do not intend to allow my little Pink Bear to be again insulted by your foolish doubts. He never makes a mistake."

"Didn't he say Ozma was in that hole in the ground?" asked Betsy.

"He did, and I am certain she was there," replied the Lavender Bear.

Scraps laughed jeeringly, and the others saw there was no use arguing with the stubborn Bear King, who seemed to have absolute faith in his Pink Bear. The Wizard, who knew that magical things can usually be depended upon and that the little Pink Bear was able to answer questions by some remarkable power of magic, thought it wise to apologize to the Lavender Bear for the unbelief of his friends, at the same time urging the King to consent to question the Pink Bear once more. Cayke and the Frogman also pleaded with the big Bear, who finally agreed, although rather ungraciously, to put the little Bear's wisdom to the test once more. So he sat the little one on his knee and turned the crank, and the Wizard himself asked the questions in a very respectful tone of voice. "Where is Ozma?" was his first query.

"Here in this room," answered the little Pink Bear.

They all looked around the room, but of course did not see her. "In what part of the room is she?" was the Wizard's next question.

"In Button-Bright's pocket," said the little Pink Bear.

This reply amazed them all, you may be sure, and although the three girls smiled and Scraps yelled "Hoo-ray!" in derision, the Wizard turned to consider the matter with grave thoughtfulness. "In which one of Button-Bright's pockets is Ozma?" he presently inquired.

"In the left-hand jacket pocket," said the little Pink Bear.

"The pink one has gone crazy!" exclaimed Button-Bright, staring hard at the little bear on the big bear's knee.

"I am not so sure of that," declared the Wizard. "If Ozma proves to be really in your pocket, then the little Pink Bear spoke truly when he said Ozma was in that hole in the ground. For at that time you were also in the hole, and after we had pulled you out of it, the little Pink Bear said Ozma was not in the hole."

"He never makes a mistake," asserted the Bear King stoutly.

"Empty that pocket, Button-Bright, and let's see what's in it," requested Dorothy.

So Button-Bright laid the contents of his left jacket pocket on the table. These proved to be a peg top, a bunch of string, a small rubber ball and a golden peach pit. "What's this?" asked the Wizard, picking up the peach pit and examining it closely.

"Oh," said the boy, "I saved that to show to the girls, and then forgot all about it. It came out of a lonesome peach that I found in the orchard back yonder, and which I ate while I was lost. It looks like gold, and I never saw a peach pit like it before."

"Nor I," said the Wizard, "and that makes it seem suspicious."

All heads were bent over the golden peach pit. The Wizard turned it over several times and then took out his pocket knife and pried the pit open. As the two halves fell apart, a pink, cloud-like haze came pouring from the golden peach pit, almost filling the big room, and from the haze a form took shape and settled beside them. Then, as the haze faded away, a sweet voice said, "Thank you, my friends!" and there before them stood their lovely girl Ruler, Ozma of Oz.

With a cry of delight, Dorothy rushed forward and embraced her. Scraps turned gleeful flipflops all around the room. Button-Bright gave a low whistle of astonishment. The Frogman took off his tall hat and bowed low before the beautiful girl who had been freed from her enchantment in so startling a manner. For a time, no sound was heard beyond the low murmur of delight that came from the amazed group, but presently the growl of the big Lavender Bear grew louder, and he said in a tone of triumph, "He never makes a mistake!"

25. Ozma of Oz

"It's funny," said Toto, standing before his friend the Lion and wagging his tail, "but I've found my growl at last! I am positive now that it was the cruel magician who stole it."

"Let's hear your growl," requested the Lion.

"G-r-r-r-r-r!" said Toto.

"That is fine," declared the big beast. "It isn't as loud or as deep as the growl of the big Lavender Bear, but it is a very respectable growl for a small dog. Where did you find it, Toto?"

"I was smelling in the corner yonder," said Toto, "when suddenly a mouse ran out—and I growled."

The others were all busy congratulating Ozma, who was very happy at being released from the confinement of the golden peach pit, where the magician had placed her with the notion that she never could be found or liberated.

"And only to think," cried Dorothy, "that Button-Bright has been carrying you in his pocket all this time, and we never knew it!"

The little Pink Bear told you," said the Bear King, "but you wouldn't believe him."

"Never mind, my dears," said Ozma graciously, "all is well that ends well, and you couldn't be expected to know I was inside the peach pit. Indeed, I feared I would remain a captive much longer than I did, for Ugu is a bold and clever magician, and he had hidden me very securely."

"You were in a fine peach," said Button-Bright, "the best I ever ate."

"The magician was foolish to make the peach so tempting," remarked the Wizard, "but Ozma would lend beauty to any transformation."

"How did you manage to conquer Ugu the Shoemaker?" inquired the girl Ruler of Oz.

Dorothy started to tell the story, and Trot helped her, and Button-Bright wanted to relate it in his own way, and the Wizard tried to make it clear to Ozma, and Betsy had to remind them of important things they left out, and all together there was such a chatter that it was a wonder that Ozma understood any of it. But she listened patiently, with a smile on her lovely face at their eagerness, and presently had gleaned all the details of their adventures.

Ozma thanked the Frogman very earnestly for his assistance, and she advised Cayke the Cookie Cook to dry her weeping eyes, for she promised to take her to the Emerald City and see that her cherished dishpan was restored to her. Then the beautiful Ruler took a chain of emeralds from around her own neck and placed it round the neck of the little Pink Bear.

"Your wise answers to the questions of my friends," said she, "helped them to rescue me. Therefore I am deeply grateful to you and to your noble King."

The bead eyes of the little Pink Bear stared unresponsive to this praise until the Big Lavender Bear turned the crank in its side, when it said in its squeaky voice, "I thank Your Majesty."

"For my part," returned the Bear King, "I realize that you were well worth saving, Miss Ozma, and so I am much pleased that we could be of service to you. By means of my Magic Wand I have been creating exact images of your Emerald City and your Royal Palace, and I must confess that they are more attractive than any places I have ever seen—not excepting Bear Center."

"I would like to entertain you in my palace," returned Ozma sweetly, "and you are welcome to return with me and to make me a long visit, if your bear subjects can spare you from your own kingdom."

"As for that," answered the King, "my kingdom causes me little worry, and I often find it somewhat tame and uninteresting. Therefore I am glad to accept your kind invitation. Corporal Waddle may be trusted to care for my bears in my absence."

"And you'll bring the little Pink Bear?" asked Dorothy eagerly.

"Of course, my dear. I would not willingly part with him."

They remained in the wicker castle for three days, carefully packing all the magical things that had been stolen by Ugu and also taking whatever in the way of magic the shoemaker had inherited from his ancestors. "For," said Ozma, "I have forbidden any of my subjects except Glinda the Good and the Wizard of Oz to practice magical arts, because they cannot be trusted to do good and not harm. Therefore Ugu must never again be permitted to work magic of any sort."

"Well," remarked Dorothy cheerfully, "a dove can't do much in the way of magic, anyhow, and I'm going to keep Ugu in the form of a dove until he reforms and becomes a good and honest shoemaker."

When everything was packed and loaded on the backs of the animals, they set out for the river, taking a more direct route than that by which Cayke and the Frogman had come. In this way they avoided the Cities of Thi and Herku and Bear Center and after a pleasant journey reached the Winkie River and found a jolly ferryman who had a fine, big boat and was willing to carry the entire party by water to a place quite near to the Emerald City.

The river had many windings and many branches, and the journey did not end in a day, but finally the boat floated into a pretty lake which was but a short distance from Ozma's home. Here the jolly ferryman was rewarded for his labors, and then the entire party set out in a grand procession to march to the Emerald City. News that the Royal Ozma had been found spread quickly throughout the neighborhood, and both sides of the road soon became lined with loyal subjects of the beautiful and beloved Ruler. Therefore Ozma's ears heard little but cheers, and her eyes beheld little else than waving handkerchiefs and banners during all the triumphal march from the lake to the city's gates.

And there she met a still greater concourse, for all the inhabitants of the Emerald City turned out to welcome her return, and all the houses were decorated with flags and bunting, and never before were the people so joyous and happy as at this moment when they welcomed home their girl Ruler. For she had been lost and was now found again, and surely that was cause for rejoicing. Glinda was at the royal palace to meet the returning party, and the good Sorceress was indeed glad to have her Great Book of Records returned to her, as well as all the precious collection of magic instruments and elixirs and chemicals that had been stolen from her castle. Cap'n Bill and the Wizard at once hung the Magic Picture upon the wall of Ozma's boudoir, and the Wizard was so light-hearted that he did several tricks with the tools in his black bag to amuse his companions and prove that once again he was a powerful wizard.

For a whole week there was feasting and merriment and all sorts of joyous festivities at the palace in honor of Ozma's safe return. The Lavender Bear and the little Pink Bear received much attention and were honored by all, much to the Bear King's satisfaction. The Frogman speedily became a favorite at the Emerald City, and the Shaggy Man and Tik-Tok and Jack Pumpkinhead, who had now returned from their search, were very polite to the big frog and made him feel quite at home. Even the Cookie Cook, because she was quite a stranger and Ozma's guest, was shown as much deference as if she had been a queen.

"All the same, Your Majesty," said Cayke to Ozma, day after day with tiresome repetition, "I hope you will soon find my jeweled dishpan, for never can I be quite happy without it."

26. Dorothy Forgives

The gray dove which had once been Ugu the Shoemaker sat on its tree in the far Quadling Country and moped, chirping dismally and brooding over its misfortunes. After a time, the Scarecrow and the Tin Woodman came along and sat beneath the tree, paying no heed to the mutterings of the gray dove. The Tin Woodman took a small oilcan from his tin pocket and carefully oiled his tin joints with it.

While he was thus engaged, the Scarecrow remarked, "I feel much better, dear comrade, since we found that heap of nice, clean straw and you stuffed me anew with it."

"And I feel much better now that my joints are oiled," returned the Tin Woodman with a sigh of pleasure. "You and I, friend Scarecrow, are much more easily cared for than those clumsy meat people, who spend half their time dressing in fine clothes and who must live in splendid dwellings in order to be contented and happy. You and I do not eat, and so we are spared the dreadful bother of getting three meals a day. Nor do we waste half our lives in sleep, a condition that causes the meat people to lose all consciousness and become as thoughtless and helpless as logs of wood."

"You speak truly," responded the Scarecrow, tucking some wisps of straw into his breast with his padded fingers. "I often feel sorry for the meat people, many of whom are my friends. Even the beasts are happier than they, for they require less to make them content. And the birds are the luckiest creatures of all, for they can fly swiftly where they will and find a home at any place they care to perch. Their food consists of seeds and grains they gather from the fields, and their drink is a sip of water from some running brook. If I could not be a Scarecrow or a Tin Woodman, my next choice would be to live as a bird does."

The gray dove had listened carefully to this speech and seemed to find comfort in it, for it hushed its moaning. And just then the Tin Woodman discovered Cayke's dishpan, which was on the ground quite near to him. "Here is a rather pretty utensil," he said, taking it in his tin hand to examine it, "but I would not care to own it. Whoever fashioned it of gold and covered it with diamonds did not add to its usefulness, nor do I consider it as beautiful as the bright dishpans of tin one usually sees. No yellow color is ever so handsome as the silver sheen of tin," and he turned to look at his tin legs and body with approval.

"I cannot quite agree with you there," replied the Scarecrow. "My straw stuffing has a light yellow color, and it is not only pretty to look at, but it crunkles most delightfully when I move."

"Let us admit that all colors are good in their proper places," said the Tin Woodman, who was too kind-hearted to quarrel, "but you must agree with me that a dishpan that is yellow is unnatural. What shall we do with this one, which we have just found?"

"Let us carry it back to the Emerald City," suggested the Scarecrow. "Some of our friends might like to have it for a foot-bath, and in using it that way, its golden color and sparkling ornaments would not injure its usefulness."

So they went away and took the jeweled dishpan with them. And after wandering through the country for a day or so longer, they learned the news that Ozma had been found. Therefore they straightway returned to the Emerald City and presented the dishpan to Princess Ozma as a token of their joy that she had been restored to them. Ozma promptly gave the diamond-studded gold dishpan to Cayke the Cookie Cook, who was delighted at regaining her lost treasure that she danced up and down in glee and then threw her skinny arms around Ozma's neck and kissed her gratefully. Cayke's mission was now successfully accomplished, but she was having such a good time at the Emerald City that she seemed in no hurry to go back to the Country of the Yips.

It was several weeks after the dishpan had been restored to the Cookie Cook when one day, as Dorothy was seated in the royal gardens with Trot and Betsy beside her, a gray dove came flying down and alighted at the girl's feet.

"I am Ugu the Shoemaker," said the dove in a soft, mourning voice, "and I have come to ask you to forgive me for the great wrong I did in stealing Ozma and the magic that belonged to her and to others."

"Are you sorry, then?" asked Dorothy, looking hard at the bird.

"I am VERY sorry," declared Ugu. "I've been thinking over my misdeeds for a long time, for doves have little else to do but think, and I'm surprised that I was such a wicked man and had so little regard for the rights of others. I am now convinced that even had I succeeded in making myself ruler of all Oz, I should not have been happy, for many days of quiet thought have shown me that only those things one acquires honestly are able to render one content."

"I guess that's so," said Trot.

"Anyhow," said Betsy, "the bad man seems truly sorry, and if he has now become a good and honest man, we ought to forgive him."

"I fear I cannot become a good MAN again," said Ugu, "for the transformation I am under will always keep me in the form of a dove. But with the kind forgiveness of my former enemies, I hope to become a very good dove and highly respected."

"Wait here till I run for my Magic Belt," said Dorothy, "and I'll transform you back to your reg'lar shape in a jiffy."

"No, don't do that!" pleaded the dove, fluttering its wings in an excited way. "I only want your forgiveness. I don't want to be a man again. As Ugu the Shoemaker I was skinny and old and unlovely. As a dove I am quite pretty to look at. As a man I was ambitious and cruel, while as a dove I can be content with my lot and happy in my simple life. I have learned to love the free and independent life of a bird, and I'd rather not change back."

"Just as you like, Ugu," said Dorothy, resuming her seat. "Perhaps you are right, for you're certainly a better dove than you were a man, and if you should ever backslide an' feel wicked again, you couldn't do much harm as a gray dove."

"Then you forgive me for all the trouble I caused you?" he asked earnestly.

"Of course. Anyone who's sorry just has to be forgiven."

"Thank you," said the gray dove, and flew away again.

The Tin Woodman Of Oz
by L. Frank Baum

A Faithful Story of the Astonishing Adventure Undertaken by the Tin Woodman, assisted by Woot the Wanderer, the Scarecrow of Oz, and Polychrome, the Rainbow's Daughter, by L. Frank Baum, "Royal Historian of Oz".

This Book is dedicated to the son of my son, Frank Alden Baum.

To My Readers

I know that some of you have been waiting for this story of the Tin Woodman, because many of my correspondents have asked me, time and again what ever became of the "pretty Munchkin girl" whom Nick Chopper was engaged to marry before the Wicked Witch enchanted his axe and he traded his flesh for tin. I, too, have wondered what became of her, but until Woot the Wanderer interested himself in the matter the Tin Woodman knew no more than we did. However, he found her, after many thrilling adventures, as you will discover when you have read this story.

I am delighted at the continued interest of both young and old in the Oz stories. A learned college professor recently wrote me to ask: "For readers of what age are your books intended?" It puzzled me to answer that properly, until I had looked over some of the letters I have received. One says: "I'm a little boy 5 years old, and I just love your Oz stories. My sister, who is writing this for me, reads me the Oz books, but I wish I could read them myself." Another letter says: "I'm a great girl 13 years old, so you'll be surprised when I tell you I am not too old yet for the Oz stories." Here's another letter: "Since I was a young girl I've never missed getting a Baum book for Christmas. I'm married, now, but am as eager to get and read the Oz stories as ever." And still another writes: "My good wife and I, both more than 70 years of age, believe that we find more real enjoyment in your Oz books than in any other books we read." Considering these statements, I wrote the college professor that my books are intended for all those whose hearts are young, no matter what their ages may be.

I think I am justified in promising that there will be some astonishing revelations about The Magic of Oz in my book for 1919. Always your loving and grateful friend,

L. Frank Baum, "Royal Historian of Oz"
"Ozcot" at Hollywood in California, 1918.

1. Woot the Wanderer

The Tin Woodman sat on his glittering tin throne in the handsome tin hall of his splendid tin castle in the Winkie Country of the Land of Oz. Beside him, in a chair of woven straw, sat his best friend, the Scarecrow of Oz. At times they spoke to one another of curious things they had seen and strange adventures they had known since first they two had met and become comrades. But at times they were silent, for these things had been talked over many times between them, and they found themselves contented in merely being together, speaking now and then a brief sentence to prove they were wide awake and attentive. But then, these two quaint persons never slept. Why should they sleep, when they never tired?

And now, as the brilliant sun sank low over the Winkie Country of Oz, tinting the glistening tin towers and tin minarets of the tin castle with glorious sunset hues, there approached along a winding pathway Woot the Wanderer, who met at the castle entrance a Winkie servant.

The servants of the Tin Woodman all wore tin helmets and tin breastplates and uniforms covered with tiny tin discs sewed closely together on silver cloth, so that their bodies sparkled as beautifully as did the tin castle — and almost as beautifully as did the Tin Woodman himself.

Woot the Wanderer looked at the manservant — all bright and glittering — and at the magnificent castle — all bright and glittering — and as he looked his eyes grew big with wonder. For Woot was not very big and not very old and, wanderer though he was, this proved the most gorgeous sight that had ever met his boyish gaze.

"Who lives here?" he asked.

"The Emperor of the Winkies, who is the famous Tin Woodman of Oz," replied the servant, who had been trained to treat all strangers with courtesy.

"A Tin Woodman? How queer!" exclaimed the little wanderer.

"Well, perhaps our Emperor is queer," admitted the servant; "but he is a kind master and as honest and true as good tin can make him; so we, who gladly serve him, are apt to forget that he is not like other people."

"May I see him?" asked Woot the Wanderer, after a moment's thought.

"If it please you to wait a moment, I will go and ask him," said the servant, and then he went into the hall where the Tin Woodman sat with his friend the Scarecrow. Both were glad to learn that a stranger had arrived at the castle, for this would give them something new to talk about, so the servant was asked to admit the boy at once.

By the time Woot the Wanderer had passed through the grand corridors — all lined with ornamental tin — and under stately tin archways and through the many tin rooms all set with beautiful tin furniture, his eyes had grown bigger than ever and his whole little body thrilled with amazement. But, astonished though he was, he was able to make a polite bow before the throne and to say in a respectful voice: "I salute your Illustrious Majesty and offer you my humble services."

"Very good!" answered the Tin Woodman in his accustomed cheerful manner. "Tell me who you are, and whence you come."

"I am known as Woot the Wanderer," answered the boy, "and I have come, through many travels and by roundabout ways, from my former home in a far corner of the Gillikin Country of Oz."

"To wander from one's home," remarked the Scarecrow, "is to encounter dangers and hardships, especially if one is made of meat and bone. Had you no friends in that corner of the Gillikin Country? Was it not homelike and comfortable?"

To hear a man stuffed with straw speak, and speak so well, quite startled Woot, and perhaps he stared a bit rudely at the Scarecrow. But after a moment he replied: "I had home and friends, your Honorable Strawness, but they were so quiet and happy and comfortable that I found them dismally stupid. Nothing in that corner of Oz interested me, but I believed that in other parts of the country I would find strange people and see new sights, and so I set out upon my wandering journey. I have been a wanderer for nearly a full year, and now my wanderings have brought me to this splendid castle."

"I suppose," said the Tin Woodman, "that in this year you have seen so much that you have become very wise."

"No," replied Woot, thoughtfully, "I am not at all wise, I beg to assure your Majesty. The more I wander the less I find that I know, for in the Land of Oz much wisdom and many things may be learned."

"To learn is simple. Don't you ask questions?" inquired the Scarecrow.

"Yes; I ask as many questions as I dare; but some people refuse to answer questions."

"That is not kind of them," declared the Tin Woodman. "If one does not ask for information he seldom receives it; so I, for my part, make it a rule to answer any civil question that is asked me."

"So do I," added the Scarecrow, nodding.

"I am glad to hear this," said the Wanderer, "for it makes me bold to ask for something to eat."

"Bless the boy!" cried the Emperor of the Winkies; "how careless of me not to remember that wanderers are usually hungry. I will have food brought you at once."

Saying this he blew upon a tin whistle that was suspended from his tin neck, and at the summons a servant appeared and bowed low. The Tin Woodman ordered food for the stranger, and in a few minutes the servant brought in a tin tray heaped with a choice array of good things to eat, all neatly displayed on tin dishes that were polished till they shone like mirrors. The tray was set upon a tin table drawn before the throne, and the servant placed a tin chair before the table for the boy to seat himself.

"Eat, friend Wanderer," said the Emperor cordially, "and I trust the feast will be to your liking. I, myself, do not eat, being made in such manner that I require no food to keep me alive. Neither does my friend the Scarecrow. But all my Winkie people eat, being formed of flesh, as you are, and so my tin cupboard is never bare, and strangers are always welcome to whatever it contains."

The boy ate in silence for a time, being really hungry, but after his appetite was somewhat satisfied, he said: "How happened your Majesty to be made of tin, and still be alive?"

"That," replied the tin man, "is a long story."

"The longer the better," said the boy. "Won't you please tell me the story?"

"If you desire it," promised the Tin Woodman, leaning back in his tin throne and crossing his tin legs. "I haven't related my history in a long while, because everyone here knows it nearly as well as I do. But you, being a stranger, are no doubt curious to learn how I became so beautiful and prosperous, so I will recite for your benefit my strange adventures."

"Thank you," said Woot the Wanderer, still eating.

"I was not always made of tin," began the Emperor, "for in the beginning I was a man of flesh and bone and blood and lived in the Munchkin Country of Oz. There I was, by trade, a woodchopper, and contributed my share to the comfort of the Oz people by chopping up the trees of the forest to make firewood, with which the women would cook their meals while the children warmed themselves about the fires. For my home I had a little hut by the edge of the forest, and my life was one of much content until I fell in love with a beautiful Munchkin girl who lived not far away."

"What was the Munchkin girl's name?" asked Woot.

"Nimmie Amee. This girl, so fair that the sunsets blushed when their rays fell upon her, lived with a powerful witch who wore silver shoes and who had made the poor child her slave. Nimmie Amee was obliged to work from morning till night for the old Witch of the East, scrubbing and sweeping her hut and cooking her meals and washing her dishes. She had to cut firewood, too, until I found her one day in the forest and fell in love with her. After that, I always brought plenty of firewood to Nimmie Amee and we became very friendly. Finally I asked her to marry me, and she agreed to do so, but the Witch happened to overhear our conversation and it made her very angry, for she did not wish her slave to be taken away from her. The Witch commanded me never to come near Nimmie Amee again, but I told her I was my own master and would do as I pleased, not realizing that this was a careless way to speak to a Witch.

"The next day, as I was cutting wood in the forest, the cruel Witch enchanted my axe, so that it slipped and cut off my right leg."

"How dreadful!" cried Woot the Wanderer.

"Yes, it was a seeming misfortune," agreed the Tin Man, "for a one-legged woodchopper is of little use in his trade. But I would not allow the Witch to conquer me so easily. I knew a very skillful mechanic at the other side of the forest, who was my friend, so I hopped on one leg to him and asked him to help me. He soon made me a new leg out of tin and fastened it cleverly to my meat body. It had joints at the knee and at the ankle and was almost as comfortable as the leg I had lost."

"Your friend must have been a wonderful workman!" exclaimed Woot.

"He was, indeed," admitted the Emperor. "He was a tinsmith by trade and could make anything out of tin. When I returned to Nimmie Amee, the girl was delighted and threw her arms around my neck and kissed me, declaring she was proud of me. The Witch saw the kiss and was more angry than before. When I went to work in the forest, next day, my axe, being still enchanted, slipped and cut off my other leg. Again I hopped — on my tin leg — to my friend the tinsmith, who kindly made me another tin leg and fastened it to my body. So I returned joyfully to Nimmie Amee, who was much pleased with my glittering legs and promised that when we were wed she would always keep them oiled and polished. But the Witch was more furious than ever, and as soon as I raised my axe to chop, it twisted around and cut off one of my arms. The tinsmith made me a tin arm and I was not much worried, because Nimmie Amee declared she still loved me."

2. The Heart of the Tin Woodman

The Emperor of the Winkies paused in his story to reach for an oil-can, with which he carefully oiled the joints in his tin throat, for his voice had begun to squeak a little. Woot the Wanderer, having satisfied his hunger, watched this oiling process with much curiosity, but begged the Tin Man to go on with his tale.

The Witch with the Silver Shoes hated me for having defied er," resumed the Emperor, his voice now sounding clear as a ell, "and she insisted that Nimmie Amee should never marry ie. Therefore she made the enchanted axe cut off my other arm, nd the tinsmith also replaced that member with tin, including iese finely-jointed hands that you see me using. But, alas! after iat, the axe, still enchanted by the cruel Witch, cut my body in wo, so that I fell to the ground. Then the Witch, who was ratching from a near-by bush, rushed up and seized the axe and hopped my body into several small pieces, after which, thinking iat at last she had destroyed me, she ran away laughing in ·icked glee.

But Nimmie Amee found me. She picked up my arms and legs nd head, and made a bundle of them and carried them to the nsmith, who set to work and made me a fine body of pure tin. Vhen he had joined the arms and legs to the body, and set my ead in the tin collar, I was a much better man than ever, for my ody could not ache or pain me, and I was so beautiful and right that I had no need of clothing. Clothing is always a uisance, because it soils and tears and has to be replaced; but iy tin body only needs to be oiled and polished.

Nimmie Amee still declared she would marry me, as she still oved me in spite of the Witch's evil deeds. The girl declared I ould make the brightest husband in all the world, which was uite true. However, the Wicked Witch was not yet defeated. Vhen I returned to my work the axe slipped and cut off my head, hich was the only meat part of me then remaining. Moreover, ie old woman grabbed up my severed head and carried it away ith her and hid it. But Nimmie Amee came into the forest and und me wandering around helplessly, because I could not see here to go, and she led me to my friend the tinsmith. The ithful fellow at once set to work to make me a tin head, and he ad just completed it when Nimmie Amee came running up with iy old head, which she had stolen from the Witch. But, on :flection, I considered the tin head far superior to the meat one - I am wearing it yet, so you can see its beauty and grace of utline — and the girl agreed with me that a man all made of tin as far more perfect than one formed of different materials. The nsmith was as proud of his workmanship as I was, and for iree whole days, all admired me and praised my beauty. "Being ow completely formed of tin, I had no more fear of the Wicked 'itch, for she was powerless to injure me. Nimmie Amee said e must be married at once, for then she could come to my ittage and live with me and keep me bright and sparkling.

I am sure, my dear Nick,' said the brave and beautiful girl — my ame was then Nick Chopper, you should be told — 'that you will iake the best husband any girl could have. I shall not be obliged · cook for you, for now you do not eat; I shall not have to make iur bed, for tin does not tire or require sleep; when we go to a ance, you will not get weary before the music stops and say you ant to go home. All day long, while you are chopping wood in ie forest, I shall be able to amuse myself in my own way — a rivilege few wives enjoy. There is no temper in your new head, · you will not get angry with me. Finally, I shall take pride in eing the wife of the only live Tin Woodman in all the world!' hich shows that Nimmie Amee was as wise as she was brave id beautiful."

think she was a very nice girl," said Woot the Wanderer. "But, ll me, please, why were you not killed when you were chopped · pieces?"

n the Land of Oz," replied the Emperor, "no one can ever be lled. A man with a wooden leg or a tin leg is still the same man;

and, as I lost parts of my meat body by degrees, I always remained the same person as in the beginning, even though in the end I was all tin and no meat."

"I see," said the boy, thoughtfully. "And did you marry Nimmie Amee?"

"No," answered the Tin Woodman, "I did not. She said she still loved me, but I found that I no longer loved her. My tin body contained no heart, and without a heart no one can love. So the Wicked Witch conquered in the end, and when I left the Munchkin Country of Oz, the poor girl was still the slave of the Witch and had to do her bidding day and night."

"Where did you go?" asked Woot.

"Well, I first started out to find a heart, so I could love Nimmie Amee again; but hearts are more scarce than one would think. One day, in a big forest that was strange to me, my joints suddenly became rusted, because I had forgotten to oil them. There I stood, unable to move hand or foot. And there I continued to stand — while days came and went — until Dorothy and the Scarecrow came along and rescued me. They oiled my joints and set me free, and I've taken good care never to rust again."

"Who was this Dorothy?" questioned the Wanderer.

"A little girl who happened to be in a house when it was carried by a cyclone all the way from Kansas to the Land of Oz. When the house fell, in the Munchkin Country, it fortunately landed on the Wicked Witch and smashed her flat. It was a big house, and I think the Witch is under it yet."

"No," said the Scarecrow, correcting him, "Dorothy says the Witch turned to dust, and the wind scattered the dust in every direction."

"Well," continued the Tin Woodman, "after meeting the Scarecrow and Dorothy, I went with them to the Emerald City, where the Wizard of Oz gave me a heart. But the Wizard's stock of hearts was low, and he gave me a Kind Heart instead of a Loving Heart, so that I could not love Nimmie Amee any more than I did when I was heartless."

"Couldn't the Wizard give you a heart that was both Kind and Loving?" asked the boy.

"No; that was what I asked for, but he said he was so short on hearts, just then, that there was but one in stock, and I could take that or none at all. So I accepted it, and I must say that for its kind it is a very good heart indeed."

"It seems to me," said Woot, musingly, "that the Wizard fooled you. It can't be a very Kind Heart, you know."

"Why not?" demanded the Emperor.

"Because it was unkind of you to desert the girl who loved you, and who had been faithful and true to you when you were in trouble. Had the heart the Wizard gave you been a Kind Heart, you would have gone back home and made the beautiful Munchkin girl your wife, and then brought her here to be an Empress and live in your splendid tin castle."

The Tin Woodman was so surprised at this frank speech that for a time he did nothing but stare hard at the boy Wanderer. But the Scarecrow wagged his stuffed head and said in a positive tone: "This boy is right. I've often wondered, myself, why you didn't go back and find that poor Munchkin girl."

Then the Tin Woodman stared hard at his friend the Scarecrow. But finally he said in a serious tone of voice: "I must admit that never before have I thought of such a thing as finding Nimmie Amee and making her Empress of the Winkies. But it is surely not too late, even now, to do this, for the girl must still be living in the Munchkin Country. And, since this strange Wanderer has reminded me of Nimmie Amee, I believe it is my duty to set out and find her. Surely it is not the girl's fault that I no longer love her, and so, if I can make her happy, it is proper that I should do so, and in this way reward her for her faithfulness."

"Quite right, my friend!" agreed the Scarecrow.

"Will you accompany me on this errand?" asked the Tin Emperor.

"Of course," said the Scarecrow.

"And will you take me along?" pleaded Woot the Wanderer in an eager voice.

"To be sure," said the Tin Woodman, "if you care to join our party. It was you who first told me it was my duty to find and marry Nimmie Amee, and I'd like you to know that Nick Chopper, the Tin Emperor of the Winkies, is a man who never shirks his duty, once it is pointed out to him."

"It ought to be a pleasure, as well as a duty, if the girl is so beautiful," said Woot, well pleased with the idea of the adventure.

"Beautiful things may be admired, if not loved," asserted the Tin Man. "Flowers are beautiful, for instance, but we are not inclined to marry them. Duty, on the contrary, is a bugle call to action, whether you are inclined to act, or not. In this case, I obey the bugle call of duty."

"When shall we start?" inquired the Scarecrow, who was always glad to embark upon a new adventure. "I don't hear any bugle, but when do we go?"

"As soon as we can get ready," answered the Emperor. "I'll call my servants at once and order them to make preparations for our journey."

3. Roundabout

Woot the Wanderer slept that night in the tin castle of the Emperor of the Winkies and found his tin bed quite comfortable. Early the next morning he rose and took a walk through the gardens, where there were tin fountains and beds of curious tin flowers, and where tin birds perched upon the branches of tin trees and sang songs that sounded like the notes of tin whistles. All these wonders had been made by the clever Winkie tinsmiths, who wound the birds up every morning so that they would move about and sing.

After breakfast the boy went into the throne room, where the Emperor was having his tin joints carefully oiled by a servant, while other servants were stuffing sweet, fresh straw into the body of the Scarecrow. Woot watched this operation with much interest, for the Scarecrow's body was only a suit of clothes filled with straw. The coat was buttoned tight to keep the packed straw from falling out and a rope was tied around the waist to hold it in shape and prevent the straw from sagging down. The Scarecrow's head was a gunnysack filled with bran, on which th[e] eyes, nose and mouth had been painted. His hands were whit[e] cotton gloves stuffed with fine straw. Woot noticed that eve[n] when carefully stuffed and patted into shape, the straw man wa[s] awkward in his movements and decidedly wobbly on his feet, s[o] the boy wondered if the Scarecrow would be able to travel wit[h] them all the way to the forests of the Munchkin Country of Oz.

The preparations made for this important journey were ver[y] simple. A knapsack was filled with food and given Woot th[e] Wanderer to carry upon his back, for the food was for his us[e] alone. The Tin Woodman shouldered an axe which was shar[p] and brightly polished, and the Scarecrow put the Emperor's oi[l] can in his pocket, that he might oil his friend's joints should the[re] need it.

"Who will govern the Winkie Country during your absence[?]" asked the boy.

"Why, the Country will run itself," answered the Emperor. "As [a] matter of fact, my people do not need an Emperor, for Ozma o[f] Oz watches over the welfare of all her subjects, including th[e] Winkies. Like a good many kings and emperors, I have a gran[d] title, but very little real power, which allows me time to amus[e] myself in my own way. The people of Oz have but one law t[o] obey, which is: 'Behave Yourself,' so it is easy for them to abid[e] by this Law, and you'll notice they behave very well. But it is tim[e] for us to be off, and I am eager to start because I suppose tha[t] that poor Munchkin girl is anxiously awaiting my coming."

"She's waited a long time already, seems to me," remarked th[e] Scarecrow, as they left the grounds of the castle and followed [a] path that led eastward.

"True," replied the Tin Woodman; "but I've noticed that the la[st] end of a wait, however long it has been, is the hardest to endur[e], so I must try to make Nimmie Amee happy as soon as possible."

"Ah; that proves you have a Kind heart," remarked th[e] Scarecrow, approvingly.

"It's too bad he hasn't a Loving Heart," said Woot. "This Tin Ma[n] is going to marry a nice girl through kindness, and not becaus[e] he loves her, and somehow that doesn't seem quite right."

"Even so, I am not sure it isn't best for the girl," said th[e] Scarecrow, who seemed very intelligent for a straw man, "for [a] loving husband is not always kind, while a kind husband is su[re] to make any girl content."

"Nimmie Amee will become an Empress!" announced the Ti[n] Woodman, proudly. "I shall have a tin gown made for her, wit[h] tin ruffles and tucks on it, and she shall have tin slippers, and t[in] earrings and bracelets, and wear a tin crown on her head. I a[m] sure that will delight Nimmie Amee, for all girls are fond [of] finery."

"Are we going to the Munchkin Country by way of the Emeral[d] City?" inquired the Scarecrow, who looked upon the Ti[n] Woodman as the leader of the party.

"I think not," was the reply. "We are engaged upon a rathe[r] delicate adventure, for we are seeking a girl who fears her forme[r] lover has forgotten her. It will be rather hard for me, you mu[st] admit, when I confess to Nimmie Amee that I have come t[o] marry her because it is my duty to do so, and therefore the few[er] witnesses there are to our meeting the better for both of us. Afte[r] I have found Nimmie Amee and she has managed to control he[r] joy at our reunion, I shall take her to the Emerald City and introduce her to Ozma and Dorothy, and to Betsy Bobbin and Tiny Trot, and all our other friends; but, if I remember rightly, poor Nimmie Amee has a sharp tongue when angry, and she may be a trifle angry with me, at first, because I have been so long in coming to her."

"I can understand that," said Woot gravely. "But how can we get to that part of the Munchkin Country where you once lived without passing through the Emerald City?"

"Why, that is easy," the Tin Man assured him.

"I have a map of Oz in my pocket," persisted the boy, "and it shows that the Winkie Country, where we now are, is at the west of Oz, and the Munchkin Country at the east, while directly between them lies the Emerald City."

"True enough; but we shall go toward the north, first of all, into the Gillikin Country, and so pass around the Emerald City," explained the Tin Woodman.

"That may prove a dangerous journey," replied the boy. "I used to live in one of the top corners of the Gillikin Country, near to Oogaboo, and I have been told that in this northland country are many people whom it is not pleasant to meet. I was very careful to avoid them during my journey south."

"A Wanderer should have no fear," observed the Scarecrow, who was wobbling along in a funny, haphazard manner, but keeping pace with his friends.

"Fear does not make one a coward," returned Woot, growing a little red in the face, "but I believe it is more easy to avoid danger than to overcome it. The safest way is the best way, even for one who is brave and determined."

"Do not worry, for we shall not go far to the north," said the Emperor. "My one idea is to avoid the Emerald City without going out of our way more than is necessary. Once around the Emerald City we will turn south into the Munchkin Country, where the Scarecrow and I are well acquainted and have many friends."

"I have traveled some in the Gillikin Country," remarked the Scarecrow, "and while I must say I have met some strange people there at times, I have never yet been harmed by them."

"Well, it's all the same to me," said Woot, with assumed carelessness. "Dangers, when they cannot be avoided, are often quite interesting, and I am willing to go wherever you two venture to go."

So they left the path they had been following and began to travel toward the northeast, and all that day they were in the pleasant Winkie Country, and all the people they met saluted the Emperor with great respect and wished him good luck on his journey. At night they stopped at a house where they were well entertained and where Woot was given a comfortable bed to sleep in.

"Were the Scarecrow and I alone," said the Tin Woodman, "we would travel by night as well as by day; but with a meat person in our party, we must halt at night to permit him to rest."

"Meat tires, after a day's travel," added the Scarecrow, "while straw and tin never tire at all. Which proves," said he, "that we are somewhat superior to people made in the common way."

Woot could not deny that he was tired, and he slept soundly until morning, when he was given a good breakfast, smoking hot.

"You two miss a great deal by not eating," he said to his companions.

"It is true," responded the Scarecrow. "We miss suffering from hunger, when food cannot be had, and we miss a stomachache, now and then."

As he said this, the Scarecrow glanced at the Tin Woodman, who nodded his assent.

All that second day they traveled steadily, entertaining one another the while with stories of adventures they had formerly met and listening to the Scarecrow recite poetry. He had learned a great many poems from Professor Wogglebug and loved to repeat them whenever anybody would listen to him. Of course Woot and the Tin Woodman now listened, because they could not do otherwise — unless they rudely ran away from their stuffed comrade.

One of the Scarecrow's recitations was like this:
"What sound is so sweet
As the straw from the wheat
When it crunkles so tender and low?
It is yellow and bright,
So it gives me delight
To crunkle wherever I go.

Sweet, fresh, golden Straw!
There is surely no flaw
In a stuffing so clean and compact.
It creaks when I walk,
And it thrills when I talk,
And its fragrance is fine, for a fact.

To cut me don't hurt,
For I've no blood to squirt,
And I therefore can suffer no pain;
The straw that I use
Doesn't lump up or bruise,
Though it's pounded again and again!

I know it is said
That my beautiful head
Has brains of mixed wheat-straw and bran,
But my thoughts are so good
I'd not change, if I could,
For the brains of a common meat man.

Content with my lot,
I'm glad that I'm not
Like others I meet day by day;
If my insides get musty,
Or mussed-up, or dusty,
I get newly stuffed right away."

4. The Loons of Loonville

Toward evening, the travelers found there was no longer a path to guide them, and the purple hues of the grass and trees warned them that they were now in the Country of the Gillikins, where strange peoples dwelt in places that were quite unknown to the other inhabitants of Oz. The fields were wild and uncultivated and there were no houses of any sort to be seen. But our friends kept on walking even after the sun went down, hoping to find a good place for Woot the Wanderer to sleep; but when it grew quite dark and the boy was weary with his long walk, they halted right in the middle of a field and allowed Woot to get his supper from the food he carried in his knapsack. Then the Scarecrow laid himself down, so that Woot could use his stuffed body as a pillow, and the Tin Woodman stood up beside them all night, so the dampness of the ground might not rust his joints or dull his brilliant polish. Whenever the dew settled on his body he carefully wiped it off with a cloth, and so in the morning the Emperor shone as brightly as ever in the rays of the rising sun.

They wakened the boy at daybreak, the Scarecrow saying to him: "We have discovered something queer, and therefore we must counsel together what to do about it."

"What have you discovered?" asked Woot, rubbing the sleep from his eyes with his knuckles and giving three wide yawns to prove he was fully awake.

"A Sign," said the Tin Woodman. "A Sign, and another path."

"What does the Sign say?" inquired the boy.

"It says that 'All Strangers are Warned not to Follow this Path to Loonville,'" answered the Scarecrow, who could read very well when his eyes had been freshly painted.

"In that case," said the boy, opening his knapsack to get some breakfast, "let us travel in some other direction."

But this did not seem to please either of his companions.

"I'd like to see what Loonville looks like," remarked the Tin Woodman.

"When one travels, it is foolish to miss any interesting sight," added the Scarecrow.

"But a warning means danger," protested Woot the Wanderer, "and I believe it sensible to keep out of danger whenever we can."

They made no reply to this speech for a while. Then said the Scarecrow: "I have escaped so many dangers, during my lifetime, that I am not much afraid of anything that can happen."

"Nor am I!" exclaimed the Tin Woodman, swinging his glittering axe around his tin head, in a series of circles. "Few things can injure tin, and my axe is a powerful weapon to use against a foe. But our boy friend," he continued, looking solemnly at Woot, "might perhaps be injured if the people of Loonville are really dangerous; so I propose he waits here while you and I, Friend Scarecrow, visit the forbidden City of Loonville."

"Don't worry about me," advised Woot, calmly. "Wherever you wish to go, I will go, and share your dangers. During my wanderings I have found it more wise to keep out of danger than to venture in, but at that time I was alone, and now I have two powerful friends to protect me."

So, when he had finished his breakfast, they all set out along the path that led to Loonville.

"It is a place I have never heard of before," remarked the Scarecrow, as they approached a dense forest. "The inhabitants may be people, of some sort, or they may be animals, but whatever they prove to be, we will have an interesting story to relate to Dorothy and Ozma on our return."

The path led into the forest, but the big trees grew so closely together and the vines and underbrush were so thick and matted that they had to clear a path at each step in order to proceed. In one or two places the Tin Man, who went first to clear the way, cut the branches with a blow of his axe. Woot followed next, and last of the three came the Scarecrow, who could not have kept the path at all had not his comrades broken the way for his straw-stuffed body.

Presently the Tin Woodman pushed his way through some heavy underbrush, and almost tumbled headlong into a vast cleared space in the forest. The clearing was circular, big and roomy, yet the top branches of the tall trees reached over and formed a complete dome or roof for it. Strangely enough, it was not dark in this immense natural chamber in the woodland, for the place glowed with a soft, white light that seemed to come from some unseen source.

In the chamber were grouped dozens of queer creatures, and these so astonished the Tin Man that Woot had to push his metal body aside, that he might see, too. And the Scarecrow pushed Woot aside, so that the three travelers stood in a row, staring with all their eyes.

The creatures they beheld were round and ball-like; round in body, round in legs and arms, round in hands and feet and round of head. The only exception to the roundness was a slight hollow on the top of each head, making it saucer-shaped instead of dome-shaped. They wore no clothes on their puffy bodies, nor had they any hair. Their skins were all of a light gray color, and their eyes were mere purple spots. Their noses were as puffy as the rest of them.

"Are they rubber, do you think?" asked the Scarecrow, who noticed that the creatures bounded, as they moved, and seemed almost as light as air.

"It is difficult to tell what they are," answered Woot, "they seem to be covered with warts."

The Loons — for so these folks were called — had been doing many things, some playing together, some working at tasks and some gathered in groups to talk; but at the sound of strange voices, which echoed rather loudly through the clearing, all turned in the direction of the intruders. Then, in a body, they all rushed forward, running and bounding with tremendous speed.

The Tin Woodman was so surprised by this sudden dash that he had no time to raise his axe before the Loons were on them. The creatures swung their puffy hands, which looked like boxing-gloves, and pounded the three travelers as hard as they could, on all sides. The blows were quite soft and did not hurt our friends at all, but the onslaught quite bewildered them, so that in a brief period all three were knocked over and fell flat upon the ground. Once down, many of the Loons held them, to prevent their getting up again, while others wound long tendrils of vines about them, binding their arms and legs to their bodies and so rendering them helpless.

"Aha!" cried the biggest Loon of all; "we've got 'em safe; so let's carry 'em to King Bal and have 'em tried, and condemned and perforated!" They had to drag their captives to the center of the domed chamber, for their weight, as compared with that of the Loons, prevented their being carried. Even the Scarecrow was much heavier than the puffy Loons. But finally the party halted before a raised platform, on which stood a sort of throne, consisting of a big, wide chair with a string tied to one arm of it.

This string led upward to the roof of the dome.

Arranged before the platform, the prisoners were allowed to sit up, facing the empty throne.

"Good!" said the big Loon who had commanded the party. "Now to get King Bal to judge these terrible creatures we have so bravely captured."

As he spoke he took hold of the string and began to pull as hard as he could. One or two of the others helped him and pretty soon, as they drew in the cord, the leaves above them parted and a Loon appeared at the other end of the string. It didn't take long to draw him down to the throne, where he seated himself and was tied in, so he wouldn't float upward again.

"Hello," said the King, blinking his purple eyes at his followers; "what's up now!"

"Strangers, your Majesty — strangers and captives," replied the big Loon, pompously

"Dear me! I see 'em. I see 'em very plainly," exclaimed the King, his purple eyes bulging out as he looked at the three prisoners. "What curious animals! Are they dangerous, do you think, my good Panta?"

"I'm 'fraid so, your Majesty. Of course, they may not be dangerous, but we mustn't take chances. Enough accidents happen to us poor Loons as it is, and my advice is to condemn and perforate 'em as quickly as possible."

"Keep your advice to yourself," said the monarch, in a peeved tone. "Who's King here, anyhow? You or Me?"

"We made you our King because you have less common sense than the rest of us," answered Panta Loon, indignantly. "I could have been King myself, had I wanted to, but I didn't care for the hard work and responsibility."

As he said this, the big Loon strutted back and forth in the space between the throne of King Bal and the prisoners, and the other Loons seemed much impressed by his defiance. But suddenly there came a sharp report and Panta Loon instantly disappeared, to the great astonishment of the Scarecrow, the Tin Woodman and Woot the Wanderer, who saw on the spot where the big fellow had stood a little heap of flabby, wrinkled skin that looked like a collapsed rubber balloon.

"There!" exclaimed the King; "I expected that would happen. The conceited rascal wanted to puff himself up until he was bigger than the rest of you, and this is the result of his folly. Get the pump working, some of you, and blow him up again."

"We will have to mend the puncture first, your Majesty," suggested one of the Loons, and the prisoners noticed that none of them seemed surprised or shocked at the sad accident to Panta.

"All right," grumbled the King. "Fetch Til to mend him."

One or two ran away and presently returned, followed by a lady Loon wearing huge, puffed-up rubber skirts. Also she had a purple feather fastened to a wart on the top of her head, and around her waist was a sash of fibre-like vines, dried and tough, that looked like strings.

"Get to work, Til," commanded King Bal. "Panta has just

exploded."

The lady Loon picked up the bunch of skin and examined it carefully until she discovered a hole in one foot. Then she pulled a strand of string from her sash, and drawing the edges of the hole together. she tied them fast with the string, thus making one of those curious warts which the strangers had noticed on so many Loons. Having done this, Til Loon tossed the bit of skin to the other Loons and was about to go away when she noticed the prisoners and stopped to inspect them.

"Dear me!" said Til; "what dreadful creatures. Where did they come from?"

"We captured them," replied one of the Loons.

"And what are we going to do with them?" inquired the girl Loon.

"Perhaps we'll condemn 'em and puncture 'em," answered the King.

"Well," said she, still eyeing the "I'm not sure they'll puncture. Let's try it, and see."

One of the Loons ran to the forest's edge and quickly returned with a long, sharp thorn. He glanced at the King, who nodded his head in assent, and then he rushed forward and stuck the thorn into the leg of the Scarecrow. The Scarecrow merely smiled and said nothing, for the thorn didn't hurt him at all.

Then the Loon tried to prick the Tin Woodman's leg, but the tin only blunted the point of the thorn.

"Just as I thought," said Til, blinking her purple eyes and shaking her puffy head; but just then the Loon stuck the thorn into the leg of Woot the Wanderer, and while it had been blunted somewhat, it was still sharp enough to hurt.

"Ouch!" yelled Woot, and kicked out his leg with so much energy that the frail bonds that tied him burst apart. His foot caught the Loon — who was leaning over him — full on his puffy stomach, and sent him shooting up into the air. When he was high over their heads he exploded with a loud "pop" and his skin fell to the ground.

"I really believe," said the King, rolling his spotlike eyes in a frightened way, "that Panta was right in claiming these prisoners are dangerous. Is the pump ready?"

Some of the Loons had wheeled a big machine in front of the throne and now took Panta's skin and began to pump air into it. Slowly it swelled out until the King cried "Stop!"

"No, no!" yelled Panta, "I'm not big enough yet." "You're as big as you're going to be," declared the King. "Before you exploded you were bigger than the rest of us, and that caused you to be proud and overbearing. Now you're a little smaller than the rest, and you will last longer and be more humble."

"Pump me up — pump me up!" wailed Panta "If you don't you'll break my heart."

"If we do we'll break your skin," replied the King.

So the Loons stopped pumping air into Panta, and pushed him away from the pump. He was certainly more humble than before his accident, for he crept into the background and said nothing more.

"Now pump up the other one," ordered the King. Til had already mended him, and the Loons set to work to pump him full of air.

During these last few moments none had paid much attention to the prisoners, so Woot, finding his legs free, crept over to the Tin Woodman and rubbed the bonds that were still around his arms and body against the sharp edge of the axe, which quickly cut them.

The boy was now free, and the thorn which the Loon had stuck into his leg was lying unnoticed on the ground, where the creature had dropped it when he exploded. Woot leaned forward and picked up the thorn, and while the Loons were busy watching the pump, the boy sprang to his feet and suddenly rushed upon the group.

"Pop" — "pop" — "pop!" went three of the Loons, when the Wanderer pricked them with his thorn, and at the sounds the others looked around and saw their danger. With yells of fear they bounded away in all directions, scattering about the clearing, with Woot the Wanderer in full chase. While they could run much faster than the boy, they often stumbled and fell, or got in one another's way, so he managed to catch several and prick them with his thorn.

It astonished him to see how easily the Loons exploded. When the air was let out of them they were quite helpless. Til Loon was one of those who ran against his thorn, and many others suffered the same fate. The creatures could not escape from the enclosure, but in their fright many bounded upward and caught branches of the trees, and then climbed out of reach of the dreaded thorn.

Woot was getting pretty tired chasing them, so he stopped and came over, panting, to where his friends were sitting, still bound.

"Very well done, my Wanderer," said the Tin Woodman. "It is evident that we need fear these puffed-up creatures no longer, so be kind enough to unfasten our bonds and we will proceed upon our journey."

Woot untied the bonds of the Scarecrow and helped him to his feet. Then he freed the Tin Woodman, who got up without help. Looking around them, they saw that the only Loon now remaining within reach was Bal Loon, the King, who had remained seated in his throne, watching the punishment of his people with a bewildered look in his purple eyes.

"Shall I puncture the King?" the boy asked his companions.

King Bal must have overheard the question, for he fumbled with the cord that fastened him to the throne and managed to release it. Then he floated upward until he reached the leafy dome, and parting the branches he disappeared from sight. But the string that was tied to his body was still connected with the arm of the throne, and they knew they could pull his Majesty down again, if they wanted to.

"Let him alone," suggested the Scarecrow. "He seems a good enough king for his peculiar people, and after we are gone, the Loons will have something of a job to pump up all those whom Woot has punctured."

"Every one of them ought to be exploded," declared Woot, who was angry because his leg still hurt him.

"No," said the Tin Woodman, "that would not be just fair. They were quite right to capture us, because we had no business to intrude here, having been warned to keep away from Loonville. This is their country, not ours, and since the poor things can't get out of the clearing, they can harm no one save those who venture here out of curiosity, as we did."

"Well said, my friend," agreed tile Scarecrow. "We really had no right to disturb their peace and comfort; so let us go away."

They easily found the place where they had forced their way into the enclosure, so the Tin Woodman pushed aside the underbrush and started first along the path. The Scarecrow followed next and last came Woot, who looked back and saw that the Loons were still clinging to their perches on the trees and watching their former captives with frightened eyes.

"I guess they're glad to see the last of us," remarked the boy, and laughing at the happy ending of the adventure, he followed his comrades along the path.

5. Mrs. Yoop, the Giantess

When they had reached the end of the path, where they had first seen the warning sign, they set off across the country in an easterly direction. Before long they reached Rolling Lands, which were a succession of hills and valleys where constant climbs and descents were required, and their journey now became tedious because on climbing each hill, they found before them nothing in the valley below it except grass, or weeds or stones.

Up and down they went for hours, with nothing to relieve the monotony of the landscape, until finally, when they had topped a higher hill than usual, they discovered a cup-shaped valley before them in the center of which stood an enormous castle built of purple stone. The castle was high and broad and long, but had no turrets and towers. So far as they could see, there was but one small window and one big door on each side of the great building.

"This is strange!" mused the Scarecrow. "I'd no idea such a big castle existed in this Gillikin Country. I wonder who lives here?"

"It seems to me, from this distance," remarked the Tin Woodman, "that it's the biggest castle I ever saw. It is really too big for any use, and no one could open or shut those big doors without a stepladder."

"Perhaps, if we go nearer, we shall find out whether anybody lives there or not," suggested Woot. "Looks to me as if nobody lived there."

On they went, and when they reached the center of the valley where the great stone castle stood, it was beginning to grow dark. So they hesitated as to what to do.

"If friendly people happen to live here," said Woot. I shall be glad of a bed; but should enemies occupy the place, I prefer to sleep upon the ground."

"And if no one at all lives here," added the Scarecrow, "we can enter, and take possession, and make ourselves at home."

While speaking he went nearer to one of the great doors, which was three times as high and broad as any he had ever seen in a house before, and then he discovered, engraved in big letters upon a stone over the doorway, the words: YOOP CASTLE

"Oho!" he exclaimed; "I know the place now. This was probably the home of Mr. Yoop, a terrible giant whom I have seen confined in a cage, a long way from here. Therefore this castle is likely to be empty and we may use it in any way we please."

"Yes, yes," said the Tin Emperor, nodding; "I also remember Mr. Yoop. But how are we to get into his deserted castle? The latch of the door is so far above our heads that none of us can reach it."

They considered this problem for a while, and then Woot said to the Tin Man: "If I stand upon your shoulders, I think I can unlatch the door."

"Climb up, then," was the reply, and when the boy was perched upon the tin shoulders of Nick Chopper, he was just able to reach the latch and raise it.

At once the door swung open, its great hinges making a groaning sound as if in protest, so Woot leaped down and followed his companions into a big, bare hallway. Scarcely were the three inside, however, when they heard the door slam shut behind them, and this astonished them because no one had touched it. It had closed of its own accord, as if by magic. Moreover, the latch was on the outside, and the thought occurred to each one of them that they were now prisoners in this unknown castle.

"However," mumbled the Scarecrow, "we are not to blame for what cannot be helped; so let us push bravely ahead and see what may be seen."

It was quite dark in the hallway, now that the outside door was shut, so as they stumbled along a stone passage they kept close together, not knowing what danger was likely to befall them.

Suddenly a soft glow enveloped them. It grew brighter, until they could see their surroundings distinctly. They had reached the end of the passage and before them was another huge door. This noiselessly swung open before them, without the help of anyone, and through the doorway they observed a big chamber, the walls of which were lined with plates of pure gold, highly polished.

This room was also lighted, although they could discover no lamps, and in the center of it was a great table at which sat an immense woman. She was clad in silver robes embroidered with gay floral designs, and wore over this splendid raiment a short apron of elaborate lace-work. Such an apron was no protection, and was not in keeping with the handsome gown, but the huge woman wore it, nevertheless. The table at which she sat was spread with a white cloth and had golden dishes upon it, so the travelers saw that they had surprised the Giantess while she was eating her supper.

She had her back toward them and did not even turn around, but taking a biscuit from a dish she began to butter it and said in a voice that was big and deep but not especially unpleasant: "Why don't you come in and allow the door to shut? You're causing a draught, and I shall catch cold and sneeze. When I sneeze, I get cross, and when I get cross I'm liable to do something wicked. Come in, you foolish strangers; come in!"

Being thus urged, they entered the room and approached the table, until they stood where they faced the great Giantess. She continued eating, but smiled in a curious way as she looked at them. Woot noticed that the door had closed silently after they had entered, and that didn't please him at all.

"Well," said the Giantess, "what excuse have you to offer?"

"We didn't know anyone lived here, Madam," explained the Scarecrow; "so, being travelers and strangers in these parts, and wishing to find a place for our boy friend to sleep, we ventured to enter your castle."

"You knew it was private property, I suppose?" said she, buttering another biscuit.

"We saw the words, 'Yoop Castle,' over the door, but we knew that Mr. Yoop is a prisoner in a cage in a far-off part of the land of Oz, so we decided there was no one now at home and that we might use the castle for the night."

"I see," remarked the Giantess, nodding her head and smiling again in that curious way — a way that made Woot shudder. "You didn't know that Mr. Yoop was married, or that after he was cruelly captured his wife still lived in his castle and ran it to suit herself."

"Who captured Mr. Yoop?" asked Woot, looking gravely at the big woman.

"Wicked enemies. People who selfishly objected to Yoop's taking their cows and sheep for his food. I must admit, however, that Yoop had a bad temper, and had the habit of knocking over a few houses, now and then, when he was angry. So one day the little folks came in a great crowd and captured Mr. Yoop, and carried him away to a cage somewhere in the mountains. I don't know where it is, and I don't care, for my husband treated me badly at times, forgetting the respect a giant owes to a giantess. Often he kicked me on my shins, when I wouldn't wait on him. So I'm glad he is gone."

"It's a wonder the people didn't capture you, too," remarked Woot.

"Well, I was too clever for them," said she, giving a sudden laugh that caused such a breeze that the wobbly Scarecrow was almost blown off his feet and had to grab his friend Nick Chopper to steady himself. "I saw the people coining," continued Mrs. Yoop, "and knowing they meant mischief I transformed myself into a mouse and hid in a cupboard. After they had gone away, carrying my shin-kicking husband with them, I transformed myself back to my former shape again, and here I've lived in peace and comfort ever since."

"Are you a Witch, then?" inquired Woot.

"Well, not exactly a Witch," she replied, "but I'm an Artist in Transformations. In other words, I'm more of a Yookoohoo than a Witch, and of course you know that the Yookoohoos are the cleverest magic-workers in the world."

The travelers were silent for a time, uneasily considering this statement and the effect it might have on their future. No doubt the Giantess had wilfully made them her prisoners; yet she spoke so cheerfully, in her big voice, that until now they had not been alarmed in the least.

By and by the Scarecrow, whose mixed brains had been working steadily, asked the woman: "Are we to consider you our friend, Mrs. Yoop, or do you intend to be our enemy?"

"I never have friends," she said in a matter-of-fact tone, "because friends get too familiar and always forget to mind their own business. But I am not your enemy; not yet, anyhow. Indeed, I'm glad you've come, for my life here is rather lonely. I've had no one to talk to since I transformed Polychrome, the Daughter of the Rainbow, into a canary-bird."

"How did you manage to do that?" asked the Tin Woodman, in amazement. "Polychrome is a powerful fairy!"

"She was," said the Giantess; "but now she's a canary-bird. One day after a rain, Polychrome danced off the Rainbow and fell asleep on a little mound in this valley, not far from my castle. The sun came out and drove the Rainbow away, and before Poly wakened, I stole out and transformed her into a canary-bird in a gold cage studded with diamonds. The cage was so she couldn't fly away. I expected she'd sing and talk and we'd have good times together; but she has proved no company for me at all. Ever since the moment of her transformation, she has refused to speak a single word."

"Where is she now?" inquired Woot, who had heard tales of lovely Polychrome and was much interested in her.

"The cage is hanging up in my bedroom," said the Giantess, eating another biscuit. The travelers were now more uneasy and suspicious of the Giantess than before. If Polychrome, the Rainbow's Daughter, who was a real fairy, had been transformed and enslaved by this huge woman, who claimed to be a Yookoohoo, what was liable to happen to them? Said the Scarecrow, twisting his stuffed head around in Mrs. Yoop's direction: "Do you know, Ma'am, who we are?"

"Of course," said she; "a straw man, a tin man and a boy."

"We are very important people," declared the Tin Woodman.

"All the better," she replied. "I shall enjoy your society the more on that account. For I mean to keep you here as long as I live, to amuse me when I get lonely. And," she added slowly, "in this Valley no one ever dies."

They didn't like this speech at all, so the Scarecrow frowned in a way that made Mrs. Yoop smile, while the Tin Woodman looked so fierce that Mrs. Yoop laughed. The Scarecrow suspected she was going to laugh, so he slipped behind his friends to escape the wind from her breath. From this safe position he said warningly: "We have powerful friends who will soon come to rescue us."

"Let them come," she returned, with an accent of scorn. "When they get here they will find neither a boy, nor a tin man, nor a scarecrow, for tomorrow morning I intend to transform you all into other shapes, so that you cannot be recognized."

This threat filled them with dismay. The good-natured Giantess was more terrible than they had imagined. She could smile and wear pretty clothes and at the same time be even more cruel than her wicked husband had been.

Both the Scarecrow and the Tin Woodman tried to think of some way to escape from the castle before morning, but she seemed to read their thoughts and shook her head.

"Don't worry your poor brains," said she. "You can't escape me, however hard you try. But why should you wish to escape? I shall give you new forms that are much better than the ones you now have. Be contented with your fate, for discontent leads to unhappiness, and unhappiness, in any form, is the greatest evil that can befall you."

"What forms do you intend to give us?" asked Woot earnestly.

"I haven't decided, as yet. I'll dream over it tonight, so in the

morning I shall have made up my mind how to transform you. Perhaps you'd prefer to choose your own transformations?"

"No," said Woot, "I prefer to remain as I am."

"That's funny," she retorted. "You are little, and you're weak; as you are, you're not much account, anyhow. The best thing about you is that you're alive, for I shall be able to make of you some sort of live creature which will be a great improvement on your present form."

She took another biscuit from a plate and dipped it in a pot of honey and calmly began eating it.

The Scarecrow watched her thoughtfully. "There are no fields of grain in your Valley," said he; "where, then, did you get the flour to make your biscuits?"

"Mercy me! do you think I'd bother to make biscuits out of flour?" she replied. "That is altogether too tedious a process for a Yookoohoo. I set some traps this afternoon and caught a lot of field-mice, but as I do not like to eat mice, I transformed them into hot biscuits for my supper. The honey in this pot was once a wasp's nest, but since being transformed it has become sweet and delicious. All I need do, when I wish to eat, is to take something I don't care to keep, and transform it into any sort of food I like, and eat it. Are you hungry?"

"I don't eat, thank you," said the Scarecrow.

"Nor do I," said the Tin Woodman.

"I have still a little natural food in my knapsack," said Woot the Wanderer, "and I'd rather eat that than any wasp's nest."

"Every one to his taste," said the Giantess carelessly, and having now finished her supper she rose to her feet, clapped her hands together, and the supper table at once disappeared.

6. The Magic of a Yookoohoo

Woot had seen very little of magic during his wanderings, while the Scarecrow and the Tin Woodman had seen a great deal of many sorts in their lives, yet all three were greatly impressed by Mrs. Yoop's powers. She did not affect any mysterious airs or indulge in chants or mystic rites, as most witches do, nor was the Giantess old and ugly or disagreeable in face or manner. Nevertheless, she frightened her prisoners more than any witch could have done.

"Please be seated," she said to them, as she sat herself down in a great arm-chair and spread her beautiful embroidered skirts for them to admire. But all the chairs in the room were so high that our friends could not climb to the seats of them. Mrs. Yoop observed this and waved her hand, when instantly a golden ladder appeared leaning against a chair opposite her own.

"Climb up," said she, and they obeyed, the Tin Man and the boy assisting the more clumsy Scarecrow. When they were all seated in a row on the cushion of the chair, the Giantess continued: "Now tell me how you happened to travel in this direction, and where you came from and what your errand is."

So the Tin Woodman told her all about Nimmie Amee, and how he had decided to find her and marry her, although he had no Loving Heart. The story seemed to amuse the big woman, who then began to ask the Scarecrow questions and for the first time in her life heard of Ozma of Oz, and of Dorothy and Jack

Pumpkinhead and Dr. Pipt and Tik-tok and many other Oz people who are well known in the Emerald City. Also Woot had to tell his story, which. was very simple and did not take long. The Giantess laughed heartily when the boy related their adventure at Loonville, but said she knew nothing of the Loons because she never left her Valley.

"There are wicked people who would like to capture me, as they did my giant husband, Mr. Yoop," said she; "so I stay at home and mind my own business."

"If Ozma knew that you dared to work magic without her consent, she would punish you severely," declared the Scarecrow, "for this castle is in the Land of Oz, and no persons in the Land of Oz are permitted to work magic except Glinda the Good and the little Wizard who lives with Ozma in the Emerald City."

"That for your Ozma!" exclaimed the Giantess, snapping her fingers in derision. "What do I care for a girl whom I have never seen and who has never seen me?"

"But Ozma is a fairy," said the Tin Woodman, and therefore she is very powerful. Also, we are under Ozma's protection, and to injure us in any way would make her extremely angry."

"What I do here, in my own private castle in this secluded Valley — where no one comes but fools like you — can never be known to your fairy Ozma," returned the Giantess. "Do not seek to frighten me from my purpose, and do not allow yourselves to be frightened, for it is best to meet bravely what cannot be avoided. I am now going to bed, and in the morning I will give you all new forms, such as will be more interesting to me than the ones you now wear. Good night, and pleasant dreams."

Saying this, Mrs. Yoop rose from her chair and walked through a doorway into another room. So heavy was the tread of the Giantess that even the walls of the big stone castle trembled as she stepped. She closed the door of her bedroom behind her, and then suddenly the light went out and the three prisoners found themselves in total darkness.

The Tin Woodman and the Scarecrow didn't mind the dark at all, but Woot the Wanderer felt worried to be left in this strange place in this strange manner, without being able to see any danger that might threaten.

"The big woman might have given me a bed, anyhow," he said to his companions, and scarcely had he spoken when he felt something press against his legs, which were then dangling from the seat of the chair. Leaning down, he put out his hand and found that a bedstead had appeared, with mattress, sheets and covers, all complete. He lost no time in slipping down upon the bed and was soon fast asleep.

During the night the Scarecrow and the Emperor talked in low tones together, and they got out of the chair and moved all about the room, feeling for some hidden spring that might open a door or window and permit them to escape.

Morning found them still unsuccessful in the quest and as soon as it was daylight Woot's bed suddenly disappeared, and he dropped to the floor with a thump that quickly wakened him. And after a time the Giantess came from her bedroom, wearing another dress that was quite as elaborate as the one in which she had been attired the evening before, and also wearing the pretty lace apron. Having seated herself in a chair, she said: "I'm hungry; so I'll have breakfast at once."

She clapped her hands together and instantly the table appeared before her, spread with snowy linen and laden with golden dishes. But there was no food upon the table, nor anything else except a pitcher of water, a bundle of weeds and a handful of pebbles. But the Giantess poured some water into her coffee-pot, patted it once or twice with her hand, and then poured out a cupful of steaming hot coffee.

"Would you like some?" she asked Woot.

He was suspicious of magic coffee, but it smelled so good that he could not resist it; so he answered: "If you please, Madam."

The Giantess poured out another cup and set it on the floor for Woot. It was as big as a tub, and the golden spoon in the saucer beside the cup was so heavy the boy could scarcely lift it. But Woot managed to get a sip of the coffee and found it delicious.

Mrs. Yoop next transformed the weeds into a dish of oatmeal, which she ate with good appetite.

"Now, then," said she, picking up the pebbles. "I'm wondering whether I shall have fish-balls or lamb-chops to complete my meal. Which would you prefer, Woot the Wanderer?"

"If you please, I'll eat the food in my knapsack," answered the boy. "Your magic food might taste good, but I'm afraid of it."

The woman laughed at his fears and transformed the pebbles into fish-balls.

"I suppose you think that after you had eaten this food it would turn to stones again and make you sick," she remarked; "but that would be impossible. Nothing I transform ever gets back to its former shape again, so these fish-balls can never more be pebbles. That is why I have to be careful of my transformations," she added, busily eating while she talked, "for while I can change forms at will I can never change them back again — which proves that even the powers of a clever Yookoohoo are limited. When I have transformed you three people, you must always wear the shapes that I have given you."

"Then please don't transform us," begged Woot, "for we are quite satisfied to remain as we are."

"I am not expecting to satisfy you, but intend to please myself," she declared, "and my pleasure is to give you new shapes. For, if by chance your friends came in search of you, not one of them would be able to recognize you."

Her tone was so positive that they knew it would be useless to protest. The woman was not unpleasant to look at; her face was not cruel; her voice was big but gracious in tone; but her words showed that she possessed a merciless heart and no pleadings would alter her wicked purpose.

Mrs. Yoop took ample time to finish her breakfast and the prisoners had no desire to hurry her, but finally the meal was concluded and she folded her napkin and made the table disappear by clapping her hands together. Then she turned to her captives and said: "The next thing on the programme is to change your forms."

"Have you decided what forms to give us?" asked the Scarecrow, uneasily.

"Yes; I dreamed it all out while I was asleep. This Tin Man seems a very solemn person " — indeed, the Tin Woodman was looking solemn, just then, for he was greatly disturbed — "so I shall change him into an Owl."

All she did was to point one finger at him as she spoke, but immediately the form of the Tin Woodman began to change and in a few seconds Nick Chopper, the Emperor of the Winkies, had been transformed into an Owl, with eyes as big as saucers and a hooked beak and strong claws. But he was still tin. He was a Tin Owl, with tin legs and beak and eyes and feathers. When he flew to the back of a chair and perched upon it, his tin feathers rattled against one another with a tinny clatter. The Giantess seemed much amused by the Tin Owl's appearance, for her laugh was big and jolly.

"You're not liable to get lost," said she, "for your wings and feathers will make a racket wherever you go. And, on my word, a Tin Owl is so rare and pretty that it is an improvement on the ordinary bird. I did not intend to make you tin, but I forgot to wish you to be meat. However, tin you were, and tin you are, and as it's too late to change you, that settles it."

Until now the Scarecrow had rather doubted the possibility of Mrs. Yoop's being able to transform him, or his friend the Tin Woodman, for they were not made as ordinary people are. He had worried more over what might happen to Woot than to himself, but now he began to worry about himself.

"Madam," he said hastily, "I consider this action very impolite. It may even be called rude, considering we are your guests."

"You are not guests, for I did not invite you here," she replied.

"Perhaps not; but we craved hospitality. We threw ourselves upon your mercy, so to speak, and we now find you have no mercy. Therefore, if you will excuse the expression, I must say it is downright wicked to take our proper forms away from us and give us others that we do not care for."

"Are you trying to make me angry?" she asked, frowning.

"By no means," said the Scarecrow; "I'm just trying to make you act more ladylike."

"Oh, indeed! In my opinion, Mr. Scarecrow, you are now acting like a bear — so a Bear you shall be!"

Again the dreadful finger pointed, this time in the Scarecrow's direction, and at once his form began to change. In a few seconds he had become a small Brown Bear, but he was stuffed with straw as he had been before, and when the little Brown Bear shuffled across the floor he was just as wobbly as the Scarecrow had been and moved just as awkwardly.

Woot was amazed, but he was also thoroughly frightened.

"Did it hurt?" he asked the little Brown Bear.

"No, of course not," growled the Scarecrow in the Bear's form; "but I don't like walking on four legs; it's undignified."

"Consider my humiliation!" chirped the Tin Owl, trying to settle its tin feathers smoothly with its tin beak. "And I can't see very well, either. The light seems to hurt my eyes."

"That's because you are an Owl," said Woot. "I think you will see better in the dark."

"Well," remarked the Giantess, "I'm very well pleased with these new forms, for my part, and I'm sure you will like them better when you get used to them. So now," she added, turning to the boy, "it is your turn."

"Don't you think you'd better leave me as I am?" asked Woot in a trembling voice.

"No," she replied, "I'm going to make a Monkey of you. I love monkeys — they're so cute! — and I think a Green Monkey will be lots of fun and amuse me when I am sad."

Woot shivered, for again the terrible magic finger pointed, and pointed directly his way. He felt himself changing; not so very much, however, and it didn't hurt him a bit. He looked down at his limbs and body and found that his clothes were gone and his skin covered with a fine, silk-like green fur. His hands and feet were now those of a monkey. He realized he really was a monkey, and his first feeling was one of anger. He began to chatter as monkeys do. He bounded to the seat of a giant chair, and then to its back and with a wild leap sprang upon the laughing Giantess. His idea was to seize her hair and pull it out by the roots, and so have revenge for her wicked transformations. But she raised her hand and said: "Gently, my dear Monkey — gently! You're not angry; you're happy as can be!"

Woot stopped short. No; he wasn't a bit angry now; he felt as good-humored and gay as ever he did when a boy. Instead of pulling Mrs. Yoop's hair, he perched on her shoulder and smoothed her soft cheek with his hairy paw. In return, she smiled at the funny green animal and patted his head.

"Very good," said the Giantess. "Let us all become friends and be happy together. How is my Tin Owl feeling?"

"Quite comfortable," said the Owl. "I don't like it, to be sure, but I'm not going to allow my new form to make me unhappy. But tell me, please: what is a Tin Owl good for?"

"You are only good to make me laugh," replied the Giantess.

"Will a stuffed Bear also make you laugh?" inquired the Scarecrow, sitting back on his haunches to look up at her.

"Of course," declared the Giantess; "and I have added a little magic to your transformations to make you all contented with wearing your new forms. I'm sorry I didn't think to do that when I transformed Polychrome into a Canary-Bird. But perhaps when she sees how cheerful you are, she will cease to be silent and sullen and take to singing. I will go get the bird and let you see her."

With this, Mrs. Yoop went into the next room and soon returned bearing a golden cage in which sat upon a swinging perch a lovely yellow Canary. "Polychrome," said the Giantess, "permit me to introduce to you a Green Monkey, which used to be a boy called Woot the Wanderer, and a Tin Owl, which used to be a Tin Woodman named Nick Chopper, and a straw-stuffed little Brown Bear which used to be a live Scarecrow."

"We already know one another," declared the Scarecrow. "The bird is Polychrome, the Rainbow's Daughter, and she and I used to be good friends."

"Are you really my old friend, the Scarecrow?" asked; the bird, in a sweet, low voice.

"There!" cried Mrs. Yoop; "that's the first time she has spoken since she was transformed."

"I am really your old friend," answered the Scarecrow; "but you must pardon me for appearing just now in this brutal form."

"I am a bird, as you are, dear Poly," said the Tin Woodman; "but, alas! a Tin Owl is not as beautiful as a Canary-Bird."

"How dreadful it all is!" sighed the Canary. "Couldn't you manage to escape from this terrible Yookoohoo?"

No," answered the Scarecrow, "we tried to escape, but failed. She first made us her prisoners and then transformed us. But how did she manage to get you, Polychrome?"'

"I was asleep, and she took unfair advantage of me," answered the bird sadly. "Had I been awake, I could easily have protected myself."

"Tell me," said the Green Monkey earnestly, as he came close to the cage, "what must we do, Daughter of the Rainbow, to escape from these transformations? Can't you help us, being a Fairy?"

"At present I am powerless to help even myself," replied the Canary.

"That's the exact truth!" exclaimed the Giantess, who seemed pleased to hear the bird talk, even though it complained; "you are all helpless and in my power, so you may as well make up your minds to accept your fate and be content. Remember that you are transformed for good, since no magic on earth can break your enchantments. I am now going out for my morning walk, for each day after breakfast I walk sixteen times around my castle for exercise. Amuse yourselves while I am gone, and when I return I hope to find you all reconciled and happy."

So the Giantess walked to the door by which our friends had entered the great hall and spoke one word: "Open!" Then the door swung open and after Mrs. Yoop had passed out it closed again with a snap as its powerful bolts shot into place. The Green Monkey had rushed toward the opening, hoping to escape, but he was too late and only got a bump on his nose as the door slammed shut.

7. The Lace Apron

"Now," said the Canary, in a tone more brisk than before, "we may talk together more freely, as Mrs. Yoop cannot hear us. Perhaps we can figure out a way to escape."

"Open!" said Woot the Monkey, still facing the door; but his command had no effect and he slowly rejoined the others.

"You cannot open any door or window in this enchanted castle unless you are wearing the Magic Apron," said the Canary.

"What Magic Apron do you mean?" asked the Tin Owl, in a curious voice.

"The lace one, which the Giantess always wears. I have been her prisoner, in this cage, for several weeks, and she hangs my cage in her bedroom every night, so that she can keep her eye on me," explained Polychrome the Canary. "Therefore I have discovered that it is the Magic Apron that opens the doors and windows, and nothing else can move them. When she goes to bed, Mrs. Yoop hangs her apron on the bedpost, and one morning she forgot to put it on when she commanded the door to open, and

the door would not move. So then she put on the lace apron and the door obeyed her. That was how I learned the magic power of the apron."

"I see — I see!" said the little Brown Bear, wagging his stuffed head. "Then, if we could get the apron from Mrs. Yoop, we could open the doors and escape from our prison."

"That is true, and it is the plan I was about to suggest," replied Polychrome the Canary-Bird. "However, I don't believe the Owl could steal the apron, or even the Bear, but perhaps the Monkey could hide in her room at night and get the apron while she is asleep."

"I'll try it!" cried Woot the Monkey. "I'll try it this very night, if I can manage to steal into her bedroom."

"You mustn't think about it, though," warned the bird, "for she can read your thoughts whenever she cares to do so. And do not forget, before you escape, to take me with you. Once I am out of the power of the Giantess, I may discover a way to save us all."

"We won't forget our fairy friend," promised the boy; "but perhaps you can tell me how to get into the bedroom."

"No," declared Polychrome, "I cannot advise you as to that. You must watch for a chance, and slip in when Mrs. Yoop isn't looking."

They talked it over for a while longer and then Mrs. Yoop returned. When she entered, the door opened suddenly, at her command, and closed as soon as her huge form had passed through the doorway. During that day she entered her bedroom several times, on one errand or another, but always she commanded the door to close behind her and her prisoners found not the slightest chance to leave the big hall in which they were confined.

The Green Monkey thought it would be wise to make a friend of the big woman, so as to gain her confidence, so he sat on the back of her chair and chattered to her while she mended her stockings and sewed silver buttons on some golden shoes that were as big as row-boats. This pleased the Giantess and she would pause at times to pat the Monkey's head. The little Brown Bear curled up in a corner and lay still all day. The Owl and the Canary found they could converse together in the bird language, which neither the Giantess nor the Bear nor the Monkey could understand; so at times they twittered away to each other and passed the long, dreary day quite cheerfully.

After dinner Mrs. Yoop took a big fiddle from a big cupboard and played such loud and dreadful music that her prisoners were all thankful when at last she stopped and said she was going to bed.

After cautioning the Monkey and Bear and Owl to behave themselves during the night, she picked up the cage containing the Canary and, going to the door of her bedroom, commanded it to open. Just then, however, she remembered she had left her fiddle lying upon a table, so she went back for it and put it away in the cupboard, and while her back was turned the Green Monkey slipped through the open door into her bedroom and hid underneath the bed. The Giantess, being sleepy, did not notice this, and entering her room she made the door close behind her and then hung the bird-cage on a peg by the window. Then she began to undress, first taking off the lace apron and laying it over the bedpost, where it was within easy reach of her hand.

As soon as Mrs. Yoop was in bed the lights all went out, and Woot the Monkey crouched under the bed and waited patiently until he heard the Giantess snoring. Then he crept out and in the dark felt around until he got hold of the apron, which he at once tied around his own waist.

Next, Woot tried to find the Canary, and there was just enough moonlight showing through the window to enable him to see where the cage hung; but it was out of his reach. At first he was tempted to leave Polychrome and escape with his other friends, but remembering his promise to the Rainbow's Daughter Woot tried to think how to save her.

A chair stood near the window, and this — showing dimly in the moonlight — gave him an idea. By pushing against it with all his might, he found he could move the giant chair a few inches at a time. So he pushed and pushed until the chair was beneath the bird-cage, and then he sprang noiselessly upon the seat — for his monkey form enabled him to jump higher than he could do as a boy — and from there to the back of the chair, and so managed to reach the cage and take it off the peg. Then down he sprang to the floor and made his way to the door. "Open!" he commanded, and at once the door obeyed and swung open, But his voice wakened Mrs. Yoop, who gave a wild cry and sprang out of bed with one bound. The Green Monkey dashed through the doorway, carrying the cage with him, and before the Giantess could reach the door it slammed shut and imprisoned her in her own bed-chamber!

The noise she made, pounding upon the door, and her yells of anger and dreadful threats of vengeance, filled all our friends with terror, and Woot the Monkey was so excited that in the dark he could not find the outer door of the hall. But the Tin Owl could see very nicely in the dark, so he guided his friends to the right place and when all were grouped before the door Woot commanded it to open. The Magic Apron proved as powerful as when it had been worn by the Giantess, so a moment later they had rushed through the passage and were standing in the fresh night air outside the castle, free to go wherever they willed.

8. The Menace of the Forest

"Quick!" cried Polychrome the Canary; "we must hurry, or Mrs. Yoop may find some way to recapture us, even now. Let us get out of her Valley as soon as possible."

So they set off toward the east, moving as swiftly as they could, and for a long time they could hear the yells and struggles of the imprisoned Giantess. The Green Monkey could run over the ground very swiftly, and he carried with him the bird-cage containing Polychrome the Rain-bow's Daughter. Also the Tin Owl could skip and fly along at a good rate of speed, his feathers rattling against one another with a tinkling sound as he moved. But the little Brown Bear, being stuffed with straw, was a clumsy traveler and the others had to wait for him to follow.

However, they were not very long in reaching the ridge that led out of Mrs. Yoop's Valley, and when they had passed this ridge and descended into the next valley they stopped to rest, for the Green Monkey was tired.

"I believe we are safe, now," said Polychrome, when her cage was set down and the others had all gathered around it, "for Mrs. Yoop dares not go outside of her own Valley, for fear of being captured by her enemies. So we may take our time to consider what to do next."

"I'm afraid poor Mrs. Yoop will starve to death, if no one lets her out of her bedroom," said Woot, who had a heart as kind as that of the Tin Woodman. "We've taken her Magic Apron away, and now the doors will never open."

"Don't worry about that," advised Polychrome. "Mrs. Yoop has plenty of magic left to console her."

"Are you sure of that?" asked the Green Monkey.

"Yes, for I've been watching her for weeks," said the Canary. "She has six magic hairpins, which she wears in her hair, and a magic ring which she wears on her thumb and which is invisible to all eyes except those of a fairy, and magic bracelets on both her ankles. So I am positive that she will manage to find a way out of her prison."

"She might transform the door into an archway," suggested the little Brown Bear.

"That would be easy for her," said the Tin Owl; "but I'm glad she was too angry to think of that before we got out of her Valley."

"Well, we have escaped the big woman, to be sure," remarked the Green Monkey, "but we still wear the awful forms the cruel yookoohoo gave us. How are we going to get rid of these shapes, and become ourselves again?"

None could answer that question. They sat around the cage, brooding over the problem, until the Monkey fell asleep. Seeing this, the Canary tucked her head under her wing and also slept, and the Tin Owl and the Brown Bear did not disturb them until morning came and it was broad daylight.

"I'm hungry," said Woot, when he wakened, for his knapsack of food had been left behind at the castle.

"Then let us travel on until we can find something for you to eat," returned the Scarecrow Bear.

"There is no use in your lugging my cage any farther," declared the Canary. "Let me out, and throw the cage away. Then I can fly with you and find my own breakfast of seeds. Also I can search for water, and tell you where to find it."

So the Green Monkey unfastened the door of the golden cage and the Canary hopped out. At first she flew high in the air and made great circles overhead, but after a time she returned and perched beside them.

"At the east in the direction we were following," announced the Canary, "there is a fine forest, with a brook running through it. In the forest there may be fruits or nuts growing, or berry bushes at its edge, so let us go that way."

They agreed to this and promptly set off, this time moving more deliberately. The Tin Owl, which had guided their way during the night, now found the sunshine very trying to his big eyes, so he shut them tight and perched upon the back of the little Brown Bear, which carried the Owl's weight with ease. The Canary sometimes perched upon the Green Monkey's shoulder and sometimes fluttered on ahead of the party, and in this manner they traveled in good spirits across that valley and into the next one to the east of it.

This they found to be an immense hollow, shaped like a saucer, and on its farther edge appeared the forest which Polychrome had seen from the sky.

Come to think of it," said the Tin Owl, waking up and blinking comically at his friends, "there's no object, now, in our traveling to the Munchkin Country. My idea in going there was to marry Nimmie Amee, but however much the Munchkin girl may have loved a Tin Woodman, I cannot reasonably expect her to marry a Tin Owl."

There is some truth in that, my friend," remarked the Brown Bear. "And to think that I, who was considered the handsomest Scarecrow in the world, am now condemned to be a scrubby, no-account beast, whose only redeeming feature is that he is stuffed with straw!"

Consider my case, please," said Woot. "The cruel Giantess has made a Monkey of a Boy, and that is the most dreadful deed of all!"

Your color is rather pretty," said the Brown Bear, eyeing Woot critically. "I have never seen a pea-green monkey before, and it strikes me you are quite gorgeous."

It isn't so bad to be a bird," asserted the Canary, fluttering from one to another with a free and graceful motion, "but I long to enjoy my own shape again."

As Polychrome, you were the loveliest maiden I have ever seen — except, of course, Ozma," said the Tin Owl; "so the Giantess did well to transform you into the loveliest of all birds, if you were to be transformed at all. But tell me, since you are a fairy, and have a fairy wisdom: do you think we shall be able to break these enchantments?"

Queer things happen in the Land of Oz," replied the Canary, again perching on the Green Monkey's shoulder and turning one bright eye thoughtfully toward her questioner. "Mrs. Yoop has declared that none of her transformations can ever be changed, even by herself, but I believe that if we could get to Glinda the Good Sorceress, she might find a way to restore us to our natural shapes. Glinda, as you know, is the most powerful Sorceress in the world, and there are few things she cannot do if she tries."

In that case," said the Little Brown Bear, "let us return southward and try to get to Glinda's castle. It lies in the Quadling Country, you know, so it is a good way from here."

First, however, let us visit the forest and search for something to eat," pleaded Woot. So they continued on to the edge of the forest, which consisted of many tall and beautiful trees. They discovered no fruit trees, at first, so the Green Monkey pushed on into the forest depths and the others followed close behind him.

They were traveling quietly along, under the shade of the trees, when suddenly an enormous jaguar leaped upon them from a limb and with one blow of his paw sent the little Brown Bear tumbling over and over until he was stopped by a tree-trunk. Instantly they all took alarm. The Tin Owl shrieked: "Hoot — hoot!" and flew straight up to the branch of a tall tree, although he could scarcely see where he was going. The Canary swiftly darted to a place beside the Owl, and the Green Monkey sprang up, caught a limb, and soon scrambled to a high perch of safety.

The Jaguar crouched low and with hungry eyes regarded the little Brown Bear, which slowly got upon its feet and asked reproachfully: "For goodness' sake, Beast, what were you trying to do?"

Trying to get my breakfast," answered the Jaguar with a snarl, "and I believe I've succeeded. You ought to make a delicious meal — unless you happen to be old and tough."

"I'm worse than that, considered as a breakfast," said the Bear, "for I'm only a skin stuffed with straw, and therefore not fit to eat."

"Indeed!" cried the Jaguar, in a disappointed voice; "then you must be a magic Bear, or enchanted, and I must seek my breakfast from among your companions."

With this he raised his lean head to look up at the Tin Owl and the Canary and the Monkey, and he lashed his tail upon the ground and growled as fiercely as any jaguar could.

"My friends are enchanted, also," said the little Brown Bear.

"All of them?" asked the Jaguar.

"Yes. The Owl is tin, so you couldn't possibly eat him. The Canary is a fairy — Polychrome, the Daughter of the Rainbow — and you never could catch her because she can easily fly out of your reach."

"There still remains the Green Monkey," remarked the Jaguar hungrily. "He is neither made of tin nor stuffed with straw, nor can he fly. I'm pretty good at climbing trees, myself, so I think I'll capture the Monkey and eat him for my breakfast."

Woot the Monkey, hearing this speech from his perch on the tree, became much frightened, for he knew the nature of jaguars and realized they could climb trees and leap from limb to limb with the agility of cats. So he at once began to scamper through the forest as fast as he could go, catching at a branch with his long monkey arms and swinging his green body through space to grasp another branch in a neighboring tree, and so on, while the Jaguar followed him from below, his eyes fixed steadfastly on his prey. But presently Woot got his feet tangled in the Lace Apron, which he was still wearing, and that tripped him in his flight and made him fall to the ground, where the Jaguar placed one huge paw upon him and said grimly: I've got you, now!" The fact that the Apron had tripped him made Woot remember its magic powers, and in his terror he cried out: "Open!" without stopping to consider how this command might save him. But, at the word, the earth opened at the exact spot where he lay under the Jaguar's paw, and his body sank downward, the earth closing over it again. The last thing Woot the Monkey saw, as he glanced upward, was the Jaguar peering into the hole in astonishment.

"He's gone!" cried the beast, with a long-drawn sigh of disappointment; "he's gone, and now I shall have no breakfast."

The clatter of the Tin Owl's wings sounded above him, and the little Brown Bear came trotting up and asked: "Where is the monkey? Have you eaten him so quickly?"

"No, indeed," answered the Jaguar. "He disappeared into the earth before I could take one bite of him!"

And now the Canary perched upon a stump, a little way from the forest beast, and said: "I am glad our friend has escaped you; but, as it is natural for a hungry beast to wish his breakfast, I will try to give you one."

"Thank you," replied the Jaguar. "You're rather small for a full meal, but it's kind of you to sacrifice yourself to my appetite."

"Oh, I don't intend to be eaten, I assure you," said the Canary, "but as I am a fairy I know something of magic, and though I am now transformed into a bird's shape, I am sure I can conjure up a breakfast that will satisfy you."

"If you can work magic, why don't you break the enchantment you are under and return to your proper form?" inquired the beast doubtingly.

"I haven't the power to do that," answered the Canary, "for Mrs. Yoop, the Giantess who transformed me, used a peculiar form of yookoohoo magic that is unknown to me. However, she could not deprive me of my own fairy knowledge, so I will try to get you a breakfast."

"Do you think a magic breakfast would taste good, or relieve the pangs of hunger I now suffer?" asked the Jaguar.

"I am sure it would. What would you like to eat?"

"Give me a couple of fat rabbits," said the beast.

"Rabbits! No, indeed. I'd not allow you to eat the dear little things," declared Polychrome the Canary.

"Well, three or four squirrels, then," pleaded the Jaguar.

"Do you think me so cruel?" demanded the Canary, indignantly. "The squirrels are my especial friends."

"How about a plump owl?" asked the beast. "Not a tin one, you know, but a real meat owl."

"Neither beast nor bird shall you have," said Polychrome in a positive voice.

"Give me a fish, then; there's a river a little way off," proposed the Jaguar.

"No living thing shall be sacrificed to feed you," returned the Canary.

"Then what in the world do you expect me to eat?" said the Jaguar in a scornful tone.

"How would mush-and-milk do?" asked the Canary.

The Jaguar snarled in derision and lashed his tail against the ground angrily

"Give him some scrambled eggs on toast, Poly," suggested the Bear Scarecrow. "He ought to like that."

"I will," responded the Canary, and fluttering her wings she made a flight of three circles around the stump. Then she flew up to a tree and the Bear and the Owl and the Jaguar saw that upon the stump had appeared a great green leaf upon which was a large portion of scrambled eggs on toast, smoking hot.

"There!" said the Bear; "eat your breakfast, friend Jaguar, and be content."

The Jaguar crept closer to the stump and sniffed the fragrance of the scrambled eggs. They smelled so good that he tasted them, and they tasted so good that he ate the strange meal in a hurry, proving he had been really hungry.

"I prefer rabbits," he muttered, licking his chops, "but I must admit the magic breakfast has filled my stomach full, and

brought me comfort. So I'm much obliged for the kindness, little Fairy, and I'll now leave you in peace."

Saying this, he plunged into the thick underbrush and soon disappeared, although they could hear his great body crashing through the bushes until he was far distant.

"That was a good way to get rid of the savage beast, Poly," said the Tin Woodman to the Canary; "but I'm surprised that you didn't give our friend Woot a magic breakfast, when you knew he was hungry."

"The reason for that," answered Polychrome, "was that my mind was so intent on other things that I quite forgot my power to produce food by magic. But where is the monkey boy?"

"Gone!" said the Scarecrow Bear, solemnly. "The earth has swallowed him up."

9. The Quarrelsome Dragons

The Green Monkey sank gently into the earth for a little way and then tumbled swiftly through space, landing on a rocky floor with a thump that astonished him. Then he sat up, found that no bones were broken, and gazed around him.

He seemed to be in a big underground cave, which was dimly lighted by dozens of big round discs that looked like moons. They were not moons, however, as Woot discovered when he had examined the place more carefully. They were eyes. The eyes were in the heads of enormous beasts whose bodies trailed far behind them. Each beast was bigger than an elephant, and three times as long, and there were a dozen or more of the creatures scattered here and there about the cavern. On their bodies were big scales, as round as pie-plates, which were beautifully tinted in shades of green, purple and orange. On the ends of their long tails were clusters of jewels. Around the great, moon-like eyes were circles of diamonds which sparkled in the subdued light that glowed from the eyes.

Woot saw that the creatures had wide mouths and rows of terrible teeth and, from tales he had heard of such beings, he knew he had fallen into a cavern inhabited by the great Dragons that had been driven from the surface of the earth and were only allowed to come out once in a hundred years to search for food. Of course he had never seen Dragons before, yet there was no mistaking them, for they were unlike any other living creatures.

Woot sat upon the floor where he had fallen, staring around, and the owners of the big eyes returned his look, silently and motionless. Finally one of the Dragons which was farthest away from him asked, in a deep, grave voice: "What was that?"

And the greatest Dragon of all, who was just in front of the Green Monkey, answered in a still deeper voice: "It is some foolish animal from Outside."

"Is it good to eat?" inquired a smaller Dragon beside the great one. "I'm hungry."

"Hungry!" exclaimed all the Dragons, in a reproachful chorus; and then the great one said chidingly: "Tut- tut, my son! You've no reason to be hungry at this time."

"Why not?" asked the little Dragon. "I haven't eaten anything in eleven years."

"Eleven years is nothing," remarked another Dragon, sleepi

opening and closing his eyes; "I haven't feasted for eighty-seven years, and I dare not get hungry for a dozen or so years to come. Children who eat between meals should be broken of the habit."

"All I had, eleven years ago, was a rhinoceros, and that's not a full meal at all," grumbled the young one. "And, before that, I had waited sixty-two years to be fed; so it's no wonder I'm hungry."

"How old are you now?" asked Woot, forgetting his own dangerous position in his interest in the conversation.

"Why, I'm — I'm — How old am I, Father?" asked the little Dragon.

"Goodness gracious! what a child to ask questions. Do you want to keep me thinking all the time? Don't you know that thinking is very bad for Dragons?" returned the big one, impatiently.

"How old am I, Father?" persisted the small Dragon.

"About six hundred and thirty, I believe. Ask your mother."

"No; don't!" said an old Dragon in the background; "haven't I enough worries, what with being wakened in the middle of a nap, without being obliged to keep track of my children's ages?"

"You've been fast asleep for over sixty years, Mother," said the child Dragon. "How long a nap do you wish?"

"I should have slept forty years longer. And this strange little green beast should be punished for falling into our cavern and disturbing us."

"I didn't know you were here, and I didn't know I was going to fall in," explained Woot.

"Nevertheless, here you are," said the great Dragon, "and you have carelessly wakened our entire tribe; so it stands to reason you must be punished."

"In what way?" inquired the Green Monkey, trembling a little.

"Give me time and I'll think of a way. You're in no hurry, are you?" asked the great Dragon.

"No, indeed," cried Woot. "Take your time. I'd much rather you'd all go to sleep again, and punish me when you wake up in a hundred years or so."

"Let me eat him!" pleaded the littlest Dragon.

"He is too small," said the father. "To eat this one Green Monkey would only serve to make you hungry for more, and there are no more."

"Quit this chatter and let me get to sleep," protested another Dragon, yawning in a fearful manner, for when he opened his mouth a sheet of flame leaped forth from it and made Woot jump back to get out of its way.

In his jump he bumped against the nose of a Dragon behind him, which opened its mouth to growl and shot another sheet of flame at him. The flame was bright, but not very hot, yet Woot screamed with terror and sprang forward with a great bound. This time he landed on the paw of the great Chief Dragon, who angrily raised his other front paw and struck the Green Monkey a fierce blow. Woot went sailing through the air and fell sprawling upon the rocky floor far beyond the place where the Dragon Tribe was grouped.

All the great beasts were now thoroughly wakened and aroused, and they blamed the monkey for disturbing their quiet. The littlest Dragon darted after Woot and the others turned their unwieldy bodies in his direction and followed, flashing from their eyes and mouths flames which lighted up the entire cavern. Woot almost gave himself up for lost, at that moment, but he scrambled to his feet and dashed away to the farthest end of the cave, the Dragons following more leisurely because they were too clumsy to move fast. Perhaps they thought there was no need of haste, as the monkey could not escape from the cave. But, away up at the end of the place, the cavern floor was heaped with tumbled rocks, so Woot, with an agility born of fear, climbed from rock to rock until he found himself crouched against the cavern roof. There he waited, for he could go no farther, while on over the tumbled rocks slowly crept the Dragons — the littlest one coming first because he was hungry as well as angry.

The beasts had almost reached him when Woot, remembering his lace apron — now sadly torn and soiled — recovered his wits and shouted: "Open!" At the cry a hole appeared in the roof of the cavern, just over his head, and through it the sunlight streamed full upon the Green Monkey

The Dragons paused, astonished at the magic and blinking at the sunlight, and this gave Woot time to climb through the opening. As soon as he reached the surface of the earth the hole closed again, and the boy monkey realized, with a thrill of joy, that he had seen the last of the dangerous Dragon family.

He sat upon the ground, still panting hard from his exertions, when the bushes before him parted and his former enemy, the Jaguar, appeared.

"Don't run," said the woodland beast, as Woot sprang up; "you are perfectly safe, so far as I am concerned, for since you so mysteriously disappeared I have had my breakfast. I am now on my way home to sleep the rest of the day."

"Oh, indeed!" returned the Green Monkey, in a tone both sorry and startled. "Which of my friends did you manage to eat?"

"None of them," returned the Jaguar, with a sly grin, "I had a dish of magic scrambled eggs on toast — and it wasn't a bad feast, at all. There isn't room in me for even you, and I don't regret it because I judge, from your green color, that you are not ripe, and would make an indifferent meal. We jaguars have to be careful of our digestions. Farewell, Friend Monkey. Follow the path I made through the bushes and you will find your friends."

With this the Jaguar marched on his way and Woot took his advice and followed the trail he had made until he came to the place where the little Brown Bear, and the Tin Owl, and the Canary were conferring together and wondering what had become of their comrade, the Green Monkey.

10. Tommy Kwikstep

"Our best plan," said the Scarecrow Bear, when the Green Monkey had related the story of his adventure with the Dragons, "is to get out of this Gillikin Country as soon as we can and try to find our way to the castle of Glinda, the Good Sorceress. There are too many dangers lurking here to suit me, and Glinda may be able to restore us to our proper forms."

"If we turn south now," the Tin Owl replied, "we might go

straight into the Emerald City. That's a place I wish to avoid, for I'd hate to have my friends see me in this sad plight," and he blinked his eyes and fluttered his tin wings mournfully.

"But I am certain we have passed *beyond* the Emerald City," the Canary assured him, sailing lightly around their heads. "So, should we turn south from here, we would pass into the Munchkin Country, and continuing south we would reach the Quadling Country where Glinda's castle is located."

"Well, since you're sure of that, let's start right away," proposed the Bear. "It's a long journey, at the best, and I'm getting tired of walking on four legs."

"I thought you never tired, being stuffed with straw," said Woot.

"I mean that it annoys me, to be obliged to go on all fours, when two legs are my proper walking equipment," replied the Scarecrow. "I consider it beneath my dignity. In other words, my remarkable brains can tire, through humiliation, although my body cannot tire."

"That is one of the penalties of having brains," remarked the Tin Owl with a sigh. "I have had no brains since I was a man of meat, and so I never worry. Nevertheless, I prefer my former manly form to this owl's shape and would be glad to break Mrs. Yoop's enchantment as soon as possible. I am so noisy, just now, that I disturb myself," and he fluttered his wings with a clatter that echoed throughout the forest.

So, being all of one mind, they turned southward, traveling steadily on until the woods were left behind and the landscape turned from purple tints to blue tints, which assured them they had entered the Country of the Munchkins.

"Now I feel myself more safe," said the Scarecrow Bear. "I know this country pretty well, having been made here by a Munchkin farmer and having wandered over these lovely blue lands many times. Seems to me, indeed, that I even remember that group of three tall trees ahead of us; and, if I do, we are not far from the home of my friend Jinjur."

"Who is Jinjur?" asked Woot, the Green Monkey.

"Haven't you heard of Jinjur?" exclaimed the Scarecrow, in surprise.

"No," said Woot. "Is Jinjur a man, a woman, a beast or a bird?"

"Jinjur is a girl," explained the Scarecrow Bear. "She's a fine girl, too, although a bit restless and liable to get excited. Once, a long time ago, she raised an army of girls and called herself 'General Jinjur.' With her army she captured the Emerald City, and drove me out of it, because I insisted that an army in Oz was highly improper. But Ozma punished the rash girl, and afterward Jinjur and I became fast friends. Now Jinjur lives peacefully on a farm, near here, and raises fields of cream-puffs, chocolate-caramels and macaroons. They say she's a pretty good farmer, and in addition to that she's an artist, and paints pictures so perfect that one can scarcely tell them from nature. She often repaints my face for me, when it gets worn or mussy, and the lovely expression I wore when the Giantess transformed me was painted by Jinjur only a month or so ago."

"It was certainly a pleasant expression," agreed Woot.

"Jinjur can paint anything," continued the Scarecrow Bear, with enthusiasm, as they walked along together. "Once, when I came

to her house, my straw was old and crumpled, so that my body sagged dreadfully. I needed new straw to replace the old, but Jinjur had no straw on all her ranch and I was really unable to travel farther until I had been restuffed. When I explained this to Jinjur, the girl at once painted a straw-stack which was so natural that I went to it and secured enough straw to fill all my body. It was a good quality of straw, too, and lasted me a long time."

This seemed very wonderful to Woot, who knew that such a thing could never happen in any place but a fairy country like Oz.

The Munchkin Country was much nicer than the Gillikin Country, and all the fields were separated by blue fences, with grassy lanes and paths of blue ground, and the land seemed well cultivated. They were on a little hill looking down upon this favored country, but had not quite reached the settled parts, when on turning a bend in the path they were halted by a form that barred their way

A more curious creature they had seldom seen, even in the Land of Oz, where curious creatures abound. It had the head of a young man — evidently a Munchkin — with a pleasant face and hair neatly combed. But the body was very long, for it had twenty legs — ten legs on each side — and this caused the body to stretch out and lie in a horizontal position, so that all the legs could touch the ground and stand firm. From the shoulders extended two small arms; at least, they seemed small beside so many legs.

This odd creature was dressed in the regulation clothing of the Munchkin people, a dark blue coat neatly fitting the long body and each pair of legs having a pair of sky-blue trousers, with blue-tinted stockings and blue leather shoes turned up at the pointed toes.

"I wonder who you are?" said Polychrome the Canary, fluttering above the strange creature, who had probably been asleep on the path.

"I sometimes wonder, myself, who I am," replied the many-legged young man; "but, in reality, I am Tommy Kwikstep, and I live in a hollow tree that fell to the ground with age. I have polished the inside of it, and made a door at each end, and that's a very comfortable residence for me because it just fits my shape."

"How did you happen to have such a shape?" asked the Scarecrow Bear, sitting on his haunches and regarding Tommy Kwikstep with a serious look. "Is the shape natural?"

"No; it was wished on me," replied Tommy, with a sigh. "I used to be very active and loved to run errands for anyone who needed my services. That was how I got my name of Tommy Kwikstep. I could run an errand more quickly than any other boy, and so I was very proud of myself. One day, however, I met an old lady who was a fairy, or a witch, or something of the sort, and she said if I would run an errand for her — to carry some magic medicine to another old woman — she would grant me just one Wish, whatever the Wish happened to be. Of course I consented and, taking the medicine, I hurried away. It was a long distance, mostly up hill, and my legs began to grow weary. Without thinking what I was doing I said aloud: 'Dear me; I wish I had twenty legs!' and in an instant I became the unusual creature you see beside you. Twenty legs! Twenty on one man! You may count them, if you doubt my word."

"You've got 'em, all right," said Woot the Monkey, who had

already counted them.

After I had delivered the magic medicine to the old woman, I returned and tried to find the witch, or fairy, or whatever she was, who had given me the unlucky wish, so she could take it away again. I've been searching for her ever since, but never can find her," continued poor Tommy Kwikstep, sadly "I suppose," said the Tin Owl, blinking at him, "you can travel very fast, with those twenty legs."

At first I was able to," was the reply; "but I traveled so much, searching for the fairy, or witch, or whatever she was, that I soon got corns on my toes. Now, a corn on one toe is not so bad, but when you have a hundred toes — as I have — and get corns on most of them, it is far from pleasant. Instead of running, I now painfully crawl, and although I try not to be discouraged I do hope I shall find that witch or fairy, or whatever she was, before long."

I hope so, too," said the Scarecrow. "But, after all, you have the pleasure of knowing you are unusual, and therefore remarkable among the people of Oz. To be just like other persons is small credit to one, while to be unlike others is a mark of distinction."

That sounds very pretty," returned Tommy Kwikstep, "but if you had to put on ten pair of trousers every morning, and tie up twenty shoes, you would prefer not to be so distinguished."

Was the witch, or fairy, or whatever she was, an old person, with wrinkled skin and half her teeth gone?" inquired the Tin Owl.

No," said Tommy Kwikstep.

Then she wasn't Old Mombi," remarked the transformed Emperor.

I'm not interested in who it wasn't, so much as I am in who it was," said the twenty-legged young man. "And, whatever or whomsoever she was, she has managed to keep out of my way."

If you found her, do you suppose she'd change you back into a two-legged boy?" asked Woot.

Perhaps so, if I could run another errand for her and so earn another wish."

Would you really like to be as you were before?" asked Polychrome the Canary, perching upon the Green Monkey's shoulder to observe Tommy Kwikstep more attentively.

I would, indeed," was the earnest reply.

Then I will see what I can do for you," promised the Rainbow's Daughter, and flying to the ground she took a small twig in her bill and with it made several mystic figures on each side of Tommy Kwikstep.

Are you a witch, or fairy, or something of the sort?" he asked as he watched her wonderingly.

The Canary made no answer, for she was busy, but the Scarecrow Bear replied: "Yes; she's something of the sort, and a bird of a magician."

The twenty-legged boy's transformation happened so queerly that they were all surprised at its method. First, Tommy Kwikstep's last two legs disappeared; then the next two, and the next, and as each pair of legs vanished his body shortened. All this while Polychrome was running around him and chirping mystical words, and when all the young man's legs had disappeared but two he noticed that the Canary was still busy and cried out in alarm: "Stop — stop! Leave me two of my legs, or I shall be worse off than before."

"I know," said the Canary. "I'm only removing with my magic the corns from your last ten toes."

"Thank you for being so thoughtful," he said gratefully, and now they noticed that Tommy Kwikstep was quite a nice looking young fellow.

"What will you do now?" asked Woot the Monkey.

"First," he answered, "I must deliver a note which I've carried in my pocket ever since the witch, or fairy, or whatever she was, granted my foolish wish. And I am resolved never to speak again without taking time to think carefully on what I am going to say, for I realize that speech without thought is dangerous. And after I've delivered the note, I shall run errands again for anyone who needs my services."

So he thanked Polychrome again and started away in a different direction from their own, and that was the last they saw of Tommy Kwikstep.

11. Jinjur's Ranch

As they followed a path down the blue-grass hillside, the first house that met the view of the travelers was joyously recognized by the Scarecrow Bear as the one inhabited by his friend Jinjur, so they increased their speed and hurried toward it.

On reaching the place, how ever, they found the house deserted. The front door stood open, but no one was inside. In the garden surrounding the house were neat rows of bushes bearing cream-puffs and macaroons, some of which were still green, but others ripe and ready to eat. Farther back were fields of caramels, and all the land seemed well cultivated and carefully tended. They looked through the fields for the girl farmer, but she was nowhere to be seen.

"Well," finally remarked the little Brown Bear, "let us go into the house and make ourselves at home. That will be sure to please my friend Jinjur, who happens to be away from home just now. When she returns, she will be greatly surprised."

"Would she care if I ate some of those ripe cream-puffs?" asked the Green Monkey.

"No, indeed; Jinjur is very generous. Help yourself to all you want," said the Scarecrow Bear.

So Woot gathered a lot of the cream-puffs that were golden yellow and filled with a sweet, creamy substance, and ate until his hunger was satisfied. Then he entered the house with his friends and sat in a rocking-chair — just as he was accustomed to do when a boy. The Canary perched herself upon the mantel and daintily plumed her feathers; the Tin Owl sat on the back of another chair; the Scarecrow squatted on his hairy haunches in the middle of the room.

"I believe I remember the girl Jinjur," remarked the Canary, in her sweet voice. "She cannot help us very much, except to direct us on our way to Glinda's castle, for she does not understand magic. But she's a good girl, honest and sensible, and I'll be glad to see her."

"All our troubles," said the Owl with a deep sigh, "arose from my foolish resolve to seek Nimmie Amee and make her Empress of the Winkies, and while I wish to reproach no one, I must say that it was Woot the Wanderer who put the notion into my head."

"Well, for my part, I am glad he did," responded the Canary. "Your journey resulted in saving me from the Giantess, and had you not traveled to the Yoop Valley, I would still be Mrs. Yoop's prisoner. It is much nicer to be free, even though I still bear the enchanted form of a Canary-Bird."

"Do you think we shall ever be able to get our proper forms back again?" asked the Green Monkey earnestly.

Polychrome did not make reply at once to this important question, but after a period of thoughtfulness she said: "I have been taught to believe that there is an antidote for every magic charm, yet Mrs. Yoop insists that no power can alter her transformations. I realize that my own fairy magic cannot do it, although I have thought that we Sky Fairies have more power than is accorded to Earth Fairies. The yookoohoo magic is admitted to be very strange in its workings and different from the magic usually practiced, but perhaps Glinda or Ozma may understand it better than I. In them lies our only hope. Unless they can help us, we must remain forever as we are."

"A Canary-Bird on a Rainbow wouldn't be so bad," asserted the Tin Owl, winking and blinking with his round tin eyes, "so if you can manage to find your Rainbow again you need have little to worry about."

"That's nonsense, Friend Chopper," exclaimed Woot. "I know just how Polychrome feels. A beautiful girl is much superior to a little yellow bird, and a boy — such as I was — far better than a Green Monkey. Neither of us can be happy again unless we recover our rightful forms."

"I feel the same way," announced the stuffed Bear. "What do you suppose my friend the Patchwork Girl would think of me, if she saw me wearing this beastly shape?"

"She'd laugh till she cried," admitted the Tin Owl. "For my part, I'll have to give up the notion of marrying Nimmie Amee, but I'll try not to let that make me unhappy. If it's my duty, I'd like to do my duty, but if magic prevents my getting married I'll flutter along all by myself and be just as contented."

Their serious misfortunes made them all silent for a time, and as their thoughts were busy in dwelling upon the evils with which fate had burdened them, none noticed that Jinjur had suddenly appeared in the doorway and was looking at them in astonishment. The next moment her astonishment changed to anger, for there, in her best rocking-chair, sat a Green Monkey. A great shiny Owl perched upon another chair and a Brown Bear squatted upon her parlor rug. Jinjur did not notice the Canary, but she caught up a broomstick and dashed into the room, shouting as she came: "Get out of here, you wild creatures! How dare you enter my house?"

With a blow of her broom she knocked the Brown Bear over, and the Tin Owl tried to fly out of her reach and made a great clatter with his tin wings. The Green Monkey was so startled by the sudden attack that he sprang into the fireplace — where there was fortunately no fire — and tried to escape by climbing up the chimney. But he found the opening too small, and so was forced to drop down again. Then he crouched trembling in the fireplace,

his pretty green hair all blackened with soot and covered with ashes. From this position Woot watched to see what would happen next.

"Stop, Jinjur — stop!" cried the Brown Bear, when the broom again threatened him. "Don't you know me? I'm your old friend the Scarecrow?"

"You're trying to deceive me, you naughty beast! I can see plainly that you are a bear, and a mighty poor specimen of a bear, too," retorted the girl.

"That's because I'm not properly stuffed," he assured her. "When Mrs. Yoop transformed me, she didn't realize I should have more stuffing."

"Who is Mrs. Yoop?" inquired Jinjur, pausing with the broom still upraised.

"A Giantess in the Gillikin Country."

"Oh; I begin to understand. And Mrs. Yoop transformed you. You are really the famous Scarecrow of Oz."

"I was, Jinjur. Just now I'm as you see me — a miserable little Brown Bear with a poor quality of stuffing. That Tin Owl is none other than our dear Tin Woodman — Nick Chopper, the Emperor of the Winkies — while this Green Monkey is a nice little boy we recently became acquainted with, Woot the Wanderer."

"And I," said the Canary, flying close to Jinjur, "am Polychrome the Daughter of the Rainbow, in the form of a bird."

"Goodness me!" cried Jinjur, amazed; "that Giantess must be a powerful Sorceress, and as wicked as she is powerful."

"She's a yookoohoo," said Polychrome. "Fortunately, we managed to escape from her castle, and we are now on our way to Glinda the Good to see if she possesses the power to restore us to our former shapes."

"Then I must beg your pardons; all of you must forgive me," said Jinjur, putting away the broom. "I took you to be a lot of wild unmannerly animals, as was quite natural. You are very welcome to my home and I'm sorry I haven't the power to help you out of your troubles. Please use my house and all that I have, as if it were your own."

At this declaration of peace, the Bear got upon his feet and the Owl resumed his perch upon the chair and the Monkey crept out of the fireplace. Jinjur looked at Woot critically, and scowled.

"For a Green Monkey," said she, "you're the blackest creature I ever saw. And you'll get my nice clean room all dirty with soot and ashes. Whatever possessed you to jump up the chimney?"

"I — I was scared," explained Woot, somewhat ashamed.

"Well, you need renovating, and that's what will happen to you right away. Come with me!" she commanded.

"What are you going to do?" asked Woot.

"Give you a good scrubbing," said Jinjur.

Now, neither boys nor monkeys relish being scrubbed, so Woot shrank away from the energetic girl, trembling fearfully. But

Jinjur grabbed him by his paw and dragged him out to the back yard, where, in spite of his whines and struggles, she plunged him into a tub of cold water and began to scrub him with a stiff brush and a cake of yellow soap.

This was the hardest trial that Woot had endured since he became a monkey, but no protest had any influence with Jinjur, who lathered and scrubbed him in a business-like manner and afterward dried him with a coarse towel.

The Bear and the Owl gravely watched this operation and nodded approval when Woot's silky green fur shone clear and bright in the afternoon sun. The Canary seemed much amused and laughed a silvery ripple of laughter as she said: "Very well done, my good Jinjur; I admire your energy and judgment. But I had no idea a monkey could look so comical as this monkey did while he was being bathed."

"I'm not a monkey!" declared Woot, resentfully; "I'm just a boy in a monkey's shape, that's all."

"If you can explain to me the difference," said Jinjur, "I'll agree not to wash you again — that is, unless you foolishly get into the fireplace. All persons are usually judged by the shapes in which they appear to the eyes of others. Look at me, Woot; what am I?"

Woot looked at her.

"You're as pretty a girl as I've ever seen," he replied.

Jinjur frowned. That is, she tried hard to frown.

"Come out into the garden with me," she said, "and I'll give you some of the most delicious caramels you ever ate. They're a new variety, that no one can grow but me, and they have a heliotrope flavor."

12. Ozma and Dorothy

In her magnificent palace in the Emerald City, the beautiful girl Ruler of all the wonderful Land of Oz sat in her dainty boudoir with her friend Princess Dorothy beside her. Ozma was studying a roll of manuscript which she had taken from the Royal Library, while Dorothy worked at her embroidery and at times stooped to pat a shaggy little black dog that lay at her feet. The little dog's name was Toto, and he was Dorothy's faithful companion.

To judge Ozma of Oz by the standards of our world, you would think her very young — perhaps fourteen or fifteen years of age — yet for years she had ruled the Land of Oz and had never seemed a bit older. Dorothy appeared much younger than Ozma. She had been a little girl when first she came to the Land of Oz, and she was a little girl still, and would never seem to be a day older while she lived in this wonderful fairyland.

Oz was not always a fairyland, I am told. Once it was much like other lands, except it was shut in by a dreadful desert of sandy wastes that lay all around it, thus preventing its people from all contact with the rest of the world. Seeing this isolation, the fairy band of Queen Lurline, passing over Oz while on a journey, enchanted the country and so made it a Fairyland. And Queen Lurline left one of her fairies to rule this enchanted Land of Oz, and then passed on and forgot all about it.

From that moment no one in Oz ever died. Those who were old remained old; those who were young and strong did not change as years passed them by; the children remained children always, and played and romped to their hearts' content, while all the babies lived in their cradles and were tenderly cared for and never grew up. So people in Oz stopped counting how old they were in years, for years made no difference in their appearance and could not alter their station. They did not get sick, so there were no doctors among them. Accidents might happen to some, on rare occasions, it is true, and while no one could die naturally, as other people do, it was possible that one might be totally destroyed. Such incidents, however, were very unusual, and so seldom was there anything to worry over that the Oz people were as happy and contented as can be.

Another strange thing about this fairy Land of Oz was that whoever managed to enter it from the outside world came under the magic spell of the place and did not change in appearance as long as they lived there. So Dorothy, who now lived with Ozma, seemed just the same sweet little girl she had been when first she came to this delightful fairyland.

Perhaps all parts of Oz might not be called truly delightful, but it was surely delightful in the neighborhood of the Emerald City, where Ozma reigned. Her loving influence was felt for many miles around, but there were places in the mountains of the Gillikin Country, and the forests of the Quadling Country, and perhaps in far-away parts of the Munchkin and Winkie Countries, where the inhabitants were somewhat rude and uncivilized and had not yet come under the spell of Ozma's wise and kindly rule. Also, when Oz first became a fairyland, it harbored several witches and magicians and sorcerers and necromancers, who were scattered in various parts, but most of these had been deprived of their magic powers, and Ozma had issued a royal edict forbidding anyone in her dominions to work magic except Glinda the Good and the Wizard of Oz. Ozma herself, being a real fairy, knew a lot of magic, but she only used it to benefit her subjects.

This little explanation will help you to understand better the story you are reaching, but most of it is already known to those who are familiar with the Oz people whose adventures they have followed in other Oz books.

Ozma and Dorothy were fast friends and were much together. Everyone in Oz loved Dorothy almost as well as they did their lovely Ruler, for the little Kansas girl's good fortune had not spoiled her or rendered her at all vain. She was just the same brave and true and adventurous child as before she lived in a royal palace and became the chum of the fairy Ozma.

In the room in which the two sat — which was one of Ozma's private suite of apartments — hung the famous Magic Picture. This was the source of constant interest to little Dorothy. One had but to stand before it and wish to see what any person was doing, and at once a scene would flash upon the magic canvas which showed exactly where that person was, and like our own moving pictures would reproduce the actions of that person as long as you cared to watch them. So today, when Dorothy tired of her embroidery, she drew the curtains from before the Magic Picture and wished to see what her friend Button Bright was doing. Button Bright, she saw, was playing ball with Ojo, the Munchkin boy, so Dorothy next wished to see what her Aunt Em was doing. The picture showed Aunt Em quietly engaged in darning socks for Uncle Henry, so Dorothy wished to see what her old friend the Tin Woodman was doing.

The Tin Woodman was then just leaving his tin castle in the company of the Scarecrow and Woot the Wanderer. Dorothy had never seen this boy before, so she wondered who he was. Also she was curious to know where the three were going, for she noticed Woot's knapsack and guessed they had started on a long journey. She asked Ozma about it, but Ozma did not know

That afternoon Dorothy again saw the travelers in the Magic Picture, but they were merely tramping through the country and Dorothy was not much interested in them. A couple of days later, however, the girl, being again with Ozma, wished to see her friends, the Scarecrow and the Tin Woodman in the Magic Picture, and on this occasion found them in the great castle of Mrs. Yoop, the Giantess, who was at the time about to transform them. Both Dorothy and Ozma now became greatly interested and watched the transformations with indignation and horror.

"What a wicked Giantess!" exclaimed Dorothy.

"Yes," answered Ozma, "she must be punished for this cruelty to our friends, and to the poor boy who is with them."

After this they followed the adventure of the little Brown Bear and the Tin Owl and the Green Monkey with breathless interest, and were delighted when they escaped from Mrs. Yoop. They did not know, then, who the Canary was, but realized it must be the transformation of some person of consequence, whom the Giantess had also enchanted.

When, finally, the day came when the adventurers headed south into the Munchkin Country, Dorothy asked anxiously: "Can't something be done for them, Ozma? Can't you change 'em back into their own shapes? They've suffered enough from these dreadful transformations, seems to me."

"I've been studying ways to help them, ever since they were transformed," replied Ozma. "Mrs. Yoop is now the only yookoohoo in my dominions, and the yookoohoo magic is very peculiar and hard for others to understand, yet I am resolved to make the attempt to break these enchantments. I may not succeed, but I shall do the best I can. From the directions our friends are taking, I believe they are going to pass by Jinjur's Ranch, so if we start now we may meet them there. Would you like to go with me, Dorothy?"

"Of course," answered the little girl; "I wouldn't miss it for anything."

"Then order the Red Wagon," said Ozma of Oz, "and we will start at once."

Dorothy ran to do as she was bid, while Ozma went to her Magic Room to make ready the things she believed she would need. In half an hour the Red Wagon stood before the grand entrance of the palace, and before it was hitched the Wooden Sawhorse, which was Ozma's favorite steed.

This Sawhorse, while made of wood, was very much alive and could travel swiftly and without tiring. To keep the ends of his wooden legs from wearing down short, Ozma had shod the Sawhorse with plates of pure gold. His harness was studded with brilliant emeralds and other jewels and so, while he himself was not at all handsome, his outfit made a splendid appearance.

Since the Sawhorse could understand her spoken words, Ozma used no reins to guide him. She merely told him where to go. When she came from the palace with Dorothy, they both climbed into the Red Wagon and then the little dog, Toto, ran up and asked:

"Are you going to leave me behind, Dorothy?" Dorothy looked at Ozma, who smiled in return and said: "Toto may go with us, if you wish him to."

So Dorothy lifted the little dog into the wagon, for, while he could run fast, he could not keep up with the speed of the wonderful Sawhorse.

Away they went, over hills and through meadows, covering the ground with astonishing speed. It is not surprising, therefore, that the Red Wagon arrived before Jinjur's house just as that energetic young lady had finished scrubbing the Green Monkey and was about to lead him to the caramel patch.

13. The Restoration

The Tin Owl gave a hoot of delight when he saw the Red Wagon draw up before Jinjur's house, and the Brown Bear grunted and growled with glee and trotted toward Ozma as fast as he could wobble. As for the Canary, it flew swiftly to Dorothy's shoulder and perched there, saying in her ear: "Thank goodness you have come to our rescue!"

"But who are you?" asked Dorothy

"Don't you know?" returned the Canary.

"No; for the first time we noticed you in the Magic Picture, you were just a bird, as you are now. But we've guessed that the giant woman had transformed you, as she did the others."

"Yes; I'm Polychrome, the Rainbow's Daughter," announced the Canary.

"Goodness me!" cried Dorothy. "How dreadful."

"Well, I make a rather pretty bird, I think," returned Polychrome, "but of course I'm anxious to resume my own shape and get back upon my rainbow."

"Ozma will help you, I'm sure," said Dorothy. "How does it feel, Scarecrow, to be a Bear?" she asked, addressing her old friend.

"I don't like it," declared the Scarecrow Bear. "This brutal form is quite beneath the dignity of a wholesome straw man."

"And think of me," said the Owl, perching upon the dashboard of the Red Wagon with much noisy clattering of his tin feathers. "Don't I look horrid, Dorothy, with eyes several sizes too big for my body, and so weak that I ought to wear spectacles?"

"Well," said Dorothy critically, as she looked him over, "you're nothing to brag of, I must confess. But Ozma will soon fix you up again."

The Green Monkey had hung back, bashful at meeting two lovely girls while in the form of a beast; but Jinjur now took his hand and led him forward while she introduced him to Ozma, and Woot managed to make a low bow, not really ungraceful, before her girlish Majesty, the Ruler of Oz.

"You have all been forced to endure a sad experience," said Ozma, "and so I am anxious to do all in my power to break Mrs. Yoop's enchantments. But first tell me how you happened to stray into that lonely Valley where Yoop Castle stands."

Between them they related the object of their journey, the Scarecrow Bear telling of the Tin Woodman's resolve to find Nimmie Amee and marry her, as a just reward for her loyalty to him. Woot told of their adventures with the Loons of Loonville, and the Tin Owl described the manner in which they had been captured and transformed by the Giantess. Then Polychrome related her story, and when all had been told, and Dorothy had several times reproved Toto for growling at the Tin Owl, Ozma remained thoughtful for a while, pondering upon what she had heard.

Finally she looked up, and with one of her delightful smiles, said to the anxious group: "I am not sure my magic will be able to restore every one of you, because your transformations are of such a strange and unusual character. Indeed, Mrs. Yoop was quite justified in believing no power could alter her enchantments. However, I am sure I can restore the Scarecrow to his original shape. He was stuffed with straw from the beginning, and even the yookoohoo magic could not alter that. The Giantess was merely able to make a bear's shape of a man's shape, but the bear is stuffed with straw, just as the man was. So I feel confident I can make a man of the bear again."

"Hurrah!" cried the Brown Bear, and tried clumsily to dance a jig of delight.

"As for the Tin Woodman, his case is much the same," resumed Ozma, still smiling. "The power of the Giantess could not make him anything but a tin creature, whatever shape she transformed him into, so it will not be impossible to restore him to his manly form. Anyhow, I shall test my magic at once, and see if it will do what I have promised."

She drew from her bosom a small silver Wand and, making passes with the Wand over the head of the Bear, she succeeded in the brief space of a moment in breaking his enchantment. The original Scarecrow of Oz again stood before them, well stuffed with straw and with his features nicely painted upon the bag which formed his head.

The Scarecrow was greatly delighted, as you may suppose, and he strutted proudly around while the powerful fairy, Ozma of Oz, broke the enchantment that had transformed the Tin Woodman and made a Tin Owl into a Tin Man again.

"Now, then," chirped the Canary, eagerly; "I'm next, Ozma!"

"But your case is different," replied Ozma, no longer smiling but wearing a grave expression on her sweet face. "I shall have to experiment on you, Polychrome, and I may fail in all my attempts."

She then tried two or three different methods of magic, hoping one of them would succeed in breaking Polychrome's enchantment, but still the Rainbow's Daughter remained a Canary-Bird. Finally, however, she experimented in another way. She transformed the Canary into a Dove, and then transformed the Dove into a Speckled Hen, and then changed the Speckled Hen into a rabbit, and then the rabbit into a Fawn. And at the last, after mixing several powders and sprinkling them upon the Fawn, the yookoohoo enchantment was suddenly broken and before them stood one of the daintiest and loveliest creatures in any fairyland in the world. Polychrome was as sweet and merry in disposition as she was beautiful, and when she danced and capered around in delight, her beautiful hair floated around her like a golden mist and her many-hued raiment, as soft as cobwebs, reminded one of drifting clouds in a summer sky.

Woot was so awed by the entrancing sight of this exquisite Sky Fairy that he quite forgot his own sad plight until be noticed Ozma gazing upon him with an intent expression that denoted sympathy and sorrow. Dorothy whispered in her friend's ear, but the Ruler of Oz shook her head sadly.

Jinjur, noticing this and understanding Ozma's looks, took the paw of the Green Monkey in her own hand and patted it softly.

"Never mind," she said to him. "You are a very beautiful color, and a monkey can climb better than a boy and do a lot of other things no boy can ever do."

"What's the matter?" asked Woot, a sinking feeling at his heart. "Is Ozma's magic all used up?"

Ozma herself answered him.

"Your form of enchantment, my poor boy," she said pityingly, "is different from that of the others. Indeed, it is a form that is impossible to alter by any magic known to fairies or yookoohoos. The wicked Giantess was well aware, when she gave you the form of a Green Monkey, that the Green Monkey must exist in the Land of Oz for all future time."

Woot drew a long sigh.

"Well, that's pretty hard luck," he said bravely, "but if it can't be helped I must endure it; that's all. I don't like being a monkey, but what's the use of kicking against my fate?"

They were all very sorry for him, and Dorothy anxiously asked Ozma: "Couldn't Glinda save him?"

"No," was the reply. "Glinda's power in transformations is no greater than my own. Before I left my palace I went to my Magic Room and studied Woot's case very carefully. I found that no power can do away with the Green Monkey. He might transfer, or exchange his form with some other person, it is true; but the Green Monkey we cannot get rid of by any magic arts known to science."

"But — see here," said the Scarecrow, who had listened intently to this explanation, "why not put the monkey's form on some one else?"

"Who would agree to make the change?" asked Ozma. "If by force we caused anyone else to become a Green Monkey, we would be as cruel and wicked as Mrs. Yoop. And what good would an exchange do?" she continued. "Suppose, for instance, we worked the enchantment, and made Toto into a Green Monkey. At the same moment Woot would become a little dog."

"Leave me out of your magic, please," said Toto, with a reproachful growl. "I wouldn't become a Green Monkey for anything."

"And I wouldn't become a dog," said Woot. "A green monkey is much better than a dog, it seems to me."

"That is only a matter of opinion," answered Toto.

"Now, here's another idea," said the Scarecrow. "My brains are working finely today, you must admit. Why not transform Toto into Woot the Wanderer, and then have them exchange forms? The dog would become a green monkey and the monkey would have his own natural shape again."

"To be sure!" cried Jinjur. "That's a fine idea."

"Leave me out of it," said Toto. "I won't do it."

"Wouldn't you be willing to become a green monkey — see what a pretty color it is — so that this poor boy could be restored to his own shape?" asked Jinjur, pleadingly

"No," said Toto.

"I don't like that plan the least bit," declared Dorothy, "for then I wouldn't have any little dog."

"But you'd have a green monkey in his place," persisted Jinjur, who liked Woot and wanted to help him.

"I don't want a green monkey," said Dorothy positively.

"Don't speak of this again, I beg of you," said Woot. "This is my own misfortune and I would rather suffer it alone than deprive Princess Dorothy of her dog, or deprive the dog of his proper shape. And perhaps even her Majesty, Ozma of Oz, might not be able to transform anyone else into the shape of Woot the Wanderer."

"Yes; I believe I might do that," Ozma returned; "but Woot is quite right; we are not justified in inflicting upon anyone — man or dog — the form of a green monkey. Also it is certain that in order to relieve the boy of the form he now wears, we must give it to someone else, who would be forced to wear it always."

"I wonder," said Dorothy, thoughtfully, "if we couldn't find someone in the Land of Oz who would be willing to become a green monkey? Seems to me a monkey is active and spry, and he can climb trees and do a lot of clever things, and green isn't a bad color for a monkey — it makes him unusual."

"I wouldn't ask anyone to take this dreadful form," said Woot; "it wouldn't be right, you know. I've been a monkey for some time, now, and I don't like it. It makes me ashamed to be a beast of this sort when by right of birth I'm a boy; so I'm sure it would be wicked to ask anyone else to take my place."

They were all silent, for they knew he spoke the truth. Dorothy was almost ready to cry with pity and Ozma's sweet face was sad and disturbed. The Scarecrow rubbed and patted his stuffed head to try to make it think better, while the Tin Woodman went into the house and began to oil his tin joints so that the sorrow of his friends might not cause him to weep. Weeping is liable to rust tin, and the Emperor prided himself upon his highly polished body — now doubly dear to him because for a time he had been deprived of it.

Polychrome had danced down the garden paths and back again a dozen times, for she was seldom still a moment, yet she had heard Ozma's speech and understood very well Woot's unfortunate position. But the Rainbow's Daughter, even while dancing, could think and reason very clearly, and suddenly she solved the problem in the nicest possible way.

Coming close to Ozma, she said: "Your Majesty, all this trouble was caused by the wickedness of Mrs. Yoop, the Giantess. Yet even now that cruel woman is living in her secluded castle, enjoying the thought that she has put this terrible enchantment on Woot the Wanderer. Even now she is laughing at our despair because we can find no way to get rid of the green monkey. Very well, we do not wish to get rid of it. Let the woman who created the form wear it herself, as a just punishment for her wickedness. I am sure your fairy power can give to Mrs. Yoop the form of Woot the Wanderer — even at this distance from her — and then it will be possible to exchange the two forms. Mrs. Yoop will become the Green Monkey, and Woot will recover his own form again."

Ozma's face brightened as she listened to this clever proposal.

"Thank you, Polychrome," said she. "The task you propose is not so easy as you suppose, but I will make the attempt, and perhaps I may succeed."

14. The Green Monkey

They now entered the house, and as an interested group watched Jinjur, at Ozma's command, build a fire and put a kettle of water over to boil. The Ruler of Oz stood before the fire silent and grave, while the others, realizing that an important ceremony of magic was about to be performed, stood quietly in the background so as not to interrupt Ozma's proceedings. Only Polychrome kept going in and coming out, humming softly to herself as she danced, for the Rainbow's Daughter could not keep still for long, and the four walls of a room always made her nervous and ill at ease. She moved so noiselessly, however, that her movements were like the shifting of sunbeams and did not annoy anyone.

When the water in the kettle bubbled, Ozma drew from her bosom two tiny packets containing powders. These powders she threw into the kettle and after briskly stirring the contents with a branch from a macaroon bush, Ozma poured the mystic broth upon a broad platter which Jinjur had placed upon the table. As the broth cooled it became as silver, reflecting all objects from its smooth surface like a mirror.

While her companions gathered around the table, eagerly attentive — and Dorothy even held little Toto in her arms that he might see — Ozma waved her wand over the mirror-like surface. At once it reflected the interior of Yoop Castle, and in the big hall sat Mrs. Yoop, in her best embroidered silken robes, engaged in weaving a new lace apron to replace the one she had lost.

The Giantess seemed rather uneasy, as if she had a faint idea that someone was spying upon her, for she kept looking behind her and this way and that, as though expecting danger from an unknown source. Perhaps some yookoohoo instinct warned her Woot saw that she had escaped from her room by some of the magical means at her disposal, after her prisoners had escaped her. She was now occupying the big hall of her castle as she used to do. Also Woot thought, from the cruel expression on the face of the Giantess, that she was planning revenge on them, as soon as her new magic apron was finished

But Ozma was now making passes over the platter with her silver Wand, and presently the form of the Giantess began to shrink in size and to change its shape. And now, in her place sat the form of Woot the Wanderer, and as if suddenly realizing her transformation Mrs. Yoop threw down her work and rushed to a looking-glass that stood against the wall of her room. When she saw the boy's form reflected as her own, she grew violently angry and dashed her head against the mirror, smashing it to atoms.

Just then Ozma was busy with her magic Wand, making strange figures, and she had also placed her left hand firmly upon the shoulder of the Green Monkey. So now, as all eyes were turned upon the platter, the form of Mrs. Yoop gradually changed again. She was slowly transformed into the Green Monkey, and at the same time Woot slowly regained his natural form.

It was quite a surprise to them all when they raised their eyes from the platter and saw Woot the Wanderer standing beside Ozma. And, when they glanced at the platter again, it reflected nothing more than the walls of the room in Jinjur's house in which they stood. The magic ceremonial was ended, and Ozma of Oz had triumphed over the wicked Giantess.

"What will become of her, I wonder?" said Dorothy, as she drew a long breath.

"She will always remain a Green Monkey," replied Ozma, "and in that form she will be unable to perform any magical arts whatsoever. She need not be unhappy, however, and as she lives all alone in her castle she probably won't mind the transformation very much after she gets used to it."

"Anyhow, it serves her right," declared Dorothy, and all agreed with her.

"But," said the kind hearted Tin Woodman, "I'm afraid the Green Monkey will starve, for Mrs. Yoop used to get her food by magic, and now that the magic is taken away from her, what can she eat?"

"Why, she'll eat what other monkeys do," returned the Scarecrow. "Even in the form of a Green Monkey, she's a very clever person, and I'm sure her wits will show her how to get plenty to eat."

"Don't worry about her," advised Dorothy. "She didn't worry about you, and her condition is no worse than the condition she imposed on poor Woot. She can't starve to death in the Land of Oz, that's certain, and if she gets hungry at times it's no more than the wicked thing deserves. Let's forget Mrs. Yoop; for, in spite of her being a yookoohoo, our fairy friends have broken all of her transformations."

15. The Man of Tin

Ozma and Dorothy were quite pleased with Woot the Wanderer, whom they found modest and intelligent and very well mannered. The boy was truly grateful for his release from the cruel enchantment, and he promised to love, revere and defend the girl Ruler of Oz forever afterward, as a faithful subject.

"You may visit me at my palace, if you wish," said Ozma, "where I will be glad to introduce you to two other nice boys, Ojo the Munchkin and Button-Bright."

"Thank your Majesty," replied Woot, and then he turned to the Tin Woodman and inquired: "What are your further plans, Mr. Emperor? Will you still seek Nimmie Amee and marry her, or will you abandon the quest and return to the Emerald City and your own castle?"

The Tin Woodman, now as highly polished and well-oiled as ever, reflected a while on this question and then answered: "Well, I see no reason why I should not find Nimmie Amee. We are now in the Munchkin Country, where we are perfectly safe, and if it was right for me, before our enchantment, to marry Nimmie Amee and make her Empress of the Winkies, it must be right now, when the enchantment has been broken and I am once more myself. Am I correct, friend Scarecrow?"

"You are, indeed," answered the Scarecrow. "No one can oppose such logic."

"But I'm afraid you don't love Nimmie Amee," suggested Dorothy.

"That is just because I can't love anyone," replied the Tin Woodman. "But, if I cannot love my wife, I can at least be kind to her, and all husbands are not able to do that."

"Do you s'pose Nimmie Amee still loves you, after all these years?" asked Dorothy

"I'm quite sure of it, and that is why I am going to her to make her happy. Woot the Wanderer thinks I ought to reward her for being faithful to me after my meat body was chopped to pieces and I became tin. What do you think, Ozma?"

Ozma smiled as she said: "I do not know your Nimmie Amee, and so I cannot tell what she most needs to make her happy. But there is no harm in your going to her and asking her if she still wishes to marry you. If she does, we will give you a grand wedding at the Emerald City and, afterward, as Empress of the Winkies, Nimmie Amee would become one of the most important ladies in all Oz."

So it was decided that the Tin Woodman would continue his journey, and that the Scarecrow and Woot the Wanderer should accompany him, as before. Polychrome also decided to join their party, somewhat to the surprise of all.

"I hate to be cooped up in a palace," she said to Ozma, "and of course the first time I meet my Rainbow I shall return to my own dear home in the skies, where my fairy sisters are even now awaiting me and my father is cross because I get lost so often. But I can find my Rainbow just as quickly while traveling in the Munchkin Country as I could if living in the Emerald City — or any other place in Oz — so I shall go with the Tin Woodman and help him woo Nimmie Amee."

Dorothy wanted to go, too, but as the Tin Woodman did not invite her to join his party, she felt she might be intruding if she asked to be taken. She hinted, but she found he didn't take the hint. It is quite a delicate matter for one to ask a girl to marry him, however much she loves him, and perhaps the Tin Woodman did not desire to have too many looking on when he found his old sweetheart, Nimmie Amee. So Dorothy contented herself with the thought that she would help Ozma prepare a splendid wedding feast, to be followed by a round of parties and festivities when the Emperor of the Winkies reached the Emerald City with his bride.

Ozma offered to take them all in the Red Wagon to a place as near to the great Munchkin forest as a wagon could get. The Red Wagon was big enough to seat them all, and so, bidding good-bye to Jinjur, who gave Woot a basket of ripe cream-puffs and caramels to take with him, Ozma commanded the Wooden Sawhorse to start, and the strange creature moved swiftly over the lanes and presently came to the Road of Yellow Bricks. This road led straight to a dense forest, where the path was too narrow for the Red Wagon to proceed farther, so here the party separated.

Ozma and Dorothy and Toto returned to the Emerald City, after wishing their friends a safe and successful journey, while the Tin Woodman, the Scarecrow, Woot the Wanderer and Polychrome, the Rainbow's Daughter, prepared to push their way through the thick forest. However, these forest paths were well known to the Tin Man and the Scarecrow, who felt quite at home among the trees.

"I was born in this grand forest," said Nick Chopper, the tin Emperor, speaking proudly, "and it was here that the Witch enchanted my axe and I lost different parts of my meat body until I became all tin. Here, also — for it is a big forest — Nimmie

Amee lived with the Wicked Witch, and at the other edge of the trees stands the cottage of my friend Ku-Klip, the famous tinsmith who made my present beautiful form."

"He must be a clever workman," declared Woot, admiringly.

"He is simply wonderful," declared the Tin Woodman.

"I shall be glad to make his acquaintance," said Woot.

"If you wish to meet with real cleverness," remarked the Scarecrow, "you should visit the Munchkin farmer who first made me. I won't say that my friend the Emperor isn't all right for a tin man, but any judge of beauty can understand that a Scarecrow is far more artistic and refined."

"You are too soft and flimsy," said the Tin Woodman.

"You are too hard and stiff," said the Scarecrow, and this was as near to quarreling as the two friends ever came. Polychrome laughed at them both, as well she might, and Woot hastened to change the subject.

At night they all camped underneath the trees. The boy ate cream-puffs for supper and offered Polychrome some, but she preferred other food and at daybreak sipped the dew that was clustered thick on the forest flowers. Then they tramped onward again, and presently the Scarecrow paused and said: "It was on this very spot that Dorothy and I first met the Tin Woodman, who was rusted so badly that none of his joints would move. But after we had oiled him up, he was as good as new and accompanied us to the Emerald City."

"Ah, that was a sad experience," asserted the Tin Woodman soberly. "I was caught in a rainstorm while chopping down a tree for exercise, and before I realized it, I was firmly rusted in every joint. There I stood, axe in hand, but unable to move, for days and weeks and months! Indeed, I have never known exactly how long the time was; but finally along came Dorothy and I was saved. See! This is the very tree I was chopping at the time I rusted."

"You cannot be far from your old home, in that case," said Woot.

"No; my little cabin stands not a great way off, but there is no occasion for us to visit it. Our errand is with Nimmie Amee, and her house is somewhat farther away, to the left of us."

"Didn't you say she lives with a Wicked Witch, who makes her a slave?" asked the boy.

"She did, but she doesn't," was the reply. "I am told the Witch was destroyed when Dorothy's house fell on her, so now Nimmie Amee must live all alone. I haven't seen her, of course, since the Witch was crushed, for at that time I was standing rusted in the forest and had been there a long time, but the poor girl must have felt very happy to be free from her cruel mistress."

"Well," said the Scarecrow, "let's travel on and find Nimmie Amee. Lead on, your Majesty, since you know the way, and we will follow."

So the Tin Woodman took a path that led through the thickest part of the forest, and they followed it for some time. The light was dim here, because vines and bushes and leafy foliage were all about them, and often the Tin Man had to push aside the branches that obstructed their way, or cut them off with his axe. After they had proceeded some distance, the Emperor suddenly stopped short and exclaimed: "Good gracious!"

The Scarecrow, who was next, first bumped into his friend and then peered around his tin body, and said in a tone of wonder: "Well, I declare!"

Woot the Wanderer pushed forward to see what was the matter, and cried out in astonishment: "For goodness' sake!"

Then the three stood motionless, staring hard, until Polychrome's merry laughter rang out behind them and aroused them from their stupor.

In the path before them stood a tin man who was the exact duplicate of the Tin Woodman. He was of the same size, he was jointed in the same manner, and he was made of shining tin from top to toe. But he stood immovable, with his tin jaws half parted and his tin eyes turned upward. In one of his hands was held a long, gleaming sword. Yes, there was the difference, the only thing that distinguished him from the Emperor of the Winkies. This tin man bore a sword, while the Tin Woodman bore an axe.

"It's a dream; it must be a dream!" gasped Woot.

"That's it, of course," said the Scarecrow; "there couldn't be two Tin Woodmen."

"No," agreed Polychrome, dancing nearer to the stranger, "this one is a Tin Soldier. Don't you see his sword?"

The Tin Woodman cautiously put out one tin hand and felt of his double's arm. Then he said in a voice that trembled with emotion: "Who are you, friend?"

There was no reply.

"Can't you see he's rusted, just as you were once?" asked Polychrome, laughing again. "Here, Nick Chopper, lend me your oil-can a minute!"

The Tin Woodman silently handed her his oil-can, without which he never traveled, and Polychrome first oiled the stranger's tin jaws and then worked them gently to and fro until the Tin Soldier said: "That's enough. Thank you. I can now talk. But please oil my other joints."

Woot seized the oil-can and did this, but all the others helped wiggle the soldier's joints as soon as they were oiled, until they moved freely.

The Tin Soldier seemed highly pleased at his release. He strutted up and down the path, saying in a high, thin voice:
"The Soldier is a splendid man
When marching on parade,
And when he meets the enemy
He never is afraid.

He rights the wrongs of nations,
His country's flag defends,
The foe he'll fight with great delight,
But seldom fights his friends."

16. Captain Fyter

"Are you really a soldier?" asked Woot, when they had all watched this strange tin person parade up and down the path and proudly flourish his sword.

I was a soldier," was the reply, "but I've been a prisoner to Mr. Rust so long that I don't know exactly what I am."

But — dear me!" cried the Tin Woodman, sadly perplexed; "how came you to be made of tin?"

That," answered the Soldier, "is a sad, sad story I was in love with a beautiful Munchkin girl, who lived with a Wicked Witch. The Witch did not wish me to marry the girl, so she enchanted my sword, which began hacking me to pieces. When I lost my legs I went to the tinsmith, Ku-Klip, and he made me some tin legs. When I lost my arms, Ku-Klip made me tin arms, and when I lost my head he made me this fine one out of tin. It was the same way with my body, and finally I was all tin. But I was not unhappy, for Ku-Klip made a good job of me, having had experience in making another tin man before me."

Yes," observed the Tin Woodman, "it was Ku-Klip who made me. But, tell me, what was the name of the Munchkin girl you were in love with?"

She is called Nimmie Amee," said the Tin Soldier.

Hearing this, they were all so astonished that they were silent for a time, regarding the stranger with wondering looks. Finally the Tin Woodman ventured to ask: "And did Nimmie Amee return your love?"

Not at first," admitted the Soldier. "When first I marched into the forest and met her, she was weeping over the loss of her former sweetheart, a woodman whose name was Nick Chopper."

That is me," said the Tin Woodman.

She told me he was nicer than a soldier, because he was all made of tin and shone beautifully in the sun. She said a tin man appealed to her artistic instincts more than an ordinary meat man, as I was then. But I did not despair, because her tin sweetheart had disappeared, and could not be found. And finally Nimmie Amee permitted me to call upon her and we became friends. It was then that the Wicked Witch discovered me and became furiously angry when I said I wanted to marry the girl. She enchanted my sword, as I said, and then my troubles began. When I got my tin legs, Nimmie Amee began to take an interest in me; when I got my tin arms, she began to like me better than ever, and when I was all made of tin, she said I looked like her dear Nick Chopper and she would be willing to marry me.

The day of our wedding was set, and it turned out to be a rainy day. Nevertheless I started out to get Nimmie Amee, because the Witch had been absent for some time, and we meant to elope before she got back. As I traveled the forest paths the rain wetted my joints, but I paid no attention to this because my thoughts were all on my wedding with beautiful Nimmie Amee and I could think of nothing else until suddenly my legs stopped moving. Then my arms rusted at the joints and I became frightened and cried for help, for now I was unable to oil myself. No one heard my calls and before long my jaws rusted, and I was unable to utter another sound. So I stood helpless in this spot, hoping some wanderer would come my way and save me. But this forest path is seldom used, and I have been standing here so long that I have lost all track of time. In my mind I composed poetry and sang songs, but not a sound have I been able to utter. But this desperate condition has now been relieved by your coming my way and I must thank you for my rescue."

This is wonderful!" said the Scarecrow, heaving a stuffy, long sigh. "I think Ku-Klip was wrong to make two tin men, just alike, and the strangest thing of all is that both you tin men fell in love with the same girl."

As for that," returned the Soldier, seriously, "I must admit I lost my ability to love when I lost my meat heart. Ku-Klip gave me a tin heart, to be sure, but it doesn't love anything, as far as I can discover, and merely rattles against my tin ribs, which makes me wish I had no heart at all."

Yet, in spite of this condition, you were going to marry Nimmie Amee?"

Well, you see I had promised to marry her, and I am an honest man and always try to keep my promises. I didn't like to disappoint the poor girl, who had been disappointed by one tin man already."

That was not my fault," declared the Emperor of the Winkies, and then he related how he, also, had rusted in the forest and after a long time had been rescued by Dorothy and the Scarecrow and had traveled with them to the Emerald City in search of a heart that could love.

If you have found such a heart, sir," said the Soldier, "I will gladly allow you to marry Nimmie Amee in my place."

If she loves you best, sir," answered the Woodman, "I shall not interfere with your wedding her. For, to be quite frank with you, I cannot yet love Nimmie Amee as I did before I became tin."

Still, one of you ought to marry the poor girl," remarked Woot; "and, if she likes tin men, there is not much choice between you. Why don't you draw lots for her?"

That wouldn't be right," said the Scarecrow.

The girl should be permitted to choose her own husband," asserted Polychrome. "You should both go to her and allow her to take her choice. Then she will surely be happy."

That, to me, seems a very fair arrangement," said the Tin Soldier.

I agree to it," said the Tin Woodman, shaking the hand of his twin to show the matter was settled. "May I ask your name, sir?" he continued.

Before I was so cut up," replied the other, "I was known as Captain Fyter, but afterward I was merely called 'The Tin Soldier.'"

Well, Captain, if you are agreeable, let us now go to Nimmie Amee's house and let her choose between us."

Very well; and if we meet the Witch, we will both fight her — you with your axe and I with my sword."

The Witch is destroyed," announced the Scarecrow, and as they walked away he told the Tin Soldier of much that had happened in the Land of Oz since he had stood rusted in the forest.

I must have stood there longer than I had imagined," he said thoughtfully

17. The Workshop of Ku-Klip

It was not more than a two hours' journey to the house where

Nimmie Amee had lived, but when our travelers arrived there they found the place deserted. The door was partly off its hinges, the roof had fallen in at the rear and the interior of the cottage was thick with dust. Not only was the place vacant, but it was evident that no one had lived there for a long time.

"I suppose," said the Scarecrow, as they all stood looking wonderingly at the ruined house, "that after the Wicked Witch was destroyed, Nimmie Amee became lonely and went somewhere else to live."

"One could scarcely expect a young girl to live all alone in a forest," added Woot. "She would want company, of course, and so I believe she has gone where other people live."

"And perhaps she is still crying her poor little heart out because no tin man comes to marry her," suggested Polychrome.

"Well, in that case, it is the clear duty of you two tin persons to seek Nimmie Amee until you find her," declared the Scarecrow.

"I do not know where to look for the girl," said the Tin Soldier, "for I am almost a stranger to this part of the country."

"I was born here," said the Tin Woodman, "but the forest has few inhabitants except the wild beasts. I cannot think of anyone living near here with whom Nimmie Amee might care to live."

"Why not go to Ku-Klip and ask him what has become of the girl?" proposed Polychrome.

That struck them all as being a good suggestion, so once more they started to tramp through the forest, taking the direct path to Ku-Klip's house, for both the tin twins knew the way, having followed it many times.

Ku-Klip lived at the far edge of the great forest, his house facing the broad plains of the Munchkin Country that lay to the eastward. But, when they came to this residence by the forest's edge, the tinsmith was not at home.

It was a pretty place, all painted dark blue with trimmings of lighter blue. There was a neat blue fence around the yard and several blue benches had been placed underneath the shady blue trees which marked the line between forest and plain. There was a blue lawn before the house, which was a good sized building. Ku-Klip lived in the front part of the house and had his workshop in the back part, where he had also built a lean-to addition, in order to give him more room.

Although they found the tinsmith absent on their arrival, there was smoke coming out of his chimney, which proved that he would soon return.

"And perhaps Nimmie Amee will be with him," said the Scarecrow in a cheerful voice.

While they waited, the Tin Woodman went to the door of the workshop and, finding it unlocked, entered and looked curiously around the room where he had been made.

"It seems almost like home to me," hie told his friends, who had followed him in. "The first time I came here I had lost a leg, so I had to carry it in my hand while I hopped on the other leg all the way from the place in the forest where the enchanted axe cut me. I remember that old Ku-Klip carefully put my meat leg into a barrel — I think that is the same barrel, still standing in the corner yonder — and then at once he began to make a tin leg for

me. He worked fast and with skill, and I was much interested in the job."

"My experience was much the same," said the Tin Soldier. "I used to bring all the parts of me, which the enchanted sword had cut away, here to the tinsmith, and Ku-Klip would put them into the barrel."

"I wonder," said Woot, "if those cast-off parts of you two unfortunates are still in that barrel in the corner?"

"I suppose so." replied the Tin Woodman. "In the Land of Oz no part of a living creature can ever be destroyed."

"If that is true, how was that Wicked Witch destroyed?" inquired Woot.

"Why, she was very old and was all dried up and withered before Oz became a fairyland," explained the Scarecrow. "Only her magic arts had kept her alive so long, and when Dorothy's house fell upon her she just turned to dust, and was blown away and scattered by the wind. I do not think, however, that the parts cut away from these two young men could ever be entirely destroyed and, if they are still in those barrels, they are likely to be just the same as when the enchanted axe or sword severed them."

"It doesn't matter, however," said the Tin Woodman; "our tin bodies are more brilliant and durable, and quite satisfy us."

"Yes, the tin bodies are best," agreed the Tin Soldier. "Nothing can hurt them."

"Unless they get dented or rusted," said Woot, but both the tin men frowned on him.

Scraps of tin, of all shapes and sizes, lay scattered around the workshop. Also there were hammers and anvils and soldering irons and a charcoal furnace and many other tools such as a tinsmith works with. Against two of the side walls had been built stout work-benches and in the center of the room was a long table. At the end of the shop, which adjoined the dwelling, were several cupboards.

After examining the interior of the workshop until his curiosity was satisfied, Woot said;

"I think I will go outside until Ku-Klip comes. It does not seem quite proper for us to take possession of his house while he is absent."

"That is true," agreed the Scarecrow, and they were all about to leave the room when the Tin Woodman said: "Wait a minute," and they halted in obedience to the command.

18. The Tin Woodman Talks to Himself

The Tin Woodman had just noticed the cupboards and was curious to know what they contained, so he went to one of them and opened the door. There were shelves inside, and upon one of the shelves which was about on a level with his tin chin the Emperor discovered a Head — it looked like a doll's head, only it was larger, and he soon saw it was the Head of some person. It was facing the Tin Woodman and as the cupboard door swung back, the eyes of the Head slowly opened and looked at him. The Tin Woodman was not at all surprised, for in the Land of Oz one runs into magic at every turn.

"Dear me!" said the Tin Woodman, staring hard. "It seems as if had met you, somewhere, before. Good morning, sir!"

"You have the advantage of me," replied the Head. "I never saw you before in my life."

"Still, your face is very familiar," persisted the Tin Woodman. "Pardon me, but may I ask if you — eh — eh — if you ever had a Body?"

"Yes, at one time," answered the Head, "but that is so long ago I can't remember it. Did you think," with a pleasant smile, "that I was born just as I am? That a Head would be created without a Body?"

"No, of course not," said the other. "But how came you to lose your body?"

"Well, I can't recollect the details; you'll have to ask Ku-Klip about it," returned the Head. "For, curious as it may seem to you, my memory is not good since my separation from the rest of me. I still possess my brains and my intellect is as good as ever, but my memory of some of the events I formerly experienced is quite hazy."

"How long have you been in this cupboard?" asked the Emperor.

"I don't know."

"Haven't you a name?"

"Oh, yes," said the Head; "I used to be called Nick Chopper, when I was a woodman and cut down trees for a living."

"Good gracious!" cried the Tin Woodman in astonishment. "If you are Nick Chopper's Head, then you are Me — or I'm You — or — or — What relation are we, anyhow?"

"Don't ask me," replied the Head. "For my part, I'm not anxious to claim relationship with any common, manufactured article, like you. You may be all right in your class, but your class isn't my class. You're tin."

The poor Emperor felt so bewildered that for a time he could only stare at his old Head in silence. Then he said: "I must admit that I wasn't at all bad looking before I became tin. You're almost handsome — for meat. If your hair was combed, you'd be quite attractive."

"How do you expect me to comb my hair without help?" demanded the Head, indignantly. "I used to keep it smooth and neat, when I had arms, but after I was removed from the rest of me, my hair got mussed, and old Ku-Klip never has combed it for me."

"I'll speak to him about it," said the Tin Woodman. "Do you remember loving a pretty Munchkin girl named Nimmie Amee?"

"No," answered the Head. "That is a foolish question. The heart in my body — when I had a body — might have loved someone, for all I know, but a head isn't made to love; it's made to think."

"Oh; do you think, then?"

"I used to think."

"You must have been shut up in this cupboard for years and years. What have you thought about, in all that time?"

"Nothing. That's another foolish question. A little reflection will convince you that I have had nothing to think about, except the boards on the inside of the cupboard door, and it didn't take me long to think of everything about those boards that could be thought of. Then, of course, I quit thinking."

"And are you happy?"

"Happy? What's that?"

"Don't you know what happiness is?" inquired the Tin Woodman.

"I haven't the faintest idea whether it's round or square, or black or white, or what it is. And, if you will pardon my lack of interest in it, I will say that I don't care."

The Tin Woodman was much puzzled by these answers. His traveling companions had grouped themselves at his back, and had fixed their eyes on the Head and listened to the conversation with much interest, but until now, they had not interrupted because they thought the Tin Woodman had the best right to talk to his own head and renew acquaintance with it.

But now the Tin Soldier remarked: "I wonder if my old head happens to be in any of these cupboards," and he proceeded to open all the cupboard doors. But no other head was to be found on any of the shelves.

"Oh, well; never mind," said Woot the Wanderer; "I can't imagine what anyone wants of a cast-off head, anyhow."

"I can understand the Soldier's interest," asserted Polychrome, dancing around the grimy workshop until her draperies formed a cloud around her dainty form. "For sentimental reasons a man might like to see his old head once more, just as one likes to revisit an old home."

"And then to kiss it good-bye," added the Scarecrow.

"I hope that tin thing won't try to kiss me good-bye!" exclaimed the Tin Woodman's former head. "And I don't see what right you folks have to disturb my peace and comfort, either."

"You belong to me," the Tin Woodman declared.

"I do not!"

"You and I are one."

"We've been parted," asserted the Head. "It would be unnatural for me to have any interest in a man made of tin. Please close the door and leave me alone."

"I did not think that my old Head could be so disagreeable," said the Emperor. "I — I'm quite ashamed of myself; meaning you."

"You ought to be glad that I've enough sense to know what my rights are," retorted the Head. "In this cupboard I am leading a simple life, peaceful and dignified, and when a mob of people in whom I am not interested disturb me, they are the disagreeable ones; not I."

With a sigh the Tin Woodman closed and latched the cupboard door and turned away.

"Well," said the Tin Soldier, "if my old head would have treated me as coldly and in so unfriendly a manner as your old head has treated you, friend Chopper, I'm glad I could not find it."

"Yes; I'm rather surprised at my head, myself," replied the Tin Woodman, thoughtfully. "I thought I had a more pleasant disposition when I was made of meat."

But just then old Ku-Klip the Tinsmith arrived, and he seemed surprised to find so many visitors. Ku-Klip was a stout man and a short man. He had his sleeves rolled above his elbows, showing muscular arms, and he wore a leathern apron that covered all the front of him, and was so long that Woot was surprised he didn't step on it and trip whenever he walked. And Ku-Klip had a gray beard that was almost as long as his apron, and his head was bald on top and his ears stuck out from his head like two fans. Over his eyes, which were bright and twinkling, he wore big spectacles. It was easy to see that the tinsmith was a kind hearted man, as well as a merry and agreeable one. "Oh-ho!" he cried in a joyous bass voice; "here are both my tin men come to visit me, and they and their friends are welcome indeed. I'm very proud of you two characters, I assure you, for you are so perfect that you are proof that I'm a good workman. Sit down. Sit down, all of you — if you can find anything to sit on — and tell me why you are here."

So they found seats and told him all of their adventures that they thought he would like to know. Ku- Klip was glad to learn that Nick Chopper, the Tin Woodman, was now Emperor of the Winkies and a friend of Ozma of Oz, and the tinsmith was also interested in the Scarecrow and Polychrome.

He turned the straw man around, examining him curiously, and patted him on all sides, and then said: "You are certainly wonderful, but I think you would be more durable and steady on your legs if you were made of tin. Would you like me to —"

"No, indeed!" interrupted the Scarecrow hastily; "I like myself better as I am."

But to Polychrome the tinsmith said: "Nothing could improve you, my dear, for you are the most beautiful maiden I have ever seen. It is pure happiness just to look at you."

"That is praise, indeed, from so skillful a workman," returned the Rainbow's Daughter, laughing and dancing in and out the room.

"Then it must be this boy you wish me to help," said Ku-Klip, looking at Woot.

"No," said Woot, "we are not here to seek your skill, but have merely come to you for information."

Then, between them, they related their search for Nimmie Amee, whom the Tin Woodman explained he had resolved to marry, yet who had promised to become the bride of the Tin Soldier before he unfortunately became rusted. And when the story was told, they asked Ku-Klip if he knew what had become of Nimmie Amee.

"Not exactly," replied the old man, "but I know that she wept bitterly when the Tin Soldier did not come to marry her, as he had promised to do. The old Witch was so provoked at the girl's tears that she beat Nimmie Amee with her crooked stick and then hobbled away to gather some magic herbs, with which she intended to transform the girl into an old hag, so that no one would again love her or care to marry her. It was while she was away on this errand that Dorothy's house fell on the Wicked Witch, and she turned to dust and blew away. When I heard this good news, I sent Nimmie Amee to find the Silver Shoes which the Witch had worn, but Dorothy had taken them with her to the Emerald City."

"Yes, we know all about those Silver Shoes," said the Scarecrow.

"Well," continued Ku-Klip, "after that, Nimmie Amee decided to go away from the forest and live with some people she was acquainted with who had a house on Mount Munch. I have never seen the girl since."

"Do you know the name of the people on Mount Munch, with whom she went to live?" asked the Tin Woodman.

"No, Nimmie Amee did not mention her friend's name, and I did not ask her. She took with her all that she could carry of the goods that were in the Witch's house, and she told me I could have the rest. But when I went there I found nothing worth taking except some magic powders that I did not know how to use, and a bottle of Magic Glue."

"What is Magic Glue?" asked Woot.

"It is a magic preparation with which to mend people when they cut themselves. One time, long ago, I cut off one of my fingers by accident, and I carried it to the Witch, who took down her bottle and glued it on again for me. See!" showing them his finger, "it is as good as ever it was. No one else that I ever heard of had this Magic Glue, and of course when Nick Chopper cut himself to pieces with his enchanted axe and Captain Fyter cut himself to pieces with his enchanted sword, the Witch would not mend them, or allow me to glue them together, because she had herself wickedly enchanted the axe and sword. Nothing remained but for me to make them new parts out of tin; but, as you see, tin answered the purpose very well, and I am sure their tin bodies are a great improvement on their meat bodies."

"Very true," said the Tin Soldier.

"I quite agree with you," said the Tin Woodman. "I happened to find my old head in your cupboard, a while ago, and certainly it is not as desirable a head as the tin one I now wear."

"By the way," said the Tin Soldier, "what ever became of my old head, Ku-Klip?"

"And of the different parts of our bodies?" added the Tin Woodman.

"Let me think a minute," replied Ku-Klip. "If I remember right, you two boys used to bring me most of your parts, when they were cut off, and I saved them in that barrel in the corner. You must not have brought me all the parts, for when I made Chopfyt I had hard work finding enough pieces to complete the job. I finally had to finish him with one arm."

"Who is Chopfyt?" inquired Woot.

"Oh, haven't I told you about Chopfyt?" exclaimed Ku- Klip. "Of course not! And he's quite a curiosity, too. You'll be interested in hearing about Chopfyt. This is how he happened:

"One day, after the Witch had been destroyed and Nimmie Amee had gone to live with her friends on Mount Munch, I was looking around the shop for something and came upon the bottle of Magic Glue which I had brought from the old Witch's house. It occurred to me to piece together the odds and ends of you two people, which of course were just as good as ever, and see if I couldn't make a man out of them. If I succeeded, I would have an assistant to help me with my work, and I thought it would be a clever idea to put to some practical use the scraps of Nick Chopper and Captain Fyter. There were two perfectly good heads in my cupboard, and a lot of feet and legs and parts of bodies in the barrel, so I set to work to see what I could do.

First, I pieced together a body, gluing it with the Witch's Magic Glue, which worked perfectly. That was the hardest part of my job, however, because the bodies didn't match up well and some parts were missing. But by using a piece of Captain Fyter here and a piece of Nick Chopper there, I finally got together a very decent body, with heart and all the trimmings complete."

Whose heart did you use in making the body?" asked the Tin Woodman anxiously.

I can't tell, for the parts had no tags on them and one heart looks much like another. After the body was completed, I glued two fine legs and feet onto it. One leg was Nick Chopper's and one was Captain Fyter's and, finding one leg longer than the other, I trimmed it down to make them match. I was much disappointed to find that I had but one arm. There was an extra leg in the barrel, but I could find only one arm. Having glued this onto the body, I was ready for the head, and I had some difficulty in making up my mind which head to use. Finally I shut my eyes and reached out my hand toward the cupboard shelf, and the first head I touched I glued upon my new man."

It was mine!" declared the Tin Soldier, gloomily.

No, it was mine," asserted Ku-Klip, "for I had given you another in exchange for it — the beautiful tin head you now wear. When the glue had dried, my man was quite an interesting fellow. I named him Chopfyt, using a part of Nick Chopper's name and a part of Captain Fyter's name, because he was a mixture of both our cast-off parts. Chopfyt was interesting, as I said, but he did not prove a very agreeable companion. He complained bitterly because I had given him but one arm — as if it were my fault! — and he grumbled because the suit of blue Munchkin clothes, which I got for him from a neighbor, did not fit him perfectly."

Ah, that was because he was wearing my old head," remarked the Tin Soldier. "I remember that head used to be very particular about its clothes."

As an assistant," the old tinsmith continued, "Chopfyt was not a success. He was awkward with tools and was always hungry. He demanded something to eat six or eight times a day, so I wondered if I had fitted his insides properly. Indeed, Chopfyt ate so much that little food was left for myself; so, when he proposed, one day, to go out into the world and seek adventures, I was delighted to be rid of him. I even made him a tin arm to take the place of the missing one, and that pleased him very much, so that we parted good friends."

What became of Chopfyt after that?" the Scarecrow inquired.

I never heard. He started off toward the east, into the plains of the Munchkin Country, and that was the last I ever saw of him."

It seems to me," said the Tin Woodman reflectively, "that you did wrong in making a man out of our cast-off parts. It is evident that Chopfyt could, with justice, claim relationship with both of us."

Don't worry about that," advised Ku-Klip cheerfully; "it is not likely that you will ever meet the fellow. And, if you should meet him, he doesn't know who he is made of, for I never told him the secret of his manufacture. Indeed, you are the only ones who know of it, and you may keep the secret to yourselves, if you wish to."

"Never mind Chopfyt," said the Scarecrow. "Our business now is to find poor Nimmie Amee and let her choose her tin husband. To do that, it seems, from the information Ku-Klip has given us, we must travel to Mount Munch."

"If that's the programme, let us start at once," suggested Woot.

So they all went outside, where they found Polychrome dancing about among the trees and talking with the birds and laughing as merrily as if she had not lost her Rainbow and so been separated from all her fairy sisters.

They told her they were going to Mount Munch, and she replied: "Very well; I am as likely to find my Rainbow there as here, and any other place is as likely as there. It all depends on the weather. Do you think it looks like rain?"

They shook their heads, and Polychrome laughed again and danced on after them when they resumed their journey.

19. The Invisible Country

They were proceeding so easily and comfortably on their way to Mount Munch that Woot said in a serious tone of voice: "I'm afraid something is going to happen."

"Why?" asked Polychrome, dancing around the group of travelers.

"Because," said the boy, thoughtfully, "I've noticed that when we have the least reason for getting into trouble, something is sure to go wrong. Just now the weather is delightful; the grass is beautifully blue and quite soft to our feet; the mountain we are seeking shows clearly in the distance and there is no reason anything should happen to delay us in getting there. Our troubles all seem to be over, and — well, that's why I'm afraid," he added, with a sigh.

"Dear me!" remarked the Scarecrow, "what unhappy thoughts you have, to be sure. This is proof that born brains cannot equal manufactured brains, for my brains dwell only on facts and never borrow trouble. When there is occasion for my brains to think, they think, but I would be ashamed of my brains if they kept shooting out thoughts that were merely fears and imaginings, such as do no good, but are likely to do harm."

"For my part," said the Tin Woodman, "I do not think at all, but allow my velvet heart to guide me at all times."

"The tinsmith filled my hollow head with scraps and clippings of tin," said the Soldier, "and he told me they would do nicely for brains, but when I begin to think, the tin scraps rattle around and get so mixed that I'm soon bewildered. So I try not to think. My tin heart is almost as useless to me, for it is hard and cold, so I'm sure the red velvet heart of my friend Nick Chopper is a better guide."

"Thoughtless people are not unusual," observed the Scarecrow, "but I consider them more fortunate than those who have useless or wicked thoughts and do not try to curb them. Your oil can, friend Woodman, is filled with oil, but you only apply the oil to your joints, drop by drop, as you need it, and do not keep spilling it where it will do no good. Thoughts should be restrained in the same way as your oil, and only applied when necessary, and for a good purpose. If used carefully, thoughts are good things to have."

Polychrome laughed at him, for the Rainbow's Daughter knew more about thoughts than the Scarecrow did. But the others were solemn, feeling they had been rebuked, and tramped on in silence. Suddenly Woot, who was in the lead, looked around and found that all his comrades had mysteriously disappeared. But where could they have gone to? The broad plain was all about him and there were neither trees nor bushes that could hide even a rabbit, nor any hole for one to fall into. Yet there he stood, alone.

Surprise had caused him to halt, and with a thoughtful and puzzled expression on his face he looked down at his feet. It startled him anew to discover that he had no feet. He reached out his hands, but he could not see them. He could feel his hands and arms and body; he stamped his feet on the grass and knew they were there, but in some strange way they had become invisible. While Woot stood, wondering, a crash of metal sounded in his ears and he heard two heavy bodies tumble to the earth just beside him.

"Good gracious!" exclaimed the voice of the Tin Woodman.

"Mercy me!" cried the voice of the Tin Soldier.

"Why didn't you look where you were going?" asked the Tin Woodman reproachfully.

"I did, but I couldn't see you," said the Tin Soldier. "Something has happened to my tin eyes. I can't see you, even now, nor can I see anyone else!"

"It's the same way with me," admitted the Tin Woodman.

Woot couldn't see either of them, although he heard them plainly, and just then something smashed against him unexpectedly and knocked him over; but it was only the straw-stuffed body of the Scarecrow that fell upon him and while he could not see the Scarecrow he managed to push him off and rose to his feet just as Polychrome whirled against him and made him tumble again.

Sitting upon the ground, the boy asked: "Can you see us, Poly?"

"No, indeed," answered the Rainbow's Daughter; "we've all become invisible."

"How did it happen, do you suppose?" inquired the Scarecrow, lying where he had fallen.

"We have met with no enemy," answered Polychrome, "so it must be that this part of the country has the magic quality of making people invisible — even fairies falling under the charm. We can see the grass, and the flowers, and the stretch of plain before us, and we can still see Mount Munch in the distance; but we cannot see ourselves or one another."

"Well, what are we to do about it?" demanded Woot.

"I think this magic affects only a small part of the plain," replied Polychrome; "perhaps there is only a streak of the country where an enchantment makes people become invisible. So, if we get together and hold hands, we can travel toward Mount Munch until the enchanted streak is passed."

"All right," said Woot, jumping up, "give me your hand,

Polychrome. Where are you?"

"Here," she answered. "Whistle, Woot, and keep whistling until I come to you."

So Woot whistled, and presently Polychrome found him and grasped his hand.

"Someone must help me up," said the Scarecrow, lying near them; so they found the straw man and sat him upon his feet after which he held fast to Polychrome's other hand.

Nick Chopper and the Tin Soldier had managed to scramble up without assistance, but it was awkward for them and the Tin Woodman said: "I don't seem to stand straight, somehow. But my joints all work, so I guess I can walk."

Guided by his voice, they reached his side, where Woot grasped his tin fingers so they might keep together.

The Tin Soldier was standing near by and the Scarecrow soon touched him and took hold of his arm.

"I hope you're not wobbly," said the straw man, "for if two of us walk unsteadily we will be sure to fall."

"I'm not wobbly," the Tin Soldier assured him, "but I'm certain that one of my legs is shorter than the other. I can't see it, to tell what's gone wrong, but I'll limp on with the rest of you until we are out of this enchanted territory."

They now formed a line, holding hands, and turning their faces toward Mount Munch resumed their journey. They had not gone far, however, when a terrible growl saluted their ears. The sound seemed to come from a place just in front of them, so they halted abruptly and remained silent, listening with all their ears.

"I smell straw!" cried a hoarse, harsh voice, with more growls and snarls. "I smell straw, and I'm a Hip-po-gy-raf who loves straw and eats all he can find. I want to eat this straw! Where is it? Where is it?"

The Scarecrow, hearing this, trembled but kept silent. All the others were silent, too, hoping that the invisible beast would be unable to find them. But the creature sniffed the odor of the straw and drew nearer and nearer to them until he reached the Tin Woodman, on one end of the line. It was a big beast and it smelled of the Tin Woodman and grated two rows of enormous teeth against the Emperor's tin body.

"Bah! that's not straw," said the harsh voice, and the beast advanced along the line to Woot.

"Meat! Pooh, you're no good! I can't eat meat," grumbled the beast, and passed on to Polychrome.

"Sweetmeats and perfume — cobwebs and dew! Nothing to eat in a fairy like you," said the creature.

Now, the Scarecrow was next to Polychrome in the line, and he realized if the beast devoured his straw he would be helpless for a long time, because the last farmhouse was far behind them and only grass covered the vast expanse of plain. So in his fright he let go of Polychrome's hand and put the hand of the Tin Soldier in that of the Rainbow's Daughter. Then he slipped back of the line and went to the other end, where he silently seized the Tin Woodman's hand.

Meantime, the beast had smelled the Tin Soldier and found he was the last of the line.

"That's funny!" growled the Hip-po-gy-raf; "I can smell straw, but I can't find it. Well, it's here, somewhere, and I must hunt around until I do find it, for I'm hungry."

His voice was now at the left of them, so they started on, hoping to avoid him, and traveled as fast as they could in the direction of Mount Munch.

"I don't like this invisible country," said Woot with a shudder. "We can't tell how many dreadful, invisible beasts are roaming around us, or what danger we'll come to next."

"Quit thinking about danger, please," said the Scarecrow, warningly.

"Why?" asked the boy.

"If you think of some dreadful thing, it's liable to happen, but if you don't think of it, and no one else thinks of it, it just can't happen. Do you see?"

"No," answered Woot. "I won't be able to see much of anything until we escape from this enchantment."

But they got out of the invisible strip of country as suddenly as they had entered it, and the instant they got out they stopped short, for just before them was a deep ditch, running at right angles as far as their eyes could see and stopping all further progress toward Mount Munch.

"It's not so very wide," said Woot, "but I'm sure none of us can jump across it."

Polychrome began to laugh, and the Scarecrow said: "What's the matter?"

"Look at the tin men!" she said, with another burst of merry laughter.

Woot and the Scarecrow looked, and the tin men looked at themselves.

"It was the collision," said the Tin Woodman regretfully. "I knew something was wrong with me, and now I can see that my side is dented in so that I lean over toward the left. It was the Soldier's fault; he shouldn't have been so careless."

"It is your fault that my right leg is bent, making it shorter than the other, so that I limp badly," retorted the Soldier. "You shouldn't have stood where I was walking."

"You shouldn't have walked where I was standing," replied the Tin Woodman.

It was almost a quarrel, so Polychrome said soothingly: "Never mind, friends; as soon as we have time I am sure we can straighten the Soldier's leg and get the dent out of the Woodman's body. The Scarecrow needs patting into shape, too, for he had a bad tumble, but our first task is to get over this ditch."

"Yes, the ditch is the most important thing, just now," added Woot

They were standing in a row, looking hard at the unexpected

barrier, when a fierce growl from behind them made them all turn quickly. Out of the invisible country marched a huge beast with a thick, leathery skin and a surprisingly long neck. The head on the top of this neck was broad and flat and the eyes and mouth were very big and the nose and ears very small. When the head was drawn down toward the beast's shoulders, the neck was all wrinkles, but the head could shoot up very high indeed, if the creature wished it to.

"Dear me!" exclaimed the Scarecrow, "this must be the Hip-po-gy-raf."

"Quite right," said the beast; "and you're the straw which I'm to eat for my dinner. Oh, how I love straw! I hope you don't resent my affectionate appetite?"

With its four great legs it advanced straight toward the Scarecrow, but the Tin Woodman and the Tin Soldier both sprang in front of their friend and flourished their weapons.

"Keep off!" said the Tin Woodman, warningly, or I'll chop you with my axe."

"Keep off!" said the Tin Soldier, "or I'll cut you with my sword."

"Would you really do that?" asked the Hip-po-gy-raf, in a disappointed voice.

"We would," they both replied, and the Tin Woodman added: "The Scarecrow is our friend, and he would be useless without his straw stuffing. So, as we are comrades, faithful and true, we will defend our friend's stuffing against all enemies."

The Hip-po-gy-raf sat down and looked at them sorrowfully.

"When one has made up his mind to have a meal of delicious straw, and then finds he can't have it, it is certainly hard luck," he said. "And what good is the straw man to you, or to himself, when the ditch keeps you from going any further?"

"Well, we can go back again," suggested Woot.

"True," said the Hip-po; "and if you do, you'll be as disappointed as I am. That's some comfort, anyhow."

The travelers looked at the beast, and then they looked across the ditch at the level plain beyond. On the other side the grass had grown tall, and the sun had dried it, so there was a fine crop of hay that only needed to be cut and stacked.

"Why don't you cross over and eat hay?" the boy asked the beast.

"I'm not fond of hay," replied the Hip-po-gy-raf; "straw is much more delicious, to my notion, and it's more scarce in this neighborhood, too. Also I must confess that I can't get across the ditch, for my body is too heavy and clumsy for me to jump the distance. I can stretch my neck across, though, and you will notice that I've nibbled the hay on the farther edge — not because I liked it, but because one must eat, and if one can't get the sort of food he desires, he must take what is offered or go hungry."

"Ah, I see you are a philosopher," remarked the Scarecrow.

"No, I'm just a Hip-po-gy-raf," was the reply.

Polychrome was not afraid of the big beast. She danced close to him and said: "If you can stretch your neck across the ditch, why not help us over? We can sit on your big head, one at a time, and then you can lift us across."

"Yes; I can, it is true," answered the Hip-po; "but I refuse to do it. Unless —" he added, and stopped short.

"Unless what?" asked Polychrome.

"Unless you first allow me to eat the straw with which the Scarecrow is stuffed."

"No," said the Rainbow's Daughter, "that is too high a price to pay. Our friend's straw is nice and fresh, for he was restuffed only a little while ago."

"I know," agreed the Hip-po-gy-raf. "That's why I want it. If it was old, musty straw, I wouldn't care for it."

"Please lift us across," pleaded Polychrome.

"No," replied the beast; "since you refuse my generous offer, I can be as stubborn as you are."

After that they were all silent for a time, but then the Scarecrow said bravely: "Friends, let us agree to the beast's terms. Give him my straw, and carry the rest of me with you across the ditch. Once on the other side, the Tin Soldier can cut some of the hay with his sharp sword, and you can stuff me with that material until we reach a place where there is straw. It is true I have been stuffed with straw all my life and it will be somewhat humiliating to be filled with common hay, but I am willing to sacrifice my pride in a good cause. Moreover, to abandon our errand and so deprive the great Emperor of the Winkies — or this noble Soldier — of his bride, would be equally humiliating, if not more so."

"You're a very honest and clever man!" exclaimed the Hip-po-gy-raf, admiringly. "When I have eaten your head, perhaps I also will become clever."

"You're not to eat my head, you know," returned the Scarecrow hastily. "My head isn't stuffed with straw and I cannot part with it. When one loses his head he loses his brains."

"Very well, then; you may keep your head," said the beast.

The Scarecrow's companions thanked him warmly for his loyal sacrifice to their mutual good, and then he laid down and permitted them to pull the straw from his body. As fast as they did this, the Hip-po-gy-raf ate up the straw, and when all was consumed Polychrome made a neat bundle of the clothes and boots and gloves and hat and said she would carry them, while Woot tucked the Scarecrow's head under his arm and promised to guard its safety.

"Now, then," said the Tin Woodman, "keep your promise, Beast, and lift us over the ditch."

"M-m-m-mum, but that was a fine dinner!" said the Hip-po, smacking his thick lips in satisfaction, "and I'm as good as my word. Sit on my head, one at a time, and I'll land you safely on the other side."

He approached close to the edge of the ditch and squatted down. Polychrome climbed over his big body and sat herself lightly upon the flat head, holding the bundle of the Scarecrow's raiment in her hand. Slowly the elastic neck stretched out until it reached the far side of the ditch, when the beast lowered his head and permitted the beautiful fairy to leap to the ground.

Woot made the queer journey next, and then the Tin Soldier and the Tin Woodman went over, and all were well pleased to have overcome this serious barrier to their progress.

"Now, Soldier, cut the hay," said the Scarecrow's head, which was still held by Woot the Wanderer.

"I'd like to, but I can't stoop over, with my bent leg, without falling," replied Captain Fyter.

"What can we do about that leg, anyhow?" asked Woot, appealing to Polychrome.

She danced around in a circle several times without replying, and the boy feared she had not heard him; but the Rainbow's Daughter was merely thinking upon the problem, and presently she paused beside the Tin Soldier and said: "I've been taught a little fairy magic, but I've never before been asked to mend tin legs with it, so I'm not sure I can help you. It all depends on the good will of my unseen fairy guardians, so I'll try, and if I fail, you will be no worse off than you are now."

She danced around the circle again, and then laid both hands upon the twisted tin leg and sang in her sweet voice:
"Fairy Powers, come to my aid!
This bent leg of tin is made;
Make it straight and strong and true,
And I'll render thanks to you."

"Ah!" murmured Captain Fyter in a glad voice, as she withdrew her hands and danced away, and they saw he was standing straight as ever, because his leg was as shapely and strong as it had been before his accident.

The Tin Woodman had watched Polychrome with much interest, and he now said: "Please take the dent out of my side, Poly, for I am more crippled than was the Soldier."

So the Rainbow's Daughter touched his side lightly and sang:
"Here's a dent by accident;
Such a thing was never meant.
Fairy Powers, so wondrous great,
Make our dear Tin Woodman straight!"

"Good!" cried the Emperor, again standing erect and strutting around to show his fine figure. "Your fairy magic may not be able to accomplish all things, sweet Polychrome, but it works splendidly on tin. Thank you very much."

"The hay — the hay!" pleaded the Scarecrow's head.

"Oh, yes; the hay," said Woot. "What are you waiting for, Captain Fyter?"

At once the Tin Soldier set to work cutting hay with his sword and in a few minutes there was quite enough with which to stuff the Scarecrow's body. Woot and Polychrome did this and as no easy task because the hay packed together more than straw and as they had little experience in such work their job, when completed, left the Scarecrow's arms and legs rather bunchy. Also there was a hump on his back which made Woot laugh and say it reminded him of a camel, but it was the best they could do and when the head was fastened on to the body they asked the Scarecrow how he felt.

"A little heavy, and not quite natural," he cheerfully replied; "but I'll get along somehow until we reach a straw-stack. Don't laugh at me, please, because I'm a little ashamed of myself and I don't want to regret a good action."

They started at once in the direction of Mount Munch, and as the Scarecrow proved very clumsy in his movements, Woot took one of his arms and the Tin Woodman the other and so helped their friend to walk in a straight line.

And the Rainbow's Daughter, as before, danced ahead of them and behind them and all around them, and they never minded her odd ways, because to them she was like a ray of sunshine.

20. Over Night

The Land of the Munchkins is full of surprises, as our travelers had already learned, and although Mount Munch was constantly growing larger as they advanced toward it, they knew it was still a long way off and were not certain, by any means, that they had escaped all danger or encountered their last adventure.

The plain was broad, and as far as the eye could see, there seemed to be a level stretch of country between them and the mountain, but toward evening they came upon a hollow, in which stood a tiny blue Munchkin dwelling with a garden around it and fields of grain filling in all the rest of the hollow.

They did not discover this place until they came close to the edge of it, and they were astonished at the sight that greeted them because they had imagined that this part of the plain had no inhabitants.

It's a very small house," Woot declared. "I wonder who lives here?"

The way to find out is to knock on the door and ask," replied the Tin Woodman. "Perhaps it is the home of Nimmie Amee."

Is she a dwarf?" asked the boy.

No, indeed; Nimmie Amee is a full sized woman."

Then I'm sure she couldn't live in that little house," said Woot.

Let's go down," suggested the Scarecrow. "I'm almost sure I can see a straw-stack in the back yard."

They descended the hollow, which was rather steep at the sides, and soon came to the house, which was indeed rather small. Woot knocked upon a door that was not much higher than his waist, but got no reply. He knocked again, but not a sound was heard.

Smoke is coming out of the chimney," announced Polychrome, who was dancing lightly through the garden, where cabbages and beets and turnips and the like were growing finely

Then someone surely lives here," said Woot, and knocked again.

Now a window at the side of the house opened and a queer head appeared. It was white and hairy and had a long snout and little round eyes. The ears were hidden by a blue sunbonnet tied under the chin.

Oh; it's a pig!" exclaimed Woot.

Pardon me; I am Mrs. Squealina Swyne, wife of Professor Grunter Swyne, and this is our home," said the one in the window. "What do you want?"

"What sort of a Professor is your husband?" inquired the Tin Woodman curiously.

"He is Professor of Cabbage Culture and Corn Perfection. He is very famous in his own family, and would be the wonder of the world if he went abroad," said Mrs. Swyne in a voice that was half proud and half irritable. "I must also inform you intruders that the Professor is a dangerous individual, for he files his teeth every morning until they are sharp as needles. If you are butchers, you'd better run away and avoid trouble."

"We are not butchers," the Tin Woodman assured her.

"Then what are you doing with that axe? And why has the other tin man a sword?"

"They are the only weapons we have to defend our friends from their enemies," explained the Emperor of the Winkies, and Woot added: "Do not be afraid of us, Mrs. Swyne, for we are harmless travelers. The tin men and the Scarecrow never eat anything and Polychrome feasts only on dewdrops. As for me, I'm rather hungry, but there is plenty of food in your garden to satisfy me."

Professor Swyne now joined his wife at the window, looking rather scared in spite of the boy's assuring speech. He wore a blue Munchkin hat, with pointed crown and broad brim, and big spectacles covered his eyes.

He peeked around from behind his wife and after looking hard at the strangers, he said: "My wisdom assures me that you are merely travelers, as you say, and not butchers. Butchers have reason to be afraid of me, but you are safe. We cannot invite you in, for you are too big for our house, but the boy who eats is welcome to all the carrots and turnips he wants. Make yourselves at home in the garden and stay all night, if you like; but in the morning you must go away, for we are quiet people and do not care for company."

"May I have some of your straw?" asked the Scarecrow.

"Help yourself," replied Professor Swyne.

"For pigs, they're quite respectable," remarked Woot, as they all went toward the straw-stack.

"I'm glad they didn't invite us in," said Captain Fyter. "I hope I'm not too particular about my associates, but I draw the line at pigs."

The Scarecrow was glad to be rid of his hay, for during the long walk it had sagged down and made him fat and squatty and more bumpy than at first.

"I'm not specially proud," he said, "but I love a manly figure, such as only straw stuffing can create. I've not felt like myself since that hungry Hip-po ate my last straw."

Polychrome and Woot set to work removing the hay and then they selected the finest straw, crisp and golden, and with it stuffed the Scarecrow anew. He certainly looked better after the operation, and he was so pleased at being reformed that he tried to dance a little jig, and almost succeeded.

"I shall sleep under the straw-stack tonight," Woot decided, after he had eaten some of the vegetables from the garden, and in fact he slept very well, with the two tin men and the Scarecrow sitting silently beside him and Polychrome away somewhere in the moonlight dancing her fairy dances.

At daybreak the Tin Woodman and the Tin Soldier took occasion to polish their bodies and oil their joints, for both were exceedingly careful of their personal appearance. They had forgotten the quarrel due to their accidental bumping of one another in the invisible country, and being now good friends the Tin Woodman polished the Tin Soldier's back for him and then the Tin Soldier polished the Tin Woodman's back.

For breakfast the Wanderer ate crisp lettuce and radishes, and the Rainbow's Daughter, who had now returned to her friends, sipped the dewdrops that had formed on the petals of the wildflowers.

As they passed the little house to renew their journey, Woot called out: "Good-bye, Mr. and Mrs. Swyne!"

The window opened and the two pigs looked out.

"A pleasant journey," said the Professor.

"Have you any children?" asked the Scarecrow, who was a great friend of children.

"We have nine," answered the Professor; "but they do not live with us, for when they were tiny piglets the Wizard of Oz came here and offered to care for them and to educate them. So we let him have our nine tiny piglets, for he's a good Wizard and can be relied upon to keep his promises."

"I know the Nine Tiny Piglets," said the Tin Woodman.

"So do I," said the Scarecrow. "They still live in the Emerald City, and the Wizard takes good care of them and teaches them to do all sorts of tricks."

"Did they ever grow up?" inquired Mrs. Squealina Swyne, in an anxious voice.

"No," answered the Scarecrow; "like all other children in the Land of Oz, they will always remain children, and in the case of the tiny piglets that is a good thing, because they would not be nearly so cute and cunning if they were bigger."

"But are they happy?" asked Mrs. Swyne.

"Everyone in the Emerald City is happy," said the Tin Woodman. "They can't help it."

Then the travelers said good-bye, and climbed the side of the basin that was toward Mount Munch.

21. Polychrome's Magic

On this morning, which ought to be the last of this important journey, our friends started away as bright and cheery as could be, and Woot whistled a merry tune so that Polychrome could dance to the music.

On reaching the top of the hill, the plain spread out before them in all its beauty of blue grasses and wildflowers, and Mount Munch seemed much nearer than it had the previous evening. They trudged on at a brisk pace, and by noon the mountain was so close that they could admire its appearance. Its slopes were partly clothed with pretty evergreens, and its foot-hills were tufted with a slender waving bluegrass that had a tassel on the end of every blade. And, for the first time, they perceived, near

the foot of the mountain, a charming house, not of great size but neatly painted and with many flowers surrounding it and vines climbing over the doors and windows.

It was toward this solitary house that our travelers now directed their steps, thinking to inquire of the people who lived there where Nimmie Amee might be found.

There were no paths, but the way was quite open and clear, and they were drawing near to the dwelling when Woot the Wanderer, who was then in the lead of the little party, halted with such an abrupt jerk that he stumbled over backward and lay flat on his back in the meadow. The Scarecrow stopped to look at the boy.

"Why did you do that?" he asked in surprise.

Woot sat up and gazed around him in amazement. "I — I don't know!" he replied.

The two tin men, arm in arm, started to pass them when both halted and tumbled, with a great clatter, into a heap beside Woot. Polychrome, laughing at the absurd sight, came dancing up and she, also, came to a sudden stop, but managed to save herself from falling.

Everyone of them was much astonished, and the Scarecrow said with a puzzled look: "I don't see anything."

"Nor I," said Woot; "but something hit me, just the same."

"Some invisible person struck me a heavy blow," declared the Tin Woodman, struggling to separate himself from the Tin Soldier, whose legs and arms were mixed with his own.

"I'm not sure it was a person," said Polychrome, looking more grave than usual. "It seems to me that I merely ran into some hard substance which barred my way. In order to make sure of this, let me try another place."

She ran back a way and then with much caution advanced in a different place, but when she reached a position on a line with the others she halted, her arms outstretched before her.

"I can feel something hard - something smooth as glass," she said, "but I'm sure it is not glass."

"Let me try," suggested Woot, getting up; but when he tried to get forward, he discovered the same barrier that Polychrome had encountered.

"No," he said, "it isn't glass. But what is it?"

"Air," replied a small voice beside him. "Solid air; that's all."

They all looked downward and found a sky-blue rabbit had stuck his head out of a burrow in the ground. The rabbit's eyes were a deeper blue than his fur, and the pretty creature seemed friendly and unafraid.

"Air!" exclaimed Woot, staring in astonishment into the rabbit's blue eyes; "whoever heard of air so solid that one cannot push it aside?"

"You can't push this air aside," declared the rabbit, "for it was made hard by powerful sorcery, and it forms a wall that is intended to keep people from getting to that house yonder."

"Oh; it's a wall, is it?" said the Tin Woodman.

"Yes, it is really a wall," answered the rabbit, "and it is fully six feet thick."

"How high is it?" inquired Captain Fyter, the Tin Soldier.

"Oh, ever so high; perhaps a mile," said the rabbit.

"Couldn't we go around it?" asked Woot.

"Of course, for the wall is a circle," explained the rabbit. "In the center of the circle stands the house, so you may walk around the Wall of Solid Air, but you can't get to the house."

"Who put the air wall around the house?" was the Scarecrow's question.

"Nimmie Amee did that."

"Nimmie Amee!" they all exclaimed in surprise.

"Yes," answered the rabbit. "She used to live with an old Witch, who was suddenly destroyed, and when Nimmie Amee ran away from the Witch's house, she took with her just one magic formula —pure sorcery it was — which enabled her to build this air wall around her house — the house yonder. It was quite a clever idea, I think, for it doesn't mar the beauty of the landscape, solid air being invisible, and yet it keeps all strangers away from the house."

"Does Nimmie Amee live there now?" asked the Tin Woodman anxiously.

"Yes, indeed," said the rabbit.

"And does she weep and wail from morning till night?" continued the Emperor.

"No; she seems quite happy," asserted the rabbit.

The Tin Woodman seemed quite disappointed to hear this report of his old sweetheart, but the Scarecrow reassured his friend, saying: "Never mind, your Majesty; however happy Nimmie Amee is now, I'm sure she will be much happier as Empress of the Winkies."

"Perhaps," said Captain Fyter, somewhat stiffly, "she will be still more happy to become the bride of a Tin Soldier."

"She shall choose between us, as we have agreed," the Tin Woodman promised; "but how shall we get to the poor girl?"

Polychrome, although dancing lightly back and forth, had listened to every word of the conversation. Now she came forward and sat herself down just in front of the Blue Rabbit, her many-hued draperies giving her the appearance of some beautiful flower. The rabbit didn't back away an inch. Instead, he gazed at the Rainbow's Daughter admiringly.

"Does your burrow go underneath this Wall of Air?" asked Polychrome.

"To be sure," answered the Blue Rabbit; "I dug it that way so I could roam in these broad fields, by going out one way, or eat the cabbages in Nimmie Amee's garden by leaving my burrow at the other end. I don't think Nimmie Amee ought to mind the little I take from her garden, or the hole I've made under her magic wall. A rabbit may go and come as he pleases, but no one who is bigger than I am could get through my burrow."

"Will you allow us to pass through it, if we are able to? " inquired Polychrome.

"Yes, indeed," answered the Blue Rabbit. "I'm no especial friend of Nimmie Amee, for once she threw stones at me, just because I was nibbling some lettuce, and only yesterday she yelled 'Shoo!' at me, which made me nervous. You're welcome to use my burrow in any way you choose."

"But this is all nonsense!" declared Woot the Wanderer. "We are every one too big to crawl through a rabbit's burrow."

"We are too big now," agreed the Scarecrow, "but you must remember that Polychrome is a fairy, and fairies have many magic powers."

Woot's face brightened as he turned to the lovely Daughter of the Rainbow.

"Could you make us all as small as that rabbit?" he asked eagerly.

"I can try," answered Polychrome, with a smile. And presently she did it — so easily that Woot was not the only one astonished. As the now tiny people grouped themselves before the rabbit's burrow the hole appeared to them like the entrance to a tunnel, which indeed it was.

"I'll go first," said wee Polychrome, who had made herself grow as small as the others, and into the tunnel she danced without hesitation. A tiny Scarecrow went next and then the two funny little tin men.

"Walk in; it's your turn," said the Blue Rabbit to Woot the Wanderer. "I'm coming after, to see how you get along. This will be a regular surprise party to Nimmie Amee."

So Woot entered the hole and felt his way along its smooth sides in the dark until he finally saw the glimmer of daylight ahead and knew the journey was almost over. Had he remained his natural size, the distance could have been covered in a few steps, but to a thumb-high Woot it was quite a promenade. When he emerged from the burrow he found himself but a short distance from the house, in the center of the vegetable garden, where the leaves of rhubarb waving above his head seemed like trees. Outside the hole, and waiting for him, he found all his friends.

"So far, so good!" remarked the Scarecrow cheerfully.

"Yes; so far, but no farther," returned the Tin Woodman in a plaintive and disturbed tone of voice. "I am now close to Nimmie Amee, whom I have come ever so far to seek, but I cannot ask the girl to marry such a little man as I am now."

"I'm no bigger than a toy soldier!" said Captain Fyter, sorrowfully. "Unless Polychrome can make us big again, there is little use in our visiting Nimmie Amee at all, for I'm sure she wouldn't care for a husband she might carelessly step on and ruin."

Polychrome laughed merrily.

"If I make you big, you can't get out of here again," said she, "and if you remain little Nimmie Amee will laugh at you. So make your choice."

"I think we'd better go back," said Woot seriously

"No," said the Tin Woodman, stoutly, "I have decided that it's my duty to make Nimmie Amee happy, in case she wishes to marry me."

"So have I," announced Captain Fyter. "A good soldier never shrinks from doing his duty."

"As for that," said the Scarecrow, "tin doesn't shrink any to speak of, under any circumstances. But Woot and I intend to stick to our comrades, whatever they decide to do, so we will ask Polychrome to make us as big as we were before."

Polychrome agreed to this request and in half a minute all of them, including herself, had been enlarged again to their natural sizes. They then thanked the Blue Rabbit for his kind assistance, and at once approached the house of Nimme Amee.

22. Nimmie Amee

We may be sure that at this moment our friends were all anxious to see the end of the adventure that had caused them so many trials and troubles. Perhaps the Tin Woodman's heart did not beat any faster, because it was made of red velvet and stuffed with sawdust, and the Tin Soldier's heart was made of tin and reposed in his tin bosom without a hint of emotion. However, there is little doubt that they both knew that a critical moment in their lives had arrived, and that Nimmie Amee's decision was destined to influence the future of one or the other.

As they assumed their natural sizes and the rhubarb leaves that had before towered above their heads now barely covered their feet, they looked around the garden and found that no person was visible save themselves. No sound of activity came from the house, either, but they walked to the front door, which had a little porch built before it, and there the two tinmen stood side by side while both knocked upon the door with their tin knuckles.

As no one seemed eager to answer the summons they knocked again; and then again. Finally they heard a stir from within and someone coughed.

"Who's there?" called a girl's voice.

"It's I!" cried the tin twins, together.

"How did you get there?" asked the voice.

They hesitated how to reply, so Woot answered for them:

"By means of magic."

"Oh," said the unseen girl. "Are you friends, or foes?"

"Friends!" they all exclaimed. Then they heard footsteps approach the door, which slowly opened and revealed a very pretty Munchkin girl standing in the doorway.

"Nimmie Amee!" cried the tin twins.

"That's my name," replied the girl, looking at them in cold surprise. "But who can you be?"

"Don't you know me, Nimmie?" said the Tin Woodman. "I'm your old sweetheart, Nick Chopper!"

"Don't you know me, my dear?" said the Tin Soldier. "I'm your old sweetheart, Captain Fyter!"

Nimmie Amee smiled at them both. Then she looked beyond them at the rest of the party and smiled again. However, she seemed more amused than pleased.

"Come in," she said, leading the way inside. "Even sweethearts are forgotten after a time, but you and your friends are welcome."

The room they now entered was cosy and comfortable, being neatly furnished and well swept and dusted. But they found someone there besides Nimmie Amee. A man dressed in the attractive Munchkin costume was lazily reclining in an easy chair, and he sat up and turned his eyes on the visitors with a cold and indifferent stare that was almost insolent. He did not even rise from his seat to greet the strangers, but after glaring at them he looked away with a scowl, as if they were of too little importance to interest him.

The tin men returned this man's stare with interest, but they did not look away from him because neither of them seemed able to take his eyes off this Munchkin, who was remarkable in having one tin arm quite like their own tin arms.

"Seems to me," said Captain Fyter, in a voice that sounded harsh and indignant, "that you, sir, are a vile impostor!"

"Gently — gently!" cautioned the Scarecrow; "don't be rude to strangers, Captain."

"Rude?" shouted the Tin Soldier, now very much provoked; "why, he's a scoundrel — a thief! The villain is wearing my own head!"

"Yes," added the Tin Woodman, "and he's wearing my right arm! I can recognize it by the two warts on the little finger."

"Good gracious!" exclaimed Woot. "Then this must be the man whom old Ku-Klip patched together and named Chopfyt."

The man now turned toward them, still scowling.

"Yes, that is my name," he said in a voice like a growl, "and it is absurd for you tin creatures, or for anyone else, to claim my head, or arm, or any part of me, for they are my personal property."

"You? You're a Nobody!" shouted Captain Fyter.

"You're just a mix-up," declared the Emperor.

"Now, now, gentlemen," interrupted Nimmie Amee, "I must ask you to be more respectful to poor Chopfyt. For, being my guests, it is not polite for you to insult my husband."

"Your husband!" the tin twins exclaimed in dismay.

"Yes," said she. "I married Chopfyt a long time ago, because my other two sweethearts had deserted me."

This reproof embarrassed both Nick Chopper and Captain Fyter. They looked down, shamefaced, for a moment, and then the Tin Woodman explained in an earnest voice: "I rusted."

"So did I," said the Tin Soldier.

I could not know that, of course," asserted Nimmie Amee. "All I knew was that neither of you came to marry me, as you had promised to do. But men are not scarce in the Land of Oz. After I came here to live, I met Mr. Chopfyt, and he was the more interesting because he reminded me strongly of both of you, as you were before you became tin. He even had a tin arm, and that reminded me of you the more.

No wonder!" remarked the Scarecrow.

But, listen, Nimmie Amee!" said the astonished Woot; "he really is both of them, for he is made of their cast-off parts."

Oh, you're quite wrong," declared Polychrome, laughing, for she was greatly enjoying the confusion of the others. "The tin men are still themselves, as they will tell you, and so Chopfyt must be someone else."

They looked at her bewildered, for the facts in the case were too puzzling to be grasped at once.

It is all the fault of old Ku-Klip," muttered the Tin Woodman. He had no right to use our castoff parts to make another man with."

It seems he did it, however," said Nimmie Amee calmly, "and I married him because he resembled you both. I won't say he is a husband to be proud of, because he has a mixed nature and isn't always an agreeable companion. There are times when I have to chide him gently, both with my tongue and with my broomstick. But he is my husband, and I must make the best of him."

If you don't like him," suggested the Tin Woodman, "Captain Fyter and I can chop him up with our axe and sword, and each take such parts of the fellow as belong to him. Then we are willing for you to select one of us as your husband."

That is a good idea," approved Captain Fyter, drawing his sword.

No," said Nimmie Amee; "I think I'll keep the husband I now have. He is now trained to draw the water and carry in the wood and hoe the cabbages and weed the flower-beds and dust the furniture and perform many tasks of a like character. A new husband would have to be scolded — and gently chided — until he learns my ways. So I think it will be better to keep my Chopfyt, and I see no reason why you should object to him. You two gentlemen threw him away when you became tin, because you had no further use for him, so you cannot justly claim him now. I advise you to go back to your own homes and forget me, as I have forgotten you."

Good advice!" laughed Polychrome, dancing.

Are you happy?" asked the Tin Soldier.

Of course I am," said Nimmie Amee; "I'm the mistress of all I survey — the queen of my little domain."

Wouldn't you like to be the Empress of the Winkies?" asked the Tin Woodman.

Mercy, no," she answered. "That would be a lot of bother. I don't care for society, or pomp, or posing. All I ask is to be left alone and not to be annoyed by visitors."

The Scarecrow nudged Woot the Wanderer. "That sounds to me like a hint," he said.

"Looks as if we'd had our journey for nothing," remarked Woot, who was a little ashamed and disappointed because he had proposed the journey.

"I am glad, however," said the Tin Woodman, "that I have found Nimmie Amee, and discovered that she is already married and happy. It will relieve me of any further anxiety concerning her."

"For my part," said the Tin Soldier, "I am not sorry to be free. The only thing that really annoys me is finding my head upon Chopfyt's body."

"As for that, I'm pretty sure it is my body, or a part of it, anyway," remarked the Emperor of the Winkies. "But never mind, friend Soldier; let us be willing to donate our cast-off members to insure the happiness of Nimmie Amee, and be thankful it is not our fate to hoe cabbages and draw water —and be chided — in the place of this creature Chopfyt."

"Yes," agreed the Soldier, "we have much to be thankful for."

Polychrome, who had wandered outside, now poked her pretty head through an open window and exclaimed in a pleased voice: "It's getting cloudy. Perhaps it is going to rain!"

23. Through the Tunnel

It didn't rain just then, although the clouds in the sky grew thicker and more threatening. Polychrome hoped for a thunder-storm, followed by her Rainbow, but the two tin men did not relish the idea of getting wet. They even preferred to remain in Nimmie Amee's house, although they felt they were not welcome there, rather than go out and face the coming storm.

But the Scarecrow, who was a very thoughtful person, said to his friends: "If we remain here until after the storm, and Polychrome goes away on her Rainbow, then we will be prisoners inside the Wall of Solid Air; so it seems best to start upon our return journey at once. If I get wet, my straw stuffing will be ruined, and if you two tin gentlemen get wet, you may perhaps rust again, and become useless. But even that is better than to stay here. Once we are free of the barrier, we have Woot the Wanderer to help us, and he can oil your joints and restuff my body, if it becomes necessary, for the boy is made of meat, which neither rusts nor gets soggy or moldy."

"Come along, then!" cried Polychrome from the window, and the others, realizing the wisdom of the Scarecrow's speech, took leave of Nimmie Amee, who was glad to be rid of them, and said good-bye to her husband, who merely scowled and made no answer, and then they hurried from the house.

"Your old parts are not very polite, I must say," remarked the Scarecrow, when they were in the garden.

"No," said Woot, "Chopfyt is a regular grouch. He might have wished us a pleasant journey, at the very least."

"I beg you not to hold us responsible for that creature's actions," pleaded the Tin Woodman. "We are through with Chopfyt and shall have nothing further to do with him."

Polychrome danced ahead of the party and led them straight to the burrow of the Blue Rabbit, which they might have had some difficulty in finding without her. There she lost no time in making them all small again. The Blue Rabbit was busy nibbling cabbage leaves in Nimmie Amee's garden, so they did not ask his permission but at once entered the burrow.

Even now the raindrops were beginning to fall, but it was quite dry inside the tunnel and by the time they had reached the other end, outside the circular Wall of Solid Air, the storm was at its height and the rain was coming down in torrents.

"Let us wait here," proposed Polychrome, peering out of the hole and then quickly retreating. "The Rainbow won't appear until after the storm and I can make you big again in a jiffy, before I join my sisters on our bow."

"That's a good plan," said the Scarecrow approvingly. "It will save me from getting soaked and soggy."

"It will save me from rusting," said the Tin Soldier.

"It will enable me to remain highly polished," said the Tin Woodman.

"Oh, as for that, I myself prefer not to get my pretty clothes wet," laughed the Rainbow's daughter.

"But while we wait I will bid you all adieu. I must also thank you for saving me from that dreadful Giantess, Mrs. Yoop. You have been good and patient comrades and I have enjoyed our adventures together, but I am never so happy as when on my dear Rainbow."

"Will your father scold you for getting left on the earth?" asked Woot.

"I suppose so," said Polychrome gaily; "I'm always getting scolded for my mad pranks, as they are called. My sisters are so sweet and lovely and proper that they never dance off our Rainbow, and so they never have any adventures. Adventures to me are good fun, only I never like to stay too long on earth, because I really don't belong here. I shall tell my Father the Rainbow that I'll try not to be so careless again, and he will forgive me because in our sky mansions there is always joy and happiness."

They were indeed sorry to part with their dainty and beautiful companion and assured her of their devotion if they ever chanced to meet again. She shook hands with the Scarecrow and the Tin Men and kissed Woot the Wanderer lightly upon his forehead.

And then the rain suddenly ceased, and as the tiny people left the burrow of the Blue Rabbit, a glorious big Rainbow appeared in the sky and the end of its arch slowly descended and touched the ground just where they stood.

Woot was so busy watching a score of lovely maidens — sisters of Polychrome — who were leaning over the edge of the bow, and another score who danced gaily amid the radiance of the splendid hues, that he did not notice he was growing big again. But now Polychrome joined her sisters on the Rainbow and the huge arch lifted and slowly melted away as the sun burst from the clouds and sent its own white beams dancing over the meadows.

"Why, she's gone!" exclaimed the boy, and turned to see his companions still waving their hands in token of adieu to the vanished Polychrome.

24. The Curtain Falls

Well, the rest of the story is quickly told, for the return Journey of our adventurers was without any important incident. The Scarecrow was so afraid of meeting the Hip-po-gy-raf, and having his straw eaten again, that he urged his comrades to select another route to the Emerald City, and they willingly consented, so that the Invisible Country was wholly avoided.

Of course, when they reached the Emerald City their first duty was to visit Ozma's palace, where they were royally entertained. The Tin Soldier and Woot the Wanderer were welcomed as warmly as any strangers might be who had been the traveling companions of Ozma's dear old friends, the Scarecrow and the Tin Woodman.

At the banquet table that evening they related the manner in which they had discovered Nimmie Amee, and told how they had found her happily married to Chopfyt, whose relationship to Nick Chopper and Captain Fyter was so bewildering that they asked Ozma's advice what to do about it.

"You need not consider Chopfyt at all," replied the beautiful girl Ruler of Oz. "If Nimmie Amee is content with that misfit man for a husband, we have not even just cause to blame Ku-Klip for gluing him together."

"I think it was a very good idea," added little Dorothy, "for if Ku Klip hadn't used up your castoff parts, they would have been wasted. It's wicked to be wasteful, isn't it?"

"Well, anyhow," said Woot the Wanderer, "Chopfyt, being kept a prisoner by his wife, is too far away from anyone to bother either of you tin men in any way. If you hadn't gone where he is and discovered him, you would never have worried about him."

"What do you care, anyhow," Betsy Bobbin asked the Tin Woodman, "so long as Nimmie Amee is satisfied?"

"And just to think," remarked Tiny Trot, "that any girl would rather live with a mixture like Chopfyt, on far-away Mount Munch, than to be the Empress of the Winkies!"

"It is her own choice," said the Tin Woodman contentedly; "and after all, I'm not sure the Winkies would care to have an Empress."

It puzzled Ozma, for a time, to decide what to do with the Tin Soldier. If he went with the Tin Woodman to the Emperor's castle, she felt that the two tin men might not be able to live together in harmony, and moreover the Emperor would not be so distinguished if he had a double constantly beside him. So she asked Captain Fyter if he was willing to serve her as a soldier, and he promptly declared that nothing would please him more. After he had been in her service for some time, Ozma sent him into the Gillikin Country, with instructions to keep order among the wild people who inhabit some parts of that unknown country of Oz.

As for Woot, being a Wanderer by profession, he was allowed to wander wherever he desired, and Ozma promised to keep watch over his future journeys and to protect the boy as well as she was able, in case he ever got into more trouble.

All this having been happily arranged, the Tin Woodman returned to his tin castle, and his chosen comrade, the Scarecrow, accompanied him on the way. The two friends were sure to pass many pleasant hours together in talking over their recent adventures, for as they neither ate nor slept they found their greatest amusement in conversation.

The Magic of Oz
by L. Frank Baum

A Faithful Record of the Remarkable Adventures of Dorothy and Trot and the Wizard of Oz, together with the Cowardly Lion, the Hungry Tiger and Cap'n Bill, in their successful search for a Magical and Beautiful Birthday Present for Princess Ozma of Oz, by L. Frank Baum, "Royal Historian of Oz".

To My Readers

Curiously enough, in the events which have taken place in the last few years in our "great outside world," we may find incidents so marvelous and inspiring that I cannot hope to equal them with stories of The Land of Oz.

However, "The Magic of Oz" is really more strange and unusual than anything I have read or heard about on our side of The Great Sandy Desert which shuts us off from The Land of Oz, even during the past exciting years, so I hope it will appeal to your love of novelty.

A long and confining illness has prevented my answering all the good letters sent me—unless stamps were enclosed—but from now on I hope to be able to give prompt attention to each and every letter with which my readers favor me.

Assuring you that my love for you has never faltered and hoping the Oz Books will continue to give you pleasure as long as I am able to write them, I am

Yours affectionately,
L. Frank Baum, "Royal Historian of Oz."
"Ozcot" at Hollywood in California, 1919

1. Mount Munch

On the east edge of the Land of Oz, in the Munchkin Country, is a big, tall hill called Mount Munch. One one side, the bottom of this hill just touches the Deadly Sandy Desert that separates the Fairyland of Oz from all the rest of the world, but on the other side, the hill touches the beautiful, fertile Country of the Munchkins.

The Munchkin folks, however, merely stand off and look at Mount Munch and know very little about it; for, about a third of the way up, its sides become too steep to climb, and if any people live upon the top of that great towering peak that seems to reach nearly to the skies, the Munchkins are not aware of the fact.

But people DO live there, just the same. The top of Mount Munch is shaped like a saucer, broad and deep, and in the saucer are fields where grains and vegetables grow, and flocks are fed, and brooks flow and trees bear all sorts of things. There are houses scattered here and there, each having its family of Hyups, as the people call themselves. The Hyups seldom go down the mountain, for the same reason that the Munchkins never climb up: the sides are too steep.

In one of the houses lived a wise old Hyup named Bini Aru, who used to be a clever Sorcerer. But Ozma of Oz, who rules everyone in the Land of Oz, had made a decree that no one should practice magic in her dominions except Glinda the Good and the Wizard of Oz, and when Glinda sent this royal command to the Hyups by means of a strong-winged Eagle, old Bini Aru at once stopped performing magical arts. He destroyed many of his magic powders and tools of magic, and afterward honestly obeyed the law. He had never seen Ozma, but he knew she was his Ruler and must be obeyed.

There was only one thing that grieved him. He had discovered a new and secret method of transformations that was unknown to any other Sorcerer. Glinda the Good did not know it, nor did the little Wizard of Oz, nor Dr. Pipt nor old Mombi, nor anyone else who dealt in magic arts. It was Bini Aru's own secret. By its means, it was the simplest thing in the world to transform anyone into beast, bird or fish, or anything else, and back again, once you know how to pronounce the mystical word: "Pyrzqxgl."

Bini Aru had used this secret many times, but not to cause evil or suffering to others. When he had wandered far from home and was hungry, he would say: "I want to become a cow—Pyrzqxgl!" In an instant he would be a cow, and then he would eat grass and satisfy his hunger. All beasts and birds can talk in the Land of Oz, so when the cow was no longer hungry, it would say: "I want to be Bini Aru again: Pyrzqxgl!" and the magic word, properly pronounced, would instantly restore him to his proper form.

Now, of course, I would not dare to write down this magic word so plainly if I thought my readers would pronounce it properly and so be able to transform themselves and others, but it is a fact that no one in all the world except Bini Aru, had ever (up to the time this story begins) been able to pronounce "Pyrzqxgl!" the right way, so I think it is safe to give it to you. It might be well, however, in reading this story aloud, to be careful not to pronounce Pyrzqxgl the proper way, and thus avoid all danger of the secret being able to work mischief.

Bini Aru, having discovered the secret of instant transformation, which required no tools or powders or other chemicals or herbs and always worked perfectly, was reluctant to have such a wonderful discovery entirely unknown or lost to all human knowledge. He decided not to use it again, since Ozma had forbidden him to do so, but he reflected that Ozma was a girl and some time might change her mind and allow her subjects to practice magic, in which case Bini Aru could again transform himself and others at will — unless, of course, he forgot how to pronounce Pyrzqxgl in the meantime.

After giving the matter careful thought, he decided to write the word, and how it should be pronounced, in some secret place, so that he could find it after many years, but where no one else could ever find it.

That was a clever idea, but what bothered the old Sorcerer was to find a secret place. He wandered all over the Saucer at the top of Mount Munch, but found no place in which to write the secret word where others might not be likely to stumble upon it. So finally he decided it must be written somewhere in his own house.

Bini Aru had a wife named Mopsi Aru who was famous for making fine huckleberry pies, and he had a son named Kiki Aru who was not famous at all. He was noted as being cross and disagreeable because he was not happy, and he was not happy because he wanted to go down the mountain and visit the big world below and his father would not let him. No one paid any attention to Kiki Aru, because he didn't amount to anything, anyway.

Once a year there was a festival on Mount Munch which all the Hyups attended. It was held in the center of the saucer-shaped country, and the day was given over to feasting and merry-making. The young folks danced and sang songs; the women spread the tables with good things to eat, and the men played on musical instruments and told fairy tales.

Kiki Aru usually went to these festivals with his parents, and then sat sullenly outside the circle and would not dance or sing or even talk to the other young people. So the festival did not make him any happier than other days, and this time he told Bini Aru and Mopsi Aru that he would not go. He would rather stay at home and be unhappy all by himself, he said, and so they gladly let him stay.

But after he was left alone Kiki decided to enter his father's private room, where he was forbidden to go, and see if he could find any of the magic tools Bini Aru used to work with when he practiced sorcery. As he went in Kiki stubbed his toe on one of the floor boards. He searched everywhere but found no trace of his father's magic. All had been destroyed.

Much disappointed, he started to go out again when he stubbed his toe on the same floor board. That set him thinking. Examining the board more closely, Kiki found it had been pried up and then nailed down again in such a manner that it was a little higher than the other boards. But why had his father taken up the board? Had he hidden some of his magic tools underneath the floor?

Kiki got a chisel and pried up the board, but found nothing under it. He was just about to replace the board when it slipped from his hand and turned over, and he saw something written on the underside of it. The light was rather dim, so he took the board to the window and examined it, and found that the writing described exactly how to pronounce the magic word Pyrzqxgl, which would transform anyone into anything instantly, and back again when the word was repeated.

Now, at first, Kiki Aru didn't realize what a wonderful secret he had discovered; but he thought it might be of use to him and so he took a piece of paper and made on it an exact copy of the instructions for pronouncing Pyrzqxgl. Then he folded the paper and put it in his pocket, and replaced the board in the floor so that no one would suspect it had been removed.

After this Kiki went into the garden and sitting beneath a tree made a careful study of the paper. He had always wanted to get away from Mount Munch and visit the big world—especially the Land of Oz—and the idea now came to him that if he could transform himself into a bird, he could fly to any place he wished to go and fly back again whenever he cared to. It was necessary, however, to learn by heart the way to pronounce the magic word, because a bird would have no way to carry a paper with it, and Kiki would be unable to resume his proper shape if he forgot the word or its pronunciation.

So he studied it a long time, repeating it a hundred times in his mind until he was sure he would not forget it. But to make safety doubly sure he placed the paper in a tin box in a neglected part of the garden and covered the box with small stones.

By this time it was getting late in the day and Kiki wished to attempt his first transformation before his parents returned from the festival. So he stood on the front porch of his home and said: "I want to become a big, strong bird, like a hawk — Pyrzqxgl!" He pronounced it the right way, so in a flash he felt that he was completely changed in form. He flapped his wings, hopped to the porch railing and said: "Caw-oo! Caw-oo!"

Then he laughed and said half aloud: "I suppose that's the funny sound this sort of a bird makes. But now let me try my wings and see if I'm strong enough to fly across the desert."

For he had decided to make his first trip to the country outside the Land of Oz. He had stolen this secret of transformation and he knew he had disobeyed the law of Oz by working magic. Perhaps Glinda or the Wizard of Oz would discover him and punish him, so it would be good policy to keep away from Oz altogether.

Slowly Kiki rose into the air, and resting on his broad wings, floated in graceful circles above the saucer-shaped mountain-top. From his height, he could see, far across the burning sands of the Deadly Desert, another country that might be pleasant to explore, so he headed that way, and with strong, steady strokes of his wings, began the long flight.

2. The Hawk

Even a hawk has to fly high in order to cross the Deadly Desert, from which poisonous fumes are constantly rising. Kiki Aru felt sick and faint by the time he reached good land again, for he could not quite escape the effects of the poisons. But the fresh air soon restored him and he alighted in a broad table-land which is called Hiland. Just beyond it is a valley known as Loland, and these two countries are ruled by the Gingerbread Man, John Dough, with Chick the Cherub as his Prime Minister. The hawk merely stopped here long enough to rest, and then he flew north and passed over a fine country called Merryland, which is ruled by a lovely Wax Doll. Then, following the curve of the Desert, he turned north and settled on a tree-top in the Kingdom of Noland.

Kiki was tired by this time, and the sun was now setting, so he decided to remain here till morning. From his tree-top he could see a house near by, which looked very comfortable. A man was milking a cow in the yard and a pleasant-faced woman came to the door and called him to supper.

That made Kiki wonder what sort of food hawks ate. He felt hungry, but didn't know what to eat or where to get it. Also he thought a bed would be more comfortable than a tree-top for sleeping, so he hopped to the ground and said: "I want to become Kiki Aru again—Pyrzqxgl!"

Instantly he had resumed his natural shape, and going to the house, he knocked upon the door and asked for some supper.

"Who are you?" asked the man of the house.

"A stranger from the Land of Oz," replied Kiki Aru.

"Then you are welcome," said the man.

Kiki was given a good supper and a good bed, and he behaved very well, although he refused to answer all the questions the good people of Noland asked him. Having escaped from his home and found a way to see the world, the young man was no longer unhappy, and so he was no longer cross and disagreeable. The people thought him a very respectable person and gave him breakfast next morning, after which he started on his way feeling quite contented.

Having walked for an hour or two through the pretty country that is ruled by King Bud, Kiki Aru decided he could travel faster and see more as a bird, so he transformed himself into a white dove and visited the great city of Nole and saw the King's palace and gardens and many other places of interest. Then he flew westward into the Kingdom of Ix, and after a day in Queen Zixi's country went on westward into the Land of Ev. Every place he visited he thought was much more pleasant than the saucer-country of the Hyups, and he decided that when he reached the finest country of all he would settle there and enjoy his future life to the utmost.

In the land of Ev he resumed his own shape again, for the cities and villages were close together and he could easily go on foot from one to another of them.

Toward evening he came to a good Inn and asked the inn-keeper if he could have food and lodging.

"You can if you have the money to pay," said the man, "otherwise you must go elsewhere."

This surprised Kiki, for in the Land of Oz they do not use money at all, everyone being allowed to take what he wishes without price. He had no money, therefore, and so he turned away to seek hospitality elsewhere. Looking through an open window into one of the rooms of the Inn, as he passed along, he saw an old man counting on a table a big heap of gold pieces, which Kiki thought to be money. One of these would buy him supper and a bed, he reflected, so he transformed himself into a magpie and, flying through the open window, caught up one of the gold pieces in his beak and flew out again before the old man could interfere. Indeed, the old man who was robbed was quite helpless, for he dared not leave his pile of gold to chase the magpie, and before he could place the gold in a sack in his pocket the robber bird was out of sight and to seek it would be folly.

Kiki Aru flew to a group of trees and, dropping the gold piece to the ground, resumed his proper shape, and then picked up the money and put it in his pocket.

"You'll be sorry for this!" exclaimed a small voice just over his head.

Kiki looked up and saw that a sparrow, perched upon a branch, was watching him.

"Sorry for what?" he demanded.

"Oh, I saw the whole thing," asserted the sparrow. "I saw you look in the window at the gold, and then make yourself into a magpie and rob the poor man, and then I saw you fly here and make the bird into your former shape. That's magic, and magic is wicked and unlawful; and you stole money, and that's a still greater crime. You'll be sorry, some day."

"I don't care," replied Kiki Aru, scowling.

"Aren't you afraid to be wicked?" asked the sparrow.

"No, I didn't know I was being wicked," said Kiki, "but if I was, I'm glad of it. I hate good people. I've always wanted to be wicked, but I didn't know how."

"Haw, haw, haw!" laughed someone behind him, in a big voice; "that's the proper spirit, my lad! I'm glad I've met you; shake hands."

The sparrow gave a frightened squeak and flew away.

. Two Bad Ones

Kiki turned around and saw a queer old man standing near. He didn't stand straight, for he was crooked. He had a fat body and thin legs and arms. He had a big, round face with bushy, white whiskers that came to a point below his waist, and white hair

that came to a point on top of his head. He wore dull-gray clothes that were tight fitting, and his pockets were all bunched out as if stuffed full of something.

"I didn't know you were here," said Kiki.

"I didn't come until after you did," said the queer old man.

"Who are you?" asked Kiki.

"My name's Ruggedo. I used to be the Nome King; but I got kicked out of my country, and now I'm a wanderer."

"What made them kick you out?" inquired the Hyup boy.

"Well, it's the fashion to kick kings nowadays. I was a pretty good King—to myself—but those dreadful Oz people wouldn't let me alone. So I had to abdicate."

"What does that mean?"

"It means to be kicked out. But let's talk about something pleasant. Who are you and where did you come from?"

"I'm called Kiki Aru. I used to live on Mount Munch in the Land of Oz, but now I'm a wanderer like yourself."

The Nome King gave him a shrewd look.

"I heard that bird say that you transformed yourself into a magpie and back again. Is that true?"

Kiki hesitated, but saw no reason to deny it. He felt that it would make him appear more important.

"Well—yes," he said.

"Then you're a wizard?"

"No; I only understand transformations," he admitted.

"Well, that's pretty good magic, anyhow," declared old Ruggedo. "I used to have some very fine magic, myself, but my enemies took it all away from me. Where are you going now?"

"I'm going into the inn, to get some supper and a bed," said Kiki.

"Have you the money to pay for it?" asked the Nome.

"I have one gold piece."

"Which you stole. Very good. And you're glad that you're wicked. Better yet. I like you, young man, and I'll go to the inn with you if you'll promise not to eat eggs for supper."

"Don't you like eggs?" asked Kiki.

"I'm afraid of 'em; they're dangerous!" said Ruggedo, with a shudder.

"All right," agreed Kiki; "I won't ask for eggs."

"Then come along," said the Nome.

When they entered the inn, the landlord scowled at Kiki and said: "I told you I would not feed you unless you had money."

Kiki showed him the gold piece.

"And how about you?" asked the landlord, turning to Ruggedo. "Have you money?"

"I've something better," answered the old Nome, and taking a bag from one of his pockets he poured from it upon the table a mass of glittering gems—diamonds, rubies and emeralds.

The landlord was very polite to the strangers after that. He served them an excellent supper, and while they ate it, the Hyup boy asked his companion: "Where did you get so many jewels?"

"Well, I'll tell you," answered the Nome. "When those Oz people took my kingdom away from me—just because it was my kingdom and I wanted to run it to suit myself— they said I could take as many precious stones as I could carry. So I had a lot of pockets made in my clothes and loaded them all up. Jewels are fine things to have with you when you travel; you can trade them for anything."

"Are they better than gold pieces?" asked Kiki.

"The smallest of these jewels is worth a hundred gold pieces such as you stole from the old man."

"Don't talk so loud," begged Kiki, uneasily. "Some one else might hear what you are saying."

After supper they took a walk together, and the former Nome King said: "Do you know the Shaggy Man, and the Scarecrow, and the Tin Woodman, and Dorothy, and Ozma and all the other Oz people?"

"No," replied the boy, "I have never been away from Mount Munch until I flew over the Deadly Desert the other day in the shape of a hawk."

"Then you've never seen the Emerald City of Oz?"

"Never."

"Well," said the Nome, "I knew all the Oz people, and you can guess I do not love them. All during my wanderings I have brooded on how I can be revenged on them. Now that I've met you I can see a way to conquer the Land of Oz and be King there myself, which is better than being King of the Nomes."

"How can you do that?" inquired Kiki Aru, wonderingly.

"Never mind how. In the first place, I'll make a bargain with you. Tell me the secret of how to perform transformations and I will give you a pocketful of jewels, the biggest and finest that I possess."

"No," said Kiki, who realized that to share his power with another would be dangerous to himself.

"I'll give you TWO pocketsful of jewels," said the Nome.

"No," answered Kiki.

"I'll give you every jewel I possess."

"No, no, no!" said Kiki, who was beginning to be frightened.

"Then," said the Nome, with a wicked look at the boy, "I'll tell the inn-keeper that you stole that gold piece and he will have you put in prison."

Kiki laughed at the threat.

"Before he can do that," said he, "I will transform myself into a lion and tear him to pieces, or into a bear and eat him up, or into a fly and fly away where he could not find me."

"Can you really do such wonderful transformations?" asked the old Nome, looking at him curiously.

"Of course," declared Kiki. I can transform you into a stick of wood, in a flash, or into a stone, and leave you here by the roadside."

"The wicked Nome shivered a little when he heard that, but it made him long more than ever to possess the great secret. After a while he said: "I'll tell you what I'll do. If you will help me to conquer Oz and to transform the Oz people, who are my enemies, into sticks or stones, by telling me your secret, I'll agree to make YOU the Ruler of all Oz, and I will be your Prime Minister and see that your orders are obeyed."

"I'll help do that," said Kiki, "but I won't tell you my secret."

The Nome was so furious at this refusal that he jumped up and down with rage and spluttered and choked for a long time before he could control his passion. But the boy was not at all frightened. He laughed at the wicked old Nome, which made him more furious than ever.

"Let's give up the idea," he proposed, when Ruggedo had quieted somewhat. "I don't know the Oz people you mention and so they are not my enemies. If they've kicked you out of your kingdom that's your affair—not mine."

"Wouldn't you like to be king of that splendid fairyland?" asked Ruggedo.

"Yes, I would," replied Kiki Aru; "but you want to be king yourself, and we would quarrel over it."

"No," said the Nome, trying to deceive him. "I don't care to be King of Oz, come to think it over. I don't even care to live in that country. What I want first is revenge. If we can conquer Oz, I'll get enough magic then to conquer my own Kingdom of the Nomes, and I'll go back and live in my underground caverns which are more home-like than the top of the earth. So here's my proposition: Help me conquer Oz and get revenge, and help me get the magic away from Glinda and the Wizard, and I'll let you be King of Oz forever afterward."

"I'll think it over," answered Kiki, and that is all he would say that evening.

In the night when all in the Inn were asleep but himself, old Ruggedo the Nome rose softly from his couch and went into the room of Kiki Aru the Hyup, and searched everywhere for the magic tool that performed his transformations. Of course, there was no such tool, and although Ruggedo searched in all the boy's pockets, he found nothing magical whatever. So he went back to his bed and began to doubt that Kiki could perform transformations.

Next morning he said: "Which way do you travel to-day?"

"I think I shall visit the Rose Kingdom," answered the boy.

"That is a long journey," declared the Nome.

"I shall transform myself into a bird," said Kiki, "and so fly to the Rose Kingdom in an hour."

"Then transform me, also, into a bird, and I will go with you," suggested Ruggedo. "But, in that case, let us fly together to the Land of Oz, and see what it looks like."

Kiki thought this over. Pleasant as were the countries he had visited, he heard everywhere that the Land of Oz was more beautiful and delightful. The Land of Oz was his own country, too, and if there was any possibility of his becoming its King, he must know something about it.

While Kiki the Hyup thought, Ruggedo the Nome was also thinking. This boy possessed a marvelous power, and although very simple in some ways, he was determined not to part with his secret. However, if Ruggedo could get him to transport the wily old Nome to Oz, which he could reach in no other way, he might then induce the boy to follow his advice and enter into the plot for revenge, which he had already planned in his wicked heart.

"There are wizards and magicians in Oz," remarked Kiki, after a time. "They might discover us, in spite of our transformations."

"Not if we are careful," Ruggedo assured him. "Ozma has a Magic Picture, in which she can see whatever she wishes to see; but Ozma will know nothing of our going to Oz, and so she will not command her Magic Picture to show where we are or what we are doing. Glinda the Good has a Great Book called the Book of Records, in which is magically written everything that people do in the Land of Oz, just the instant they do it."

"Then," said Kiki, "there is no use our attempting to conquer the country, for Glinda would read in her book all that we do, and as her magic is greater than mine, she would soon put a stop to our plans."

"I said 'people,' didn't I?" retorted the Nome. "The book doesn't make a record of what birds do, or beasts. It only tells the doings of people. So, if we fly into the country as birds, Glinda won't know anything about it."

"Two birds couldn't conquer the Land of Oz," asserted the boy, scornfully.

"No; that's true," admitted Ruggedo, and then he rubbed his forehead and stroked his long pointed beard and thought some more.

"Ah, now I have the idea!" he declared. "I suppose you can transform us into beasts as well as birds?"

"Of course."

"And can you make a bird a beast, and a beast a bird again, without taking a human form in between?"

"Certainly," said Kiki. "I can transform myself or others into anything that can talk. There's a magic word that must be spoken in connection with the transformations, and as beasts and birds and dragons and fishes can talk in Oz, we may become any of these we desire to. However, if I transformed myself into a tree, I would always remain a tree, because then I could not utter the magic word to change the transformation."

"I see; I see," said Ruggedo, nodding his bushy, white head until the point of his hair waved back and forth like a pendulum. "That fits in with my idea, exactly. Now, listen, and I'll explain to you my plan. We'll fly to Oz as birds and settle in one of the thick forests in the Gillikin Country. There you will transform us into powerful beasts, and as Glinda doesn't keep any track of the doings of beasts we can act without being discovered."

"But how can two beasts raise an army to conquer the powerful people of Oz?" inquired Kiki.

"That's easy. But not an army of PEOPLE, mind you. That would be quickly discovered. And while we are in Oz you and I will never resume our human forms until we've conquered the country and destroyed Glinda, and Ozma, and the Wizard, and Dorothy, and all the rest, and so have nothing more to fear from them."

"It is impossible to kill anyone in the Land of Oz," declared Kiki.

"It isn't necessary to kill the Oz people," rejoined Ruggedo.

"I'm afraid I don't understand you," objected the boy. "What will happen to the Oz people, and what sort of an army could we get together, except of people?"

"I'll tell you. The forests of Oz are full of beasts. Some of them, in the far-away places, are savage and cruel, and would gladly follow a leader as savage as themselves. They have never troubled the Oz people much, because they had no leader to urge them on, but we will tell them to help us conquer Oz and as a reward we will transform all the beasts into men and women, and let them live in the houses and enjoy all the good things; and we will transform all the people of Oz into beasts of various sorts, and send them to live in the forests and the jungles. That is a splendid idea, you must admit, and it's so easy that we won't have any trouble at all to carry it through to success."

"Will the beasts consent, do you think?" asked the boy.

"To be sure they will. We can get every beast in Oz on our side—except a few who live in Ozma's palace, and they won't count."

4. Conspirators

Kiki Aru didn't know much about Oz and didn't know much about the beasts who lived there, but the old Nome's plan seemed to him to be quite reasonable. He had a faint suspicion that Ruggedo meant to get the best of him in some way, and he resolved to keep a close watch on his fellow-conspirator. As long as he kept to himself the secret word of the transformations, Ruggedo would not dare to harm him, and he promised himself that as soon as they had conquered Oz, he would transform the old Nome into a marble statue and keep him in that form forever.

Ruggedo, on his part, decided that he could, by careful watching and listening, surprise the boy's secret, and when he had learned the magic word he would transform Kiki Aru into a bundle of faggots and burn him up and so be rid of him.

This is always the way with wicked people. They cannot be trusted even by one another. Ruggedo thought he was fooling Kiki, and Kiki thought he was fooling Ruggedo; so both were pleased.

"It's a long way across the Desert," remarked the boy, "and the sands are hot and send up poisonous vapors. Let us wait until evening and then fly across in the night when it will be cooler."

The former Nome King agreed to this, and the two spent the rest of that day in talking over their plans. When evening came they paid the inn-keeper and walked out to a little grove of trees that stood near by.

"Remain here for a few minutes and I'll soon be back," said Kiki, and walking swiftly away, he left the Nome standing in the grove. Ruggedo wondered where he had gone, but stood quietly in his place until, all of a sudden, his form changed to that of a great eagle, and he uttered a piercing cry of astonishment and flapped his wings in a sort of panic. At once his eagle cry was answered from beyond the grove, and another eagle, even larger and more powerful than the transformed Ruggedo, came sailing through the trees and alighted beside him.

"Now we are ready for the start," said the voice of Kiki, coming from the eagle.

Ruggedo realized that this time he had been outwitted. He had thought Kiki would utter the magic word in his presence, and so he would learn what it was, but the boy had been too shrewd for that.

As the two eagles mounted high into the air and began their flight across the great Desert that separates the Land of Oz from all the rest of the world, the Nome said: "When I was King of the Nomes I had a magic way of working transformations that I thought was good, but it could not compare with your secret word. I had to have certain tools and make passes and say a lot of mystic words before I could transform anybody."

"What became of your magic tools?" inquired Kiki.

"The Oz people took them all away from me—that horrid girl, Dorothy, and that terrible fairy, Ozma, the Ruler of Oz—at the time they took away my underground kingdom and kicked me upstairs into the cold, heartless world."

"Why did you let them do that?" asked the boy.

"Well," said Ruggedo, "I couldn't help it. They rolled eggs at me—EGGS—dreadful eggs!—and if an egg even touches a Nome, he is ruined for life."

"Is any kind of an egg dangerous to a Nome?"

"Any kind and every kind. An egg is the only thing I'm afraid of."

5. A Happy Corner of Oz

There is no other country so beautiful as the Land of Oz. There are no other people so happy and contented and prosperous as the Oz people. They have all they desire; they love and admire their beautiful girl Ruler, Ozma of Oz, and they mix work and play so justly that both are delightful and satisfying and no one has any reason to complain. Once in a while something happens in Oz to disturb the people's happiness for a brief time, for so rich and attractive a fairyland is sure to make a few selfish and greedy outsiders envious, and therefore certain evil-doers have treacherously plotted to conquer Oz and enslave its people and destroy its girl Ruler, and so gain the wealth of Oz for themselves. But up to the time when the cruel and crafty Nome, Ruggedo, conspired with Kiki Aru, the Hyup, all such attempts had failed. The Oz people suspected no danger. Life in the world's nicest fairyland was one round of joyous, happy days.

In the center of the Emerald City of Oz, the capital city of Ozma's dominions, is a vast and beautiful garden, surrounded by a wall inlaid with shining emeralds, and in the center of this garden stands Ozma's Royal Palace, the most splendid building ever constructed. From a hundred towers and domes floated the banners of Oz, which included the Ozmies, the Munchkins, the Gillikins, the Winkies and the Quadlings. The banner of the Munchkins is blue, that of the Winkies yellow; the Gillikin banner is purple, and the Quadling's banner is red. The colors of the Emerald City are of course green. Ozma's own banner has a green center, and is divided into four quarters. These quarters are colored blue, purple, yellow and red, indicating that she rules over all the countries of the Land of Oz.

This fairyland is so big, however, that all of it is not yet known to its girl Ruler, and it is said that in some far parts of the country, in forests and mountain fastnesses, in hidden valleys and thick jungles, are people and beasts that know as little about Ozma as she knows of them. Still, these unknown subjects are not nearly so numerous as the known inhabitants of Oz, who occupy all the countries near to the Emerald City. Indeed, I'm sure it will not be long until all parts of the fairyland of Oz are explored and their peoples made acquainted with their Ruler, for in Ozma's palace are several of her friends who are so curious that they are constantly discovering new and extraordinary places and inhabitants.

One of the most frequent discoverers of these hidden places in Oz is a little Kansas girl named Dorothy, who is Ozma's dearest friend and lives in luxurious rooms in the Royal Palace. Dorothy is, indeed, a Princess of Oz, but she does not like to be called a princess, and because she is simple and sweet and does not pretend to be anything but an ordinary little girl, she is called just "Dorothy" by everybody and is the most popular person, next to Ozma, in all the Land of Oz.

One morning Dorothy crossed the hall of the palace and knocked on the door of another girl named Trot, also a guest and friend of Ozma. When told to enter, Dorothy found that Trot had company, an old sailor-man with one wooden leg and one meat leg, who was sitting by the open window puffing smoke from a corn-cob pipe. This sailor-man was named Cap'n Bill, and he had accompanied Trot to the Land of Oz and was her oldest and most faithful comrade and friend. Dorothy liked Cap'n Bill, too, and after she had greeted him, she said to Trot: "You know, Ozma's birthday is next month, and I've been wondering what I can give here as a birthday present. She's so good to us all that we certainly ought to remember her birthday."

"That's true," agreed Trot. "I've been wondering, too, what I could give Ozma. It's pretty hard to decide, 'cause she's got already all she wants, and as she's a fairy and knows a lot about magic, she could satisfy any wish."

"I know," returned Dorothy, "but that isn't the point. It isn't that Ozma NEEDS anything, but that it will please her to know we've remembered her birthday. But what shall we give her?"

Trot shook her head in despair.

"I've tried to think and I can't," she declared.

"It's the same way with me," said Dorothy.

"I know one thing that 'ud please her," remarked Cap'n Bill, turning his round face with its fringe of whiskers toward the two girls and staring at them with his big, light-blue eyes wide open.

"What is it, Cap'n Bill?"

"It's an Enchanted Flower," said he. "It's a pretty plant that stands in a golden flower-pot an' grows all sorts o' flowers, one after another. One minute a fine rose buds an' blooms, an' then a tulip, an' next a chrys—chrys—"

"—anthemum," said Dorothy, helping him.

"That's it; and next a dahlia, an' then a daffydil, an' on all through the range o' posies. Jus' as soon as one fades away, another comes, of a different sort, an' the perfume from 'em is mighty snifty, an' they keeps bloomin' night and day, year in an' year out."

"That's wonderful!" exclaimed Dorothy. "I think Ozma would like it."

"But where is the Magic Flower, and how can we get it?" asked Trot.

"Dun'no, zac'ly," slowly replied Cap'n Bill. "The Glass Cat tol' me 'bout it only yesterday, an' said it was in some lonely place up at the nor'east o' here. The Glass Cat goes travelin' all around Oz, you know, an' the little critter sees a lot o' things no one else does."

"That's true," said Dorothy, thoughtfully. "Northeast of here must be in the Munchkin Country, and perhaps a good way off, so let's ask the Glass Cat to tell us how to get to the Magic Flower."

So the two girls, with Cap'n Bill stumping along on his wooden leg after them, went out into the garden, and after some time spent in searching, they found the Glass Cat curled up in the sunshine beside a bush, fast sleep.

The Glass Cat is one of the most curious creatures in all Oz. It was made by a famous magician named Dr. Pipt before Ozma had forbidden her subjects to work magic. Dr. Pipt had made the Glass Cat to catch mice, but the Cat refused to catch mice and was considered more curious than useful.

This astonished cat was made all of glass and was so clear and transparent that you could see through it as easily as through a window. In the top of its head, however, was a mass of delicate pink balls which looked like jewels but were intended for brains. It had a heart made of blood-red ruby. The eyes were two large emeralds. But, aside from these colors, all the rest of the animal was of clear glass, and it had a spun-glass tail that was really beautiful.

"Here, wake up," said Cap'n Bill. "We want to talk to you."

Slowly the Glass Cat got upon its feed, yawned and then looked at the three who stood before it.

"How dare you disturb me?" it asked in a peevish voice. "You ought to be ashamed of yourselves."

"Never mind that," returned the Sailor. "Do you remember tellin' me yesterday 'bout a Magic Flower in a Gold Pot?"

"Do you think I'm a fool? Look at my brains—you can see 'em work. Of course I remember!" said the cat.

"Well, where can we find it?"

"You can't. It's none of your business, anyhow. Go away and let me sleep," advised the Glass Cat.

"Now, see here," said Dorothy; "we want the Magic Flower to give to Ozma on her birthday. You'd be glad to please Ozma, wouldn't you?"

"I'm not sure," replied the creature. "Why should I want to please anybody?"

"You've got a heart, 'cause I can see it inside of you," said Trot.

"Yes; it's a pretty heart, and I'm fond of it," said the cat, twisting around to view its own body. "But it's made from a ruby, and it's hard as nails."

"Aren't you good for ANYthing?" asked Trot.

"Yes, I'm pretty to look at, and that's more than can be said of you," retorted the creature.

Trot laughed at this, and Dorothy, who understood the Glass Cat pretty well, said soothingly: "You are indeed beautiful, and if you can tell Cap'n Bill where to find the Magic Flower, all the people in Oz will praise your cleverness. The Flower will belong to Ozma, but everyone will know the Glass Cat discovered it."

This was the kind of praise the crystal creature liked.

"Well," it said, while the pink brains rolled around, "I found the Magic Flower way up in the north of the Munchkin Country where few people live or ever go. There's a river there that flows through a forest, and in the middle of the forest there is a small island on which stands the gold pot in which grows the Magic Flower."

"How did you get to the island?" asked Dorothy. "Glass cats can't swim."

"No, but I'm not afraid of water," was the reply. "I just walked across the river on the bottom."

"Under the water?" exclaimed Trot.

The cat gave her a scornful look.

"How could I walk OVER the water on the BOTTOM of the river? If you were transparent, anyone could see YOUR brains were not working. But I'm sure you could never find the place alone. It has always been hidden from the Oz people."

"But you, with your fine pink brains, could find it again, I s'pose," remarked Dorothy.

"Yes; and if you want that Magic Flower for Ozma, I'll go with you and show you the way."

"That's lovely of you!" declared Dorothy. "Trot and Cap'n Bill will go with you, for this is to be their birthday present to Ozma. While you're gone I'll have to find something else to give her."

"All right. Come on, then, Cap'n," said the Glass Cat, starting to move away.

"Wait a minute," begged Trot. "How long will we be gone?"

"Oh, about a week."

"Then I'll put some things in a basket to take with us," said the girl, and ran into the palace to make her preparations for the journey.

6. Ozma's Birthday Presents

When Cap'n Bill and Trot and the Glass Cat had started for the hidden island in the far-off river to get the Magic Flower, Dorothy wondered again what she could give Ozma on her birthday. She met the Patchwork Girl and said: "What are you going to give Ozma for a birthday present?"

"I've written a song for her," answered the strange Patchwork Girl, who went by the name of "Scraps," and who, through stuffed with cotton, had a fair assortment of mixed brains. "It's a splendid song and the chorus runs this way:
I am crazy;
You're a daisy,
Ozma dear;

I'm demented;
You're contented,
Ozma dear;

I am patched and gay and glary;
You're a sweet and lovely fairy;
May your birthdays all be happy, Ozma dear!"

"How do you like it, Dorothy?" inquired the Patchwork Girl.

"Is it good poetry, Scraps?" asked Dorothy, doubtfully.

"It's as good as any ordinary song," was the reply. "I have given it a dandy title, too. I shall call the song: 'When Ozma Has a Birthday, Everybody's Sure to Be Gay, for She Cannot Help the Fact That She Was Born.'"

"That's a pretty long title, Scraps," said Dorothy.

"That makes it stylish," replied the Patchwork Girl, turning a somersault and alighting on one stuffed foot. "Now-a-days the titles are sometimes longer than the songs."

Dorothy left her and walked slowly toward the place, where she met the Tin Woodman just going up the front steps.

"What are you going to give Ozma on her birthday?" she asked.

"It's a secret, but I'll tell you," replied the Tin Woodman, who was Emperor of the Winkies. "I am having my people make Ozma a lovely girdle set with beautiful tin nuggets. Each tin nugget will be surrounded by a circle of emeralds, just to set it off to good advantage. The clasp of the girdle will be pure tin! Won't that be fine?"

"I'm sure she'll like it," said Dorothy. "Do you know what I can give her?"

"I haven't the slightest idea, Dorothy. It took me three months to think of my own present for Ozma."

The girl walked thoughtfully around to the back of the palace, and presently came upon the famous Scarecrow of Oz, who has having two of the palace servants stuff his legs with fresh straw.

"What are you going to give Ozma on her birthday?" asked Dorothy.

"I want to surprise her," answered the Scarecrow.

"I won't tell," promised Dorothy.

"Well, I'm having some straw slippers made for her—all straw, mind you, and braided very artistically. Ozma has always admired my straw filling, so I'm sure she'll be pleased with these lovely straw slippers."

"Ozma will be pleased with anything her loving friends give her," said the girl. "What I'M worried about, Scarecrow, is what to give Ozma that she hasn't got already."

"That's what worried me, until I thought of the slippers," said the Scarecrow. "You'll have to THINK, Dorothy; that's the only way to get a good idea. If I hadn't such wonderful brains, I'd never have thought of those straw foot-decorations."

Dorothy left him and went to her room, where she sat down and tried to think hard. A Pink Kitten was curled up on the window-sill and Dorothy asked her: "What can I give Ozma for her birthday present?"

"Oh, give her some milk," replied the Pink Kitten; "that's the nicest thing I know of."

A fuzzy little black dog had squatted down at Dorothy's feet and now looked up at her with intelligent eyes.

"Tell me, Toto," said the girl; "what would Ozma like best for a birthday present?"

The little black dog wagged his tail.

"Your love," said he. "Ozma wants to be loved more than anything else."

"But I already love her, Toto!"

"Then tell her you love her twice as much as you ever did before."

"That wouldn't be true," objected Dorothy, "for I've always loved her as much as I could, and, really, Toto, I want to give Ozma some PRESENT, 'cause everyone else will give her a present."

"Let me see," said Toto. "How would it be to give her that useless Pink Kitten?"

"No, Toto; that wouldn't do."

"Then six kisses."

"No; that's no present."

"Well, I guess you'll have to figure it out for yourself, Dorothy," said the little dog. "To MY notion you're more particular than Ozma will be."

Dorothy decided that if anyone could help her it would be Glinda the Good, the wonderful Sorceress of Oz who was Ozma's faithful subject and friend. But Glinda's castle was in the Quadling Country and quite a journey from the Emerald City.

So the little girl went to Ozma and asked permission to use the Wooden Sawhorse and the royal Red Wagon to pay a visit to Glinda, and the girl Ruler kissed Princess Dorothy and graciously granted permission.

The Wooden Sawhorse was one of the most remarkable

creatures in Oz. Its body was a small log and its legs were limbs of trees stuck in the body. Its eyes were knots, its mouth was sawed in the end of the log and its ears were two chips. A small branch had been left at the rear end of the log to serve as a tail.

Ozma herself, during one of her early adventures, had brought this wooden horse to life, and so she was much attached to the queer animal and had shod the bottoms of its wooden legs with plates of gold so they would not wear out. The Sawhorse was a swift and willing traveler, and though it could talk if need arose, it seldom said anything unless spoken to. When the Sawhorse was harnessed to the Red Wagon there were no reins to guide him because all that was needed was to tell him where to go.

Dorothy now told him to go to Glinda's Castle and the Sawhorse carried her there with marvelous speed.

"Glinda," said Dorothy, when she had been greeted by the Sorceress, who was tall and stately, with handsome and dignified features and dressed in a splendid and becoming gown, "what are you going to give Ozma for a birthday present?"

The Sorceress smiled and answered: "Come into my patio and I will show you."

So they entered a place that was surrounded by the wings of the great castle but had no roof, and was filled with flowers and fountains and exquisite statuary and many settees and chairs of polished marble or filigree gold. Here there were gathered fifty beautiful young girls, Glinda's handmaids, who had been selected from all parts of the Land of Oz on account of their wit and beauty and sweet dispositions. It was a great honor to be made one of Glinda's handmaidens.

When Dorothy followed the Sorceress into this delightful patio all the fifty girls were busily weaving, and their shuttles were filled with a sparkling green spun glass such as the little girl had never seen before.

"What is it, Glinda?" she asked.

"One of my recent discoveries," explained the Sorceress. "I have found a way to make threads from emeralds, by softening the stones and then spinning them into long, silken strands. With these emerald threads we are weaving cloth to make Ozma a splendid court gown for her birthday. You will notice that the threads have all the beautiful glitter and luster of the emeralds from which they are made, and so Ozma's new dress will be the most magnificent the world has ever seen, and quite fitting for our lovely Ruler of the Fairyland of Oz."

Dorothy's eyes were fairly dazed by the brilliance of the emerald cloth, some of which the girls had already woven.

"I've never seen ANYthing so beautiful!" she said, with a sigh. "But tell me, Glinda, what can I give our lovely Ozma on her birthday?"

The good Sorceress considered this question for a long time before she replied. Finally she said: "Of course there will be a grand feast at the Royal Palace on Ozma's birthday, and all our friends will be present. So I suggest that you make a fine big birthday cake of Ozma, and surround it with candles."

"Oh, just a CAKE!" exclaimed Dorothy, in disappointment.

"Nothing is nicer for a birthday," said the Sorceress.

"How many candles should there be on the cake?" asked the girl.

"Just a row of them," replied Glinda, "for no one knows how old Ozma is, although she appears to us to be just a young girl—as fresh and fair as if she had lived but a few years."

"A cake doesn't seem like much of a present," Dorothy asserted.

"Make it a surprise cake," suggested the Sorceress. "Don't you remember the four and twenty blackbirds that were baked in a pie? Well, you need not use live blackbirds in your cake, but you could have some surprise of a different sort."

"Like what?" questioned Dorothy, eagerly.

"If I told you, it wouldn't be YOUR present to Ozma, but MINE," answered the Sorceress, with a smile. "Think it over, my dear, and I am sure you can originate a surprise that will add greatly to the joy and merriment of Ozma's birthday banquet."

Dorothy thanked her friend and entered the Red Wagon and told the Sawhorse to take her back home to the palace in the Emerald City.

On the way she thought the matter over seriously of making a surprise birthday cake and finally decided what to do.

As soon as she reached home, she went to the Wizard of Oz, who had a room fitted up in one of the high towers of the palace, where he studied magic so as to be able to perform such wizardry as Ozma commanded him to do for the welfare of her subjects.

The Wizard and Dorothy were firm friends and had enjoyed many strange adventures together. He was a little man with a bald head and sharp eyes and a round, jolly face, and because he was neither haughty nor proud he had become a great favorite with the Oz people.

"Wizard," said Dorothy, "I want you to help me fix up a present for Ozma's birthday."

"I'll be glad to do anything for you and for Ozma," he answered. "What's on your mind, Dorothy?"

"I'm going to make a great cake, with frosting and candles, and all that, you know."

"Very good," said the Wizard.

"In the center of this cake I'm going to leave a hollow place, with just a roof of the frosting over it," continued the girl.

"Very good," repeated the Wizard, nodding his bald head.

"In that hollow place," said Dorothy, "I want to hide a lot of monkeys about three inches high, and after the cake is placed on the banquet table, I want the monkeys to break through the frosting and dance around on the table-cloth. Then, I want each monkey to cut out a piece of cake and hand it to a guest."

"Mercy me!" cried the little Wizard, as he chuckled with laughter. "Is that ALL you want, Dorothy?"

"Almost," said she. "Can you think of anything more the little monkeys can do, Wizard?"

"Not just now," he replied. "But where will you get such tiny monkeys?"

"That's where you're to help me," said Dorothy. "In some of those wild forests in the Gillikin Country are lots of monkeys."

"Big ones," said the Wizard.

"Well, you and I will go there, and we'll get some of the big monkeys, and you will make them small—just three inches high—by means of your magic, and we'll put the little monkeys all in a basket and bring them home with us. Then you'll train them to dance—up here in your room, where no one can see them—and on Ozma's birthday we'll put 'em into the cake and they'll know by that time just what to do."

The Wizard looked at Dorothy with admiring approval, and chuckled again.

"That's really clever, my dear," he said, "and I see no reason why we can't do it, just the way you say, if only we can get the wild monkeys to agree to it."

"Do you think they'll object?" asked the girl.

"Yes; but perhaps we can argue them into it. Anyhow it's worth trying, and I'll help you if you'll agree to let this Surprise Cake be a present to Ozma from you and me together. I've been wondering what I could give Ozma, and as I've got to train the monkeys as well as make them small, I think you ought to make me your partner."

"Of course," said Dorothy; "I'll be glad to do so."

"Then it's a bargain," declared the Wizard. "We must go to seek those monkeys at once, however, for it will take time to train them and we'll have to travel a good way to the Gillikin forests where they live."

"I'm ready to go any time," agreed Dorothy. "Shall we ask Ozma to let us take the Sawhorse?"

The Wizard did not answer that at once. He took time to think of the suggestion.

"No," he answered at length, "the Red Wagon couldn't get through the thick forests and there's some danger to us in going into the wild places to search for monkeys. So I propose we take the Cowardly Lion and the Hungry Tiger. We can ride on their backs as well as in the Red Wagon, and if there is danger to us from other beasts, these two friendly champions will protect us from all harm."

"That's a splendid idea!" exclaimed Dorothy. "Let's go now and ask the Hungry Tiger and the Cowardly Lion if they will help us. Shall we ask Ozma if we can go?"

"I think not," said the Wizard, getting his hat and his black bag of magic tools. "This is to be a surprise for her birthday, and so she mustn't know where we're going. We'll just leave word, in case Ozma inquires for us, that we'll be back in a few days."

7. The Forest of Gugu

In the central western part of the Gillikin Country is a great tangle of trees called Gugu Forest. It is the biggest forest in all Oz and stretches miles and miles in every direction—north, south, east and west. Adjoining it on the east side is a range of rugged mountains covered with underbrush and small twisted trees. You can find this place by looking at the Map of the Land of Oz.

Gugu Forest is the home of most of the wild beasts that inhabit Oz. These are seldom disturbed in their leafy haunts because there is no reason why Oz people should go there, except on rare occasions, and most parts of the forest have never been seen by any eyes but the eyes of the beasts who make their home there. The biggest beasts inhabit the great forest, while the smaller ones live mostly in the mountain underbrush at the east.

Now, you must know that there are laws in the forests, as well as in every other place, and these laws are made by the beasts themselves, and are necessary to keep them from fighting and tearing one another to pieces. In Gugu Forest there is a King—an enormous yellow leopard called "Gugu"—after whom the forest is named. And this King has three other beasts to advise him in keeping the laws and maintaining order—Bru the Bear, Loo the Unicorn and Rango the Gray Ape—who are known as the King's Counselors. All these are fierce and ferocious beasts, and hold their high offices because they are more intelligent and more feared then their fellows.

Since Oz became a fairyland, no man, woman or child ever dies in that land nor is anyone ever sick. Likewise the beasts of the forests never die, so that long years add to their cunning and wisdom, as well as to their size and strength. It is possible for beasts—or even people—to be destroyed, but the task is so difficult that it is seldom attempted. Because it is free from sickness and death is one reason why Oz is a fairyland, but it is doubtful whether those who come to Oz from the outside world, as Dorothy and Button-Bright and Trot and Cap'n Bill and the Wizard did, will live forever or cannot be injured. Even Ozma is not sure about this, and so the guests of Ozma from other lands are always carefully protected from any danger, so as to be on the safe side.

In spite of the laws of the forests there are often fights among the beasts; some of them have lost an eye or an ear or even had a leg torn off. The King and the King's Counselors always punish those who start a fight, but so fierce is the nature of some beasts that they will at times fight in spite of laws and punishment.

Over this vast, wild Forest of Gugu flew two eagles, one morning, and near the center of the jungle the eagles alighted on a branch of a tall tree.

"Here is the place for us to begin our work," said one, who was Ruggedo, the Nome.

"Do many beasts live here?" asked Kiki Aru, the other eagle.

"The forest is full of them," said the Nome. "There are enough beasts right here to enable us to conquer the people of Oz, if we can get them to consent to join us. To do that, we must go among them and tell them our plans, so we must now decide on what shapes we had better assume while in the forest."

"I suppose we must take the shapes of beasts?" said Kiki.

"Of course. But that requires some thought. All kinds of beasts live here, and a yellow leopard is King. If we become leopards, the King will be jealous of us. If we take the forms of some of the other beasts, we shall not command proper respect."

"I wonder if the beasts will attack us?" asked Kiki.

"I'm a Nome, and immortal, so nothing can hurt me," replied Ruggedo.

"I was born in the Land of Oz, so nothing can hurt me," said Kiki.

"But, in order to carry out our plans, we must win the favor of all the animals of the forest."

"Then what shall we do?" asked Kiki.

"Let us mix the shapes of several beasts, so we will not look like any one of them," proposed the wily old Nome. "Let us have the heads of lions, the bodies of monkeys, the wings of eagles and the tails of wild asses, with knobs of gold on the end of them instead of bunches of hair."

"Won't that make a queer combination?" inquired Kiki.

"The queerer the better," declared Ruggedo.

"All right," said Kiki. "You stay here, and I'll fly away to another tree and transform us both, and then we'll climb down our trees and meet in the forest."

"No," said the Nome, "we mustn't separate. You must transform us while we are together."

"I won't do that," asserted Kiki, firmly. "You're trying to get my secret, and I won't let you."

The eyes of the other eagle flashed angrily, but Ruggedo did not dare insist. If he offended this boy, he might have to remain an eagle always and he wouldn't like that. Some day he hoped to be able to learn the secret word of the magical transformations, but just now he must let Kiki have his own way.

"All right," he said gruffly; "do as you please."

So Kiki flew to a tree that was far enough distant so that Ruggedo could not overhear him and said: "I want Ruggedo, the Nome, and myself to have the heads of lions, the bodies of monkeys, the wings of eagles and the tails of wild asses, with knobs of gold on the ends of them instead of bunches of hair—*yrzqxgl!*"

He pronounced the magic word in the proper manner and at once his form changed to the one he had described. He spread his eagle's wings and finding they were strong enough to support his monkey body and lion head he flew swiftly to the tree where he had left Ruggedo. The Nome was also transformed and was climbing down the tree because the branches all around him were so thickly entwined that there was no room between them to fly.

Kiki quickly joined his comrade and it did not take them long to reach the ground.

8. The Li-Mon-Eags Make Trouble

There had been trouble in the Forest of Gugu that morning. Chipo the Wild Boar had bitten the tail off Arx the Giraffe while the latter had his head among the leaves of a tree, eating his breakfast. Arx kicked with his heels and struck Tirrip, the great Kangaroo, who had a new baby in her pouch. Tirrip knew it was the Wild Boar's fault, so she knocked him over with one powerful blow and then ran away to escape Chipo's sharp tusks. In the chase that followed a giant porcupine stuck fifty sharp quills into the Boar and a chimpanzee in a tree threw a cocoanut at the porcupine that jammed its head into its body.

All this was against the Laws of the Forest, and when the excitement was over, Gugu the Leopard King called his royal Counselors together to decide how best to punish the offenders.

The four lords of the forest were holding solemn council in a small clearing when they saw two strange beasts approaching them—beasts the like of which they had never seen before.

Not one of the four, however, relaxed his dignity or showed by a movement that he was startled. The great Leopard crouched at full length upon a fallen tree-trunk. Bru the Bear sat on his haunches before the King; Rango the Gray Ape stood with his muscular arms folded, and Loo the Unicorn reclined, much as a horse does, between his fellow-councillors. With one consent they remained silent, eyeing with steadfast looks the intruders, who were making their way into their forest domain.

"Well met, Brothers!" said one of the strange beasts, coming to a halt beside the group, while his comrade with hesitation lagged behind.

"We are not brothers," returned the Gray Ape, sternly. "Who are you, and how came you in the forest of Gugu?"

"We are two Li-Mon-Eags," said Ruggedo, inventing the name. "Our home is in Sky Island, and we have come to earth to warn the forest beasts that the people of Oz are about to make war upon them and enslave them, so that they will become beasts of burden forever after and obey only the will of their two-legged masters."

A low roar of anger arose from the Council of Beasts.

"WHO'S going to do that?" asked Loo the Unicorn, in a high, squeaky voice, at the same time rising to his feet.

"The people of Oz," said Ruggedo.

"But what will WE be doing?" inquired the Unicorn.

"That's what I've come to talk to you about."

"You needn't talk! We'll fight the Oz people!" screamed the Unicorn. "We'll smash 'em; we'll trample 'em; we'll gore 'em; we'll—"

"Silence!" growled Gugu the King, and Loo obeyed, although still trembling with wrath. The cold, steady gaze of the Leopard wandered over the two strange beasts. "The people of Oz," said he, "have not been our friends; they have not been our enemies. They have let us alone, and we have let them alone. There is no reason for war between us. They have no slaves. They could not use us as slaves if they should conquer us. I think you are telling us lies, you strange Li-Mon-Eag—you mixed-up beast who are neither one thing nor another."

"Oh, on my word, it's the truth!" protested the Nome in the beast's shape. "I wouldn't lie for the world; I—"

"Silence!" again growled Gugu the King; and somehow, even Ruggedo was abashed and obeyed the edict.

"What do you say, Bru?" asked the King, turning to the great Bear, who had until now said nothing.

"How does the Mixed Beast know that what he says is true?" asked the Bear.

"Why, I can fly, you know, having the wings of an Eagle,"

explained the Nome. "I and my comrade yonder," turning to Kiki, "flew to a grove in Oz, and there we heard the people telling how they will make many ropes to snare you beasts, and then they will surround this forest, and all other forests, and make you prisoners. So we came here to warn you, for being beasts ourselves, although we live in the sky, we are your friends."

The Leopard's lip curled and showed his enormous teeth, sharp as needles. He turned to the Gray Ape.

"What do YOU think, Rango?" he asked.

"Send these mixed beasts away, Your Majesty," replied the Gray Ape. "They are mischief-makers."

"Don't do that—don't do that!" cried the Unicorn, nervously. "The stranger said he would tell us what to do. Let him tell us, then. Are we fools, not to heed a warning?"

Gugu the King turned to Ruggedo.

"Speak, Stranger," he commanded.

"Well," said the Nome, "it's this way: The Land of Oz is a fine country. The people of Oz have many good things—houses with soft beds, all sorts of nice-tasting food, pretty clothes, lovely jewels, and many other things that beasts know nothing of. Here in the dark forests the poor beasts have hard work to get enough to eat and to find a bed to rest in. But the beasts are better than the people, and why should they not have all the good things the people have? So I propose that before the Oz people have the time to make all those ropes to snare you with, that all we beasts get together and march against the Oz people and capture them. Then the beasts will become the masters and the people their slaves."

"What good would that do us?" asked Bru the Bear.

"It would save you from slavery, for one thing, and you could enjoy all the fine things of Oz people have."

"Beasts wouldn't know what to do with the things people use," said the Gray Ape.

"But this is only part of my plan," insisted the Nome. "Listen to the rest of it. We two Li-Mon-Eags are powerful magicians. When you have conquered the Oz people we will transform them all into beasts, and send them to the forests to live, and we will transform all the beasts into people, so they can enjoy all the wonderful delights of the Emerald City."

For a moment no beast spoke. Then the King said: "Prove it."

"Prove what?" asked Ruggedo.

"Prove that you can transform us. If you are a magician transform the Unicorn into a man. Then we will believe you. If you fail, we will destroy you."

"All right," said the Nome. "But I'm tired, so I'll let my comrade make the transformation."

Kiki Aru had stood back from the circle, but he had heard all that was said. He now realized that he must make good Ruggedo's boast, so he retreated to the edge of the clearing and whispered the magic word.

Instantly the Unicorn became a fat, chubby little man, dressed in the purple Gillikin costume, and it was hard to tell which was the more astonished, the King, the Bear, the Ape or the former Unicorn.

"It's true!" shorted the man-beast. "Good gracious, look what I am! It's wonderful!"

The King of Beasts now addressed Ruggedo in a more friendly tone.

"We must believe your story, since you have given us proof of your power," said he. "But why, if you are so great a magician, cannot you conquer the Oz people without our help, and so save us the trouble?"

"Alas!" replied the crafty old Nome, "no magician is able to do everything. The transformations are easy to us because we are Li-Mon-Eags, but we cannot fight, or conquer even such weak creatures as the Oz people. But we will stay with you and advise and help you, and we will transform all the Oz people into beasts, when the time comes, and all the beasts into people."

Gugu the King turned to his Counselors.

"How shall we answer this friendly stranger?" he asked.

Loo the former Unicorn was dancing around and cutting capers like a clown.

"On my word, your Majesty," he said, "this being a man is more fun than being a Unicorn."

"You look like a fool," said the Gray Ape.

"Well, I FEEL fine!" declared the man-beast.

"I think I prefer to be a Bear," said Big Bru. "I was born a Bear and I know a Bear's ways. So I am satisfied to live as a Bear lives."

"That," said the old Nome, "is because you know nothing better. When we have conquered the Oz people, and you become a man, you'll be glad of it."

The immense Leopard rested his chin on the log and seemed thoughtful.

"The beasts of the forest must decide this matter for themselves," he said. "Go you, Rango the Gray Ape, and tell your monkey tribe to order all the forest beasts to assemble in the Great Clearing at sunrise to-morrow. When all are gathered together, this mixed up Beast who is a magician shall talk to them and tell them what he has told us. Then, if they decide to fight the Oz people, who have declared war on us, I will lead the beasts to battle."

Rango the Gray Ape turned at once and glided swiftly through the forest on his mission. The Bear gave a grunt and walked away. Gugu the King rose and stretched himself. Then he said to Ruggedo: "Meet us at sunrise to-morrow," and with stately stride vanished among the trees.

The man-unicorn, left alone with the strangers, suddenly stopped his foolish prancing.

"You'd better make me a Unicorn again," he said. "I like being a man, but the forest beasts won't know I'm their friend, Loo, and they might tear me in pieces before morning."

So Kiki changed him back to his former shape, and the Unicorn departed to join his people.

Ruggedo the Nome was much pleased with his success.

"To-morrow," he said to Kiki Aru, "we'll win over these beasts and set them to fight and conquer the Oz people. Then I will have my revenge on Ozma and Dorothy and all the rest of my enemies."

"But I am doing all the work," said Kiki.

"Never mind; you're going to be King of Oz," promised Ruggedo.

"Will the big Leopard let me be King?" asked the boy anxiously.

The Nome came close to him and whispered: "If Gugu the Leopard opposes us, you will transform him into a tree, and then he will be helpless."

"Of course," agreed Kiki, and he said to himself: "I shall also transform this deceitful Nome into a tree, for he lies and I cannot trust him."

9. The Isle of the Magic Flower

The Glass Cat was a good guide and led Trot and Cap'n Bill by straight and easy paths through all the settled part of the Munchkin Country, and then into the north section where there were few houses, and finally through a wild country where there were no houses or paths at all. But the walking was not difficult and at last they came to the edge of a forest and stopped there to make camp and sleep until morning.

From branches of trees Cap'n Bill made a tiny house that was just big enough for the little girl to crawl into and lie down. But first they ate some of the food Trot had carried in the basket.

"Don't you want some, too?" she asked the Glass Cat.

"No," answered the creature.

"I suppose you'll hunt around an' catch a mouse," remarked Cap'n Bill.

"Me? Catch a mouse! Why should I do that?" inquired the Glass Cat.

"Why, then you could eat it," said the sailor-man.

"I beg to inform you," returned the crystal tabby, "that I do not eat mice. Being transparent, so anyone can see through me, I'd look nice, wouldn't I, with a common mouse inside me? But the fact is that I haven't any stomach or other machinery that would permit me to eat things. The careless magician who made me didn't think I'd need to eat, I suppose."

"Don't you ever get hungry or thirsty?" asked Trot.

"Never. I don't complain, you know, at the way I'm made, for I've never yet seen any living thing as beautiful as I am. I have the handsomest brains in the world. They're pink, and you can see 'em work."

"I wonder," said Trot thoughtfully, as she ate her bread and jam, "if MY brains whirl around in the same way yours do."

"No; not the same way, surely," returned the Glass Cat; "for, in that case, they'd be as good as MY brains, except that they're hidden under a thick, boney skull."

"Brains," remarked Cap'n Bill, "is of all kinds and work different ways. But I've noticed that them as thinks that their brains is best is often mistook."

Trot was a little disturbed by sounds from the forest, that night, for many beasts seemed prowling among the trees, but she was confident Cap'n Bill would protect her from harm. And in fact, no beast ventured from the forest to attack them.

At daybreak they were up again, and after a simple breakfast Cap'n Bill said to the Glass Cat: "Up anchor, Mate, and let's forge ahead. I don't suppose we're far from that Magic Flower, are we?"

"Not far," answered the transparent one, as it led the way into the forest, "but it may take you some time to get to it."

Before long they reached the bank of a river. It was not very wide, at this place, but as they followed the banks in a northerly direction it gradually broadened.

Suddenly the blue-green leaves of the trees changed to a purple hue, and Trot noticed this and said: "I wonder what made the colors change like that?"

"It's because we have left the Munchkin Country and entered the Gillikin Country," explained the Glass Cat. "Also it's a sign our journey is nearly ended."

The river made a sudden turn, and after the travelers had passed around the bend, they saw that the stream had now become as broad as a small lake, and in the center of the Lake they beheld a little island, not more than fifty feet in extent, either way. Something glittered in the middle of this tiny island, and the Glass Cat paused on the bank and said: "There is the gold flower-pot containing the Magic Flower, which is very curious and beautiful. If you can get to the island, your task is ended—except to carry the thing home with you."

Cap'n Bill looked at the broad expanse of water and began to whistle a low, quavering tune. Trot knew that the whistle meant that Cap'n Bill was thinking, and the old sailor didn't look at the island as much as he looked at the trees upon the bank where they stood. Presently he took from the big pocket of his coat an axe-blade, wound in an old cloth to keep the sharp edge from cutting his clothing. Then, with a large pocket knife, he cut a small limb from a tree and whittled it into a handle for his axe.

"Sit down, Trot," he advised the girl, as he worked. "I've got quite a job ahead of me now, for I've got to build us a raft."

"What do we need a raft for, Cap'n?"

"Why, to take us to the island. We can't walk under water, in the river bed, as the Glass Cat did, so we must float atop the water."

"Can you make a raft, Cap'n Bill?"

"O' course, Trot, if you give me time."

The little girl sat down on a log and gazed at the Island of the Magic Flower. Nothing else seemed to grow on the tiny isle. There was no tree, no shrub, no grass, even, as far as she could make out from that distance. But the gold pot glittered in the rays of the sun, and Trot could catch glimpses of glowing colors above it, as the Magic Flower changed from one sort to another.

"When I was here before," remarked the Glass Cat, lazily reclining at the girl's feet, "I saw two Kalidahs on this very bank, where they had come to drink."

"What are Kalidahs?" asked the girl.

"The most powerful and ferocious beasts in all Oz. This forest is their especial home, and so there are few other beasts to be found except monkeys. The monkeys are spry enough to keep out of the way of the fierce Kalidahs, which attack all other animals and often fight among themselves."

"Did they try to fight you when you saw 'em?" asked Trot, getting very much excited.

"Yes. They sprang upon me in an instant; but I lay flat on the ground, so I wouldn't get my legs broken by the great weight of the beasts, and when they tried to bite me I laughed at them and jeered them until they were frantic with rage, for they nearly broke their teeth on my hard glass. So, after a time, they discovered they could not hurt me, and went away. It was great fun."

"I hope they don't come here again to drink,—not while we're here, anyhow," returned the girl, "for I'm not made of glass, nor is Cap'n Bill, and if those bad beasts bit us, we'd get hurt."

Cap'n Bill was cutting from the trees some long stakes, making them sharp at one end and leaving a crotch at the other end. These were to bind the logs of his raft together. He had fashioned several and was just finishing another when the Glass Cat cried: "Look out! There's a Kalidah coming toward us."

Trot jumped up, greatly frightened, and looked at the terrible animal as if fascinated by its fierce eyes, for the Kalidah was looking at her, too, and its look wasn't at all friendly. But Cap'n Bill called to her: "Wade into the river, Trot, up to your knees—an' stay there!" and she obeyed him at once. The sailor-man hobbled forward, the stake in one hand and his axe in the other, and got between the girl and the beast, which sprang upon him with a growl of defiance.

Cap'n Bill moved pretty slowly, sometimes, but now he was quick as could be. As the Kalidah sprang toward him he stuck out his wooden leg and the point of it struck the beast between the eyes and sent it rolling upon the ground. Before it could get upon its feet again the sailor pushed the sharp stake right through its body and then with the flat side of the axe he hammered the stake as far into the ground as it would go. By this means he captured the great beast and made it harmless, for try as it would, it could not get away from the stake that held it.

Cap'n Bill knew he could not kill the Kalidah, for no living thing in Oz can be killed, so he stood back and watched the beast wriggle and growl and paw the earth with its sharp claws, and then, satisfied it could not escape, he told Trot to come out of the water again and dry her wet shoes and stockings in the sun.

"Are you sure he can't get away?" she asked.

"I'd bet a cookie on it," said Cap'n Bill, so Trot came ashore and took off her shoes and stockings and laid them on the log to dry, while the sailor-man resumed his work on the raft.

The Kalidah, realizing after many struggles that it could not escape, now became quiet, but it said in a harsh, snarling voice:

"I suppose you think you're clever, to pin me to the ground in this manner. But when my friends, the other Kalidahs, come here, they'll tear you to pieces for treating me this way."

"P'raps," remarked Cap'n Bill, coolly, as he chopped at the logs, "an' p'raps not. When are your folks comin' here?"

"I don't know," admitted the Kalidah. "But when they DO come, you can't escape them."

"If they hold off long enough, I'll have my raft ready," said Cap'n Bill.

"What are you going to do with a raft?" inquired the beast.

"We're goin' over to that island, to get the Magic Flower."

The huge beast looked at him in surprise a moment, and then it began to laugh. The laugh was a good deal like a roar, and it had a cruel and derisive sound, but it was a laugh nevertheless.

"Good!" said the Kalidah. "Good! Very good! I'm glad you're going to get the Magic Flower. But what will you do with it?"

"We're going to take it to Ozma, as a present on her birthday."

The Kalidah laughed again; then it became sober. "If you get to the land on your raft before my people can catch you," it said, "you will be safe from us. We can swim like ducks, so the girl couldn't have escaped me by getting into the water; but Kalidahs don't go to that island over there."

"Why not?" asked Trot.

The beast was silent.

"Tell us the reason," urged Cap'n Bill.

"Well, it's the Isle of the Magic Flower," answered the Kalidah, "and we don't care much for magic. If you hadn't had a magic leg, instead of a meat one, you couldn't have knocked me over so easily and stuck this wooden pin through me."

"I've been to the Magic Isle," said the Glass Cat, "and I've watched the Magic Flower bloom, and I'm sure it's too pretty to be left in that lonely place where only beasts prowl around it and no else sees it. So we're going to take it away to the Emerald City."

"I don't care," the beast replied in a surly tone. "We Kalidahs would be just as contented if there wasn't a flower in our forest. What good are the things anyhow?"

"Don't you like pretty things?" asked Trot.

"No."

"You ought to admire my pink brains, anyhow," declared the Glass Cat. "They're beautiful and you can see 'em work."

The beast only growled in reply, and Cap'n Bill, having now cut all his logs to a proper size, began to roll them to the water's edge and fasten them together.

10. Stuck Fast

The day was nearly gone when, at last, the raft was ready.

"It ain't so very big," said the old sailor, "but I don't weigh much, an' you, Trot, don't weigh half as much as I do, an' the glass pussy don't count."

"But it's safe, isn't it?" inquired the girl.

"Yes; it's good enough to carry us to the island an' back again, an' that's about all we can expect of it."

Saying this, Cap'n Bill pushed the raft into the water, and when it was afloat, stepped upon it and held out his hand to Trot, who quickly followed him. The Glass Cat boarded the raft last of all.

The sailor had cut a long pole, and had also whittled a flat paddle, and with these he easily propelled the raft across the river. As they approached the island, the Wonderful Flower became more plainly visible, and they quickly decided that the Glass Cat had not praised it too highly. The colors of the flowers that bloomed in quick succession were strikingly bright and beautiful, and the shapes of the blossoms were varied and curious. Indeed, they did not resemble ordinary flowers at all.

So intently did Trot and Cap'n Bill gaze upon the Golden Flower-pot that held the Magic Flower that they scarcely noticed the island itself until the raft beached upon its sands. But then the girl exclaimed: "How funny it is, Cap'n Bill, that nothing else grows here excep' the Magic Flower."

Then the sailor glanced at the island and saw that it was all bare ground, without a weed, a stone or a blade of grass. Trot, eager to examine the Flower closer, sprang from the raft and ran up the bank until she reached the Golden Flower-pot. Then she stood beside it motionless and filled with wonder. Cap'n Bill joined her, coming more leisurely, and he, too, stood in silent admiration for a time.

"Ozma will like this," remarked the Glass Cat, sitting down to watch the shifting hues of the flowers. "I'm sure she won't have as fine a birthday present from anyone else."

"Do you 'spose it's very heavy, Cap'n? And can we get it home without breaking it?" asked Trot anxiously.

"Well, I've lifted many bigger things than that," he replied; "but let's see what it weighs."

He tried to take a step forward, but could not lift his meat foot from the ground. His wooden leg seemed free enough, but the other would not budge.

"I seem stuck, Trot," he said, with a perplexed look at his foot. "It ain't mud, an' it ain't glue, but somethin's holdin' me down."

The girl attempted to lift her own feet, to go nearer to her friend, but the ground held them as fast as it held Cap'n Bill's foot. She tried to slide them, or to twist them around, but it was no use; she could not move either foot a hair's breadth.

"This is funny!" she exclaimed. "What do you 'spose has happened to us, Cap'n Bill?"

"I'm tryin' to make out," he answered. "Take off your shoes, Trot. 'Raps it's the leather soles that's stuck to the ground."

She leaned down and unlaced her shoes, but found she could not pull her feet out of them. The Glass Cat, which was walking round as naturally as ever, now said: "Your foot has got roots to it, Cap'n, and I can see the roots going into the ground, where they spread out in all directions. It's the same way with Trot. That's why you can't move. The roots hold you fast."

Cap'n Bill was rather fat and couldn't see his own feet very well, but he squatted down and examined Trot's feet and decided that the Glass Cat was right.

"This is hard luck," he declared, in a voice that showed he was uneasy at the discovery. "We're pris'ners, Trot, on this funny island, an' I'd like to know how we're ever goin' to get loose, so's we can get home again."

"Now I know why the Kalidah laughed at us," said the girl, "and why he said none of the beasts ever came to this island. The horrid creature knew we'd be caught, and wouldn't warn us."

In the meantime, the Kalidah, although pinned fast to the earth by Cap'n Bill's stake, was facing the island, and now the ugly expression which passed over its face when it defied and sneered at Cap'n Bill and Trot, had changed to one of amusement and curiosity. When it saw the adventurers had actually reached the island and were standing beside the Magic Flower, it heaved a breath of satisfaction—a long, deep breath that swelled its deep chest until the beast could feel the stake that held him move a little, as if withdrawing itself from the ground.

"Ah ha!" murmured the Kalidah, "a little more of this will set me free and allow me to escape!"

So he began breathing as hard as he could, puffing out his chest as much as possible with each indrawing breath, and by doing this he managed to raise the stake with each powerful breath, until at last the Kalidah—using the muscles of his four legs as well as his deep breaths—found itself free of the sandy soil. The stake was sticking right through him, however, so he found a rock deeply set in the bank and pressed the sharp point of the stake upon this rock until he had driven it clear through his body. Then, by getting the stake tangled among some thorny bushes, and wiggling his body, he managed to draw it out altogether.

"There!" he exclaimed, "except for those two holes in me, I'm as good as ever; but I must admit that that old wooden-legged fellow saved both himself and the girl by making me a prisoner."

Now the Kalidahs, although the most disagreeable creatures in the Land of Oz, were nevertheless magical inhabitants of a magical Fairyland, and in their natures a certain amount of good was mingled with the evil. This one was not very revengeful, and now that his late foes were in danger of perishing, his anger against them faded away.

"Our own Kalidah King," he reflected, "has certain magical powers of his own. Perhaps he knows how to fill up these two holes in my body."

So without paying any more attention to Trot and Cap'n Bill than they were paying to him, he entered the forest and trotted along a secret path that led to the hidden lair of all the Kalidahs.

While the Kalidah was making good its escape Cap'n Bill took his pipe from his pocket and filled it with tobacco and lighted it. Then, as he puffed out the smoke, he tried to think what could be done.

"The Glass Cat seems all right," he said, "an' my wooden leg didn't take roots and grow, either. So it's only flesh that gets caught."

"It's magic that does it, Cap'n!"

"I know, Trot, and that's what sticks me. We're livin' in a magic country, but neither of us knows any magic an' so we can't help ourselves."

"Couldn't the Wizard of Oz help us—or Glinda the Good?" asked the little girl.

"Ah, now we're beginnin' to reason," he answered. "I'd probably thought o' that, myself, in a minute more. By good luck the Glass Cat is free, an' so it can run back to the Emerald City an' tell the Wizard about our fix, an' ask him to come an' help us get loose."

"Will you go?" Trot asked the cat, speaking very earnestly.

"I'm no messenger, to be sent here and there," asserted the curious animal in a sulky tone of voice.

"Well," said Cap'n Bill, "you've got to go home, anyhow, 'cause you don't want to stay here, I take it. And, when you get home, it wouldn't worry you much to tell the Wizard what's happened to us."

"That's true," said the cat, sitting on its haunches and lazily washing its face with one glass paw. "I don't mind telling the Wizard—when I get home."

"Won't you go now?" pleaded Trot. "We don't want to stay here any longer than we can help, and everybody in Oz will be interested in you, and call you a hero, and say nice things about you because you helped your friends out of trouble."

That was the best way to manage the Glass Cat, which was so vain that it loved to be praised.

"I'm going home right away," said the creature, "and I'll tell the Wizard to come and help you."

Saying this, it walked down to the water and disappeared under the surface. Not being able to manage the raft alone, the Glass Cat walked on the bottom of the river as it had done when it visited the island before, and soon they saw it appear on the farther bank and trot into the forest, where it was quickly lost to sight among the trees.

Then Trot heaved a deep sigh.

"Cap'n," said she, "we're in a bad fix. There's nothing here to eat, and we can't even lie down to sleep. Unless the Glass Cat hurries, and the Wizard hurries, I don't know what's going to become of us!"

11. The Beasts of the Forest of Gugu

There was a wonderful gathering of wild animals in the Forest of Gugu next sunrise. Rango, the Gray Ape, had even called his monkey sentinels away from the forest edge, and every beast, little and big, was in the great clearing where meetings were held on occasions of great importance.

In the center of the clearing stood a great shelving rock, having a flat, inclined surface, and on this sat the stately Leopard Gugu, who was King of the Forest. On the ground beneath him squatted Bru the Bear, Loo the Unicorn, and Rango the Gray Ape, the King's three Counselors, and in front of them stood the two strange beasts who had called themselves Li-Mon-Eags, but were really the transformations of Ruggedo the Nome, and Kiki Aru the Hyup.

Then came the beasts—rows and rows and rows of them! The smallest beasts were nearest the King's rock throne; then there were wolves and foxes, lynxes and hyenas, and the like; behind them were gathered the monkey tribes, who were hard to keep in order because they teased the other animals and were full of mischievous tricks. Back of the monkeys were the pumas, jaguars, tigers and lions, and their kind; next the bears, all sizes and colors; after them bisons, wild asses, zebras and unicorns; farther on the rhinoceri and hippopotami, and at the far edge of the forest, close to the trees that shut in the clearing, was a row of thick-skinned elephants, still as statues but with eyes bright and intelligent.

Many other kinds of beasts, too numerous to mention, were there, and some were unlike any beasts we see in the menageries and zoos in our country. Some were from the mountains west of the forest, and some from the plains at the east, and some from the river; but all present acknowledged the leadership of Gugu, who for many years had ruled them wisely and forced all to obey the laws.

When the beasts had taken their places in the clearing and the rising sun was shooting its first bright rays over the treetops, King Gugu rose on his throne. The Leopard's giant form, towering above all the others, caused a sudden hush to fall on the assemblage.

"Brothers," he said in his deep voice, "a stranger has come among us, a beast of curious form who is a great magician and is able to change the shapes of men or beasts at his will. This stranger has come to us, with another of his kind, from out of the sky, to warn us of a danger which threatens us all, and to offer us a way to escape from that danger. He says he is our friend, and he has proved to me and to my Counselors his magic powers. Will you listen to what he has to say to you—to the message he has brought from the sky?"

"Let him speak!" came in a great roar from the great company of assembled beasts.

So Ruggedo the Nome sprang upon the flat rock beside Gugu the King, and another roar, gentle this time, showed how astonished the beasts were at the sight of his curious form. His lion's face was surrounded by a mane of pure white hair; his eagle's wings were attached to the shoulders of his monkey body and were so long that they nearly touched the ground; he had powerful arms and legs in addition to the wings, and at the end of his long strong tail was a golden ball. Never had any beast beheld such a curious creature before, and so the very sight of the stranger who was said to be a great magician, filled all present with awe and wonder.

Kiki stayed down below and, half hidden by the shelf of rock, was scarcely noticed. The boy realized that the old Nome was helpless without his magic power, but he also realized that Ruggedo was the best talker. So he was willing the Nome should take the lead.

"Beasts of the Forest of Gugu," began Ruggedo the Nome, "my comrade and I are your friends. We are magicians, and from our home in the sky we can look down into the Land of Oz and see everything that is going on. Also we can hear what the people below us are saying. That is how we heard Ozma, who rules the Land of Oz, say to her people: 'The beasts in the Forest of Gugu are lazy and are of no use to us. Let us go to their forest and make them all our prisoners. Let us tie them with ropes, and beat them with sticks, until they work for us and become our willing slaves.' And when the people heard Ozma of Oz say this, they were glad and raised a great shout and said: 'We will do it! We will make the beasts of the Forest of Gugu our slaves!'"

The wicked old Nome could say no more, just then, for such a fierce roar of anger rose from the multitude of beasts that his voice was drowned by the clamor. Finally the roar died away, like distant thunder, and Ruggedo the Nome went on with his speech.

"Having heard the Oz people plot against your liberty, we watched to see what they would do, and saw them all begin making ropes—ropes long and short—with which to snare our friends the beasts. You are angry, but we also were angry, for when the Oz people became the enemies of the beasts they also became our enemies; for we, too, are beasts, although we live in the sky. And my comrade and I said: 'We will save our friends and have revenge on the Oz people,' and so we came here to tell you of your danger and of our plan to save you."

"We can save ourselves," cried an old Elephant. "We can fight."

"The Oz people are fairies, and you can't fight against magic unless you also have magic," answered the Nome.

"Tell us your plan!" shouted the huge Tiger, and the other beasts echoed his words, crying: "Tell us your plan."

"My plan is simple," replied Ruggedo. "By our magic we will transform all you animals into men and women—like the Oz people—and we will transform all the Oz people into beasts. You can then live in the fine houses of the Land of Oz, and eat the fine food of the Oz people, and wear their fine clothes, and sing and dance and be happy. And the Oz people, having become beasts, will have to live here in the forest and hunt and fight for food, and often go hungry, as you now do, and have no place to sleep but a bed of leaves or a hole in the ground. Having become men and women, you beasts will have all the comforts you desire, and having become beasts, the Oz people will be very miserable. That is our plan, and if you agree to it, we will all march at once into the Land of Oz and quickly conquer our enemies."

When the stranger ceased speaking, a great silence fell on the assemblage, for the beasts were thinking of what he had said. Finally one of the walruses asked: "Can you really transform beasts into men, and men into beasts?"

"He can—he can!" cried Loo the Unicorn, prancing up and down in an excited manner. "He transformed ME, only last evening, and he can transform us all."

Gugu the King now stepped forward.

"You have heard the stranger speak," said he, "and now you must answer him. It is for you to decide. Shall we agree to this plan, or not?"

"Yes!" shouted some of the animals.

"No!" shouted others.

And some were yet silent.

Gugu looked around the great circle.

"Take more time to think," he suggested. "Your answer is very important. Up to this time we have had no trouble with the Oz people, but we are proud and free, and never will become slaves. Think carefully, and when you are ready to answer, I will hear you."

12. Kiki Uses His Magic

Then arose a great confusion of sounds as all the animals began talking to their fellows. The monkeys chattered and the bears growled and the voices of the jaguars and lions rumbled, and the wolves yelped and the elephants had to trumpet loudly to make their voices heard. Such a hubbub had never been known in the forest before, and each beast argued with his neighbor until it seemed the noise would never cease.

Ruggedo the Nome waved his arms and fluttered his wings to try to make them listen to him again, but the beasts paid no attention. Some wanted to fight the Oz people, some wanted to be transformed, and some wanted to do nothing at all.

The growling and confusion had grown greater than ever when in a flash silence fell on all the beasts present, the arguments were hushed, and all gazed in astonishment at a strange sight.

For into the circle strode a great Lion—bigger and more powerful than any other lion there—and on his back rode a little girl who smiled fearlessly at the multitude of beasts. And behind the Lion and the little girl came another beast—a monstrous Tiger, who bore upon his back a funny little man carrying a black bag. Right past the rows of wondering beasts the strange animals walked, advancing until they stood just before the rock throne of Gugu.

Then the little girl and the funny little man dismounted, and the great Lion demanded in a loud voice: "Who is King in this forest?"

"I am!" answered Gugu, looking steadily at the other. "I am Gugu the Leopard, and I am King of this forest."

"Then I greet Your Majesty with great respect," said the Lion. "Perhaps you have heard of me, Gugu. I am called the 'Cowardly Lion,' and I am King of all Beasts, the world over."

Gugu's eyes flashed angrily.

"Yes," said he, "I have heard of you. You have long claimed to be King of Beasts, but no beast who is a coward can be King over me."

"He isn't a coward, Your Majesty," asserted the little girl, "He's just cowardly, that's all."

Gugu looked at her. All the other beasts were looking at her, too.

"Who are you?" asked the King.

"Me? Oh, I'm just Dorothy," she answered.

"How dare you come here?" demanded the King.

"Why, I'm not afraid to go anywhere, if the Cowardly Lion is with me," she said. "I know him pretty well, and so I can trust him. He's always afraid, when we get into trouble, and that's why he's cowardly; but he's a terrible fighter, and that's why he isn't a coward. He doesn't like to fight, you know, but when he HAS to, there isn't any beast living that can conquer him."

Gugu the King looked at the big, powerful form of the Cowardly Lion, and knew she spoke the truth. Also the other Lions of the forest now came forward and bowed low before the strange Lion.

"We welcome Your Majesty," said one. "We have known you many years ago, before you went to live at the Emerald City, and we have seen you fight the terrible Kalidahs and conquer them, so we know you are the King of all Beasts."

"It is true," replied the Cowardly Lion; "but I did not come here to rule the beasts of this forest. Gugu is King here, and I believe he is a good King and just and wise. I come, with my friends, to be the guest of Gugu, and I hope we are welcome."

That pleased the great Leopard, who said very quickly: "Yes; you, at least, are welcome to my forest. But who are these strangers with you?"

"Dorothy has introduced herself," replied the Lion, "and you are sure to like her when you know her better. This man is the Wizard of Oz, a friend of mine who can do wonderful tricks of magic. And here is my true and tried friend, the Hungry Tiger, who lives with me in the Emerald City."

"Is he ALWAYS hungry?" asked Loo the Unicorn.

"I am," replied the Tiger, answering the question himself. "I am always hungry for fat babies."

"Can't you find any fat babies in Oz to eat?" inquired Loo, the Unicorn.

"There are plenty of them, of course," said the Tiger, "but unfortunately I have such a tender conscience that it won't allow me to eat babies. So I'm always hungry for 'em and never can eat 'em, because my conscience won't let me."

Now of all the surprised beasts in that clearing, not one was so much surprised at the sudden appearance of these four strangers as Ruggedo the Nome. He was frightened, too, for he recognized them as his most powerful enemies; but he also realized that they could not know he was the former King of the Nomes, because of the beast's form he wore, which disguised him so effectually. So he took courage and resolved that the Wizard and Dorothy should not defeat his plans.

It was hard to tell, just yet, what the vast assemblage of beasts thought of the new arrivals. Some glared angrily at them, but more of them seemed to be curious and wondering. All were interested, however, and they kept very quiet and listened carefully to all that was said.

Kiki Aru, who had remained unnoticed in the shadow of the rock, was at first more alarmed by the coming of the strangers than even Ruggedo was, and the boy told himself that unless he acted quickly and without waiting to ask the advice of the old Nome, their conspiracy was likely to be discovered and all their plans to conquer and rule Oz be defeated. Kiki didn't like the way Ruggedo acted either, for the former King of the Nomes wanted to do everything his own way, and made the boy, who alone possessed the power of transformations, obey his orders as if he were a slave.

Another thing that disturbed Kiki Aru was the fact that a real Wizard had arrived, who was said to possess many magical powers, and this Wizard carried his tools in a black bag, and was the friend of the Oz people, and so would probably try to prevent war between the beasts of the forest and the people of Oz.

All these things passed through the mind of the Hyup boy while the Cowardly Lion and Gugu the King were talking together, and that was why he now began to do several strange things.

He had found a place, near to the point where he stood, where there was a deep hollow in the rock, so he put his face into this hollow and whispered softly, so he would not be heard: "I want the Wizard of Oz to become a fox—Pyrzqxgl!"

The Wizard, who had stood smilingly beside his friends, suddenly felt his form change to that of a fox, and his black bag fell to the ground. Kiki reached out an arm and seized the bag, and the Fox cried as loud as it could: "Treason! There's a traitor here with magic powers!"

Everyone was startled at this cry, and Dorothy, seeing her old friend's plight, screamed and exclaimed: "Mercy me!"

But the next instant the little girl's form had changed to that of a lamb with fleecy white wool, and Dorothy was too bewildered to do anything but look around her in wonder.

The Cowardly Lion's eyes now flashed fire; he crouched low and lashed the ground with his tail and gazed around to discover who the treacherous magician might be. But Kiki, who had kept his face in the hollow rock, again whispered the magic word, and the great lion disappeared and in his place stood a little boy dressed in Munchkin costume. The little Munchkin boy was as angry as the lion had been, but he was small and helpless.

Ruggedo the Nome saw what was happening and was afraid Kiki would spoil all his plans, so he leaned over the rock and shouted: "Stop, Kiki—stop!"

Kiki would not stop, however. Instead, he transformed the Nome into a goose, to Ruggedo's horror and dismay. But the Hungry Tiger had witnessed all these transformations, and he was watching to see which of those present was to blame for them. When Ruggedo spoke to Kiki, the Hungry Tiger knew that he was the magician, so he made a sudden spring and hurled his great body full upon the form of the Li-Mon-Eag crouching against the rock. Kiki didn't see the Tiger coming because his face was still in the hollow, and the heavy body of the tiger bore him to the earth just as he said "Pyrzqxgl!" for the fifth time.

So now the tiger which was crushing him changed to a rabbit, and relieved of its weight, Kiki sprang up and, spreading his eagle's wings, flew into the branches of a tree, where no beast could easily reach him. He was not an instant too quick in doing this, for Gugu the King had crouched on the rock's edge and was about to spring on the boy.

From his tree Kiki transformed Gugu into a fat Gillikin woman, and laughed aloud to see how the woman pranced with rage, and how astonished all the beasts were at their King's new shape.

The beasts were frightened, too, fearing they would share the fate of Gugu, so a stampede began when Rango the Gray Ape sprang into the forest, and Bru the Bear and Loo the Unicorn followed as quickly as they could. The elephants backed into the forest, and all the other animals, big and little, rushed after them, scattering through the jungles until the clearing was far behind. The monkeys scrambled into the trees and swung themselves from limb to limb, to avoid being trampled upon by the bigger beasts, and they were so quick that they distanced all the rest. A panic of fear seemed to have overtaken the forest people and they got as far away from the terrible Magician as they possibly could.

But the transformed ones stayed in the clearing, being so astonished and bewildered by their new shapes that they could only look at one another in a dazed and helpless fashion, although each one was greatly annoyed at the trick that had been played on him.

"Who are you?" the Munchkin boy asked the Rabbit; and "Who are you?" the Fox asked the Lamb; and "Who are you?" the Rabbit asked the fat Gillikin woman.

"I'm Dorothy," said the woolly Lamb.

"I'm the Wizard," said the Fox.

"I'm the Cowardly Lion," said the Munchkin boy.

"I'm the Hungry Tiger," said the Rabbit.

"I'm Gugu the King," said the fat Woman.

But when they asked the Goose who he was, Ruggedo the Nome would not tell them.

"I'm just a Goose," he replied, "and what I was before, I cannot remember."

3. The Loss of the Black Bag

Kiki Aru, in the form of the Li-Mon-Eag, had scrambled into the high, thick branches of the tree, so no one could see him, and there he opened the Wizard's black bag, which he had carried away in his flight. He was curious to see what the Wizard's magic tools looked like, and hoped he could use some of them and so secure more power; but after he had taken the articles, one by one, from the bag, he had to admit they were puzzles to him. For, unless he understood their uses, they were of no value whatever. Kiki Aru, the Hyup boy, was no wizard or magician at all, and could do nothing unusual except to use the Magic Word he had stolen from his father on Mount Munch. So he hung the Wizard's black bag on a branch of the tree and then climbed down to the lower limbs that he might see what the victims of his transformations were doing.

They were all on top of the flat rock, talking together in tones so low that Kiki could not hear what they said.

"This is certainly a misfortune," remarked the Wizard in the Fox's form, "but our transformations are a sort of enchantment which is very easy to break—when you know how and have the tools to do it with. The tools are in my Black Bag; but where is the Bag?"

No one knew that, for none had seen Kiki Aru fly away with it.

"Let's look and see if we can find it," suggested Dorothy the Lamb.

So they left the rock, and all of them searched the clearning high and low without finding the Bag of Magic Tools. The Goose searched as earnestly as the others, for if he could discover it, he meant to hide it where the Wizard could never find it, because if the Wizard changed him back to his proper form, along with the others, he would then be recognized as Ruggedo the Nome, and they would send him out of the Land of Oz and so ruin all his hopes of conquest.

Ruggedo was not really sorry, now that he thought about it, that Kiki had transformed all these Oz folks. The forest beasts, it was true, had been so frightened that they would now never consent to be transformed into men, but Kiki could transform them against their will, and once they were all in human forms, it would not be impossible to induce them to conquer the Oz people.

So all was not lost, thought the old Nome, and the best thing for him to do was to rejoin the Hyup boy who had the secret of the transformations. So, having made sure the Wizard's black bag was not in the clearing, the Goose wandered away through the trees when the others were not looking, and when out of their hearing, he began calling, "Kiki Aru! Kiki Aru! Quack—quack! Kiki Aru!"

The Boy and the Woman, the Fox, the Lamb, and the Rabbit, not being able to find the bag, went back to the rock, all feeling exceedingly strange.

"Where's the Goose?" asked the Wizard.

"He must have run away," replied Dorothy. "I wonder who he was?"

"I think," said Gugu the King, who was the fat Woman, "that the Goose was the stranger who proposed that we make war upon the Oz people. If so, his transformation was merely a trick to deceive us, and he has now gone to join his comrade, that wicked Li-Mon-Eag who obeyed all his commands."

"What shall we do now?" asked Dorothy. "Shall we go back to the Emerald City, as we are, and then visit Glinda the Good and ask her to break the enchantments?"

"I think so," replied the Wizard Fox. "And we can take Gugu the King with us, and have Glinda restore him to his natural shape. But I hate to leave my Bag of Magic Tools behind me, for without it I shall lose much of my power as a Wizard. Also, if I go back to the Emerald City in the shape of a Fox, the Oz people will think I'm a poor Wizard and will lose their respect for me."

"Let us make still another search for your tools," suggested the Cowardly Lion, "and then, if we fail to find the Black Bag anywhere in this forest, we must go back home as we are."

"Why did you come here, anyway?" inquired Gugu.

"We wanted to borrow a dozen monkeys, to use on Ozma's birthday," explained the Wizard. "We were going to make them small, and train them to do tricks, and put them inside Ozma's birthday cake."

"Well," said the Forest King, "you would have to get the consent of Rango the Gray Ape, to do that. He commands all the tribes of monkeys."

"I'm afraid it's too late, now," said Dorothy, regretfully. "It was a splendid plan, but we've got troubles of our own, and I don't like being a lamb at all."

"You're nice and fuzzy," said the Cowardly Lion.

"That's nothing," declared Dorothy. "I've never been 'specially proud of myself, but I'd rather be the way I was born than anything else in the whole world."

* * * * *

The Glass Cat, although it had some disagreeable ways and manners, nevertheless realized that Trot and Cap'n Bill were its friends and so was quite disturbed at the fix it had gotten them into by leading them to the Isle of the Magic Flower. The ruby heart of the Glass Cat was cold and hard, but still it was a heart, and to have a heart of any sort is to have some consideration for others. But the queer transparent creature didn't want Trot and Cap'n Bill to know it was sorry for them, and therefore it moved very slowly until it had crossed the river and was out of sight among the trees of the forest. Then it headed straight toward the Emerald City, and trotted so fast that it was like a crystal streak crossing the valleys and plains. Being glass, the cat was tireless, and with no reason to delay its journey, it reached Ozma's palace in wonderfully quick time.

"Where's the Wizard?" it asked the Pink Kitten, which was curled up in the sunshine on the lowest step of the palace entrance.

"Don't bother me," lazily answered the Pink Kitten, whose name was Eureka.

"I must find the Wizard at once!" said the Glass Cat.

"Then find him," advised Eureka, and went to sleep again.

The Glass Cat darted up the stairway and came upon Toto, Dorothy's little black dog.

"Where's the Wizard?" asked the Cat.

"Gone on a journey with Dorothy," replied Toto.

"When did they go, and where have they gone?" demanded the Cat.

"They went yesterday, and I heard them say they would go to the Great Forest in the Munchkin Country."

"Dear me," said the Glass Cat; "that is a long journey."

"But they rode on the Hungry Tiger and the Cowardly Lion," explained Toto, "and the Wizard carried his Black Bag of Magic Tools."

The Glass Cat knew the Great Forest of Gugu well, for it had traveled through this forest many times in its journeys through the Land of Oz. And it reflected that the Forest of Gugu was nearer to the Isle of the Magic Flower than the Emerald City was, and so, if it could manage to find the Wizard, it could lead him across the Gillikin Country to where Trot and Cap'n Bill were prisoned. It was a wild country and little traveled, but the Glass Cat knew every path. So very little time need be lost, after all.

Without stopping to ask any more questions the Cat darted out of the palace and away from the Emerald City, taking the most direct route to the Forest of Gugu. Again the creature flashed through the country like a streak of light, and it would surprise you to know how quickly it reached the edge of the Great Forest.

There were no monkey guards among the trees to cry out a warning, and this was so unusual that it astonished the Glass Cat. Going farther into the forest it presently came upon a wolf, which at first bounded away in terror. But then, seeing it was only a Glass Cat, the Wolf stopped, and the Cat could see it was trembling, as if from a terrible fright.

"What's the matter?" asked the Cat.

"A dreadful Magician has come among us!" exclaimed the Wolf "and he's changing the forms of all the beasts—quick as a wink—and making them all his slaves."

The Glass Cat smiled and said: "Why, that's only the Wizard o Oz. He may be having some fun with you forest people, but the Wizard wouldn't hurt a beast for anything."

"I don't mean the Wizard," explained the Wolf. "And if the Wizard of Oz is that funny little man who rode a great Tiger into the clearing, he's been transformed himself by the terrible Magician."

"The Wizard transformed? Why, that's impossible," declared the Glass Cat.

"No; it isn't. I saw him with my own eyes, changed into the form of a Fox, and the girl who was with him was changed to a woolly Lamb."

The Glass Cat was indeed surprised.

"When did that happen?" it asked.

"Just a little while ago in the clearing. All the animals had me there, but they ran away when the Magician began hi transformations, and I'm thankful I escaped with my natura shape. But I'm still afraid, and I'm going somewhere to hide."

With this the Wolf ran on, and the Glass Cat, which knew where the big clearing was, went toward it. But now it walked mor slowly, and its pink brains rolled and tumbled around at a grea rate because it was thinking over the amazing news the Wolf had told it.

When the Glass Cat reached the clearing, it saw a Fox, a Lamb, Rabbit, a Munchkin boy and a fat Gillikin woman, all wanderin around in an aimless sort of way, for they were again searchin for the Black Bag of Magic Tools.

The Cat watched them a moment and then it walked slowly int the open space. At once the Lamb ran toward it, crying: "Oh Wizard, here's the Glass Cat!"

"Where, Dorothy?" asked the Fox.

"Here!"

The Boy and the Woman and the Rabbit now joined the Fox an the Lamb, and they all stood before the Glass Cat and speakin together, almost like a chorus, asked: "Have you seen the Blac Bag?"

"Often," replied the Glass Cat, "but not lately."

"It's lost," said the Fox, "and we must find it."

"Are you the Wizard?" asked the Cat.

"Yes."

"And who are these others?"

"I'm Dorothy," said the Lamb.

"I'm the Cowardly Lion," said the Munchkin boy.

"I'm the Hungry Tiger," said the Rabbit.

"I'm Gugu, King of the Forest," said the fat Woman.

The Glass Cat sat on its hind legs and began to laugh. "My, what a funny lot!" exclaimed the Creature. "Who played this joke on you?"

"It's no joke at all," declared the Wizard. "It was a cruel, wicked transformation, and the Magician that did it has the head of a lion, the body of a monkey, the wings of an eagle and a round ball on the end of his tail."

The Glass Cat laughed again. "That Magician must look funnier than you do," it said. "Where is he now?"

"Somewhere in the forest," said the Cowardly Lion. "He just jumped into that tall maple tree over there, for he can climb like a monkey and fly like an eagle, and then he disappeared in the forest."

"And there was another Magician, just like him, who was his friend," added Dorothy, "but they probably quarreled, for the wickedest one changed his friend into the form of a Goose."

"What became of the Goose?" asked the Cat, looking around.

"He must have gone away to find his friend," answered Gugu the King. "But a Goose can't travel very fast, so we could easily find him if we wanted to."

"The worst thing of all," said the Wizard, "is that my Black Bag is lost. It disappeared when I was transformed. If I could find it I could easily break these enchantments by means of my magic, and we would resume our own forms again. Will you help us search for the Black Bag, Friend Cat?"

"Of course," replied the Glass Cat. "But I expect the strange Magician carried it away with him. If he's a magician, he knows you need that Bag, and perhaps he's afraid of your magic. So he's probably taken the Bag with him, and you won't see it again unless you find the Magician."

"That sounds reasonable," remarked the Lamb, which was Dorothy. "Those pink brains of yours seem to be working pretty well to-day."

"If the Glass Cat is right," said the Wizard in a solemn voice, "there's more trouble ahead of us. That Magician is dangerous, and if we go near him he may transform us into shapes not as nice as these."

"I don't see how we could be any WORSE off," growled Gugu, who was indignant because he was forced to appear in the form of a fat woman.

"Anyway," said the Cowardly Lion, "our best plan is to find the Magician and try to get the Black Bag from him. We may manage to steal it, or perhaps we can argue him into giving it to us."

"Why not find the Goose, first?" asked Dorothy. "The Goose will be angry at the Magician, and he may be able to help us."

"That isn't a bad idea," returned the Wizard. "Come on, Friends; let's find that Goose. We will separate and search in different directions, and the first to find the Goose must bring him here, where we will all meet again in an hour."

14. The Wizard Learns the Magic Word

Now, the Goose was the transformation of old Ruggedo, who was at one time King of the Nomes, and he was even more angry at Kiki Aru than were the others who shapes had been changed. The Nome detested anything in the way of a bird, because birds lay eggs and eggs are feared by all the Nomes more than anything else in the world. A goose is a foolish bird, too, and Ruggedo was dreadfully ashamed of the shape he was forced to wear. And it would make him shudder to reflect that the Goose might lay an egg!

So the Nome was afraid of himself and afraid of everything around him. If an egg touched him he could then be destroyed, and almost any animal he met in the forest might easily conquer him. And that would be the end of old Ruggedo the Nome.

Aside from these fears, however, he was filled with anger against Kiki, whom he had meant to trap by cleverly stealing from him the Magic Word. The boy must have been crazy to spoil everything the way he did, but Ruggedo knew that the arrival of the Wizard had scared Kiki, and he was not sorry the boy had transformed the Wizard and Dorothy and made them helpless. It was his own transformation that annoyed him and made him indignant, so he ran about the forest hunting for Kiki, so that he might get a better shape and coax the boy to follow his plans to conquer the Land of Oz.

Kiki Aru hadn't gone very far away, for he had surprised himself as well as the others by the quick transformations and was puzzled as to what to do next. Ruggedo the Nome was overbearing and tricky, and Kiki knew he was not to be depended on; but the Nome could plan and plot, which the Hyup boy was not wise enough to do, and so, when he looked down through the branches of a tree and saw a Goose waddling along below and heard it cry, "Kiki Aru! Quack—quack! Kiki Aru!" the boy answered in a low voice, "Here I am," and swung himself down to the lowest limb of the tree.

The Goose looked up and saw him.

"You've bungled things in a dreadful way!" exclaimed the Goose. "Why did you do it?"

"Because I wanted to," answered Kiki. "You acted as if I was your slave, and I wanted to show these forest people that I am more powerful than you."

The Goose hissed softly, but Kiki did not hear that.

Old Ruggedo quickly recovered his wits and muttered to himself: "This boy is the goose, although it is I who wear the goose's shape. I will be gentle with him now, and fierce with him when I have him in my power."

Then he said aloud to Kiki: "Well, hereafter I will be content to acknowledge you the master. You bungled things, as I said, but we can still conquer Oz."

"How?" asked the boy.

"First give me back the shape of the Li-Mon-Eag, and then we can talk together more conveniently," suggested the Nome.

"Wait a moment, then," said Kiki, and climbed higher up the tree. There he whispered the Magic Word and the Goose became a Li-Mon-Eag, as he had been before.

"Good!" said the Nome, well pleased, as Kiki joined him by dropping down from the tree. "Now let us find a quiet place where we can talk without being overheard by the beasts."

So the two started away and crossed the forest until they came to a place where the trees were not so tall nor so close together, and among these scattered trees was another clearing, not so large as the first one, where the meeting of the beasts had been held. Standing on the edge of this clearing and looking across it, they saw the trees on the farther side full of monkeys, who were chattering together at a great rate of the sights they had witnessed at the meeting.

The old Nome whispered to Kiki not to enter the clearing or allow the monkeys to see them.

"Why not?" asked the boy, drawing back.

"Because those monkeys are to be our army—the army which will conquer Oz," said the Nome. "Sit down here with me, Kiki, and keep quiet, and I will explain to you my plan."

Now, neither Kiki Aru nor Ruggedo had noticed that a sly Fox had followed them all the way from the tree where the Goose had been transformed to the Li-Mon-Eag. Indeed, this Fox, who was none other than the Wizard of Oz, had witnessed the transformation of the Goose and now decided he would keep watch on the conspirators and see what they would do next.

A Fox can move through a forest very softly, without making any noise, and so the Wizard's enemies did not suspect his presence. But when they sat down by the edge of the clearing, to talk, with their backs toward him, the Wizard did not know whether to risk being seen, by creeping closer to hear what they said, or whether it would be better for him to hide himself until they moved on again.

While he considered this question he discovered near him a great tree which had a hollow trunk, and there was a round hole in this tree, about three feet above the ground. The Wizard Fox decided it would be safer for him to hide inside the hollow tree, so he sprang into the hole and crouched down in the hollow, so that his eyes just came to the edge of the hole by which he had entered, and from here he watched the forms of the two Li-Mon-Eags.

"This is my plan," said the Nome to Kiki, speaking so low that the Wizard could only hear the rumble of his voice. "Since you can transform anything into any form you wish, we will transform these monkeys into an army, and with that army we will conquer the Oz people."

"The monkeys won't make much of an army," objected Kiki.

"We need a great army, but not a numerous one," responded the Nome. "You will transform each monkey into a giant man, dressed in a fine uniform and armed with a sharp sword. There are fifty monkeys over there and fifty giants would make as big an army as we need."

"What will they do with the swords?" asked Kiki. "Nothing can kill the Oz people."

"True," said Ruggedo. "The Oz people cannot be killed, but they can be cut into small pieces, and while every piece will still be alive, we can scatter the pieces around so that they will be quite helpless. Therefore, the Oz people will be afraid of the swords of our army, and we will conquer them with ease."

"That seems like a good idea," replied the boy, approvingly. "And in such a case, we need not bother with the other beasts of the forest."

"No; you have frightened the beasts, and they would no longer consent to assist us in conquering Oz. But those monkeys are foolish creatures, and once they are transformed to Giants, they will do just as we say and obey our commands. Can you transform them all at once?"

"No, I must take one at a time," said Kiki. "But the fifty transformations can be made in an hour or so. Stay here, Ruggedo, and I will change the first monkey—that one at the left, on the end of the limb—into a Giant with a sword."

"Where are you going?" asked the Nome.

"I must not speak the Magic Word in the presence of another person," declared Kiki, who was determined not to allow his treacherous companion to learn his secret, "so I will go where you cannot hear me."

Ruggedo the Nome was disappointed, but he hoped still to catch the boy unawares and surprise the Magic Word. So he merely nodded his lion head, and Kiki got up and went back into the forest a short distance. Here he spied a hollow tree, and by chance it was the same hollow tree in which the Wizard of Oz, now in the form of a Fox, had hidden himself.

As Kiki ran up to the tree the Fox ducked its head, so that it was out of sight in the dark hollow beneath the hole, and then Kiki put his face into the hole and whispered: "I want that monkey on the branch at the left to become a Giant man fifty feet tall, dressed in a uniform and with a sharp sword—Pyrzqxgl!"

Then he ran back to Ruggedo, but the Wizard Fox had heard quite plainly every word that he had said.

The monkey was instantly transformed into the Giant, and the Giant was so big that as he stood on the ground his head was higher than the trees of the forest. The monkeys raised a great chatter but did not seem to understand that the Giant was one of themselves.

"Good!" cried the Nome. "Hurry, Kiki, and transform the others."

So Kiki rushed back to the tree and putting his face to the hollow, whispered: "I want the next monkey to be just like the first—Pyrzqxgl!"

Again the Wizard Fox heard the Magic Word, and just how it was pronounced. But he sat still in the hollow and waited to hear it again, so it would be impressed on his mind and he would not forget it.

Kiki kept running to the edge of the forest and back to the hollow tree again until he had whispered the Magic Word six times and six monkeys had been changed to six great Giants. Then the Wizard decided he would make an experiment and use the Magic Word himself. So, while Kiki was running back to the Nome, the Fox stuck his head out of the hollow and said softly: "I want that creature who is running to become a hickory-nut—Pyrzqxgl!"

Instantly the Li-Mon-Eag form of Kiki Aru the Hyup disappeared and a small hickory-nut rolled upon the ground a moment and then lay still.

The Wizard was delighted, and leaped from the hollow just as Ruggedo looked around to see what had become of Kiki. The Nome saw the Fox but no Kiki, so he hastily rose to his feet. The Wizard did not know how powerful the queer beast might be, so he resolved to take no chances.

"I want this creature to become a walnut—Pyrzqxgl!" he said aloud. But he did not pronounce the Magic Word in quite the right way, and Ruggedo's form did not change. But the Nome knew at once that "Pyrzqxgl!" was the Magic Word, so he rushed at the Fox and cried: "I want you to become a Goose—Pyrzqxgl!"

But the Nome did not pronounce the word aright, either, having never heard it spoken but once before, and then with a wrong accent. So the Fox was not transformed, but it had to run away to escape being caught by the angry Nome.

Ruggedo now began pronouncing the Magic Word in every way he could think of, hoping to hit the right one, and the Fox, hiding in a bush, was somewhat troubled by the fear that he might succeed. However, the Wizard, who was used to magic arts, remained calm and soon remembered exactly how Kiki Aru had pronounced the word. So he repeated the sentence he had before uttered and Ruggedo the Nome became an ordinary walnut.

The Wizard now crept out from the bush and said: "I want my own form again—Pyrzqxgl!"

Instantly he was the Wizard of Oz, and after picking up the hickory-nut and the walnut, and carefully placing them in his pocket, he ran back to the big clearing.

Dorothy the Lamb uttered a bleat of delight when she saw her old friend restored to his natural shape. The others were all here, not having found the Goose. The fat Gillikin woman, the Munchkin boy, the Rabbit and the Glass Cat crowded around the Wizard and asked what had happened.

Before he explained anything of his adventure, he transformed them all—except, of course, the Glass Cat—into their natural shapes, and when their joy permitted them to quiet somewhat, he told how he had by chance surprised the Magician's secret and been able to change the two Li-Mon-Eags into shapes that could not speak, and therefore would be unable to help themselves. And the little Wizard showed his astonished friends the hickory-nut and the walnut to prove that he had spoken the truth.

"But—see here!"—exclaimed Dorothy. "What has become of those Giant Soldiers who used to be monkeys?"

"I forgot all about them!" admitted the Wizard; "but I suppose they are still standing there in the forest."

5. The Lonesome Duck

Trot and Cap'n Bill stood before the Magic Flower, actually rooted to the spot.

"Aren't you hungry, Cap'n?" asked the little girl, with a long sigh, for she had been standing there for hours and hours.

"Well," replied the sailor-man, "I ain't sayin' as I couldn't EAT, Trot—if a dinner was handy—but I guess old folks don't get as hungry as young folks do."

"I'm not sure 'bout that, Cap'n Bill," she said thoughtfully. "Age MIGHT make a diff'rence, but seems to me SIZE would make a bigger diff'rence. Seeing you're twice as big as me, you ought to be twice as hungry."

"I hope I am," he rejoined, "for I can stand it a while longer. I do hope the Glass Cat will hurry, and I hope the Wizard won't waste time a-comin' to us."

Trot sighed again and watched the wonderful Magic Flower, because there was nothing else to do. Just now a lovely group of pink peonies budded and bloomed, but soon they faded away, and a mass of deep blue lilies took their place. Then some yellow chrysanthemums blossomed on the plant, and when they had opened all their petals and reached perfection, they gave way to a lot of white floral balls spotted with crimson—a flower Trot had never seen before.

"But I get awful tired watchin' flowers an' flowers an' flowers," she said impatiently.

"They're might pretty," observed Cap'n Bill.

"I know; and if a person could come and look at the Magic Flower just when she felt like it, it would be a fine thing, but to HAVE TO stand and watch it, whether you want to or not, isn't so much fun. I wish, Cap'n Bill, the thing would grow fruit for a while instead of flowers."

Scarcely had she spoken when the white balls with crimson spots faded away and a lot of beautiful ripe peaches took their place. With a cry of mingled surprise and delight Trot reached out and plucked a peach from the bush and began to eat it, finding it delicious. Cap'n Bill was somewhat dazed at the girl's wish being granted so quickly, so before he could pick a peach they had faded away and bananas took their place. "Grab one, Cap'n!" exclaimed Trot, and even while eating the peach she seized a banana with her other hand and tore it from the bush.

The old sailor was still bewildered. He put out a hand indeed, but he was too late, for now the bananas disappeared and lemons took their place.

"Pshaw!" cried Trot. "You can't eat those things; but watch out, Cap'n, for something else."

Coconuts next appeared, but Cap'n Bill shook his head.

"Ca'n't crack 'em," he remarked, "'cause we haven't anything handy to smash 'em with."

"Well, take one, anyhow," advised Trot; but the coconuts were gone now, and a deep, purple, pear-shaped fruit which was unknown to them took their place.

Again Cap'n Bill hesitated, and Trot said to him: "You ought to have captured a peach and a banana, as I did. If you're not careful, Cap'n, you'll miss all your chances. Here, I'll divide my banana with you."

Even as she spoke, the Magic Plant was covered with big red apples, growing on every branch, and Cap'n Bill hesitated no longer. He grabbed with both hands and picked two apples, while Trot had only time to secure one before they were gone.

"It's curious," remarked the sailor, munching his apple, "how these fruits keep good when you've picked 'em, but dis'pear inter thin air if they're left on the bush."

"The whole thing is curious," declared the girl, "and it couldn't exist in any country but this, where magic is so common. Those are limes. Don't pick 'em, for they'd pucker up your mouth and—Ooo! here come plums!" and she tucked her apple in her apron pocket and captured three plums—each one almost as big as an egg—before they disappeared. Cap'n Bill got some too, but both were too hungry to fast any longer, so they began eating their apples and plums and let the magic bush bear all sorts of fruits, one after another. The Cap'n stopped once to pick a fine cantaloupe, which he held under his arm, and Trot, having finished her plums, got a handful of cherries and an orange; but when almost every sort of fruit had appeared on the bush, the crop ceased and only flowers, as before, bloomed upon it.

"I wonder why it changed back," mused Trot, who was not worried because she had enough fruit to satisfy her hunger.

"Well, you only wished it would bear fruit 'for a while,'" said the sailor, "and it did. P'raps if you'd said 'forever,' Trot, it would have always been fruit."

"But why should MY wish be obeyed?" asked the girl. "I'm not a fairy or a wizard or any kind of a magic-maker."

"I guess," replied Cap'n Bill, "that this little island is a magic island, and any folks on it can tell the bush what to produce, an' it'll produce it."

"Do you think I could wish for anything else, Cap'n and get it?" she inquired anxiously.

"What are you thinkin' of, Trot?"

"I'm thinking of wishing that these roots on our feet would disappear, and let us free."

"Try it, Trot."

So she tried it, and the wish had no effect whatever.

"Try it yourself, Cap'n," she suggested.

Then Cap'n Bill made the wish to be free, with no better result.

"No," said he, "it's no use; the wishes only affect the Magic Plant; but I'm glad we can make it bear fruit, 'cause now we know we won't starve before the Wizard gets to us."

"But I'm gett'n' tired standing here so long," complained the girl. "If I could only lift one foot, and rest it, I'd feel better."

"Same with me, Trot. I've noticed that if you've got to do a thing, and can't help yourself, it gets to be a hardship mighty quick."

"Folks that can raise their feet don't appreciate what a blessing it is," said Trot thoughtfully. "I never knew before what fun it is to raise one foot, an' then another, any time you feel like it."

"There's lots o' things folks don't 'preciate," replied the sailor-man. "If somethin' would 'most stop your breath, you'd think breathin' easy was the finest thing in life. When a person's well, he don't realize how jolly it is, but when he gets sick he 'members the time he was well, an' wishes that time would come back. Most folks forget to thank God for givin' 'em two good legs, till they lose one o' 'em, like I did; and then it's too late, 'cept to praise God for leavin' one."

"Your wooden leg ain't so bad, Cap'n," she remarked, looking at

it critically. "Anyhow, it don't take root on a Magic Island, like our meat legs do."

"I ain't complainin'," said Cap'n Bill. "What's that swimmin towards us, Trot?" he added, looking over the Magic Flower and across the water.

The girl looked, too, and then she replied.

"It's a bird of some sort. It's like a duck, only I never saw a duck have so many colors."

The bird swam swiftly and gracefully toward the Magic Isle, and as it drew nearer its gorgeously colored plumage astonished them. The feathers were of many hues of glistening greens and blues and purples, and it had a yellow head with a red plume and pink, white and violet in its tail. When it reached the Isle, i came ashore and approached them, waddling slowly and turning its head first to one side and then to the other, so as to see the girl and the sailor better.

"You're strangers," said the bird, coming to a halt near them "and you've been caught by the Magic Isle and made prisoners."

"Yes," returned Trot, with a sigh; "we're rooted. But I hope w won't grow."

"You'll grow small," said the Bird. "You'll keep growing smalle every day, until bye and bye there'll be nothing left of you. That' the usual way, on this Magic Isle."

"How do you know about it, and who are you, anyhow?" asked Cap'n Bill.

"I'm the Lonesome Duck," replied the bird. "I suppose you'v heard of me?"

"No," said Trot, "I can't say I have. What makes you lonesome?"

"Why, I haven't any family or any relations," returned the Duck.

"Haven't you any friends?"

"Not a friend. And I've nothing to do. I've lived a long time, an I've got to live forever, because I belong in the Land of Oz, wher no living thing dies. Think of existing year after year, with n friends, no family, and nothing to do! Can you wonder I'r lonesome?"

"Why don't you make a few friends, and find something to do? inquired Cap'n Bill.

"I can't make friends because everyone I meet—bird, beast, o person—is disagreeable to me. In a few minutes I shall be unabl to bear your society longer, and then I'll go away and leave you, said the Lonesome Duck. "And, as for doing anything, there's n use in it. All I meet are doing something, so I have decided it' common and uninteresting and I prefer to remain lonesome."

"Don't you have to hunt for your food?" asked Trot.

"No. In my diamond palace, a little way up the river, food i magically supplied me; but I seldom eat, because it is s common."

"You must be a Magician Duck," remarked Cap'n Bill.

"Why so?"

"Well, ordinary ducks don't have diamond palaces an' magic food, like you do."

"True; and that's another reason why I'm lonesome. You must remember I'm the only Duck in the Land of Oz, and I'm not like any other duck in the outside world."

"Seems to me you LIKE bein' lonesome," observed Cap'n Bill.

"I can't say I like it, exactly," replied the Duck, "but since it seems to be my fate, I'm rather proud of it."

"How do you s'pose a single, solitary Duck happened to be in the Land of Oz?" asked Trot, wonderingly.

"I used to know the reason, many years ago, but I've quite forgotten it," declared the Duck. "The reason for a thing is never so important as the thing itself, so there's no use remembering anything but the fact that I'm lonesome."

"I guess you'd be happier if you tried to do something," asserted Trot. "If you can't do anything for yourself, you can do things for others, and then you'd get lots of friends and stop being lonesome."

"Now you're getting disagreeable," said the Lonesome Duck, "and I shall have to go and leave you."

"Can't you help us any," pleaded the girl. "If there's anything magic about you, you might get us out of this scrape."

"I haven't any magic strong enough to get you off the Magic Isle," replied the Lonesome Duck. "What magic I possess is very simple, but I find it enough for my own needs."

"If we could only sit down a while, we could stand it better," said Trot, "but we have nothing to sit on."

"Then you will have to stand it," said the Lonesome Duck.

"P'raps you've enough magic to give us a couple of stools," suggested Cap'n Bill.

"A duck isn't supposed to know what stools are," was the reply.

"But you're diff'rent from all other ducks."

"That is true." The strange creature seemed to reflect for a moment, looking at them sharply from its round black eyes. Then it said: "Sometimes, when the sun is hot, I grow a toadstool to shelter me from its rays. Perhaps you could sit on toadstools."

"Well, if they were strong enough, they'd do," answered Cap'n Bill.

"Then, before I do I'll give you a couple," said the Lonesome Duck, and began waddling about in a small circle. It went around the circle to the right three times, and then it went around to the left three times. Then it hopped backward three times and forward three times.

"What are you doing?" asked Trot.

"Don't interrupt. This is an incantation," replied the Lonesome Duck, but now it began making a succession of soft noises that sounded like quacks and seemed to mean nothing at all. And it kept up these sounds so long that Trot finally exclaimed: "Can't you hurry up and finish that 'cantation? If it takes all summer to make a couple of toadstools, you're not much of a magician."

"I told you not to interrupt," said the Lonesome Duck, sternly. "If you get TOO disagreeable, you'll drive me away before I finish this incantation."

Trot kept quiet, after the rebuke, and the Duck resumed the quacky muttering. Cap'n Bill chuckled a little to himself and remarked to Trot in a whisper: "For a bird that ain't got anything to do, this Lonesome Duck is makin' consider'ble fuss. An' I ain't sure, after all, as toadstools would be worth sittin' on."

Even as he spoke, the sailor-man felt something touch him from behind and, turning his head, he found a big toadstool in just the right place and of just the right size to sit upon. There was one behind Trot, too, and with a cry of pleasure the little girl sank back upon it and found it a very comfortable seat—solid, yet almost like a cushion. Even Cap'n Bill's weight did not break his toadstool down, and when both were seated, they found that the Lonesome Duck had waddled away and was now at the water's edge.

"Thank you, ever so much!" cried Trot, and the sailor called out: "Much obliged!"

But the Lonesome Duck paid no attention. Without even looking in their direction again, the gaudy fowl entered the water and swam gracefully away.

16. The Glass Cat Finds the Black Bag

When the six monkeys were transformed by Kiki Aru into six giant soldiers fifty feet tall, their heads came above the top of the trees, which in this part of the forest were not so high as in some other parts; and, although the trees were somewhat scattered, the bodies of the giant soldiers were so big that they quite filled the spaces in which they stood and the branches pressed them on every side.

Of course, Kiki was foolish to have made his soldiers so big, for now they could not get out of the forest. Indeed, they could not stir a step, but were imprisoned by the trees. Even had they been in the little clearing they could not have made their way out of it, but they were a little beyond the clearing. At first, the other monkeys who had not been enchanted were afraid of the soldiers, and hastily quitted the place; but soon finding that the great men stood stock still, although grunting indignantly at their transformation, the band of monkeys returned to the spot and looked at them curiously, not guessing that they were really monkeys and their own friends.

The soldiers couldn't see them, their heads being above the trees; they could not even raise their arms or draw their sharp swords, so closely were they held by the leafy branches. So the monkeys, finding the giants helpless, began climbing up their bodies, and presently all the band were perched on the shoulders of the giants and peering into their faces.

"I'm Ebu, your father," cried one soldier to a monkey who had perched upon his left ear, "but some cruel person has enchanted me."

"I'm your Uncle Peeker," said another soldier to another monkey.

So, very soon all the monkeys knew the truth and were sorry for their friends and relations and angry at the person—whoever it was—who had transformed them. There was a great chattering among the tree-tops, and the noise attracted other monkeys, so that the clearing and all the trees around were full of them.

Rango the Gray Ape, who was the Chief of all the monkey tribes of the forest, heard the uproar and came to see what was wrong with his people. And Rango, being wiser and more experienced, at once knew that the strange magician who looked like a mixed-up beast was responsible for the transformations. He realized that the six giant soldiers were helpless prisoners, because of their size, and knew he was powerless to release them. So, although he feared to meet the terrible magician, he hurried away to the Great Clearing to tell Gugu the King what had happened and to try to find the Wizard of Oz and get him to save his six enchanted subjects.

Rango darted into the Great Clearing just as the Wizard had restored all the enchanted ones around him to their proper shapes, and the Gray Ape was glad to hear that the wicked magician-beast had been conquered.

"But now, O mighty Wizard, you must come with me to where six of my people are transformed into six great giant men," he said, "for if they are allowed to remain there, their happiness and their future lives will be ruined."

The Wizard did not reply at once, for he was thinking this a good opportunity to win Rango's consent to his taking some monkeys to the Emerald City for Ozma's birthday cake.

"It is a great thing you ask of me, O Rango the Gray Ape," said he, "for the bigger the giants are the more powerful their enchantment, and the more difficult it will be to restore them to their natural forms. However, I will think it over."

Then the Wizard went to another part of the clearing and sat on a log and appeared to be in deep thought.

The Glass Cat had been greatly interested in the Gray Ape's story and was curious to see what the giant soldiers looked like. Hearing that their heads extended above the tree-tops, the Glass Cat decided that if it climbed the tall avocado tree that stood at the side of the clearing, it might be able to see the giants' heads. So, without mentioning her errand, the crystal creature went to the tree and, by sticking her sharp glass claws in the bark, easily climbed the tree to its very top and, looking over the forest, saw the six giant heads, although they were now a long way off. It was, indeed, a remarkable sight, for the huge heads had immense soldier caps on them, with red and yellow plumes and looked very fierce and terrible, although the monkey hearts of the giants were at that moment filled with fear.

Having satisfied her curiosity, the Glass Cat began to climb down from the tree more slowly. Suddenly she discerned the Wizard's black bag hanging from a limb of the tree. She grasped the black bag in her glass teeth, and although it was rather heavy for so small an animal, managed to get it free and to carry it safely down to the ground. Then she looked around for the Wizard and seeing him seated upon the stump she hid the black bag among some leaves and then went over to where the Wizard sat.

"I forgot to tell you," said the Glass Cat, "that Trot and Cap'n Bill are in trouble, and I came here to hunt you up and get you to go and rescue them."

"Good gracious, Cat! Why didn't you tell me before?" exclaimed the Wizard.

"For the reason that I found so much excitement here that I forgot Trot and Cap'n Bill."

"What's wrong with them?" asked the Wizard.

Then the Glass Cat explained how they had gone to get the Magic Flower for Ozma's birthday gift and had been trapped by the magic of the queer island. The Wizard was really alarmed, but he shook his head and said sadly: "I'm afraid I can't help my dear friends, because I've lost my black bag."

"If I find it, will you go to them?" asked the creature.

"Of course," replied the Wizard. "But I do not think that a Glass Cat with nothing but pink brains can succeed when all the rest of us have failed."

"Don't you admire my pink brains?" demanded the Cat.

"They're pretty," admitted the Wizard, "but they're not regular brains, you know, and so we don't expect them to amount to much."

"But if I find your black bag—and find it inside of five minutes—will you admit my pink brains are better than your common human brains?"

"Well, I'll admit they're better HUNTERS," said the Wizard, reluctantly, "but you can't do it. We've searched everywhere, and the black bag isn't to be found."

"That shows how much you know!" retorted the Glass Cat, scornfully. "Watch my brains a minute, and see them whirl around."

The Wizard watched, for he was anxious to regain his black bag, and the pink brains really did whirl around in a remarkable manner.

"Now, come with me," commanded the Glass Cat, and led the Wizard straight to the spot where it had covered the bag with leaves. "According to my brains," said the creature, "your black bag ought to be here."

Then it scratched at the leaves and uncovered the bag, which the Wizard promptly seized with a cry of delight. Now that he had regained his Magic Tools, he felt confident he could rescue Trot and Cap'n Bill.

Rango the Gray Ape was getting impatient. He now approached the Wizard and said: "Well, what do you intend to do about those poor enchanted monkeys?"

"I'll make a bargain with you, Rango," replied the little man. "If you will let me take a dozen of your monkeys to the Emerald City, and keep them until after Ozma's birthday, I'll break the enchantment of the six Giant Soldiers and return them to their natural forms."

But the Gray Ape shook his head.

"I can't do it," he declared. "The monkeys would be very lonesome and unhappy in the Emerald City and your people would tease them and throw stones at them, which would cause them to fight and bite."

"The people won't see them till Ozma's birthday dinner," promised the Wizard. "I'll make them very small—about four inches high, and I'll keep them in a pretty cage in my own room, where they will be safe from harm. I'll feed them the nicest kind of food, train them to do some clever tricks, and on Ozma's birthday I'll hide the twelve little monkeys inside a cake. When Ozma cuts the cake the monkeys will jump out on to the table and do their tricks. The next day I will bring them back to the forest and make them big as ever, and they'll have some exciting stories to tell their friends. What do you say, Rango?"

"I say no!" answered the Gray Ape. "I won't have my monkeys enchanted and made to do tricks for the Oz people."

"Very well," said the Wizard calmly; "then I'll go. Come, Dorothy," he called to the little girl, "let's start on our journey."

"Aren't you going to save those six monkeys who are giant soldiers?" asked Rango, anxiously.

"Why should I?" returned the Wizard. "If you will not do me the favor I ask, you cannot expect me to favor you."

"Wait a minute," said the Gray Ape. "I've changed my mind. If you will treat the twelve monkeys nicely and bring them safely back to the forest, I'll let you take them."

"Thank you," replied the Wizard, cheerfully. "We'll go at once and save those giant soldiers."

So all the party left the clearing and proceeded to the place where the giants still stood among the trees. Hundreds of monkeys, apes, baboons and orangoutangs had gathered round, and their wild chatter could be heard a mile away. But the Gray Ape soon hushed the babel of sounds, and the Wizard lost no time in breaking the enchantments. First one and then another giant soldier disappeared and became an ordinary monkey again, and the six were shortly returned to their friends in their proper forms.

This action made the Wizard very popular with the great army of monkeys, and when the Gray Ape announced that the Wizard wanted to borrow twelve monkeys to take to the Emerald City for a couple of weeks, and asked for volunteers, nearly a hundred offered to go, so great was their confidence in the little man who had saved their comrades.

The Wizard selected a dozen that seemed intelligent and good-tempered, and then he opened his black bag and took out a queerly shaped dish that was silver on the outside and gold on the inside. Into this dish he poured a powder and set fire to it. It made a thick smoke that quite enveloped the twelve monkeys, as well as the form of the Wizard, but when the smoke cleared away the dish had been changed to a golden cage with silver bars, and the twelve monkeys had become about three inches high and were all seated comfortably inside the cage.

The thousands of hairy animals who had witnessed this act of magic were much astonished and applauded the Wizard by barking aloud and shaking the limbs of the trees in which they sat. Dorothy said: "That was a fine trick, Wizard!" and the Gray Ape remarked: "You are certainly the most wonderful magician in all the Land of Oz!"

"Oh, no," modestly replied the little man. "Glinda's magic is better than mine, but mine seems good enough to use on ordinary occasions. And now, Rango, we will say good-bye, and I promise to return your monkeys as happy and safe as they are now."

The Wizard rode on the back of the Hungry Tiger and carried the cage of monkeys very carefully, so as not to joggle them. Dorothy rode on the back of the Cowardly Lion, and the Glass Cat trotted, as before, to show them the way.

Gugu the King crouched upon a log and watched them go, but as he bade them farewell, the enormous Leopard said: "I know now that you are the friends of beasts and that the forest people may trust you. Whenever the Wizard of Oz and Princess Dorothy enter the Forest of Gugu hearafter, they will be as welcome and as safe with us as ever they are in the Emerald City."

17. A Remarkable Journey

"You see," explained the Glass Cat, "that Magic Isle where Trot and Cap'n Bill are stuck is also in this Gillikin Country—over at the east side of it, and it's no farther to go across-lots from here than it is from here to the Emerald City. So we'll save time by cutting across the mountains."

"Are you sure you know the way?" asked Dorothy.

"I know all the Land of Oz better than any other living creature knows it," asserted the Glass Cat.

"Go ahead, then, and guide us," said the Wizard. "We've left our poor friends helpless too long already, and the sooner we rescue them the happier they'll be."

"Are you sure you can get 'em out of their fix?" the little girl inquired.

"I've no doubt of it," the Wizard assured her. "But I can't tell what sort of magic I must use until I get to the place and discover just how they are enchanted."

"I've heard of that Magic Isle where the Wonderful Flower grows," remarked the Cowardly Lion. "Long ago, when I used to live in the forests, the beasts told stories about the Isle and how the Magic Flower was placed there to entrap strangers—men or beasts."

"Is the Flower really wonderful?" questioned Dorothy.

"I have heard it is the most beautiful plant in the world," answered the Lion. "I have never seen it myself, but friendly beasts have told me that they have stood on the shore of the river and looked across at the plant in the gold flower-pot and seen hundreds of flowers, of all sorts and sizes, blossom upon it in quick succession. It is said that if one picks the flowers while they are in bloom they will remain perfect for a long time, but if they are not picked they soon disappear and are replaced by other flowers. That, in my opinion, make the Magic Plant the most wonderful in existence."

"But these are only stories," said the girl. "Has any of your friends ever picked a flower from the wonderful plant?"

"No," admitted the Cowardly Lion, "for if any living thing ventures upon the Magic Isle, where the golden flower-pot stands, that man or beast takes root in the soil and cannot get away again."

"What happens to them, then?" asked Dorothy.

"They grow smaller, hour by hour and day by day, and finally disappear entirely."

"Then," said the girl anxiously, "we must hurry up, or Cap'n Bill an' Trot will get too small to be comf'table."

They were proceeding at a rapid pace during this conversation, for the Hungry Tiger and the Cowardly Lion were obliged to move swiftly in order to keep pace with the Glass Cat. After leaving the Forest of Gugu they crossed a mountain range, and then a broad plain, after which they reached another forest, much smaller than that where Gugu ruled.

"The Magic Isle is in this forest," said the Glass Cat, "but the river is at the other side of the forest. There is no path through the trees, but if we keep going east, we will find the river, and then it will be easy to find the Magic Isle."

"Have you ever traveled this way before?" inquired the Wizard.

"Not exactly," admitted the Cat, "but I know we shall reach the river if we go east through the forest."

"Lead on, then," said the Wizard.

The Glass Cat started away, and at first it was easy to pass between the trees; but before long the underbrush and vines became thick and tangled, and after pushing their way through these obstacles for a time, our travelers came to a place where even the Glass Cat could not push through.

"We'd better go back and find a path," suggested the Hungry Tiger.

"I'm s'prised at you," said Dorothy, eyeing the Glass Cat severely.

"I'm surprised, myself," replied the Cat. "But it's a long way around the forest to where the river enters it, and I thought we could save time by going straight through."

"No one can blame you," said the Wizard, "and I think, instead of turning back, I can make a path that will allow us to proceed."

He opened his black bag and after searching among his magic tools drew out a small axe, made of some metal so highly polished that it glittered brightly even in the dark forest. The Wizard laid the little axe on the ground and said in a commanding voice:
"Chop, Little Axe, chop clean and true;
A path for our feet you must quickly hew.
Chop till this tangle of jungle is passed;
Chop to the east, Little Axe — chop fast!"

Then the little axe began to move and flashed its bright blade right and left, clearing a way through vine and brush and scattering the tangled barrier so quickly that the Lion and the Tiger, carrying Dorothy and the Wizard and the cage of monkeys on their backs, were able to stride through the forest at a fast walk. The brush seemed to melt away before them and the little axe chopped so fast that their eyes only saw a twinkling of the blade. Then, suddenly, the forest was open again, and the little axe, having obeyed its orders, lay still upon the ground.

The Wizard picked up the magic axe and after carefully wiping it with his silk handkerchief put it away in his black bag. Then they went on and in a short time reached the river.

"Let me see," said the Glass Cat, looking up and down the stream, "I think we are below the Magic Isle; so we must go up the stream until we come to it."

So up the stream they traveled, walking comfortably on the river bank, and after a while the water broadened and a sharp bend appeared in the river, hiding all below from their view. They walked briskly along, however, and had nearly reached the bend when a voice cried warningly: "Look out!"

The travelers halted abruptly and the Wizard said: "Look out for what?"

"You almost stepped on my Diamond Palace," replied the voice, and a duck with gorgeously colored feathers appeared before them. "Beasts and men are terribly clumsy," continued the Duck in an irritated tone, "and you've no business on this side of the River, anyway. What are you doing here?"

"We've come to rescue some friends of ours who are stuck fast on the Magic Isle in this river," explained Dorothy.

"I know 'em," said the Duck. "I've been to see 'em, and they're stuck fast, all right. You may as well go back home, for no power can save them."

"This is the Wonderful Wizard of Oz," said Dorothy, pointing to the little man.

"Well, I'm the Lonesome Duck," was the reply, as the fowl strutted up and down to show its feathers to best advantage. "I'm the great Forest Magician, as any beast can tell you, but even I have no power to destroy the dreadful charm of the Magic Isle."

"Are you lonesome because you're a magician?" inquired Dorothy.

"No; I'm lonesome because I have no family and no friends. But I like to be lonesome, so please don't offer to be friendly with me. Go away, and try not to step on my Diamond Palace."

"Where is it?" asked the girl.

"Behind this bush."

Dorothy hopped off the lion's back and ran around the bush to see the Diamond Palace of the Lonesome Duck, although the gaudy fowl protested in a series of low quacks. The girl found, indeed, a glistening dome formed of clearest diamonds, neatly cemented together, with a doorway at the side just big enough to admit the duck.

"Where did you find so many diamonds?" asked Dorothy wonderingly.

"I know a place in the mountains where they are thick as pebbles," said the Lonesome Duck, "and I brought them here in my bill, one by one and put them in the river and let the water run over them until they were brightly polished. Then I built this palace, and I'm positive it's the only Diamond Palace in all the world."

"It's the only one I know of," said the little girl; "but if you live in it all alone, I don't see why it's any better than a wooden palace or one of bricks or cobble-stones."

"You're not supposed to understand that," retorted the Lonesome Duck. "But I might tell you, as a matter of education, that a home of any sort should be beautiful to those who live in it, and should not be intended to please strangers. The Diamond Palace is my home, and I like it. So I don't care a quack whether YOU like it or not."

"Oh, but I do!" exclaimed Dorothy. "It's lovely on the outside, but—" Then she stopped speaking, for the Lonesome Duck had entered his palace through the little door without even saying good-bye. So Dorothy returned to her friends and they resumed their journey.

"Do you think, Wizard, the Duck was right in saying no magic can rescue Trot and Cap'n Bill?" asked the girl in a worried tone of voice.

"No, I don't think the Lonesome Duck was right in saying that," answered the Wizard, gravely, "but it is possible that their enchantment will be harder to overcome than I expected. I'll do my best, of course, and no one can do more than his best."

That didn't entirely relieve Dorothy's anxiety, but she said nothing more, and soon, on turning the bend in the river, they came in sight of the Magic Isle.

"There they are!" exclaimed Dorothy eagerly.

"Yes, I see them," replied the Wizard, nodding. "They are sitting on two big toadstools."

"That's queer," remarked the Glass Cat. "There were no toadstools there when I left them."

"What a lovely flower!" cried Dorothy in rapture, as her gaze fell on the Magic Plant.

"Never mind the Flower, just now," advised the Wizard. "The most important thing is to rescue our friends."

By this time they had arrived at a place just opposite the Magic Isle, and now both Trot and Cap'n Bill saw the arrival of their friends and called to them for help.

"How are you?" shouted the Wizard, putting his hands to his mouth so they could hear him better across the water.

"We're in hard luck," shouted Cap'n Bill, in reply. "We're anchored here and can't move till you find a way to cut the hawser."

"What does he mean by that?" asked Dorothy.

"We can't move our feet a bit!" called Trot, speaking as loud as she could.

"Why not?" inquired Dorothy.

"They've got roots on 'em," explained Trot.

It was hard to talk from so great a distance, so the Wizard said to the Glass Cat: "Go to the island and tell our friends to be patient, for we have come to save them. It may take a little time to release them, for the Magic of the Isle is new to me and I shall have to experiment. But tell them I'll hurry as fast as I can."

So the Glass Cat walked across the river under the water to tell Trot and Cap'n Bill not to worry, and the Wizard at once opened his black bag and began to make his preparations.

18. The Magic of the Wizard

He first set up a small silver tripod and placed a gold basin at the top of it. Into this basin he put two powders—a pink one and a sky-blue one—and poured over them a yellow liquid from a crystal vial. Then he mumbled some magic words, and the powders began to sizzle and burn and send out a cloud of violet smoke that floated across the river and completely enveloped both Trot and Cap'n Bill, as well as the toadstools on which they sat, and even the Magic Plant in the gold flower-pot. Then, after the smoke had disappeared into air, the Wizard called out to the prisoners:

"Are you free?"

Both Trot and Cap'n Bill tried to move their feet and failed.

"No!" they shouted in answer.

The Wizard rubbed his bald head thoughtfully and then took some other magic tools from the bag.

First he placed a little black ball in a silver pistol and shot it toward the Magic Isle. The ball exploded just over the head of Trot and scattered a thousand sparks over the little girl.

"Oh!" said the Wizard, "I guess that will set her free."

But Trot's feet were still rooted in the ground of the Magic Isle, and the disappointed Wizard had to try something else.

For almost an hour he worked hard, using almost every magic tool in his black bag, and still Cap'n Bill and Trot were not rescued.

"Dear me!" exclaimed Dorothy, "I'm 'fraid we'll have to go to Glinda, after all."

That made the little Wizard blush, for it shamed him to think that his magic was not equal to that of the Magic Isle.

"I won't give up yet, Dorothy," he said, "for I know a lot of wizardry that I haven't yet tried. I don't know what magician enchanted this little island, or what his powers were, but I DO know that I can break any enchantment known to the ordinary witches and magicians that used to inhabit the Land of Oz. It's like unlocking a door; all you need is to find the right key."

"But 'spose you haven't the right key with you." suggested Dorothy; "what then?"

"Then we'll have to make the key," he answered.

The Glass Cat now came back to their side of the river, walking under the water, and said to the Wizard: "They're getting frightened over there on the island because they're both growing smaller every minute. Just now, when I left them, both Trot and Cap'n Bill were only about half their natural sizes."

"I think," said the Wizard reflectively, "that I'd better go to the shore of the island, where I can talk to them and work to better advantage. How did Trot and Cap'n Bill get to the island?"

"On a raft," answered the Glass Cat. "It's over there now on the beach."

"I suppose you're not strong enough to bring the raft to this side, are you?"

"No; I couldn't move it an inch," said the Cat.

"I'll try to get it for you," volunteered the Cowardly Lion. "I'm dreadfully scared for fear the Magic Isle will capture me, too; but I'll try to get the raft and bring it to this side for you."

"Thank you, my friend," said the Wizard.

So the Lion plunged into the river and swam with powerful strokes across to where the raft was beached upon the island. Placing one paw on the raft, he turned and struck out with his other three legs and so strong was the great beast that he managed to drag the raft from off the beach and propel it slowly to where the Wizard stood on the river bank.

"Good!" exclaimed the little man, well pleased.

"May I go across with you?" asked Dorothy.

The Wizard hesitated.

"If you'll take care not to leave the raft or step foot on the island, you'll be quite safe," he decided. So the Wizard told the Hungry Tiger and the Cowardly Lion to guard the cage of monkeys until he returned, and then he and Dorothy got upon the raft. The paddle which Cap'n Bill had made was still there, so the little Wizard paddled the clumsy raft across the water and ran it upon the beach of the Magic Isle as close to the place where Cap'n Bill and Trot were rooted as he could.

Dorothy was shocked to see how small the prisoners had become, and Trot said to her friends: "If you can't save us soon, there'll be nothing left of us."

"Be patient, my dear," counseled the Wizard, and took the little axe from his black bag.

"What are you going to do with that?" asked Cap'n Bill.

"It's a magic axe," replied the Wizard, "and when I tell it to chop, it will chop those roots from your feet and you can run to the raft before they grow again."

"Don't!" shouted the sailor in alarm. "Don't do it! Those roots are all flesh roots, and our bodies are feeding 'em while they're growing into the ground."

"To cut off the roots," said Trot, "would be like cutting off our fingers and toes."

The Wizard put the little axe back in the black bag and took out a pair of silver pincers.

"Grow—grow—grow!" he said to the pincers, and at once they grew and extended until they reached from the raft to the prisoners.

"What are you going to do now?" demanded Cap'n Bill, fearfully eyeing the pincers.

"This magic tool will pull you up, roots and all, and land you on this raft," declared the Wizard.

"Don't do it!" pleaded the sailor, with a shudder. "It would hurt us awfully."

"It would be just like pulling teeth to pull us up by the roots," explained Trot.

"Grow small!" said the Wizard to the pincers, and at once they became small and he threw them into the black bag.

"I guess, friends, it's all up with us, this time," remarked Cap'n Bill, with a dismal sigh.

"Please tell Ozma, Dorothy," said Trot, "that we got into trouble trying to get her a nice birthday present. Then she'll forgive us. The Magic Flower is lovely and wonderful, but it's just a lure to catch folks on this dreadful island and then destroy them. You'll have a nice birthday party, without us, I'm sure; and I hope, Dorothy, that none of you in the Emerald City will forget me—or dear ol' Cap'n Bill."

19. Dorothy and the Bumble Bees

Dorothy was greatly distressed and had hard work to keep the tears from her eyes.

"Is that all you can do, Wizard?" she asked the little man.

"It's all I can think of just now," he replied sadly. "But I intend to keep on thinking as long—as long—well, as long as thinking will do any good."

They were all silent for a time, Dorothy and the Wizard sitting thoughtfully on the raft, and Trot and Cap'n Bill sitting thoughtfully on the toadstools and growing gradually smaller and smaller in size.

Suddenly Dorothy said: "Wizard, I've thought of something!"

"What have you thought of?" he asked, looking at the little girl with interest.

"Can you remember the Magic Word that transforms people?" she asked.

"Of course," said he.

"Then you can transform Trot and Cap'n Bill into birds or bumblebees, and they can fly away to the other shore. When they're there, you can transform 'em into their reg'lar shapes again!"

"Can you do that, Wizard?" asked Cap'n Bill, eagerly.

"I think so."

"Roots an' all?" inquired Trot.

"Why, the roots are now a part of you, and if you were transformed to a bumblebee the whole of you would be transformed, of course, and you'd be free of this awful island."

"All right; do it!" cried the sailor-man.

So the Wizard said slowly and distinctly: "I want Trot and Cap'n Bill to become bumblebees—Pyrzqxgl!"

Fortunately, he pronounced the Magic Word in the right way, and instantly Trot and Cap'n Bill vanished from view, and up from the places where they had been flew two bumblebees.

"Hooray!" shouted Dorothy in delight; "they're saved!"

"I guess they are," agreed the Wizard, equally delighted.

The bees hovered over the raft an instant and then flew across the river to where the Lion and the Tiger waited. The Wizard picked up the paddle and paddled the raft across as fast as he could. When it reached the river bank, both Dorothy and the Wizard leaped ashore and the little man asked excitedly: "Where are the bees?"

"The bees?" inquired the Lion, who was half asleep and did not know what had happened on the Magic Isle.

"Yes; there were two of them."

"Two bees?" said the Hungry Tiger, yawning. "Why, I ate one of them and the Cowardly Lion ate the other."

"Goodness gracious!" cried Dorothy horrified.

"It was little enough for our lunch," remarked the Tiger, "but the bees were the only things we could find."

"How dreadful!" wailed Dorothy, wringing her hands in despair. "You've eaten Trot and Cap'n Bill."

But just then she heard a buzzing overhead and two bees alighted on her shoulder.

"Here we are," said a small voice in her ear. "I'm Trot, Dorothy."

"And I'm Cap'n Bill," said the other bee.

Dorothy almost fainted, with relief, and the Wizard, who was close by and had heard the tiny voices, gave a laugh and said: "You are not the only two bees in the forest, it seems, but I advise you to keep away from the Lion and the Tiger until you regain your proper forms."

"Do it now, Wizard!" advised Dorothy. "They're so small that you never can tell what might happen to 'em."

So the Wizard gave the command and pronounced the Magic Word, and in the instant Trot and Cap'n Bill stood beside them as natural as before they had met their fearful adventure. For they were no longer small in size, because the Wizard had transformed them from bumblebees into the shapes and sizes that nature had formerly given them. The ugly roots on their feet had disappeared with the transformation.

While Dorothy was hugging Trot, and Trot was softly crying because she was so happy, the Wizard shook hands with Cap'n Bill and congratulated him on his escape. The old sailor-man was so pleased that he also shook the Lion's paw and took off his hat and bowed politely to the cage of monkeys.

Then Cap'n Bill did a curious thing. He went to a big tree and, taking out his knife, cut away a big, broad piece of thick bark. Then he sat down on the ground and after taking a roll of stout cord from his pocket—which seemed to be full of all sorts of things—he proceeded to bind the flat piece of bark to the bottom of his good foot, over the leather sole.

"What's that for?" inquired the Wizard.

"I hate to be stumped," replied the sailor-man; "so I'm goin' back to that island."

"And get enchanted again?" exclaimed Trot, with evident disapproval.

"No; this time I'll dodge the magic of the island. I noticed that my wooden leg didn't get stuck, or take root, an' neither did the glass feet of the Glass Cat. It's only a thing that's made of meat—like man an' beasts—that the magic can hold an' root to the ground. Our shoes are leather, an' leather comes from a beast's hide. Our stockin's are wool, an' wool comes from a sheep's back. So, when we walked on the Magic Isle, our feet took root there an' held us fast. But not my wooden leg. So now I'll put a wooden bottom on my other foot an' the magic can't stop me."

"But why do you wish to go back to the island?" asked Dorothy.

"Didn't you see the Magic Flower in the gold flower-pot?" returned Cap'n Bill.

"Of course I saw it, and it's lovely and wonderful."

"Well, Trot an' I set out to get the magic plant for a present to Ozma on her birthday, and I mean to get it an' take it back with us to the Emerald City."

"That would be fine," cried Trot eagerly, "if you think you can do it, and it would be safe to try!"

"I'm pretty sure it is safe, the way I've fixed my foot," said the sailor, "an' if I SHOULD happen to get caught, I s'pose the Wizard could save me again."

"I suppose I could," agreed the Wizard. "Anyhow, if you wish to try it, Cap'n Bill, go ahead and we'll stand by and watch what happens."

So the sailor-man got upon the raft again and paddled over to the Magic Isle, landing as close to the golden flower-pot as he could. They watched him walk across the land, put both arms around the flower-pot and lift it easily from its place. Then he carried it to the raft and set it down very gently. The removal did not seem to affect the Magic Flower in any way, for it was growing daffodils when Cap'n Bill picked it up and on the way to the raft it grew tulips and gladioli. During the time the sailor was paddling across the river to where his friends awaited him, seven different varieties of flowers bloomed in succession on the plant.

"I guess the Magician who put it on the island never thought that any one would carry it off," said Dorothy.

"He figured that only men would want the plant, and any man who went upon the island to get it would be caught by the enchantment," added the Wizard.

"After this," remarked Trot, "no one will care to go on the island, so it won't be a trap any more."

"There," exclaimed Cap'n Bill, setting down the Magic Plant in triumph upon the river bank, "if Ozma gets a better birthday present than that, I'd like to know what it can be!"

"It'll s'prise her, all right," declared Dorothy, standing in awed wonder before the gorgeous blossoms and watching them change from yellow roses to violets.

"It'll s'prise ev'rybody in the Em'rald City," Trot asserted in glee, "and it'll be Ozma's present from Cap'n Bill and me."

"I think I ought to have a little credit," objected the Glass Cat. "I discovered the thing, and led you to it, and brought the Wizard here to save you when you got caught."

"That's true," admitted Trot, "and I'll tell Ozma the whole story, so she'll know how good you've been."

20. The Monkeys Have Trouble

"Now," said the Wizard, "we must start for home. But how are we going to carry that big gold flower-pot? Cap'n Bill can't lug it all the way, that's certain."

"No," acknowledged the sailor-man; "it's pretty heavy. I could carry it for a little while, but I'd have to stop to rest every few minutes."

"Couldn't we put it on your back?" Dorothy asked the Cowardly Lion, with a good-natured yawn.

"I don't object to carrying it, if you can fasten it on," answered the Lion.

"If it falls off," said Trot, "it might get smashed an' be ruined."

"I'll fix it," promised Cap'n Bill. "I'll make a flat board out of one of these tree trunks, an' tie the board on the lion's back, an' set the flower-pot on the board." He set to work at once to do this, but as he only had his big knife for a tool his progress was slow.

So the Wizard took from his black bag a tiny saw that shone like silver and said to it:
"Saw, Little Saw, come show your power;
Make us a board for the Magic Flower."

And at once the Little Saw began to move and it sawed the log so fast that those who watched it work were astonished. It seemed to understand, too, just what the board was to be used for, for when it was completed it was flat on top and hollowed beneath in such a manner that it exactly fitted the Lion's back.

"That beats whittlin'!" exclaimed Cap'n Bill, admiringly. "You don't happen to have TWO o' them saws; do you, Wizard?"

"No," replied the Wizard, wiping the Magic Saw carefully with his silk handkerchief and putting it back in the black bag. "It's the only saw of its kind in the world; and if there were more like it, it wouldn't be so wonderful."

They now tied the board on the Lion's back, flat side up, and Cap'n Bill carefully placed the Magic Flower on the board.

"For fear o' accidents," he said, "I'll walk beside the Lion and hold onto the flower-pot."

Trot and Dorothy could both ride on the back of the Hungry Tiger, and between them they carried the cage of monkeys. But this arrangement left the Wizard, as well as the sailor, to make the journey on foot, and so the procession moved slowly and the Glass Cat grumbled because it would take so long to get to the Emerald City.

The Cat was sour-tempered and grumpy, at first, but before they had journeyed far, the crystal creature had discovered a fine amusement. The long tails of the monkeys were constantly sticking through the bars of their cage, and when they did, the Glass Cat would slyly seize the tails in her paws and pull them. That made the monkeys scream, and their screams pleased the Glass Cat immensely. Trot and Dorothy tried to stop this naughty amusement, but when they were not looking the Cat would pull the tails again, and the creature was so sly and quick that the monkeys could seldom escape. They scolded the Cat angrily and shook the bars of their cage, but they could not get out and the Cat only laughed at them.

After the party had left the forest and were on the plains of the Munchkin Country, it grew dark, and they were obliged to make camp for the night, choosing a pretty place beside a brook. By means of his magic the Wizard created three tents, pitched in a row on the grass and nicely fitted with all that was needful for the comfort of his comrades. The middle tent was for Dorothy and Trot, and had in it two cosy white beds and two chairs. Another tent, also with beds and chairs, was for the Wizard and Cap'n Bill, while the third tent was for the Hungry Tiger, the Cowardly Lion, the cage of Monkeys and the Glass Cat. Outside the tents the Wizard made a fire and placed over it a magic kettle from which he presently drew all sorts of nice things for their supper, smoking hot.

After they had eaten and talked together for a while under the twinkling stars, they all went to bed and the people were soon asleep. The Lion and the Tiger had almost fallen asleep, too, when they were roused by the screams of the monkeys, for the Glass Cat was pulling their tails again. Annoyed by the uproar, the Hungry Tiger cried: "Stop that racket!" and getting sight of the Glass Cat, he raised his big paw and struck at the creature. The cat was quick enough to dodge the blow, but the claws of the Hungry Tiger scraped the monkey's cage and bent two of the bars.

Then the Tiger lay down again to sleep, but the monkeys soon discovered that the bending of the bars would allow them to squeeze through. They did not leave the cage, however, but after whispering together they let their tails stick out and all remained quiet. Presently the Glass Cat stole near the cage again and gave a yank to one of the tails. Instantly the monkeys leaped through the bars, one after another, and although they were so small the entire dozen of them surrounded the Glass Cat and clung to her claws and tail and ears and made her a prisoner. Then they forced her out of the tent and down to the banks of the stream. The monkeys had noticed that these banks were covered with thick, slimy mud of a dark blue color, and when they had taken the Cat to the stream, they smeared this mud all over the glass body of the cat, filling the creature's ears and eyes with it, so that she could neither see nor hear. She was no longer transparent and so thick was the mud upon her that no one could see her pink brains or her ruby heart.

In this condition they led the pussy back to the tent and then got inside their cage again.

By morning the mud had dried hard on the Glass Cat and it was a dull blue color throughout. Dorothy and Trot were horrified, but the Wizard shook his head and said it served the Glass Cat right for teasing the monkeys.

Cap'n Bill, with his strong hands, soon bent the golden wires of the monkeys' cage into the proper position and then he asked the Wizard if he should wash the Glass Cat in the water of the brook.

"Not just yet," answered the Wizard. "The Cat deserves to be punished, so I think I'll leave that blue mud—which is as bad a paint—upon her body until she gets to the Emerald City. The silly creature is so vain that she will be greatly shamed when the Oz people see her in this condition, and perhaps she'll take the lesson to heart and leave the monkeys alone hereafter."

However, the Glass Cat could not see or hear, and to avoid carrying her on the journey the Wizard picked the mud out of her eyes and ears and Dorothy dampened her handkerchief and washed both the eyes and ears clean.

As soon as she could speak the Glass Cat asked indignantly: "Aren't you going to punish those monkeys for playing such a trick on me?"

"No," answered the Wizard. "You played a trick on them by pulling their tails, so this is only tit-for-tat, and I'm glad the monkeys had their revenge."

He wouldn't allow the Glass Cat to go near the water, to wash herself, but made her follow them when they resumed their journey toward the Emerald City.

"This is only part of your punishment," said the Wizard, severely. "Ozma will laugh at you, when we get to her palace, and so will the Scarecrow, and the Tin Woodman, and Tik-Tok, and the Shaggy Man, and Button-Bright, and the Patchwork Girl, and—"

"And the Pink Kitten," added Dorothy.

That suggestion hurt the Glass Cat more than anything else. The Pink Kitten always quarreled with the Glass Cat and insisted that flesh was superior to glass, while the Glass Cat would jeer at the Pink Kitten, because it had no pink brains. But the pink brains were all daubed with blue mud, just now, and if the Pink Kitten should see the Glass Cat in such a condition, it would be dreadfully humiliating.

For several hours the Glass Cat walked along very meekly, but toward noon it seized an opportunity when no one was looking and darted away through the long grass. It remembered that there was a tiny lake of pure water near by, and to this lake the Cat sped as fast as it could go.

The others never missed her until they stopped for lunch, and then it was too late to hunt for her.

"I s'pect she's gone somewhere to clean herself," said Dorothy.

"Never mind," replied the Wizard. "Perhaps this glass creature has been punished enough, and we must not forget she saved both Trot and Cap'n Bill."

"After first leading 'em onto an enchanted island," added Dorothy. "But I think, as you do, that the Glass Cat is punished enough, and p'raps she won't try to pull the monkeys' tails again."

The Glass Cat did not rejoin the party of travelers. She was still resentful, and they moved too slowly to suit her, besides. When they arrived at the Royal Palace, one of the first things they saw was the Glass Cat curled up on a bench as bright and clean and transparent as ever. But she pretended not to notice them, and they passed her by without remark.

21. The College of Athletic Arts

Dorothy and her friends arrived at the Royal Palace at an opportune time, for Ozma was holding high court in her Throne Room, where Professor H. M. Wogglebug, T.E., was appealing to her to punish some of the students of the Royal Athletic College, of which he was the Principal.

This College is located in the Munchkin Country, but not far from the Emerald City. To enable the students to devote their entire time to athletic exercises, such as boating, football, and the like, Professor Wogglebug had invented an assortment of Tablets of Learning. One of these tablets, eaten by a scholar after breakfast, would instantly enable him to understand arithmetic or algebra or any other branch of mathematics. Another tablet eaten after lunch gave a student a complete knowledge of geography. Another tablet made it possible for the eater to spell the most difficult words, and still another enabled him to write a beautiful hand. There were tablets for history, mechanics, home cooking and agriculture, and it mattered not whether a boy or a girl was stupid or bright, for the tablets taught them everything in the twinkling of an eye.

This method, which is patented in the Land of Oz by Professor Wogglebug, saves paper and books, as well as the tedious hours devoted to study in some of our less favored schools, and it also allows the students to devote all their time to racing, baseball, tennis and other manly and womanly sports, which are greatly interfered with by study in those Temples of Learning where Tablets of Learning are unknown.

But it so happened that Professor Wogglebug (who had invented so much that he had acquired the habit) carelessly invented a Square-Meal Tablet, which was no bigger than your little finger-nail but contained, in condensed form, the equal of a bowl of soup, a portion of fried fish, a roast, a salad and a dessert, all of which gave the same nourishment as a square meal.

The Professor was so proud of these Square-Meal Tablets that he began to feed them to the students at his college, instead of other food, but the boys and girls objected because they wanted food that they could enjoy the taste of. It was no fun at all to swallow a tablet, with a glass of water, and call it a dinner; so they refused to eat the Square-Meal Tablets. Professor Wogglebug insisted, and the result was that the Senior Class seized the learned Professor one day and threw him into the river—clothes and all. Everyone knows that a wogglebug cannot swim, and so the inventor of the wonderful Square-Meal Tablets lay helpless on the bottom of the river for three days before a fisherman caught one of his legs on a fishhook and dragged him out upon the bank.

The learned Professor was naturally indignant at such treatment, and so he brought the entire Senior Class to the Emerald City and appealed to Ozma of Oz to punish them for their rebellion.

I do not suppose the girl Ruler was very severe with the rebellious boys and girls, because she had herself refused to eat the Square-Meal Tablets in place of food, but while she was listening to the interesting case in her Throne Room, Cap'n Bill managed to carry the golden flower-pot containing the Magic Flower up to Trot's room without it being seen by anyone except Jellia Jamb, Ozma's chief Maid of Honor, and Jellia promised not to tell.

Also the Wizard was able to carry the cage of monkeys up to one of the top towers of the palace, where he had a room of his own, to which no one came unless invited. So Trot and Dorothy and Cap'n Bill and the Wizard were all delighted at the successful end of their adventure. The Cowardly Lion and the Hungry Tiger went to the marble stables behind the Royal Palace, where they lived while at home, and they too kept the secret, even refusing to tell the Wooden Sawhorse, and Hank the Mule, and the Yellow Hen, and the Pink Kitten where they had been.

Trot watered the Magic Flower every day and allowed no one in her room to see the beautiful blossoms except her friends, Betsy Bobbin and Dorothy. The wonderful plant did not seem to lose any of its magic by being removed from its island, and Trot was sure that Ozma would prize it as one of her most delightful treasures.

Up in his tower the little Wizard of Oz began training his twelve tiny monkeys, and the little creatures were so intelligent that they learned every trick the Wizard tried to teach them. The Wizard treated them with great kindness and gentleness and gave them the food that monkeys love best, so they promised to do their best on the great occasion of Ozma's birthday.

22. Ozma's Birthday Party

It seems odd that a fairy should have a birthday, for fairies, they say, were born at the beginning of time and live forever. Yet, on the other hand, it would be a shame to deprive a fairy, who has so many other good things, of the delights of a birthday. So we need not wonder that the fairies keep their birthdays just as other folks do, and consider them occasions for feasting and rejoicing.

Ozma, the beautiful girl Ruler of the Fairyland of Oz, was a real fairy, and so sweet and gentle in caring for her people that she was greatly beloved by them all. She lived in the most magnificent palace in the most magnificent city in the world, but that did not prevent her from being the friend of the most humble person in her dominions. She would mount her Wooden Sawhorse, and ride out to a farm house and sit in the kitchen to talk with the good wife of the farmer while she did her family baking; or she would play with the children and give them rides on her famous wooden steed; or she would stop in a forest to speak to a charcoal burner and ask if he was happy or desired anything to make him more content; or she would teach young girls how to sew and plan pretty dresses, or enter the shops where the jewelers and craftsmen were busy and watch them at their work, giving to each and all a cheering word or sunny smile.

And then Ozma would sit in her jeweled throne, with her chosen courtiers all about her, and listen patiently to any complaint brought to her by her subjects, striving to accord equal justice to all. Knowing she was fair in her decisions, the Oz people never murmured at her judgments, but agreed, if Ozma decided against them, she was right and they wrong.

When Dorothy and Trot and Betsy Bobbin and Ozma were together, one would think they were all about of an age, and the fairy Ruler no older and no more "grown up" than the other three. She would laugh and romp with them in regular girlish fashion, yet there was an air of quiet dignity about Ozma, even in her merriest moods, that, in a manner, distinguished her from the others. The three girls loved her devotedly, but they were never able to quite forget that Ozma was the Royal Ruler of the wonderful Fairyland of Oz, and by birth belonged to a powerful race.

Ozma's palace stood in the center of a delightful and extensive garden, where splendid trees and flowering shrubs and statuary and fountains abounded. One could walk for hours in this fascinating park and see something interesting at every step. In one place was an aquarium, where strange and beautiful fish swam; at another spot all the birds of the air gathered daily to a great feast which Ozma's servants provided for them, and were so fearless of harm that they would alight upon one's shoulders and eat from one's hand. There was also the Fountain of the Water of Oblivion, but it was dangerous to drink of this water, because it made one forget everything he had ever before known, even to his own name, and therefore Ozma had placed a sign of warning upon the fountain. But there were also fountains that were delightfully perfumed, and fountains of delicious nectar, cool and richly flavored, where all were welcome to refresh themselves.

Around the palace grounds was a great wall, thickly encrusted with glittering emeralds, but the gates stood open and no one was forbidden entrance. On holidays the people of the Emerald City often took their children to see the wonders of Ozma's gardens, and even entered the Royal Palace, if they felt so inclined, for they knew that they and their Ruler were friends, and that Ozma delighted to give them pleasure.

When all this is considered, you will not be surprised that the people throughout the Land of Oz, as well as Ozma's most intimate friends and her royal courtiers, were eager to celebrate her birthday, and made preparations for the festival weeks in advance. All the brass bands practiced their nicest tunes, for they were to march in the numerous processions to be made in the Winkie Country, the Gillikin Country, the Munchkin Country and the Quadling Country, as well as in the Emerald City. Not all the people could go to congratulate their Ruler, but all could celebrate her birthday, in one way or another, however far distant from her palace they might be. Every home and building throughout the Land of Oz was to be decorated with banners and bunting, and there were to be games, and plays, and a general good time for every one.

It was Ozma's custom on her birthday to give a grand feast at the palace, to which all her closest friends were invited. It was a queerly assorted company, indeed, for there are more quaint and unusual characters in Oz than in all the rest of the world, and Ozma was more interested in unusual people than in ordinary ones—just as you and I are.

On this especial birthday of the lovely girl Ruler, a long table was set in the royal Banquet Hall of the palace, at which were place-cards for the invited guests, and at one end of the great room was a smaller table, not so high, for Ozma's animal friends, whom she never forgot, and at the other end was a big table where all of the birthday gifts were to be arranged.

When the guests arrived, they placed their gifts on this table and then found their places at the banquet table. And, after the guests were all placed, the animals entered in a solemn procession and were placed at their table by Jellia Jamb. Then, while an orchestra hidden by a bank of roses and ferns played a march composed for the occasion, the Royal Ozma entered the Banquet Hall, attended by her Maids of Honor, and took her seat at the head of the table.

She was greeted by a cheer from all the assembled company, the animals adding their roars and growls and barks and mewing and cackling to swell the glad tumult, and then all seated themselves at their tables.

At Ozma's right sat the famous Scarecrow of Oz, whose straw-stuffed body was not beautiful, but whose happy nature and shrewd wit had made him a general favorite. On the left of the Ruler was placed the Tin Woodman, whose metal body had been brightly polished for this event. The Tin Woodman was the Emperor of the Winkie Country and one of the most important persons in Oz.

Next to the Scarecrow, Dorothy was seated, and next to her was Tik-Tok, the Clockwork Man, who had been wound up as tightly as his clockwork would permit, so he wouldn't interrupt the festivities by running down. Then came Aunt Em and Uncle Henry, Dorothy's own relations, two kindly old people who had a cozy home in the Emerald City and were very happy and contented there. Then Betsy Bobbin was seated, and next to her the droll and delightful Shaggy Man, who was a favorite wherever he went.

On the other side of the table, opposite the Tin Woodman was placed Trot, and next to her, Cap'n Bill. Then was seated Button-Bright and Ojo the Lucky, and Dr. Pipt and his good wife Margalot, and the astonishing Frogman, who had come from the Yip country to be present at Ozma's birthday feast.

At the foot of the table, facing Ozma, was seated the queenly Glinda, the good Sorceress of Oz, for this was really the place of honor next to the head of the table where Ozma herself sat. On Glinda's right was the little Wizard of Oz, who owed to Glinda all of the magical arts he knew. Then came Jinjur, a pretty girl farmer of whom Ozma and Dorothy were quite fond. The adjoining seat was occupied by the Tin Soldier, and next to him was Professor H. M. Wogglebug, T.E., of the Royal Athletic College.

On Glinda's left was placed the jolly Patchwork Girl, who was a little afraid of the Sorceress and so was likely to behave herself pretty well. The Shaggy Man's brother was beside the Patchwork Girl, and then came that interesting personage, Jack Pumpkinhead, who had grown a splendid big pumpkin for a new head to be worn on Ozma's birthday, and had carved a face on it that was even jollier in expression than the one he had last worn. New heads were not unusual with Jack, for the pumpkins did not keep long, and when the seeds—which served him as brains—began to get soft and mushy, he realized his head would soon spoil, and so he procured a new one from his great field of pumpkins—grown by him so that he need never lack a head.

You will have noticed that the company at Ozma's banquet table was somewhat mixed, but every one invited was a tried and trusted friend of the girl Ruler, and their presence made her quite happy.

No sooner had Ozma seated herself, with her back to the birthday table, than she noticed that all present were eyeing with curiosity and pleasure something behind her, for the gorgeous Magic Flower was blooming gloriously and the mammoth blossoms that quickly succeeded one another on the plant were beautiful to view and filled the entire room with their delicate fragrance. Ozma wanted to look, too, to see what all were staring at, but she controlled her curiosity because it was not proper that she should yet view her birthday gifts.

So the sweet and lovely Ruler devoted herself to her guests, several of whom, such as the Scarecrow, the Tin Woodman, the Patchwork Girl, Tik-Tok, Jack Pumpkinhead and the Tin Soldier, never ate anything but sat very politely in their places and tried to entertain those of the guests who did eat.

And, at the animal table, there was another interesting group, consisting of the Cowardly Lion, the Hungry Tiger, Toto—Dorothy's little shaggy black dog—Hank the Mule, the Pink Kitten, the Wooden Sawhorse, the Yellow Hen, and the Glass Cat. All of these had good appetites except the Sawhorse and the Glass Cat, and each was given a plentiful supply of the food it liked best.

Finally, when the banquet was nearly over and the ice-cream was to be served, four servants entered bearing a huge cake, all frosted and decorated with candy flowers. Around the edge of the cake was a row of lighted candles, and in the center were raised candy letters that spelled the words:
OZMA'S Birthday Cake from Dorothy and the Wizard

"Oh, how beautiful!" cried Ozma, greatly delighted, and Dorothy said eagerly: "Now you must cut the cake, Ozma, and each of us will eat a piece with our ice-cream."

Jellia Jamb brought a large golden knife with a jeweled handle, and Ozma stood up in her place and attempted to cut the cake. But as soon as the frosting in the center broke under the pressure of the knife there leaped from the cake a tiny monkey three inches high, and he was followed by another and another, until twelve monkeys stood on the tablecloth and bowed low to Ozma.

"Congratulations to our gracious Ruler!" they exclaimed in a chorus, and then they began a dance, so droll and amusing that all the company roared with laughter and even Ozma joined in the merriment. But after the dance the monkeys performed some wonderful acrobatic feats, and then they ran to the hollow of the cake and took out some band instruments of burnished gold—cornets, horns, drums, and the like—and forming into a procession the monkeys marched up and down the table playing a jolly tune with the ease of skilled musicians.

Dorothy was delighted with the success of her "Surprise Cake," and after the monkeys had finished their performance, the banquet came to an end.

Now was the time for Ozma to see her other presents, so Glinda the Good rose and, taking the girl Ruler by her hand, led her to the table where all her gifts were placed in magnificent array. The Magic Flower of course attracted her attention first, and Trot had to tell her the whole story of their adventures in getting it. The little girl did not forget to give due credit to the Glass Cat and the little Wizard, but it was really Cap'n Bill who had bravely carried the golden flower-pot away from the enchanted Isle.

Ozma thanked them all, and said she would place the Magic Flower in her boudoir where she might enjoy its beauty and fragrance continually. But now she discovered the marvelous gown woven by Glinda and her maidens from strands drawn from pure emeralds, and being a girl who loved pretty clothes, Ozma's ecstasy at being presented with this exquisite gown may well be imagined. She could hardly wait to put it on, but the table was loaded with other pretty gifts and the night was far spent before the happy girl Ruler had examined all her presents and thanked those who had lovingly donated them.

23. The Fountain of Oblivion

The morning after the birthday fete, as the Wizard and Dorothy were walking in the grounds of the palace, Ozma came out and joined them, saying: "I want to hear more of your adventures in the Forest of Gugu, and how you were able to get those dear little monkeys to use in Dorothy's Surprise Cake."

So they sat down on a marble bench near to the Fountain of the Water of Oblivion, and between them Dorothy and the Wizard related their adventures.

"I was dreadfully fussy while I was a woolly lamb," said Dorothy, "for it didn't feel good, a bit. And I wasn't quite sure, you know, that I'd ever get to be a girl again."

"You might have been a woolly lamb yet, if I hadn't happened to have discovered that Magic Transformation Word," declared the Wizard.

"But what became of the walnut and the hickory-nut into which you transformed those dreadful beast magicians?" inquired Ozma.

"Why, I'd almost forgotten them," was the reply; "but I believe they are still here in my pocket."

Then he searched in his pockets and brought out the two nuts and showed them to her.

Ozma regarded them thoughtfully.

"It isn't right to leave any living creatures in such helpless forms," said she. "I think, Wizard, you ought to transform them into their natural shapes again."

"But I don't know what their natural shapes are," he objected, "for of course the forms of mixed animals which they had assumed were not natural to them. And you must not forget, Ozma, that their natures were cruel and mischievous, so if I bring them back to life they might cause us a great deal of trouble."

"Nevertheless," said the Ruler of Oz, "we must free them from their present enchantments. When you restore them to their natural forms we will discover who they really are, and surely we need not fear any two people, even though they prove to be magicians and our enemies."

"I am not so sure of that," protested the Wizard, with a shake of his bald head. "The one bit of magic I robbed them of—which was the Word of Transformation—is so simple, yet so powerful, that neither Glinda nor I can equal it. It isn't all in the word, you know, it's the way the word is pronounced. So if the two strange magicians have other magic of the same sort, they might prove very dangerous to us, if we liberated them."

"I've an idea!" exclaimed Dorothy. "I'm no wizard, and no fairy, but if you do as I say, we needn't fear these people at all."

"What is your thought, my dear?" asked Ozma.

"Well," replied the girl, "here is this Fountain of the Water of Oblivion, and that's what put the notion into my head. When the Wizard speaks that ter'ble word that will change 'em back to their real forms, he can make 'em dreadful thirsty, too, and we'll put a cup right here by the fountain, so it'll be handy. Then they'll drink the water and forget all the magic they ever knew—and everything else, too."

"That's not a bad idea," said the Wizard, looking at Dorothy approvingly.

"It's a very GOOD idea," declared Ozma. "Run for a cup, Dorothy."

So Dorothy ran to get a cup, and while she was gone the Wizard said: "I don't know whether the real forms of these magicians are those of men or beasts. If they're beasts, they would not drink from a cup but might attack us at once and drink afterward. So it might be safer for us to have the Cowardly Lion and the Hungry Tiger here to protect us if necessary."

Ozma drew out a silver whistle which was attached to a slender gold chain and blew upon the whistle two shrill blasts. The sound, though not harsh, was very penetrating, and as soon as it reached the ears of the Cowardly Lion and the Hungry Tiger, the two huge beasts quickly came bounding toward them. Ozma explained to them what the Wizard was about to do, and told them to keep quiet unless danger threatened. So the two powerful guardians of the Ruler of Oz crouched beside the

fountain and waited.

Dorothy returned and set the cup on the edge of the fountain. Then the Wizard placed the hickory-nut beside the fountain and said in a solemn voice: "I want you to resume your natural form and to be very thirsty—Pyrzqxgl!"

In an instant there appeared, in the place of the hickory-nut, the form of Kiki Aru, the Hyup boy. He seemed bewildered, at first, as if trying to remember what had happened to him and why he was in this strange place. But he was facing the fountain, and the bubbling water reminded him that he was thirsty. Without noticing Ozma, the Wizard and Dorothy, who were behind him, he picked up the cup, filled it with the Water of Oblivion, and drank it to the last drop.

He was now no longer thirsty, but he felt more bewildered than ever, for now he could remember nothing at all—not even his name or where he came from. He looked around the beautiful garden with a pleased expression, and then, turning, he beheld Ozma and the Wizard and Dorothy regarding him curiously and the two great beasts crouching behind them.

Kiki Aru did not know who they were, but he thought Ozma very lovely and Dorothy very pleasant. So he smiled at them—the same innocent, happy smile that a baby might have indulged in and that pleased Dorothy, who seized his hand and led him to a seat beside her on the bench.

"Why, I thought you were a dreadful magician," she exclaimed "and you're only a boy!"

"What is a magician?" he asked, "and what is a boy?"

"Don't you know?" inquired the girl.

Kiki shook his head. Then he laughed.

"I do not seem to know anything," he replied.

"It's very curious," remarked the Wizard. "He wears the dress of the Munchkins, so he must have lived at one time in the Munchkin Country. Of course the boy can tell us nothing of his history or his family, for he has forgotten all that he ever knew."

"He seems a nice boy, now that all the wickedness has gone from him," said Ozma. "So we will keep him here with us and teach him our ways—to be true and considerate of others."

"Why, in that case, it's lucky for him he drank the Water of Oblivion," said Dorothy.

"It is indeed," agreed the Wizard. "But the remarkable thing, to me, is how such a young boy ever learned the secret of the Magic Word of Transformation. Perhaps his companion, who is at present this walnut, was the real magician, although I seem to remember that it was this boy in the beast's form who whispered the Magic Word into the hollow tree, where I overheard it."

"Well, we will soon know who the other is," suggested Ozma. "He may prove to be another Munchkin boy."

The Wizard placed the walnut near the fountain and said, as slowly and solemnly as before: "I want you to resume your natural form, and to be very thirsty—Pyrzqxgl!"

Then the walnut disappeared and Ruggedo the Nome stood in its place. He also was facing the fountain, and he reached for the cup, filled it, and was about to drink when Dorothy exclaimed: "Why, it's the old Nome King!"

Ruggedo swung around and faced them, the cup still in his hand.

"Yes," he said in an angry voice, "it's the old Nome King, and I'm going to conquer all Oz and be revenged on you for kicking me out of my throne." He looked around a moment, and then continued: "There isn't an egg in sight, and I'm stronger than all of you people put together! I don't know how I came here, but I'm going to fight the fight of my life—and I'll win!"

His long white hair and beard waved in the breeze; his eyes flashed hate and vengeance, and so astonished and shocked were they by the sudden appearance of this old enemy of the Oz people that they could only stare at him in silence and shrink away from his wild glare.

Ruggedo laughed. He drank the water, threw the cup on the ground and said fiercely: "And now—and now—and—"

His voice grew gentle. He rubbed his forehead with a puzzled air and stroked his long beard.

"What was I going to say?" he asked, pleadingly.

"Don't you remember?" said the Wizard.

"No; I've forgotten."

"Who ARE you?" asked Dorothy.

He tried to think. "I—I'm sure I don't know," he stammered.

"Don't you know who WE are, either?" questioned the girl.

"I haven't the slightest idea," said the Nome.

"Tell us who this Munchkin boy is," suggested Ozma.

Ruggedo looked at the boy and shook his head.

"He's a stranger to me. You are all strangers. I—I'm a stranger to myself," he said.

Then he patted the Lion's head and murmured, "Good doggie!" and the Lion growled indignantly.

"What shall we do with him?" asked the Wizard, perplexed.

"Once before the wicked old Nome came here to conquer us, and then, as now, he drank of the Water of Oblivion and became harmless. But we sent him back to the Nome Kingdom, where he soon learned the old evil ways again.

"For that reason," said Ozma, "we must find a place for him in the Land of Oz, and keep him here. For here he can learn no evil and will always be as innocent of guile as our own people."

And so the wandering ex-King of the Nomes found a new home, a peaceful and happy home, where he was quite content and passed his days in innocent enjoyment.

Glinda Of Oz
by L. Frank Baum

In which are related the Exciting Experiences of Princess Ozma of Oz, and Dorothy, in their hazardous journey to the home of the Flatheads, and to the Magic Isle of the Skeezers, and how they were rescued from dire peril by the sorcery of Glinda the Good, by L. Frank Baum, "Royal Historian of Oz".

This Book is Dedicated to My Son, Robert Stanton Baum.

1. The Call to Duty

Glinda, the good Sorceress of Oz, sat in the grand court of her palace, surrounded by her maids of honor — a hundred of the most beautiful girls of the Fairyland of Oz. The palace court was built of rare marbles, exquisitely polished. Fountains tinkled musically here and there; the vast colonnade, open to the south, allowed the maidens, as they raised their heads from their embroideries, to gaze upon a vista of rose-hued fields and groves of trees bearing fruits or laden with sweet-scented flowers. At times one of the girls would start a song, the others joining in the chorus, or one would rise and dance, gracefully swaying to the music of a harp played by a companion. And then Glinda smiled, glad to see her maids mixing play with work.

Presently among the fields an object was seen moving, threading the broad path that led to the castle gate. Some of the girls looked upon this object enviously; the Sorceress merely gave it a glance and nodded her stately head as if pleased, for it meant the coming of her friend and mistress — the only one in all the land that Glinda bowed to.

Then up the path trotted a wooden animal attached to a red wagon, and as the quaint steed halted at the gate there descended from the wagon two young girls, Ozma, Ruler of Oz, and her companion, Princess Dorothy. Both were dressed in simple white muslin gowns, and as they ran up the marble steps of the palace they laughed and chatted as gaily as if they were not the most important persons in the world's loveliest fairyland.

The maids of honor had risen and stood with bowed heads to greet the royal Ozma, while Glinda came forward with outstretched arms to greet her guests.

"We've just come on a visit, you know," said Ozma. "Both Dorothy and I were wondering how we should pass the day when we happened to think we'd not been to your Quadling Country for weeks, so we took the Sawhorse and rode straight here."

"And we came so fast," added Dorothy, "that our hair is blown all fuzzy, for the Sawhorse makes a wind of his own. Usually it's a day's journey from the Em'rald City, but I don't s'pose we were two hours on the way."

"You are most welcome," said Glinda the Sorceress, and led them through the court to her magnificent reception hall. Ozma took the arm of her hostess, but Dorothy lagged behind, kissing some of the maids she knew best, talking with others, and making them all feel that she was their friend. When at last she joined Glinda and Ozma in the reception hall, she found them talking earnestly about the condition of the people, and how to make them more happy and contented — although they were already the happiest and most contented folks in all the world.

This interested Ozma, of course, but it didn't interest Dorothy very much, so the little girl ran over to a big table on which was lying open Glinda's Great Book of Records.

This Book is one of the greatest treasures in Oz, and the Sorceress prizes it more highly than any of her magical possessions. That is the reason it is firmly attached to the big marble table by means of golden chains, and whenever Glinda leaves home she locks the Great Book together with five jeweled padlocks, and carries the keys safely hidden in her bosom.

I do not suppose there is any magical thing in any fairyland to compare with the Record Book, on the pages of which are constantly being printed a record of every event that happens in any part of the world, at exactly the moment it happens. And the records are always truthful, although sometimes they do not give as many details as one could wish. But then, lots of things happen, and so the records have to be brief or even Glinda's Great Book could not hold them all.

Glinda looked at the records several times each day, and Dorothy, whenever she visited the Sorceress, loved to look in the Book and see what was happening everywhere. Not much was recorded about the Land of Oz, which is usually peaceful and uneventful, but today Dorothy found something which interested her. Indeed, the printed letters were appearing on the page even while she looked.

"This is funny!" she exclaimed. "Did you know, Ozma, that there were people in your Land of Oz called Skeezers?"

"Yes," replied Ozma, coming to her side, "I know that on Professor Wogglebug's Map of the Land of Oz there is a place marked 'Skeezer,' but what the Skeezers are like I do not know. No one I know has ever seen them or heard of them. The Skeezer Country is 'way at the upper edge of the Gillikin Country, with the sandy, impassable desert on one side and the mountains of Oogaboo on another side. That is a part of the Land of Oz of which I know very little."

"I guess no one else knows much about it either, unless it's the Skeezers themselves," remarked Dorothy. "But the Book says: 'The Skeezers of Oz have declared war on the Flatheads of Oz, and there is likely to be fighting and much trouble as the result.'"

"Is that all the Book says?" asked Ozma.

"Every word," said Dorothy, and Ozma and Glinda both looked at the Record and seemed surprised and perplexed.

"Tell me, Glinda," said Ozma, "who are the Flatheads?"

"I cannot, your Majesty," confessed the Sorceress. "Until now I never heard of them, nor have I ever heard the Skeezers mentioned. In the faraway corners of Oz are hidden many curious tribes of people, and those who never leave their own countries and never are visited by those from our favored part of Oz, naturally are unknown to me. However, if you so desire, I can learn through my arts of sorcery something of the Skeezers and the Flatheads."

"I wish you would," answered Ozma seriously. "You see, Glinda, if these are Oz people they are my subjects and I cannot allow any wars or troubles in the Land I rule, if I can possibly help it."

"Very well, your Majesty," said the Sorceress, "I will try to get some information to guide you. Please excuse me for a time, while I retire to my Room of Magic and Sorcery."

"May I go with you?" asked Dorothy, eagerly.

'No, Princess," was the reply. "It would spoil the charm to have anyone present."

So Glinda locked herself in her own Room of Magic and Dorothy and Ozma waited patiently for her to come out again.

In about an hour Glinda appeared, looking grave and thoughtful.

'Your Majesty," she said to Ozma, "the Skeezers live on a Magic Isle in a great lake. For that reason — because the Skeezers deal in magic — I can learn little about them."

'Why, I didn't know there was a lake in that part of Oz," exclaimed Ozma. "The map shows a river running through the Skeezer Country, but no lake."

'That is because the person who made the map never had visited that part of the country," explained the Sorceress. "The lake surely is there, and in the lake is an island — a Magic Isle — and on that island live the people called the Skeezers."

'What are they like?" inquired the Ruler of Oz.

'My magic cannot tell me that," confessed Glinda, "for the magic of the Skeezers prevents anyone outside of their domain knowing anything about them."

'The Flatheads must know, if they're going to fight the Skeezers," suggested Dorothy

'Perhaps so," Glinda replied, "but I can get little information concerning the Flatheads, either. They are people who inhabit a mountain just south of the Lake of the Skeezers. The mountain has steep sides and a broad, hollow top, like a basin, and in this basin the Flatheads have their dwellings. They also are magic-workers and usually keep to themselves and allow no one from outside to visit them. I have learned that the Flatheads number about one hundred people — men, women and children — while the Skeezers number just one hundred and one."

'What did they quarrel about, and why do they wish to fight one another?" was Ozma's next question.

'I cannot tell your Majesty that," said Glinda.

'But see here!" cried Dorothy, "it's against the law for anyone but Glinda and the Wizard to work magic in the Land of Oz, so if these two strange people are magic-makers they are breaking the law and ought to be punished!" Ozma smiled upon her little friend.

'Those who do not know me or my laws," she said, "cannot be expected to obey my laws. If we know nothing of the Skeezers or the Flatheads, it is likely that they know nothing of us."

'But they ought to know, Ozma, and we ought to know. Who's going to tell them, and how are we going to make them behave?"

'That," returned Ozma, "is what I am now considering. What would you advise, Glinda?"

'he Sorceress took a little time to consider this question, before she made reply. Then she said: "Had you not learned of the existence of the Flatheads and the Skeezers, through my Book of Records, you would never have worried about them or their quarrels. So, if you pay no attention to these peoples, you may never hear of them again."

'But that wouldn't be right," declared Ozma. "I am Ruler of all the Land of Oz, which includes the Gillikin Country, the Quadling Country, the Winkie Country and the Munchkin Country, as well as the Emerald City, and being the Princess of this fairyland it is my duty to make all my people — wherever they may be — happy and content and to settle their disputes and keep them from quarreling. So, while the Skeezers and Flatheads may not know me or that I am their lawful Ruler, I now know that they inhabit my kingdom and are my subjects, so I would not be doing my duty if I kept away from them and allowed them to fight."

'That's a fact, Ozma," commented Dorothy. "You've got to go up to the Gillikin Country and make these people behave themselves and make up their quarrels. But how are you going to do it?"

'That is what is puzzling me also, your Majesty," said the Sorceress. "It may be dangerous for you to go into those strange countries, where the people are possibly fierce and warlike."

'I am not afraid," said Ozma, with a smile.

'"Tisn't a question of being 'fraid," argued Dorothy. "Of course we know you're a fairy, and can't be killed or hurt, and we know you've a lot of magic of your own to help you. But, Ozma dear, in spite of all this you've been in trouble before, on account of wicked enemies, and it isn't right for the Ruler of all Oz to put herself in danger."

'Perhaps I shall be in no danger at all," returned Ozma, with a little laugh. "You mustn't imagine danger, Dorothy, for one should only imagine nice things, and we do not know that the Skeezers and Flatheads are wicked people or my enemies. Perhaps they would be good and listen to reason."

'Dorothy is right, your Majesty," asserted the Sorceress. "It is true we know nothing of these faraway subjects, except that they intend to fight one another, and have a certain amount of magic power at their command. Such folks do not like to submit to interference and they are more likely to resent your coming among them than to receive you kindly and graciously, as is your due."

'If you had an army to take with you," added Dorothy, "it wouldn't be so bad; but there isn't such a thing as an army in all Oz."

'I have one soldier," said Ozma.

'Yes, the soldier with the green whiskers; but he's dreadful 'fraid of his gun and never loads it. I'm sure he'd run rather than fight. And one soldier, even if he were brave, couldn't do much against two hundred and one Flatheads and Skeezers."

'What then, my friends, would you suggest?" inquired Ozma.

'I advise you to send the Wizard of Oz to them, and let him inform them that it is against the laws of Oz to fight, and that you command them to settle their differences and become friends," proposed Glinda. "Let the Wizard tell them they will be punished if they refuse to obey the commands of the Princess of all the Land of Oz."

Ozma shook her head, to indicate that the advice was not to her satisfaction.

'If they refuse, what then?" she asked. "I should be obliged to carry out my threat and punish them, and that would be an unpleasant and difficult thing to do. I am sure it would be better for me to go peacefully, without an army and armed only with my authority as Ruler, and plead with them to obey me. Then, if they prove obstinate I could resort to other means to win their obedience."

"It's a ticklish thing, anyhow you look at it," sighed Dorothy. "I'm sorry now that I noticed the Record in the Great Book."

"But can't you realize, my dear, that I must do my duty, now that I am aware of this trouble?" asked Ozma. "I am fully determined to go at once to the Magic Isle of the Skeezers and to the enchanted mountain of the Flatheads, and prevent war and strife between their inhabitants. The only question to decide is whether it is better for me to go alone, or to assemble a party of my friends and loyal supporters to accompany me."

"If you go I want to go, too," declared Dorothy. "Whatever happens it's going to be fun — 'cause all excitement is fun — and I wouldn't miss it for the world!"

Neither Ozma nor Glinda paid any attention to this statement, for they were gravely considering the serious aspect of this proposed adventure.

"There are plenty of friends who would like to go with you," said the Sorceress, "but none of them would afford your Majesty any protection in case you were in danger. You are yourself the most powerful fairy in Oz, although both I and the Wizard have more varied arts of magic at our command. However, you have one art that no other in all the world can equal — the art of winning hearts and making people love to bow to your gracious presence. For that reason I believe you can accomplish more good alone than with a large number of subjects in your train."

"I believe that also," agreed the Princess. "I shall be quite able to take care of myself, you know, but might not be able to protect others so well. I do not look for opposition, however. I shall speak to these people in kindly words and settle their dispute — whatever it may be — in a just manner."

"Aren't you going to take me?" pleaded Dorothy. "You'll need some companion, Ozma."

The Princess smiled upon her little friend.

"I see no reason why you should not accompany me," was her reply. "Two girls are not very warlike and they will not suspect us of being on any errand but a kindly and peaceful one. But, in order to prevent war and strife between these angry peoples, we must go to them at once. Let us return immediately to the Emerald City and prepare to start on our journey early tomorrow morning."

Glinda was not quite satisfied with this plan, but could not think of any better way to meet the problem. She knew that Ozma, with all her gentleness and sweet disposition, was accustomed to abide by any decision she had made and could not easily be turned from her purpose. Moreover she could see no great danger to the fairy Ruler of Oz in the undertaking, even though the unknown people she was to visit proved obstinate. But Dorothy was not a fairy; she was a little girl who had come from Kansas to live in the Land of Oz. Dorothy might encounter dangers that to Ozma would be as nothing but to an "Earth child" would be very serious.

The very fact that Dorothy lived in Oz, and had been made a

Princess by her friend Ozma, prevented her from being killed or suffering any great bodily pain as long as she lived in that fairyland. She could not grow big, either, and would always remain the same little girl who had come to Oz, unless in some way she left that fairyland or was spirited away from it. But Dorothy was a mortal, nevertheless, and might possibly be destroyed, or hidden where none of her friends could ever find her. She could, for instance be cut into pieces, and the pieces, while still alive and free from pain, could be widely scattered; or she might be buried deep underground or "destroyed" in other ways by evil magicians, were she not properly protected. These facts Glinda was considering while she paced with stately tread her marble hall.

Finally the good Sorceress paused and drew a ring from her finger, handing it to Dorothy.

"Wear this ring constantly until your return," she said to the girl. "If serious danger threatens you, turn the ring around on your finger once to the right and another turn to the left. That will ring the alarm bell in my palace and I will at once come to your rescue. But do not use the ring unless you are actually in danger of destruction. While you remain with Princess Ozma I believe she will be able to protect you from all lesser ills."

"Thank you, Glinda," responded Dorothy gratefully, as she placed the ring on her finger. "I'm going to wear my Magic Belt which I took from the Nome King, too, so I guess I'll be safe from anything the Skeezers and Flatheads try to do to me."

Ozma had many arrangements to make before she could leave her throne and her palace in the Emerald City, even for a trip of a few days, so she bade goodbye to Glinda and with Dorothy climbed into the Red Wagon. A word to the wooden Sawhorse started that astonishing creature on the return journey, and so swiftly did he run that Dorothy was unable to talk or do anything but hold tight to her seat all the way back to the Emerald City.

2. Ozma and Dorothy

Residing in Ozma's palace at this time was a live Scarecrow, a most remarkable and intelligent creature who had once ruled the Land of Oz for a brief period and was much loved and respected by all the people. Once a Munchkin farmer had stuffed an old suit of clothes with straw and put stuffed boots on the feet and used a pair of stuffed cotton gloves for hands. The head of the Scarecrow was a stuffed sack fastened to the body, with eyes, nose, mouth and ears painted on the sack. When a hat had been put on the head, the thing was a good imitation of a man. The farmer placed the Scarecrow on a pole in his cornfield and it came to life in a curious manner. Dorothy, who was passing by the field, was hailed by the live Scarecrow and lifted him off his pole. He then went with her to the Emerald City, where the Wizard of Oz gave him some excellent brains, and the Scarecrow soon became an important personage.

Ozma considered the Scarecrow one of her best friends and most loyal subjects, so the morning after her visit to Glinda she asked him to take her place as Ruler of the Land of Oz while she was absent on a journey, and the Scarecrow at once consented without asking any questions.

Ozma had warned Dorothy to keep their journey a secret and say nothing to anyone about the Skeezers and Flatheads until their return, and Dorothy promised to obey. She longed to tell her girl friends, tiny Trot and Betsy Bobbin, of the adventure they were undertaking, but refrained from saying a word on the subject although both these girls lived with her in Ozma's palace.

Indeed, only Glinda the Sorceress knew they were going, until after they had gone, and even the Sorceress didn't know what their errand might be.

Princess Ozma took the Sawhorse and the Red Wagon, although she was not sure there was a wagon road all the way to the Lake of the Skeezers. The Land of Oz is a pretty big place, surrounded on all sides by a Deadly Desert which it is impossible to cross, and the Skeezer Country, according to the map, was in the farthest northwestern part of Oz, bordering on the north desert. As the Emerald City was exactly in the center of Oz, it was no small journey from there to the Skeezers.

Around the Emerald City the country is thickly settled in every direction, but the farther away you get from the city the fewer people there are, until those parts that border on the desert have small populations. Also those faraway sections are little known to the Oz people, except in the south, where Glinda lives and where Dorothy has often wandered on trips of exploration.

The least known of all is the Gillikin Country, which harbors many strange bands of people among its mountains and valleys and forests and streams, and Ozma was now bound for the most distant part of the Gillikin Country.

"I am really sorry," said Ozma to Dorothy, as they rode away in the Red Wagon, "not to know more about the wonderful Land I rule. It is my duty to be acquainted with every tribe of people and every strange and hidden country in all Oz, but I am kept so busy at my palace making laws and planning for the comforts of those who live near the Emerald City, that I do not often find time to make long journeys."

"Well," replied Dorothy, "we'll prob'bly find out a lot on this trip, and we'll learn all about the Skeezers and Flatheads, anyhow. Time doesn't make much diff'rence in the Land of Oz, 'cause we don't grow up, or get old, or become sick and die, as they do other places; so, if we explore one place at a time, we'll by-an'-by know all about every nook and corner in Oz."

Dorothy wore around her waist the Nome King's Magic Belt, which protected her from harm, and the Magic Ring which Glinda had given her was on her finger. Ozma had merely slipped a small silver wand into the bosom of her gown, for fairies do not use chemicals and herbs and the tools of wizards and sorcerers to perform their magic. The Silver Wand was Ozma's one weapon of offense and defense and by its use she could accomplish many things.

They had left the Emerald City just at sunrise and the Sawhorse traveled very swiftly over the roads towards the north, but in a few hours the wooden animal had to slacken his pace because the farm houses had become few and far between and often there were no paths at all in the direction they wished to follow. At such times they crossed the fields, avoiding groups of trees and fording the streams and rivulets whenever they came to them. But finally they reached a broad hillside closely covered with scrubby brush, through which the wagon could not pass.

"It will be difficult even for you and me to get through without tearing our dresses," said Ozma, "so we must leave the Sawhorse and the Wagon here until our return."

"That's all right," Dorothy replied, "I'm tired riding, anyhow. Do you s'pose, Ozma, we're anywhere near the Skeezer Country?"

"I cannot tell, Dorothy dear, but I know we've been going in the right direction, so we are sure to find it in time."

The scrubby brush was almost like a grove of small trees, for it reached as high as the heads of the two girls, neither of whom was very tall. They were obliged to thread their way in and out, until Dorothy was afraid they would get lost, and finally they were halted by a curious thing that barred their further progress. It was a huge web — as if woven by gigantic spiders — and the delicate, lacy film was fastened stoutly to the branches of the bushes and continued to the right and left in the form of a half circle. The threads of this web were of a brilliant purple color and woven into numerous artistic patterns, but it reached from the ground to branches above the heads of the girls and formed a sort of fence that hedged them in.

"It doesn't look very strong, though," said Dorothy. "I wonder if we couldn't break through." She tried but found the web stronger than it seemed. All her efforts could not break a single thread.

"We must go back, I think, and try to get around this peculiar web," Ozma decided.

So they turned to the right and, following the web found that it seemed to spread in a regular circle. On and on they went until finally Ozma said they had returned to the exact spot from which they had started. "Here is a handkerchief you dropped when we were here before," she said to Dorothy.

"In that case, they must have built the web behind us, after we walked into the trap," exclaimed the little girl.

"True," agreed Ozma, "an enemy has tried to imprison us."

"And they did it, too," said Dorothy. "I wonder who it was."

"It's a spider-web, I'm quite sure," returned Ozma, "but it must be the work of enormous spiders."

"Quite right!" cried a voice behind them. Turning quickly around they beheld a huge purple spider sitting not two yards away and regarding them with its small bright eyes.

Then there crawled from the bushes a dozen more great purple spiders, which saluted the first one and said: "The web is finished, O King, and the strangers are our prisoners."

Dorothy did not like the looks of these spiders at all. They had big heads, sharp claws, small eyes and fuzzy hair all over their purple bodies.

"They look wicked," she whispered to Ozma. "What shall we do?"

Ozma gazed upon the spiders with a serious face.

"What is your object in making us prisoners?" she inquired.

"We need someone to keep house for us," answered the Spider King. "There is sweeping and dusting to be done, and polishing and washing of dishes, and that is work my people dislike to do. So we decided that if any strangers came our way we would capture them and make them our servants."

"I am Princess Ozma, Ruler of all Oz," said the girl with dignity.

"Well, I am King of all Spiders," was the reply, "and that makes me your master. Come with me to my palace and I will instruct you in your work."

"I won't," said Dorothy indignantly. "We won't have anything to do with you."

"We'll see about that," returned the Spider in a severe tone, and the next instant he made a dive straight at Dorothy, opening the claws in his legs as if to grab and pinch her with the sharp points. But the girl was wearing her Magic Belt and was not harmed. The Spider King could not even touch her. He turned swiftly and made a dash at Ozma, but she held her Magic Wand over his head and the monster recoiled as if it had been struck.

"You'd better let us go," Dorothy advised him, "for you see you can't hurt us."

"So I see," returned the Spider King angrily. "Your magic is greater than mine. But I'll not help you to escape. If you can break the magic web my people have woven you may go; if not you must stay here and starve." With that the Spider King uttered a peculiar whistle and all the spiders disappeared.

"There is more magic in my fairyland than I dreamed of," remarked the beautiful Ozma, with a sigh of regret. "It seems that my laws have not been obeyed, for even these monstrous spiders defy me by means of Magic."

"Never mind that now," said Dorothy; "let's see what we can do to get out of this trap."

They now examined the web with great care and were amazed at its strength. Although finer than the finest silken hairs, it resisted all their efforts to work through, even though both girls threw all their weight against it.

"We must find some instrument which will cut the threads of the web," said Ozma, finally. "Let us look about for such a tool."

So they wandered among the bushes and finally came to a shallow pool of water, formed by a small bubbling spring. Dorothy stooped to get a drink and discovered in the water a green crab, about as big as her hand. The crab had two big, sharp claws, and as soon as Dorothy saw them she had an idea that those claws could save them.

"Come out of the water," she called to the crab; "I want to talk to you."

Rather lazily the crab rose to the surface and caught hold of a bit of rock. With his head above the water he said in a cross voice: "What do you want?"

"We want you to cut the web of the purple spiders with your claws, so we can get through it," answered Dorothy. "You can do that, can't you?"

"I suppose so," replied the crab. "But if I do what will you give me?"

"What do you wish?" Ozma inquired.

"I wish to be white, instead of green," said the crab. "Green crabs are very common, and white ones are rare; besides the purple spiders, which infest this hillside, are afraid of white crabs. Could you make me white if I should agree to cut the web for you?"

"Yes," said Ozma, "I can do that easily. And, so you may know I am speaking the truth, I will change your color now."

She waved her silver wand over the pool and the crab instantly became snow-white — all except his eyes, which remained black. The creature saw his reflection in the water and was so delighted that he at once climbed out of the pool and began moving slowly toward the web, by backing away from the pool. He moved so very slowly that Dorothy cried out impatiently: "Dear me, this will never do!" Caching the crab in her hands she ran with him to the web.

She had to hold him up even then, so he could reach with his claws strand after strand of the filmy purple web, which he was able to sever with one nip.

When enough of the web had been cut to allow them to pass, Dorothy ran back to the pool and placed the white crab in the water, after which she rejoined Ozma. They were just in time to escape through the web, for several of the purple spiders now appeared, having discovered that their web had been cut, and had the girls not rushed through the opening the spiders would have quickly repaired the cuts and again imprisoned them.

Ozma and Dorothy ran as fast as they could and although the angry spiders threw a number of strands of web after them, hoping to lasso them or entangle them in the coils, they managed to escape and clamber to the top of the hill.

3. The Mist Maidens

From the top of the hill Ozma and Dorothy looked down into the valley beyond and were surprised to find it filled with a floating mist that was as dense as smoke. Nothing in the valley was visible except these rolling waves of mist, but beyond, on the other side, rose a grassy hill that appeared quite beautiful.

"Well," said Dorothy, "what are we to do, Ozma? Walk down into that thick fog, an' prob'bly get lost in it, or wait till it clears away?"

"I'm not sure it will clear away, however long we wait," replied Ozma, doubtfully. "If we wish to get on, I think we must venture into the mist."

"But we can't see where we're going, or what we're stepping on," protested Dorothy. "There may be dreadful things mixed up in that fog, an' I'm scared just to think of wading into it."

Even Ozma seemed to hesitate. She was silent and thoughtful for a little while, looking at the rolling drifts that were so gray and forbidding. Finally she said: "I believe this is a Mist Valley, where these moist clouds always remain, for even the sunshine above does not drive them away. Therefore the Mist Maids must live here, and they are fairies and should answer my call."

She placed her two hands before her mouth, forming a hollow with them, and uttered a clear, thrilling, bird-like cry. It floated far out over the mist waves and presently was answered by a similar sound, as of a far-off echo.

Dorothy was much impressed. She had seen many strange things since coming to this fairy country, but here was a new experience. At ordinary times Ozma was just like any little girl one might chance to meet — simple, merry, lovable as could be — yet with a certain reserve that lent her dignity in her most joyous moods. There were times, however, when seated on her throne and commanding her subjects, or when her fairy powers were called into use, when Dorothy and all others about her stood in awe of their lovely girl Ruler and realized her superiority.

Ozma waited. Presently out from the billows rose beautiful forms, clothed in fleecy, trailing garments of gray that could scarcely be distinguished from the mist. Their hair was mist-color, too; only their gleaming arms and sweet, pallid faces proved they were living, intelligent creatures answering the call of a sister fairy.

Like sea nymphs they rested on the bosom of the clouds, their eyes turned questioningly upon the two girls who stood upon the bank. One came quite near and to her Ozma said: "Will you please take us to the opposite hillside? We are afraid to venture into the mist. I am Princess Ozma of Oz, and this is my friend Dorothy, a Princess of Oz."

The Mist Maids came nearer, holding out their arms. Without hesitation Ozma advanced and allowed them to embrace her and Dorothy plucked up courage to follow. Very gently the Mist Maids held them. Dorothy thought the arms were cold and misty – they didn't seem real at all — yet they supported the two girls above the surface of the billows and floated with them so swiftly to the green hillside opposite that the girls were astonished to find themselves set upon the grass before they realized they had fairly started.

Thank you!" said Ozma gratefully, and Dorothy also added her thanks for the service.

The Mist Maids made no answer, but they smiled and waved their hands in good-bye as again they floated out into the mist and disappeared from view.

4. The Magic Tent

Well," said Dorothy with a laugh, "that was easier than I expected. It's worth while, sometimes, to be a real fairy. But I wouldn't like to be that kind, and live in a dreadful fog all the time."

They now climbed the bank and found before them a delightful plain that spread for miles in all directions. Fragrant wild flowers were scattered throughout the grass; there were bushes bearing lovely blossoms and luscious fruits; now and then a group of stately trees added to the beauty of the landscape. But there were no dwellings or signs of life.

The farther side of the plain was bordered by a row of palms, and just in front of the palms rose a queerly shaped hill that towered above the plain like a mountain. The sides of this hill were straight up and down; it was oblong in shape and the top seemed flat and level.

Oh, ho!" cried Dorothy; "I'll bet that's the mountain Glinda told us of, where the Flatheads live."

If it is," replied Ozma, "the Lake of the Skeezers must be just beyond the line of palm trees. Can you walk that far, Dorothy?"

Of course, in time," was the prompt answer. "I'm sorry we had to leave the Sawhorse and the Red Wagon behind us, for they'd come in handy just now; but with the end of our journey in sight a tramp across these pretty green fields won't tire us a bit."

It was a longer tramp than they suspected, however, and night overtook them before they could reach the flat mountain. So Ozma proposed they camp for the night and Dorothy was quite ready to approve. She didn't like to admit to her friend she was tired, but she told herself that her legs "had prickers in 'em,"

meaning they had begun to ache.

Usually when Dorothy started on a journey of exploration or adventure, she carried with her a basket of food, and other things that a traveler in a strange country might require, but to go away with Ozma was quite a different thing, as experience had taught her. The fairy Ruler of Oz only needed her silver wand — tipped at one end with a great sparkling emerald — to provide through its magic all that they might need. Therefore Ozma, having halted with her companion and selected a smooth, grassy spot on the plain, waved her wand in graceful curves and chanted some mystic words in her sweet voice, and in an instant a handsome tent appeared before them. The canvas was striped purple and white, and from the center pole fluttered the royal banner of Oz.

"Come, dear," said Ozma, taking Dorothy's hand, "I am hungry and I'm sure you must be also; so let us go in and have our feast."

On entering the tent they found a table set for two, with snowy linen, bright silver and sparkling glassware, a vase of roses in the center and many dishes of delicious food, some smoking hot, waiting to satisfy their hunger. Also, on either side of the tent were beds, with satin sheets, warm blankets and pillows filled with swansdown. There were chairs, too, and tall lamps that lighted the interior of the tent with a soft, rosy glow.

Dorothy, resting herself at her fairy friend's command, and eating her dinner with unusual enjoyment, thought of the wonders of magic. If one were a fairy and knew the secret laws of nature and the mystic words and ceremonies that commanded those laws, then a simple wave of a silver wand would produce instantly all that men work hard and anxiously for through weary years. And Dorothy wished in her kindly, innocent heart, that all men and women could be fairies with silver wands, and satisfy all their needs without so much work and worry, for then, she imagined, they would have all their working hours to be happy in.

But Ozma, looking into her friend's face and reading those thoughts, gave a laugh and said: "No, no, Dorothy, that wouldn't do at all. Instead of happiness your plan would bring weariness to the world. If every one could wave a wand and have his wants fulfilled there would be little to wish for. There would be no eager striving to obtain the difficult, for nothing would then be difficult, and the pleasure of earning something longed for, and only to be secured by hard work and careful thought, would be utterly lost. There would be nothing to do you see, and no interest in life and in our fellow creatures. That is all that makes life worth our while — to do good deeds and to help those less fortunate than ourselves."

"Well, you're a fairy, Ozma. Aren't you happy?" asked Dorothy

"Yes, dear, because I can use my fairy powers to make others happy. Had I no kingdom to rule, and no subjects to look after, I would be miserable. Also, you must realize that while I am a more powerful fairy than any other inhabitant of Oz, I am not as powerful as Glinda the Sorceress, who has studied many arts of magic that I know nothing of. Even the little Wizard of Oz can do some things I am unable to accomplish, while I can accomplish things unknown to the Wizard. This is to explain that I'm not all-powerful, by any means. My magic is simply fairy magic, and not sorcery or wizardry."

"All the same," said Dorothy, "I'm mighty glad you could make this tent appear, with our dinners and beds all ready for us."

Ozma smiled.

"Yes, it is indeed wonderful," she agreed. "Not all fairies know that sort of magic, but some fairies can do magic that fills me with astonishment. I think that is what makes us modest and unassuming — the fact that our magic arts are divided, some being given each of us. I'm glad I don't know everything, Dorothy, and that there still are things in both nature and in wit for me to marvel at."

Dorothy couldn't quite understand this, so she said nothing more on the subject and presently had a new reason to marvel. For when they had quite finished their meal table and contents disappeared in a flash.

"No dishes to wash, Ozma!" she said with a laugh. "I guess you'd make a lot of folks happy if you could teach 'em just that one trick."

For an hour Ozma told stories, and talked with Dorothy about various people in whom they were interested. And then it was bedtime, and they undressed and crept into their soft beds and fell asleep almost as soon as their heads touched their pillows.

5. The Magic Stairway

The flat mountain looked much nearer in the clear light of the morning sun, but Dorothy and Ozma knew there was a long tramp before them, even yet. They finished dressing only to find a warm, delicious breakfast awaiting them, and having eaten they left the tent and started toward the mountain which was their first goal. After going a little way Dorothy looked back and found that the fairy tent had entirely disappeared. She was not surprised, for she knew this would happen.

"Can't your magic give us a horse an' wagon, or an automobile?" inquired Dorothy.

"No, dear; I'm sorry that such magic is beyond my power," confessed her fairy friend.

"Perhaps Glinda could," said Dorothy thoughtfully.

"Glinda has a stork chariot that carries her through the air," said Ozma, "but even our great Sorceress cannot conjure up other modes of travel. Don't forget what I told you last night, that no one is powerful enough to do everything."

"Well, I s'pose I ought to know that, having lived so long in the Land of Oz," replied Dorothy; "but I can't do any magic at all, an' so I can't figure out e'zactly how you an' Glinda an' the Wizard do it."

"Don't try," laughed Ozma. "But you have at least one magical art, Dorothy: you know the trick of winning all hearts."

"No, I don't," said Dorothy earnestly. "If I really can do it, Ozma, I am sure I don't know how I do it."

It took them a good two hours to reach the foot of the round, flat mountain, and then they found the sides so steep that they were like the wall of a house.

"Even my purple kitten couldn't climb 'em," remarked Dorothy, gazing upward.

"But there is some way for the Flatheads to get down and up

again," declared Ozma; "otherwise they couldn't make war with the Skeezers, or even meet them and quarrel with them."

"That's so, Ozma. Let's walk around a ways; perhaps we'll find a ladder or something."

They walked quite a distance, for it was a big mountain, and as they circled around it and came to the side that faced the palm trees, they suddenly discovered an entrance way cut out of the rock wall. This entrance was arched overhead and not very deep because it merely led to a short flight of stone stairs.

"Oh, we've found a way to the top at last," announced Ozma, and the two girls turned and walked straight toward the entrance. Suddenly they bumped against something and stood still, unable to proceed farther.

"Dear me!" exclaimed Dorothy, rubbing her nose, which had struck something hard, although she could not see what it was; "this isn't as easy as it looks. What has stopped us, Ozma? Is it magic of some sort?"

Ozma was feeling around, her hands outstretched before her.

"Yes, dear, it is magic," she replied. "The Flatheads had to have a way from their mountain top from the plain below, but to prevent enemies from rushing up the stairs to conquer them, they have built, at a small distance before the entrance a wall of solid stone, the stones being held in place by cement, and then they made the wall invisible."

"I wonder why they did that?" mused Dorothy. "A wall would keep folks out anyhow, whether it could be seen or not, so there wasn't any use making it invisible. Seems to me it would have been better to have left it solid, for then no one would have seen the entrance behind it. Now anybody can see the entrance, as we did. And prob'ly anybody that tries to go up the stairs gets bumped, as we did."

Ozma made no reply at once. Her face was grave and thoughtful.

"I think I know the reason for making the wall invisible," she said after a while. "The Flatheads use the stairs for coming down and going up. If there was a solid stone wall to keep them from reaching the plain they would themselves be imprisoned by the wall. So they had to leave some place to get around the wall, and if the wall was visible, all strangers or enemies would find the place to go around it and then the wall would be useless. So the Flatheads cunningly made their wall invisible, believing that everyone who saw the entrance to the mountain would walk straight toward it, as we did, and find it impossible to go any farther. I suppose the wall is really high and thick, and can't be broken through, so those who find it in their way are obliged to go away again."

"Well," said Dorothy, "if there's a way around the wall, where is it?"

"We must find it," returned Ozma, and began feeling her way along the wall. Dorothy followed and began to get discouraged when Ozma had walked nearly a quarter of a mile away from the entrance. But now the invisible wall curved in toward the side of the mountain and suddenly ended, leaving just space enough between the wall and the mountain for an ordinary person to pass through.

The girls went in, single file, and Ozma explained that they were now behind the barrier and could go back to the entrance. They met no further obstructions.

"Most people, Ozma, wouldn't have figured this thing out the way you did," remarked Dorothy. "If I'd been alone the invisible wall surely would have stumped me."

Reaching the entrance they began to mount the stone stairs. They went up ten stairs and then down five stairs, following a passage cut from the rock. The stairs were just wide enough for the two girls to walk abreast, arm in arm. At the bottom of the five stairs the passage turned to the right, and they ascended ten more stairs, only to find at the top of the flight five stairs leading straight down again. Again the passage turned abruptly, this time to the left, and ten more stairs led upward.

The passage was now quite dark, for they were in the heart of the mountain and all daylight had been shut out by the turns of the passage. However, Ozma drew her silver wand from her bosom and the great jewel at its end gave out a lustrous, green-tinted light which lighted the place well enough for them to see their way plainly.

Ten steps up, five steps down, and a turn, this way or that. That was the program, and Dorothy figured that they were only gaining five stairs upward each trip that they made.

"Those Flatheads must be funny people," she said to Ozma. "They don't seem to do anything in a bold straightforward manner. In making this passage they forced everyone to walk three times as far as is necessary. And of course this trip is just as tiresome to the Flatheads as it is to other folks."

"That is true," answered Ozma; "yet it is a clever arrangement to prevent their being surprised by intruders. Every time we reach the tenth step of a flight, the pressure of our feet on the stone makes a bell ring on top of the mountain, to warn the Flatheads of our coming."

"How do you know that?" demanded Dorothy, astonished.

"I've heard the bell ever since we started," Ozma told her. "You could not hear it, I know, but when I am holding my wand in my hand I can hear sounds a great distance off."

"Do you hear anything on top of the mountain 'cept the bell?" inquired Dorothy

"Yes. The people are calling to one another in alarm and many footsteps are approaching the place where we will reach the flat top of the mountain."

This made Dorothy feel somewhat anxious. "I'd thought we were going to visit just common, ordinary people," she remarked, "but they're pretty clever, it seems, and they know some kinds of magic, too. They may be dangerous, Ozma. P'raps we'd better stayed at home."

Finally the upstairs-and-downstairs passage seemed coming to an end, for daylight again appeared ahead of the two girls and Ozma replaced her wand in the bosom of her gown. The last ten steps brought them to the surface, where they found themselves surrounded by such a throng of queer people that for a time they halted, speechless, and stared into the faces that confronted them.

Dorothy knew at once why these mountain people were called Flatheads. Their heads were really flat on top, as if they had been cut off just above the eyes and ears. Also the heads were bald, with no hair on top at all, and the ears were big and stuck straight out, and the noses were small and stubby, while the mouths of the Flatheads were well shaped and not unusual. Their eyes were perhaps their best feature, being large and bright and a deep violet in color.

The costumes of the Flatheads were all made of metals dug from their mountain. Small gold, silver, tin and iron discs, about the size of pennies, and very thin, were cleverly wired together and made to form knee trousers and jackets for the men and skirts and waists for the women. The colored metals were skillfully mixed to form stripes and checks of various sorts, so that the costumes were quite gorgeous and reminded Dorothy of pictures she had seen of Knights of old clothed armor.

Aside from their flat heads, these people were not really bad looking. The men were armed with bows and arrows and had small axes of steel stuck in their metal belts. They wore no hats nor ornaments.

6. Flathead Mountain

When they saw that the intruders on their mountain were only two little girls, the Flatheads grunted with satisfaction and drew back, permitting them to see what the mountain top looked like. It was shaped like a saucer, so that the houses and other buildings — all made of rocks — could not be seen over the edge by anyone standing in the plain below.

But now a big fat Flathead stood before the girls and in a gruff voice demanded: "What are you doing here? Have the Skeezers sent you to spy upon us?"

"I am Princess Ozma, Ruler of all the Land of Oz."

"Well, I've never heard of the Land of Oz, so you may be what you claim," returned the Flathead.

"This is the Land of Oz — part of it, anyway," exclaimed Dorothy. "So Princess Ozma rules you Flathead people, as well as all the other people in Oz."

The man laughed, and all the others who stood around laughed, too. Some one in the crowd called: "She'd better not tell the Supreme Dictator about ruling the Flatheads. Eh, friends?"

"No, indeed!" they all answered in positive tones.

"Who is your Supreme Dictator?" answered Ozma.

"I think I'll let him tell you that himself," answered the man who had first spoken. "You have broken our laws by coming here; and whoever you are the Supreme Dictator must fix your punishment. Come along with me."

He started down a path and Ozma and Dorothy followed him without protest, as they wanted to see the most important person in this queer country. The houses they passed seemed pleasant enough and each had a little yard in which were flowers and vegetables. Walls of rock separated the dwellings, and all the paths were paved with smooth slabs of rock. This seemed their only building material and they utilized it cleverly for every purpose.

Directly in the center of the great saucer stood a larger building which the Flathead informed the girls was the palace of the Supreme Dictator. He led them through an entrance hall into a big reception room, where they sat upon stone benches and awaited the coming of the Dictator. Pretty soon he entered from another room — a rather lean and rather old Flathead, dressed much like the others of this strange race, and only distinguished from them by the sly and cunning expression of his face. He kept his eyes half closed and looked through the slits of them at Ozma and Dorothy, who rose to receive him.

"Are you the Supreme Dictator of the Flatheads?" inquired Ozma.

"Yes, that's me," he said, rubbing his hands slowly together. "My word is law. I'm the head of the Flatheads on this flat headland."

"I am Princess Ozma of Oz, and I have come from the Emerald City to —"

"Stop a minute," interrupted the Dictator, and turned to the man who had brought the girls there. "Go away, Dictator Felo Flathead!" he commanded. "Return to your duty and guard the Stairway. I will look after these strangers."

The man bowed and departed, and Dorothy asked wonderingly: "Is he a Dictator, too?"

"Of course," was the answer. "Everybody here is a dictator of something or other. They're all office holders. That's what keeps them contented. But I'm the Supreme Dictator of all, and I'm elected once a year. This is a democracy, you know, where the people are allowed to vote for their rulers. A good many others would like to be Supreme Dictator, but as I made a law that I am always to count the votes myself, I am always elected."

"What is your name?" asked Ozma.

"I am called the Su-dic, which is short for Supreme Dictator. I sent that man away because the moment you mentioned Ozma of Oz, and the Emerald City, I knew who you are. I suppose I'm the only Flathead that ever heard of you, but that's because I have more brains than the rest."

Dorothy was staring hard at the Su-dic.

"I don't see how you can have any brains at all," she remarked, "because the part of your head is gone where brains are kept."

"I don't blame you for thinking that," he said. "Once the Flatheads had no brains because, as you say, there is no upper part to their heads, to hold brains. But long, long ago a band of fairies flew over this country and made it all a fairyland, and when they came to the Flatheads the fairies were sorry to find them all very stupid and quite unable to think. So, as there was no good place in their bodies in which to put brains the Fairy Queen gave each one of us a nice can of brains to carry in his pocket and that made us just as intelligent as other people. See," he continued, "here is one of the cans of brains the fairies gave us." He took from a pocket a bright tin can having a pretty red label on it which said: Concentrated Brains, Extra Quality."

"And does every Flathead have the same kind of brains?" asked Dorothy.

"Yes, they're all alike. Here's another can." From another pocket he produced a second can of brains.

"Did the fairies give you a double supply?" inquired Dorothy.

"No, but one of the Flatheads thought he wanted to be the Su-dic and tried to get my people to rebel against me, so I punished him by taking away his brains. One day my wife scolded me severely, so I took away her can of brains. She didn't like that and went out and robbed several women of their brains. Then I made a law that if anyone stole another's brains, or even tried to borrow them, he would forfeit his own brains to the Su-dic. So each one is content with his own canned brains and my wife and I are the only ones on the mountain with more than one can. I have three cans and that makes me very clever — so clever that I'm a good Sorcerer, if I do say it myself. My poor wife had four cans of brains and became a remarkable witch, but alas! that was before those terrible enemies, the Skeezers, transformed her into a Golden Pig."

"Good gracious!" cried Dorothy; "is your wife really a Golden Pig?"

"She is. The Skeezers did it and so I have declared war on them. In revenge for making my wife a Pig I intend to ruin their Magic Island and make the Skeezers the slaves of the Flatheads!"

The Su-dic was very angry now; his eyes flashed and his face took on a wicked and fierce expression. But Ozma said to him, very sweetly and in a friendly voice: "I am sorry to hear this. Will you please tell me more about your troubles with the Skeezers? Then perhaps I can help you."

She was only a girl, but there was dignity in her pose and speech which impressed the Su-dic.

"If you are really Princess Ozma of Oz," the Flathead said, "you are one of that band of fairies who, under Queen Lurline, made all Oz a Fairyland. I have heard that Lurline left one of her own fairies to rule Oz, and gave the fairy the name of Ozma."

"If you knew this why did you not come to me at the Emerald City and tender me your loyalty and obedience?" asked the Ruler of Oz.

"Well, I only learned the fact lately, and I've been too busy to leave home," he explained, looking at the floor instead of into Ozma's eyes.

She knew he had spoken a falsehood, but only said: "Why did you quarrel with the Skeezers?"

"It was this way," began the Su-dic, glad to change the subject. "We Flatheads love fish, and as we have no fish on this mountain we would sometimes go to the Lake of the Skeezers to catch fish. This made the Skeezers angry, for they declared the fish in their lake belonged to them and were under their protection and they forbade us to catch them. That was very mean and unfriendly in the Skeezers, you must admit, and when we paid no attention to their orders they set a guard on the shore of the lake to prevent our fishing.

"Now, my wife, Rora Flathead, having four cans of brains, had become a wonderful witch, and fish being brain food, she loved to eat fish better than any one of us. So she vowed she would destroy every fish in the lake, unless the Skeezers let us catch what we wanted. They defied us, so Rora prepared a kettleful of magic poison and went down to the lake one night to dump it all in the water and poison the fish. It was a clever idea, quite worthy of my dear wife, but the Skeezer Queen — a young lady named Coo-ee-oh — hid on the bank of the lake and taking Rora unawares, transformed her into a Golden Pig. The poison was spilled on the ground and wicked Queen Coo-ee-oh, not content with her cruel transformation, even took away my wife's four cans of brains, so she is now a common grunting pig without even brains enough to know her own name."

"Then," said Ozma thoughtfully, "the Queen of the Skeezers must be a Sorceress."

"Yes," said the Su-dic, "but she doesn't know much magic, after all. She is not as powerful as Rora Flathead was, nor half as powerful as I am now, as Queen Coo-ee-oh will discover when we fight our great battle and destroy her."

"The Golden Pig can't be a witch any more, of course," observed Dorothy.

"No; even had Queen Coo-ee-oh left her the four cans of brains, poor Rora, in a pig's shape, couldn't do any witchcraft. A witch has to use her fingers, and a pig has only cloven hoofs."

"It seems a sad story," was Ozma's comment, "and all the trouble arose because the Flatheads wanted fish that did not belong to them."

"As for that," said the Su-dic, again angry, "I made a law that any of my people could catch fish in the Lake of the Skeezers, whenever they wanted to. So the trouble was through the Skeezers defying my law."

"You can only make laws to govern your own people," asserted Ozma sternly. "I, alone, am empowered to make laws that must be obeyed by all the peoples of Oz."

"Pooh!" cried the Su-dic scornfully. "You can't make me obey your laws, I assure you. I know the extent of your powers, Princess Ozma of Oz, and I know that I am more powerful than you are. To prove it I shall keep you and your companion prisoners in this mountain until after we have fought and conquered the Skeezers. Then, if you promise to be good, I may let you go home again."

Dorothy was amazed by this effrontery and defiance of the beautiful girl Ruler of Oz, whom all until now had obeyed without question. But Ozma, still unruffled and dignified, looked at the Su-dic and said: "You did not mean that. You are angry and speak unwisely, without reflection. I came here from my palace in the Emerald City to prevent war and to make peace between you and the Skeezers. I do not approve of Queen Coo-ee-oh's action in transforming your wife Rora into a pig, nor do I approve of Rora's cruel attempt to poison the fishes in the lake. No one has the right to work magic in my dominions without my consent, so the Flatheads and the Skeezers have both broken my laws — which must be obeyed."

"If you want to make peace," said the Su-dic, "make the Skeezers restore my wife to her proper form and give back her four cans of brains. Also make them agree to allow us to catch fish in their lake."

"No," returned Ozma, "I will not do that, for it would be unjust. I will have the Golden Pig again transformed into your wife Rora, and give her one can of brains, but the other three cans must be restored to those she robbed. Neither may you catch fish in the lake of the Skeezers, for it is their lake and the fish belong to them. This arrangement is just and honorable, and you must agree to it."

"Never!" cried the Su-dic. Just then a pig came running into the room, uttering dismal grunts. It was made of solid gold, with joints at the bends of the legs and in the neck and jaws. The Golden Pig's eyes were rubies, and its teeth were polished ivory.

"There!" said the Su-dic, "gaze on the evil work of Queen Coo-ee-oh, and then say if you can prevent my making war on the Skeezers. That grunting beast was once my wife — the most beautiful Flathead on our mountain and a skillful witch. Now look at her!"

"Fight the Skeezers, fight the Skeezers, fight the Skeezers!" grunted the Golden Pig.

"I will fight the Skeezers," exclaimed the Flathead chief, "and if a dozen Ozmas of Oz forbade me I would fight just the same."

"Not if I can prevent it!" asserted Ozma.

"You can't prevent it. But since you threaten me, I'll have you confined in the bronze prison until the war is over," said the Su-dic. He whistled and four stout Flatheads, armed with axes and spears, entered the room and saluted him. Turning to the men he said: "Take these two girls, bind them with wire ropes and cast them into the bronze prison."

The four men bowed low and one of them asked: "Where are the two girls, most noble Su-dic?"

The Su-dic turned to where Ozma and Dorothy had stood but they had vanished!

7. The Magic Isle

Ozma, seeing it was useless to argue with the Supreme Dictator of the Flatheads. had been considering how best to escape from his power. She realized that his sorcery might be difficult to overcome, and when he threatened to cast Dorothy and her into a bronze prison she slipped her hand into her bosom and grasped her silver wand. With the other hand she grasped the hand of Dorothy, but these motions were so natural that the Su-dic did not notice them. Then when he turned to meet his four soldiers, Ozma instantly rendered both herself and Dorothy invisible and swiftly led her companion around the group of Flatheads and out of the room. As they reached the entry and descended the stone steps, Ozma whispered: "Let us run, dear! We are invisible, so no one will see us."

Dorothy understood and she was a good runner. Ozma had marked the place where the grand stairway that led to the plain was located, so they made directly for it. Some people were in the paths but these they dodged around. One or two Flatheads heard the pattering of footsteps of the girls on the stone pavement and stopped with bewildered looks to gaze around them, but no one interfered with the invisible fugitives.

The Su-dic had lost no time in starting the chase. He and his men ran so fast that they might have overtaken the girls before they reached the stairway had not the Golden Pig suddenly run across their path. The Su-dic tripped over the pig and fell flat, and his four men tripped over him and tumbled in a heap. Before they could scramble up and reach the mouth of the passage it was too late to stop the two girls.

There was a guard on each side of the stairway, but of course they did not see Ozma and Dorothy as they sped past and descended the steps. Then they had to go up five steps and down another ten, and so on, in the same manner in which they had climbed to the top of the mountain. Ozma lighted their way with her wand and they kept on without relaxing their speed until they reached the bottom. Then they ran to the right and turned the corner of the invisible wall just as the Su-dic and his followers rushed out of the arched entrance and looked around in an attempt to discover the fugitives.

Ozma now knew they were safe, so she told Dorothy to stop and both of them sat down on the grass until they could breathe freely and become rested from their mad flight.

As for the Su-dic, he realized he was foiled and soon turned and climbed his stairs again. He was very angry — angry with Ozma and angry with himself — because, now that he took time to think, he remembered that he knew very well the art of making people invisible, and visible again, and if he had only thought of it in time he could have used his magic knowledge to make the girls visible and so have captured them easily. However, it was now too late for regrets and he determined to make preparations at once to march all his forces against the Skeezers.

"What shall we do next?" asked Dorothy, when they were rested.

"Let us find the Lake of the Skeezers," replied Ozma. "From what that dreadful Su-dic said I imagine the Skeezers are good people and worthy of our friendship, and if we go to them we may help them to defeat the Flatheads."

"I s'pose we can't stop the war now," remarked Dorothy reflectively, as they walked toward the row of palm trees.

"No; the Su-dic is determined to fight the Skeezers, so all we can do is to warn them of their danger and help them as much as possible."

"Of course you'll punish the Flatheads," said Dorothy.

"Well, I do not think the Flathead people are as much to blame as their Supreme Dictator," was the answer. "If he is removed from power and his unlawful magic taken from him, the people will probably be good and respect the laws of the Land of Oz, and live at peace with all their neighbors in the future."

"I hope so," said Dorothy with a sigh of doubt

The palms were not far from the mountain and the girls reached them after a brisk walk. The huge trees were set close together, in three rows, and had been planted so as to keep people from passing them, but the Flatheads had cut a passage through this barrier and Ozma found the path and led Dorothy to the other side.

Beyond the palms they discovered a very beautiful scene. Bordered by a green lawn was a great lake fully a mile from shore to shore, the waters of which were exquisitely blue and sparkling, with little wavelets breaking its smooth surface where the breezes touched it. In the center of this lake appeared a lovely island, not of great extent but almost entirely covered by a huge round building with glass walls and a high glass dome which glittered brilliantly in the sunshine. Between the glass building and the edge of the island was no grass, flowers or shrubbery, but only an expanse of highly polished white marble. There were no boats on either shore and no signs of life could be seen anywhere on the island.

"Well," said Dorothy, gazing wistfully at the island, we've found the Lake of the Skeezers and their Magic Isle. I guess the Skeezers are in that big glass palace, but we can't get at 'em."

8. Queen Coo-ee-oh

Princess Ozma considered the situation gravely. Then she tied her handkerchief to her wand and, standing at the water's edge, waved the handkerchief like a flag, as a signal. For a time they could observe no response.

"I don't see what good that will do," said Dorothy. "Even if the Skeezers are on that island and see us, and know we're friends, they haven't any boats to come and get us."

But the Skeezers didn't need boats, as the girls soon discovered. For on a sudden an opening appeared at the base of the palace and from the opening came a slender shaft of steel, reaching out slowly but steadily across the water in the direction of the place where they stood. To the girls this steel arrangement looked like a triangle, with the base nearest the water. It came toward them in the form of an arch, stretching out from the palace wall until its end reached the bank and rested there, while the other end still remained on the island.

Then they saw that it was a bridge, consisting of a steel footway just broad enough to walk on, and two slender guide rails, one on either side, which were connected with the footway by steel bars. The bridge looked rather frail and Dorothy feared it would not bear its weight, but Ozma at once called, "Come on!" and started to walk across, holding fast to the rail on either side. So Dorothy summoned her courage and followed after. Before Ozma had taken three steps she halted and so forced Dorothy to halt, for the bridge was again moving and returning to the island.

"We need not walk after all," said Ozma. So they stood still in their places and let the steel bridge draw them onward. Indeed, the bridge drew them well into the glass-domed building which covered the island, and soon they found themselves standing in a marble room where two handsomely dressed young men stood on a platform to receive them.

Ozma at once stepped from the end of the bridge to the marble platform, followed by Dorothy, and then the bridge disappeared with a slight clang of steel and a marble slab covered the opening from which it had emerged.

The two young men bowed profoundly to Ozma, and one of them said: "Queen Coo-ee-oh bids you welcome, O Strangers. Her Majesty is waiting to receive you in her palace."

"Lead on," replied Ozma with dignity.

But instead of "leading on," the platform of marble began to rise carrying them upward through a square hole above which just fitted it. A moment later they found themselves within the great glass dome that covered almost all of the island.

Within this dome was a little village, with houses, streets, gardens and parks. The houses were of colored marbles, prettily designed, with many stained-glass windows, and the streets and gardens seemed well cared for. Exactly under the center of the lofty dome was a small park filled with brilliant flowers, with an elaborate fountain, and facing this park stood a building large and more imposing than the others. Toward this building the young men escorted Ozma and Dorothy.

On the streets and in the doorways or open windows of the houses were men, women and children, all richly dressed. These were much like other people in different parts of the Land of Oz except that instead of seeming merry and contented they all wore expressions of much solemnity or of nervous irritation They had beautiful homes, splendid clothes, and ample food, but Dorothy at once decided something was wrong with their lives and that they were not happy. She said nothing, however, but looked curiously at the Skeezers.

At the entrance of the palace Ozma and Dorothy were met by two other young men, in uniform and armed with queer weapons that seemed about halfway between pistols and guns, but were like neither. Their conductors bowed and left them, and the two in uniforms led the girls into the palace.

In a beautiful throne room, surrounded by a dozen or more young men and women, sat the Queen of the Skeezers, Coo-ee-oh. She was a girl who looked older than Ozma or Dorothy — fifteen or sixteen, at least — and although she was elaborately dressed as if she were going to a ball she was too thin and plain of feature to be pretty. But evidently Queen Coo-ee-oh did not realize this fact, for her air and manner betrayed her as proud and haughty and with a high regard for her own importance. Dorothy at once decided she was "snippy" and that she would not like Queen Coo-ee-oh as a companion.

The Queen's hair was as black as her skin was white and her eyes were black, too. The eyes, as she calmly examined Ozma and Dorothy, had a suspicious and unfriendly look in them, but she said quietly: "I know who you are, for I have consulted my Magic Oracle, which told me that one calls herself Princess Ozma, the Ruler of all the Land of Oz, and the other is Princess Dorothy of Oz, who came from a country called Kansas. I know nothing of the Land of Oz, and I know nothing of Kansas."

"Why, this is the Land of Oz!" cried Dorothy. "It's a part of the Land of Oz, anyhow, whether you know it or not."

"Oh, in-deed!" answered Queen Coo-ee-oh, scornfully. "I suppose you will claim next that this Princess Ozma, ruling the Land of Oz, rules me!"

"Of course," returned Dorothy. "There's no doubt of it."

The Queen turned to Ozma.

"Do you dare make such a claim?" she asked.

By this time Ozma had made up her mind as to the character of this haughty and disdainful creature, whose self-pride evidently led her to believe herself superior to all others.

"I did not come here to quarrel with your Majesty," said the girl Ruler of Oz, quietly. "What and who I am is well established, and my authority comes from the Fairy Queen Lurline, of whose band I was a member when Lurline made all Oz a Fairyland. There are several countries and several different peoples in this broad land, each of which has its separate rulers, Kings, Emperors and Queens. But all these render obedience to my laws and acknowledge me as the supreme Ruler."

"If other Kings and Queens are fools that does not interest me in the least," replied Coo-ee-oh, disdainfully. "In the Land of the Skeezers I alone am supreme. You are impudent to think I would defer to you — or to anyone else."

"Let us not speak of this now, please," answered Ozma. "Your island is in danger, for a powerful foe is preparing to destroy it."

"Pah! The Flatheads. I do not fear them."

"Their Supreme Dictator is a Sorcerer."

"My magic is greater than his. Let the Flatheads come! They will never return to their barren mountain-top. I will see to that."

Ozma did not like this attitude, for it meant that the Skeezers were eager to fight the Flatheads, and Ozma's object in coming here was to prevent fighting and induce the two quarrelsome neighbors to make peace. She was also greatly disappointed in Coo-ee-oh, for the reports of Su-dic had led her to imagine the Queen more just and honorable than were the Flatheads. Indeed Ozma reflected that the girl might be better at heart than her self-pride and overbearing manner indicated, and in any event it would be wise not to antagonize her but to try to win her friendship.

"I do not like wars, your Majesty," said Ozma. "In the Emerald City, where I rule thousands of people, and in the countries near to the Emerald City, where thousands more acknowledge my rule, there is no army at all, because there is no quarreling and no need to fight. If differences arise between my people, they come to me and I judge the cases and award justice to all. So, when I learned there might be war between two faraway people of Oz, I came here to settle the dispute and adjust the quarrel."

"No one asked you to come," declared Queen Coo-ee-oh. "It is my business to settle this dispute, not yours. You say my island is a part of the Land of Oz, which you rule, but that is all nonsense, for I've never heard of the Land of Oz, nor of you. You say you are a fairy, and that fairies gave you command over me. I don't believe it! What I do believe is that you are an impostor and have come here to stir up trouble among my people, who are already becoming difficult to manage. You two girls may even be spies of the vile Flatheads, for all I know, and may be trying to trick me. But understand this," she added, proudly rising from her jeweled throne to confront them, "I have magic powers greater than any fairy possesses, and greater than any Flathead possesses. I am a Krumbic Witch — the only Krumbic Witch in the world — and I fear the magic of no other creature that exists! You say you rule thousands. I rule one hundred and one Skeezers. But every one of them trembles at my word. Now that Ozma of Oz and Princess Dorothy are here, I shall rule one hundred and three subjects, for you also shall bow before my power. More than that, in ruling you I also rule the thousands you say you rule."

Dorothy was very indignant at this speech.

"I've got a pink kitten that sometimes talks like that," she said, "but after I give her a good whipping she doesn't think she's so high and mighty after all. If you only knew who Ozma is you'd be scared to death to talk to her like that!"

Queen Coo-ee-oh gave the girl a supercilious look. Then she turned again to Ozma.

"I happen to know," said she, "that the Flatheads intend to attack us tomorrow, but we are ready for them. Until the battle is over, I shall keep you two strangers prisoners on my island, from which there is no chance for you to escape."

She turned and looked around the band of courtiers who stood silently around her throne.

"Lady Aurex," she continued, singling out one of the young women, "take these children to your house and care for them, giving them food and lodging. You may allow them to wander anywhere under the Great Dome, for they are harmless. After I have attended to the Flatheads I will consider what next to do with these foolish girls."

She resumed her seat and the Lady Aurex bowed low and said in a humble manner: "I obey your Majesty's commands." Then to

Ozma and Dorothy she added, "Follow me," and turned to leave the throne room.

Dorothy looked to see what Ozma would do. To her surprise and a little to her disappointment Ozma turned and followed Lady Aurex. So Dorothy trailed after them, but not without giving a parting, haughty look toward Queen Coo-ee-oh, who had her face turned the other way and did not see the disapproving look

9. Lady Aurex

Lady Aurex led Ozma and Dorothy along a street to a pretty marble house near to one edge of the great glass dome that covered the village. She did not speak to the girls until she had ushered them into a pleasant room, comfortably furnished, nor did any of the solemn people they met on the street venture to speak.

When they were seated Lady Aurex asked if they were hungry, and finding they were summoned a maid and ordered food to be brought.

This Lady Aurex looked to be about twenty years old, although in the Land of Oz where people have never changed in appearance since the fairies made it a fairyland — where no one grows old or dies — it is always difficult to say how many years anyone has lived. She had a pleasant, attractive face, even though it was solemn and sad as the faces of all Skeezers seemed to be, and her costume was rich and elaborate, as became a lady in waiting upon the Queen.

Ozma had observed Lady Aurex closely and now asked her in a gentle tone:

"Do you, also, believe me to be an impostor?"

"I dare not say," replied Lady Aurex in a low tone.

"Why are you afraid to speak freely?" inquired Ozma.

"The Queen punishes us if we make remarks that she does not like."

"Are we not alone then, in this house?"

"The Queen can hear everything that is spoken on this island — even the slightest whisper," declared Lady Aurex. "She is a wonderful witch, as she has told you, and it is folly to criticise her or disobey her commands."

Ozma looked into her eyes and saw that she would like to say more if she dared. So she drew from her bosom her silver wand, and having muttered a magic phrase in a strange tongue, she left the room and walked slowly around the outside of the house, making a complete circle and waving her wand in mystic curves as she walked. Lady Aurex watched her curiously and, when Ozma had again entered the room and seated herself, she asked: "What have you done?"

"I've enchanted this house in such a manner that Queen Coo-ee-oh, with all her witchcraft, cannot hear one word we speak within the magic circle I have made," replied Ozma. "We may now speak freely and as loudly as we wish, without fear of the Queen's anger."

Lady Aurex brightened at this.

"Can I trust you?" she asked.

"Ev'rybody trusts Ozma," exclaimed Dorothy. "She is true and honest, and your wicked Queen will be sorry she insulted the powerful Ruler of all the Land of Oz."

"The Queen does not know me yet," said Ozma, "but I want you to know me, Lady Aurex, and I want you to tell me why you, and all the Skeezers, are unhappy. Do not fear Coo-ee-oh's anger, for she cannot hear a word we say, I assure you."

Lady Aurex was thoughtful a moment; then she said: "I shall trust you, Princess Ozma, for I believe you are what you say you are — our supreme Ruler. If you knew the dreadful punishments our Queen inflicts upon us, you would not wonder we are so unhappy. The Skeezers are not bad people; they do not care to quarrel and fight, even with their enemies the Flatheads; but they are so cowed and fearful of Coo-ee-oh that they obey her slightest word, rather than suffer her anger."

"Hasn't she any heart, then?" asked Dorothy.

"She never displays mercy. She loves no one but herself," asserted Lady Aurex, but she trembled as she said it, as if afraid even yet of her terrible Queen.

"That's pretty bad," said Dorothy, shaking her head gravely. "I see you've a lot to do here, Ozma, in this forsaken corner of the Land of Oz. First place, you've got to take the magic away from Queen Coo-ee-oh, and from that awful Su-dic, too. My idea is that neither of them is fit to rule anybody, 'cause they're cruel and hateful. So you'll have to give the Skeezers and Flatheads new rulers and teach all their people that they're part of the Land of Oz and must obey, above all, the lawful Ruler, Ozma of Oz. Then, when you've done that, we can go back home again."

Ozma smiled at her little friend's earnest counsel, but Lady Aurex said in an anxious tone: "I am surprised that you suggest these reforms while you are yet prisoners on this island and in Coo-ee-oh's power. That these things should be done, there is no doubt, but just now a dreadful war is likely to break out, and frightful things may happen to us all. Our Queen has such conceit that she thinks she can overcome the Su-dic and his people, but it is said Su-dic's magic is very powerful, although not as great as that possessed by his wife Rora, before Coo-ee-oh transformed her into a Golden Pig."

"I don't blame her very much for doing that," remarked Dorothy, "for the Flatheads were wicked to try to catch your beautiful fish and the Witch Rora wanted to poison all the fishes in the lake."

"Do you know the reason?" asked the Lady Aurex.

"I don't s'pose there was any reason, 'cept just wickedness," replied Dorothy.

"Tell us the reason," said Ozma earnestly.

"Well, your Majesty, once — a long time ago — the Flatheads and the Skeezers were friendly. They visited our island and we visited their mountain, and everything was pleasant between the two peoples. At that time the Flatheads were ruled by three Adepts in Sorcery, beautiful girls who were not Flatheads, but had wandered to the Flat Mountain and made their home there. These three Adepts used their magic only for good, and the mountain people gladly made them their rulers. They taught the Flatheads how to use their canned brains and how to work metals into clothing that would never wear out, and many other things that added to their happiness and content.

"Coo-ee-oh was our Queen then, as now, but she knew no magic and so had nothing to be proud of. But the three Adepts were very kind to Coo-ee-oh. They built for us this wonderful dome of glass and our houses of marble and taught us to make beautiful clothing and many other things. Coo-ee-oh pretended to be very grateful for these favors, but it seems that all the time she was jealous of the three Adepts and secretly tried to discover their arts of magic. In this she was more clever than anyone suspected. She invited the three Adepts to a banquet one day, and while they were feasting Coo-ee-oh stole their charms and magical instruments and transformed them into three fishes — a gold fish, a silver fish and a bronze fish. While the poor fishes were gasping and flopping helplessly on the floor of the banquet room one of them said reproachfully: 'You will be punished for this, Coo-ee- oh, for if one of us dies or is destroyed, you will become shrivelled and helpless, and all your stolen magic will depart from you.' Frightened by this threat, Coo-ee-oh at once caught up the three fish and ran with them to the shore of the lake, where she cast them into the water. This revived the three Adepts and they swam away and disappeared.

"I, myself, witnessed this shocking scene," continued Lady Aurex, "and so did many other Skeezers. The news was carried to the Flatheads, who then turned from friends to enemies. The Su-dic and his wife Rora were the only ones on the mountain who were glad the three Adepts had been lost to them, and they at once became Rulers of the Flatheads and stole their canned brains from others to make themselves the more powerful. Some of the Adepts' magic tools had been left on the mountain, and these Rora seized and by the use of them she became a witch.

"The result of Coo-ee-oh's treachery was to make both the Skeezers and the Flatheads miserable instead of happy. Not only were the Su-dic and his wife cruel to their people, but our Queen at once became proud and arrogant and treated us very unkindly. All the Skeezers knew she had stolen her magic powers and so she hated us and made us humble ourselves before her and obey her slightest word. If we disobeyed, or did not please her, or if we talked about her when we were in our own homes she would have us dragged to the whipping post in her palace and lashed with knotted cords. That is why we fear her so greatly."

This story filled Ozma's heart with sorrow and Dorothy's heart with indignation.

"I now understand," said Ozma, "why the fishes in the lake have brought about war between the Skeezers and the Flatheads."

"Yes," Lady Aurex answered, "now that you know the story it is easy to understand. The Su-dic and his wife came to our lake hoping to catch the silver fish, or gold fish, or bronze fish — any one of them would do — and by destroying it deprive Coo-ee-oh of her magic. Then they could easily conquer her. Also they had another reason for wanting to catch the fish — they feared that in some way the three Adepts might regain their proper forms and then they would be sure to return to the mountain and punish Rora and the Su-dic. That was why Rora finally tried to poison all the fishes in the lake, at the time Coo-ee-oh transformed her into a Golden Pig. Of course this attempt to destroy the fishes frightened the Queen, for her safety lies in keeping the three fishes alive."

"I s'pose Coo-ee-oh will fight the Flatheads with all her might," observed Dorothy.

"And with all her magic," added Ozma, thoughtfully.

"I do not see how the Flatheads can get to this island to hurt us," said Lady Aurex.

"They have bows and arrows, and I guess they mean to shoot the arrows at your big dome, and break all the glass in it," suggested Dorothy.

But Lady Aurex shook her head with a smile.

"They cannot do that," she replied.

"Why not?"

"I dare not tell you why, but if the Flatheads come to-morrow morning you will yourselves see the reason."

"I do not think they will attempt to harm the island," Ozma declared. "I believe they will first attempt to destroy the fishes, by poison or some other means. If they succeed in that, the conquest of the island will not be difficult."

"They have no boats," said Lady Aurex, "and Coo-ee-oh, who has long expected this war, has been preparing for it in many astonishing ways. I almost wish the Flatheads would conquer us, for then we would be free from our dreadful Queen; but I do not wish to see the three transformed fishes destroyed, for in them lies our only hope of future happiness."

"Ozma will take care of you, whatever happens," Dorothy assured her. But the Lady Aurex, not knowing the extent of Ozma's power — which was, in fact, not so great as Dorothy imagined — could not take much comfort in this promise.

It was evident there would be exciting times on the morrow, if the Flatheads really attacked the Skeezers of the Magic Isle.

10. Under Water

When night fell all the interior of the Great Dome, streets and houses, became lighted with brilliant incandescent lamps, which rendered it bright as day. Dorothy thought the island must look beautiful by night from the outer shore of the lake. There was revelry and feasting in the Queen's palace, and the music of the royal band could be plainly heard in Lady Aurex's house, where Ozma and Dorothy remained with their hostess and keeper. They were prisoners, but treated with much consideration.

Lady Aurex gave them a nice supper and when they wished to retire showed them to a pretty room with comfortable beds and wished them a good night and pleasant dreams.

"What do you think of all this, Ozma?" Dorothy anxiously inquired when they were alone.

"I am glad we came," was the reply, "for although there may be mischief done to-morrow, it was necessary I should know about these people, whose leaders are wild and lawless and oppress their subjects with injustice and cruelties. My task, therefore, is to liberate the Skeezers and the Flatheads and secure for them freedom and happiness. I have no doubt I can accomplish this in time."

"Just now, though, we're in a bad fix," asserted Dorothy. "If Queen Coo-ee-oh conquers to-morrow, she won't be nice to us, and if the Su-dic conquers, he'll be worse."

"Do not worry, dear," said Ozma, "I do not think we are in

danger, whatever happens, and the result of our adventure is sure to be good."

Dorothy was not worrying, especially. She had confidence in her friend, the fairy Princess of Oz, and she enjoyed the excitement of the events in which she was taking part. So she crept into bed and fell asleep as easily as if she had been in her own cosy room in Ozma's palace.

A sort of grating, grinding sound awakened her. The whole island seemed to tremble and sway, as it might do in an earthquake. Dorothy sat up in bed, rubbing her eyes to get the sleep out of them, and then found it was daybreak.

Ozma was hurriedly dressing herself.

"What is it?" asked Dorothy, jumping out of bed.

"I'm not sure," answered Ozma "but it feels as if the island is sinking."

As soon as possible they finished dressing, while the creaking and swaying continued. Then they rushed into the living room of the house and found Lady Aurex, fully dressed, awaiting them.

"Do not be alarmed," said their hostess. "Coo-ee-oh has decided to submerge the island, that is all. But it proves the Flatheads are coming to attack us."

"What do you mean by sub-sub-merging the island?" asked Dorothy.

"Come here and see," was the reply.

Lady Aurex led them to a window which faced the side of the great dome which covered all the village, and they could see that the island was indeed sinking, for the water of the lake was already half way up the side of the dome. Through the glass could be seen swimming fishes, and tall stalks of swaying seaweeds, for the water was clear as crystal and through it they could distinguish even the farther shore of the lake.

"The Flatheads are not here yet," said Lady Aurex. "They will come soon, but not until all of this dome is under the surface of the water."

"Won't the dome leak?" Dorothy inquired anxiously.

"No, indeed."

"Was the island ever sub-sub-sunk before?"

"Oh, yes; on several occasions. But Coo-ee-oh doesn't care to do that often, for it requires a lot of hard work to operate the machinery. The dome was built so that the island could disappear. I think," she continued, "that our Queen fears the Flatheads will attack the island and try to break the glass of the dome."

"Well, if we're under water, they can't fight us, and we can't fight them," asserted Dorothy.

"They could kill the fishes, however," said Ozma gravely

"We have ways to fight, also, even though our island is under water," claimed Lady Aurex. "I cannot tell you all our secrets, but this island is full of surprises. Also our Queen's magic is astonishing."

"Did she steal it all from the three Adepts in Sorcery that are now fishes?"

"She stole the knowledge and the magic tools, but she has used them as the three Adepts never would have done."

By this time the top of the dome was quite under water and suddenly the island stopped sinking and became stationary.

"See!" cried Lady Aurex, pointing to the shore. "The Flatheads have come."

On the bank, which was now far above their heads, a crowd o dark figures could be seen.

"Now let us see what Coo-ee-oh will do to oppose them, continued Lady Aurex, in a voice that betrayed her excitement.

* * * * * * * *

The Flatheads, pushing their way through the line of palm trees had reached the shore of the lake just as the top of the island' dome disappeared beneath the surface. The water now flowe from shore to shore, but through the clear water the dome wa still visible and the houses of the Skeezers could be dimly see through the panes of glass.

"Good!" exclaimed the Su-dic, who had armed all his follower and had brought with him two copper vessels, which he carefull set down upon the ground beside him. "If Coo-ee-oh wants t hide instead of fighting our job will be easy, for in one of thes copper vessels I have enough poison to kill every fish in th lake."

"Kill them, then, while we have time, and then we can go hom again," advised one of the chief officers.

"Not yet," objected the Su-dic. "The Queen of the Skeezers ha defied me, and I want to get her into my power, as well as t destroy her magic. She transformed my poor wife into a Golde Pig, and I must have revenge for that, whatever else we do."

"Look out!" suddenly exclaimed the officers, pointing into th lake; "something's going to happen."

From the submerged dome a door opened and something blac shot swiftly out into the water. The door instantly closed behin it and the dark object cleaved its way through the water, withou rising to the surface, directly toward the place where th Flatheads were standing.

"What is that?" Dorothy asked the Lady Aurex.

"That is one of the Queen's submarines," was the reply. "It is a enclosed, and can move under water. Coo-ee-oh has several o these boats which are kept in little rooms in the basement und our village. When the island is submerged, the Queen uses thes boats to reach the shore, and I believe she now intends to figh the Flatheads with them."

The Su-dic and his people knew nothing of Coo-ee-oh' submarines, so they watched with surprise as the underwate boat approached them. When it was quite near the shore it ros to the surface and the top parted and fell back, disclosing a boa full of armed Skeezers. At the head was the Queen, standing u in the bow and holding in one hand a coil of magic rope tha gleamed like silver.

The boat halted and Coo-ee-oh drew back her arm to throw the silver rope toward the Su-dic, who was now but a few feet from her. But the wily Flathead leader quickly realized his danger and before the Queen could throw the rope he caught up one of the copper vessels and dashed its contents full in her face!

11. The Conquest of the Skeezers

Queen Coo-ee-oh dropped the rope, tottered and fell headlong into the water, sinking beneath the surface, while the Skeezers in the submarine were too bewildered to assist her and only stared at the ripples in the water where she had disappeared. A moment later there arose to the surface a beautiful White Swan. This Swan was of large size, very gracefully formed, and scattered all over its white feathers were tiny diamonds, so thickly placed that as the rays of the morning sun fell upon them the entire body of the Swan glistened like one brilliant diamond. The head of the Diamond Swan had a bill of polished gold and its eyes were two sparkling amethysts.

"Hooray!" cried the Su-dic, dancing up and down with wicked glee. "My poor wife, Rora, is avenged at last. You made her a Golden Pig, Coo-ee-oh, and now I have made you a Diamond Swan. Float on your lake forever, if you like, for your web feet can do no more magic and you are as powerless as the Pig you made of my wife!

"Villain! Scoundrel!" croaked the Diamond Swan. "You will be punished for this. Oh, what a fool I was to let you enchant me!

"A fool you were, and a fool you are!" laughed the Su-dic, dancing madly in his delight. And then he carelessly tipped over the other copper vessel with his heel and its contents spilled on the sands and were lost to the last drop.

The Su-dic stopped short and looked at the overturned vessel with a rueful countenance.

"That's too bad — too bad!" he exclaimed sorrowfully. "I've lost all the poison I had to kill the fishes with, and I can't make any more because only my wife knew the secret of it, and she is now a foolish Pig and has forgotten all her magic."

"Very well," said the Diamond Swan scornfully, as she floated upon the water and swam gracefully here and there. I'm glad to see you are foiled. Your punishment is just beginning, for although you have enchanted me and taken away my powers of sorcery you have still the three magic fishes to deal with, and they'll destroy you in time, mark my words."

The Su-dic stared at the Swan a moment. Then he yelled to his men: "Shoot her! Shoot the saucy bird!"

They let fly some arrows at the Diamond Swan, but she dove under the water and the missiles fell harmless. When Coo-ce-oh rose to the surface she was far from the shore and she swiftly swam across the lake to where no arrows or spears could reach her.

The Su-dic rubbed his chin and thought what to do next. Nearby floated the submarine in which the Queen had come, but the Skeezers who were in it were puzzled what to do with themselves. Perhaps they were not sorry their cruel mistress had been transformed into a Diamond Swan, but the transformation had left them quite helpless. The under-water boat was not operated by machinery, but by certain mystic words uttered by Coo-ee-oh. They didn't know how to submerge it, or how to make the water-tight shield cover them again, or how to make the boat go back to the castle, or make it enter the little basement room where it was usually kept. As a matter of fact, they were now shut out of their village under the Great Dome and could not get back again. So one of the men called to the Supreme Dictator of the Flatheads, saying: "Please make us prisoners and take us to your mountain, and feed and keep us, for we have nowhere to go."

Then the Su-dic laughed and answered: "Not so. I can't be bothered by caring for a lot of stupid Skeezers. Stay where you are, or go wherever you please, so long as you keep away from our mountain." He turned to his men and added: "We have conquered Queen Coo-ee-oh and made her a helpless swan. The Skeezers are under water and may stay there. So, having won the war, let us go home again and make merry and feast, having after many years proved the Flatheads to be greater and more powerful than the Skeezers."

So the Flatheads marched away and passed through the row of palms and went back to their mountain, where the Su-dic and a few of his officers feasted and all the others were forced to wait on them.

"I'm sorry we couldn't have roast pig," said the Su-dic, "but as the only pig we have is made of gold, we can't eat her. Also the Golden Pig happens to be my wife, and even were she not gold I am sure she would be too tough to eat."

12. The Diamond Swan

When the Flatheads had gone away the Diamond Swan swam back to the boat and one of the young Skeezers named Ervic said to her eagerly: "How can we get back to the island, your Majesty?"

"Am I not beautiful?" asked Coo-ee-oh, arching her neck gracefully and spreading her diamond-sprinkled wings. "I can see my reflection in the water, and I'm sure there is no bird nor beast, nor human as magnificent as I am!"

"How shall we get back to the island, your Majesty?" pleaded Ervic.

"When my fame spreads throughout the land, people will travel from all parts of this lake to look upon my loveliness," said Coo-ee-oh, shaking her feathers to make the diamonds glitter more brilliantly.

"But, your Majesty, we must go home and we do not know how to get there," Ervic persisted.

"My eyes," remarked the Diamond Swan, "are wonderfully blue and bright and will charm all beholders."

"Tell us how to make the boat go — how to get back into the island," begged Ervic and the others cried just as earnestly: "Tell us, Coo-ee-oh; tell us!"

"I don't know," replied the Queen in a careless tone.

"You are a magic-worker, a sorceress, a witch!"

"I was, of course, when I was a girl," she said, bending her head over the clear water to catch her reflection in it; "but now I've forgotten all such foolish things as magic. Swans are lovelier than girls, especially when they're sprinkled with diamonds. Don't you think so?" And she gracefully swam away, without seeming to care whether they answered or not.

Ervic and his companions were in despair. They saw plainly that Coo-ee-oh could not or would not help them. The former Queen had no further thought for her island, her people, or her wonderful magic; she was only intent on admiring her own beauty.

"Truly," said Ervic, in a gloomy voice, "the Flatheads have conquered us!"

* * * * * * * *

Some of these events had been witnessed by Ozma and Dorothy and Lady Aurex, who had left the house and gone close to the glass of the dome, in order to see what was going on. Many of the Skeezers had also crowded against the dome, wondering what would happen next. Although their vision was to an extent blurred by the water and the necessity of looking upward at an angle, they had observed the main points of the drama enacted above. They saw Queen Coo-ee-oh's submarine come to the surface and open; they saw the Queen standing erect to throw her magic rope; they saw her sudden transformation into a Diamond Swan, and a cry of amazement went up from the Skeezers inside the dome.

"Good!" exclaimed Dorothy. "I hate that old Su-dic, but I'm glad Coo-ee-oh is punished."

"This is a dreadful misfortune!" cried Lady Aurex, pressing her hands upon her heart.

"Yes," agreed Ozma, nodding her head thoughtfully; "Coo-ee-oh's misfortune will prove a terrible blow to her people."

"What do you mean by that?" asked Dorothy in surprise. "Seems to me the Skeezers are in luck to lose their cruel Queen."

"If that were all you would be right," responded Lady Aurex; "and if the island were above water it would not be so serious. But here we all are, at the bottom of the lake, and fast prisoners in this dome."

"Can't you raise the island?" inquired Dorothy.

"No. Only Coo-ee-oh knew how to do that," was the answer.

"We can try," insisted Dorothy. "If it can be made to go down, it can be made to come up. The machinery is still here, I suppose.

"Yes; but the machinery works by magic, and Coo-ee-oh would never share her secret power with any one of us."

Dorothy's face grew grave; but she was thinking.

"Ozma knows a lot of magic," she said.

"But not that kind of magic," Ozma replied.

"Can't you learn how, by looking at the machinery?"

"I'm afraid not, my dear. It isn't fairy magic at all; it is witchcraft."

"Well," said Dorothy, turning to Lady Aurex, "you say there are other sub-sub-sinking boats. We can get in one of those, and shoot out to the top of the water, like Coo-ee-oh did, and so escape. And then we can help to rescue all the Skeezers down here."

"No one knows how to work the under-water boats but the Queen," declared Lady Aurex.

"Isn't there any door or window in this dome that we could open?"

"No; and, if there were, the water would rush in to flood the dome, and we could not get out."

"The Skeezers," said Ozma, "could not drown; they only get wet and soggy and in that condition they would be very uncomfortable and unhappy. But you are a mortal girl, Dorothy, and if your Magic Belt protected you from death you would have to lie forever at the bottom of the lake."

"No, I'd rather die quickly," asserted the little girl. "But there are doors in the basement that open — to let out the bridges and the boats — and that would not flood the dome, you know."

"Those doors open by a magic word, and only Coo-ee-oh knows the word that must be uttered," said Lady Aurex.

"Dear me!" exclaimed Dorothy, "that dreadful Queen's witchcraft upsets all my plans to escape. I guess I'll give it up, Ozma, and let you save us."

Ozma smiled, but her smile was not so cheerful as usual. The Princess of Oz found herself confronted with a serious problem, and although she had no thought of despairing she realized that the Skeezers and their island, as well as Dorothy and herself, were in grave trouble and that unless she could find a means to save them they would be lost to the Land of Oz for all future time.

"In such a dilemma," said she, musingly, "nothing is gained by haste. Careful thought may aid us, and so may the course of events. The unexpected is always likely to happen, and cheerful patience is better than reckless action."

"All right," returned Dorothy; "take your time, Ozma; there's no hurry. How about some breakfast, Lady Aurex?"

Their hostess led them back to the house, where she ordered her trembling servants to prepare and serve breakfast. All the Skeezers were frightened and anxious over the transformation of their Queen into a swan. Coo-ee-oh was feared and hated, but they had depended on her magic to conquer the Flatheads and she was the only one who could raise their island to the surface of the lake again.

Before breakfast was over several of the leading Skeezers came to Aurex to ask her advice and to question Princess Ozma, of whom they knew nothing except that she claimed to be a fairy and the Ruler of all the land, including the Lake of the Skeezers.

"If what you told Queen Coo-ee-oh was the truth," they said to her, "you are our lawful mistress, and we may depend on you to get us out of our difficulties."

"I will try to do that" Ozma graciously assured them, "but you must remember that the powers of fairies are granted them to bring comfort and happiness to all who appeal to them. On the contrary, such magic as Coo-ee-oh knew and practiced is unlawful witchcraft and her arts are such as no fairy would condescend to use. However, it is sometimes necessary to consider evil in order to accomplish good, and perhaps by studying Coo-ee-oh's tools and charms of witchcraft I may be able to save us. Do you promise to accept me as your Ruler and to obey my commands?"

They promised willingly.

"Then," continued Ozma, "I will go to Coo-ee-oh's palace and take possession of it. Perhaps what I find there will be of use to me. In the meantime tell all the Skeezers to fear nothing, but have patience. Let them return to their homes and perform their daily tasks as usual. Coo-ee-oh's loss may not prove a misfortune, but rather a blessing."

This speech cheered the Skeezers amazingly. Really, they had no one now to depend upon but Ozma, and in spite of their dangerous position their hearts were lightened by the transformation and absence of their cruel Queen.

They got out their brass band and a grand procession escorted Ozma and Dorothy to the palace, where all of Coo-ee-oh's former servants were eager to wait upon them. Ozma invited Lady Aurex to stay at the palace also, for she knew all about the Skeezers and their island and had also been a favorite of the former Queen, so her advice and information were sure to prove valuable.

Ozma was somewhat disappointed in what she found in the palace. One room of Coo-ee-oh's private suite was entirely devoted to the practice of witchcraft, and here were countless queer instruments and jars of ointments and bottles of potions labeled with queer names, and strange machines that Ozma could not guess the use of, and pickled toads and snails and lizards, and a shelf of books that were written in blood, but in a language which the Ruler of Oz did not know.

"I do not see," said Ozma to Dorothy, who accompanied her in her search, "how Coo-ee-oh knew the use of the magic tools she stole from the three Adept Witches. Moreover, from all reports these Adepts practiced only good witchcraft, such as would be helpful to their people, while Coo-ee-oh performed only evil."

"Perhaps she turned the good things to evil uses?" suggested Dorothy.

"Yes, and with the knowledge she gained Coo-ee-oh doubtless invented many evil things quite unknown to the good Adepts, who are now fishes," added Ozma. "It is unfortunate for us that the Queen kept her secrets so closely guarded, for no one but herself could use any of these strange things gathered in this room."

"Couldn't we capture the Diamond Swan and make her tell the secrets?" asked Dorothy.

"No; even were we able to capture her, Coo-ee-oh now has forgotten all the magic she ever knew. But until we ourselves escape from this dome we could not capture the Swan, and were we to escape we would have no use for Coo-ee-oh's magic."

"That's a fact," admitted Dorothy. "But — say, Ozma, here's a good idea! Couldn't we capture the three fishes — the gold and silver and bronze ones, and couldn't you transform 'em back to their own shapes, and then couldn't the three Adepts get us out of here?"

"You are not very practical, Dorothy dear. It would be as hard for us to capture the three fishes, from among all the other fishes in the lake, as to capture the Swan."

"But if we could, it would be more help to us," persisted the little girl.

"That is true," answered Ozma, smiling at her friend's eagerness. "You find a way to catch the fish, and I'll promise when they are caught to restore them to their proper forms."

"I know you think I can't do it," replied Dorothy, "but I'm going to try."

She left the palace and went to a place where she could look through a clear pane of the glass dome into the surrounding water. Immediately she became interested in the queer sights that met her view.

The Lake of the Skeezers was inhabited by fishes of many kinds and many sizes. The water was so transparent that the girl could see for a long distance and the fishes came so close to the glass of the dome that sometimes they actually touched it. On the white sands at the bottom of the lake were star-fish, lobsters, crabs and many shell fish of strange shapes and with shells of gorgeous hues. The water foliage was of brilliant colors and to Dorothy it resembled a splendid garden.

But the fishes were the most interesting of all. Some were big and lazy, floating slowly along or lying at rest with just their fins waving. Many with big round eyes looked full at the girl as she watched them and Dorothy wondered if they could hear her through the glass if she spoke to them. In Oz, where all the animals and birds can talk, many fishes are able to talk also, but usually they are more stupid than birds and animals because they think slowly and haven't much to talk about.

In the Lake of the Skeezers the fish of smaller size were more active than the big ones and darted quickly in and out among the swaying weeds, as if they had important business and were in a hurry. It was among the smaller varieties that Dorothy hoped to spy the gold and silver and bronze fishes. She had an idea the three would keep together, being companions now as they were in their natural forms, but such a multitude of fishes constantly passed, the scene shifting every moment, that she was not sure she would notice them even if they appeared in view. Her eyes couldn't look in all directions and the fishes she sought might be on the other side of the dome, or far away in the lake.

"P'raps, because they were afraid of Coo-ee-oh, they've hid themselves somewhere, and don't know their enemy has been transformed," she reflected.

She watched the fishes for a long time, until she became hungry and went back to the palace for lunch. But she was not discouraged.

"Anything new, Ozma?" she asked.

"No, dear. Did you discover the three fishes?"

"Not yet. But there isn't anything better for me to do, Ozma, so I guess I'll go back and watch again."

13. The Alarm Bell

Glinda, the Good, in her palace in the Quadling Country, had many things to occupy her mind, for not only did she look after the weaving and embroidery of her bevy of maids, and assist all those who came to her to implore her help — beasts and birds as well as people — but she was a close student of the arts of sorcery and spent much time in her Magical Laboratory, where she strove to find a remedy for every evil and to perfect her skill in magic.

Nevertheless, she did not forget to look in the Great Book of Records each day to see if any mention was made of the visit of Ozma and Dorothy to the Enchanted Mountain of the Flatheads and the Magic Isle of the Skeezers. The Records told her that Ozma had arrived at the mountain, that she had escaped, with her companion, and gone to the island of the Skeezers, and that Queen Coo-ee-oh had submerged the island so that it was entirely under water. Then came the statement that the Flatheads had come to the lake to poison the fishes and that their Supreme Dictator had transformed Queen Coo-ee-oh into a swan.

No other details were given in the Great Book and so Glinda did not know that since Coo-ee-oh had forgotten her magic none of the Skeezers knew how to raise the island to the surface again. So Glinda was not worried about Ozma and Dorothy until one morning, while she sat with her maids, there came a sudden clang of the great alarm bell. This was so unusual that every maid gave a start and even the Sorceress for a moment could not think what the alarm meant.

Then she remembered the ring she had given Dorothy when she left the palace to start on her venture. In giving the ring Glinda had warned the little girl not to use its magic powers unless she and Ozma were in real danger, but then she was to turn it on her finger once to the right and once to the left and Glinda's alarm bell would ring.

So the Sorceress now knew that danger threatened her beloved Ruler and Princess Dorothy, and she hurried to her magic room to seek information as to what sort of danger it was. The answer to her question was not very satisfactory, for it was only: "Ozma and Dorothy are prisoners in the great Dome of the Isle of the Skeezers, and the Dome is under the water of the lake."

"Hasn't Ozma the power to raise the island to the surface?" inquired Glinda.

"No," was the reply, and the Record refused to say more except that Queen Coo-ee-oh, who alone could command the island to rise, had been transformed by the Flathead Su-dic into a Diamond Swan.

Then Glinda consulted the past records of the Skeezers in the Great Book. After diligent search she discovered that Coo-ee-oh was a powerful sorceress who had gained most of her power by treacherously transforming the Adepts of Magic, who were visiting her, into three fishes — gold, silver and bronze — after which she had them cast into the lake.

Glinda reflected earnestly on this information and decided that someone must go to Ozma's assistance. While there was no great need of haste, because Ozma and Dorothy could live in a submerged dome a long time, it was evident they could not get out until someone was able to raise the island.

The Sorceress looked through all her recipes and books of sorcery, but could find no magic that would raise a sunken island. Such a thing had never before been required in sorcery. Then Glinda made a little island, covered by a glass dome, and sunk it in a pond near her castle, and experimented in magical ways to bring it to the surface. She made several such experiments, but all were failures. It seemed a simple thing to do, yet she could not do it.

Nevertheless, the wise Sorceress did not despair of finding a way to liberate her friends. Finally she concluded that the best thing to do was to go to the Skeezer country and examine the lake. While there she was more likely to discover a solution to the problem that bothered her, and to work out a plan for the rescue of Ozma and Dorothy.

So Glinda summoned her storks and her aerial chariot, and telling her maids she was going on a journey and might not soon return, she entered the chariot and was carried swiftly to the Emerald City.

In Princess Ozma's palace the Scarecrow was now acting as Ruler of the Land of Oz. There wasn't much for him to do, because all the affairs of state moved so smoothly, but he was there in case anything unforeseen should happen.

Glinda found the Scarecrow playing croquet with Trot and Betsy Bobbin, two little girls who lived at the palace under Ozma's protection and were great friends of Dorothy and much loved by all the Oz people.

"Something's happened!" cried Trot, as the chariot of the Sorceress descended near them. "Glinda never comes here 'cept something's gone wrong."

"I hope no harm has come to Ozma, or Dorothy," said Betsy anxiously, as the lovely Sorceress stepped down from her chariot.

Glinda approached the Scarecrow and told him of the dilemma of Ozma and Dorothy and she added: "We must save them somehow, Scarecrow."

"Of course," replied the Scarecrow, stumbling over a wicket and falling flat on his painted face.

The girls picked him up and patted his straw stuffing into shape and he continued, as if nothing had occurred: "But you'll have to tell me what to do, for I never have raised a sunken island in all my life."

"We must have a Council of State as soon as possible," proposed the Sorceress. "Please send messengers to summon all of Ozma's counsellors to this palace. Then we can decide what is best to be done."

The Scarecrow lost no time in doing this. Fortunately most of the royal counsellors were in the Emerald City or near to it, so they all met in the throne room of the palace that same evening.

14. Ozma's Counsellors

No Ruler ever had such a queer assortment of advisers as the Princess Ozma had gathered about her throne. Indeed, in no other country could such amazing people exist. But Ozma loved them for their peculiarities and could trust every one of them.

First there was the Tin Woodman. Every bit of him was tin, brightly polished. All his joints were kept well oiled and moved smoothly. He carried a gleaming axe to prove he was a woodman, but seldom had cause to use it because he lived in a magnificent tin castle in the Winkie Country of Oz and was the Emperor of all the Winkies. The Tin Woodman's name was Nick Chopper. He had a very good mind, but his heart was not of much account, so he was very careful to do nothing unkind or to hurt anyone's feelings.

Another counsellor was Scraps, the Patchwork Girl of Oz, who was made of a gaudy patchwork quilt, cut into shape and stuffed with cotton. This Patchwork Girl was very intelligent, but so full of fun and mad pranks that a lot of more stupid folks thought she must be crazy. Scraps was jolly under all conditions, however grave they might be, but her laughter and good spirits were of value in cheering others and in her seemingly careless remarks much wisdom could often be found.

Then there was the Shaggy Man — shaggy from head to foot, hair and whiskers, clothes and shoes — but very kind and gentle and one of Ozma's most loyal supporters.

Tik-Tok was there, a copper man with machinery inside him, so cleverly constructed that he moved, spoke and thought by three separate clock-works. Tik-Tok was very reliable because he always did exactly what he was wound up to do, but his machinery was liable to run down at times and then he was quite helpless until wound up again.

A different sort of person was Jack Pumpkinhead, one of Ozma's oldest friends and her companion on many adventures. Jack's body was very crude and awkward, being formed of limbs of trees of different sizes, jointed with wooden pegs. But it was a substantial body and not likely to break or wear out, and when it was dressed the clothes covered much of its roughness. The head of Jack Pumpkinhead was, as you have guessed, a ripe pumpkin, with the eyes, nose and mouth carved upon one side. The pumpkin was stuck on Jack's wooden neck and was liable to get turned sidewise or backward and then he would have to straighten it with his wooden hands.

The worst thing about this sort of a head was that it did not keep well and was sure to spoil sooner or later. So Jack's main business was to grow a field of fine pumpkins each year, and always before his old head spoiled he would select a fresh pumpkin from the field and carve the features on it very neatly, and have it ready to replace the old head whenever it became necessary. He didn't always carve it the same way, so his friends never knew exactly what sort of an expression they would find on his face. But there was no mistaking him, because he was the only pumpkin-headed man alive in the Land of Oz.

A one-legged sailor-man was a member of Ozma's council. His name was Cap'n Bill and he had come to the Land of Oz with Trot, and had been made welcome on account of his cleverness, honesty and good nature. He wore a wooden leg to replace the one he had lost and was a great friend of all the children in Oz because he could whittle all sorts of toys out of wood with his big jack-knife.

Professor H. M. Wogglebug, T. E., was another member of the council. The "H. M." meant Highly Magnified, for the Professor was once a little bug, who became magnified to the size of a man and always remained so. The "T. E." meant that he was Thoroughly Educated. He was at the head of Princess Ozma's Royal Athletic College, and so that the students would not have to study and so lose much time that could be devoted to athletic sports, such as football, baseball and the like, Professor Wogglebug had invented the famous Educational Pills. If one of the college students took a Geography Pill after breakfast, he knew his geography lesson in an instant; if he took a Spelling Pill he at once knew his spelling lesson, and an Arithmetic Pill enabled the student to do any kind of sum without having to think about it.

These useful pills made the college very popular and taught the boys and girls of Oz their lessons in the easiest possible way. In spite of this, Professor Wogglebug was not a favorite outside his college, for he was very conceited and admired himself so much and displayed his cleverness and learning so constantly, that no one cared to associate with him. Ozma found him of value in her councils, nevertheless.

Perhaps the most splendidly dressed of all those present was a great frog as large as a man, called the Frogman, who was noted for his wise sayings. He had come to the Emerald City from the Yip Country of Oz and was a guest of honor. His long-tailed coat was of velvet, his vest of satin and his trousers of finest silk. There were diamond buckles on his shoes and he carried a gold-headed cane and a high silk hat. All of the bright colors were represented in his rich attire, so it tired one's eyes to look at him for long, until one became used to his splendor.

The best farmer in all Oz was Uncle Henry, who was Dorothy's own uncle, and who now lived near the Emerald City with his wife Aunt Em. Uncle Henry taught the Oz people how to grow the finest vegetables and fruits and grains and was of much use to Ozma in keeping the Royal Storehouses well filled. He, too, was a counsellor.

The reason I mention the little Wizard of Oz last is because he was the most important man in the Land of Oz. He wasn't a big man in size but he was a man in power and intelligence and second only to Glinda the Good in all the mystic arts of magic. Glinda had taught him, and the Wizard and the Sorceress were the only ones in Oz permitted by law to practice wizardry and sorcery, which they applied only to good uses and for the benefit of the people.

The Wizard wasn't exactly handsome but he was pleasant to look at. His bald head was as shiny as if it had been varnished; there was always a merry twinkle in his eyes and he was as spry as a schoolboy. Dorothy says the reason the Wizard is not as powerful as Glinda is because Glinda didn't teach him all she knows, but what the Wizard knows he knows very well and so he performs some very remarkable magic. The ten I have mentioned assembled, with the Scarecrow and Glinda, in Ozma's throne room, right after dinner that evening, and the Sorceress told them all she knew of the plight of Ozma and Dorothy

"Of course we must rescue them," she continued, "and the sooner they are rescued the better pleased they will be; but what we must now determine is how they can be saved. That is why I have called you together in council."

"The easiest way," remarked the Shaggy Man, "is to raise the sunken island of the Skeezers to the top of the water again."

"Tell me how?" said Glinda.

"I don't know how, your Highness, for I have never raised a sunken island."

"We might all get under it and lift," suggested Professor Wogglebug.

"How can we get under it when it rests on the bottom of the lake?" asked the Sorceress.

"Couldn't we throw a rope around it and pull it ashore?" inquired Jack Pumpkinhead.

"Why not pump the water out of the lake?" suggested the Patchwork Girl with a laugh.

"Do be sensible!" pleaded Glinda. "This is a serious matter, and we must give it serious thought."

"How big is the lake and how big is the island?" was the Frogman's question.

"None of us can tell, for we have not been there."

"In that case," said the Scarecrow, "it appears to me we ought to go to the Skeezer country and examine it carefully."

"Quite right," agreed the Tin Woodman.

"We-will-have-to-go-there-any-how," remarked Tik-Tok in his jerky machine voice.

"The question is which of us shall go, and how many of us?" said the Wizard.

"I shall go of course," declared the Scarecrow.

"And I," said Scraps.

"It is my duty to Ozma to go," asserted the Tin Woodman.

"I could not stay away, knowing our loved Princess is in danger," said the Wizard.

"We all feel like that," Uncle Henry said.

Finally one and all present decided to go to the Skeezer country, with Glinda and the little Wizard to lead them. Magic must meet magic in order to conquer it, so these two skillful magic-workers were necessary to insure the success of the expedition.

They were all ready to start at a moment's notice, for none had any affairs of importance to attend to. Jack was wearing a newly made Pumpkin-head and the Scarecrow had recently been stuffed with fresh straw. Tik-Tok's machinery was in good running order and the Tin Woodman always was well oiled.

"It is quite a long journey," said Glinda, "and while I might travel quickly to the Skeezer country by means of my stork chariot the rest of you will be obliged to walk. So, as we must keep together, I will send my chariot back to my castle and we will plan to leave the Emerald City at sunrise to-morrow."

15. The Great Sorceress

Betsy and Trot, when they heard of the rescue expedition, begged the Wizard to permit them to join it and he consented. The Glass Cat, overhearing the conversation, wanted to go also and to this the Wizard made no objection.

This Glass Cat was one of the real curiosities of Oz. It had been made and brought to life by a clever magician named Dr. Pipt, who was not now permitted to work magic and was an ordinary citizen of the Emerald City. The cat was of transparent glass, through which one could plainly see its ruby heart beating and its pink brains whirling around in the top of the head.

The Glass Cat's eyes were emeralds; its fluffy tail was of spun glass and very beautiful. The ruby heart, while pretty to look at, was hard and cold and the Glass Cat's disposition was not pleasant at all times. It scorned to catch mice, did not eat, and was extremely lazy. If you complimented the remarkable cat on her beauty, she would be very friendly, for she loved admiration above everything. The pink brains were always working and their owner was indeed more intelligent than most common cats.

Three other additions to the rescue party were made the next morning, just as they were setting out upon their journey. The first was a little boy called Button Bright, because he had no other name that anyone could remember. He was a fine, manly little fellow, well mannered and good humored, who had only one bad fault. He was continually getting lost. To be sure, Button Bright got found as often as he got lost, but when he was missing his friends could not help being anxious about him.

"Some day," predicted the Patchwork Girl, "he won't be found, and that will be the last of him." But that didn't worry Button Bright, who was so careless that he did not seem to be able to break the habit of getting lost.

The second addition to the party was a Munchkin boy of about Button Bright's age, named Ojo. He was often called "Ojo the Lucky," because good fortune followed him wherever he went. He and Button Bright were close friends, although of such different natures, and Trot and Betsy were fond of both.

The third and last to join the expedition was an enormous lion, one of Ozma's regular guardians and the most important and intelligent beast in all Oz. He called himself the Cowardly Lion, saying that every little danger scared him so badly that his heart thumped against his ribs, but all who knew him knew that the Cowardly Lion's fears were coupled with bravery and that however much he might be frightened he summoned courage to meet every danger he encountered. Often he had saved Dorothy and Ozma in times of peril, but afterward he moaned and trembled and wept because he had been so scared.

"If Ozma needs help, I'm going to help her," said the great beast. "Also, I suspect the rest of you may need me on the journey — especially Trot and Betsy — for you may pass through a dangerous part of the country. I know that wild Gillikin country pretty well. Its forests harbor many ferocious beasts."

They were glad the Cowardly Lion was to join them, and in good spirits the entire party formed a procession and marched out of the Emerald City amid the shouts of the people, who wished them success and a safe return with their beloved Ruler.

They followed a different route from that taken by Ozma and Dorothy, for they went through the Winkie Country and up north toward Oogaboo. But before they got there they swerved to the left and entered the Great Gillikin Forest, the nearest thing to a wilderness in all Oz. Even the Cowardly Lion had to admit that certain parts of this forest were unknown to him, although he had often wandered among the trees, and the Scarecrow and Tin Woodman, who were great travelers, never had been there at all.

The forest was only reached after a tedious tramp, for some of the Rescue Expedition were quite awkward on their feet. The Patchwork Girl was as light as a feather and very spry; the Tin Woodman covered the ground as easily as Uncle Henry and the Wizard; but Tik-Tok moved slowly and the slightest obstruction in the road would halt him until the others cleared it away. Then, too, Tik-Tok's machinery kept running down, so Betsy and Trot took turns in winding it up.

The Scarecrow was more clumsy but less bother, for although he often stumbled and fell he could scramble up again and a little patting of his straw-stuffed body would put him in good shape again.

Another awkward one was Jack Pumpkinhead, for walking would jar his head around on his neck and then he would be likely to go in the wrong direction. But the Frogman took Jack's arm and then he followed the path more easily.

Cap'n Bill's wooden leg didn't prevent him from keeping up with the others and the old sailor could walk as far as any of them.

When they entered the forest the Cowardly Lion took the lead. There was no path here for men, but many beasts had made paths of their own which only the eyes of the Lion, practiced in woodcraft, could discern. So he stalked ahead and wound his way in and out, the others following in single file, Glinda being next to the Lion.

There are dangers in the forest, of course, but as the huge Lion headed the party he kept the wild denizens of the wilderness from bothering the travelers. Once, to be sure, an enormous leopard sprang upon the Glass Cat and caught her in his powerful jaws, but he broke several of his teeth and with howls of pain and dismay dropped his prey and vanished among the trees.

"Are you hurt?" Trot anxiously inquired of the Glass Cat.

"How silly!" exclaimed the creature in an irritated tone of voice; "nothing can hurt glass, and I'm too solid to break easily. But I'm annoyed at that leopard's impudence. He has no respect for beauty or intelligence. If he had noticed my pink brains work, I'm sure he would have realized I'm too important to be grabbed in a wild beast's jaws."

"Never mind," said Trot consolingly; "I'm sure he won't do it again."

They were almost in the center of the forest when Ojo, the Munchkin boy, suddenly said: "Why, where's Button Bright?"

They halted and looked around them. Button Bright was not with the party.

"Dear me," remarked Betsy, "I expect he's lost again!"

"When did you see him last, Ojo?" inquired Glinda.

"It was some time ago," replied Ojo. "He was trailing along at the end and throwing twigs at the squirrels in the trees. Then I went to talk to Betsy and Trot, and just now I noticed he was gone."

"This is too bad," declared the Wizard, "for it is sure to delay our journey. We must find Button Bright before we go any farther, for this forest is full of ferocious beasts that would not hesitate to tear the boy to pieces."

"But what shall we do?" asked the Scarecrow. "If any of us leaves the party to search for Button Bright he or she might fall a victim to the beasts, and if the Lion leaves us we will have no protector.

"The Glass Cat could go," suggested the Frogman. "The beasts can do her no harm, as we have discovered."

The Wizard turned to Glinda.

"Cannot your sorcery discover where Button Bright is?" he asked.

"I think so," replied the Sorceress.

She called to Uncle Henry, who had been carrying her wicker box, to bring it to her, and when he obeyed she opened it and drew out a small round mirror. On the surface of the glass she dusted a white powder and then wiped it away with her handkerchief and looked in the mirror. It reflected a part of the forest, and there, beneath a wide-spreading tree, Button Bright was lying asleep. On one side of him crouched a tiger, ready to spring; on the other side was a big gray wolf, its bared fangs glistening in a wicked way.

"Goodness me!" cried Trot, looking over Glinda's shoulder. "They'll catch and kill him sure."

Everyone crowded around for a glimpse at the magic mirror.

"Pretty bad — pretty bad!" said the Scarecrow sorrowfully.

"Comes of getting lost!" said Cap'n Bill, sighing.

"Guess he's a goner!" said the Frogman, wiping his eyes on his purple silk handkerchief.

"But where is he? Can't we save him?" asked Ojo the Lucky.

"If we knew where he is we could probably save him," replied the little Wizard, "but that tree looks so much like all the other trees, that we can't tell whether it's far away or near by."

"Look at Glinda!" exclaimed Betsy

Glinda, having handed the mirror to the Wizard, had stepped aside and was making strange passes with her outstretched arms and reciting in low, sweet tones a mystical incantation. Most of them watched the Sorceress with anxious eyes, despair giving way to the hope that she might be able to save their friend. the Wizard, however, watched the scene in the mirror, while over his shoulders peered Trot, the Scarecrow and the Shaggy Man.

What they saw was more strange than Glinda's actions. The tiger started to spring on the sleeping boy, but suddenly lost its power to move and lay flat upon the ground. The gray wolf seemed unable to lift its feet from the ground. It pulled first at one leg and then at another, and finding itself strangely confined to the spot began to back and snarl angrily. They couldn't hear the barkings and snarls, but they could see the creature's mouth open and its thick lips move. Button Bright, however, being but a few feet away from the wolf, heard its cries of rage, which wakened him from his untroubled sleep. The boy sat up and looked first at the tiger and then at the wolf. His face showed that for a moment he was quite frightened, but he soon saw that the beasts were unable to approach him and so he got upon his feet and examined them curiously, with a mischievous smile upon his face. Then he deliberately kicked the tiger's head with his foot and catching up a fallen branch of a tree he went to the wolf and gave it a good whacking. Both the beasts were furious at such treatment but could not resent it.

Button Bright now threw down the stick and with his hands in his pockets wandered carelessly away.

"Now," said Glinda, "let the Glass Cat run and find him. He is in that direction," pointing the way, "but how far off I do not know. Make haste and lead him back to us as quickly as you can."

The Glass Cat did not obey everyone's orders, but she really feared the great Sorceress, so as soon as the words were spoken the crystal animal darted away and was quickly lost to sight.

The Wizard handed the mirror back to Glinda, for the woodland scene had now faded from the glass. Then those who cared to rest sat down to await Button Bright's coming. It was not long before be appeared through the trees and as he rejoined his friends he said in a peevish tone: "Don't ever send that Glass Cat to find me again. She was very impolite and, if we didn't all know that she had no manners, I'd say she insulted me."

Glinda turned upon the boy sternly.

"You have caused all of us much anxiety and annoyance," said she. "Only my magic saved you from destruction. I forbid you to get lost again."

"Of course," he answered. "It won't be my fault if I get lost again; but it wasn't my fault this time."

16. The Enchanted Fishes

I must now tell you what happened to Ervic and the three other Skeezers who were left floating in the iron boat after Queen Coo-ee-oh had been transformed into a Diamond Swan by the magic of the Flathead Su-dic.

The four Skeezers were all young men and their leader was Ervic. Coo-ee-oh had taken them with her in the boat to assist her if she captured the Flathead chief, as she hoped to do by means of her silver rope. They knew nothing about the witchcraft that moved the submarine and so, when left floating upon the lake, were at a loss what to do. The submarine could not be submerged by them or made to return to the sunken island. There were neither oars nor sails in the boat, which was not anchored but drifted quietly upon the surface of the lake.

The Diamond Swan had no further thought or care for her people. She had sailed over to the other side of the lake and all the calls and pleadings of Ervic and his companions were unheeded by the vain bird. As there was nothing else for them to do, they sat quietly in their boat and waited as patiently as they could for someone to come to their aid.

The Flatheads had refused to help them and had gone back to their mountain. All the Skeezers were imprisoned in the Great Dome and could not help even themselves. When evening came, they saw the Diamond Swan, still keeping to the opposite shore of the lake, walk out of the water to the sands, shake her diamond-sprinkled feathers, and then disappear among the bushes to seek a resting place for the night.

"I'm hungry," said Ervic.

"I'm cold," said another Skeezer.

"I'm tired," said a third.

"I'm afraid," said the last one of them.

But it did them no good to complain. Night fell and the moon rose and cast a silvery sheen over the surface of the water.

"Go to sleep," said Ervic to his companions. "I'll stay awake and watch, for we may be rescued in some unexpected way.

So the other three laid themselves down in the bottom of the boat and were soon fast asleep.

Ervic watched. He rested himself by leaning over the bow of the boat, his face near to the moonlit water, and thought dreamily of the day's surprising events and wondered what would happen to the prisoners in the Great Dome.

Suddenly a tiny goldfish popped its head above the surface of the lake, not more than a foot from his eyes. A silverfish then raised its head beside that of the goldfish, and a moment later a bronzefish lifted its head beside the others. The three fish, all in a row, looked earnestly with their round, bright eyes into the astonished eyes of Ervic the Skeezer.

"We are the three Adepts whom Queen Coo-ee-oh betrayed and wickedly transformed," said the goldfish, its voice low and soft but distinctly heard in the stillness of the night.

"I know of our Queen's treacherous deed," replied Ervic, "and I am sorry for your misfortune. Have you been in the lake ever since?"

"Yes," was the reply.

"I — I hope you are well — and comfortable," stammered Ervic, not knowing what else to say.

"We knew that some day Ooo-ee-oh would meet with the fate she so richly deserves," declared the bronzefish. "We have waited and watched for this time. Now if you will promise to help us and will be faithful and true, you can aid us in regaining our natural forms, and save yourself and all your people from the dangers that now threaten you."

"Well," said Ervic, "you can depend on my doing the best I can But I'm no witch, nor magician, you must know."

"All we ask is that you obey our instructions," returned the silverfish. "We know that you are honest and that you served Coo-ee-oh only because you were obliged to in order to escape her anger. Do as we command and all will be well."

"I promise!" exclaimed the young man. "Tell me what I am to do first."

"You will find in the bottom of your boat the silver cord which dropped from Coo-ee-oh's hand when she was transformed," said the goldfish. "Tie one end of that cord to the bow of your boat and drop the other end to us in the water. Together we will pull your boat to the shore."

Ervic much doubted that the three small fishes could move so heavy a boat, but he did as he was told and the fishes all seized their end of the silver cord in their mouths and headed toward the nearest shore, which was the very place where the Flatheads had stood when they conquered Queen Coo-ee-oh.

At first the boat did not move at all, although the fishes pulled with all their strength. But presently the strain began to tell Very slowly the boat crept toward the shore, gaining more speed at every moment. A couple of yards away from the sandy beach the fishes dropped the cord from their mouths and swam to one side, while the iron boat, being now under way, continued to move until its prow grated upon the sands.

Ervic leaned over the side and said to the fishes: "What next?"

"You will find upon the sand," said the silverfish, "a copper kettle, which the Su-dic forgot when he went away. Cleanse it thoroughly in the water of the lake, for it has had poison in it When it is cleaned, fill it with fresh water and hold it over the side of the boat, so that we three may swim into the kettle. W will then instruct you further."

"Do you wish me to catch you, then?" asked Ervic in surprise.

"Yes," was the reply.

So Ervic jumped out of the boat and found the copper kettle. Carrying it a little way down the beach, he washed it well, scrubbing away every drop of the poison it had contained with sand from the shore

Then he went back to the boat.

Ervic's comrades were still sound asleep and knew nothing of the three fishes or what strange happenings were taking place about them. Ervic dipped the kettle in the lake, holding fast to the handle until it was under water. The gold and silver and bronze fishes promptly swam into the kettle. The young Skeezer then lifted it, poured out a little of the water so it would not spill over the edge, and said to the fishes: "What next?"

"Carry the kettle to the shore. Take one hundred steps to the east, along the edge of the lake, and then you will see a path leading through the meadows, up hill and down dale. Follow the path until you come to a cottage which is painted a purple color with white trimmings. When you stop at the gate of this cottage we will tell you what to do next. Be careful, above all, not to stumble and spill the water from the kettle, or you would destroy us and all you have done would be in vain."

The goldfish issued these commands and Ervic promised to be careful and started to obey. He left his sleeping comrades in the boat, stepping cautiously over their bodies, and on reaching the shore took exactly one hundred steps to the east. Then he looked for the path and the moonlight was so bright that he easily discovered it, although it was hidden from view by tall weeds until one came full upon it. This path was very narrow and did not seem to be much used, but it was quite distinct and Ervic had no difficulty in following it. He walked through a broad meadow, covered with tall grass and weeds, up a hill and down into a valley and then up another hill and down again.

It seemed to Ervic that he had walked miles and miles. Indeed the moon sank low and day was beginning to dawn when finally he discovered by the roadside a pretty little cottage, painted purple with white trimmings. It was a lonely place — no other buildings were anywhere about and the ground was not tilled at all. No farmer lived here, that was certain. Who would care to dwell in such an isolated place?

But Ervic did not bother his head long with such questions. He went up to the gate that led to the cottage, set the copper kettle carefully down and bending over it asked: "What next?"

17. Under the Great Dome

When Glinda the Good and her followers of the Rescue Expedition came in sight of the Enchanted Mountain of the Flatheads, it was away to the left of them, for the route they had taken through the Great Forest was some distance from that followed by Ozma and Dorothy.

They halted awhile to decide whether they should call upon the Supreme Dictator first, or go on to the Lake of the Skeezers.

"If we go to the mountain," said the Wizard, "we may get into trouble with that wicked Su-dic, and then we would be delayed in rescuing Ozma and Dorothy. So I think our best plan will be to go to the Skeezer Country, raise the sunken island and save our friends and the imprisoned Skeezers. Afterward we can visit the mountain and punish the cruel magician of the Flatheads."

"That is sensible," approved the Shaggy Man. "I quite agree with you."

The others, too, seemed to think the Wizard's plan the best, and Glinda herself commended it, so on they marched toward the line of palm trees that hid the Skeezers' lake from view.

Pretty soon they came to the palms. These were set closely together, the branches, which came quite to the ground, being so tightly interlaced that even the Glass Cat could scarcely find a place to squeeze through. The path which the Flatheads used was some distance away.

"Here's a job for the Tin Woodman," said the Scarecrow.

So the Tin Woodman, who was always glad to be of use, set to work with his sharp, gleaming axe, which he always carried, and in a surprisingly short time had chopped away enough branches to permit them all to pass easily through the trees.

Now the clear waters of the beautiful lake were before them and by looking closely they could see the outlines of the Great Dome of the sunken island, far from shore and directly in the center of the lake.

Of course every eye was at first fixed upon this dome, where Ozma and Dorothy and the Skeezers were still fast prisoners. But soon their attention was caught by a more brilliant sight, for here was the Diamond Swan swimming just before them, its long neck arched proudly, the amethyst eyes gleaming and all the diamond-sprinkled feathers glistening splendidly under the rays of the sun.

"That," said Glinda, "is the transformation of Queen Coo-ee-oh, the haughty and wicked witch who betrayed the three Adepts at Magic and treated her people like slaves."

"She's wonderfully beautiful now," remarked the Frogman.

"It doesn't seem like much of a punishment," said Trot. "The Flathead Su-dic ought to have made her a toad."

"I am sure Coo-ee-oh is punished," said Glinda, "for she has lost all her magic power and her grand palace and can no longer misrule the poor Skeezers."

"Let us call to her, and hear what she has to say," proposed the Wizard.

So Glinda beckoned the Diamond Swan, which swam gracefully to a position near them. Before anyone could speak Coo-ee-oh called to them in a rasping voice — for the voice of a swan is always harsh and unpleasant — and said with much pride: "Admire me, Strangers! Admire the lovely Coo-ee-oh, the handsomest creature in all Oz. Admire me!"

"Handsome is as handsome does," replied the Scarecrow. "Are your deeds lovely, Coo-ee-oh?"

"Deeds? What deeds can a swan do but swim around and give pleasure to all beholders?" said the sparkling bird.

"Have you forgotten your former life? Have you forgotten your magic and witchcraft?" inquired the Wizard.

"Magic — witchcraft? Pshaw, who cares for such silly things?" retorted Coo-ee-oh. "As for my past life, it seems like an unpleasant dream. I wouldn't go back to it if I could. Don't you admire my beauty, Strangers?"

"Tell us, Coo-ee-oh," said Glinda earnestly, "if you can recall enough of your witchcraft to enable us to raise the sunken island to the surface of the lake. Tell us that and I'll give you a string of pearls to wear around your neck and add to your beauty."

"Nothing can add to my beauty, for I'm the most beautiful creature anywhere in the whole world."

"But how can we raise the island?"

"I don't know and I don't care. If ever I knew I've forgotten, and I'm glad of it," was the response. "Just watch me circle around and see me glitter!

"It's no use," said Button Bright; "the old Swan is too much in love with herself to think of anything else."

"That's a fact," agreed Betsy with a sigh; "but we've got to get Ozma and Dorothy out of that lake, somehow or other."

"And we must do it in our own way," added the Scarecrow.

"But how?" asked Uncle Henry in a grave voice, for he could not bear to think of his dear niece Dorothy being out there under water; "how shall we do it?"

"Leave that to Glinda," advised the Wizard, realizing he was helpless to do it himself.

"If it were just an ordinary sunken island," said the powerful sorceress, "there would be several ways by which I might bring it to the surface again. But this is a Magic Isle, and by some curious art of witchcraft, unknown to any but Queen Coo-ee-oh, it obeys certain commands of magic and will not respond to any other. I do not despair in the least, but it will require some deep study to solve this difficult problem. If the Swan could only remember the witchcraft that she invented and knew as a woman, I could force her to tell me the secret, but all her former knowledge is now forgotten."

"It seems to me," said the Wizard after a brief silence had followed Glinda's speech, "that there are three fishes in this lake that used to be Adepts at Magic and from whom Coo-ee-oh stole much of her knowledge. If we could find those fishes and return them to their former shapes, they could doubtless tell us what to do to bring the sunken island to the surface."

"I have thought of those fishes," replied Glinda, "but among so many fishes as this lake contains how are we to single them out?"

You will understand, of course, that had Glinda been at home in her castle, where the Great Book of Records was, she would have known that Ervic the Skeezer already had taken the gold and silver and bronze fishes from the lake. But that act had been recorded in the Book after Glinda had set out on this journey, so it was all unknown to her.

"I think I see a boat yonder on the shore," said Ojo the Munchkin boy, pointing to a place around the edge of the lake. "If we could get that boat and row all over the lake, calling to the magic fishes, we might be able to find them."

"Let us go to the boat," said the Wizard.

They walked around the lake to where the boat was stranded upon the beach, but found it empty. It was a mere shell of blackened steel, with a collapsible roof that, when in position, made the submarine watertight, but at present the roof rested in slots on either side of the magic craft. There were no oars or sails, no machinery to make the boat go, and although Glinda promptly realized it was meant to be operated by witchcraft, she was not acquainted with that sort of magic.

"However," said she, "the boat is merely a boat, and I believe I can make it obey a command of sorcery, as well as it did the command of witchcraft. After I have given a little thought to the matter, the boat will take us wherever we desire to go."

"Not all of us," returned the Wizard, "for it won't hold so many. But, most noble Sorceress, provided you can make the boat go, of what use will it be to us?"

"Can't we use it to catch the three fishes?" asked Button Bright.

"It will not be necessary to use the boat for that purpose," replied Glinda. "Wherever in the lake the enchanted fishes may be, they will answer to my call. What I am trying to discover is how the boat came to be on this shore, while the island on which it belongs is under water yonder. Did Coo-ee-oh come here in the boat to meet the Flatheads before the island was sunk, or afterward?"

No one could answer that question, of course; but while they pondered the matter three young men advanced from the line of trees, and rather timidly bowed to the strangers.

"Who are you, and where did you come from?" inquired the Wizard.

"We are Skeezers," answered one of them, "and our home is on the Magic Isle of the Lake. We ran away when we saw you coming, and hid behind the trees, but as you are Strangers and seem to be friendly we decided to meet you, for we are in great trouble and need assistance."

"If you belong on the island, why are you here?" demanded Glinda.

So they told her all the story: How the Queen had defied the Flatheads and submerged the whole island so that her enemies could not get to it or destroy it; how, when the Flatheads came to the shore, Coo-ee-oh had commanded them, together with their friend Ervic, to go with her in the submarine to conquer the Su-dic, and how the boat had shot out from the basement of the sunken isle, obeying a magic word, and risen to the surface, where it opened and floated upon the water.

Then followed the account of how the Su-dic had transformed Coo-ee-oh into a swan, after which she had forgotten all the witchcraft she ever knew. The young men told how, in the night when they were asleep, their comrade Ervic had mysteriously disappeared, while the boat in some strange manner had floated to the shore and stranded upon the beach.

That was all they knew. They had searched in vain for three days for Ervic. As their island was under water and they could not get back to it, the three Skeezers had no place to go, and so had waited patiently beside their boat for something to happen.

Being questioned by Glinda and the Wizard, they told all they knew about Ozma and Dorothy and declared the two girls were still in the village under the Great Dome. They were quite safe and would be well cared for by Lady Aurex, now that the Queen who opposed them was out of the way.

When they had gleaned all the information they could from these Skeezers, the Wizard said to Glinda: "If you find you can make this boat obey your sorcery, you could have it return to the island, submerge itself, and enter the door in the basement from which it came. But I cannot see that our going to the sunken island would enable our friends to escape. We would only join them as prisoners."

"Not so, friend Wizard," replied Glinda. "If the boat would obey my commands to enter the basement door, it would also obey my commands to come out again, and I could bring Ozma and Dorothy back with me."

"And leave all of our people still imprisoned?" asked one of the Skeezers reproachfully.

"By making several trips in the boat, Glinda could fetch all your people to the shore," replied the Wizard.

"But what could they do then?" inquired another Skeezer. "They would have no homes and no place to go, and would be at the mercy of their enemies, the Flatheads."

"That is true," said Glinda the Good. "And as these people are Ozma's subjects, I think she would refuse to escape with Dorothy and leave the others behind, or to abandon the island which is the lawful home of the Skeezers. I believe the best plan will be to summon the three fishes and learn from them how to raise the island."

The little Wizard seemed to think that this was rather a forlorn hope.

"How will you summon them," he asked the lovely Sorceress, "and how can they hear you?"

"That is something we must consider carefully," responded stately Glinda, with a serene smile. "I think I can find a way."

All of Ozma's counsellors applauded this sentiment, for they knew well the powers of the Sorceress.

"Very well," agreed the Wizard. "Summon them, most noble Glinda."

18. The Cleverness of Ervic

We must now return to Ervic the Skeezer, who, when he had set down the copper kettle containing the three fishes at the gate of the lonely cottage, had asked, "What next?"

The goldfish stuck its head above the water in the kettle and said in its small but distinct voice: "You are to lift the latch, open the door, and walk boldly into the cottage. Do not be afraid of anything you see, for however you seem to be threatened with dangers, nothing can harm you. The cottage is the home of a powerful Yookoohoo, named Reera the Red, who assumes all sorts of forms, sometimes changing her form several times in a day, according to her fancy. What her real form may be we do not know. This strange creature cannot be bribed with treasure, or coaxed through friendship, or won by pity. She has never assisted anyone, or done wrong to anyone, that we know of. All her wonderful powers are used for her own selfish amusement.

She will order you out of the house but you must refuse to go. Remain and watch Reera closely and try to see what she uses to accomplish her transformations. If you can discover the secret whisper it to us and we will then tell you what to do next."

"That sounds easy," returned Ervic, who had listened carefully. "But are you sure she will not hurt me, or try to transform me?"

"She may change your form," replied the goldfish, "but do not worry if that happens, for we can break that enchantment easily. You may be sure that nothing will harm you, so you must not be frightened at anything you see or hear."

Now Ervic was as brave as any ordinary young man, and he knew the fishes who spoke to him were truthful and to be relied upon, nevertheless he experienced a strange sinking of the heart as he picked up the kettle and approached the door of the cottage. His hand trembled as he raised the latch, but he was resolved to obey his instructions. He pushed the door open, took three strides into the middle of the one room the cottage contained, and then stood still and looked around him.

The sights that met his gaze were enough to frighten anyone who had not been properly warned. On the floor just before Ervic lay a great crocodile, its red eyes gleaming wickedly and its wide open mouth displaying rows of sharp teeth. Horned toads hopped about; each of the four upper corners of the room was festooned with a thick cobweb, in the center of which sat a spider as big around as a washbasin, and armed with pincher-like claws; a red-and-green lizard was stretched at full length on the window-sill and black rats darted in and out of the holes they had gnawed in the floor of the cottage.

But the most startling thing was a huge gray ape which sat upon a bench and knitted. It wore a lace cap, such as old ladies wear, and a little apron of lace, but no other clothing. Its eyes were bright and looked as if coals were burning in them. The ape moved as naturally as an ordinary person might, and on Ervic's entrance stopped knitting and raised its head to look at him.

"Get out!" cried a sharp voice, seeming to come from the ape's mouth.

Ervic saw another bench, empty, just beyond him, so he stepped over the crocodile, sat down upon the bench and carefully placed the kettle beside him.

"Get out!" again cried the voice.

Ervic shook his head.

"No," said he, "I'm going to stay."

The spiders left their four corners, dropped to the floor and made a rush toward the young Skeezer, circling around his legs with their pinchers extended. Ervic paid no attention to them. An enormous black rat ran up Ervic's body, passed around his shoulders and uttered piercing squeals in his ears, but he did not wince. The green-and-red lizard, coming from the window-sill, approached Ervic and began spitting a flaming fluid at him, but Ervic merely stared at the creature and its flame did not touch him.

The crocodile raised its tail and, swinging around, swept Ervic off the bench with a powerful blow. But the Skeezer managed to save the kettle from upsetting and he got up, shook off the horned toads that were crawling over him and resumed his seat on the bench.

All the creatures, after this first attack, remained motionless, as if awaiting orders. The old gray ape knitted on, not looking toward Ervic now, and the young Skeezer stolidly kept his seat. He expected something else to happen, but nothing did. A full hour passed and Ervic was growing nervous.

"What do you want?" the ape asked at last.

"Nothing," said Ervic.

"You may have that!" retorted the ape, and at this all the strange creatures in the room broke into a chorus of cackling laughter.

Another long wait.

"Do you know who I am?" questioned the ape.

"You must be Reera the Red — the Yookoohoo," Ervic answered.

"Knowing so much, you must also know that I do not like strangers. Your presence here in my home annoys me. Do you not fear my anger?"

"No," said the young man.

"Do you intend to obey me, and leave this house?" "No," replied Ervic, just as quietly as the Yookoohoo had spoken.

The ape knitted for a long time before resuming the conversation.

"Curiosity," it said, "has led to many a man's undoing. I suppose in some way you have learned that I do tricks of magic, and so through curiosity you have come here. You may have been told that I do not injure anyone, so you are bold enough to disobey my commands to go away. You imagine that you may witness some of the rites of witchcraft, and that they may amuse you. Have I spoken truly?"

"Well," remarked Ervic, who had been pondering on the strange circumstances of his coming here, "you are right in some ways, but not in others. I am told that you work magic only for your own amusement. That seems to me very selfish. Few people understand magic. I'm told that you are the only real Yookoohoo in all Oz. Why don't you amuse others as well as yourself?"

"What right have you to question my actions?"

"None at all."

"And you say you are not here to demand any favors of me?"

"For myself I want nothing from you."

"You are wise in that. I never grant favors."

"That doesn't worry me," declared Ervic.

"But you are curious? You hope to witness some of my magic transformations?"

"If you wish to perform any magic, go ahead," said Ervic. "It may interest me and it may not. If you'd rather go on with your knitting, it's all the same to me. I am in no hurry at all."

This may have puzzled Red Reera, but the face beneath the lace cap could show no expression, being covered with hair. Perhaps

in all her career the Yookoohoo had never been visited by anyone who, like this young man, asked for nothing, expected nothing, and had no reason for coming except curiosity. This attitude practically disarmed the witch and she began to regard the Skeezer in a more friendly way. She knitted for some time, seemingly in deep thought, and then she arose and walked to a big cupboard that stood against the wall of the room. When the cupboard door was opened Ervic could see a lot of drawers inside, and into one of these drawers — the second from the bottom — Reera thrust a hairy hand.

Until now Ervic could see over the bent form of the ape, but suddenly the form, with its back to him, seemed to straighten up and blot out the cupboard of drawers. The ape had changed to the form of a woman, dressed in the pretty Gillikin costume, and when she turned around he saw that it was a young woman, whose face was quite attractive.

"Do you like me better this way?" Reera inquired with a smile.

"You look better," he said calmly, "but I'm not sure I like you any better."

She laughed, saying: "During the heat of the day I like to be an ape, for an ape doesn't wear any clothes to speak of. But if one has gentlemen callers it is proper to dress up."

Ervic noticed her right hand was closed, as if she held something in it. She shut the cupboard door, bent over the crocodile and in a moment the creature had changed to a red wolf. It was not pretty even now, and the wolf crouched beside its mistress as a dog might have done. Its teeth looked as dangerous as had those of the crocodile.

Next the Yookoohoo went about touching all the lizards and toads, and at her touch they became kittens. The rats she changed into chipmunks. Now the only horrid creatures remaining were the four great spiders, which hid themselves behind their thick webs.

"There!" Reera cried, "now my cottage presents a more comfortable appearance. I love the toads and lizards and rats, because most people hate them, but I would tire of them if they always remained the same. Sometimes I change their forms a dozen times a day."

"You are clever," said Ervic. "I did not hear you utter any incantations or magic words. All you did was to touch the creatures."

"Oh, do you think so?" she replied. "Well, touch them yourself, if you like, and see if you can change their forms."

"No," said the Skeezer, "I don't understand magic and if I did I would not try to imitate your skill. You are a wonderful Yookoohoo, while I am only a common Skeezer."

This confession seemed to please Reera, who liked to have her witchcraft appreciated.

"Will you go away now?" she asked. "I prefer to be alone."

"I prefer to stay here," said Ervic.

"In another person's home, where you are not wanted?"

"Yes."

"Is not your curiosity yet satisfied?" demanded Reera, with a smile.

"I don't know. Is there anything else you can do?"

"Many things. But why should I exhibit my powers to a stranger?"

"I can think of no reason at all," he replied.

She looked at him curiously.

"You want no power for yourself, you say, and you're too stupid to be able to steal my secrets. This isn't a pretty cottage, while outside are sunshine, broad prairies and beautiful wildflowers. Yet you insist on sitting on that bench and annoying me with your unwelcome presence. What have you in that kettle?"

"Three fishes," he answered readily.

"Where did you get them?"

"I caught them in the Lake of the Skeezers."

"What do you intend to do with the fishes?"

"I shall carry them to the home of a friend of mine who has three children. The children will love to have the fishes for pets."

She came over to the bench and looked into the kettle, where the three fishes were swimming quietly in the water.

"They're pretty," said Reera. "Let me transform them into something else."

"No," objected the Skeezer.

"I love to transform things; it's so interesting. And I've never transformed any fishes in all my life."

"Let them alone," said Ervic.

"What shapes would you prefer them to have? I can make them turtles, or cute little sea-horses; or I could make them piglets, or rabbits, or guinea-pigs; or, if you like I can make chickens of them, or eagles, or bluejays."

"Let them alone!" repeated Ervic.

"You're not a very pleasant visitor," laughed Red Reera. "People accuse me of being cross and crabbed and unsociable, and they are quite right. If you had come here pleading and begging for favors, and half afraid of my Yookoohoo magic, I'd have abused you until you ran away; but you're quite different from that. You're the unsociable and crabbed and disagreeable one, and so I like you, and bear with your grumpiness. It's time for my midday meal; are you hungry?"

"No," said Ervic, although he really desired food.

"Well, I am," Reera declared and clapped her hands together. Instantly a table appeared, spread with linen and bearing dishes of various foods, some smoking hot. There were two plates laid, one at each end of the table, and as soon as Reera seated herself all her creatures gathered around her, as if they were accustomed to be fed when she ate. The wolf squatted at her right hand and the kittens and chipmunks gathered at her left.

"Come, Stranger, sit down and eat," she called cheerfully, "and while we're eating let us decide into what forms we shall change your fishes."

"They're all right as they are," asserted Ervic, drawing up his bench to the table. "The fishes are beauties — one gold, one silver and one bronze. Nothing that has life is more lovely than a beautiful fish."

"What! Am I not more lovely?" Reera asked, smiling at his serious face.

"I don't object to you — for a Yookoohoo, you know," he said, helping himself to the food and eating with good appetite.

"And don't you consider a beautiful girl more lovely than a fish, however pretty the fish may be?"

"Well," replied Ervic, after a period of thought, "that might be. If you transformed my three fish into three girls — girls who would be Adepts at Magic, you know they might please me as well as the fish do. You won't do that of course, because you can't, with all your skill. And, should you be able to do so, I fear my troubles would be more than I could bear. They would not consent to be my slaves — especially if they were Adepts at Magic — and so they would command me to obey them. No, Mistress Reeraq, let us not transform the fishes at all."

The Skeezer had put his case with remarkable cleverness. He realized that if he appeared anxious for such a transformation the Yookoohoo would not perform it, yet he had skillfully suggested that they be made Adepts at Magic.

19. Red Reera, the Yookoohoo

After the meal was over and Reera had fed her pets, including the four monster spiders which had come down from their webs to secure their share, she made the table disappear from the floor of the cottage.

"I wish you'd consent to my transforming your fishes," she said, as she took up her knitting again.

The Skeezer made no reply. He thought it unwise to hurry matters. All during the afternoon they sat silent. Once Reera went to her cupboard and after thrusting her hand into the same drawer as before, touched the wolf and transformed it into a bird with gorgeous colored feathers. This bird was larger than a parrot and of a somewhat different form, but Ervic had never seen one like it before.

"Sing!" said Reera to the bird, which had perched itself on a big wooden peg — as if it had been in the cottage before and knew just what to do.

And the bird sang jolly, rollicking songs with words to them — just as a person who had been carefully trained might do. The songs were entertaining and Ervic enjoyed listening to them. In an hour or so the bird stopped singing, tucked its head under its wing and went to sleep. Reera continued knitting but seemed thoughtful.

Now Ervic had marked this cupboard drawer well and had concluded that Reera took something from it which enabled her to perform her transformations. He thought that if he managed to remain in the cottage, and Reera fell asleep, he could slyly open the cupboard, take a portion of whatever was in the drawer, and by dropping it into the copper kettle transform the three fishes into their natural shapes. Indeed, he had firmly resolved to carry out this plan when the Yookoohoo put down her knitting and walked toward the door.

"I'm going out for a few minutes," said she; "do you wish to go with me, or will you remain here?"

Ervic did not answer but sat quietly on his bench. So Reera went out and closed the cottage door.

As soon as she was gone, Ervic rose and tiptoed to the cupboard.

"Take care! Take care!" cried several voices, coming from the kittens and chipmunks. "If you touch anything we'll tell the Yookoohoo!"

Ervic hesitated a moment but, remembering that he need not consider Reera's anger if he succeeded in transforming the fishes, he was about to open the cupboard when he was arrested by the voices of the fishes, which stuck their heads above the water in the kettle and called out: "Come here, Ervic!"

So he went back to the kettle and bent over it

"Let the cupboard alone," said the goldfish to him earnestly. "You could not succeed by getting that magic powder, for only the Yookoohoo knows how to use it. The best way is to allow her to transform us into three girls, for then we will have our natural shapes and be able to perform all the Arts of Magic we have learned and well understand. You are acting wisely and in the most effective manner. We did not know you were so intelligent, or that Reera could be so easily deceived by you. Continue as you have begun and try to persuade her to transform us. But insist that we be given the forms of girls."

The goldfish ducked its head down just as Reera re-entered the cottage. She saw Ervic bent over the kettle, so she came and joined him.

"Can your fishes talk?" she asked.

"Sometimes," he replied, "for all fishes in the Land of Oz know how to speak. Just now they were asking me for some bread. They are hungry."

"Well, they can have some bread," said Reera. "But it is nearly supper-time, and if you would allow me to transform your fishes into girls they could join us at the table and have plenty of food much nicer than crumbs. Why not let me transform them?"

"Well," said Ervic, as if hesitating, "ask the fishes. If they consent, why — why, then, I'll think it over."

Reera bent over the kettle and asked:

"Can you hear me, little fishes?"

All three popped their heads above water.

"We can hear you," said the bronzefish.

"I want to give you other forms, such as rabbits, or turtles or girls, or something; but your master, the surly Skeezer, does not wish me to. However, he has agreed to the plan if you will consent."

"We'd like to be girls," said the silverfish.

"No, no!" exclaimed Ervic.

"If you promise to make us three beautiful girls, we will consent," said the goldfish.

"No, no!" exclaimed Ervic again.

"Also make us Adepts at Magic," added the bronzefish.

"I don't know exactly what that means," replied Reera musingly, "but as no Adept at Magic is as powerful as Yookoohoo, I'll add that to the transformation."

"We won't try to harm you, or to interfere with your magic in any way," promised the goldfish. "On the contrary, we will be your friends."

"Will you agree to go away and leave me alone in my cottage, whenever I command you to do so?" asked Reera.

"We promise that," cried the three fishes.

"Don't do it! Don't consent to the transformation," urged Ervic.

"They have already consented," said the Yookoohoo, laughing in his face, "and you have promised me to abide by their decision. So, friend Skeezer, I shall perform the transformation whether you like it or not."

Ervic seated himself on the bench again, a deep scowl on his face but joy in his heart. Reera moved over to the cupboard, took something from the drawer and returned to the copper kettle. She was clutching something tightly in her right hand, but with her left she reached within the kettle, took out the three fishes and laid them carefully on the floor, where they gasped in distress at being out of water.

Reera did not keep them in misery more than a few seconds, for she touched each one with her right hand and instantly the fishes were transformed into three tall and slender young women, with fine, intelligent faces and clothed in handsome, clinging gowns. The one who had been a goldfish had beautiful golden hair and blue eyes and was exceedingly fair of skin; the one who had been a bronzefish had dark brown hair and clear gray eyes and her complexion matched these lovely features. The one who had been a silverfish had snow-white hair of the finest texture and deep brown eyes. The hair contrasted exquisitely with her pink cheeks and ruby-red lips, nor did it make her look a day older than her two companions.

As soon as they secured these girlish shapes, all three bowed low to the Yookoohoo and said: "We thank you, Reera."

Then they bowed to the Skeezer and said:

"We thank you, Ervic."

"Very good!" cried the Yookoohoo, examining her work with critical approval. "You are much better and more interesting than fishes, and this ungracious Skeezer would scarcely allow me to do the transformations. You surely have nothing to thank him for. But now let us dine in honor of the occasion."

She clapped her hands together and again a table loaded with food appeared in the cottage. It was a longer table, this time, and places were set for the three Adepts as well as for Reera and Ervic.

"Sit down, friends, and eat your fill," said the Yookoohoo, but instead of seating herself at the head of the table she went to the cupboard, saying to the Adepts: "Your beauty and grace, my fair friends, quite outshine my own. So that I may appear properly at the banquet table I intend, in honor of this occasion, to take upon myself my natural shape."

Scarcely had she finished this speech when Reera transformed herself into a young woman fully as lovely as the three Adepts. She was not quite so tall as they, but her form was more rounded and more handsomely clothed, with a wonderful jeweled girdle and a necklace of shining pearls. Her hair was a bright auburn red, and her eyes large and dark.

"Do you claim this is your natural form?" asked Ervic of the Yookoohoo.

"Yes," she replied. "This is the only form I am really entitled to wear. But I seldom assume it because there is no one here to admire or appreciate it and I get tired admiring it myself."

"I see now why you are named Reera the Red," remarked Ervic.

"It is on account of my red hair," she explained smiling. "I do not care for red hair myself, which is one reason I usually wear other forms."

"It is beautiful," asserted the young man; and then remembering the other women present he added: "But, of course, all women should not have red hair, because that would make it too common. Gold and silver and brown hair are equally handsome."

The smiles that he saw interchanged between the four filled the poor Skeezer with embarrassment, so he fell silent and attended to eating his supper, leaving the others to do the talking. The three Adepts frankly told Reera who they were. how they became fishes and how they had planned secretly to induce the Yookoohoo to transform them. They admitted that they had feared, had they asked her to help, that she would have refused them.

"You were quite right," returned the Yookoohoo. "I make it my rule never to perform magic to assist others, for if I did there would always be crowd at my cottage demanding help and I hate crowds and want to be left alone."

However, now that you are restored to your proper shapes, I do not regret my action and I hope you will be of use in saving the Skeezer people by raising their island to the surface of the lake, where it really belongs. But you must promise me that after you go away you will never come here again, nor tell anyone what I have done for you."

The three Adepts and Ervic thanked the Yookoohoo warmly. They promised to remember her wish that they should not come to her cottage again and so, with a good-bye, took their departure.

20. A Puzzling Problem

Glinda the Good, having decided to try her sorcery upon the abandoned submarine, so that it would obey her commands, asked all of her party, including the Skeezers, to withdraw from the shore of the lake to the line of palm trees. She kept with her only the little Wizard of Oz, who was her pupil and knew how to assist her in her magic rites.

When they two were alone beside the stranded boat, Glinda said to the Wizard: "I shall first try my magic recipe No. 1163, which is intended to make inanimate objects move at my command. Have you a skeropythrope with you?"

"Yes, I always carry one in my bag," replied the Wizard. He opened his black bag of magic tools and took out a brightly polished skeropythrope, which he handed to the Sorceress. Glinda had also brought a small wicker bag, containing various requirements of sorcery, and from this she took a parcel of powder and a vial of liquid. She poured the liquid into the skeropythrope and added the powder. At once the skeropythrope began to sputter and emit sparks of a violet color, which spread in all directions. The Sorceress instantly stepped into the middle of the boat and held the instrument so that the sparks fell all around her and covered every bit of the blackened steel boat. At the same time Glinda crooned a weird incantation in the language of sorcery, her voice sounding low and musical.

After a little the violet sparks ceased, and those that had fallen upon the boat had disappeared and left no mark upon its surface. The ceremony was ended and Glinda returned the skeropythrope to the Wizard, who put it away in his black bag.

"That ought to do the business all right," he said confidently

"Let us make a trial and see," she replied.

So they both entered the boat and seated themselves.

Speaking in a tone of command the Sorceress said to the boat: "Carry us across the lake, to the farther shore."

At once the boat backed off the sandy beach, turned its prow and moved swiftly over the water.

"Very good — very good indeed!" cried the Wizard, when the boat slowed up at the shore opposite from that whence they had departed. "Even Coo-ee-oh, with all her witchcraft, could do no better."

The Sorceress now said to the boat: "Close up, submerge and carry us to the basement door of the sunken island — the door from which you emerged at the command of Queen Coo-ee-oh."

The boat obeyed. As it sank into the water the top sections rose from the sides and joined together over the heads of Glinda and the Wizard, who were thus enclosed in a water-proof chamber. There were four glass windows in this covering, one on each side and one on either end, so that the passengers could see exactly where they were going. Moving under water more slowly than on the surface, the submarine gradually approached the island and halted with its bow pressed against the huge marble door in the basement under the Dome. This door was tightly closed and it was evident to both Glinda and the Wizard that it would not open to admit the underwater boat unless a magic word was spoken by them or someone from within the basement of the island. But what was this magic word? Neither of them knew.

"I'm afraid," said the Wizard regretfully, "that we can't get in, after all. Unless your sorcery can discover the word to open the marble door."

"That is probably some word only known to Coo-ee-oh," replied the Sorceress. "I may be able to discover what it is, but that will require time. Let us go back again to our companions."

"It seems a shame, after we have made the boat obey us, to be balked by just a marble door," grumbled the Wizard.

At Glinda's command the boat rose until it was on a level with the glass dome that covered the Skeezer village, when the Sorceress made it slowly circle all around the Great Dome.

Many faces were pressed against the glass from the inside, eagerly watching the submarine, and in one place were Dorothy and Ozma, who quickly recognized Glinda and the Wizard through the glass windows of the boat. Glinda saw them, too, and held the boat close to the Dome while the friends exchanged greetings in pantomime. Their voices, unfortunately, could not be heard through the Dome and the water and the side of the boat. The Wizard tried to make the girls understand, through signs, that he and Glinda had come to their rescue, and Ozma and Dorothy understood this from the very fact that the Sorceress and the Wizard had appeared. The two girl prisoners were smiling and in safety, and knowing this Glinda felt she could take all the time necessary in order to effect their final rescue.

As nothing more could be done just then, Glinda ordered the boat to return to shore and it obeyed readily. First it ascended to the surface of the water, then the roof parted and fell into the slots at the side of the boat, and then the magic craft quickly made the shore and beached itself on the sands at the very spot from which it had departed at Glinda's command. All the Oz people and the Skeezers at once ran to the boat to ask if they had reached the island, and whether they had seen Ozma and Dorothy. The Wizard told them of the obstacle they had met in the way of a marble door, and how Glinda would now undertake to find a magic way to conquer the door.

Realizing that it would require several days to succeed in reaching the island raising it and liberating their friends and the Skeezer people, Glinda now prepared a camp half way between the lake shore and the palm trees.

The Wizard's wizardry made a number of tents appear and the sorcery of the Sorceress furnished these tents all complete, with beds, chairs, tables, flags, lamps and even books with which to pass idle hours. All the tents had the Royal Banner of Oz flying from the centerpoles and one big tent, not now occupied, had Ozma's own banner moving in the breeze.

Betsy and Trot had a tent to themselves, and Button Bright and Ojo had another. The Scarecrow and the Tin Woodman paired together in one tent and so did Jack Pumpkinhead and the Shaggy Man, Cap'n Bill and Uncle Henry, Tik-Tok and Professor Wogglebug. Glinda had the most splendid tent of all, except that reserved for Ozma, while the Wizard had a little one of his own. Whenever it was meal time, tables loaded with food magically appeared in the tents of those who were in the habit of eating, and these complete arrangements made the rescue party just as comfortable as they would have been in their own homes.

Far into the night Glinda sat in her tent studying a roll of mystic scrolls in search of a word that would open the basement door of the island and admit her to the Great Dome. She also made many magical experiments, hoping to discover something that would aid her. Yet the morning found the powerful Sorceress still unsuccessful.

Glinda's art could have opened any ordinary door, you may be sure, but you must realize that this marble door of the island had been commanded not to open save in obedience to one magic word, and therefore all other magic words could have no effect upon it. The magic word that guarded the door had probably been invented by Coo-ee-oh, who had now forgotten it. The only

way, then, to gain entrance to the sunken island was to break the charm that held the door fast shut. If this could be done no magic would be required to open it.

The next day the Sorceress and the Wizard again entered the boat and made it submerge and go to the marble door, which they tried in various ways to open, but without success.

"We shall have to abandon this attempt, I think," said Glinda. "The easiest way to raise the island would be for us to gain admittance to the Dome and then descend to the basement and see in what manner Coo-ee-oh made the entire island sink or rise at her command. It naturally occurred to me that the easiest way to gain admittance would be by having the boat take us into the basement through the marble door from which Coo-ee-oh launched it. But there must be other ways to get inside the Dome and join Ozma and Dorothy, and such ways we must find by study and the proper use of our powers of magic."

"It won't be easy," declared the Wizard, "for we must not forget that Ozma herself understands considerable magic, and has doubtless tried to raise the island or find other means of escape from it and failed."

"That is true," returned Glinda, "but Ozma's magic is fairy magic, while you are a Wizard and I am a Sorceress. In this way the three of us have a great variety of magic to work with, and if we should all fail it will be because the island is raised and lowered by a magic power none of us is acquainted with. My idea therefore is to seek — by such magic as we possess — to accomplish our object in another way."

They made the circle of the Dome again in their boat, and once more saw Ozma and Dorothy through their windows and exchanged signals with the two imprisoned girls.

Ozma realized that her friends were doing all in their power to rescue her and smiled an encouragement to their efforts. Dorothy seemed a little anxious but was trying to be as brave as her companion.

After the boat had returned to the camp and Glinda was seated in her tent, working out various ways by which Ozma and Dorothy could be rescued, the Wizard stood on the shore dreamily eying the outlines of the Great Dome which showed beneath the clear water, when he raised his eyes and saw a group of strange people approaching from around the lake. Three were young women of stately presence, very beautifully dressed, who moved with remarkable grace. They were followed at a little distance by a good-looking young Skeezer.

The Wizard saw at a glance that these people might be very important, so he advanced to meet them. The three maidens received him graciously and the one with the golden hair said: "I believe you are the famous Wizard of Oz, of whom I have often heard. We are seeking Glinda, the Sorceress, and perhaps you can lead us to her."

"I can, and will, right gladly," answered the Wizard. "Follow me please."

The little Wizard was puzzled as to the identity of the three lovely visitors but he gave no sign that might embarrass them.

He understood they did not wish to be questioned, and so he made no remarks as he led the way to Glinda's tent.

With a courtly bow the Wizard ushered the three visitors into the gracious presence of Glinda, the Good.

21. The Three Adepts

The Sorceress looked up from her work as the three maidens entered, and something in their appearance and manner led her to rise and bow to them in her most dignified manner. The three knelt an instant before the great Sorceress and then stood upright and waited for her to speak.

"Whoever you may be," said Glinda, "I bid you welcome."

"My name is Audah," said one.

"My name is Aurah," said another.

"My name is Aujah," said the third.

Glinda had never heard these names before, but looking closely at the three she asked: "Are you witches or workers in magic?"

"Some of the secret arts we have gleaned from Nature," replied the brownhaired maiden modestly, "but we do not place our skill beside that of the Great Sorceress, Glinda the Good."

"I suppose you are aware it is unlawful to practice magic in the Land of Oz, without the permission of our Ruler, Princess Ozma?"

"No, we were not aware of that," was the reply. "We have heard of Ozma, who is the appointed Ruler of all this great fairyland, but her laws have not reached us, as yet."

Glinda studied the strange maidens thoughtfully; then she said to them: "Princess Ozma is even now imprisoned in the Skeezer village. for the whole island with its Great Dome, was sunk to the bottom of the lake by the witchcraft of Coo-ee-oh, whom the Flathead Su-dic transformed into a silly swan. I am seeking some way to overcome Coo-ee-oh's magic and raise the isle to the surface again. Can you help me do this?"

The maidens exchanged glances, and the white-haired one replied, "We do not know; but we will try to assist you."

"It seems," continued Glinda musingly, "that Coo-ee-oh derived most of her witchcraft from three Adepts at Magic, who at one time ruled the Flatheads. While the Adepts were being entertained by Coo-ee-oh at a banquet in her palace, she cruelly betrayed them and after transforming them into fishes cast them into the lake.

"If I could find these three fishes and return them to their natural shapes — they might know what magic Coo-ee-oh used to sink the island. I was about to go to the shore and call these fishes to me when you arrived. So, if you will join me, we will try to find them."

The maidens exchanged smiles now, and the golden- haired one, Audah, said to Glinda: "It will not be necessary to go to the lake. We are the three fishes."

"Indeed!" cried Glinda. "Then you are the three Adepts at Magic, restored to your proper forms?"

"We are the three Adepts," admitted Aujah.

"Then," said Glinda, "my task is half accomplished. But who destroyed the transformation that made you fishes?"

"We have promised not to tell," answered Aurah; "but this young Skeezer was largely responsible for our release; he is brave and clever, and we owe him our gratitude."

Glinda looked at Ervic, who stood modestly behind the Adepts, hat in hand. "He shall be properly rewarded," she declared, "for in helping you he has helped us all, and perhaps saved his people from being imprisoned forever in the sunken isle."

The Sorceress now asked her guests to seat themselves and a long talk followed, in which the Wizard of Oz shared.

"We are quite certain," said Aurah, "that if we could get inside the Dome we could discover Coo-ee-oh's secrets, for in all her work, after we became fishes, she used the formulas and incantations and arts that she stole from us. She may have added to these things, but they were the foundation of all her work."

"What means do you suggest for our getting into the Dome?" inquired Glinda.

The three Adepts hesitated to reply, for they had not yet considered what could be done to reach the inside of the Great Dome. While they were in deep thought, and Glinda and the Wizard were quietly awaiting their suggestions, into the tent rushed Trot and Betsy, dragging between them the Patchwork Girl.

"Oh, Glinda," cried Trot, "Scraps has thought of a way to rescue Ozma and Dorothy and all of the Skeezers."

The three Adepts could not avoid laughing merrily, for not only were they amused by the queer form of the Patchwork Girl, but Trot's enthusiastic speech struck them as really funny. If the Great Sorceress and the famous Wizard and the three talented Adepts at Magic were unable as yet to solve the important problem of the sunken isle, there was little chance for a patched girl stuffed with cotton to succeed.

But Glinda, smiling indulgently at the earnest faces turned toward her, patted the children's heads and said: "Scraps is very clever. Tell us what she has thought of, my dear."

"Well," said Trot, "Scraps says that if you could dry up all the water in the lake the island would be on dry land, an' everyone could come and go whenever they liked."

Glinda smiled again, but the Wizard said to the girls: "If we should dry up the lake, what would become of all the beautiful fishes that now live in the water?"

"Dear me! That's so," admitted Betsy, crestfallen; "we never thought of that, did we Trot?"

"Couldn't you transform 'em into polliwogs?" asked Scraps, turning a somersault and then standing on one leg. "You could give them a little, teeny pond to swim in, and they'd be just as happy as they are as fishes."

"No indeed!" replied the Wizard, severely. "It is wicked to transform any living creatures without their consent, and the lake is the home of the fishes and belongs to them."

"All right," said Scraps, making a face at him; "I don't care."

"It's too bad," sighed Trot, "for I thought we'd struck a splendid idea."

"So you did," declared Glinda, her face now grave and thoughtful. "There is something in the Patchwork Girl's idea that may be of real value to us."

"I think so, too," agreed the golden-haired Adept. "The top of the Great Dome is only a few feet below the surface of the water. If we could reduce the level of the lake until the Dome sticks a little above the water, we could remove some of the glass and let ourselves down into the village by means of ropes."

"And there would be plenty of water left for the fishes to swim in," added the white-haired maiden.

"If we succeed in raising the island we could fill up the lake again," suggested the brown-haired Adept.

"I believe," said the Wizard, rubbing his hands together in delight, "that the Patchwork Girl has shown us the way to success."

The girls were looking curiously at the three beautiful Adepts, wondering who they were, so Glinda introduced them to Trot and Betsy and Scraps, and then sent the children away while she considered how to carry the new idea into effect.

Not much could be done that night, so the Wizard prepared another tent for the Adepts, and in the evening Glinda held a reception and invited all her followers to meet the new arrivals. The Adepts were greatly astonished at the extraordinary personages presented to them, and marveled that Jack Pumpkinhead and the Scarecrow and the Tin Woodman and Tik-Tok could really live and think and talk just like other people. They were especially pleased with the lively Patchwork Girl and loved to watch her antics.

It was quite a pleasant party, for Glinda served some dainty refreshments to those who could eat, and the Scarecrow recited some poems, and the Cowardly Lion sang a song in his deep bass voice. The only thing that marred their joy was the thought that their beloved Ozma and dear little Dorothy were yet confined in the Great Dome of the Sunken island.

22. The Sunken Island

As soon as they had breakfasted the next morning, Glinda and the Wizard and the three Adepts went down to the shore of the lake and formed a line with their faces toward the submerged island. All the others came to watch them, but stood at a respectful distance in the background.

At the right of the Sorceress stood Audah and Aurah, while at the left stood the Wizard and Aujah. Together they stretched their arms over the water's edge and in unison the five chanted a rhythmic incantation.

This chant they repeated again and again, swaying their arms gently from side to side, and in a few minutes the watchers behind them noticed that the lake had begun to recede from the shore. Before long the highest point of the dome appeared above the water. Gradually the water fell, making the dome appear to rise. When it was three or four feet above the surface Glinda gave the signal to stop, for their work had been accomplished.

The blackened submarine was now entirely out of the water, but Uncle Henry and Cap'n Bill managed to push it into the lake. Glinda, the Wizard, Ervic and the Adepts got into the boat, taking with them a coil of strong rope, and at the command of

the Sorceress the craft cleaved its way through the water toward the part of the Dome which was now visible.

"There's still plenty of water for the fish to swim in," observed the Wizard as they rode along. "They might like more but I'm sure they can get along until we have raised the island and can fill up the lake again."

The boat touched gently on the sloping glass of the Dome, and the Wizard took some tools from his black bag and quickly removed one large pane of glass, thus making a hole large enough for their bodies to pass through. Stout frames of steel supported the glass of the Dome, and around one of these frames the Wizard tied the end of a rope.

"I'll go down first," said he, "for while I'm not as spry as Cap'n Bill I'm sure I can manage it easily. Are you sure the rope is long enough to reach the bottom?"

"Quite sure," replied the Sorceress.

So the Wizard let down the rope and climbing through the opening lowered himself down, hand over hand, clinging to the rope with his legs and feet. Below in the streets of the village were gathered all the Skeezers, men, women and children, and you may be sure that Ozma and Dorothy, with Lady Aurex, were filled with joy that their friends were at last coming to their rescue.

The Queen's palace, now occupied by Ozma, was directly in the center of the Dome, so that when the rope was let down the end of it came just in front of the palace entrance. Several Skeezers held fast to the rope's end to steady it and the Wizard reached the ground in safety. He hugged first Ozma and then Dorothy, while all the Skeezers cheered as loud as they could.

The Wizard now discovered that the rope was long enough to reach from the top of the Dome to the ground when doubled, so he tied a chair to one end of the rope and called to Glinda to sit in the chair while he and some of the Skeezers lowered her to the pavement. In this way the Sorceress reached the ground quite comfortably and the three Adepts and Ervic soon followed her.

The Skeezers quickly recognized the three Adepts at Magic, whom they had learned to respect before their wicked Queen betrayed them, and welcomed them as friends. All the inhabitants of the village had been greatly frightened by their imprisonment under water, but now realized that an attempt was to be made to rescue them.

Glinda, the Wizard and the Adepts followed Ozma and Dorothy into the palace, and they asked Lady Aurex and Ervic to join them. After Ozma had told of her adventures in trying to prevent war between the Flatheads and the Skeezers, and Glinda had told all about the Rescue Expedition and the restoration of the three Adepts by the help of Ervic, a serious consultation was held as to how the island could be made to rise.

"I've tried every way in my power," said Ozma, "but Coo-ee-oh used a very unusual sort of magic which I do not understand. She seems to have prepared her witchcraft in such a way that a spoken word is necessary to accomplish her designs, and these spoken words are known only to herself."

"That is a method we taught her," declared Aurah the Adept.

"I can do no more, Glinda," continued Ozma, "so I wish you would try what your sorcery can accomplish."

"First, then," said Glinda, "let us visit the basement of the island, which I am told is underneath the village."

A flight of marble stairs led from one of Coo-ee-oh's private rooms down to the basement, but when the party arrived all were puzzled by what they saw. In the center of a broad, low room, stood a mass of great cog-wheels, chains and pulleys, all interlocked and seeming to form a huge machine; but there was no engine or other motive power to make the wheels turn.

"This, I suppose, is the means by which the island is lowered or raised," said Ozma, "but the magic word which is needed to move the machinery is unknown to us."

The three Adepts were carefully examining the mass of wheels, and soon the golden-haired one said: "These wheels do not control the island at all. On the contrary, one set of them is used to open the doors of the little rooms where the submarines are kept, as may be seen from the chains and pulleys used. Each boat is kept in a little room with two doors, one to the basement room where we are now and the other letting into the lake.

"When Coo-ee-oh used the boat in which she attacked the Flatheads, she first commanded the basement door to open and with her followers she got into the boat and made the top close over them. Then the basement door being closed, the outer door was slowly opened, letting the water fill the room to float the boat, which then left the island, keeping under water."

"But how could she expect to get back again?" asked the Wizard.

"Why the boat would enter the room filled with water and after the outer door was closed a word of command started a pump which pumped all the water from the room. Then the boat would open and Coo-ee-oh could enter the basement."

"I see," said the Wizard. "It is a clever contrivance, but won't work unless one knows the magic words."

"Another part of this machinery," explained the white-haired Adept, "is used to extend the bridge from the island to the mainland. The steel bridge is in a room much like that in which the boats are kept, and at Coo-ce-oh's command it would reach out, joint by joint, until its far end touched the shore of the lake. The same magic command would make the bridge return to its former position. Of course the bridge could not be used unless the island was on the surface of the water."

"But how do you suppose Coo-ee-oh managed to sink the island, and make it rise again?" inquired Glinda.

This the Adepts could not yet explain. As nothing more could be learned from the basement they mounted the steps to the Queen's private suite again, and Ozma showed them to a special room where Coo-ee-oh kept her magical instruments and performed all her arts of witchcraft.

23. The Magic Words

Many interesting things were to be seen in the Room of Magic, including much that had been stolen from the Adepts when they were transformed to fishes, but they had to admit that Coo-ee-oh had a rare genius for mechanics, and had used her knowledge in inventing a lot of mechanical apparatus that ordinary witches, wizards and sorcerers could not understand.

They all carefully inspected this room, taking care to examine every article they came across.

"The island," said Glinda thoughtfully, "rests on a base of solid marble. When it is submerged, as it is now, the base of the island is upon the bottom of the lake. What puzzles me is how such a great weight can be lifted and suspended in the water, even by magic."

"I now remember," returned Aujah, "that one of the arts we taught Coo-ee-oh was the way to expand steel, and I think that explains how the island is raised and lowered. I noticed in the basement a big steel pillar that passed through the floor and extended upward to this palace. Perhaps the end of it is concealed in this very room. If the lower end of the steel pillar is firmly embedded in the bottom of the lake, Coo-ee-oh could utter a magic word that would make the pillar expand, and so lift the entire island to the level of the water."

"I've found the end of the steel pillar. It's just here," announced the Wizard, pointing to one side of the room where a great basin of polished steel seemed to have been set upon the floor.

They all gathered around, and Ozma said: "Yes, I am quite sure that is the upper end of the pillar that supports the island. I noticed it when I first came here. It has been hollowed out, you see, and something has been burned in the basin, for the fire has left its marks. I wondered what was under the great basin and got several of the Skeezers to come up here and try to lift it for me. They were strong men, but could not move it at all."

"It seems to me," said Audah the Adept, "that we have discovered the manner in which Coo-ee-oh raised the island. She would burn some sort of magic powder in the basin, utter the magic word, and the pillar would lengthen out and lift the island with it."

"What's this?" asked Dorothy, who had been searching around with the others, and now noticed a slight hollow in the wall, near to where the steel basin stood. As she spoke Dorothy pushed her thumb into the hollow and instantly a small drawer popped out from the wall.

The three Adepts, Glinda and the Wizard sprang forward and peered into the drawer. It was half filled with a grayish powder, the tiny grains of which constantly moved as if impelled by some living force.

"It may be some kind of radium," said the Wizard.

"No," replied Glinda, "it is more wonderful than even radium, for I recognize it as a rare mineral powder called Gaulau by the sorcerers. I wonder how Coo-ee-oh discovered it and where she obtained it."

"There is no doubt," said Aujah the Adept, "that this is the magic powder Coo-ee-oh burned in the basin. If only we knew the magic word, I am quite sure we could raise the island."

"How can we discover the magic word?" asked Ozma, turning to Glinda as she spoke.

"That we must now seriously consider," answered the Sorceress.

So all of them sat down in the Room of Magic and began to think. It was so still that after a while Dorothy grew nervous. The little girl never could keep silent for long, and at the risk of displeasing her magic-working friends she suddenly said: "Well, Coo-ee-oh used just three magic words, one to make the bridge work, and one to make the submarines go out of their holes, and one to raise and lower the island. Three words. And Coo-ee-oh's name is made up of just three words. One is 'Coo,' and one is 'ee,' and one is 'oh.'

The Wizard frowned but Glinda looked wonderingly at the young girl and Ozma cried out: "A good thought, Dorothy dear! You may have solved our problem."

"I believe it is worth a trial," agreed Glinda. "It would be quite natural for Coo-ee-oh to divide her name into three magic syllables, and Dorothy's suggestion seems like an inspiration."

The three Adepts also approved the trial but the brown-haired one said: "We must be careful not to use the wrong word, and send the bridge out under water. The main thing, if Dorothy's idea is correct, is to hit upon the one word that moves the island."

"Let us experiment," suggested the Wizard.

In the drawer with the moving gray powder was a tiny golden cup, which they thought was used for measuring. Glinda filled this cup with the powder and carefully poured it into the shallow basin, which was the top of the great steel pillar supporting the island. Then Aurah the Adept lighted a taper and touched it to the powder, which instantly glowed fiery red and tumbled about the basin with astonishing energy. While the grains of powder still glowed red the Sorceress bent over it and said in a voice of command: "Coo!"

They waited motionless to see what would happen. There was a grating noise and a whirl of machinery, but the island did not move a particle.

Dorothy rushed to the window, which overlooked the glass side of the dome.

"The boats!" she exclaimed. "The boats are all loose an' sailing under water."

"We've made a mistake," said the Wizard gloomily.

"But it's one which shows we are on the right track," declared Aujah the Adept. "We know now that Coo-ee-oh used the syllables of her name for the magic words."

"If 'Coo' sends out the boats, it is probable that ee' works the bridge," suggested Ozma. "So the last part of the name may raise the island."

"Let us try that next then," proposed the Wizard.

He scraped the embers of the burned powder out of the basin and Glinda again filled the golden cup from the drawer and placed it on top the steel pillar. Aurah lighted it with her taper and Ozma bent over the basin and murmured the long drawn syllable: "Oh-h-h!"

Instantly the island trembled and with a weird groaning noise it moved upward — slowly, very slowly, but with a steady motion, while all the company stood by in awed silence. It was a wonderful thing, even to those skilled in the arts of magic, wizardry and sorcery, to realize that a single word could raise that great, heavy island, with its immense glass Dome.

"Why, we're way above the lake now!" exclaimed Dorothy from the window, when at last the island ceased to move.

"That is because we lowered the level of the water," explained Glinda.

They could hear the Skeezers cheering lustily in the streets of the village as they realized that they were saved.

"Come," said Ozma eagerly, "let us go down and join the people."

"Not just yet," returned Glinda, a happy smile upon her lovely face, for she was overjoyed at their success. "First let us extend the bridge to the mainland, where our friends from the Emerald City are waiting."

It didn't take long to put more powder in the basin, light it and utter the syllable "EE!" The result was that a door in the basement opened and the steel bridge moved out, extended itself joint by joint, and finally rested its far end on the shore of the lake just in front of the encampment.

"Now," said Glinda, "we can go up and receive the congratulations of the Skeezers and of our friends of the Rescue Expedition."

Across the water, on the shore of the lake, the Patchwork Girl was waving them a welcome.

24. Glinda's Triumph

Of course all those who had joined Glinda's expedition at once crossed the bridge to the island, where they were warmly welcomed by the Skeezers. Before all the concourse of people Princess Ozma made a speech from a porch of the palace and demanded that they recognize her as their lawful Ruler and promise to obey the laws of the Land of Oz. In return she agreed to protect them from all future harm and declared they would no longer be subjected to cruelty and abuse.

This pleased the Skeezers greatly, and when Ozma told them they might elect a Queen to rule over them, who in turn would be subject to Ozma of Oz, they voted for Lady Aurex, and that same day the ceremony of crowning the new Queen was held and Aurex was installed as mistress of the palace.

For her Prime Minister the Queen selected Ervic, for the three Adepts had told of his good judgment, faithfulness and cleverness, and all the Skeezers approved the appointment.

Glinda, the Wizard and the Adepts stood on the bridge and recited an incantation that quite filled the lake with water again, and the Scarecrow and the Patchwork Girl climbed to the top of the Great Dome and replaced the pane of glass that had been removed to allow Glinda and her followers to enter.

When evening came Ozma ordered a great feast prepared, to which every Skeezer was invited. The village was beautifully decorated and brilliantly lighted and there was music and dancing until a late hour to celebrate the liberation of the people For the Skeezers had been freed, not only from the water of the lake but from the cruelty of their former Queen.

As the people from the Emerald City prepared the next morning to depart, Queen Aurex said to Ozma: "There is only one thing I now fear for my people, and that is the enmity of the terrible Su-dic of the Flatheads. He is liable to come here at any time and try to annoy us, and my Skeezers are peaceful folks and unable to fight the wild and wilful Flatheads."

"Do not worry," returned Ozma, reassuringly. "We intend to stop on our way at the Flatheads' Enchanted Mountain and punish the Su-dic for his misdeeds."

That satisfied Aurex and when Ozma and her followers trooped over the bridge to the shore, having taken leave of their friends, all the Skeezers cheered them and waved their hats and handkerchiefs, and the band played and the departure was indeed a ceremony long to be remembered.

The three Adepts at Magic, who had formerly ruled the Flatheads wisely and considerately, went with Princess Ozma and her people, for they had promised Ozma to stay on the mountain and again see that the laws were enforced.

Glinda had been told all about the curious Flatheads and she had consulted with the Wizard and formed a plan to render them more intelligent and agreeable.

When the party reached the mountain Ozma and Dorothy showed them how to pass around the invisible wall — which had been built by the Flatheads after the Adepts were transformed — and how to gain the up-and-down stairway that led to the mountain top.

The Su-dic had watched the approach of the party from the edge of the mountain and was frightened when he saw that the three Adepts had recovered their natural forms and were coming back to their former home. He realized that his power would soon be gone and yet he determined to fight to the last. He called all the Flatheads together and armed them, and told them to arrest all who came up the stairway and hurl them over the edge of the mountain to the plain below. But although they feared the Supreme Dictator, who had threatened to punish them if they did not obey his commands, as soon as they saw the three Adepts they threw down their arms and begged their former rulers to protect them.

The three Adepts assured the excited Flatheads that they had nothing to fear.

Seeing that his people had rebelled the Su-dic ran away and tried to hide, but the Adepts found him and had him cast into a prison, all his cans of brains being taken away from him.

After this easy conquest of the Su-dic, Glinda told the Adepts of her plan, which had already been approved by Ozma of Oz, and they joyfully agreed to it. So, during the next few days, the great Sorceress transformed, in a way, every Flathead on the mountain.

Taking them one at a time, she had the can of brains that belonged to each one opened and the contents spread on the flat head, after which, by means of her arts of sorcery, she caused the head to grow over the brains — in the manner most people wear them — and they were thus rendered as intelligent and good looking as any of the other inhabitants of the Land of Oz.

When all had been treated in this manner there were no more Flatheads at all, and the Adepts decided to name their people Mountaineers. One good result of Glinda's sorcery was that no one could now be deprived of the brains that belonged to him and each person had exactly the share he was entitled to.

Even the Su-dic was given his portion of brains and his flat head made round, like the others, but he was deprived of all power to work further mischief, and with the Adepts constantly watching him he would be forced to become obedient and humble.

The Golden Pig, which ran grunting about the streets, with no brains at all, was disenchanted by Glinda, and in her woman's form was given brains and a round head. This wife of the Su-dic had once been even more wicked than her evil husband, but she had now forgotten all her wickedness and was likely to be a good woman thereafter.

These things being accomplished in a satisfactory manner, Princess Ozma and her people bade farewell to the three Adepts and departed for the Emerald City, well pleased with their interesting adventures.

They returned by the road over which Ozma and Dorothy had come, stopping to get the Sawhorse and the Red Wagon where they had left them.

"I'm very glad I went to see these peoples," said Princess Ozma, "for I not only prevented any further warfare between them, but they have been freed from the rule of the Su-dic and Coo-ee-oh and are now happy and loyal subjects of the Land of Oz. Which proves that it is always wise to do one's duty, however unpleasant that duty may seem to be."

CPSIA information can be obtained at www.ICGtesting.com
Printed in the USA
LVOW110810021012

300992LV00003BA/16/A